CARL HIAASEN OMNIBUS 2

Carl Hiaasen is the author of nine brilliant
black comic capers among which are *Tourist Season*,
Skin Tight, *Lucky You* and *Sick Puppy*. He is a journalist
and lives with his family in the Florida Keys.

Native Tongue

'Tirelessly inventive screwball thiller in which
valiant-for-truth PR man outfaces sexually deviant
dolphin, man-eating pet whale, and sub-moronic
goon addicted to steriods. Aaagh!'
Guardian

Strip Tease

'Sharp-eyed, sharp-tongued, wickedly inventive
– laughs all the way to the blood bank'
Independent on Sunday

Stormy Weather

'The great absurdist on peak form'
Literary Review

Also by Carl Hiaasen

Fiction

Sick Puppy

Lucky You

Skin Tight

Double Whammy

Tourist Season

Basket Case

Carl Hiaasen Omnibus 1
Tourist Season, Double Whammy, Skin Tight

Non-fiction

Paradise Screwed: Selected Columns
(edited by Diane Stevenson)

Kick Ass: Selected Columns
(edited by Diane Stevenson)

Team Rodent: How Disney Devours the World

CARL HIAASEN OMNIBUS 2

NATIVE TONGUE

STRIP TEASE

STORMY WEATHER

PICADOR

Native Tongue first published 1991 by Alfred A. Knopf, Inc., New York
First published in Great Britain 1992 by Macmillan
and in paperback 1992 by Pan Books

Strip Tease first published 1993 by Alfred A. Knopf, Inc., New York
First published in Great Britain 1993 by Macmillan
and in paperback 1994 by Pan Books

Stormy Weather first published 1995 by Alfred A. Knopf, Inc., New York
First published in Great Britain 1995 by Macmillan
and in paperback 1996 by Pan Books

This omnibus edition published 2005 by Picador
an imprint of Pan Macmillan Ltd
20 New Wharf Road, London N1 9RR
Basingstoke and Oxford
Associated companies throughout the world
www.panmacmillan.com

ISBN 0 330 43217 6

9 8 7 6 5 4 3 2 1

A CIP catalogue record for this book is available from
the British Library.

Typeset by SetSystems Ltd, Saffron Walden, Essex
Printed and bound in Great Britain by
Mackays of Chatham plc, Chatham, Kent

Contents

NATIVE TONGUE

For my brother Rob

This is a work of fiction. The events described are imaginary.

However, the depiction of aberrant sexual behaviour by bottle-nosed dolphins is based on true cases on file with the Florida state marine laboratory in St. Petersburg.

1

On July 16, in the aching torpid heat of the South Florida summer, Terry Whelper stood at the Avis counter at Miami International Airport and rented a bright red Chrysler LeBaron convertible. He had originally signed up for a Dodge Colt, a sensible low-mileage compact, but his wife had told him go on, be sporty for once in your life. So Terry Whelper got the red LeBaron plus the extra collision coverage, in anticipation of Miami drivers. Into the convertible he inserted the family—his wife Gerri, his son Jason, his daughter Jennifer—and bravely set out for the turnpike.

The children, who liked to play car games, began counting all the other LeBarons on the highway. By the time the Whelpers got to Snapper Creek, the total was up to seventeen. 'And they're all rentals,' Terry muttered. He felt like a fool; every tourist in Miami was driving a red LeBaron convertible.

'But look at all this legroom,' said his wife.

From the back seat came Jennifer's voice: 'Like, what if it rains?'

'Like, we put up the top,' Terry said.

His wife scolded him for being sarcastic with their daughter. 'She's only eleven, for heaven's sake.'

'Sorry,' said Terry Whelper. Then louder, over his shoulder: 'Jenny, I'm sorry.'

'For what?'

Terry shook his head. 'Nothing, hon.'

It started raining near Florida City, and of course the convertible top wouldn't go up; something was stuck, or maybe Terry wasn't pushing the right button on the dash. The Whelpers sought shelter at an Amoco station, parked near the full-service pumps and waited for the cloudburst to stop. Terry was dying to tell his wife I-told-you-so, sporty my ass, but she wouldn't look up from the paperback that she was pretending to read.

Jennifer asked, 'Like, what if it rains all day and all night?'

'It won't,' said Terry, trying hard to be civil.

The shower stopped in less than an hour, and the Whelpers were off again. While the kids used beach towels to dry off the interior of the convertible, Gerri passed around cans of Pepsi-Cola and snacks from the gas station vending machine. In vain Terry fiddled with the buttons on the car radio, trying to find a station that played soft rock.

The Whelpers were halfway down Card Sound Road when a blue pickup truck passed them the other way doing at least eighty. Without warning, something flew out of the truck driver's window and landed in the back seat of the LeBaron. Terry heard Jason yell; then Jennifer started to wail.

'Pull over!' Gerri cried.

'Easy does it,' said her husband.

The convertible skidded to a halt in a spray of grass and gravel. The Whelpers scrambled from the car, checked themselves for injuries and reassembled by the side of the road.

'It was two guys,' Jason declared, pointing down the road. 'White guys, too.'

'Are you sure?' asked his mother. The family had been on guard for possible trouble from blacks and Hispanics; a neighbor in Dearborn had given them the scoop on South Florida.

'They looked white to me,' Jason said of the assailants.

Terry Whelper frowned. 'I don't care if they were purple. Just tell me, what did they throw?'

Jennifer stopped crying long enough to say: 'I dunno, but it's alive.'

Terry said, 'For Christ's sake.' He walked over to the convertible and leaned inside for a look. 'I don't see anything.'

Jennifer cried even harder, a grating subhuman bray. 'You . . . don't . . . believe . . . me!' she said, sobbing emphatically with each word.

'Of course we believe you,' said her mother.

'I saw it, too,' said Jason, who rarely took his sister's side on anything. 'Try down on the floor, Dad.'

Terry Whelper got into the back of the LeBaron, squeezed down to his knees and peered beneath the seat. The children heard him say, 'Holy shit,' then he leapt out of the car.

'What is it?' asked his wife.

'It's a rat,' said Terry Whelper. 'The ugliest goddamn rat I ever saw.'

'They threw a rat in our car?'

'Apparently.'

Jason said, 'Too bad we didn't bring Grandpa's gun.'

Gerri Whelper looked shaken and confused. 'Why would they throw a rat in our car? Is it alive?'

'Very much so,' Terry reported. 'It's eating from a bag of Raisinets.'

'Those are mine!' Jennifer cried.

The Whelpers stood there discussing the situation for fifteen minutes before a highway patrol car pulled up, and a young state trooper asked what was the matter. He listened sympathetically to the story about the rat in the rented LeBaron.

'You want me to call the Avis people?' he asked. 'Maybe they'll send another car.'

'Actually, we're on a pretty tight schedule,' explained Gerri Whelper. 'We've got reservations at a motor lodge in Key Largo. They said we had to be there by five or else we lose the rooms.'

Jennifer, who had almost stopped crying, said: 'I don't care about the motel, I want a different car.'

Terry Whelper said to the trooper, 'If you could just help me get rid of it.'

'The rat?'

'It's a big one,' Terry said.

'Well, I can probably shoot it.'

'Could you?' Gerri said. 'Please?'

The trooper said, 'Technically, it's against regulations. But since you're from out of town . . .'

He stepped out of the patrol car and unsnapped the holster strap on his .357.

'Wow!' said Jason.

Jennifer put her arms around her mother's waist. Terry Whelper manfully directed his brood to move safely out of the line of fire. The state trooper approached the LeBaron with the calm air of a seasoned lawman.

'He's under the seat,' Terry advised.

'Yeah, I see him.'

The trooper fired three times. Then he holstered the gun, reached into the convertible and picked up what remained of the creature by what remained of its tail. He tossed the misshapen brown lump into some holly bushes.

'Thank you so much,' said Gerri Whelper.

'You say it was a blue pickup. You didn't happen to see the license plate?'

'No,' said Terry. He was wondering what to tell Avis about the bullet holes in the floorboard. When the kids climbed back in the rental car, their mother said, 'Don't touch any of those raisins! We'll get more candy when we get to the Amazing Kingdom.'

'Good, I want a Petey Possum Popsicle,' Jennifer said, nearly recovered from the trauma. Jason asked if he could keep one of the empty shell casings out of the state trooper's revolver, and the trooper said sure.

Terry Whelper grimly contemplated the upcoming journey in the red, rat-befouled LeBaron. He felt fog-headed and emotionally drained. To think, just that morning he'd been safe and sound in his bed back in Michigan.

'Don't forget to buckle up,' said the trooper, holding the door open.

Terry said, 'This ever happen before?'

'What do you mean?'

'This rat business.'

'I'm sure it has. We don't hear about everything.' The trooper smiled as he closed Terry Whelper's door. 'Now, you all have a nice vacation.'

In the blue pickup truck, still heading north, Danny Pogue said, 'That was the damnedest thing I ever saw.'

Bud Schwartz, who was driving, said, 'Yeah, that was some shot. If I do say so.'

'There was kids in that car.'

'It was just a mouse, for Chrissakes.'

'It wasn't a mouse, it was a rat.' Danny Pogue poked his partner in the shoulder. 'What if those was your kids? You like it, somebody throws a fucking rat in their laps?'

Bud Schwartz glanced at the place on his shoulder where Danny Pogue had touched him. Then he looked back at the highway. His bare bony arms got rigid on the steering wheel. 'I wasn't exactly aiming for the kids.'

'Were too.'

After a few strained moments, Bud Schwartz said, 'You don't see that many convertibles anymore.'

'So when you finally see one, you throw a rat in it? Is that the deal?' Danny Pogue picked at a pair of ripe pimples on the peak of his Adam's apple.

'Let's just drop it,' said Bud Schwartz.

But Danny Pogue remained agitated all the way to Florida City. He told Bud Schwartz to let him off in front of the Long John Silver's.

'No way,' said Bud Schwartz.

'Then I'll jump outta the goddamn truck.'

Danny Pogue would damn sure try it, too, Bud thought. Jump out of the damn truck purely on principles.

Bud Schwartz said, 'Hey, you don't want to do that. We've gotta go get your money.'

'I'll find my own ride.'

'It'll look hinky, we don't show up together.'

Danny Pogue said, 'I'm not riding nowhere with a guy that throws rats on little kids. Understand?'

'What if I said I was sorry,' Bud Schwartz said. 'I'm sorry, all right? It was a shitty thing to do. I feel terrible, Danny, honest to God. I feel like a shit.'

Danny Pogue gave him a sideways look.

'I mean it,' said Bud Schwartz. 'You got me feeling so bad I got half a mind to cry. Swear to God, look here—my eyes are all watered up. For a second I was thinking of Bud, Jr., about what I'd do, some asshole threw a rat or any other damn animal at my boy. Probably kill him, that's what I'd do.'

As he spun through this routine, Bud Schwartz was thinking: The things I do to keep him steady.

And it seemed to work. In no time Danny Pogue said, 'It's all right, Bud. Least nobody got hurt.'

'That's true.'

'But don't scare no more little kids, understand?'

Bud Schwartz said, 'I won't, Danny. That's a promise.'

Ten minutes later, stopped at a traffic light in Cutler Ridge, Danny Pogue turned in the passenger seat and said, 'Hey, it just hit me.'

He was grinning so wide that you could count all the spaces where teeth used to be.

'What?' said Bud Schwartz.

'I remember you told me that Bud Schwartz wasn't your real name. You said your real name was Mickey Reilly.'

'Mike. Mike Reilly,' said Bud Schwartz, thinking, Here we go.

'Okay, then how could you have a kid named Bud, Jr.?'

'Well—'

'If your name's Mike.'

'Simple. I changed the boy's name when I changed mine.'

Danny Pogue looked skeptical. Bud Schwartz said, 'A boy oughta have the same name as his daddy, don't you agree?'

'So his real name was—'

'Mike, Jr. Now it's Bud, Jr.'

'You say so,' said Danny Pogue, grinning again, a jack-o'-lantern with volcanic acne.

'What, you don't believe me?'

'No, I don't believe you,' said Danny Pogue, 'but it was a damn good story. Whatever your fucking name is.'

'Bud is just fine. Bud Schwartz. And let's not fight no more, we're gonna be rich.'

Danny Pogue got two beers out of the Styrofoam cooler in the back of the cab. He popped one of the cans for his partner and handed it to him. 'I still can't believe they're payin' us ten grand apiece to steal a boxful of rats.'

'This is Miami,' said Bud Schwartz. 'Maybe they're voodoo rats. Or maybe they're fulla dope. I heard where they smuggle coke in French rubbers, so why not rats.'

Danny Pogue lifted the box from behind the front seat and placed it carefully on his lap. He leaned down and put his ear to the lid. 'Wonder how many's in there,' he said.

Bud Schwartz shrugged. 'Didn't ask.'

The den box was eighteen inches deep, and twice the size of a briefcase. It was made of plywood, painted dark green, with small hinged doors on each end. Air holes had been drilled through the side panels; the holes were no bigger than a dime, but somehow one of the animals had managed to squeeze out. Then it had scaled the front seat and perched on Danny Pogue's headrest, where it had balanced on its hind legs and wiggled its velvety snout in the air. Laughing, Bud Schwartz had deftly snatched it by the tail and dangled it in his partner's face. Over Danny Pogue's objections, Bud Schwartz had toyed with the rodent for six or seven miles, until he'd spotted the red convertible coming the other way down the road. Then he had said, 'Watch this,' and had tossed the animal out the window, into the passing car.

Now Danny Pogue lifted the green box off his lap and said, 'Sure don't weigh much.'

Bud Schwartz chuckled. 'You want a turn, is that it? Well, go ahead then, grab one.'

'But I don't wanna get bit.'

'You got to do it real fast, way I did. Hurry now, here comes one of them Winnebagos. I'll slow down when we go by.'

Danny Pogue said, 'The top of this box ain't even locked.'

'So what're you waiting for?' said his partner. 'Pop goes the weasel.'

After the rat attack, the Whelper family rode in edgy silence until they arrived at the Amazing Kingdom of Thrills. They parked the

red LeBaron in the Mr. Bump-a-Rump lot, Section Jellybean,
and took the tram to the main gate. There they came upon a
chaotic scene: police cars, an ambulance, TV trucks, news photographers. The ticket turnstiles were all blocked.

'Swell,' said Terry Whelper. 'Beautiful.'

'Maybe they're filming a movie,' his wife suggested. 'Maybe
it's not real.'

But it was. The center of attention was a supremely tanned
young man in a blue oxford shirt with a dark red club tie,
loosened fashionably at the throat. Once all the TV lights were
on, the man started to read from a typed sheet of paper. He said
he was a spokesperson for the company.

'This is a message for all our friends and visitors to the Amazing
Kingdom of Thrills,' the man began. 'We deeply regret the
incident that disturbed today's Summerfest celebration. We are
proud of our security arrangements here at the park, and proud
of our safety record. Up until today, there had been—and I say
this unequivocally—no serious crimes committed within our
friendly gates.'

In the swell of the crowd, Terry Whelper felt his wife's chin
digging into his shoulder blade. 'What do you suppose he's
talking about?' she said.

The man in the oxford shirt continued: 'We believe there was
no way to anticipate, much less prevent, what happened this
afternoon in the Rare Animal Pavilion.'

Terry Whelper said, 'This oughta be good.' A large woman
wearing a damp cotton blouse and a Nikkormat around her neck
turned and shot him a dirty look.

The man at the TV microphones was saying, 'At approximately
2.15 p.m., two men entered the compound and attacked one of
the wildlife exhibits with a sledgehammer, breaking the glass.
One of our park employees courageously tried to stop the
intruders, but was overpowered and beaten. The two men then
grabbed a box of specimens from the exhibit arena and ran. In
the confusion, the suspects managed to escape from the park,
apparently by mingling with ordinary tourists aboard the Jungle
Jerry Amazon Boat Cruise.'

Jason Whelper said, 'Specimens? What kinda specimens?'

Jennifer announced, 'I don't want to go on the Jungle Jerry anymore.'

Terry Whelper told the children to be quiet and listen. The tanned man in the blue shirt was saying that the park employee who had so bravely tried to stop the crime was being rushed to the hospital for X-rays.

'Hey, look!' said Jason, pointing.

Somebody in an oversized polyester animal outfit was being loaded into the ambulance.

'That's Robbie Raccoon!' cried Jennifer Whelper. 'He must be the one who got hurt.'

All around them in the crowd, other tourist children began to whimper and sniffle at the sight of Robbie Raccoon on the stretcher. Jason swore he saw some blood on Robbie Raccoon's nose.

'No, he's going to be fine,' said Gerri Whelper. 'See there, he's waving at us!'

And, indeed, whoever was inside the Robbie Raccoon costume managed a weak salute to the crowd before the ambulance doors swung closed.

'It's gotta be ninety-eight degrees out here,' marveled Terry Whelper. 'You'd think they'd get the poor guy out of that raccoon getup.'

Terry Whelper's wife whispered urgently to the nape of his neck, 'Not in front of Jennifer. She thinks he's real.'

'Oh, you're kidding,' Terry said.

Under the TV lights, the tan young spokesperson finally was revealing what had been stolen in the daring robbery.

'As many of you know,' he said, 'the Amazing Kingdom of Thrills is home to several endangered varieties of wildlife. Unfortunately, the animals that were stolen this afternoon are among the rarest, and most treasured, in our live-animal collection. In fact, they were believed to be the last two surviving specimens of the blue-tongued mango vole.' Here the handsome spokesman paused dramatically. Then: 'The animals were being kept here in a specially climatized habitat, in the hope that they might breed and keep the species alive. Tragically, that dream came to an end this afternoon.'

'Mango voles!' exclaimed Jason Whelper. 'Dad, did you hear? Maybe that's what landed in our car. Maybe those guys in the pickup truck were the crooks!'

Terry Whelper took his son by the arm and led him back toward the tram, away from the tourist crowd. Gerri and Jennifer followed steadfastly.

Gerri whispered to her husband: 'What do you think? Maybe Jason is right.'

'I don't know what to think. You were the one who wanted to come to Florida.'

Jason cut in: 'Dad, there was only two of those mangos left in the whole-wide world. And we shot one!'

'No, we didn't. The policeman did.'

'But we told him to!'

Terry Whelper said, 'Be quiet, son. We didn't know.'

'Your father's right,' added Gerri. 'How were we to know?'

Jennifer hugged her mother fiercely around the waist. 'I'm so scared—can we drive to Epcot instead?'

'Excellent idea,' said Terry Whelper. Like a cavalry commander, he raised his right arm and cocked two fingers toward the parking lot. 'Everybody back to the car.'

2

As soon as Charles Chelsea got back to the Publicity Department, he took a poll of the secretaries. 'How was I?' he asked. 'How'd I do? What about the necktie?'

The secretaries told Chelsea that he looked terrific on television, that loosening the necktie was a nifty touch, that overall it was quite a solid performance. Chelsea asked if Mr. Kingsbury had called, but the secretaries said he hadn't.

'Wonder why not,' said Chelsea.

'He's playing golf up at Ocean Reef.'

'Yeah, but he's got a cellular. He could've called.' Chelsea told one of the secretaries to get Joe Winder, and then went into his private office and closed the door.

Ten minutes later, when Joe Winder got there, Charles Chelsea was watching himself on the VCR, reliving the press conference.

'Whadja think?' he asked, motioning at the television screen in the cabinet.

'I missed it,' said Joe Winder.

'You missed it? It was your bloody speech—how'd you miss it?'

'I heard you were dynamite.'

Charles Chelsea broke into a grin. 'Yeah? Who said?'

'Everybody,' lied Joe Winder. 'They said you're another Mario Cuomo.'

'Well, your speech had something to do with it.'

It wasn't a speech, Winder thought; it was a *statement*. Forty lines, big deal.

'It was a great speech, Joe,' Chelsea went on, 'except for one part. *Specially climatized habitat.* That's a mouthful. Maybe we should've tried something else.' With pursed lips he repeated the culprit phrase: 'Climatized habitat—when I was trying to say it, I accidentally spit on that girl from Channel 10. The cute one. Next time be more careful, okay? Don't sneak in any zingers without me knowing.'

Joe Winder said, 'I was in a hurry.' The backs of his eyeballs were starting to throb. Sinus headache: Chelsea always gave him one. But Winder had to admit, the guy looked like a million bucks in an oxford shirt. He looked like a vice president in charge of public relations, which he was.

Chelsea was saying, 'I don't even know what it means, climatized habitat.'

'That's the beauty of it,' Winder said.

'Now, now.' Chelsea wagged a well-tanned finger. 'None of that, Joey. There's no place for cynics here at the Amazing Kingdom. You know what Kingsbury says.'

'Yeah. We're all little kids.' Winder kneaded his skull with both hands, trying to squeeze out the pain.

'Children,' Charles Chelsea said. He turned off the VCR and spun his chair to face Joe Winder. 'The moment we walk through that gate, we're all children. We see the world through children's eyes; we cry children's tears, we laugh children's laughter. We're all innocent again, Joe, and where there's innocence there can't be cynicism. Not here in the Amazing Kingdom.'

Joe Winder said, 'You're giving me a fucking headache. I hope you're happy.'

Charles Chelsea's blue eyes narrowed and darkened. 'Look, we hired you because you're good and you're fast. But this isn't a big-city newsroom, you can't use that type of coarse language. Children don't talk like that, Joe. That's gutter language.'

'Sorry,' said Winder, concealing his amusement. Gutter language, that was a good one.

'When's the last time you heard a child say that word?'

'Which word, Charlie?'

'You know. The 'F' word.'

'I've heard children say it. Plenty of times.'

'Not here, you haven't.' Charles Chelsea sat up straight, trying to radiate authority. 'This is a major event for us, Joey. We've had a robbery on the premises. Felons invaded the theme park. Somebody could've been hurt.'

'Rat-nappers,' Winder remarked. 'Not exactly Ted Bundy.'

'Hey,' Chelsea said, tapping a lacquered fingernail on the desk. 'Hey, this is serious. Mr. X is watching very closely to see how we do. All of us, Joe, all of us in Publicity are on red alert until this thing blows over. We mishandle it, and it blows up into a story about crime at the Amazing Kingdom. If we can spin it around, it's a story about a crime against Nature. Nature with a capital 'N.' The annihilation of an entire species. Where's your notebook?'

'Downstairs, on my desk.'

'Listen, you're my ace in the hole. Whatever gets dumped in my lap gets dumped in yours.'

Joe Winder's sinuses hurt so much he thought his eyeballs must be leaking from the inside. He didn't want to be Chelsea's ace in the hole.

Chelsea said, 'And, Joe, while we're at it, what'd I tell you about the hair? No braids.'

'But it's all the rage,' Winder said.

'Get it cut before Kingsbury sees you. Please, Joe, you look like a Navajo nightmare.'

'Nice talk, Charlie.'

'Sit down,' said Chelsea, 'and put on your writing cap.'

'I'd love to look as spiffy as you, but you bought up all the oxford shirts in Miami. Either that or you wear the same one every day.'

Chelsea wasn't listening. 'Before we begin, there's some stuff you need to know.'

'Like what?'

'Like their names.'

'Whose names?'

'The voles,' Charles Chelsea said. 'Vance and Violet—two helpless, adorable, fuzzy little furballs. Mated for life. The last of their species, Joey.'

With a straight face, Winder repeated the names of the missing creatures. 'Vance and Violet Vole. That's lovely.' He glanced at his wristwatch, and saw that it was half past five. 'Charlie,' he said, 'you don't happen to have any Darvons?'

Chelsea said, 'I wish you were writing this stuff down.'

'What the hell for?'

'For the story. The story of how Francis X. Kingsbury tried everything in his power to save the blue-tongued mango voles from extinction.'

'Only to be thwarted by robbers?'

'You got it,' said Charles Chelsea. 'Stay late if necessary and take a comp day next week—I need a thousand words by tomorrow morning. I promised Corporate a press kit.' He stood up and waited for Joe Winder to do the same. 'Get with Koocher for more background on the missing animals. He's got reams of pictures, too, in case you need inspiration. By the way, did you ever get to see them?'

Winder felt oddly detached. 'The voles? No, not in person,' he said. 'I wasn't even aware they had actual names.'

'They do now.'

At the door, Charles Chelsea winked and shook Joe Winder's hand. 'You know, Joe, some people in the organization weren't too thrilled when we brought you aboard. I mean, after what happened up at Disney.'

Winder nodded politely. Chelsea's hand felt moist and lifeless, like a slab of cold grouper.

'But, by God, I knew you'd be fine. That speech today was masterful, Joey, a classic.'

'A classic.'

'I need you on this one. The other kids are fine, they can turn a phrase. But they're right out of school, most of them, and they're not ready for something so big. For this I need somebody with scars. Combat experience.'

With effort, Joe Winder said, 'Guess I'm your man.'

Charles Chelsea chucked him on the arm and opened the door.

'What about a reward?' Winder asked. 'In the press release, should I say we're offering a reward?'

Thinking about it, Chelsea nearly rubbed the tan off his chin. 'I guess it couldn't hurt,' he said finally. 'What do you think?'

'For two rats? Ten grand is good.'

'Voles, Joe. Don't ever say rats. And five grand is plenty.'

Winder shrugged. 'The park netted forty-two million dollars last year. I know a few reporters who'd be happy to remind us.'

'All right, go for ten,' said Charles Chelsea. 'But don't overplay it. Otherwise every geek in Miami is going to show up at the gate with shoe boxes full of God knows what.'

The thought of it made Joe Winder smile for the first time all day.

One of the few things Winder liked about his new job was the golf cart he got to drive around the Amazing Kingdom of Thrills. It was a souped-up Cushman with an extra set of twelve-volts, and headlights scavenged off a real Jeep. It was the closest thing to a company car that Joe Winder had ever had, and sometimes (especially on that long downhill stretch between Magic Mansion and the Wet Willy) he could stomp on the tiny accelerator and forget what exactly he did for a living.

At night Joe Winder tried to drive more carefully, because it was harder to watch out for the tourists. The tourists at the Amazing Kingdom seldom paid attention to where they were going; they wandered and weaved, peered and pointed. And who could blame them? There were so many colorful and entertaining distractions. Before Charles Chelsea had given Joe Winder the keys to the Cushman, he had warned him to be wary when driving near the tourists. 'Whatever you do, don't hit one,' Chelsea had said. 'If you're going to crash, aim for a building,' he had advised, 'or even a park employee. Anything but a paying customer.'

So Joe Winder drove with extra caution in the golf cart at night. He arrived at the Rare Animal Pavilion shortly after eight, and parked in the back. Dr. Will Koocher, the vole man, was waiting inside with handouts and glossy photographs. Winder sat on a lab stool and skimmed the material.

Koocher said, 'We kept the information fairly general. They tell me the pictures usually go over big.'

As Winder studied the photographs, he said, 'Cute little buggers.'

'They're just rodents,' the doctor noted, without malice.

'You don't understand,' Winder said, 'Cuteness is vital for a story like this.' He explained how newspapers and television stations got much more excited about animal stories when the animal came across as cuddly and lovable. 'I'm not saying it's good or bad, but that's the way it is.'

Will Koocher nodded. 'Like with the manatees—everybody wants to save the manatees, but nobody gives a hoot about the poor crocodiles.'

'Because they're not particularly cute,' Winder said. 'Who wants to hug a reptile?'

'I see your point.' Will Koocher was a gaunt young man with the longest neck that Joe Winder had ever seen. He seemed painfully earnest and shy, and Winder liked him immediately.

'I'll tell you what I can,' Koocher said, 'but I've only been here a month.'

Like everything else at the Amazing Kingdom, the Vole Project had begun as a scheme to compete with Walt Disney World. Years earlier, Disney had tried to save the dusky seaside sparrow, a small marsh bird whose habitat was being wiped out by overdevelopment along Florida's coastline. With much fanfare, Disney had unveiled a captive-breeding program for the last two surviving specimens of the dusky. Unfortunately, the last two surviving specimens were both males, and even the wizards of Disney could not induce the scientific miracle of homosexual procreation. Eventually the sparrow fell to extinction, but the Disney organization won gobs of fawning publicity for its conservation efforts.

Not to be outdone (although he invariably was), Francis X. Kingsbury had selected another endangered species and commanded that his staff save it, ASAP. And so the Vole Project was born.

Koocher had gotten the phone call while finishing his thesis at Cornell. 'I'd published two field studies on the genus *Microtus*, so I suppose that's where they got my name. Anyway, this guy Chelsea calls and asks if I'd heard of *Microtus mango*, and I said no, all my work was on the northern species. He sent me a scientific paper that had been published, and offered me a job. Forty grand a year.'

'That's good money right out of school.'

'Tell me about it. I burned up the interstate getting down here.'

'And that's when you met Violet and Vance.'

'Who's that?'

'The voles,' Winder said. 'They've got names now.'

'Really?' Will Koocher looked doubtful. 'I always called them Male One and Female One.'

'Not anymore. Kingsbury's got big plans, PR-wise. The little mango cuties are going to be famous—don't be surprised if the networks show up tomorrow.'

'Is that so,' Koocher said, with not the wildest enthusiasm. Winder sensed that the scientist disapproved of anthropomorphizing rodents, so he decided to lay off the Vance-and-Violet routine. Instead he asked about the tongue.

'Well, it really is blue,' Koocher said stiffly. 'Remarkably blue.'

'Could I say indigo?' Joe Winder was taking notes.

'Yeah,' said Koocher, 'that's about right.' He started to say something more, but caught himself.

Joe Winder asked: 'So what killed off the rest of them? Was it disease?'

'No, same old story. The encroachment of mankind.' Koocher unfolded a map that illustrated how the mango vole had once ranged from the Middle Keys up to Palm Beach. As the coastline surrendered to hotels, subdivisions and condominiums, the voles' territory shrank. 'They tell me the last known colony was here, on North Key Largo. One of Kingsbury's foremen found it in

1988, but so did a hungry barn owl. They were lucky to save the two that they did.'

'And they mated for life?' said Winder.

Koocher seemed amused. 'Who told you that?'

'Chelsea.'

'That figures. Voles don't mate for life. They mate for fun, and they mate with just about anything that resembles another vole.'

Winder said, 'Then here's another dumb question: Why were there only two in our exhibit? They'd been together, what, a year? So where're all the bouncing baby voles?'

Edgily, Koocher said, 'That's been our biggest disappointment.'

'I did some reading up on it,' Winder said. 'With your typical *Microtus*, the female gives birth every two months. Each litter's got eight or nine babies—at that rate, you could replenish the whole species in a year.'

Will Koocher shifted uncomfortably. 'Female One was not receptive,' he said. 'Do you understand what that means?'

'Do I ever.'

'This was an extreme case. The female nearly killed the male on several occasions. We had to hire a Wackenhut to watch the cage.'

'A guard?' said Joe Winder.

'To make sure she didn't hurt him.'

Winder swallowed a laugh. Apparently, Koocher saw no humor in the story. He said, 'I felt sorry for the little guy. The female was much larger, and extremely hostile. Every time the male would attempt to mount her, she would attack.'

Joe Winder put his notebook away. He'd think of a way to write around the reproduction question.

Koocher said: 'The female vole wasn't quite right.'

'In what way?'

But Koocher was staring past him. Winder turned and saw Charles Chelsea on the other side of the glass door. Chelsea gave a chipper, three-fingered salute and disappeared.

The doctor said, 'Now's not a terrific time to get into all this. Can we talk later?'

'You bet. I'll be in the publicity office.'

'No, not here. Can I call you at home in a day or two?'

Winder said sure. 'But I've got to write the press release tonight. If there's something I ought to know, please tell me before I make an ass of myself.'

Koocher stood up and smoothed the breast of his lab coat. 'That business about the networks coming—were you serious?'

'Cute sells,' Winder said. 'You take an offbeat animal story on a slow news day, we're talking front page.'

'Christ.' Koocher sighed.

'Hey, I'm sorry,' Winder said. He hadn't meant to come off as such a coldhearted prick. 'I know what these little critters meant to you.'

Will Koocher smiled ruefully. He folded the habitat map and put it away. He looked tired and sad, and Winder felt bad for him. 'It's all right,' the young scientist said. 'They were doomed, no matter what.'

'We're all doomed,' said Joe Winder, 'if you really think about it.' Which he tried not to.

Bud Schwartz parked the pickup truck under an immense ficus tree. He told Danny Pogue not to open the doors right away, because of all the mosquitoes. The insects had descended in a sibilant cloud, bouncing off the windows and the hood and the headlights.

'I bet we don't have no bug spray,' said Danny Pogue.

Bud Schwartz pointed at the house. 'On the count of three, make a run for it.'

Danny Pogue remarked that the old place was dark. 'She saving on the electricity, or what? I bet she's not even home. I bet she was hoping we got caught, so she wouldn't have to pay us.'

'You got no faith,' said Bud Schwartz. 'You're the most negative fucking person I ever met. That's why your skin's broke out all the time—all those negative thoughts is like a poison in your bloodstream.'

'Wait a minute, now. Everybody gets pimples.'

Bud Schwartz said, 'You're thirty-one years old. Tell me that's normal.'

'Do we got bug spray or not?'

'No.' Bud Schwartz unlocked his door. 'Now let's go—one, two, three!'

They burst out of the pickup and bolted for the house, flailing at mosquitoes as they ran. When they got inside the screened porch, the two men took turns swatting the insects off each other. A light came on, and Molly McNamara poked out of the door. Her white hair was up in curlers, her cheeks were slathered in oily yellow cream and her broad, pointy-shouldered frame was draped in a blue terry-cloth bathrobe.

'Get inside,' she said to the two men.

Immediately Bud Schwartz noticed how grim the woman looked. The curlers, cream and bathrobe didn't help.

The house was all mustiness and shadows, made darker and damper by the ubiquitous wood paneling. The living room smelled of jasmine, or some other old-woman scent. It reminded Bud Schwartz of his grandmother's sewing room.

Molly McNamara sat down in a rocker. Bud Schwartz and Danny Pogue just stood there like the hired help they were.

'Where are they?' Molly demanded. 'Where's the box?'

Danny Pogue looked at Bud Schwartz, who said, 'They got away.'

Molly folded her hands across her lap. She said, 'You're lying to me.'

'No, ma'am.'

'Then tell me what happened.'

Before Bud Schwartz could stop him, Danny Pogue said, 'There was holes in the box. That's how they got out.'

Molly McNamara's right hand slipped beneath her bathrobe and came out holding a small black pistol. Without saying a word she shot Danny Pogue twice in the left foot. He fell down, screaming, on the smooth pine floor. Bud Schwartz couldn't believe it; he tried to speak, but there was no air in his lungs.

'You boys are lying,' Molly said. She got up from the rocker and left the room. She came back with a towel, chipped ice, bandages and a roll of medical adhesive tape. She told Bud Schwartz to patch up his partner before the blood got all over everything. Bud Schwartz knelt on the floor next to Danny Pogue and tried to calm him. Molly sat down and started rocking.

'The towel is for his mouth,' she said, 'so I don't have to listen to all that yammering.'

And it was true, Danny Pogue's wailing was unbearable, even allowing for the pain. It reminded Bud Schwartz of the way his first wife had sounded during the thrashings of childbirth.

Molly said, 'It's been all over the news, so at least I know that you went ahead and did it. I suppose I'm obliged to pay up.'

Bud Schwartz was greatly relieved; she wouldn't pay somebody she was about to kill. The thought of being murdered by a seventy-year-old woman in pink curlers was harrowing on many levels.

'Tell me if I'm wrong,' Molly said. 'Curiosity got the best of you, right? You opened the box, the animals escaped.'

'That's about the size of it,' said Bud Schwartz, wrapping a bandage around Danny Pogue's foot. He had removed the sneaker and the sock, and examined the wounds. Miraculously (or maybe by design) both bullets had missed the bones, so Danny Pogue was able to wiggle all his toes. When he stopped whimpering, Bud Schwartz removed the towel from his mouth.

'So you think they're still alive,' Molly said.

'Why not? Who'd be mean enough to hurt 'em?'

'This is important,' said Molly. The pistol lay loose on her lap, looking as harmless as a macramé.

Danny Pogue said, 'We didn't kill them things, I swear to God. They just scooted out of the damn truck.'

'They're awful fast,' added Bud Schwartz.

'Oh, please,' said Molly McNamara, shaking her head. Even Danny Pogue picked up on the sarcasm.

'We didn't know there was only two,' he said. 'We thought there must be a whole bunch in a box that size. That's how come we wasn't so worried when they got away—see, we thought there was more.'

Molly started rocking a little faster. The rocking chair didn't squeak a bit on the varnished pine. She said, 'I'm very disappointed in the both of you.'

Bud Schwartz helped his partner limp to an ottoman. All he wanted was to get the money and get the hell out of this spooky old house, away from this crazy witch.

'Here's the really bad news,' said Molly McNamara. 'It's your truck—only about a thousand people saw you drive away. Now, I don't know if they got the license tag, but they sure as hell got a good description. It's all over the TV.'

'Shit,' said Bud Schwartz.

'So you're going to have to keep a low profile for a while.'

Still breathing heavily, Danny Pogue said, 'What's that mean?'

Molly stopped rocking and sat forward. 'For starters, say good-bye to the pickup truck. Also, you can forget about going home. If the police got your tag, they'll be waiting.'

'I'll take my chances,' said Bud Schwartz.

'No, you won't,' said Molly. 'I'll give you a thousand dollars each. You'll get the rest in two weeks, if things die down. Meanwhile, I've arranged a place for you boys to stay.'

'Here?' asked Danny Pogue in a fretful, pain-racked voice.

'No, not here,' Molly said. 'Not on your life.'

She stood up from the rocker. The pistol disappeared again into a fuzzy pocket of the blue robe. 'Your foot's going to be fine,' she announced to Danny Pogue. 'I hope I made my point.'

The bafflement on the two men's faces suggested otherwise.

Molly McNamara said, 'I chose you for a reason.'

'Come on,' said Bud Schwartz, 'we're just burglars.'

'And don't you ever forget it,' Molly said.

Danny Pogue couldn't believe she was talking to them this way. He couldn't believe he was being terrorized by an old lady in a rocking chair.

'There's something else you should know,' said Molly McNamara. 'There are others.'

Momentarily Bud Schwartz's mind had stuck on that thousand dollars she'd mentioned. He had been thinking: Screw the other nine, just grab the grand and get lost. Now she was saying something about others—what others?

'Anything happens to me,' Molly said, 'there's others that know who you are. Where you live. Where you hang out. Everything.'

'I don't get it,' muttered Danny Pogue.

'Burglars get shot sometimes,' Molly McNamara said. 'Nobody says boo about it, either. Nobody gets arrested or investigated or anything else. In this country, you kill a burglar and the Kiwanis gives you a plaque. That's the point I was trying to make.'

Danny Pogue turned to Bud Schwartz, who was staring down at his partner's swollen foot and wondering if it was too late to make a run for it. Finally he said, 'Lady, we're very sorry about your animals.'

'They're not my animals,' said Molly, 'any more than you are.'

3

At half past ten Joe Winder went down to The Catacombs, the underground network of service roads that ran beneath the Amazing Kingdom of Thrills. It was along these winding cart paths, discreetly out of view from visitors, that the food, merchandise, money and garbage were moved throughout the sprawling amusement park. It was also along these secret subterranean passageways that the kiddie characters traveled, popping up suddenly at strategic locations throughout the Amazing Kingdom and imploring tourists to snap their picture. No customers ('guests' was the designated term) ever were allowed to venture into The Catacombs, lest they catch a glimpse of something that might tarnish their image of the Amazing Kingdom—a dog rooting through a dumpster, for example. Or one of Uncle Ely's Elves smoking a joint.

Which is what Joe Winder saw when he got to the bottom of the stairs.

'I'm looking for Robbie Raccoon,' he said to the elf, who wasn't particularly jolly or gnomelike.

The elf belched blue smoke and asked which Robbie Raccoon he was looking for, since there were three.

'The one who was on duty this afternoon,' Winder said. 'The one who fought with the rat robbers.'

The big elf pointed with the smoldering end of the joint. 'Okay, there's a locker room on the west side. Just follow the orange signs.' He took another drag. 'I'd offer you a hit, but I got this nasty chest virus. Hate to pass it along.'

'Sure,' said Joe Winder. 'No problem.'

The lockers were at the end of a damp concrete tunnel that smelled of stale laundry and ammonia. Robbie Raccoon was straddling the bench, trying to unzip his head. Winder introduced himself, and explained that he was from the Publicity Department.

'I'm writing a press release about what happened earlier today,' he said. 'A few quick questions is all.'

'Fire away,' said Robbie Raccoon. The words came out muffled, from a small opening in the neck of the costume.

Winder said, 'I can barely hear you.'

With a grunt Robbie Raccoon removed his head, which was as large as a beach ball. Joe Winder was startled by what he saw beneath it: long shimmering blond hair, green eyes and mascara. Robbie Raccoon was a woman.

She said, 'If you're going to make a joke, get it over with.'

'No, I wasn't.'

'Don't think this is my life ambition or anything.'

'Of course not,' said Joe Winder.

The woman said her name was Carrie Lanier. 'And I got my SAG card,' she said, still somewhat defensive. 'That's the only reason I took this stupid job. I'm going to be an actress.'

Mindlessly Winder said, 'You've got to start somewhere.'

'Darn right.'

He waited for Carrie Lanier to remove the rest of the raccoon outfit, but she didn't. He took out his notebook and asked her to describe what had happened at the Rare Animal Pavilion.

Carrie shrugged in an exaggerated way, as if she were still in character. 'It was two men, we're talking white trash. One of them has a sledgehammer, and they're both walking real fast. I start to follow, don't ask me why—I just had a hunch. All of a sudden the one with the hammer smashes out the glass in one of the exhibits.'

'And you tried to stop him?'

'Yeah, I jumped the guy. Climbed on his back. He turned around and clobbered me pretty solid. Thank God for this.' Carrie knocked on the crown of the raccoon head, which was propped face-up on the bench. Her fist made a sharp hollow sound. 'Chicken wire, plaster and Kevlar,' she explained. 'They say it's bulletproof.'

Joe Winder wrote this down, even though Charles Chelsea

would never let him use it in the press release. At the Amazing Kingdom, each publicity announcement was carefully purged of all intriguing details. Winder was having a tough time kicking the habit of taking good notes.

Carrie Lanier said, 'He knocked me down pretty hard, but that's about it. There was a tour group from Taiwan, Korea, someplace like that. They helped me off the ground, but by then the two dirtbags were long gone. I could've done without the ambulance ride, but Risk Management said I had to.'

'Can I say you suffered a slight head injury?' Joe Winder asked, pen poised.

'No,' said Carrie Lanier. 'As soon as the X-rays came out negative, they hauled me back to work. I'm fine.'

That wouldn't go over well with Charles Chelsea; the vole story was infinitely more dramatic if a park employee had been wounded in the rescue attempt.

'Not even a headache?' Winder persisted.

'Yeah, I've got a headache,' Carrie said. 'I've always got a headache. Take a whiff of this place.' She stood up and yanked on the fluffy striped raccoon tail, which was attached to the rump of the costume by a Velcro patch. The tail made a ripping sound when Carrie took it off. She tossed it in her locker and said, 'Why would anyone steal rats?'

'Voles,' said Joe Winder.

'The guys who did it, boy, what a pair. Scum of the earth.'

Again Winder didn't bother to write this down.

'It's crazy,' said Carrie Lanier. She reached beneath her left armpit and found, deep in the fur, another zipper. Carefully she unzipped the costume lengthwise down to her ankle. She did the same on the other side. As she stepped out of the animal outfit, Winder saw that she was wearing only a bra and panties. He tried not to stare.

Carrie hung the costume on a pair of hooks in the locker. She said, 'This damn thing weighs a ton, I wish you'd write that down. It's about a hundred twenty degrees inside, too. OSHA made them put in air conditioners, but they're always broken.'

Winder stepped closer to examine the raccoon costume, not

Carrie Lanier in her bra (which was the type that unhooked in the front; pink with lacy cups). Winder held up the animal suit and said, 'Where's the AC?'

'In the back. Here, look.' Carrie showed him. 'The batteries last about two hours max, then forget about it. We tried to call the feds and complain—what a joke. They haven't been out here since the day Petey Possum died.'

'Do I want to hear this story?'

'Heart attack,' Carrie Lanier went on. 'This was Sessums. Billy Sessums. The very first Petey Possum. He'd been twenty-two years with Disneyland—Goofy, Pluto, you name it. Billy was a pro. He taught me plenty.'

'So what happened?'

'One of those days. Ninety-two in the shade, one twelve inside the possum suit. The AC went out, and so did Billy.' Carrie Lanier paused reflectively. 'He was an older fella but still . . .'

'I'm sorry,' said Joe Winder. He put his notebook away. He was starting to feel prickly and claustrophobic.

Carrie said, 'You're gonna put my name in the press release?'

'I'm afraid not. It's company policy not to identify the actors who portray the animal characters. Mr. Kingsbury says it would spoil the illusion for the children.'

Carrie laughed. 'Some illusion. I've had kids grab my boobs, right through the costume. One time there was a Shriner, tried to goose me in the Magic Mansion.'

Winder said, 'How'd they know you were a woman?'

'That's the scary part.' Her eyes flashed mischievously. 'What if they didn't know I was a woman? What if they thought I was a real raccoon? What would Mr. Francis X. Kingsbury say about that?' She took a pair of blue jeans out of the locker and squirmed into them. 'Anyhow, I don't want my name in any stupid press release,' she said. 'Not for this place.'

'Maybe not, but you did a brave thing,' said Winder.

As Carrie buttoned her blouse, she said, 'I don't want my folks knowing what I do. You blame me?'

'You make lots of little children happy. What's wrong with that?'

She looked at him evenly. 'You're new here, aren't you?'

'Yeah,' Joe Winder said.

'My job's crummy, but you know what? I think your job is worse.'

Joe Winder wrote the press release in forty minutes. 'Theft of Rare Animals Stuns Amazing Kingdom.' Ten paragraphs on the crime itself, with a nod to the heroics of Robbie Raccoon ('who barely escaped serious injury'). Three paragraphs of official reaction ('a sad and shocking event') from Francis X. Kingsbury, chairman and president of the park. Three grafs more of scientific background on the blue-tongued mango vole, with a suitable quote from Dr. Will Koocher. A hundred words about the $10,000 reward, and a hundred more announcing new beefed-up security precautions at the park.

Winder put the press release on Charles Chelsea's desk and went home. By the time he called Nina, it was nearly one in the morning. He dialed the number and hoped she would be the one to answer.

'Hello, sugar,' Nina said.

'It's me.'

'God, I need to talk to a real man,' she said. 'I had a fantasy that got me so hot. We were on the bow of a sailboat. Making love in the sun. I was on top. Suddenly a terrible storm came—'

'Nina, it's me!'

'—but instead of hiding in the cabin, we lashed each other to the deck and kept on doing it in the lightning and thunder. Afterwards the warm rain washed the salt off our bodies. . . .'

'For Christ's sake.'

'Joe?'

'Yeah, it's me. Why don't you ever listen?'

'Because they don't pay me to listen,' Nina said. 'They pay me to talk.'

'I wish you'd get a normal job.'

'Joe, don't start.'

Nina was a voice for one of those live dial-a-fantasy telephone services. She worked nights, which put a strain on her personal relationships. Also, every time Joe Winder called, it cost him four bucks. At least the number was easy to remember: 976-COME.

Nina said, 'What do you think about the lightning-and-thunder business? I added it to the script myself.'

'What was it before—something about whales, right?'

'Porpoises, Joe. *A school of friendly porpoises leaped and frolicked in the water while we made love. Our animal cries only seemed to arouse them.*'

Nina had a wonderful voice, Winder had to admit. 'I like the new stuff better,' he agreed. 'The storm idea is good—you wrote that yourself?'

'Don't sound so surprised.' She asked him how his day had gone, and he told her about the stolen voles.

Nina said, 'See? And you thought you were going to be bored.'

'I am bored. Most of the time.'

'Joe, it's never going to be like the old days.'

He wasn't in the mood to hear it. He said, 'How's it going with you?'

'Slow,' Nina said. 'Beverly went home early. It's just me and Miriam.'

'Any creeps call in?' Of course creeps had called—who else would bother?

'The usual jack-off artists,' Nina reported. 'They're harmless, Joe, don't worry. I just give a straight read, no moans or groans, and still they get off in about thirty seconds. I had one guy fall asleep afterwards. Snoring like a baby.'

Sometimes she talked about her job as if it were a social service, like UNICEF or Meals on Wheels.

'When will you be home?' Winder asked.

The usual, Nina said, meaning four in the morning. 'Want me to wake you up?'

'Sure.' She had loads of energy, this girl. Winder needed somebody with energy, to help him use up his own. One of the drawbacks of his high-paying bullshit PR job was that it took absolutely nothing out of him, except his pride.

Hurriedly Nina said, 'Joe, I got another call waiting.'

'Make it short and sweet.'

'I'll deal with you later, sailor boy.'

And then she hung up.

Winder couldn't sleep, so he put a Warren Zevon tape in the stereo and made himself a runny cheese omelet. He ate in the living room, near the speakers, and sat on a box because there were no chairs in the apartment. The box was filled with old newspaper clippings, his own, as well as plaques and certificates from various journalism awards that he had received over the years. The only important journalism award that wasn't in the box was the single one that impressed anybody—the Pulitzer Prize, which Joe Winder had never won.

When he was first interviewed for the publicitywriting job at the Amazing Kingdom of Thrills, Joe Winder had been asked if he'd ever gotten a Pulitzer. When he answered no, Charles Chelsea had threatened to put him on the polygraph machine.

'I never won,' Winder insisted. 'You can look it up.'

And Charles Chelsea did. A Pulitzer on the wall would have disqualified Joe Winder from the PR job just as surely as flunking a urinalysis for drugs.

'We're not in the market for aggressive, hard-bitten newshounds,' Chelsea had warned him. 'We're looking for writers with a pleasing, easygoing style. We're looking for a certain attitude.'

'I'm flexible,' Joe Winder had said. 'Especially my attitude.'

Chelsea had grilled him about the other journalism awards, then about the length of his hair, then about the thin pink scar along his jawline.

Eyeing Winder's face at close range, the publicity man had said, 'You look like a bar fighter. Did you get that scar in a fight?'

'Car accident,' Joe Winder had lied, figuring what the hell, Chelsea must've known the truth. One phone call to the newspaper, and any number of people would've been happy to drop the dime.

But Chelsea never said another word about the scar, never gave a hint that he'd even picked up the rumor. It was Joe Winder's journalism achievements that seemed to disturb the publicity man, although these concerns were ultimately outweighed by the discovery that Winder had been born and raised in Florida. The Publicity Department at the Amazing Kingdom was desperate for native talent, somebody who understood the mentality of tourists and crackers alike.

The Disney stint hadn't hurt Joe Winder's chances, either; he had worked among the enemy, and learned many of their professional secrets. So Charles Chelsea had set aside his doubts and hired him.

That was two weeks ago. It was still too early for Winder to compare the new job with the one at Disney World. Certainly Disney was slicker and more efficient than the Amazing Kingdom, but it was also more regimented and impersonal. The Disney bureaucracy, and its reach, was awesome. In retrospect Joe Winder wasn't sure how he had lasted as long as he did, six months, before he was caught having sex on Mr. Toad's Wild Ride and fired for not wearing his ID card. Winder felt especially bad that the young woman with whom he'd been dallying, a promising understudy to Cinderella, had also been dismissed over the incident; she for leaving Main Street during Mickey's Birthday Parade.

During the job interview at the Amazing Kingdom, Charles Chelsea had told him: 'You work for us, you'd better keep it in your pants, understand?'

'I've got a girlfriend now,' Joe Winder had said.

'Don't think you won't be tempted around here.'

Winder hadn't been tempted once, until today. Now he was thinking about Carrie Lanier, the fearless beauty inside a seven-foot raccoon suit.

This is what happens when you turn thirty-seven, Winder thought; the libido goes blind with fever. What else could explain his attraction to Nina? Or her attraction to him?

Being a newspaper reporter had left Joe Winder no time for such reckless attachments. Being a flack left him all the time in the world. Now that he was forbidden to write about trouble, he seemed determined to experience it.

He finished his omelet and opened a beer and slumped down on the floor, between the stereo speakers. Something had been nagging at him all afternoon, ever since the insufferable Chelsea had drafted him to help with the robbery crisis. In the push toward his deadline, it was clear to Joe Winder that none of his writing skills had eroded—his speed at the keyboard, his facile vocabulary, his smooth sense of pacing and transition. Yet something from the old days was missing.

Curiosity. The most essential and feral of reporters' instincts, the urge to pursue. It was dead. Or dying.

Two strangers had invaded a family theme park in broad daylight and kidnapped a couple of obscure rodents from an animal exhibit. Winder had thoroughly and competently reported the incident, but had made no effort to explore the fascinating possibilities. Having established the *what*, he had simply ignored the *why*.

Even by South Florida standards the crime was perverse, and the old Joe Winder would have reveled energetically in its mysteries. The new Joe Winder had merely typed up his thousand words, and gone home.

Just as he was supposed to do.

So this is how it feels, he thought. This is how it feels to sell out. On the stereo, Warren Zevon was singing about going to the Louvre museum and throwing himself against the wall. To Joe Winder it sounded like a pretty good idea.

He closed his eyes tightly and thought: Don't tell me I'm getting used to this goddamn zombie job. Then he thought: Don't tell me I'm getting drunk on one lousy beer.

He crawled across the carpet to the phone, and tried to call Nina at the service. The woman named Miriam answered instead, and launched into a complicated fantasy involving trampolines and silver ankle bracelets. Miriam was struggling so valiantly in broken English ('Ooooh, bebee, chew make me comb so many time!') that Joe Winder didn't have the heart to interrupt.

What the hell, it was only four bucks. He could certainly afford it.

4

On the morning of July 17, Danny Pogue awoke in a cold sweat, his T-shirt soaked from neck to navel. He kicked the covers off the bed and saw the lump of gauze around his foot. It wasn't a dream. He limped to the window and from there he could see everything: the Olympic-sized swimming pool, the freshly painted tennis courts, the shady shuffleboard gazebo. Everywhere he looked there were old people with snowy heads and pale legs and fruit-colored Bermuda shorts. All the men wore socks with their sandals, and all the women wore golf visors and oversized sunglasses.

'Mother of Christ,' said Danny Pogue. He hollered for his partner to come quick.

Bud Schwartz ambled in, looking settled and well rested. He was spooning out half a grapefruit, cupped in the palm of one hand. 'Do you believe this fucking place?' he said to Danny Pogue. 'What a gas.'

'We gotta get out.'

'How come?'

'Just look.' Danny Pogue pointed out the window.

'So now you got a problem with senior citizens? What—they don't have the right to have fun? Besides, there's some young people that live here, too. I saw a couple a hot ones out by the swimming pool. Major titties.'

'I don't care,' mumbled Danny Pogue.

'Hey,' Bud Schwartz said. 'She shot your foot, not your weenie.'

'Where is she?'

'Long gone. You want some lunch? She loaded up at the Publix, you should see. Steaks, chops, beer—we're set for a couple a weeks, easy.'

Danny Pogue hopped back to the bed and peeled off the damp shirt. He spotted a brand-new pair of crutches propped in the corner. He said, 'Bud, I'm gonna split. Seriously, I'm taking off.'

'I can give you ten thousand reasons not to.'

'Speaking of which.'

'She's bringing a grand for each of us, just like she promised,' said Bud Schwartz. 'Good faith money is what she called it.'

'Invisible is what I call it.'

'Hey, lighten the fuck up. She's an old lady, Danny. Old ladies never lie.' Bud Schwartz lobbed the grapefruit skin into some kind of designer wastebasket. 'What's wrong with you, man? This is like a vacation, all expenses paid. Look at this freaking condo—two bedrooms, two bathrooms. Microwave in the kitchen, Cinemax on the cable. Say what you will, the old geezer knows how to live.'

'Who is she?' Danny Pogue asked.

'Who cares?'

'I care. She shot me.'

Bud Schwartz said, 'Just some crazy, rich old broad. Don't worry about it.'

'It's not you that got shot.'

'She won't do it again, Danny. She got it out of her system.' Bud Schwartz wiped his hands on the butt of his jeans to get the grapefruit juice off. He said, 'She was pissed, that's all. On account of us losing the rats.'

Danny Pogue said, 'Well, screw that deal. I'm leaving.' He made a move for the crutches but faltered, hot and dizzy. Molly McNamara had fed him some pain pills late last night; that much he remembered.

'I don't know where you think you're going,' said Bud Schwartz. 'The truck's history.'

'I'll hitch,' said Danny Pogue woozily.

'Look in the mirror. Your own mother wouldn't pick you up. The Hell's Fucking Angels wouldn't pick you up.'

'Somebody'll stop,' Danny Pogue said. 'Especially with me on them crutches.'

'Oh, sure.'

'Maybe even some girls.' Danny Pogue eased himself back on the pillow. He took deep breaths and tried to blink away the haze in his brain.

'Have another codeine,' said Bud Schwartz. 'Here, she got a whole bottle.' He went to the kitchen and came back with a cold Busch.

Danny Pogue swallowed two more pills and slurped at the beer can noisily. He closed his eyes and said, 'She ain't never gonna pay us, Bud.'

'Sure she is,' said his partner. 'She's loaded, just look at this place. You should see the size of the TV.'

'We better get away while we can.'

'Go back to sleep,' said Bud Schwartz. 'I'll be down at the pool.'

The Mothers of Wilderness met every other Tuesday at a public library in Cutler Ridge. This week the main item on the agenda was the proposed bulldozing of seventy-three acres of mangroves to make room for the back nine of a championship golf course on the shore of North Key Largo. The Mothers of Wilderness strenuously opposed the project, and had begun to map a political strategy to obstruct it. They pursued such crusades with unflagging optimism, despite the fact that they had never succeeded in stopping a single development. Not one. The builders ignored them. Zoning boards ignored them. County commissioners listened politely, nodded intently, then ignored them, too. Of all the environmental groups fighting to preserve what little remained of Florida, the Mothers of Wilderness was regarded as the most radical and shrill and intractable. It was also, unfortunately, the smallest of the groups and thus the easiest to brush off.

Still, the members were nothing if not committed. Molly McNamara steadfastly had refused all offers to merge her organization with the Audubon Society or the Sierra Club or the Friends of the Everglades. She wanted no part of coalitions because coalitions compromised. She enjoyed being alone on the fringe, enjoyed being the loose cannon that establishment environmentalists feared. The fact that the Mothers of Wilderness was politically impotent did not diminish Molly McNamara's passion, though occasionally it ate at her pride.

She ran the meetings with brusque efficiency, presiding over a membership that tended to be retired and liberal and well-to-do. For its size, the Mothers of Wilderness was exceedingly well financed; Molly knew this was why the other environmental groups wooed her, in hopes of a merger. The Mothers had bucks.

They had hired a hotshot Miami land-use lawyer to fight the golf course project, which was called Falcon Trace. The lawyer, whose name was Spacci, stood up at the meeting to update the Mothers on the progress of the lawsuit, which, typically, was about to be thrown out of court. The case was being heard in Monroe County—specifically, Key West—where many of the judges were linked by conspiracy or simple inbreeding to the crookedest politicians. Moreover, the zoning lawyer admitted he was having a terrible time ascertaining the true owners of the Falcon Trace property; he had gotten as far as a blind trust in Dallas, then stalled.

Molly McNamara thanked Spacci for his report and made a motion to authorize another twenty thousand dollars for legal fees and investigative expenses. It passed unanimously.

After the meeting, Molly took the lawyer aside and said, 'Next time I want to see some results. I want the names of these bastards.'

'What about the lawsuit?'

'File a new one,' Molly said. 'You ever considered going federal?'

'How?' asked Spacci. 'On what grounds?'

Pinching his elbow, Molly led him to an easel behind the rostrum. Propped on the easel was an aerial map of North Key Largo. Molly pointed and said, 'See? There's where they want the golf course. And right here is a national wildlife refuge. That's your federal jurisdiction, Counselor.'

The lawyer plucked a gold pen from his breast pocket and did some pointing of his own. 'And right here, Ms. McNamara, is a two-thousand-acre amusement park that draws three million tourists every year. We'd be hard pressed to argue that one lousy golf course would be more disruptive to the habitat than what's already there—a major vacation resort.'

Molly snapped, 'You're the damn attorney. Think of something.'

Bitterly she remembered the years she had fought the Kingsbury project; the Mothers of Wilderness had been the only group that had never given up. Audubon and the others had realized immediately that protest was futile; the prospect of a major theme park to compete with Disney World carried an orgasmic musk to local chambers of commerce. The most powerful of powerful civic leaders clung to the myth that Mickey Mouse was responsible for killing the family tourist trade in South Florida, strangling the peninsula so that all southbound station wagons stopped in Orlando. What did Miami have to offer as competition? Porpoises that could pitch a baseball with their blowholes? Wisecracking parrots on unicycles? Enjoyable diversions, but scarcely in the same high-tech league with Disney. The Mouse's sprawling self-contained empire sucked tourists' pockets inside out; they came, they spent until there was nothing left to spend; then they went home *happy*. To lifelong Floridians it was a dream concept: fleecing a snowbird in such a way that he came back for more. Astounding! So when Francis X. Kingsbury unveiled his impressive miniature replica of the Amazing Kingdom of Thrills—the Wet Willy water flume, the Magic Mansion, Orky the Killer Whale, Jungle Jerry, and so on—roars of exultation were heard from Palm Beach to Big Pine. The only cry of dismay came from the Mothers of Wilderness, who were (as usual) ignored.

'No golf course,' Molly told Spacci the lawyer, 'and no more chickenshit excuses from you.' She sent him away with the wave of a blue-veined hand.

After the rank and file had gone home, Molly gathered the board of directors in the back of the library. Five women and two men, all nearly as gray as Molly, they sat in molded plastic chairs and sipped herbal tea while Molly told them what had happened.

It was a bizarre and impossible scheme, but no one asked Molly why she had done it. They knew why. In a fussy tone, one of the Mothers said: 'This time you went too far.'

'It's under control,' Molly insisted.

'Except for the voles. They're not under control.'

Another Mother asked: 'Any chance of finding them?'

'You never know,' said Molly.

'Horseshit,' said the first Mother. 'They're gone for good. Dead, alive, it doesn't matter if we can't locate the damn things.'

Molly said, 'Please. Keep your voice down.'

The second Mother: 'What about these two men? Where are they now?'

'My condo,' Molly replied. 'Up at Eagle Ridge.'

'Lord have mercy.'

'That's enough,' said Molly sharply. 'I said it's under control, and it's under control.'

A silence fell over the small group. No one wished to challenge her authority, but this time things had really gotten out of hand. This time there was a chance they could all go to jail. 'I'll have some more tea,' the first Mother said finally, 'and then I'd love to hear your new plan. You do have one?'

'Of course I do,' said Molly McNamara. 'For heaven's sake.'

When Joe Winder got to work, Charles Chelsea was waiting in yet another blue oxford shirt. He was sitting on the edge of Winder's desk in a pose of casual superiority. A newspaper was freshly folded under one arm. 'Fine job on the press release,' Chelsea said. 'I changed a word or two, but otherwise it went out just like you wrote it.'

Calmly Joe Winder said, 'Which word or two did you change?'

'Oh, I improved Mr. Kingsbury's comments. Couple of adverbs here and there.'

'Fine.' Winder wasn't so surprised. It was well known that Chelsea invented all of Francis X. Kingsbury's quotes. Kingsbury was one of those men who rarely spoke in complete sentences. Didn't have to. For publicity purposes this made him perfectly useless and unquotable.

Chelsea said, 'I also updated the info on Robbie Raccoon. Turns out he got a mild concussion from that blow to the head.'

Winder forced a smile and set his briefcase on the desk. 'It's a she, Charlie. And she was fine when I spoke to her last night. Not even a bruise.'

Chelsea's voice took on a scolding tone. 'Joey, you know the gender rule. If it's a male character, we always refer to it with masculine pronouns—regardless of who's inside the costume. I explained all this the day you were hired. It comes straight from Mr. X. Speaking of which, weren't you supposed to get a haircut?'

'Don't be a dork, Charlie.'

'What's a dork?'

'You're not serious.'

Charles Chelsea said, 'Really, tell me. You called me a dork, I'd like to know what exactly that is.'

'It's a Disney character,' said Joe Winder. 'Daffy Dork.' He opened the briefcase and fumbled urgently for his sinus medicine. 'Anyway, Charlie, the lady in the coon suit didn't have a concussion. That's a lie, and it's a stupid lie because it's so easy to check. Some newspaper reporter is going to make a few calls and we're going to look sleazy and dishonest, all because you had to exaggerate.'

'No exaggeration,' Charles Chelsea said, stiffening. 'I spoke with Robbie Raccoon myself, first thing this morning. He said he got dizzy and sick overnight. Doctor said it's probably a concussion.'

Winder popped two pills into his mouth and said, 'You're amazing.'

'We'll have a neurologist's report this afternoon, in case anybody wants to see. Notarized, too.' Chelsea looked pleased with himself. 'Mild concussion, Joe. Don't believe me, just ask Robbie.'

'What'd you do, threaten to fire her? Bust her down to the elf patrol?'

Charles Chelsea stood up, shot his cuffs, gave Joe Winder his coldest, hardest look. 'I came down here to thank you for doing such outstanding work, and look what I get. More of your cynicism. Just because you had a rotten night, Joey, it's no reason to rain on everyone else's parade.'

Did the man really say that? Winder wondered. Did he really accuse me of raining on his parade? 'That's the only reason you're here?' Winder said. 'To thank me?'

'Well, not entirely.' Charles Chelsea removed the newspaper from under his arm, unfolded it and handed it to Joe Winder. 'Check the last three paragraphs.'

It was the story about the theft of the blue-tongued mango voles. The *Herald* had stripped it across the top of the Local News page, a feature play. 'Hey,' Winder said brightly, 'they even used one of our pictures.'

'Never mind that, just read the last three grafs.'

The newspaper story ended like this:

> An anonymous caller identifying himself as an animal-rights activist telephoned the Miami office of the Associated Press late Monday and took credit for the incident at the popular theme park. The caller claimed to be a member of the radical Wildlife Rescue Corps.
>
> 'We freed the voles because they were being exploited,' he said. 'Francis Kingsbury doesn't care about saving the species, he just wanted another stupid tourist attraction.'
>
> Officials at the Amazing Kingdom of Thrills were unavailable for comment late Monday night.

Joe Winder gave the newspaper back to Charles Chelsea and said, 'What a kick in the nuts. I'll bet the boss man is going batshit.'

'You find this amusing?'

'Don't you?' Winder asked. 'I guess not.'

'No,' said Chelsea. He refolded the newspaper and returned it to his armpit. 'What do you suggest in the way of a response?'

'I suggest we forget the fucking voles and get on with our lives.'

'This is serious.'

Winder said, 'So I was right, Kingsbury's on a tear. Then I would suggest you tell him that we're waiting to see if there's any truth to this claim. Tell him that if we say anything now, it might turn around and bite us in the rat hole.'

Chelsea started rubbing his chin, a sign of possible cognition. 'Go on,' he told Winder. 'I'm listening.'

'For instance, suppose the real Wildlife Rescue Corps calls up and denies any involvement. Hell, Charlie, there's a good chance the caller was a crank. Had nothing to do with the group. To play it safe, we don't respond for now. We say absolutely nothing.'

'But if it turns out to be true?'

'Then,' said Joe Winder, 'we express outrage that any organization, no matter how worthy its cause, would commit a violent felony and endanger the lives of innocent bystanders.'

Chelsea nodded enthusiastically; he liked what he was hearing. 'Not just any bystanders,' he said. 'Tourists.'

Winder went on: 'We would also recount Mr. Kingsbury's many philanthropic gifts to the ASPCA, the World Wildlife Fund, Save the Beavers, whatever. And we would supply plenty of testimonial quotes from eminent naturalists supporting our efforts on behalf of the endangered mango vole.'

'Excellent,' Charles Chelsea said. 'Joe, that's perfect.'

'Pure unalloyed genius,' Winder said.

'Let's hope it doesn't come to that,' Chelsea said. 'You don't want to spend the rest of the week writing about rodents. Too much like covering City Hall, right?'

Joe Winder chuckled politely. He could tell Chelsea was worried about pitching it to Kingsbury.

In a hopeful voice, Chelsea said, 'You think the guy was really just a nut? This guy who called the AP?'

'Who knows,' Winder said. 'We've certainly got our share.'

Charles Chelsea nodded hopefully. A simple nut would be fine with him, PR-wise; it's the zealots you had to worry about.

'The only thing to do is wait,' said Joe Winder. Already he could feel his sinuses drying up. He felt suddenly clearheaded, chipper, even optimistic. Maybe it was the medicine flushing his head, or maybe it was something else.

Like having a real honest-to-God story, for a change. A story getting good and hot.

Just like the old days.

5

Chelsea had a stark, irrational fear of Francis X. Kingsbury. It was not Kingsbury's physical appearance (for he was gnomish and flabby) but his volcanically profane temper that caused Chelsea so much anxiety. Kingsbury long ago had practically ceased speaking in complete sentences, but his broken exclamations could be daunting and acerbic. The words struck venomously at Charles Chelsea's insecurities, and made him tremble.

On the afternoon of July 17, Chelsea finished his lunch, threw up, flossed his teeth and walked briskly to Kingsbury's office. Kingsbury was leaning over the desk; the great man's sleeves were rolled up to reveal the famous lewd tattoo on his doughy left forearm. The other arm sparkled with a gold Robbie Raccoon wristwatch, with emerald insets. Today's surfer-blond hairpiece was longish and curly.

Kingsbury grunted at Charles Chelsea and said: 'Wildlife Rescue Corps?' He raised his hands. 'Well?'

Chelsea said, 'The group exists, but the phone call could be a crank. We're checking it out.'

'What's this exploitation—shit, we're talking about, what, some kind of rodent or such goddamn thing.'

Not even close to a quotable sentence, Chelsea thought. It was astounding—the man spoke in over-torqued, expletive-laden fragments that somehow made perfect sense. At all times, Charles Chelsea knew exactly what Francis X. Kingsbury was talking about.

The publicity man said, 'Don't worry, sir, the situation is being contained. We're ready for any contingency.'

Kingsbury made a small fist. 'Damage control,' he said.

'Our top gun,' Chelsea said. 'His name is Joe Winder, and he's a real pro. Offering the reward money was his idea, sir. The AP led with it this morning, too.'

Kingsbury sat down. He fingered the florid tip of his bulbous nose. 'These animals, there's still a chance maybe?'

Chelsea could feel a chilly dampness spreading in deadly crescents from his armpits. 'It's unlikely, sir. One of them is dead for sure. Shot by the highway patrol. Some tourists apparently mistook it for a rat.'

'Terrific,' said Kingsbury.

'The other one, likewise. The bandits threw it in the window of a Winnebago camper.'

Kingsbury peered from beneath dromedary lids. 'Don't,' he said, exhaling noisily. 'This is like . . . no, don't bother.'

'You might as well know,' said Chelsea. 'It was a church group from Boca Raton in the Winnebago. They beat the poor thing to death with a golf umbrella. Then they threw it off the Card Sound Bridge.'

There, Chelsea thought. He had done it. Stood up and delivered the bad news. Stood up like a man.

Francis X. Kingsbury entwined his hands and said: 'Who knows about this? Knows that *we* know? Anybody?'

'You mean anybody on the outside? No.' Charles Chelsea paused. 'Well, except the highway patrol. And I took care of them with some free passes to the Kingdom.'

'But civilians?'

'No, sir. Nobody knows that we know the voles are dead.'

'Fine,' said Francis X. Kingsbury. 'Good time to up the reward.'

'Sir?'

'Make it a million bucks. Six zeros, if I'm not mistaken.'

Chelsea took out a notebook and a Cross pen, and began to write. 'That's one million dollars for the safe return of the missing voles.'

'Which are dead.'

'Yes, sir.'

'Simple, hell. Very simple.'

'It's a most generous offer,' said Charles Chelsea.

'Bullshit,' Kingsbury said. 'It's PR, whatever. Stuff for the fucking AP.'

'But your heart's in the right place.'

Impatiently Kingsbury pointed toward the door. 'Fast,' he said. 'Before I get sick.'

Chelsea was startled. Backing away from Kingsbury's desk, he said, 'I'm sorry, sir. Is it something I said?'

'No, something you are.' Kingsbury spoke flatly, with just a trace of disgust.

On the way back to his office, Charles Chelsea stopped in the executive washroom and threw up again.

Like many wildly successful Floridians, Francis X. Kingsbury was a transplant. He had moved to the Sunshine State in balding middle age, alone and uprooted, never expecting that he would become a multimillionaire.

And, like so many new Floridians, Kingsbury was a felon on the run. Before arriving in Miami, he was known by his real name of Frankie King. Not Frank, but Frankie; his mother had named him after the singer Frankie Laine. All his life Frankie King had yearned to change his name to something more distinguished, something with weight and social bearing. A racketeering indictment (twenty-seven counts) out of Brooklyn was as good an excuse as any.

Once he was arrested, Frankie King exuberantly began ratting on his co-conspirators, which included numerous high-ranking members of the John Gotti crime organization. Frankie's testimony conveniently glossed the fact that it was he, not the surly Zuboni brothers, who had personally flown to San Juan and picked up the twenty-seven crate-loads of bootleg 'educational' videotapes that were eventually sold to the New York City school system for $119.95 apiece. Under oath, Frankie King indignantly blamed the Zubonis and, indirectly, John Gotti himself for failing to inspect the shipment once it had arrived at JFK. On the witness stand, Frankie expressed tearful remorse that, in TV classrooms from Queens to Staten Island, students expecting to see 'Kermit's Wild West Adventure' were instead exposed to a mattress-level montage of Latin porn star Pina Kolada deep-throating a semi-pro soccer team.

The Zuboni brothers and a cluster of dull-eyed knee-cappers were swiftly convicted by a horrified jury. The reward for Frankie King's cooperation was a suspended sentence, ten years' probation and a new identity of his choosing: Francis X. Kingsbury. Frankie felt the 'X' was a classy touch; he decided it should stand for Xavier.

When the man from the Witness Relocation Program told him that Miami would be his new home, Frankie King thought he had died and gone to heaven. *Miami!* Frankie couldn't believe his good fortune; he had no idea the U.S. government could be so generous. What Frankie did not know was that Miami was the prime relocation site for scores of scuzzy federal snitches (on the theory that South Florida was a place where just about any dirtbag would blend in smoothly with the existing riffraff). Frankie King continued to entertain the false notion that he was somebody special in the witness program, a regular Joe Valachi, until he saw the accommodations provided by his government benefactors: a one-bedroom apartment near the railroad tracks in beautiful downtown Naranja.

When Frankie complained about the place, FBI agents reminded him that the alternative was to return to New York and take his chances that John Gotti was a compassionate and forgiving fellow. With this on his mind, Francis X. Kingsbury began a new life.

Like all Floridians with time on their hands, he went to night school and got his real-estate license. It was an entirely new racket, and Frankie worked at it tirelessly; first he specialized in small commercial properties, then citrus groves and farmlands. Doggedly he worked his way east toward the good stuff—oceanfront, the Big O. He went from condos to prime residential estates in no time flat.

Francis X. Kingsbury had found a new niche. He was, undeniably, a whiz at selling Florida real estate. In five short years he had accumulated more money than in an entire lifetime of mob bunko, jukebox skimming and mail fraud. He had a home down on Old Cutler, a beautiful young wife and a closetful of mustard blazers. But he wanted more.

One day he walked into the boardroom of Kingsbury Realty and announced that he was selling the business. 'I'm ready to move up in the world,' he told his startled partners. 'I'm ready to become a developer.'

Six months later, Kingsbury stood before a luncheon meeting of the Greater Miami Chamber of Commerce and unveiled his model of the Amazing Kingdom of Thrills. It was the first time in his life that Frankie had gotten a standing ovation. He blushed and said: 'Florida is truly the land of opportunity.'

His probation officer, standing near the salad bar, had to bite back tears.

'This is a very bad idea, Charlie.' Joe Winder was talking about the phony million-dollar reward. 'A very bad idea. And cynical, I might add.'

Over the phone, Chelsea said: 'Don't give me any lectures. I need five hundred words by tomorrow morning.'

'This is nuts.'

'And don't overdo it.'

'This is not just dumb,' continued Joe Winder, 'it's dishonest. The blue-tongued mango voles are dead, Charlie. Everybody at the park is talking about it.'

Chelsea said, 'Mr. X is adamant. He considers the money a symbolic gesture of his commitment to preserving the environment.'

'Did you write that yourself?' Winder asked. 'That's fucking awful, Charlie. *Symbolic gesture!* You ought to be shot.'

'Joey, don't talk to me that way. This thing was your idea, offering a reward.'

'I was wrong,' Winder said. 'It was a big mistake.'

'No, it was genius. The AP had it all over the wires.'

'Look, I'm trying to save your ass,' Winder said. 'And mine, too. Listen to me. This morning, a man with a cardboard box showed up at the front gate of the Amazing Kingdom. Said he'd found the missing voles. Said he'd come to collect his ten-thousand-dollar reward. Listen to me, Charlie. Know what was in the box? Rabbits. Two baby rabbits.'

'So what? They don't look anything like a vole.'

'They do when you cut their ears off, Charlie. That's what the sonofabitch had done. Cut the ears off a couple of little tiny bunny rabbits.'

Charles Chelsea gasped.

'I know, I know,' Winder said, 'Think about what's going to happen we dangle a million bucks out there. Think of the freaks and sadists and degenerates stampeding this place.'

'Holy Christ,' said Chelsea.

'Now,' said Joe Winder, 'think of the headlines.'

'I'll talk to Kingsbury.'

'Good.'

'Maybe I'll bring you along.'

'No thank you.'

'You owe me,' said Chelsea. 'Please. I've been good to you, Joe. Remember who hired you in the first place.'

Thanks for reminding me, Winder thought, for the two-thousandth time. 'I'm not the right man to deal with Mr. X,' he said. 'I make a lousy first impression.'

'You're right,' said Chelsea, rethinking his plan. 'Tell me one thing—that sicko with the bunny rabbits . . . what happened?'

'Don't worry,' said Winder. 'We paid him to go away.'

'How much? Not the whole ten grand?'

'No, not ten grand.' Winder sighed. 'Try fifty bucks. And he was delighted, Charlie. Positively thrilled.'

'Thank God for that.' There was a brittle pause on Chelsea's end. 'Joe?'

'What?'

'This is turning into something real bad, isn't it?'

Late in the afternoon, Joe Winder decided to drive down to the Rare Animal Pavilion and find out more about the voles. He needed someone to take his mind off the rabbit episode, which made him heartsick. He should've seen it coming—naturally some greedy psychopath would mutilate helpless bunny rabbits for ten lousy thousand fucking dollars. It's South Florida, isn't it? Winter should've anticipated the worst. That's why Chelsea had hired him, for his native instinct.

The door to the vole lab was locked but the lights were on. Winder knocked twice and got no answer. He could hear a telephone ringing on the other side of the door. It stopped briefly, then began ringing again. He used his car keys to rap sharply on the glass, but there was no sign of Koocher. Winder figured the doctor was taking a late lunch.

He strolled out to the pavilion, where he found a group of tourists milling around the empty mango-vole exhibit. A tarpaulin had been hung to cover the mess, but somebody had lifted a corner to peek inside the enclosure, which was littered with glass and smudged with fingerprint dust. A yellow police ribbon lay crumpled like a dead snake on the porch of the vole hutch. Some of the tourists were snapping pictures of the scene of the crime.

A voice behind Joe Winder said, 'You work here?'

It was an old woman wearing a floppy pink Easter hat and a purse the size of a saddlebag. She eyed Joe Winder's ID badge, which was clipped to his belt.

'You a security man?' the woman asked.

Winder tried to remember what Chelsea had told him about speaking to park visitors; some gooey greeting that all employees were supposed to say. *Welcome to the Amazing Kingdom. How can I help you?* Or was it: *How may I help you?* No, that wasn't it. *How can we help you?*

Eventually Joe Winder said, 'I work in Publicity. Is something wrong?'

The old lady made a clucking noise and foraged in her enormous purse. 'I've got a little something for you.'

In a helpful tone Winder said, 'The Lost and Found is down by the killer-whale tank.'

'This isn't lost and it isn't found.' The old lady produced an envelope. 'Here,' she said, pressing it into Joe Winder's midsection. 'And don't try to follow me.'

She turned and scuttled off, one hand atop her head, holding the Easter hat in place. Winder stuffed the envelope into his pocket and started after her. 'Hey! Wait a second.'

He had taken only three steps when a fist came out of somewhere and smashed him behind the right ear. He pitched forward on the walkway, skidding briefly on his face. When he awoke, Joe Winder was staring at shoes: Reeboks, loafers, sandals, Keds, orthopedics, Hush Puppies, flip-flops. The tourists had gathered in a murmuring semicircle around him. A young man knelt at his side, asking questions in German.

Winder sat up. 'Did anybody see who hit me?' His cheek stung, and he tasted blood on his lower lip.

'Beeg orange!' sputtered a woman wearing two cameras around her neck. 'Beeg orange man!'

'Swell,' Winder said. 'Did he have a cape? A ray gun?'

The young German tourist patted him on the shoulder and said: 'You okay, *ja*?'

'Yah,' Winder muttered. 'Fall down go boom.'

He picked himself up, waved idiotically at his audience and retreated to the men's room. There he tore open the old lady's envelope and studied the message, which was typed double-spaced on ordinary notebook paper. It said: 'WE DID IT. we're glad. long live the voles.'

It was signed by the Wildlife Rescue Corps.

With copies, Joe Winder noted glumly, to every major news organization on the planet.

Bud Schwartz shook Danny Pogue awake and said, 'Look who's here. I told you not to worry.'

Molly McNamara was in the kitchen, fussing around. Danny Pogue was on the sofa in the living room. He had fallen asleep watching *Lady Chatterley IV* on Cinemax.

Bud Schwartz sat down, grinning. 'She brought the money, too,' he said.

'All of it?'

'No, just the grand. Like she said before.'

'You mean the two grand,' Danny Pogue said. 'One for each of us.' He didn't entirely trust his partner.

Bud Schwartz said, 'Yeah, that's what I meant. A thousand bucks each.'

'Then let's see it.'

Molly came in, drying her hands on a flowered towel. She looked at Danny Pogue as if he were a dog that was supposed to stay off the good furniture. She said, 'How's that foot?'

'Hurts.' Danny Pogue frowned. 'Hurts like a bitch.'

'He's all out of them pills,' added Bud Schwartz.

'Already?' Molly sounded concerned. 'You finished the whole bottle?'

'Danny's got what you call a high resistance to pharmaceuticals,' Bud Schwartz said. 'We had to double the dose.'

'Bull,' said Danny Pogue. 'Bud here just helped hisself.'

'Is that true?' asked Molly McNamara. 'Did you take some of your friend's pills?'

'Aw, come on,' said Bud Schwartz. 'Jesus Christ, there's nothing else to do around here. I was bored stiff.'

'That was prescription medicine,' Molly said sternly.

She went back to the kitchen and got her handbag. It was the largest handbag that Bud Schwartz or Danny Pogue had ever seen. Molly took out another plastic bottle of codeine pills and handed them to Danny Pogue. Then she took out her gun and shot Bud Schwartz once in the left hand.

He fell down, shaking his arm as if it were on fire.

In a whisper Danny Pogue said, 'Oh Lord Jesus.' He felt the blood flooding out of his brain, and saw the corners of the room get fuzzy.

Molly said, 'Am I getting through to you fellows?' She returned the gun to her purse. 'There will be no illegal drug activity in this condominium, is that clear? The owners' association has very strict rules. Here, take this.' She handed Danny Pogue two packets of cash. Each packet was held together with a fresh bank wrapper.

'That's one thousand each, just like I promised,' she said. Then, turning to Bud Schwartz: 'Does it hurt?'

'The fuck do you think?' He was squeezing the wounded purple hand between his knees. 'Damn right it hurts!'

'In that case, you may borrow your friend's pills. But only as needed.' Then Molly McNamara put on her floppy pink Easter hat and said good night.

Nina was naked, kneeling on Joe Winder's back and rubbing his shoulders. 'See, isn't this better than sex?'

'No,' he said, into the pillow. 'Good, but not better.'

'It's my night off,' Nina said. 'All week long, all I do is talk about it.'

'We don't have to talk,' Joe Winder mumbled. 'Let's just do.'

'Joe, I need a break from it.' She kneaded his neck so ferociously that he let out a cry. 'You understand, don't you?'

'Sure,' he said. It was the second time in a week that they'd had this conversation. Winder had a feeling that Nina was burning out on her job; practically nothing aroused her lately. All she wanted to do was sleep, and of course she talked in her sleep, said the most tantalizing things.

It was driving Joe Winder crazy. 'I had a particularly lousy day,' he said. 'I was counting on you to wear me out.'

Nina climbed off his back. 'I love you,' she said, slipping her long legs under the sheets, 'but at this moment I don't have a single muscle that's the least bit interested.'

This, from the same wonderful woman who once left fingernail grooves in the blades of a ceiling fan. Winder groaned in self-pity.

From the other side of the bed came Nina's delicious voice: 'Tell me the weirdest thing that happened to you today.'

It was a bedtime ritual, exchanging anecdotes about work. Joe Winder said: 'Some creep claimed he found the missing voles, except they weren't voles. They were baby rabbits. He was trying to con us.' Winder left out the grisly details.

'That's a tough one to beat,' Nina remarked.

'Also, I got slugged in the head.'

'Really?' she said. 'Last night I had a caller jerk himself off in eleven seconds flat. Miriam said it might be a new world's record.'

'You timed it?'

'Sort of.' Playfully she reached between his legs and tweaked him. 'Miriam has an official Olympic stopwatch.'

'Nina, I want you to get another job. I'm serious.'

She said, 'That reminds me—some strange guy phoned for you this afternoon. A doctor from the park. He called twice.'

'Koocher?'

'Yeah,' said Nina. 'Interesting name. Anyway, he made it sound important. I told him to try you at the office, but he said no. He wouldn't leave a message, either, just said he'd call back. The second time he said to tell you a man from Security was in the lab.'

Joe Winder lifted his head off the pillow. 'A man from Security?'

'That's what he said.'

'Anything else?' Winder was thinking about the empty laboratory: lights on, phone ringing. Maybe he should've tried the back door.

'I told him you'd be home soon, but he said he couldn't call back. He said he was leaving with the guy from Security.' Nina propped herself on one elbow. 'Joe, what's going on over there?'

'I thought I knew,' said Winder, 'but obviously I don't.'

With a fingertip she traced a feathery line down his cheek. 'Do me a favor,' she said.

'I know what you're going to say.'

She scooted closer, under the covers, and pressed against him. 'But things are going so great.'

Winder kissed her on the tip of the nose, and started to roll out of bed.

'Joe, don't go crazy on me,' Nina said. 'Please.'

He rolled back, into her arms. 'All right,' he said. 'Not just yet.'

6

The next morning, in the hallway by the water fountain, Charles Chelsea seized Joe Winder by the sleeve and tugged him into the office. Two men shared opposite ends of Chelsea's leather sofa—one was the immense Pedro Luz, chief of Security for the Amazing Kingdom, and the other was a serious-looking fellow with a square haircut and a charcoal suit.

'Joe,' Chelsea said, 'this gentleman is from the FBI.'

'I can see that.'

Chelsea cleared his throat. 'This is Agent Hawkins.'

Joe Winder stuck out his hand. 'Billy, isn't it? You worked a Coral Gables Savings job about four years back.'

The agent smiled cautiously. 'And you were with the *Herald*.'

'Right.'

'Dated one of the tellers.'

'Right again.'

Charles Chelsea was trying to set some sort of record for clearing his throat. 'What a coincidence that you two guys know each other.'

Joe Winder sat down and stretched his legs. 'Bank robbery. Billy here was the lead agent. Funny story, too—it was the Groucho guy.'

'Yeah,' said Hawkins, loosening up. 'Wore the big nose and the eyebrows, even carried a cigar. We finally caught up with him in Clearwater.'

'No kidding?' Winder said, knowing that it was driving Chelsea crazy, all this friendly conversation with a real FBI man. 'All the way up in Clearwater?'

'Gentlemen,' Chelsea cut in, 'if you don't mind.'

'What is it, Charlie?'

'Agent Hawkins is here at Mr. Kingsbury's personal request.' Chelsea lowered his voice. 'Joe, there were three notes delivered to employees in the park. Each was signed by this Wildlife Rescue Corps.'

Winder reached in his pocket. 'You mean like this?' He handed his copy to Billy Hawkins. He told him what had happened at the Rare Animal Pavilion—the old lady in the Easter bonnet, the phantom punch. Hawkins took it all down in a notebook.

Chelsea tried to contain his irritation. 'Why didn't you report this to Security?' he asked Joe Winder.

'Because I didn't want to interrupt Pedro's nap.'

Pedro Luz darkened. Every now and then he dozed off in the security office. 'All you had to do was ring the buzzer,' he snapped at Winder. He glanced at the FBI man, whose expression remained impassive and nonjudgmental. 'I've had a touch of the flu,' Pedro Luz added defensively. 'The medicine makes me sleepy.' For a large man he had a high tinny voice.

'Never mind,' said Charles Chelsea. 'The point is, everybody's calling up for comment. The networks. The wires. We're under siege, Joe.'

Winder felt his headache coming back. Agent Billy Hawkins admitted that the federal government didn't know much about the Wildlife Rescue Corps.

'Most of these groups seem to specialize in rodents,' the agent said. 'Laboratory rats, mostly. Universities, pharmaceutical houses—those are the common targets. What usually happens, they break in at night and free the animals.'

'But we weren't doing experiments.' Chelsea was exasperated. 'We treated Vance and Violet as royalty.'

'Who?' the agent said.

'The voles,' Joe Winder explained cheerfully.

Charles Chelsea continued to whine. 'Why have they singled out the Amazing Kingdom? We didn't abuse these creatures. Quite the opposite.'

'You do any vivisections here?' asked Agent Hawkins. 'These groups are quite vocal against vivisection.'

Chelsea paled. 'Vivisection? Christ, we gave the little bastards fresh corn on the cob every morning. Sometimes even citrus!'

'Well, this is what we've got.' Hawkins flipped backwards in his notebook. 'Two white males ages twenty-five to thirty-five, fleeing the scene in a 1979 blue Ford pickup, license GPP-Bo6. The registration comes back to a convicted burglar whose current alias is Buddy Michael Schwartz. I might add that Mr. Schwartz's rap sheet shows no history of a social conscience with regard to animal rights, or any other.'

'Somebody hired him,' Joe Winder said.

'Most likely,' agreed the FBI man. 'Anyway, they dragged the truck out of a rock pit this morning. No bodies.'

'Any sign of the voles?'

Billy Hawkins allowed himself a slight frown. 'We believe the animals are dead.' He handed Winder copies of the highway patrol reports, which described the incident with the tourist family in the red LeBaron, as well as the subsequent Winnebago attack. As Winder scanned the reports, Charles Chelsea reminded him to keep the news under his hat.

Agent Hawkins said, 'I heard something on the radio about a million-dollar reward.'

'Right!' Winder said.

'How can you do that,' the FBI man said, 'when you know these animals are dead?'

Joe Winder was having a wonderful time. 'Go ahead,' he said to Charles Chelsea. 'Explain to the gentleman.'

'Where's Koocher?' Chelsea grumbled. 'I left about a dozen messages.'

'Let's ask Pedro,' said Joe Winder. 'He sent one of his boys over to the lab yesterday. Must've had a reason.'

Charles Chelsea folded his hands on the desk, waiting. Agent Billy Hawkins turned slightly on the couch to get a better angle on the security chief. Joe Winder arched his eyebrows and said, 'How about it, Pedro? Something else happen at the Rare Animal Pavilion?'

Pedro Luz scowled, his tiny black eyes receding under the ledge of his forehead. 'I don't know what you're talking about,' he said. 'Nothing happened nowhere.' He fumbled with his clipboard. 'See? There is no report.'

The Security Department at the Amazing Kingdom of Thrills was staffed exclusively by corrupt ex-policemen, of which there was a steady supply in South Florida. The chief of Security, Pedro Luz, was a black-haired pinheaded giant of a young man who had been fired from the Miami Police for stealing cash and cocaine from drug dealers, then pushing them out of a Beechcraft high over the Everglades. Pedro Luz's conviction had been over-turned by an appeals court, and the charges ultimately dropped when the government's key witness failed to appear for the new trial. The witness's absence was later explained when bits and pieces of his body were found in a shrimper's net off Key West, although there was no evidence linking this sad turn of events to Pedro Luz himself.

Once the corruption and murder charges had been dis-missed, Pedro Luz promptly sued the police department to reclaim his old job, plus back wages and vacation time. Mean-while, to keep his hand in law enforcement, Pedro Luz went to work at Francis X. Kingsbury's vacation theme park. The pay was only $8.50 an hour, but as a perk Pedro was given free access to the executive gym, where he spent hours of company time lifting weights and taking anabolic steroids. This leisurely regimen was interrupted by the embarrassing daylight theft of the prized voles—and a personal communication of urgency from Francis X. Kingsbury himself. Chief Pedro Luz immediately put the security staff on double shifts, and rented a cot for him-self in the office.

Which is where he snoozed at one-thirty in the afternoon when he heard a knock on the bulletproof glass.

Pedro Luz sat up slowly and swung his thick legs off the bed. He stood up, strapped on his gun, straightened the shoulders of his uniform shirt. The knocking continued.

Through the glass, Pedro Luz saw a wiry brown man in a sweaty tank top. The man battled a spastic tic on one side of his face; it looked as if a wasp were loose in one cheek.

Pedro Luz opened the door and said, 'What do you want?'

'I'm here for the money,' the man said, twitching. He clutched a grocery bag to his chest. 'The million dollars.'

'Go away,' said Pedro Luz.

'Don't you even want to see?'

'The voles are dead.'

The wiry man said, 'But I heard on the news—'

'Go away,' said Pedro Luz, 'before I break your fucking legs.'

'But I found the mango voles. I want my money.'

Pedro Luz stepped out of the office and closed the door. He stood a full foot taller than the man with the grocery bag, and outweighed him by a hundred pounds.

'You don't listen so hot,' Pedro Luz said.

The man's face twitched uncontrollably as he tried to open the bag. 'Just one look,' he said, 'please.'

Pedro Luz seized the man by the throat and shook him like a doll. The grocery bag fell to the ground and tore open. Pedro Luz was so involved in assaulting the derelict that he didn't notice what came out of the bag: two half-starved, swaybacked ferrets, eyes glazed and bluish, lips flecked with foam. Instantly they settled in chewing on Pedro Luz's right ankle, and did not stop until he tore them off, bare-handed, and threw them with all his might against the nearest wall.

One hour later, the Publicity Department of the Amazing Kingdom of Thrills faxed the following statement to all media, under the caption 'Rare Voles Now Believed Dead':

> Police authorities reported today that the bluetongued mango voles stolen this week from the Amazing Kingdom of Thrills are probably dead. According to the Florida Highway Patrol and the Federal Bureau of Investigation, the rare mammals—believed to be the last of the species—were killed while crossing a highway after being abandoned by the robbers who took them.
>
> Francis X. Kingsbury, founder and chairman of the Amazing Kingdom, expressed shock and sorrow at the news. 'This is a tragedy for all of us at the park,' he said Wednesday.

'We had come to love and admire Vance and Violet. They were as much a part of our family as Robbie Raccoon or Petey Possum.'

Mr. Kingsbury, who had offered $1 million for the safe return of the missing animals, said he will use part of the money as a reward for information leading to the arrest and conviction of those responsible for the crime.

A radical outlaw group calling itself the Wildlife Rescue Corps has claimed responsibility for the robbery at the popular amusement resort. Mr. Kingsbury said he was 'shocked and dismayed that anyone claiming to support such a cause would commit crimes of violence—crimes that ultimately led not only to the animals' deaths, but to the extinction of an entire species.'

Charles Chelsea, vice president in charge of public relations, said that the blue-tongued mango voles were provided with the best possible care while in captivity at the Amazing Kingdom. Only last year, the Florida Audubon Society praised the Vole Project as 'a shining example of private enterprise using its vast financial resources to save a small but precious resource of nature.'

Next week, the Amazing Kingdom of Thrills will present a multi-media retrospective featuring slides and videotapes of the voles during their time at the park. Entitled 'Vance and Violet: The Final Days,' the presentation will be shown three times daily at the Rare Animal Pavilion.

Tickets will be $4 for adults, $2.75 for children and senior citizens.

In the cafeteria, Charles Chelsea handed Joe Winder the fax and said, 'Nice job, big guy.'

Winder stopped on the last sentence. 'You're charging money? For a goddamn slide show?'

'Joey, we're running a business here. We're not the *National Geographic*, okay? We're not a charity.'

'A rodent slide show.' Joe Winder wadded up the press release. 'The amazing thing is not that you'd do it, because I think you'd charge tourists twenty bucks to watch the pelicans fuck, if they'd let you. The amazing thing is, people will actually come and pay.' He clapped his hands once, loudly. 'I love this business, Charlie. Every day I learn something new.'

Chelsea tightened his necktie. 'Christ, here we go again. I try to pay you a compliment, and you twist it into some sort of cynical . . . *commentary*.'

'Sorry,' said Winder. He could feel his sinuses filling up like a bathtub.

'For your information,' said Chelsea, 'I got people calling all the way from Alaska, wanting to buy Vance-and-Violet T-shirts.' Chelsea sighed, to show how disappointed he was in Joe Winder's attitude. Then he said, with an edge of reluctance, 'You did some nice writing on this piece, Joe. Got us all off the hook.'

'Thanks, boss. And you're right—it was a piece.'

Chelsea sat down, eyeing the fast-food debris on Joe Winder's tray. One of Uncle Ely's Elves, sitting at the other end of the table, belched sonorously. Charles Chelsea pretended not to notice. He said, 'Not to brag, Joey, but I think I did a pretty fair job with this ditty myself. Mr. X loved his quotes. He said I made him sound like a real human being.'

With the tips of his fingers, Joe Winder began to rub both his temples in a ferocious circular motion.

Chelsea asked, 'Now what's the matter?'

'Headache.' Winder squinted as tightly as he could, to wring the pain out of his eyeballs. 'Listen, I called Dr. Koocher's house. He didn't go home last night. His wife is scared out of her mind.'

'Maybe he just got depressed and tied one on. Or maybe he's got a girlfriend.'

Joe Winder decided not to tell Chelsea that Koocher had tried to reach him. 'His wife's eight months pregnant, Charlie. She says he usually calls about nineteen times an hour, but she hasn't heard a word since yesterday.'

'What would you like me to do?'

'Worry like hell,' said Winder. He stood up. 'Also, I'd like your permission to talk to Pedro Luz. I think he's hiding something.'

Charles Chelsea said, 'You can't talk to him, Joe. He's in the hospital.' He paused wearily and shook his head. 'Don't ask.'

'Come on, Charlie.'

'For rabies shots.'

'I should've guessed,' Winder said. 'My condolences to the dog.'

'It wasn't a dog,' Chelsea said. 'Can't this wait till tomorrow? Pedro's in a lot of pain.'

'No,' said Joe Winder, 'that's perfect.'

Pedro Luz had been taken to the closest emergency room, which was Mariners' Hospital down on Plantation Key. The nurse on duty remembered Pedro Luz very well, and directed Joe Winder to a private room on the second floor.

He didn't bother to knock, just eased the door open. The impressive bulk of Pedro Luz was propped up in bed, watching a Spanish-language soap opera on Channel 23. He was sucking on one end of the plastic IV tube, which he had yanked out of his arm.

'That doesn't go in your mouth,' Winder told him.

'Yeah, well, I'm thirsty.'

'You're bleeding all over the place.'

'What do you care?' said Pedro Luz. With a corner of the sheet he swabbed the blood from his arm. 'You better get out of here. I mean right now.'

Joe Winder pulled a chair close to the bed and sat down. Pedro Luz smelled like a fifty-five-gallon drum of rubbing alcohol. His luxuriant hair stood in oily black spikes, and his massive neck was covered with angry purple acne, a side effect of the fruit-and-steroid body-building diet.

'You like your job?' Winder asked him.

'What do you mean—at the Kingdom? Sure, I guess.' The security man pulled the covers off his legs, so Joe Winder could see the bandages on his ferret-gnawed ankle. 'Except for shit like this,' said Pedro Luz. 'Otherwise, it's an okay job most of the time.'

Winder said, 'So you really wouldn't want to get fired.'

'The hell are you talking about?'

'For lying. I think you're lying.'

'What about?'

Joe Winder said, 'Don't play dumb with me.' As if the guy had a choice. 'Tell me why you sent a man to Koocher's lab yesterday. I know you did, because he called me about it.'

Pedro Luz got red in the cheeks. The cords in his neck stood out like a rutting bull's. 'I already told you,' he said. 'I don't have no report on that guy.'

'He's missing from the park.'

'Then I'll do up a report,' Pedro Luz said. He breathed deeply, as if trying to calm himself. 'Soon as I get outta here, I'll make a report.' He took the IV tube out of his mouth. 'This stuff's not so bad,' he said thoughtfully. 'Tastes like sugar syrup.' He replaced the tube between his lips and sucked on it loudly.

Joe Winder said, 'You're a moron.'

'What did you say?'

'Make that a submoron.'

Pedro Luz shrugged. 'I'd beat the piss out of you, if I didn't feel so bad. They gave me about a million shots.' He leered woozily and opened his gown. 'See, they broke two needles on my stomach.'

Joe Winder couldn't help but admire Pedro Luz's physique. He could see the bright crimson spots where the hypodermics had bent against the muscle.

'Least I won't get the rabies,' said Pedro Luz, drawing merrily on the tube. 'You oughta take off, before I start feeling better.'

Winder stood up and slid the chair back to its corner. 'Last chance, Hercules. Tell me why you sent a man to the lab yesterday.'

'Or else what?'

'Or we play *"This Is Your Life, Pedro Dipshit."* I tell Kingsbury's people all about your sterling employment record with the Miami Police Department. I might even give them a copy of the indictment. A spine-chilling saga, Pedro. Not for the meek and mild.'

Pedro Luz removed the tube and wiped his lips on the sleeve of his gown. He looked genuinely puzzled. 'But they know,' he said. 'They know all about it.'

'And they hired you anyway?'

''Course,' said Pedro Luz. 'It was Kingsbury himself. He said every man deserves a second chance.'

'I admire that philosophy,' Joe Winder said, 'most of the time.'

'Yeah, well, Mr. X took a personal liking to me. That's why I'm not too worried about all your bullshit.'

'Yes,' said Joe Winder. 'I'm beginning to understand.'

'Because you couldn't get me fired no matter what,' said Pedro Luz. 'And you know what else? Don't never call me a moron again, if you know what's good for you.'

'I guess I don't,' said Joe Winder. 'Obviously.'

7

The ticket taker at the Wet Willy attraction was trying to control his temper. *Firm, but friendly.* That's how you deal with difficult customers; that's what they taught in ticket-taker training.

The young man, who was new to the job, said, 'I'm sorry, sir, but you can't cut to the front of the line. These other people have been waiting for a long time.'

'These other people,' the man said; 'tell me, do they own this fucking joint?'

The ticket taker did not recognize Francis X. Kingsbury, who wore thong sandals, baggy pastel swim trunks and no shirt. He also had a stopwatch hanging from a red lanyard around his neck.

'Now, you don't want me to call Security,' the ticket taker said.

'Nothing but idiots,' Kingsbury muttered, pushing his pallid belly through the turnstile. He shuffled up two flights of stairs to the launching ramp, and dropped to all fours.

The Wet Willy ride was one of the Amazing Kingdom's most popular thrill attractions, and one of the cheapest to operate. A marvel of engineering simplicity, it was nothing but a long translucent latex tube. The inside was painted in outrageous psychedelic hues, and kept slippery with drain water diverted at no cost from nearby drinking fountains. The narrow tube descended from a height of approximately six stories, with riders plunging downhill at an average angle of twenty-seven exhilarating degrees.

Francis X. Kingsbury was exceptionally proud of the Wet Willy because the whole contraption had been his idea, his concept. The design engineers at the Amazing Kingdom had wanted something to compete with Disney's hugely successful Space Mountain ride. Kingsbury had collected all the press clippings about Space Mountain and used a bright yellow marker to emphasize his contempt for the project, particularly the development cost. 'Seventeen million bucks,' he had scoffed, 'for a frigging roller ride in the dark.'

The engineers had earnestly presented several options for the Amazing Kingdom—Jungle Coaster, Moon Coaster, Alpine Death Coaster—but Kingsbury rejected each for the obvious reason that roller-coaster cars and roller-coaster tracks cost money. So did the electricity needed to run them.

'Gravity!' Kingsbury had grumped. 'The most underused energy source on the planet.'

'So you're suggesting a slide,' ventured one of the engineers. 'Maybe a water slide.'

Kingsbury had shaken his head disdainfully. Slides *look* cheap, he'd complained, we're not running a goddamn State Fair. A tube would be better, a sleek space-age tube.

'Think condom,' he had advised the engineers. 'A three-hundred-foot condom.'

And so the Wet Willy was erected. Instantly it had become a sensation among tourists at the park, a fact that edified Kingsbury's belief that the illusion of quality is more valuable than quality itself.

Lately, though, ridership figures for the Wet Willy had shown a slight but troubling decline. Francis X. Kingsbury decided to investigate personally, without notifying the engineers, the ticket takers, the Security Department or anyone else at the park. He wanted to test his theory that the ride had become less popular because it had gotten slower. The stopwatch would tell the story.

The way the Wet Willy was designed, a 110-pound teenager would be able to slide headlong from the ramp to the gelatin-filled landing sac in exactly 22.7 seconds. Marketing specialists had calibrated the time down to the decimal point—the ride needed to be long enough to make customers think they were getting their money's worth, yet fast enough to seem dangerous and exciting.

Francis X. Kingsbury weighed considerably more than 110 pounds as he crawled into the slippery chute. Ahead of him, he saw the wrinkled bare soles of a child disappear swiftly into the tube, as if flushed down a rubber commode. Kingsbury pressed the button on the stop-watch, eased to his belly and pushed off. He held his arms at his sides, like an otter going down a riverbank. In this case, an overweight otter in a ridiculous Jack Kemp hairpiece.

Kingsbury grimaced as he swooshed downward, skimming on a thin plane of clammy water. He thought: This is supposed to be fun? The stopwatch felt cold and hard against his breastbone. The bright colors on the walls of the tube did little to lift his spirits; he noticed that some of the reds had faded to pink, and the blues were runny. Not only that, sections of the chute seemed irregular and saggy, as if the latex were giving way.

He took his eyes off the fabric long enough to notice, with alarm, that he was gaining on the youngster who had entered the Wet Willy ahead of him. Being so much heavier, Francis X. Kingsbury was plummeting earth-bound at a much faster speed. Suddenly he was close enough to hear the child laughing, oblivious to the danger—no! Close enough to make out the grinning, bewhiskered visage of Petey Possum waving from the rump of the youngster's swimming trunks.

'Shit,' said Kingsbury. Feverishly he tried to brake, digging into the rubber with his toes and fingernails. It was no use: gravity ruled the Wet Willy.

Kingsbury overtook the surprised child and they became one, hurtling down the slick pipe in a clumsy union of tangled torsos.

'Hey!' the kid cried. 'You're smushing me!' It was a boy, maybe nine or ten, with bright red hair and freckless all over his neck. Francis X. Kingsbury now steered the kid as if he were a toboggan.

They hit the gelatin sac at full speed and disengaged. The boy came out of the goo bawling, followed by Kingsbury, who was studying the dial of the stopwatch and frowning. He seemed not to notice the solemn group waiting outside the exit: the earnest young ticket taker, plus three uniformed security men. All were breathing heavily, as if they had run the whole way.

The ticket taker pointed at Kingsbury and said, 'That's him. Except he wasn't bald before.'

The security men, all former crooked cops recruited by Pedro Luz, didn't move. They recognized Mr. X right away.

The ticket taker said, 'Get him, why don't you!'

'Yeah,' said the red-haired tourist kid. 'He hurt me.'

'Mildew,' said Francis X. Kingsbury, still preoccupied. 'Fucking mildew under my fingernails.' He looked up and, to no one in particular, said: 'Call Maintenance and have them Lysol the Willy, A-S-A-P.'

The tourist kid raised the pitch of his whining so that it was impossible to ignore. 'That's the man who tried to smush me. On my bottom!'

'Give the little turd a free pass to the Will Bill Hiccup,' said Francis X. Kingsbury. 'And *him*,' pointing at the ticket taker, 'throw his ass, I mean it, off the property.'

The boy with the Petey Possum swimsuit ran off, sniffling melodramatically. As the security men surrounded the ticket taker, Kingsbury said, 'What, like it takes three of you monkeys?'

The men hesitated. All were reluctant to speak.

'You,' Kingsbury said, nodding at the smallest of the guards. 'Go back up and slide this goddamn tube. Yeah, you heard me. See if you can beat twenty-seven-point-two.'

The security man nodded doubtfully. 'All right, sir.'

'Yeah, and my hair,' said Kingsbury, 'it's up there somewhere. Grab it on the way down.'

Bud Schwartz paused at the door and looked back. 'It don't seem right,' he said. 'Maybe just the VCR.'

'Forget it.' Danny Pogue was rocking on his crutches down by the elevator. 'Where we gonna hide anything? Come on, Bud, let's just go.'

The elevator came and Danny Pogue clumped in. With one crutch he held the elevator door and waited for his partner. Bud

Schwartz was trying to tear himself away from Molly McNamara's fancy condo. 'Look at all this shit we're leaving behind,' he said longingly. 'We could probably get five hundred easy for the Dolbys.'

Danny Pogue leaned out of the elevator. 'And how the fuck we supposed to carry 'em? Me with these toothpicks and you with one good arm. Would you get your ass moving, please, before the bitch comes back?'

As they rode to the first floor, Danny Pogue said, 'Besides, we got no car.'

Bud Schwartz grunted sourly, wondering what became of the blue pickup. 'I feel like she owes us.'

'She does owe us. She owes us nine grand, to be exact. But we agreed it wasn't worth waiting, right?'

'I mean, owes us for this.' Bud Schwartz brandished a gauze-wrapped hand. 'Shooting us, for no good reason.'

'She's a nut case. She don't need a reason.' They got off the elevator and for once Danny Pogue led the way, swinging on his crutches.

They could see the gatehouse at the main entrance, on the other side of the condominium complex. Rather than follow the sidewalks, they decided to shorten the trip by cutting across the grounds, which were sparsely landscaped and dimly lit. In the still of the evening, the high-rise community of Eagle Ridge was at rest, except for a noisy bridge tournament being held in the rec room. On the screened porches of ground-floor apartments, couples could be seen watering their plants or feeding their cats.

As the two outsiders made their way across the darkened, shuffle-board courts, Danny Pogue's left crutch gave out and he went down with a cry.

'Goddamn,' he said, splayed on the concrete. 'Look here, somebody left a puck on the court.'

Bud Schwartz said, 'It's not a puck. Pucks are for hockey.'

Danny Pogue held the plastic disk like a Danish. 'Then what do you call it?'

'I don't know what you call it,' said Bud Schwartz, 'but people are staring, so why don't you get up before some fucking Good Samaritan calls 911.'

'I ought to sue the assholes for leaving this damn thing lying around.'

'Good idea, Danny. We'll go see a lawyer first thing in the morning. We'll sue the bastards for a jillion trillion dollars. Then we'll retire down to Club Med.' With great effort, Bud Schwartz helped Danny Pogue off the cement and steadied him on the crutches.

'So who's watching us?'

'There.' Bud Schwartz raised his eyes toward a third-floor balcony, where three women stood and peered, arms on their hips, like cranky old cormorants drying their wings.

'Hey!' Danny Pogue yelled. 'Get a life!'

The women retreated into the apartment, and Danny Pogue laughed. Bud Schwartz didn't think it was all that funny; he'd been in a rotten frame of mind ever since Molly McNamara had shot him in the hand.

As they approached the gatehouse, Danny Pogue said, 'So where's the taxi?'

'First things first,' said Bud Schwartz. Then, in a whisper: 'Remember what we talked about. The girl's name is Annie. Annie Lefkowitz.'

He had met her that afternoon by the swimming pool and gotten nowhere—but that's who they were visiting, if anybody asked. No way would they mention Molly McNamara; never heard of her.

A rent-a-cop came out of the gatehouse and nodded neutrally at the two men. He was a young muscular black with a freshly pressed uniform and shiny shoes. Over his left breast pocket was a patch that said, in navy-blue stitching: 'Eagle Ridge Security.' Danny Pogue and Bud Schwartz were surprised to see what appeared to be a real Smith & Wesson on his hip.

The rent-a-cop said: 'Looks like you guys had a rough night.'

'Barbecue blew up,' said Bud Schwartz. 'Ribs all over the place.'

Danny Pogue extended his wounded foot, as if offering it for examination. 'Burns is all,' he said. 'We'll be okay.'

The rent-a-cop didn't seem in a hurry to move out of the way. He asked for their names, and Bud Schwartz made up a couple of beauts. Ron Smith and Dick Jones.

'Where are you staying?' the rent-a-cop said. 'Which building?'

'With Amy Leibowitz,' answered Danny Pogue.

'Lefkowitz,' said Bud Schwartz, grinding his molars. 'Annie *Lefkowitz*. Building K.'

'Which unit?' asked the rent-a-cop.

'We're visiting from up North,' said Bud Schwartz. 'We're not related or anything. She's just a friend, if you know what I mean.'

'But which unit?'

Bud Schwartz made a sheepish face. 'You know, I don't even remember. But her last name's Lefkowitz, you can look it up.'

The rent-a-cop said: 'There are four different Lefkowitzes that live here. Hold tight, I'll be right back.'

The guard went back inside, and Danny Pogue leaned closer to his partner. The gatehouse cast just enough light to reveal a change in Bud Schwartz's expression.

'So help me God,' said Danny Pogue, 'if you leave me here, I'll go to the cops.'

'What're you talking about?'

'You're gonna run, goddamn you.'

'No, I'm not,' said Bud Schwartz, although that was precisely what he was considering. He had spotted the yellow taxi, parked near a mailbox across the street.

'Don't even think about it,' said Danny Pogue. 'You're still on probation.'

'And you're on parole,' Bud Schwartz snapped. Then he thought: Hell, what are we worried about? We're not even arrested. And this jerk-off's not even a real cop.

'This guy, he can't stop us from leaving,' said Bud Schwartz. 'He can stop us from trying to get in, but he can't stop us from getting out.'

Danny Pogue thought about this. 'You're right,' he said. 'Why don't we just take off?'

'Taking off is not how I'd describe it, considering the shape we're in. Limping off is more like it.'

'I wonder if that gun's loaded,' said Danny Pogue. 'Or if he's allowed to use it.'

Bud Schwartz told him not to worry, they could still talk their way out of it. When the rent-a-cop came out of the gatehouse, he held a clipboard in one hand and a big ugly Maglite in the other.

'Miss Lefkowitz says she's had no visitors.'

Bud Schwartz looked stunned. 'Annie? Are you sure you got the right one?' He stuck with it, digging them in even deeper. 'She's probably just pissed off 'cause we're leaving, that's all. Got a good taste and doesn't want to let go.'

The rent-a-cop pointed the white beam of the Maglite at Bud Schwartz's face and said, 'Why don't you fuckheads come with me.'

Danny Pogue retreated a couple of steps. 'We didn't do nothin' wrong.'

'You lied,' said the rent-a-cop. 'That's wrong.'

Half-blind from the flashlight, Bud Schwartz shielded his eyes and said, 'Look, I can explain about Annie.' He was ummming and awwwwing, trying to come up with something, when he heard a shuffling noise off to his left. The rent-a-cop aimed the flashlight toward Danny Pogue, but Danny Pogue was gone.

Bud Schwartz said, 'I'm not believing this.'

The rent-a-cop seemed mildly annoyed. They could hear the frantic thwuck-thwuck of the crutches, heading down the unlit road.

'Bastard,' said Bud Schwartz. He felt sharp fingers—impressively strong—seize the loose span of flesh where his neck met his shoulder.

'Before I go get the gimper,' said the rent-a-cop, pinching harder, 'how about you telling me some portion of the truth.'

'Really I can't,' said Bud Schwartz. 'I'd like to, but it's just not possible.'

Then the Maglite came down against the top of his forehead, and the shutters of his brain slammed all at once, leaving the interior of his skull very cool, black, empty.

Joe Winder parked at the end of the gravel road and changed out of his work clothes. The necktie was the first thing to come off. He put on a pair of cutoffs, slipped into some toeless sneakers, slathered on some Cutter's and grabbed his spinning rod out of the car. He found the path through the mangroves—his path, to the water's edge. He came here almost every day after work, depending on how badly the wind was blowing. Sometimes he fished, sometimes he sat and watched.

Today he made his way quickly, worried about missing the best of the tide. When he got to the shoreline, he put on the Polaroids and swept the shallow flats with his eyes. He spotted a school of small bonefish working against the current, puffing mud about forty yards out. He grinned and waded out purpose-fully, sliding his feet silently across the marly bottom. A small plane flew over and the rumble of the engine flushed the fish. Joe Winder cursed, but kept his gaze on the nervous wake, just in case. Sure enough, the bonefish settled down and started feeding again. As he edged closer, he counted five in all, small black torpedoes.

As Joe Winder lifted his arm to cast, he heard a woman call out his name. The distraction was sufficient to ruin his aim; the small pink jig landed smack in the middle of the school, causing the fish to depart at breakneck speed for Andros Island and beyond. An absolutely terrible cast.

He turned and saw Nina waving from the shore. She was climbing out of her blue jeans, which was no easy task.

'I'm coming out,' she called.

'I can see that.'

And out she came, in an aqua T-shirt, an orange Dolphins cap, black panties and white Keds. Under these circumstances, it was impossible for Joe Winder to stay angry about the bonefish.

Nina was laughing like a child when she reached him. 'The water's so warm,' she said. 'Makes me want to dive in.'

He gave her a left-handed hug. 'Did you put on some bug spray?' he asked.

'Designer goo,' said Nina. 'Some sort of weird enzyme. The bugs gag on it.'

Joe Winder pointed with the tip of the fishing rod. 'See that? They're mocking me.' Another school of bonefish cavorted, tails flashing, far out of human casting range.

'I'll take your word for it,' said Nina, squinting. 'Joe, what'd you do to your hair?'

'Cut it.'

'With what?'

'A steak knife. I couldn't find the scissors.'

Nina reached up and touched what was left. 'For God's sake, why?'

'Chelsea said I looked like one of the Manson family.'

Nina frowned. 'Since when do you give a hoot what Charlie Chelsea thinks?'

'It's part of the damn dress code. Kingsbury's cracking down, or so Charlie says. I was trying to be a team player, like you wanted.' Joe Winder spotted a small bonnet shark cruising the shallows, and cast the jig for the hell of it. The shark took one look and swam away arrogantly.

Joe Winder said, 'So now I look like a Nazi.'

'No,' said Nina, 'the Nazis had combs.'

'How's the new routine coming? I assume that's why you're here.' It was the time of the week when the girls on the sex-phone line had to update their shtick.

'Tell me what you think.' Nina reached into the breast pocket of the T-shirt and pulled out a folded piece of notebook paper. Carefully she unfolded it. 'Now, be honest,' she said to Winder.

'Always.'

''Kay, here goes.' She cleared her throat. 'You say "Hello."'

'Hello!' Joe Winder sang out.

'*Hi, there,*' said Nina, reading. '*I was just thinking about you. I was thinking it would be so nice to go on a train, just you and me. A long, romantic train ride. I love the way trains rock back and forth. At first they start out so slow and hard, but then*'—here Nina had scripted a pause—'*but then they get faster and stronger. I love the motion of a big locomotive, it gets me so hot.*'

'Gets me going,' suggested Joe Winder. 'Hot is a cliché.'

Nina nodded in agreement. 'That's better, yeah. *I love the motion of a big locomotive, it really gets me going.*'

Joe Winder noticed that the tide was slowing. These fish would be gone soon.

But there was Nina in her black panties. Knee deep in the Atlantic. Blond hair tied back under her cap with a pink ribbon. Reading some damn nonsense about sex on the Amtrak, in that killer voice of hers. The words didn't matter, it was all music to Joe Winder; he was stirred by the sight of her in the water with the sun dropping behind the Keys. At times like this he sure loved Florida.

Nina told him to quit staring at her all sappy and listen, so he did.

'*Sometimes, late at night, I dream that you're a locomotive. And I'm riding you on top, stretched out with my legs around your middle. First we go uphill, real slow and hard and rough. Then all of a sudden I'm riding the engine down, faster and harder and hotter until . . .*'

'Until what?' Joe Winder said.

'Until whatever,' said Nina with a shrug. 'I figure I'd just leave the rest to their imagination.'

'No,' said Winder. 'A metaphor like that, you need a big ending.' He slapped a mosquito that had penetrated the sheen of Cutter's on his neck. 'How about: *We're going downhill, out of control, faster and hotter. I scream for you to stop but you keep pumping and pumping until I explode, melting against you.*'

From someplace—her bra?—Nina produced a ballpoint pen and began to scribble. 'The pumping business is a bit much,' she said, 'but I like the melting part. That's good imagery, Joe, thanks.'

'Any time.'

'Miriam's writing up another hot-tub blowjob.'

'Not again,' said Joe Winder.

'She says it's going to be a series.' Nina folded up the notebook paper and slipped it back in the pocket of her shirt. 'I'm going to be late to work if I don't get a move on. You coming in?'

'No, there's another school working that deep edge. I'm gonna try not to brain 'em with this feather.'

Nina said good luck and sloshed back toward shore. Halfway there, she turned and said, 'My God, I almost forgot. I got one of those phone calls at home.'

Winder stopped tracking the fish. He closed the bail on his spinning reel, and tucked the rod in the crook of an elbow. 'Was it Koocher?' he asked, across the flat.

Nina shook her head. 'It was a different voice from last time.' She took a half-dozen splashy steps toward him, so she wouldn't have to yell so far. 'But that's what I wanted to tell you. The guy today said he was Dr. Koocher, only he wasn't. It was the wrong voice from before.'

Joe Winder said, 'You're sure?'

'It's my business, Joe. It's what I do all night, listen to grown men lie.'

'What exactly did he say, Nina? The guy who called. Besides that he was Koocher.'

'He said all hell was breaking loose at the park.'

'All hell,' repeated Winder.

'And he said he wanted to meet you tonight at the Card Sound Bridge.'

'When?'

'Midnight sharp.' Nina shifted her weight from one leg to the other, rippling the water. 'You're not going,' she said. 'Please?'

Joe Winder looked back across the flats, lifeless in the empty auburn dusk. 'No sign of those fish,' he said. 'I believe this tide is officially dead.'

8

Bud Schwartz didn't have to open his eyes to know where he was; the scent of jasmine room freshener assailed his nostrils. He was in Molly McNamara's place, lying on the living-room sofa. He could feel her stare, unblinking, like a stuffed owl.

'I know you're awake,' she said.

He elected not to open his eyes right away.

'Son, I know you're there.'

It was the same tone she had used the first time they met, at one of the low points in Bud Schwartz's burglary career; he had been arrested after his 1979 Chrysler Cordoba stalled in the middle of 163rd Street, less than a block from the duplex apartment he had just burglarized with his new partner, Danny Pogue. The victim of the crime had been driving home when he saw the stalled car, stopped to help and immediately recognized the Sony television, Panasonic clock radio, Amana microwave and Tandy laptop computer stacked neatly in the Cordoba's back seat. The reason the stuff was lying in the back seat was because the trunk was full of stolen Neil Diamond cassettes that the burglars could not, literally, give away.

Bud Schwartz had been smoking in a holding cell of the Dade County Jail when Molly McNamara arrived. At the time, she was a volunteer worker for Jackson Memorial Hospital and the University of Miami Medical School; her job was recruiting jail inmates as subjects for medical testing, a task that suited her talent for maternal prodding. She had entered the holding cell wearing white rubber-soled shoes, a polyester nurse's uniform and latex gloves.

'I'm insulted,' Bud Schwartz had said.

Molly McNamara had eyed him over the top of her glasses and said, 'I understand you're looking at eighteen months.'

'Twelve, tops,' Bud Schwartz had said.

'Well, I'm here to offer you a splendid opportunity.'

'And I'm here to listen.'

Molly had asked if Bud Schwartz was interested in testing a new ulcer drug for the medical school.

'I don't have no ulcers.'

'It doesn't matter,' Molly had said. 'You'd be in the control group.' A pill a day for three months, she had explained. Sign up now, the prosecutor asks the judge to chop your time in half.

'Your friend's already agreed to it.'

'That figures,' Bud Schwartz had said. 'I end up with ulcers, he'll be the cause of it.'

When he'd asked about possible side effects, Molly read from a printed page: headaches, high blood pressure, urinary-tract infections.

'Run that last one by me again.'

'It's unlikely you'll experience any problems,' Molly had assured him. 'They've been testing this medication for almost two years.'

'Thanks, just the same.'

'I know you're smarter than this,' Molly had told him in a chiding tone.

'If I was really smart,' Bud Schwartz had said, 'I'd a put new plugs in the car.'

A week later she had returned, this time without the rubber gloves. Pulled his rap sheet out of her purse, held it up like the Dead Sea Scrolls.

'I've been looking for a burglar,' she had said.

'What for?'

'Ten thousand dollars.'

'Very funny,' Bud Schwartz had said.

'Call me when you get out. You and your friend.'

'You serious?'

'It's not what you think,' Molly had said.

'I can't think of anything. Except maybe you're some kinda snitch for the cops.'

'Be serious, young man.' Again with the needle in her voice, worse than his mother. 'Don't mention this to anyone.'

'Who the hell would believe it? Ten grand, I swear.'

'Call me when you get out.'

'Be a while,' he said. 'Hey, is it too late to get me in on that ulcer deal?'

That was six months ago.

Bud Schwartz touched the place on his brow where the rent-a-cop's flashlight had clobbered him. He could feel a scabby eruption the size of a golf ball. 'Damn,' he said, opening his eyes slowly.

Molly McNamara moved closer and stood over him. She was wearing her reading glasses with the pink roses on the frames. She said, 'Your friend is in the bedroom.'

'Danny's back?'

'I was on my way here when I spotted him at the Farm Stores. He tried to get away, but—'

'You didn't shoot him again?' Bud Schwartz was asking more out of curiosity than concern.

'No need to,' said Molly. 'I had the Cadillac. I think your friend realized there's no point in getting run over.'

With a wheeze, Bud Schwartz sat up. His ears pounded and stomach juices bubbled up sourly in his throat. As always, Molly was prompt with the first aid. She handed him a towel filled with chipped ice and told him to pack it against his wound.

Danny Pogue clumped into the living room and sat on the other end of the sofa. 'You look like shit,' he said to Bud Schwartz.

'Thank you, Tom Selleck.' From under the towel Bud Schwartz glared with one crimson eye.

Molly McNamara said, 'That's enough, the both of you. I can't begin to tell you how much trouble you've caused.'

'We was trying to get out of your hair is all,' said Danny Pogue. 'Why're you keeping us prisoners?'

Molly said, 'Aren't we being a bit melodramatic? You are not prisoners. You're simply two young men in my employ until I decide otherwise.'

'In case you didn't hear,' said Bud Schwartz, 'Lincoln freed the slaves a long time ago.'

Molly McNamara ignored the remark. 'At the gatehouse I had to tell Officer Andrews a lie. I told him you were my nephews visiting from Georgia. I told him we'd had a fight and that's why you were trying to sneak out of Eagle Ridge. I told him your parents died in a plane crash when you were little, and I was left responsible for taking care of you.'

'Pitiful,' said Bud Schwartz.

'I told him you both had emotional problems.'

'We're heading that direction,' Bud Schwartz said.

'I don't like to lie,' Molly added sternly. 'Normally I don't believe in it.'

'But shooting people is okay?' Danny Pogue cackled bitterly. 'Lady, pardon me for saying, but I think you're goddamn fucking nutso.'

Molly's eyes flickered. In a frozen voice she said, 'Please don't use that word in my presence.'

Danny Pogue mumbled that he was sorry. He wasn't sure which word she meant.

'I'm not certain Officer Andrews believed any of it,' Molly went on. 'I wouldn't be surprised if he reported the entire episode to the condominium association. You think you've got problems now! Oh, brother, just wait.'

Bud Schwartz removed the towel from his forehead and examined it for bloodstains. Molly said, 'Are you listening to me?'

'Hanging on every word.'

'Because I've got some very bad news. For all of us.'

Bud Schwartz grunted wearily. What now? What the hell now?

'It was on the television tonight,' Molly McNamara said. 'The mango voles are dead. Killed on the highway.'

Nervously Danny Pogue glanced at his partner, whose eyes

were fixed hard on the old woman. Waiting, no doubt, to see if she pulled that damn pistol from her sweater.

Molly said, 'I don't know all the details, but I suppose it's not important. I feel absolutely sick about this.'

Good, thought Bud Schwartz, maybe she's not blaming us.

But she was. 'If only I'd known how careless and irresponsible you were, I would never have recruited you for this job.' Molly took off her rose-framed glasses and folded them meticulously. Her gray eyes were misting.

'The blue-tongued mango voles are extinct because of me,' she said, blinking, 'and because of you.'

Bud Schwartz said, 'We're real sorry.'

'Yeah,' agreed Danny Pogue. 'It's too bad they died.'

Molly was downcast. 'This is an unspeakable sin against Nature. The death of these dear animals, I can't tell you—it goes against everything I've worked for, everything I believe in. I was so stupid to entrust this project to a couple of reckless, clumsy criminals.'

'That's us,' said Bud Schwartz.

Danny Pogue didn't like his partner's casual tone. He said to Molly, 'We didn't know they was so important. They looked like regular old rats.'

The old woman absently fondled the buttons of her sweater. 'There's no point belaboring it. The damage is done. Now we've got to atone.'

'Atone,' said Bud Schwartz suspiciously.

'What does that mean?' asked Danny Pogue. 'I don't know that word.'

Molly said, 'Tell him, Bud.'

'It means we gotta do something to make up for all this.'

Molly nodded. 'That's right. Somehow we must redeem ourselves.'

Bud Schwartz sighed. He wondered what crazy lie she'd told the rent-a-cop about their gunshot wounds. And this condo association—what's she so worried about?

'Have you ever heard of the Mothers of Wilderness?' asked Molly McNamara.

'No,' said Bud Schwartz, 'can't say that I have.' Danny Pogue said he'd never heard of them, either.

'No matter,' said Molly, brightening, 'because as of tonight, you're our newest members. Congratulations, gentlemen!'

Restlessly Danny Pogue squeezed a pimple on his neck. 'Is it like a nature club?' he said. 'Do we get T-shirts and stuff?'

'Oh, you'll enjoy it,' said Molly. 'I've got some pamphlets in my briefcase.'

Bud Schwartz clutched at the damp towel. This time he pressed it against his face. 'Cut to the chase,' he muttered irritably. 'What the hell is it you want us to do?'

'I'm coming to that,' said Molly McNamara. 'By the way, did I mention that Mr. Kingsbury is offering a reward to anyone who turns in the vole robbers?'

'Oh, no,' said Danny Pogue.

'Quite an enormous reward, according to the papers.'

'How nice,' said Bud Schwartz, his voice cold.

'Oh, don't worry,' Molly said. 'I wouldn't dream of saying anything to the authorities.'

'How could you?' Danny Pogue exclaimed. 'You're the one asked us to rob the place!'

Molly's face crinkled in thought. 'That'd be awfully hard to swallow, that an old retired woman like myself would get involved in such a distasteful crime. I suppose the FBI would have to decide whom to believe—two young fellows with your extensive criminal pasts, or an older woman like myself who's never even had a parking ticket.'

Danny Pogue angrily pounded the floor with one of his crutches. 'For someone who don't like to lie, you sure do make a sport of it.'

Bud Schwartz stretched out on the sofa, closed his eyes and smiled in resignation. 'You're a piece a work,' he said to Molly McNamara. 'I gotta admit.'

The Card Sound Bridge is a steep two-lane span that connects the northern tip of Key Largo with the South Florida mainland. Joe Winder got there two hours early, at ten o'clock. He parked half a mile down the road and walked the rest of the way. He staked out a spot on some limestone boulders, which formed a jetty under the eastern incline of the bridge. From there Winder could watch for the car that would bring the mystery caller to this meeting.

He knew it wouldn't be Dr. Will Koocher; Nina was never wrong about phone voices. Joe Winder had no intention of confronting the impostor, but at least he wanted to get a good look, maybe even a tag number.

Not much was biting under the bridge. Effortlessly Winder cast the same pink wiggle-jig he'd been using on the bonefish flats. He let it sink into the fringe of the sea grass, then reeled in slowly, bouncing the lure with the tip of his rod. In this fashion he picked up a couple of blue runners and a large spiny pinfish, which he tossed back. The other fishermen were using dead shrimp with similar unexciting results. By eleven most of them had packed up their buckets and rods and gone home, leaving the jetty deserted except for Joe Winder and two other diehards.

The other men stood side by side, conversing quietly in Spanish. As Joe Winder watched them more closely, it seemed that the men were doing more serious talking than fishing. They were using Cuban yo-yo rigs, twirling the lines overhead and launching the baits with a loud plop into the water. Once in a while they'd pull in the lines and cast out again, usually without even checking the hooks.

One of the men was a husky no-neck in long canvas pants. The other was short and wiry, and as dark as coffee. Both wore baseball caps and light jackets, which was odd, considering the heat. Every few minutes a pair of headlights would appear down Card Sound Road, and Joe Winder would check to see if the car stopped at the foot of the bridge. After a while, he noticed that the two other fishermen were doing the same. This was not a good sign.

As midnight approached, the other men stopped pretending to fish and concentrated on the road. Joe Winder realized that he was stranded on the jetty with two goons who probably were waiting to ambush him. Worse, they stood squarely between Winder and the relative safety of the island. The most obvious means of escape would be jumping into Card Sound; while exceptionally dramatic, such a dive would prove both stupid and futile. The bay was shallow and provided no cover; if the goons had guns, they could simply shoot him like a turtle.

Joe Winder's only hope was that they wouldn't recognize him in the dark with his hair hacked off. It was a gray overcast night, and he was doing a creditable impersonation of a preoccupied angler. Most likely the goons would be expecting him at twelve sharp, some dumb shmuck hollering Koocher's name under the bridge.

The strategy of staying invisible might have worked if only a powerful fish had not seized Joe Winder's lure. The strike jolted his arms, and reflexively he yanked back hard to set the hook. The fish streaked toward the rock, then back out again toward open water. The buzz of Winder's reel cut like a saw through the stillness of the bay. The two goons stopped talking and looked up to see what was happening.

Joe Winder knew. It was a snook, a damn big one. Any other night he would have been thrilled to hook such a fish, but not now. From the corner of his eye he could see the goons rock-hopping down the jetty so they could better view the battle. Near a piling the fish broke to the surface, shaking its gills furiously before diving in a frothy silver gash. The goons pointed excitedly at the commotion, and Winder couldn't blame them; it was a grand fish.

Joe Winder knew what to do, but he couldn't bring himself to do it. Palm the spool. Break the damn thing off, before the two guys got any closer. Instead Joe Winder was playing the fish like a pro, horsing it away from the rocks and pilings, letting it spend itself in short hard bursts. What am I, crazy? Winder thought. From up here I could never land this fish alone. The goons would want to help, sure they would, and then they'd see who I was and that would be it. One dead snook and one dead flack.

Again the fish thrust its underslung snout from the water and splashed. Even in the tea-colored water the black lateral stripe was visible along its side. Twelve pounds easy, thought Winder. A fine one.

One of the goons clapped his hands and Joe Winder looked up. 'Nize goying,' the man said. 'Dat's some fugging fish.' It was the short wiry one.

'Thanks,' said Winder. Maybe he was wrong. Maybe these weren't the bad guys, after all. Or maybe they hadn't come to hurt him; maybe they just wanted to talk. Maybe they had Koocher and were scheming for a ransom.

After five minutes of back-and-forth, the snook was tiring. Twenty yards from the jetty it glided to the surface and flopped its tail once, twice. Not yet, Winder thought; don't give up yet, you marvelous bastard.

He heard their heavy footsteps on the rocks. Now they were behind him. He heard their breathing. One of them was chewing gum. Joe Winder smelled hot spearmint and beer.

'What're you waiting for?' asked the big one.

'He's not ready,' Winder said, afraid to turn and give them a look at his face. 'He's still got some gas.'

'No, look at the fugging thin,' said the little one. 'He juice about dead, mang.'

The snook was dogging it on top, barely putting a bend in Joe Winder's fishing rod.

'That's some good eating,' the big no-neck goon remarked.

Winder swallowed dryly and said, 'Too bad they're out of season.'

He heard both of the men laugh. 'Hey, you don't want him, we'll take it off your hands. Fry his ass up in a minute. Right, Angel?'

The little one, Angel, said, 'Yeah, I go down and grab hole the fugging thin.' He took off his baseball cap and scrabbled noisily down the rocks.

Joe Winder got a mental picture of these two submorons in yellowed undershirts—swilling beer, watching 'Wheel' on the tube—cooking up the snook on a cheap gas stove in some rathole Hialeah duplex. The thought of it was more than he could stand.

He placed his hand on the spool of the reel and pulled once, savagely.

The snook had one good powerful surge left in its heart, and the fishing line snapped like a rifle shot. Joe Winder fell back, then steadied himself. 'Goddammit,' he said, trying to sound disappointed.

'That was really stupid,' said the big goon. 'You don't know shit about fighting a fish.'

'I guess not.'

The wiry one had been waiting by the water when the fish got off. Cursing in Spanish, he monkeyed back up the rocks. To guide himself, he held a small flashlight in one hand. The beam caught Joe Winder flush in the face; there was nothing he could do.

Instantly the big goon grabbed him by the shoulder. 'Hey! You work at the park.'

'What park?'

The wiry one said, 'Doan tell me he's the guy.'

'Yup,' said the big one, tightening his grip.

The men edged closer. Joe Winder could sense they were angry about not recognizing him sooner.

'Mr. Fisherman,' said the big one acidly.

'That's me,' said Winder. 'You must be the one who wanted to talk about Dr. Koocher.'

The goon named Angel turned off the flashlight and buried it in his jacket. 'Two hours with these damn mosquitoes and you standing right here, the whole fugging tine!' He punched Joe Winder ferociously in the kidney.

As Winder fell, he thought: So they're not here to chat.

His head bounced against limestone and he began to lose consciousness. Then he felt himself being lifted by the armpits, which hurt like hell. They were carrying him somewhere in a hurry.

The husky one, Spearmint Breath, was talking in Joe Winder's ear. 'What'd he say on the phone?'

'Who?'

'The rat doctor.'

'Nothing.' Winder was panting.

'Aw, bullshit.'

'I swear. He left a message, that's all.' Winder tried to walk but felt his legs pedaling air, being swept along. 'Just a message was all,' he said again. 'He wanted to see me but he didn't say why.'

In his other ear, Joe Winder heard the wiry one call him a stinken fugging liar.

'No, I swear.'

They had him up against the side of a truck. Bronco. White. Rusty as hell. Ford Bronco, Winder thought. In case I live through this.

In case anybody might be interested.

The big goon spun Joe Winder around and pinned his arms while the one named Angel slugged him on the point of the jaw. Then he hit him once in each eye. Winder felt his face start to bloat and soften, like a melon going bad. With any luck, total numbness would soon follow.

Angel was working up a sweat. Every time he threw a punch, he let out a sharp yip, like a poodle. It would have been hilarious except for the pain that went with it.

Finally, Spearmint Breath said, 'I don't think he knows jack shit.' Then he said something in Spanish.

Angel said, 'Chur he does, the cokesucker.' This time he hit Joe Winder in the gut.

Perfect. Can't breathe. Can't see. Can't talk.

The big goon let go, and Winder fell limp across the hood of the truck.

The man named Angel said, 'Hey, what the fug.' There was something new in his voice; he sounded very confused. Even in a fog, Joe Winder could tell that the little creep wasn't talking to him—or to Spearmint Breath, either.

Suddenly a great turmoil erupted around the truck, and the man named Angel gave out a scream that didn't sound anything like a little dog. The scream made Joe Winder raise his head off the fender and open what was left of his eyelids.

Through misty slits he saw the husky no-neck goon running toward the bridge. Running away as fast as he could.

Where was Angel?

Something lifted Joe Winder off the truck and laid him on the gravel. He struggled to focus on the face. Face? Naw, had to be a mask. A silvery beard of biblical proportions. Mismatched eyes: one as green as mountain pines, the other brown and dead. Above that, a halo of pink flowers. Weird. The mask leaned closer and whispered in Joe Winder's ear.

The words tumbled around like dice in his brainpan. Made no damn sense. The stranger bent down and said it again.

'I'll get the other one later.'

Joe Winder tried to speak but all that came out was a gulping noise. He heard a car coming down the old road and turned his head to see. Soon he became mesmerized by the twin beams of yellow light, growing larger and larger; lasers shooting out of the mangroves. Or was it a spaceship?

When Winder turned back, he was alone. The man who had saved his life was gone.

The car went by in a rush of noise. Joe Winder watched the taillights vanish over the crest of the bridge. It was an hour before he could get to his feet, another twenty minutes before he could make them move in any sensible way.

As he staggered along the pavement, he counted the cars to keep his mind off the pain. Seven sped past without stopping to help. Winder was thinking, Maybe I feel worse than I look. Maybe the blood doesn't show up so well in the dark. Two or three drivers actually touched the brakes. One honked and hurled a Heineken bottle at him.

The eighth car went by doing seventy at least, heading eastbound to the island. Joe Winder saw the brake lights wink and heard the tires squeal. Slowly the car backed up. The door on the passenger side swung open.

A voice said: 'My God, are you all right?'

'Not really,' said Joe Winder. Half-blind, he was trying to fit himself into the car when he encountered something large and fuzzy on the upholstery.

It was an animal head. He hoped it was not real.

Carrie Lanier picked it up by the snout and tossed it into the back seat. She took Joe Winder's elbow and helped him sit down. Reaching across his lap, she slammed the car door and locked it. 'I can't believe this,' she said, and stepped on the accelerator.

To Joe Winder it felt as if they were going five hundred miles an hour, straight for the ocean.

Carrie Lanier kept glancing over at him, probably to make sure he was still breathing. After a while she said, 'I'm sorry, what was your name again?'

'Joe. Joe Winder.'

'Joe, I can't believe they did this to you.'

Winder raised his head. 'Who?' he said. 'Who did this to me?'

9

Carrie Lanier pulled off Joe Winder's shoes and said, 'You want me to call your girlfriend?'

Winder said no, don't bother. 'She'll be home in a couple hours.'

'What does she do? What kind of work?'

'She talks dirty,' said Joe Winder, 'on the phone.'

Carrie sat on the edge of the bed. She put a hand on his forehead and felt for fever.

He said, 'Thanks for cleaning me up.'

'It's all right. You want more ginger ale?'

'No, but there's some Darvocets in the medicine cabinet.'

'I think Advils will do just fine.'

Winder grunted unhappily. 'Look at me. You ever see a face like this on an Advil commercial?'

She brought him one lousy Darvocet and he swallowed it dry. He felt worse than he could remember ever feeling, and it wasn't only the pain. It was anger, too.

'So who beat me up?' he said.

'I don't know,' said Carrie Lanier. 'I imagine it was somebody from the park. I imagine you stuck your nose where it doesn't belong.'

'I didn't,' Joe Winder said, 'not yet.'

He felt her rise from the bed, and soon heard her moving around the apartment. He called her name and she came back to the bedroom, sitting in the same indentation on the mattress.

'I was looking for something to bandage those ribs.'

'That's okay,' said Winder. 'It only hurts when I breathe.'

Carrie said, 'Maybe I don't need to tell you this, but the

Amazing Kingdom is not what it seems. It's not fun and games, there's a ton of money at stake.'

'You mean it's a scam?'

'Hey, everything's a scam when you get down to it.' Her voice softened. 'All I'm saying is, stick to your job. I know it's boring as hell, but stick to it anyway. You shouldn't go poking around.'

Joe Winder said, 'My poking days are over.'

'Then what were you doing out there tonight?'

'Meeting someone at the bridge. What about you?'

'I had a free-lance gig,' Carrie said. 'A birthday party up in South Miami. Mummy and Daddy wanted Junior to meet Robbie Raccoon in person. What the heck, it was an easy five hundred. And you should've seen the house. Or should I say mansion.'

Floating, Joe Winder said: 'What do you have to do at these parties?'

'Dance with the kiddies. Waggle my coon tail. Juggle marshmallows, whatever. And pose for pictures, of course. Everybody wants a picture.'

She touched his brow again. 'You're still hot. Maybe I ought to call your girlfriend at work.'

'Don't do that,' said Joe Winder, 'please.' He didn't want Carrie to hook up with Miriam by accident. Miriam and her hot-tub 'blow-yobs.'

'This is important,' he said. 'Did you see anyone else on the road out there? Like maybe a circus-type person.'

'You're not well,' said Carrie Lanier.

'No, I mean it. Big guy with a beard. Flowers on his head.' It sounded so ridiculous, maybe he'd hallucinated the whole thing.

'That's not a circus person you're describing. That's Jesus. Or maybe Jerry García.'

'Whatever,' Joe Winder said. 'Did you see anybody on the road? That's all I'm asking.'

'Nope,' Carrie said. 'I really ought to be on my way. What'd you decide about calling the cops?'

'Not a good idea,' said Winder. 'Especially with Dr. Koocher still missing. Maybe the bad guys'll call back.'

'The creeps who did this to you?' Carrie sounded incredulous. 'I don't think so, Joe.'

She didn't say anything for several moments. Joe Winder tried to read her expression but she had turned away.

'How much does she make, your girlfriend, talking sexy on the phone?'

'Not much. Two hundred a week, sometimes two fifty. They get a bonus for selling videos. And panties, too. Twenty bucks a pair. They buy 'em wholesale from Zayre's.'

'Two fifty, that stinks,' said Carrie Lanier. 'But, hey, I've been there. You do what you have to.'

'Nina's got no complaints,' said Joe Winder. 'She says there's a creative component to every job; the trick is finding it.'

Carrie turned around, glowing. 'She's absolutely right, your girlfriend is. You know what I did before I got my SAG card? I worked in a cough-drop factory. Wrapping the lozenges in foil, one at a time. The only way I kept from going crazy—each cough drop, I'd make a point to wrap it differently from the others. One I'd do in squares, the next I'd do in a triangle, the one after that I'd fold into a rhombus or something. Believe me, it got to be a challenge, especially at thirty lozenges per minute. That was our quota, or else we got docked.'

Joe Winder said the first dumb thing that popped into his brain. 'I wonder if Nina has a quota.'

'She sounds like she's doing just fine,' Carrie said. 'Listen, Joe, I think you ought to know. There's a rumor going around about the rat doctor. Supposedly they found a note.'

'Yeah?'

'You know what kind of note I mean. The bad kind. Good-bye, cruel world, and all that. Supposedly they found it in his desk at the lab.'

Joe Winder said, 'What exactly did it say, this supposed note?'

'I don't know all the details.' Carrie Lanier stood up to go. 'Get some rest. It's just a rumor.'

'Give me another pill, and sit down for a second.'

'Nope, I can't.'

'Get me another goddamn pill!'

'Go to sleep, Joe.'

By eight the next morning, a crowd had gathered beneath the Card Sound Bridge to see the dead man hanging from the center span. From a distance it looked like a wax dummy with an elongated neck. Up close it looked much different.

The crowd was made up mostly of tourist families on their way down to the Florida Keys. They parked haphazardly on the shoulder of the road and clambered down to where the police cars and marine patrols were positioned, blue lights flashing in that insistent syncopation of emergency. A few of the tourist husbands took out portable video cameras to record the excitement, but the best vantage was from the decks of the yachts and sleek sailboats that had dropped anchor in the channel near the bridge. The mast of one of the sloops had snagged on the hanging dead man and torn off his trousers as the vessel had passed through the bridge at dawn. By now everyone had noticed that the corpse wore no underwear.

A man from the Dade County Medical Examiner's Office stood on the jetty and looked up at the dead body swinging in the breeze, forty feet over the water. Standing next to the man from the medical examiner's was FBI Agent Billy Hawkins, who was asking lots of questions that the man from the medical examiner's didn't answer. He was keenly aware that the FBI held absolutely no authority in this matter.

'I was on my way to the park,' Agent Hawkins was saying, 'and I couldn't help but notice.'

With cool politeness, the man from the medical examiner's office said: 'Not much we can tell you at the moment. Except he's definitely dead, that much is obvious.' The coroner knew that most FBI agents went their whole careers without ever setting eyes on an actual corpse. The way Billy Hawkins was staring, he hadn't seen many.

'The poor bastard has no pants,' the agent observed. 'What do you make of that?'

'Sunburned testicles is what I make of that. If we don't haul him down soon.'

Agent Hawkins nodded seriously. He gave the coroner a card. The feds, they loved to hand out cards.

The man from the medical examiner's played along. 'I'll call if anything turns up,' he lied. The FBI man said thanks and headed back toward his car; he was easy to track—a blocky gray suit moving through a bright sea of Hawaiian prints and Day-Glo surfer shorts. A dog in a flower bed.

The amused coroner soon was joined by an equally amused trooper from the Florida Highway Patrol.

'Nice day for a hangin',' drawled the trooper. His name was Jim Tile. He wore the standard mirrored sunglasses with gold wire frames.

'I don't see a rope,' said the coroner, gesturing at the dead man high above them. 'What the hell's he hanging with?'

'That would be fishing line,' Jim Tile said.

The coroner thought about it for several moments. Then he said, 'All right, Jim, what do you think?'

'I think it's a pretty poor excuse for a suicide,' said the trooper.

A tanned young man in a crisp blue shirt and a red necktie worked his way out of the crowd. The man walked up to the coroner and somberly extended his right hand. He wore some kind of plastic ID badge clipped to his belt. The coroner knew that the tanned young man wasn't a cop, because his ID badge was in the shape of an animal head, possibly a raccoon or a small bear.

Charles Chelsea gestured toward the dead man without looking. In a voice dripping with disgust, he said, 'Can't you guys do something about that?'

'We're working on it,' replied the coroner.

'Well, work a little faster.'

The man from the medical examiner's looked down at Charles Chelsea's animal-head ID and smiled. 'These things can't be hurried,' he said.

A jurisdictional dispute had delayed the removal of the offending body for most of the morning. It was a tricky geographic dilemma. The middle of the Card Sound Bridge marked the boundary line between Dade and Monroe counties. The Monroe County medical examiner's man had arrived first on the scene, and decided that the dead man was hanging in Dade County airspace and therefore was not his responsibility. The Dade County medical examiner's man had argued vigorously that the victim had most certainly plummeted from the Monroe County side of the bridge. Besides which the Dade County morgue was already packed to the rafters with homicides, and it wouldn't kill Monroe County to take just one. Neither coroner would budge, so the dead body just hung there for four hours until the Monroe County medical examiner announced that he was needed at a fatal traffic accident in Marathon, and scurried away, leaving his colleague stuck with the corpse—and now some whiny pain-in-the-ass PR man.

The coroner said to Charles Chelsea: 'We've got to get some pictures. Take some measurements. Preserve the scene, just in case.'

'In case of what? The poor jerk killed himself.' Chelsea sounded annoyed. Preserving the scene was the opposite of what he wanted.

Trooper Jim Tile removed his sunglasses and folded them into a breast pocket. 'I guess I can go home. Now that we got an expert on the case.'

Charles Chelsea started to rebuke this impertinent flatfoot, but changed his mind when he took a good look. The trooper was very tall and very muscular and very black, all of which made Chelsea edgy. He sensed that Jim Tile was not the sort to be impressed by titles, but nonetheless he introduced himself as a vice president at the Amazing Kingdom of Thrills.

'How nifty,' said the trooper.

'Yes, it is,' Chelsea said pleasantly. Then, lowering his voice: 'But, to be frank, we could do without this kind of spectacle.' His golden chin pointed up at the hapless corpse. Then he jerked a thumb over his shoulder at the chattering throng of onlookers.

'All these people,' Chelsea said urgently, 'were on their way to our theme park.'

'How do you know?' asked Jim Tile.

'Look around here—where else would they be going? What else is there to see?'

'In other words, you would like us to remove the deceased as quickly as possible.'

'Yes, exactly,' said Charles Chelsea.

'Because it's competition.'

The publicity man's eyes narrowed. Frostily he said, 'That's not at all what I meant.' Giving up on the black policeman, he appealed to the coroner's sense of propriety: 'All the young children hanging around—they shouldn't be witness to something like this. Vacations are for fun and fantasy, not for looking at dead bodies.'

Jim Tile said, 'They seem to be enjoying it.'

'We didn't ask for an audience,' the coroner added. He was accustomed to gawkers in Miami. Shopping malls were the worst; drug dealers were always leaving murdered rivals in the trunks of luxury automobiles at shopping malls. The crowds were unbelievable, pushing and shoving, everybody wanting a peek at the stiff.

The coroner told Charles Chelsea: 'This always happens. It's just a sick fact of human nature.'

'Well, can't you hurry up and get him—it—down? The longer it stays up there, the more people will stop.' Chelsea paused to survey the size of the crowd. 'This is horrible,' he said, 'right in the middle of Summerfest. It's giving all these folks the wrong idea.'

Jim Tile couldn't wait to hear more. 'The wrong idea about what?'

'About Florida,' said Charles Chelsea. The indignation in his tone was authentic. 'This is not the image we're trying to promote. Surely you can understand.'

Grimly he turned and disappeared into the gallery of onlookers.

The coroner once again fixed his attention on what was hanging from the Card Sound Bridge. He asked Jim Tile, 'So what do you think about getting him down from there?'

'Easy,' said the trooper. 'I'll go up and cut the line.'

'You really think that's safe?'

Jim Tile looked at him curiously.

'With all these people milling around,' said the coroner. 'What if he hits somebody? Look at all these damn boats.' He frowned and shook his head. 'I think we've got a serious liability risk here. Somebody could be injured or killed.'

'By a falling corpse,' said Jim Tile thoughtfully.

'You betcha. Look at all these damn tourists.'

Jim Tile took out a bullhorn and ordered the boats to weigh anchor. He also instructed the bystanders to get off the jetty under threat of arrest. Then he went to the top of the bridge and quickly found what he was looking for: a nest of heavy monofilament fishing line tangled around the base of a concrete column. One end of the monofilament was attached to the type of flat plastic spool used by Cuban handline fishermen. The other end of the line led over the side of the bridge, and was attached to the dead man's neck.

The trooper got a 35-millimeter camera out of the patrol car and took pictures of the column and the knot. Then he got down on his belly and extended his head over the side of the bridge and snapped several aerial-type photographs of the hanging corpse.

After Jim Tile put the camera away, he waved twice at the coroner, still standing on the rocks below. Then, when the coroner gave the signal, the trooper unfolded his pocketknife and cut through the monofilament fishing line.

He heard the crowd go *ooooohhhh* before he heard the splash. A marine patrol boat idled up to the dead man and fished him out of the water with a short-handled gaff.

They were loading the body into the van when the coroner told his theory to Jim Tile. 'I don't think it's a suicide,' he said.

'What, somebody was using him for bait?'

'No, this is what I think happened,' said the coroner, demon-

strating with his arms. 'You know how these Cuban guys twirl
the fishlines over their heads real fast to make a long cast? It
looks to me like he messed up and wrapped the damn thing tight
around his neck, like a bolo. That's what I think.' He picked up a
clipboard and began to write. 'What was the color of his eyes?
Brown, I think.'

'I didn't look,' said Jim Tile. He wasn't crazy about dead bodies.

The man from the medical examiner's reached into the van
and tugged at the woolen blanket, revealing the dead man's
features.

'I was right,' said the coroner, scribbling again. 'Brown they
are.'

Jim Tile stared at the rictus face and said, 'Damn, I know that
guy.' He wasn't a fisherman.

'A name would be nice,' the coroner said. 'He lost his wallet
when he lost his pants.'

Angel, the trooper said. Angel Gaviria. 'Don't ask me how to
spell it.'

'Where do you know him from?'

'He used to be a cop.' Jim Tile yanked the blanket up to cover
the dead man's face. 'Before he got convicted.'

'Convicted of what?'

'Everything short of first-degree murder.'

'Jesus Christ. And here he is, out of the slammer already.'

'Yeah,' said Jim Tile. 'Modeling neckwear.'

Bud Schwartz had been a two-bit burglar since he was seventeen
years old. He was neither proud of it nor ashamed. It was what
he did, period. It suited his talents. Whenever his mother gave
him a hard time about getting an honest job, Bud Schwartz
reminded her that he was the only one of her three children
who was not in psychoanalysis. His sister was a lawyer and his
brother was a stockbroker, and both of them were miserably
fucked up. Bud Schwartz was a crook, sure, but at least he was
at peace with himself.

He considered himself a competent burglar who was swift,
thorough and usually cautious. The times he'd been caught—five

in all—these were flukes. A Rottweiler that wasn't in the yard the night before. A nosy neighbor, watering her begonias at three in the goddamn morning. A getaway car with bad plugs. That sort of thing. Occupational hazards, in Bud Schwartz's opinion—plain old lousy luck.

Normally he was a conservative guy who played the odds and didn't like unnecessary risks. Why he ever accepted the rat-napping job from Molly McNamara, he couldn't figure. Broad daylight, thousands of people, the middle of a fucking theme park. Jesus! Maybe he did it just to break the monotony. Or maybe because ten grand was ten grand.

Definitely a score. In his entire professional burgling career, Bud Schwartz had never stolen anything worth ten thousand dollars. The one time he'd pinched a Rolex Oyster, it turned out to be fake. Another time he got three diamond rings from a hotel room on Key Biscayne—a big-time movie actress, too—and the fence informed him it was all zircon. Fucking paste. Or so said the fence.

Who could blame him for saying yes to Molly McNamara, or at least checking it out? So when he gets out of jail, he rounds up Danny Pogue—Danny, who's really nothing but a pair of hands; somebody you drag along to help carry the shit to the car. But reliable, as far as that goes. Not really smart enough to pull anything.

So together they meet the old lady once, twice. Get directions, instructions. Go over the whole damn thing until they're bored to tears, except for the part about what to do with the voles. Bud Schwartz had assumed the whole point was to free the damn things, the way Molly talked. 'Liberate' was the word she'd used. Of course, if he'd known then what he knew now, he wouldn't have chucked that one little rat into the red convertible. If he'd known there were only two of the damn things left on the whole entire planet, he wouldn't ever have let Danny take a throw at the Winnebago.

Now the voles were gone, and Bud Schwartz and Danny Pogue were nursing their respective gunshot wounds in the old lady's apartment.

Watching a slide show about endangered species.

'This formidable fellow,' Molly McNamara was saying, 'is the North American crocodile.'

Danny Pogue said, 'Looks like a gator.'

'No, it's a different animal entirely,' said Molly. 'There's only a few dozen left in the wild.'

'So what?' said Danny Pogue. 'You got tons of gators. So many they went and opened a hunting season. I can't see gettin' all worked up about crocodiles dyin' off, not when they got a season on gators. It don't make sense.'

Molly said, 'You're missing the point.'

'He can't help it,' said Bud Schwartz. 'Just go on to the next slide.'

Molly clicked the remote. 'This is the Schaus' swallowtail butterfly.'

'Now that's pretty,' said Danny Pogue. 'I can see wanting to save somethin' like that. Isn't that a pretty butterfly, Bud?'

'Beautiful,' said Bud Schwartz. 'Really gorgeous. Next?'

Molly asked why he was in such a hurry.

'No reason,' he replied.

Danny Pogue snickered. 'Maybe 'cause there's a movie he wants to see on cable.'

'Really?' Molly said. 'Bud, you should've told me. We can always continue the orientation tomorrow.'

'That's okay,' Bud Schwartz said. 'Go on with the program.'

'*Amazon Cheerleaders*,' said Danny Pogue. 'We seen the ending the other night.'

Molly said, 'I don't believe I've heard of that one.'

'Get on with the slides,' said Bud Schwartz gloomily. Of all the partners he'd ever had, Danny Pogue was turning out to be the dumbest by a mile.

A picture of something called a Key Largo wood rat appeared on the slide screen, and Danny exclaimed: 'Hey, it looks just like one a them voles!'

'Not really,' said Molly McNamara patiently. 'This hardy little fellow is one of five endangered species native to the North Key Largo habitat.' She went on to explain the uniqueness of the island—hardwood hammocks, brackish lakes and acres of precious mangroves. And, only a few miles offshore, the only living coral reef in North America. 'Truly a tropical paradise,' said Molly McNamara, 'which is why it's worth fighting for.'

As she clicked through the rest of the slides, Bud Schwartz was thinking: How hard would it be to overpower the old bat and escape? Two grown men with six functional limbs, come on. Just grab the frigging purse, take the gun—what could she do?

The trouble was, Bud Schwartz wasn't fond of guns. He didn't mind stealing them, but he'd never pointed one at anybody, never fired one, even at a tin can. Getting shot by Molly McNamara had only reinforced his view that guns were a tool for the deranged. He knew the law, and the law smiled on harmless unarmed house burglars. A burglar with a gun wasn't a burglar anymore, he was a robber. Not only did robbers get harder time, but the accommodations were markedly inferior. Bud Schwartz had never been up to Raiford but he had a feeling he wouldn't like it. He also had a hunch that if push came to shove, Danny Pogue would roll over like a big dumb puppy. Do whatever the cops wanted, including testify.

Bud Schwartz decided he needed more time to think.

A new slide came up on the screen and he told Molly McNamara to wait a second. 'Is that an endangered species, too?' he asked.

'Unfortunately not,' Molly said. 'That's Francis X. Kingsbury, the man who's destroying the island.'

Danny Pogue lifted his chin out of his hands and said, 'Yeah? How?'

'Mr. Kingsbury is the founder and chief executive officer of the Amazing Kingdom of Thrills—the so-called amusement park you boys raided the other day. It's a tourist trap, plain and simple. It brings traffic, garbage, litter, air pollution, effluent—Kingsbury cares nothing about preserving the habitat. He's a developer.'

The word came out as an epithet.

Bud Schwartz studied the jowly middle-aged face on the

screen. Kingsbury was smiling, and you could tell it was killing him. His nose was so large that it seemed three-dimensional, a huge mottled tuber of some kind, looming out of the wall.

'Public enemy number one,' said Molly. She glared at the picture on the screen. 'Yes, indeed. The park is only a smoke-screen. We've got reason to believe that Mr. Kingsbury holds the majority interest in a new golfing resort called Falcon Trace, which abuts the Amazing Kingdom. We have reason to believe that Kingsbury's intention is to eventually bulldoze every square inch of ocean waterfront. You know what that means?'

Danny Pogue pursed his lips. Bud Schwartz said nothing; he was trying to guess where the old coot was heading with this.

Molly said, 'It means no more crocodiles, no more wood rats, no more swallowtail butterflies.'

'No more butterflies?' Danny Pogue looked at her with genuine alarm. 'What kinda bastard would do something like that?'

'This kind,' said Molly, aiming a stern papery finger at the screen.

'But we can stop him, right?' Bud Schwartz was smiling.

'You can help, yes.'

'How?' Danny Pogue demanded. 'What do we do?'

Molly said, 'I need to know the full extent of Mr. Kingsbury's financial involvement—you see, there are legal avenues we could pursue, if only we knew.' She flicked off the slide projector and turned on a pair of brass table lamps. 'Unfortunately,' she said, 'Mr. Kingsbury is a very secretive man. Every document we've gotten, we've had to sue for. He is extremely wealthy and hires only the finest attorneys.'

From his expression it was clear that Danny Pogue was struggling to keep up. 'Go on,' he said.

Bud Schwartz inhaled audibly, a reverse sigh. 'Danny, we're burglars, remember? What do burglars do?'

Danny Pogue glanced at Molly McNamara, who said, 'Your partner's got the right idea.'

'Wait a second,' said Danny Pogue. 'More voles?'

'Jesus Christ, no,' Bud Schwartz said. 'No more voles.'

By now he was planning ahead again, feeling better about his prospects. He was wondering about Francis X. Kingsbury's money, and thinking what a shame that a bunch of greedy lawyers should get so much of it, all for themselves.

10

Nina didn't believe him, not for a second.

'You were drinking. You opened your big fat mouth and somebody smacked you.'

'No,' Joe Winder said. 'That's not what happened.'

Well, the truth would only frighten her. He sat up and squinted brutally at the sunlight.

'I'm so disappointed in you,' Nina said. She studied the bruises on his face, and not out of concern; she was looking for clues.

'I wasn't drinking,' said Joe Winder. That much he had to assert, out of pride. 'They were muggers, that's all.'

Nina pointed to his wallet, which was on the dresser. 'Muggers, Joe? Some muggers.'

'A car scared them off.'

She rolled her eyes. 'You're only making it worse.'

'What happened to trust?' Winder said. 'What happened to true goddamn love?' He got out of bed and tested his legs. Nina watched reproachfully.

'I smell perfume,' she said. 'Did you bring a woman home last night?'

'No, a woman brought *me*. She saw me on Card Sound Road and wanted to go to the police. I told her to bring me here so I could be with the love of my life.'

'Did you screw her?'

'Only six or seven times.' He went to the bathroom and stuck his face under the shower and screamed at the top of his lungs, it hurt so bad. He screamed until his ears reverberated. Then he came out, dripping, and said: 'Nina, be reasonable. Who'd make love with me, looking like this?'

'Not me.'

'Not anybody. Besides, I was half blind. I probably would've stuck it in her ear by mistake.'

Nina smiled. Finally.

Winder asked her who'd called so damn early. The phone is what woke him up.

'Your employer, Mr. Charles Chelsea. He wanted you to know there was a dead person hanging from the bridge this morning.'

Joe Winder shuffled back to the shower. This time he stepped all the way in and braced his forehead against the tile. He made the water as hot as he could bear. Maybe the dead man was Angel, he thought, or maybe it was the big guy who'd saved him from Angel.

When Winder got out, Nina stood poised with a towel in her hand. She wore a white halter top and no panties. Winder took the towel and draped it over his head.

'Why do you do this to me,' he mumbled.

'Did you hear what I said? About the dead man?' She peeled off the halter and climbed in the shower. 'Did you save me some hot water? I've got to shave my legs.' She turned the faucet handles and cursed the cold.

'Sorry,' said Joe Winder. Raising his voice over the beating of the water: 'So why is Chelsea calling me, just because there's some dead guy? The bridge is five miles from the Kingdom.'

Nina didn't answer; just filed the question away and kept on shaving. Joe Winder sat down on the toilet and watched the fixtures fog up. Plenty of hot water, he thought; no problem.

When she came out, he remarked how beautiful she looked. 'Like a sleek arctic seal.'

'Oh stop it.'

'Don't dry off, please. Don't ever dry off.'

'Get your hand away from there.' Nina slapped him sharply. 'Put your clothes on. Chelsea's waiting at the office.'

Joe Winder said, 'I'm phoning in sick.'

'No, you're not. You can't.' She wrapped the towel around her hair and left the rest bare. 'He wasn't calling about the dead person on the bridge, he was calling about the whale.'

'Orky?'

Nina opened the bathroom door to let out the steamy humidity. Joe Winder impulsively clutched her around the waist. He pressed his cheek against her damp thigh, and began to hum the tune of 'Poor Pitiful Me.' Nina pried him loose and said, 'I'm glad you don't get beat up every day.'

Something was out of alignment in Winder's brain. He blinked three or four times, slowly, but even as the steam cleared it didn't go away. Double vision! The bastards had pounded him that badly. Nina's bare bottom appeared to him as four gleaming porcelain orbs.

Distractedly, he said, 'Go on. Something about the whale?'

'Yes,' said Nina. She stood before the mirror, checking her armpits for stubble. 'Chelsea said the whale is dead.'

'Hmmm,' said Joe Winder. Orky the Killer Whale.

'And?' he said.

'And, I don't know.' Nina stepped into her panties. 'He said for you to come right away. He said it was an emergency.'

'First let's go to bed.' Winder came up behind her. In the mirror he saw two pairs of hands cupping two pairs of nipples. He saw two faces that looked just like his—lumpy, lacerated, empurpled—nuzzling the tan silky slopes of two feminine necks.

'All right, Joe,' Nina said, turning around. 'But I've got to be honest: I'm very disappointed in you—'

'It wasn't what you think.'

'—and I'm only doing this because you're in pain.' Mechanically Nina took his hand and led him toward the bed. She kicked off her underwear and unwrapped the towel from her hair. Winder was grinning like an idiot.

'I'm warning you,' Nina said, 'this isn't an act of passion, it's an act of pity.'

'I'll take it,' said Joe Winder. 'But, please, no more talking for a while.'

'All right,' she said. 'No more talking.'

Orky the Killer Whale had come to the Amazing Kingdom of Thrills under clouded circumstances. His true name (or the name bestowed by his human captors off the coast of British Columbia) was Samson. Delivered in a drugged stupor to a north California marine park, he was measured at twenty-nine feet and seven inches, a robust male example of the species *orca*. Samson was larger than the other tame killer whales in the tank, and proved considerably more recalcitrant and unpredictable. In his first six months of captivity he mauled two trained porpoises and chomped the tail off a popular sea lion named Mr. Mugsy. Trainers worked overtime trying to teach their new star the most rudimentary of whale tricks—leaping through a plastic hoop, or snatching a dead mackerel from the fingers of a pretty model—with minimal success. One day he would perform like a champ, the next he would sink to the bottom of the tank and fart belligerently, launching balloon-sized bubbles of fishy gas to the surface. The audience seldom found this entertaining. Eventually most of the seasoned whale trainers refused to enter the water with Samson. Those who tried to ride his immense black dorsal were either whiplashed or pretzeled or corkscrewed into semi-consciousness.

Quite by accident, it was discovered that Samson was enraged by the color green. This became evident on the day that the human trainers switched to vivid Kelly-green tank suits without telling the other performing mammals. Samson was supposed to open the first show by fetching an inflatable topless mermaid and gaily delivering it to a young man on a ladder, in exchange for a fistful of smelts. On this particular morning, Samson retrieved the toy, carried it across the water on his snout, flipped it into the bleachers, snatched the green-clad trainer off the ladder, flipped *him* into the bleachers, then dived to the bottom of the tank and began to pass gas relentlessly. Each time somebody tried to lure him up, Samson shot from the depths with his mouth open, the great black-and-white jaws clacking like a truck door. The crowd loved it. They thought it was part of the act.

Reluctantly the curators of the California marine park concluded that this whale was one dangerous rogue. They attempted to peddle him to another marine park, far away on the western coast of Florida, but first they changed his name to Ramu. The transaction took place at a time when ocean-theme parks around the country were reporting various troubles with trained killer whales, and animal-rights groups were seeking legislation to prevent capturing them for exhibit. Word of Samson's behavioral quirks had spread throughout the marine-park industry, which is why it was necessary to change his name before trying to sell him.

The day the deal was done, Samson was tranquilized, lashed to a canvas litter and placed aboard a chartered Sikorsky helicopter. There workers took turns sponging him with salt water during the arduous cross-country flight, which lasted seventeen hours, including stops for refueling. By the time Samson arrived in Sarasota, he was in a vile and vindictive mood. During his first fifteen minutes in the new tank, he savagely foreshortened a pectoral fin on another male *orca* and destroyed the floating basket through which he was supposed to slam-dunk beach balls. Weeks passed with little improvement in the new whale's temperament. One fateful Sunday, the animal abruptly awakened from its funk, tail-walked across the tank and did a dazzling double somersault before hundreds of delighted tourists. When a stubby woman in a green plaid sundress leaned too close with her Nikon, the whale seized her in his teeth, dragged her once around the tank, then spit her out like an olive pit.

It was then that Samson's new owners realized that they had been duped; they'd bought themselves a bum whale. Ramu was in fact the infamous and incorrigible Samson. Immediately the beast was quarantined as a repeat offender, while the Sarasota theme park made plans to resell him under the misleadingly gentle name of Orky.

Francis X. Kingsbury was the ideal chump. The soon-to-be-opened Amazing Kingdom of Thrills was shopping for a major ocean attraction to compete with Disney World's 'living reef.' Kingsbury saw the Orky offer as a bargain of a lifetime—a trained killer whale for only nine hundred bucks, plus freight! Kingsbury snapped at it.

Orky was more than a disappointment, he was a dud. No one at the Amazing Kingdom could train the whale to do a single trick on cue; capable of wondrous gymnastic feats, the animal remained oblivious of regimen and performed only when he damn well felt like it. Often he did his best work in the middle of the night, when the stadium was empty. But on those nocturnal occasions, when the park was closed and there was no one to reward him with buckets of dead mullet, Orky furiously would ram the sides of the whale tank until the Plexiglas cracked and the plaster buckled.

Because it was impossible to predict his moods, Orky's shows were not posted in a regular schedule. Tourists paid their money, took their seats and hoped for the best. Once in a great while, the killer whale would explode in exuberant ballet, but more often he just sulked or blew water aimlessly.

One time Francis X. Kingsbury had suggested punishing the mammoth creature by withholding supper. Orky retaliated by breaking into the pelican pool and wolfing down nine of the slow-moving birds. After that, Kingsbury said to hell with the goddamn whale and gave up on training the beast. He knew he'd been scammed but was too proud to admit it. Kingsbury's corporate underlings sensed that Orky was a sore spot with the boss, and avoided mentioning the whale exhibit in his presence.

Until today.

With Orky unexpectedly dead, the subject was bound to come up. Charles Chelsea decided on a pre-emptive strike. He broke the news as Francis Kingsbury was munching his regular breakfast bagel. 'Good,' Kingsbury said, spraying crumbs. 'Hated that fucking load.'

'Sir, it's not good,' said Charles Chelsea, 'publicity-wise.'

'How do you figure,' Kingsbury said. 'I mean, shit, what's a lousy whale to these people. You know who I mean—the media.'

Charles Chelsea said he would try to explain it on the way to the autopsy.

Joe Winder's vision returned to normal after making love to Nina; he regarded this as providential. He took a cab to Card Sound Road and retrieved his car. When he got back to the apartment, he changed to a long-sleeved shirt, charcoal trousers and a navy necktie, in the hope that high fashion would divert attention from his pulverized face. When he got to the Amazing Kingdom, he saw he had nothing to worry about. Everybody was staring at the dead killer whale.

They had hauled the remains to one of the parking lots, and roped a perimeter to keep out nosy customers. To conceal Orky's corpse, which was as large as a boxcar, Charles Chelsea had rented an immense tent from an auto dealership in Homestead. The tent was brilliantly striped and decorated with the legend 'SOUTH FLORIDA TOYOTA-THON.' A dozen or so electric fans had been requisitioned to circulate the air, which had grown heavy with the tang of dead whale. The staff veterinarian, a man named Kukor, was up to his knees in Orky's abdomen when Joe Winder arrived.

'Joe, thank God,' said Chelsea, with an air of grave urgency. He led Winder to a corner and said, 'Mr. X is here, to give you some idea.'

'Some idea of what?'

'Of how serious this is.'

Joe Winder said, 'Charlie, I don't mean to be disrespectful but I'm not sure why I'm needed.' Over his shoulder, he heard somebody crank up a chain saw.

'Joey, think! First the damn mango voles and now Orky. It's gonna look like we're neglecting the wildlife. And this whole killer-whale thing, it's gotten very controversial. There was a piece in *Newsweek* three weeks ago.' Charles Chelsea was sweating extravagantly, and Winder assumed it had something to do with the presence of Francis X. Kingsbury.

Chelsea went on, 'I know it's unpleasant, Joe, but you can leave as soon as Doc Kukor gives us a cause of death.'

Joe Winder nodded. 'How many words?'

'Three hundred. And I need it for the early news.'

'Fine, Charlie. Later you and I need to talk.'

Chelsea was peering through the flaps in the tent, making sure that no gawkers had sneaked past the security men.

'Listen to me,' Joe Winder said. 'There's some big trouble in this park. I got the shit kicked out of me last night because of it.'

For the first time Chelsea noticed the battered condition of Joe

Winder's face. He said, 'What the hell happened? No, wait, not now. Not with Mr. X around. We'll chat later, I promise.'

Winder grabbed his elbow. 'I need to know everything about the dead man at the bridge.'

Chelsea shook free and said, 'Later, Joe, for heaven's sake. Let's tackle the crisis at hand, shall we?'

Together they returned to the autopsy. Instead of concentrating on Orky's entrails, Joe Winder scanned the small group of official observers: a state wildlife officer, taking notes; the tow-truck drivers who had hauled the whale corpse to the tent; three of Uncle Ely's Elves, apparently recruited as extra manpower; and Francis X. Kingsbury himself, mouthing obscenities over the gruesome ceremony.

Nervously Chelsea directed Joe Winder to Kingsbury's side and introduced him. 'This is the fellow I told you about,' said the PR man. 'Our ace in the hole.'

Kingsbury chuckled darkly. 'Blame us for this? Some fucking fish croaks, how can they blame us?'

Joe Winder shrugged. 'Why not?' he said.

Cutting in quickly, Chelsea said: 'Don't worry, sir, it'll die down. It's just the crazy pro-animal types, that's all.' He planted a moist hand on Winder's shoulder. 'Joe's got the perfect touch for this.'

'Hope so,' said Francis X. Kingsbury. 'Meanwhile, the stink, holy Christ! Don't we have some Glade. I mean, this is fucking rank.'

'Right away,' said Chelsea, dashing off in search of air freshener.

Kingsbury gestured at the billowing tent, the murmuring onlookers, the husk of deceased behemoth. 'You believe this shit?' he said to Joe Winder. 'I'm a goddamn real-estate man is all. I don't know from animals.'

'It's a tricky business,' Winder agreed.

'Who'd believe it, I mean, looking at this thing.'

It was quite a strange scene, Joe Winder had to admit. 'I'm sure they can find a new whale for the show.'

'This time mechanical,' Kingsbury said, jabbing a finger at Orky's lifeless form. 'No more real ones. Computerized, that'd be the way to go. That's how Disney would handle it, eh?'

'Either that or a hologram,' said Joe Winder with a wink. 'Think of all the money you'd save on whale food.'

Just then Dr. Kukor, the veterinarian, tripped on something and fell down inside Orky's closet-sized stomach cavity. Two of Uncle Ely's Elves bravely charged forward to help, hoisting the doctor to his feet.

'Oh my,' Kukor said, pointing. The elves ran away frantically, their huge curly-toed shoes slapping noisily on the blood-slickened asphalt.

'What?' barked Francis X. Kingsbury. 'What is it?'

'I don't believe this,' said the veterinarian.

Kingsbury stepped forward to see for himself and Joe Winder followed, though he was sorry he did.

'Call somebody,' wheezed Dr. Kukor.

'Looks like a human,' Kingsbury remarked. He turned to stare at Winder because Winder was clinging to his arm. 'Don't puke on me or you're fired,' said Kingsbury.

Joe Winder was trying not to pass out. The corpse wasn't in perfect condition, but you could tell who it was.

A wan and shaky Dr. Kukor stepped out of Orky's excavated carcass. 'Asphyxiation,' he declared numbly. 'The whale choked to death.'

'Well, damn,' said Francis X. Kingsbury.

Joe Winder thought: Choked to death on Will Koocher. Koocher, in a mint-green golf shirt.

'Somebody call somebody,' Kukor said. 'This is way out of my field.'

Winder reeled away from the scene. In a croaky voice he said, 'That's the worst thing I ever saw.'

'You?' Kingsbury laughed harshly. 'Three fucking tons of whale meat, talk about a nightmare.'

'Yes,' Joe Winder said, gasping for fresh air.

'I'm thinking South Korea or maybe the Sudan,' Kingsbury

was saying. 'Stamp it "Tuna," who the hell would ever know? Those little fuckers are starving.'

'What?' said Winder. 'What did you say?'

'Providing I can get some goddamn ice, pronto.'

11

Charles Chelsea decreed that there should be no mention of Dr. Will Koocher in the press release. 'Stick to Orky,' he advised Joe Winder. 'Three hundred words max.'

'You're asking me to lie.'

'No, I'm asking you to omit a few superfluous details. The whale died suddenly overnight, scientists are investigating, blah, blah, blah. Oh, and be sure to include a line that Mr. Francis X. Kingsbury is shocked and saddened.' Chelsea paused, put a finger to his chin. 'Scratch the "shocked," he said. ' "Saddened" is plenty. "Shocked" makes it sound like something, I don't know, something—'

'Out of the ordinary?' said Joe Winder.

'Right. Exactly.'

'Charlie, you are one sorry bucket of puss.'

Chelsea steepled his hands on his chest. Then he unfolded them. Then he folded them once more and said, 'Joe, this is a question of privacy, not censorship. Until Dr. Koocher's wife is officially notified, the least we can do is spare her the agony of hearing about it on the evening news.'

For a moment, Winder saw two Charles Chelseas instead of one. Somewhere in the cacophonous gearbox of his brain, he heard the hiss of a petcock, blowing off steam. 'Charlie,' he said blankly, 'the man was eaten by a fucking thirty-foot leviathan. This isn't going to remain our little secret very long.'

Chelsea's brow wrinkled. 'Eventually, yes, I suppose we'll have to make some sort of public statement. Seeing as it was our whale.'

Joe Winder leaned forward on one elbow. 'Charlie, I'm going to be honest.'

'I appreciate that.'

'Very soon I intend to kick the living shit out of you.'

Chelsea stiffened. He shifted in his chair. 'I don't know what to make of a remark like that.'

Joe Winder imagined his eyeballs pulsating in the sockets, as if jolted by a hot wire.

Charles Chelsea said, 'You mean, punch me? Actually punch me?'

'Repeatedly,' said Winder, 'until you are no longer conscious.'

The publicity man's voice was plaintive, but it held no fear. 'Do you know what kind of day I've had? I've dealt with two dead bodies—first the man on the bridge, and now the vole doctor. Plus I've been up to my knees in whale guts. I'm drained, Joe, physically and emotionally drained. But if it makes you feel better to beat me up, go ahead.'

Joe Winder said he was a reasonable man. He said he would reconsider the beating if Charles Chelsea would show him the suicide note allegedly written by Dr. Will Koocher.

Chelsea unlocked a file drawer and took out a sheet of paper with block printing on it. 'It's only a Xerox,' he said, handing it to Winder, 'but still it breaks your heart.'

It was one of the lamest suicide notes that Joe Winder had ever seen. In large letters it said: 'TO MY FRIENDS AND FAMILY, I SORRY BUT I CAN'T GO ON. NOW THAT MY WORKS IS OVER, SO AM I.'

The name signed at the bottom was '*William Bennett Koocher, PhD.*'

Winder stuffed the Xerox copy in his pocket and said, 'This is a fake.'

'I know what you're thinking, Joey, but it wasn't only the voles that got him down. There were problems at home, if you know what I mean.'

'My goodness.' Winder whistled. 'Problems at home. I had no idea.'

Chelsea continued: 'And I know what else you're thinking. Why would anybody kill himself in this . . . *extreme* fashion? Jumping in a whale tank and all.'

'It struck me as a bit unorthodox, yes.'

'Well, me too,' said Chelsea, regaining some of his starch, 'until I remembered that Koocher couldn't swim a lick. More to the point, he was deathly afraid of sharks. It's not so surprising that he chose to drown himself here, indoors, rather than the ocean.'

'And the green shirt?'

'Obviously he wasn't aware of Orky's, ah, problem.'

Joe Winder blinked vigorously in an effort to clear his vision. He said, 'The man's spine was snapped like a twig.'

'I am told,' said Charles Chelsea, 'that it's not as bad as it appears. Very quick, and nearly painless.' He took out a handkerchief and discreetly dried the palms of his hands. 'Not everyone has the stomach for using a gun,' he said. 'Myself, I'd swallow a bottle of roach dust before I'd resort to violence. But, anyway, I was thinking: Maybe this was Koocher's way of joining the lost voles. A symbolic surrender to Nature, if you will. Sacrificing himself to the whale.'

Chelsea squared the corners of the handkerchief and tucked it into a pants pocket. He looked pleased with his theory. Sagely he added, 'In a sense, what happened that night in Orky's tank was a purely natural event: Dr. Koocher became part of the food chain. Who's to say he didn't plan it that way?'

Joe Winder stood up, clutching the corners of Charles Chelsea's desk. 'It wasn't a suicide,' he said, 'and it wasn't an accident.'

'Then what, Joe?'

'I believe Koocher was murdered.'

'Oh, for God's sake. At the Amazing Kingdom?'

Again Winder felt the sibilant whisper from a valve letting off pressure somewhere deep inside his skull. He reached across the desk and got two crisp fistfuls of Chelsea's blue oxford shirt. *'I sorry but I can't go on?'*

Perplexed, Chelsea shook his head.

Joe Winder said, 'The man was a PhD, Charlie. *I sorry but I can't go on?* Tonto might write a suicide note like that, but not Dr. Koocher.'

Chelsea pulled himself free of Winder's grip and said: 'It was probably just a typo, Joe. Hell, the man was terribly depressed and upset. Who proofreads their own damn suicide note?'

Pressing his knuckles to his forehead, Winder said, 'A typo? With a Magic Marker, Charlie? *I sorry* is not a bummed-out scientist making a mistake; it's an illiterate moron trying to fake a suicide note.'

'I've heard just about enough.' Chelsea circled the desk and made for the door. He stepped around Winder as if he were a rattlesnake.

Chelsea didn't leave the office. He held the door open for Joe Winder, and waited.

'I see,' said Winder. On his way out, he stopped to smooth the shoulders of Chelsea's shirt, where he had grabbed him.

'No more talk of murder,' Charles Chelsea said. 'I want you to promise me.'

'All right, but on the more acceptable subject of suicide—who was the dead guy hanging from the Card Sound Bridge?'

'I've no idea, Joe. It doesn't concern us.'

'It concerns me.'

'Look, I'm starting to worry. First you threaten me with physical harm, now you're blabbing all these crazy theories. It's alarming, Joe. I hope I didn't misjudge your stability.'

'I suspect you did.'

Warily, Chelsea put a hand on Winder's arm. 'We've got a tough week ahead. I'd like to be able to count on you.'

'I'm a pro, Charlie.'

'That's my boy. So you'll give me Orky by four o'clock?'

'No sweat,' Winder said. 'Three hundred words.'

'Max,' reminded Charles Chelsea, 'and keep it low key.'

'My middle name,' said Joe Winder.

In the first draft of the press release, he wrote: *Orky the killer whale, a popular but unpredictable performer at the Amazing Kingdom of Thrills, died suddenly last night after asphyxiating on a foreign object.*

Chelsea sent the press release back, marked energetically in red ink.

In the second draft, Joe Winder wrote: *Orky the whale, one of the most colorful animal stars at the Amazing Kingdom of Thrills, passed away last night of sudden respiratory complications.*

Chelsea returned it with a few editing suggestions in blue ink.

In the third draft, Winder began: *Lovable Orky the whale, one of the most colorful and free-spirited animal stars at the Amazing Kingdom of Thrills, was found dead in his tank this morning.*

While pathologists conducted tests to determine the cause of death, Francis X. Kingsbury, founder of the popular family theme park, expressed deep sorrow over the sudden loss of this majestic creature.

'We had come to love and admire Orky,' Kingsbury said. 'He was as much a part of our family as Robbie Raccoon or Petey Possum.'

Joe Winder sent the press release up to Charles Chelsea's office and decided not to wait for more revisions. He announced that he was going home early to have his testicles reattached.

Before leaving the park, Winder stopped at a pay phone near the Magic Mansion and made a few calls. One of the calls was to an old newspaper source who worked at the Dade County Medical Examiner's Office. Another call was to the home of Mrs. Will Koocher, where a friend said she'd already gone back to Ithaca to await her husband's coffin. A third phone call went to Nina at home, who listened to Joe Winder's sad story of the dead vole doctor, and said: 'So the new job isn't working out, is that what you're saying?'

'In a nutshell, yes.'

'If you ask me, your attitude is contributing to the problem.'

Joe Winder spotted the acne-speckled face of Pedro Luz, peering suspiciously from behind a Snappy-the-Troll photo gazebo, where tourists were lined up to buy Japanese film and cameras. Pedro Luz was again sucking on the business end of an intravenous tube; the tube snaked up to a bottle that hung from a movable metal sling. Whenever Pedro Luz took a step, the IV rig would roll after him. The liquid dripping from the bottle was the color of weak chicken soup.

Joe Winder said to Nina: 'My attitude is not a factor.'

'Joe, you sound . . .'

'Yes?'

'Different. You sound different.'

'Charlie made me lie in the press release.'

'And this comes as a shock? Joe, it's a whole different business from before. We talked about this at length when you took the job.'

'I can fudge the attendance figures and not lose a minute of sleep. Covering up a murder is something else.'

On Nina's end he heard the rustling of paper. 'I want to read you something,' she said.

'Not now, please.'

'Joe, it's the best thing I've ever done.'

Winder glanced over toward the Snappy photo gazebo, but Pedro Luz had slipped out of sight.

Nina began to read: *Last night I dreamed I fell asleep on a diving board; the highest one, fifty meters. It was a hot steamy day, so I took my top off and lay down. I was so high up that no one but the sea gulls could see me. The sun felt wonderful. I closed my eyes and drifted off to sleep—*

'Not *"meters,"* ' Winder cut in. ' *"Meters"* is not a sexy word.'

Nina kept going: *When I awoke, you were standing over me, naked and brown from the sun. I tried to move but I couldn't—you had used the top of my bikini to tie my hands to the board. I was helpless, yet afraid to struggle . . . we were up so high. But then you knelt between my legs and told me not to worry. Before long, I forgot where we were. . . .*

'Not bad.' Joe Winder tried to sound encouraging, but the thought of trying to have sex on a high diving board made his stomach pitch.

Nina said: 'I want to leave something to the imagination. Not like Miriam, she's unbelievable. *I took chew in my mouth and sock like a typhoon.*'

Winder conceded that this was truly dreadful.

'I've got to listen to that pulp all night long,' Nina said. 'While she's clipping her toenails!'

'And I thought I had problems.'

She said, 'Was that sarcasm? Because if it was—'

The telephone receiver was getting heavy in Joe Winder's hand. He wedged it in the crook of his shoulder and said, 'Can I tell you what I was thinking just now? I was thinking about the gastric secretions inside a killer whale's stomach. I was thinking how unbelievably powerful the digestive juices must be in order for a whale to be able to eat swordfish beaks and seal bones and giant squid gizzards and the like.'

In a flat voice, Nina said, 'I have to go now, Joe. You're getting morbid again.'

'I guess I am.'

The click on the other end seemed an appropriate punctuation.

On the way home he decided to stop and try some bonefishing at his secret spot. He turned off County Road 905 and came to the familiar gravel path that led through the hardwoods to the mangrove shore.

Except the woods were gone. The buttonwoods, the mahogany, the gumbo-limbos—all obliterated. So were the mangroves.

Joe Winder got out of his car and stared. The hammock had been flattened; he could see all the way to the water. It looked as if a twenty-megaton bomb had gone off. Bulldozers had piled the dead trees in mountainous tangles at each corner of the property.

Several hundred yards from Joe Winder's car, in the center of what was now a vast tundra of scrabbled dirt, a plywood stage had been erected. The stage was filled with men and women, all dressed up in the dead of summer. A small crowd sat in folding chairs laid out in rows in front of the stage. Joe Winder could hear the brassy strains of 'America the Beautiful' being played by a high-school band, its lone tuba glinting in the afternoon sun. The song was followed by uneven applause. Then a man stood up at a microphone and began to speak, but Joe Winder was too far away to hear what was being said.

In a daze, Winder kicked out of his trousers and changed into his cutoffs. He got his fly rod out of the trunk of the car and assembled it. To the end of the monofilament leader he attached a small brown epoxy fly that was intended to resemble a crustacean. The tail of the fly was made from deer hair; Winder examined it to make sure it was bushy enough to attract fish.

Then he tucked the fly rod under his left arm, put on his Polaroid sunglasses and marched across the freshly flattened field toward the stage. Absolutely nothing of logic went through his mind.

The man at the microphone turned out to be the mayor of Monroe County, Florida. It was largely a ceremonial title that was passed in odd-numbered years from one county commissioner to another, a tradition interrupted only by death or indictment. The current mayor was a compact fellow with silvery hair, olive skin and the lean fissured face of a chain-smoker.

'This is a grand day for the Florida Keys,' the mayor was saying. 'Nine months from today, this will be a gorgeous fairway.' A burst of masculine clapping. 'The sixteenth fairway, if I'm not mistaken. A four-hundredand-twenty-yard par-four dogleg toward the ocean. Is that about right, Jake?'

A heavyset man sitting behind the mayor grinned enormously in acknowledgment. He had squinty eyes and a face as brown as burned walnut. He waved at the audience; the hearty and well-practiced wave of a sports celebrity. Joe Winder recognized the squinty-eyed man as Jake Harp, the famous professional golfer. He looked indefensibly ridiculous in a bright lemon blazer, brown beltless slacks, shiny white loafers and no socks.

At the microphone, the mayor was going on about the championship golf course, the lighted tennis courts, the his-and-her spas, the posh clubhouse with its ocean view and, of course, the exclusive luxury waterfront homesites. The mayor was effervescent in his presentation, and the small overdressed audience seemed to share his enthusiasm. The new development was to be called Falcon Trace.

'And the first phase,' said the mayor, 'is already sold out. We're talking two hundred and two units!'

Joe Winder found an empty chair and sat down. He propped the fly rod in his lap so that it rose like a nine-foot CB antenna out of his crotch. He wondered why he hadn't heard about this project, considering that the property abutted the southern boundary of the Amazing Kingdom of Thrills. He didn't remember seeing anything in the newspapers about a new country club. He felt a homicidal churning in his belly.

Not again, he thought. Not again, not again, not again.

The mayor introduced Jake Harp—'one of the greatest cross-handed putters of all time'—and the audience actually rose to its feet and cheered.

Jake Harp stood at the podium and waved ebulliently. Waved and waved, as if he were the bloody pope.

'Welcome to Falcon Trace,' he began, reading off an index card. 'Welcome to my new home.'

More clapping as everyone settled back in their chairs.

'You know, I've won the PGA three times,' said Jake Harp, 'and finished third in the Masters twice. But I can honestly say that I was never so honored as when y'all selected me as the touring pro for beautiful Falcon Trace.'

A voice piped up near the stage: 'You rot in hell!'

A strong empassioned voice—a woman. The crowd murmured uncomfortably. Jake Harp nervously cleared his throat, a tubercular grunt into the microphone.

Again the woman's voice rose: 'We don't need another damn golf course. Why don't you go back to Palm Springs with the rest of the gangsters!'

Now she was standing. Joe Winder craned to get a good look.

The famous golfer tried to make a joke. Painfully he said, 'I guess we got ourselves a golf widow in the audience.'

'No,' the woman called back, 'a real widow.'

On stage, Jake Harp bent over and whispered something to the mayor, who was smoking fiercely. Someone signaled to the conductor of the high-school band, which adroitly struck up a Michael Jackson dance number. Meanwhile three uniformed sheriff's deputies materialized and edged toward the rude protester. The woman stood up, shook a fist above the silvery puff that was her head and said something that Joe Winder couldn't quite hear, except for the word 'bastard.'

Then she put on a floppy pink Easter bonnet and permitted herself to be arrested.

Well, hello, thought Winder. The lady from the Wildlife Rescue Corps, the one who'd slipped him the note at the Amazing
Kingdom.

Joe Winder watched the deputies lead the old woman away.
He wanted to follow and ask what in the hell was going on, but
she was quickly deposited in the back of a squad car, which sped
off toward Key Largo. As Jake Harp resumed his speech, Winder
got up and walked past the stage toward the ocean. In a few
minutes he found the familiar stretch of shoreline where he
usually searched for bonefish, but the water was too milky to see
over the tops of his own sneakers. As he waded into the flats, he
could hear the high-school band begin to play 'The Star Spangled
Banner,' signaling the climax of the groundbreaking ceremony.

As he slid his feet across the rocks and sea grass, Joe Winder
started false-casting his fly, stripping out the line as he moved
forward. The water was murky, roiled, just a mess. There would
be no fish here, Winder knew, but still he drove the meat of the
line seventy feet hard into the wind, and watched the tiny plop
of the fly when it landed.

Joe Winder fished in manic motion because he knew time was
running out. Before long, this fine little bay would be a stagnant
ruin and the only fish worth catching would be gone, spooked
by jet skis, sailboarders, motorboats and plumes of rank sewage
blossoming from submerged drainage pipes.

Welcome to Falcon Trace.

He took another step and felt something seize his right ankle.
When he tried to pull free, he lost his balance and fell down
noisily in the water. He landed on his ass but quickly rolled to
his knees, careful to hold the expensive Seamaster fly reel high
and dry. Irritably Winder groped beneath the surface for the
thing that had tripped him.

His fingers closed around the slick branch of a freshly cut tree.
He lifted it out of the water, examined it, then let it drop again.
A red mangrove, bulldozed, ripped out by the roots and dumped
on the flats. Illegal as hell, but who besides the fish would ever
know?

Joe Winder knelt in the shallows and thought about what to do next. Back on the soon-to-be-sixteenth hole, the band played on. After a while, the music stopped and voices could be heard, collegial chamber-of-commerce good-old-boy voices, dissipating in the afternoon breeze. Not long afterward came the sounds of luxury cars being started.

Eventually the place got quiet, and Joe Winder knew he was alone again in his favorite fishing spot. He stayed on his knees in the water until the sun went down.

In the evening he drove out to the Card Sound Bridge and parked. He got a flashlight from the trunk and began to walk along the road, keeping close to the fringe of the trees and playing the light along the ground. Soon he found the place where he had been beaten by the two goons, Angel and Spearmint Breath. Here Joe Winder slowed his pace and forced himself to concentrate.

He knew what he was looking for: a trail.

He'd spent most of his childhood outdoors, cutting paths to secret hideaways in the hammocks, glades and swamps. At a young age he had become an expert woodsman, a master of disappearing into impenetrable pockets where no one else wanted to go. Every time his father bought a new piece of property, Joe Winder set out to explore each acre. If there was a big pine, he would climb it; if there was a lake or a creek, he'd fish it. If there was a bobcat, he'd track it; a snake, he'd catch it.

He would pursue these solitary adventures relentlessly until the inevitable day when the heavy machinery appeared, and the guys in the hard hats would tell him to beat it, not knowing he was the boss's kid.

On those nights, lying in his bed at home, he would wait for his mother to come in and console him. Often she would suggest a new place for his expeditions, a mossy parcel off Old Cutler Road, or twenty acres in the Gables, right on the bay. Pieces his father's company had bought, or was buying, or was considering.

Raw, tangled, hushed, pungent with animals, buzzing with

insects, glistening with extravagant webs, pulsing, rustling and doomed. And always the portal to these mysterious places was a trail.

Which is what Winder needed on this night.

Soon he found it: an ancient path of scavengers, flattened by raccoons and opossums but widened recently by something much larger. As Winder slipped into the woods, he felt ten years old again. He followed the trail methodically but not too fast, though his heart was pounding absurdly in his ears. He tried to travel quietly, meticulously ducking boughs and stepping over rotted branches. Every thirty or so steps, he would turn off the flashlight, hold his breath and wait. Before long, he could no longer hear the cars passing on Card Sound Road. He was so deep in the wetlands that a shout or a scream would be swallowed at once, eternally.

He walked for fifteen minutes before he came upon the remains of a small campfire. Joe Winder knelt and sniffed at the half-burned wood; somebody had doused it with coffee. He poked at the acrid remains of something wild that had been cooked in a small rusty pan. He swung the flashlight in a semi-circle and spotted a dirty cooler, some lobster traps and a large cardboard box with the letters 'EDTIAR' stamped on the side. On the ground, crumpled into a bright pile, was a fluorescent orange rainsuit. Winder unfolded it, held it up to gauge the size. Then he put it back the way he found it.

Behind him, a branch snapped and a voice said, 'How do you like the new pants?'

Winder wheeled around and pointed the flashlight as if it were a pistol.

The man was eating—and there was no mistaking it—a fried snake on a stick.

'Cottonmouth,' he said, crunching off a piece. 'Want some?'

'No thanks.'

'Then we've got nothing to talk about.'

Joe Winder politely took a bite of snake. 'Like chicken,' he said.

The man was cleaning his teeth with a fishhook. He looked almost exactly as Joe Winder remembered, except that the beard was now braided into numerous silvery sprouts that drooped here and there from the man's jaw. He was probably in his early fifties, although it was impossible to tell. The mismatched eyes unbalanced his face and made his expression difficult to read; the snarled eyebrows sat at an angle of permanent scowl. He wore a flowered pink shower cap, sunglasses on a lanyard, a heavy red plastic collar and no shirt. At first Joe Winder thought that the man's chest was grossly freckled, but in the flashlight's trembling beam the freckles began to hover and dance: mosquitoes, hundreds of them, feasting on his blood.

In a strained voice Joe Winder said, 'I can't help but notice that thing on your neck.'

'Radio collar.' The man lifted his chin so Winder could see it. 'Made by Telonics. A hundred fifty megahertz. I got it off a dead panther.'

'Does it work?' Winder asked.

'Like a charm.' The man snorted. 'Why else would I be wearing it?'

Joe Winder decided this was something they could chat about later. He said, 'I didn't mean to bother you. I just wanted to thank you for what you did the other night.'

The stranger nodded. 'No problem. Like I said, I got a pair of pants out of the deal.' He slapped himself on the thigh. 'Canvas, too.'

'Listen, that little guy—Angel Gaviria was his name. They found him hanging under the bridge.' Winder's friend at the medical examiner's office had confirmed the identity.

'What do you know,' the stranger said absently.

'I was wondering about the other one, too,' said Winder, 'since they were trying to kill me.'

'Don't blame you for being curious. By the way, they call me Skink. And I already know who you are. And your daddy, too, goddamn his soul.'

He motioned for Joe Winder to follow, and crashed down a

trail that led away from the campfire. 'I went through your wallet the other night,' Skink was saying, 'to make sure you were worth saving.'

'These days I'm not so sure.'

'Shit,' said Skink. 'Don't start with that.'

After five minutes they broke out of the hardwoods into a substantial clearing. A dump, Joe Winder noticed.

'Yeah, it's lovely,' muttered Skink. He led Winder to the oxidized husk of an abandoned Cadillac, and lifted the trunk hatch off its hinges. The nude body of Spearmint Breath had been fitted inside, folded as neatly as a beach chair.

'Left over from the other night,' Skink explained. 'He ran out of steam halfway up the big bridge. Then we had ourselves a talk.'

'Oh Jesus.'

'A bad person,' Skink said. 'He would've brought more trouble.'

An invisible cloud of foul air rose from the trunk. Joe Winder attempted to breathe through his mouth.

Skink played the beam of the flashlight along the dead goon's swollen limbs. 'Notice the skeeters don't go near him,' he said, 'so in one sense, he's better off.'

Joe Winder backed away, speechless. Skink handed him the light and said, 'Don't worry, this is only temporary.' Winder hoped he wasn't talking to the corpse.

Skink replaced the trunk hatch on the junked Cadillac. 'Asshole used to work Security at the Kingdom. He and Angel baby. But I suppose you already knew that.'

'All I know,' said Winder, 'is that everything's going bad and I'm not sure what to do.'

'Tell me about it. I still can't believe they shot John Lennon and it's been—what, ten years?' He sat down heavily on the trunk of the car. 'You ever been to the Dakota?'

'Once,' Joe Winder said.

'What's it like?'

'Sad.'

Skink twirled the fishhook in his mouth, bit off the barb, and spit it out savagely. 'Some crazy shithead with a .38—it's the story of America, isn't it?'

'We live in violent times. That's what they say.'

'Guys like that, they give violence a bad name.' Skink stretched out on the trunk, and stared at the stars. 'Sometimes I think about that bastard in jail, how he loves all the publicity. Went from being nobody to The Man Who Shot John Lennon. I think some pretty ugly thoughts about that.'

'It was a bad day,' Joe Winder agreed. He couldn't tell if the man was about to sleep or explode.

Suddenly Skink sat up. With a blackened fingernail he tapped the radio collar on his neck. 'See, it's best to keep moving. If you don't move every so often, a special signal goes out. Then they think the panther's dead and they all come searching.'

'Who's they?'

'Rangers,' Skink replied. 'Game and Fish.'

'But the panther *is* dead.'

'You're missing the whole damn point.'

As usual. Joe Winder wondered which way to take it, and decided he had nothing to lose. 'What exactly are you doing out here?' he asked.

Skink grinned, a stunning, luminous movie-star grin.

'Waiting,' he said.

12

On the morning of July 21, a Saturday, Molly McNamara drove Bud Schwartz and Danny Pogue to the Amazing Kingdom of Thrills for the purpose of burglarizing the office of Francis X. Kingsbury.

'All you want is files?' asked Bud Schwartz.

'As many as you can fit in the camera bag,' Molly said. 'Anything to do with Falcon Trace.'

Danny Pogue, who was sitting in the back seat of the El Dorado, leaned forward and said, 'Suppose there's some other good stuff. A tape deck or a VCR, maybe some crystal. Is it okay we grab it?'

'No, it is not,' Molly replied. 'Not on my time.'

She parked in the Cindy-the-Sun-Queen lot and left the engine running. The radio was tuned to the classical station, and Bud Schwartz asked if Molly could turn it down a notch or two. She went searching through her immense handbag and came out with a Polaroid camera. Without saying a word, she snapped a photograph of Bud Schwartz, turned halfway in the seat and snapped one of Danny Pogue. The flashbulb caused him to flinch and make a face. Molly plucked the moist negatives from the slot in the bottom of the camera and slipped them into the handbag.

'What's that all about?' said Danny Pogue.

'In case you get the itch to run away,' Molly McNamara said, 'I'd feel compelled to send your photographs to the authorities. They are still, I understand, quite actively investigating the theft of the mango voles.'

'Pictures,' said Bud Schwartz. 'That's cute.'

Molly smiled pleasantly and told both men to listen closely. 'I rented you a blue Cutlass. It's parked over by the tram station. Here are the keys.'

Bud Schwartz put them in his pocket. 'Something tells me we won't be cruising down to Key West.'

'Not if you know what's good for you,' Molly said.

Danny Pogue began to whine again. 'Ma'am, I don't know nothin' about stealing files,' he said. 'Now I'm a regular bear for tape decks and Camcorders and shit like that, but frankly I don't do much in the way of, like, *reading*. It's just not my area.'

Molly said, 'You'll do fine. Get in, grab what you can and get out.'

'And hope that nobody recognizes us from before.' Bud Schwartz arched his eyebrows. 'What happens then? Or didn't you think of that.'

Molly chuckled lightly. 'Don't be silly. No one will recognize you dressed the way you are.'

She had bought them complete golfing outfits, polyester down to the matching socks. Danny Pogue's ensemble was raspberry red and Bud Schwartz's was baby blue. The pants were thin and baggy; the shirts had short sleeves and loud horizontal stripes and a tiny fox stitched on the left breast.

Bud Schwartz said, 'You realize we look like total dipshits.'

'No, you look like tourists.'

'It's not that bad,' agreed Danny Pogue.

'Listen,' Molly said again. 'When you're done with the job, get in the Cutlass and come straight back to my place. The phone will ring at one sharp. If you're not there, I'm going directly to the post office and mail these snapshots to the police, along with your names. Do you believe me?'

'Yeah, sure,' said Bud Schwartz.

She got out of the Cadillac and opened the doors for the burglars. 'How is your hand?' she asked Bud Schwartz. 'Better let your friend carry the camera bag.'

She held Danny Pogue's crutch (mending quickly, he was down to one) while he slipped the camera bag over his right shoulder. 'The tram's coming,' she announced. 'Better get moving.'

As the men hobbled away, Molly called out cheerfully and waved good-bye, as if she were their mother, or a loving old aunt.

With a trace of fondness, Danny Pogue said, 'Look at her.'

'Look at *us*,' said Bud Schwartz. 'Real fucking pros.'

'Well, at least it's for a good cause. You know, saving them butterflies.'

Bud Schwartz eyed his partner in a clinical way. 'Danny, you ever had a CAT scan?'

'A what?'

'Nothing.'

The burglars were huffing pretty heavily by the time they made it to the tram. They climbed on the last car, along with a family of nine from Minneapolis. Every one of them had sandy hair and Nordic-blue eyes and eyebrows so blond they looked white in the sunlight.

A little girl of about seven turned to Danny Pogue and asked what had happened to his foot.

'I got shot,' he said candidly.

The little girl flashed a glance at her mother, whose eyes widened.

'A tetanus shot,' said Bud Schwartz. 'He stepped on a rusty nail.'

The mother's eyes softened with relief. 'Where are you from?' she asked the men.

'Portugal,' said Danny Pogue, trying to live up to the tourist act.

'Portugal, Ohio,' Bud Schwartz said, thinking: There is no hope for this guy; he simply can't be allowed to speak.

The tiny blond girl piped up: 'We heard on the radio that the whale died yesterday. Orky the whale.'

'Oh no,' said Danny Pogue. 'You sure?'

The tram rolled to a stop in front of the main gate, where the burglars got off. Nodding good-bye to the blond Minneapolitans, Bud Schwartz and Danny Pogue slipped into the throng and located the shortest line at the ticket turnstiles.

In a gruff tone, Bud Schwartz said, '*Portugal*? What kind of fuckhead answer is that?'

'I don't know, Bud. I don't know a damn thing about tourists or where they come from.'

'Then don't say anything, you understand?' Bud Schwartz got out the money that Molly had given them to buy the admission tickets. He counted out thirty-six dollars and handed the cash to his partner.

'Just hold up one finger, that's all you gotta do,' said Bud Schwartz. 'One finger means one ticket. Don't say a goddamn thing.'

'All right,' Danny Pogue said. 'Man, I can't believe the whale croaked, can you?'

'Shut up,' said Bud Schwartz. 'I'm not kidding.'

Danny Pogue didn't seem the least bit nervous about returning to the scene of their crime. To him the Amazing Kingdom of Thrills was a terrific place, and he strutted around with a permanent grin. Bud Schwartz thought: He's worse than these damn kids.

Outside the Magic Mansion, Danny Pogue stopped to shake hands with Petey Possum. A tourist lady from Atlanta took a photograph, and Danny Pogue begged her to send him a copy. At this point Bud Schwartz considered ditching the dumb shit altogether and pulling the job alone.

Golf duds and all, Bud Schwartz was antsy about being back on the premises so soon after the rat-napping; it went against his long-standing aversion to dumb risk. He wanted to hurry up and get the hell out.

It wasn't easy locating Francis X. Kingsbury's office because it didn't appear on any of the colorful maps or diagrams posted throughout the amusement park. Bud Schwartz and Danny Pogue checked closely; there was the Cimarron Trail Ride, Orky's Undersea Paradise, the Wet Willy, the Jungle Jerry Amazon Boat Cruise, Bigfoot Mountain, Excitement Boulevard, and so on, with no mention of the administration building. Bud Schwartz decided Kingsbury's headquarters must be somewhere in the geographic center of the Amazing Kingdom of Thrills, and for security reasons probably wasn't marked.

'Why don't we ask somebody?' Danny Pogue suggested.

'Very smart,' said Bud Schwartz. 'I got a better idea. Why don't we just paint the word "thief" in big red letters on our goddamn foreheads?'

Danny Pogue wasn't sure why his partner was in such a lousy mood. The Kingdom was awesome, fantastic, sensational. Everywhere they went, elves and fairy princesses and happy animal characters waved or shook hands or gave a hug.

'I never seen so much friendliness,' he remarked.

'It's the crutch,' said Bud Schwartz.

'No way.'

'It's the damn crutch, I'm tellin' you. They're only being nice because they got to, Danny. Anytime there's a customer on crutches, they make a special point. You know, in case he's dying a some fatal disease.'

Danny Pogue said, 'You go to hell.'

'Ten bucks says it's right in the training manual.'

'Bud, I swear to God.'

'Gimme the crutch and I'll prove it.'

Danny Pogue said, 'You're the one's always on my ass about attitude. And now just listen to yourself—all because people're actin' nice to me and not to you.'

'That's not it,' said Bud Schwartz, but when he turned around his partner was gone. He found him on line at the Wild Bill Hiccup rodeo ride; Danny Pogue had stashed his crutch in the men's room and was determined to give Wild Bill Hiccup a go. Bud Schwartz was tired of bickering.

The ride was set up in an indoor corral that had been laboriously fabricated, from the brown-dyed dirt to the balsa fence posts to the polyethylene cowshit that lay in neat regular mounds, free of flies. Twenty-five mechanical bulls (only the horns were real) jumped and bucked on hidden tracks while a phony rodeo announcer described the action through a realistically tinny megaphone.

During this particular session, the twenty-five bulls were mounted by twenty-three tourists and two professional crooks. Before the ride began, Bud Schwartz leaned over to Danny Pogue and told him to be sure and fall off.

'What?'

'You heard me. And make it look good.'

When the bell rang, Bud Schwartz hung on with his good hand and bounced back and forth for maybe a minute without feeling anything close to excitement. Danny Pogue, however, was launched almost instantly from the sponge hump of his motorized Brahma—a tumble so spectacular that it brought three Company Cowpokes out of the bronco chute at a dead run. They surrounded Danny Pogue, measured his blood pressure, palpated his ribs and abdomen, listened to his heart, shined a light in his eyeballs and finally shoved a piece of paper under his nose.

'Why don't you put your name on this, li'l pardner?' said one of the Cowpokes.

Danny Pogue examined the document, shook his head and handed it to Bud Schwartz for interpretation.

'Release of liability,' Bud Schwartz said. He looked up with a dry smile. 'This means we can't sue, right?'

'Naw,' said the solicitous Cowpoke. 'All it means is your buddy's not hurt.'

'Says who?' said Bud Schwartz. 'Bunch a dumb cowboy shit-kickers. Thanks, but I think we'll try our luck with an actual doctor.'

The Cowpokes didn't look so amiable anymore, or so Western. In fact, they were starting to look like pissed-off Miami insurance men. Danny Pogue got to his feet, dusted off his butt and said, 'Hell, Bud, it's my fault anyhow—'

'Not another word.' Bud Schwartz seized his partner by the elbow, as if to prop him up. Then he announced to the Cowpokes: 'We'd like to file a complaint about this ride. Where exactly is the administration office?'

The Cowpoke in charge of the blood-pressure cuff said, 'It's closed today.'

'Then we'll come back Monday,' said Bud Schwartz. 'Where is the office, please?'

'Over Sally's Saloon,' the Cowpoke answered. 'Upstairs, ask for Mr. Dexter in Risk Management.'

'And he'll be in Monday?'

'Nine sharp,' muttered the Cowpoke.

The other tourists watched curiously as Bud Schwartz led Danny Pogue haltingly out of the corral. By this time the Wild Bill Hiccup attraction had come to a complete and embarrassing stop (a man with a sprocket wrench had beheaded Danny Pogue's bull), and Bud Schwartz wanted to depart the arena before his partner spoiled the plan by saying something irretrievably stupid.

Into Danny Pogue's ear he said, 'You're doing fine.'

'It wasn't on purpose.'

'Yeah, I had a feeling.'

As they watched Danny Pogue's genuine hobble, the three Cowpokes from Risk Management began to worry that they might have missed something during their quickie medical exam.

One of them called out: 'Hey, how about a wheelchair?'

Without turning around, Bud Schwartz declined the offer with the wave of an arm.

'No thanks, li'l pardner,' he called back.

The same tool that picked the lock on Francis X. Kingsbury's office did the job on the rosewood file cabinet.

'So now what?' Danny Pogue said.

'We read.' Bud Schwartz divided the files into two stacks. He showed his partner how to save time by checking the index labels.

'Anything to do with banks and property, put it in the bag. Also, anything that looks personal.'

'What about Falcon Trace?' asked Danny Pogue. 'That's what Mrs. McNamara said to get.'

'That, too.'

They used pocket flashlights to examine the files because Bud

Schwartz didn't want to turn on the lights in Kingsbury's office. They were on the third floor of the administration building, above Sally's Cimarron Saloon. Through the curtains Bud Schwartz could watch the Wild West show on the dusty street below. Tourists shrieked as two scruffy bank robbers suddenly opened fire on the sheriff; bloodied, the sheriff managed to shoot both bandits off their horses as they tried to escape. The tourists cheered wildly. Bud Schwartz grunted and said, 'Now there's a job for you. Fallin' off horses.'

Sitting on the floor amid Kingsbury's files, Danny Pogue looked orphaned. He said, 'I know lawyers that couldn't make sense a this shit.' He couldn't take his eyes off a portable Canon photocopier: seventy-five bucks, staring him in the face.

'We'll give it an hour,' said Bud Schwartz, but it didn't take him that long to realize that his partner was right. The files were impenetrable, stuffed with graphs and pie charts and computer printouts that meant nothing to your average break-in artist. The index tabs were marked with hopelessly stilted titles like 'Bermuda Intercontinental Services, Inc.,' and 'Ramex Global Trust, N.A.,' and 'Jersey Premium Market Research.'

Bud Schwartz arbitrarily selected the three thickest files and stuffed them in the camera bag. This would keep the old bat busy for a while.

'Look here,' said Danny Pogue, holding up a thin file. 'Credit cards.'

The index tab was marked 'Personal Miscellany.' Inside was a folder from the American Express Company that listed all the activity on Francis X. Kingsbury's Platinum Card for the previous twelve months. Bud Schwartz's expression warmed as he skimmed the entries.

Reading over his shoulder, Danny Pogue said. 'The guy sure knows how to eat.'

'He knows how to buy jewelry, too.' Bud Schwartz pointed at some large numbers. 'Look here.'

'Yeah,' said Danny Pogue, catching on. 'I wonder where he keeps it, all that jewelry.'

Bud Schwartz slipped Kingsbury's American Express folder into the camera bag. 'This one's for us,' he told his partner. 'Don't show the old lady unless I say so.'

Danny Pogue said, 'I heard a that place in New York. Cartier's.' He pronounced it 'Car-teer's.' 'That's some expensive shit they sell.'

'You bet,' said Bud Schwartz. Another thin file had caught his attention. He opened it on his lap, using his good hand to hold the flashlight while he read. The file contained Xeroxed copies of numerous old newspaper clippings, and three or four letters from somebody at the U.S. Department of Justice. The letterhead was embossed, and it felt important.

'Jesus,' said Bud Schwartz, sizing things up.

'What is it?'

He thrust the file at Danny Pogue. 'Put this in the damn bag, and let's get going.'

Danny Pogue peered at the index tab and said, 'So what does it mean?'

'It means we're gonna be rich, li'l pardner.'

Danny Pogue contemplated the name on the file folder. 'So how do you pronounce it anyway?'

'Gotti,' said Bud Schwartz. 'Rhymes with body.'

13

Rummaging through a dead man's belongings at midnight was not Joe Winder's idea of fun. The lab was as cold and quiet as a morgue. Intimate traces of the late Will Koocher were everywhere: a wrinkled lab coat hung on the back of a door; a wedding picture in a brass frame on a corner of his desk; a half-eaten roll of cherry-flavored Tums in the drawer; Koocher's final paycheck, endorsed but never cashed.

Winder shivered and went to work. Methodically he pored through the vole file, and quickly learned to decipher Koocher's daily charts: size, weight, feeding patterns, sleeping patterns, stool patterns. Some days there was blood work, some days there were urine samples. The doctor's notes were clinical, brief and altogether unenlightening. Whatever had bothered Koocher about the mango-vole program, he hadn't put it in the charts.

It was an hour before Joe Winder found something that caught his eyes: a series of color photographs of the voles. These were different from the glossy publicity pictures—these were extreme close-ups taken from various angles to highlight anatomical characteristics. Typed labels identified the animals as either 'Male One' or 'Female One.' Several pictures of the female had been marked up in red wax pencil, presumably by Will Koocher. In one photograph, an arrow had been drawn to the rump of the mango vole, accompanied by the notation 'CK. TAIL LENGTH.' On another, Koocher had written: 'CK. MICROTUS FUR COLOR—IS THERE BLOND PHASE?' In a third photograph, the animal's mouth had carefully been propped open with a Popsicle stick, which allowed a splendid frontal view of two large yellow incisors and a tiny indigo tongue.

Obviously the female vole had troubled Koocher, but why? Winder slipped the photos into his briefcase, and turned to the next file. It contained a muddy Xerox of a research paper titled, 'Habitat Loss and the Decline of *Microtus mango* in Southeastern Florida.' The author of the article was listed as Dr. Sarah Hunt, PhD, of Rollins College. In red ink Koocher had circled the woman's name, and put a question mark next to it. The research paper was only five pages long, but the margins were full of Koocher's scribbles. Winder was trying to make sense of them when he heard a squeaking noise behind him.

In the doorway stood Pedro Luz—pocked, bloated, puffy-eyed Pedro. 'The fuck are you doing?' he said.

Joe Winder explained that a janitor had been kind enough to loan him a key to the lab.

'What for?' Pedro Luz demanded.

'I need some more information on the voles.'

'Haw,' said Pedro Luz, and stepped inside the lab. The squeaking came from the wheels of his mobile steroid dispenser, the IV rig he had swiped from the hospital. A clear tube curled from a hanging plastic bag to a scabby junction in the crook of Pedro Luz's left arm; the needle was held in place by several cross-wraps of cellophane tape.

The idea had come to him while he was hospitalized with the ferret bites. He had been so impressed with the wonders of intravenous refueling that he'd decided to try it with his anabolic steroids. Whether this method was effective, or even safe, were questions that Pedro Luz hadn't considered because the basic theory seemed unassailable: straight from bottle to vein, just like a gasoline pump. No sooner had he hung the first bag than he had felt the surge, the heat, the tingling glory of muscles in rapture. Even at ease, his prodigious biceps twitched and rippled as if prodded by invisible electrodes.

Joe Winder wondered why Pedro Luz kept staring down at himself, smiling as he admired the dimensions of his own broad chest and log-sized arms.

'Are you feeling all right?' Winder asked.

Pedro Luz looked up from his reverie and blinked, toadlike.

Affably, Winder remarked, 'You're working mighty late tonight.'

Pedro Luz grunted: 'I feel fine.' He walked up to the desk and grabbed the briefcase. 'You got no authorization to be here after hours.'

'Mr. Chelsea won't mind.'

Invoking Charlie's name made no impression on Pedro Luz, who plucked a leaf out of Joe Winder's hair. 'Look at this shit on your head!'

'I spent some time in the mangroves,' Winder said. 'Ate snake-on-a-stick.'

Pedro Luz announced: 'I'm keeping your damn briefcase.' He tucked it under his right arm. 'Until I see some fucking authorization.'

'What's in the IV bag?' Joe Winder asked.

'Vitamins,' said Pedro Luz. 'Now get the hell out.'

'You know what I think? I think Will Koocher was murdered.'

Pedro Luz scrunched his face as if something toxic were burning his eyes. His jaw was set so rigidly that Joe Winder expected to hear the teeth start exploding one by one, like popcorn.

Winder said, 'Well, I guess I'll be going.'

Pedro Luz followed him out the door, the IV rig squeaking behind them. To the back of Winder's neck, he growled, 'You dumb little shit, now I gotta do a whole report.'

'Pedro, you need some rest.'

'The doctor wasn't murdered. He killed hisself.'

'I don't think so.'

'Man, I used to be a cop. I know the difference between murder and suicide.'

Pedro Luz turned around to lock the laboratory door. Joe Winder thought it would be an excellent moment to snatch his briefcase from the security man and make a run for it. He figured Pedro Luz could never catch him as long as he was attached to the cumbersome IV rig.

Winder pondered the daring maneuver too long. Pedro Luz glanced over his shoulder and caught him staring at the briefcase. 'Go ahead,' the big man taunted. 'Just go ahead and try.'

Francis X. Kingsbury and Jake Harp had an early starting time at the Ocean Reef Club, up the road a few miles from the Amazing Kingdom of Thrills. Kingsbury played golf two or three times a week at Ocean Reef, even though he was not a member and would never be a member. A most exclusive outfit, the Ocean Reef board had voted consistently to blackball Kingsbury because it could not verify several important details of his biography, beginning with his name. Infuriated by the rejection, Kingsbury made himself an unwelcome presence by wheedling regular golf invitations from all acquaintances who happened to be members, including the famous Jake Harp.

Reluctantly Jake Harp had agreed to play nine holes. He didn't like golf with rich duffers but it was part of the deal; playing with Francis X. Kingsbury, though, was a special form of torture. All he talked about was Disney this and Disney that. If the stock had dropped a point or two, Kingsbury was euphoric; if the stock was up, he was bellicose and depressed. He referred to the Disney mascot as Mickey Ratface, or sometimes simply The Rat. 'The Rat's updating his pathetic excuse for a jungle cruise,' Kingsbury would report with a sneer. 'The fake hippos must be rusting out.' Another time, while Jake Harp was lining up a long putt for an eagle, Kingsbury began to cackle. 'The Rat's got a major problem at the Hall of the Presidents! Heard they had to yank the Nixon robot because his jowls were molting!'

Jake Harp, a lifelong Republican, had suppressed the urge to take a Ping putter and clobber Francis X. Kingsbury into a deep coma. Jake Harp had to remain civil because of the Falcon Trace gig. It was his second chance at designing a golf course and he didn't want to screw up again; over on Sanibel they were still searching for that mysterious fourteenth tee, the one Jake Harp's architects had mistakenly located in the middle of San Carlos Bay.

As for his title of Falcon Trace 'touring pro,' it was spending money, that's all—tape a couple of television spots, get your face on a billboard, play a couple of charity tournaments in the winter. Hell, no one seriously expected you to actually show up and give golf lessons. Not the great Jake Harp.

In the coffee shop Francis X. Kingsbury announced that he was in a hurry because he was leaving town later in the day. The sooner the better, thought Jake Harp.

Standing on the first tee, Kingsbury spotted two of the Ocean Reef board members waiting in a foursome behind them. The men smiled thinly and nodded at him. Kingsbury placidly flipped them the finger. Jake Harp grimaced and reached for his driver.

'Love it,' said Kingsbury. 'Think they're such hot snots.'

Jake Harp knocked the ball two hundred and sixty yards down the left side of the fairway. Kingsbury hit it about half as far and shrugged as if he didn't care. Once he got in the golf cart, he drove like a maniac and cursed bitterly.

'Our club'll make this place look like a buffalo latrine.' The cart jounced heedlessly along the asphalt path. 'Like fucking Goony Golf—I can't wait.'

Jake Harp, who was badly hung over, said: 'Let's take it easy, Frank.'

'They're dying to know how I did it,' Kingsbury went on, full tilt. 'This island, it's practically a goddamn nature preserve. I mean, you can't mow your lawn without a permit from the fucking EPA.'

He stomped the brake, got out and lined up his second shot. Jake Harp asked: 'You gonna use the driver again?'

Kingsbury swung like a canecutter, topping the ball noisily. It skidded maybe eighty yards, cutting a bluish vector through the dew-covered grass.

'Keep your head down,' advised Jake Harp.

Kingsbury hopped back in the cart and said: 'Grandfathering, that's how I did it. The guy I bought from, he'd had his permits since '74. I'm talking Army Corps, Fish and Wildlife, even Interior. The state—well, yeah, that was a problem. For that I had to spread a little here and there. And Monroe County, forget it.'

He shut up long enough to get out and hit again. This time he switched to a four-wood, which he skied into a liver-shaped bunker. 'Fuck me,' muttered Francis Kingsbury. He remained silent as Jake Harp casually knocked his second shot thirty feet from the pin.

'What was that, a five-iron? A six?'

'A six,' replied Jake Harp, pinching the bridge of his nose. He figured if he could just cut off circulation, it would starve the pain behind his eyeballs and make his hangover go away.

Kingsbury punched the accelerator and they were off again. 'You know how I got the county boys? The ones giving me a bad time, I promised 'em units. Not raw lots, no fucking way—town houses is all, the one-bedrooms with no garage.'

'Oh,' said Jake Harp, feeling privileged. He'd been given a double lot, oceanfront, plus first option on one of the spec homes.

'Townhouses,' Kingsbury repeated with a laugh. 'And they were happy as clams. All I got to do, it's easy, is sit on the titles until Phase One is built. You know, keep it off the tax rolls for a few months. 'Case some damn reporter shows up at the court-house and starts looking up names.'

Jake Harp didn't understand the nuances of Francis Kingsbury's scheme. The man was proud of himself, that much was obvious.

When they pulled up to the sand trap, they saw that Kingsbury's golf ball was practically buried under the lip. It appeared to have landed at the approximate speed and trajectory of a mortar round.

Kingsbury stood over the ball for a long time, as if waiting for it to make a move. Finally he said to Jake Harp: 'You're the pro. What the hell now, a wedge? A nine, maybe?'

'Your only prayer,' said Jake Harp, forcing a rheumy chuckle, 'is a stick of dynamite.' Miraculously, Kingsbury needed only three swings to blast out of the bunker, and two putts to get down.

While waiting on the next tee, Jake Harp said he thought it

would be better if he didn't do any more speaking engagements on behalf of Falcon Trace.

Kingsbury scowled. 'Yeah, I heard what happened, some broad.'

'I'm not comfortable in those situations, Frank.'

'Well, who the hell is? We got her name, the old bitch.' Kingsbury took out a wood and started whisking the air with violent practice swings. Jake Harp could scarcely stand to look.

'One of those damn bunny huggers,' Kingsbury was saying. 'Anti this and anti that. Got some group, the Mothers of some fucking thing.'

'It doesn't really matter,' said Jake Harp.

'The hell it doesn't.' Francis X. Kingsbury stopped swinging and pointed the polished head of the driver at Jake Harp's chest. 'Now that we know who she is, don't you worry. This shit'll stop—it's been taken care of. You'll be fine from now on.'

'I'm a golfer is all. I don't do speeches.'

Kingsbury wasn't listening. 'Maybe these assholes'll let us play through.' He hollered down the fairway toward the other golfers, but they seemed not to hear. Kingsbury teed up a ball. He said, 'Fine, they want to be snots.'

'Don't,' pleaded Jake Harp. The slow-playing four-some was well within the limited range of Kingsbury's driver. 'Frank, what's the hurry?'

Kingsbury had already coiled into his backswing. 'Yuppie snots,' he said, following through with a ferocious grunt. The ball took off like a missile, low and true.

Terrific, thought Jake Harp. The one time he keeps his left arm straight.

The other golfers scattered and watched the ball streak past. They reassembled in the middle of the fairway, shook their fists at Kingsbury and began a swift march back toward the tee.

'Shit,' said Jake Harp. He didn't have the energy for a fistfight; he didn't even have the energy to watch.

Francis X. Kingsbury put the wood in his bag, and sat down behind the steering wheel of the golf cart. The angry players were advancing in an infantry line that was the color of lollipops. Where Kingsbury came from, it would be hard to regard such men as dangerous.

'Aw, let's go,' said Jake Harp.

Kingsbury nodded and turned the golf cart around. 'Trying to make a point is all,' he said. 'Etiquette, am I right? Have some fucking common courtesy for other players.'

Jake Harp said, 'I think they got the message.' He could hear the golfers shouting and cursing as they drove away. He hoped none of them had recognized him.

On the drive back to the clubhouse, Francis Kingsbury asked Jake Harp for the name of the restaurant manager at Ocean Reef.

'I've got no idea,' Jake Harp said.

'But you're a member here.'

'Frank, I'm a member of seventy-four country clubs all over the damn country. Some I've never even played.'

Kingsbury went on: 'The reason I asked, I got a line on a big shipment of fish. Maybe they'd want to buy some.'

'I'll ask around. What kind of fish?'

'Tuna, I think. Maybe king mackerel.'

'You don't know?'

'Hell, Jake, I'm a real-estate man, not a goddamn chef. It's a trailer full of fish is all I know. Maybe six thousand pounds.'

Jake Harp said, 'Holy Jesus.'

Francis Kingsbury wasn't about to get into the whole messy story. He'd been having a devil of a time penetrating the Sudanese bureaucracy; UNICEF was no better. *Yes, of course we'd welcome any famine relief, but first you'll have to fill out some forms and answer some questions. . . .* Meanwhile, no one at the Amazing Kingdom seemed to know how long whale meat would stay fresh.

From the back of the golf cart came a high-pitched electronic beeping. Kingsbury quickly pulled off the path and parked in a stand of Australian pines. He unzipped his golf bag and removed a cellular telephone.

When he heard who was on the other end, he lowered his

voice and turned away. Jake Harp took the hint; he slipped into the trees to get rid of the two Bloody Marys he'd had for breakfast. It was several seconds before he realized he was pissing all over somebody's brand-new Titleist. He carefully wiped it dry with a handkerchief and dropped it in his pocket.

Francis X. Kingsbury was punching a new number into the phone when Jake Harp returned to the golf cart.

'Get me that dildo Chelsea,' he was saying. 'No . . . who? I don't care—where did you say he is? Twenty minutes, he's not in my office and that's it. And get that fucking Pedro, he's in his car. Keep him on the line till—right—I get back.'

He touched a button and the cellular phone made a burp. Kingsbury put it away. He was steaming mad.

Jake Harp said, 'More problems?'

'Yeah, a major goddamn problem,' said Kingsbury. 'Only this one works for me.'

'So fire him.'

'Oh, I am,' Kingsbury said, 'and that's just for starters.'

14

Molly McNamara came out of the kitchen carrying a silver teapot on a silver tray.

'No thank you,' said Agent Billy Hawkins.

'It's herbal,' Molly said, pouring a cup. 'Now I want you to try this.'

Hawkins politely took a drink. It tasted like cider.

'There now,' said Molly. 'Isn't that good?'

Hiding behind the door of the guest bedroom, Bud Schwartz and Danny Pogue strained to hear what was going on. They couldn't believe she was serving tea to an FBI man.

'I'd like to ask you a few questions,' Billy Hawkins was saying.

Molly cocked her head pleasantly. 'Of course. Fire away.'

'Let's begin with the Mothers of Wilderness. You're the president?'

'And founder, yes. We're just a small group of older folks who are deeply concerned about the future of the environment.' She held her teacup steady. 'I'm sure you know all this.'

Agent Hawkins went on: 'What about the Wildlife Rescue Corps? What can you tell me about it?'

Molly McNamara was impressed by the FBI man's grammar; most people would have used 'them' instead of 'it.'

'Just what I've read in the papers,' she said, sipping. 'That's the organization that is taking credit for freeing the mango voles, is that correct?'

'Right.'

'I'm assuming this is what gives you jurisdiction in this matter—the fact that the voles are a federally protected endangered species.'

'Right again,' said Hawkins. She was a sharp one.

Behind the bedroom door, Bud Schwartz was ready to yank his hair out. The crazy old twat was screwing with the FBI, and enjoying it!

Danny Pogue looked as confused as ever. He leaned close and whispered: 'I thought sure he was after you and me.'

'Shut up,' Bud Schwartz said. He was having a hard enough time hearing the conversation in the living room.

The FBI man was saying: 'We have reason to suspect a connection between the Wildlife Rescue Corps and the Mothers of Wilderness—'

'That's outlandish,' said Molly McNamara.

Agent Hawkins let the idea hang. He just sat there with his square shoulders and his square haircut, looking impassive and not the least bit accusatory.

Molly asked: 'What evidence do you have?'

'No evidence, just indications.'

'I see.' Her tone was one of pleasant curiosity.

Billy Hawkins opened his briefcase and took out two shiny pieces of paper. Xeroxes. 'Last month the Mothers of Wilderness put out a press release. Do you remember?'

'Certainly,' said Molly. 'I wrote it myself. We were calling for an investigation of zoning irregularities at Falcon Trace. We thought the grand jury should call a few witnesses.'

The FBI agent handed her the papers. 'That one's a copy of your press release. The other is a note delivered to the Amazing Kingdom of Thrills soon after the theft of the blue-tongued mango voles.'

Molly held both documents in her lap. 'It looks like they were done on the same typewriter,' she remarked.

In the bedroom, Bud Schwartz slumped to his knees when he heard what Molly said. He thought: She's insane. She's crazy as a goddamn bedbug. *We're all going to jail!*

Back in the living room, Molly was saying, 'I'm no expert, but the typing looks very similar.'

If Agent Billy Hawkins was caught off guard, he masked it well.

'You're right,' he said without expression. 'Both of these

papers were typed on a Smith-Corona model XD 5500 electronic. We don't know yet if they came out of the same machine, but they were definitely done on the same model.'

Molly cheerfully took the half-empty teapot back to the kitchen. Hawkins heard a faucet running, the sound of silverware clanking in the sink. In the bedroom, Danny Pogue put his mouth to Bud Schwartz's ear and said: 'What if she shoots him?'

Bud Schwartz hadn't thought of that. Christ, she couldn't be that loony, to kill an FBI man in her own apartment! Unless she planned to pin it on a couple of dirtbag burglars in the bedroom. . . .

When Molly came bustling out again, Billy Hawkins said: 'We've sent the originals to Washington. Hopefully they'll be able to say conclusively if it was the same typewriter.'

Molly sat down. 'It's quite difficult to tell, isn't it? With these new electronic typewriters, I mean. The key strokes are not as distinct. I read that someplace.'

The FBI man smiled confidently. 'Our lab is very, very good. Probably the best in the world.'

Molly McNamara took out a pale blue tissue and began to clean her eyeglasses: neat, circular swipes. 'I suppose it's possible,' she said, 'that somebody in our little group has gotten carried away.'

'It's an emotional issue,' agreed Billy Hawkins, 'this animal-rights thing.'

'Still, I cannot believe any of the Mothers would commit a crime. I simply cannot believe they would steal those creatures.'

'Perhaps they hired somebody to do it.'

Hawkins went into the briefcase again and came out with a standard police mug shot. He handed it to Molly and said: 'Buddy Michael Schwartz, a convicted felon. His pickup truck was seen leaving the Amazing Kingdom shortly after the theft. Two white males inside.'

Behind the bedroom door, Bud Schwartz steadied himself. His gut churned, his throat turned to chalk. Danny Pogue looked frozen and glassy-eyed, like a rabbit trapped in the diamond lane of I-95. 'Bud,' he said. 'Oh shit.' Bud Schwartz clapped a hand over his partner's mouth.

They could hear Molly saying, 'He looks familiar, but I just can't be sure.'

The hair prickled on Bud Schwartz's arms. The old witch was going to drop the dime. Unbelievable.

Agent Hawkins was saying, 'Do you know him personally?'

There was a pause that seemed to last five minutes. Molly nudged her eyeglasses up the bridge of her nose. She held the photograph near a lamp, and examined it from several angles.

'No,' she said finally. 'He looks vaguely familiar, but I really can't place the face.'

'Do me a favor. Think about it.'

'Certainly,' she said. 'May I keep the picture?'

'Sure. And think about the Wildlife Rescue Corps, too.'

Molly liked the way this fellow conducted an interview. He knew precisely how much to say without giving away the good stuff—and he certainly knew how to listen. He was a pro.

'Talk to your friends,' said Billy Hawkins. 'See if they have any ideas.'

'You're putting me in a difficult position. These are fine people.'

'I'm sure they are.' The FBI man stood up, straight as a flagpole. He said, 'It would be helpful if I could borrow that Smith-Corona—the one that was used for your press announcements. And the ribbon cartridge as well.'

Molly said, 'Oh dear.'

'I can get a warrant, Mrs. McNamara.'

'That's not it,' she said. 'You see, the typewriter's been stolen.'

Billy Hawkins didn't say anything.

'Out of my car.'

'That's too bad,' the agent said.

'The trunk of my car,' Molly added. 'While I was grocery-shopping.'

She walked the FBI man to the front door. 'Can I ask you something, Agent Hawkins? Are you fellows investigating the death of the killer whale, as well?'

'Should we?'

'I think so. It looks like a pattern, doesn't it? Terrible things are happening at that park.' Molly looked at him over the tops of her glasses. He felt as if he were back in elementary school. She said, 'I know the mango voles are important, but if I may make a suggestion?'

'Sure,' said Hawkins.

'Your valuable time and talents would be better spent on a thorough investigation of the Falcon Trace resort. It's a cesspool down there, and Mr. Francis X. Kingsbury is the root of the cess. I trust the FBI is still interested in bribery and public corruption.'

'We consider it a priority.'

'Then you'll keep this in mind.' Molly's eyes lost some of their sparkle. 'They've up and bulldozed the whole place,' she said. 'The trees, everything. It's a crime what they did. I drove by it this morning.'

For the first time Billy Hawkins heard a trembling in her voice. He handed her a card. 'Anything solid, we'll look into it. And thank you very much for the tea.'

She held the door open. 'You're a very polite young man,' she said. 'You renew my faith in authority.'

'We'll be talking soon,' said Agent Hawkins.

As soon as he was gone, Molly McNamara heard a whoop from the bedroom. She found Danny Pogue dancing a one-legged jig, ecstatic that he was not in federal custody. Bud Schwartz sat on the edge of the bed, nervously pounding his fist in a pillow.

Danny Pogue took Molly by the arms and said: 'You did good. You stayed cool!'

Bud Schwartz said, 'Cool's not the word for it.'

Molly handed him the mug shot. 'Next time comb your hair,' she said. 'Now then—let's have a look at those files you boys borrowed from Mr. Kingsbury.'

Joe Winder took Nina's hand and led her down the trail. 'You're gonna love this guy,' he said.

'What happened to the movie?'

'Later,' Winder said. 'There's a ten-o'clock show.' He hated going to the movies. Hated driving all the way up to Homestead.

Nina said, 'Don't you have a flashlight?'

'We've got a good hour till dusk. Come on.'

'It's my night off,' she said. 'I wanted to go someplace.'

Winder pulled her along through the trees. 'Just you wait,' he said.

They found Skink shirtless, skinning a raccoon at the campsite. He grunted when Joe Winder said hello. Nina wondered if the plastic collar around his neck was from a prison or some other institution. She stepped closer to get a look at the dead raccoon.

'Import got him,' Skink said, feeling her stare. 'Up on 905 about two hours ago. Little guy's still warm.'

Winder cleared a spot for Nina to sit down. 'How do you know it was a foreign car?' he asked. He truly was curious.

'Low bumper broke his neck, that's how I know. Usually it's the tires that do the trick. That's because the rental companies prefer mid-sized American models. Fords and Chevys. We get a ton of rentals up and down this stretch.'

He stripped the skin off the animal and laid it to one side. To Nina he said: 'They call me Skink.'

She took a small breath. 'I'm Nina. Joe said you were the governor of Florida.'

'Long time ago.' Skink frowned at Winder. 'No need to bring it up.'

The man's voice was a deep, gentle rumble. Nina wondered why the guys who phoned the sex line never sounded like that. She shivered and said: 'Joe told me you just vanished. Got up and walked away from the job. It was in all the papers.'

'I'm sure. Did he also tell you that I knew his daddy?'

'Ancient history,' Winder cut in. 'Nina, I wanted you to meet this guy because he saved my life the other night.'

Skink sliced the hindquarters off the dead raccoon and placed them side by side in a large fry pan. He said to Nina: 'Don't believe a word of it, darling. The only reason he wanted you to meet me was so you'd understand.'

'Understand what?'

'What's about to happen.'

Nina looked uncomfortable. With one hand she began twisting the ends of her hair into tiny braids.

'Don't be nervous,' Joe Winder said, touching her knee.

'Well, what's he talking about?'

Skink finished with the raccoon carcass and slopped the innards into a grocery bag, which he buried. After he got the fire going, he wiped his palms on the seat of his new canvas trousers, the ones he'd taken off Spearmint Breath. He watched, satisfied as the gray meat began to sizzle and darken in the fry pan.

'I don't suppose you're hungry,' Skink said.

'We've got other plans.' Nina was cordial but firm.

Skink foraged through a rubble of old crates and lobster traps, mumbled, stomped into the woods. He came back carrying a dirty blue Igloo cooler. He took out three beers, opened one and gave the other two to Nina and Joe Winder.

Before taking a drink, Nina wiped the top of the can on the sleeve of Winder's shirt. She touched a hand to her neck and said, 'So what's with the collar?'

'Telemetry.' Skink pointed a finger at the sky. 'Every week or so, a plane comes around.'

'They think he's a panther,' Joe Winder explained. 'See, it's a radio collar. He took it off a dead panther.'

Skink quickly added: 'But I'm not the one who killed it. It was a liquor truck out of Marathon. Didn't even stop.'

Nina wasn't plugging in. After a pause she said, 'Joe, don't forget about our movie.'

Winder nodded. Sometimes he felt they were oceans apart. 'The panther's all but extinct,' he said. 'Maybe two dozen left alive. The Game and Fish Department uses radio collars to keep track of where they are.'

Skink drained his beer. 'Two nights later, here comes the liquor truck again. Only this time he blows a tire on some barbed wire.'

'In the middle of the road?' Nina said.

'Don't ask me how it got there. Anyway, I had a good long talk with the boy.'

Winder said, 'Jesus, don't tell me.'

'Cat's blood was still on the headlights. Fur, too.' Skink spat into the fire. 'Cracker bastard didn't seem to care.'

'You didn't . . .'

'No, nothing permanent. Nothing his insurance wouldn't cover.'

In her smoothest voice Nina asked, 'Did you eat the panther, too?'

'No, ma'am,' said Skink. 'I did not.'

The big cat was buried a half-mile up the trail, under brilliant bougainvilleas that Skink himself had planted. Joe Winder thought about showing Nina the place, but she didn't act interested. Darkness was settling in, and the mosquitoes had arrived by the billions. Nina slapped furiously at her bare arms and legs, while Joe Winder shook his head to keep the little bloodsuckers out of his ears.

Skink said, 'I got some goop if you want it. Great stuff.' He held his arms out in the firelight. The left one was engulfed by black mosquitoes; the right one was untouched.

'It's called EDTIAR,' Skink said. 'Extended Duration Topical Insect/Arthropod Repellent. I'm a field tester for the U.S. Marines; they pay me and everything.' Studiously he began counting the bites on his left arm.

Nina, on the shrill edge of misery, whacked a big fat arthropod on Joe Winder's cheek. 'We've got to get going,' she said.

'They're nasty tonight,' Skink said sympathetically. 'I just took seventeen hits in thirty seconds.'

Winder himself was getting devoured. He stood up, flailing his own torso. The bugs were humming in his eyes, his mouth, his nostrils.

'Joe, what's the point of all this?' Nina asked.

'I'm waiting for him to tell me who killed Will Koocher.'

'Oh, for God's sake.'

Skink said, 'We're in dangerous territory now.'

'I don't care,' Winder said. 'Tell me what happened. It had something to do with the mango voles, I'm sure.'

'Yes,' said Skink.

Nina announced that she was leaving. 'I'm getting eaten alive, and we're going to miss the movie.'

'Screw the movie,' said Joe Winder, perhaps too curtly.

For Nina was suddenly gone—down the trail, through the woods. Snapping twigs and muffled imprecations divulged her path.

'Call me Mr. Charm,' Winder said.

Skink chuckled. 'You'd better go. This can wait.'

'I want to know more.'

'It's the voles, like you said.' He reached into his secondhand trousers and took out a bottle so small it couldn't have held more than four ounces. He pressed it into the palm of Joe Winder's right hand.

'Ah, the magic bug goop!'

'No,' Skink said. 'Now take off, before Snow White gets lost in the big bad forest.'

Blindly Winder jogged down the trail after his girlfriend. He held one arm across his face to block the branches from slashing him, and weaved through the low viny trees like a halfback slipping tacklers.

Nina had given up her solo expedition forty yards from Skink's campsite, and that's where Winder found her, leaning against the slick red trunk of a gumbo-limbo.

'Get us out of here,' she said, brushing a squadron of plump mosquitoes from her forehead.

Out of breath, Winder gave her a hug. She didn't exactly melt in his arms. 'You were doing fine,' he said. 'You stayed right on the trail.'

They were in the car, halfway to Homestead, when she spoke again: 'Why can't you leave it alone? The guy's nothing but trouble.'

'He's not crazy, Nina.'

'Oh right.'

'A man was murdered. I can't let it slide.'

She picked a buttonwood leaf from her sleeve, rolled down the window and flicked the leaf away. She said, 'If he's not crazy, then how come he lives the way he does? How come he wears that electric collar?'

'He says it keeps him on his toes.' Joe Winder plugged a Zevon tape in the stereo. 'Look, I'm not saying he's normal. I'm just saying he's not crazy.'

'Like you would know,' Nina said.

15

On Sunday, July 22, Charles Chelsea got up at eight-thirty, showered, shaved, dressed (navy slacks, Cordovan loafers, blue oxford shirt, burgundy necktie), trimmed his nose hairs, splashed on about three gallons of Aramis and drove off to work in his red Mazda Miata, for which he had paid thirty-five hundred dollars over dealer invoice.

Chelsea had two important appointments at the Amazing Kingdom of Thrills. One of them would be routine, and one promised to be unpleasant. He had not slept well, but he didn't feel exceptionally tired. In fact, he felt surprisingly confident, composed, tough; if only he could remain that way until his meeting with Joe Winder.

A crew from Channel 7 was waiting outside the main gate. The reporter was an attractive young Latin woman wearing oversized sunglasses. Chelsea greeted her warmly and told her she was right on time. They all got in a van, which was driven by a man wearing a costume of bright neoprene plumes. The man introduced himself as Baldy the Eagle, and said he was happy to be their host. He began a long spiel about the Amazing Kingdom of Thrills until Charles Chelsea flashed his ID badge, at which point the bird man shrugged and shut up. Chelsea slapped his arm when he tried to bum a Marlboro off the Channel 7 cameraman.

When they arrived at the killer-whale tank, Chelsea stepped from the van and held the door for the reporter, whose first name was Maria. Chelsea led the way inside the marine stadium, where the TV crew unpacked and began to set up the equipment. Chelsea sat next to Maria in the front row, facing the empty blue pool. Above them, men on scaffolds were sandblasting the word 'Orky' from the coral-colored wall.

Chelsea said, 'I guess the others will be along soon.'

Maria removed her sunglasses and brushed her hair. She took out a spiral notebook and flipped to a blank page.

'The other stations,' Chelsea said, 'they must be running a little late.'

Five others had received the same fax as Channel 7 had. Surely more crews would show up—it was Sunday, after all, the slowest news day of the week.

Maria said, 'Before we go on the air—'

'You want some background,' Chelsea said helpfully. 'Well, to be perfectly frank, Orky's death left us with a rather large vacancy. Here we have this beautiful saltwater tank, as you see, and a scenic outdoor stadium. A facility like this is too special to waste. We thought about getting another whale, but Mr. Kingsbury felt it would be inappropriate. He felt Orky was irreplaceable.'

Charles Chelsea glanced over Maria's shoulder to see the Minicam pointed at him. Its red light winked innocuously as the tape rolled. The cameraman was on his knees. Squinting through the viewfinder, he signaled for Chelsea to keep talking.

'Are we on?' the PR man said. 'What about the mike? I don't have a mike.'

The cameraman pointed straight up. Chelsea raised his eyes. A gray boom microphone, the size of a fungo bat, hung over his head. The boom was controlled by a sound man standing to Chelsea's right. The man wore earphones and a Miami Dolphins warm-up jacket.

Maria said, 'You mentioned Orky. Could you tell us what your staff has learned about the whale's death? What exactly killed it?'

Chelsea fought to keep his Adam's apple from bobbing spasmodically, as it often did when he lied. 'The tests,' he said, 'are still incomplete.'

Maria's warm brown eyes blinked inquisitively. 'There's a rumor that the whale died during an encounter with an employee of the Amazing Kingdom.'

'Oh, that's a good one.' Chelsea laughed stiffly. 'Where did you hear that?'

'Is it true?'

The camera's blinking red light no longer seemed harmless. Charles Chelsea said, 'I'm not going to dignify such a question by responding.'

The reporter said nothing, just let the tape roll. Let him choke on the silence. It worked.

'We did have a death that night,' Chelsea admitted, toying with his cuffs. 'An employee of the park apparently took his own life. It was very, very tragic—'

'What was the name of this employee?'

Chelsea's tone became cold, reproachful. 'It is our strict policy not to discuss such matters publicly. There is an issue of privacy, and respect for the family.'

Maria said, 'The rumor is—'

'We don't respond to rumors, Ms. Rodríguez.' Now Chelsea was leaning forward, lecturing. The boom mike followed him. 'Would you like to hear about our newest attraction, or not?'

She smiled like a moray eel. 'That's why we're here.'

Oh no it isn't, thought Chelsea, trying not to glare, trying not to perspire, trying not to look like the unvarnished shill he was.

'I brought a bathing suit,' Maria said, 'as you suggested.'

'Maybe we should wait for the others.'

'I think we're it, Mr. Chelsea. I don't think any of the other stations are coming.'

'Fine.' He tried not to sound disappointed.

The cameraman stopped taping. Chelsea dabbed his forehead in relief; he needed to collect himself, recover from the ambush. Everybody wants to be Mike Wallace, he thought bitterly. Everybody's a hardass.

Maria picked up a tote bag and asked directions to the lady's room. When she returned, she was wearing a tight melon-colored tonga that required continual adjustment. At the sight of her, Charles Chelsea inadvertently licked the corners of his mouth. It wasn't so bad after all, coming to work on a Sunday.

'Should I get in?' Maria asked.

'Sure.' Chelsea signaled across the pool to a young man dressed in khaki shorts. This was one of the trainers.

Maria slipped into the whale pool, dipped her head underwater, and smoothed her hair straight back. The tape was rolling again.

Eyes twinkling, she smiled up at the camera. The guy with the boom mike leaned over the wall of the tank to capture her words.

'Hi, this is Maria Rodríguez. Today we're visiting the Amazing Kingdom of Thrills in North Key Largo. As you can see, it's a gorgeous summer day—'

Chelsea was thinking: Good girl, stick to the fluff.

'—and we're about to meet the newest star of the Kingdom's outdoor marine show. His name is Dickie the Dolphin . . . cut! Hold it, Jimmy.'

The cameraman stopped the tape. Bobbing in the whale pool, Maria groped beneath the surface, frowned and spun away. Chelsea could see that she was struggling to realign the bathing suit.

'Damn thing's riding up my crack.'

'Take your time,' said the cameraman. 'We got plenty of light.'

Moments later, Maria was ready again; fresh, sleek, languid. She splashed herself lightly in the face so that droplets glistened in her eyelashes; Charles Chelsea was transfixed.

'Hi, this is Maria Rodríguez reporting from the Amazing Kingdom of Thrills in North Key Largo. As you can see, it's a gorgeous summer day in South Florida—perfect for a swim with the newest star of the Amazing Kingdom's marine show. His name is Dickie the Dolphin and, starting tomorrow, you can swim with him, too!'

Chelsea cued the trainer, who pulled the pin on the gate to the whale pool. Pushing a V-shaped wake, the dolphin charged from the holding tank and sounded.

The TV reporter continued: 'It's the latest concept in marine theme parks—customer participation. Instead of sitting in the bleachers and watching these remarkable mammals do tricks, you can actually get in the water and play with them. It costs a little more, but—believe me—it's worth it.'

A few yards behind her, Dickie the Dolphin rolled, blowing air noisily. Maria kept her poise, glancing over one shoulder with a breezy, affectionate smile. Chelsea was impressed; she had the whole script memorized.

Turning back to the camera, Maria said: 'To be in the water with these gentle, intelligent creatures is an experience you'll never forget. Scientists say the dolphin's brain is actually larger than ours, and much of their complex social behavior remains a mystery. . . .'

Dickie the Dolphin surfaced lazily near Maria, who grabbed its dorsal fin with both hands. Chelsea stood up quickly and waved a warning, but it was too late. The dolphin carried the TV reporter across the top of the water; she closed her eyes and squealed with child-like excitement.

'Great fucking video,' remarked Jimmy the cameraman, panning expertly with the action.

The boom man said, 'She's getting out of range.'

Charles Chelsea cupped his hands and shouted. 'Let go! No rides allowed!'

Maria couldn't hear a word. She was holding her breath underwater while the dolphin imitated a torpedo. Every few seconds her long brown legs would slice the surface as she was dragged along, like the tail of a kite. Chelsea bit his lip and watched in queasy silence. Finally Maria splashed to the surface—and she was laughing, thank God! She thought it was all in fun, and maybe it was.

The sound man scurried along the rim of the tank and repositioned the boom. Giggling, short of breath, Maria's eyes found the camera. She said, 'Folks, this is unbelievable. Bring the family, you're gonna love it!' Dickie the Dolphin appeared at her side, and she stroked its sleek flank. Wondrously, it seemed to nuzzle her bosom with its snout.

'He's so *adorable*!' Maria exclaimed.

From the feeding platform on the side of the tank, the trainer called out, 'Hey, be careful!' Then he started peeling off his khakis.

'Such friendly animals,' Maria was saying. 'Notice how they always look like they're smiling!'

Dickie the Dolphin slapped its tail on the surface and pushed even closer. Maria threw both arms around the slippery mammal, which obligingly rolled on its back.

Chelsea saw the trainer dive in. He saw Maria's expression change from tenderness to awe. Then he saw the dolphin hook her with its flippers and drag her down.

When she broke to the top, Maria's giggle had become a low fearful moan. As the dolphin's dark form appeared beneath her, she seemed to rise from the water. Then, just as slowly, the creature drew her under.

The cameraman muttered that he was running out of tape. A voice behind him said: 'You'll miss the best part.'

It was Joe Winder. He stood next to Charles Chelsea, who was clutching the rail with knuckles as pink as shrimp. In the water, the trainer was trying without much success to separate the dolphin from the TV reporter.

Chelsea said to Winder: 'Maybe it's a new trick—'

'It's no trick. He's trying to boink her.'

'That's not funny, Joe.'

Winder pointed. 'What do you think *that* is? See?'

'I—I don't know.'

'It's a dolphin shlong, Charlie. One of Nature's marvels.'

Chelsea began to stammer.

'They get in moods,' Joe explained. 'Same as dogs.'

'My God.'

'Don't worry, Charlie, it'll pass.'

With the trainer's help, Maria Rodríguez finally broke free from Dickie the Dolphin's embrace. Cursing, tugging at her tonga, she paddled furiously toward the ladder on the wall of the tank.

'Faster!' Charles Chelsea hollered. 'Here he comes again!'

Two hours later, he was still trying to apologize without admitting the truth. 'Sometimes they play too rough, that's all.'

'Playing?' Maria sniffed sarcastically. 'Excuse me, Mr. Chelsea, but I know a dick when I see one.' She had changed back to TV clothes, although her hair was still wrapped in a towel. 'I ought to sue your ass,' she said.

They were sitting in Chelsea's office—the reporter, Charles Chelsea, and Joe Winder. The crew had returned to the truck to put the dish up, just in case.

'Come on,' Winder said to Maria, 'be a sport.'

'What?' She gave him an acid glare. 'What did you say?' She whipped the towel off her head and tossed it on the floor.

Very impolite, Winder thought, and unprofessional. 'Take it easy,' he said. 'Nothing unspeakable happened.'

Maria pointed a finger in his face and said, 'Someone could get killed out there.'

Charles Chelsea was miserable. 'How can we make it up to you?' he asked Maria Rodríguez. 'How about we comp you some passes to the Wild Bill Hiccup show?'

She was gone before he could come up with something better. On her way out, she kicked at the towel.

Joe Winder said, 'Don't worry, she won't sue.'

'How do you know?'

'It's too embarrassing. Hell, she'll probably destroy the tape on the way back to Miami.'

Defensively Chelsea said, 'She wasn't supposed to grab the dolphin. No touching is allowed—swimming only.'

'This was a terrible idea, Charlie. Who thought of it?'

'Fifty bucks a head. They've got a bunch of these places in the Keys.'

Joe Winder asked where Kingsbury had purchased the new dolphin.

'How should I know?' Chelsea snapped. 'A dolphin's a dolphin, for Christ's sake. They don't come with a pedigree.'

'This one needs a female,' Winder said, 'before you let tourists in the water.'

'Thank you, Doctor Cousteau.' The publicity man got up and closed the door. He looked gravely serious when he returned to the desk.

Joe Winder said, 'I hope you're not going to make me write a press release about this. I've got more important things to do.'

'Me, too.' To steel himself, Charles Chelsea tightened his stomach muscles. 'Joe, we're going to have to let you go.'

'I see.'

Chelsea studied his fingernails, trying not to make eye contact with Winder. 'It's a combination of things.'

'My attitude, I suppose.'

'That's a factor, yes. I tried to give some latitude. The hair. The casual clothing.'

Winder said, 'Anything else?'

'I understand you broke into the vole lab.'

'Would you like to hear what I found?'

'Not particularly,' Chelsea said.

'A paper written about the blue-tongued mango voles. The one you sent to Will Koocher when you were recruiting him.'

Chelsea gave Winder a so-what look. 'That it?'

'Funny thing, Charlie. The person who supposedly wrote that paper, this Dr. Sarah Hunt? Rollins College never heard of her.' Winder raised his palms in mock puzzlement. 'Never on the faculty, never graduated, never even attended—what do you make of that, Charlie?'

'Pedro told me of your ridiculous theory.' Chelsea's lips barely moved when he spoke; he looked like a goldfish burping. 'Dr. Koocher wasn't murdered, Joe, but in your twisted brain I'm sure you've made some connection between his unfortunate death and this . . . this typographical error.'

Winder laughed. 'A typo? You're beautiful, Charlie. The paper's a goddamn fake.'

Chelsea rolled his eyes. 'And I suppose a simpler explanation is impossible—that perhaps the author's name was misspelled by the publisher, or that the university was misidentified. . . .'

'No way.'

'You're not a well person,' Chelsea said. 'And now I learn that you've telephoned Koocher's widow in New York. That's simply inexcusable.' The way he spit out the word was meant to have a lacerating effect.

'What's inexcusable,' said Winder, 'is the way you lied.'

'It was a judgment call.' Chelsea's cheek twitched. 'We were trying to spare the woman some grief.'

'I told her to get a lawyer.'

Chelsea's tan seemed to fade.

Joe Winder went on: 'The newspapers are bound to find out the truth. 'Man Gobbled by Whale. Modern-Day Jonah Perishes in Freak Theme Park Mishap.' Think about it, Charlie.'

'The coroner said he drowned. We've never denied it.'

'But they didn't say *how* he drowned. Or why.'

Charles Chelsea began to rock back and forth. 'This is all academic, Joey. As of this moment, you no longer work here.'

'And here I thought I was your ace in the hole.'

Chelsea extended a hand, palm up. 'The keys to the Cushman, please.'

Winder obliged. He said, 'Charlie, even though you're an obsequious dork, I'd like to believe you're not a part of this. I'd like to believe that you're just incredibly dim.'

'Go clean out your desk.'

'I don't have to. There's nothing in it.'

Chelsea looked momentarily confused.

Winder waved his arms. 'Desks are places to keep facts, Charlie. Who needs a desk when the words simply fly off the tops of our heads! Hell, I've done my finest work for you while sitting on the toilet.'

'If you're trying to insult me, it won't work.' Chelsea lowered his eyelids in lizardly disinterest. 'We all fudge the truth when it suits our purposes, don't we? Like when you told me you got that scar in a car accident.'

So he knew all along, just as Joe Winder had suspected.

'I heard it was a fight in the newsroom,' Chelsea said, 'a fistfight with one of your editors.'

'He had it coming,' said Winder. 'He screwed up a perfectly good news story.'

The story concerned Joe Winder's father bribing a county commissioner in exchange for a favorable vote on a zoning variance. Winder had written the story himself after digging through a stack of his father's canceled checks and finding five made out to the commissioner's favorite bagman.

Though admiring of Winder's resourcefulness, the editor had

said it created an ethical dilemma; he decided that someone else would have to write the piece. You're too emotionally involved, the editor had told him.

So Winder had gotten a firm grip on the editor's head and rammed it through the screen of the word processor, cutting himself spectacularly in the struggle that followed.

'I'm sorry, Charlie,' he said. 'Maybe you shouldn't have hired me.'

'The understatement of the year.'

'Before I go, may I show you something?' He took out the small bottle that Skink had given him and placed it in the center of Chelsea's desk blotter.

The publicity man examined it and said, 'It's food coloring, so what?'

'Look closer.'

'Betty Crocker food coloring. What's the point, Joe?'

'And what color?'

'Blue.' Chelsea was impatient. 'The label says blue.'

Winder twisted the cap off the bottle. He said, 'I believe this came from the vole lab, too. You might ask Pedro about it.'

Baffled, Charles Chelsea watched Joe Winder toss back his head and empty the contents of the bottle into his mouth. He sloshed the liquid from cheek to cheek, then swallowed.

'Ready?' Winder said. He stuck out his tongue, which now was the color of indigo dye.

'That's a very cute trick.' Chelsea sounded nervous.

Joe Winder climbed onto the desk on his hands and knees. 'The voles were phony, Charlie. Did you know that?' He extended his tongue two inches from Chelsea's nose, then sucked it back in. He said, 'There's no such thing as a blue-tongued mango vole. Kingsbury faked the whole deal. Invented an entire species!'

'You're cracking up,' Chelsea said thinly.

Winder grabbed him by the collar. 'You fucker, did you know all along?'

'Get out, or I'm calling Security.'

'That's why Will Koocher was killed. He'd figured out every-thing. He was going to rat, so to speak, on the upstanding Mr. Kingsbury.'

Chelsea's upper lip was a constellation of tiny droplets. He tried to pull away. 'Let me go, Joe. If you know what's good for you.'

'They painted their tongues, Charlie. Think of it. They took these itty-bitty animals and dyed their tongues blue, all in the name of tourism.'

Straining against Winder's grasp, Chelsea said, 'You're talking crazy.'

Joe Winder licked him across the face.

'Stop it!'

Winder slurped him again. 'It's your color, Charlie. Very snappy.'

His tongue waggled in mockery; Chelsea eyed the fat blue thing as if it were a poisonous slug.

'You can fire me,' Winder announced, 'but I won't go away.'

He climbed off the desk, careful not to drop the bottle of food coloring. Chelsea swiftly began plucking tissues from a silver box and wiping his face, examining each crumpled remnant for traces of the dye. His fingers were shaking.

'I should have you arrested,' he hissed.

'But you won't,' Winder said. 'Think of the headlines.'

He was halfway to the door when Chelsea said, 'Wait a minute, Joey. What is it you want?'

Winder kept walking, and began to laugh. He laughed all the way down the hall, a creepy melodic warble that made Charles Chelsea shudder and curse.

16

As a reward for the successful theft of Francis X. Kingsbury's files, Molly McNamara allowed Bud Schwartz and Danny Pogue to keep the rented Cutlass for a few days.

On the evening of July 22, they drove down Old Cutler Road, where many of Miami's wealthiest citizens lived. The homes were large and comfortable-looking, and set back impressively from the tree-shaded road. Danny Pogue couldn't get over the size of the yards, the tall old pines and colorful tropical shrubbery; it was beautiful, yet intimidating.

'They got those Spanish bayonets under the windows,' he reported. 'God, I hate them things.' Wicked needles on the end of every stalk—absolute murder, even with gloves.

Bud Schwartz said, 'Don't sweat it, we'll find us a back door.'

'For sure they got alarms.'

'Yeah.'

'And a goddamn dog, too.'

'Probably so,' said Bud Schwartz, thinking: Already the guy's a nervous wreck.

'You ever done a house like this?'

'Sure.' Bud Schwartz was lying. Mansions, that's what these were, just like the ones on 'Miami Vice.' The bandage on his bad hand was damp with perspiration. Hunched over the steering wheel, he thought: Thank God for the rental—at least we got a car that'll move.

To cut the tension, he said: 'Ten bucks it's a Dobie.'

'No way,' said Danny Pogue. 'I say Rottweiler, that's the dog nowadays.'

'For the Yuppies, sure, but not this guy. I'm betting on a Dobie.'

Danny Pogue fingered a pimple on his neck. 'Okay, but give me ten on the side.'

'For what?'

'Give me ten on the color.' Danny Pogue slugged him softly on the shoulder. 'Black or brown?'

Bud Schwartz said, 'I'll give you ten if it's brown.'

'Deal.'

'You're a sucker. Nobody in this neighborhood's got a brown Doberman.'

'We'll see,' said Danny Pogue. He pointed as they passed a crimson Porsche convertible parked on a cobbler drive. A beautiful dark-haired girl, all of seventeen, was washing the sports car under a quartet of halogen spotlights. The girl wore a dazzling green bikini and round reflector sunglasses. The sun had been down for two hours.

Danny Pogue clapped his hands. 'Jesus, you see that?'

'Yeah, hosing down her Targa. And here we are in the middle of a drought.' Bud Schwartz braked softly to peer at the name on a cypress mailbox. 'Danny, what's that house number? I can't see it from here.'

'Four-oh-seven.'

'Good. We're almost there.'

'I was wondering,' said Danny Pogue.

'Yeah, what else is new.'

'Do I get twenty bucks if it's a brown Rottweiler?'

'They don't come in brown,' said Bud Schwartz. 'I thought you knew.'

It wasn't a Doberman pinscher or a Rottweiler.

'Maybe some type of weasel,' whispered Danny Pogue. 'Except it's got a collar on it.'

They were kneeling in the shadow of a sea-grape tree. 'One of them beady-eyed dogs from Asia,' said Bud Schwartz, 'or maybe it's Africa.' Dozing under the electric bug lamp, the animal showed no reaction to the sizzle and zap of dying moths.

Carefully Bud Schwartz inserted four Tylenol No. 3 tablets into a ten-ounce patty of prime ground sirloin. With his good hand he lobbed the meat over the fence. It landed with a wet slap on the patio near the pool. The weasel-dog lifted its head, barked once sharply and got up.

Danny Pogue said, 'That's the ugliest goddamn thing I ever saw.'

'Like you're Mel Gibson, right?'

'No, but just look.'

The dog found the hamburger and gulped it in two bites. When its front legs began to wobble, Danny Pogue said, 'Jesus, what'd you use?'

'About a hundred milligrams of codeine.'

Soon the animal lay down, snuffling into a stupor. Bud Schwartz hopped the fence and helped his crutchless partner across. The two burglars crab-walked along a low cherry hedge until they reached the house. Through a glass door they saw that all the kitchen lights were on; in fact, lamps glowed in every window. Bud Schwartz heard himself take a short breath; he was acting against every instinct, every fundamental rule of the trade. Never *ever* break into an occupied dwelling—especially an occupied dwelling protected by four thousand dollars' worth of electronic burglar alarm.

Bud Schwartz knew the screens would be wired, so busting the windows was out of the question. He knew he couldn't jimmy the sliding door because that would trip the contact, also setting off the alarm. The best hope was cutting the glass door in such a way that it wouldn't trigger the noise detectors; he could see one of the matchbook-sized boxes mounted on a roof beam in the kitchen. Its tiny blue eye winked insidiously at him.

'What's the plan?' asked Danny Pogue.

Bud Schwartz took the glass cutter out of his pocket and showed it to his partner, who hadn't the faintest idea what it was. Bud Schwartz got to his knees. 'I'm going to cut a square,' he said, 'big enough to crawl through.'

'Like hell.' Danny Pogue was quite certain they would be arrested any moment.

Bud Schwartz dug the blades of the glass cutter into the door and pressed with the full strength of his good arm. The door began to slide on its rollers. 'Damn,' said Bud Schwartz. Cold air rushed from the house and put goose bumps on his arms.

Danny Pogue said: 'Must not be locked.'

The door coasted open. No bells or sirens went off. The only sound came from a television, probably upstairs.

They slipped into the house. Bud Schwartz's sneakers squeaked on the kitchen tile; hopping on one leg, Danny Pogue followed his partner through the living room, which was deco-rated hideously in black and red. The furniture was leather, the carpeting a deep stringy shag. On a phony brick wall over the fireplace hung a painting that was, by Bud Schwartz's astonished calculation, larger than life-sized. The subject of the painting was a nude blond with a Pepsodent smile and breasts the size of soccer balls. She wore a yellow visored cap, and held a flagstick over her shoulder. A small brass plate announced the title of the work: 'My Nineteenth Hole.'

It was unspeakably crude, even to two men who had spent most of their adult lives in redneck bars and minimum-security prisons. Bud Schwartz gazed at the painting and said: 'I'll bet it's the wife.'

'No way,' said Danny Pogue. He couldn't imagine being mar-ried to somebody who would do such a thing.

As they moved cautiously through the house, Bud Schwartz couldn't help but notice there wasn't much worth stealing, even if they'd wanted to. Oh, the stuff was expensive enough, but tacky as hell. A Waterford armadillo—how could millionaires have such lousy taste?

The burglars followed the sound of the television down a hallway toward a bedroom. Bud Schwartz had never been so jittery. *What if the asshole has a gun?* This had been Danny Pogue's question, and for once Bud Schwartz couldn't answer. The asshole probably *did* have a gun; it was Miami, after all. Probably something in a semi-automatic, a Mini-14 or a MAC-11. Christ, there's a pleasant thought. Ten, fifteen rounds a second. Hardly time to piss in your pants.

Danny Pogue's whiny breathing seemed to fill the hallway. Bud

Schwartz glared, held a finger to his lips. The door to the bedroom was wide open; somebody was switching the channels on the television. Momentously, Bud Schwartz smoothed his hair; Danny Pogue did the same. Bud Schwartz nodded and motioned with an index finger; Danny Pogue gave a constipated nod in return.

When they stepped into the room, they saw the blond woman from the golf painting. She was lying naked on the bed; two peach-colored pillows were tucked under her head, and the remote control was propped on her golden belly. At the sight of the burglars, the woman covered her chest. Excitedly she tried to speak—no sounds emerged, though her jaws moved vigorously, as if she were chewing a wad of bubble gum.

Inanely, Bud Schwartz said, 'Don't be afraid.'

The woman forced out a low guttural cry that lasted several seconds. She sounded like a wildcat in labor.

'Enough a that,' said Danny Pogue tensely.

Suddenly a door opened and a porky man in powder-blue boxer shorts stepped out of the bathroom. He was short and jowly, with skin like yellow lard. Tattooed on his left forearm was a striking tableau: Minnie Mouse performing oral sex on Mickey Mouse. At least that's what it looked like to Danny Pogue and Bud Schwartz, who couldn't help but stare. Mickey was wearing his sorcerer's hat from *Fantasia*, and appeared to be whistling a happy tune.

Danny Pogue said, 'That'd make a great T-shirt.'

With fierce reddish eyes, the man in the boxer shorts studied the two intruders.

'Honey!' cried the woman on the bed.

The man scowled impatiently. 'Well, shit, get it over with. Take, you know, whatever the hell.'

Bud Schwartz said, 'We didn't mean to scare you, Mr. Kingsbury.'

'Don't fucking flatter yourself. And, Penny, watch it with that goddamn thing!'

Still recumbent, the naked Mrs. Kingsbury now was aiming a small chrome-plated pistol at Danny Pogue's midsection.

'I knew it,' muttered Bud Schwartz. He hated the thought of

getting shot twice in the same week, especially by women. This one must've had it under the damn pillows, or maybe in the sheets.

Danny Pogue's lips were quivering, as if he were about to cry. He held out his arms beseechingly.

Quickly Bud Schwartz said: 'We're not here to rob you. We're here to talk business.'

Kingsbury hooked his nubby thumbs into the elastic waistband of his underpants. 'Make me laugh,' he said. 'Break into my house like a couple of putzes.'

'We're pros,' said Bud Schwartz.

Kingsbury cackled, snapping the elastic. 'Two hands, babe,' he reminded his wife.

Danny Pogue said, 'Bud, make her drop it!'

'It's only a .25,' said Kingsbury. 'She's been out to the range—what?—a half-dozen times. Got the nerves for it, apparently.'

Bud Schwartz tried to keep his voice level and calm. He said to Kingsbury: 'Your office got hit yesterday, right?'

'As a matter of fact, yeah.'

'You're missing some files.'

The naked Mrs. Kingsbury said, 'Frankie, you didn't tell me.' Her arms were impressively steady with the gun.

Kingsbury took his hands out of his underwear and folded them in a superior way across his breasts, which were larger than those of a few women whom Danny Pogue had known.

'Not exactly the Brink's job,' Kingsbury remarked.

'Well, we got your damn files,' said Bud Schwartz.

'That was you? Bullshit.'

'Maybe you need some proof. Maybe you need to see some credit-card slips.'

Kingsbury hesitated. 'Selling them back, is that the idea?'

Some genius businessman, thought Bud Schwartz. The guy was a bum, a con. You could tell right away.

'Tell your wife to drop the piece.'

'Penny, you heard the man.'

'And tell her to go lock herself in the john.'

'What?'

The wife said, 'Frankie, I don't like this.' Carefully she placed the gun on the nightstand next to a bottle of Lavoris mouthwash. A tremor of relief passed through Danny Pogue, starting at the shoulders. He hopped across the room and sat down on the corner of the bed.

'It's better if she's in the john,' Bud Schwartz said to Francis X. Kingsbury. 'Or maybe you don't care.'

Kingsbury gnawed his upper lip. He was thinking about the files, and what was in them.

His wife wrapped herself in a sheet. 'Frank?'

'Do what he said,' Kingsbury told her. 'Take a magazine, something. A book if you can find one.'

'Fuck you,' said Penny Kingsbury. On her way to the bathroom, she waved a copy of GQ in his face.

'At Doral is where I met her. Selling golf shoes.'

'How nice,' said Bud Schwartz.

'Fuzzy Zoeller, Tom Kite, I'm not kidding. Penny's customers.' Kingsbury had put on a red bathrobe and turned up the television, in case his wife was at the door trying to eavesdrop. Bud Schwartz lifted the handgun from the nightstand and slipped it into his pocket; the cold weight of the thing in his pants, so close to his privates, made him shudder. God, how he hated guns.

Kingsbury said, 'The painting in the big room—you guys get a look at it?'

'Yeah, boy,' answered Danny Pogue.

'We did that up on the Biltmore. Number seven or ten, I can't remember. Some par three. Anyway, I had to lease the whole fucking course for a day, that's how long it took. Must've been two hundred guys standing around, staring at her boobs. Penny didn't mind, she's proud of 'em.'

'And who wouldn't be,' said Bud Schwartz, tight as a knot. 'Can we get to it, please? We got plenty to talk about.'

Francis X. Kingsbury said, 'I'm trying to remember. You got the Ramex Global file. Jersey Premium. What else?'

'You know what else.'

Kingsbury nodded. 'Start with the American Express. Give me a number.'

Bud Schwartz sat down in a high-backed colonial chair. From memory he gave Kingsbury an inventory: 'We got a diamond tennis necklace in New York, earrings in Chicago. Yeah, and an emerald stickpin in Nassau of all places, for like three grand.' He motioned to Danny Pogue, who hobbled over to Mrs. Kingsbury's dresser and began to look through the boxes.

Dispiritedly, Kingsbury said, 'Forget it, you won't find it there.'

'So who got it all?'

'Friends. It's not important.'

'Not to us, maybe.' Bud Schwartz nodded toward the bathroom. 'I got a feeling your old lady might be interested.'

Kingsbury lowered his voice. 'The reason I use the credit card, hell, who carries that much cash?'

'Plus the insurance,' said Danny Pogue, pawing through Mrs. Kingsbury's jewelry. 'Stuff gets broke or stolen, they replace it, no questions. It's a new thing.'

Great, Bud Schwartz thought; now he's doing commercials.

'There's some excellent shit here. Very nice.' Danny Pogue held up a diamond solitaire and played it off the light. 'I'm guessin' two carats.'

'Try one-point-five,' said Kingsbury.

'There were some dinners on your card,' Bud Schwartz said. 'And plane tickets, too. It's handy how they put it all together at the end of the year where you can check it.'

Kingsbury asked him how much.

'Five grand,' Bud Schwartz said, 'and we won't say a word to the wife.'

'The file, Jesus, I need it back.'

'No problem. Now let's talk about serious money.'

Kingsbury frowned. He pulled on the tip of his nose with a thumb and forefinger, as if he were straightening it.

Bud Schwartz said, 'The Gotti file, Mr. King.'

'Mother of Christ.'

"Frankie, The Ferret, King.' That's what the indictment said.'

'You got me by surprise,' Kingsbury said.

Danny Pogue looked up from an opal bracelet he was admiring. 'So who's this Gotti dude again? Some kinda gangster is what Bud said.'

'How much?' said Kingsbury. He leaned forward and put his hands on his bare knees. 'Don't make it, like . . . a game.'

Bud Schwartz detected visceral fear in the man's voice; it gave him an unfamiliar feeling of power. On the other side of the bathroom door, Francis Kingsbury's wife shouted something about wanting to get out. Kingsbury ignored her.

'The banks that made the loans on Falcon Trace, do they know who you are?' Bud Schwartz affected a curious tone. 'Do they know you're a government witness? A mob guy?'

Kingsbury didn't bother to reply.

'I imagine they gave you shitloads a money,' Bud Schwartz went on, 'and I imagine they could call it back.'

Francis Kingsbury went to the bathroom door and told Penny to shut up and sit her sweet ass on the can. He turned back to the burglars and said: 'So what's the number, the grand total? For Gotti, I mean.'

Danny Pogue resisted the urge to enter the negotiation; expectantly he looked at his partner. Bud Schwartz smoothed his hair, pursed his mouth. He wanted to hear what kind of bullshit offer Kingsbury would make on his own.

'I'm trying to think what's fair.'

'Give me a fucking number,' said Kingsbury, 'and I'll goddamn tell you if it's fair.'

What the hell, thought Bud Schwartz. 'Fifty grand,' he said calmly. 'And we toss in Ramex and the rest for free.'

Excitedly Danny Pogue began excavating a new pimple.

Kingsbury eyed the men suspiciously. 'Fifty, you said? As in five-oh?'

'Right.' Bud Schwartz gave half a grin. 'That's fifty to give back the Gotti file . . .'

'And?'

'Two hundred more to forget what was in it.'

Kingsbury chuckled bitterly. 'So I was wrong,' he said. 'You're not such a putz.'

Danny Pogue was so overjoyed that he could barely control himself on the ride back to Molly's condominium. 'We're gonna be rich,' he said, pounding both hands on the upholstery. 'You're a genius, man, that's what you are.'

'It went good,' Bud Schwartz agreed. Better than he had ever imagined. As he drove, he did the arithmetic in his head. Five thousand for the American Express file, fifty for the Gotti stuff, another two hundred in hush money . . . rich was the word for it. 'Early retirement,' he said to Danny Pogue. 'No more damn b-and-e's.'

'You don't think he'll call the cops?'

'That's the last place he'd call. Guy's a scammer, Danny.'

They stopped at a U-Tote-Em and bought two six-packs of Coors and a box of jelly doughnuts. In the parking lot they rolled down the windows and turned up the radio and stuffed themselves in jubilation. It was an hour until curfew; if they weren't back by midnight, Molly had said, she would call the FBI and say her memory had returned.

'I bet she'll cut us some slack,' said Danny Pogue, 'if we're a little late.'

'Maybe.' Bud Schwartz opened the door and rolled an empty beer can under the car. He said, 'I'm sure gettin' tired of being her pet burglar.'

'Well, then, let's go to a tittie bar and celebrate.' Danny Pogue said he knew of a place where the girls danced naked on the tables, and let you grab their ankles for five bucks.

Bud Schwartz said not tonight. There would be no celebration until they broke free from the old lady. Tonight he would make a pitch for the rest of the ten grand that she'd promised. Surely they were square by now; Molly had been so thrilled by the contents of the Ramex file that she'd given him a hug. Then she'd gone out and had eight copies made. What more could she want of them?

Back on the road, Bud Schwartz said: 'Remember, don't say a damn thing about what we done tonight.'

'You told me a hundred times.'

'Well, it'll screw up everything. I mean it, don't tell her where we been.'

'No reason,' said Danny Pogue. 'It's got nothin' to do with the butterflies, right?'

'No, it sure does not.'

Danny Pogue said he was hungry again, so they stopped to pick up some chicken nuggets. Again they ate in the parking lot, listening to a country station. Bud Schwartz had never before driven an automobile with a working clock, so he was surprised to glance at the dashboard of the Cutlass and find that it was half past twelve, and counting.

'Better roll,' Danny Pogue said, 'just in case.'

'I got a better idea—gimme a quarter.' Bud Schwartz got out and walked to a pay telephone under a streetlight. He dialed the number of Molly McNamara's condominium and let it ring five minutes. He hung up, retrieved the quarter and dialed again. This time he let it ring twice as long.

In the car, speeding down U.S. 1, Danny Pogue said, 'I can't believe she'd do it—maybe she went someplace else. Maybe she left us a note.'

Bud Schwartz gripped the wheel with both hands; the bullet wound was numb because he had forgotten about it. Escape was on his mind—what if the old bitch had run to the feds? Worse, what if she'd found the Gotti file? What if she'd gone snooping through the bedroom and found it hidden between the mattress and the box spring, which in retrospect was probably not the cleverest place of concealment.

'Shit,' he said, thinking of the bleak possibilities.

'Don't jump the gun,' said Danny Pogue, for once the optimist.

They made it back to the condo in twenty-two minutes, parked the rental car and went upstairs. The door to Molly's apartment was unlocked. Bud Schwartz knocked twice anyway. 'It's just us,' he announced lightly, 'Butch and Sundance.'

When he went in, he saw that the place had been torn apart. 'Oh Jesus,' he said.

Danny Pogue pushed him with the crutch. 'I can't fucking believe it,' he said. 'Somebody hit the place.'

'No,' said Bud Schwartz, 'it's more than that.'

The sofas had been slit, chairs broken, mirrors shattered. A ceramic Siamese cat had been smashed face-first through the big-screen television. While Danny Pogue hopscotched through the rubble, Bud Schwartz went directly to the bedroom, which also had been ransacked and vandalized. He reached under the mattress and found the Kingsbury files exactly where he had left them. Whoever did the place hadn't been looking very hard, if it all.

A hoarse shout came from the kitchen.

Bud Schwartz found Danny Pogue on his knees next to Molly McNamara. She lay on her back, with one leg folded crookedly under the other. Her housecoat, torn and stained with something dark, was bunched around her hips. Her face had been beaten to pulp; beads of blood glistened like holly berries in her snowy hair. Her eyes were closed and her lips were gray, but she was breathing—raspy, irregular gulps.

Danny Pogue took Molly's wrist. 'God Almighty,' he said, voice quavering. 'What—who do we call?'

'Nobody.' Bud Schwartz shook his head ruefully. 'Don't you understand, we can't call nobody.' He bent down and put his bandaged hand on Molly's forehead. 'Who the hell would do this to an old lady?'

'I hope she don't die.'

'Me, too,' said Bud Schwartz. 'Honest to God, this ain't right.'

17

Joe Winder's trousers were soaked from the thighs down. Nina took a long look and said: 'You've been fishing.'

'Yes.'

'In the middle of the day.'

'The fish are all gone,' Winder said dismally. 'Ever since they bulldozed the place.'

Nina sat cross-legged on the floor. She wore blue-jean shorts and a pink cotton halter; the same outfit she'd been wearing the day he'd met her, calling out numbers at the Seminole bingo hall. Joe Winder had gone there to meet an Indian named Sammy Deer, who purportedly was selling an airboat, but Sammy Deer had hopped over to Freeport for the weekend, leaving Joe Winder stuck with three hundred chain-smoking white women in the bingo hall. Halfway out the door, he'd heard Nina's voice ('Q 34; Q, as in "quicksilver," 34!'), spun around and went back to see if she looked as lovely as she sounded, and she had. Nina informed him that she was part-timing as a bingo caller until the telephone gig came through, and he confided to her that he was buying an airboat so he could disappear into the Everglades at will. He changed his plans after their first date.

Now, analyzing her body language, Joe Winder knew that he was in danger of losing Nina's affections. A yellow legal pad was propped on her lap. She tapped on a bare knee with her felt-tipped pen, which she held as a drummer would.

'What happened to your big meeting?' she said. 'Why aren't you at the Kingdom?'

He pretended not to hear. He said, 'They dumped a ton of fill in the cove. The bottom's mucky and full of cut trees.' He removed his trousers and arranged them crookedly on a wire hanger. 'All against the law, of course. Dumping in a marine sanctuary.'

Nina said, 'You got canned, is that it?'

'A mutual parting of the ways, and not a particularly amicable one.' Joe Winder sat down beside her. He sensed a lecture coming on.

'Put on some pants,' she said.

'What's the point?'

Nina asked why his tongue was blue, and he told her the story of the bogus mango voles. She said she didn't believe a word.

'Charlie practically admitted everything.'

'I don't really care,' Nina said. She stopped drumming on her kneecap and turned away.

'What is it?'

'Look, I can't afford to support you.' When she looked back at him, her eyes were moist and angry. 'Things were going so well,' she said.

Winder was stunned. Was she seriously worried about the money? 'Nina, there's a man dead. Don't you understand? I can't work for a murderer.'

'Stop it!' She shook the legal pad in front of his nose. 'You know what I've been working on? Extra scripts. The other girls like my stuff so much they offered to buy, like, two or three a week. Twenty-five bucks each, it could really add up.'

'That's great.' He was proud of her, that was the hell of it. She'd never believe that he could be proud of her.

Pen in mouth, Nina said: 'I wrote about an out-of-body experience. Like when you're about to die and you can actually see yourself lying there—but then you get saved at the very last minute. Only my script was about making love, about floating out of yourself just as you're about to come. *Suspended in air, I looked down at the bed and saw myself shudder violently, my fingernails raking across your broad tan shoulders.* I gave it to the new girl, Addie, and she tried it Friday night. One guy, she said, he called back eleven times.'

'Is that a new record?'

'It just so happens, yes. But the point is, I'm looking at a major opportunity. If I start selling enough scripts, maybe I can get off the phones. Just stay home and write—wouldn't that be better?'

'Sure would.' Winder put his arm around her. 'You can still do that, honey. It would be great.'

'Not with you sitting here every day. Playing your damn Warren Zevon.'

'I'll get another job.'

'No, Joe, it'll be the same old shit.' She pulled away and got up from the floor. 'I can't write when my life is in turmoil. I need a stabilizer. Peacefulness. Quiet.'

Winder felt wounded. 'For God's sake, Nina, I know a little something about writing. This place is plenty quiet.'

'There is tension,' she said grimly, 'and don't deny it.'

'Writers thrive on domestic tension. Look at Poe, Hemingway—and Mailer in his younger days, you talk about tense.' He hoped Nina would appreciate being included on such an eminent roster, but she didn't. Impatiently he said, 'It isn't exactly epic literature, anyway. It's phone porn.'

Her expression clouded. 'Phone porn? Thanks, Joe.'

'Well, Christ, that's what it is.'

Coldly she folded her arms and leaned against one of the tall speakers. 'It's still writing, and writing is hard work. If I'm going to make a go of it, I need some space. And some security.'

'If you're talking about groceries, don't worry. I intend to pull my own weight.'

Nina raised her hands in exasperation. 'Where can you find another job that pays so much?'

Joe Winder couldn't believe what he was hearing. Why the sudden anxiety? The laying on of guilt? If he'd known he was in for a full-blown argument, he indeed would have put on some pants.

Nina said, 'It's not just the money. I need someone reliable, someone who will be here for me.'

'Have I ever let you down?'

'No, but you will.'

Winder didn't say anything because she was absolutely correct; nothing in his immediate plans would please her.

'I know you,' Nina added, in a sad voice. 'You aren't going to let go of this thing.'

'Probably not.'

'Then I think we're definitely heading in different directions. I think you're going to end up in jail, or maybe dead.'

'Have some faith,' Joe Winder said.

'It's not that easy.' Nina stalked to the closet, flung open the door and stared at the clutter. 'Where'd you put my suitcase?'

In the mid-1970s, Florida elected a crusading young governor named Clinton Tyree, an ex-football star and Vietnam War veteran. At six feet six, he was the tallest chief executive in the history of the state. In all likelihood he was also the most honest. When a ravenous and politically connected land-development company attempted to bribe Clinton Tyree, he tape-recorded their offers, turned the evidence over to the FBI and volunteered to testify at the trial. By taking a public stand against such omnipotent forces, Clinton Tyree became something of a folk hero in the Sunshine State and beyond. The faint scent of integrity attracted the national media, which roared into Florida and anointed the young governor a star of the new political vanguard.

It was, unfortunately, a vanguard of one. Clinton Tyree spoke with a blistering candor that terrified his fellow politicians. While others reveled in Florida's boom times, Clinton Tyree warned that the state was on the brink of an environmental cataclysm. The Everglades were drying up, the coral reefs were dying, Lake Okeechobee was choking on man-made poisons and the bluegills were loaded with mercury. While other officeholders touted Florida as a tropical dreamland, the governor called it a toxic dump with palm trees. On a popular call-in radio show, he asked visitors to stay away for a couple of years. He spoke not of managing the state's breakneck growth, but of halting it altogether. This, he declared, was the only way to save the place.

The day Clinton Tyree got his picture on the cover of a national newsmagazine, some of the most powerful special interests in Florida—bankers, builders, highway contractors, sugar barons, phosphate-mining executives—congealed in an informal conspiracy to thwart the new governor's reforms by stepping around him, as if he were a small lump of dogshit on an otherwise luxuriant carpet.

Bypassing Clinton Tyree was relatively easy to do; all it took was money. In a matter of months, everyone who could be compromised, intimidated or bought off was. The governor found himself isolated from even his own political party, which had no stake in his radical bluster because it was alienating all the big campaign contributors. Save Florida? Why? And from what? The support that Clinton Tyree enjoyed among voters didn't help him one bit in the back rooms of Tallahassee; every bill he wanted passed got gutted, buried or rebuffed. The fact that he was popular with the media didn't deter his enemies; it merely softened their strategy. Rather than attack the governor's agenda, they did something worse—they ignored it. Only the most gentlemanly words were publicly spoken about young Clint, the handsome war hero, and about his idealism and courage to speak out. Any reporter who came to town could fill two or three notebooks with admiring quotes—so many (and so effusive) that someone new to the state might have assumed that Clinton Tyree had already died, which he had, in a way.

On the morning the Florida Cabinet decided to shut down a coastal wildlife preserve and sell it dirt cheap to a powerful land-sales firm, the lone dissenting vote trudged from the Capitol Building in disgust and vanished from the political landscape in the back of a limousine.

At first authorities presumed that the governor was the victim of a kidnapping or other foul play. A nationwide manhunt was suspended only after a notarized resignation letter was analyzed by the FBI and found to be authentic. It was true; the crazy bastard had up and quit.

Journalists, authors and screenwriters flocked to Florida with hopes of securing exclusive rights to the renegade governor's story, but none could find him. Consequently, nothing was written that even bordered on the truth.

Which was this: Clinton Tyree now went by the name of Skink, and lived in those steamy clawing places where he was least likely to be bothered by human life-forms. For fifteen years the governor had been submerged in an expatriation that was deliberately remote and anonymous, if not entirely tranquil.

Joe Winder wanted to talk about what happened in Tallahassee. 'I read all the stories,' he said. 'I went back and looked up the microfiche.'

'Then you know all there is to know.' Skink was on his haunches, poking the embers with a stick. Winder refused to look at what was frying in the pan.

He said, 'All this time and they never found you.'

'They quit searching,' Skink said. A hot ash caught in a wisp of his beard. He snuffed it with two fingers. 'I don't normally eat soft-shell turtle,' he allowed.

'Me neither,' said Joe Winder.

'The flavor makes up for the texture.'

'I bet.' Winder knelt on the other side of the fire.

Out of the blue Skink said, 'Your old man wasn't a bad guy, but he was in a bad business.'

Winder heard himself agree. 'He never understood what was so wrong about it. Or why I was so goddamn mad. He died not having a clue.'

Skink lifted the turtle by the tail and stuck a fork in it. 'Ten more minutes,' he said, 'at least.'

It wasn't easy trying to talk with him this way, but Winder wouldn't give up: 'It's been an interesting day. In the space of two hours I lost my job and my girlfriend.'

'Christ, you sound like Dobie Gillis.'

'The job was shit, I admit. But I was hoping Nina would stay strong. She's one in a million.'

'Love,' said Skink, 'it's just a kiss away.'

Dejectedly, Winder thought: I'm wasting my time. The man

couldn't care less. 'I came to ask about a plan,' Winder said. 'I've been racking my brain.'

'Come on, I want to show you something.' Skink rose slowly and stretched, and the blaze-orange rainsuit made a crackling noise. He pulled the shower cap tight on his skull and, in high steps, marched off through the trees. To the west, the sky boiled with fierce purple thunderheads.

'Keep it moving,' Skink advised, over his shoulder.

Joe Winder followed him to the same dumpsite where the corpse of Spearmint Breath had been hidden. When they walked past the junker Cadillac, Winder noted that the trunk was open, and empty. He didn't ask about the body. He didn't want to know.

Skink led him through a hazardous obstacle course of discarded household junk—shells of refrigerators, ripped sofas, punctured mattresses, crippled Barca-loungers, rusty barbecue grills, disemboweled air conditioners—until they came to a very old Plymouth station wagon, an immense egg-colored barge with no wheels and no windshield. A yellow beach umbrella sprouted like a giant marigold from the dashboard, and offered minimal protection from blowing rain or the noonday sun. Skink got in the car and ordered Joe Winder to do the same.

The Plymouth was full of books—hundreds of volumes arranged lovingly from the tailgate to the front. With considerable effort, Skink turned completely in the front seat; he propped his rear end on the warped steering wheel. 'This is where I come to read,' he said. 'Believe it or not, the dome light in this heap still works.'

Joe Winder ran a finger along the spines of the books, and found himself smiling at the exhilarating variety of writers: Churchill, Hesse, Sandburg, Steinbeck, Camus, Paine, Wilde, Vonnegut, de Tocqueville, Salinger, García Márquez, even Harry Crews.

'I put a new battery in this thing,' Skink was saying. 'This time of year I've got to run the AC at least two, three hours a day. To stop the damn mildew.'

'So there's gas in this car?' Winder asked.

'Sure.'

'But no wheels.'

Skink shrugged. 'Where the hell would I be driving?'

A cool stream of wind rushed through the open windshield, and overhead the yellow beach umbrella began to flap noisily. A fat drop of rain splatted on the hood, followed by another and another.

'Damn,' said Skink. He put a shoulder to the door and launched himself out of the station wagon, 'Hey, Flack, you coming or not?'

The storm came hard and they sat through it, huddled like Sherpas. The campfire washed out, but the soft-shelled turtle was cooked to perfection. Skink chewed intently on its tail and blinked the raindrops from his good eye; the other one fogged up like a broken headlight. Water trickled down his bronze cheeks, drenching his beard. Lightning cracked so close they could smell it—Winder ducked, but Skink showed no reaction, even when thunder rattled the coffeepot.

He adjusted the blaze weather suit to cover the electronic panther collar on his neck. 'They say it's waterproof, but I don't know.'

Winder could scarcely hear him over the drum of the rain against the trees. Lightning flashed again, and reflexively he shut his eyes.

Skink raised his voice: 'You know about that new golf resort?'

'I saw where they're putting it.'

'No!' Skink was shouting now. 'You know who's behind it? That fucking Kingsbury!'

The wind was getting worse, if that was possible. With his free hand, Skink wrung out the tendrils of his beard. 'Goddammit, man, are you listening? It all ties together.'

'What—with Koocher's death?'

'Everything—' Skink paused for another white sizzle of lightning. 'Every damn thing.'

It made sense to Winder. A scandal at the Amazing Kingdom

would not only be bad for business, it might jeopardize Francis Kingsbury's plans for developing Falcon Trace. If anyone revealed that he'd lied about the 'endangered' voles, the feds might roll in and halt the whole show. The EPA, the Army Corps of Engineers, the Department of Interior—they could jerk Kingsbury around until he died of old age.

'Look at the big picture,' Skink said. With a tin fork he cleaned out the insides of the turtle shell. The wind was dying quickly, and the rain was turning soft on the leaves. The clouds broke out west, revealing raspberry patches of summer sunset. The coolness disappeared and the air turned muggy again.

Skink put down the fry pan and wiped his mouth on the sleeve of his rainsuit. 'It's beautiful out here,' he remarked. 'That squall felt damn good.'

'It might be too late,' Joe Winder said. 'Hell, they've started clearing the place.'

'I know.' The muscles in Skink's neck tightened. 'They tore down an eagle nest the other day. Two little ones, dead. That's the kind of bastards we're talking about.'

'Did you see—'

'I got there after the fact,' Skink said. 'Believe me, if I could've stopped them . . .'

'What if we're too late?'

'Are you in or not? That's all I need to know.'

'I'm in,' said Winder. 'Of course I am. I'm just not terribly optimistic.'

Skink smiled his matinee smile, the one that had gotten him elected so many years before. 'Lower your sights, boy,' he said to Joe Winder. 'I agree, justice is probably out of the question. But we can damn sure ruin their day.'

He reached under the flap of his rainsuit, grunted, fumbled inside his clothing. Finally his hand came out holding a steel-blue semi-automatic pistol.

'Don't worry,' he said. 'I've got an extra one for you.'

The woman who called herself Rachel Lark was receiving a vigorous massage when Francis X. Kingsbury phoned. She'd been expecting to hear from him ever since she'd read in the *Washington Post* about the theft of the blue-tongued mango voles in Florida. Her first thought, a natural one, was that Kingsbury would try to talk her into giving some of the money back. Rachel Lark braced for the worst as she sat up, naked, and told the masseur to give her the damn telephone.

On the other end, Kingsbury said: 'Is this my favorite redhead?'

'Forget it,' said the woman who called herself Rachel Lark, though it was not her true name.

Kingsbury said, 'Can you believe it, babe? My luck, the god-damn things get swiped.'

'I've already spent the money,' Rachel Lark said, 'and even if I didn't, a deal's a deal.'

Instead of protesting, Kingsbury said, 'Same here. I spent mine, too.'

'Then it's a social call, is it?'

'Not exactly. Are you alone, babe?'

'Me and a nice young man named Sven.'

The image gave Kingsbury a tingle. Rachel was an attractive woman, a bit on the heavy side, but a very hot dresser. They had met years before in the lobby of a prosecutor's office in Camden, where both of them were waiting to cut deals allowing them to avert unpleasant prison terms. Frankie King had chosen to drop the dime on the Zubonis, while the woman who now called herself Rachel Lark (it was Sarah Hunt at that time) was pre-paring to squeal on an ex-boyfriend who had illegally imported four hundred pounds of elephant ivory. In the lobby that day, the two informants had amiably traded tales about life on the lam. Later they'd exchanged phone numbers and a complete list of aliases, and promised to keep in touch.

Rachel's specialty was wildlife, and Kingsbury phoned her soon after opening the Amazing Kingdom of Thrills. Before then, he had never heard of the Endangered Species Act, never dreamed that an obscure agency of the federal government would casually fork over two hundred thousand dollars in grant money for the purpose of preserving a couple of lousy rodents.

Rachel Lark had offered to provide the animals and the documentation, and Kingsbury was so intrigued by the plan—not just the dough, but the radiant publicity for the Amazing Kingdom—that he didn't bother to inquire if the blue-tongued mango voles were real.

The government check had arrived on time, they'd split it fifty-fifty and that was that. Francis Kingsbury paid no further attention to the creatures until customers started noticing that the voles' tongues were no longer very blue. Once children openly began grilling the Amazing Kingdom tour guides about how the animals got their name, Kingsbury ordered Pedro Luz to get some food coloring and touch the damn things up. Unfortunately, Pedro had neither the patience nor the gentle touch required to be an animal handler, and one of the voles—the female—was crushed accidentally during a tongue-painting session. Afraid for his job, Pedro Luz had told no one of the mishap. To replace the deceased vole, he had purchased a dwarf hamster for nine dollars from a pet store in Perrine. After minor modifications, the hamster had fooled both the customers and the male vole, which repeatedly attempted to mount its chubby new companion. Not only had the hamster rejected these advances, it had counterattacked with such ferocity that Pedro Luz had been forced to hire a night security guard to prevent a bloodbath.

Matters were further complicated by the appearance of an ill-mannered pinhead from U.S. Fish and Wildlife, who had barged into the theme park and demanded follow-up data from the 'project manager.' Of course there was no such person because there was no project to manage; research consisted basically of making sure that the rodents were still breathing every morning before the gates were opened. With the feds suddenly asking questions, Charles Chelsea had quietly put out an all-points bulletin for a legitimate biologist—a recruiting effort that eventually induced Dr. Will Koocher to come to the Amazing Kingdom of Thrills.

Kingsbury decided not to burden Rachel Lark with the details of the doctor's grisly demise; it was irrelevant to the purpose of his call.

'Forget the money,' Kingsbury told her.

'I must be hearing things.'

'No, I mean it.'

'Then what do you want?'

'More voles.'

'You're joking.'

'My customers, hell, they go nuts for the damn things. Now I got spin-offs, merchandise—a major warehouse situation, if you follow me.'

'Sorry,' Rachel Lark said, 'it was a one-time deal.' She'd pulled off the endangered-species racket on two other occasions—once for a small Midwestern zoo, and once for a disreputable reptile farm in South Carolina. Neither deal made as much money as the mango-vole scam, but neither had wound up in the headlines of the *Washington Post*, either.

Kingsbury said, 'Look, I know there's no more mango voles—'

'Hey, sport, there never *were* any mango voles.'

'So what you're saying, we defrauded the government.'

'God, you're quick.'

'I'm wondering,' said Kingsbury, 'those fucking furballs I paid for—what were they? Just out of curiosity.'

Rachel Lark said, 'Give me some credit, Frankie. They were voles. *Microtus pitymys*. Common pine voles.'

'Not endangered?'

'There's billions of the darn things.'

It figures, Kingsbury thought. The blue tongues were a neat touch. 'So get me some more,' he said. 'We'll call 'em something else, banana voles or whatever. The name's not important, long as they're cute.'

The woman who called herself Rachel Lark said: 'Look, I can get you other animals—rare, not endangered—but my advice is to stay away from the feds for a while. You put in for another big grant, it's a swell way to get audited.'

Again Kingsbury agreed without objection. 'So what else have you got, I mean, in the way of a species?'

'Lizards are your best bet.' Rachel Lark stretched on her belly and motioned the masseur, whose real name was Ray, to do her spine.

'Christ on a Harley, who wants goddamn lizards!' Kingsbury cringed at the idea; he had been thinking more along the lines of a panda or a koala bear. 'I need something, you know, soft and furry and all that. Something the kiddies'll want to take home.'

Rachel Lark explained that the Florida Keys were home to a very limited number of native mammals, and the sudden discovery of a new species (so soon after the mango-vole announcement) would attract more scientific scrutiny than the Amazing Kingdom could withstand.

'You're saying, I take it, forget about pandas.'

'Frank, they'd die of heatstroke in about five minutes.'

Exasperated, Kingsbury said, 'I got problems down here you wouldn't believe.' He nearly told her about the blackmailing burglars.

'A new lizard you can get away with,' she said, 'especially in the tropics.'

'Rachel, what'd I just say? Fuck the lizards. I can't market lizards.'

Rachel Lark moaned blissfully as the masseur kneaded the muscles of her neck. 'My advice,' she said into the phone, 'is stay away from mammals and birds—it's too risky. Insects are another story. Dozens of species of insects are discovered every year. Grasshoppers, doodlebugs, you name it.'

There was a grumpy pause on the other end. Finally, Francis X. Kingsbury said, 'Getting back to the lizards. I mean, for the sake of argument . . .'

'They're very colorful,' said the woman who called herself Rachel Lark.

'Ugly is out of the question,' Kingsbury stated firmly. 'Ugly scares the kiddies.'

'Not all reptiles are ugly, Frankie. In fact, some are very beautiful.'

'All right,' he said. 'See what you can do.'

The woman who called herself Rachel Lark hung up the phone and closed her eyes. When she awoke, the masseur was gone and the man from Singapore was knocking on the door. In one hand was a small bouquet of yellow roses, and in the other was a tan briefcase holding a large down payment for a shipment of rare albino scorpions. Real ones.

18

On the morning of July 23, a semi-tractor truck leaving North Key Largo lost its brakes on the Card Sound Bridge. The truck plowed through the tollbooth, jack-knifed and overturned, blocking both lanes of traffic and effectively severing the northern arm of the island from the Florida mainland. The gelatinous contents of the container were strewn for ninety-five yards along the road, and within minutes the milky-blue sky filled with turkey buzzards—hundreds of them, wheeling counterclockwise lower and lower; only the noisy throng of gawkers kept the hungry scavengers from landing on the crash site. The first policeman to arrive was Highway Patrol Trooper Jim Tile, who nearly flipped his Crown Victoria cruiser when he tried to stop on the freshly slickened pavement. The trooper tugged the truck driver from the wreckage and, while splinting the man's arm, demanded to know what godforsaken cargo he'd been hauling.

'A dead whale,' moaned the driver, 'and that's all I'm saying.'

Charles Chelsea was summoned to Francis X. Kingsbury's office at the unholy hour of seven in the morning. Kingsbury looked as if he hadn't slept since Easter. He asked Chelsea how long it would take to get the TV stations out to the Amazing Kingdom of Thrills.

'Two hours,' Chelsea said confidently.

'Do it.' Kingsbury blew his nose. 'On the horn, now.'

'What's the occasion, if I might ask?'

Kingsbury held up five fingers. 'Today's the big day. Our five-millionth visitor. Arrange something, a fucking parade, I don't care.'

Charles Chelsea felt his stomach yaw. 'Five million visitors,' he said. 'Sir, I didn't realize we'd reached that milestone.'

'We haven't.' Kingsbury hacked ferociously into a monogrammed handkerchief. 'Damn my hay fever, I think it's the mangroves. Every morning my whole head's fulla snot.' He pushed a copy of the *Wall Street Journal* at Chelsea. A column on the front page announced that Walt Disney World was expanding its empire to build a mammoth retail shopping center, one of the largest in the Southeastern United States.

'See, we can't just sit here,' Kingsbury said. 'Got to come back strong. Big media counterpunch.'

Chelsea skimmed the *Journal* article and laid it on his lap. Tentatively he said, 'It's hard to compete with something like this. I mean, it goes so far beyond the realm of a family theme park—'

'Bullshit,' said Kingsbury. 'The Miami-Lauderdale TV market is—what, three times the size of Orlando. Plus CNN, don't they have a bureau down here?' Kingsbury spun his chair and gazed out the window. 'Hell, that new dolphin I bought—can't you work him into the piece? Say he rescued somebody who fell in the tank. A pregnant lady or maybe an orphan. Rescued them from drowning—that's your story! "Miracle Dolphin Saves Drowning Orphan."'

'I don't know if that's such a good plan,' said Chelsea, though inwardly he had to admit it would have been one helluva headline.

'This celebration, make it for noon,' Kingsbury said. 'Whoever comes through the turnstiles, strike up the band. But make sure it's a tourist, no goddamn locals. Number five million, okay? In giant letters.'

His gut tightening, Chelsea said, 'Sir, it might be wiser to go with two million. It's closer to the real number . . . just in case somebody makes an issue of it.'

'No, two is—chickenshit, really. Five's better. And the parade, too, I'm serious.' Kingsbury stood up. He was dressed for golf. 'A parade, that's good video,' he said. 'Plenty of time to get it for the six-o'clock news. That's our best demographic, am I right? Fucking kids, they don't watch the eleven.'

Chelsea nodded. 'What do we give the winner? Mr. Five Million, I mean.'

'A car, Jesus Christ.' Kingsbury looked at him as if he were an idiot. A few years earlier, Disney World had given away an automobile every day for an entire summer. Kingsbury had never gotten over it. 'Make it a Corvette,' he told Chelsea.

'All right, but you're looking at forty thousand dollars. Maybe more.'

Kingsbury extended his lower lip so far that it seemed to touch his nose; for a moment he wore the pensive look of a caged orangutan. 'Forty grand,' he repeated quietly. 'That's brand new, I suppose.'

'When you give one away, yes. Ordinarily the cars should be new.'

'Unless they're classics.' Kingsbury winked. 'Make it a classic. Say, a 1964 Ford Falcon. You don't see many of those babies.'

'Sure don't.'

'A Falcon convertible, geez, we could probably pick one up for twenty-five hundred.'

'Probably,' agreed Chelsea, not even pretending enthusiasm.

'Well, move on it.' Francis X. Kingsbury thumbed him out of the office. 'And tell Pedro, get his ass in here.'

Pedro Luz was in the executive gym, bench-pressing a bottle of stanozolol tablets. He was letting the tiny pink pills drop one by one into his mouth.

A man named Churrito, lounging on a Nautilus, said: 'Hiss very bad for liver.'

'Very good for muscles,' said Pedro Luz, mimicking the accent.

Churrito was his latest hire to the security squad at the Amazing Kingdom of Thrills. He had accompanied Pedro Luz on his mission to Miami, but had declined to participate in the beating. Pedro Luz was still miffed about what had happened— the old lady chomping off the top joint of his right index finger.

'You're useless,' he had told Churrito afterward.

'I am a soldier,' Churrito had replied. 'I dun hit no wooman.'

Unlike the other security guards hired by Pedro Luz, Churrito had not been a crooked cop. He was a Nicaraguan *contra* who had moved to Florida when things were bleak, and had not gotten around to moving back. While Churrito was pleased at the prospect of democracy taking seed in his homeland, he suspected that true economic prosperity was many years away. Elections notwithstanding, Churrito's buddies were still stuck in the border hills, frying green bananas and dynamiting the rivers for fish. Meanwhile his uncle, formerly a sergeant in Somoza's National Guard, now lived with a twenty-two-year-old stewardess in a high-rise condo on Key Biscayne. To Churrito, this seemed like a pretty good advertisement for staying right where he was.

Pedro Luz had hired him because he looked mean, and because he'd said he had killed people.

'*Comunistas*,' Churrito had specified, that night at the old lady's apartment. 'I only kill commoonists. And I dun hit no wooman.'

And now here he was, lecturing Pedro Luz about the perils of anabolic steroids.

'Make you face like balloon.'

'Shut up,' said Pedro Luz. He was wondering if the hospital in Key Largo would sell him extra bags of dextrose water for the IV. Grind up the stanozolols, drop them in the mix and everything would be fine again.

'Make you bulls shrink, too.'

'That's enough,' Pedro Luz said.

Churrito held up two fingers. 'Dis big. Like BBs.'

'Quiet,' said Pedro Luz, 'or I call a friend a mine at INS.' He couldn't decide whether to fire the guy or beat him up. He knew which would give more pleasure.

'They got, like, three flights a day to Managua,' he said to Churrito. 'You getting homesick?'

The Nicaraguan grimaced.

'I didn't think so,' said Pedro Luz. 'So shut up about my medicines.'

Charles Chelsea appeared at the foot of the weight bench. He had never seen Pedro Luz without a shirt, and couldn't conceal his awe at the freakish physique—the hairless bronze trunk of a chest, cantaloupe biceps, veins as thick as a garden hose. Chelsea didn't recognize the other fellow—shorter and sinewy, with skin the color of nutmeg.

'I'm working out,' said Pedro Luz.

'Mr. Kingsbury needs to see you.'

'Who ees that?' Churrito said.

Pedro Luz sat up. 'That be the boss.'

'Right away,' said Charles Chelsea.

'Can I go?' asked Churrito. He didn't want to miss an opportunity to meet the boss; according to his uncle, that's what success in America was all about. Kissing ass.

'I'm sorry,' Chelsea said, 'but Mr. Kingsbury wants to see Chief Luz alone.'

'Yeah,' said Pedro Luz. As he rolled off the bench, he made a point of clipping Churrito with a casual forearm. Churrito didn't move, didn't make a sound. His eyes grew very small and he stared at Pedro Luz until Pedro Luz spun away, pretending to hunt for his sweatshirt.

Churrito pointed at the scarlet blemishes on Pedro Luz's shoulder blades and said: 'You all broke out, man.'

'Shut up before I yank your nuts off.'

Backing away, Charles Chelsea thought: Where do they get these guys?

Francis X. Kingsbury offered a Bloody Mary to Pedro Luz, who guzzled it like Gatorade.

'So, Pedro, the job's going all right?'

The security chief was startled at Kingsbury's genial tone. A ration of shit was what he'd expected; the old fart had been livid since the burglary of his private office. The crime had utterly baffled Pedro Luz, who hadn't the first notion of how to solve it. He had hoped that the mission to Eagle Ridge would absolve him.

'I took care of that other problem,' he announced to Kingsbury.

'Fine. Excellent.' Kingsbury was swiveling back and forth in his chair. He didn't look so good: nervous, ragged, droopy-eyed, his fancy golf shirt all wrinkled. Pedro Luz wondered if the old fart was doing coke. The very idea was downright hilarious.

'She won't bother you no more,' he said to Kingsbury.

'You made it look, what—like muggers? Crack fiends?'

'Sure, that's what the cops would think. If she calls them, which I don't think she will. I made it clear what could happen.'

'Fine. Excellent.' Kingsbury propped his elbows on the desk in a way that offered Pedro Luz an unobstructed view of the lurid mouse tattoo.

'Two things—' Kingsbury paused when he spotted the bandage on Pedro Luz's finger.

'Hangnail,' said the security chief.

'Whatever,' Kingsbury said. 'Two things—some assholes, the guys who stole my files, they're blackmailing me. You know, shaking me down.'

Pedro Luz asked how much money he had promised them.

'Never mind,' Kingsbury replied. 'Five grand so far is what I paid. But the files, see, I can't just blow 'em off. I need the files.'

'Who are these men?'

Francis Kingsbury threw up his hands. 'That's the thing—just ordinary shitheads. White trash. I can't fucking believe it.'

Pedro Luz had never understood the concept of white trash, or how it differed from black trash or Hispanic trash or any other kind of criminal dirtbag. He said, 'You want the files but you don't want to pay.'

'Exacto!' said Kingsbury. 'In fact, the five grand—I wouldn't mind getting it back.'

Pedro Luz laughed sharply. Months go by and the job's a snooze—now suddenly all this dirty work. Oh well, Pedro thought, it beats painting rat tongues. He hadn't shed a tear when the mango voles were stolen.

Kingsbury was saying, 'The other thing, I fired a guy from Publicity.'

'Yeah?' Watching that damn tattoo, it was driving Pedro silly.

Minnie on her knees, polishing Mickey's knob—whoever did the drawing was damn good, almost Disney caliber.

'You need to go see this guy I fired,' Kingsbury was saying. 'Find out some things.'

Pedro Luz asked what kind of things.

Kingsbury moved his lips around, like a camel getting ready to spit. Eventually he said, 'The problem we had before? This is worse, okay. The guy I mentioned, we're talking major pain in the rectum.'

'Okay.'

'As long as he worked for us, we had some control. On the outside, hell, he's a major pain. I just got a feeling.'

Pedro Luz gave him a thumbs-up. 'Don't worry.'

'Carefully,' Kingsbury added. 'Same as before would be excellent. Except no dead whales this time.'

God, thought Pedro Luz, what a fuckup *that* was.

'Do I know him?' he asked Kingsbury.

'From Publicity. Joe Winder's his name.'

'Oh.' Pedro Luz perked up. Winder was the smartass who'd been hassling him about Dr. Koocher. The same guy he'd sent Angel and Big Paulie to teach a lesson, only something went sour and Angel ended up dead and Paulie must've took off. Next thing Pedro knows, here's this smartass Winder snooping around the animal lab in the middle of the night.

Mr. X was right about the guy. Now that he was fired, he might go hog-wild. Start talking crazy shit all over the place.

'You look inspired,' Kingsbury said.

Pedro Luz smiled crookedly. 'Let's just say I got some ideas.'

When Molly McNamara opened her eyes, she was surprised to see Bud Schwartz and Danny Pogue at her bedside.

'I thought you boys would be long gone.'

'No way,' said Danny Pogue. His eyes were large and intent, like a retriever's. His chin was in his hands, and he was sitting very close to the bed. He patted Molly's brow with a damp washcloth.

'Thank you,' she said. 'I'm very thirsty.'

Danny Pogue bolted to the kitchen to get her a glass of ginger ale. Bud Schwartz took a step closer. He said, 'What happened? Can you remember anything?'

'My glasses,' she said, pointing to the nightstand.

'They got busted,' said Bud Schwartz. 'I used some Scotch tape on the nose part.'

Molly McNamara put them on, and said, 'Two men. Only one did the hitting.'

'Why? What'd they want—money?'

Molly shook her head slowly. Danny Pogue came back with the ginger ale, and she took two small sips. 'Thank you,' she said. 'No, they didn't want money.'

Danny Pogue said, 'Who?'

'The men who came. They said it was a warning.'

'Oh Christ.'

'It's none of your concern,' said Molly.

Grimly Bud Schwartz said, 'They were after the files.'

'No. They never mentioned that.'

Bud Schwartz was relieved; he had worried that Francis X. Kingsbury had somehow identified them, connected them to Molly and sent goons to avenge the burglary. It was an irrational fear, he knew, because even the powerful Kingsbury couldn't have done it so quickly after their blackmail visit.

Still, it was discouraging to see how they had battered Molly McNamara. These were extremely bad men, and Bud Schwartz doubted they would have allowed him and Danny Pogue to survive the encounter.

'I think we ought to get out of here,' he said to Molly. 'Take you back to the big house.'

'That's a sensible plan,' Molly agreed, 'but you boys don't have to stay.'

'Like hell,' Danny Pogue declared. 'Look at you, all busted up. You'll be needing some help.'

'You got some bad bruises,' agreed Bud Schwartz. 'Your right knee's twisted, too, but I don't think it's broke. Plus they knocked out a couple teeth.'

Molly ran her tongue around her gums and said, 'I was the only one in this building who still had their own.'

Danny Pogue paced with a limp. 'I wanted to call an ambulance or somebody, only Bud decided we better not.'

Molly said that was a smart decision, considering what the three of them had been up to lately. She removed the damp cloth from her forehead and folded it on the nightstand.

Danny Pogue wanted to know all about the attackers—how big they were, what they looked like. 'I bet they was niggers,' he said.

Molly raised herself off the pillow, cocked her arm and slapped him across the face. Incredulous, Danny Pogue rubbed his cheek.

She said, 'Don't you ever again use that word in my presence.'

'Christ, I didn't mean nothin'.'

'Well, it just so happens these men were white. White Hispanic males. The one who beat me up was very large and muscular.'

'My question,' said Bud Schwartz, 'is how they slipped past that crack security guard. What's his name, Andrews, the ace with the flashlight.'

Molly said: 'You won't believe it. The big one had a badge. A police badge, City of Miami.'

'Wonderful,' Bud Schwartz said.

'I saw it myself,' Molly said. 'Why do you think I even opened the door? He said they were plainclothes detectives. Once they had me down, I couldn't get to my purse.'

Danny Pogue looked at his partner with the usual mix of confusion and concern. Bud Schwartz said, 'It sounds like some serious shitkickers. You say they were Cubans?'

'Hispanics,' Molly said.

'Did they speak American?' asked Danny Pogue.

'The big one did all the talking, and his English was quite competent. Especially his use of four-letter slang.'

Danny Pogue rocked on his good leg, and slammed a fist against the wall. 'I'll murder the sumbitch!'

'Sure you will,' said his partner. 'You're a killer and I'm the next quarterback for the Dolphins.'

'I mean it, Bud. Look what he done to her.'

'I see, believe me.' Bud Schwartz gave Molly McNamara two Percodans and said it would help her sleep. She swallowed the pills in one gulp and thanked the burglars once again. 'It's very kind of you to look after me,' she said.

'Only till you're feeling better,' said Bud Schwartz. 'We got some business that requires our full attention.'

'Of course, I understand.'

'We made five grand tonight!' said Danny Pogue. Quickly he withered under his partner's glare.

'Five thousand is very good,' Molly said. 'Add the money I still owe you, and that's quite a handsome nest egg.' She slid deeper into the sheets, and pulled the blanket to her chin.

'Get some rest,' Bud Schwartz said. 'We'll take you to the house in the morning.'

'Yeah, get some sleep.' Danny Pogue gazed at her dolorously. Bud Schwartz wondered if he was about to cry.

'Bud?' Molly spoke in a fog.

'Yeah.'

'Did you boys happen to find a piece of finger on the floor?'

'No,' said Bud Schwartz. 'Why?'

'Would you check in the kitchen, please?'

'No problem.' He wondered how the pills could mess her up so quickly. 'You mean, like a human finger?'

But Molly's eyes were already closed.

19

Charles Chelsea worked feverishly all morning. By half past eleven the parade was organized. The gateway to the Amazing Kingdom of Thrills was festooned with multi-colored streamers and hundreds of Mylar balloons. Cheerleaders practiced cart-wheels over the turnstiles while the Tavernier High School band rehearsed the theme from *Exodus*. Several of the most popular animal characters—Robbie Raccoon, Petey Possum and Barney the Bison—were summoned from desultory lunch breaks in The Catacombs to greet and be photographed with the big winner. Above a hastily constructed stage, a billowy hand-painted banner welcomed 'OUR FIVE-MILLIONTH SPECIAL GUEST!!!'

And there, parked in the courtyard, was a newly restored 1966 Chevrolet Corvair, one of Detroit's most venerated deathtraps. Charles Chelsea had been unable to locate a mint-condition Falcon, and the vintage Mustangs were beyond Francis Kingsbury's budget. The Corvair was Chelsea's next choice as the giveaway car because it was a genuine curiosity, and because it was cheap. The one purchased by Chelsea had been rear-ended by a dairy tanker in 1972, and the resulting explosion had wiped out a quartet of home-appliance salesmen. The rebuilt Corvair was seven inches shorter from bumper to bumper than the day it had rolled off the assembly line, but Charles Chelsea was certain no one would notice. Two extra coats of cherry paint and the Corvair shouted classic. It was exactly the sort of campy junk-mobile that some dumb Yuppie would love.

The scene was set for the coronation of the alleged five-millionth visitor to the Amazing Kingdom. The only thing missing from the festive tableau, Chelsea noted lugubriously, was customers. The park had opened more than two hours ago, yet not a single carload of tourists had arrived. The trams were empty, the cash registers mute; no one had passed through the ticket gates. Chelsea couldn't understand it—the place had not experienced such a catastrophic attendance drop since salmonella had felled a visiting contingent of Rotarians at Sally's Cimarron Saloon.

Chelsea prayed with all his heart that some tourists would show up before the television vans. He did not know, and could not have envisioned, that an eighteen-wheeler loaded with the decomposing remains of Orky the Whale had flipped on Card Sound Road and paralyzed all traffic heading toward the Amazing Kingdom. The highway patrol diligently had set up a road-block at the junction near Florida City, where troopers were advising all buses, campers and rental cars filled with Francis X. Kingsbury's customers to turn around and return to Miami. The beleaguered troopers did not consider it their sworn duty to educate the tourists about an alternate route to the Amazing Kingdom—taking Highway 1 south past Jewfish Creek, then backtracking up County Road 905 to the park. The feeling among the troopers (based on years of experience) was that no matter how simple and explicit they made the directions, many of the tourists would manage to get lost, run out of gas and become the victims of some nasty roadside crime. A more sensible option was simply to tell them to go back, there'd been a bad accident.

Consequently Charles Chelsea stood in eery solitude on the makeshift stage, the cheery banner flapping over his head as he stared at the empty parking lot and wondered how in the hell he would break the news to Francis X. Kingsbury. Today there would be no celebration, no parade, no five-millionth visitor. There were no visitors at all.

Joe Winder felt like a damn redneck—he hadn't been to a firing range in ten or twelve years, and that was to shoot his father's revolver, an old Smith. The gun Skink had given him was a thin foreign-made semi-automatic. It didn't have much weight, but Skink promised it would do the job, whatever job needed doing.

Winder had decided to keep it for ornamental purposes. It lay under the front seat as he drove south on County Road 905.

He stopped at a pay phone, dialed the sex-talk number and billed it to his home. Miriam answered and started in with a new routine, something about riding bareback on a pony. When Winder broke in and asked for Nina, Miriam told him she wasn't there.

'Tell her to call me, please.'

'Hokay, Joe.'

'On second thought, never mind.'

'Whatever chew say. You like the horsey business?'

'Yes, Miriam, it's very good.'

'Nina wrote it. Want me do the end?'

'No thank you.'

'Is hot stuff, Joe. Cheese got some mansionation.'

'She sure does.'

Joe Winder drove until he reached the Falcon Trace construction site. He parked on the side of the road and watched a pair of mustard-colored bulldozers plow a fresh section of hammock, creating a tangled knoll of uprooted tamarinds, buttonwoods, pigeon plums and rouge-berry. Each day a few more acres were being destroyed in the name of championship golf.

A team of surveyors worked the distant end of the property, near Winder's fishing spot. He assumed they were marking off the lots where the most expensive homes would be built—the more ocean frontage, the higher the price. This was how Francis X. Kingsbury would make his money—the golf course itself was never meant to profit; it was a real-estate tease, plain and simple. The links would be pieced together in the middle of the development on whatever parcels couldn't be peddled as residential waterfront. Soon, Winder knew, they'd start blasting with dynamite to dig fairway lakes in the ancient reef rock.

He saw that both bulldozers had stopped, and that the drivers had gotten down from the cabs to look at something in the trees. Joe Winder stepped out of the car and started running. He remembered what Skink had told him about the baby eagles.

He shouted at the men and saw them turn. One folded his arms and slouched against his dozer.

Winder covered the two hundred yards in a minute. When he reached the men, he was panting too hard to speak.

One of them said: 'What's your problem?'

Winder flashed his Amazing Kingdom identification badge, which he had purposely neglected to turn in upon termination of employment. The lazy bulldozer driver, the one leaning against his machine, studied the badge and began to laugh. 'What the hell is this?'

When Joe Winder caught his breath, he said: 'I work for Mr. Kingsbury. He owns this land.'

'Ain't the name on the permit. The permit says Ramex Global.'

The other driver spoke up: 'Anyway, who gives a shit about some goddamn wolves?'

'Yeah,' the first driver said. 'Bury 'em.'

'No,' said Joe Winder. They weren't wolves, they were gray foxes—six of them, no larger than kittens. The bulldozers had uprooted the den tree. Half-blind, the little ones were crawling all over each other, squeaking and yapping in toothless panic.

Winder said, 'If we leave them alone, the mother will probably come back.'

'What is this, "Wild Kingdom"?'

'At least help me move them out of the way.'

'Forget it,' the smartass driver said. 'I ain't in the mood for rabies. Come on, Bobby, let's roll it.'

The men climbed back in the dozers and seized the gear sticks. Instinctively Joe Winder positioned himself between the large machines and the baby foxes. The drivers began to holler and curse. The smartass lowered the blade of his bulldozer and inched forward, pushing a ridge of moist dirt over the tops of Joe Winder's shoes. The driver grinned and whooped at his own cleverness until he noticed the gun pointed up at his head.

He quickly turned off the engine and raised his hands. The other driver did the same. In a scratchy whine he said, 'Geez, what's your problem?'

Winder held the semi-automatic steady. He was surprised at

how natural it felt. He said, 'Is this what it takes to have a civilized conversation with you shitheads?'

Quickly he checked over his shoulder to make sure the kits hadn't crawled from the den. The outlandishness of the situation was apparent, but he'd committed himself to melodrama. With the gun on display, he was already deep into felony territory.

The smartass driver apologized profusely for burying Winder's shoes. 'I'll buy you some new ones,' he offered.

'Oh, that's not necessary.' Winder yearned to shoot the bulldozers but he didn't know where to begin; the heavy steel thoraxes looked impervious to cannon fire.

The lazy driver said: 'You want us to get down?'

'Not just yet,' said Joe Winder, 'I'm thinking.'

'Hey, there's no need to shoot. Just tell us what the hell you want.'

'I want you to help me fuck up these machines.'

It was nine o'clock when the knock came. Joe Winder was sitting in the dark on the floor of the apartment. He had the clip out of the gun, and the bullets out of the clip. A full load, too, sixteen rounds; he had lined up the little rascals side by side on a windowsill, a neat row of identical copper-headed soldiers.

The knocking wouldn't go away. Winder picked up the empty gun. He went to the door and peeked out of the peephole. He saw an orb of glistening blond; not Nina-style blond, this was lighter. When the woman turned around, Winder flung open the door and pulled her inside.

In the darkness Carrie Lanier took a deep breath and said: 'I hope that's you.'

'It's me,' Joe Winder said.

'Was that a gun I saw?'

'I'm afraid so. My situation has taken a turn for the worse.'

Carrie said, 'That's why I came.'

Winder led her back to the living room, where they sat between two large cardboard boxes. The only light was the amber glow from the stereo receiver; Carrie Lanier could barely hear the music from the speakers.

'Where's your girlfriend?' she asked.

'Moved out.'

'I'm sorry.' She paused; then, peering at him: 'Is that a beret?'

'Panties,' Joe Winder said. 'Can you believe it—that's all she left me. Cheap ones, too. The mail-order crap she sold over the phone.' He pulled the underwear off his head to show her the shoddy stitching.

'You've had a rough time,' said Carrie Lanier. 'I didn't know she'd moved out.'

'Yeah, well, I'm doing just fine. Adjusting beautifully to the single life. Sitting here in a dark apartment with a gun in my lap and underpants on my head.'

Carrie squeezed his arm. 'Joe, are you on drugs?'

'Nope,' he said. 'Pretty amazing, isn't it?'

'I think you should come home with me.'

'Why?'

'Because bad things will happen if you stay here.'

'Ah.' Winder scooped the bullets off the windowsill and fed them into the gun clip. 'You must be talking about Pedro Luz.'

'It's all over the Magic Kingdom,' Carrie said, 'about the reasons you were fired.'

'Mr. X doesn't kill his former employees, does he?'

She leaned closer. 'It's no joke. The word is, you're number one on Pedro's list.'

'So that's the word.'

'Joe, I get around. Spend the day in a raccoon suit, people forget there's a real person inside. I might as well be invisible—the stuff I pick up, you wouldn't believe.'

'The spy wore a tail! And now you hear Pedro's irritated.'

'I got it from two of the other guards on lunch break. They were doing blow behind the Magic Mansion.'

Winder was struck by how wonderful Carrie looked, her eyes all serious in the amber light. Impulsively he kissed her on the cheek. 'Don't worry about me,' he said. 'You can go home.'

'You aren't listening.'

'Yes, I—'

'No, you aren't.' Her tone was one of motherly disapproval.

'I warned you about this before. About sticking your nose where it doesn't belong.'

'You did, yes.'

'Last time you were lucky. You truly were.'

'I suppose so.' Joe Winder felt oppressively tired. Suddenly the handgun weighed a ton. He slid it across the carpet so forcefully that it banged into the baseboard of the opposite wall.

Carrie Lanier told him to hurry and pack some clothes.

'I can't leave,' he said. 'Nina might call.'

'Joe, it's not just Pedro you've got to worry about. It's the police.'

Winder's chin dropped to his chest. 'Already?'

'Mr. X swore out a warrant this afternoon,' Carrie said. 'I heard it from his secretary.'

Francis Kingsbury's secretary was a regular visitor to The Catacombs, where she was conducting an athletic love affair with the actor who portrayed Bartholomew, the most shy and bookish of Uncle Ely's Elves.

Carrie said, 'She mentioned something about destruction of private property.'

'There was an incident,' Joe Winder acknowledged, 'but no shots were fired.'

Under his supervision, the two bulldozers had torn down the three-dimensional billboard that proclaimed the future home of the Falcon Trace Golf and Country Club. The bulldozers also had demolished the air-conditioned double-wide trailer (complete with beer cooler and billiard table) that served as an on-site office for the construction company. They had even wrecked the Port-O-Lets, trapping one of the foremen with his anniversary issue of *Hustler* magazine.

Afterwards Joe Winder had encouraged the bulldozer operators to remove their clothing, which he'd wadded in the neck of the gas tanks. Then—after borrowing the smartass driver's cigarette lighter—Joe Winder had suggested that the men aim their powerful machines toward the Atlantic Ocean, engage the forward gear and swiftly exit the cabs. Later he had proposed a friendly wager on which of the dozers would blow first.

'They spotted the flames all the way from Homestead Air Base,' Carrie Lanier reported. 'Channel 7 showed up in a helicopter, so Kingsbury made Chelsea write up a press release.'

'A freak construction accident, no doubt.'

'Good guess. I've got a Xerox in my purse.'

'No thanks.' Joe Winder wasn't in the mood for Chelsea's golden lies. He stood up and stretched; joints and sockets popped in protest. Lights began to flash blue, green and red on the bare wall, and Winder assumed it was fatigue playing tricks with his vision.

He squinted strenuously, and the lights disappeared. When he opened his eyes, the lights were still strobing. 'Shit, here we go.' Winder went to the window and peeked through the curtain.

'How many?' Carrie asked.

'Two cops, one car.'

'Is there another way out?'

'Sure,' he said.

They heard the tired footsteps on the front walk, the deep murmur of conversation, the crinkle of paper. In the crack beneath the door they saw the yellow flicker of flashlight as the policemen examined the warrant one more time, probably double-checking the address.

Winder picked up the semi-automatic and arranged it in his waistband. Carrie Lanier followed him to the kitchen, where they slipped out the back door just as the cops got serious with their knocking. Once outside, in the pale blue moonlight, she deftly grabbed the gun from Joe Winder's trousers and put it in her handbag.

'In case you go stupid on me,' she whispered.

'No chance of that,' he said. 'None at all.'

20

A thin coil of copper dangled by a string from Carrie Lanier's rearview mirror. Joe Winder asked if it was some type of hieroglyphic emblem.

'It's an IUD,' said Carrie, without taking her eyes off the road. 'A reminder of my ex-husband.'

'I like it.' Winder tried to beef up the compliment. 'It's better than fuzzy dice.'

'He wanted to have babies,' Carrie explained, shooting into the left lane and passing a cement truck. 'A baby boy and a baby girl. House with a white picket fence and big backyard. Snapper riding mower. Golden retriever named Champ. He had it all planned.'

Joe Winder said, 'Sounds pretty good, except for the golden. Give me a Lab any day.'

'Well, he wanted to get me pregnant,' Carrie went on. 'Every night, it was like a big routine. So I'd say sure, Roddy, whatever you want, let's make a baby. I never told him about wearing the loop. And every month he'd want to know. "Did we do it, sweetie? Is there a zygote?" And I'd say "Sorry, honey, guess we'd better try harder."'

'Roddy was his name? That's a bad sign right there.'

'He was a screamer, all right.'

'What happened?' Winder asked. 'Is he still around?'

'No, he's not.' Carrie hit the intersection at Highway 1 without touching the brakes, and merged neatly into the northbound traffic. She said, 'Roddy's up at Eglin doing a little time.'

'Which means he's either a drug dealer or a crooked lawyer.'

'Both,' she said. 'Last month he sent a Polaroid of him with a tennis trophy. He said he can't wait to get out and start trying for a family again.'

'The boy's not well.'

'It's all Oedipal, that's my theory.' Carrie nodded at the IUD and said, 'I keep it there to remind myself that you can't be too careful when it comes to men. Here's Roddy with his Stanford diploma and his fancy European car and his heavy downtown law firm, everything in the whole world going for him. Turns out he's nothing but a dipshit, and a dumb dipshit to boot.'

Winder said she'd been smart to take precautions.

'Yeah, well, I had my career to consider.' Carrie turned a corner into a trailer park, and coasted the car to the end of a narrow gravel lane. 'Home sweet home,' she said. 'Be sure to lock your door. This is not a wonderful neighborhood.'

Joe Winder said, 'Why are you doing this for me?'

'I'm not sure. I'm really not.' She tossed him the keys and asked him to get the raccoon costume from the trunk of the car.

Bud Schwartz and Danny Pogue helped Molly McNamara up the steps of the old house in South Miami. They eased her into the rocker in the living room, and opened the front windows to air the place out. Bud Schwartz's hand still throbbed from the gunshot wound, but his fingers seemed to be functioning.

Danny Pogue said, 'Ain't it good to be home?'

'Indeed it is,' said Molly. 'Could you boys fix me some tea?'

Bud Schwartz looked hard at his partner. 'I'll do it,' said Danny Pogue. 'It don't bother me.' Cheerfully he hobbled toward the kitchen.

'He's not a bad young man,' Molly McNamara said. 'Neither of you are.'

'Model citizens,' said Bud Schwartz. 'That's us.'

He lowered himself into a walnut captain's chair but stood again quickly, as if the seat were hot. He'd forgotten about the damn thing in his pocket until it touched him in the right testicle. Irritably he removed it from his pants and placed it on an end table. He had wrapped it in a blue lace doily.

He said, 'Can we do something with this, please?'

'There's a Mason jar in the cupboard over the stove,' Molly said, 'and some pickle juice in the refrigerator.'

'You're kidding.'

'This is important, Bud. It's evidence.'

In the hall he passed Danny Pogue carrying a teapot on a silver tray. 'You believe this shit?' Bud Schwartz said. He held up the doily.

'What now?'

'She wants me to pickle the goddamn thing!'

Danny Pogue made a squeamish face. 'What for?' When he returned to the living room, Molly was rocking tranquilly in the chair. He poured the tea and said, 'You must be feeling better.'

'Better than I look.' She drank carefully, watching Danny Pogue over the rim of the cup. In a tender voice she said: 'You don't know what this means to me, the fact that you stayed to help.'

'It wasn't just me. It was Bud, too.'

'He's not a bad person,' Molly McNamara allowed. 'I suspect he's a man of principle, deep down.'

Danny Pogue had never thought of his partner as a man of principle, but maybe Molly had spotted something. While Bud was an incorrigible thief, he played by a strict set of rules. No guns, no violence, no hard drugs—Danny Pogue supposed that these could be called principles. He hoped that Molly recognized that he, too, had his limits—moral borders he would not cross. Later on, when she was asleep, he would make a list.

He said, 'So what are you gonna do now? Stay at it?'

'To tell the truth, I'm not certain.' She put down the teacup and dabbed her swollen lips with a napkin. 'I've had some experts go over Kingsbury's files. Lawyers, accountants, people sympathetic to the cause. They made up a cash-flow chart, ran the numbers up and down and sideways. They say it's all very interesting, these foreign companies, but it would probably take months for the IRS and Customs to sort it out; another year for an indictment. We simply don't have that kind of time.'

'Shoot,' said Danny Pogue. He hadn't said 'shoot' since the third grade, but he'd been trying to clean up his language in Molly's presence.

'I'm a little discouraged,' she went on. 'I guess I'd gotten my hopes up prematurely.'

Danny Pogue felt so lousy that he almost told her about the other files, about the blackmail scam that he and Bud Schwartz were running on the great Francis X. Kingsbury.

He said, 'There's nothing we can do? Just let him go ahead and murder off them butterflies and snails?' Molly had given him a magazine clipping about the rare tropical snails of Key Largo.

She said, 'I didn't say we're giving up—'

'Because we should talk to Bud. He'll think a something.'

'Every day we lose precious time,' Molly said. 'Every day they're that much closer to pouring the concrete.'

Danny Pogue nodded. 'Let's talk to Bud. Bud's sharp as a tack about stuff like this—'

Molly stopped rocking and raised a hand. 'I heard something, didn't you?'

From the kitchen came muffled percussions of a struggle— men grunting, something heavy hitting a wall, a jar breaking.

Danny Pogue was shaking when he stood up. The bum foot made him think twice about running.

'Hand me the purse,' Molly said. 'I'll need my gun.'

But Danny Pogue was frozen to the pine floor. His eyelids fluttered and his arms stiffened at his side. All he could think was: *Somebody's killing Bud!*

'Danny, did you hear me? Get me my purse!'

A block of orange appeared in the hallway. It was a tall man in a bright rainsuit and a moldy-looking shower cap. He had a damp silvery beard and black wraparound sunglasses and some-thing red fastened to his neck. The man carried Bud Schwartz in a casual way, one arm around the midsection. Bud Schwartz was limp, gasping, flushed in the face.

Danny Pogue's tongue was as dry as plaster when the stranger stepped out of the shadow.

'Oh, it's you,' Molly McNamara said. 'Now be careful, don't hurt that young man.'

The stranger dropped Bud Schwartz butt-first on the pine and said, 'I caught him putting somebody's fingertip in a Mason jar.'

'I'm the one who told him to,' said Molly. 'Now, Governor, you just settle down.'

'What happened to you?' the stranger demanded. 'Who did this to you, Miss McNamara?'

He took off the sunglasses and glared accusingly at Danny Pogue, who emitted a pitiful hissing noise as he shook his head. Bud Schwartz, struggling to his feet, said: 'It wasn't us, it was some damn Cuban.'

'Tell me a name,' said the stranger.

'I don't know,' said Molly McNamara, 'but I got a good bite out of him.'

'The finger,' Bud Schwartz explained, still gathering his breath.

The stranger knelt beside the rocking chair and gently examined the raw-looking cuts and bruises on Molly's face. 'This is . . . intolerable.' He was whispering to himself and no one else. 'This is barbarism.'

Molly touched the visitor's arm and said, 'I'll be all right. Really.'

Bud Schwartz and Danny Pogue had seen men like this only in prison, and not many. Wild was the only way to describe the face . . . wild and driven and fearless, but not necessarily insane. It would be foolish, perhaps even fatal, to assume the guy was spaced.

He turned to Bud Schwartz and said, 'How about giving me that Cuban's nub.'

'I dropped it on the floor.' Bud Schwartz thought: Christ, he's *not* going to make me go pick it up, is he?

Danny Pogue said, 'No sweat, I'll find it.'

'No,' said the man in the orange rainsuit. 'I'll grab it on the way out.' He squeezed Molly's hands and stood up. 'Will you be all right?'

'Yes, they're taking good care of me.'

The stranger nodded at Bud Schwartz, who couldn't help but notice that one of the man's eyes was slipping out of the socket. The man calmly reinserted it.

'I didn't mean to hurt you,' he said to Bud Schwartz. 'Well, actually, I *did* mean to hurt you.'

Molly explained: 'He didn't know you fellows were my guests, that's all.'

'I'll be in touch,' said the stranger. He kissed Molly on the cheek and said he would check on her in a day or two. Then he was gone.

Bud Schwartz waited until he heard the door slam. Then he said: 'What the hell was that?'

'A friend,' Molly replied. They had known each other a long time. She had worked as a volunteer in his guber-natorial campaign, whipping up both the senior-citizen vote and the environmental coalitions. Later, when he quit office and vanished, Molly was one of the few who knew what happened, and one of the few who understood. Over the years he had kept in touch in his own peculiar way—sometimes a spectral glimpse, sometimes a sensational entrance; jarring cameos that were as hair-raising as they were poignant.

'Guy's big,' said Danny Pogue. 'Geez, he looks like—did he do time? What's his story?'

'We don't want to know,' Bud Schwartz said. 'Am I right?'

'You're absolutely right,' said Molly McNamara.

Shortly before midnight on July 23, Jim Tile received a radio call that an unknown individual was shooting at automobiles on Card Sound Road. The trooper told the dispatcher he was en route, and that he'd notify the Monroe County Sheriff's Office if he needed back-ups—which he knew he wouldn't.

The cars were lined up on the shoulder of the road a half-mile east of the big bridge. Jim Tile took inventory from the stickers on the bumpers: two Alamos, a Hertz, a National and an Avis. The rental firms had started putting bumper plates on all their automobiles, which served not only as advertisement but as a warning to local drivers that a disoriented tourist was nearby. On this night, though, the bright stickers had betrayed their unsuspecting drivers. Each of the vehicles bore a single .45-caliber bullet hole in the left-front fender panel.

Jim Tile knew exactly what had happened. He took brief statements from the motorists, who seemed agitated by the suggestion that anyone would fire at them simply because they were tourists. Jim Tile assured them that this sort of thing didn't happen every day. Then he called Homestead for tow trucks to get the three rental cars whose engine blocks had been mortally wounded by the sniper in the mangroves.

One of the drivers, a French-Canadian textile executive, used a cellular phone to call the Alamo desk at Miami International Airport and explain the situation. Soon new cars were on the way.

It took Jim Tile several hours to clear the scene. A pair of Monroe County deputies stopped by and helped search for shell casings until the mosquitoes drove them away. After the officers had fled, and after the tourists had motored north in a wary caravan of Thunderbirds, Skylarks and Zephyrs, Jim Tile got in his patrol car and mashed on the horn with both fists. Then he rolled up the windows, turned up the air conditioner and waited for his sad old friend to come out of the swamp.

'I'm sorry.' Skink offered the trooper a stick of EDTIAR insect repellent.

'You promised to behave,' said Jim Tile. 'Now you've put me in a tough position.'

'Had to blow off some steam,' Skink said. 'Anyway, I didn't hurt anybody.' He took off his sunglasses and tinkered unabashedly with the fake eyeball. 'Haven't you ever had days like this? Days where you just had to go out and shoot the shit out of something, didn't matter what?'

Jim Tile sighed. 'Rental cars?'

'Why the hell not.'

The tension dissolved into weary silence. The men had talked of such things before. When Clinton Tyree was the governor of Florida, Jim Tile had been his chief bodyguard—an unusually prestigious assignment for a black state trooper. After Clinton Tyree resigned, Jim Tile immediately lost his job on the elite security detail. The new governor, it was explained, felt more comfortable around peckerwoods. By the end of that fateful week, Jim Tile had found himself back on road patrol, Harney County, night shifts.

Over the years he had stayed close to Clinton Tyree, partly out of friendship, partly out of admiration and partly out of certitude that the man would need police assistance now and then, which he had. Whenever Skink got restless and moved his hermitage to deeper wilderness, Jim Tile would quietly put in for a transfer and move, too. This meant more rural two-lanes, more night duty and more ignorant mean-eyed crackers—but the trooper knew that his friend would have done the same for him, had fortunes been reversed. Besides, Jim Tile was confident of his own abilities and believed that one day he'd be in charge of the entire highway patrol—dishing out a few special night shifts himself.

Usually Skink kept to himself, except for the occasional public sighting when he dashed out of the pines to retrieve a fresh opossum or squirrel off the road. Once in a while, though, something triggered him in a tumultuous way and the results were highly visible. Standing on the crowded Fort Lauderdale beach, he'd once put four rounds into the belly of an inbound Eastern 727. Another time he'd crashed the Miss Florida pageant and tearfully heaved a dead baby manatee on stage to dramatize the results of waterfront development. It was fortunate, in such instances, that no one had recognized the hoary cyclopic mad-man as Clinton Tyree; it was even more fortunate that Jim Tile had been around to help the ex-governor slip away safely and collect what was left of his senses.

Now, sitting in the trooper's patrol car, Skink polished his glass eye with a bandanna and apologized for causing his friend so much inconvenience. 'If you've got to arrest me,' he said, 'I'll understand.'

'Wouldn't do a damn bit of good,' said Jim Tile. 'But I tell you what—I'd appreciate if you'd let me know what's going on down here.'

'The usual,' Skink said. 'The bad guys are kicking our collective ass.'

'We got a dead body off the bridge, a guy named Angel Gaviria.

You know about that, right?' The trooper didn't wait for an answer. 'The coroner is saying suicide or accident, but I was there and I don't think it's either one. The deceased was a well-known scum-bucket and they don't usually have the decency to kill themselves. Usually someone else does the honor.'

'Jim, we live in troubled times.'

'The other day I pull over a blue Ford sedan doing eighty-six down the bridge. Turns out to be a Feeb.'

'FBI?' Skink perked up. 'All the way down here?'

'Hawkins was his name. He badges me, we get to chatting. Turns out he's working a case at the Amazing Kingdom. Something to do with militant bunny huggers and missing blue-tongued rats.' Jim Tile gave a lazy laugh. 'Now this is the FBI, interviewing elves and cowboys and fairy princesses. I don't suppose you can fill me in.'

Skink was pleased that the feds had taken notice of events in North Key Largo. He said, 'All I know is bits and pieces.'

'Speaking of which, what can you tell me about killer whales? This morning a semi rolls over and I got stinking gobs of dead whale all over my nice clean blacktop. I'm talking tonnage.'

Skink said, 'That would explain the buzzard shit on this state vehicle.' Secretly he wished he could have been there to witness the spectacle.

'You think it's funny?'

'I think,' said Skink, 'you should prepare for the worst.'

Jim Tile took off his Stetson and lowered his face in front of the dashboard vents; the cool air felt good on his cheeks. A gumdrop-shaped sports car blew by doing ninety-plus, and the trooper barely glanced up. He radioed the dispatcher in Miami and announced he was going off duty. 'I'm tired,' he said to Skink.

'Me, too. You haven't seen anybody from Game and Fish, have you?'

'The panther patrol? No, I haven't.' Jim Tile sat up. 'I haven't seen the plane in at least a month.'

Skink said, 'Must've broken down. Else they're working the Fokahatchee.'

'Listen,' the trooper said, 'I won't ask about the dead guy on the bridge, and I won't ask about the whale—'

'I had nothing whatsoever to do with the whale.'

'Fair enough,' said Jim Tile, 'but what about torching those bulldozers up on 905? Were you in on that?'

Skink looked at him blankly. The trooper described what had happened that very afternoon at the Falcon Trace construction project. 'They're looking for a guy who used to work at the Kingdom. They say he's gone nuts. They say he's got a gun.'

'Is that right?' Skink tugged pensively at his beard.

'Do you know this person?'

'Possibly.'

'Then could you *possibly* get him a message to stop this shit before it gets out of hand?'

'It's already out of hand,' Skink said. 'The sons-of-bitches are beating up little old ladies.'

'Damn.' The trooper stared out the window of the car. A trio of mosquitoes bounced off the glass and circled his head. Skink reached over and snatched the insects out of the air. Then he opened the window and let them buzz away into the thick fragrant night.

Jim Tile said, 'I'm worried about you.'

Skink grinned. 'That's a good one.'

'Maybe I should haul you in after all.'

'Wouldn't stick. No one saw me do it, and no one found the gun. Hell, they wouldn't even hold me overnight.'

'Yeah, they would,' Jim Tile said, 'on my word.'

Skink's smile went away.

The trooper said, 'The charge wouldn't stick, that's true. But I could take you out of circulation for a month or two. Let the situation simmer down.'

'Why?' Skink demanded. 'You know I'm right. You know what I'm doing is right.'

'Not shooting rental cars.'

'A lapse of judgment,' Skink admitted. 'I said I was sorry, for God's sake.'

Jim Tile put a hand on his friend's shoulder. 'I know you think it's the right thing, and the cause is good. But I'm afraid you're gonna lose.'

'Maybe not,' Skink said. 'I think the Mojo's rising.'

The trooper always got lost when Skink started quoting old rock-and-roll songs; someday he was going to sit Skink's shiny ass down and make him listen to Aretha. Put some soul in his system. Jim Tile said, 'I've got a life, too. Can't spend the rest of it looking out for you.'

Skink sagged against the car door. 'Jim, they're paving the goddamn island.'

'Not the whole thing—'

'But this is how it begins,' Skink said. 'Jesus Christ, you ought to know. This is how it begins!'

There was no point in pushing it. The state had bought up nearly all North Key Largo for preservation; the Amazing Kingdom and the Falcon Trace property were essentially all that remained in private hands. Still, Skink was not celebrating.

Jim Tile said, 'This guy you recruited—'

'I didn't recruit him.'

'Whatever. He's in it, that's the main thing.'

'Apparently so,' Skink said. 'Apparently he's serious.'

'So locking you up won't do any good, will it? Not with him still out there.' The trooper put on his hat and adjusted it out of habit. In the darkness of the car, Skink couldn't read the expression on his friend's face. Jim Tile said, 'Promise me one thing, all right? Talk some sense to the boy. He's new at it, Governor, and he could get hurt. That stunt with the bulldozers, it's not cool.'

'I know,' said Skink, 'but it's got a certain flair.'

'Listen to me,' Jim Tile said sternly. 'Already he's got some serious people after his ass, you understand? There's things I can help with and things I can't.'

Skink nodded. 'I'll talk to him, I promise. And thanks.'

Then he was gone. Jim Tile reached across to shut the door and his arm instantly was enveloped by an influx of mosquitoes. Frenzied humming filled the car.

He stomped the accelerator and the big Crown Victoria sprayed a fusillade of gravel into the mangroves. Westbound at a hundred fifteen miles an hour, the trooper rolled down the windows to let the wind suck the bugs from the car.

'Two of them.' His words were swallowed in the roar of the open night. 'Now I got two of the crazy bastards.'

21

Carrie Lanier's place was furnished as exquisitely as any mobile home. It had a microwave, an electric can opener, a stove, a nineteen-inch color TV, two paddle fans and a Naugahyde convertible sofa where Joe Winder slept. But there was no music, so on his third day as a fugitive Winder borrowed Carrie's car and went back to the apartment to retrieve his stereo system and rock tapes. He was not totally surprised to find that his place had been broken, entered and ransacked; judging by the viciousness of the search, Pedro Luz was the likely intruder. The inventory of losses included the portable television, three champagne glasses, a tape recorder, the plumbing fixtures, the mattress, a small Matisse print and the toaster. One of Nina's pink bras, which she had forgotten, had been desecrated ominously with cigarette burns, and hung from a Tiffany lamp. Also, the freshwater aquarium had been shattered, and the twin Siamese fighting fish had been killed. It appeared to Joe Winder that their heads were pinched off.

The stereo tuner and tape deck escaped harm, though the turntable was in pieces. A pair of hedge clippers protruded from one of the speakers; the other, fortunately, was undamaged.

'It's better than nothing,' Joe Winder said when he got back to the trailer. 'Low fidelity is better than no fidelity.'

While he reassembled the components, Carrie Lanier explored the box of cassettes. Every now and then she would smile or go 'Hmmm' in an amused tone.

Finally Winder looked up from the nest of colored wires and said, 'You don't like my music?'

'I like it just fine,' she said. 'I'm learning a lot about you. We've got The Kinks. Seeger live at Cobo Hall. Mick and the boys.'

'Living in the past, I know.'

'Oh, baloney.' She began to stack the tapes alphabetically on a shelf made from raw plywood and cinder blocks.

'Do you have a typewriter?' he asked.

'In the closet,' Carrie said. 'Are you going to start writing again?'

'I wouldn't call it writing.'

She got out the typewriter, an old Olivetti manual, and made a place for it on the dinette. 'This is a good idea,' she said to Joe Winder. 'You'll feel much better. No more shooting at heavy machinery.'

He reminded her that he hadn't actually pulled the trigger on the bulldozers. Then he said, 'I stopped writing a long time ago. Stopped being a journalist, anyway.'

'But you didn't burn out, you sold out.'

'Thanks,' Winder said, 'for the reminder.'

It was his fault for staggering down memory lane in the first place. Two nights earlier, Carrie had quizzed him about the newspaper business, wanted to know what kind of stories he'd written. So he'd told her about the ones that had stuck with him. The murder trial of a thirteen-year-old boy who'd shot his little sister because she had borrowed his Aerosmith album without asking. The marijuana-smuggling ring led by a fugitive former justice of the Florida Supreme Court. The bribery scandal in which dim-witted Dade County building inspectors were caught soliciting Lotto tickets as payoffs. The construction of a $47 million super-highway by a Mafia contractor whose formula for high-grade asphalt included human body parts.

Joe Winder did not mention the story that had ended his career. He offered nothing about his father. When Carrie Lanier had asked why he'd left the newspaper for public relations, he simply said, 'Because of the money.' She had seemed only mildly interested in his short time as a Disney World flack, but was impressed by the reckless sexual behavior that had gotten him fired. She said it was a healthy sign that he had not become a corporate drone, that the spark of rebellion still glowed in his soul.

'Maybe in my pants,' Winder said, 'not in my soul.'

Carrie repeated what she had told him the first night: 'You could always go back to being a reporter.'

'No, I'm afraid not.'

'So what is it you want to type—love letters? Maybe a confession?' Mischievously she tapped the keys of the Olivetti; two at a time, as if she were playing 'Chopsticks.'

The trailer was getting smaller and smaller. Joe Winder felt the heat lick at his eardrums. He said, 'There's a reason you've hidden that gun.'

'Because it's not your style.' Carrie slapped the carriage and made the typewriter ring. 'God gave you a talent for expression, a gift with the language.'

Winder moaned desolately. 'Have you ever read a single word I've written?'

'No,' she admitted.

'So my alleged talent for expression, this gift—'

'I'm giving you the benefit of the doubt,' she said. 'The fact is, I don't trust you with a firearm. Now come help me open the wine.'

Every evening at nine sharp, visitors to the Amazing Kingdom of Thrills gathered on both sides of Kingsbury Lane, the park's main thoroughfare, to buy overpriced junk food and await the rollicking pageant that was the climax of the day's festivities. All the characters in the Kingdom were expected to participate, from the gunslingers to the porpoise trainers to the elves. Sometimes a real marching band would accompany the procession, but in the slow months of summer the music was usually canned, piped in through the garbage chutes. Ten brightly colored floats comprised the heart of the parade, although mechanical problems frequently reduced the number of entries by half. These were organized in a story line based loosely on the settlement of Florida, going back to the days of the Spaniards. The plundering, genocide, defoliation and gang rape that typified the peninsula's past had been toned down for the sake of Francis X. Kingsbury's younger, more impressionable customers; also, it would have been difficult to find a musical score suitable to accompany a mass disemboweling of French Huguenots.

For the feel-good purposes of the Amazing Kingdom's nightly pageant, the sordid history of Florida was compressed into a series of amiable and bloodless encounters. Floats celebrated such fabricated milestones as the first beachfront Thanksgiving, when friendly settlers and gentle Tequesta Indians shared wild turkey and fresh coconut milk under the palms. It was a testament to Charles Chelsea's imagination (and mortal fear of Kingsbury) that even the most shameful episodes were reinterpreted with a positive commercial spin. A float titled 'Migrants on a Mission' depicted a dozen cheery, healthful farm workers singing Jamaican folk songs and swinging their machetes in a precisely choreographed break-dance through the cane fields. Tourists loved it. So did the Okeechobee Sugar Federation, which had bankrolled the production in order to improve its image.

One of the highlights of the pageant was the arrival of 'the legendary Seminole maiden' known as Princess Golden Sun. No such woman and no such lore ever existed; Charles Chelsea had invented her basically as an excuse to show tits and ass, and pass it off as ethnic culture. Traditional Seminole garb was deemed too dowdy for the parade, so Princess Golden Sun appeared in a micro-bikini made of simulated deerskin. The authentic Green Corn Dance, a sacred Seminole rite, was politely discarded as too solemn and repetitious; instead Golden Sun danced the *lambada*, a pelvic-intensive Latin step. Surrounded by ersatz Indian warriors wearing bright Brazilian slingshots, the princess proclaimed in song and mime her passionate love for the famous Seminole chieftain Osceola. At the news of his death, she broke into tears and vowed to haunt the Everglades forever in search of his spirit. The peak of the drama, and the parade, was the moment when Golden Sun mounted a wild panther (in this case, a heavily drugged African lioness) and disappeared from sight in a rising fog of dry ice.

It was the role most coveted among the female actors employed at the Amazing Kingdom, and for six months it had belonged to Annette Fury, a dancer of mountainous dimensions whose previous job was as a waitress at a topless doughnut shop in Fort Lauderdale. A competent singer, Miss Fury had done so well with the role of Princess Golden Sun that the newspaper in Key Largo had done a nice write-up, including a photograph of Miss Fury straddling the bleary-eyed cat. The reporter had been careful to explain that the spavined animal was not actually a Florida panther, since real panthers were all but extinct. Given Princess Golden Sun's appearance, it was doubtful that a single reader even noticed the lion in the picture. Miss Fury's pose—head flung back, eyes closed, tongue between the teeth—was suggestive enough to provoke indignant outcries from a fundamentalist church in Big Pine Key, as well as the entire Seminole Nation, or what was left of it. At the first whiff of controversy, Charles Chelsea swiftly purchased the negatives from the newspaper and converted the most provocative one to a color postcard, which went on sale for $1.95 in all gift shops in the Amazing Kingdom of Thrills. As far as Chelsea was concerned, a star had been born.

On the night of July 25, however, Annette Fury's stint as Princess Golden Sun ended abruptly in a scandal that defied even Chelsea's talents for cosmetic counter-publicity. Shortly before the pageant, the dancer had ingested what were probably the last three Quaalude tablets in the entire continental United States. She had scrounged the dusty pills from the stale linty recesses of her purse, and washed them down with a warm bottle of Squirt. They had kicked in just as the float made the wide horseshoe turn onto Kingsbury Lane. By the time it rolled past the Cimarron Saloon, Annette Fury was bottomless, having surrendered her deerskin costume to a retired postal worker who had brought his wife and family all the way from Providence, Rhode Island. By the time the float reached the Wet Willy, the stone-faced Indian entourage of Princess Golden Sun had been augmented by nine rowdy Florida State fraternity men, who were taking turns balancing the drowsy young maiden on their noses, or so it must have appeared to the children in the audience. Afterwards, several parents threatened to file criminal obscenity charges against the park. They were appeased by a prompt written apology signed by Francis X. Kingsbury, and a gift of laminated lifetime passes to the Amazing Kingdom. Reluctantly, Charles Chelsea advised the Talent Manager to inform Annette Fury that her services were no longer required. The following day, Carrie Lanier was told that the role of Princess Golden Sun was hers if she wanted it. This was after they'd asked for her measurements.

So tonight she'd splurged on a bottle of Mondavi.

'To the late Robbie Raccoon,' Carrie said, raising her glass.

'No one did him better,' said Joe Winder.

He put on a tape of Dire Straits and they both agreed that it sounded pretty darn good, even with only one speaker. The wine was tolerable, as well.

Carrie said, 'I told them I want a new costume.'

'Something in beads and grass would be authentic.'

'Also, no lip-synching,' she said. 'I don't care if the music's canned, but I want to do my own singing.'

'What about the lion?' Joe Winder asked.

'They swear she's harmless.'

'Tranked out of her mind is more like it. I'd be concerned, if I were you.'

'If she didn't maul Annette, I can't imagine why she'd go after me.'

A police siren penetrated the aluminium husk of the trailer; Joe Winder could hear it even over the guitar music and the tubercular groan of the ancient air conditioner. Parting the drapes, he watched one Metro squad car, and then another, enter the trailer park at high speed. Throwing dust, they sped past the turnoff to Carrie's place.

'Another domestic,' Winder surmised.

'We average about four a week.' Carrie refilled the wine-glasses. 'People who take love too damn seriously.'

'Which reminds me.' He opened his wallet and removed twelve dollars and placed it on a wicker table. 'I was a very bad boy. I called her three times.'

'You shmuck.'

The Nina Situation. Every time he picked up the phone, it

added four bucks to Carrie Lanier's bill. Worse, Nina pretended not to recognize his voice—stuck to the script to the bitter end, no matter how much he pleaded for her to shut up and listen.

'It is pathetic,' Winder conceded.

'No other word for it.'

'Haven't you ever been like this?' Obsessed is what he meant.

'Nope.' Carrie shrugged. 'I've got to be honest.'

'So what's the matter with me?'

'You're just having a bad week.'

She went to the bedroom and changed to a lavender nightshirt that came down to the knees—actually, a good four inches above the knees. Her hair was pulled back in a loose, sandy-colored ponytail.

Winder said, 'You look sixteen years old.' Only about three dozen other guys must have told her the same thing. His heart was pounding a little harder than he expected. 'Tomorrow I'll get a motel room,' he said.

'No, you're staying here.'

'I appreciate it but—'

'Please,' Carrie said. 'Please stay.'

'I've got serious plans. You won't approve.'

'How do you know? Besides, I'm a little nervous about this new job. It's nice to have someone here at the end of the day, someone to talk with.'

Gazing at her, Winder thought: God, don't do this to me. Don't make me say it.

But he did: 'You just want to keep an eye on me. You're afraid I'll screw everything up.'

'You're off to a pretty good start.'

'It's only fair to warn you: I'm going after Kingsbury.'

'That's what I figured, Joe. Call it a wild hunch.' She took his hand and led him toward the bedroom.

I'm not ready for this, Winder thought. Sweat broke out in a linear pattern on the nape of his neck. He felt as if he were back in high school, the day the prettiest cheerleader winked at him in biology class; at the time, he'd been examining frog sperm under a microscope, and the wink from Pamela Shaughnessy had fractured his concentration. It had taken a month or two for Joe Winder to recover, and by then Pámela was knocked up by the co-captain of the junior wrestling squad. The teacher said that's what she got for not paying attention in class.

The sheets in Carrie Lanier's bedroom were rose, the blanket was plum. A novel by Anne Tyler was open on the bedstand, next to a bottle of nose drops.

A fuzzy stuffed animal sat propped on the pillow: shoe-button eyes, round ears and short whiskers. Protruding slightly from its upturned, bucktoothed mouth was a patch of turquoise cotton that could only be a tongue.

'Violet the Vole,' Carrie explained. 'Note the sexy eyelashes.'

'For Christ's sake,' Joe Winder said.

'The Vance model comes with a tiny cigar.'

'How much?' Winder asked.

'Eighteen ninety-five, plus tax. Mr. X ordered a shipment of three thousand.' Carrie stroked his arm. 'Come on, I feel like cuddling.'

Wordlessly, Winder moved the toy mango vole off the bed. The tag said it was manufactured in the People's Republic of China. What must they think of us on the assembly line? Winder wondered. Stuffed rats with cigars!

Carrie Lanier said, 'I've got the jitters about singing in the parade. I don't look much like a Seminole.'

Winder assured her she would do just fine. 'Listen, I need to ask a favor. If you say no, I'll understand.'

'Shoot.'

'I need you to steal something for me,' he said.

'Sure.'

'Just like that?'

Carrie said, 'I trust you. I want to help.'

'Do you see the possibilities?'

'Surprise me,' she said.

'Don't worry, it won't be dangerous. A very modest effort, as larcenies go.'

'Sure. First thing tomorrow.'

'Why are you doing this?' he asked.

'Because it's a fraud, the whole damn place. But mainly because an innocent man is dead. I liked Will Koocher.' She paused. 'I like his wife, too.'

She didn't have to add the last part, but Winder was glad she did. He said, 'You might lose your job.'

Carrie smiled. 'There's always dinner theater.'

It seemed a good time to break the ice, so he tried—a brotherly peck on the cheek.

'Joe,' she murmured, 'you kiss like a parakeet.'

'I'm slightly nervous myself.'

Slowly she levered him to the bed, pinning his arms. 'Why,' she said, giggling, 'why are you so nervous, little boy?'

'I really don't know.' Her breasts pressed against his ribs, a truly wonderful sensation. Winder decided he could spend the remainder of his life in that position.

Carrie said, 'Lesson Number One: How to smooch an Indian maiden.'

'Go ahead,' said Winder. 'I'm all lips.'

'Now do as I say.'

'Anything,' he agreed. 'Anything at all.'

As they kissed, an unrelated thought sprouted like a mushroom in the only dim crevice of Joe Winder's brain that was not fogged with lust.

The thought was: If I play this right, we won't need the gun after all.

22

Pedro Luz was in Francis Kingsbury's den when the blackmailers called. He listened to Kingsbury's half of the conversation, a series of impatient grunts, and said to Churrito, 'Looks like we're in business.'

Kingsbury put down the phone and said, 'All set. Monkey Mountain at four sharp. In front of the baboons.'

Monkey Mountain was a small animal park off Krome Avenue, a cut-rate imitation of the venerable Monkey Jungle. To Pedro Luz, it didn't sound like an ideal place to kill a couple of burglars.

With a snort, Kingsbury said, 'These assholes, who knows where they get these cute ideas. Watching television, maybe.'

'What is this monkey place?' Churrito asked.

'For Christ's sake, like the name says, it's basically monkeys. Two thousand of the damn things running all over creation.' Kingsbury disliked monkeys and had summarily vetoed plans for a Primate Pavilion at the Amazing Kingdom of Thrills. He felt that apes had limited commercial appeal; Disney had steered clear of them, too, for what that was worth.

'For one thing, they bite. And, two, they shit like a sewer pipe.' Kingsbury put the issue to rest. 'If they're so damn smart, how come they don't hold it. Like people.'

'They tasty good,' Churrito remarked, licking his lips. 'Squirrel monkey is best, where I come from.'

Pedro Luz sucked noisily on the open end of the IV tube. He had purchased a dozen clear bags of five-percent dextrose solution from a wholesale medical shop in Perrine. The steroid pills he pulverized with the butt of his Colt, and funneled the powder into the bags. No one at the gym had ever heard of getting stoked by this method; Pedro Luz boasted that it was all his idea, he'd never even checked with a doctor. The only part that bothered him was using the needle—a problematic endeavor, since anabolic steroids were usually injected into muscle, not veins. Whenever Pedro Luz was having second thoughts, he'd yank out the tube and insert it directly in his mouth.

Sitting in Kingsbury's house, it gave him great comfort to feel again these magnificent potent chemicals flooding his system. With nourishment came strength, and with strength came confidence. Pedro Luz was afraid of nothing. He felt like stepping in front of a speeding bus, just to prove it.

Churrito pointed at the intravenous rig and said: 'Even monkeys aren't that stupid.'

'Put a lid on it,' Pedro growled. He thought: No wonder these dorks lost the war.

'Stuff make you bulls shrink up. Dick get leetle tiny.' Churrito seemed unconcerned by the volcanic mood changes that swept over Pedro Luz every few hours. To Francis Kingsbury he said, 'Should see the zits on his cholders.'

'Some other time,' Kingsbury said. 'You guys, now, don't get into it. There's work to do—I want these assholes off my back, these fucking burglars, and I want the files. So don't start up with each other, I mean, save your energy for the job.'

Pedro Luz said, 'Don't worry.'

The phone rang and Kingsbury snatched it. The call obviously was long-distance because Kingsbury began to shout. Something about a truck accident ruining an important shipment of fish. The caller kept cutting in on Kingsbury, and Kingsbury kept making half-assed excuses, meaning some serious money already had changed hands.

When Kingsbury hung up, he said, 'That was Hong Kong. Some cat-food outfit, I set up this deal and it didn't work out. What the hell, they'll get their dough back.'

'My uncle had a fish market,' remarked Pedro Luz. 'It's a very hard business.'

Without warning Mrs. Kingsbury came into the room. She wore terry-cloth tennis shorts and the top half of a lime-colored bikini. She nodded at Churrito, who emitted a low tomcat rumble. Pedro Luz glowered at him.

She said, 'Frankie, I need some money for my lessons.'

Under his breath, Churrito said, 'I give her some lessons. Chew bet I will.'

Kingsbury said, 'I just gave you—was it yesterday?—like two hundred bucks.'

'That was yesterday.' Mrs. Kingsbury's eyes shifted to Pedro Luz, and the bottle of fluid on the hanger.

'What's the matter with him?' she asked.

'One of them crash diets,' said her husband.

Churrito said, 'Yeah, make your muscles get big and your dick shrivel up like a noodle.'

Pedro Luz reddened. 'It's vitamins, that's all.' He gnawed anxiously on the end of the tube, as if it were a piece of beef jerky.

'What kind of vitamins?' asked Kingsbury's wife.

'For men,' said Pedro Luz. 'Men-only vitamins.'

As always, it was a test to be in the same room with Mrs. Kingsbury and her phenomenal breasts. Pedro Luz had given up sex three years earlier in the misinformed belief that ejaculation was a waste of precious hormones. Somehow, Pedro Luz had acquired the false notion that semen was one-hundred-percent pure testosterone, and consequently he was distraught when a popular weightlifter magazine reported that the average sexually active male would squirt approximately 19.6 gallons in a lifetime. For a fitness fiend such as Pedro Luz, the jism statistic was a shocker. To expend a single pearly drop of masculine fuel on a recreational pleasure was frivolous and harmful and plainly against God's plan; how could it do anything but weaken the body?

As it happened, Pedro Luz's fruit-and-steroid diet had taken the edge off his sex drive anyway. Abstinence had not proved to be difficult, except when Mrs. Kingsbury was around.

'I don't like needles,' she announced. 'I don't like the way they prick.'

Again Churrito began to growl lasciviously. Pedro Luz said,

'After a while, you don't even notice.' He showed Mrs. Kingsbury how the IV rig moved on wheels.

'Like a shopping cart,' she said gaily. Her husband handed her a hundred-dollar bill and she waved goodbye.

'There she goes,' Kingsbury said. 'Pedro, did you show your little buddy the golf painting? The one we did at Biltmore?'

'I saw,' Churrito said. 'In the living room.'

'Those are the real McCoys,' said Kingsbury.

Churrito looked perplexed. 'McCoys?'

'Her tits, I mean. How you say, *hoot-aires*?' Kingsbury cackled. 'Now, about this afternoon, these assholes—I'm not interested in details. Not at all interested.'

That was fine with Pedro Luz. He'd skipped the details the last time, too, when they had roughed up the old lady at the condo. Although Churrito had nagged him to lighten up, the beating had been therapeutic for Pedro, a venting of toxic brain fumes. Like the rush he got while pinching the heads off Joe Winder's goldfish.

'I doubt this monkey place will be crowded,' Kingsbury was saying, 'except for the baboons.'

'We'll be careful,' Pedro Luz assured him.

'You get caught, no offense, but I don't know you. Never seen you bastards before in my life.'

'We won't get caught.'

Kingsbury snapped his fingers. 'The files, I'll give you a list. Don't do anything till you get my files back. After that, it's your call.'

Pedro Luz looked at his wristwatch and said it was time to go. The wheels on the IV rig twittered as it followed him to the door.

'I wanted to ask,' Churrito said, 'is it okay I look at the pitcher again? The one with your wife and those real McCoys.'

'Be my guest,' said Kingsbury, beaming. 'That's what it's there for.'

One problem, Bud Schwartz realized, was that he and his partner had never done a blackmail before. In fact, he wasn't sure if it was blackmail or extortion, technically speaking.

'Call it a trade,' said Danny Pogue.

Bud Schwartz smiled. Not bad, he thought. A trade it is.

They were waiting in the rented Cutlass in the parking lot of Monkey Mountain. Mrs. Kingsbury's chrome-plated pistol lay on the seat between them. Neither of them wanted to handle it.

'Christ, I hate guns,' said Bud Schwartz.

'How's your hand?'

'Getting there. How's your foot?'

'Pretty good.' Danny Pogue opened a bag of Burger King and the oily smell of hot fries filled the car. Bud Schwartz rolled down the window and was counter-assailed by the overpowering odor of monkeys.

Chewing, Danny Pogue said, 'I can't get over that guy in the house, Molly's friend. Just come right in.'

'Bigfoot,' said Bud Schwartz, 'without the manners.'

'I just hope he don't come back.'

'You and me both.'

Bud Schwartz was watching out for Saabs. Over the phone Kingsbury had told him he'd be driving a navy Saab with tinted windows; so far, no sign of the car.

He asked his partner: 'You ever done a Saab?'

'No, they all got alarms,' said Danny Pogue. 'Like radar is what I heard. Just look at 'em funny, and they go off. Same with the Porsches, I fucking whisper just walkin' by the damn things.'

At two minutes after four, Bud Schwartz said it was time to get ready. Gingerly he put the gun in his pocket. 'Leave the files under the seat,' he said. 'We'll make the trade after we got the money.'

At the ticket window they got a map of Monkey Mountain. It wasn't exactly a sprawling layout.

'Hey, they even got a gorilla,' said Danny Pogue, 'name of Brutus. From the picture it looks like an African silverback.'

'Fascinating,' Bud Schwartz said. He'd had about enough of animal lore. Lately Danny Pogue had been spending too many hours watching wildlife documentaries on the Discovery Channel. It was all he talked about, he and Molly, and it was driving Bud Schwartz up the wall. One night, instead of the Cubs game, he had to sit through ninety minutes of goddamn hummingbirds. To Bud Schwartz they resembled moths with beaks; he got dizzy watching the damn things, even the slow-motion parts. Danny Pogue, on the other hand, had been enthralled. The fact that hummingbirds also inhabited North Key Largo heightened his sense of mission against Francis X. Kingsbury.

As they set out for the Baboon Tree, Danny Pogue said, 'Why'd you pick this place, Bud?'

''Cause it's out in public. That's how you do these things, extortions.'

'Are you sure?'

The visitor paths through Monkey Mountain were enclosed by chicken wire, giving the effect that it was the humans who were encaged while the wild beasts roamed free. Bud Schwartz was uncomfortable with this arrangement. Above his head, screeching monkeys loped along the mesh, begging for peanuts and crackers that Bud Schwartz had neglected to purchase at the concession stand. The impatient animals—howlers, gibbons, rhesus and spider monkeys—got angrier by the second. They bared yellow teeth and spit maliciously and shook the chicken wire. When Danny Pogue reached up to give one of them a shiny dime, it defecated in his hair.

'You happy now?' said Bud Schwartz.

'Damn, I can't believe it.' Danny Pogue stopped to stick his head under a water fountain. 'Don't they ever feed these goddamn things?' he said.

Above them, the gang of furry, shrieking, incontinent beggars had swollen to three dozen. Bud Schwartz and Danny Pogue shielded their heads and jogged the rest of the way to the Baboon Tree, an ancient ficus in the hub of a small plaza. Bud Schwartz was relieved to escape the yammering din and the rain of monkey feces. With a sigh he sat next to a Japanese family on a concrete bench. A moat of filmy brown water separated them from the bustling baboon colony in the big tree.

Danny Pogue said: 'Know why they don't let the other monkeys together with the baboons?'

'Why not?'

'Because the baboons'd eat 'em.'

'What a loss that would be.'

'Let's go see Brutus.'

'Danny, we're here on business. Now shut the fuck up, if you don't mind.'

The Japanese husband apparently understood at least one word of English, because he gave Bud Schwartz a sharp look. The Japanese wife, who hadn't heard the profane remark, signaled that she would like a photograph of the whole family in front of the moat. Bud Schwartz motioned that his partner would do the honors; Danny Pogue had stolen many Nikons, but he'd never gotten a chance to use one. He arranged the Japanese in a neat row according to height, and snapped several pictures. In the background were many wild-eyed baboons, including a young male gleefully abusing itself.

Bud Schwartz was glad the children weren't watching. After the Japanese had moved on, Danny Pogue said: 'That was two hundred bucks right there, a Nikon with autofocus. I got a guy in Carol City fences nothing but cameras.'

'I told you,' said Bud Schwartz, 'we're through with that. We got a new career.' He didn't sound as confident as he would've liked. Where the hell was Kingsbury?

Danny Pogue joined him on the concrete bench. 'So how much is he gonna bring?'

'Fifty is what I told him.' Bud Schwartz couldn't get the tremor out of his voice. 'Fifty thousand, if he ever shows up.'

In the parking lot, Pedro Luz and Churrito got into a heated discussion about bringing the IV rack. Churrito prevailed on the grounds that it would attract too much attention.

The first thing they noticed about Monkey Mountain was the stink, which Churrito likened to that of a mass grave. Next came the insistent clamor of the creatures themselves, clinging to the chicken wire and extending miniature brown hands in hopes of food. Churrito lit up a Marlboro and handed it to a rhesus, who took a sniff and hurled it back at him. Pedro Luz didn't think it was the least bit funny; he was sinking into one of his spells—

every heartbeat sent cymbals crashing against his brainpan. An act of irrational violence was needed to calm the mood. It was fortunate, then, that the monkeys were safely on the other side of the chicken wire. Every time one appeared on the mesh over his head, Pedro Luz would jump up and smash at it savagely with his knuckles. This exercise was repeated every few seconds, all the way to the Baboon Tree.

The burglars—and it *had* to be them, greasy-looking rednecks—were sitting on a bench. Nobody else was around.

Pedro Luz whispered to Churrito: 'Remember to get their car keys. They left the damn files in the car.'

'What if they dint?'

'They did. Now be quiet.'

Danny Pogue wasn't paying attention. He was talking about a TV program that showed a male baboon killing a zebra, that's how strong they were. A monkey that could kill something as big as a horse! Bud Schwartz was tuned out entirely; he was sizing up the two new men. The tall one, God Almighty, he was trouble. Built like a grizzly but that wasn't the worst of it; the worst was the eyes. Bud Schwartz could spot a doper two miles away; this guy was buzzing like a yellow jacket. The other one was no prize, dull-eyed and cold, but at least he was of normal dimensions. What caught Bud Schwartz's eye was the Cordovan briefcase that the smaller man was carrying.

'Get ready,' he said to Danny Pogue.

'But that ain't Kingsbury.'

'You don't miss a trick.'

'Bud, I don't like this.'

'Really? I'm having the time of my life.' Bud Schwartz stood up and approached the two strangers. 'Where's the old man?'

'Where's the files?' asked Pedro Luz.

'Where's the money?'

Churrito held up the briefcase. It was plainly stuffed with something, possibly fifty thousand in cash.

'Now,' said Pedro Luz, 'where's the damn files?'

'We give 'em to the old man and nobody else.'

Pedro Luz checked over both shoulders to make sure there

were no tourists around. In the same motion his right hand casually fished into the waistband of his trousers for the Colt. Before he could get to it, something dug into his right ear. It was another gun. *A burglar with a gun*! Pedro Luz was consumed with fury.

Bud Schwartz said, 'Don't move.' The words fluttered out. Danny Pogue gaped painfully.

Churrito laughed. 'Good work,' he said to Pedro Luz. 'Excellent.'

'I'm gonna be straight about this,' said Bud Schwartz, 'I don't know shit about guns.'

The veins in Pedro Luz's neck throbbed like a tangle of snakes. He was seething, percolating in hormones, waiting for the moment. The gun barrel cut into his earlobe but he didn't feel a thing. Trying not to snarl, he said, 'Don't push it, *chico*.'

'I ain't kidding,' Bud Schwartz said in a voice so high he didn't recognize it as his own. 'You even fart, I may blow your brains out. Explain that to your friend.'

Churrito seemed indifferent to the idea. He shrugged and handed the briefcase to Danny Pogue.

'Open it,' Bud Schwartz told him.

Again Pedro Luz asked, 'Where are the files?' He anticipated that the burglars would soon be unable to answer the question, since he intended to kill them. And possibly Churrito while he was in the mood.

Even the baboons sensed trouble, for they had fallen silent in the boughs of the ficus. Danny Pogue opened the Cordovan briefcase and showed Bud Schwartz what was inside: sanitary napkins.

'Too bad,' said Bud Schwartz. And it was too bad. He had no clue what to do next. Danny Pogue took one of the maxi-pads out of the briefcase and examined it, as if searching for insight.

Pedro Luz's steroid-marinated glands were starting to cook. Infused with the strength of a thousand warriors, he announced that he wouldn't let a mere bullet spoil Mr. Kingsbury's plan. He told Bud Schwartz to go ahead and fire, and went so far as to reach up and seize the burglar's arm.

As they struggled, Pedro Luz said, 'Shoot me, you pussy! Shoot me now!'

Out of the corner of his eye, Bud Schwartz spotted Danny Pogue running away in the general direction of the gorilla compound—moving impressively for someone fresh off crutches.

Just as Pedro Luz was preparing to snap Bud Schwartz's arm like a matchstick, Mrs. Kingsbury's chrome-plated pistol shook loose from the burglar's fingers and flew over the moat. The gun landed in a pile of dead leaves at the foot of the ficus tree, where it was retrieved by a laconic baboon with vermilion buttocks. Bud Schwartz wasn't paying attention, what with Pedro Luz hurling him to the ground and kneeling on his neck and trying to twist his head off. Meanwhile the other man was going through Bud Schwartz's trousers in search of the car keys.

When Bud Schwartz tried to shout for help, Pedro Luz slapped a large moist hand over his mouth. It was then that Bud Schwartz spotted the bandaged nub of the right index finger, and assimilated in his dying deoxygenated consciousness the probability that this was the same goon who had brutalized Molly McNamara. The burglar decided, in the hastening gray twilight behind his eyeballs, that the indignity of being found mugged and dead in a monkey park might be mitigated by a final courageous deed, such as disfiguring a murderous steroid freak—which Bud Schwartz attempted to do by sucking Pedro Luz's hand into his jaws and chomping down with heedless ferocity.

The wailing of Pedro Luz brought the baboon colony to life, and a hellish chorus enveloped the three men as they fought on the ground. A gunshot was heard, and the monkeys scattered adroitly to the highest branches of the graceful old tree.

Pedro Luz rolled off Bud Schwartz and groped with his bloody paw for the Colt. It was still in his waistband. Only two things prevented him from shooting the burglar: the sight of fifty chattering children skipping toward him down the monkey trail, and the sight of Churrito lying dead with a grape-sized purple hole beneath his left eye.

Pedro Luz pushed himself to his feet, stepped over the body and ran. Bud Schwartz did the same—much more slowly and in the opposite direction—but not before pausing to contemplate the visage of the dead Nicaraguan. Judging by the ironic expression on Churrito's face, he knew exactly what had happened to him.

Now the killer was halfway up the ficus tree, barking and slobbering and shaking the branches. Mrs. Kingsbury's gun glinted harmlessly in the brackish shallows, where the startled baboon had dropped it.

The oxygen returning to Bud Schwartz's head brought a chilling notion that maybe the monkey had been aiming the damn thing. Maybe he'd even done it before. Stranger things had occurred in Miami.

Bud Schwartz lifted the keys to the Cutlass from the dead man's hand and jogged away just as Miss Juanita Pedrosa's kindergarten class marched into the plaza.

23

Francis X. Kingsbury was on the thirteenth green at the Ocean Reef Club when Charles Chelsea caught up with him and related the problem.

'Holy piss,' said Kingsbury as Jake Harp was about to putt. 'If it's not one thing, it's—hell, you deal with it, Charlie. Isn't that what I pay you for, to deal with this shit?'

Jake Harp pushed the putt to the right. He looked up stonily and said, 'Thank you both very much.'

'Sorry,' Chelsea said. 'We've got a little emergency here.'

Kingsbury said, 'If you're gonna be a crybaby, Jake, then do it over. Take another putt. And you, Charlie, what emergency? This is nothing, a goddamn prank.'

Charles Chelsea suggested that it was considerably more serious than a prank. 'Every television station in South Florida received a copy, Mr. Kingsbury. Plus the *Herald* and the *New York Times*. We'll be getting calls all day, I expect.'

He followed Kingsbury and Jake Harp to the fourteenth tee. 'The reason I say it's serious, we've got less than a week until the Summerfest Jubilee.' It was set for August 6, the day Kingsbury had rescheduled the arrival of the phony five-millionth visitor to the Amazing Kingdom of Thrills. The postponement caused by the truck accident had been a blessing in one way—it had given Charles Chelsea time to scout for a flashy new giveaway car. The 'classic' Corvair had been junked in favor of a jet-black 300-Z, which had been purchased at bargain price from the estate of a murdered amphetamine dealer. Chelsea was further buoyed by the news that NBC weatherman Willard Scott had tentatively agreed to do a live broadcast from the Kingdom on Jubilee morning, as long as Risk Management cleared it with the network.

Overall, the publicity chief had been feeling fairly positive about Summerfest until some worm from the *Herald* called up to bust his hump about the press release.

What press release? Chelsea had asked.

The one about hepatitis, said the guy from the newspaper. The hepatitis epidemic among Uncle Ely's Elves.

In his smoothest, most controlled tone, Chelsea had asked the newspaper guy to please fax him a copy. The sight of it creeping off the machine had sent a prickle down the ridge of his spine.

As Jake Harp prepared to tee off, Chelsea showed the press release to Francis X. Kingsbury and said, 'It's ours.'

'What the hell you—I don't get it. Ours?'

'Meaning it's the real thing. The stationery is authentic.'

Kingsbury frowned at the letterhead. 'Jesus Christ, then we got some kinda mole. That what you're saying? Somebody on the inside trying to screw with our plans?'

'Not necessarily,' Chelsea said.

Jake Harp hooked his drive into a fairway bunker. He said, 'Don't you boys know when to shut up?'

This time Charles Chelsea didn't bother to apologize. He itched to remind Jake Harp that dead silence hadn't helped him one bit in the '78 Masters, when he'd four-putted the third hole at Augusta and let Nicklaus, Floyd, everybody and their mothers blow right past him.

Kingsbury said, 'Probably it's some bastard from Disney. A ringer, hell, I should've known. Somebody they sent just to screw me up for the summer.'

'It's nobody on the inside,' said Chelsea. 'It wasn't done on one of our typewriters.'

'Who then? I mean, why in the name of fuck?'

Jake Harp marveled at the inventive construction of Kingsbury's profanity. He imagined how fine it would feel to take a two-iron and pulverize the man's skull into melon rind. Instead he said, 'You're up, Frank.'

Charles Chelsea stood back while Kingsbury took a practice swing. It was not a thing of beauty. From the safety of the cart path, Chelsea said, 'I think it's Joe Winder. The fellow we fired last week. The one we've had some trouble with.'

'What makes you so sure—wait, Christ, didn't he used to work for The Rat?'

'Yes, briefly. Anyway, there's some stationery missing from Publicity. I thought you ought to know.'

'How much?'

'Two full boxes,' Chelsea replied. Enough to do one fake press release every day for about three years. Or one hundred a day until the Summerfest Jubilee.

Kingsbury knocked his drive down the left side of the fairway and grunted in approval. He plopped his butt in the golf cart and said to Chelsea: 'Let me see it one more time.'

Chelsea gave him the paper and climbed on the back of the cart, wedging himself between the two golf bags. He wondered if this was how the Secret Service rode when the President was playing.

Pointing over Kingsbury's shoulder, Chelsea said, 'It's definitely Winder's style. I recognize some of the dry touches.'

The press release said:

> Medical authorities at the Amazing Kingdom of Thrills announced today that the outbreak of viral hepatitis that struck the popular theme park this week is 'practically under control.'
>
> Visitors to the Amazing Kingdom are no longer in immediate danger of infection, according to specialists who flew in from the National Center for Disease Control in Atlanta. So far, five cases of hepatitis have been positively diagnosed. All the victims were actors who portray Uncle Ely's Elves, a troupe of mischievous trolls who frolic and dance in daily performances throughout the park.
>
> Experts say there is no reason to suspect that the highly contagious disease is being transmitted in the food and beverages being served at the Amazing Kingdom. A more likely source is the vending machine located in a dressing room often used by Uncle Ely's Elves and several other performers.
>
> Charles Chelsea, vice president in charge of publicity, said:

'We know that the candy machine down there hadn't been serviced for about seven months. There are serious questions regarding the freshness and edibility of some of the chocolate products, as well as the breath mints. All items have been removed from the machine and are presently being tested for contamination.'

Although no cases of hepatitis have been reported among visitors to the Amazing Kingdom, Monroe County health officials advise testing for anyone who has had recent contact with any of Uncle Ely's Elves—or food products handled by the elves. This advisory applies to all persons who might have posed for photographs or danced with one of the little people during the Nightly Pageant of Tropics.

Moe Strickland, the veteran character actor who popular-ized the role of Uncle Ely, said the stricken performers are resting quietly at Baptist Hospital in Miami, and are expected to recover. He added, 'I'm worried about what the kids will think when they don't see us around the park for a few weeks. I guess we'll have to tell them that Uncle Ely took the elves on a summer vacation to Ireland, or wherever it is that elves go.'

Chelsea said there are no plans to close the Amazing Kingdom to the public. 'This was a freakish incident, and we are confident that the worst is over,' he said. 'From now on, we get back to the business of having fun.'

Beginning tonight, the Amazing Kingdom of Thrills will present a multi-media tribute to Vance and Violet, the last surviving blue-tongued mango voles. The gentle animals were stolen from the park ten days ago in a daring daylight robbery, and later died tragically.

The show will be presented at 8 p.m. in the Rare Animal Pavilion, and will feature color slides, video-tapes, rare out-door film footage and a Claymation exhibit. Admission is $4 for adults, $2.50 for children.

Kingsbury reread the press release as they jolted down the cart path with Jake Harp at the wheel. When they stopped next to his golf ball, Kingsbury shoved the paper back at Chelsea. 'It sounds awfully damn . . . what's the word?'

'Authentic, sir. This is what we're up against.'

'I mean, hell, it sure puts me off the candy machines.'

'It's fooling the reporters, too,' Chelsea said.

'You say this maniac's got—what, two goddamn boxes?'

'That's what's missing.'

Jake Harp said, 'If you're not going to play that lie, pick the damn thing up.'

Kingsbury paid no attention. 'I guess we'll need—obviously, what am I saying!—get a new letterhead for Publicity.'

'I ordered it this morning,' Chelsea reported. 'I'm afraid it won't be ready for two weeks.'

'Don't tell me—God, two weeks. So what do we do if your theory's right? If it's Winder, I mean.' Kingsbury took his stance and rifled a six–iron dead into the heart of a tea-colored pond.

'See what happens when you run your mouth,' said Jake Harp.

'The options are limited,' Chelsea told Kingsbury. 'Do we come right out and admit it's a fake? A disgruntled former employee, blah, blah, blah. Or do we roll with it? Take the hit and hope it's over.'

'Is that your advice? Roll with it?'

'For now, yes.'

'Me, too,' Francis Kingsbury said. 'Besides, Pedro's on the case.' A brand-new golf ball appeared in Kingsbury's right hand, and he dropped it with a flourish on the fairway. This time he nailed the six–iron to the center of the green, fifteen feet from the flag.

Jake Harp blinked sullenly and said nothing.

A duel.

That's how Charles Chelsea saw it. The ultimate test of skills. He warmed up the word processor and began to write:

> The outbreak of viral hepatitis among performers at the Amazing Kingdom of Thrills was not as serious as first believed, according to a respected epidemiologist who visited the popular tourist attraction Friday.
>
> The disease was confined to only four persons, none of whom became seriously ill, according to Dr. Neil Shulman, an international expert on liver pathology.

'Visitors to the Amazing Kingdom are in absolutely no danger,' Dr. Shulman declared. 'There's no evidence that the disease originated here. The food and beverages I've sampled are perfectly safe—and tasty, too!'

Initially it was believed that five persons were infected with hepatitis. Later, however, it was determined that one of the ill employees was actually suffering from gallstones, a common and non-transmittable disorder.

The four men who were diagnosed with hepatitis all began showing symptoms on Wednesday morning. Contrary to earlier reports, however, the victims did not contrac the virus from contaminated candy purchased at a vending machine in the Amazing Kingdom. It is now believed that the men—all of whom portray members of Uncle Ely's Elves—became infected during a recent promotional trip to the Caribbean aboard a Nassau-based cruise ship.

Moe Strickland, the crusty character actor who immortalized the character of Uncle Ely, recalled how some of his troupe had complained of 'funky-tasting lobster' during the four-day excursion. Viral hepatitis has an incubation period of 15 to 45 days.

Those who were stricken spent only one night in the hospital, and are now resting comfortably at home. Although their conditions are good, they will not return to work until doctors are sure that they are not contagious.

Dr. Shulman, who has written extensively for national medical journals, said he is certain that the disease has been contained, and that no other employees or visitors to the Amazing Kingdom are in jeopardy. 'It's as safe as can be,' he said. 'In fact, I'm staying over the weekend myself so I can ride the new porpoise!'

Skimming the text, Charles Chelsea changed the word 'outbreak' to 'incidence.' Then, with uncharacteristic fire, he punched the Send button.

To an invisible enemy he snarled, 'All right, Joey. It's go time.'

The queasy feeling that always accompanied the prospect of bad publicity had given way to a fresh sense of challenge; Chelsea felt he'd been training his whole professional life for such a test.

He was up against an opponent who was talented, ruthless and quite possibly insane.

As much as Chelsea feared and distrusted Winder, he respected his creative skills: the vocabulary, so rich in adjectives; the glib turn of an alliterative phrase—and, of course, the speed. Joe Winder was the fastest writer that Chelsea had ever seen.

Now it was just the two of them: Winder, holed up God knows where, hammering out inflammatory libels as fast as his fingers could fly. And on the other end, Chelsea himself, waiting to catch these malicious grenades and smother them. The alternative—meaning, to tell the truth—was unthinkable. To admit a hoaxster was loose, forging demented fantasies on Amazing Kingdom letterhead . . . what a story *that* would make. In their excitement the media would come all over themselves. Even worse, each publicity announcement from the theme park would be scrutinized severely by reporters and editors, whose careers are seldom enhanced by getting duped into print. One thing that Charles Chelsea (or any PR flack) didn't need was a more toxic level of skepticism and suspicion among the journalists he was supposed to manipulate.

So telling the truth about Joe Winder was out of the question. Whatever revolting fable Winder concocted next, Chelsea would be ready to extinguish it with press releases that were both calm and plausible. One pack of lies softening another.

It was going to be one roaring hell of a battle.

As the Publicity Department's fax machines were launching Chelsea's counterattack against the hepatitis scare, Moe Strickland arrived to bitch about sick pay and what the almighty Screen Actors Guild would say.

He lit up a cigar and said, 'The union would go nuts.'

'We don't recognize the union,' Chelsea said coolly. 'I really don't understand your objections, Moe. Most people would kill for two weeks off.'

Moe Strickland protested with a wet cough. 'You're docking us sick days, that's the objection. Because we're not really sick.'

'That's something to be taken up with Personnel. It's simply not my bailiwick.' Charles Chelsea waved his hands to clear the rancid smoke. The office was starting to smell like dead mice.

'I don't see why they can't just give us two weeks paid,' said Moe Strickland, 'and leave us our sick days. Whatever happened, it's sure not our fault.'

'No, it's not,' Chelsea agreed. 'Listen to me, Moe. Uncle Ely and the Elves are on vacation, all right? They went to Ireland. That's the official story.'

'For Christ's sake—Ireland? Does Ely sound like an Irish name?' Moe Strickland sneered in contempt.

'I'm not here to argue,' Chelsea said. 'But I do wish to caution you against speaking to the media. All interview requests are to be routed through me, understand?'

'You mean like the newspapers.'

'Newspapers, television, anybody asking questions about a cruise. You tell them to call me. And make sure the elves do the same.'

'What, now you don't trust us?'

'No interviews, Moe. The order comes straight from Mr. X.'

'Figures,' said Moe Strickland. 'What's the name of that disease? Tell me again.'

'Viral hepatitis.'

'Sounds terrible.'

'It's a nasty one,' Chelsea conceded.

'Who in hell would make up a story like that?' The actor smacked on the soggy stump of cigar. 'What kind of sick bastard would say such a thing?'

Chelsea did not reply. He was watching a string of brown drool make its way down Moe Strickland's snowy beard.

'I feel like suing the sonofabitch,' Moe Strickland remarked.

Chelsea said, 'Don't take it personally. It's got nothing to do with you.'

'I never had hepatitis. Is it some kind of dick disease? Because if it is, we're definitely suing the bastard. The boys're as clean as a whistle down there and they can sure prove it.'

'Moe,' said Chelsea, 'please settle down.'

'Does this mean we can't march in the Jubilee?'

'Not as Uncle Ely and the Elves. We'll get you some other costumes—gunslingers, how about that?'

'Oh great, midget gunslingers. No thanks.' On his way out the door, Moe Strickland spit something heavy into Charles Chelsea's wastebasket.

That night, Channel 7 devoted forty seconds to the hepatitis scare, closing the piece with a sound-bite from Charles Chelsea, cool in a crisp blue oxford shirt and tortoiseshell eyeglasses. The glasses were a new touch.

Not bad, thought Joe Winder, if you like the George Will look.

He was watching the news with a notebook on his lap. He called toward the kitchen: 'He got the number of victims down from five to four. Plus he's planted the idea that the disease was picked up in the Caribbean, not at the Amazing Kingdom. Pretty damn slick on short notice!'

Carrie Lanier was fixing popcorn. 'So they're toughing it out,' she said.

'Looks that way.'

She came out and placed the bowl on the sofa between them. 'They've got to be worried.'

'I hope so.' Joe Winder thanked her again for stealing the letterhead paper from the stockroom in the Publicity Department. 'And for renting the fax,' he added. 'I'll pay you back.'

'Not necessary, sir. Hey, I heard somebody shot up some rental cars on Card Sound Road.'

'Yeah, it was on the news.'

'Did they catch the guy?'

'No,' he said, 'and they won't.' He wondered if Skink's sniper attack was the beginning of a major offensive.

Carrie pointed at the television. 'Hey, look, it's Monkey Mountain!'

A blue body bag was being carried out of the amusement park. A florid middle-aged schoolteacher, a Miss Pedrosa, was being interviewed about what happened. She said her students thought the man was merely sleeping, not dead. The news reporter said the victim was believed to be a recent immigrant, a Latin male in his mid-thirties. A police detective at the scene of the shooting said it appeared to be a suicide. The detective's voice was nearly drowned out by the jabbering of angry baboons in a tree behind him.

Carrie said, 'Well, Mr. X ought to be happy. Finally someplace else is getting bad press.'

'Strange place for a suicide,' observed Joe Winder.

Carrie Lanier stuffed a handful of popcorn into his mouth. 'They gave me my new costume today. You're gonna die.'

'Let's see.'

It was a white fishnet tank suit. Carrie put it on and struck a Madonna pose. 'Isn't it awful?' she said.

Joe Winder said she looked irresistibly slutty. 'The Indians aren't going to like it, though.'

'I've got a headband, too. And a black wig.'

'The Seminoles didn't wear fishnets; they used them on bass. By the way, are those your nipples?'

'Who else's would they be?'

'What I mean is, isn't there supposed to be something underneath?'

'A tan body stocking,' Carrie said. 'I must've forgot to put it on.'

Winder told her not to bother. Exuberantly she positioned herself on his lap and fastened her bare legs around his waist. 'Before we make love,' Carrie said, 'you've got to hear the song.'

It was a bastardized version of the famous production number in *Evita*. They both burst out laughing when she did the refrain. 'I can't believe it,' Joe Winder said.

Carrie kept singing, 'Don't Cry for Me, Osceola!' Winder buried his face in her breasts. Unconsciously he began nibbling through the fishnet suit.

'Now stop.' Carrie clutched the back of his head. 'I've forgotten the rest of the words.'

Still gnawing, Winder said, 'I feel like a shark.'

'You do indeed.' She pulled him even closer. 'I know a little boy who forgot to shave this morning, didn't he?'

'I was busy writing.' A muffled voice rising out of her cleavage.

Carrie smiled. 'I know you were writing, and I'm proud of you. What's the big news at the Kingdom tomorrow—typhoid? Trichinosis?'

He lifted his head. 'No more diseases. From now on, it's the heavy artillery.'

She kissed him on the nose. 'You're a very sick man. Why do I like you so much?'

'Because I'm full of surprises.'

'Oh, like this?' Carrie grabbed him and gave a little tug. 'Is this for me?'

'If you're not careful.'

'Hold still,' she told him.

'Aren't you going to take off that outfit?'

'What for? Look at all these convenient holes. We've just got to get you lined up.'

'It's a good thing,' Joe Winder said, 'it doesn't have gills.'

He held his breath as Carrie Lanier worked on the delicate alignment. Then she adjusted the Naugahyde sofa cushion behind his head, and braced her hands on the windowsill. The lights from the highway skipped in her eyes, until she closed them. Slowly she started rocking and said, 'Tonight we're shooting for four big ones.'

'Excuse me?'

'I told you, Joe, I'm a very goal-oriented person.'

'I think I'm tangled.'

'You're doing fine,' she said.

He was still hanging on, minutes later, when Carrie stopped moving.

'What is it?'

'Joe, did you go back to the apartment tonight?' She was whispering.

'Just for a minute. I needed some clothes.'

'Oh boy.'

'What's the matter?'

Carrie said, 'Somebody's watching us. Somebody followed you

here.' She lowered herself until she was flat against him, so she couldn't be seen from the window. 'It's a man,' she said. 'He's just standing out there.'

'What's he look like?'

'Very large.'

'Guess I'd better do something.'

'Such as?'

'I'm not exactly sure,' Joe Winder said. 'I need to refocus here.'

'In other words, you want me to climb off.'

'Well, I think the mood has been broken.'

'The thing is—'

'I know. We'll need scissors.' His fingers, his chin, everything was tangled in the netting.

Outside the trailer, something moved. A shadow flickering across the windowpane. Footsteps crunching on the gravel. Then a hand on the doorknob, testing the lock.

Carrie's muscles tightened. She put her lips to his ear. 'Joe, are we going to die like this?'

'There are worse ways,' he said.

And then the door buckled.

24

Skink said he was sorry, and turned away. Joe Winder and Carrie Lanier scrambled to disengage, tearing the fishnet suit to strings.

'I heard noises,' said Skink. 'Thought there might be trouble.'

The adrenaline ebbed in a cold tingle from Winder's veins. Breathlessly he said, 'How'd you know I was here?'

'Followed you from the apartment.'

'In what—the bookmobile?'

'I've got friends,' Skink said.

While Joe Winder fastened his trousers, Carrie Lanier dived into a University of Miami football jersey. Skink turned to face them, and Carrie gamely shook his hand. She said, 'I didn't catch your name.'

'Jim Morrison,' said Skink. '*The* Jim Morrison.'

'No, he's not,' Winder said irritably.

Carrie smiled. 'Nice to meet you, Mr. Morrison.' Winder considered her cordiality amazing in view of Skink's menacing appearance.

Skink said, 'I suppose he told you all about me.'

'No,' Carrie replied. 'He didn't say a word.'

Skink seemed impressed by Joe Winder's discretion. To Carrie he said: 'Feel free to stare.'

'I am staring, Mr. Morrison. Is that a snake you're eating?'

'A mud snake, yes. Medium-rare.' He took a crackling bite and moved through the trailer, turning off the television and all the lights. 'A precaution,' he explained, peeking out a window.

In the darkness Carrie found Joe Winder's hand and squeezed it. Winder said, 'This is the man who saved my life a couple weeks ago—the night I got beaten up, and you gave me a lift.'

'I live in the hammocks,' Skink interjected. 'The heavy rains have brought out the snakes.'

Winder wondered when he would get to the point.

Carrie said, 'Can I ask about the red collar? Is it some sort of neck brace?'

'No, it isn't.' Skink crouched on his haunches in front of them, beneath the open window. The highway lights twinkled in his sunglasses.

'Events are moving haphazardly,' he said, gnawing a piece of the cooked reptile. 'There needs to be a meeting. A confluence, if you will.'

'Of whom?' Winder asked.

'There are others,' Skink said. 'They don't know about you, and you don't know about them.' He paused, cocking an ear toward the ceiling. 'Hear that? It's the plane. They've been tracking me all damn day.'

Carrie gave Joe Winder a puzzled look. He said, 'The rangers from Game and Fish—it's a long story.'

'Government,' Skink said. 'A belated pang of conscience, at tax-payer expense. But Nature won't be fooled, the damage is already done.'

Sensing trouble, Winder lurched in to change the subject. 'So who are these mysterious others?'

'Remember that afternoon at the Amazing Kingdom, when a stranger gave you something?'

'Yeah, some old lady at the Rare Animal Pavilion. She handed me a note and then I got my lights punched out.'

Skink said, 'That was me who slugged you.'

'What an odd relationship,' Carrie remarked.

'My specialty,' Joe Winder said. Then to Skink: 'Can I ask why you knocked the door down tonight? Your timing stinks, by the way.'

Skink was at the window again, lurking on the edge of the shadow. 'Do you know anyone who drives a blue Saab?'

'No—'

'Because he was waiting at your apartment this morning. Big Cuban meathead who works at the park. He saw you arrive.'

Skink dropped down again. He said to Winder, 'You were driving the young lady's car, right?'

'She loaned it to me. So what?'

'So it's got a parking sticker on the rear bumper.'

'Oh shit, you're right.' Joe Winder had completely forgotten; employees of the Amazing Kingdom were issued Petey Possum parking permits. Each decal bore an identification number. It was a simple matter to trace the car to Carrie Lanier.

'I need to go to fugitive school,' Winder said. 'This was really stupid.'

Carrie asked Skink about the man in the blue Saab. 'Did he follow Joe, too? Is he out there now?'

'He was diverted,' Skink said, 'but I'm sure he'll be here eventually. That's why we're leaving.'

'No,' Winder said, 'I can't.'

Skink asked Carrie Lanier for a paper napkin. Carefully he wrapped the uneaten segment of mud snake and placed it in a pocket of his blaze rainsuit.

He said, 'There'll be trouble if we stay.'

'I can't go,' Winder insisted. 'Look, the fax lines are already set up. Everything's in place right here.'

'So you've got something more in mind?'

'You know I do. In fact, you've given me a splendid inspiration.'

'All right, we'll wait until daybreak. Can you type in the dark?'

'It's been a while, but sure.' Back in the glory days, Winder had once written forty inches in the blackness of a Gulfport motel bathroom—a Royal manual typewriter balanced on his lap. This was during Hurricane Frederic.

Skink said, 'Get busy, genius. I'll watch the window.'

'What can I do to help?' Carrie asked.

'Put on some Stones,' said Skink.

'And some panties,' Winder whispered.

She told him to hush and quit acting like an old prude.

While the tow truck hooked up the Saab, Pedro Luz forced himself to reflect on events.

There he was, waiting for Winder to come out of the apartment when here comes this big spade highway patrolman knocking on the window of the car.

'Hey, there,' he says from behind those damn reflector shades.

'Hey,' says Pedro Luz, giving him the slight macho nod that says, I'm one of you, brother.

But the spade doesn't go for it. Asks for Pedro's driver's license and also for the registration of the Saab. Looks over the papers and says, 'So who's Ramex Global?'

'Oh, you know,' Pedro says, flashing his old Miami PD badge.

Trooper goes 'Hmmm.' Just plain 'Hmmm.' And then the fucker jots down the badge number, like he's going to check it out!

Pedro resists the urge to reach under the seat for his gun. Instead he says, 'Man, you're burning me. I'm sitting on a dude out here.'

'Yeah? What's his name?'

Pedro Luz says, 'Smith. José Smith.' It's the best he can do on short notice, with his brain twitching all crazy inside his skull. 'Man, you and that marked unit are burning me bad.'

Trooper doesn't act too damn concerned. 'So you're a police officer, is that right?'

'Hell,' Pedro says, 'you saw the badge.'

'Yes, I sure did. You're a long way from the city.'

'Hey, *chico*, we're in a war, remember.'

'Narcotics?' The trooper sounds positively intrigued. 'This man Smith, he's some big-time dope smuggler, eh?'

'Was,' Pedro says. 'He sees your car sitting out here, he's back in wholesale footwear.'

'Hmmm,' the spade trooper says again. Meanwhile Pedro's fantasizing about grabbing him around the middle and squeezing his guts out both ends, like a very large tube of licorice toothpaste.

'Don't tell me you're gonna run my tag,' Pedro says.

'Nah.' But the trooper's still leaning his thick black arms against the door of the Saab, his face not a foot from Pedro's, so

that Pedro can see himself twice in the mirrored sunglasses. Now
the trooper says: 'What happened to your finger?'

'Cat bite.'

'Looks like it took the whole top joint.'

'That's right,' says Pedro, aching all over, wishing he'd brought
his intravenous bag of Winstrol-V. Talking high-octane. Same
stuff they use on horses. One thousand dollars a vial, and worth
every penny.

Trooper says, 'Must've been some cat to give you a bite like
that.'

'Yeah, I ought to put the damn thing to sleep.'

'Sounds like a smart idea,' says the trooper, 'before he bites
you someplace else.'

And then the sonofabitch touches the brim of his Stetson and
says so long. Like John Fucking Wayne.

And here comes Winder, cruising out of the apartment with
an armful of clothes. Gets in the car—not his car, somebody
else's; somebody with an employee sticker from the Kingdom—
and drives off with the radio blasting.

Pedro Luz lays back cool and sly, maybe half a mile, waiting
until the cocky bastard reaches that long empty stretch on Card
Sound Road, south of the Carysfort Marina. That's where Pedro
aims to make the big move.

Until the Saab dies. Grinds to a miserable wheezing halt. A
Saab!

Pedro Luz is so pissed he yanks the steering wheel off its
column and heaves it into a tamarind tree. Only afterwards does
it dawn on him that Mr. X isn't going to appreciate having a
$35,000 automobile and no way to steer it.

An hour later, here comes Pascual's Wrecker Service. Guy
lifts the hood, can't find a thing. Slides underneath, zero. Then
he says maybe Pedro ran out of gas, and Pedro says don't be
an asshole. Guy pulls off the gas cap, closes one eye and looks
inside, like he can actually *see* something.

Then he sniffs real hard, rubs his nose, sniffs again. Then he
starts laughing like a fruit.

'Your friends fucked you up real good,' he says.

'What are you talking about?'

'Come here and take a whiff.'

'No, thanks,' Pedro says.

Guy hoots. 'Now I seen everything.'

Pedro's trying to figure out when it happened. Figures some-body snuck up and did it while he was talking to that hardass trooper. Which means the trooper was in on it.

'Did a number on your engine,' says the tow-truck man, chuckling way too much.

Pedro Luz grabs him by the arm until his fingers lock on bone. He says, 'So tell me. What exactly's in the gas tank?'

'Jack Daniels,' the guy says. 'I know that smell anywhere.'

So now Pedro's watching him put the hook to Mr. Kingsbury's Saab and wondering what else could go wrong. Thinking about the monkeys and shithead burglars and what happened to Chur-rito. Thinking about the black state trooper busting his balls for no reason, and how somebody managed to pour booze in the tank without Pedro even knowing it.

Pedro thinks he'd better shoot some horse juice in his arms as soon as possible, and get tight on Joe Winder's ass.

In one of his pockets he finds the scrap of paper where he wrote the decal number off the car Winder was driving. It's not much, but it's the only thing he's got to show for a long sorry morning.

So Pedro tells the tow-truck guy he's going to ride in the busted Saab on the way to the shop. Use Kingsbury's car phone to make a few calls.

Guy says no way, it's against company policy. Gotta sit up front in the truck.

Which is not what Pedro wants to hear after such a shitty day. So he tackles the guy and yanks his arms out of the sockets one at a time, pop-pop. Leaves him thrashing in the grass by the side of the road.

Jumps in the tow truck and heads for the Amazing Kingdom of Thrills.

*

The Mothers of Wilderness listened solemnly as Molly McNamara recounted the brutal assault. They were gathered in the Florida room of Molly's old house, where a potluck supper had been arranged on a calico tablecloth. Normally a hungry bunch, the Mothers scarcely touched the food; a huge bacon-cheese ball lay undisturbed on a sterling platter—a sure sign that the group was distracted.

And no wonder: Molly's story was appalling. No one dreamed that the battle against Falcon Trace would ever come to violence. That Molly had been attacked by thugs in her own apartment was horrifying; equally unsettling was her lurid description of the finger-biting episode. In disbelief, several of the older members fiddled frenetically with the controls to their hearing aids.

'Obviously we've struck a nerve with Kingsbury,' Molly was saying. 'Finally he considers us a serious threat.'

One of the Mothers asked why Molly had not called the police.

'Because I couldn't prove he was behind it,' she replied. 'They'd think I was daffy.'

The members seemed unsatisfied by this explanation. They clucked and whispered among themselves until Molly cut in and asked for order. The lawyer, Spacci, stood up and said it was a mistake not to notify the authorities.

'You're talking about a felony,' he said. 'Aggravated assault, possibly even attempted murder.'

One of the Mothers piped up: 'It's not worth dying for, Molly. They're already clearing the land.'

Molly's gray eyes flashed angrily. 'It is not too late!' She wheeled on Spacci. 'Did you file in federal court?'

'These things take time.'

'Can you get an injunction?'

'No,' said the lawyer. 'You mean, to stop construction? No, I can't.'

Molly drummed her fingers on the portable podium. Spacci was preparing to sit down when she jolted him back to attention: 'Give us a report on the blind trust.'

'Yes, well, I talked to a fellow over in Dallas. He tells me the paperwork comes back to a company called Ramex Global, which is really Francis Kingsbury—'

'We *know*.'

'—but the bulk of the money isn't his. It's from some S & L types. Former S & L types, I should say. Apparently they were in a hurry to invest.'

'I'll bet,' said one of the Mothers in the front row.

'They moved the funds through Nassau,' Spacci said. 'Not very original, but effective.'

Molly folded her arms. 'Perfect,' she said. 'Falcon Trace is being built with stolen savings accounts. And you people are ready to give up!'

'Our options,' the lawyer noted, 'are extremely limited.'

'No, they're not. We're going to kill this project.'

A worried murmuring swept through the Mothers. 'How?' one asked. 'How can we stop it now?'

'Sabotage,' Molly McNamara answered. 'Don't you people have any imagination?'

Immediately Spacci began waving his arms and whining about the ramifications of criminal misconduct.

Molly said: 'If it makes you feel better, Mr. Spacci, get yourself a plate of the chicken Stroganoff and go out on the patio. And take your precious ethics with you.'

Once the lawyer was gone, Molly asked if anyone else was having doubts about the Falcon Trace campaign. One board member, a devout Quaker, fluttered his hand and said yes, he was afraid of more bloodshed. Then he made a motion (quickly seconded) that the Mothers telephone the police to report the two men who had attacked Molly.

'We don't need the police,' she said. 'In fact, I've already retained the services of two experienced security men.' With both hands she motioned to the back of the room, where Bud Schwartz and Danny Pogue stood near an open door. Danny Pogue flushed at the introduction and puffed his chest, trying to look like a tough customer. Bud Schwartz focused sullenly on an invisible tarantula, dangling directly over Molly McNamara's hair.

Eventually the Mothers of Wilderness quit staring at the burglars-turned-bodyguards, and Molly resumed her pep talk. Danny Pogue picked up a spoon and sidled over to the cheese ball. Bud Schwartz slipped out the door.

In a butcher shop near Howard Beach, Queens, a man known as The Salamander picked up the telephone and said: 'Talk.'

'Jimmy gave me the number. Jimmy Noodles.'

'I'm listening,' said The Salamander, whose real name was Salvatore Delicato.

'I got Jimmy's number from Gino Ricci's brother.'

The Salamander said, 'Fine. Didn't I already say I was listening? So talk.'

'In case you wanna check it out—I'm calling from Florida. I did time with Gino's brother.'

'How thrilling for you. Now I'm hangin' up, asshole.'

'Wait,' said the voice. 'You been lookin' for a certain rat. I know where he is. The man who did the Zubonis.'

The Salamander slammed down his cleaver. 'Gimme a number I can call you back,' he said. 'Don't say another word, just tell me a number.'

The caller from Florida repeated it twice. Sal Delicato used a finger to write the numerals in pig blood on a butcher block. Then he untied his apron, washed his hands, combed his hair, snatched a roll of quarters from the cash register and walked three blocks to a pay phone.

'All right, smart guy,' he said when the man answered in Florida. 'First off, I don't know any Zuboni brothers.'

'I never said they was brothers.'

'You didn't?' Shit, thought The Salamander, I gotta pay closer attention. 'Look, never mind. Just hurry up and tell me what's so important.'

'There's this creep in the Witness Relocation Program, you know who I'm talking about. He testified against the Zuboni brothers, the ones you never heard of. Anyway, they gave this creep a new name, new Social Security, the whole nine yards. He's doing real nice for himself. In fact, he's worth a couple million bucks is what I hear.'

Sal Delicato said, 'You're a dreamer.'

'Well, maybe I got the wrong man. Maybe I got some bad information. I was under the impression you people were looking for Frankie King, am I wrong?'

'I don't know no Frankie King.'

'Fine. Nice talkin' with you—'

'Hold on,' said The Salamander. 'I probably know somebody who might be interested. What'd you say your name was?'

'Schwartz. Buddy Schwartz. I was with Gino's brother at Lake Butler, Florida. You can check it out.'

'I will.'

'In the meantime, you oughta talk to Mr. Gotti.'

'I don't know no Gotti,' said The Salamander. 'I definitely don't know no fucking Gotti.'

'Whatever.'

Over the phone Bud Schwartz heard the din of automobile horns and hydraulic bus brakes and jackhammers and police sirens. He felt glad he was in Miami instead of on a street corner in Queens. At the other end, Sal Delicato cleared his throat with a series of porcine grunts. 'You said they gave him a new name, right? This Frankie King.'

'Yep,' said Bud Schwartz.

'Well, what name does he got at the moment?'

'See, this is what I wanna talk about.'

'Sounds like you're playin' games, huh?'

Bud Schwartz said, 'No, sir. This ain't no game.'

'All right, all right. Tell you what to do: First off, you might already got some problems. The phone lines to my shop aren't so clean, understand?'

Bud Schwartz said, 'I'll be gone from here in a few days.'

'Be that as it may,' said The Salamander, 'next time you call me at the shop, do it from a pay booth—they got pay booths in Florida, right? And don't say shit, either. Just say you want five dozen lamb chops, all right? That's how I know it's you—five dozen lamb chops.'

'No problem,' said Bud Schwartz.

'Thirdly, it don't matter what phones we're on, don't ever mention that fucking name.'

'Frankie King?'

'No, the other one. The one starts with "G." '

'The one you never heard of?'

'Right,' said Salvatore (The Salamander) Delicato. 'That's the one.'

Later, drinking a beer on the porch, Danny Pogue said, 'I can't believe you done that.'

'Why not?' said Bud Schwartz. 'The asshole doublecrossed us. Tried to rip us off.'

'Plus what he done to Molly.'

'Yeah, there's that.'

Danny Pogue said, 'Do you think they'll kill him?'

'Something like that. Maybe worse.'

'Jesus, Bud, I wouldn't know how to call up the Mafia, my life depended on it. The Mafia!'

'It wasn't easy finding the right people. They're not in the Yellow Pages, that's for sure.'

Danny Pogue laughed uproariously, exposing cheese-spackled teeth. 'You're a piece a work,' he said.

'Yeah, well.' Bud Schwartz had surprised himself with the phone call. He had remained cool and composed even with a surly mob heavyweight on the other end of the line. Bud Schwartz felt he had braved a higher and more serious realm of criminality; what's more, he had single-handedly set in motion a major event.

Danny Pogue said, 'How much'll they give us for turning the bastard in?'

'Don't know,' said Bud Schwartz. 'The man's checking it out.'

Danny Pogue drained his beer and stared at his dirty tennis shoes. In a small voice he said, 'Bud, I'm really sorry I ran away at the monkey place.'

'Yeah, what a surprise. You taking off and leaving me alone to get my brains knocked out. Imagine that.'

'I got scared is all.'

'Obviously.' What the hell could he expect? Like all thieves, Danny Pogue was low on valor and high on self-preservation.

He said, 'It's okay if you killed that guy. I mean, it was definitely self-defense. No jury in the world would send you up on that one.'

Great, Bud Schwartz thought, now he's Perry Mason. 'Danny, I'm gonna tell you one more time: it wasn't me, it was a damn baboon.'

Here was something Danny Pogue admired about his partner; most dirtbags would have lied about what happened so they could take credit for the shooting. Not Bud—even if a monkey was involved. That was Danny Pogue's idea of class.

'I got a feeling they meant to kill us,' Bud Schwartz said. He had replayed the scene a hundred times in his head, and it always added up to a murderous rip-off. It made him furious to think that Francis Kingsbury would try it . . . so furious that he'd tracked down his old cellmate Mario, who steered him to Jimmy Noodles, who gave him the number of the butcher shop in Queens.

Nothing but revenge was on Bud Schwartz's mind. 'I want them to know,' he said to Danny Pogue, 'that they can't screw with us just 'cause we're burglars.'

The screen door squeaked open and Molly McNamara joined the men on the porch. Her eyes looked puffy and tired. She asked Danny Pogue to fix her a glass of lemonade, and he dashed to the kitchen. She adjusted her new dentures and said, 'The meeting went poorly. There's not much support for my ideas.'

One hand moved to her chest, and she took a raspy, labored breath.

Bud Schwartz said, 'You ain't feeling so good, huh?'

'Not tonight, no.' She placed a tiny pill under her tongue and closed her eyes. A flash of distant lightning announced a thunderstorm sweeping in from the Everglades. Bud Schwartz spotted a mosquito on Molly's cheek, and he brushed it away.

She blinked her eyes and said, 'You boys have been up to something, I can tell.'

'It's going to be a surprise.'

'I'm too old for surprises,' said Molly.

'This one you'll like.'

'Be careful, please.' She leaned forward and dropped her voice. 'For Danny's sake, be careful. He's not as sharp as you are.'

Bud Schwartz said, 'We look out for each other.' Unless there's trouble, then the little dork runs for the hills.

'There's a reason I can't spill everything,' Bud Schwartz said to Molly, 'but don't you worry.' She was in a mood, all right. He'd never seen her so worn out and gloomy.

Danny Pogue returned with a pitcher of lemonade. Molly thanked him and held her glass with both hands as she drank. 'I'm afraid we won't be able to count on the Mothers of Wilderness,' she said. 'I sensed an alarming lack of resolve in the meeting tonight.'

'You mean, they wimped out.'

'Oh, they offered to picket Falcon Trace. And sign a petition, of course. They're very big on petitions.' Molly sighed and tilted her head. The oncoming thunder made the pine planks rumble beneath their feet.

'Maybe it's me. Maybe I'm just a batty old woman.'

Danny Pogue said, 'No, you're not!'

Yes, she is, thought Bud Schwartz. But that was all right. She was entitled.

Molly gripped the arms of the chair and pulled herself up. 'We'll probably get a visitor soon,' she said. 'The tall fellow with the collar on his neck.'

'Swell,' Bud Schwartz muttered. His ribs still throbbed from last time.

'He's not to be feared,' Molly McNamara said. 'We should hear what he has to say.'

This ought to be good, thought Bud Schwartz. This ought to be priceless.

25

Early on the morning of July 29, a Sunday, the fax machine in the wire room of the *Miami Herald* received the following transmission:

REPTILE SCARE CLOSES THEME PARK;
HIGH WATER BLAMED

The Amazing Kingdom of Thrills will be closed Sunday, July 29, due to an infestation of poisonous snakes caused by heavy summer rains and flooding. Cottonmouth moccasins numbering 'in the low hundreds' swarmed the popular South Florida theme park over the weekend, according to Charles Chelsea, vice president of publicity.

Several workers and visitors were bitten Saturday, but no deaths were reported. 'Our medical-emergency personnel responded to the crisis with heroic efficiency,' Chelsea stated.

Reptile experts say snakes become more active in times of heavy rainfall, and travel great distances to seek higher ground. Even the so-called water moccasin, which thrives in canals and brackish lagoons, becomes uncommonly restless and aggressive during flood-type conditions.

The cottonmouth is a pit viper known for its large curved fangs and whitish mouth. While extremely painful, the bite of the snake is seldom fatal if medical treatment is administered quickly. However, permanent damage to muscle and soft tissue often occurs.

The moccasin is prevalent throughout South Florida, although it is rare to find more than two or three snakes together at a time. Cluster migrations are a rarity in nature. 'They appeared to be hunting for toads,' Chelsea explained.

Officials ordered the theme park to be closed temporarily

> while teams of armed hunters captured and removed the wild reptiles, some of which were nearly six feet in length.
>
> Chelsea said that the Amazing Kingdom will reopen Tuesday morning with a full schedule of events. He added: 'While we are confident that the grounds will be perfectly safe and secure, we are also suggesting, as a precaution, that our visitors wear heavy rubber boots. These will be available in all sizes, for a nominal rental fee.'

Reporters began calling before eight o'clock. Charles Chelsea was summoned from home; he arrived bleary-eyed and tieless. Clutching a Styrofoam cup of black coffee, he hunched over the desk to examine Joe Winder's newest atrocity.

'Wicked bastard,' he said after reading the last line.

A secretary told him about the TV helicopters. 'We've counted five so far,' she reported. 'They're trying to get an aerial shot of the snakes.'

'The snakes!' Chelsea laughed dismally.

To ignite his competitive spirit, the secretary said, 'I can't believe they'd fall for a dumb story like this.'

'Are you kidding?' Chelsea buried his hands in his hair. 'Snakes are dynamite copy. Anything with a snake, the media eats it up.' A law of journalism of which Joe Winder, the ruthless sonofabitch, was well aware.

Chelsea sucked down the dregs of the coffee and picked up the phone. Francis X. Kingsbury answered on the seventeenth ring.

'I've got some extremely bad news,' Chelsea said.

'Horseshit, Charlie, if you get my drift.' It sounded as if Kingsbury's hay fever was acting up. 'Calling me at home, Christ, what's your job description anyway—*professional pussy?* Is that what I hired you for?'

'No, sir.' The publicity man gritted his teeth and told Kingsbury what had happened. There was a long unpleasant silence, followed by the sound of a toilet being flushed.

'I'm in the can,' Kingsbury said. 'That's what you get for calling me at home.'

'Sir, did you hear what I said? About the snake story that Winder put out?'

'Yes, hell, I'm not deaf. Hold on.' Chelsea heard the toilet flush again. Grimly he motioned for his secretary to get him another cup of coffee.

On the other end, Kingsbury said, 'All right, so on this snake thing, what do you think?'

'Close the park for a day.'

'Don't be an idiot.'

'There's no choice, Mr. Kingsbury. Even if we came clean and admitted the press release was fake, nobody's going to believe it. They'll think we're covering up.' That was the insidious genius of Joe Winder's strategy.

Kingsbury said: 'Close the goddamn park, are you kidding? What about business?'

'Business is shot,' Chelsea replied. 'Nobody but reptile freaks would show up today. We're better off closing the Kingdom and taking our lumps.'

'Un-fucking-real, this is.'

'I forgot to mention, we'll also need to purchase some boots. Several hundred pairs.' Chelsea's fingers began to cramp on the telephone receiver. He said, 'Don't worry, I'll put something out on the wires right away.'

'Everything's under control, blah, blah, blah.'

'Right,' said Chelsea. Now he could hear the water running in Francis Kingsbury's sink.

'I bruffing my teef,' Kingsbury gargled.

Chelsea waited for the sound of spitting. Then he said, 'I'll call a press conference for noon. We'll get somebody, some scientist, to say the snakes are almost gone. Then we'll reopen tomorrow.'

Kingsbury said, 'Four hundred grand is what this fucking clown is costing me, you realize? A whole day's receipts.'

'Sir, it could get worse.'

'Don't say that, Charlie.'

In a monotone Chelsea read the phony press release to Francis Kingsbury, who said: 'Christ Almighty, they get six feet long! These poison cottonheads do?'

'I don't know. I don't know how big they get.' Chelsea wanted to tell Kingsbury that it really didn't matter if the imaginary snakes were two feet or twenty feet, the effect on tourists was the same.

Over the buzz of his electric razor, Kingsbury shouted, 'What does he want—this prick Winder—what's he after?'

'Nothing we can give him,' Chelsea said.

'It's got to stop or he'll kill our business.'

'Yes, I know.'

'And I'll tell you what else,' Francis Kingsbury said. 'I'm very disappointed in that fucking Pedro.'

Molly McNamara was writing a letter to her daughter in Minneapolis when Danny Pogue rushed into the den. Excitedly he said: 'I just saw on the news about all them snakes!' His Adam's apple juked up and down.

'Yes,' Molly said, 'it's very odd.'

'Maybe you could get your people together. The Mothers of Wilderness. Maybe go down to Key Largo and demonstrate.'

'Against what?'

'Well, it said on the news they're killing 'em all. The snakes, I mean. That don't seem right—it ain't their fault about the high water.' Danny Pogue was rigid with indignation, and Molly hated to dampen the fervor.

Gently she said, 'I don't know that they're actually killing the snakes. The radio said something about capture teams.'

'No, unh-uh, I just saw on the TV. A man from the Amazing Kingdom said they were killing the ones they couldn't catch. Especially the preggy ones.' He meant 'pregnant.' 'It's that Kingsbury asshole, pardon my French.'

Molly McNamara capped her fountain pen and turned the chair toward Danny Pogue. She told him she understood how he felt. 'But we've got to choose our battles carefully,' she said, 'if we hope to get the public on our side.'

'So?'

'So there's not much sympathy for poisonous snakes.'

Danny Pogue looked discouraged. Molly said, 'I'm sorry, Danny, but it's true. Nobody's going to care if they use flame-throwers, as long as they get rid of the cottonmouths.'

'But it ain't right.'

Molly patted his knee. 'There's plenty of snakes out there. Not like the mango voles, where there were only two left in the entire world.'

With those words she could have hammered an icepick into Danny Pogue's heart. Morosely he bowed his head. As his environmental consciousness had been awakened, the vole theft had begun to weigh like a bleak ballast on his soul; he'd come to feel personally responsible for the extinction of the voles, and had inwardly promised to avenge his crime.

He said to Molly: 'What's that word you used before—"*atome*"?'

'Atone, Danny. A-t-o-n-e. It means making amends.'

'Yeah, well, that's me.'

Molly smiled and removed her reading glasses. 'Don't worry, we've all made mistakes in our lives. We've all committed errors of judgment.'

'Like when you shot me and Bud. Before you got to know us better.'

'No, Danny, that wasn't a mistake. I'd do the same thing all over again, if it became necessary.'

'You would?'

'Oh, now, don't take it the wrong way. Come here.' Molly reached out and took him by the shoulders. Firmly she pulled his greasy head to her breast. The heavy jasmine scent brought the tickle of a sneeze to Danny Pogue's nostrils.

Molly gave him a hug and said, 'Both you boys mean so much to me.' Danny Pogue might have been moved to tears, except for the familiar bluish glint of the pistol tucked in the folds of Molly's housedress.

He said, 'You want some tea?'

'That would be lovely.'

As soon as Carrie Lanier left for work, Skink curled up in the shower, turned on the cold water and went to sleep.

Joe Winder kept writing for thirty minutes, until his will dissolved and he could no longer concentrate. He dialed Miriam's house and asked for Nina.

'It's six-dirty inna morning,' Miriam complained.

'I know what time it is. May I speak to her, please?'

'What if chee no here?'

'Miriam, I swear to God—'

'All rye, Joe. Chew wait.'

When Nina came on the line, she sounded wide awake. 'This is very rude of you,' she said crossly, 'waking Miriam.'

'What about you?'

'I was writing.'

'Me, too,' Joe Winder said. 'You were working on your phone fantasies?'

'My stories, yes.'

'That's the main reason for the call. I had an idea for you.'

Nina said, 'I've got some good news, Joe. I'm getting syndicated.'

'Hey, that's great.' Syndicated? What the hell was she talking about. Ann Landers was *syndicated*. Ellen Goodman was syndicated. Not women who write about bondage on Olympic diving boards.

'There's a company called Hot Talk,' Nina said. 'They own, like, two hundred of these adult phone services. They're going to buy my scripts and market them all over. Chicago, Denver, even Los Angeles.'

'That's really something.'

'Yeah, in a few months I'll be able to get off the phones and write full-time. It's like a dream come true.'

She asked about Joe's idea for a fantasy and he described it. 'Not bad,' Nina admitted. 'It just might work.'

'Oh, it'll work,' Winder said, but Nina didn't take the bait. She expressed no curiosity. 'Remember,' he added, 'it has to be a fishnet suit with absolutely nothing underneath.'

'Joe, please. I understand the principle.'

He was hoping she would ask how he was doing, what he'd been up to, and so on. Instead she told him she'd better go because she didn't want to keep Miriam awake.

Winder fought for more time. 'Basically, I called to see how you're doing. I admit it.'

'Well, I'm doing fine.'

'Things might get crazy in the next week or so. I didn't want you to worry.'

'I'll try not to.' Her tone was disconcertingly sincere. Winder waited for a follow-up question, but none came.

He blurted: 'Are you seeing anybody?'

'Not exactly.'

'Oh?'

'What I mean is, there's a man.'

'Oh, ho!' A hot stab in the sternum.

'But we're not exactly seeing each other,' Nina said. 'He calls up and we talk.'

'He calls on the 976 number? You mean he's a customer?'

'It's not like the others. We talk about deep things, personal things—I can't describe it, you wouldn't understand.'

'And you've never actually met him?'

'Not face-to-face, no. But you can tell a lot from the way a person talks. I think he must be very special.'

'What if he's a hunchback? What if he's got pubic lice?' Joe Winder was reeling. 'Nina, don't you see how sick this is? You're falling in love with a stranger's voice!'

'He's very sensual, Joe. I can tell.'

'For God's sake, the man's calling on the come line. What does that tell you?'

'I don't want to get into it,' Nina said. 'You asked if I was interested in anyone, and I told you. I should've known you'd react this way.'

'Just tell me, is he paying for the telephone calls?'

'We've agreed to split the cost.'

'Sweet Jesus.'

'And we're meeting for dinner Tuesday up in the Gables.'

'Wonderful,' said Joe Winder. 'What color trench coat did he say he'd be wearing?'

'I hate you,' Nina remarked.

They hung up on each other at precisely the same instant.

Pedro Luz slithered beneath Carrie's mobile home. Lying on his back in the cool dirt, he listened to the shower running and laughed giddily. He placed both hands on a wooden floor beam and pushed with all his strength; he was certain that he felt the double-wide rise above him, if only a few millimeters. With a bullish snort, he tried again. To bench-press a mobile home! Pedro Luz grimaced in ecstasy.

He was proud of himself for tracing the car, even if the detective work entailed only the pushing of three lousy buttons on a computer. He was equally proud of himself for locating the address in the dark and remaining invisible to the occupants of the trailer. At dawn he had watched the woman drive off to work, leaving him alone with that crazy doomed bastard, Joe Winder.

Pedro Luz had spent a long time fueling himself for the task. He had strung the intravenous rigs in the storage room of the Security Department at the Amazing Kingdom of Thrills. There, stretched on a cot, he had dripped large quantities of horse steroids into both arms. Afterwards, Pedro Luz had guzzled nine Heinekens and studied himself naked in a full-length mirror.

The mirror examination had become a ritual to make sure that his penis and testicles were not shrinking, as Churrito had warned they would. Pedro Luz had become worried when his security-guard uniform had gotten baggy in the crotch, so every night he took a measuring tape and checked his equipment. Then he would leaf through some pornographic magazines to make sure he could still get a hard-on; on some evenings, when he was particularly anxious, he would even measure the angle of his erection.

On the night he went after Joe Winder, the angle was exactly zero degrees. Pedro Luz blamed it on the beer.

Inside the trailer, Winder finished typing another counterfeit press release, which said:

> The widow of a young scientist killed at the Amazing King-dom of Thrills has been offered a settlement of $2.8 million, officials of the popular amusement park have announced.
> The payment would be made in a single installment to

Deborah Koocher, age 31, of New York. Her husband, Dr. William Bennett Koocher, was a noted wildlife biologist who helped supervise the Endangered Species Program at the Amazing Kingdom. Dr. Koocher died two weeks ago in a tragic drowning at the park's outdoor whale tank. That incident is still under investigation.

Charles Chelsea, vice president of publicity, said the cash offer to Mrs. Koocher 'demonstrates our sense of loss and sorrow over the untimely death of her husband.'

Added Chelsea: 'Will was instrumental in our rare-animal programs, and his heroic efforts to save the blue-tongued mango vole won international acclaim.'

In a statement released Sunday morning, Francis X. Kingsbury, founder and chairman of the Amazing Kingdom, said that Dr. Koocher's death 'was a tragedy for all of us at the park. We had come to love and admire Will, who was as much a part of our family as Robbie Raccoon or Petey Possum.'

The $2.8 million settlement offer is 'a gesture not only of compassion, but fairness,' Mr. Kingsbury added. 'If Dr. Koocher's family isn't satisfied, we would certainly consider increasing the payment.'

Joe Winder reread the announcement, inserted the word 'completely' before 'satisfied,' and fed the paper into the fax machine. He considered phoning Nina again, but decided it was no use; the woman was groping recklessly for male companionship. What else could explain her irrational attraction to a disembodied masculine voice?

Besides, Joe had Carrie now—or she had him. The dynamics of the relationship had yet to be calibrated.

Winder was in the mood for acoustic guitar, so he put on some Neil Young and fixed himself four eggs, scrambled, and two English muffins with tangerine marmalade. Glancing out the kitchen window, he noticed a tow truck parked crookedly on the shoulder of the dirt lane. He didn't see a driver.

The shower had been running for some time. Winder cracked the door and saw Skink curled in a fetal snooze, cold water slapping on the blaze weather suit. Winder decided not to wake him.

Suddenly he heard a pop like a car backfiring, and a hole the size of a nickel appeared in the tile six inches above Skink's face. Then came another bang, another hole.

Joe Winder yelled and dived out of the doorway.

In a way, Carrie Lanier was glad that the Amazing Kingdom was closed. It meant an extra day to work on her singing, which was still rusty, and to design a new costume for Princess Golden Sun.

Driving back toward the mainland, she couldn't wait to tell Joe about all the TV trucks and helicopters at the park's main gate. A reporter from Channel 10 had approached the car and thrust a microphone in her face and asked if she had seen any snakes. Quickly Carrie had improvised a story about a teeming herd—she wasn't sure it was the right term—slithering across County Road 905 near Carysfort. The fellow from Channel 10 had marshaled his camera crew and sprinted off toward the van.

Carrie was impressed by the immediate and dramatic effect of Joe Winder's hoax: everyone was wearing sturdy rubber hip boots.

On the way home, she practiced another song from the show.

> 'You took our whole Indian nation,
> Stuck us on this reservation.
> Took away our way of life,
> The garfish gig and the gator knife.
> Seminole people! Seminole tribe!'

'YIt was a variation of a song called 'Indian Reservation,' which was recorded by Paul Revere and the Raiders, a band not generally remembered for its biting social commentary. Carrie Lanier thought the new lyrics were insipid, but she liked the simple tune and tom-tom rhythms. She was singing the third verse when she turned into the trailer park and spotted a bloated body-builder firing a pistol into the side of her double-wide.

Without hesitating, without even honking the horn, Carrie Lanier took aim.

Pedro Luz was so thoroughly engrossed in assassinating Joe Winder in the shower that he didn't hear the 1979 Buick Electra until it mowed a row of garbage cans ten feet behind him. Pedro Luz started to run but tripped over a garden hose and pitched forward, arms outstretched; it seemed as if he were tumbling in slow motion. When he stopped, the Buick was parked squarely on his left foot.

He lay there for a full minute, bracing for agony that never came: Each of the twenty-six bones in Pedro Luz's foot had been pulverized, yet the only sensation was a mildly annoying throb. Four thousand pounds of ugly Detroit steel on his toes and not even a twinge of pain. Incredible, Pedro thought; the ultimate result of supreme physical conditioning! Or possibly the drugs.

Apparently the driver had abandoned the Buick with the engine running. Steroids and all, Pedro Luz could not budge the sedan by himself. Meanwhile, the gunfire and crash had awakened other denizens of the trailer park; bulldogs yapped, doors slammed, babies wailed, a rooster cackled. Probably somebody had phoned the police.

Pedro Luz probed at the bloody burrito that was now his left foot, protruding beneath a Goodyear whitewall, and made a fateful decision.

What the hell, he mused. Long as I'm feeling no pain.

Dr. Richard Rafferty's assistant called him at home to say there was an emergency, he'd better come right away. When he arrived at the office, the doctor sourly observed a tow truck parked in the handicapped zone. Inside the examining room, a husky one-eyed man with a radio collar lay prone on the steel table.

Dr. Rafferty said: 'Is this some kind of joke?'

The couple who had brought the injured man said he had been shot at least twice.

'Then he's got a big problem,' said Dr. Rafferty, 'because I'm a veterinarian.'

The couple seemed to know this already. 'He won't go to a regular doctor,' Joe Winder explained.

Carrie Lanier added, 'We took him to the hospital but he refused to get out of the truck.'

Dr. Rafferty's assistant pulled him aside. 'I believe I saw a gun,' he whispered.

Skink opened his good eye and turned toward the vet. 'Richard, you remember me?'

'I'm not sure.'

'The night that panther got nailed by the liquor truck.'

Dr. Rafferty leaned closer and studied the face. 'Lord, yes,' he said. 'I do remember.' It was the same fellow who'd charged into the office with a hundred-pound wildcat in his bare arms. The doctor remembered how the dying panther had clawed bloody striations on the man's neck and shoulders.

Skink said, 'You did a fine job, even though we lost the animal.'

'We gave it our best.'

'How about another try?'

'Look, I don't work on humans.'

'I won't tell a soul,' Skink said.

'Please,' Joe Winder cut in, 'you're the only one he'll trust.'

Skink's chest heaved, and he let out a groan.

'He's lost some blood,' Carrie said.

Dr. Rafferty slipped out of his jacket and told the assistant to prepare a surgical tray. 'Oh, we've got plenty of blood,' the doctor said, 'but unless you're a schnauzer, it won't do you much good.'

'Whatever,' Skink mumbled, drifting light-headedly. 'If you can't fix me up, then put me to sleep. Like you would any old sick dog.'

26

Charles Chelsea decided that 'dapper' was too strong a word for Francis X. Kingsbury's appearance; 'presentable' was more like it.

Kingsbury wore a gray silk necktie, and a long-sleeved shirt to conceal the lewd mouse tattoo. The reason for the sartorial extravagance was an invitation to address the Tri-County Chamber of Commerce luncheon; Kingsbury intended to use the occasion to unveil a model of the Falcon Trace Golf and Country Club Resort Community.

Impatiently he pointed at Charles Chelsea's belly and said: 'So? The damn snake situation—let's hear it.'

'The worst is over,' said Chelsea, with genuine confidence. He had countered Joe Winder's moccasin attack with a publicity blurb announcing that most of the reptiles had turned out to be harmless banded water snakes that only *looked* like deadly cottonmouths. For reinforcement Chelsea had released videotape of a staged capture, peppered with reassuring comments from a local zoologist.

'By the end of the week, we can send back all those boots,' Chelsea said in conclusion.

'All right, that's fine.' Kingsbury swiveled toward the window, then back again. Restlessly he kneaded the folds of his neck. 'Item Number Two,' he said. 'This shit with the doctor's widow, is that cleared up yet?'

Here Chelsea faltered, for Joe Winder had stymied him with the Koocher gambit. The publicity man was at a loss for remedies. There was no clever or graceful way to recant a $2.8 million settlement offer for a wrongful death.

Anxiety manifested itself in a clammy deluge from Chelsea's armpits. 'Sir, this one's a stumper,' he said.

'I don't want to hear it!' Kingsbury clasped his hands in a manner suggesting that he was trying to control a homicidal rage. 'What was it, two-point-eight? There's no fucking way—what, do I look like Onassis?'

Chelsea's jaws ached from nervous clenching. He pushed onward: 'To rescind the offer could have very grave consequences, publicity-wise. The fallout could be ugly.'

'Grave consequences? I'll give you grave, Charlie. Two million simoleons outta my goddamn pocket, how's that for grave?'

'Perhaps you should talk to the insurance company.'

'Ha!' Kingsbury tossed back his head and snorted insanely. 'They just jack the rates, those assholes, every time some putz from Boise stubs his little toe. No way, Charlie, am I talking to those damn insurance people.'

In recent years the insurance company had tripled its liability premium for the Amazing Kingdom of Thrills. This was due to the unusually high incidence of accidents and injuries on the main attractions; the Wet Willy water slide alone had generated seventeen lawsuits, and out-of-court settlements totaling nearly three-quarters of a million dollars. Even more costly was the freakish malfunction of a mechanical bull at the Wild Bill Hiccup Corral—an elderly British tourist had been hospitalized with a 90-degree crimp in his plastic penile implant. The jury's seven-figure verdict had surprised no one.

There was no point rehashing these sad episodes with Francis Kingsbury, for it would only appear that Charles Chelsea was trying to defend the insurance company.

'I think you should be aware,' he said, 'Mrs. Koocher has retained an attorney.'

'Good for her,' Kingsbury rumbled. 'Let her explain to a judge what the hell her old man was doing, swimming with a damn killer whale in the middle of the night.'

Chelsea was now on the precipice of anger himself. 'If we drag this out, the *Herald* and the TV will be all over us. Do we really want a pack of reporters investigating the doctor's death?'

Kingsbury squinted suspiciously. 'What are you getting at?'

'I'm simply advising you to take time and think about this. Let me stall the media.'

The swiveling started again, back and forth, Kingsbury fidgeting like a hyperactive child. 'Two-point-eight-million dollars! Where the hell did that crazy number come from? I guess he couldn't of made it a hundred grand, something do-able.'

'Winder? No, sir, he tends to think big.'

'He's trying to put me out of business, isn't he?' Francis Kingsbury stopped spinning the chair. He planted his elbows on the desk and dug his polished fingernails into his jowls. 'The fucker, this is my theory, the fucker's trying to put me under.'

'You might be right,' Chelsea admitted.

'What's his—you hired him, Charlie—what's his angle?'

'I couldn't begin to tell you. For now, my advice is to get the insurance company in touch with Mrs. Koocher's lawyer. Before it blows up even worse.'

Kingsbury gave an anguished moan. 'Worse? How is that possible?'

'Anything's possible.' Chelsea was alarmed by the weariness in his own voice. He wondered if the tempest of bad news would ever abate.

The phone buzzed and Kingsbury plucked it off the hook. He listened, grunted affirmatively and hung up. 'Pedro's on his way in,' he said. 'And it better be good news or I'm gonna can his fat ass.'

Pedro Luz did not look like a cheery bundle of good tidings. The wheelchair was one clue. The missing foot was another.

Kingsbury sighed. 'Christ, now what?' He saw a whopper of a worker's comp claim coming down the pike.

'An accident,' Pedro Luz said, wheeling to a stop in front of Kingsbury's desk. 'Hey, it's not so bad.'

Chelsea noticed that the security man's face was swollen and mottled like a rotten melon, and that his massive arms had exploded in fresh acne sores.

Kingsbury drummed on a marble paperweight. 'So? Let's hear it.'

Pedro Luz said, 'I shot the bastard.'

'Yeah?'

'You better believe it.'

Charles Chelsea deftly excused himself, talk of felonies made him uncomfortable. He closed the door softly and nearly sprinted down the hall. He was thinking: Thank God it's finally over. No more dueling flacks.

Kingsbury grilled Pedro Luz on the details of the Joe Winder murder, but the security man edited selectively.

'He was in the shower. I fired eleven times, so I know damn well I hit him. Besides, I heard the shouts.'

Kingsbury asked, 'How do you know he's dead?'

'There was lots of blood,' said Pedro Luz. 'And like I told you, I fired almost a dozen goddamn rounds. Later I set the place on fire.'

'Yeah?' Kingsbury had seen footage of a trailer blaze on Channel 4; there had been no mention of bodies.

Pedro Luz said, 'It went up like a damn torch. One of them cheap mobile homes.'

'You're sure the bastard was inside?'

'Far as I know. And the bitch, too.'

Francis Kingsbury said, 'Which bitch? You're losing me here.'

'The dumb bitch he was staying with. The one who ran me over.'

Pedro Luz gestured at the bandaged stump on the end of his leg. 'That's what she did to me.'

The puffy slits made it difficult to read the expression in Pedro Luz's eyes. Kingsbury said, 'She hit you with a car?'

'More than that, she ran me down. Parked right on top of me.'

'On your foot? Jesus Christ.' Kingsbury winced sympathetically.

Pedro Luz said: 'Good thing I'm in shape.' Selfconsciously he folded his bulging arms and spread his hands in a way that covered the pimples.

Kingsbury said, 'So what happened?'

'What do you mean? I told you what happened.'

'No, I mean with the car on your foot. How'd you get free?'

'Oh, I chewed it off,' said Pedro Luz, 'right below the ankle.'

Kingsbury stared at the stump. He couldn't think of anything to say.

'Animals do it all the time,' Pedro Luz explained, 'when they get caught in traps.'

Francis Kingsbury nodded unconsciously. His eyes roamed the office, searching for a convenient place to throw up.

'The hard part wasn't the pain. The hard part was the reach.' Pedro Luz bent down to demonstrate.

'Oh Lord,' Kingsbury muttered.

'Like I said, it's a good thing I'm in shape.'

At the campsite, Joe Winder told Molly McNamara it was nice to see her again. Molly congratulated Joe for blowing up Kingsbury's bulldozers. Skink thanked Molly for the bottle of Jack Daniels, and briefly related how it had been utilized. Carrie Lanier was introduced to the burglars, whom she instantly recognized as the scruffy vole robbers. Bud Schwartz and Danny Pogue were stunned to learn that Robbie Raccoon was a woman, and apologized for knocking Carrie down during the heist.

The heat was throbbing and the hammock steamed. No breeze stirred off the water. A high brown haze of African dust muted the hues of the broad summer sky. Skink handed out cold sodas and tended the fire; he wore cutoff jeans, the panther collar and a thick white vest of tape and bandages.

'You were lucky,' Molly told him.

'Guy was aiming high,' Skink said. 'He assumed I'd be standing up.'

As most people do in the shower, thought Joe Winder. 'He also assumed that you were me,' he said.

'Maybe so.' Skink smeared a stick of EDTIAR bug repellent on both arms. Then he sat down under a buttonwood tree to count the mosquitoes biting his legs.

Carrie Lanier told the others about the breakneck ride to the veterinarian. 'Dr. Rafferty did a great job. We're lucky he knew somebody over at the Red Cross.'

Between insect frenzies, Danny Pogue struggled to follow the conversation. 'You got shot?' he said to Skink. 'So did me and Bud!'

Sharply, Molly cut in: 'It wasn't the same.'

'Like hell,' mumbled Bud Schwartz miserably. The humidity made him dizzy, and his arms bled from scratching the bugs. In addition, he wasn't thrilled about the lunch menu, which included fox, opossum and rabbit—Skink's road-kill bounty from the night before.

Joe Winder was in a lousy mood, too. The sight of Carrie's burned-out trailer haunted him. The fax machine, the Amazing Kingdom stationery, his stereo—all lost. Neil Young, melting in the flames. Helpless, helpless, helpless, helpless.

Skink said, 'It's time to get organized. Those damn John Deeres are back.' He looked at Winder. 'Now they've got cops on the site.'

'What can we blow up next?' Molly asked.

Skink shook his head. 'Let's try to be more imaginative.'

'All the building permits are in Kingsbury's name,' Winder noted. 'If he goes down, the project goes under.'

Carrie wondered what Joe meant by 'goes down.'

'You mean, if he dies?'

'Or gets bankrupt,' Winder said.

'Or lost,' added Skink, glancing up from his mosquito census.

Danny Pogue elbowed Bud Schwartz, who kept his silence. He had spoken again to the butcher in Queens, who had relayed an offer from unnamed friends of the Zubonis: fifty thousand for the whereabouts of Frankie King. Naturally Bud Schwartz had agreed to the deal; now, sitting in the wilderness among these idealistic crusaders, he felt slightly guilty. Maybe he should've ratted on Kingsbury for free.

'Mr. X had a terrible run of luck the last few days,' Carrie was saying, 'thanks to Joe.'

Skink got up to check the campfire. He said, 'It's time for a full-court press.'

'Each day is precious,' agreed Molly McNamara. She dabbed her forehead with a linen handkerchief. 'I think we should move against Mr. Kingsbury as soon as possible.'

Bud Schwartz crumpled a soda can. 'Why don't we hold off a week or so?'

'No.' Skink offered him a shank of opossum on a long-handled fork. He said, 'Every hour that passes, we lose more of the island.'

'Kingsbury's got worse problems than all of us put together,' said Bud Schwartz. 'If we can just lay back a few days.'

Joe Winder urged him to elaborate.

'Tell him, Bud, go on!' Danny Pogue was nearly bursting.

'I wish I could.'

Skink fingered the silvery tendrils of his beard. Towering over the burglar, he said, 'Son, I'm not fond of surprises.'

'This is serious shit.' Bud Schwartz was pleading. 'You gotta understand—heavy people from up North.'

Wiping the condensation from her eyeglasses, Molly said, 'Bud, what on earth are you talking about?'

Winder leaned toward Carrie and whispered: 'This is getting interesting.'

'No damn surprises,' Skink repeated balefully. 'We act in confluence, you understand?'

Reluctantly Bud Schwartz took a bite of fried opossum. He scowled as the warm juices dripped down his chin.

'Is that blood?' asked Danny Pogue.

Skink nodded and said, 'Nature's gravy.'

Suddenly he turned his face to the sky, peered toward the lemon sun and cursed vehemently. Then he was gone, running barefoot into the bright tangles of the hammock.

The others looked at one another in utter puzzlement.

Joe Winder was the first to stand. 'When in Rome,' he said, reaching for Carrie's hand.

Humanity's encroachment had obliterated the Florida panther so thoroughly that numerals were assigned to each of the few surviving specimens. In a desperate attempt to save the species, the Game and Fresh Water Commission had embarked on a program of monitoring the far-roaming panthers and tracking their movements by radio telemetry. Over a period of years most of the cats were treed, tranquilized and fitted with durable plastic collars that emitted a regular electronic signal on a frequency of 150 megahertz. The signals could be followed by rangers on the ground or, when the animal was deep in the swamp, by air. Using this system, biologists were able to map the territories traveled by individual cats, chart their mating habits and even locate new litters of kittens. Because the battery-operated collars were activated by motion, it was also possible for rangers to know when a numbered panther was sick or even dead; if a radio collar was inert for more than a few hours, it automatically began sending a distress signal.

No such alarm was transmitted if an animal became abnormally active, but the rangers were expected to notice any strange behavior and react accordingly. For instance, a panther that was spending too much time near populated areas was usually captured and relocated for its own safety; the cats had a long and dismal record of careless prowling along busy highways.

Sergeant Mark Dyerson had retrieved too many dead panthers that had been struck by trucks and automobiles. Recently the ranger had become certain that if something wasn't done soon, Panther 17 would end up the same way. The Game and Fish files indicated that the animal was a seven-year-old male whose original range stretched from Homestead south to Everglades National Park, and west all the way to Card Sound. Because this area was crisscrossed by high-speed roads, the rangers paid special attention to the travels of Number 17.

For months the cat had seemed content to hunker in the deep upland hammocks of North Key Largo, which made sense, considering the dicey crossing to the mainland. But Sergeant Dyerson had grown concerned when, two weeks earlier, radio readings on Number 17 began to show extraordinary, almost unbelievable movement. Intermittent flyovers had pinpointed the cat variously at Florida City, North Key Largo, Homestead, Naranja and South Miami—although Sergeant Dyerson believed the latter coordinates were a mistake, probably a malfunction of the radio tracking unit. South Miami was simply an impossible destination; not only was it well out of the panther's range, but the animal would have had to travel at a speed of sixty-five miles an hour to be there when the telemetry said it was. Unlike the cheetah, panthers prefer loping to racing. The only way Number 17 could go that far, Sergeant Dyerson joked to his pilot, is if it took a bus.

Even omitting South Miami from the readings, the cat's travels were inexplicably erratic. The rangers were concerned at the frequency with which Number 17 crossed Card Sound between Key Largo and the mainland. The only two possible routes—by water or the long bridge—were each fraught with hazards. It was Sergeant Dyerson's hope that Number 17 chose to swim the bay rather than risk the run over the steep concrete span, where the animal stood an excellent chance of getting creamed by a speeding car.

On July 29, the ranger took up the twin Piper to search for the wandering panther. The homing signal didn't come to life until the plane passed low over a trailer park on the outskirts of Homestead. It was not a safe place for humans, much less wild animals, and the panther's presence worried Sergeant Dyerson. Though the tawny cats were seldom visible from the Piper, the ranger half-expected to see Number 17 limping down the center lane of U.S. Highway 1.

Later that afternoon, Sergeant Dyerson went up again; this time he marked the strongest signal in thick cover near Steamboat Creek, on North Key Largo. The ranger couldn't believe it— twenty-nine miles in one day! This cat was either manic, or chained to the bumper of a Greyhound.

When Sergeant Dyerson landed in Naples, he asked an electrician to double-check the antenna and receiver of the telemetry unit. Every component tested perfectly.

That night, the ranger phoned his supervisor in Tallahassee and reviewed the recent radio data on Number 17. The supervisor agreed that he'd never heard of a panther moving such a great distance, so fast.

'Send me a capture team as soon as possible,' Sergeant Dyerson said. 'I'm gonna dart this sonofabitch and find out what's what.'

*

The twin Piper made three dives over the campsite. Joe Winder and Carrie Lanier watched from the bank of Steamboat Creek.

'Game and Fish,' Winder said, 'just what we need.'

'What do we do?' Carrie asked.

'Follow the water.'

They didn't get far. A tall uniformed man materialized at the edge of the tree line. He carried an odd small-bore rifle that looked like a toy. When he motioned to Joe and Carrie, they obediently followed him through the hammock out to the road. Molly McNamara and the two burglars already had been rounded up; another ranger, with a clipboard, was questioning them. There was no sign of Skink.

Sergeant Mark Dyerson introduced himself and asked to see some identification. Joe Winder and Carrie Lanier showed him their driver's licenses. The ranger was copying down their names when a gaunt old cracker, pulled by three lean hounds, came out of the woods.

'Any luck?' Sergeant Dyerson asked.

'Nope,' said the tracker. 'And I lost me a dog.'

'Maybe the panther got him.'

'They ain't no panther out there.'

'Hell, Jackson, the radio don't lie.' The ranger turned back to Joe Winder and Carrie Lanier. 'And I suppose you're bird-watchers, too. Just like Mrs. McNamara and her friends.'

Beautiful, thought Winder. We're bird-watchers now.

Playing along, Carrie informed the ranger they were following a pair of nesting kestrels.

'No kidding?' Sergeant Dyerson said. 'I've never met a birder who didn't carry binoculars—and here I get five of 'em, all at one time.'

'We're thinking of forming a club,' said Carrie. Joe Winder bit his lip and looked away. Molly's Cadillac took off, eastbound—a crown of white hair behind the wheel, the burglars slouched in the back seat.

'I'll give you this much,' the ranger said, 'you sure don't look like poachers.' A Florida Highway Patrol car pulled up and parked beside Sergeant Dyerson's Jeep. A muscular black trooper got out and tipped his Stetson at the ranger.

'Whatcha know?' the trooper said affably.

'Tracking a panther. These folks got in the way.'

'A panther? You *got* to be kidding.' The trooper's laughter boomed. 'I've been driving this stretch for three years and never saw a bobcat, much less a panther.'

'They're very secretive,' Sergeant Dyerson said. 'You wouldn't necessarily spot them.' He wasn't in the mood for a nature lesson. He turned to the old tracker and told him to run the frigging dogs one more time.

'Ain't no point.'

'Humor me,' said Sergeant Dyerson. 'Come on, let's go find your other hound.'

Once the wildlife officers were gone, the trooper's easygoing smile dissolved. 'You folks need a lift.'

'No, thanks,' Joe Winder said.

'It wasn't a question, friend.' The trooper opened the back door of the cruiser, and motioned them inside.

27

The trooper took them to lunch at the Ocean Reef Club. The clientele seemed ruffled by the sight of a tall black man with a sidearm.

'You're making the folks nervous,' Joe Winder observed.

'Must be the uniform.'

Carrie popped a shrimp into her mouth. 'Are we under arrest?'

'I'd be doing all three of us a favor,' Jim Tile said, 'but no, unfortunately, you're not under arrest.'

Winder was working on a grouper sandwich. Jim Tile had ordered the fried dolphin and conch fritters. The dining room was populated by rich Republican golfers with florid cheeks and candy-colored Izod shirts. The men shot anxious squinty-eyed glances toward the black trooper's table.

Jim Tile motioned for iced tea. 'I can't imagine why I've never gotten a membership application. Maybe it got lost in the mail.'

'What's the point of all this?' Winder asked.

'To have a friendly chat.'

'About what?'

Jim Tile shrugged. 'Flaming bulldozers. Dead whales. One-eyed woodsmen. You pick the subject.'

'So we've got a mutual friend.'

'Yes, we do.' The trooper was enjoying the fish platter immensely; despite the stares, he seemed in no hurry to finish. He said, 'The plane scared him off, right?'

'It doesn't make sense,' Winder said. 'They're not after him, they're after a cat. Why does he run?'

Jim Tile put down the fork and wiped his mouth. 'My own opinion—he feels a duty to hide because that's what the panther would've done. He wears that damn collar like a sacred obligation.'

'To the extreme.'

'Yeah,' the trooper said. 'I don't expect they'll find that missing dog. You understand?'

Carrie said, 'He's a very interesting person.'

'A man to be admired but not imitated.' Jim Tile paused. 'I say that with no disrespect.'

Winder chose not to acknowledge the warning. 'Where do you think he went?' he asked the trooper.

'I'm not sure, but it's a matter of concern.'

The manager of the restaurant appeared at the table. He was a slender young man with bleached hair and pointy shoulders and brand new teeth. In a chilly tone he asked Jim Tile if he were a member of the club, and the trooper said no, not yet. The manager started to say something else but changed his mind. Jim Tile requested a membership application, and the manager said he'd be back in a jiffy.

'That's the last we'll see of him,' the trooper predicted.

Joe Winder wanted to learn more about Skink. He decided it was safe to tell Jim Tile what the group had been doing in the hammock before the airplane came: 'We were hatching quite a plot.'

'I figured as much,' the trooper said. 'You know much about rock and roll?'

Carrie pointed at Winder and said, 'Hard core.'

'Good,' said Jim Tile. 'Maybe you can tell me what's a Mojo? The other day he was talking about a Mojo flying.'

'*Rising*,' Winder said. 'Mojo rising. It's a line from The Doors— I believe it's got phallic connotations.'

'No,' Carrie jumped in. 'I think it's about drugs.'

The trooper looked exasperated. 'White people's music, I swear to God. Sinatra's all right, but you can keep the rest of it.'

'Shall we discuss rap?' Joe Winder said sharply. 'Shall we examine the lyrical genius of, say, 2 Live Crew?' He could be very defensive when it came to rock. Carrie reached under the table and pinched his thigh. She told him to lighten up.

'Rikers Island,' Jim Tile said. 'Is there a song about Rikers Island?'

Winder couldn't think of one. 'You sure it's not Thunder Island?'

'No.' Jim Tile shook his head firmly. 'Our friend said he'd be leaving Florida one day. Go up to Rikers Island and see to some business.'

'But that's a prison,' Carrie said.

'Yeah. A prison in New York City.'

Joe Winder remembered something Skink had told him the first day at the campsite. If it was a clue, it foreshadowed a crime of undiluted madness.

Winder said, 'Rikers is where they keep that idiot who shot John Lennon.' He cocked an eyebrow at Jim Tile. 'You *do* know who John Lennon was?'

'Yes, I do.' The trooper's shoulders sagged. 'This could be trouble,' he added emptily.

'Our mutual friend never got over it,' Winder said. 'The other night, he asked me about the Dakota.'

'Wait a minute.' Carrie Lanier made a time-out signal with her hands. 'You guys aren't serious.'

Gloomily Jim Tile stirred the ice in his tea. 'The man gets his mind set on things. And these days, I've been noticing he doesn't handle stress all that well.'

Joe Winder said, 'Christ, it was only an airplane. It's gone now, he'll calm down.'

'Let's hope.' The trooper called for the check.

Carrie looked sadly at Winder. 'And here I thought *you* were bonkers,' she said.

Agent Billy Hawkins told Molly McNamara that the house was simply beautiful. Old-time Florida, you don't see pine floors like this anymore. Dade County pine.

Molly said, 'I've got carpenter ants in the attic. All this wet weather's got 'em riled.'

'You'd better get that seen to, and soon. They can be murder on the beams.'

'Yes, I know. How about some more lemonade?'

'No, thank you,' said Agent Hawkins. 'We really need to talk about this telephone call.'

Molly began to rock slowly. 'I'm completely stumped. As I told you before, I don't know a living soul in Queens.'

Hawkins held a notebook on his lap, a blue Flair pen in his right hand. He said, 'Salvatore Delicato is an associate of the John Gotti crime family.'

'Goodness!' Molly exclaimed.

'Prior arrests for racketeering, extortion and income-tax evasion. The phone call to his number was made from here. It lasted less than a minute.'

'There must be some mistake. Did you check with Southern Bell?'

'Miss McNamara,' Hawkins said, 'can we please cut the crap.'

Molly's grandmotherly expression turned glacial. 'Watch your language, young man.'

Flushing slightly, the agent continued: 'Have you ever met a Jimmy Nardoni, otherwise known as Jimmy Noodles? Or a man named Gino Ricci, otherwise known as Gino The Blade?'

'Such colorful names,' Molly remarked. 'No, I've never heard of them. Do you have my telephone bugged, Agent Hawkins?'

He resisted the impulse to tell her that Sal Delicato's telephone was tapped by a squadron of eavesdroppers—not only the FBI, but the New York State Police, the U.S. Drug Enforcement Administration, the Tri-State Task Force on Organized Crime and the Bureau of Alcohol, Tobacco and Firearms. The New York Telephone box on the utility pole behind The Salamander's butcher shop sprouted so many extra wires, it looked like a pigeon's nest.

'Let me give you a scenario,' Agent Hawkins said to Molly. 'A man used your phone to call Sal Delicato for the purpose of revealing the whereabouts of a federally protected witness now living in Monroe County, Florida.'

'That's outlandish,' Molly said. 'Who is this federal witness?'

'I imagine you already know.' Hawkins jotted something in

the notebook. 'The man who made the phone call, we believe, was Buddy Michael Schwartz. I showed you his photograph the last time we visited. You said he looked familiar.'

'I vaguely remember.'

'He has other names,' Hawkins said. 'As I told you before, Schwartz is wanted in connection with the animal theft from the Amazing Kingdom.'

'Wanted?'

'For questioning,' the agent said. 'Anyway, we believe the events are connected.' The ominous wiretap conversation had elevated the vole investigation from zero-priority to high-priority. Billy Hawkins had been yanked off a bank-robbery case and ordered to find out why anyone would be setting up Francis X. Kingsbury, aka Frankie King. The Justice Department had pretty much forgotten about Frankie The Ferret until the phone call to Sal Delicato. The renewed interest in Washington was not a concern for Frankie's well-being so much as fear of a potential publicity nightmare; the murder of a protected government informant would not enhance the reputation of the Witness Relocation Program. It could, in fact, have a profoundly discouraging effect on other snitches. Agent Hawkins was told to track down Buddy Michael Schwartz and then call for backup.

Molly McNamara said, 'You think this man might have broken into my house to use the phone!'

'Not exactly,' Hawkins said.

She peered at him skeptically. 'How do you know it was he on the line? Did you use one of those voice-analyzing machines?'

The FBI man chuckled. 'No, we didn't need a machine. The caller identified himself.'

'By name?' The blockhead! Molly thought.

'No, not by name. He told Mr. Delicato that he was an acquaintance of Gino Ricci's brother. It just so happens that Buddy Michael Schwartz served time with Mario Ricci at the Lake Butler Correctional Institute.'

Molly McNamara said, 'Could be a coincidence.'

'They shared a cell. Buddy and Gino's brother.'

'But still—'

'Would you have a problem,' the agent said, 'if I asked you to come downtown and take a polygraph examination?'

Molly stopped rocking and fixed him with an indignant glare. 'Are you saying you don't believe me?'

'Call it a hunch.'

'Agent Hawkins, I'm offended.'

'And I'm tired of this baloney.' He closed the notebook and capped the pen. 'Where is he?'

'I don't know what you're talking about.'

Hawkins stood up, pocketed his notebook, straightened his tie. 'Let's go for a ride,' he said. 'Come on.'

'No!'

'Don't make it worse for yourself.'

'You're not paying attention,' Molly said. 'I thought G-men were trained to be observant.'

Billy Hawkins laughed. 'G-men? I haven't heard that one in a long—'

It was then he noticed the pistol. The old lady held it impassively, with both hands. She was pointing it directly at his crotch.

'This is amazing,' said the agent. 'The stuff of legends.' Wait till the tough guys at Quantico hear about it.

Molly asked Billy Hawkins to raise his hands.

'No, ma'am.'

'And why not?'

'Because you're going to give me the gun now.'

'No,' said Molly, 'I'm going to shoot you.'

'Lady, gimme the goddamn gun!'

Calmly she shot him in the thigh, two and one-quarter inches below the left hip. The FBI man went down with a howl, clawing at the burning hole in his pants.

'I told you to watch your language,' Molly said.

The pop of the pistol brought Danny Pogue and Buddy Schwartz scrambling down the stairs. From a living-room window they cautiously surveyed the scene on the porch: Molly rocking placidly, a man in a gray suit thrashing on the floor.

Danny Pogue cried, 'She done it again!'

'Christ on a bike,' said Bud Schwartz, 'it's that dick from the FBI.'

The burglars cracked the door and peeked out. Molly assured them the situation was under control.

'Flesh wound,' she reported. 'Keep an eye on this fellow while I get some ice and bandages.' She confiscated Billy Hawkins's Smith & Wesson and gave it to Bud Schwartz, who took it squeamishly, like a dog turd, in his hands.

'It works best when you aim it,' Molly chided.

Danny Pogue reached for the barrel. 'I'll do it!'

'Like hell,' said Bud Schwartz, spinning away. He sat in the rocker and braced the pistol on his knee. The air smelled pungently of gunpowder; it brought back the memory of Monkey Mountain and the trigger-happy baboon.

Watching the gray-suited man squirm in pain, Bud Schwartz fought the urge to get up and run. What was the old bat thinking this time? Nothing good could come of shooting an FBI man. Surely she understood the consequences.

Danny Pogue opened the front door for Molly, who disappeared into the house with a pleasant wave. Danny Pogue sat down, straddling an iron patio chair. 'Take it easy,' he told the agent. 'You ain't hurt so bad.'

Billy Hawkins grunted up at him: 'What's your name?'

'Marcus Welby,' Bud Schwartz cut in. 'Don't he look like a doctor?'

'I know who *you* are,' the agent said. It felt as if a giant wasp were boring into his thigh. Billy Hawkins unbuckled his trousers and grimaced at the sight of his Jockey shorts soaked crimson.

'You assholes are going to jail,' he said, pinching the pale flesh around the bullet wound.

'We're just burglars,' said Danny Pogue.

'Not anymore.' Hawkins attempted to rise to his feet, but Bud Schwartz wiggled the gun and told him to stay where he was. The agent's forehead was sprinkled with sweat, and his lips were gray. 'Hey, Bud,' he said, 'I've seen your jacket, and this isn't your style. Assault on a federal officer, man, you're looking at Atlanta.'

Bud Schwartz was deeply depressed to hear the FBI man call him by name. 'You don't know shit about me,' he snapped.

'Suppose you tell me what the hell's going on out here. What's your beef with Frankie King?'

Bud Schwartz said, 'I don't know who you're talkin' about.'

Miraculously, Danny Pogue caught on before saying something disastrous. He flashed a checkerboard grin and said, 'Yeah, who's Frankie King? We never heard a no Frankie King.'

'Bullshit,' Agent Billy Hawkins growled. 'Go ahead and play it stupid. You're all going to prison, anyhow. You and that crazy old lady.'

'If it makes you feel any better,' said Danny Pogue, 'she shot us, too.'

The campsite was . . . gone.

'I'm not surprised,' Joe Winder said. He took Carrie's hand and kept walking. A light rain was falling, and the woods smelled cool.

Carrie asked, 'What do we do if he's really gone?'

'I don't know.'

Ten minutes later she asked if they were lost.

'I got turned around,' Winder admitted. 'It can't be too far.'

'Joe, where are we going?'

The rain came down harder, and the sky blackened. From the west came a roll of thunder that shook the leaves. The birds fell silent; then the wind began to race across the island, and Joe Winder could taste the storm. He dropped Carrie's hand and started to jog, slapping out a trail with his arms. He called over his shoulder, urging Carrie to keep up.

It took fifteen more minutes to find the junkyard where the ancient Plymouth station wagon sat on rusty bumpers. The yellow beach umbrella—still stuck in the dashboard—fluttered furiously in the gale.

Joe Winder pulled Carrie inside the car, and hugged her so tightly she let out a cry. 'My arms are tingling,' she said. 'The little hairs on my arms.'

He covered her ears. 'Hold on, it's lightning.'

It struck with a white flash and a deafening rip. Twenty yards away, a dead mahogany tree split up the middle and dropped a huge leafless branch. 'God,' Carrie whispered. 'That was close.'

Raindrops hammered on the roof. Joe Winder turned around in the seat and looked in the back of the car. 'They're gone,' he said.

'What, Joe?'

'The books. This is where he kept all his books.'

She turned to see. Except for several dead roaches and a yellowed copy of the *New Republic*, the station wagon had been cleaned out.

Winder was vexed. 'I don't know how he did it. You should've seen—there were hundreds in here. Steinbeck, Hemingway. Jesus, Carrie, he had García Márquez in Spanish. First editions! Some of the greatest books ever written.'

'Then he's actually gone.'

'It would appear to be so.'

'Think we should call somebody?'

'What?'

'Somebody up in New York,' Carrie said, 'at the prison. I mean, just in case.'

'Let me think about this.'

'I can't believe he'd try it.'

The thunderstorm moved quickly over the island and out to sea. Soon the lightning stopped and the downpour softened to a drizzle. Carrie said, 'The breeze felt nice, didn't it?'

Joe Winder wasn't listening. He was trying to decide if they should keep looking or not. Without Skink, new choices lay ahead: bold and serious decisions. Winder suddenly felt responsible for the entire operation.

Carrie turned to kiss him and her knee hit the glove compartment, which popped open. Curiously she poked through the contents—a flashlight, a tire gauge, three D-sized batteries and what appeared to be the dried tail of a squirrel.

And one brown envelope with Joe Winder's name printed in small block letters.

He tore it open. Reading the note, he broke into a broad smile. 'Short and to the point,' he said.

Carrie read it:

> Dear Joe,
> You make one hell of an oracle.
> Don't worry about me, just keep up the fight.
> We all shine on!

Carrie folded the note and returned it to the envelope. 'I assume this means something.'

'Like the moon and the stars and the sun,' Joe Winder said. He felt truly inspired.

28

The Amazing Kingdom of Thrills reopened with only a minimal drop in attendance, thanks to a three-for-one ticket promotion that included a free ride on Dickie the Dolphin, whose amorous behavior was now inhibited by four trainers armed with electric stun guns. Francis X. Kingsbury was delighted by the crowds, and emboldened by the fact that many customers actually complained about the absence of wild snakes. Kingsbury regarded it as proof that closing the Amazing Kingdom had been unnecessary, a costly overestimation of the average tourist's brainpower. Obviously the yahoos were more curious than afraid of lethal reptiles. A thrill is a thrill, Kingsbury said.

The two persons forced to sit through this speech were Pedro Luz and Special Agent Ron Donner of the U.S. Marshal Service. Agent Donner had come to notify Francis X. Kingsbury of a possible threat against his life.

'Ho! From who?'

'Elements of organized crime,' the marshal said.

'Well, fuck em.'

'Excuse me?'

'This is just, I mean really, the word is horseshit!' Kingsbury flapped his arms like a tangerine-colored buzzard. He was dressed for serious golf; even his cleats were orange.

Agent Donner said: 'We think it would be wise if you left town for a few weeks.'

'Oh, you do? Leave town, like hell I will.'

Pedro Luz spun his wheelchair slightly toward the marshal. 'Organized crime,' he said. 'You mean the Mafia?'

'We're taking it very seriously,' said Agent Donner, thinking: Who's the freak with the IV bag?

With the proud sweep of a hand, Francis Kingsbury introduced his chief of Security. 'He handles everything for the park and so on. Personal affairs, as well. You can say anything in front of him, understand? He's thoroughly reliable.'

Pedro Luz casually adjusted the drip valve on the intravenous tube.

The marshal asked, 'What happened to your foot?'

'Never mind!' blurted Kingsbury.

'Car accident,' Pedro Luz volunteered affably. 'I had to chew the damn thing off.' He pointed with a swathed, foreshortened index finger. 'Right there above the anklebone, see?'

'Tough luck,' said Agent Donner, thinking: Psycho City.

'It's what animals do,' Pedro Luz added, 'when they get caught in traps.'

Kingsbury clapped his hands nervously. 'Hey, hey! Can we get back to the issue, please, this Godfather thing. For the record, I'm not going anyplace.'

The marshal said, 'We can have you safely in Bozeman, Montana, by tomorrow afternoon.'

'What, do I look like fucking Grizzly Adams? Listen to me— *Montana*, don't even joke about something like that.'

Pedro Luz said, 'Why would the Mafia want to kill Mr. Kingsbury? I don't exactly make the connection.' Then his chin dropped, and he appeared to drift off.

Agent Donner said, 'I wish you'd consider the offer.'

'Two words.' Kingsbury held up two fingers as if playing charades. 'Summerfest Jubilee. One of our biggest days, receipt-wise, of the whole damn year. Parades, clowns, prizes. We're giving away . . . I forget, some kinda car.'

'And I suppose you need to be here.'

'Yeah, damn right. It's my park and my show. And know what else? You can't make me go anywhere. I kept my end of the deal. I'm free and clear of you people.'

'You're still on probation,' said the marshal. 'But you're right, we can't force you to go anyplace. This visit is a courtesy—'

'And I appreciate the information. I just don't happen to

believe it.' But a part of Francis Kingsbury did believe it. What if the men who stole his files had given up on the idea of blackmail? What if the damn burglars had somehow made touch with the Gotti organization? It strained Kingsbury's imagination because they'd seemed like such jittery putzes that night at the house. Yet perhaps he'd misjudged them.

'Where'd you get the tip?' he demanded.

Agent Donner was briefly distracted by the cartoon depiction of rodent fellatio that adorned Kingsbury's forearm. Eventually the marshal looked up and said, 'It surfaced during another investigation. I can't go into details.'

'But, really, you guys think it's on the level? You think some guineas are coming after me?' Kingsbury struggled to maintain an air of amused skepticism.

Soberly the marshal said, 'The FBI is checking it out.'

'Well, regardless, I'm not going to Montana. Just thinking about it hurts my mucous membranes—I got the world's worst hay fever.'

'So your mind is made up.'

'Yep,' said Kingsbury. 'I'm staying put.'

'Then let us provide you with protection here at the park. A couple of men, at least.'

'Thanks, but no thanks. I got Pedro.'

At the mention of his name, Pedro Luz's swollen eyelids parted. He reached up and squeezed the IV bag. Then he tugged the tube out of the needle in his arm, and fitted the end into the corner of his mouth. The sound of energetic sucking filled Francis Kingsbury's office.

Agent Donner was dumbfounded. In a brittle voice he assured Kingsbury that the marshals would be extremely discreet, and would in no way interfere with the Summerfest Jubilee events. Kingsbury, in a tone approaching politeness, declined the offer of bodyguards. The last thing he needed was federal dicks nosing around the Amazing Kingdom.

'Besides, like I mentioned, there's Pedro. He's as tough as they come.'

'All right,' said Agent Donner, casting his eyes once again on the distended, scarified, cataleptic, polypheaded mass that was Pedro Luz.

Kingsbury said, 'I know what you're thinking but, hell, he's worth ten of yours. Twenty of yours! Any sonofabitch that would bite off his own damn leg—you tell me, is that tough or what?'

The marshal rose stiffly to leave. 'Tough isn't the word for it,' he said.

The trailer fire had left Carrie Lanier with only three possessions: her Buick Electra, the gun she had taken from Joe Winder and the newly retired raccoon suit. The costume and the gun had been stowed in the trunk of the car. Everything else had been destroyed in the blaze.

Molly McNamara offered her a bedroom on the second floor of the old house. 'I'd loan you the condo but the cleaners are in this week,' Molly said. 'It's hard to rent out a place with blood-stains in the carpet.'

'What about Joe?' Carrie said, 'I'd like him to stay with me.'

Molly clucked. 'Young lady, I really can't approve. Two unmarried people—'

'But under the circumstances,' Carrie persisted, 'with all that's happened.'

'Oh . . . I suppose it's all right.' Molly had a sparkle in her eyes. 'I was teasing, darling. Besides, you act as if you're in love.'

Carrie said it was a long shot. 'We're both very goal-oriented, and very stubborn. I'm not sure we're heading in the same direction.' She paused and looked away. 'He doesn't seem to fit anywhere.'

'You wouldn't want him if he did,' Molly said. 'The world is full of nice boring young men. The crazy ones are hard to find and harder to keep, but it's worth it.'

'Your husband was like that?'

'Yes. My lovers, too.'

'But crazy isn't the word for it, is it?'

Molly smiled pensively. 'You're a smart cookie.'

'Did you know that Joe's father built Seashell Estates?'

'Oh dear,' Molly said. A dreadful project: six thousand units on eight hundred acres, plus a golf course. Wiped out an egret rookery. A mangrove estuary. And too late it was discovered that the fairways were leaching fertilizer and pesticides directly into the waters of Biscayne Bay.

Molly McNamara said, 'Those were the bad old days.'

'Joe's still upset.'

'But it certainly wasn't his fault. He must've been barely a teenager when Seashell was developed.'

'He's got a thing about his father,' Carrie said.

'Is that what this is all about?'

'He hears bulldozers in his sleep.'

Molly said, 'It's not as strange as you might imagine. The question is, can you take it? Is this the kind of fellow you want?'

'That's a tough one,' Carrie said. 'He could easily get himself killed this week.'

'Take the blue bedroom at the end of the hall.'

'Thank you, Miss McNamara.'

'Just one favor,' Molly said. 'The headboard—it's an antique. I found it at a shop in Williamsburg.'

'We'll be careful,' Carrie promised.

That night they made love on the bare pine floor. Drenched in sweat, they slid like ice cubes across the slick varnished planks. Eventually they wound up wedged headfirst in a corner, where Carrie fell asleep with Joe Winder's earlobe clenched tenderly in her teeth. He was starting to doze himself when he heard Molly's voice in the adjoining bedroom. She was talking sternly to a man who didn't sound like either Skink or the two redneck burglars.

When Winder heard the other door close, he delicately extricated himself from Carrie's bite and lifted her to the bed. Then he wrapped himself in an old quilt and crept into the hall to see who was in the next room.

The last person he expected to find was Agent Billy Hawkins of the Federal Bureau of Investigation. Trussed to a straight-backed chair, Hawkins wore someone else's boxer shorts and black nylon socks. A bandage was wadded around one bare thigh, and two strips of hurricane tape crisscrossed his mouth. He reeked of antiseptic.

Joe Winder slipped into the room and twisted the lock behind him. Gingerly he peeled the heavy tape from the agent's face.

'Fancy meeting you here.'

'Nice getup,' Billy Hawkins remarked. 'Would you please untie me?'

'First tell me what happened.'

'What does it look like? The old bird shot me.'

'Any particular reason?'

'Just get me loose, goddammit.'

Winder said, 'Not until I hear the story.'

Reluctantly, Hawkins told him about Bud Schwartz and the long-distance phone call to Queens and the possible exposure of a federally protected witness.

'Who's the flip?'

'I can't tell you *that*.'

Joe Winder pressed the hurricane tape over Hawkins's lips—then fiercely yanked it away. Hawkins yelped. Tears of pain sprang to his eyes. In colorful expletives he offered the opinion that Winder had gone insane.

The excruciating procedure was repeated on one of Billy Hawkins's bare nipples and nearly uprooted a cluster of curly black hairs. 'I can do this all night,' Winder said. 'I'm way past the point of caring.'

The agent took a long bitter moment to compose himself. 'You could go to prison,' he mumbled.

'For assaulting you with adhesive tape? I don't think so.' Winder placed one gummy strip along the line of soft hair that trailed southward from Billy Hawkins's navel. The agent gaped helplessly as Winder jerked hard; the tape came off with a sibilant rip.

'You—you're a goddamn lunatic!'

'But I'm your only hope. Who's going to believe you were shot and abducted by an elderly widow? And if they should believe it, what would that do to your career?' Joe Winder spread the quilt on the floor and sat cross-legged in front of the hog-tied agent.

'Blaine, Washington,' Winder said. 'Isn't that the FBI's equivalent of Siberia?'

Hawkins conceded the point silently. The political cost of prosecuting a grandmother and a pair of candyass burglars would be high. The Bureau was hypersensitive to incidents incongruous with the lantern-jawed crime-buster image promoted by J. Edgar Hoover; for an FBI agent to be overpowered by a doddering senior citizen was a disgrace. An immediate transfer to some godforsaken cowtown would be a certainty.

'So what can *you* do?' Hawkins asked Winder sourly.

'Maybe nothing. Maybe save your skin. Did Molly make you call the office?'

The agent nodded. 'At gunpoint. I told them I was taking a couple of sick days.'

'They ask about this Mafia thing?'

'I told them it wasn't panning out. Looked like a bullshit shakedown.' Hawkins sounded embarrassed. 'That's what she made me say. Threatened to shoot me again if I didn't go along with the routine—and it didn't sound like a bluff.'

'You did the right thing,' Joe Winder said. 'No sense chancing it.' He stood up and rewrapped himself in the quilt. 'You'll have to stay like this a while,' he told the agent. 'It's the only way.'

'I don't get it. What's your connection to these crackpots?'

'Long story.'

'Winder, don't be a jackass. This isn't a game.' Hawkins spoke sternly for a man in his ridiculous predicament. 'Somebody could get killed. That's not what you want, is it?'

'Depends. Tell me the name of this precious witness.'

'Frankie King.'

Joe Winder shrugged. 'Never heard of him.'

'Moved down from New York after he snitched on some of Gotti's crowd. This was a few years back.'

'Swift move. What's he calling himself these days?'

'That I can't possibly tell you.'

'Then you're on your own, Billy. Think about it. Your word against Grandma Moses. Picture the headlines: "Sharpshooter Widow Gunned Me Down, Nude G-Man Claims." '

Hawkins sagged dispiritedly. He said, 'The flip's name is Francis Kingsbury. You happy now?'

'Kingsbury?' Joe Winder raised his eyes to the heavens and cackled raucously. 'The Mafia is coming down here to whack Mr. X!'

'Hey,' Billy Hawkins said, 'it's not funny.'

But it was very funny to Joe Winder. 'Francis X. Kingsbury. Millionaire theme-park developer and real-estate mogul, darling of the Chamber of Commerce, 1988 Rotarian Citizen of the Year. And you're telling me he's really a two-bit jizzbag on the run from the mob?'

Ecstatically, Joe Winder hopped from foot to foot, spinning in a circle and twirling Molly's quilt like a calico cape.

'Oh, Billy boy,' he sang, 'isn't this a great country!'

They were thirty minutes late to the airport because Danny Pogue insisted on watching the end of a *National Geographic* television documentary about rhinoceros poachers in Africa.

In the car he couldn't stop talking about the program. 'The only reason they kill 'em, see, what they're after is the horns. Just the horns!' He put his fist on his nose to simulate a rhinoceros snout. 'In some places they use 'em for sex potions.'

'Get off it,' said Bud Schwartz.

'No shit. They grind the horns into powder and put it in their tea.'

'Does it work?'

'I don't know,' Danny Pogue said. 'The TV didn't say.'

'Like, it gives you a super big boner or what?'

'I don't know, Bud, the TV didn't say. They just talked about how much the powder goes for in Hong Kong, stuff like that. Thousands of bucks.'

Bud Schwartz said, 'You ask me, they left out the most important part of the show. Does it work or not?'

He drove into one of the airport garages and snatched a ticket from the machine. He parked on Level M, as always. 'M' for Mother; it was the only way Bud Schwartz could remember how to find his car. He was annoyed that his partner wasn't sharing in the excitement of the moment: they were about to be rich.

'After today, you can retire,' Bud Schwartz said. 'No more b-and-e's. Man, we should throw us a party tonight.'

Danny Pogue said, 'I ain't in the mood.'

They stepped onto the moving sidewalk and rode in silence to the Delta Airlines concourse. The plane had arrived on time, so the visitor already was waiting outside the gate. As promised, he was carrying a blue umbrella; otherwise Bud Schwartz would never have known that he was the hit man. He stood barely five feet tall and weighed at least two hundred pounds. He had thinning brown hair, small black eyes and skin that was the color of day-old lard. Under a herringbone sport coat he wore a striped polyester shirt, open at the neck, with a braided gold chain. The hit man seemed fond of gold; a bracelet rattled on his wrist when he shook Bud Schwartz's hand.

'Hello,' said the burglar.

'You call me Lou.' The hit man spoke in a granite baritone that didn't match the soft roly-polyness of his figure.

'Hi, Lou,' said Danny Pogue. 'I'm Bud's partner.'

'How nice for you. Where's the car?' He pointed to a Macy's shopping bag near his feet. 'That's yours. Now, where's the car?'

On the drive south, Danny Pogue peeked in the Macy's bag and saw that it was full of cash. Lou was up in the front seat next to Bud Schwartz.

'I wanna do this tomorrow,' he was saying. 'I gotta get home for my wife's birthday. She's forty.' Then he farted loudly and pretended not to hear it.

'Forty? No kidding?' said Bud Schwartz. He had been expecting something quite different in the way of a mob assassin. Perhaps it wasn't fair, but Bud Schwartz was disappointed in Lou's appearance. For Francis Kingsbury's killer, he had envisioned someone taut, snake-eyed and menacing—not fat, balding and flatulent.

Just goes to show, thought Bud Schwartz, these days every-thing's hype. Even the damn Mafia.

From the back seat, Danny Pogue asked: 'How're you gonna do it? What kinda gun?'

Lou puffed out his cheeks and said, 'Brand X. The fuck do you care, what kinda gun?'

'Danny,' Bud Schwartz said, 'let's stay out of the man's private business, okay?'

'I didn't mean nothin'.'

'You usually don't.'

The man named Lou said, 'This the neighborhood?'

'We're almost there,' said Bud Schwartz.

'I can't get over all these trees,' Lou said. 'Parts a Jersey look like this. My wife's mother lives in Jersey, a terrific old lady. Seventy-seven years old, she bowls twice a week! In a league!'

Bud Schwartz smiled weakly. Perfect. A hit man who loves his mother-in-law. What next—he collects for the United Way?

The burglar said to Lou: 'Maybe it's better if you rent a car. For tomorrow, I mean.'

'Sure. Usually I do my own driving.'

Danny Pogue tapped his partner on the shoulder and said, 'Slow down, Bud, it's up here on the right.'

Kingsbury's estate was bathed in pale orange lights. Gray sedans with green bubble lights were parked to block both ends of the driveway. Three men sat in each sedan; two more, in security-guard uniforms, were posted at the front door. It was, essentially, the complete private security force of the Amazing Kingdom of Thrills—except for Pedro Luz, who was inside the house, his wheelchair parked vigilantly at Francis Kingsbury's bedroom door.

Bud Schwartz drove by slowly. 'Look at this shit,' he muttered. Once they had passed the house, he put some muscle into the accelerator.

'An army,' Lou said, 'that's what it was.'

Danny Pogue sank low in the back seat. With both hands he clutched the Macy's bag to his chest. 'Let's just go,' he said. 'Bud, let's just haul ass.'

29

On the morning of August 2, Jake Harp crawled into the back of a white limousine and rode in a dismal gin-soaked stupor to the construction site on North Key Largo. There he was met by Charles Chelsea, Francis X. Kingsbury and a phalanx of armed security men whose crisp blue uniforms failed to mitigate their shifty felonious smirks. The entourage moved briskly across a recently bulldozed plateau, barren except for a bright green hillock that was cordoned with rope and ringed by reporters, photographers and television cameramen. Kingsbury took Jake Harp by the elbow and, ascending the grassy knob, waved mechanically; it reminded Charles Chelsea of the rigidly determined way that Richard Nixon had saluted before boarding the presidential chopper for the final time. Except that, compared to Francis Kingsbury, Nixon was about as tense as Pee Wee Herman.

Jake Harp heard himself pleading for coffee, please God, even decaf, but Kingsbury seemed not to hear him. Jake Harp blinked amphibiously and struggled to focus on the scene. It was early. He was outdoors. The sun was intensely bright. The Atlantic Ocean murmured at his back. And somebody had dressed him: Izod shirt, Sansibelt slacks, tasseled Footjoy golf shoes. What could this be! Then he heard the scratchy click of a portable microphone and the oily voice of Charles Chelsea.

'Welcome, everybody. We're standing on what will soon be the first tee of the Falcon Trace Championship Golf Course. As you can see, we've got a little work ahead of us. . . .'

Laughter. These numbnuts are laughing, thought Jake Harp. He squinted at the white upturned faces and recognized one or two as sportswriters.

More from Chelsea: '. . . and we thought it would be fun to inaugurate the construction of this magnificent golfing layout with a hitting clinic.'

Jake Harp's stomach clenched as somebody folded a three-wood into his fingers. The golf pro stared in disgust: a graphite head. They expect me to hit with metal!

Charles Chelsea's well-tanned paw settled amiably on Jake Harp's shoulder; the stench of Old Spice was overpowering.

'This familiar fellow needs no introduction,' Chelsea was saying. 'He's graciously agreed to christen the new course by hitting a few balls into the ocean—since we don't actually have a fairway yet.'

Laughter again. Mysterious, inexplicable laughter. Jake Harp swayed, bracing himself with the three-wood. What had he been drinking last night? Vodka sours? Tanqueray martinis? Possibly both. He remembered dancing with a banker's wife. He remembered telling her how he'd triple-bogeyed the Road Hole and missed the cut at the British Open; missed the damn cut, all because some fat Scotsman booted the ball. . . .

Jake Harp also remembered the banker's wife whispering something about a blowjob—but did it happen? He hoped so, but he truly couldn't recall. One thing was ertain: today he was physically incapable of swinging a golf club; it was simply out of the question. He wondered how he would break the news to Francis Kingsbury, who was bowing to the photographers in acknowledgment of Charles Chelsea's effusive introduction.

'Frank,' said Jake Harp. 'Where am I?'

With a frozen smile, Kingsbury remarked that Jake Harp looked about as healthy as dog barf.

'A bad night,' the golfer rasped. 'I'd like to go home and lie down.'

Then came an acrid gust of cologne as Chelsea leaned in: 'Hit a few, Jake, okay? No interviews, just a photo op.'

'But I can't use a fucking graphite wood. This is Jap voodoo, Frank, I need my MacGregors.'

Francis Kingsbury gripped Jake Harp by the shoulders and

turned him toward the ocean. 'And would you please, for Christ's sake, try not to miss the goddamn ball?'

Chelsea cautioned Kingsbury to keep his voice down. The sportswriters were picking up on the fact that Jake Harp was seriously under the weather.

'Coffee's on the way,' Chelsea chirped lightly.

'You want me to hit it in the ocean?' Jake Harp said. 'This is nuts.'

One of the news photographers shouted for the security officers to get out of the way, they were blocking the picture. Kingsbury commanded the troops of Pedro Luz to move to one side; Pedro Luz himself was not present, having refused with vague mutterings to exit the storage room and join the phony golf clinic at Falcon Trace. His men, however, embraced with gusto and amusement the task of guarding Francis X. Kingsbury from assailants unknown.

Having cleared the security force to make an opening for Jake Harp, Kingsbury ordered the golfer to swing away.

'I can't, Frank.'

'What?'

'I'm hung over. I can't lift the bloody club.'

'Assume the position, Jake. You're starting to piss me off.'

Tottering slightly, Jake Harp slowly arranged himself in the familiar stance that *Golf Digest* once hailed as 'part Hogan, part Nicklaus, part Baryshnikov'—chin down, feet apart, shoulders square, left arm straight, hands interlocked loosely on the shaft of the club.

'There,' Jake Harp said gamely.

Charles Chelsea cleared his throat. Francis Kingsbury said, 'A golf ball would help, Jake.'

'Oh Jesus, you're right.'

'You got everything but a goddamn ball.'

Under his breath, Jake Harp said, 'Frank, would you do me a favor? Tee it up?'

'What?'

'I can't bend down. I'm too hung over, Frank. If I try to bend, I'll fall on my face. I swear to God.'

Francis Kingsbury dug in his pocket and pulled out a scuffed Maxfli and a plastic tee that was shaped like a naked woman. 'You're quite an athlete, Jake. A regular Jim Fucking Thorpe.'

Gratefully Jake Harp watched Kingsbury drop to one knee and plant the tee. Then suddenly the sun exploded, and a molten splinter tore a hole in the golfer's belly, spinning him like a tenpin and knocking him flat. A darkening puddle formed as he lay there and floundered, gulping for breath through a mouthful of fresh Bermuda sod. Jake Harp was not too hung over to realize he could be dying, and it bitterly occurred to him that he would rather leave his mortal guts on the fairways of Augusta or Muirfield or Pebble Beach.

Anywhere but here.

Bud Schwartz and Danny Pogue had driven up to Kendall to break into a house. The house belonged to FBI Agent Billy Hawkins, who was still tied up as Molly McNamara's prisoner.

'Think he's got a dog?' said Danny Pogue.

Bud Schwartz said probably not. 'Guys like that, they think dogs are for pussies. It's a cop mentality.'

But Bud Schwartz was wrong. Bill Hawkins owned a German shepherd. The burglars could see the animal prowling the fence in the backyard.

'Guess we gotta do the front-door routine,' said Bud Schwartz. What a way to end a career: breaking into an FBI man's house in broad daylight. 'I thought we retired,' Bud Schwartz complained. 'All that dough we got, tell me what's the point if we're still pullin' these jobs.'

Danny Pogue said, 'Just this one more. And besides, what if Lou takes the money back?'

'No way.'

'If he can't get to the guy, yeah, he might. Already he thinks we tipped Kingsbury off, on account of all those rent-a-cops.'

Bud Schwartz said he wasn't worried about Lou going back on the deal. 'These people are pros, Danny. Now gimme the scroogie.' They were poised at Billy Hawkins's front door. Danny

Pogue checked the street for cars or pedestrians; then he handed Bud Schwartz a nine-inch screwdriver.

Skeptically Danny Pogue said, 'Guy's gotta have a deadbolt. Anybody works for the FBI, probably he's got an alarm, too. Maybe even lasers.'

But there was no alarm system. Bud Schwartz pried the doorjamb easily. He put his shoulder to the wood and pushed it open. 'You believe that?' he said to his partner. 'See what I mean about cop mentality. They think they're immune.'

'Yeah,' said Danny Pogue. 'Immune.' Later he'd ask Molly McNamara what it meant.

They closed the door and entered the empty house. Bud Schwartz would never have guessed that a federal agent lived there. It was a typical suburban Miami home: three bedrooms, two baths, nothing special. Once they got used to the idea, the burglars moved through the rooms with casual confidence—wife at work, kids at school, no sweat.

'Too bad we're not stealin' anything,' Bud Schwartz mused.

'Want to?' said his partner. 'Just for old times' sake.'

'What's the point?'

'I saw one of the kids has a CD player.'

'Wow,' said Bud Schwartz acidly. 'What's that, like, thirty bucks. Maybe forty?'

'No, man, it's a Sony.'

'Forget it. Now gimme the papers.'

In captivity Billy Hawkins had agreed to notify his family that he was out of town on a top-secret assignment. However, the agent had displayed a growing reluctance to call the FBI office and lie about being sick. To motivate him, Molly McNamara had composed a series of cryptic notes and murky correspondence suggesting that Hawkins was not the most loyal of government servants. Prominently included in the odd jottings were the telephone numbers of the Soviet Embassy and the Cuban Special Interest Section in Washington, D.C. For good measure, Molly had included a bank slip showing a suspicious $25,000 deposit to Agent Billy Hawkins's personal savings account—a deposit that

Molly herself had made at the South Miami branch of Unity National Savings & Loan. The purpose of these maneuvers was to create a shady portfolio that, despite its sloppiness, Billy Hawkins would not wish to try to explain to his colleagues at the FBI.

Who would definitely come to the house in search of clues, if Agent Hawkins failed to check in.

Molly McNamara had entrusted the bank receipt, phone numbers and other manufactured evidence to Bud Schwartz and Danny Pogue, whose mission was to conceal the material in a semi-obvious location in Billy Hawkins's bedroom.

Bud Schwartz chose the second drawer of the nightstand. He placed the envelope under two unopened boxes of condoms. 'Raspberry-colored,' he marveled. 'FBI man uses raspberry rubbers!' Another stereotype shattered.

Danny Pogue was admiring a twelve-inch portable television as if it were a rare artifact. 'Jesus, Bud, you won't believe this.'

'Don't tell me it's a black-and-white.'

'Yep. You know the last time I saw one?'

'Little Havana,' said Bud Schwartz, 'that duplex off Twelfth Avenue. I remember.'

'Remember what we got for it.'

'Yeah. Thirteen goddamn dollars.' The fence was a man named Fat Jack on Seventy-ninth Street, near the Boulevard. Bud Schwartz couldn't stand Fat Jack not only because he was cheap but because he smelled like dirty socks. One day Bud Schwartz had boosted a case of Ban Extra Dry Roll-on Deodorant sticks from the back of a Publix truck, and given it to Fat Jack as a hint. Fat Jack had handed him eight bucks and said that nobody should ever use roll-ons because they cause cancer of the armpits.

'I don't get it,' said Danny Pogue. 'I thought the FBI paid big bucks—what's a baby Magnavox go for, two hundred retail? You'd think he could spring for color.'

'Who knows, maybe he spends it all on clothes. Come on, let's take off.' Bud Schwartz wanted to be long gone before the mailman arrived and noticed what had happened to the front door.

Danny Pogue turned on the portable TV and said, 'That's not a bad picture.' The noon news was just starting.

'I said let's go, Danny.'

'Wait, look at this!'

A video clip showed a heavyset man in golf shoes being hoisted on a stretcher. The man's shirt was drenched in blood, but his eyelids were half open. A plastic oxygen mask covered the man's face and nose, but the jaw moved as if he were trying to speak. The newscaster reported that the shooting had taken place at a new resort development called Falcon Trace, near Key Largo.

'Lou! He did it!' exclaimed Danny Pogue. 'You were right.'

'Only trouble is, that ain't Mr. Kingsbury.'

'You sure?'

Bud Schwartz sat down in front of the television. The anchorman had tossed the sniper story to a sportscaster, who was somberly recounting the stellar career of Jake Harp. The golfer's photograph, taken in happier times, popped up on a wide green mat behind the sports desk.

Danny Pogue said, 'Who the hell's that?'

'Not Kingsbury,' grunted Bud Schwartz. The mishap confirmed his worst doubts about Lou's qualifications as a hit man. It was unbelievable. The asshole had managed to shoot the wrong guy.

'Know what?' said Danny Pogue. 'There's a Jake Harp Cadillac in Boca Raton where I swiped a bunch of tape decks once. Is that the same guy? This golfer?'

Bud Schwartz said, 'I got no earthly idea.' What was all this crap the TV guy was yakking about—career earnings, number of Top Ten finishes, average strokes per round, percentage of greens hit in regulation. To Bud Schwartz, golf was as foreign as polo. Except you didn't see so many fat guys playing polo.

'The main thing is, did they catch the shooter?'

'Nuh-huh.' Danny Pogue had his nose to the tube. 'They said he got away in a boat. No arrests, no motives is what they said.'

Bud Schwartz was trying to picture Lou from Queens at the helm of a speedboat, racing for the ocean's horizon.

'He's gonna be pissed,' Danny Pogue said.

'Yeah, well, I don't guess his boss up North is gonna be too damn thrilled, either. Whackin' the wrong man.'

'He ain't dead yet. Serious but stable is what they said.'

Bud Schwartz said it didn't really matter. 'Point is, it's still a fuckup. A major *major* fuckup.'

The Mafia had gunned down a life member of the Professional Golfers Association.

Pedro Luz finally emerged from the storage room, where he had been measuring his penis. He rolled the wheelchair out to Kingsbury Lane for the morning rehearsal of the Summerfest Jubilee, a greatly embellished version of the nightly musical pageant. Pedro Luz needed something to lift his spirits. His leg had begun to throb in an excruciating way; no combination of steroids and analgesics put a dent in the pain. To add psychic misery to the physical, Pedro Luz had now documented the fact that his sexual wand was indeed shrinking as a result of prolonged steroid abuse. At first, Pedro Luz had assured himself that it was only an optical illusion; the more swollen his face and limbs became, the smaller everything else appeared to be. But weeks of meticulous calibrations had produced conclusive evidence: His wee-wee had withered from 10.4 centimeters to 7.9 centimeters in its flaccid state. Worse, it seemed to Pedro Luz (although there was no painless way to measure) that his testicles had also become smaller—not yet as tiny as BBs, as Churrito had predicted, but more like gumballs.

These matters weighed heavily on his mind as Pedro Luz sat in the broiling sun and watched the floats rumble by. He was hoping that the sight of Annette Fury's regal bosom would buoy his mood, and was disappointed to see that she had been replaced as Princess Golden Sun. The new actress looked familiar, but Pedro Luz couldn't place the face. She was a very pretty girl, but the black wig needed some work, as did the costume— buckskin culottes and a fringed halter top. Her singing was quite lovely, much better than Annette's, but Pedro Luz would've preferred larger breasts. The lioness that shared the Seminole float was in no condition to rehearse; panting miserably in the humidity, the animal sprawled half-conscious on one side, thus thwarting the cat-straddling exit that culminated the princess's dramatic performance.

As the parade disbanded, Pedro Luz eased the wheelchair off the curb and approached the Seminole float. The pretty young singer was not to be seen; there was only the driver of the float and Dr. Kukor, the park veterinarian, who had climbed aboard to revive the heatstruck lioness. Dr. Kukor was plainly flabbergasted by the sight of Pedro Luz.

'I lost my foot in an accident,' the security chief explained.

Dr. Kukor hadn't noticed the missing foot. It was the condition of Pedro Luz's face, so grossly inflated, that had generated the horror. The man looked like a blow-fish: puffed cheeks, bulging lips, teeny eyes wedged deep under a pimpled, protuberant brow.

To Pedro Luz, Dr. Kukor directed the most inane inquiry of a long and distinguished career: 'Are you all right?'

'Just fine. Where's the young lady?'

Dr. Kukor pointed, and Pedro Luz spun the wheelchair to see: Princess Golden Sun stood behind him. She was zipping a black Miami Heat warm-up jacket over the halter.

Pedro Luz introduced himself and said, 'I've seen you before, right?'

'It's possible,' said Carrie Lanier, who recognized him instantly as the goon who shot up her double-wide, the creep she'd run over with the car. She noticed the bandaged trunk of his leg, and felt a pang of guilt. It passed quickly.

'You sing pretty nice,' Pedro Luz said, 'but you could use a couple three inches up top. If you get my meaning.'

'Thanks for the advice.'

'I know a doctor who specializes in that sort of thing. Maybe I could get you a discount.'

'Actually,' said Carrie, patting her chest, 'I kind of like the little fellas just the way they are.'

'Suit yourself.' Pedro Luz scratched brutally at a raw patch on his scalp. 'I'm trying to figure where I saw you before. Take off the wig for a second, okay?'

Carrie Lanier pressed her hands to her eyes and began to cry

—plaintive, racking sobs that attracted the concern of tourists and the other pageant performers.

Pedro Luz said, 'Hey, what's the matter?'

'It's not a wig!' Carrie cried. 'It's my real hair.' She turned and scampered down a stairwell into The Catacombs.

'Geez, I'm sorry,' said Pedro Luz, to no one. Flustered, he rolled full tilt toward the security office. Speeding downhill past the Wet Willy, he chafed his knuckles trying to brake the wheelchair. When he reached the chilled privacy of the storage room, he slammed the door and drove the bolt. In the blackness Pedro Luz probed for the string that turned on the ceiling's bare bulb; he found it and jerked hard.

The white light revealed a shocking scene. Someone had entered Pedro's sanctuary and destroyed the delicate web of sustenance. Sewing shears had snipped the intravenous tubes into worthless inch-long segments, which littered the floor like plastic rice. The same person had sliced open every one of Pedro's unused IV bags; the wheelchair rested, literally, in a pond of liquid dextrose.

But by far the worst thing to greet Pedro Luz was the desolate sight of brown pill bottles, perhaps a half-dozen, open and empty on the floor. Whoever he was, the sonofabitch had flushed Pedro's anabolic steroids down the john. The ceramic pestle with which he had so lovingly powdered his Winstrols lay shattered beneath the toilet tank.

And, on the wall, a message in coral lipstick. Pedro Luz groaned and backed the wheelchair so he could read it easier. A wild rage heaved through his chest and he began to snatch items from the storage shelves and hurl them against the cinder block: nightsticks, gas masks, flashlights, handcuffs, cans of Mace, pistol grips, boxes of bullets.

Only when there was nothing left to throw did Pedro Luz stop to read the words on the wall again. Written in a loopy flamboyant script, the message said:

> *Good morning, Dipshit!*
> *Just wanted you to know I'm not dead.*
> *Have a nice day, and don't forget your Wheaties!*

It was signed, 'Yours truly, J. Winder.'

Pedro Luz emitted a feral cry and aimed himself toward the executive gym, where he spent the next two hours alone on the bench press, purging the demons and praying for his testicles to grow back.

30

Somehow Charles Chelsea summoned the creative energy necessary for fabrication:

> Golf legend Jake Harp was accidentally shot Thursday during groundbreaking ceremonies for the new Falcon Trace Golf and Country Club Resort on North Key Largo.
>
> The incident occurred as Mr. Harp was preparing to hit a ball off what will be the first tee of the 6,970-yard championship golf course, which Mr. Harp designed himself. The golfer apparently was struck by a stray bullet from an unidentified boater, who may have been shooting at nearby sea gulls.
>
> Mr. Harp was listed in serious but stable condition after undergoing surgery at South Miami Hospital.
>
> 'This is a tragedy for the entire golfing world, professionals and amateurs alike,' said Francis X. Kingsbury, the developer of Falcon Trace, and a close personal friend of Mr. Harp.
>
> 'We're all praying for Jake to pull through,' added Kingsbury, who is also the founder and chairman of the Amazing Kingdom of Thrills, the popular family theme park adjacent to the sprawling Falcon Trace project.
>
> By mid-afternoon Thursday, police had not yet arrested any suspects in the shooting. Charles Chelsea, vice president of publicity for Falcon Trace Ltd., disputed accounts by some reporters on the scene who claimed that Mr. Harp was the victim of a deliberate sniper attack.
>
> 'There's no reason to believe that this terrible event was anything but a freak accident,' Chelsea said.

Kingsbury approved the press release with a disgusted flick of his hand. He drained a third martini and asked Chelsea if he had ever before witnessed a man being shot.

'Not that I can recall, sir.'

'Close up, I mean,' Kingsbury said. 'Dead bodies are one thing—car wrecks, heart attacks—I'm not counting those. What I mean is, *bang*!'

Chelsea said, 'It happened so damn fast.'

'Well, you know who they were aiming at? *Moi*, that's who. How about that!' Kingsbury pursed his lips and drummed his knuckles.

'You?' Chelsea said. 'Who would try to kill you?' He instantly thought of Joe Winder.

But Kingsbury smiled drunkenly and began to hum the theme from *The Godfather*.

Chelsea said, 'There's something you're not telling me.'

'Of course there's something I'm not telling you. There's tons of shit I'm not telling you. What, I look like a total moron?'

Watching Francis Kingsbury pour another martini, Chelsea felt like seizing the bottle and guzzling himself into a Tanqueray coma. The time had come to look for another job; the fun had leaked out of this one. A malevolent force, unseen and uncontrollable, had perverted Chelsea's role from cheery town crier to conniving propagandist. Reflecting on the past weeks, he realized he should've quit on the day the blue-tongued voles were stolen, the day innocence was lost.

We are all no longer children, Chelsea thought sadly. We are potential co-defendants.

'No offense,' Kingsbury was saying, 'but you're just a flack. I only tell you what I've absolutely got to tell you. Which is precious damned little.'

'That's the way it should be,' Chelsea said lifelessly. 'Right! Loose dicks sink ships. Or whatever.' Kingsbury slurped at the gin like a thirsty mutt. 'Anyhow, don't worry about me. I'm taking—well, let's just say, the necessary precautions. You can be goddamn sure.'

'That's wise of you.'

'Meanwhile, sharpen your pencil. I ordered us more animals.' Kingsbury wistfully studied his drink. 'Who's the guy in the Bible, the one with the ark. Was it Moses?'

'Noah,' Chelsea said. Boy, was the old man smashed.

'Yeah, Noah, that's who I feel like. Me and these fucking critters. Anyhow, we're back in the endangered-species business, saving the animals. There oughta be some publicity when they get here. You see to it.'

The woman named Rachel Lark had phoned all the way from New Zealand. She said she'd done her best on such short notice, and said Kingsbury would be pleased when he saw the new attractions for the Rare Animal Pavilion. I hope so, he'd told her, because we could damn sure use some good news.

Fearing the worst, Charles Chelsea said, 'What kind of animals are we talking about?'

'Cute is what I ordered. Thirty-seven hundred dollars' worth of cute.' Kingsbury snorted. 'Could be anything. The point is, we've got to rebound, Charlie. We got a fucking void to fill.'

'Right.'

'Speaking of which, we also need another golfer. In case Jake croaks, God forbid.'

Chelsea recoiled at the cold-bloodedness of the assignment. 'It won't look good, sir, not with what happened this morning. It's best if we stick by Jake.'

'Sympathy's all fine and dandy, Charlie, but we got more than golf at stake here. We got waterfront to sell. We got patio homes. We got club memberships. Can Jake Harp—don't get me wrong—but in his present situation can Jake do promotional appearances? TV commercials? Celebrity programs? We don't even know if Jake can still breathe, much less swing a fucking five-iron.'

For once Francis Kingsbury expressed himself in nearly cogent syntax. It must be excellent gin, Chelsea thought.

'I want you to call Nicklaus,' Kingsbury went on. 'Tell him money is no problem.'

'Jack Nicklaus,' the publicity man repeated numbly.

'No, *Irving* Nicklaus. Who the hell do you think! And if you can't get the Bear, try Palmer. And if you can't get Annie, you try Trevino. And if you can't get the Mex, try the Shark. And so on. The bigger the better, but make it quick.'

Knowing it would do no good, Chelsea reminded Kingsbury

that he had tried to recruit the top golfing names when he was first planning Falcon Trace, and that they'd all said no. Only Jake Harp had the stomach to work for him.

'I don't care what they said before,' Kingsbury growled, 'you call 'em again. Money is no problem, all right?'

'Again, I'd just like to caution you about how this might appear to people—'

'I need a hotshot golfer, Charlie. The hell do you guys call it— a media personality?' Kingsbury raised one plump fist and let it fall heavily on the desk. 'I can't sell a golf resort when my star golfer's on a goddamn respirator. Don't you understand? Don't you know a goddamn thing about Florida real estate?'

They rode to the airport in edgy silence. Danny Pogue was waiting for Lou to say something. Like it was all *their* fault. Like the people in Queens wanted their money back.

Earlier Bud Schwartz had pulled his partner aside and said, look, they want the dough, we give it back. This is the mob, he said, and we're not playing games with the mob. But it's damned important, Bud Schwartz had said, that Lou and his Mafia people know that we didn't tip off Kingsbury. How the hell he found out about the hit, it don't matter. It wasn't us and we gotta make that clear, okay? Danny Pogue agreed whole-heartedly. Like Bud Schwartz, he didn't want to go through the rest of life having somebody else start his car every morning. Or peeking around corners, watching out for inconspicuous fat guys like Lou.

So when they got to the Delta Airlines terminal, Danny Pogue shook Lou's hand and said he was very sorry about what had happened. 'Honest to God, we didn't tell nobody.'

'That's the truth,' said Bud Schwartz.

Lou shrugged. 'Probably a wire. Don't sweat it.'

'Thanks,' said Danny Pogue, flushed with relief. He pumped Lou's pudgy arm vigorously. 'Thanks for—well, just thanks is all.'

Lou nodded. His nose and cheeks were splashed pink with raw sunburn. He wore the same herringbone coat and striped shirt that he had when he'd gotten off the airplane. There was still no sign of the gun, but the burglars knew he was carrying it somewhere on his corpulent profile.

Lou said, 'Since I know you're dyin' to ask, what happened was this: the asshole bent over. Don't ask me why, but he bent over just as I pulled the trigger.'

'Bud thought you probably got the two guys mixed up—'

'I didn't get nobody mixed up.' Lou's upper lip curled when he directed this bulletin toward Bud Schwartz. 'The guy leaned over is all. Otherwise he'd be dead right now, trust me.'

Despite his doubts about Lou's marksmanship, Bud Schwartz didn't want him to leave Miami with hard feelings. He didn't want any hit man, even a clumsy one, to be sore at him.

'Could've happened to anybody,' Bud Schwartz said supportively. 'Sounds like one hell of a tough shot from the water, anyway.'

A voice on the intercom announced that the Delta flight to LaGuardia was boarding at Gate 7. Lou said, 'The guy that got hit, I heard he's hanging on.'

'Yeah, some golfer named Harp,' said Danny Pogue. 'Serious but stable.'

'Maybe he'll make it,' Lou said. 'That would be good.'

Bud Schwartz asked what would happen when Lou returned to Queens.

'Have a sitdown with my people. Find out what they want to do next. Then I got this big birthday party for my wife's fortieth. I bought her one a them electric woks—she really likes Jap food, don't ask me why.'

Danny Pogue said, 'Are you in big trouble?'

Lou's chest bounced when he laughed. 'With my wife or the boys? Ask me which is worse.'

He picked up his carry-on and the blue umbrella, and waddled for the gate.

Bud Schwartz waved. 'Sorry it got so screwed up.'

'What the hell,' said Lou, still laughing. 'I got me a nice boat ride outta the deal.'

*

Joe Winder and Carrie Lanier met Trooper Jim Tile at the Snapper Creek Plaza on the Turnpike extension. They took a booth at the Roy Rogers and ordered burgers and shakes. Winder found the atmosphere more pleasant than it had been at Ocean Reef. Carrie asked Jim Tile if he had phoned Rikers Island.

'Yeah, I called,' the trooper said. 'They thought it was crazy, but they said they'd watch for anything out of the ordinary.'

'Out of the ordinary hardly begins to describe him.'

'New Yorkers,' said Jim Tile, 'think they've cornered the market on psychopaths. They don't know Florida.'

Joe Winder said, 'I don't think he's going to Rikers Island. I think he's still here.'

'I heard about Harp,' said Jim Tile, 'and my opinion is no, it wasn't the governor. I'll put money on it.'

'How can you be so sure?' asked Carrie.

'Because (a) it's not his style, and (b) he wouldn't have missed.'

Winder said, 'Mr. X was the target.'

'Had to be,' agreed Jim Tile. 'Who'd waste a perfectly good bullet on a golfer?'

Carrie speculated that it could have been a disgruntled fan. Joe Winder threw an arm around her and gave her a hug. He'd been in a good mood since trashing Pedro Luz's steroid den.

The trooper was saying Skink might've headed upstate. 'This morning somebody shot up a Greyhound on the interstate outside Orlando. Sixty-seven Junior Realtors on their way to Epcot.'

Panic at Disney World! Winder thought. Kingsbury will come in his pants.

'Nobody was hurt,' Jim Tile said, 'which leads me to believe it was you-know-who.' He pried the plastic cap off his milkshake and spooned out the ice cream. 'Eight rounds into a speeding bus and nobody even gets nicked. That's one hell of a decent shot.'

Carrie said, 'I'm assuming they didn't catch the culprit.'

'Vanished without a trace,' said the trooper. 'If it's him, they'll never even find a footprint. He knows that area of the state very well.'

Winder said it was a long way to go for a man with two fresh gunshot wounds.

Jim Tile shrugged. 'I called Game and Fish. The panther plane hasn't picked up the radio signal for days.'

'So he's really gone,' Carrie said.

'Or hiding in a bomb shelter.'

'Joe thinks we should go ahead and make a move. He's got a plan all worked out.'

Jim Tile raised a hand. 'Don't tell me, please. I don't want to hear it.'

'Fair enough,' Winder said, 'but I've got to ask a small favor.'

'The answer is no.'

'But it's nothing illegal.'

The trooper used the corner of a paper napkin to polish the lenses of his sunglasses. 'This falls into the general category of pressing your luck. Just because the governor gets away, don't think it's easy. Or even right.'

'Please,' said Carrie, 'just listen.'

'What is it you want me to do?'

'Your job,' Joe Winder replied. 'That's all.'

Later, in the rental boat, Joe Winder said he almost felt sorry for Charles Chelsea. 'Getting your sports celebrity shot with the press watching, that's tough.'

Carrie Lanier agreed that Chelsea was earning his salary. She was at the helm of the outboard, expertly steering a course toward the ocean shore of North Key Largo. A young man named Oscar sat shirtless on the bow, dangling his brown legs and drinking a root beer.

Carrie told Joe he had some strange friends.

'Oscar thinks he owes me a favor, that's all. Years ago I left his name out of a newspaper article and it wound up saving his life.'

Carrie looked doubtful, but said nothing. Her hair was tied back in a ponytail. She wore amber sunglasses with green Day-Glo frames and a silver one-piece bathing suit. Oscar didn't stare, not even once. His mind was on business, and the soccer game he was missing on television. Most Thursdays he was on his way to Belize, only this morning there'd been a minor problem with Customs, and the flight was canceled. When Joe Winder called him at the warehouse, Oscar felt honor-bound to lend a hand.

'He thinks I cut him a break,' Winder whispered to Carrie, 'but the fact is, I *did* use his name in the story. It just got edited out for lack of space.'

'What was the article about?'

'Gunrunning.'

From the bow, Oscar turned and signaled that they were close enough now. Kneeling on the deck, he opened a canvas duffel and began to arrange odd steel parts on a chamois cloth. The first piece that Carrie saw was a long gray tube.

'Oscar's from Colombia,' Joe Winder explained. 'His brother's in the M-19. They're leftist rebels.'

'Thank you, Professor Kissinger.' Carrie smeared the bridge of her nose with mauve-colored zinc oxide. It was clear from her attitude that she had reservations about this phase of the plan.

She said, 'What makes you think Kingsbury needs another warning? I mean, he's got the mob after him, Joe. Why should he care about a couple of John Deeres?'

'He's a developer. He'll care.' Winder leaned back and squinted at the sun. 'Keep the pressure on, that's the key.'

Carrie admired the swiftness with which Oscar went about his task. She said to Winder: 'Tell me again what they call that.'

'An RPG. Rocket-propelled grenade.'

'And you're positive no one's going to get hurt?'

'It's lunch hour, Carrie. You heard the whistle.' He took out a pair of waterproof Zeiss binoculars and scanned the shoreline until he found the stand of pigeon plums that Molly McNamara had told him about. The dreaded bulldozers had multiplied from two to five; they were parked in a semicircle, poised for the mission against the plum trees.

'Everybody's on their break,' Winder reported. 'Even the deputies.' At the other end of the boat, Oscar assembled the grenade launcher in well-practiced silence.

Carrie cut the twin Evinrudes and let the currents nudge the boat over the grassy shallows. She took the field glasses and tried to spot the bird nest that Molly had mentioned. She couldn't see anything, the hardwoods were so dense.

'I'm not sure I understand the significance of this gesture,' she said. 'Mockingbirds aren't exactly endangered.'

'These ones are.' Winder peeled off his T-shirt and tied it around his forehead like a bandanna. The air stuck to his chest like a hot rag; the temperature on the water was ninety-four degrees, and no breeze. 'You don't approve,' he said to Carrie. 'I can tell.'

'What bothers me is the lack of imagination, Joe. You could be blowing up bulldozers the rest of your life.'

The words stung, but she was right. Clever this was not, merely loud. 'I'm sorry,' he said, 'but there wasn't time to come up with something more creative. The old lady said they were taking out the plum trees this afternoon, and it looks like she was right.'

Oscar gave the okay sign from the bow. The boat had drifted close enough so they could hear the voices and lunchtime banter of the Falcon Trace construction crew.

'Which dozer you want?' Oscar inquired, raising the weapon to his shoulder.

'Take your pick.'

'Joe, wait!' Carrie handed him the binoculars. 'Over there, check it out.'

Winder beamed when he spotted it. 'Looks like they're pouring the slab for the clubhouse.'

'That's a large cement mixer,' Carrie noted.

'Sure is. A *very* large cement mixer.' Joe Winder snapped his fingers and motioned to Oscar. Spying the new target, the young Colombian smiled broadly and readjusted his aim.

In a low voice Carrie said, 'I take it he's done this sort of thing before.'

'I believe so, yes.'

Oscar grunted something in Spanish, then pulled the trigger. The RPG took out the cement truck quite nicely. An orange gout of flame shot forty feet into the sky, and warm gray gobs of cement rained down on the construction workers as they sprinted for their cars.

'See,' Carrie said. 'A little variety's always nice.'

Joe Winder savored the smoky scent of chaos and wondered what his father would have thought.

We all shine on.

That night Carrie banished him from the bedroom while she practiced her songs for the Jubilee. At first he listened in dreamy amazement at the door; her voice was crystalline, delicate, soothing. After a while Bud Schwartz and Danny Pogue joined him in the hallway, and Carrie's singing seemed to soften their rough convict features. Danny Pogue lowered his eyes and began to hum along; Bud Schwartz lay on the wooden floor with hands behind his head and gazed at the high pine beams. Molly McNamara even unlocked the door to the adjoining bedroom so that Agent Billy Hawkins, gagged but alert, could enjoy the beautiful musical interlude.

Eventually Joe Winder excused himself and slipped downstairs to make a call. He went through three telephone temptresses before they switched him to Nina's line.

'I'm glad it's you,' she said. 'There's something you've got to hear.'

'I'm honestly not in the mood—'

'This is different, Joe. It took three nights to write.'

What could he possibly say? 'Go ahead, Nina.'

'Ready?' She was so excited. He heard the rustle of paper. Then she took a breath and began to read:

> 'Your hands find me in the night, burrow for my
>   warmth.
> Lift me, turn me, move me apart.
> The language of blind insistence,
> You speak with a slow tongue on my belly,
> An eyelash fluttering against my nipple.
> This is the moment of raw cries and murmurs when

Nothing matters in the vacuum of passion
But passion itself.'

He wasn't sure if she had finished. It sounded like a big ending, but he wasn't sure.

'Nina?'

'What do you think?'

'It's . . . vivid.'

'Poetry. A brand-new concept in phone sex.'

'Interesting.' God, she's making a career of this.

'Did it arouse you?'

'Definitely,' he said. 'My loins surge in wild tumescence inside my jeans.'

'Stop it, Joe!'

'I'm sorry. Really it's quite good.' And maybe it was. He knew next to nothing about poetry.

'I wanted to try something different,' Nina said, 'something literate. A few of the girls complained—Miriam, of course. She's more comfortable with the old sucky-fucky.'

'Well,' Winder said, 'it's all in the reading.'

'My editor wants to see more.'

'You have an editor?'

'For the syndication deal, Joe. What'd you think of the last part? *Nothing matters in the vacuum of passion but passion itself.*'

He said, ' "Abyss" is better than "vacuum." '

'The abyss of passion! You're right, Joe, that's much better.'

'It's a long way from dry-humping on the Amtrak.'

Nina laughed. He had almost forgotten how wonderful it sounded.

'So how was your hot date with The Voice?'

'It was very enjoyable. He's an exceptional man.'

'What does he do?'

Without skipping a beat: 'He markets General Motors products.'

'Cars? He sells cars! That *is* exceptional.'

Nina said, 'I don't want to talk about this.'

'Buicks? Pontiacs? Oldsmobiles? Or perhaps all three?'

'He is a surprisingly cultured man,' Nina said. 'An educated man. And it's Chevrolets, for your information. The light-truck division.'

'Boy.' Winder felt exhausted. First the poetry, now this. 'Nina, I've got to ask. Does the face match the voice?'

'There's nothing wrong with the way he looks.'

'Say no more.'

'You can be such a prick,' she observed.

'You're right. I'm sorry—again.'

'He wants to marry me.'

'Showing excellent taste,' Winder said. 'He'd be nuts if he didn't.'

There was a brief pause, then Nina asked: 'Are you the one who shot the golfer?'

'Nope. But I don't blame you for wondering.'

'Please don't kill anybody, Joe. I know how strongly you feel about these issues, but please don't murder anyone.'

'I'll try not to.'

'Better sign off,' she said. 'I'm tying up the phone.'

'Hey, I'm a paying customer.'

'You really liked the poem?'

'It was terrific, Nina. I'm very proud.'

He could tell she was pleased. 'Any more suggestions?' she said.

'Well, the line about the nipple.'

'Yes. *An eyelash fluttering against my nipple.*'

'The imagery is nice,' Winder said, 'but it makes it sound like you've got just one. Nipple, I mean.'

'Hmm,' said Nina. 'That's a good point.'

'Otherwise it's great.'

'Thanks, Joe,' she said. 'Thanks for everything.'

31

Joe Winder held Carrie in his arms and wondered why the women he loved were always a step or two ahead of him.

'So what are you planning?' he asked.

She stirred but didn't answer. Her cheek felt silky and warm against his chest. When would he ever learn to shut up and enjoy the moment?

'Carrie, I know you're not asleep.'

Her eyes opened. Even in the darkness he could feel the liquid stare. 'You're the only man I've ever been with,' she said, 'who insists on talking afterward.'

'You inspire me, that's all.'

'Aren't you exhausted?' She raised her head. 'Was I hallucinating, or did we just fuck our brains out?'

Winder said, 'I'm nervous as hell. I've been rehearsing it all in my head.'

She told him to stop worrying and go to sleep. 'What's the worst thing that could happen?'

'Jail is a distinct possibility. Death is another.'

Carrie turned on her belly and slid between his legs. Then she propped her elbows on his rib cage, and rested her chin on her hands.

'What are you smiling at?' Winder said.

'It's all going to work out. I've got faith in you.'

'But you're planning something, just the same.'

'Joe, it might be my only chance.'

'At what?'

'Singing. I mean really singing. Am I hurting you?'

'Oh, no, you're light as a feather.'

'You asshole,' she giggled, and began to tickle him ferociously.

Winder locked his legs around her thighs and flipped her over in the sheets.

They were kissing when he felt compelled to pull back and say, 'I'm sorry I dragged you into this mess.'

'What mess? And, besides, you're doing the honest thing. Even if it's slightly mad.'

'You're speaking of the major felonies?'

'Of course,' Carrie said. 'But your motives are absolutely pure and unassailable. I'll be cheering for you, Joe.'

'Clinical insanity isn't out of the question,' he said. 'Just thinking about Kingsbury and that damn golf course, I get noises inside my skull.'

'What kind of noises?'

'Hydraulic-type noises. Like the crusher on a garbage truck.'

Carrie looked concerned, and he couldn't blame her. 'It goes back to my old man,' he said.

'Don't think about it so much, Joe.'

'I'd feel better if the governor were here. Just knowing I wasn't the only lunatic—'

'I had a dream about him,' she said quietly. 'I dreamed he broke into prison and killed that guy—what's his name?'

'Mark Chapman,' said Winder. 'Mark David Chapman.'

She heard sadness in the reply, sadness because she didn't remember the details. 'Joe, I was only fourteen when it happened.'

'You're right.'

'Besides, I've always been lousy with names. Oswald, Sirhan, Hinkley—it's easy to lose track of these idiots.'

'Sure is,' Winder agreed.

Carrie tenderly laced her hands on the back of his neck. 'Everything's going to be fine. And no, you're not crazy. A little zealous is all.'

'It's not a bad plan,' he said.

'Joe, it's a terrific plan.'

'And if all goes well, you'll still have your job.'

'No, I don't think so. I'm not much of a Seminole go-go dancer.'

Now it was his turn to smile. 'I take it there may be some last-minute changes in the musical program.'

'Quite possibly,' Carrie said.

He kissed her softly on the forehead. 'I'll be cheering for you, too.'

'I know you will, Joe.'

As far as Bud Schwartz was concerned, he'd rather be in jail than in a hospital. Practically everyone he ever knew who died—his mother, his brother, his uncles, his first probation officer—had died in hospital beds. In fact, Bud Schwartz couldn't think of a single person who'd come out of a hospital in better shape than when they'd gone in.

'What about babies?' Danny Pogue said.

'Babies don't count.'

'What about your boy? Mike, Jr., wasn't he borned in a hospital?'

'Matter of fact, no. It was the back of a Bronco. And his name is *Bud*, Jr., like I told you.' Bud Schwartz rolled down the window and tried to spit the toothpick from the corner of his mouth. It landed on his arm. 'A hospital's the last place for a sick person to go,' he said.

'You think she'll die there?'

'No. I don't wanna set foot in the place is all.'

'Jesus, you're a cold shit.'

Bud Schwartz was startled by his partner's anger. Out of pure guilt he relented and agreed to go, but only for a few minutes. Danny Pogue seemed satisfied. 'Let's get some roses on the way.'

'Fine. A lovely gesture.'

'Hey, it'll mean a lot to her.'

'Danny, this is the same woman who shot us. And you're talking flowers.'

Molly McNamara had driven herself to Baptist Hospital after experiencing mild chest pains. She had a private room with a gorgeous view of a parking deck.

When he saw her shriveled in the bed, Danny Pogue gulped desperately to suppress the tears. Bud Schwartz also was jarred by the sight—she looked strikingly pallid and frail. And small. He'd never thought of Molly McNamara as a small woman, but that's how she appeared in the hospital: small and caved-in. Maybe because all that glorious white hair was stuffed under a paper cap.

'The flowers are splendid,' she said, lifting the thin plastic tube that fed extra oxygen to her nostrils.

Danny Pogue positioned the vase on the bedstand, next to the telephone. 'American Beauty roses,' he said.

'So I see.'

The burglars stood on opposite sides of the bed. Molly reached out and held their hands.

She said, 'A touch of angina, that's all. I'll be as good as new in a few days.'

Danny Pogue wondered if angina was contagious; it sounded faintly sexual. 'The house is fine,' he said. 'The disposal jammed this morning, but I fixed it myself.'

'A spatula got stuck,' Bud Schwartz added. 'Don't ask how.'

Molly said, 'How is Agent Hawkins?'

'Same as ever.'

'Are you feeding him?'

'Three times a day, just like you told us.'

'Are his spirits improved?'

'Hard to tell,' Bud Schwartz said. 'He don't talk much with all that tape on his face.'

'I heard about the golfer being shot,' said Molly. 'Mr. Kingsbury's had quite a run of bad luck, wouldn't you say?' She asked the question with a trace of a smile. Danny Pogue glanced down at his shoes.

To change the subject, Bud Schwartz asked if there was a cafeteria in the hospital. 'I could sure use a Coke.'

'Make that two,' said Danny Pogue. 'And a lemonade for Molly.'

'Yes, that would hit the spot. Or maybe a ginger ale, something carbonated.' She patted Danny Pogue's hand. Again he looked as if he were about to weep.

In the elevator Bud Schwartz couldn't shake the vision of the old woman sunken in bed. It was all Kingsbury's fault—Molly hadn't felt right since those bastards beat her up at the condo. That one of them had been gunned down later by a baboon was only a partial consolation; the other goon, the one with nine fingertips, was still loose. Joe Winder had said don't worry, they'll all pay—but what did Winder know about the law of the street? He was a writer, for Chrissakes. A goddamn dreamer. Bud Schwartz had agreed to help but he couldn't pretend to share Winder's optimism. As a lifelong criminal, he knew for a fact that the bad guys seldom get what they deserve. More often they just plain get away, even assholes who beat up old ladies.

Bud Schwartz was so preoccupied that he got off on the wrong floor and found himself standing amidst throngs of cooing relatives at the window of the nursery. He couldn't believe the number of newborn babies—it baffled him, left him muttering while others clucked and pointed and sighed. In a world turning to shit, why were so many people still having children? Maybe it was a fad, like CB radios and Cabbage Patch dolls. Or maybe these men and women didn't understand the full implications of reproduction.

More victims, thought Bud Schwartz, the last damn thing we need. He gazed at the rows of sleeping infants, crinkly and squinty-eyed and blissfully innocent, and silently foretold their future. They would grow up to have automobiles and houses and apartments that would all, eventually, be burglarized by lowlifes such as himself.

When Bud Schwartz returned to Molly McNamara's room, he sensed he was interrupting something private. Danny Pogue, who had been talking in a low voice, became silent at the sight of his partner.

Molly thanked Bud Schwartz for the cup of ginger ale. 'Danny's got something to tell you,' she said.

'Yeah?'

'I must admit,' Molly said, 'he left me speechless.'

'So let's hear it already.'

Danny Pogue lifted his chin and thrust out his bony chest. 'I decided to give my share of the money to Molly.'

'Not to me personally,' she interjected. 'To the Mothers of Wilderness.'

'And the Wildlife Rescue Corps!'

'Unofficially, yes,' she said.

'The mob money,' Danny Pogue explained.

Bud Schwartz didn't know whether to laugh or scream. 'Twenty-five grand? You're just givin' it away?'

Molly beamed. 'Isn't that a magnificent gesture?'

'Oh, magnificent,' said Bud Schwartz. Magnificently stupid.

Danny Pogue picked up on his partner's sarcasm and tried to mount a defense. He said, 'It's just somethin' I wanted to do, okay?'

'Fine by me.'

Molly said, 'It automatically makes him a Golden Lifetime Charter Member!'

'It also automatically makes him broke.'

'Come on,' Danny Pogue said, 'it's for a good cause.'

Bud Schwartz's eyes narrowed. 'Don't even think about asking.'

'Danny, he's right,' said Molly. 'It's not fair to pressure a friend.'

Warily Bud Schwartz scanned Molly's bed sheets for any lumps that might reveal the outline of a pistol. He said, 'Look, I wanna go straight. That money's my future.'

Danny Pogue rolled his eyes and snorted. 'Cut the bull—I mean, don't kid yourself. All we're ever gonna be is thieves.'

'Now there's a happy thought. That's what I mean about you and your fucking attitude.'

To Danny Pogue's relief, Molly barely flinched at the profane adjective. She said, 'Bud, I respect your ambitions. I really do.'

But Danny Pogue wasn't finished whining. 'Man, at least can't you spare *some*thing?'

For several moments the only sound was the muted whistle of Molly's oxygen machine. Finally she said, in a voice creaky with fatigue, 'Even a small donation would be appreciated.'

Bud Schwartz ground his molars. 'How does a grand sound? Is

that all right?' Christ, he must be insane. One thousand dollars to a bunch of blue-haired bunny huggers!

Molly McNamara smiled kindly. Danny Pogue exuberantly chucked him on the shoulder.

Bud Schwartz said, 'Why don't I feel wonderful about this?'

'You will,' Molly replied, 'someday.'

Among the men hired by Pedro Luz as security officers was Diamond J. Love, Diamond being his given name and the 'J' standing for Jesus. As was true with most of the guards at the Amazing Kingdom of Thrills, Diamond J. Love's personal history was investigated with only enough diligence to determine the absence of outstanding felony warrants. It was a foregone conclusion that Diamond J. Love's career in law enforcement had been derailed by unpleasant circumstances; there was no other logical reason for applying as a private security guard at a theme park.

Initially, Diamond J. Love was apprehensive about his employment chances at the Amazing Kingdom. He knew that Disney World and other family resorts were scrupulous about hiring clean-cut, enthusiastic, All-American types; Diamond J. Love was worried because in all ways he defied the image, but he need not have worried. Nobody from the Amazing Kingdom bothered to check with previous employers, such as the New York City Police Department, to inquire about allegations of bribery, moral turpitude, substance abuse, witness tampering and the unnecessary use of deadly force, to wit, the pistol-whipping of a young man suspected of shoplifting a bag of cheese-flavored Doritos.

Diamond J. Love was elated to be hired for the security force at the Amazing Kingdom, and pleased to find himself surrounded with colleagues of similarly checkered backgrounds. On slow days, when they weren't breaking into the RVs of tourists, they'd sit around and swap stories about the old police days—tales of stacking the civil-service boards to beat a brutality rap; perjuring themselves silly before grand juries; rounding up hookers on phony vice sweeps just to cop a free hummer; switching kilos of baking soda for cocaine in the evidence rooms. Diamond J. Love enjoyed these bull sessions, and he enjoyed his job. For the most part.

The only area of concern was the boss himself, a monster steroid freak whose combustible mood swings had prompted several of his own officers to leave their holsters permanently unsnapped, just in case. Some days Pedro Luz was reasonable and coherent, other days he was a drooling psycho. The news that he had chewed off his own foot only heightened the anxiety level on the security squad; even the potheads were getting jumpy.

Which is why Diamond J. Love did not wish to be late for work on this very important morning, and why he reacted with exceptionally scathing impudence to the mild-mannered inquiry of a black state trooper who had pulled over his car on County Road 905.

'May I see your driver's license, please?'

'Get serious, Uncle Ben.'

From there it went downhill. The trooper was singularly unimpressed by Diamond J. Love's expired NYPD police badge; nor was he particularly understanding on the issue of Diamond J. Love's outdated New York driver's license. Or the fact that, according to some computer, the serial numbers on Diamond J. Love's Camaro matched precisely those of a Camaro stolen eight months earlier in New Smyrna Beach.

'That's bullshit,' suggested Diamond J. Love.

'Please get out of the car,' the trooper said.

At which point Diamond J. Love attempted to speed away, and instead felt himself dragged by the collar through the window and deposited face-first on the macadam. Upon regaining consciousness, Diamond J. Love discovered Plasticuffs cinched painfully to his wrists and ankles. He further was surprised to see that he shared his predicament with several other security guards, who had apparently encountered the highway patrol on the predawn journey to the Amazing Kingdom of Thrills. There sat Ossie Cano, former Seattle robbery detective-turned-fence; William Z. Ames, former Orlando patrolman-turned-pornographer; Neal

'Bart' Bartkowski, former sergeant with the Atlanta police, currently appealing a federal conviction for tax evasion.

'The hell's going on here?' demanded Diamond J. Love.

'Roadblock,' Cano replied.

'A one-man roadblock?'

'I heard him radio for backup.'

'But still,' said Diamond J. Love. 'One guy?'

By sunrise there were nine of them handcuffed or otherwise detained, a row of sullen penguins lined up along County Road 905. Basically it was the Amazing Kingdom's entire security force, except for Pedro Luz and one other guard, who had spent the night at the amusement park.

Trooper Jim Tile was impressed by the accuracy of Joe Winder's intelligence, particularly the make and license numbers of the guards' personal cars—information pilfered by Carrie Lanier from the files of the Personnel Department. Jim Tile was also impressed that not a single one of the guards had a clean record; to a man there arose problems with driver's licenses, expired registration stickers, doctored title certificates or unpaid traffic tickets. Each of the nine attempted to slide out of the road check by flashing outdated police ID—'badging,' in cop vernacular. Two of the nine had offered Jim Tile a whispered inducement of either cash or narcotics; three others had sealed their fate by making racial remarks. All had been disarmed and handcuffed so swiftly, and with such force, that physical resistance had been impossible.

When the van from the Monroe County Sheriff's Office arrived, the deputy's eyes swept from Jim Tile to the cursing horde of prisoners and back again.

The deputy said, 'Jimmy, you do this all by yourself?'

'One at a time,' the trooper answered. 'A road check, that's all.'

'I know some of these boys.'

'Figured you might.'

'We lookin' at anything serious?'

'We're considering it.'

From the end of the line came an outcry from Diamond J. Love: 'Dwight, you gonna let this nigger get away with it?'

Jim Tile gave no indication of hearing the remark. The deputy named Dwight did, however. 'Damndest thing,' he said in a hearty voice. 'The air-conditioning broke down in the paddy wagon. Just now happened.'

The trooper said, 'What a shame.'

'Gonna be a long trip back to the substation.'

'Probably gets hot as hell inside that van.'

'Like an oven,' Dwight agreed with a wink.

'Fuck you!' shouted Diamond J. Love. 'Fuck the both of you.'

The phone bleeped in Charles Chelsea's apartment at seven-fifteen. It might as well have been a bomb.

'That fucking Pedro, I can't find him!' Who else but Francis X. Kingsbury.

'Have you tried the gym?' Chelsea said foggily.

'I tried everywhere, hell, you name it. And there's no guards! I waited and waited, finally said fuck it and drove myself to work.' He was on the speaker phone, hollering as he stormed around the office.

'The security men never showed up?'

'Wake up, dicklick! I'm alone, *comprende?* No Pedro, no guards, *nada.*'

Dicklick? Charles Chelsea sat up in bed and shook his head like a spaniel. Do I really deserve to be called a dicklick? Is that what I get for all my loyalty?

Kingsbury continued to fulminate: 'So where in the name of Christ Almighty is everybody? Today of all days—is there something you're not telling me, Charlie?'

'I haven't heard a thing, sir. Let me check into it.' 'You do that!' And he was gone.

Chelsea dragged himself to the kitchen and fine-tuned the coffee-maker. In less than two hours, some lucky customer would breach the turnstiles at the Amazing Kingdom of Thrills and be proclaimed the Five-Millionth Visitor. Officially, at least.

Chelsea was fairly certain that at least one enterprising journalist would take the time to add up the park's true attendance figures and expose the promotion for the hoax that it was. The scene was set for a historic publicity disaster; already the national newsmagazines and out-of-state papers were snooping around, waiting for poor Jake Harp to expire. In recent days Chelsea's office had been deluged with applications for media credentials from publications that previously had displayed no interest in covering the Amazing Kingdom's Summerfest Jubilee. Chelsea wasn't naive enough to believe that the New York *Daily News* was seriously interested in a feature profile of the engineer who'd designed the Wet Willy water slide; no, their presence was explained by pure rampant bloodlust. The kidnapped mango voles, the dead scientist, the dead Orky, the nearly dead Jake Harp, flaming bulldozers, phony snake invasions, exploding cement trucks—an irresistible convergence of violence, mayhem and mortality!

Charles Chelsea understood that the dispatches soon to be filed from the Amazing Kingdom of Thrills wouldn't be bright or warm or fluffy. They would be dark and ominous and chilling. They would describe a screaming rupture of the civil order, a culture in terminal moral hemorrhage.

And this would almost certainly have a negative effect on tourism. Oh well, Chelsea thought, I gave it my best.

He foraged in the refrigerator, unearthed a stale bagel and began gnawing dauntlessly. Hearing a knock at the door, he assumed that the pathologically impatient Kingsbury had sent a car for him.

'Just a second!' Chelsea called, and went to put on a robe.

When he opened the door, he faced the immutable, bewhiskered grin of Robbie Raccoon.

Who was holding, in his three-fingered polyester paw, a gun.

Which was pointed at Charles Chelsea's throat.

'What's this?' croaked the publicity man.

'Show time,' said Joe Winder.

32

The raccoon suit was musty and stifling, but it smelled reassuringly of Carrie's hair and perfume. Even the lint seemed familiar. Through slits in the cheeks Joe Winder was able to see the procession: Bud Schwartz, Danny Pogue and the captive Charles Chelsea, entering the gates of the Amazing Kingdom of Thrills.

To affect Robbie Raccoon's most recognizable mannerisms, Winder took floppy exaggerated steps (the way Carrie had showed him) and jauntily twirled the bushy tail. In spite of the serious circumstances, he felt a bolt of childlike excitement as the amusement park prepared to open for the Summerfest Jubilee. Outside, the trams were delivering waves of eager tourists—the children stampeding rabidly toward the locked turnstiles; the women bravely toting infants and designer baby bags; the men with shoulder-mounted Camcorders aimed at anything that moved. Fruity-colored balloons decorated every lamppost, every shrubbery, every concession; Broadway show tunes blasted through tinny public-address speakers. Mimes and jugglers and musicians rehearsed on street corners while desultory maintenance crews collected cigarette butts, Popsicle sticks and gum wrappers off the pavement. A cowboy from the Wild Bill Hiccup show tested his six-shooter by firing blanks at Petey Possum's scraggly bottom.

'Show business,' said Joe Winder, 'is my life.' The words echoed inside the plaster animal head.

If the costume had a serious flaw (besides the non-functioning air conditioner), it was a crucial lack of peripheral vision. The slits, located several inches below Robbie Raccoon's large plastic eyes, were much too narrow. Had the openings been wider, Winder would have spotted the fleshy pale hand in time to evade it.

It was the hand of famed TV weatherman Willard Scott, and it dragged Joe Winder in front of a camera belonging to the National Broadcasting Company. Danny Pogue, Bud Schwartz and Charles Chelsea stopped in their tracks: Robbie Raccoon was on the 'Today Show.' *Live*. Willard flung one meaty arm around Winder's shoulders, and the other around a grandmother from Hialeah who said she was 107 years old. The old woman was telling a story about riding Henry Flagler's railroad all the way to Key West.

'A hunnert and seven!' marveled Danny Pogue.

Charles Chelsea shifted uneasily. Bud Schwartz shot him a look. 'What, she's lying?'

Morosely the publicity man confessed. 'She's a complete fake. A ringer. I arranged the whole thing.' The burglars stared as if he were speaking another language. Chelsea lowered his voice: 'I *had* to do it. Willard wanted somebody over a hundred years old, they told me he might not come, otherwise. But I couldn't find anyone over a hundred—ninety-one was the best I could do, and the poor guy was completely spaced. Thought he was Rommel.'

Danny Pogue whispered, 'So who's she?'

'A local actress,' Chelsea said. 'Age thirty-eight. The makeup is remarkable.'

'Christ, this is what you do for a living?' Bud Schwartz turned to his partner. 'And I thought *we* were scumballs.'

To the actress, Willard Scott was saying: 'You're here to win that 300-Z, aren't you, sweetheart? In a few minutes the park opens and the first lucky customer through the gate will be Visitor Number Five Million. They'll get the new sports car and all kinds of great prizes!'

'I'm so excited!' the actress proclaimed.

'You run along now, but be careful getting in line. The folks are getting pretty worked up out there. Good luck, sweetheart!' Then Willard Scott gave the bogus 107-year-old grandmother a slurpy smooch on the ear. As he released his grip on the woman, he tightened his hug on Joe Winder.

And an awakening nation heard the famous weatherman

say: 'This ring-tailed rascal is one of the most popular characters here at the Amazing Kingdom of Thrills. Go ahead, tell us your name.'

And in a high squeaky voice, Joe Winder gamely replied: 'Hi, Willard! My name is Robbie Raccoon.'

'You're certainly a big fella, Robbie. Judging by the size of that tummy, I'd say you've been snooping through a few garbage cans!'

To which Robbie Raccoon responded: 'Look who's talking, lard-ass.'

Briefly the smile disappeared from Willard's face, and his eyes searched desperately off-camera for the director. A few feet away, Charles Chelsea tasted bile creeping up his throat. The burglars seemed pleased to be standing so close to a genuine TV star.

A young woman wearing earphones and a jogging suit held up a cue card, and valiantly the weatherman attempted to polish off the segment: 'Well, spirits are obviously running high for the big Summerfest Jubilee, so pack up the family and come down to'—here Willard paused to find his place on the card—'Key Largo, Florida, and enjoy the fun! You can swim with a real dolphin, or go sliding headfirst down the Wet Willy or bust some broncos with Wild Bill Hiccup. And you kids can get your picture taken with all your favorite animal characters, even Robbie Raccoon.'

Obligingly Joe Winder cocked his head and twirled his tail. Willard appeared to regain his jolly demeanor. He prodded at something concealed under one of the fuzzy raccoon arms. 'It looks like our ole pal Robbie's got a surprise for Uncle Willard, am I right?'

From Winder came a strained chirp: ''Fraid not, Mr. Scott.'

'Aw, come on. Whatcha got in that paw?'

'*Nothing.*'

'Let's see it, you little scamp. Is it candy? A toy? Whatcha got there?'

And seventeen million Americans heard Robbie Raccoon say: 'That would be a gun, Willard.'

Chelsea's ankles got rubbery and he began to sway. The burglars each grabbed an elbow.

'My, oh, my,' Willard Scott said with a nervous chuckle. 'It even *looks* like a real gun.'

'Doesn't it, though,' said the giant raccoon.

Please, thought Bud Schwartz, not on national TV. Not with little kids watching.

But before anything terrible could happen, Willard Scott adroitly steered the conversation from firearms to a tropical depression brewing in the eastern Caribbean. Joe Winder was able to slip away when the weatherman launched into a laxative commercial.

On the path to the Cimarron Saloon, Charles Chelsea and the burglars heard howling behind them; a rollicking if muffled cry that emanated from deep inside the globular raccoon head.

'Aaaahhh-ooooooooooo,' Joe Winder sang. 'We're the were-wolves of Florida! Aaaahhh-ooooooooooo!'

The smoke from Moe Strickland's cigar hung like a purple shroud in The Catacombs. Uncle Ely's Elves had voted unanimously to boycott the Jubilee, and Uncle Ely would honor their decision.

'The cowboy getups look stupid,' he agreed.

The actor who played the elf Jeremiah, and sometimes Dumpling, lit a joint to counteract the stogie fumes. He declared, 'We're not clowns, we're actors. So fuck Kingsbury.'

'That's right,' said another elf. 'Fuck Mr. X.'

Morale in the troupe had been frightfully low since the newspapers had picked up the phony story about a hepatitis outbreak. Several of the actor-elves had advocated changing the name of the act to escape the stigma. Others wanted to hire a Miami attorney and file a lawsuit.

Moe Strickland said, 'I heard they're auditioning up at Six Flags.'

'Fuck Six Flags,' said Jeremiah-Dumpling elf. 'Probably another damn midget routine.'

'Our options are somewhat limited,' Moe Strickland said, trying to put it as delicately as possible.

'So fuck our options.'

The mood began to simmer after they'd passed the joint around about four times. Moe Strickland eventually stubbed out the cigar and began to enjoy himself. On the street above, a high-school marching band practiced the theme from *2001: A Space Odyssey*. Filtered through six feet of stone, it didn't sound half bad.

One of the actor-elves said, 'Did I mention there's a guy living in our dumpster?'

'You're kidding,' said Moe Strickland.

'No, Uncle Ely, it's true. We met him yesterday.'

'In the dumpster?'

'He fixed it up nice like you wouldn't believe. We gave him a beer.'

Moe Strickland wondered how a homeless person could've found a way into The Catacombs, or why he'd want to stay where it was so musty and humid and bleak.

'A nice guy,' said the actor-elf. 'A real gentleman.'

'We played poker,' added Jeremiah-Dumpling. 'Cleaned his fucking clock.'

'But he was a sport about it. A gentleman, like I said.'

Again Moe Strickland raised the subject of Six Flags. 'Atlanta's a great town,' he said. 'Lots of pretty women.'

'We'll need some new songs.'

'That's okay,' said Moe Strickland. 'Some new songs would be good. We'll have the whole bus ride to work on the arrangements. Luther can bring his guitar.'

'Why not?' said Jeremiah-Dumpling. 'Fuck Kingsbury anyhow.'

'That's the spirit,' Moe Strickland said.

From the end of the tunnel came the sound of boots on brick. A man bellowed furiously.

'Damn,' said one of the actor-elves. He dropped the nub of the joint and ground it to ash under a long, curly-toed, foam-rubber foot.

The boots and the bellowing belonged to a jittery Spence Mooher, who was Pedro Luz's right-hand man. Mooher was agitated because none of the other security guards had shown up for work on this, the busiest day of the summer. Mooher had been up all night patrolling the Amazing Kingdom, and now it looked as if he'd be up all day.

'I smell weed,' he said to Moe Strickland.

In this field Mooher could honestly boast of expertise; he had served six years with the U.S. Drug Enforcement Administration until he was involuntarily relieved of duty. There had been vague accusations of unprofessional conduct in Puerto Rico— something about a missing flash roll, twenty or thirty thousand dollars. As Spence Mooher was quick to point out, no charges were ever filed.

He shared his new boss's affinity for anabolic steroids, but he strongly disapproved of recreational drugs. Steroids hardened the body, but pot and cocaine softened the mind.

'Who's got the weed?' he demanded of Uncle Ely's Elves.

'Lighten up, Spence,' sighed Moe Strickland.

'Why aren't you shitheads up top in rehearsal? Everybody's supposed to be there.'

'Because we're boycotting,' said Jeremiah-Dumpling. 'We're not going to be in the damn show.'

Mooher's mouth twisted. 'Yes, you are,' he said. 'This is the Summerfest Jubilee!'

'I don't care if it's the second coming of Christ,' said Jeremiah-Dumpling. 'We're not performing.'

Moe Strickland added, 'It's a labor action, Spence. Nothing you can do.'

'No?' With one hand Mooher grabbed the veteran character actor by the throat and slammed him against a row of tall lockers. The actor-elves could only cry out helplessly as the muscular security officer banged Uncle Ely's head again and again, until blood began to trickle from his ears. The racket of bone against metal was harrowing, and amplified in the bare tunnel.

Finally Spence Mooher stopped. He held Moe Strickland at arm's length, three feet off the ground; the actor kicked spasmodically.

'Have you reconsidered?' Mooher asked. Moe Strickland's eyelids drooped, but he managed a nod.

A deep voice down the passageway said, 'Let him go.'

Spence Mooher released Uncle Ely and wheeled to face . . . a bum. An extremely tall bum, but a bum nonetheless. It took the security guard a few moments to make a complete appraisal: the damp silver beard, braided on one cheek only; the flowered plastic rain hat pulled taut over the scalp; the broad tan chest wrapped in heavy copper-stained bandages; a red plastic collar around the neck; one dead eye steamed with condensation, the other alive and dark with anger; the mouthful of shiny white teeth.

Here, thought Spence Mooher, was a bum to be reckoned with. He came to this conclusion approximately one second too late, for the man had already seized Mooher's testicles and twisted with such forcefulness that all strength emptied from Mooher's powerful limbs; quivering, he felt a rush of heat down his legs as he soiled himself. When he tried to talk, a weak croaking noise came out of his mouth.

'Time to go night-night,' said the bum, twisting harder. Spence Mooher fell down unconscious.

With a slapping of many oversized feet, the actor-elves scurried toward the slack figure of Moe Strickland, who was awake but in considerable pain. Jeremiah-Dumpling lifted Moe's bloody head and said, 'This is the guy we told you about. The one in the dumpster.'

Skink bent down and said, 'Pleased to meet you, Uncle Ely. I think your buddies better get you to the vet.'

Charles Chelsea tested the door to Francis X. Kingsbury's office and found it locked. He tapped lightly but received no reply.

'I know he's in there,' Chelsea said.

Danny Pogue said, 'Allow us.' He produced a small screwdriver and easily popped the doorjamb.

'Like ridin' a bicycle,' said Bud Schwartz.

From inside the raccoon costume came a hollow command.

The others stood back while Joe Winder opened the door. Upon viewing the scene, he clapped his paws and said: 'Perfect.'

Francis X. Kingsbury was energetically fondling himself in front of a television set. On the screen, a dark young man in a torn soccer jersey was copulating with a wild-haired brunette woman, who was moaning encouragement in Spanish. Other video cassettes were fanned out like a poker hand on the desk.

Kingsbury halted mid-pump and wheeled to confront the intruders. The boxer shorts around his ankles greatly diminished his ability to menace. Today's hair-piece was a silver Kenny Rogers model.

'Get out,' Kingsbury snarled. He fumbled for the remote control and turned off the VCR. He seemed unaware that the Amazing Kingdom's stalwart mascot, Robbie Raccoon, was pointing a loaded semi-automatic at him. Joe Winder tucked the gun under one arm while he unzipped his head and removed it.

'So you're alive,' Kingsbury hissed. 'I had a feeling, goddammit.'

Bud Schwartz laughed and pointed at Kingsbury, who shielded his receding genitals. The burglar said, 'The asshole's wearing golf shoes!'

'For traction,' Joe Winder theorized.

Charles Chelsea looked disgusted. Danny Pogue tossed a package on the desk. 'Here,' he said to Kingsbury, 'even though you tried to kill us.'

'What's this?'

'The files we swiped. Ramex, Gotti, it's all there.'

Kingsbury was confused. Why would they return the files now? Bud Schwartz read his expression and said, 'You were right. It was out of our league.'

Which was baloney. The true reason for returning the files was to ensure that no one would come searching for them later. Like the police or the FBI.

'I suppose you want, what, a great big thank-you or some such goddamn thing.' Francis X. Kingsbury tugged the boxer shorts high on his gelatinous waist. The indignity of the moment finally had sunk in. 'Get out or I'm calling Security!'

'You've got no Security,' Winder informed him.

'Charlie?'

'I'm afraid that's right, sir. I'll explain later.'

Bud Schwartz said to his partner, 'This is pathetic. Let's go.'

'Wait.' Danny Pogue stepped up to Kingsbury and said: 'Beating up an old lady, what's the matter with you?'

'What the hell do you care.' By now Kingsbury had more or less focused on Joe Winder's gun, so he spoke to Danny Pogue without looking at him. 'That fucking Pedro, he gets carried away. Not a damn thing I can do.'

'She's a sick old woman, for Chrissake.'

'What's your point, Jethro?'

'My point is this,' said Danny Pogue, and ferociously punched Francis Kingsbury on the chin. Kingsbury's golf cleats snagged on the carpet as he toppled.

Surveying the messy scene, Charles Chelsea felt refreshingly detached. He truly didn't care anymore. Outside, a roar of thousands swept the Amazing Kingdom, followed by gay cheers and applause. Chelsea went to the window and parted the blinds. 'What do you know,' he said. 'Our five-millionth customer just walked through the gate.'

With gray hands Kingsbury clutched the corner of the desk and pulled himself to his feet. In this fashion he was also able to depress a concealed alarm button that rang in the Security Office.

But Schwartz said, 'We'll be saying good-bye now.'

'You're welcome to stay,' offered Joe Winder.

'No thanks.' Danny Pogue examined his knuckles for bruises and abrasions. He said, 'Molly's having surgery this afternoon. We promised to be at the hospital.'

'I understand,' Winder said. 'You guys want to take anything?' He motioned with his gun paw around the lavish office. 'The VCR? Some tapes? How about a cellular phone for the car?'

'The phone might be good,' said Danny Pogue. 'What'd you think, Bud? You could call your little boy from the road, wouldn't that be cool?'

'Let's roll,' Bud Schwartz said.

Later they were driving on Card Sound Road, halfway back to

the mainland, when Bud Schwartz motioned with a thumb and said: 'Right about here's where it all started, Danny. Me throwin' that damn rat in the convertible.'

'It was a vole,' said Danny Pogue. 'A blue-tongued mango vole. *Microtus mango*. That's the Latin name.'

Bud Schwartz laughed. 'Whatever you say.' There was no denying he was impressed. How many burglars knew Latin?

A few more miles down the road, Danny Pogue again brought up the topic of portable phones. 'If we had us one right now, we could call the hospital and see how she's doin'.'

'You know the problem with cellulars,' said Bud Schwartz.

'The reception?'

'Besides the reception,' Bud Schwartz said. 'The problem with cellulars is, people always steal the damn things.'

'Yeah,' said his partner. 'I hadn't thought about that.' The emergency buzzer awakens Pedro Luz in the storage room. He sits up and blinks. Blinks at the bare light bulb. Blinks at the pitted walls. Blinks at the empty intravenous bags on the hangers. He thinks, What the hell was it this time? Stanozolol, yeah. He'd pilfered a half-dozen tabs from Spence Mooher's locker. Ground them up with the toe of a boot, stirred it in the bag with the dextrose.

Feeling good. Feeling just fine. The beer sure helped.

Then comes Kingsbury's alarm and it sounds like a dental drill. Better get up now. Better get moving.

Pedro Luz pulls the tubes from his arms and tries to stand. Whoa, hoss! He forgot all about his foot, the fact that it was missing.

He grabs a wooden crutch and steadies himself. Facing the mirror, Pedro notices he's buck naked from the waist down. The image shocks him; his legs are as thick as oaks, but his penis is no larger than a peanut. Hastily he scrambles into the trousers of his guard uniform, the gun belt, one sock, one shoe.

Time to go to work. It's the Summerfest Jubilee and Mr. Kingsbury's in some kind of trouble.

And the damn door won't open.

Pedro can't fucking believe it. Okay, now somebody's either

locked the damn thing from the outside, which don't make sense, or maybe welded it shut, which is even crazier. Pedro lowers one shoulder and hits the door like a tackle dummy. *Nada.* Now he's getting pissed. Through the steel he yells for Cano or Spence or Diamond J. Love, and gets no answer. 'Where the hell *is* everybody?' hollers Pedro Luz.

Next logical step is using his skull as a battering ram. Wedging the crutch against the baseboard, he uses it to vault himself headfirst at the door. Amazing thing is, it don't hurt after a while. Tense the neck muscles just before impact and it acts like a spring. Boom, boom, boom. Boing, boing, boing.

No more door! Flattened.

What a fine feeling, to be free again.

The Security Office is empty, which is a mystery. Pedro checks the time cards and sees that none of the other guards have clocked in; something's going on here. Outside, the morning sun burns through a milky August haze, and the park is crawling with customers. There's a middle-aged lady at the security window complaining how somebody swiped her pocketbook off the tram. Behind her is some guy from Wisconsin, red hair and freckles, says he locked his keys in the rental car. And behind him is some bony old man with a shnoz that could cut glass. Claims one of the animals is walking around the park with a gun. Which one? Pedro asks. The possum? The raccoon? We got bunches of animals, says Pedro Luz. And the old guy scratches his big nose and says he don't know the difference from animals. Was Wally Wolverine for all he knows, but it damn sure was a gun in its paw. Sure, says Pedro, whatever you say. Here's a form to fill out. I'll be back in a few minutes.

Between the whiny tourists and all that banging with his head, Pedro's finally waking up. On the floor near the broken door he spots something shiny, and checks it out: a new Master padlock, still fastened to the broken hasp.

Pedro never would've imagined it was the lovely Princess Golden Sun who'd locked him in the storage room with his drugs and beer. He figured it was Spence Mooher or one of the other security guards, playing a joke.

He could deal with those jerk-offs later. Now it was time to haul ass over to Mr. Kingsbury's office and see what was wrong. For a moment Pedro Luz thought he heard the alarm go off again, but then he realized no, it was just the regular buzzing in his eardrums. Only it seemed to be getting louder.

33

'First things first,' Joe Winder said. 'Who killed Will Koocher?'

Francis X. Kingsbury was rolling a shiny new Titleist from hand to hand across the top of his desk. The brassy strains of a marching band rose from the street below; the Summerfest Jubilee was in full swing.

'This Koocher,' Kingsbury said, 'he was threatening to go public about the voles. Pangs of conscience, whatever. So what I did, I told that fucking Pedro to go talk sense with the boy. See, it would've been a disaster—and Charlie'll back me up on this— a goddamn mess if it came out the voles were fake. Especially after the stupid things got stolen—talk about embarrassing.'

Winder said, 'So the answer to the question is Pedro. That's who committed the murder.'

Kingsbury smothered his nose with a handkerchief and snuffled like a boar. 'Damn hay fever!' The handkerchief puckered with each breath. 'Far as I'm concerned, Koocher drowned in the Orky tank. Plain and simple. Case closed.'

'But everyone knew the truth.'

'No!' Chelsea protested. 'I swear to God, Joey.'

'Tell me about the blue-tongued mango voles,' said Joe Winder. 'Whose clever idea was that?'

From behind the veil of the soggy hanky, Kingsbury said: 'I figured wouldn't it be fantastic if the Amazing Kingdom had an animal we could save. Like Disney tried to do with the dusky sparrow, only I was thinking in terms of a panda bear. People, I've seen this, they go fucking nuts for pandas. Only come to find out it's too hot down here, they'd probably croak in the sun.

'So I call this connection I got, this old friend, and I ask her what's endangered in Florida and she says all the good ones are taken—the panthers and manatees and so forth. She says it'd be better to come up with an animal nobody else had or even knew about. She says we might even get a government grant, which it turns out we did. Two hundred grand!'

Chelsea tried to act appalled; he even made a sound like a gasp. Impatiently, Winder said, 'Charlie, this might come as a shock, but I don't care how much you knew and how much you didn't. For the purposes of settling this matter, you've become superfluous. Now show Mr. Kingsbury what we've prepared.'

From an inside pocket Chelsea withdrew a folded sheet of Amazing Kingdom stationery. He handed it across the desk to Francis X. Kingsbury, who set aside both the handkerchief and the golf ball in order to read.

'It's a press release,' Chelsea said.

'I see what it is. Horseshit is what it is.' Kingsbury scanned it several times, including once from the bottom up. His mouth moved in twitchy circles, like a mule chewing a carrot.

'You ought to consider it,' Winder advised him, 'if you want to stay out of jail.'

'Oh, so now it's blackmail?'

'No, sir, it's the cold fucking hand of fate.'

Nervously Kingsbury fingered the bridge of his nose. 'The hell is your angle, son?'

'You arranged an elaborate scientific fraud for the purposes of profit. An ingenious fraud, to be sure, but a felony nonetheless. Two hundred thousand is just about enough to interest the U.S. Attorney's Office.'

Kingsbury shrugged in mockery. 'Is that, what, like the end of the world?'

'I forgot,' Winder said, 'you're an expert on indictments. Aren't you, Frankie?'

Kingsbury turned color.

'Frankie King,' said Winder. 'That's your real name, in case you don't remember.'

Kingsbury shrank into the chair. Winder turned to Charles Chelsea and said, 'I think somebody's finally in the mood to talk.'

'Can I leave?'

'Certainly, Charlie. And thanks for a terrific job on the publicity release.'

'Yeah, right.'

'I mean it,' Winder said. 'It's seamless.'

Chelsea eyed him warily. 'You're just being sarcastic.'

'No, it was perfect. You've got a definite flair.'

'Thanks, Joe. And I mean it, too.'

The rescue of Francis Kingsbury was further delayed when a disturbance broke out near the front gate of the Amazing Kingdom; a tense and potentially violent dispute over the distribution of prizes, specifically a Nissan 300-Z.

The security-guard uniform is what gave Pedro Luz away. As he crutched toward Kingsbury's office, he was spotted and intercepted by a flying wedge of disgruntled customers. Something about the Summerfest contest being rigged. Pedro Luz insisted he didn't know about any damn contest, but the customers were loud and insistent. They led the security man back to the stage, where a short plump tourist named Rossiter had just been presented the keys to the sleek new sports car. Draped around Mr. Rossiter's neck was a shiny streamer that said: 'OUR FIVE-MILLIONTH SPECIAL GUEST!' In response to questions from a tuxedoed emcee, Mr. Rossiter said he was visiting the Amazing Kingdom with his wife and mother-in-law. He said it was only his second trip to Florida.

Mr. Rossiter gave the car keys to his wife, who squeezed her torso into the driver's seat and happily posed for pictures. Several persons in the crowd began to hiss and boo. Somebody threw a cup of frozen yogurt, which splattered against one of the car's wire wheels.

This was too much for Pedro Luz's jangled, hormone-flooded sensory receptors. He grabbed the microphone from the emcee and said, 'Next person that throws food, I break their fucking spine.'

Instantly a lull came over the mob. Pedro Luz said, 'Now somebody explain what's going on.'

At first no one spoke up, but there was a good bit of whispering about the bloody purple knots on the security chief's forehead. Finally a man in the crowd pointed at the Rossiters and shouted, 'They cheated, that's what!'

Another male voice: 'He cut in line!'

Pedro Luz said, 'Jesus, I can't believe you people.' He turned to the Rossiters. 'Is it true? Did you cut in line?'

'No, Officer,' Mr. Rossiter answered. 'We got here first, fair and square.'

Mrs. Rossiter popped her head from the car and said, 'They're just a bunch of sore losers.' Mrs. Rossiter's mother, a stubby woman wearing sandals and a Petey Possum T-shirt, said she'd never seen such rude people in all her life.

Pedro Luz didn't know what to do next; for one pleasantly deranged moment, he considered throwing the Rossiters off the stage and claiming the 300-Z for himself. *Daring* anyone to try to take it away from him. Then Charles Chelsea materialized and Pedro Luz gratefully surrendered the microphone. His ears buzzed and his head clanged and all he really wanted to do was limp to the gymnasium and pump some iron.

'Ladies and gentlemen,' Chelsea intoned, 'please settle down.' He looked smooth and confident in a crisp blue oxford shirt and a wine-colored tie. He looked as if he could talk his way out of practically anything.

'I've reviewed the tapes from our security cameras,' Chelsea told the crowd, 'and whether you like it or not, Mr. Rossiter and his family were clearly the first ones through the turnstiles this morning—'

'But he threatened me!' yelled a teenager in the crowd. 'I was here first but he said he'd kill me!'

A middle-aged woman in a straw Orky hat hollered: 'Me, too! And I was ahead of that kid—'

The crowd surged toward the stage until Pedro Luz drew his revolver and aimed it toward the sky. Seeing the gun, the tourists grew quiet and rippled back a few steps.

'Thank you,' Chelsea said to Pedro Luz.

'I got an emergency.'

'You can go now. I'll be fine.'

'You need a gun?'

'No,' said Chelsea, 'but thanks just the same.'

'You got something against fun.'

Francis Kingsbury made it an indictment. 'What, you got something against little children? Little cutey pies having a good time?'

Joe Winder said: 'You can keep the park, Frankie. The park is already built. It's the golf resort that's eighty-sixed, as of today.'

'Oh, ho,' said Kingsbury. 'So you got something against golf?'

'That's the deal. Take it or leave it.'

'You think you can scare me? Hell, I got gangsters shooting at me. Professionals.' Kingsbury cut loose an enormous sneeze, and promptly plugged his nostrils with the handkerchief.

Winder said, 'I was hoping to appeal to the pragmatic side of your nature.'

'Listen, I know how to handle this situation from up North. The way to handle it is, I cut the wop bastards in. The Zubonis, I'm talking about. I cut 'em in on Falcon Trace, you'd be surprised how fast they let bygones be bygones. You watch what good friends we are once I start using Zuboni roofers, Zuboni drywall, Zuboni plumbing.' Kingsbury looked positively triumphant. 'Blackmail, my ass. The fuck are you going to blackmail me with now?'

'I believe you misunderstood the offer,' Joe Winder said. 'I'm not planning to go to the mob. I'm planning to go to the media.'

Defiantly Kingsbury snatched the hanky from his nose. 'Jesus, you're pissing me off.' He picked up the phone and commanded the operator to connect him with Security. Joe Winder took two steps toward the desk, raised his paw and shot the telephone console to pieces.

Impressed, Kingsbury probed at the tangle of wires and broken plastic. 'Goddamn lunatic,' he said.

Winder sat down and tucked the gun into the furry folds of the costume. 'Think in terms of headlines,' he said. 'Imagine what'll happen when the newspapers find out the Amazing

Kingdom of Thrills is run by a Mafia snitch. You'll be famous, Frankie. Wouldn't you love to be interviewed by Connie Chung?'

'Let me just say, fuck you.'

Winder frowned. 'Don't make me shoot up more office equipment. Stop and consider the facts. You obtained the bank notes and financing for Falcon Trace under false pretenses; to wit, using a false name and phony credit references. Ditto on your construction permits. Ditto on your performance bond. Once the money boys find out who you really are, once they read about it on the front page of the *Wall Street Journal*, not only is Falcon Trace dead, you can look forward to spending the rest of your natural life at the courthouse, getting your fat ass sued off. Everybody'll want a piece, Frankie. We're talking cluster-fuck.'

He now had Francis X. Kingsbury's undivided attention. 'And last but not least,' Winder said, 'is the criminal situation. If I'm not mistaken, you're still on probation.'

'Yeah, so?'

'So the terms of probation strictly prohibit consorting with known felons and other unsavory dirtbags. However, a review of your Security Department indicates you're not only consorting with known criminals, you've surrounded yourself with them.'

'This isn't Orlando,' Kingsbury said. 'Down here it's not so easy to get good help. If I was as strict as Disney, I'd have nobody working for me. What, maybe altar boys? Mormons and Brownie Scouts? This is Miami, for Chrissakes, I got a serious recruiting problem here.'

'Nonetheless,' Joe Winder said, 'you've gone out of your way to dredge up extremely primitive life-forms.'

'What's wrong with giving a guy a second chance?' Kingsbury paused for a second, then said, 'I'm the first to admit, hell, Pedro was a bad choice. I didn't know about the damn drugs.' Speaking of Pedro, he thought, where the hell is he?

'What's done is done,' Winder said. He fanned himself with his spare paw, it was wretchedly hot inside the costume. 'Frankie, this is a matter for you and the probation bureau. Between us boys, I wouldn't be surprised if they packed you off to Eglin for six or eight months. You do play tennis, don't you?'

The haughtiness ebbed from Kingsbury's face. Pensively he traced a pudgy finger along the lines of his infamous rodent tattoo. 'Winder, what exactly is your problem?'

'The problem is you're mutilating a fine chunk of island so a bunch of rich people have a warm place to park their butts in the winter. You couldn't have picked a worse location, Frankie, the last green patch of the Keys. You're bulldozing next door to a national wildlife refuge. And offshore, in that magnificent ocean, is the only living coral reef in North America. I believe that's where you intended to flush your toilets—'

'No!' Kingsbury snapped. 'We'll have deep-well sewage injection. High-tech facilities—no runoff, no outfall.'

'Imagine,' Winder mused, 'the shit of millionaires dappling our azure waters.'

Kingsbury reddened and clenched his fists. 'If I go along with this deal, what, it's some major victory for the environment? You think the ghost of Henry Fucking Thoreau is gonna pin a medal or some such goddamn thing on your chest?'

Joe Winder smiled at the thought. 'I've got no illusions,' he said. 'One less golf course is one less golf course. I'll settle for that.'

'The lots, Jesus, they're worth millions. That's what this goddamn piece of paper'll cost me.'

'I'll settle for that, too.'

Kingsbury was still stymied. He glared furiously at Charles Chelsea's final publicity release.

'You'll never understand,' Winder said, 'because you weren't born here. Compared to where you came from, this is always going to look like paradise. Hell, you could wipe out every last bird and butterfly, and it's still better than Toledo in the dead of winter.'

With a dark chuckle, Kingsbury said, 'No kidding.'

'Don't read too much into this operation, Frankie. I'm just sick of asshole carpetbaggers coming down here and fucking up the place. Nothing personal.'

It came out of the blue, Kingsbury saying, 'There was a guy named Jack Winder. Big-time land developer, this goes back a few years, before I was selling waterfront. Winder Planned Communities was the company.'

'My father.'

'What?' said Kingsbury. 'Quit whispering.'

'Jack Winder was my father.'

'Then what the hell are you doing? Biting the hand is what I'd call it. Dishonoring the family name.'

'Depends on your point of view.'

Kingsbury sneered. 'I hear this line of bullshit all the time: "We got our slice of sunshine, fine, now it's time to close the borders." Selfish is what you are.'

'Maybe so,' Winder said. 'I'd like to fish that shoreline again, that's for sure. I'd like to see some tarpon out there next spring.'

Dramatically, Francis Kingsbury straightened in the chair. He began talking with his eyes and hands, unmistakably a sales pitch: 'People come to the Amazing Kingdom, they might like to play some golf. Mommy takes the kids to the theme park, Daddy hits the fairways. So what?'

Winder said nothing. Kingsbury began to knead his jowls in exasperation. 'What the hell's so wrong with that picture? Eighteen lousy holes, I just don't see the crime. It's what Disney did. It's what everybody does with prime acreage. This is Florida, for Chrissakes.'

'Not the way it ought to be, Frankie.'

'Then you're living in what they call a dreamworld. This ain't Oz, son, and there's no fairy wizard to make things right again. Down here the brick road's not yellow, it's green. Plain and simple. Case closed.'

But Joe Winder wasn't changing his mind. 'I hope the papers get your name right,' he said.

Bleakly Kingsbury thought of front-page headlines and multi-million-dollar lawsuits and minimum-security prisons with no driving range. 'All right,' he said to Winder, 'let's talk.'

'You've got my offer. Read the press release, it's all tied up with a pretty ribbon. You shut down Falcon Trace for the noblest of reasons and you're a hero, Frankie. Isn't that what you want?'

'I'd rather have my oceanfront lots.'

Then the door flew open and there, bug-eyed and seething, was Pedro Luz. He aimed a large blue handgun at Joe Winder and grunted something unintelligible.

'Nice of you to put in an appearance,' Kingsbury remarked. His eyes flooded with a mixture of rage and relief. 'This asshole, get him out of my sight! For good this time.'

'Drop the gun,' Pedro Luz told Winder. 'And put on your goddamn head.'

Winder did as he was told. Zipping himself in, he felt cumbersome and helpless and feverishly short of breath.

Kingsbury said, 'He doesn't leave the park alive, you understand?'

'No problem,' said Pedro Luz.

'No *problem*,' mimicked Kingsbury. 'No problem, my ass. This is Mr. Crackerjack Bodyguard, right? Mr. Lightning Response Time.'

For a moment Pedro Luz felt an overwhelming urge to turn the pistol on Francis X. Kingsbury; something told him it would be every bit as satisfying as shooting Joe Winder. Maybe another time, he decided. After payday.

A muted voice inside the raccoon head said: 'This is a big mistake, Frankie.'

Kingsbury laughed mordantly and blew his nose. 'Pedro, it's your last fucking chance. I hope you still got enough brain cells to do this one simple chore.'

'No problem.' With the crutch he roughly shoved Joe Winder toward the door.

'Hey, Pedro.'

'What, Mr. Kingsbury?'

'That's a six-hundred-dollar animal costume. Try not to mess it up.'

34

Carrie Lanier was practicing a song at the mirror as she dressed for the pageant. The door opened behind her, and she saw a flash of orange.

'Hey! We thought you were headed for New York.'

'I seriously considered it.' Skink shut the door with his foot.

'Your friend Officer Tile mentioned Orlando. Somebody shot up a tour bus, he figured it might be you.'

'Another pale imitation, that's all. Where's your boyfriend?'

Carrie described Winder's plan to confront Francis Kingsbury. 'Joe's got all the bases covered.'

Skink shook his head. 'It'll never work.'

'Where have you been, anyway?'

'Down here in the underground, away from all radio beams. I needed a break from that damn plane.'

Carrie moved closer to the mirror and began to put on her makeup. 'What's with the gas cans?' she asked.

Skink carried one in each hand. 'Let's pretend you didn't see these,' he said. 'I just want to make sure you've got a way out of the park.'

'When?'

'Whenever.'

'What about Joe?'

'I expect he's in some trouble,' Skink said. 'I've got a chore to do, then I'll check around.'

'Don't worry, Pedro's locked in the storage room.'

'How? With what?'

When Carrie told him, Skink frowned. 'I guess I'd better get going.'

She said, 'Can you zip me up? There's a little hook at the top.'

Skink set down the gas cans and fastened the back of her gown. He wondered what had happened to the Indian theme.

'When do you go on?' he asked.

'Half an hour.'

'The dress is lovely,' he said, stepping back. 'Half an hour it is.'

'Thanks. Wish me luck.'

'You'll do fine.'

Carrie turned from the mirror. 'Should I wait for Joe?'

'Of course,' said Skink, 'but not too long.'

When they got to the security office, Pedro Luz ordered Joe Winder to remove the raccoon costume and hang it neatly in the uniform closet. Then Pedro Luz dragged Winder into the storage room, clubbed him to the floor and beat him seven or eight times with the crutch—Joe Winder lost count. Every time Pedro Luz struck a blow, he emitted a queer high-pitched peep that sounded like a baby sparrow. When he finally stopped to rest, he was panting heavily and his face shone with damp splotches. Spying from a fetal position on the floor, Joe Winder watched Pedro Luz swallow two handfuls of small orange tablets. Winder assumed these were not muscle relaxants.

'I can kill you with my bare hands,' Pedro Luz said informatively.

Winder sat up, hugging his own chest to prevent pieces of broken ribs from snapping off like dead twigs. He couldn't figure out why Pedro Luz kept a full-length mirror in the storage room.

'It's raining outside,' Pedro Luz said.

'That's what we're waiting for?'

'Yeah. Soon as it stops, I'll take you out and kill you.'

Pedro Luz stripped off his shirt and began to work out with a pair of heavy dumbbells; he couldn't take his eyes off his own glorious biceps. The syncopation of Pedro's breathing and pumping put Joe Winder to sleep. When he awoke much later, still on the floor, he saw that Pedro Luz had put on a fresh uniform. The security man rose unsteadily and reached for the crutch; his hands trembled and his eyelids were mottled and puffy.

'The parade starts soon,' he said. 'Everyone in the park goes to watch—that's when you're gonna break into the ticket office to rip off the cashboxes.'

'And you're going to catch me in the act, and shoot me.'

'Yeah,' Pedro Luz wheezed, 'in the back.'

'Pretty sloppy. The cops'll have plenty of questions.'

'I'm still thinking it through.' His head lolled and he shut his eyes. Joe Winder sprang for the door and regretted it instantly. Pedro Luz was on him like a mad bear; he grabbed Winder at the base of the neck and hurled him backward into the stock shelves.

'And that was one-handed,' Pedro Luz bragged. 'How much do you weigh?'

Winder answered, with a groan, 'One seventy-five.'

The security man beamed. 'Light as a feather. No problem.'

'I'd like to speak with your boss one more time.'

'No way.' Pedro Luz hoisted Winder from a tangle of intravenous tubes and set him down in a bare corner. He said, 'Remember, I still got that gun you were carrying—I figure that's my throwdown. The story is, I had to shoot you because of the gun.'

Winder nodded. 'I'm assuming there'll be no witnesses.'

'Course not. They'll all be at the parade.'

'What about the rain, Pedro? What if the parade's washed out?'

'It's August, asshole. The rain don't last long.' Pedro Luz hammered the heel of his hand against the side of his skull, as if trying to knock a wasp out of his ear. 'God, it's loud in here.'

'I don't mean to nag,' Joe Winder said, 'but you ought to lay off the steroids.'

'Don't start with me!' Pedro Luz cracked the door and poked his head out. 'See, it's stopped already. Just a drizzle.' He gripped Joe Winder by the shoulder. 'Let's go, smartass.'

But Winder could barely walk for the pain. Outside, under a low muddy sky, the tourists rushed excitedly toward Kingsbury Lane, where a band had begun to play. Pedro Luz marched Winder against the flow of yammering, gummy-faced children and their anxious, umbrella-wielding parents. The ticket office was on the other side of the park, a long hike, and Joe Winder had planned to use the time to devise a plan for escape. Instead his thoughts meandered inanely; he noticed, for example, what a high percentage of the Amazing Kingdom's tourists were clinically overweight. Was this a valid cross-section of American society? Or did fat people travel to Florida more frequently than thin people? Three times Winder slowed to ponder the riddle, and three times Pedro Luz thwacked the back of his legs with the dreaded crutch. No one stopped to interfere; most likely they assumed that Winder was a purse snatcher or some other troublemaker being rousted by Security.

Eventually the crowds thinned and the light rain stopped. The two men were alone, crossing the walkway that spanned the dolphin tank. The swim-along attraction had closed early because the trainers were needed at the parade, in case the lion got testy. Joe Winder heard a burst of applause across the amusement park—fireworks blossoming over Kingsbury Lane. The pageant had begun!

Winder thought of Carrie Lanier, and hoped she had the good sense not to come looking for him. He felt Pedro Luz's crutch jab him between the shoulder blades. 'Hold it,' the security man commanded.

A hoary figure appeared at the end of the walkway ahead of them. It was a tall man carrying two red containers.

'Now what?' said Pedro Luz.

Joe Winder's heart sank. Skink didn't see them. He went down two flights of stairs and stacked the gas cans on the back of a Cushman motor cart. He ran back up the steps, disappeared through an unmarked door near the Rare Animal Pavilion and quickly emerged with two more cans of gasoline.

'The Catacombs,' Pedro Luz said, mainly to himself.

Joe Winder heard him unsnap the holster. He turned and told Pedro Luz not to do anything crazy.

'Shut up, smartass.'

As they watched Skink load the second pair of cans onto the Cushman, Winder realized his own mistake: he had tried too hard to be reasonable and civilized and possibly even clever.

Such efforts were wasted on men such as Francis X. Kingsbury. Skink had the right idea.

Pedro Luz aimed his .45 and shouted, 'Freeze right there!' Skink stopped at the top of the steps. Pedro Luz ordered him to raise his hands, but Skink acted as if he didn't hear.

'Don't I know you?' Skink said, coming closer.

Pedro Luz found it difficult to look directly at the bearded stranger because one of the man's eyeballs seemed dislodged from the socket. As Skink approached, he gave no indication of recognizing Joe Winder.

'Hello, gentlemen,' he said. Casually he bent to examine the taped stump of Pedro Luz's leg. 'Son, you're dropping more parts than a Ford Pinto.'

Flustered, Pedro Luz fell back on standard hardass-cop colloquy: 'Lemme see some ID.'

Skink reached into the blaze-orange weather suit and came out with a small kitchen jar. He handed it to the security man and said, 'I believe this belongs to you.'

Pedro Luz felt his stomach quake. At the bottom of the jar, drifting in pickle juice, was the tip of his right index finger. It looked like a cube of pink tofu.

'The old woman bit it off,' Skink reminded him, 'while you were beating her up.'

Beautiful, Joe Winder thought. We're both going to die long horrible deaths.

Hoarsely, Pedro Luz said, 'Who the hell are you?'

Skink gestured at the soiled bandages around his chest. 'I'm the one you shot at the trailer!'

All three of them jumped as a Roman candle exploded high over Kingsbury Lane. A band was playing the theme from *2001: A Space Odyssey*. It sounded dreadful.

In the tank below, Dickie the Dolphin rolled twice and shot a light spray of water from his blowhole. A few drops sprinkled the barrel of Pedro Luz's gun, and he wiped it nervously on the front of his trousers. The circuits of his brain were becoming badly overloaded; assimilating new information had become a struggle—the drugs, the finger in the jar, the one-eyed stoner with the gas cans, the fireworks, the god-awful music. It was time to kill these sorry bastards and go to the gym.

'Who first?' he asked. 'Who wants it first?'

Joe Winder saw no evidence of urgency in Skink's demeanor, so he took it upon himself to ram an elbow into the soft declivity beneath Pedro Luz's breastbone. Winder was stunned to see the bodybuilder go down, and idiotically he leapt upon him to finish the job. Winder's punching ability was hampered by the searing pain in his rib cage, and though Pedro Luz was gagging and drooling and gulping to catch his wind, it was a relatively simple exercise to lock his arms around all hundred and seventy-five pounds of Joe Winder and squeeze the breath out of him. The last thing Winder heard, before blacking out, was a splash in the tank below.

He hoped like hell it was the pistol.

Marine biologists debate the relative intelligence of the Atlantic bottle-nosed dolphin, but it is generally accepted that the grace-ful mammal is extremely smart; that it is able to communicate using sophisticated underwater sonics; that it sometimes appears capable of emotions, including grief and joy. Noting that the dolphin's brain is proportionally larger and more fully developed than that of human beings, some experts contend that the animals are operating in a superior cognitive realm that we simply cannot comprehend.

A more skeptical view (and one endorsed by Joe Winder) is that dolphins probably aren't quite as smart as tourist lore suggests. Otherwise why would they allow themselves to be so easily captured, subjugated, trained and put on public display? It seemed to Winder that somersaulting through hula hoops in exchange for a handful of sardines was not proof of high intellect. Given fins and some Milk-Bones, your average French poodle could master the same feat.

It is certainly true, however, that captive dolphins exhibit distinct and complex personalities. Some are gregarious and easily tamed, while others are aloof and belligerent; some are happy to perform stunts for cheering tourists, while others get ulcers. Because each dolphin is so sensitive and unique, curators must be extremely careful when selecting the animals for commercial aquarium shows.

When it came to jumping hula hoops, Dickie the Dolphin was competent if unspectacular. The same could be said for his tail-walking, his backward flips and his mastery of the beach ball. While most spectators thought he was a lovable ham, experienced dolphin trainers could see he was just going through the motions. Ever since replacing the deceased Orky as the Amazing Kingdom's aquatic star, Dickie had approached each performance with the same sullen indifference. He took a similar attitude into the swim-along sessions, where he habitually kept a large distance between himself and whatever loud pale humanoid had been suckered into entering the tank.

The exception, of course, was when Dickie the Dolphin got into one of his 'moods.' Then he would frolic and nuzzle and rub eagerly against the swimmer, who inevitably mistook these gestures for honest affection. Dolphin researchers have documented numerous sexual advances upon human beings of both genders, but they cannot agree on the animal's intention in these circumstances. If dolphins truly are second to people on the intelligence scale, then they most certainly would not mistake a bikini-clad legal secretary for a member of their own species. Which raises a more intriguing hypothesis: that captive male dolphins attempt these outrageous liaisons out of mischief, or perhaps even revenge. The truth is locked deep inside the dolphin's large and complicated cerebrum, but the phenomenon has been widely reported.

On the evening of August 6, Dickie the Dolphin was in a state of high agitation as he circled the darkened whale tank at the Amazing Kingdom of Thrills. Perhaps it was the percussion of the nearby fireworks that disrupted the powerful creature's peace, or perhaps it was the effect of a long and lonely confinement. Although the trained seals and pelicans could be entertaining, Dickie the Dolphin probably would have preferred the companionship of a female partner. And he would have had one if Francis X. Kingsbury had not been so cheap. In any event, the solitary dolphin was keeping a sharp and wily eye on the commotion taking place along the walkway above.

At the first splash, Dickie swiftly sounded, tracking a small steel object to the bottom of his tank. He never considered retrieving the item, as there would be no reward for his effort—the buckets of cut fish had been hauled away hours ago. So the dolphin disregarded Pedro Luz's gun, glided slowly to the surface and waited.

The second splash was different.

Pedro Luz was astonished by the strength of the one-eyed man. He took a punch as well as anyone that Pedro Luz had ever assaulted, plus he was quick. Every time Pedro Luz swung and missed, the bearded stranger hit him two or three times in the gut. It was starting to hurt immensely.

Having lost his own gun, Pedro Luz tried to retrieve the spare—Joe Winder's gun—from the pocket of his trousers. Every attempt brought a new flurry of punches from the one-eyed hobo, so Pedro Luz abandoned the plan. With a bellowing lunge, he was able to get a grip on the stranger's collar—an animal collar!—and pull him close. Pedro Luz preferred squeezing to boxing, and was confident he could end the fight (and the big freak's life) with a vigorous hug. That's when somebody grabbed Pedro Luz's hair from behind, and yanked his head back so fiercely that a popping noise came from his neck. Next thing he knew, his pants were off and he was thrashing in the warm water. Above him stood Joe Winder and the stranger, peering over the rail.

Swimming is an exercise that depends more on style than muscle, and Pedro Luz was plainly a terrible swimmer. The throbbing of his truncated leg added pain to ineptitude as he paddled the tank haplessly in search of a ladder. When the massive dolphin rolled beside him in the dark, Pedro Luz cursed and splashed his arms angrily. He was not the least bit afraid of stupid fish; perhaps he was deceived by the dolphin's friendly smile, or misled by childhood memories of the hokey 'Flipper' television series. In any event, Pedro Luz struck out at the creature with the misguided assumption that he could actually hurt it, and that it was too tame and good-natured to retaliate. Pedro's drug-inflamed brain failed to register the fact that Dickie the Dolphin was a more attuned physiological specimen than Pedro Luz himself, and about five hundred pounds larger. When the animal nudged him playfully with its snout, Pedro Luz balled his fists and slugged its silky gray flank.

'Be careful,' Joe Winder advised from the walkway, but Pedro Luz paid no attention. The damn fish would not go away! Using its pectoral flippers almost as arms, it held Pedro Luz in a grasp that was gentle yet firm.

Spitting curses, he kicked the dolphin savagely and pushed away. Stroking clumsily for the wall of the tank, he saw the long sleek form rise beneath him. A fin found Pedro Luz's armpit and spun him roughly. He came up choking, but again the creature tugged him down. Once more Pedro Luz fought his way to the top, and this time Dickie the Dolphin began to nip mischievously—tiny needle-like teeth raking Pedro's neck, his shoulders, his bare thighs. Then the dolphin rolled languidly on its side and gave a soft inquisitive whistle, the same sound Flipper used to make at the end of the TV show when he waved at the camera. Pedro Luz tried not to be afraid, but he couldn't understand what this dolphin was trying to say, or do. The salt water stung his eyes and his throat, and the stump of his leg felt as if it were on fire.

Again Pedro Luz felt cool fins slide under his arms as the dolphin gradually steered him toward the deepest part of the tank. The security man tried to break free, but it did no good. Something else propelled him now—a formidable protuberance that left no doubt as to Dickie the Dolphin's true purpose.

Pedro Luz was awestruck and mortified. The long pale thing loomed from the gray water and touched him—hooking, in fact, around his buttocks. The amphibious prodding brought an unfamiliar plea to Pedro Luz's lips: 'Help!'

Watching events unfold in the tank below, Skink agreed it was an extraordinary scene.

'I told you,' said Joe Winder. 'It's one of Nature's marvels.'

Pedro Luz began to whimper. No regimen of weight training and pharmaceutical enhancement could have prepared him, or any mortal man, for an all-out sexual attack by a healthy bottle-nosed dolphin. Pedro Luz had never felt so helpless, exhausted and inadequate; desperately he punched at the prodigious inquiring tuber, only to be rebuked by a well-placed slap from Dickie's sinewy fluke.

Leaning over the rail, Joe Winder offered more advice: 'Just roll with it. Don't fight him.'

But the futility of resistance was already clear to Pedro Luz, who found himself—for the first time in his adult life—completely out of strength. As he was pulled underwater for the final time, terror gave way to abject humiliation: he was being fucked to death by a damn fish.

35

Nina asked where he was calling from.

'Charlie's office,' Winder said. 'Here's what I'm going to do: I'll leave the phone off the hook all night. That way you can work on your poetry and still make money.'

'Joe, that'll cost him a fortune. It's four bucks a minute.'

'I know the rates, Nina. Don't worry about it.'

'You ready for the latest?'

'Just one verse. Time's running out.'

'Here goes,' she said, and began to recite:

> 'You flooded me with passions
> Hard and lingering.
> You took me down again
> Pumping breathless, biting blind.
> Hot in your bloodrush, I dreamed of more.'

'Wow,' Winder said. Obviously things were going gangbusters between Nina and the light-truck salesman.

'You really like it? Or are you patronizing me again?'

'Nina, you're breaking new ground.'

'Guess what the moron at the phone syndicate wants. Limericks! Sex limericks, like they publish in *Playboy*. That's his idea of erotic poetry!'

'Stick to your guns,' Winder said.

'You bet I will.'

'The reason I called was to say good-bye.'

'So tonight's the night,' she said. 'Will I be seeing you on the news?'

'I hope not.' He thought: What the hell. 'I met a woman,' he said.

'I'm very happy for you.'

'Aw, Nina, don't say that.'

'I *am*. I think it's great.'

'Christ Almighty, aren't you the least bit jealous?'

'Not really.'

God, she was a pisser. 'Then lie to me,' Winder said. 'Have mercy on my lunatic soul and lie to me. Tell me you're mad with jealousy.'

'You win, Joe. You saw through my act.'

'Was that a giggle I heard?'

'No!' Nina said. The giggle burst into a full-blown laugh. 'I'm dying here. I might just leap off the building, I'm so damn jealous. Who is she? Who is this tramp?'

Now Winder started laughing, too. 'I'd better go,' he said, 'before I say something sensible.'

'Call me, Joe. Whatever happens, I'd love to get a phone call.'

'I know the number by heart,' he said. 'Me and every pervert on the Gold Coast.'

'You go to hell,' Nina teased. 'And be careful, dammit.'

He said good-bye and placed the receiver on Charles Chelsea's desk.

Skink mulched a cotton candy and said, 'These are excellent seats.'

'They ought to be.' Joe Winder assumed Francis X. Kingsbury would arrive at any moment; it was his private viewing box, after all—leather swivel chairs, air-conditioning, video monitors, a wet bar. Thirty rows up, overlooking the parade route.

'What will you do when he gets here?' Skink asked.

'I haven't decided. Maybe he'd like to go swimming with Pedro's new friend.'

The grandstand was packed, and Kingsbury Lane was lined five deep with eager spectators. As the history of Florida unfolded in song and skit, Joe Winder imagined that the Stations of the Cross could be similarly adapted and set to music, if the audience would only forgive a few minor revisions. Every float in the

Summerfest pageant was greeted with the blind and witless glee displayed by people who have spent way too much money and are determined to have fun. They cheered at the sight of a bootless Ponce de León, an underaged maiden on each arm, wading bawdily into the Fountain of Youth; they roared as the pirate Black Caesar chased a concubine up the mizzenmast while his men plundered a captured galleon; they gasped as the Killer Hurricane of 1926 tore the roof off a settler's cabin and the smock off his brave young wife.

Skink said, 'I never realized cleavage played such an important role in Florida history.' Joe Winder told him to just wait for the break-dancing migrants.

Carrie Lanier gave a cassette of the new music to the driver, and took her place on the last float. The Talent Manager showed up and demanded to know why she wasn't wearing the Indian costume.

'That wasn't an Indian costume,' Carrie said, 'unless the Seminoles had streetwalkers.'

The Talent Manager, a middle-aged woman with sweeping peroxide hair and ropes of gold jewelry, informed Carrie that a long gown was unsuitable for the Jubilee parade.

'It's ideal for what I'm singing,' Carrie replied.

'And what would that be?'

'That would be none of your business.' She adjusted the microphone, which was clipped into the neck of her dress.

The Talent Manager became angry. 'Paul Revere and the Raiders isn't good enough for you?'

'Go away,' said Carrie.

'And where's our lion?'

'The lion is taking the night off.'

'No, missy,' the Talent lady said, shaking a finger. 'Thousands of people out there are waiting to see Princess Golden Sun ride a wild lion through the Everglades.'

'The lion has a furball. Now get lost.'

'At least put on the wig,' the Talent lady pleaded. 'There's no such thing as a blond Seminole. For the sake of authenticity, put on the damn wig!'

'Toodle-loo,' said Carrie. And the float began to roll.

At first, Sergeant Mark Dyerson thought the telemetry was on the fritz again. How could the panther get back on the island? No signal had been received for days, then suddenly there it was, beep-beep-beep. Number 17. The sneaky bastard was at it again!

Sergeant Dyerson asked the pilot to keep circling beneath the clouds until he got a more precise fix on the transmitter. The greenish darkness of the hammocks and the ocean suddenly was splayed by a vast sparkling corridor of lights—the Amazing Kingdom of Thrills. The plane banked high over a confetti of humanity.

'Damn,' said the ranger. Sharply he tapped the top of the radio receiver. 'This can't be right. Fly me over again.'

But the telemetry signals were identical on the second pass, and the third and the fourth. Sergeant Dyerson peered out the window of the Piper and thought, He's down there. He's inside the goddamn park!

The ranger told the pilot to call Naples. 'I need some backup,' he said, 'and I need the guy with the dogs.'

'Should I say which cat we're after?'

'No, don't,' Sergeant Dyerson said. The top brass of the Game and Fish Department was tired of hearing about Number 17. 'Tell them we've got a panther in trouble,' said Sergeant Dyerson, 'that's all you need to say.'

The pilot reached for the radio. 'What the hell's it doing in the middle of an amusement park?'

'Going crazy,' said the ranger. 'That's all I can figure.'

The break-dancing migrant workers were a sensation with the crowd. Skink covered his face during most of the performance; it was one of the most tasteless spectacles he had ever seen. He asked Joe Winder if he wished to help with the gasoline.

'No, I'm waiting for Kingsbury.'

'What for?'

'To resolve our differences as gentlemen. And possibly pound him into dog chow.'

'Forget Kingsbury,' Skink advised. 'There's your girl.'

Carrie's float appeared at the end of the promenade; a spotlight found her in a black sequined evening gown, posed among ersatz palms and synthetic cypress. She was perfectly dazzling, although the crowd reacted with confused and hesitant applause—they'd been expecting a scantily clad Indian princess astride a snarling wildcat.

Joe Winder tried to wave, but it hurt too much to raise his arms. Carrie didn't see him. She folded her hands across her midriff and began to sing:

> *'Vissi d'arte, vissi d'amore*
> *Non feci mai male ad animal viva!*
> *Con man furtiva*
> *Quante miserie conobbi, aiutai. . . .'*

Winder was dazed, and he was not alone; a restless murmuring swept through the stands and rippled along the promenade.

'Magnificent!' Skink said. His good eye ablaze, he clutched Winder's shoulder: 'Isn't she something!'

'What is that? What's she singing?'

Skink shook him with fierce exuberance. 'My God, man, it's Puccini. It's *Tosca*!'

'I see.' It was a new wrinkle: opera.

And Carrie sang beautifully; what her voice lacked in strength it made up in a flawless liquid clarity. The aria washed sorrowfully across the Amazing Kingdom and, like a chilly rain, changed the mood of the evening.

Skink put his mouth to Winder's ear and whispered: 'This takes place in the second act, where Tosca has just seen her lover tortured by the ruthless police chief and sentenced to death by a firing squad. In her failed effort to save him, Tosca herself becomes a murderess. Her song is a lamentation on life's tragic ironies.'

'I'd never have guessed,' Winder said.

As the float passed the Magic Mansion, Carrie sang:

> 'Nell'ora del dolore
> Perchè, perchè, Signore,
> Perchè me ne rimuneri così?'

Skink closed his eyes and swayed. 'Ah, why, dear Lord,' he said. 'Ah, why do you reward your servant so?'

Winder said the audience seemed fidgety and disturbed.

'Disturbed?' Skink was indignant. 'They ought to be distraught. Mournful. They ought to be *weeping*.'

'They're only tourists,' Joe Winder said. 'They've been waiting all afternoon to see a lion.'

'Cretins.'

'Oh, she knew,' Winder said fondly. 'She knew they wouldn't like it one bit.'

Skink grinned. 'Bless her heart.' He began to applaud rambunctiously, 'Bravo! Bravo!' His clapping and shouting caught the attention of spectators in the lower rows, who looked up toward the VIP box with curious annoyance. Carrie spotted both of them in Kingsbury's booth, and waved anxiously. Then she gathered herself and, with a deep breath, began the first verse again.

'What a trouper.' Joe Winder was very proud.

Skink straightened his rain cap and said, 'Go get her.'

'Now?'

'Right now. It's time.' Skink reached out to shake Winder's hand. 'You've got about an hour,' he said.

Winder told him to be careful. 'There's lots of kids out there.'

'Don't you worry.'

'What about Kingsbury?'

Skink said, 'Without the park, he's finished.'

'I intended to make him famous. You should've heard my plan.'

'Some other time,' Skink said. 'Now go. And tell her how great she was. Tell her it was absolutely wonderful. Giacomo would've been proud.'

'*Arrivederci!*' said Joe Winder.

*

From his third-floor office above Sally's Cimarron Saloon, Francis X. Kingsbury heard the parade go by. Only Princess Golden Sun's dolorous aria brought him to the window, where he parted the blinds to see what in the name of Jesus H. Christ had gone wrong. The disposition of the crowd had changed from festive to impatient. Unfuckingbelievable, thought Kingsbury. It's death, this music. And what's with the evening gown, the Kitty Carlisle number. Where's the buckskin bikini? Where's the tits and ass? The tourists looked ready to bolt.

Carrie hit the final note and held it—held it forever, it seemed to Kingsbury. The girl had great pipes, he had to admit, but it wasn't the time or place for Italian caterwauling. And God, this song, when would it end?

As the float trundled by, Kingsbury was surprised to see that Princess Golden Sun wasn't singing anymore; in fact, she was drinking from a can of root beer. Yet her final melancholy note still hung in the air!

Or was it something else now?

The fire alarm, for instance.

Kingsbury thought: Please, don't let it be. He tried to call Security but no one answered—that fucking Pedro, he should've been back from his errand hours ago.

Outside, the alarm had tripped a prerecorded message on the public-address system, urging everyone to depart the Amazing Kingdom in a calm and orderly fashion. When Kingsbury peeked out the window again, he saw customers streaming like ants for the exits; the performers and concessionaires ran, as well. Baldy the Eagle ripped off his wings and sprinted from the park at Olympic speed; the animal trainers fled together in a hijacked Cushman, but not before springing the hinge on the lion's cage and shooing the wobbly, tranquilized beast toward the woods.

Kingsbury ran, too. He ran in search of Pedro Luz, the only man who knew how to turn off the fire alarm. Golf spikes clacking on the concrete, Kingsbury jogged from the security office to King Arthur's Food Court to The Catacombs, where he found Spence Mooher limping in mopey addled circles, like a dog who'd been grazed by a speeding bus.

But there was no trace of Pedro, and despair clawed at Kingsbury's gut. People now were pouring out of the park, and taking their money with them. Even if they had wished to stop and purchase one last overpriced souvenir, no one was available to sell it to them.

Chickenshits! Kingsbury raged inwardly. All this panic, and no fire. *Can't you idiots see it's a false alarm?*

Then came the screams.

Kingsbury's throat tightened. He ducked into a photo kiosk and removed the laminated ID card from his belt. Why risk it if the crowd turned surly?

The screaming continued. In a prickly sweat, Kingsbury tracked the disturbance to the whale tank, where something had caught the attention of several families on their way out of the park. They lined the walkway, and excitedly pointed to the water. Assuming the pose of a fellow tourist, Kingsbury nonchalantly joined the others on the rail. He overheard one man tell his wife that there wasn't enough light to use the video camera; she encouraged him to try anyway. A young girl cried and clutched at her mother's leg; her older brother told her to shut up, it's just a plastic dummy.

It wasn't a dummy. It was the partially clothed body of Pedro Luz, facedown in the Orky tank. His muscular buttocks mooned the masses, and indeed it was this sight—not the fact he was dead—that had shocked customers into shrieking.

Francis X. Kingsbury glared spitefully at the corpse. Pedro's bobbing bare ass seemed to mock him—a hairy faceless smile, taunting as it floated by. So this is how it goes, thought Kingsbury. Give a man a second chance, this is how he pays you back.

Suddenly, and without warning, Dickie the Dolphin rocketed twenty feet out of the water and performed a perfect triple-reverse somersault.

The tourists, out of pure dumb reflex, broke into applause.

The Amazing Kingdom of Thrills emptied in forty minutes. Two hook-and-ladder rigs arrived from Homestead, followed by a small pumper truck from the main fire station in lower Key

Largo. The fire fighters unrolled the hoses and wandered around the park, but found no sign of a fire. They were preparing to leave when three green Jeeps with flashing lights raced into the empty parking lot. The fire fighters weren't sure what to make of the Game and Fish officers; an amusement park seemed an unlikely hideout for gator poachers. Sergeant Mark Dyerson flagged down one of the departing fire trucks and asked the captain if it was safe to take dogs into the area. The captain said sure, be my guest. Almost immediately the hounds struck a scent, and the old tracker turned them loose. The wildlife officers loaded up the dart guns and followed.

Francis Kingsbury happened to be staring out the window when he spotted the lion loping erratically down Kingsbury Lane; a pack of dogs trailed closely, snapping at its tail. The doped-up cat attempted to climb one of the phony palm trees, but fell when its claws pulled loose from the Styrofoam bark. Swatting at the hounds, the cat rose and continued its disoriented escape.

Lunacy, thought Kingsbury.

Someone knocked twice on the office door and came in—a short round man with thin brown hair and small black eyes. A hideous polyester-blend shirt identified him as a valued customer. Pinned diagonally across the man's chest was a wrinkled streamer that said 'OUR FIVE-MILLIONTH SPECIAL GUEST!' In the crook of each arm sat a stuffed toy animal with reddish fur, pipestem whiskers and a merry turquoise tongue.

Vance and Violet Vole.

'For my nieces,' the man explained. 'I got so much free stuff I can hardly fit it in the car.'

Kingsbury smiled stiffly. 'The big winner, right? That's you.'

'Yeah, my wife can't fuckin' believe it.'

'Didn't you hear it, the fire alarm? Everybody else, I mean, off they went.'

'But I didn't see no fire,' the man said. 'No smoke, neither.' He arranged the stuffed animals side by side on Kingsbury's sofa.

The guy's a total yutz, Kingsbury thought. Does he want my autograph or what? Maybe a snapshot with the big cheese.

'What's that you got there?' the man asked. 'By the way, the name's Rossiter.' He nodded toward a plaid travel bag that lay open on Kingsbury's desk. The bag was full of cash, mostly twenties and fifties.

The man said, 'Looks like I wasn't the only one had a lucky day.'

Kingsbury snapped the bag closed. 'I'm very busy, Mr. Rossiter. What's the problem—something with the new car, right? The color doesn't match your wife's eyes or whatever.'

'No, the car's great. I got no complaints about the car.'

'Then what?' Kingsbury said. 'The parade, I bet. That last song, I swear to Christ, I don't know where that shit came from—'

'You kiddin' me? It was beautiful. It was Puccini.'

Kingsbury threw up his hands. 'Whatever. Not to be rude, but what the fuck do you want?'

The man said, 'I got a confession to make. I cheated a little this morning.' He shrugged sheepishly. 'I cut in line so we could be the first ones through the gate. That's how I won the car.'

It figures, thought Kingsbury. Your basic South Florida clientele.

The man said, 'I felt kinda lousy, but what the hell. Opportunity knocks, right? I mean, since I had to be here anyway—'

'Mr. Rossiter, do I look like a priest? All this stuff, I don't need to hear it—'

'Hey, call me Lou,' the man said, 'and I'll call *you* Frankie.' From his Sansibelt slacks he withdrew a .38-caliber pistol with a silencer.

Francis Kingsbury's cheeks went from pink to gray. 'Don't tell me,' he said.

'Yeah,' said Lou, 'can you believe it?'

36

Francis X. Kingsbury asked the hit man not to shoot.

'Save your breath,' said Lou.

'But, look, a fantastic new world I built here. A place for little tykes, you saw for yourself—roller coasters and clowns and talking animals. Petey Possum and so forth. I did all this myself.'

'What a guy,' said Lou.

Kingsbury was unaccustomed to such bald sarcasm. 'Maybe I make a little dough off the operation, so what? Look at all the fucking happiness I bring people!'

'I enjoyed myself,' Lou admitted. 'My wife, she's crazy about the Twirling Teacups. She and her mother both. I almost spit up on the damn thing, to be honest, but my wife's got one a them cast-iron stomachs.'

Kingsbury brightened. 'The Twirling Teacups, I designed those myself. The entire ride from scratch.'

'No shit?'

The hit man seemed to soften, and Kingsbury sensed an opening. 'Look, I got an idea about paying back the Zubonis. It's a big construction deal, we're talking millions. They'd be nuts to pass it up—can you make a phone call? Tell 'em it's once in a lifetime.'

Lou said, 'Naw, I don't think so.'

'Florida waterfront—that's all you gotta say. Florida fucking waterfront, and they'll be on the next plane from Newark, I promise.'

'You're a good salesman,' said the hit man, 'but I got a contract.'

Kingsbury nudged the plaid travel bag across the desk. 'My old lady, she wanted me to go on a trip—Europe, the whole nine yards. I was thinking why not, just for a couple months. She's never been there.'

Lou nodded. 'Now's a good time to go. The crowds aren't so bad.'

'Anyhow, I emptied the cash registers after the parade.' Kingsbury patted the travel bag. 'This is just from ticket sales, not concessions, and still you're talking three hundred and forty thousand. Cash-ola.'

'Yeah? That's some vacation, three hundred forty grand.'

'And it's all yours if you forget about the contract.'

'Hell,' said Lou, 'it's mine if I don't.'

Outside there was a bang, followed by a hot crackling roar. When Kingsbury spun his chair toward the window, his face was bathed in flickering yellow light.

'Lord,' he said.

The Wet Willy was on fire—hundreds of feet of billowed latex, squirming and thrashing like an eel on a griddle. White sparks and flaming bits of rubber hissed into the tropical sky, and came down as incendiary rain upon the Amazing Kingdom of Thrills. Smaller fires began to break out everywhere.

Francis Kingsbury shivered under his hairpiece.

Lou went to the window and watched the Wet Willy burn. 'You know what it looks like?'

'Yes,' Kingsbury said.

'A giant Trojan.'

'I know.'

'It ain't up to code, that's for sure. You must've greased some county inspectors.'

'Another good guess,' Kingsbury said. Why did the alarm cut off? he wondered. Where did all the firemen go?

Lou farted placidly as he walked back to the desk. 'Well, I better get a move on.'

Kingsbury tried to hand him the telephone. 'Please,' he begged, 'call the Zuboni brothers.'

'A deal's a deal,' Lou said, checking the fit of the silencer.

'But you saw for yourself!' Kingsbury cried. 'Another five years, goddamn, I'll be bigger than Disney.'

Lou looked doubtful. 'I wasn't gonna say anything, but what the hell. The car and the prizes are great, don't get me wrong, but the park's got a long ways to go.'

Petulantly, Kingsbury said, 'Fine, let's hear it.'

'It's the bathrooms,' said Lou. 'The fuckin' Port Authority's got cleaner bathrooms.'

'Is that so?'

'Yeah, and it wouldn't hurt to keep an extra roll a toilet paper in the stalls.'

'Is that it? That's your big gripe?'

Lou said, 'People notice them things, they really do.' Then he stepped toward Francis X. Kingsbury and raised the pistol.

Joe Winder led her through the dense hammock, all the way to the ocean's edge. It took nearly an hour because Carrie wore high heels. The gown kept snagging on branches, and the insects were murder.

'I'm down two pints,' she said, scratching at her ankles.

'Take off the shoes. Hurry.' He held her hand and waded into the water.

'Joe!' The gown rose up around her hips; the sequins sparkled like tiny minnows.

'How deep are we going?' she asked.

At first the turtle grass tickled her toes, then it began to sting. Winder kept walking until the water was up to his chest.

'See? No more bugs.'

'You're full of tricks,' Carrie said, clinging to his arm. From the flats it was possible to see the entire curving shore of the island, including the naked gash made by the bulldozers at Falcon Trace. She asked if the trees would ever come back.

'Someday,' Joe Winder said, 'if the bastards leave it alone.'

Stretching toward the horizon was a ribbon of lights from the cars sitting bumper-to-bumper on County Road 905—the exodus of tourists from the Amazing Kingdom. Winder wondered if Skink had waited long enough to make his big move.

He listened for the distant sound of sirens as he moved through the shallows, following the shoreline south. The warm hug of the tide soothed the pain in his chest. He pointed at a pair of spotted leopard rays, pushing twin wakes.

'What else do you see?' Carrie said.

'Turtles. Jellyfish. A pretty girl with no shoes.' He kissed her on the neck.

'How far can we go like this?' she asked.

'Big Pine, Little Torch, all the way to Key West if you want.'

She laughed. 'Joe, that's a hundred miles.' She kicked playfully into the deeper water. 'It feels so good.'

'You sang beautifully tonight. Watch out for the coral.'

When Carrie stood up, the water came to her chin. Blowing bubbles, she said, 'I didn't know you liked opera.'

'I hate opera,' Winder said, 'but you made it wonderful.'

She splashed after him, but he swam away.

They didn't leave the ocean until the road was clear and the island was dark. They agreed it would be best to get out of Monroe County for a while, so they took Card Sound Road toward the mainland. The pavement felt cool under their feet. They wanted to hold hands, but it hampered their ability to defend themselves against the swarming mosquitoes. Every few minutes Winder would stop walking and check the sky for a change in the light. One time he was sure he heard a helicopter.

Carrie said, 'What's your feeling about all this?'

'Meaning Kingsbury and the whole mess.'

'Exactly.'

'There's thousands more where he came from.'

'Oh, brother,' Carrie said. 'I was hoping you'd gotten it all out of your system.'

'Never,' said Winder, 'but I'm open to suggestions.'

'All right, here's one: Orlando.'

'God help us.'

'Now wait a second, Joe. They're shooting commercials at those new studios up there. I've got my first audition lined up for next week.'

'What kind of commercial?'

'The point is, it's national exposure.'

'Promise me something,' Winder said. 'Promise it's not one of those personal-hygiene products.'

'Fabric softener. The script's not bad, all things considered.'

'And will there be singing?'

'No singing,' Carrie said, picking up the pace. 'They've got newspapers in Orlando, don't they?'

'Oh no, you don't.'

'It'd be good for you, Joe. Write about the important things, whatever pisses you off. Just write *something*. Otherwise you'll make me crazy, and I'll wind up killing you in your sleep.'

The Card Sound Bridge rose steeply ahead. A handful of crabbers and snapper fishermen sleepily tended slack lines. Joe and Carrie took the sidewalk. For some reason she stopped and gave him a long kiss.

Halfway up the rise, she tugged on his hand and told him to turn around.

There it was: the eastern sky aglow, fat clouds roiling unnaturally under a pulsing halo of wild pink and orange. Baleful columns of tarry smoke rose from the Amazing Kingdom of Thrills.

Joe Winder whistled in amazement. 'There's arson,' he said, 'and then there's arson.'

Bud Schwartz and Danny Pogue were surprised to find Molly McNamara wide awake, propped up with a stack of thin hospital pillows. She was brushing her snowy hair and reading the *New Republic* when the burglars arrived.

'Pacemaker,' Molly reported. 'A routine procedure.'

'You look so good,' said Danny Pogue. 'Bud, don't she look good?'

'Hush now,' Molly said. 'Sit down here, the news is coming on. There's a story you'll both find interesting.' Without being asked, Danny Pogue switched the television to Channel 10, Molly's favorite.

Bud Schwartz marveled at the old woman in bed. Days earlier, she had seemed so weak and withered and close to death. Now the gray eyes were as sharp as a hawk's, her cheeks shone, and her voice rang strong with maternal authority.

She said, 'Danny, did you get the bullets?'

'Yes, ma'am.' He handed Molly the yellow box.

'These are .22-longs,' she said. 'I needed shorts. That's what the gun takes.'

Danny Pogue looked lamely toward his partner. Bud Schwartz said, 'Look, we just asked for .22s. The guy didn't say nothin' about long or short.'

'It's all right,' Molly McNamara said. 'I'll pick up a box at the range next week.'

'We don't know diddly about guns,' Danny Pogue reiterated. 'Neither of us do.'

'I know, and I think it's precious.' Molly put on her rose-framed glasses and instructed Bud Schwartz to adjust the volume on the television. A nurse came in to check the dressing on Molly's stitches, but Molly shooed her away. She pointed at the TV and said, 'Look here, boys.'

The news opened with videotape of a colossal raging fire. The scene had been recorded at a great distance, and from a helicopter. When the TV reporter announced what was burning, the burglars simultaneously looked at one another and mouthed the same profane exclamation.

'Yes,' Molly McNamara said rapturously. 'Yes, indeed.'

Danny Pogue felt mixed emotions as he watched the Amazing Kingdom burn. He recalled the gaiety of the promenade, the friendliness of the animal characters, the circus colors and brassy music, the wondrous sensation of being inundated with fun. Then he thought of Francis X. Kingsbury killing off the butterflies and crocodiles, and the conflagration seemed more like justice than tragedy.

Bud Schwartz was equally impressed by the destruction of the theme park—not as a moral lesson, but as a feat of brazen criminality. The torch artist had been swift and thorough; the place was engulfed in roaring, implacable flames, and there was no saving it. The man on TV said he had never witnessed such a fierce, fast-moving blaze. Bud Schwartz felt relieved and lucky and wise.

'And you wanted to stay,' he said to Danny Pogue. 'You wanted to ride the Jungle Jerry again.'

Danny Pogue nodded solemnly and slid the chair close to the television. 'We could be dead,' he murmured.

'Fried,' said his partner. 'Fried clams.'

'Hush now,' Molly said. 'There's no call for melodrama.'

She announced that she wasn't going to ask why they'd gone to the Amazing Kingdom that night. 'I don't like to pry,' she said. 'You're grown men, you've got your own lives.'

Danny Pogue said, 'It wasn't us who torched the place.'

Molly McNamara smiled as if she already knew. 'How's your foot, Danny?'

'It don't hardly hurt at all.'

Then to Bud Schwartz: 'And your hand? Is it better?'

'Gettin' there,' he said, flexing the fingers.

Molly removed her glasses and rested her head against the pillows. 'Nature is a wonder,' she said. 'Such power to renew, or to destroy. It's an awesome paradox.'

'A what?' said Danny Pogue.

Molly told them to think of the fire as a natural purge, a cyclical scouring of the land. Bud Schwartz could hardly keep a straight face. He jerked his chin toward the flickering images on television, and said, 'So maybe it's spontaneous combustion, huh? Maybe a bolt a lightning?'

'Anything's possible,' Molly said with a twinkle. She asked Danny Pogue to switch to the Discovery Channel, which just happened to be showing a documentary about endangered Florida manatees. A mating scene was in progress as Danny Pogue adjusted the color tint.

Not tonight, thought Bud Schwartz, and got up to excuse himself.

Molly said, 'There's a Dodgers game on ESPN. You can watch across the hall in Mr. McMillan's room—he is in what they call a nonresponsive state, so he probably won't mind.'

'Swell,' Bud Schwartz muttered. 'Maybe we'll go halfsies on a keg.'

Danny Pogue heard none of this; he was already glued to the tube. Bud Schwartz pointed at his partner and grinned. 'Look what you done to him.'

Molly McNamara winked. 'Go on now,' she said. 'I think Ojeda's pitching.'

Trooper Jim Tile braked sharply when he saw the three green Jeeps. The wildlife officers had parked in a precise triangle at the intersection of Card Sound Road and County 905.

'We'll be out of the way in a minute,' said Sergeant Mark Dyerson.

The rangers had gathered between the trucks in the center of the makeshift triangle. Jim Tile joined them. He noticed dogs pacing in the back of one of the Jeeps.

'Look at this,' Sergeant Dyerson said.

In the middle of the road, illuminated by headlights, was a battered red collar. Jim Tile crouched to get a closer look.

'Our transmitter,' the ranger explained. Imprinted on the plastic was the name 'Telonics MOD-500.'

'What happened?' Jim Tile asked.

'The cat tore it off. Somehow.'

'That's one tough animal.'

'It's a first,' Sergeant Dyerson said. 'We've never had one that could bust the lock on the buckle.'

Another officer asked, 'What now?' It was the wretched plea of a man being devoured by insects.

'If the cat wants out this bad,' said Sergeant Dyerson, 'I figure we'll let him be.'

From the south came the oscillating whine of a fire truck. Sergeant Dyerson retrieved the broken panther collar and told his men to move the Jeeps off the road. Minutes later, a hook-and-ladder rig barreled past.

Jim Tile mentioned that the theme park was on fire.

'It's breaking my heart,' Sergeant Dyerson said. He handed the trooper a card. 'Keep an eye out. My home number is on the back.'

Jim Tile said, 'All my life, I've never seen a panther.'

'You probably never will,' said the ranger, 'and that's the crime of it.' He tossed the radio collar in the back of the truck and slid behind the wheel.

'Not all the news is bad,' he said. 'Number Nine's got a litter of kittens over in the Fokahatchee.'

'Yeah?' Jim Tile admired the wildlife officer's outlook and dedication. He was sorry his old friend had caused the man so much trouble and confusion. He said, 'So this is all you do— track these animals?'

'It's all I do,' Sergeant Dyerson said.

To Jim Tile it sounded like a fine job, and an honorable one. He liked the notion of spending all day in the deep outdoors, away from the homicidal masses. He wondered how difficult it would be to transfer from the highway patrol to the Game and Fish.

'Don't you worry about this cat,' he told Sergeant Dyerson.

'I worry about all of them.'

'This one'll be all right,' the trooper said. 'You've got my word.'

As soon as he spotted the police car, Joe told Carrie to hike up her gown and run. She followed him down the slope of the bridge and into a mangrove creek. Breathlessly they clung to the slippery roots; only their heads stayed dry.

'Don't move,' Joe Winder said.

'There's a june bug in your ear.'

'Yes, I'm aware of that.' He quietly dunked his face, and the beetle was swept away by the milky-blue current.

She said, 'May I raise the subject of snakes?'

'We're fine.' He wrapped his free arm around her waist, to hold her steady against the tide. 'You're certainly being a good sport about all this,' he said.

'Will you think about Orlando?'

'Sure.' It was the least he could do.

The metronomic blink of the blue lights grew stronger, and soon tires crunched the loose gravel on the road; the siren died with a tremulous moan.

Winder chinned up on a mangrove root for a better view. He saw a highway patrol cruiser idling at an angle on the side of the road. The headlights dimmed, and the trooper honked three times. They heard a deep voice, and Winder recognized it: Jim Tile.

'We lucked out,' he said to Carrie. 'Come on, that's our ride.' They climbed from the creek and sloshed out of the mangroves. Before reaching the road, they heard another man's voice and the slam of a door.

Then the patrol car started to roll.

Joe Winder sprinted ahead, waving both arms and shouting for the trooper to stop. Jim Tile calmly swerved around him and, by way of a farewell, flicked his brights as he drove past.

Winder clutched his aching rib cage and cursed spiritedly at the speeding police car. Carrie joined him on the centerline, and together they watched the flashing blue lights disappear over the crest of the Card Sound Bridge.

'Everyone's a comedian,' Joe Winder said.

'Didn't you see who was in the back seat?'

'I didn't see a damn thing.'

Carrie laughed. 'Look what he threw out the window.' She held up a gooey stick of insect repellent. The top-secret military formula.

'Do me first,' she said. 'Every square inch.'

Epilogue

A team of police divers recovered the body of PEDRO LUZ from the whale tank at the Amazing Kingdom of Thrills. The Monroe County medical examiner ruled drowning as the official cause of death, although the autopsy revealed 'minor bite marks, contusions and chafing of a sexual nature.'

JAKE HARP recovered from his gunshot wound and rejoined the professional golfing circuit, although he never regained championship form. His next best finish was a tie for 37th place at the Buick Open, and subsequently he set a modern PGA record by missing the cut in twenty-two consecutive tournaments. Eventually he retired to the Seniors' Tour, where he collapsed and died of a cerebral hemorrhage on the first hole of a sudden-death play-off with Billy Casper.

With his payoff money from the mob, BUD SCHWARTZ started a private security company that specializes in high-tech burglar-alarm systems for the home, car and office. Bearing a letter of recommendation from Molly McNamara, DANNY POGUE moved to Tanzania, where he is training to be a game warden at the Serengeti National Park.

After Francis X. Kingsbury's murder, AGENT BILLY HAWKINS was docked a week's pay, and given a written reprimand for taking an unauthorized leave of absence. A month later he was transferred to the FBI office in Sioux Falls, South Dakota. He endured one winter before resigning from the Bureau and returning to Florida as an executive consultant to Schwartz International Security Services Ltd.

NINA WHITMAN quit the phone-sex syndicate after three of her poems were published in the *New Yorker*. A later collection of prose and short fiction was praised by Erica Jong as a 'fresh and vigorous reassessment of the female sexual dynamic.' Shortly after receiving the first royalty statement from her publisher, Nina gave up poetry and moved to Westwood, California, where she now writes motion-picture screenplays. Her husband owns the second-largest Chevrolet dealership in Los Angeles County.

The estate of FRANCIS X. KINGSBURY, aka FRANKIE KING, was sued by the Walt Disney Corporation for copyright infringement on the characters of Mickey and Minnie Mouse. The lawsuit was prompted by accounts of a pornographic tattoo on the decedent's left forearm, as described by newspaper reporters attending the opencasket funeral. After deliberating only thirty-one minutes (and reviewing a coroner's photograph of the disputed etching), an Orlando jury awarded the Disney company $1.2 million in actual and punitive damages. PENNY KINGSBURY is appealing the decision.

CHARLES CHELSEA accepted a job as executive vice president of public relations for Monkey Mountain. Four months later, disaster struck when a coked-up podiatrist from Ann Arbor, Michigan, jumped a fence and attempted to leg-wrestle a male chacma baboon. The podiatrist was swiftly killed and dismembered, and the animal park was forced to close. Chelsea retired from the public-relations business, and is now said to be working on a novel with Gothic themes.

At his own request, TROOPER JIM TILE was reassigned to Liberty County in the Florida Panhandle. With only 5.1 persons per square mile, it is the least densely populated region of the state.

DICKIE THE DOLPHIN survived the fire that destroyed the Amazing Kingdom of Thrills, and was temporarily relocated to a holding pen at an oceanfront hotel near Marathon. Seven months later, a bankruptcy judge approved the sale of the frisky mammal to a marine attraction in Hilton Head, South Carolina. No swimming is allowed in Dickie's new tank.

After the Amazing Kingdom closed, UNCLE ELY'S ELVES never worked together again. Veteran character actor MOE STRICK-LAND branched into drama, taking minor roles in television soap operas before miraculously landing the part of Big Daddy in a Scranton dinnertheater production of *Cat on a Hot Tin Roof*. A freelance critic for the *Philadelphia Inquirer* described Strickland's performance as 'gutsy and brooding.'

Several weeks after fire swept through Francis X. Kingsbury's theme park, a piano-sized crate from Auckland, New Zealand, was discovered outside the padlocked gate. No one was certain how long the crate had been there, but it was empty by the time a security guard found it; whatever was inside had clawed its way out. Soon residents of the nearby Ocean Reef Club began reporting the disappearance of pet cats and small dogs at a rate of two per week—a mystery that remains unsolved. Meanwhile, Kingsbury's estate received a handwritten invoice from a person calling herself RACHEL LARK. The bill, excluding shipping, amounted to $3,755 for 'miscellaneous wildlife.'

The widow of DR. WILL KOOCHER hired a Miami lawyer and filed a wrongful-death action against the Amazing Kingdom of Thrills, Ramex Global Trust, N.A. and Bermuda Intercontinental Services, Inc. The insurance companies hastily settled the lawsuit out of court for approximately $2.8 million. The gutted ruins of the Amazing Kingdom were razed, and the land was replanted with native trees, including buttonwoods, pigeon plums, torch-woods, brittle palms, tamarinds, gumbo-limbos and mangroves. This restoration was accomplished in spite of rigid opposition from the Monroe County Commission, which had hoped to use the property as a public dump.

The surviving owners of the FALCON TRACE golf resort sold all construction permits and building rights to a consortium of Japanese investors who had never set foot in South Florida. However, the project stalled once again when environmentalists surveying the Key Largo site reported the presence of at least two blue-tongued mango voles, previously thought to be extinct.

According to an unsigned press release faxed to all major newspapers and wire services, the tiny mammals were spotted at Falcon Trace during a nature hike by MOLLY MCNAMARA and the Mothers of Wilderness, who immediately reported the sighting to the U.S. Department of Interior.

Eventually the Falcon Trace and Amazing Kingdom properties were purchased from bankruptcy by the state of Florida, and became part of a preserve on NORTH KEY LARGO. In the spring of 1991, a *National Geographic* photographer set out to capture on film the last surviving pair of blue-tongued mango voles. After two months in the woods, the photographer contracted mosquito-borne encephalitis and was airlifted to Jackson Memorial Hospital, where he spent three weeks on clear fluids. He never got a glimpse of the shy and nocturnal creatures, although he returned to New York with a cellophane packet of suspect rodent droppings and a pledge to keep searching.

STRIP
TEASE

For the amazing Esther Newberg

1

On the night of September sixth, the eve of Paul Guber's wedding, his buddies took him to a strip joint near Fort Lauderdale for a bachelor party. The club was called the Eager Beaver, and it was famous county-wide for its gorgeous nude dancers and watered-down rum drinks. By midnight Paul Guber was very drunk and hopelessly infatuated with eight or nine of the strippers. For twenty dollars they would perch on Paul's lap and let him nuzzle their sweet-smelling cleavage; he was the happiest man on the face of the planet.

Paul's friends carried on with rowdy humor, baying witlessly and spritzing champagne at the stage. At first the dancers were annoyed about being sprayed, but eventually they fell into the spirit of the celebration. Slick with Korbel, they formed a laughing chorus line and high-kicked their way through an old Bob Seger tune. Bubbles sparkled innocently in their pubic hair. Paul Guber and his pals cheered themselves hoarse with lust.

At half-past two, a fearsome-looking bouncer announced the last call. While Paul's buddies pooled their cash to pay the exorbitant tab, Paul quietly crawled on stage and attached himself to one of the performers. Too drunk to stand, he balanced on his knees and threw a passionate hug around the woman's bare waist. She smiled good-naturedly and kept moving to the music. Paul hung on like a drowning sailor. He pressed his cheek to the woman's tan belly and closed his eyes. The dancer, whose name was Erin, stroked Paul's hair and told him to go home, sugar, get some rest before the big day.

A man yelled for Paul to get off the stage, and Paul's friends assumed it was the bouncer. The club had a strict rule against touching the dancers for free. Paul Guber himself heard no warning—he appeared comatose with bliss. His best friend Richard, with whom Paul shared a cubicle at the brokerage house, produced a camera and began taking photographs of Paul and the naked woman. Blackmail, he announced playfully. Pay up, or I mail these snapshots to your future mother-in-law! Everyone in the club seemed to be enjoying themselves. That's why Paul's friends were so shocked to see a stranger jump on stage and begin beating him with an empty champagne bottle.

Three, four, five hard blows to the head, and still Paul Guber would not release the dancer, who was trying her best to avoid being struck. The bottle-wielding man was tall and paunchy, and wore an expensive suit. His hair was silver, although his bushy mustache was black and crooked. No one in Paul Guber's bachelor party recognized him.

Raw sucking noises came from the man's throat as he pounded on the stockbroker's skull. The bouncer got there just as the champagne bottle shattered. He grabbed the silver-haired man under the arms and prepared to throw him off the stage in a manner that would have fractured large bones. But the bouncer alertly noticed that the silver-haired man had a companion, and the companion had a gun that might or might not be loaded. Having the utmost respect for Colt Industries, the bouncer carefully released the silver-haired man and allowed him to flee the club with his armed friend.

Amazingly, Paul Guber never fell down. The paramedics had to pry his fingers off the dancer's buttocks before hauling him to the hospital. In the emergency room, his worried buddies gulped coffee and cooked up a story to tell Paul's fiancée.

By the time the police arrived, the Eager Beaver lounge was empty. The bouncer, who was mopping blood off the stage, insisted he hadn't seen a thing. The cops clearly were disappointed that the nude women had gone home, and showed little enthusiasm for investigating a drunken assault with no victim present. All that remained of the alleged weapon was a pile of sparkling green shards. The bouncer asked if it was okay to toss them in the dumpster, and the cops said sure.

Paul Guber's wedding was postponed indefinitely. His friends told Paul's bride-to-be that he had been mugged in the parking lot of a synagogue.

In the car, speeding south on Federal Highway, Congressman David Lane Dilbeck rubbed his temples and said: 'Was it a bad one, Erb?'

And Erb Crandall, the congressman's loyal executive assistant and longtime bagman, said: 'One of the worst.'

'I don't know what came over me.'

'You assaulted a man.'

'Democrat or Republican?'

Crandall said, 'I have no earthly idea.'

Congressman Dilbeck gasped when he noticed the pistol on his friend's lap. 'Jesus, Mary and Joseph! Don't tell me.'

Without emotion, Crandall said, 'I had no choice. You were about to be maimed.'

Five minutes passed before the congressman spoke again. 'Erb,' he said, 'I love naked women, I truly do.'

Erb Crandall nodded neutrally. He wondered about the congressman's driver. Dilbeck had assured him that the man understood no English, only French and Creole. Still, Crandall studied the back of the driver's black head and wondered if the man was listening. These days, anyone could be a spy.

'All men have weaknesses,' Dilbeck was saying. 'Mine is of the fleshly nature.' He peeled off the phony mustache. 'Let's have it, Erb. What exactly did I do?'

'You jumped on stage and assaulted a young man.'

Dilbeck winced. 'In what manner?'

'A bottle over the head,' Crandall said. 'Repeatedly.'

'And you didn't stop me! That's your goddamn job, Erb, to get me out of those situations. Keep my name out of the papers.'

Crandall explained that he was in the john when it happened.

'Did I touch the girl?' asked the congressman.

'Not this time.'

In French, Crandall asked the Haitian driver to stop the car and wait. Crandall motioned for Dilbeck to get out. They walked to an empty bus bench and sat down.

The congressman said, 'What's all this nonsense? You can talk freely in front of Pierre.'

'We've got a problem.' Crandall steepled his hands. 'I think we should call Moldy.'

Dilbeck said no way, absolutely not.

'Somebody recognized you tonight,' said Crandall. 'Somebody in that strip joint.'

'God.' Dilbeck shut his eyes and pinched the bridge of his nose. 'It's an election year, Erb.'

'Some little twerp, I didn't get the name. He was standing by the back door when we ran out. Some skinny jerk-off with Coke-bottle glasses.'

'What'd he say?'

'"Attaboy, Davey." He was looking right at you.'

'But the mustache—'

'Then he said, '"Chivalry ain't dead."' Crandall looked very grim.

Congressman Dilbeck said, 'Did he seem like the type to stir up trouble?'

It was all Crandall could do to keep from laughing. 'Looks are deceiving, David. I'll be calling Moldy in the morning.'

Back in the car, heading south again, Dilbeck asked about the condition of the man he'd attacked.

'I have no earthly idea,' Crandall said. He would phone the hospital later.

'Did he seem dead?'

'Couldn't tell,' replied Crandall. 'Too much blood.'

'Lord,' said the congressman. 'Lord, I've got to get a grip on this. Erb, let's you and me pray. Give me your hands.' He reached across the seat for Crandall, who shook free of the congressman's clammy fervent paws.

'Knock it off,' Crandall snapped.

'Please, Erb, let's join hands.' Dilbeck flexed his fingers beseechingly. 'Join together and pray with me now.'

'No fucking way,' said the bagman. 'You pray for both of us, David. Pray like hell.'

*

The next night, Erin was taking off her clothes, getting ready, when she told Shad that she'd checked with the hospital. 'They said he's out of intensive care—the man who got hurt.'

Shad's eyes never looked up from the card table. 'Thank God,' he said. 'Now I can sleep nights.'

'The gun frightened me.' Erin was changing into her show bra. 'He sure didn't look like a bodyguard, did he? The one with the gun?'

Shad was deeply absorbed. Using a surgical hemostat, he was trying to peel the aluminum safety seal from a four-ounce container of low-fat blueberry yogurt. The light was poor in the dressing room, and Shad's eyesight wasn't too sharp. He hunched over the yogurt like a watchmaker.

'I gotta concentrate,' he said gruffly to Erin.

By now she'd seen the dead cockroach, a hefty one even by Florida standards. Legs in the air, the roach lay on the table near Shad's left elbow.

Erin said, 'Let me guess. You've had another brainstorm.'

Shad paused, rolling a cigarette from one side of his mouth to the other. He sucked hard, then blew the smoke to twin plumes from his nostrils.

'The hell does it look like?' he said.

'Fraud,' said Erin. She stepped behind a door and slipped out of her skirt. 'Fraud is what it looks like to me.'

Triumphantly, Shad lifted the foil (intact!) from the yogurt container. Carefully he placed it on the table. Then, with the hemostat, he lifted the dead cockroach by one of its brittle brown legs.

'Isn't that your music?' he said to Erin. 'Van Morrison. You better get your ass out there.'

'In a minute,' Erin said. She put on her G-string, the red one with seahorses. When Erin first bought it, she'd thought the design was paisley. One of the other dancers had noticed that the pattern was actually seahorses. Laughing seahorses.

Erin came out from behind the door. Shad didn't look up.

'Have the police been around?' she asked.

'Nope.' Shad smiled to himself. Cops—they usually got about

as far as the front bar and then forgot why they'd come. They'd wander through the Eager Beaver bug-eyed and silly, like little kids at Disney World. Cops were absolute saps when it came to bare titties.

Erin said she'd never seen a man get hit so hard with anything as the bachelor who got clobbered with the champagne bottle. 'It's a miracle there wasn't brain damage,' she said.

Shad took this as criticism of his response time. 'I got up there as quick as I could.' His tone was mildly defensive.

'Don't worry about it,' Erin told him.

'He didn't look the type. Of all the ones to go batshit.'

Erin agreed. The man wielding the Korbel bottle was not your typical strip-show creep. He wore a silk tie and passed out twenties like gumdrops.

Erin checked her stiletto pumps for bloodstains. 'This is a lousy business,' she remarked.

'No shit. Why'd you think I'm sitting here fucking with a dead roach? This little bugger is my ticket out.'

As steady as a surgeon, Shad positioned the cockroach in the low-fat blueberry yogurt. With the beak of the hemostat, he pressed lightly. Slowly the insect sunk beneath the creamy surface, leaving no trace.

Erin said, 'You big crazy dreamer.'

Shad absorbed the sarcasm passively. 'Do you get the *Wall Street Journal*?'

'No.' She wondered where he was heading now.

'According to the *Journal*,' Shad said, 'the Delicato Dairy Company is worth one hundred eighty-two million dollars, on account of Delicato Fruity Low-Fat Yogurt being the fastest-selling brand in the country. The stock's at an all-time high.'

Erin said, 'Shad, they won't fall for this.' She couldn't believe he was trying it again.

'You're late, babe.' Shad jerked a thumb toward the stage. 'Your fans are waiting.'

'I've got time. It's a long number.' Erin slipped into her teddy (which would come off after the first number) and her heels (which would stay on all night).

Shad said, 'That song, how come you like it so much? You don't even got brown eyes.'

'Nobody looks at my eyes,' Erin said. 'It's a good dancing song, don't you think?'

Shad was scrutinizing the yogurt. A hairy copper-colored leg had emerged from the creamy bog. Was it moving? Shad said to Erin: 'You ever see *Deliverance*? The movie, not the book. That last scene, where the shriveled dead hand comes out from the water? Well, come here and look at this fucking roach.'

'No thanks.' Erin asked if Mr Peepers was in the audience tonight. That was the nickname for one of her regulars, a bony bookish man with odd rectangular eyeglasses. He usually sat at table three.

Shad said, 'What, all of a sudden I'm supposed to take roll?'

'He called and left a message,' Erin said. 'Said he had a big surprise for me, which is just what I need.' She dabbed on some perfume—why, she had no idea. Nobody got close enough to smell it. Unlike the other strippers, Erin refused to do table dances. Ten bucks was ridiculous, she thought, to let some drunk breathe on your knees.

Shad said, 'You want me to, I'll throw his ass out.'

'No, if you could just hang close,' said Erin, 'especially after what happened last night.'

'No sweat.'

'It's probably nothing,' Erin said. Next came the lipstick. The boss preferred candy-apple red but Erin went with a burgundy rose. She'd hear about it from the other dancers, but what the hell.

Shad sat back from the yogurt project and said, 'Hey, come and see. It's just like new!'

'They could put you in jail. It's called product tampering.'

'It's called genius,' Shad said, 'and for your information, I already got a lawyer can't wait to take the case. And a Palm Beach shrink who swears I'm totally fucking traumatized since I opened a yogurt and found this damn cockroach—'

Erin laughed. 'Traumatized? You don't even know what that means.'

'Grossed out is what it means. And look here—' Shad lifted the foil seal with the hemostat. 'Perfect! Not even a rip. So the bastards can't say someone broke into the grocery and messed with the carton.'

'Clever,' Erin said. She checked her hair in the mirror. Most of the dancers wore wigs, but Erin felt that a wig slowed her down, limited her moves. Losing a wig was one of the worst things to happen on stage. That, and getting your period.

'How's my bottom?' she asked Shad. 'Is my crack showing?'

'Naw, babe, you're covered.'

'Thanks,' Erin said. 'Catch you later.'

'Go on and laugh. I'm gonna be rich.'

'Nothing would surprise me.' She couldn't help but envy Shad's optimism.

'The way it goes,' he said, 'them really big companies don't go to trial on stuff like this, on account of the negative publicity. They just pay off the plaintiff is what the lawyer told me. Major bucks.'

Erin said, 'The customer's name is Killian. Table three. Let me know if he comes in.' Then she was gone. He could hear the heels clicking on stage, the applause, the gin-fueled hoots.

Shad peered into the container. The roach leg had resubmerged: the surface of the yogurt looked smooth and undisturbed. A masterful job of sabotage! Shad placed the foil seal in a Ziploc bag and closed it by sliding his thumb and forefinger along the seam: evidence. Gingerly he carried the yogurt container to the dancers' refrigerator. He placed it on the second tray, between a six-pack of Diet Sprite and bowl of cottage cheese. Over the Delicato yogurt label he taped a hand-written warning:

'Do Not Eat or Else.'

He reread the note two or three times, decided it wasn't stern enough. He wrote out another and taped it beneath the first: 'Property of Shad.'

Then he went out to the lounge to see if any asses needed kicking. Sure enough, at table eight a pie-eyed Volvo salesman was trying to suck the toes off a cocktail waitress. Effortlessly

Shad heaved him out the back door. He dug a Pepsi out of the cooler and took a stool at the bar.

At midnight, the skinny guy with the square glasses came in and staked out his usual chair at table three. Shad strolled over and sat down beside him.

On stage, Erin was grinding her heart out.

She's wrong about one thing, Shad thought. *I* notice her eyes, every night I do. And they're definitely green.

2

Malcolm J. Moldowsky did not hesitate to address United States Congressman Dave Dilbeck as 'a card-carrying shithead'.

To which Dilbeck, mindful of Moldowsky's influence and stature, responded: 'I'm sorry, Malcolm.'

Pacing the congressman's office, Moldowsky cast a cold scornful eye on every plaque, every commemorative paperweight, every pitiable tin memento of Dilbeck's long and undistinguished political career.

'I see problems,' said Malcolm Moldowsky. He was a fixer's fixer, although it was not the occupation listed on his income-tax forms.

There's no problem, Dilbeck insisted, none at all. 'We were gone before the police showed up.'

Moldowsky was a short man, distractingly short, but he made up for it by dressing like royalty and slathering himself with expensive cologne. It was easy to be so impressed by Moldy's fabulous wardrobe and exotic aroma that one might overlook his words, which invariably were important.

'Are you listening?' he asked Dave Dilbeck.

'You said there's a problem, I said I don't see any problem.'

Moldowsky's upper lip curled, exposing the small and pointy dentition of a lesser primate. He stepped closer to Dilbeck and said, 'Do de name Gary Hart ring a bell? Fuckups 101—you need a refresher course?'

'That was different,' the congressman said.

'Indeed. Mr Hart did not send anyone to the emergency room.'

Dilbeck felt the heat of Moldowsky pressing closer—smelled the sharp minty breath and inhaled the imported Italian musk, which was strong enough to gas termites. Dilbeck quickly stood up. He was more at ease speaking to the crown of the man's head, instead of eye to eye. The congressman said, 'It won't happen again, that's for sure.'

'Really?'

The acid in Moldowsky's remark made the congressman nervous. 'I've been doing some soul-searching.'

Moldowsky stepped back so Dilbeck could see his face. 'David, the problem is not in your soul. It's in your goddamn trousers.'

The congressman shook his head solemnly. 'Weakness is spiritual, Malcolm. Only the manifestation is physica—'

'You are so full of shit—'

'Hey, I can conquer this,' Dilbeck said. 'I can control these animal urges, you just watch.'

Moldowsky raised his hands impatiently. 'You and your damn urges. It's an election year, Davey. That's number one. Only a card-carrying shithead would show his face at a nudie joint in an election year. Number two, your man pulls a gun, which happens to be a felony.'

'Malcolm, don't blame Erb.'

'And number three,' Moldowsky went on, 'during the commission of the act, you are recognized by a patron of this fine establishment. Which raises all sorts of possibilities, none of them good.'

'Whoa, whoa, whoa.' Dilbeck wedged his hands to signal time-out, like a football coach. 'Let's not jump to conclusions.'

Malcolm Moldowsky laughed harshly. 'That's my job, Congressman.' Once again he started to pace. 'Why did you hit that man with the bottle? Don't tell me—you got something going with the stripper, right? She's carrying your love child, perhaps?'

Dilbeck said, 'I don't even know her name.'

'But still you felt this uncontrollable impulse to defend her honor, such as it is. I understand, David, I understand perfectly.'

'It's a sickness, that's all. I should never be around naked women.'

All the fight had gone out of the congressman. Moldowsky circled the desk and approached him. In a softer voice: 'You don't need this shit right now. You got the campaign. You got the sugar vote coming up. You got a committee to run.' Moldowsky tried to chuck the congressman on the shoulder but wasn't quite tall enough. He wound up patting him on the elbow. 'I'll take care of this,' he said.

'Thanks, Mmm—Malcolm.' Dilbeck almost slipped and called him Moldy, which is what everyone called Moldowsky behind his back. Fanatically hygienic, Moldowsky hated the nickname.

'One more request,' he said. 'Keep David Jr in your pants until November. As a personal favor to me.'

Dilbeck's cheeks flushed.

'Because,' Moldowsky went on, 'I'd hate to think how your constituents would look upon such behavior—all those senior citizens in those condos, those conservative Cubans down on Eighth Street, those idealist young yupsters on the beach. What would they think if Congressman Davey got busted with a bunch of go-go dancers. How'd you suppose that would play?'

'Poorly,' admitted the congressman. He needed a drink.

'You still an elder in the church?'

'A deacon,' Dilbeck said.

'Is that a fact?' Malcolm Moldowsky wore a savage grin. 'You get the urge to chase pussy, call me. I'll set something up.' He dropped his voice. 'It's an election year, deacon, you gotta be careful. If it's a party you need, we'll bring it to you. That sound like a deal?'

'Deal,' the congressman said. When Moldy had gone, he cranked open a window and gulped for fresh air.

Every few years, the Congress of the United States of America voted generous price supports for a handful of agricultural millionaires in the great state of Florida. The crop that made them millionaires was sugar, the price of which was grossly inflated and guaranteed by the US government. This brazen act of plunder accomplished two things: it kept American growers very wealthy, and it undercut the struggling economies of poor Caribbean nations, which couldn't sell their own bounties of cane to the United States at even half the bogus rate.

For political reasons, the government's payout to the sugar

industry was patriotically promoted as aid to the struggling family farmer. True, some of the big sugar companies were family-owned, but the family members themselves seldom touched the soil. The closest most of them got to the actual crop were the cubes that they dropped in their coffee at the Bankers' Club. The scions of sugar growers wouldn't be caught dead in a broiling cane field, where the muck crawled with snakes and insects. Instead the brutal harvest was left to Jamaican and Dominican migrant workers, who were paid shameful wages to swing machetes all day in the sweltering sun.

It had been this way for an eternity, and men like Malcolm Moldowsky lost no sleep over it. His task, one of many, was making sure that Big Sugar's price supports passed Congress with no snags. To make that happen, Moldowsky needed senators and representatives who were sympathetic to the growers. Fortunately, sympathy was still easy to buy in Washington: all it took was campaign contributions.

So Moldowsky could always round up the votes. That was no problem. But the votes didn't do any good unless the sugar bill made it out of committee, and this year the committee of the House was in bitter turmoil over issues having nothing to do with agriculture. No fewer than three formerly pliant congressmen had been stricken with mysterious attacks of conscience, and announced they would vote against the sugar price supports. Ostensibly they were protesting the plight of the migrants and the disastrous pollution of the Everglades, into which the growers regularly dumped billions of gallons of waste water.

Malcolm Moldowsky knew the dissenting congressmen couldn't care less about the wretched cane workers, nor would they mind if the Everglades caught fire and burned to cinders. In truth, the opposition to the sugar bill was retaliation against the chairman of the committee, one David Dilbeck, who had cast the deciding vote that killed a hefty twenty-two-percent pay raise for himself and his distinguished colleagues in the House.

Dilbeck had committed this unforgivable sin by pure accident; he had been drunk, and had simply pushed the wrong lever when the matter of the pay raise was called to the floor. In his pickled condition, it was miraculous that Dilbeck had found the way back to his own desk, let alone connected with the tote machine. The following noon, the bleary congressman turned on the television to see George Will praising him for his courage. Dilbeck had no idea why; he remembered nothing of the night before. When staff members explained what he'd done, he crawled to a wastebasket and spit up.

Rather than admit the truth—that full credit for the deed belonged to the distillers of Barbancourt rum—David Dilbeck went on 'Nightline' and said he was proud of voting the way he did, said it was no time for Congress to go picking the public's pocket. Privately, Dilbeck was furious at himself; he'd needed the extra dough worse than anybody.

And now his fellow politicians were striking back. They knew Dilbeck depended on Big Sugar for his campaign contributions, and they knew Big Sugar relied upon Dave Dilbeck for the price supports. So the House members decided to screw with him in a major way; they aimed to teach him a lesson.

Malcolm J. Moldowsky saw the ugliness unfolding. It would require all his subterranean talents to save the sugar bill, and he couldn't do it if Dilbeck got caught in a sex scandal. After years of slithering through political gutters, Moldowsky was still amazed at how primevally stupid most politicians could be, on any given night. He hadn't a shred of pity for Congressman Dilbeck, but he would help him anyway.

Millions upon millions of dollars were at stake. Moldy would do whatever had to be done, at whatever the cost.

The other dancers knew something was bothering Erin. It showed in her performance.

'Darrell again,' said Urbana Sprawl, by far the largest and most gorgeous of the dancers. Urbana was Erin's best friend at the Eager Beaver lounge.

'No, it's not Darrell,' Erin said. 'Well, it is and it isn't.'

Darrell Grant was Erin's former husband. They were divorced after five rotten years of marriage and one wonderful child, a daughter. The court battle was protracted and very expensive, so

Erin decided to try out as an exotic dancer, which paid better than clerical work. There was nothing exotic about the new job, but it wasn't as sleazy as she had feared. The money just about covered her legal fees.

Then Darrell got cute. He filed a petition charging that Erin was an unfit mother, and invited the divorce judge to come see for himself what the future ex-Mrs Grant did for a living. The judge sat through seven dance numbers and, being a born-again Christian, concluded that Erin's impressionable young daughter was better off in the custody of her father. That Darrell Grant was a pillhead, a convict and a dealer in stolen wheelchairs didn't bother the judge as much as the fact that Erin took her undies off in public. The judge gave her a stern lecture on decency and morality, and told her she could see the child every third weekend, and on Christmas Eve. Her lawyer was appealing the custody ruling, and Erin needed dancing money now more than ever. In the meantime, the divorce judge had become a regular at the Eager Beaver lounge, sitting in a dim booth near the Foosball machines. Erin never said a word to the man, but Shad always made a point of secretly pissing in the Jack Daniels he served him.

Urbana Sprawl said to Erin: 'Come on, don't make me beat it out of you.' They were taking off their makeup, sharing the chipped mirror in the dressing room.

A customer, Erin admitted. 'Mr Peepers, I call him. His real name is Killian.'

'Table three,' said another dancer, who was known as Monique Jr. There were two Moniques dancing at the club, and neither would change her name. 'I know the guy,' Monique Jr said. 'Funny glasses, bad necktie, shitty tipper.'

Urbana Sprawl said to Erin: 'He giving you a problem?'

'He's missed a couple of nights is all.'

'Wow,' said Monique Jr. 'Call the fucking FBI.'

'You don't understand. It's about my case.' Erin opened her purse and took out a cocktail napkin, which was folded into a tiny square. She handed it to Monique Jr. 'He gave me this the other night. He wanted to talk, but Shad was sitting right there, so he wrote it down instead.'

Monique Jr read the note silently. Then she passed it to Urbana Sprawl. Mr Killian had printed carefully, in small block letters, with an obvious effort to be neat:

> *I can help get your daughter back. I ask nothing in return but a kind smile. Also, could you add ZZ Top to your routine? Any song from the first album would be fine.*
> *Thank you.*

'Men will try anything,' Monique Jr said, skeptically. 'Anything for pussy.'

Erin thought it was worth listening to Killian's pitch. 'What if he's for real?'

Urbana Sprawl folded the note and gave it back. 'Erin, how does he know about Angela?'

'He knows everything.' It was her first experience with a customer who'd gone off the deep end. For three weeks straight Killian had been swooning at table three. 'He says he loves me,' Erin said. 'I haven't encouraged him. I haven't told him anything personal.'

'This happens,' Urbana said. 'Nothing to do but stay cool.'

Erin said he seemed fairly harmless. 'It can't hurt to listen. I'm at the point where I'll try anything.'

Monique Jr said, 'Tell you one thing. The little prick needs to learn how to tip.'

Shad poked his head in the doorway. 'Staff meeting,' he announced, coughing. 'Five minutes, in the office.'

'Beat it,' snapped Urbana Sprawl, who was largely nude. Shad truly didn't notice. Eleven years of strip joints had made him numb to the sight of bare breasts. An occupational hazard, Shad figured. One more reason to get the hell out, before it was too late.

Erin said, 'Tell Mr Orly we're on the way.'

Shad withdrew, shutting the door. To Erin, he resembled a snapping turtle—his vast knobby head was moist and hairless, and his nose beaked sharply to meet the thin severe line of his lips, forming a lethal-looking overbite. From what Erin could see, Shad also had no eyebrows and no eyelashes.

'Creep,' Monique Jr said.

'He's not so bad.' Erin slipped into a blue terrycloth robe and a pair of sandals. She told the other dancers about Shad's plan for the dead roach.

'Yogurt!' Monique Jr cried. 'God, that's disgusting.'

Urbana Sprawl said, 'I hope it works. I hope he gets a million bucks and goes off to live in Tahiti.'

Dream on, thought Erin. Shad wasn't going anywhere unless Mr Orly told him to go.

Orly's office was done in imitation red velvet. He hated it as much as anyone. The vivid decor had been the choice of the club's previous owner, before he was shot and dumped in the diamond lane of Interstate 95. Orly said the crime had nothing to do with the man's taste for imitation velvet, but rather with his inability to account for gross profits in a timely fashion. Meaning he'd skimmed. The imitation velvet remained on Orly's walls to remind employees that, unless one is very good at it, one does not skim from professional skimmers.

As the dancers assembled before Orly's desk, he became overwhelmed by the commingling of fruity perfumes, and began to sneeze and cough spasmodically. Shad brought a box of tissues and a can of Dr Pepper. Orly made quite a spectacle of blowing his nose and then examining the tissue, to see what had been expelled. Erin looked at Urbana Sprawl and rolled her eyes. The man was a pig.

'All right,' Orly began. 'Tonight let's talk about the dancing. I been hearing complaints.'

None of the strippers said a word. Orly shrugged, and went on: 'Basically, here's the problem: You girls gotta move more. By that, I mean your asses and also your boobs. I was watching tonight and some of you, I swear, it's like watchin' a corpse rot. Not even a twitch.' Orly paused and popped open the Dr Pepper, which foamed out of the can. When he licked the rim with his tongue, several of the dancers groaned.

Orly glanced up and said, 'Has somebody got a problem? Because if they do, let's hear it.'

Erin raised a hand. 'Mr Orly, the style of our dancing depends on the music.'

Orly motioned with the can. 'Go on.'

Erin said, 'If the songs are fast, we dance fast. If the songs are slow, we dance slow—'

'We been through this before,' he cut in. 'You wanted to pick your own songs, and I says fine on the condition that they're good hot dance songs. But some a this shit, I swear, it's elevator music.'

Urbana Sprawl said, 'Janet Jackson, Madonna—I don't call that elevator music. Paula Abdul? Come on.'

This was the wrong approach with Orly, who didn't know Janet Jackson from Bo Jackson. He put down the soft drink and rubbed the moisture into his palms. 'All I know is, tonight I see a guy sleeping like a baby at table four. *Sleeping!* His face is maybe twelve inches from Sabrina's fur pie, and the guy is fucking snoring. With my own eyes I gotta see this.' Orly sat forward and raised his voice. 'Tell me what kind of a stripper puts a customer to sleep!'

Sabrina, who was combing a chestnut wig on her lap, said nothing. The dancers preferred not to argue with Mr Orly, who was boastful about his connections to organized crime. Besides, some of the women weren't very good on stage, and they knew it. Listless was a charitable way to describe their dancing. Erin tried to help with the routines, but generally the other dancers were not keen on rehearsals.

Orly said, 'Fast, slow or in between—it doesn't matter. The point is to take what God gave you and move it around.' He sneezed suddenly, reached for a tissue and plugged it into both nostrils. He continued speaking, the tissue fluttering with each word: 'Think of it as humping. Humping to music. What counts is not the goddamn speed, it's the motion, for Christ's sake, it's the attitude. I don't pay you girls to bore my customers, understand? A man who's sleeping isn't buying any of my booze, and he sure as hell ain't stuffing any cash in your garters.'

It was Erin who spoke up again. 'Mr Orly, you mentioned

attitude. I agree we've got a morale problem here at the club, but I think I know why.'

This got everybody's attention. Even Shad perked up.

'It's the name,' Erin said. 'Eager Beaver—it's a very crude name.'

Orly yanked the tissue out of his nose. Normally he would've fired a woman for such a remark, but Erin brought in lots of business for the club. She was one of the few dancers who could actually dance.

'I like '"Eager Beaver,"' Orly said. 'It's catchy and it's clever and it damn near rhymes.'

Erin said it was crude and demeaning. 'And it's bad for morale. It gives the impression we're a bunch of whores, which we're not.'

Orly told her to lighten up. 'It's a tease, darling. We're a strip joint, for Christ's sake, who's gonna pay a seven-dollar cover to watch *nice* girls?'

The man had a point, yet Erin persisted. 'I'm aware of the nature of our business, but it doesn't mean we can't have some pride. When friends and relatives ask where we work, some of us lie about it. Some of us are embarrassed to say the name.'

Orly seemed more amused than offended. He looked at the other dancers and asked, 'This true?'

A few nodded. Orly turned to Shad. 'How about you? You embarrassed to work here?'

'Oh no,' Shad said. 'It's my life's ambition.' He winked at Erin, who tried not to laugh.

Orly rocked back in the chair and folded his hands behind his head. His white shirt was stained the color of varnish at both armpits. 'The name stays,' he announced.

'What about a contest?' Erin suggested. 'To come up with a better one.'

'No!'

Urbana Sprawl said, 'I remember when it was the Pleasure Palace. And before that, the Booby Hatch.'

Monique Jr said, 'And I remember when it was Gentleman's Choice, until the state shut it down for prostitution.'

Orly cringed at the word. 'Well, now it's the Eager Beaver, and it will stay the Eager Beaver as long as I say so.' He still owed two grand on the new marquee.

'Fine,' said Erin, 'Eager Beaver it stays. Very classy.'

He ignored her. 'The bottom line is, work on your goddamn dancing.' He opened a drawer and pulled out a stack of video-tapes. 'This is from a joint in Dallas. Take it home, study how good these girls move. Three, four hundred a night in tips is what they make, and I'm not surprised.'

Shad handed a cassette to each of the dancers.

Urbana Sprawl said, 'Mr Orly, I don't have a VCR.'

'I got one you can rent.'

Erin said, 'Four hundred a night, huh? Maybe it's worth a trip to Dallas. Maybe they've got some openings.'

Again, Orly ignored her. 'One more item,' he said, 'then you can all go home. It's about what happened the other night. The fight on stage.'

Monique Jr said it wasn't much of a fight, just some guy swinging a bottle.

'Whatever,' said Orly. 'You didn't see a damn thing, OK? Anybody asks about it, you go tell Shad.'

Erin was surprised by these instructions. Fights broke out frequently at the Eager Beaver, but Mr Orly seldom took an interest. 'What's going on?' she asked. 'Is it the police?'

'The bottom line is, you don't get paid to answer questions. You get paid to take off your clothes.' He drained the Dr Pepper, burped and tossed the can at Shad, who caught it effortlessly. Orly said, 'Now. We all clear on this?'

The strippers muttered apathetically.

'Good,' said Orly. He started a sneeze, but caught himself. The dancer named Sabrina shyly raised a hand. Orly told her to make it quick.

She said, 'The guy who was sleeping at table four? That wasn't really my fault, Mr Orly. He was on pills.'

'Darling, I don't care if he was on a fucking respirator. In my club, I want their eyes open. Understand?'

The dancers rose and, in an arresting gust of perfume, bustled out of the office. Orly told Erin to hang around for a minute. When they were alone, he said, 'That guy didn't hurt you the other night, did he?'

'Which guy—the one who grabbed me or the one with the champagne bottle?'

'Either,' Orly said. 'I mean, if you got hurt, let me know. Cuts, bruises, whatever, we'll get you to a doctor. It's on the house.'

On the house? Erin was stunned. She told Orly she was fine.

'Good,' he said, 'but just so you know: it won't happen again. Shad's been spoken to.'

'It wasn't his fault—'

He cut her off with the wave of a hand. 'A bouncer's job is to bounce. I pay that asshole good money.'

Erin stood up to leave.

Orly said, 'One more thing. I wasn't talking about you in here tonight. When it comes to the dancing and all—you're the last girl needs to look at some frigging video. You're one a the best we ever had.'

'Thank you, Mr Orly.'

'The music I don't get. It's awful damn soft but, hey, you make it work. They can't take their eyes off you.'

'Thank you,' she said again.

'Keep it up,' Orly said. 'You need anything, I mean *anything*, lemme know.'

Erin walked out of the office absolutely certain that she was in the middle of trouble.

When she got to the car, the man she called Mr Peepers was waiting.

3

When Paul Guber regained consciousness, the first thing he saw at the foot of the hospital bed was a lawyer. He knew without being told; it was a man who could've had no other purpose in a three-piece suit.

'My name is Mordecai,' the lawyer said. Over a vast belly he clutched a thin burgundy valise, brushed leather. 'I'm here to help in any way I can.'

Paul Guber's brainpan sloshed with morphine. He tried to speak but it felt as if he were spitting ash. His field of vision was narrow and electrical around the edges, like a cheap television. A woman came into the picture, her lips moving.

'Darling, how do you feel?'

It was Joyce, his fiancée. Paul Guber saw her reach out and touch a lump in the blanket—his left foot. Paul Guber was pleased to discover that he wasn't paralyzed.

Mordecai said, 'Your friends told me what happened. I was sickened, to be very honest. Such a world we live in.'

Paul Guber blinked rapidly to improve his focus.

'You are lucky to be alive,' confided Mordecai.

Paul wasn't so sure. He wondered what Richard and the others had said to Joyce about the bachelor party. The appearance of a lawyer in his hospital room caused him to suspect the worst.

He opened his mouth to launch a provisional defense, but Mordecai halted him with a flabby pink palm. 'It would be better if you didn't,' the lawyer said, smiling like a wolf.

By way of introduction, Joyce said, 'Mordecai is my cousin. Uncle Dan's oldest son—you met Uncle Dan. I called him the minute I heard what happened.'

She didn't seem the least bit homicidal. Paul Guber was relieved, but wary.

Mordecai said, 'You probably don't remember much. That's to be expected.'

But Paul remembered everything. Joyce patted his shins under the bedcovers. 'Oh Paul,' she said. 'I can't believe such a thing could happen.'

'In my game,' said Mordecai, 'it's known as gross negligence.'

Paul coughed. It felt like someone had taken a cheese grater to his throat.

'Don't try to speak,' the lawyer advised again. 'You've been beaten severely, resulting in physical and emotional damage. *Permanent* damage, as a result of gross negligence.'

The words came out of a tunnel, but Paul got the general idea. The lawyer was itching to sue somebody. Paul wanted to nip that scheme in the bud—prolonged litigation against a strip joint would please neither his employer nor his future in-laws.

'We're not interested in who did this,' Mordecai was saying. 'We're interested in how it was allowed to happen. Accountability, in other words. We're interested in compensation of a magnitude that no simple street thug could afford.'

Joyce moved to the front of the bed and began stroking Paul's forehead. 'Someone's got to pay for this,' she said quietly.

Mordecai was quick with the follow-through. 'You are not the only aggrieved party, Mr Guber. The cancellation of a wedding is a heart-wrenching event for all concerned. I'm thinking of the bride-to-be.'

'All those engraved invitations,' Joyce elaborated. 'The musicians, the florists, the deposit on the reception hall. The Hyatt's not exactly cheap.'

Paul shut his eyes. Maybe it was all a dream. Maybe there was no naked lady dancing to Van Morrison.

The lawyer said, 'I could scarcely believe it when your friend Richard described the circumstances. Getting mugged on the grounds of a synagogue!'

Paul groaned involuntarily.

'Don't worry, we intend to pursue an action,' Mordecai said.

'You can depend on it.' He raised the briefcase as if it held some secret power.

'Unh—' said Paul, but Joyce pressed two fingers to his lips.

'Rest now,' she whispered. 'We'll come back later.'

'And not a word to anyone,' said Mordecai the lawyer. 'In my game, the best client is a helpless client.'

Paul Guber felt a stab in his arm, and he opened his eyes to see a beautiful nurse injecting him with drugs. He was so grateful he could've kissed her on the lips.

Erin's mother lived in California with her fifth husband. She wrote biweekly letters to Erin—richly detailed accounts of shopping sprees. Always the letters ended with a plea: 'Quit that awful job! Leave that awful place! Come live with us!'

Erin's mother didn't approve of nude dancing as an occupation. Erin didn't approve of marrying men for their money. The two women seldom conversed without argument. Each of Erin's successive stepfathers had offered financial assistance, but Erin wouldn't take a dime. It infuriated her mother. Money was the name of the game, she would say. We girls ought to stick together!

Erin's real father, who was also rich, had died in an automobile accident when she was young. One night he got drunk and drove his Eldorado into a drainage canal. The three young women in the back seat managed to climb out and swim to shore. It was just as well for Erin's father that he did not.

On the way to the funeral, her mother said it was a shame the sonofabitch hadn't lived, so she could've divorced him in a manner consistent with his sins. Over the years, Erin's mother came to be an expert at divorce, and also at widowhood. It was no coincidence that each of Erin's stepfathers was wealthier and more elderly than his predecessor. As Erin grew older, she accepted the fact that her mother was a restless gold digger who would never be happy, never be satisfied. On the other hand, her husbands knew exactly what they were getting, and didn't seem to care. It taught Erin one of life's great lessons: an attractive woman could get whatever she wanted, because men were so laughably weak. They would do *anything* for even the distant promise of sex.

Erin had almost forgotten this precept until her marriage broke up, and she was left broke and fighting for her daughter. It hit her on the day her divorce lawyer explained what it might cost to gain permanent custody of Angela. Erin was dumbstruck at the figure, which was more money than an office secretary would earn in two or three years. It all depended, said the lawyer, on how big of a prick her ex-husband Darrell intended to be. The biggest, Erin replied.

She knew then that a regular nine-to-five job wouldn't do, that she'd have to find another way. That night she'd gone home and stood at the bedroom mirror and slowly removed her clothes, starting with the blouse. It looked ridiculous. She put on some music, Mitch Ryder and the Detroit Wheels, and tried again. Erin had always been a good dancer, but she'd never seen herself dancing in a full-length mirror, stark naked. Even though she had a good figure, she felt silly. She thought: Who in the world would pay to see this?

The next night Erin went to the Eager Beaver to get a sense of the atmosphere. The place was crowded and the music was very loud. It took about an hour before she relaxed enough to take inventory of both the talent and the clientele. Erin noticed that many of the women were extremely poor dancers who tried to compensate with stage gimmicks. A common move was to wheel around, bend over and show off one's buttocks. Another trick, when hopelessly out of rhythm, was to halt midstep and lick one's own index finger in a salacious way. It spurred the male audience from boredom to wild cheers. Erin watched in amusement as customers lurched toward the stage, whistling and waving beer-soaked currency. How easily amused they are! she thought. There was little difference between this and what her mother did; it was the same game of tease, the same basic equation. Use what you've got to get what you want.

The following morning, Erin drank two cups of black coffee and phoned her mother in San Diego. 'Guess what?' Erin said, and delivered the news in a chirpy tone.

Erin's mother disapproved. She said it was a tawdry way to make a living, even for a few months. She said it was no place to meet high-class guys.

'The money's good,' Erin said, 'and I think I can do it.'

'Not with those tits,' said her mother.

The modest dimensions of Erin's breasts had been an issue for a long time. Erin's mother (who was on her third set of saline implants) believed that surgical enhancement would increase Erin's chances of attracting a good man. She pointed to Darrell Grant as an example of the lowlife trash that was drawn to small-bosomed women. She insisted there was a mathematical corollary between the size of one's boobs and the financial viability of one's suitors.

Erin said she was satisfied with the God-given size of her breasts, and confident that customers would find her sexy.

'Ha!' Erin's mother said. 'You'll see, young lady. You'll see who gets the biggest tips—the girls with the knockers, that's who!'

Erin's mother was wrong. Her daughter was quite a dancer.

Erin was startled to meet Jerry Killian in the parking lot of the Eager Beaver lounge. He handed her a bouquet of yellow roses, and a small box containing a diamond lavaliere. Then he told her that he loved her more than life itself.

'Try to get a grip,' Erin said.

'I am lost.'

'Obviously.'

'Lost in love!'

Erin said, 'You don't know me. If you're in love with anything, it's my dancing. And possibly the fact that I was naked at the time.'

Killian's face twisted in pain. 'I would love you as much,' he said, 'if you were a bank teller.'

'Fully clothed?'

'In a potato sack,' he declared.

Erin accepted the roses but gave back the diamond necklace.

She unlocked the car and laid the bouquet on the front seat. She felt around on the floorboard for the .32, just in case.

'Erin, I know all about you. Did you read my note?'

'Anybody can go down to the courthouse, Mr Killian. It's all in the files.'

Abruptly Killian dropped to one knee, on the pavement. 'I'm a serious man.'

'Don't do this,' Erin said, wearily.

'I love you. I can fix the custody case.' His voice was burning. 'I can get your child back.'

Stay cool, thought Erin. She was dying to ask him how it would work, how he would do it. 'Mr Killian, get up. You're ruining a perfectly good pair of pants.'

Killian maintained his genuflection. He folded his hands at his breast, as if praying. 'The judge has aspirations for higher office. He has an eye on the federal bench.'

'And I suppose you've got connections.'

Killian glowed. 'One phone call, and he will see your case in a different light.'

'I'll tell you about this judge,' Erin said. 'He comes to the club, sits in the back and doodles with himself while I'm dancing.'

Killian said, 'That's good information. We can use that.'

'Forget it—'

'Please,' he cut in, 'don't underestimate me.'

Erin was thinking, What if he can do this thing? What if he's really got some pull?

'Tell me about your connections. Why should a call from you make a difference?'

Killian said, 'Not from me. From a certain United States congressman.'

Erin took the car keys from her purse and jangled them impatiently.

Killian merrily went on: 'Think about it, Erin. A US congressman asks a favor. Would you dare say no? Not if you had hopes of getting a federal judgeship. Not if you needed some pull in Washington.'

He touched her arm lightly, and she noticed that his fingers were shaking. He said, 'Your little girl—her name is Angela. She belongs with you.'

Erin felt a hitch in her breath. The sound of her daughter's name, coming from this stranger, filled her with sorrow.

'I'm single myself,' Killian said.

'Don't get carried away.'

'You're right, Erin. I'm very sorry.' He stood up, brushed the dirt from his trousers. 'I've been working on this plan, making progress. Give me another week and you'll have a new court date. And I think you'll find the judge to be much more open-minded about the case.'

He was bowing to kiss her hand when Shad tackled him from the side. It hardly qualified as a scuffle, as there was no resistance from Killian. He seemed to go limp. When his eyeglasses flew off, a dreamy look came to his face.

Erin told Shad not to hurt him.

'Why not?'

Killian was stretched out on the damp asphalt. When he raised his head, pebbles stuck comically to one cheek. 'I'm a man of my word,' he said in a marbly voice.

Shad pointed at him. 'Don't come back, you little dork.'

'Do you speak for the management?' Killian inquired.

Shad placed a size-thirteen shoe on his windpipe.

'Be careful,' Erin said again.

'It's so tempting.'

'But I love her,' Killian croaked. 'I am lost in love.'

Shad shook his head. 'You're pathetic,' he told Killian. 'But you got good taste.'

'Don't underestimate me. I am not without influence.'

Shad looked at Erin, who shrugged.

'Be my wife,' Killian cried.

Shad leaned over and seized him by the collar. 'That's enough a that,' he said.

Erin started the car. Shad didn't let Jerry Killian off the ground until she had gone.

*

The next night, in the dressing room, Monique Sr announced that Carl Perkins was sitting at table seven.

Erin, who was repairing a heel, glanced up and said, 'Carl Perkins the guitarist?'

Monique Sr beamed. 'Is there another?' She regularly spotted celebrities in the audience. Last Tuesday it was William Kunstler, the renowned attorney. A week before, Martin Balsam, the actor.

The sightings were imaginary, but none of the other dancers made an issue of it. Each had a private trick for self-motivation, some inner force that pushed her toward the stage when the music came on. For Monique Sr, the inspiration came from believing that someone famous was in the club, someone who might be impressed by her moves, someone who could whisk her away and change her life for ever. Erin thought it clever of Monique Sr to choose personalities whose names were well known, but whose faces were not exactly national emblems. Carl Perkins, for instance, was a stroke of genius. In the smoky blue shadows of the Eager Beaver, a dozen customers might resemble the legendary musician. It was a bullet-proof fantasy, and Erin admired it.

'Old Carl tipped me forty bucks,' Monique Sr was saying. 'Not that he can't afford it. He only wrote ' "Blue Suede Shoes".'

'Great song,' said Erin, tapping the new heel in place. Monique Sr was an encyclopedia when it came to rock 'n' roll.

Shad entered the dressing room without knocking. He handed Erin a wrinkled envelope, marked up with red postal ink: her most recent letter to Angela, returned as undeliverable.

Urbana Sprawl said, 'Oh no.'

Erin bitterly crumpled the letter in the palm of her hand. The bastard Darrell had done it again—moved away without telling her. And taken Angie.

'No forwarding address?' Monique Sr asked.

Erin cursed acidly. The man was such a despicable asshole. How had she ever fallen for him?

Shad said, 'Take the night off, babe.'

'I can't.' Erin whipped out her lipstick and hairbrush, and got busy in front of the mirror. 'Dance, dance, dance,' she said, softly to herself.

Monique Sr had fictitious celebrities to motivate her; Erin had Darrell Grant. The divorce judge had ordered him not to go anywhere, but it was like talking to a tomcat. Every time her ex-husband went mobile, Erin saw her legal fees go up another five grand. Finding the bastard, then serving him with new papers, cost a fortune.

'Your lucky night,' Shad told her. He held another envelope; it was crisp and lavender, with familiar block lettering. 'I took the liberty,' he said.

'You opened it?'

'After what happened, yeah. You're damn right.'

Erin said, 'I told you, he's harmless.'

'If he's not,' said Shad, 'he will be.'

Erin read the message twice:

> *The plan is in motion. Soon my devotion to you will be proven.*
> *Still awaiting the smile, and the ZZ Top.*

The other dancers clamored to see the note, but Erin tucked it in her purse. 'No, this one's private.'

'One thing—he doesn't listen so good,' Shad said. He'd warned Mr Peepers that his attentions were unwelcome.

Erin was determined not to get her hopes up. Monique Jr was probably right; Killian was probably trying to get in her pants, nothing more. Maybe the business with the congressman and the judge was hot air. Maybe it wasn't. The question was, How far would Killian go to impress her?

She began brushing her hair, with long even strokes, and listened for her song on the speakers. She was due up next on stage.

Malcolm J. Moldowsky had no qualms about dealing with the owner of a mob strip joint. It was better than dealing with congressmen and senators.

At first, Orly was cagey and snide. He asked why a bigshot congressman's office should give a rat's ass about who hangs out at a nudie joint. But as soon as Moldowsky raised the subject of liquor licenses and the renewal thereof, Orly became a model of friendliness and cooperation. He identified the customer at table three from credit card receipts and then, when the customer returned to the club, Orly phoned promptly with the news. By that time, of course, Moldowsky knew the man's identity. By that time the man had made contact with Congressman David Lane Dilbeck.

Still, Moldowsky was grateful for Orly's information. It was good to know Jerry Killian's movements.

'Nothing happened,' Orly said. 'My help got there first.'

'The young lady wasn't hurt?'

'Not at all. But the bottom line is, I can't have some horny creepoid chasing my best dancer.'

'I understand, Mr Orly.'

'See, I got prettier girls. Longer legs, bigger tits. This one, she ain't even a blonde. But she can dance like I don't know what, and she's built up a good clientele, which is what pays the freight in my business.'

'It won't happen again,' Moldowsky assured him.

'This girl, pass her on the street and you wouldn't look twice. But the moves she's got, I swear to Christ.'

'Natural talent is rare,' Moldowsky said, 'in my line of work, as well.'

'You understand, I can't have guys hanging in the parking lot, waiting for the girls. Some hardass cop shows up and it's loitering for the purpose of solicitation. I been through that before. Like you say, I got a license to think about.'

'Mr Killian's been having some personal problems.'

'Who doesn't,' Orly said. 'It's a fucked-up world, no?'

'Yes, it is.' Again Moldowsky praised Orly for his assistance and discretion. 'If there's anything we can do to repay the favor, please let us know.'

'Just put in a good word,' Orly said.

A good word? For who—the Gambino family? Moldowsky smiled to himself. 'Done,' he said to Orly.

'Also, my brother's got a little trouble with the IRS. Maybe you know somebody over there.'

Nothing's ever simple, Moldowsky thought. 'I can't promise any miracles,' he said. 'But I'll make a few calls.'

Orly thanked him, and added, 'I'm not looking to give this Killian guy any trouble. I'm trying to save him some. My man Shad, he's in a mood to break the fucker in two.'

Moldowsky said, 'Mr Killian won't be back.'

'Whatever.'

Orly didn't ask for details. And Moldowsky had no intention of telling him.

4

Darrell Grant had been living in a suburb called Lauderhill, which offered an exceptionally wide selection of rundown apartments. He'd rented a furnished duplex on a dead-end street where every front lawn, without exception, had an automobile on blocks. Erin wondered if it was a zoning requirement.

In front of Darrell Grant's apartment was a rusted Buick Riviera with a holly tree sprouting from its dashboard. The license plate revealed that the car had been there since 1982, long before Darrell Grant's arrival. Why he hadn't moved it was no great riddle: tow trucks cost money.

The other half of Darrell's grim duplex was occupied by two young Mormon missionaries, who greeted Erin politely as she came up the sidewalk. The missionaries were oiling their bicycles in preparation for another journey among South Florida's sinners. Erin admired their high spirits and fortitude; it was a tough neighborhood for proselytizing.

'Have you seen Mr Grant today?' she asked.

The missionaries said no, Mr Grant hadn't been around in a week or so. Erin went through the motion of knocking on the door. Darrell had taped aluminum foil over the inside windows, so nothing was visible from the front. As Erin headed toward the rear of the duplex, one of the young Mormons warned her to be careful because the yard was full of wheelchair parts.

Erin carefully stepped through an obstacle course of rusting rims, loose spokes, brakes, frames and footrests. She surmised that the wheelchair-stealing business must be doing pretty well for Darrell Grant to abandon so much valuable inventory—that, or the cops were on his back again, forcing a hasty departure.

Typically, Darrell had left the back door of the apartment

unlocked. When Erin opened it, she saw that her ex-husband truly was gone. As was his custom, he had stolen everything that wasn't nailed down, plus several items that were. Furniture, carpets, appliances, lamps, plumbing fixtures, ceiling fans, water heater, phone jacks, even the toilet tank was missing. Darrell Grant was nothing if not a master scavenger; he had painstakingly pried the tiles off the kitchen floor. Erin couldn't believe there was a big market for second-hand linoleum, but it was possible that Darrell was ahead of the curve. The commerce of stolen property wasn't immune to recessionary trends.

Darrell had cleaned out every room except one: Angie's bedroom. Erin gasped when she walked in.

The walls were bare except for a dozen old nails and a heart-shaped mirror. The floor was strewn with broken dolls: beheaded Barbies, dismembered Muppets, eviscerated Cabbage Patch Kids. The dolls had something in common: each had been a gift to Angela from Erin.

That was Darrell Grant's way. Weak in the verbal skills, he was inclined to express himself with displays of idiotic violence.

Erin's heart pounded in anger. She envisioned Darrell in their daughter's room, methodically separating the dolls from Angela's other toys, then attacking with a steak knife or pruning shears or God knows what . . . and leaving the mirror up so he could watch his own performance.

No! Erin thought. That wasn't the reason for the mirror. He'd left it for Erin, so she could see herself at the moment of discovery, could see the shock on her own face when she found what he'd done in Angie's bedroom. Could see herself crying.

But she didn't cry.

Touching nothing, she backed out of the room. Then she hurried outside and asked the friendly Mormons if she could borrow a camera.

Darrell Grant's sister lived in a trailer park thirty miles south of Miami. She shared a doublewide with a man who worked nights as a security guard at the Turkey Point nuclear power plant. The guard's name was Alberto Alonso. He greeted Erin warmly at the front door. The fact she was a professional stripper made him absolutely giddy.

'Come in, come in!' Alberto sang out. He opened his arms and attempted a hug; more of a lunge, actually. Erin deftly skirted his grasp.

'Where is Rita?' she asked.

'Out with the cubs,' Alberto said. 'Lupa's new litter—you want to come look? We got an albino.'

'Maybe later,' Erin said. Lupa was the family pet, a fifty-fifty cross between a German shepherd and a wild Mt McKinley timber wolf. At regular intervals, Rita bred Lupa with other wolves. She was able to sell the cubs for three hundred dollars each, sometimes more. It was the newest rage in macho dogs, since pit bulls had gone out of fashion.

'Six babies,' Alberto reported, 'and the only male is albino. You should see the size of his balls!'

Erin said, 'You must be very proud.'

'I'm trying to get the power company interested.'

'In what?'

'Wolf dogs, what else?' Alberto's grin revealed many crooked gaps. Erin didn't know how anyone could invest full confidence in a security guard with so many teeth missing.

'Think about it,' Alberto was saying. 'Packs of wolves patrolling the perimeter. There goes your terrorist threat. There goes your sabotage.'

The screen door opened and Rita charged in. 'Al, how many times I tole you—they ain't no guard dogs. They don't got the disposition for it.'

She wore a housedress, thong slippers, a catcher's mask, and canvas logging gloves that went up to the elbows. The sight of her reminded Erin that none of Darrell's siblings had grown up to be remotely normal or well-adjusted. In the Grant family, procreation had become a game of genetic roulette.

'Hello, Rita,' said Erin.

'Oh. Hi there.' Rita took off the catcher's mask, revealing a nasty track of fresh stitches from the midpoint of her forehead to the bridge of her nose. 'Lupa,' she explained. 'She damn jumpy around those cubs.'

Alberto said, 'Erin, honey, how about a drink?'

'Water would be fine.'

'No, I mean a *drink*.'

Rita said, 'Make that two.'

'Just water,' Erin said. 'I can't stay long.'

Alberto was plainly disappointed. He shuffled to the refrigerator and began grappling with an ice tray. Rita tugged off the logging gloves and said, 'Well, this is quite a surprise.'

Erin said, 'It's about Darrell. He's gone again.'

'Now don't get all worked up.'

'You know where he is?'

'No, ma'am, I do not.' Rita lowered herself onto a black Naugahyde sofa, which hissed beneath her weight. She said, 'You still workin' at that tittie place?'

Rita wasn't going to be easy; playing dumb was her life's work. Alberto was the weaker link.

'I hear the money is good,' Rita remarked. 'But it damn well ought to be.'

Erin said, 'When's the last time you talked to your brother?'

'Lord, I'm sure I don't remember.'

Alberto reappeared with water for Erin and a bourbon for Rita, both served in Fred Flintstone jelly jars. Out of the blue, Alberto said, 'What about private parties? Some of the boys at the plant were asking. They were talking about getting a banquet room at the Ramada.'

'I don't do private parties,' Erin told him. 'I dance at the club. That's it.'

'What about the other girls?'

'You'd have to ask them, Alberto.'

Rita said, 'He's been up to your place. What's the name again?'

'The Eager Beaver,' said Alberto, helpfully.

Rita furrowed her brow. 'I thought it was the Flesh Farm.'

Alberto said. 'No, that's another one.'

'Well, anyhoo, he's seen you dance.'

'Really?' Erin didn't like the idea of Alberto tiptoeing into the club, sneaking a peek. She could picture him giving a full report to the guys down at Turkey Point. It was pathetic, really. Erin was the closest thing to a celebrity that Alberto would ever know.

'I hope it was a good show,' she said sweetly. 'I hope you got your money's worth.'

'Gawd.' Rita lit a cigarette. 'It's all he talked about for weeks after. You'd think he ain't never seen pubic hairs before.'

Alberto Alonso reddened, finally. Erin said, 'You should've told me you were coming. I would've sent some champagne to the table.'

'Are you kidding? Pink champagne?'

A howling commotion erupted in the backyard. Rita grabbed the catcher's mask and hurried out the screen door.

'Careful now!' Alberto shouted after her.

Erin motioned him to sit down. 'We don't get to visit much anymore,' she said.

'Well, the divorce and all.'

'Doesn't mean we can't still be friends,' Erin said.

'I'd like that,' said Alberto. He scooted the chair closer. 'Friends it is. You and me!' His breathing had become audibly heavy, and his eyebrows looked moist.

Erin didn't often see men sweating from their eyebrows. 'There's two sides to every story,' she went on. 'Darrell had his faults.'

'Now that's a fact. He is no saint.'

From outside, they heard Rita shouting curses at the wolf dog. Then came a chilling feral scream.

'Damn,' Alberto said. 'Another cat, I'll bet.'

Erin lightly touched his knee. 'I need to find Darrell. It's very important.'

'He moved away, Erin.'

'I know that.'

'Don't worry, honey.' Alberto flopped a fat moist hand upon hers. Clumsily he tried to intertwine fingers, but Erin pulled away.

'Where is he, Alberto?'

'Rita would kill me.'

'It's my daughter we're talking about.'

Alberto nervously glanced toward the screen door. 'Look, he calls here a couple, three times a week. Needing money, per the usual. But I'm not sure where he's at.' Alberto attempted another hand-holding, but Erin shook him off.

'Anything would be a help,' she said. 'State, county, whatever. I'll settle for an area code.'

Alberto said, 'Rita's the one he talks to, not me. Darrell never told me anything about anything. He don't trust law enforcement, period.'

It was a reach for Alberto Alonso to classify himself as law enforcement, but Erin let it slide. Alberto's job applications had been rejected by every municipal police department in the southeastern United States. Though he had the heart of a lawman, he did not have the acceptable psychological profile. 'Squirrelly' was the term most commonly heard when Alberto's file came up for consideration.

He told Erin: 'Don't worry, I'm sure Angie's fine.'

'She's not fine, Alberto. She's with that fuckhead ex-husband of mine.'

Alberto was shocked into silence. Outside, the chaos in the backyard abated suddenly. Rita poked her head in the screen door. 'Where's the damn shovel?'

Alberto said, 'I thought it was with the rakes.'

'Well, it ain't!' The door slammed.

Erin asked Alberto for some aspirin.

'You got a headache?'

'A killer,' she said.

'Poor thing.' He stood up and cupped her face in his hands. 'You feel hot, honey.'

'Alberto, it's not a fever. It's a headache.'

'I'll get you some Bayers. Be right back.' He went to the bathroom and began searching the cabinet. 'I got Advil!' he called out. 'Tylenols. Anacins. Excedrin PMs. You prefer tablets or them new gel-caps?'

Alberto returned to the living room with an armful of pills, powders and capsules. Rita was there, settling into the Naugahyde, sucking fiercely on a cigarette. Erin was gone.

'Well, well.' Rita's voice cut like a blade. 'If it ain't Marcus Welby.'

Erin was fully aware that the theft of US mail was a federal offense, punishable by fines, imprisonment or both. She was also aware that in the Southern District of Florida, the United States Attorney spent exactly zero man-hours in pursuit of mail thieves, as the government's time was consumed by the prosecution of drug dealers, gunrunners, deposed foreign dictators, savings-and-loan executives, corrupt local politicians and crooked cops of all ranks.

The workings of the federal justice system were well known to Erin because her previous job, before becoming a nude dancer, was typing and filing intelligence reports for the Federal Bureau of Investigation. Erin was efficient, precise and perceptive. In some ways she was sharper than the FBI agent to whom she reported. Although his filing system was flawless, his street instincts were shaky. Erin liked him and tried to help, but the agent was young, inexperienced and hopelessly Midwestern in his approach; South Florida ate him alive.

When Erin was dismissed from her job, the agent (whose name was Cleary) was more distraught than she was. He tried everything within bounds of the Bureau's turgid hierarchy to reverse the decision, but it was no use. Erin had been reclassified as a security risk after her husband had been charged with the fourth felony of his life: the grand theft of eleven wheelchairs from the Sunshine Groves Retirement Village. It didn't matter that Erin was separated from Darrell Grant at the time—he'd phoned her from jail, and that was that. Phoned her at work, the moron! Told her to hurry and ditch the Camaro and for God's sake don't let the cops look in the trunk. Darrell Grant, yelling these instructions, forgetting that most phone calls out of the Broward County Jail (and all phone calls into the FBI building) were automatically recorded.

Erin herself was never suspected of complicity, for on both audio tapes her words to Darrell Grant were clear.

'You asshole. Where's my daughter?'

Although she didn't want to leave the job, Erin wasn't bitter. She understood the problem. Nobody should be married to a career criminal, but it was especially important for employees of the FBI. Agent Cleary was crestfallen, and wrote a glowing letter of reference, To Whom It May Concern, on official FBI stationery. For him that was quite a daring gesture. As it turned out, the letter was not needed when Erin applied for work at the Eager Beaver lounge. 'Show me your boobs,' Mr Orly had said. 'Fine. When can you start?' Erin didn't have the heart to tell Agent Cleary of her new occupation.

Ironically, the felony charge against Darrell Grant was dropped, as he'd agreed to become a secret informant for the sheriff's department. His first task was ratting out three of his scumdog thief friends; for this, Darrell was rewarded with a pristine new past, courtesy of the DELETE button on the sheriff's crime computer. The vaporizing of Darrell's prior record was egregiously illegal but not without precedent; if questioned, Darrell's handlers could always claim it was an accident. Crime computers were famous for spontaneous erasures.

In the subsequent battle for custody of Angela, Erin found herself fighting not just Darrell Grant, model citizen, but the detectives who so foolishly believed that he was working on their behalf. 'Whenever a new court date was set, the detectives conveniently arranged for Darrell Grant to be out of town on an undercover assignment. Affidavits attesting to the urgency of the mission were available by the handful. On the rare occasions when Darrell actually showed his face in court, not a soul came forward who would swear to his felonious exploits. The file room had been purged as neatly as the computer's memory. On the issue of Darrell Grant's criminal character, the judge was left only with Erin's word, which he coolly rejected.

Broke and discouraged, Erin refused to give up. She planned to pursue Darrell Grant through the legal system for as long and as far as necessary. Angela was in peril not because Darrell was abusive, but because he was unfailingly careless. It was only a matter of time before something bad happened to him, and then the real nightmare would begin. Then Erin's daughter would be delivered into the custody of the great state of Florida, which was not known for its attentiveness toward children.

Angie would never be a foster child. Erin wouldn't let it happen. To save the girl, she would do anything, including stealing Rita Grant's mail off the kitchen counter.

Erin put on a Jimmy Buffett tape, lay down on the bed and went through Rita's letters. She wore cutoff jeans and a baggy Hawaiian shirt and wraparound shades, electric blue. Her hair was in a ponytail, tucked under a pink cotton baseball cap. Her bare feet bounced to the music, and she was feeling better about her prospects.

Most of the stolen mail was worthless to Erin's private investigation—the electric bill, a Penthouse subscription reminder, a homesick letter from yet another wayward sibling (Darrell's youngest brother, feigning insanity at the state hospital in Chattahoochee), and a membership notice from the National Rifle Association, to which both Rita and Alberto had hopefully applied.

Only one item was of interest to Erin: the telephone bill. FBI training wasn't necessary to scan the long-distance entries and pinpoint Darrell Grant's location. He hadn't run far: Erin counted seven collect phone calls from a number in Deerfield Beach. It made perfect sense. Deerfield Beach was overwhelmingly populated by retirees. Where you had retirees, you had wheelchairs.

Erin turned down the stereo and picked up the phone. Her hand trembled as she dialed—not from nerves, but from anger. It rang six times before he answered. Erin used her old-lady voice. She said she was calling from the St Vitus Society, collecting donations for the homeless.

Darrell Grant said: 'Donations of what?'

'Anything you can spare. Food, clothing, medical equipment.'

'Like wheelchairs?' Darrell Grant asked.

Erin listened for the sound of a child in the background. She heard only a television, tuned to a talk show.

Darrell Grant said: 'Hello? You mean like wheelchairs?'

'Actually, we've got plenty of wheelchairs and gurneys. But any other medical equipment would be most appreciated.'

'That's too bad,' said Darrell Grant. 'I got some used wheelchairs in pretty good shape.'

Erin resisted the urge to scream something terrible into the phone. Still using the old-lady voice, she said, 'Well, we've just received a shipment of brand-new ones donated by the hospital district. But thank you anyway.'

'Yeah? What kind?'

'I really couldn't say. Can I put you down for some canned goods or bedding?'

'Sure,' Darrell Grant said. 'Better yet, I'll haul the stuff over there myself. Gimme your address. And spell the name a that saint again, would you?'

Erin smiled. What a champ.

5

Moldowsky didn't know that Jerry Killian was crazy drooling mad with love. Not that it mattered; blackmail was blackmail.

'Where's Dilbeck?' Killian demanded.

'I'm here as the congressman's personal representative.' Malcolm Moldowsky took out a monogrammed notebook. From an inside pocket came a gold fountain pen. 'All right, let's have the terms.'

'Not so quick.'

They were seated on the top deck of the *Jungle Queen*, a gaudy ersatz paddlewheeler that motored up and down the Intracoastal Waterway in Fort Lauderdale. It was Killian's idea to meet there, safely surrounded by yammering tourists and conventioneers.

He said, 'I specifically asked to meet the congressman.'

Moldowsky sighed a patient sigh. 'Mr Dilbeck is very busy. This morning he's touring Little Haiti. This afternoon he will dedicate a domino park in Little Havana. This evening he'll be speaking to the Democratic Sons and Daughters of Nicaragua in Exile.'

Killian whistled derisively. Malcolm Moldowsky said, 'It's an election year, my friend.'

'He has nothing to fear from me.'

'He's a busy man is all I'm saying.'

Killian folded his arms. 'So he sends a guy who smells like a Bangkok bidet.'

'You're referring to my cologne?'

'No offense. I'm a Brut man myself.'

Moldowsky doodled placidly on the notepad. 'No offense taken.'

'He's an excitable boy, your congressman. Beat the living Jesus out of that schmo in the dance club.' Killian awaited an explanation, but Moldowsky continued to draw, saying nothing.

'He's got a problem around the ladies,' Killian went on. 'I think he needs help, before word gets out.'

Moldowsky said, 'May we get down to business?'

'The only reason I mention it is I'm concerned. He could hurt somebody, or get hurt. They're tough places, those dance bars.'

'I'll pass that along. Can we begin now?'

Point by point, Killian explained his demands. There were only two. Moldowsky listened impassively and took notes. When the blackmailer finished, Moldowsky looked up and said, 'This is completely outrageous.'

The *Jungle Queen* blew four long whistles. The captain was trying to get the attention of a bridgetender.

Killian said, 'Which part is outrageous?'

'The money, of course. A million dollars!'

'Forget the money. What about the other part?'

Moldowsky eyed him. 'Forget the money?'

'Sure. I was just busting your balls.' Killian gave a hearty laugh. He signaled a waiter for two more beers.

Moldowsky said, 'Just so I've got this clear: You don't want any money. Not a dime.'

Killian removed his thick eyeglasses and held them to the sunlight, inspecting for smudges. He said, 'For a guy who dresses so sharp, you're thick as a brick. No, Mr Personal Representative, I don't want money. All I want him to do is fix a simple court case.'

'Keep your voice down.'

'*Grant* versus *Grant.*'

'Yes, I got it the first time,' Moldowsky said. 'A custody matter. What's your interest in the case?'

'None of your business,' Killian replied. 'And if you pursue that line of inquiry, I will go instantly to the police and report what I saw at the Eager Beaver. Headlines are certain to follow.'

Finally the drawbridge opened to let the *Jungle Queen* pass, and the tourists broke into silly tourist applause. A waiter appeared with beers. Moldowsky and Killian drank in silence until the merriment subsided on deck.

'This is a great boat ride,' Killian said brightly. 'They've got one like this down in Miami, right?'

'In Biscayne Bay. A tour of celebrity homes.' Moldowsky remained polite even though he'd decided that Jerry Killian was a flake. Flakes could still cause trouble.

'Like who? Which celebrities?' Killian asked.

'The Bee Gees.'

'Which Bee Gees?'

'The whole damn bunch. They've all got mansions on the water.'

'Is Madonna's house on the tour?'

'Undoubtedly,' Moldowsky said, with a sigh. He steered the conversation back to blackmail. 'What makes you think Congressman Dilbeck can influence a local divorce judge? I mean, even if he wanted to.'

'Easy. The divorce judge is sick of being a divorce judge. He wants to move up in the world, namely a seat on the federal bench. For that he needs political connections.'

Moldowsky frowned. 'But it's the Senate that confirms—'

'I know that!' Killian angrily gripped the edge of the table. 'I *know*, you pompous fuck. I know it's the Senate that confirms. But a letter from a congressman would be helpful, would it not? It might carry weight with certain senators on the Judiciary Committee, correct?'

'Sure,' Moldowsky said. 'You're right.' His eyes were on Killian's ratty necktie, which was soaking in his beer mug. Killian noticed and removed it quickly. If he was embarrassed, he didn't let it show.

'The judge would be impressed to hear from a United States congressperson. That's the point, that's what we're talking about, Mr Personal Representative—not influence so much as the appearance thereof. Who cares if this hayseed ever makes it to the federal bench? We want him to think he can. We want him to think Dilbeck has the clout to make or break. And I've got a feeling you're just the sneaky little maggot to deliver that message.'

Sometimes Malcolm Moldowsky regretted his own coolness. After so many years as a political fixer, he'd lost the capacity to be personally insulted; virtually nothing provoked him. In his line of work, emotions were risky. They distorted the senses, led to grave miscalculations and foolhardy impulses. Naturally it would've been fun to punch Jerry Killian so hard that he puked up blood, but it also would've been counter-productive. The man was motivated by forces deeper and more urgent than greed, and that made him dangerous indeed.

So Moldowsky said: 'I'll see what I can do.'

'I thought you would.'

'In the meantime, you can't go back to that strip club.' Moldowsky closed his notebook and capped his pen. 'If you show your face in the place, the deal's off. Got it?'

'Fair enough,' Killian said. 'I can handle that.' But his heart ached at the thought.

Suing a synagogue was challenging under the best of circumstances. Mordecai was having difficulty finding guidance. His law books were barren of precedents. Enthusiasm was equally hard to come by. When he told his mother of the case, she slapped him across the face with an oven mitt. It was her way of reminding him that two of his uncles were Orthodox rabbis.

Mordecai's plan for the Paul Guber case was further hindered by the victim's own friends, who couldn't recall the name or location of the synagogue at which the savage attack had occurred. The young men blamed their confusion on darkness, the late hour and alcohol, but Mordecai knew better. Collective amnesia was a sure sign of conspiracy. He considered asking Paul Guber for the true details of the incident, but that would've required Paul to open his mouth and speak, thus ruining a key plank of Mordecai's legal strategy. He wanted the jury to behold a stockbroker rendered mute and helpless by violent trauma. A stockbroker who could still work the phones wasn't nearly so pitiable a plaintiff. Mordecai's plan called for poor Mr Guber to remain silent.

The lawyer decided to try visual aids. He got a map of Broward County and attached it to a tall easel. With colored pins he marked the location of every synagogue from Tamarac to Hallandale. Mordecai's idea was to assemble Paul Guber and his buddies in front of the map; either it would jog their memories, or help them agree on a plausible story. Synagogues in the most affluent neighborhoods were denoted by shiny green pins—Mordecai's subtle way of suggesting a suitably prosperous defendant.

The map was brought to Paul Guber's hospital room, and his friends gathered on each side of the bed. Mordecai stood back and waited. The men squinted at the map. They mumbled. They pointed. They rubbed their chins in feigned concentration. It was a dreadful scene. After an hour, Mordecai ordered them all to go home and think about it.

Outside the hospital room, Paul's fiancée said, 'What does it mean?'

'It means I'm losing interest,' the lawyer replied.

Back at the office, Mordecai's secretary seemed relieved to see him, which was unusual. She took him to the conference room, where a new client was waiting. It took all of Mordecai's courage to shake the man's hand.

'I'm Shad,' the man said. 'We talked on the phone.'

The man was broad, bumpy and hairless. He wore a tank top, parachute pants and black Western boots. He had the grip of a wrestler.

Mordecai's secretary vanished. The lawyer took a seat at the table and motioned for Shad to do the same.

'You got a fridge?' Shad said.

'Pardon?'

Shad opened a brown grocery sack and took out the Ziploc pouch containing the undamaged foil seal; this he held up, dramatically, for Mordecai to see. Then Shad reached in the sack and removed the container of Delicato Fruity Low-Fat Yogurt. 'Blueberry,' he announced, removing the Glad Wrap.

'Ah yes,' said Mordecai. 'You're the one with the insect.'

'Roach,' Shad said, firmly. He pushed the yogurt across the table. Mordecai examined it tentatively, finding nothing.

'It's in here?' He peered at the flawless creaminess.

'You bet,' Shad said. 'We're talking jumbo.'

Mordecai lifted the wax carton up to the light. 'I wish I could see it.'

Shad offered him a spoon and said, 'Happy hunting.'

The lawyer hesitated. 'First we should get some pictures.' He buzzed the secretary and told her to bring the camera. Moments later, she buzzed back to report it was out of film.

Shad said, 'Hope you got a fridge.'

'Well, of course.'

'And I'd like a receipt.'

Mordecai was offended. 'You don't trust me?'

'Not yet,' said Shad.

'Don't worry. We'll have a contract.'

'Still, I'd like a receipt. That's my future there.' He pointed at the yogurt carton. 'That's my retirement.'

Mordecai explained the customary arrangement in such cases. When he got to the part about the contingency fee, he saw Shad stiffen.

'Forty percent? That's what you get?'

'It's standard, Mr Shad. You can check around.'

'Forty motherfucking percent!'

'Most attorneys quote similar rates.'

'Is that so?' Shad lowered his head and leaned across the table. 'I had a guy took a rat case for thirty-three, plus expenses.'

'Well,' said Mordecai, unsettled, 'my forty includes all costs.' He didn't want to hear about the other case, but he needed to know. 'When you say rat . . .'

'Baby Norway.' With his hands Shad indicated the size. 'About yea long. It was up at the Beef N' Reef in Wilton Manors. I open the steak sauce and there she comes, bingo, a rat! Lying there on my Rib-eye Special. Talk about traumatized.'

The image made Mordecai pause. 'And you filed suit?'

'Yeah, but something happened. The other side . . . I really don't know. They sued me back, believe it or not, and my lawyer said I was better off to forget the whole thing.' Shad spoke of the experience bitterly. 'I never paid the bastard a nickel,' he added pointedly. 'That was the deal.'

'It's the usual contingency contract.' Mordecai felt better now, back in familiar territory. 'Suing a big corporation isn't easy. It's hard work. Expensive, too.'

'On the phone you said they'd settle.'

'They probably will, Mr Shad, but not without a fight. That's where I'll earn my forty percent—if we win.'

Mordecai wasn't displaying the fiery optimism that Shad would have liked. He wondered if he'd made the right choice in attorneys. 'How long does yogurt stay good?' he asked.

The lawyer said he didn't know.

'You better find out.' Shad held up the carton. 'When this shit starts to turn, watch out, Mother. The stink is so bad it peels wallpaper.'

Mordecai said, 'We'll freeze it if necessary.'

'It ain't lunch,' said Shad, 'it's evidence. So don't go fucking up the chain of custody.'

'Certainly not.' Mordecai thought: Chain of custody? What's the story on this guy?

Shad said, 'Tell me about your ace shrink.'

'A good man. I've used him on other cases. You should start seeing him as soon as possible, and as often as possible.'

'And who pays for that?'

Mordecai smiled paternally. 'Don't you worry. Eventually the Delicato company will take care of all expenses. In the meantime, we need to build up a detailed medical record.'

Shad said, 'I never been to a shrink. I got a feeling I won't like it.'

'It's important to document your pain and suffering. It will help determine the final damages.'

'The money, you mean.'

'Exactly. The court needs to know the ordeal you've been through. You might even consider quitting your job.'

'Can't do that,' Shad said flatly.

'Lost income would greatly enhance a jury award. How about taking a leave of absence?'

Shad said no, he couldn't quit work. Mordecai backed off. They could discuss it another time. 'What kind of job do you have?' he asked.

'I'm in the entertainment business,' Shad said.

'Really?' Mordecai couldn't imagine it. 'Are you a . . . performer?' He was thinking: Circus.

Shad shook his head. 'Security. I provide security.'

'May I ask where?'

'At a bottomless joint.'

Mordecai took a deep breath. He imagined jurors would do the same. He imagined how it would be in court, watching helplessly as the sympathy drained from their eyes. Mordecai felt very sorry for himself; it had been such a crummy day. First the Paul Guber debacle and now this. Why didn't he ever snare the choice plaintiffs—the adorable little kids, the winsome young widows, the sad but plucky pensioners?

Not me, thought Mordecai. I get a bouncer from a tittie bar. Not a normal-looking bouncer either; some hairless pop-eyed 'Star Trek' reject.

The man named Shad said, 'The hell's the matter? If your heart's not in it, just say so.' He probed the yogurt with the spoon. 'I want you to see this.'

'Not necessary,' the lawyer protested. 'I believe you.'

Mordecai kicked with both feet, rolling the chair back from the conference table. He got up just as Shad struck paydirt.

'Ha!'

'My God,' said Mordecai.

'Did I tell you? Is that a fucking roach or what?'

The prehistoric pest filled the spoon. Shad raised it to the level of Mordecai's eyes. The lawyer gaped in revulsion. Wings askew, the dead cockroach knelt in a creamy blue puddle. Its yogurt-flecked antennae drooped lifelessly.

Shad was very proud. 'Well?'

'Put it back,' the lawyer rasped.

'Just think,' Shad said, 'sittin' down to breakfast and—'

'No!'

'Makes you want to gag, don't it?'

'Yes,' Mordecai whispered. For balance he clutched the corner of the table. 'Put it away now, please.'

Shad carefully dropped the insect into the yogurt and stirred gently. Soon the crispy corpse disappeared from view. 'There,' he said. 'Now, where's that fridge?'

'I'll get Beverly to show you.' The lawyer mopped his jowls with a handkerchief.

'Does this mean we got a deal?'

'It does,' said Mordecai.

Times were tough, and a roach was a roach.

6

Monique Sr announced that Alan Greenspan was drinking a beer at table fourteen.

Orly clapped his fat hands together. 'See! Another reason you gotta work.' He didn't want Erin to take the night off. 'Famous comedian in the audience, you shouldn't miss the chance.'

'Alan Greenspan,' Erin said pleasantly, 'is an economist.'

'That's the one.' Monique Sr stuck by her claim. 'Check him out yourself. Corona from the bottle, no lime.'

'Not to mention it's Tuesday,' Orly carped. 'Tuesday being oil wrestling. Only one of our busiest nights.'

'I don't wrestle,' Erin reminded him. 'Not in oil, not in custard, not in mud. No wrestling for me.'

Nude oil wrestling was a tradition at the Eager Beaver, but Erin declined to participate. In her view, professional dancers shouldn't roll around in a wet tub with shirtless, semi-tumescent drunks. As a secondary issue, Erin didn't like the looks of the oil. Orly was vague about the brand; one day he'd say it was Wesson, another day he'd swear it was Mazola. Erin had a hunch it was neither. Once a health inspector showed up for an on-site bacterial census. Amazingly, not a single living microbe was found in the wrestling vat. The mystery was explained later the same evening, when the health inspector returned with four of his civil service buddies. They shared a front-row table and all the Amaretto they could drink, courtesy of Mr Orly.

'Tuesday is a big night,' Orly was saying. 'Bottom line is, we need all our best dancers.'

'Please, Mr Orly. It's personal.'

'Tell me.'

'I'm meeting my ex-husband,' Erin said, 'to discuss future custody arrangements for our daughter.'

Here Urbana Sprawl interjected her opinion of Darrell Grant, describing him so vividly that Mr Orly immediately offered to have him killed.

Erin said, 'That's not necessary.'

'Beat up? Crippled? You gives the word.' Orly pantomimed dialing a telephone. 'That's how easy it is when you know the right people.'

'Thanks, but I can handle it myself.' Erin played along with Mr Orly's Mafia routine as a matter of politeness. He looked about as Sicilian as David Letterman.

Urbana Sprawl urged Orly to give Erin the night off for the sake of her lost little daughter. Orly wasn't the least bit moved. He said, 'Promise me this is really a domestic-type deal. Promise you're not sneaking down the street for an audition.'

'Oh right,' said Erin. 'My lifelong dream is to work for those freaks.'

Mr Orly was paranoid about losing his best strippers to the Flesh Farm, which recruited aggressively with signing bonuses. The owners recently introduced Friction Dancing Night to compete with Nude Oil Wrestling Night at the Eager Beaver. Friction dancing was not so much dancing as it was rubbing, vigorously, against the frontal surfaces of fully clothed customers. It was demonstrably more erotic than oil wrestling, and not nearly as messy. Orly was definitely feeling the pressure.

'Tell me the truth,' he said to Erin.

'I told you the truth. I'm meeting my ex-husband.' She picked up her purse to indicate the conversation was over. 'If you don't believe me, ask Shad. He's coming along.'

'My Shad?' Orly's eyebrows twitched with concern.

'As a favor to me,' Erin explained. 'There could be trouble.'

'Then be damn careful.'

'I will.'

'Because good bouncers are hard to find,' Orly said. 'Harder than dancers, believe it or not.'

*

Erin first met Darrell Grant at Broward General Hospital, where her mother was recuperating from an operation in which her navel had been cosmetically inverted. Erin's mother had paid a plastic surgeon $1,500 to transform her 'outie' bellybutton to an 'innie'. Erin was unaware that such a procedure was available, but her mother assured her that all the big-name fashion models had it done.

Erin was standing at her mother's bed, admiring the surgeon's work, when Darrell Grant appeared with fresh linens and a clean bedpan. He worked as an orderly at the hospital and, as Erin later learned, it was there he acquired his taste for narcotics and his aptitude for boosting wheelchairs. In appearance, though, Darrell seemed anything but a criminal. Erin was still naïve enough to believe that all crooks had bad teeth, greasy hair and jailhouse tattoos. She assumed that cleancut, good-looking men possessed the same natural advantage as cleancut, good-looking women: the world treated you better, and consequently there was no reason for unwholesome behavior.

And Darrell Grant was uncommonly handsome, with a lean face and bright mischievous eyes. He took her to the hospital cafeteria and charmed her with a hastily fabricated story of his life. The centerpiece of the yarn was an authentic Bronze Star, which Darrell Grant kept in the breast pocket of his hospital garb. He told Erin he'd won it for killing a Cuban sniper during the invasion of Grenada. Erin chose not to question Darrell's tale, knowing the Pentagon had given out about a hundred thousand medals in appreciation for making the tiny spice island safe once again for Holiday Inns. Much later in their relationship Erin would learn that Darrell had actually acquired the Bronze Star, along with two cases of Michelob, in the burglary of an American Legion post.

They dated for six months, to the horror of Erin's mother. She had steered a long line of doctors, lawyers and accountants in her daughter's direction, and Erin had found them all too serious and self-absorbed. Some of them were old enough to be her father. Darrell Grant was impulsive, full of tricks, and he made her laugh. At the time, that seemed important. Erin's decision to marry him was sudden and cataclysmic, and it had the desired effect of freeing her from the clutches of her mother.

The sociopathic side of Darrell Grant didn't surface for about eighteen months, until he abandoned all pretense of honest labor and devoted himself full time to larceny. To explain the odd hours and fluctuating income, he told Erin he was selling medical equipment. Darrell's boyish wit and warmth evaporated dramatically under the icy twin spells of amphetamines and methaqualone; he was either a dervish or a zombie, depending on the chemical cycle. Newly pregnant, Erin didn't want to bail out of the marriage without giving Darrell Grant a chance to reform. The thought of divorce was almost as daunting as the thought of her mother's shrill I-told-you-so.

When he learned that Erin was expecting a child, Darrell vowed to change his ways. He got off the pills, removed all stolen property from the garage and took a job selling rustproofing at a Chrysler dealership. He was a new man, for about a month. One Thursday, Erin returned home from work and found Darrell in the living room, chiseling the serial numbers off a pediatric wheelchair. Confronted, he broke into a rage and slapped Erin twice across the face. The amusement ended abruptly when Erin punched him in the larynx, pushed him to the floor and whacked him in the testicles with a mop handle. It was Darrell's first glimpse of his wife's temper, and it made an impression. From then on he never laid a finger on her; instead, he vented his feelings by destroying things that she valued—artworks, furniture, photo albums, her favorite clothes. By the time Angela was born, the marriage was irretrievably pulverized.

Erin didn't torment herself with remorse. She'd gotten conned, and learned a lesson. Now it was time to concentrate on getting Angela back.

Waiting in the car with Shad, Erin outlined the latest plan.

'So it's a trap,' he said.

'Exactly.'

'He won't be bringing no wheelchairs for the poor.'

'No,' said Erin, 'he'll be looking to steal some.'

Shad spit something out the window. 'And you were married to this asswipe?'

'We all make mistakes.'

'Don't you hate it,' Shad said, 'when love turns around and bites you like a damn rattlesnake? It happens, by God. Happens every day.'

Erin showed him the photographs of the mangled dolls in Angie's bedroom. 'Christ almighty,' he said.

'My daughter is the one I'm concerned about. That's what this is all about.'

Shad said nothing for several minutes. Then he asked Erin if she was satisfied with her lawyer. 'I'm not so sure about mine,' he added. 'He needs some firing up.'

Erin said, 'My lawyer's all right. It's the system that's so frustrating.'

'Tell me about it.' Shad was glad to chat with Erin about these matters; he felt they were warriors on the same battlefield. 'If there's such a thing as true justice,' he said, 'you'll get your little girl, and I'll get rich off my dead roach.'

'That would be nice,' Erin said quietly.

The car was in the farthest, darkest corner of a parking lot attached to a strip shopping mall in Oakland Park. The address Erin had given Darrell Grant belonged to a bankrupt video store, located at the other end of the plaza. A few movie posters remained in the window; from the car, Erin could make out the blown-up likeness of Arnold Schwarzenegger in sunglasses.

Shad said, 'How do you know he's coming tonight?'

'Because I told him they ship the wheelchairs every Wednesday morning. He'll be looking to load up on inventory.'

'Any particular model?'

'He favors Everest-and-Jennings,' Erin said. 'Rolls and Theradynes are good, too.'

Shad was intrigued. He'd assumed all wheelchairs were pretty much the same. 'Rolls as in Royce?'

Erin said no, it was a different company. Shad asked why her ex-husband didn't steal cars like everybody else.

'Because he couldn't hotwire a goddamn toaster,' said Erin. 'Cars are too complicated for Darrell Grant.'

Shad spit out the window again. He seemed to be aiming at a particular curbstone. 'You want me to—do what exactly? When he gets here, I mean.'

Erin said, 'Let's play it by ear.'

'I could break something. Maybe start with a finger.' Shad wiggled one of his pinkies. 'Depends how serious you are.'

'I just want to talk with the man.' Erin leaned against the headrest and closed her eyes. She thought about the young bachelor beaten senseless on stage at the Eager Beaver—was he still in the hospital? She remembered the rabid expression on the face of his attacker, the wheezy primal grunts as he swung the champagne bottle.

Erin thought: Is it me? Do I bring that out in men?

Then here's Orly, now Shad, offering to maim her ex-husband. A casual favor, like jumping the car battery or hooking up the stereo.

'The ulna is a good one,' Shad was saying. He tapped Erin's forearm to show her the spot. 'A crowbar right about there, we'll have his attention.'

Erin sat up. 'Can I ask you something? Do I seem the type of woman to be impressed by violence?'

He grunted non-committally.

'I'm serious, Shad. Is that your opinion of me?'

He cocked his huge head and stared at her curiously. In the darkness he resembled a shaved bear. 'It's what I know best, that's all—kicking ass. On account of my job.'

'Then it's not me?'

'Ha! No, it ain't you.'

'Because I am *not* impressed by that sort of thing.'

'Is that why there's a gun under the seat?'

Erin couldn't think of a sharp retort.

Shad grinned. 'It's all right, babe. You're entitled.'

'I've never used it,' she told him.

'But you might.' Shad folded his arms. 'All I'm saying is,

violence can be helpful. Sometimes it's the best way to make your point.'

'Not with Darrell.' Erin's ex-husband would cherish an injury. What better proof that she was hanging out with a rotten crowd, and was unfit to care for Angela! Darrell, the conniving bastard, would milk a broken limb for all it was worth. He'd wear the cast until the plaster rotted off his arm.

'Your call,' Shad said.

'I just want to talk with the man.'

'Fine.'

But deep inside, Erin briefly savored a vision of Shad pounding Darrell Grant into dogmeat. She probably should've been ashamed by the feeling, but she wasn't.

Especially when she thought of what he'd done to Angie's dolls.

At midnight Shad went looking for a Coke machine. Erin put on a Buffett tape and turned the volume low. She liked the Caribbean songs the best. Her imagination set sail, and before long she was dreaming of pearly beaches and secluded harbors. She was barefoot in the surf, wiggling her toes into the sand.

When she opened her eyes, her shoes were gone. Both doors on the old Fairlane had been opened. When she got out of the car, she stepped on something plastic, which cracked into sharp pieces. The Buffett cassette on the pavement.

Erin froze. 'Shad?'

A hand grabbed her by the hair, twisting hard, jerked her head back so that all she saw was sky. She felt something sharp against her throat.

'You still snore like a pig.' It was Darrell Grant.

Erin shook uncontrollably. It was embarrassing to let him see her so afraid.

He said, 'I can't believe you tried to set me up. I can't fucking believe it.'

'What?' Erin didn't recognize the pitch of her own voice.

Darrell Grant slapped a hand across her mouth, told her to

shut the hell up. They both heard the footsteps. 'Your boyfriend,' Darrell whispered. 'This'll be choice.'

Shad came out of the shadows with a Diet Coke in one hand and an unopened can of Canada Dry in the other. He put both cans down as soon as he saw the long knife at Erin's neck. Darrell Grant told him not to try anything stupid. Shad's expression remained invisible in the darkness.

'I got an idea,' Darrell said. He told Shad to lie on his belly or else get a bucket to catch Erin's blood. Shad nodded and got down on the ground. Darrell Grant released Erin and immediately pounced on the bouncer, digging his knees into the other man's enormous shoulder blades. Laughing, Darrell managed to cinch Shad's thick wrists with a pair of flexible plastic handcuffs.

'Knock it off,' Erin said, still shaky.

With both hands Darrell Grant poised the dagger at the crest of Shad's bare skull; the smooth flesh dimpled under the pressure of the blade.

Again Erin told him to stop, and again her ex-husband cackled. He rolled the knife handle back and forth in his palms, so that the point twirled against Shad's skin. Erin saw the first drop of blood, blackish in the dim light.

'That hurt?' Darrell Grant asked.

'Nope,' Shad replied, truthfully. He felt little in the way of physical pain. The doctors didn't seem to know why.

Erin said, 'Since when do you carry a knife?'

'Since when do you hang out with ugly bald-headed Amazons?' Darrell Grant got up and whipped the dagger like a sword through the air. He was batty on speed. 'I suppose it's just a coincidence that you're here in this very parking lot tonight? *En garde!*' He slashed a Z in the air. 'What, you think I'm blind? I saw your car from three blocks away, Erin. Jesus, you'd make a great spy. Maybe next time you can set off fireworks.'

She said, 'You're such an asshole.'

Darrell Grant grinned crookedly. 'Is that how they speak at the St Vitus Society? That *was* you on the phone, right? Talking about all those brand-new wheelchairs.'

'You've lost your mind.'

'Then explain this!' Accusingly, he pointed the dagger at the Fairlane. 'And this!' He poked Shad with the toe of a tan cowboy boot. 'You fucking set me up!'

Erin said: 'Darrell, I'm keeping a list: assault with a deadly weapon, false imprisonment, burglary, possession of narcotics—'

'Shut up,' he snapped. 'What'm I supposed to believe, that you and Igor stopped here to make out? I know you're lonely, Erin, but this is ridiculous. I seen handsomer iguanas.'

She thought of the gun in the car, gauged the steps back to the driver's side. Then she pushed the idea from her mind. Shooting Darrell would mean she'd never see Angie again. The judge would make sure of it.

'Junior?' It was Shad, speaking from the side of his mouth. He had no choice, being face down on the asphalt. 'Junior, listen up. The lady and I work together. She was giving me a lift home when this piece a shit excuse for a Ford overheated. We pulled in to let the radiator cool, and that's it. That's the whole story.'

Darrell Grant dropped to his haunches and tweaked Shad's nose. 'Well, I'll be damned. It talks.'

Wonder drugs, thought Erin. 'What's with your hair?' she asked. Darrell flared at her caustic tone. For a man whose profession was stealing from invalids, he was surprisingly vain about his appearance.

He said, 'I lightened it a touch. So?'

'And the stubble,' Erin said. 'Come here, let's see.'

'No way.' He stood up, sullenly.

'Is this your Don Johnson period?'

'Shut up, Erin.'

She was trying to take his mind off Shad and further mischief with the knife. 'I'll bet you got yourself a white linen Armani to go with the hair.'

Darrell Grant said, 'Fuck you.' When he put the dagger in his belt, Erin felt slightly better about the situation. She hoped he was downgearing for a simple argument.

Then he stood on Shad's head with the heels of his cowboy boots.

'Get off!' Erin cried.

'Make me.'

'Darrell, stop!'

Shad made no sounds. Erin wasn't sure if he was still conscious.

'I like it up here,' Darrell Grant chirped. He balanced on Shad's skull as if it were a cypress stump.

'Don't,' Erin pleaded.

'What's it worth to you? How about a twenty?'

Erin looked at Shad's face under the boots. His eyes were closed but his jaw was set.

'Twenty bucks,' Darrell Grant repeated. 'Hurry, hurry.'

He had tossed Erin's purse under the car. She had to crawl for it. Darrell Grant leered as he watched her down on all fours. 'I like that,' he said. 'Brings back memories.'

Mechanically Erin fumbled in the purse for her cash. She found a twenty-dollar bill and handed it to her ex-husband. He sniffed it as if it were cognac. 'Amazing,' he said. 'All you gotta do is flash your twat and men throw money. Isn't it a great country, Erin? Aren't you proud to be an American?'

At that moment, the only person she hated more than Darrell Grant was herself, for marrying him. 'Get off the man,' she said coldly. Darrell hopped from Shad's head.

'Where's Angie?'

'Safe and sound,' said Darrell Grant. 'If you're a good mummy, I'll let her call on Christmas Day.'

'We're going back to court.' Erin's voice trembled. 'You've already violated the judge's order.'

'Back to court!' Darrell Grant's hooting filled the night. 'Back to court! I love it.'

'What's happened to you, Darrell?' She really wanted to know. He was worse than she'd ever seen him.

He yanked the knife from his belt and bent over Shad. For a moment Erin feared that he would slit Shad's throat. She had an image of herself hanging on Darrell's back, digging her fingernails into his eye sockets.

'Don't do it,' she said.

'Do what?'

Using the dagger as a pen, Darrell playfully etched the letter G into the crown of Shad's naked scalp. Blood trickled down his head and puddled in the folds of muscle at the base of his neck. Erin felt woozy and chilled. Shad remained silent, although his eyes had opened.

'There.' Darrell Grant stood back and admired his work.

Erin said, 'What does that prove?'

'We're not going back to court.'

'You're wrong, Darrell.'

'I won, sweetheart. All the marbles, remember?'

'What'd you do with my shoes?'

Again came the hooting laughter. 'Wake up, little Dorothy,' he said. 'You're not in Kansas any more!'

Darrell Grant circled Erin's car, puncturing each tire with a thrust of the knife. Then he kicked each of the soda cans and sauntered off across the parking lot. As he disappeared in the darkness, Erin could hear him singing, 'Somewhere Over the Rainbow'.

At her feet, Shad rolled over and blinked up at the stars.

'Nice guy,' he said. 'Too bad it didn't work out for you two.'

7

The next night, Erin danced to ZZ Top.

Her record store didn't stock the band's first album, so she bought one of the newer releases. Kevin, the club's disc jockey, was pleased with the hard guitar and fast bass beat. Her regular customers didn't seem to mind the change of pace.

The one she called Mr Peepers was not in the audience. Erin feared that Shad had scared him away from the Eager Beaver for ever. Either that, or he'd given up the hustle.

So much for love.

Against her better judgment, Jerry Killian had become a reed of hope for Erin in her battle for Angela. Dealing with Darrell Grant was impossible, but maybe Killian could get to the judge. Maybe political pressure was the way to go. Erin needed to know more about Killian's connection, the congressman.

His name, for starters.

She danced out of the spotlights long enough to shield her eyes and scout the back rows. The judge was in his customary booth near the Foosball machines. Monique Sr was on the tabletop, bouncing up a storm. The judge watched droopy-eyed and inert. Erin figured his hands were busy under the table.

After the set, Mr Orly came to the dressing room and announced that he approved of the new music. 'Faster the better,' he said.

Urbana Sprawl said ZZ Top was hazardous to her health. 'My tits are killing me.'

'Hey,' Orly said, 'we put up with your rap crap. Ice Puke or whatever.'

'Ice Cube!'

'Bottom line is, you can tolerate eight minutes of hard rock.'

'Instant stretch marks,' Urbana complained.

Erin said, 'I'll find some slower cuts.'

'Don't!' Orly protested. 'Fast is good. Everybody sweats, everybody drinks.'

'And everybody tips,' said Monique Sr, waving a fifty. The other dancers whistled.

'Case closed,' said Orly, and he was gone.

When the shift was over, Erin scrubbed off her makeup and dressed quickly. Urbana asked what was the hurry.

'I've got an errand.'

'Three in the morning?'

'Meeting somebody.'

'Tell me it's not Darrell.' Urbana and the other dancers knew about the harrowing incident at Erin's car. They'd seen the dagger cuts on Shad's bald head.

'Don't worry,' Erin said. 'It's only Jerry Killian.' She zipped her jeans and stepped into a pair of sandals.

'Mr Peepers?' Monique Jr said. 'Why?'

'To talk.'

'Bad idea,' said Monique Sr.

'Not many good ones at three in the morning.' Erin checked herself in the mirror. 'Desperate times call for desperate measures.'

'Be patient,' Urbana Sprawl advised. 'He'll be back. Especially you keep playing his songs.'

'I can't wait,' Erin said.

'How you gonna find him?'

'He's found.'

Urbana Sprawl smiled. 'The phone book!'

'Nope,' said Erin. 'Unlisted, unpublished.'

'Then how'd you find him?'

'Research,' Erin explained, enigmatically. Erin couldn't tell them the truth. One phone call had sent Agent Cleary to the computer keyboard. He was glad to help, and asked few questions; he still felt bad about her dismissal.

Monique Jr told Erin that it was crazy to call on Mr Peepers in the middle of the night. 'He could be a psycho slasher for all you know.'

'Oh, I believe he's harmless.'

'That's what they said about Ted Bundy.'

'Thank you,' said Erin, gathering her purse and dancing clothes, 'for the peace of mind.'

Without much effort, Urbana Sprawl blocked the door. 'Give him till the weekend,' she said.

Erin felt a wave of fatigue. She was losing the energy to argue. Her friends were right: it was craziness.

'Patience,' Urbana said.

'Until the weekend,' Erin promised. 'If you can stand the new music that long.'

Monique Jr said the ZZ Top was dynamite. She said she'd never dance to rap again. She wanted a white top hat and tails as a costume for 'Sharp-Dressed Man'.

Frowning, Urbana hoisted a titanic breast in each hand. 'Try jumping around with *these* suckers and you'd be in traction. So screw your ZZ and gimme that slow Cube.'

Erin was sympathetic. She couldn't imagine going through life with a bosom so large. None of the dancers doubted the rumor that Urbana had once smothered a man on a convertible sofa. It was completely plausible.

'See you tomorrow,' Erin told her friends.

'You headed home?' Monique Sr asked. 'Be honest.'

'Home,' Erin said.

Shad followed in his own car, just to make sure.

Moldowsky found the congressman in a state of massage. A redheaded woman in a gold tank suit straddled his back, chopping at his pale shoulder blades. The woman had very long fingernails for a masseuse.

'Say hi to Eve.' Dilbeck's words thrummed comically with each chop.

'Hello, Eve,' Moldowsky said. 'We need a moment of privacy. Do you mind?'

Eve said that was perfectly fine. She spoke with a light British accent.

'Go hop in the shower,' Dilbeck told her. 'I'll be there in a flash.'

When she was out of the room, Moldowsky said, 'David, where is your wife?'

'Shopping, I think.'

'You think?'

'Yes, shopping. I told Pierre to drive slow.'

Moldowsky said, 'You are a hopeless shithead.'

Dilbeck sat up and covered himself with the towel.

'What'd I do now, Malcolm? Hell, you're acting like my mother.'

They heard the faucets turn in the shower down the hall.

Moldowsky motioned with his chin. 'Is she a hooker?'

'I don't know yet,' said the congressman. 'And even if she is, so what? She's got no earthly idea who I am, Malcolm. She just moved here from London.'

'Beautiful. Hands across the water.'

'What's the matter with you?'

'The sugar bill, Davey. Your colleagues are playing it tough, and my clients are deeply concerned. They want to know if they've got their money on the wrong horse.'

'Relax. I'm entertaining young Christopher tonight.'

Relax? Moldowsky thought. The moron has a prostitute in the tub, an assault victim in the hospital and a blackmailer who's ready to call the newspapers. 'Did you speak with the judge?' he asked.

Dilbeck nodded. 'Yes, we had lunch.'

'Well?'

'He was grateful for my interest in his career. He does, as you say, have his heart on the federal bench.' Dilbeck stood up and adjusted the towel. He looked longingly down the hall, toward the gentle sounds of the shower.

Moldowsky said, 'And what about *Grant* versus *Grant*?'

'Oh, we talked it over.' Dilbeck began to move around the

room, trying to get upwind of Moldy's cologne. 'The judge is deeply religious,' Dilbeck said, 'or at least he pretends to be.'

'Born again, I suppose.'

'Several times. He feels strongly that he made the correct decision in the custody case. He seems to have a personal interest in the situation.'

'True enough,' Moldowsky said.

'He said the mother is a harlot. Is that right, Malcolm?'

'I haven't the faintest idea.'

'There's something you're not telling me.'

'There's lots I don't tell you, David.'

'I've got a soft spot when it comes to harlots.'

'Don't even think about it.' Moldowsky wasn't giving Dilbeck anything. The less he knew, the better. 'So what's the punch line? What did the judge say?'

'He doesn't need me, Malcolm. He plays golf with a fucking senator.'

Moldowsky cursed dispiritedly.

'—a senator on the Judiciary Committee. The next time there's an opening in our district, the judge has got it locked. He doesn't need us, is what I'm saying.'

'So he won't fix the case,' Moldowsky said, 'even as a favor.'

'"The woman is a tramp and a sinner. She is unfit to raise a child." Those are his words, Malcolm. Plus he quotes the Bible.'

'This is bad news.'

'Yes,' Dilbeck said. 'It was not a productive lunch.'

Moldowsky ground his knuckles together in agitation. 'Would he go for a bribe? Straight cash?'

'It's against his principles,' David Dilbeck said. 'But he's amenable to a free blowjob.'

A pulse became visible in Moldowsky's neck. 'Let's see if I understand: only if the lady goes down on the judge does she get custody of her child—'

'He says he'll consider it. That's all. '"Brownie points" is the way he put it.'

'David, I'll say this. You're one terrific negotiator. They needed you at the fucking SALT talks.' Moldowsky began to pace and rant, 'Who is this jizzbag judge? Bible quotes—from what, the Book of Dick?'

'Hey,' the congressman said, 'we're talking one lousy blowjob.'

Moldowsky cornered David Dilbeck and seized him by the arms. 'Killian won't go for it. The mother won't go for it. Hell, Davey, I got no morals whatsoever and I wouldn't go for it. It's the worst goddamn thing I ever heard.'

The vapors from Moldy's cologne made the congressman's eyes water. 'The judge won't take cash, Malcolm. I tried.'

'That's a disgrace.'

'Not even for his campaign,' Dilbeck said. 'I offered to funnel it through a PAC but he said no. See, that's the main reason he's angling for a federal gig, so he won't have to run for office any more. He has a very shitty opinion of politicians.'

The plumbing emitted a metallic screech as the shower stopped. Dilbeck turned sharply at the noise. His expression was a familiar glaze of sexual distraction.

'You're hopeless,' Moldowsky grumbled.

'What?' Dilbeck licked his lower lip.

'I said you're hopeless. Go check on your friend. I'll let myself out.'

'Thanks, Malcolm.'

'And stay out of trouble tonight.'

'Of course,' said the congressman. 'Erb will be there.'

'Fine,' said Moldowsky. Erb Crandall was good, but he was only one man. On some nights Dilbeck needed double-teaming.

As Moldowsky stalked down the hall, the bathroom door flung open and he was enveloped in a cloud of sweet-smelling steam. Eve stood there, sleek and wet and flushed in the cheeks. If Moldowsky was the least bit dazzled, it didn't show. He courteously stepped to the side and motioned for her to pass.

'You've got soap on your ears,' he said.

Less than two hours later, Congressman David Lane Dilbeck was a portrait of male contentment and relaxation. He smiled, he blew smoke rings, he tapped his shoes, he hummed to the music.

A fresh rum-and-Coke appeared inches from his fingers, further improving his mood. Sitting to his right was Erb Crandall, who was huddled anxiously over an orange juice. Every so often he glanced toward the door in anticipation of a raid. Sitting to the congressman's left, a man named Christopher Rojo folded a fifty-dollar bill into an airplane and sailed it toward the stage, where a woman danced cautiously with a nine-foot Burmese python. The reptile's jaws were secured with Scotch tape, and someone had painted a bottlebrush mustache on its snout. Erb Crandall figured it was some kind of Hitler joke.

'This is so wonderful,' said Dilbeck. 'Isn't she something, Erb? How about that damn snake!'

'Yeah,' Crandall said, 'what a life.'

The woman, whose stage name was Lorelei, had arranged the python in an intriguing way. The tail followed the crease of her bare buttocks downward through her legs, curling out to the crotch.

'That's a well-trained animal,' the congressman observed.

Christopher Rojo was similarly impressed. He was making a new paper airplane with a one hundred-dollar bill. Rojo was a wealthy young man with few ambitions and plenty of spare time. His family owned a large sugarcane operation on the southern shore of Lake Okeechobee. Christopher had never been to the farm, but he'd seen photographs. The cane fields looked like a stinking hellhole; he was astounded at the fortune they produced. There was so much money that one couldn't possibly spend it all. Heaven knows he was trying.

'Here, Davey,' he said. 'Your turn.'

Dilbeck took the paper airplane and tossed it toward the python dancer. It landed between her feet. She gave the men a slow wink, and scissored elegantly into a split. Picking up the money, she pretended to show it to the snake. Dilbeck laughed and laughed. Lorelei sprung to her feet, waved once and disappeared offstage. The set was over.

Erb Crandall sagged with relief. Maybe they'd get through the evening without incident.

Rojo said to Dilbeck: 'What's your bet?'

The congressman sipped his rum thoughtfully. 'Thirty-eight B,' he said. 'Nature's own.'

'And I,' said Rojo, waving more cash, 'say she's thirty-six inches of plastic fantastic.' He smoothed a fifty on the table. David Dilbeck did the same. They turned toward Crandall, who signaled himself out of the wager. They'd been at it all night, every time a new dancer came on stage. There were two parts to the bet: the size of the breasts, and whether or not they were surgically enhanced. Rojo was getting creamed, and Crandall wasn't surprised. The congressman had an unfailing eye for the female form; it was his life's passion, graft being a close second.

Rojo rose drunkenly and called for a man named Ling. Soon a small Oriental in a black tuxedo and a Yankees cap appeared at the table. He didn't look like the co-owner of a strip joint, but he was.

'Mr Ling!' Rojo said, opening his arms. 'Give us the scoop on Python Lady.'

'Her name is Lorelei,' said Dilbeck. 'Have some respect.'

Rojo sat down. Dilbeck pointed at the cash. 'Mr Ling, you see what's at stake.'

Ling nodded tolerantly. 'You want the knocker report?'

'Indeed we do.'

'Miss Lorelei is a thirty-eight B.'

'Ha!' Dilbeck crowed.

He grabbed for the money but Christopher Rojo caught his arm. 'Implants!' the young man hissed. 'Tell him, Mr Ling. Tell him it's implants, and we halve the bet.'

'No, sir,' Ling said. 'Lorelei is all Lorelei.'

'*Mierda*,' said Rojo.

The congressman gloated as he scooped up the cash.

Ling said, 'Only the best at Flesh Farm. Only the finest.'

'Top of the line,' agreed Dilbeck.

'Where else you see a snake so big?' Ling bragged. 'Snake like that could eat a pony.'

'So could Lorelei, I'll bet.' Dilbeck chuckled at his own incredible wit. It wasn't a light breezy chuckle, though. It was deep and ominous. Erb Crandall went on full alert.

He said, 'Davey, it's getting late.'

'Nonsense.' The congressman lit a cigarette. 'Mr Ling, I would like to meet the python princess.'

'Me, too,' said Christopher Rojo.

Ling shrugged. 'With or without the snake?'

'Without,' Dilbeck said. 'Tell her I've got one of my own.'

Rojo busted a gut. Erb Crandall shifted uneasily. This wasn't a smart idea, not at all. He said, 'Come on, Davey, you've got a speech in the morning.'

The congressman postured idiotically. 'Four score and seven years ago, our foreskins brought forth a new nation . . .'

Crandall didn't smile. Dilbeck said, 'All right, Erb, who the hell is it?'

'Chamber of Commerce.'

'Shit.' Dilbeck slapped Rojo's shoulder. 'Chris, you've never seen such stiffs. The Chamber of Cadavers is more like it.'

'Still,' said Crandall, 'it's for seven-thirty sharp.'

'We'll get him there,' Rojo promised.

'So,' said Ling, mildly impatient, 'you want a friction dance or what?'

The congressman spread his arms. 'Sounds enchanting, Brother Ling. Go fetch what's-her-face.'

'Miss Lorelei?'

'Absolutely.'

Crandall edged closer to Dilbeck and spoke sternly into his right ear. Dilbeck shook his head back and forth, keeping the drink to his lips the whole time. 'One little frictionating *lambada*,' he said with a slurp. 'What harm could it do?'

'Yeah,' said Rojo. 'Let the poor man have some fun.'

It was useless to object. Crandall removed all loose bottles and other potential weapons from the table. Then he made a slow pass through the club to see if he recognized anyone. He wasn't worried about the press, because reporters didn't make enough money to hang out in places like the Flesh Farm. Republicans were what Erb Crandall feared—all it took was one, spying from the shadows, and the Hon. David Lane Dilbeck was cooked. The crummy wig and dark glasses only made him more conspicuous; the chauffeur's cap, borrowed from the taciturn Pierre, was at least three sizes too small. To keep it from falling off, Dilbeck had pinned it to his wig; every time the cap moved, the hair moved with it. Not even Christopher Rojo seemed to notice. That was one good thing about Dilbeck's little problem; customers in nudie joints didn't spend much time scrutinizing each other. The dancers got all the attention.

Tonight the club was scarcely half full, and Crandall spotted no one from the wonderful world of politics. When he returned to the table, the congressman's chair was empty. Rojo pointed to the rear of the club, where a row of gilded booths lined one wall. The booths were reserved for friction dancing and other private interludes.

'I slipped him two hundred,' Rojo said. 'He wanted three but I made it two.'

'Two's plenty.' Crandall sat down and checked his wristwatch. He'd give it ten minutes.

Rojo said, 'I'm tired, man.' He reached into his coat and took out a tiny foil packet. 'You want some blow?'

Erb Crandall felt exhausted. 'That's brilliant, Chris. What a nifty idea. May I?' He unfolded the foil and examined the powder. Rojo smiled encouragingly. Crandall smiled back. Then he hawked up a glob and spit all over Christopher Rojo's dope.

'Jesus!' Rojo cried.

Crandall pushed the foil across the table. 'Get rid of it,' he said, 'on your way out the door.'

'You crazy mother!'

'Chris, listen. You're not gone in thirty seconds, I'll tell your old man about this. First thing *mañana*.'

Rojo saw the family trust fund evaporating before his eyes. He hastily wrapped the spit-soaked cocaine in a monogrammed handkerchief. 'There,' he said to Crandall. 'You happy now?'

'I said get lost.'

'But what about my turn?'

Crandall didn't understand the whining.

'With the snake lady, Erb. I'm next after Davey!'

'Take a rain check,' Crandall told him. He got up to search for the congressman.

Nothing took David Dilbeck's mind off his troubles like friction dancing. The sugar vote, the re-election campaign, the wife, the blackmail—who cared? He was alone with the python princess. They were swaying to imaginary Johnny Mathis tunes. The congressman had his hands on Lorelei's bottom. She was rubbing her delightfully natural protuberances against his middle-aged flab. Her voice sounded sweet and sincere. Her hair smelled like orchids. Dilbeck was getting hard. Life was good.

When he tried to unsnap Lorelei's top, she blocked the move.

'That's a no-no,' she whispered.

'What!'

'It's the law, baby.'

'Don't worry about it,' he said.

'Look, if you want to slow dance, I can't be naked. That's the law. I'm naked, you can't touch me anywhere.'

Dilbeck had a passing knowledge of the county obscenity ordinances.

Lorelei said, 'I'm sorry, baby.' She moved her hips against him in sinuous rhythm. 'That's not so bad, is it?' She had him pinned against the door to the booth.

'I've got an idea,' Dilbeck said.

'Yeah?'

'What if you get half naked? Then I can touch the part that's not.'

'Nice try,' Lorelei said, 'but it's all or nothing.'

So they continued dancing until Dilbeck felt himself poking her through his pants. In a low voice, he said, 'And what are we going to do about *him*?'

'Admire it,' Lorelei said, 'but that's all.'

Dilbeck gazed at his groin forlornly.

'Look,' she told him, 'you could be a cop for all I know.'

He whipped off the cap and the hairpiece, and presented his

true self to the python lady. 'I'm not a policeman. I'm a United States congressman.'

'Yeah, and I'm Gloria Steinem.'

Dilbeck sensed from Lorelei's demeanor that the friction dance would soon be finished.

'How much time do we have?' he asked.

'About forty-five seconds, baby.'

David Dilbeck hurriedly unbuttoned his shirt, dropped to the floor and lay on his back. Lorelei studied him guardedly.

'Dance on me,' he said.

'How much?'

'Two hundred bucks.'

'Heels or bare feet?'

'One of each,' said the congressman, shutting his eyes.

Carefully, Lorelei stepped on his chest. 'What's that scar?'

'Double bypass,' Dilbeck replied with a grunt. 'Don't worry, I'm good as new. Now dance, please.'

'Jesus,' mumbled the python woman.

'Oh yeah. Good girl.'

'Let me know if it hurts.'

'I'll let you know if it doesn't,' said the congressman.

Lorelei had difficulty keeping her balance, as Dilbeck's topography was spongy and uneven.

'You're a wonderful talent,' Dilbeck said, groaning pleasurably under the weight. His hands crept spiderlike toward his crotch.

'Oh, no you don't.' Lorelei stepped hard on his wrists. 'That's not allowed.'

'Stop, mommy.'

'You wanna play with yourself, go home and do it.'

David Dilbeck cried out once. Next came a series of wet suckling noises. Then he began to thrash epileptically beneath the astonished dancer; legs kicking stiffly, mad-dog eyes rolling back and forth.

Lorelei was afraid to take her feet off the man's arms. Inwardly she berated herself for not demanding payment up front; if the jerk croaked, she'd have to go through his pockets.

Dilbeck began to buck as if jolted by a hot wire. To keep from falling, Lorelei braced both arms against the walls of the booth. The door flew open and a stranger took her under the arms. He carried her out and asked if she was hurt. She said she'd left a shoe inside. The man said she probably wouldn't want it back, all things considered. He handed her three hundred dollars.

'Thanks,' Lorelei said. 'Will he be OK?'

'Don't you worry.'

The dancer's hands were shaking as she folded the money. 'You know what he told me? He told me he was a congressman.'

Erb Crandall laughed. 'Some guys,' he said, 'will try anything.' He dug into his pocket for another hundred-dollar bill.

8

The next day, Malcolm Moldowsky made the call. The meeting was set at a bowling alley on Sunrise Boulevard. 'Grab any lane you can,' the man said. 'It's League Night.'

Moldowsky's feet were so small he had to rent women's shoes. He got a nine-pound ball and tried to clean the germy holes with his monogrammed handkerchief. He willed himself to not think about those who had fingered the ball before him.

He bowled alone for an hour until the man showed up. He was as big as a wine keg, and wore a brown UPS shirt. He scanned Moldowsky's scores and said, 'Not bad.'

'I cheated,' Moldy said, tossing a gutter ball. He had knocked down maybe forty pins in all. On the score pad he had given himself a 164.

The man put on his bowling shoes and bowled strike–spare–strike. 'You picked a good lane,' he said to Moldowsky.

A waitress came by and the man waved her away. Moldowsky handed him a thick brown envelope. 'It's all there,' he told him. 'The tickets, too. Check for yourself.'

'Nuh-uh,' said the bowler. 'I don't care what's inside. I'm just the delivery boy.'

He rolled a snapping curve that left the seven-ten combination. 'Are you a gambling man?' he asked Moldowsky. 'Wait, that's a dumb question. Of course you're a gambling man. Otherwise you wouldn't be involved.'

'Good thinking.'

'Five bucks says I make this split.'

'Sure,' said Moldy. 'Five it is.' His lack of interest would've been obvious to a three-year-old.

The big man made it look easy, nicking the seven-pin just

enough to kick across and take out the ten. 'That's the toughest split in bowling,' he said. 'Did you know that?'

'Amazing,' said Moldowsky with a yawn. He gave the man five ones. 'Ask your people to move as quickly as possible. We're up against a deadline.'

'I don't know what the hell you're talking about,' the man said, 'but I'll be happy to pass it along. Your turn, sport.'

Unhappily, Moldowsky positioned himself at the head of the lane. He made three tiny, stiff steps and heaved the ball down the alley. Somehow he got a strike.

'Pure luck,' Moldy admitted.

'The best kind,' said the man in the UPS shirt. 'You go on home now, OK? Everything's under control.'

A single piece of rotten news affirmed the leaden sense of futility that had burdened Mordecai every day since his graduation from law school, 207th in a class of 212.

The setback was especially cruel, coming at a rare moment of optimism. A lawyer from the Delicato Dairy Company had arrived at Mordecai's office to discuss a possible settlement in the case of the roach-tainted blueberry yogurt. For Mordecai, the company's willingness to negotiate (without the customary exchange of nasty correspondence) was a glorious surprise. An out-of-court agreement would have spared him long hours of excruciating preparation for a trial; it would also have saved him from exposing a jury to the sight of his client, Shad the bouncer.

The informality of the meeting had sent Mordecai's hopes soaring. The attorney from the Delicato Dairy Company had been civil, sensible and not given to bluster. He was keenly aware of the public-relations consequences of a high-profile insect trial. The central concern was television: in Florida, TV cameras are allowed in court. The two men agreed that color videotape of a cockroach being plucked from a Delicato container could have a negative impact on consumer confidence. The extent of damage, sales-wise, would depend on how many major markets picked up the satellite feed from the courtroom. The attorney's eagerness to avoid such a risk was obvious by the size of his initial offer—a settlement in 'the mid-six figures'. Mordecai struggled to mask his elation.

Of course, the Delicato attorney requested to see Shad's roach. Just a formality, he assured Mordecai. The attorney had brought a 35 millimeter camera to document the contamination. Photographs would be important, he explained, should his clients challenge the wisdom of settling. A brief slide show in the boardroom would turn them around.

Mordecai was impressed by the attorney's thoroughness. He could see how product liability might be an attractive field of practice, if one could avoid the courthouse.

He wished Beverly were there to share the triumph, but she was out with one of her three-day migraines. Mordecai was using a temp named Rachel, whose unflagging bubbliness compensated for her lack of shorthand skills and slothful pace at the typewriter. Mordecai called Rachel into his office and told her to fetch the blueberry yogurt from the refrigerator. The smile left her face instantly, and Mordecai knew.

'I'll get some more,' she said quickly, 'on my lunch hour.'

Mordecai found no words to express his dismay. The Delicato attorney politely excused himself to use the telephone in the other room.

'Oh Rachel,' said Mordecai, abjectly.

'I'll buy the variety pack. Eight kinds of tropical fruit.'

'Rachel!'

'Yes, sir?'

'What possessed you?'

'I was hungry.'

'Did you not notice that the carton was open?'

'I thought it was Bev's. I didn't want it to sit there and go sour.'

'Rachel,' said Mordecai. 'You don't understand.'

'I'm very, very sorry.' She began to weep.

'Shut up,' Mordecai said. 'Shut up this instant.' When he thought of Shad, the flesh on his neck got damp. How would he tell him? What bloody havoc would ensue? Mordecai also mourned his own financial loss: forty percent of zero was zero. His vast stomach pitched.

'I didn't know it was yours,' Rachel slobbered. 'I didn't know you liked yogurt.'

'I hate yogurt. It gives me the runs.'

The secretary's remorse clouded with confusion. 'Then why are you so upset?'

'Because you swallowed my evidence.' Mordecai spoke in an odd singsong voice. 'So how was it, Rachel?'

'The yogurt?'

'Yes, the yogurt. A little chunky, perhaps?'

'Now that you mention it.' She sounded worried.

'Are you going to fire me?'

'Oh, worse than that,' said Mordecai. 'Please sit down.'

'What are you going to do?'

'Something that will give me great pleasure. I'm going to tell you exactly what you ate.'

Visitation day.

Erin waited under cloudy skies at Holiday Park. She chose a bench near the public tennis courts where Chris Evert had learned to play. Today it was a doubles match among French Canadian tourists. They had the whitest skin and the bluest veins that Erin had ever seen.

Darrell Grant always kept Erin waiting because it gave him a feeling of power, knowing how she lived for these afternoons. Today he arrived forty-five minutes late, pushing Angela in a wheelchair.

'Momma, look what we got at the hospital!'

Erin lifted her daughter to the sidewalk and told Darrell Grant to get lost.

'How's your butt-ugly boyfriend?' he said.

'Momma's got a boyfriend?' asked Angela.

'No, baby, I don't.'

Erin was furious that Darrell was using Angie in his wheelchair heists. If he were caught, the consequences would be terrible—

the state authorities would take the little girl for good. Erin felt perfectly entitled to scream at Darrell and tell him what a reckless idiot he was, but she didn't want to spoil her brief time with Angela.

Darrell Grant said, 'I see you got new tires.'

Erin ignored him. She checked her daughter's dress and socks and underpants, to make sure they were clean. For a sociopath, Darrell was good about doing the laundry.

'Take care of my pretty little partner,' he said, and pushed the empty wheelchair back to his van, where he waited. On visitation days, he never let Erin and Angela out of his sight. Given an opportunity, Erin surely would try to run away with the girl. Darrell knew it for a fact.

Erin held her daughter's hand and they began to walk.

'How are you, baby?'

'Just OK.'

'Are you making new friends?'

'I spent Friday at Aunt Rita's. She's got a real wolf!'

Terrific, thought Erin. Crazy Rita and her cuddly carnivores. 'Stay away from the wolf, Angela. They can be mean sometimes.'

'She said I can have one of the babies, Momma.'

'No, we'll get you a real puppy—'

'But Daddy said no. He said maybe a bird.'

'A bird?' Erin said. Just what every four-year-old wants.

'A talking one,' Angie said. 'Like Big Bird, only littler.'

'Would you like that?'

'He said we can call it Humpy. Is that a good name?'

'No,' said Erin. 'Not really.'

They walked the perimeter of the park. Darrell Grant followed slowly in his van. Erin fixed a picnic under the trees. She and Angela ate peanut butter sandwiches and sang songs from 'The Electric Company'. A gray squirrel appeared and they fed it Cheese Doodles.

At ten minutes to three, Darrell began honking the horn. When Erin didn't react, he leaned on it annoyingly. The blare drowned the gentle sounds of the park. The Canadians stopped playing tennis and began cursing at Darrell Grant in French.

'For God's sake,' said Erin.

'Is Daddy making that noise?'

'I'm afraid so.' Erin gave her daughter a hug and a kiss. She smelled Darrell's goddamn cigarettes in the girl's hair.

'Momma, I forgot to tell you.'

'What, honey?'

'I lost all my dolls.'

'I'm so sorry.'

'When we moved. Daddy said he couldn't find them.'

'I'll get you some new ones,' Erin promised. She would never reveal to Angela what her father had done. Such a thing could not be explained.

'I love you, Angie.'

'Love you, too, Momma. Can I tell Daddy about the new dolls?'

'Let's keep it a surprise.'

From Agent Cleary, Erin had learned the following basic information about Jerry Killian: he was five-foot-nine, 140 pounds, 48 years old and divorced. He worked as a videotape editor at the local CBS affiliate. He was a registered Democrat. He drove a 1988 Chevrolet Caprice. He purchased his eyeglasses from a discount optician. He subscribed to *Newsweek*, *Harper's*, *The New Yorker*, *Rolling Stone*, *Consumer Reports* and *Hustler*. His ex-wife recently opened a macramé shop in a suburb of Atlanta, and he co-signed the loan. They had two daughters at Georgia State University. He owned season tickets to the Miami Dolphins. He rented every movie that Debra Winger ever made. He carried a $3,000 credit limit on his Visa card. In the fall he went trout fishing in western Montana, and always rented a compact car. In his entire life he had never been arrested for anything.

And he lived in Apartment 317 at 4566 Green Duck Parkway, Fort Lauderdale, Florida.

Erin phoned ahead. Killian was flabbergasted to hear her voice. He put on a coat and a tie to meet her at the door.

'In my purse,' said Erin, 'is a loaded gun.'

'So be it.'

'I'm here on business only.'

'Understood,' Killian said.

She had expected his apartment to be tidy, and it was. The place smelled of Lemon Pledge. They sat in opposing chairs at an oval-shaped dining table.

'I just wanted to thank you,' she said. 'That music you suggested is great for stage dancing.'

Killian glowed. 'You tried it? I'm so pleased.'

'You should come by the club to see. I told Shad it's fine if you do.'

'Really?' He looked wistful. 'Maybe later down the road.'

'Why later? Why not now?'

'The deal is cooking. Part of the agreement is for me to steer clear of the Eager Beaver.' Killian paused. 'It's the hardest thing I've ever done. I miss you so much.'

Here we go, Erin thought. Get the hose.

She said, 'May I call you Jerry?'

'I'd be in heaven if you did—'

'Jerry, look. I need to know more about this so-called deal. It's my life we're talking about. My little girl.'

'Naturally you don't trust me.'

'I don't *know* you.'

'Erin,' he said, 'I would do nothing to put you or your daughter in jeopardy. My devotion is complete and enduring and pure. I am consumed by it, day and night. I am lost in love.'

Erin's heart didn't flutter even slightly. She said, 'Jerry, who is this congressman?'

'His district is elsewhere. You wouldn't know his name.'

'Try me. I read the newspapers.'

'The name is unimportant,' Killian said. 'The key fact is, he's got a serious problem with the ladies. I'd feel uncomfortable going into details.'

'Oh please.'

'I'm a gentleman. That's how I was raised.'

'And I'm a stripper, Jerry. Once I had a customer eat the G-string off the crack of my ass—chew it up, swallow it, wash it down with Southern Comfort. Then he burped the elastic.'

Killian's ears turned red.

'The point is,' Erin said, 'nothing a man does can shock me. I have an ex-husband who carves his initials into other people's scalps. Is your congressman that much fun?'

'I'm not protecting him,' Jerry Killian said. 'I'm protecting you.'

'In case there's trouble?'

Killian got up and said, 'Come with me.'

Erin followed him through the apartment. The purse was tucked tightly under her left arm, so she could feel the gun through the fabric. Killian opened the door to a small guest bedroom, which he had converted to a private hall of fame. The walls were decorated with publicity pictures of local nude dancers. Interestingly, the photographs were all standard head-and-shoulder shots; one could have shown them to a kindergarten without fear of corruption. Erin's publicity photo was framed in wood and centered prominently in the pantheon. It was illuminated by its own brass lamp.

Scanning his collection, Killian said, 'Nothing is more beautiful than a woman's smile.'

'Oh really,' said Erin. 'That's why you come to the Eager Beaver—for our smiles?'

'It's the portal to true love and serenity. Without a smile, what's the rest of it? Just boobs and a patch of hair.'

'Jerry?'

'Yes.'

'You're giving me the creeps.'

'Well, Erin, I'm lost. I admit it.'

'You know all these girls?'

'I knew them. Befriended them. And whenever I could, I helped them.' He pointed to a platinum blonde with a sharp nose and spiky greased eyelashes. 'Allison had a substance problem. I got her into a very fine program, and today she's clean.'

Erin asked if she was still dancing.

'No, she's not.' Killian stepped close to the photograph, contemplating each detail as if it were a Monet. 'A week after she got out of treatment, she married a tree surgeon and moved to

Tallahassee. I never even got a postcard.' He turned to Erin and brightened. 'But that's all right! I ask for nothing.'

'Except a smile.'

'When it's from the heart.'

Erin turned off the light and directed Killian back to the living room. She sat beside him on a deacon's bench, and spoke to him as if he were a small boy.

'This is not a game,' she said.

'I heard they call me Mr Peepers.'

'We all like you, Jerry. It's an affectionate nickname.'

'I do have a frail and bookish appearance.'

'Scholarly is the way I'd describe it.'

'Don't be fooled, Erin. I can play hardball.'

She took both his hands—a standard move, to keep them from wandering. 'Exactly what've you got on the congressman?'

Killian said he couldn't tell her. He pulled one hand free and made a zipping motion across his lips.

'It must be good,' Erin coaxed, 'to make him lean on a judge.'

'I can't discuss it,' Killian repeated. 'It's man's work.'

Erin sighed and relaxed her grip. 'Here's my problem, Jerry. Do I believe your story? Do I get my hopes up for nothing? The whole thing with Angie and Darrell has been a nightmare.'

'I understand,' he said. 'I read through the files at the court-house. That's how I got the judge's name.'

'If I knew more, maybe I could help set this up.'

'It's set up just fine,' said Killian.

He wouldn't budge. Usually a soft hand-holding would do the trick, but not this time. Erin rose and said, 'All right, Jerry. How long will it take?'

'I'm expecting a phone call this afternoon.'

'Congressmen work on Sundays?'

'They do when their careers are at stake.'

Erin stood at the door, searching for a humane way to say what had to be said. 'If this works out, if I get Angela back . . . well, I can't give you anything, Jerry. You should know that.'

'By anything, you mean—'

'You know what I mean,' Erin said. 'I'll be eternally grateful for your kindness. That's the most I can promise.'

'Do I look crushed?'

'Slightly.'

'Well, who wouldn't be?' He chuckled softly. 'I bet you'll quit the club, too.'

'Absolutely. Once I get Angie back, I'm gone.'

'Then there's one thing you can do for me.' He went to the stereo and picked through a stack of CDs. 'Just a second,' he called to Erin. 'Please!'

Soon the apartment filled with heavy rock—'Legs', by ZZ Top. Erin gave Killian a look of mock disapproval.

'Let me guess,' she said.

'Do you mind?'

'Just one dance,' Erin said. Urbana would've wrung her neck.

The first time she went on stage at the club, Erin vomited before and after the performance. Urbana Sprawl took her aside: 'It's like wing-walking, OK? You're fine, long as you don't look down.' Monique Jr hugged her and whispered: 'It's a slumber party, hon. That's how come we're in our nighties.' And Monique Sr said: 'Quit crying, for God's sake. Bobby Knight is at table nine!'

It had taken Erin a week to find a method that worked. Whenever she froze and found herself asking why—why am I doing this!—she thought of Angie. Once on stage, the trick was to dream herself away with the music. That's why she was so picky about the selections: the songs had to mean something. If things felt right, the awful anxiety would melt away and Erin would become wondrously detached from the surroundings. She'd forget she was jumping around in her birthday suit before a roomful of drunks. In Erin's fantasy, the men in the audience were cheering the high kicks and fluid turns, and not the shape of her ass.

Smiling was a struggle at first, because Erin wasn't particularly ecstatic about the work. Moreover, she'd noticed that many of the customers didn't smile, either. Instead they watched with studious and impassive expressions, like judges at a cattle auction. Again, Urbana had offered valuable counsel: 'A nice smile beats forty-inch jugs any day!'

So Erin made herself smile, and the money got better. The men came forward and folded ten-dollar bills into her garters or the elastic of her G-string. Many customers were nervous about standing so close, and plainly terrified of touching a foreign thigh. Erin was constantly reminded of the ridiculous power of sex: routine female nakedness reduced some men to stammering, clammy-fingered fools. For the bolder clientele, Shad's spooky presence discouraged groping and crude solicitation.

Erin had conquered her shyness in about a month. Unlike some of the dancers, she would never be totally comfortable on stage. There was a small thrill to the tease, but no hot rush from the cheers and whistles of strangers. By contrast, the two Moniques loved the boisterous attention, because it made them feel like glamorous stars. The wilder the audience, the wilder their performance. Erin didn't play to the crowd. The music was her master, and also her escape. When Van Morrison sang, Erin *was* dancing in the moonlight.

But that was in the club, not in a customer's apartment.

Still, she wasn't afraid. Mr Peepers obviously was helpless in her presence; he would have inserted his tongue in a light socket if she'd told him to. Erin further neutralized the man by asking about the sepia portrait of a curly-haired woman, gazing up at them from the credenza. It was, as Erin had surmised, Jerry's dear departed mother. Erin felt safer under the late Mrs Killian's watchful eye.

Killian cleared the oval table and helped Erin climb up. She handed him her sandals and her purse. By then Killian had already forgotten about the gun, the congressman, the blackmail, what day it was . . .

The wood was slick and cool under Erin's feet. She danced for four minutes and never even removed her sweater. Killian was dazzled. 'Splendid,' he said over and over, to himself.

As the song ended, he tucked something into the back pocket of Erin's jeans. It wasn't a tip.

At the door she gave him a sisterly peck on the cheek. Killian jumped at the moment of contact. He said, 'If I have good news, you'll see me outside the club.'

'Be careful,' said Erin, although she wasn't seriously concerned. The worst that could happen was that the congressman would tell Killian to blow off.

He waved fondly from the doorstep as Erin walked to her car. She waved back and gave him one of her best smiles. She had decided that he was basically a good person.

When Erin got home, she took the note from her pocket and unfolded it on the kitchen counter. It said:

> *Thank you for saving my soul.*

That night, Erin worked a double shift at the Eager Beaver in the hopes that Jerry Killian would show up. He didn't. The following morning, she phoned his apartment and got no answer. When she tried the TV station, the news director told her that Mr Killian had gone on vacation. He was expected back in two weeks.

At the club, Erin switched back to her familiar dancing routines—Clapton, Credence Clearwater, the Allman Brothers. Soon she got lost in the blues guitar, and the world seemed like a better place, even though it wasn't.

She never saw Jerry Killian again.

9

On the evening of September sixteenth, at a tavern called the Lozeau Lounge in western Montana, the Skyler brothers drank six beers apiece, threw darts at a stuffed elk and argued over the cosmic meaning of a Randy Travis song.

Then they headed for home, which was a valley in the Bitterroot Mountains. Johnny Skyler drove because brother Faron's license had been suspended four times and revoked twice permanently. That was no small achievement in the great and free state of Montana, where driving and drinking are regarded as inalienable rights.

Johnny Skyler followed the dirt road toward the Clark Fork River and the one-lane steel bridge that would carry them to their respective wives and children, waiting in identical double-wide trailers that had been purchased for twenty percent off at a spring trade show in Spokane. The money that the Skyler brothers saved on the mobile homes had been put to good use: a large satellite dish was wired to the earth on a flat clearing between the two doublewides. A parabolic eyesore among the regal vectors of Douglas firs and Ponderosa pines, the TV dish was still the finest investment that Johnny and Faron had ever made: Wrestlemania! Japanese game shows! One night, flipping channels, they'd stumbled onto a guy talking with real Playboy bunnies! The interviewer was so tan that the Skylers speculated he might be an Indian, except he talked too fast and laughed too loud. Around the man's neck hung a gold medallion as thick as a goose turd. Johnny and Faron couldn't get over it.

No doubt about it: satellite TV preserved the Skyler family units. In the long bleak stretch of winter, it was all that kept the men from going mad with boredom. In the summer, it entertained the wives and kids so that Faron and Johnny could stay out extra late: crack open another Rolling Rock, kick back, watch the sun drop down over the mountaintops.

On this night, though, a storm was rolling in hard from Idaho. There would be no sunset, just an ominous and sudden darkening. Bruised clouds stacked up over the Bitterroots, and a cool wind chased down the river. It rattled the tin price sign that hung over the gas pump outside the Lozeau Lounge. Inside, Johnny Skyler reared back and heaved one more dart at the taxidermied elk, yanked his brother off the bar stool and said they'd better get on home, while they could still see the way.

The dirt road fed straight downhill to the old steel span across the river. Fat raindrops began to slap against the Bronco, dimpling the chalky brown dust on the tinted windshield. Mindful of the strong wind, Johnny Skyler took it slowly. First gear. High beams. Both hands on the wheel. Approaching the bridge, he was careful to line up the truck's wheels on the twin wooden planks, already slickened by the drizzle.

Halfway across, Faron Skyler said, 'Hold up.'

His brother braked the truck to a stop, idling.

'Out there,' Faron said.

'On the river?'

'Yeah. I seen a raft.'

'No way,' said Johnny Skyler. He lowered the window. It was too dark to see anything on the Clark Fork.

His brother said, 'Wait for the lightning.'

Up the valley it came, an ultraviolet burst that illuminated the river for a fraction of a second. In that blink of a moment, Johnny Skyler spotted the raft, twenty yards downstream from the bridge.

'There—against the gravel bar,' Faron said.

'Yeah, I saw it.'

'Did you see the guy?'

'No.' Johnny dimmed the headlights and squinted into the thickening night. The rain was coming down pretty good, soaking the sleeve of his left arm. Johnny spit hard, and the wind hurled it back in his face.

Another rip of lightning, high and far away. A purple strobe brightened the valley, then it was dark again. But the scene was stamped in Johnny's eyes: a red raft, oars askew, gliding sideways along a narrow gravel spit that briefly split the river in two. The man in the raft had his back to the bridge. He wore an olive vest and an updowner-style cap, either of which marked him definitively as an out-of-towner. His arms were straight at his sides. A fishing rod lay across his lap.

'Crazy bastard,' said Faron Skyler.

'Think he needs help?'

'Hell, yes, he needs help. He needs his damn head examined. Crazy bastard trout fiend.'

Johnny wasn't sure what to do next, wasn't sure what could be done. As the sizzling electrified maw of the storm boiled down on them, a steel bridge seemed not such a smart place to be. Thunder had begun to shake the struts.

'He better get off the water,' Johnny Skyler remarked, staring at the place where the rafter had last appeared in a blast of light. Johnny briefly considered the logistics of a rescue, then pushed the notion out of his head. Here the banks of the Clark Fork were rocky and steep, and of course the Skyler brothers were full of beer. Disaster was the word that came to Johnny's mind.

He cupped his hands to his mouth and shouted against the wind: 'Hey out there!'

Faron said, 'Forget it, man. He can't hear you.'

Johnny tried again: 'Hey you!'

Another flash, another glimpse of the raft, slipping farther downstream. The fisherman appeared not to have heard the shouts. The rod still lay across the man's lap; the oar handles remained unattended—one pointing upriver and the other pointing the opposite way.

'There's one crazy bastard,' Faron reiterated.

'Somethin' ain't right.'

Lightning exploded nearby, and the brothers covered their heads. They heard the crash of a lodgepole pine, breaking in three pieces.

'Time to go,' Faron said. 'Would you agree?'

Johnny Skyler had a bad feeling in his gut. He gazed down the Clark Fork, waiting for more lightning, for one more look at the lunatic trout fiend.

'He'll be all right, Johnny. The river slicks out for the next mile. A blind dog could make it to shore.'

'I suppose.' Johnny had never seen a raft on this leg of the Clark Fork so late in the evening. The next takeout was twelve miles downriver. And who the hell goes fishing at night in a thunderstorm?

'Would you please fucking step on it?' Faron Skyler was saying. 'I don't feel like gettin' barbecued up here on this damn bridge. Besides, we're missing the ballgame.'

Ever since Denver had gotten a major-league franchise, Faron had become a baseball fanatic. His brother could take it or leave it. Football was something else. With the dish they could even pull in the Argonauts.

'It's nine-thirty,' Johnny Skyler noted. 'Game's almost over.'

'Well, shit.'

'Faron, I can't see him no more.'

'Maybe he turned the big bend.'

'Not without rowing he didn't. Not unless he's got an Evinrude on that raft.'

Faron said, 'All he's got to do is hang on, he'll be OK. Now let's go.'

'Just a minute.' The rain came down in sheets, thrumming on the roof of the Bronco. Johnny finally rolled up the window but he didn't take his eyes off the water.

Sky crackled and the river became a pink mirror. This time the brothers had no difficulty spotting the small red raft, turning in the slow current as it floated downstream.

'Oh my Lord,' Johnny Skyler said.

Faron grabbed the dashboard with both hands. 'Crazy goddamn bastard,' he said.

The raft was empty. The man was gone.

The Skylers hopped from the truck and ran for the river.

*

The rain stopped two hours later. By then the Mineral County Sheriff's Office had arrived with a motorboat and a bona fide scuba diver. The US Forestry Service had promised to send four rangers and a helicopter, providing the weather didn't act up again. A few residents turned out with rafts, rowboats and waterproof flashlights. The small riverside campground at Forest Grove served as headquarters for the search, which by local standards was heroic and exhaustive.

By dawn, the raft had been found, wedged sideways under a piling of the I-90 bridge, due west of Lozeau. The oars had been lost, and the raft contained no clues to the identity of the missing angler. An empty can of Colt 45 and a crumpled Snickers wrapper were the only evidence of a human passenger.

The search for the body lasted eighteen hours, and proved fruitless. A reporter from the *Missoulian* arrived at Forest Grove and interviewed the Skyler brothers, who gave a richly embroidered account of what they'd seen on the river during the thunderstorm. Then they posed for pictures next to the Forestry Service helicopter. For the next several days the brothers faithfully watched C-Span on the satellite dish, but saw no mention of the Clark Fork rescue effort or their role in it. Fame embraced the Skylers in more modest ways; it was years before they had to pay for their own beers at the Lozeau Lounge.

The children of Al García's second wife called him Al, and that was fine. 'Dad' was out of the question. The kids already had a dad, who was in prison because of Al García.

That was how García had met his second wife—while arresting her husband for a drug murder. There were no hard feelings. Six months after the trial, she filed for divorce and married Al.

From hash dealer to homicide detective, García had told her, you're moving up in the world. Not by much, Donna had said. Quick on the draw, that was Donna. The children were all right, too: a boy and a girl, ages eight and nine, or nine and ten— García had trouble remembering. Overall he was very fond of the kids, and didn't feel the least bit guilty about the circumstances.

The first time the boy asked when his real dad was getting out of jail, Al García took the small hand and said: 'Never, Andy.' When the boy asked why, García said: 'Because your daddy shot a man between the eyes.' Andy appreciated the seriousness of the situation. His sister, Lynne, who was either a year older or a year younger said maybe her dad had a good reason for shooting the other guy. A hundred thousand reasons, Al García had said, but none good enough. Just then Donna had come storming in from the kitchen and ordered them all to hush up, or else.

When it came time for their first family vacation, Donna chose western Montana because she and the kids had never seen mountains. It sounded fine to Al García. He made a few calls and found out that Montana, for all its Wild West lore, was a safe and tranquil place; there were traffic intersections in Dade County with higher murder rates.

Donna arranged to rent a small log house on the Clark Fork River, about sixty miles outside of Missoula. García was no outdoorsman, but a cabin on the water seemed like a splendid idea. He promised Andy and Lynne he would help them catch a big rainbow trout and they could fry it up for supper. He promised Donna he wouldn't talk about his job and wouldn't call Miami, not even once, to check on his open cases.

In fourteen years as a homicide detective, Sgt Al García had personally investigated 1,092 murders. It was his curse to remember every one; the oddest details, too. 'Rescue 911' playing on the television while they chalked the body. The counterfeit Rolex worn by the victim. The smell of burned biscuits in the kitchen. A photograph in the hall, the dead man whooping it up at Disney World. Al García hated the unfailing thoroughness of his memory; it made him an excellent detective but a deeply troubled person.

Montana turned out to be better than he had expected; wide-open and friendly, with a few exceptions. A desk clerk at the motel in Missoula shot him a hard look when she saw the name on the credit card. Being a García from Miami wasn't easy these days. Some people automatically assumed you had six kilos in the trunk and a loaded Uzi under the front seat.

The next day, when they got to the log house on the river, Al García nearly forgot where he'd come from and what he did for a living. Standing on the wooden deck, he thought the river valley was the most peaceful place he'd ever seen. He drank the piney air, closed his eyes and easily lost himself in the silence of the surrounding woods. The first day, Andy spotted two deer. The second night, Lynne found a small bleached skull from a dead skunk; she wanted to take it home to Florida, but Donna said no, give it a decent burial in the garden.

On the third day, Andy came running up the bank so fast that García thought a bear was chasing him. The boy was shouting: 'Al, you better come! You better come fast!'

García told him to slow down, take a breather. Andy grabbed his arm and tugged hard. 'Come on. Down to the river.'

'What is it, son?'

'A floater!' Andy exclaimed.

García felt a sour knotting in his gut. Living with a homicide cop had given Donna's youngsters a gruesome vocabulary. They knew all about trunk jobs, John Does, Juan Does, gunshots, accidentals and naturals.

And floaters, of course.

García followed the boy down the hill to the river's edge. The detective waded into the water, skating his tennis shoes across the gravel bottom. The body floated face-up, tangled in a shallow brushpile. The face was violet and bloated, the eyes springing out in a cartoonish way.

'Is he dead, Al?' Andy stood on the bank; he folded his small arms across his chest, looking very serious. 'He's dead, isn't he?'

'Extremely,' García said.

'I told you!'

The dead man wore heavy rubber trousers and an olive vest with many small pockets. García unzipped the one over the left breast, and removed a wallet. The wallet held three one hundred-dollar bills, a half-dozen traveler's checks and a laminated driver's license with familiar colors.

García said, 'Goddammit to hell.'

The boy shouted, 'Who is he, Al?'

'Go tell your mother to call the police.'

The boy ran off. The dead man's face stared up googly-eyed from the hissing river.

'You're a prick,' Al García said to the corpse. 'You're a prick for spoiling my vacation.'

He looked again at the dead man's license and cursed acidly. The sonofabitch was from Fort Lauderdale, Florida.

Why? García wondered. Why won't they let me be?

10

Shad was intrigued by the psychiatrist's eyebrows, lush and multi-hued.

'Those real?' he asked.

'Please,' said the doctor, recoiling. 'No touching.'

It was Shad's first visit to a shrink—Mordecai's man. His name was Vibbs, Palm Beach sharpie and plaintiff's best friend. A laminated diploma from Yale University hung on one wall. Shad was more interested in a jar of hard candy on the doctor's desk. He filled his cheeks and began to chew.

'Tell me about the roach,' Dr Vibbs said.

'Big fucker.' The words crackled out of Shad's mouth.

'Did it upset you?'

Shad's laugh exposed a wet maw of peppermints and butterscotch. 'Upset? Hell, I'm traumatized. Write that down.'

Dr Vibbs was rattled by Shad's hairless, hulking presence. Most of Mordecai's referrals had nothing wrong with them; this one was different. When the hairless man bent to pick up a candy wrapper, the psychiatrist noticed a 'G' carved into his scalp. He assumed that Shad had done it to himself.

Vibbs probed with caution. 'I need to ask some personal questions—it's standard for these evaluations.'

'Evaluate away,' said Shad. 'I told you I was fucking traumatized. What more do you want?'

'Are you having bad dreams?'

'Nope.'

'Not even about the roach? Try to remember.'

'Ah,' Shad said. He was catching on. 'Now that you mention it, I been havin' fearsome nightmares.'

'That's understandable,' said the psychiatrist, scribbling up a storm. 'Tell me about them.'

'I get chased down Sunrise Boulevard by a giant cockroach with yogurt dripping from its eyeball sockets.'

'I see,' the psychiatrist said. He scarcely glanced up from his notes. Shad took this as a signal to try harder.

'Yeah, so this monster roach is chasin' me back and forth, drooling and growling like a thousand tigers. The fucker's as big as a tanker truck. Plus it's got a dead baby in its teeth.'

'I see.'

'And when it gets real close . . . it turns into my mom!'

'Good,' said Dr Vibbs, without emotion. 'So tell me more about your mother.'

'Eh?'

'Please. I'm interested in your relationship with your mother.'

'You are?' An odd light flickered in Shad's eyes. He dragged Dr Vibbs out of the chair and put him face down on the floor. Then he took a handsome pair of wood-handled scissors and sliced the psychiatrist's clothing from neck to buttocks. On the desk Shad found a rotating tray of rubber stamps. He selected a red one that said NO INSURANCE, and stamped it all over Dr Vibbs's naked torso. It was quite some time before Shad ran out of ink. Meanwhile, sad puppy noises rose from the doctor's throat.

'What a phony,' Shad complained. He tossed the stamp on the desk and grabbed a handful of hard candies, for the road.

'You're disturbed!' Vibbs cried.

'I ain't disturbed. The word is fucking traumatized. You should've wrote it down.'

'Go away,' said Vibbs.

Shad stood over him. 'Not until you spell it.'

'What?'

'Come on, wigpicker. *Trau-ma-tized.* I'll even spot you the goddamn T.'

In a shaky but defiant voice, the psychiatrist spelled the word perfectly.

'Proud of you,' Shad said, stepping across him. 'And forget that business about my mom. I don't know what got into me.'

To quell employee unrest at the Eager Beaver, it was Orly's custom to pound on the desk and invoke the Mafia. He would brag of lifelong bonds with Angelo Bruno, Nicky Scarfo, Fat Tony Salerno and other famous gangsters whose names he'd clipped from crime magazines. He would talk of blood oaths, and the certain death awaiting those who violated them. Orly's performance usually had the desired effect of stanching demands for pay raises, health benefits or the slightest improvement in work conditions at the club. In truth, he had no connections whatsoever to organized crime. The mob wasn't interested in the Eager Beaver because strip joints got too much heat from police. Orly heard this first-hand from the only genuine Mafioso he'd ever met, a loan shark on trial for breaking the thumbs of a delinquent Chrysler salesman. Orly had gone to court as personal research, to learn how the mob actually operated. During a recess he approached the loan shark and struck up a friendly conversation. When Orly asked if the loan shark knew anyone in the market for a nude dance club, the man frowned and said no fucking way, there's too much heat. Now video arcades, the mob guy said, that's a whole other deal. A video arcade would be very attractive, investment-wise. Orly was disappointed, but out of politeness he hung around to hear the verdict. Not guilty, it turned out. The jurors (among them, several recent purchasers of Chrysler products) were visibly unmoved by the victim's tale of woe. Orly noticed a few of them smiling as the salesman described his hands being placed in the doorjamb of a steel-blue New Yorker sedan. All that muscle over a six hundred-dollar debt! Orly was impressed. He clung to his dream that someday the Mafia would make him a partner.

For now, though, the illusion would have to suffice. Orly faced a roomful of disgruntled dancers. As usual, Erin spoke for the group.

'Item Number One,' she began. 'The air conditioning.'

Orly scowled. 'So what about it?'

'It's way too cold,' said Erin.

Urbana Sprawl spoke up. 'Thermostat's on sixty-eight degrees. That's awful cool.'

Orly turned to Shad, who stood expressionless in a corner. 'You chilly?'

'No,' said Shad, 'but I don't feel much in the way of hot and cold.'

'Well,' Orly said, 'I'm quite comfy at sixty-eight.'

Because you're a reptile, Erin thought. She said, 'You're wearing a cardigan, Mr Orly. We, on the other hand, are freezing our bare butts.'

Orly rubbed his palms together. 'The cold makes you look sexier. Makes those nipples good and hard. Customers go for that, am I right?'

The room got tense. Erin said to Orly, 'Congratulations. You've hit a new low.'

'Watch it,' he warned. 'You just watch how you talk.'

Monique Jr, normally timid, said: 'I don't believe it—that's why you made it so cold? So we'd get hard?'

'Nipples,' Orly declared, 'are a mighty important part of this enterprise.'

In the corner, Shad muffled a laugh.

Erin said, 'Turn up the thermostat, or we don't dance.'

'I'll pretend I didn't hear that,' said Orly.

Erin picked up a ballpoint pen and wrote on the blotter: 72 DEGREES OR NO DANCING!

Orly said, 'I'll pretend I didn't see that.' He was waiting for Erin to back down. So were the other dancers. Orly adopted a menacing tone: 'Insubordination can be dangerous, young lady. Remember what happened to poor Gonzalo.'

Poor Gonzalo was the Eager Beaver's previous owner, whose bullet-riddled corpse had been dumped on the interstate— punishment, Orly claimed, for filching from the coin boxes on the Foosball machines.

'Bottom line is, Fat Tony likes things to run smooth,' Orly said.

Erin suspected that Fat Tony and the Mafia had nothing to do with Gonzalo's death. More likely, it was a dispute between Gonzalo and one of his many PCP suppliers.

'Tell you what,' said Erin. 'Why don't you ask Fat Tony to stop by the club tonight?'

Orly was dumbstruck. He rocked precariously in his roost.

'I want him to strip down,' Erin said. 'See if he doesn't freeze his saggy old Mafia tits.'

The other dancers murmured in amazement. What had gotten into this girl?

'Well?' Erin said. 'Give the man a call.'

Orly looked whipped. 'You're on very thin ice,' he said weakly.

Erin smiled. 'I bet it's warm and cozy down at the Flesh Farm.'

'Oh Christ,' said Orly. 'Don't even think about it.'

She turned to the other dancers. 'Show of hands?' One by one, the women joined up.

'No!' cried Orly. 'You stay away from those fucking Lings!'

'Then turn up the damn thermostat,' said Urbana Sprawl, freshly emboldened. 'Fat Tony don't want his dancers out sick with a chest cold.'

The two Moniques began to giggle. Shad turned toward the imitation red velvet wall, to hide his grin. He knew there was no Fat Tony and no mob connection. The principal investors in the Eager Beaver were a group of relatively harmless orthopedic surgeons from Lowell, Massachusetts.

A reluctant Orly said he'd raise the temperature in the main lounge to seventy degrees. Erin held out for seventy-one.

'All right,' Orly agreed, 'but I want to see some rockhard cherries. I mean it!'

Erin proceeded with Item Two on the agenda. 'We've been kicking around some ideas for a new name.'

'Forget it,' Orly sniffed. 'I already said no.'

'Something classy.'

'You want classy? Teach these fucking bimbos how to dance. *Then* maybe we'll talk about a classy name. For now, the Eager Beaver is perfect.'

'Candy Rockers,' Erin said. 'Sexy but not crude. What do you think?'

'I think,' Orly said, 'that I give these girls a video from only the hottest joint in Dallas, right? All they gotta do is pop it in the VCR and watch the mother-fucking tape. I mean, a chimpanzee could pick up some a these steps—'

'It takes time,' said Erin.

'Like hell.' Orly pointed at Sabrina, who was absorbed in polishing her toenails. 'You watch that tape?'

Sabrina bowed her head and said no.

'Case closed.' Orly slammed his hand on the arm of the chair. 'Case closed. We'll switch to a classy name when I see some classy dancing.'

Urbana Sprawl waved. 'Mr Orly, I looked at that video. I believe those Dallas girls were high on crack.'

'Oh, is *that* it?' Orly laid on the sarcasm.

'Candy Rockers,' Erin said again. 'Think about it, OK?'

Someone knocked quietly on the door. Orly motioned to Shad, who went to the back of the office and positioned himself strategically at the doorway.

'Who's there?' he asked.

A thick voice on the other side said: 'Police.'

Shad looked to his boss for instructions.

'Shit,' Orly said. 'What now?' His face turned the color of spackle.

Erin wasn't sure what to make of Sgt Al García. She didn't know if he was a good policeman or a lousy policeman, but she knew he'd never make it in the FBI. He was not an assiduous note-taker.

However, other factors worked in his favor. Eleven whole minutes had passed and Al García hadn't yet propositioned her, or even asked if she was married. That set him apart from most cops who dropped by the Eager Beaver.

He sat across from Erin in a back booth. Orly, citing phony flu symptoms, had slithered out the front exit. Shad was at the bar, haggling with a wholesaler over two cases of Haitian rum. On stage, Urbana Sprawl danced to a dirty rap song.

Erin wore a lace teddy, a white G-string and high heels—not

ideal attire for a police interview. García smoked a cigar and paid no attention to the perfumed surroundings. He handed Erin a Xeroxed copy of a Florida driver's license. When she saw the photograph of Jerry Killian, she knew she was looking at a dead man. García had already told her.

'Exactly what happened?' Her mouth had gone dry and her eardrums buzzed faintly.

'Drowned,' the detective said. 'Your picture is hanging in his apartment.'

'Mine and a dozen others.'

'I found a stack of cocktail napkins on the bedstand. Did you know about that? Eager Beaver cocktail napkins.'

With extreme firmness, Erin said: 'I never saw his bedroom.'

'He wrote notes on these damn napkins. Notes to himself, notes to his kids, notes to you.' García paused. 'Is the smoke bothering you?'

'No,' said Erin, 'it's my all-time favorite aroma. That and gum turpentine.'

Without apologizing, the detective extinguished the cigar.

'Tell me what happened,' Erin said. It was still sinking in—Mr Peepers was dead. This was too much. 'I want to know everything,' she said.

'What happened is, your friend floated up deceased in the Clark Fork River and spoiled my trout fishing. You ever been there—the Clark Fork?' García reached in his jacket and took out an envelope of family snapshots. He found one photo showing the river and the mountains and he handed it to Erin. 'Mineral County, Montana. Beautiful country, no?'

Erin agreed. In the foreground of the photograph was an attractive woman and two children. They looked perfectly normal, Al García's family.

'Not many homicides in Mineral County,' the detective was saying. 'The coroner takes one look at Mr Tourist, all dressed up in his L.L. Beans, and says Accidental Drowning. Being the hardass ill-mannered big-city Cuban that I am, I politely request to peek inside Mr Tourist's chest. The coroner, nice guy, says sure. Unzips 'em right on the spot.'

Erin's low-cal lunch did a slow somersault in her stomach. She asked García what was found inside Jerry Killian.

'Not much.' García held his dead cigar poised, like a paintbrush. 'A little water in the lungs. That's to be expected. But when a man drowns in a lake or a river, he also tends to suck up grass, bugs, sand—you'd be surprised. One night we got a floater off Key Biscayne, had a baby queen angelfish in his bronchioles!'

Al García spoke loudly to be heard over the dance music. 'You don't look so hot. Want me to come back some other time?'

'Could you get to the punch line,' Erin said, impatiently. 'In ten minutes it's my set.'

'Sure,' said García. 'Here's the deal. The Clark Fork was full of bugs and leaves—dip a bucket in the river and you'd see what I mean. But the water in Killian's body was amazingly clean.'

'Tap water,' Erin said.

'You're a smart girl.'

'So somebody killed him?'

'Probably in a bathtub,' García said, 'if I had to guess.'

'Can we go outside?' Erin asked.

'Only if you let me smoke.'

Shad followed them to the parking lot. Erin motioned him to go away. Al García acted as if he didn't care one way or the other. He lit his cigar and leaned up against his car, an unmarked blue Caprice.

Erin said, 'You're serious about Jerry being murdered?'

'His ex says he went fishing out West every year. This time was different in one respect: when he got there, he never took out a fishing license. That's damn strange.' García turned away and blew smoke into the darkness. 'Two local boys saw him going downriver on a raft, alone in a rainstorm.'

'Alive?'

'I doubt it. You got any ideas, Mrs Grant?'

Erin said, 'Let me think on it. Things are complicated.' Maternal instinct told her to avoid the subject of Angela, and Jerry Killian's promise. It was possible that García already knew.

'For the record,' he said, 'you didn't kill him, did you?'

Erin laughed in bitter astonishment. 'No, sir. I didn't love him, I didn't sleep with him, and I most definitely didn't kill him.'

'I believe you,' García said. 'But I'm a sucker for high heels.'

He gave her his card. She studied it curiously. 'This says Dade County.'

'Yeah, that's a problem. We're in Broward, aren't we?' García rolled the stogie back and forth in his mouth. 'Montana's a long way off, Mrs Grant. It may take me a while to drum up local interest.'

'But technically it's not your jurisdiction.'

'That's right,' he said, agreeably. 'I'm meddling, pure and simple.'

'Why?' Erin asked.

'Because my boy is the one who found him.' García took out his car keys. 'You got children, you'll understand.'

'Is he all right—your son?'

'Sure. He just wants to know what happened, and I'd prefer to tell him the truth. Anyway, floaters happen to be right up my alley, I'm proud to say.'

Al García's voice trailed off. He looked tired and preoccupied and ten years older than he probably was. Erin fought back an urge to tell him everything.

'I'd like to help,' she said, 'but I doubt if I can. Mr Killian was a customer, that's all. I hardly knew the man.'

García flicked the cigar. It landed with a hiss in a puddle.

After he got in the car, Erin motioned him to roll down the window. She stepped up to the door and said, 'If it's not an official investigation, how'd you get inside his apartment?'

'All I did was ask the super.' García winked. 'A badge is a badge.' He started the car. 'Get back inside,' he told Erin, 'before you catch cold.'

'Will there be a service?' she asked.

'For Killian? Not for a while. The coroner promised he won't sign the papers for a week or so, until I check around.'

'So where's Jerry's body?'

'In a freezer in downtown Missoula,' García said. 'Him and two tons of dead elk.'

Cousin Joyce wasn't the very last person in the world that Mordecai wanted to see, but she was high on the list.

'Disaster,' she said, dropping a stack of color slides on his desk. 'I found these in Paul's underwear drawer.'

'And how is Paul?' asked Mordecai.

'Feeling better,' Joyce said. 'Temporarily.'

'Any luck locating the phantom synagogue?'

'There was no synagogue,' she said. 'Look at the slides, Mordecai.'

They were the photographs taken by Paul Guber's friend at the ill-fated bachelor party. The lawyer went through the slides methodically, holding each one up to a goosenecked lamp.

Joyce sat down and began to sniffle. 'That's the man I wanted to marry.'

As Mordecai peered at the pictures, he longed for a projector and a screen. The women were happy-looking, gorgeous and nude. The lawyer pitied Paul Guber, for there was no mistaking his youthful face, buried serenely in the bare loins of a brunette. The effect was to give him a curly goatee.

'Obviously alcohol was involved,' Mordecai said. 'Too much alcohol.'

'Don't make excuses. I want you to sue the bastard.'

'For what? You're not married yet.'

'Some lawyer,' she said, blowing her nose.

'What's this?' Mordecai was examining the last slide, which differed in content from the others. In it, a paunchy silver-haired man loomed over the still-kneeling Paul Guber. With both hands the stranger was raising a green bottle over his head, as if swinging an ax. His face was twisted with rage. Behind the stranger was the figure of a larger man lunging with outstretched arms, trying to stop the attack.

'Dynamite,' Mordecai said. He took a magnifying glass from the top drawer and hunched over the slide.

'I'm so glad you're amused,' said Joyce. 'My future is in shambles, but thank God you're enjoying yourself.'

'Joyce?'

'What?'

'Shut up, please.'

The sniffling stopped. His cousin's expression turned cold and spiteful.

Mordecai glowed as he looked up from the pictures. 'I *know* these guys!'

'Who? What are you smiling about?'

'Joyce, go home immediately. Take care of your fiancé.'

'I can't. He's playing golf.'

'No!' Mordecai exclaimed. 'He can't possibly be playing golf. He's a very sick man. He's got cluster migraines. Blackouts. Double vision. Go find him, Joyce. Tend to him.'

The lawyer hustled her toward the door. 'I'll be out to see you tomorrow. We've much to talk about.'

Joyce balked. 'And what about me? I'm expected to forget what I saw on those pictures? My fiancé, the man I planned to marry, licking at the belly of some sleazy whore. I'm supposed to put that awful image out of my mind!'

'If you're smart, yes,' the lawyer said, 'because we've still got one hell of a case.'

'Suing a nudie bar?'

'Don't be silly.' Mordecai held his cousin by the shoulders. 'First rule of torts: always go after the deepest pockets—in this case, the fellow who assaulted Paul.'

'So who is he?' Joyce demanded.

'We'll discuss it later.'

'A celebrity?' She was hoping for a movie star. 'Let's see that picture again.'

'Later,' said Mordecai, aiming her toward the door.

'He's got money? You're absolutely sure?'

'Oh, I'm certain he can get it,' the lawyer said. 'I'm as certain as I can be.'

Mordecai thought: Finally it pays to be a Democrat!

11

Midnight found Congressman Dilbeck and Christopher Rojo in high spirits at the Flesh Farm. They were celebrating Dilbeck's good news, as related by Malcolm Moldowsky via Erb Crandall: the blackmail threat was vanquished! The elated congressman sought no details, and none were offered. Moldy was a magician, his tricks meant to be secret and mystical. Dilbeck and Rojo drank a toast to the greasy little ratfucker, then turned their attentions toward the dance stage. Soon the blue haze filled with paper airplanes made from US currency. By closing time, Dilbeck and Rojo were fast friends with two of the Flesh Farm dancers.

Dawn found the foursome eighty miles away, on a levee on the southeastern shore of Lake Okeechobee. Wearing only knee socks and jockey shorts, Chris Rojo was orating the history of sugar cultivation and Congressman Dilbeck's role in it. The dancers complained of being chewed by fire ants, and retreated on four-inch heels to the air-conditioned comfort of the limousine, where Pierre prepared Bloody Marys.

Rojo paced the dike and chattered nonstop, a typically brilliant cocaine monologue. 'Two hundred thousand acres of muck, glorious muck,' he said. 'Sweet sugarcane, far as the eye can see . . .'

Dilbeck's gin-clouded retinas barely saw past the laces of his shoes. The first rays of sunlight warmed his bare shoulders and ignited an itchy prickle of insect tracks. Dilbeck rocked from one leg to the other, as if he'd spent the night on a very small boat. 'I may puke,' he announced to Rojo.

It was the young millionaire's first visit to the fields where his family fortune was sown. He raised lean brown arms to the sky and cried: 'Twenty-three cents a pound!' The bleating caused

Dilbeck to wince. 'Twenty-three cents!' Rojo yowled again. 'Thank you, *Tio Sam*! Thank you, Davey.'

Twenty-three cents per pound was the average wholesale price of the sugar grown by Christopher Rojo's family corporation. The inflated figure was set by the United States Congress and monitored by the Commodity Credit Corporation, an arm of the Department of Agriculture. Rojo had good reason to be thankful: cane sugar from the Caribbean sold for only twelve cents per pound on the world market. Strict import quotas kept most foreign sugar out of America, thus allowing the Rojos to maintain their fixed price and, thus, their grossly excessive lifestyle. Whenever the import quotas came under attack from international trade groups, Congress charged to the rescue. Dilbeck was one of Big Sugar's best friends, and Chris Rojo never missed an opportunity to demonstrate his gratitude. Now, standing on the levee, he locked the congressman in a ferociously sloppy embrace.

Dilbeck felt himself teetering, and pulled free. 'I don't feel so good. Where are the girls?'

'Who knows,' said Rojo. 'Relax, my friend. There will always be girls.'

The congressman squinted into the sun. 'Did we get laid last night?'

'I haven't a clue.'

'Me neither,' Dilbeck said. 'I'm assuming we did.'

'For a thousand dollars, I certainly hope so.'

Dilbeck grimaced at the sum. 'That's what you paid?'

'Five hundred each. So what?' Chris Rojo's voice was dry and high-pitched. 'It's nothing to me,' he said. 'Just money.'

Dilbeck felt his body heat rise with the sun. He touched the back of his neck and found it damp. He wondered what had happened to his shirt. He hoped that one of Mr Ling's dancers had chewed it off in a sexual frenzy.

Rojo said, 'It's a crazy world, Davey. I give some girl five hundred bucks just to go for a ride, OK? The poor fucks who cut this cane'—he waved toward the fields—'that's three weeks' pay.'

'Are you serious?' Dilbeck said.

'This is some country, my friend. Now I must find my pants.'

By the time they returned to the limousine, Christopher Rojo had come down hard from the coke, and David Dilbeck wobbled on the brink of heatstroke. Pierre held the door as the two men tumbled into the backseat. The dancers were asleep, a bright tangle of blonde, lace and Spandex. Dilbeck's shirt and Rojo's trousers lay crumpled on the floor of the car. The congressman dug a handful of ice from the portable refrigerator and packed it to his forehead.

'It's so fucking hot,' he said.

Chris Rojo grunted. 'Florida, man.'

In the driver's seat, mute Pierre turned to receive directions.

'Civilization,' Rojo commanded. 'And step on it.'

Dilbeck watched the flat brown acres fly by at ninety miles an hour, tall stalks of cane stretching to the horizon. He couldn't believe that human beings worked in such suffocating heat from dawn to dusk. He'd heard it was bad but, Christ Almighty, he'd never imagined it like this.

'How much do you pay them?' he asked Rojo.

'The girls? I told you, Davey—five each.'

'No, I mean the migrants.'

'Oh, that.' Rojo was struggling to fit his legs into the wrinkled trousers. 'My father says it's up to thirty dollars a day. All depends if the foreman's in a good mood. But when you subtract room and board, booze and smokes—who knows? And medical care isn't cheap, either.'

'Jesus,' said the congressman.

'Hey, they keep coming back. Compared to Santo Domingo, this is fucking Club Med.'

'How long do they work?'

'Until it's done,' Rojo said. 'My father says a good hand cuts a ton of cane every hour. You believe that? A whole goddamn ton—amazing what a man can do when he's properly motivated.'

David Dilbeck turned from the window and closed his eyes. It made him dizzy and sick, just thinking about it.

*

The judge was startled when Erin sat down at the table.

She said, 'You remember me? The unfit mother.'

The judge stiffly drained his Jack Daniels. 'I was hoping this was a social visit,' he said.

Erin fought to steady herself. She'd had two martinis during her break—a rare indulgence while performing. The problem was Jerry Killian being dead. Even peripheral involvement with a murder could ruin her chance of getting Angie back. In his lovestruck quest to help, Killian might've provoked the wrong people. How far had he taken his screwball scheme? Had he actually tried extortion on a US congressman? Erin needed to know more, before she told Al García about her own supporting role. The judge was her strongest lead, and also the riskiest.

Erin feinted in the obvious direction. 'I'd like you to hear my side of the case.'

'I already have,' the judge said, 'in court.'

A waitress brought a fresh drink, which the judge eyed long-ingly but did not sip. Erin wondered if Shad had defiled it in the usual way.

'Thanks to you,' she said, 'my daughter is in the custody of an incorrigible felon.'

'The record reflected no such thing.'

'The record was sanitized, Your Honor. Darrell Grant is a paid informant for the sheriff's office, and you know it. They purged his rap sheet.'

Fidgeting in a dark booth, the judge wasn't nearly as imposing as he was in the courtroom. Here at the Eager Beaver, he was just another horny old fart with impossible fantasies.

Erin said, 'My ex-husband deals in stolen wheelchairs. He's made an accomplice of our daughter.'

The judge told her that he based his opinion on the known facts of the case; that's the law. 'But it's also true that a decision can be reversed.' He twirled the ice cubes counterclockwise in the bourbon. 'Are you going to dance on my table?'

'I don't do that.'

'The others do.'

'Not I,' said Erin.

'Then perhaps something else?' The judge clutched his glass with both hands, as if it were a sacred chalice. His voice took on a sly tone: 'I mentioned one particular idea to your friend.'

'Which friend was that?'

'Your ' "special" friend.'

Naturally, Erin thought. 'I've got lots of special friends,' she said, 'with lots of special ideas.'

The judge pursed his wormy lips and said: 'You're playing games.' He fumbled under the table as if scratching himself, but brought forth a Bible. 'I come here often to pray for sinners like you.'

'Oh, that's a good one.'

'I keep the Good Book on my lap at all times.'

'I'll bet,' Erin said. 'Levitating?'

'Fighting the devil on his own turf.'

'Whatever,' she said.

'Good versus evil, evil versus good. It's an eternal struggle.' The judge found a dry corner of the cocktail table and placed the Bible there. Then he treated himself to a noisy gulp of bourbon. On stage, the two Moniques danced as gunslingers: fringed boots, stetsons, holsters and a silver star on each bare breast. The judge was briefly transported.

'Time to get ready,' Erin said, slipping out of the booth.

The judge snapped to attention. 'Does this mean the answer is no?'

'What did my special friend say my answer would be?'

'Mr Dilbeck wasn't sure.'

Finally, Erin thought: Jerry's congressman.

'We talked about your custody case,' the judge said. 'I suggested an oral settlement. Didn't he tell you?'

Oral settlement. How incredibly clever! A regular Noel Coward, this one. 'Your Honor,' Erin said, 'I don't know anyone named Dilbeck. And whatever you suggested to him, I promise that my answer would be no.'

The judge seemed more perplexed than humiliated. 'All right,' he said, stirring the ice, 'but perhaps we could pray together some fine Sunday morning.'

The lawyer, grinning like an imbecile, was waiting at the door. 'Come in, come in, come in!'

Shad distrusted joviality. 'I heard you the first time. What's the news from Delicato Dairy?'

Mordecai led him to the conference room. 'Coffee, Mr Shad?'

'Answers, Mr Mordecai.'

From his waistband Shad pulled a Black & Decker cordless drill with a ¼-inch steel bit. Without a word he began to cut numerous holes in Mordecai's favorite Matisse print. 'The new pointillism,' Shad explained to the stupefied lawyer.

Soon the painting fell off the wall, exposing an identical pattern of fresh holes in the plaster. Mordecai's secretary pounded urgently on the door and Shad instructed her to go away. Mordecai dropped to his knees and began begging for mercy. He'd been rehearsing ever since Dr Vibbs had phoned, weepy on Nembutals. His session with Shad had gone quite badly.

'Don't kill me,' Mordecai pleaded. 'I'll do anything.'

Shad tucked the drill under his arm. 'Start at the beginning, fuckhead.'

The lawyer's story came out in whimpers: The yogurt had been stored securely in the office refrigerator. One day Beverly was out sick. The temp helped herself, never asked . . . ate the whole damn thing, roach and all. You believe that dumb twat?

Shad's amphibian eyes closed slowly, and remained that way for a long time. He was thinking that he should have left the warning note on the yogurt carton.

The lawyer's knees ached, but he was too frightened to move. Beverly rapped on the door again, and this time Mordecai was startled to hear his own voice telling her to relax, everything's OK.

Just another narcoleptic sociopath in need of legal advice.

'You all right?' the lawyer asked Shad.

The hairless giant opened his eyes. His face showed nothing. From a breast pocket he scooped a handful of crispy dead insects

—cockroaches, grasshoppers, june bugs, Japanese beetles, even a scorpion—which he organized on the table for Mordecai's inspection.

'This time,' Shad said, 'no fuckups.'

The lawyer rose to his feet. He circled the table slowly, pretending to admire Shad's collection.

'We should discuss this,' Mordecai said.

'Nothing to discuss, partner. Send your girl off to the supermarket. Fruit flavors only.'

'You don't understand—'

'And tell her to check the date on the cartons. I ain't stickin' my pinkies in expired yogurt. No way.' Shad sat back and waited for Mordecai to get rolling.

The lawyer said, 'But this is fraud. I could be disbarred.'

'You could be dis*membered*,' said Shad, 'if you don't move your fat ass.'

Mordecai felt the blood rush from his legs. Soon he lost all feeling below the waist. His throat tightened. 'I . . . have . . . another plan.'

'Sure you do.'

'I . . . d-d-do!'

With a single punch to the shoulder, Shad knocked the lawyer down. Mordecai wailed. Shad told him to shut up, don't be such a pussy. Mordecai wailed louder.

Shad stood over him, taking aim. All he said was: 'Pitiful.' Then he dropped the dead scorpion into Mordecai's open mouth. Instantly the lawyer stopped crying, in order to gag.

'There's more where that came from,' Shad said.

Suddenly Mordecai's secretary came through the door. It was a half-hearted charge. For a weapon Beverly had chosen a cheap gold-plated letter opener, which crumpled like foil against Shad's massive rib cage. He calmly disarmed the woman, and directed her to fetch a glass of water for the boss.

Later, after Mordecai had regurgitated the scorpion and everyone had settled down, Beverly confirmed the lawyer's version of what had happened to Shad's evidentiary cockroach: the temp had scarfed it down.

'Mmmmm,' Shad said, 'I smell malpractice.' He arranged the other dead insects in military formation on the table.

Mordecai said, 'Please. It was an accident.'

'That fucking roach was my retirement. Understand?'

'You want to retire a rich man, Mr Shad, then listen to my offer.' Mordecai signaled for his secretary to leave the room. 'Please pay attention,' he said to Shad.

Shad held a grasshopper and a Japanese beetle delicately in between the thumb and forefinger of each hand. He was making the dead bugs dance a little jig on the table. 'Go ahead,' he told the lawyer. 'I'm perfectly tuned in.'

Mordecai unveiled the color slide from Paul Guber's bachelor party. 'Take a look.'

'What is it?'

'Here. Hold it by the corner.'

Shad put the insects back in formation, and turned his scrutiny to the slide. He held it to the lamp, and squinted with one eye at the stamp-size image.

He said, 'Well, lookie there.'

'Do you know where that photo was taken?'

'Sure. At the club.'

'And who's in the picture?'

'Me and Erin and a couple asshole drunks.'

'Erin would be the stripper?'

Shad's head turned slowly. 'She would be a dancer. The best.'

His voice was murderous. Mordecai thought: Good Christ, now I've insulted the monster's girlfriend. Can anything else possibly go wrong?

The lawyer hesitantly moved on: 'The young man's name is Paul Guber. He's my client.'

'Then God help him.'

'The older man, the one swinging the wine bottle—do you recognize him?'

Shad glanced at the picture again. 'Nope. And it's a champagne bottle. Korbel, I would guess.'

'The man's name is David Dilbeck. Do you follow politics, Mr Shad?'

'Do I *look* like I follow politics?'

'Mr Dilbeck is a United States congressman.'

Shad thought about that as he studied the slide once more. He said, 'Man's put himself in one helluva posture. I'm guessing you're gonna sue his ass.'

'It may come to that,' Mordecai said. 'However, I'm hoping the matter can be settled privately, in a reasonable atmosphere.'

'"However?"' Shad disapproved of snooty verbiage. He pinched one of Mordecai's plump cheeks and said: 'I liked you better with the scorpion in your gullet.'

'Quit!' the lawyer cried out.

Shad released him. 'So how do I fit in? And no more shrinks. I've had it with phonies.'

Mordecai rubbed the sting from his face. 'You saw everything, Mr Shad, the entire assault. When Dilbeck's people learn I've got an eye-witness, they will—pardon the expression—shit a brick.'

'Tell me,' Shad said. 'How much money can a lousy congressman have?'

'Trust me. The lousier they are, the more they have.' Mordecai eased himself out of Shad's lunging range. 'The thing to remember, always, is that we're not after Dilbeck. The serious money is with the men who own his soul.'

Shad was toying with his dead insects again. 'I should try this on a chessboard,' he remarked.

'Please,' said Mordecai. 'Trust me. I know about Dilbeck—both of us were Mondale delegates back in '84.'

Shad said, 'I may just cry.'

'We're talking millions of dollars!'

The man appeared to be serious. Shad postponed his decision to stomp the shit out of him.

'Millions,' Mordecai repeated, huskily. 'The people who own David Dilbeck, the people who'd do *anything* to keep him in office—they're some of the richest bastards in Florida. They've got money to burn.'

'In that case,' Shad said, 'let's burn some.'

12

Orly hired a new dancer whose stage name was Marvela. She was a tall strawberry blonde with a lovely figure, and she knew how to move. On her first night working the birdcage, she doubled Erin in tips.

Later, over a tub of vanilla Häagen-Dazs, Urbana Sprawl told Erin that it was about time she had some competition.

'An off night,' Erin muttered. She had danced poorly, with a smile so forced and insincere that only the drunkest customers wouldn't have noticed. 'My concentration's shot,' she said.

'You wanna talk about it?'

'Mr Peepers is dead.'

Urbana whispered, 'Oh my Lord.'

'Possibly murdered.'

'Sweet Jesus.'

Until now, Erin had told no one the true reason for Sgt Al García's visit to the Eager Beaver. The other dancers had assumed that the topic was Erin's ex-husband, in whom many police agencies had expressed interest.

Urbana Sprawl begged for the details of Jerry Killian's death.

'It's a long story,' Erin said, 'and I think I'm in the middle.' She reached back and locked the dressing room door. 'Apparently somebody drowned the little guy.'

'Because of you?'

'Indirectly.'

'Then you'd better hide, girl. Come stay with me and Roy.' Urbana's boyfriend, Roy, was a mechanic for an outlaw motorcycle gang. He and Urbana specialized in unexpected house guests. Erin said thanks, anyway.

'I was you, I'd be on the first plane out.'

'Not without Angela. And first I need more money.' Her options were limited, and all were expensive.

Urbana suggested table dances and private parties.

'You're the only one who won't.'

'It may come to that.'

'There's other ways, too,' Urbana said, gravely. 'I know you wouldn't, but some girls do. It's all according to what you need, and how bad.'

Erin patted her friend's hand and told her not to worry. 'I'll rob Jiffy Marts before I'll turn tricks. Urbana, would you tell Mr Orly I'm knocking off early tonight?'

Erin was too tired to scrub her makeup or take off the dancing clothes. Over the red teddy and G-string, she put on gray sweats and a baggy T-shirt. She tied her hair in a loose ponytail, folded the tip money in her purse and put her pumps in a Penney's bag. She looked at the hollow-eyed face in the mirror and said, 'What a hot number I am.'

'Anything I can do to help,' Urbana said, 'you name it.'

'Break Marvela's legs?'

'Go home now, honey. Get some sleep.'

'Sleep? What's that?' Erin said goodbye and unlocked the dressing room door. Monique Sr was in the dim hallway, struggling to repair a broken garter.

'Of all nights,' she said. 'John Chancellor's at table eleven.'

'Yeah?' Erin said. 'I'm a Brokaw fan, myself.'

Erin went home and fixed herself a martini. She put Tom Petty full blast on the tape deck and took off her clothes. Lying on the bed, she contemplated familiar gaunt faces on the wall—posters of legendary rock stars, including a few who were still alive. The posters were a gift from one of Erin's ardent customers, a concert promoter. He was so eager to impress her that he once forged Peter Frampton's autograph on a compact disc. It was beyond pathetic.

Erin's apartment was decorated minimally because it was a temporary stop. She refused to invest in anything that wasn't plastic and portable and couldn't be moved in one day by a woman laboring alone. Even the sound system, Erin's only extravagance, broke down into four lightweight boxes.

Nothing connected her soul to the place, not even memories. The three men who'd been in the bedroom were as forgettable as the discount decor. One of them hadn't gotten his pants off before Erin told him to get lost. She'd been watching '60 Minutes', her favorite TV program, when the young visitor remarked that he didn't like the show because 'there was too much talking.' Erin ordered him to button his trousers and hit the bricks. Never again would she date a baseball player—at least, nothing below Triple A.

She bunched a pillow under her head. Acidly she thought: Quite a life I've made for myself!

The telephone looked red-hot on the bedstand; so many possibilities. Call Mom and borrow money for more lawyers? Perhaps when Biscayne Bay freezes over.

Call García and spill everything? Erin doubted the detective would be moved to tears by a recounting of her domestic problems. He would, however, be greatly intrigued by the weird details of Jerry Killian's blackmail plot. A homicide with political connections would be a welcome break from the drudgery of domestics and drug murders.

Maybe that was the phone call to make, Erin thought. Get it over with.

She changed her mind and put the empty martini glass on the floor. Jimi Hendrix loomed over the headboard, tonguing his left-handed Stratocaster. Dead at twenty-seven. Erin thought: Not me, buster.

She took the telephone off the bedstand and balanced it on her tummy. She punched a number in Deerfield Beach and closed her eyes, thinking *please, please, please*.

Angela answered on the third ring.

'Baby?'

'Momma?'

'It's me. Did I wake you?'

'Where are you, Momma?'

'Is your father there? Talk softly if he is.'

'Can you come see us? Every day we go for rides in the hospital.'

'Which hospital, baby?'

'Different ones. Daddy dresses up like Doctor Shaw.'

'Oh God,' Erin said.

'Then he puts me in a wheelchair and pushes real fast. Can you come see us? We go real fast—you can push, too.'

'Angela, listen to me.'

'I think I gotta go. Love you, Momma.'

'Angela—'

Long silence. Somebody breathing. Then a wet cough.

'Angie?'

Darrell Grant laughed, high-pitched and juiced by speed. 'I gotta get this number changed.'

Erin said, 'You are one dumb shit. If you get caught using that little girl—'

'Hell, I won't get caught. It's a dream setup, didn't she tell you? I stole a doctor's jacket, a real stethoscope, the works. Man, I look so legit! Fact, I'm thinking seriously about trying some gynecology on the side—'

'Darrell, they'll take her away! The HRS will take her away from both of us. For ever.'

'Lord, you *do* worry. I already told you, I won't get caught. The setup is, I dress Angie in pajamas so she looks like a real patient. Her Cookie Monster pajamas, remember? The ones with the little feetsies in the bottom—'

'You asshole.'

'Now, don't be judgmental. You, who flashes her tits for a living. Don't fucking judge me, sweetcakes—'

Erin hurled the phone to the floor. She was too mad to cry, too upset to sleep. She pulled on a sweat-shirt and blue jeans, and grabbed car keys off the dresser.

Special Agent Tom Cleary wore a burgundy bathrobe and brown floppy bedroom slippers. To Erin, he looked practically adorable.

She'd never seen him rumpled and ungroomed. Sleep had sculpted his sandy hair into a sharp peak, like the crest of a cardinal.

'Coffee?' he croaked.

They sat in the kitchen and spoke in low tones while Cleary's wife heated a bottle for the baby, who was yowling upstairs. It was the couple's fourth child in six years and the stress of fecundity was taking a toll. When Erin apologized for the lateness of the hour, Mrs Cleary said it was no problem. No problem at all! She was about to explode with artificial politeness. The moment she went upstairs, her husband sagged with relief.

'I need some help,' Erin said, leaning forward.

'Darrell again?'

'Naturally.' She told him about her ex-husband becoming a police informant, about the expensive court fight, about Darrell Grant's wheelchair scam with Angela as a human prop—

'Back up,' the agent interjected. 'He's got custody? That doesn't seem possible.'

Erin's throat felt chalky. 'The judge says I'm an unfit mother. How 'bout them apples?'

Cleary was incredulous. 'Unfit?' The word came out in a horrified whisper, as if he spoke of a dreaded disease. 'What in the world . . . Erin, did something happen?'

She thought: I can't tell him about the job. The Eager Beaver he would never understand.

'It's a long story,' she said.

'Darrell got to the judge?'

'Well, something did.'

The coffee was ready. Cleary poured. Upstairs, the baby finally stopped crying. Erin said, 'Tom, he's turning my daughter into a gypsy.'

The FBI man nodded soberly. 'The problem is, we can't stretch jurisdiction.' She started to say something but Cleary cut her off. 'Let me finish, Erin. Your divorce, that's a civil matter, totally out of our scope. But if you've got proof the judge is corrupt, then maybe we can do business—'

'I don't have proof,' Erin said sharply. 'I thought that was your department.'

Cleary's eyes flashed but he continued: 'The wheelchair racket—now I agree it's despicable. But basically you're talking grand larceny, which the Bureau won't touch.'

'But the locals have Darrell on the damn payroll!'

'Listen,' Cleary said, 'if I tried to run this one past my supervisor—well, there's no chance in hell. He'd throw it right back in my face.'

The agent was rueful but unwavering. Erin felt whipped. 'A phone call from you and the cops would drop him like a rock,' she said. 'One lousy phone call, Tom.'

'I don't work that way. Rules are rules.'

'But you helped me before.'

'I ran a name. That's easy, Erin.' Cleary took off his glasses and kneaded his temples. 'What I cannot do,' he said wearily, 'is open a federal case on your ex-husband. I'm very sorry.'

'Me, too,' Erin mumbled into her coffee cup.

The agent asked if the information about Jerry Killian had been helpful. Oh yes, Erin said, very helpful. She thanked him for the coffee and rose quickly to leave, but not before Cleary asked: 'How does he fit into all this? Killian, I mean.'

'Another long story,' Erin said. Cleary would panic if he knew Jerry Killian was dead. Automatically he would connect the murder to his own leak of the computer check. Next he'd feel compelled to confess the breach of regulations. Several cubic yards of paperwork would accumulate before an actual field investigation of Killian's drowning began. Meanwhile, Tom Cleary most certainly would be transferred to the FBI equivalent of Siberia, where his wife would ponder a future of frigid winters and limited day-care possibilities. Eventually the Bureau might sort out the facts of Killian's death and exonerate the exiled Cleary. By that time, though, Darrell Grant could be safely in Tasmania, or anywhere, with Angela.

Erin had no time to wait for the FBI. And she wanted Agent Tom Cleary in Miami, in case she needed him.

As he walked her to the door, Cleary asked where she was working.

'A dive,' Erin replied, 'tending bar.' Not an unmanageable lie. The same one she told her grandparents.

Cleary said. 'Which dive?'

'You don't know the place, Tom. It's definitely not in your jurisdiction.'

The agent accepted the sarcasm impassively. He said he hated to think of her slinging drinks. Erin said the money wasn't bad.

Cleary, his voice heavy with guilt: 'On this Darrell thing, I wish I could bend the rules, but I can't. I simply can't.'

'I understand, Tom.' Erin checked discreetly for the wife, then pecked him on the cheek. 'Thanks, anyway,' she said.

When she got home, Mexican championship boxing was on ESPN. The face of one fighter was purple and pulped, blood trickling from what appeared to be three nostrils. The other boxer aimed meticulous jabs at the man's fractured nose, until the bleeding got so bad that the referee lost his footing on the slippery canvas.

At one time in her life, Erin couldn't have comprehended how a human being could inflict such misery on an opponent he scarcely knew. Now, thinking of her ex-husband, Erin began to understand the boxer's drive: a simple transfer of aggression, from real life to the ring.

By morning, she had cooled off. She did one hundred sit-ups, reassembled the telephone and tried another phone call. This, too, was a long shot.

Erb Crandall noticed something new in the front hallway of Malcolm J. Moldowsky's penthouse. It was a color portrait of John Mitchell, former attorney general and convicted felon.

'A dear friend and mentor,' Moldy explained. 'Savagely maligned, long before your time. An American tragedy.'

'I know all about him, Malcolm.'

'Political genius,' said Moldowsky. 'Misplaced loyalty was his fatal flaw. He took the fall for Nixon.'

'Who didn't?' Erb Crandall had been in college during the

Watergate hearings. He remembered John Mitchell as a surly old dog who couldn't lie his way out of a paper bag.

'The ultimate insider,' Moldy said, aglow. He stroked the frame of the portrait in a tender manner that worried Crandall.

'Don't you have a hero?' Moldowsky asked.

'Nope.'

'That's very cynical, Erb.'

'People with heroes usually believe in something. How about you?'

Moldy thought about it while he poured two cognacs. He handed one to Crandall and said, 'I believe in influence for the sake of influence.'

'Pushing buttons.'

'It's a kick—wouldn't you agree?'

Crandall said, 'To be honest, some days it sucks.'

'You're still in the trenches, Erb. Be patient.'

'You mean someday I could end up like . . . *him*?' He pointed at John Mitchell's toady visage. 'Gee, Malcolm, I can hardly wait.'

'You are one cynical fuck.'

They sat in Moldowsky's plush living room, which featured a panoramic vista of the Atlantic Ocean. Distant lights of freighters and cruise ships winked at them from the Gulf Stream. Crandall was soothed by the view and warmed by the cognac.

Moldowsky asked for an update on the re-election campaign. He was pleased to hear that David Dilbeck's Republican opponent, a right-wing appliance dealer, had raised only sixty thousand dollars to date. The hapless yutz was spending most of his days fending off the press, and trying to explain two long-ago convictions for mail fraud back in Little Rock, Arkansas. Moldy himself had unearthed the obscure rap sheet, and passed it along to a friendly Miami columnist.

On the home front, Erb Crandall reported that every living Rojo, including scores of far-flung cousins, had dutifully sent cashier's checks for the maximum allowable contribution to the Re-elect Dave Dilbeck Committee. Additional thousands of dollars were pouring in from supposedly ordinary citizens wishing to support the congressman's exemplary work. Cross-checking those contributors' names with voter rolls, or even with the telephone book, would have been useless. The names belonged to Caribbean farm workers, imported by the sugar industry to work the cane fields. It was Moldowsky's inspired idea to use the untraceable migrants as a cover for illegal Rojo donations.

'Davey still doesn't know,' Crandall said.

'Don't tell him,' said Moldy.

'He thinks he's adored by the masses.'

'Encourage that notion, Erb. We like a candidate with confidence.'

'Oh, he's confident,' Crandall said. 'He's so goddamn confident I can't control him.' He handed Moldy the congressman's most recent tab from the Flesh Farm. Mr Ling had boldly tacked on forty bucks for 'replacement of damaged pasties'.

'And where were *you*?' Moldowsky demanded of Crandall.

'He went out the back door, Malcolm. Chris Rojo sent the car.'

'I said, where were you?'

'Asleep in the living room.'

'Nice work.'

'Fuck off,' Crandall said. 'Tonight *you* can tuck him in. That I'd pay to see.'

Moldowsky was disturbed to hear that Dilbeck was up to his old licentious tricks. Obviously the idiot had learned nothing from the Eager Beaver episode.

Erb Crandall said, 'Can we put something in his food? I was thinking saltpeter.'

'Yeah? I was thinking thorazine.' Moldowsky was astounded by the congressman's stupidity. Didn't he realize how close he'd come to disaster? Jerry Killian was gone, but there would be other Killians, other dangerous blackmailers, if Dilbeck didn't steer clear of the tittie bars.

'There's something else,' Crandall said.

Moldowsky loosened his necktie vigorously, as if escaping a noose.

'Let me guess: he's gone and knocked up a cheerleader. Make that an underaged cheerleader. Catholic girls' school?'

'You told me to keep you posted in the weirdo department.'

'So post me, Erb. Before I die of fucking suspense.'

Crandall popped a cough drop into his mouth. 'The congressman got an unusual phone call this morning.'

'Here, or in the Washington office?'

'Washington. One of the secretaries took the message.' As he spoke, Erb Crandall clacked the lozenge from cheek to cheek. He said, 'It was a woman calling.'

'There's a shocker.'

'Said she was a friend of Jerry Killian.'

'You're shitting me.' Moldy's jaw hung. 'Erb, this better be a joke.'

'You see me laughing?'

'What else?' Moldowsky barked. 'What else did she say?'

'That's it, Malcolm. She didn't leave a name or a number. Very polite, according to the secretary. Said she'd call back another time, when the congressman was available.'

Moldowsky ran his fingernails raggedly through his hair—that's how Crandall knew he was upset. Impeccable grooming was one of Moldy's trademarks.

'Did you tell Davey?' he asked.

'Of course not.'

'Which secretary took the call?'

'The older one—Beth Ann. Don't worry, she doesn't know a thing. The name Killian meant zero to her.' Crandall noisily chewed the cough drop and washed it down with cognac. 'Malcolm, it's about time you filled me in.'

'Be glad I haven't.'

'But you said it was taken care of.'

Moldowsky stared out to sea. 'I thought it was.'

At the moment his pager beeped, Sgt Al García was sitting on a meat freezer, chewing gum, filling out paperwork. Inside the freezer were Ira and Stephanie Fishman, ages eighty-one and seventy-seven, folded up like patio furniture. They had passed away within two days of each other in the month of July during the first full year of Gerald Ford's presidency. Daughter Audrey, their only child, had placed the dead Fishmans in a Sears industrial-size deep freeze, which she'd purchased especially for that purpose. Between them, Ira and Stephanie Fishman had been collecting about $1,700 a month in Social Security, disability and veteran's benefits. Being chronically unemployed and without prospects, Audrey felt no urgency to inform the government or anyone else that her parents had died. Friends assumed that the couple had grown tired of the hot weather and moved back to Long Island. No one but Audrey knew that Ira and Stephanie lay perfectly preserved beneath three dozen Swanson frozen dinners, mostly Salisbury steaks. The Social Security checks kept coming, and for all these years Audrey cashed them.

Her secret was safe until this day. She got up early and took the church bus to Seminole bingo, as usual. At about noon, a young outlaw named Johnnie Wilkinson broke a bedroom window and entered the Fishman residence in search of cash, handguns, credit cards and stereo equipment. Curiosity (or perhaps hunger) attracted Johnnie Wilkinson to the big freezer, and his subsequent screams were heard by a passing postal carrier. Audrey returned to find the small house swarming with cops. She was immediately taken into custody, but detectives were unsure what charges should be filed.

Days would pass before the Fishmans defrosted enough for a proper autopsy, although it appeared to García that they'd died of natural causes. Florida had no specific law against freezing one's own dead relatives, but Audrey had committed numerous misdemeanors by failing to report her parents' deaths, and by storing the bodies in a residentially zoned neighborhood. As for her Social Security flimflam, that was a federal crime. Al García had no jurisdiction, or interest. He was rather pleased when his pager went off.

Erin met him at a Denny's on Biscayne Boulevard. They took the farthest booth from the frozen pie display. When García attempted to light a cigar, Erin plucked it from his mouth and doused it in a cup of coffee.

'Unnecessary,' the detective groused.

'Get out your notebook,' she said.

Al García smiled. 'Good old FBI training.'

'You know about that?'

'I'm not as slow as I look.' A waitress appeared, and García ordered a burger and fries. Erin asked for a salad.

She said, 'What else do you know?'

'You went through a blonde phase.'

Erin laughed. 'God. Not my driver's license!'

'You look better as a brunette.' Al García took out the notebook. He clenched the cap of his pen in his teeth, to compensate for the missing cigar. He said, 'All I got really is the basics. Height, weight, marital status. Big fat zilch on the FCIC, which is good. Oh yeah, you're overextended about a hundred bucks on your Visa card. Boy, do I know *that* drill.'

'I'm impressed,' Erin said.

'Don't be.'

'You know about Darrell?'

'He's a hard one to miss. But let's hear about the late Mr Killian.'

The more Erin talked, the better she felt. García acted as if he believed every word, although she wondered if it was part of the routine. The detective was non-threatening to a fault. He made notes in sloppy cop shorthand, careful not to let the transcribing interfere with the eating of his hamburger. Predictably, he perked up when he heard that Killian had boasted of a pipeline to a congressman. 'I got the name from the judge,' Erin said. She watched as the detective printed the word DILBECK in neat block letters in his notebook.

She added: 'Whatever Jerry tried, I'm praying that it isn't what got him killed.'

'Love can be a dangerous item,' García said.

'I didn't stop him because—OK, I figured there was an outside chance to get my daughter back. I know it sounds a little crazy.'

'Not to me,' said García. 'I read the divorce.'

'Wonderful,' Erin said. The file was a trove of slander. Darrell Grant had invented lurid lies about her sexual appetite, and bribed two of his pals to corroborate the fiction. Then there were the cutting words of the judge himself, pontificating on

Erin's unfitness for motherhood. She looked hard at García. 'I wouldn't hurt my daughter for the world.'

'I know you wouldn't.'

Erin went for the salad with a vengeance. It tasted like wet napkins.

'What I meant,' García said, 'is it doesn't sound so crazy, your going along with Mr Killian's scheme. Your ex-husband is a shitbird, if I can be blunt. He's got no business raising the girl. It's Angela, right?'

'What he told the judge, the stuff in the files—'

'Forget about it,' García said.

'It's lies.'

'I said don't worry. How about some Key lime pie?'

Erin had a piece. Al García ate two. Then he unwrapped a fresh cigar, holding it safely out of Erin's reach. 'Please,' he said, 'I beg of you.' She found herself smiling. As García clipped off the butt, Erin picked up his lighter and flicked it open. She reached across the table and lit the cigar.

'They shipped the body back from Montana,' García said, puffing out the words. 'Back to Atlanta, I should say. Killian's ex-wife wants to bury him up there.'

'What about the murder investigation?'

'They don't like that word out in Mineral County. *Murder*, I mean. *Unclassified* was the best they could do. The coroner says he'll reopen the case if I turn up something new. Something besides a few drops of tap water in the lungs.'

'You'll keep at it?'

'In my spare time, sure.' García leaned back in a pose of total relaxation. He asked Erin if anything unusual had happened at the Eager Beaver lately. 'Think hard,' he said.

'Things stay quiet. We've got a pretty large floor manager.'

'No incidents? No bad fights?'

Erin mentioned the lunatic drunk with the champagne bottle. 'He sent a young man to the hospital,' she said. 'I'm sure there's a record.'

'So where was your bigshot ' "floor manager"?'

'He couldn't do much. They had a gun on him.'

'Don't stop now,' García said.

'It wasn't the guy swinging the bottle. It was his bodyguard who had the gun.'

'You get lots of bodyguards in the Eager Beaver?'

'No shots were fired,' Erin said. 'The whole thing was over in five minutes.'

'And you didn't recognize this particular drunk.'

'I had another one attached to my thigh. The guy with the Korbel came out of nowhere.'

García leaned forward. 'Did you see his face? Would you know him if you saw him again?'

'Maybe.' Erin paused. 'Shad got a better look than I did.'

'The bouncer?'

'Don't ever call him that. ' "Floor Manager" is the title.'

García said, 'I need to chat with him.'

Erin was skeptical. 'He's the strong, silent type.' She chose not to burden García with Shad's opinion of cops.

'I'll come by the club some night,' the detective said. 'You make the introductions and we'll play it by ear. All he can do is say no.'

Wrong, thought Erin. That's not all he can do.

García asked if Jerry Killian had been in the audience on the night of the champagne-bottle attack. Erin didn't remember; she said she'd check with the other dancers.

'This is probably a dumb question,' Al García said, 'but it'll save me some time: Was anybody arrested?'

Erin giggled. She couldn't help it.

'I'll take that as a no,' said the detective. He signaled for the check.

Erin said that there was something else he should know. 'Today I called the congressman's office. I told them I was a close friend of Jerry Killian.'

'Cute,' García said. 'I'm guessing he didn't take the call.'

'Right.'

'And I'm praying you didn't leave your name.'

'Right,' Erin said. 'Want me to try again?'

'Please don't.' García slid out of the booth and went to pay the bill. Erin waited by the front door, then followed him out. A light summery rain was falling. The palm trees along the boulevard looked droopy and anemic.

García stood beneath the Denny's awning and jotted on a piece of paper. He gave it to Erin and said, 'My home number. Guard it with your life.'

Erin put the number in her purse. 'Does your wife know what you're working on?'

'Don't worry about it. You call anytime.' He shielded his cigar from the rain and walked Erin to her car.

'Donna'll understand. Trust me.'

Erin said, 'I'll bet she had a Darrell, too.'

'A world-class Darrell. Makes yours look like an altar boy.'

'What happened?'

'First, I put his ass in jail,' García said, 'then I married his wife.'

'Now that's style,' said Erin.

'Yup. That's what Donna says, too.'

13

On the morning of September twenty-fifth, a breezy autumn day, Jerry Killian was laid to rest at Decatur Memorial Gardens, a few miles outside Atlanta. Burial followed a small ceremony attended by Killian's ex-wife, his daughters and nine friends from the television station in Florida. All who came to the funeral were secretly photographed by a man concealed forty-five yards away in a vale of young Georgia pines. The man wore the drab overalls of a gravedigger, but he worked for Malcolm J. Moldowsky. He used a Leica 35 millimeter camera with a long lens and a motordrive, and bracketed the exposures just to be safe. By midafternoon, six strips of black-and-white negatives were sitting on Moldowsky's desk in Miami. Every person in every frame had been identified; none seemingly could have connected the late Mr Killian to Congressman David Lane Dilbeck.

Moldy was convinced that the woman who'd phoned Dilbeck's office was not present at the funeral. Who was she—a mistress? A secret partner in the blackmail scheme? Finding her wouldn't be easy. Had Killian worked any place but a TV station, Moldowsky could've sent a discreet private investigator to chat up his pals and colleagues. In this case it was too risky. Press people tended to be cranky and suspicious, and a visit from a PI would only stir things up. The safest strategy was to wait. Maybe the mystery woman would call again, maybe she wouldn't.

Either way, Malcolm J. Moldowsky couldn't relax. It was like having a cobra loose in the house. Eventually you're bound to step on it. The only question was: when?

Darrell Grant was loading wheelchairs when Merkin and Picatta arrived, unannounced. The Broward robbery detectives got out of the unmarked car and walked slowly around the U-Haul three times. Finally one of them asked Darrell Grant what the fuck he was doing.

'Business,' he said.

'You steal these?' Merkin asked.

'Of course not.' Darrell Grant was twitchy and freckled with sweat.

Picatta said, 'What's the substance of the day, tiger?'

'Folger's,' Darrell Grant said, rolling an Everest-and-Jennings up the ramp. 'You wanna move please so I can finish here? Please?' He was worrying about something Erin had said—about what might happen to Angie if he got popped again.

Picatta and Merkin were exchanging cop-style glances, which increased Darrell Grant's nervousness. He ran a long bungie cord through the spokes of the stolen wheelchairs, and hooked it to a ring on the wall of the U-Haul; that way, they wouldn't roll all over creation every time he took a corner.

Picatta said, 'What about your van?'

'What about it?'

'Why rent the truck, is what I mean.'

'Van's too small,' Darrell Grant said. 'That should be obvious.'

'Yeah,' said Merkin. 'This broken wheelchair business is going gangbusters. Pretty soon you'll be franchising.'

Picatta laughed. Darrell Grant locked up the U-Haul and sat down on the bumper.

'Ain't like stealin' cars,' Picatta said. 'Cars got a VIN number you can check.'

'And registration,' said his partner.

'And a license tag, too,' Picatta said. 'That's the beauty of wheelchairs. They're pretty much untraceable.'

Darrell Grant took out the dagger and began cleaning his fingernails, wiping the blade on his jeans. The cops couldn't believe the balls on this guy.

'You think I stole these?' Darrell said. 'Let me put it another way: Do you want the honest-to-God truth? If I did steal these goddamn chairs, would you guys really want to know?'

'No,' Merkin said. 'We wouldn't.'

'Then stop these bullshit head games, OK?'

Picatta said, 'Funny, we were about to make the same request of you.'

Darrell Grant looked up, feigning innocence.

'You gave us a grand total of three tips this month.' Picatta paused. 'Three red-hot leads. You ready for the box score, tiger? No hits, no runs, nobody left on base.'

Darrell tapped the knife on his kneecap. 'You know how it goes,' he said. 'Win some, lose some.'

'You,' Merkin said, 'are a fucking fountain of wisdom.'

The detectives ran through a list of Darrell's bum tips: An alleged coke peddler turned out to be dealing uncut grams of Tide laundry detergent. An alleged bigtime bank robber turned out to be a teenager who vandalized (but seldom penetrated) suburban ATM machines. And a ring of allegedly sophisticated foreign-car thieves turned out to be a trio of hapless hubcap boosters.

'Bad luck streak,' said Darrell Grant, pondering his sneakers.

Picatta crouched down to eye level. 'Look at me, handsome, I'm speaking to you.'

'I got lousy information, that's all.'

'We stuck our necks out for you, tiger.'

'And I appreciate it—'

'Not once, but twice we stuck our necks out. Where's your little girl?'

Darrell Grant went rigid. The knife fell out of his hand. 'None a your goddamn business,' he said.

Merkin grabbed him roughly by the forelock. 'Blondie, lemme 'splain de facts o' life. Everything you do is our business: What you drive, what you eat, where you sleep, what you steal or don't steal. Whether you wipe your ass with your left hand or your right hand. It's all our business.'

'She's in the day care,' Darrell Grant said. 'She's fine.' He knocked Merkin's hand away and smoothed his hair. When he bent down to pick up the knife. Picatta kicked it away.

'We could always call that judge.'

'Fuck the both of you,' said Darrell Grant.

'Then give us some cases,' Merkin said. '*Good* cases.'

'Which means,' Picatta said, 'you need to be out on the street, with those pretty blue eyes wide open. Lay off the wheelchairs, tiger.'

'And the dope,' Merkin added. 'Think of it like this: What if that judge suddenly hauls you in to drop urine? You want to keep custody of that little girl, you better clean up.'

'Speed freaks make lousy parents,' Picatta said. 'That's a well-known fact.'

Darrell Grant stood up. 'Thank you, Dr Spock.' Sullenly he picked up the dagger and climbed into the cab of the U-Haul. 'I'll be in touch,' he said.

As the truck pulled away, Merkin frowned. 'You hate to see that—so much bitterness in such a young man.'

'What'd you expect from a career asshole.'

'Yeah,' Merkin said, 'but he's *our* asshole.'

Shad was short-tempered and withdrawn. Undoubtedly it was the job—the drunks, the unpredictable girls, Orly, the whole damn shooting match. Now Kevin, the disc jockey, was on a Hammer spree: twenty solid minutes of the most annoying music Shad had ever heard. Finally he couldn't stand it. He vaulted into the booth, knocked Kevin aside and tore the compact disc from the CD player. The Eager Beaver was plunged into silence—the dancers stopped moving, mid-thrust. Customers murmured worriedly. A Peruvian tourist, anticipating a raid, bolted for the door; from his abandoned tabletop came a curse of self-pity from Monique Jr. The fleeing Peruvian had been trimming her garter with twenty-dollar bills.

Shad chewed up the Hammer CD like a big shiny wafer, never feeling the sharp pieces cut his tongue and gums. He spit the whole bloody mess on Kevin's mike stand, and commanded him to play Bob Seger or die. Watching from the rear of the club, Orly silently retreated to his imitation red velvet sanctuary.

Erin waited about an hour for Shad to settle down. When she

approached him he was sitting alone in the corner booth, reading a large-print edition of Kafka's 'The Metamorphosis'.

'Good book?' she asked.

Shad looked up. 'I'm startin' to feel sorry for cockroaches.'

'I've been meaning to ask,' Erin said. 'How's the lawsuit?'

Shad shook his head glumly. 'On to other projects, babe.'

'Like what?'

How Shad had fretted over this moment: Should he include Erin in Mordecai's scheme? She was Shad's friend, or the closest he had to one. Wouldn't she be surprised to learn that the drunken lunatic with the champagne bottle was a congressman! It was almost worth telling her, just to see that beautiful smile.

On the other hand, a potentially mountainous sum of money was at stake. The more participants in Mordecai's shakedown enterprise, the smaller everyone's cut. There were times, Shad reasoned, when financial exigencies overshadowed friendship.

'I'm sworn to secrecy,' he said. 'Nothing personal.'

'Is there a yogurt angle?'

He laughed, loosening up. 'No yogurt, no fucking insects.'

Erin inquired about the scalp wound. Shad lowered his head to show her how Darrell Grant's dagger mark was healing. 'The scar's fading,' he said. 'I'm a little disappointed.'

For the fiftieth time, Erin apologized for what happened.

'Forget it,' Shad said. 'I imagine we'll meet again, me and your ex.'

'Not if I can help it,' said Erin. She had a fleeting image of Darrell Grant being loaded into an ambulance.

The new dancer, Marvela, came out on the main stage. With both hands she seized one of the gold poles, straightened her long legs and leaned back at a languorous slant. She began tossing her head like a mop, around and around in time to the music. The men in the front row crowed enthusiastically.

'What do you think?' Erin asked Shad. 'Is it the boobs or the hair?'

'Hair, definitely.'

'Supposedly she cleared four hundred the other night.'

'Oh yeah?' Shad made a mental note to speak with this upstart Marvela; she'd only tipped him out five bucks. 'You're still the best,' he told Erin.

'I don't know. She can really dance.'

'Not like you.' He went back to his Kafka.

Erin knew she should've been up dancing, making a few bucks, but it felt good to take a break. She was comfortable sitting in the dark booth with Shad.

'I've got a small problem,' she told him.

'What'sa matter?' He glanced up from the book.

'I need you to talk to somebody.'

'Who?'

'He's all right. I think he can help me.'

'I said, who?'

When Erin told him it was a cop, Shad snorted. 'You got more than a small problem.'

'Well, yes. It's a homicide detective.'

'Christ Almighty.'

'It's not as bad as it sounds.' But when Erin related what had happened to Mr Peepers, it sounded bad indeed. Shad didn't understand why anyone would bother to kill the little guy, and he didn't honestly care. He was more worried about Erin.

'Aren't you due for a vacation?' he said. 'I recommend Mars.'

'The detective wants to know about that night a few weeks ago, when the guy pulled a gun on you.'

'I don't remember. Sorry.'

'Come on,' Erin said, pinching his arm. 'It'll help with Angela. Everything's connected.'

'How?' Shad asked. 'Your daughter's involved—how'd you manage that?' He couldn't believe Erin had dug herself into such a mess.

'Shhh,' she said.

Monique Jr approached the booth and said Mr Orly wanted to speak with Shad. She said Kevin was demanding an apology. Shad said he'd be glad to apologize as soon as Kevin displayed a trace of good taste in music. Monique Jr cheerlessly agreed to take that message back to Mr Orly.

After she was gone, Shad turned to Erin and said the floor manager's job was getting to him. 'I definitely need a new career.'

'Me, too,' Erin said. 'A job where I could wear under-pants again.'

Shad put his hands on his head and squeezed lightly, as if testing a cantaloupe for ripeness. He squinted hard, then blinked repeatedly. 'I ain't noticing ordinary things anymore, that's what's got me worried. For instance, it just now hit me that your boobs are hangin' out.'

Erin covered up. 'Jeez, I'm sorry. I was in the middle of a set—'

'Point is, I should've picked up on that. Don't you agree?'

'But you see so much of it—'

'Exactly! Too much of it. I need to get out.' Shad pointed at the book on the cocktail table. 'The guy in this story, he turns into a motherfucking centipede. Wakes up one morning and bingo, he's a bug. Sounds asinine but it sure makes you think. People change overnight, they're not careful.'

Erin said, 'Maybe *you* need the vacation.'

'Yeah, maybe so.' Shad drummed his fists softly on the table. 'OK, I'll talk to your damn detective. But as I mentioned, my memory ain't so hot.'

Erin leaned over and kissed his vast forehead.

Shad said, 'Hey, that's a new G-string.'

'Sure is.'

'Very snazzy.'

'Look here. Velcro instead of snaps.' Erin demonstrated how it worked.

'I'll be damned.' Shad studied the plastic patch thoughtfully. 'Whoever dreamed that up, he probably made a bundle.'

'*She* probably made a bundle.'

Shad shrugged. 'One thing's for sure, we're in the wrong end a this business.'

'Amen,' said Erin.

*

When David Dilbeck heard the latest fund-raising figures, he told Erb Crandall to summon the limousine. It was time to celebrate! Crandall said absolutely not, tonight we stay home.

'Erb,' said the congressman, 'look at the day I had. *Three* goddamn anti-Castro rallies. Fidel is a tyrant. Fidel is a bum. Fidel is a monster—'

'Every politician's got to sing that tune.'

'It's tiresome, Erb. A man needs to unwind.'

'Out of the question, Davey.'

'I've bought a new wig—'

'Forget it.'

'We'll sit way in the back, Erb. No friction dancing, on God's word. Call the Lings and get us a table.'

Crandall offered an alternate plan. The congressman looked intrigued.

'Where's Pamela?' Crandall inquired.

'In Virginia. One of the Kennedys is having a benefit for some disease. I'm not sure which one.'

'Which Kennedy?'

'No, which disease,' Dilbeck said. 'Some kind of anemia.'

'But Pamela definitely won't be home tonight?'

'Not until Sunday.'

'So it's safe to have visitors.'

The congressman beamed. 'The more, the merrier.'

At half-past nine, the dancers from the Flesh Farm arrived. They brought their own music. Erb Crandall directed the two women toward a teak coffee table in the den. Dilbeck appeared in a loose white robe and sat cross-legged on the floor. He asked Crandall to fetch a bottle of Korbel from the refrigerator. The dancers expressed concern about damaging the fine wood, so Dilbeck encouraged them to remove their high heels and go barefoot. Erb Crandall returned with the champagne. He poured three glasses, iced the bottle and left the room. He pulled a chair into the hallway, and positioned himself near the doorway of the den. The music throbbed through the walls, unbearably monotonous. After about an hour, Erb Crandall went to Pamela Dilbeck's medicine cabinet in search of migraine relief. He lucked into a bottle of Darvons, and swallowed two with a glass of bitter orange juice from the kitchen.

When he got back to his post, the dance music seemed louder than ever. Crandall noticed that the door of the den was ajar. Before he could peek inside, one of the dancers emerged from a bathroom across the hall. In one hand she carried a curly black wig, in the other a damp towel. She seemed in a hurry.

'Everything OK?' Crandall asked.

'Peachy,' the dancer said. 'I hope you know CPR.'

In the den, there was no sign of the second dancer. The congressman lay unconscious next to the teak coffee table. His robe was open, exposing pink belly lard and silk paisley boxer shorts. Erb Crandall knelt down and placed a hand on David Dilbeck's chest, which rose and fell rapidly.

'Heart attack,' Crandall speculated.

'Wrong,' said the wigless dancer. She told Crandall what had happened.

He said, 'Jesus Christ. Where'd she hit him?'

'Between the eyes.'

'With what?'

'Right cross.'

'Her fist?' Erb Crandall found this amazing. He carefully examined Dilbeck's pallid face. A nasty blue knot was rising between the congressman's eyebrows. In the center of the bruise was a microscopic indentation, perfectly rectangular.

'She's wearing a ring,' Crandall observed.

'Aquamarine,' the wigless dancer said. 'Her birthstone.'

Erb Crandall placed a pillow under Dilbeck's head, and fashioned the damp towel around his neck. The dancer offered to call 911, but Crandall said no.

'Where's your partner?' he asked.

'Out in the car. She's scared shitless.'

Dilbeck stirred slightly, emitting a gerbil-like squeak. Crandall put his lips near the congressman's ear, and said: 'Davey, wake up!' Dilbeck grew quiet again. Crandall went to the desk and found the number of Dilbeck's private physician. He dialed rigidly, leaving an emergency message with the service.

The wigless dancer said, 'Better get him to a hospital.'

'Sure,' Erb Crandall said, caustically. Show up at Mt Sinai and tomorrow it's all over the papers.

CONGRESSMAN INJURED BY MYSTERY BLOW TO HEAD
Aides Mum Over Late-Night Incident –
Dilbeck Re-election Campaign on Hold.

Crandall gazed at the coldcocked candidate with alternating fury and panic. Whether Dilbeck lived or died, Malcolm Moldowsky would be enraged—and the blame would again fall on Crandall. It wasn't fair. Short of house arrest, it seemed impossible to control Dilbeck's carnal appetites.

'He looks bad,' said the dancer, now dressed in street clothes. 'What if he croaks?'

'Then the country loses another great leader. How much do we owe you?'

'Mr Ling said five each.'

Erb Crandall got two thousand cash from an envelope locked in the usual place, the bottom-right drawer of Dilbeck's desk. Crandall gave the money to the wigless dancer and said: 'You weren't here tonight, you never saw me, you never saw him. Same goes for the other girl, OK? You don't know this man.'

'But I *don't* know this man. I really don't.'

'God bless you,' Erb Crandall said.

'He shouldn't have done what he did. No matter who he is.'

'For that, we're truly sorry. If you count the money, I think you'll see how sorry we are.'

Something moved on the floor: the congressman's right leg, kicking out at unseen demon dogs.

The wigless dancer put the money away, strapped the purse over her shoulder. She said, 'There's no call for what he did. Everything was going fine, a nice little party. I don't know what got into him.'

'Beats me,' Crandall said. Where was the doctor?

'Maybe he should lay off the champagne.'

'Yeah, that's it. The champagne.'

The dancer stepped closer for a final look at the bruise between

Dilbeck's eyebrows. 'Damn,' she said. 'That's a big stone she's wearing.'

'Goodbye,' said Erb Crandall.

'Can we take the limo back to Lauderdale?'

'Sure,' he said. 'Take the limo. Have a ball.'

14

Paul Guber wasn't gushing enthusiasm about Mordecai's plan. 'I want no part of it,' he said.

The lawyer clucked disapprovingly. 'This is a rare opportunity.'

'I heard you before. The answer is no.'

Joyce, sitting with her fiancé, prodded forcefully. 'It's our future we're talking about, Paul. We'll be set for life.'

From the young man's bleak expression, it was plain he didn't wish to be set for a life with Joyce. Mordecai sensed his gossamer skein unraveling and acted swiftly to save it.

'Come,' he said to the troubled couple. 'Let's go for a ride.'

An hour later, they were in a northbound Lincoln on a two-lane truck route known as Bloody 27. Mordecai maintained a steady monologue to mask his nervousness on the highway. Joyce had forgotten what a terrible driver her cousin was; poor vision, sluggish reflexes, and limited range of motion behind the wheel due to excessive girth. Paul Guber was a basket case by the time they reached Clewiston. Mordecai parked the car with a jolt and extricated himself from the front seat.

'Where are we?' Paul asked.

'Sugar mill,' said the lawyer. 'Ever seen one?'

The mill was a sprawling collection of irregular barns, smokestacks and warehouses. Harvest season was weeks away, so the millworks were quiet except for the clatter of pneumatic wrenches; groups of shirtless mechanics worked on tractors, flatbeds and migrant buses. A flaking blue-and-white sign, planted by the road, said ROJO FARMS. In smaller letters:

Division of Sweetheart Sugar Corp.

'Well,' Mordecai said. 'Shall we request a tour?'

'We shall not,' Paul said. Joyce concurred, fearing that offensive agricultural aromas might taint the fabric of her imported blouse.

The lawyer sagged heavily against the fender of the car. 'Fine,' he said. 'As you wish.'

Joyce crossed her arms impatiently. 'It's sticky out here. Can you get to the point?'

Mordecai sighed like a tortoise. 'The purpose of this field trip was to illustrate the financial dimensions of your case. The Rojo family'—nodding toward the sign—'is worth approximately $400 million.'

'Hmmmm,' Joyce said.

'Conservatively.'

'We aren't suing the Rojos,' Paul Guber noted.

'True,' the lawyer said, 'but we're suing their favorite congressman, the fellow who makes all this wealth possible. Are you beginning to understand? Sugar money.'

'Look, I got clobbered in a strip joint. That's all.'

'The short view,' Mordecai scolded.

'I'm damn lucky my boss hasn't found out. If this thing goes to court, I'm out of a job.'

'Paul, you won't need a job,' the lawyer said. 'You'll need a Brink's truck. Tell him, Joyce.'

The sting of the bachelor-party photos had apparently abated, for Joyce wholeheartedly supported her cousin's scheme. 'Mordecai swears it'll never get to trial. Remember, darling, this is an election year.'

'Which means,' the lawyer cut in, 'the settlement will be timely, substantial and extremely secret. The congressman, too, has much to lose.'

'Paul Guber replied with a skeptical grunt.

'We're talking two, three million dollars,' Mordecai said. 'That's a handsome nest egg for two young newly-weds.' He chose not to mention Shad's role in the enterprise, or his percentage.

Paul kicked idly at pebbles while a big jet passed overhead, drowning the conversation. When it was quiet again, he turned to Joyce and Mordecai. 'The answer is still no,' he said.

'Sleep on it,' the lawyer advised. He winked instructively at Joyce. 'You two should discuss it alone.'

Paul said he didn't need to sleep on it, didn't need to discuss it: he flatly refused to sue anybody. 'What happened just happened. There's no permanent damage—heck, my insurance covered the hospital bills.' He broke into a series of jumping jacks, causing Joyce to gasp in concern.

'See?' said Paul breathless. 'I'll be back at the brokerage house next week.'

In exasperation, Mordecai slapped a fleshy hand on the hood of the Lincoln. 'There's a legal term for your condition,' he told Paul. 'It's called '"diminished capacity". Which means the injury to your head is affecting your judgment.'

Joyce nodded. 'He hasn't been sleeping well.'

Paul Guber stopped jumping and let his arms fall slack. 'You two are incredible,' he said, panting. Joyce's glare failed to intimidate him. 'It must run in the family,' he said, 'this conniving.'

'Is that what you call it?' Joyce's voice was taut.

Mordecai moved between them. 'Come now. Let's have a nice peaceful ride home.'

Joyce insisted on driving. Mordecai wedged into the Lincoln beside her. Paul Guber rode in the backseat alone; he fell asleep before they got to the I-595 interchange. His snores brought a mirthless chuckle from Mordecai.

'Young Paul is being foolish,' he said.

'Tell me about it.'

'This is such an opportunity,' the lawyer said. 'Such a rare, rare opportunity.'

Joyce glanced back at her snoozing husband-to-be. It was not a look of pure, unconditional love.

She said, 'I was thinking . . .'

'Go on.'

'Do we need him? I mean, when all is said and done . . .' She pretended to concentrate on the highway. 'Supposing they agree to a settlement right off the bat—then you wouldn't even need to file court papers, is that right?'

'Correct. A few phone calls, a few meetings, a cashier's check made out to a trust account—that's the simplest way, for all concerned.'

Joyce lowered her voice. 'So . . . do we really need him?'

The lawyer fingered the multiple clefts of his chin and pondered the innocent snores of his client. 'That's a good question,' he told his cousin. 'A very good question.'

When Erin arrived at the Eager Beaver, she saw a crew of workmen on the roof, dismantling the fluorescent sign. Orly and Shad stood in the parking lot, deep in discussion. As Erin got out of the car, Orly waved for her to join them.

'Well, you get your wish,' he said.

'You're changing the name?'

'Got to,' Shad said. He seemed to be enjoying himself.

Orly told Erin not to get a swelled head. The decision had nothing to do with the dancers' complaints; it was strictly a legal matter.

'Don't tell me,' said Erin. 'There's another strip joint with the same awful name.'

'Not a strip joint,' Orly said, 'a chainsaw.'

Shad bit his lower lip, trying not to laugh. Erin was on the verge of exploding. With a straight face, she said, 'Mr Orly, I've never heard of Eager Beaver Chainsaws.'

He sneered. 'Me, neither. Apparently they're very big in New England, like I give a shit.'

Shad said, 'They sent a registered letter. Threatened to sue.'

'You believe that?' Orly threw his hands in the air. 'They said I'm hurting their corporate image, on account of using the name to promote sex and nudity. Fucking asshole lawyers!'

A liquor truck pulled in, and Shad excused himself to check the shipment. Up on the roof, the last plastic vestige of BEAVER fell to a workman's wrench. Orly winced at the sight, as he still had three remaining payments on the lettering.

'How,' he mused, 'can you slander a fucking garden tool?'

Erin said she was impressed that the Eager Beaver Chainsaw Company had heard about Orly's club, so far away. Orly said it was reported by a vacationing chainsaw salesman. 'Supposedly he just drove by and noticed the name.'

'Oh sure,' Erin said. 'He just drove by.'

'Anyway, my asshole lawyers talked to their asshole lawyers and the upshot is, it's easier to switch the goddamn sign than go to court.'

Erin couldn't resist a Mafia dig. 'I never imagined the mob would be scared off by a lawsuit.'

'Scared's got nothing to do with it,' Orly grumped. She'd nailed him good this time. 'Little Nicky, guys like him, they don't like publicity. Case like this could wind up on the front page.'

'I hadn't thought of that.'

'So their attitude is screw it, just change the name.'

'The end of an era,' Erin said, with mock wistfulness.

'You know me. I'd love to fight the bastards!'

'But they could drag it out for years,' she said. 'It's best to be practical.'

Orly rubbed his nose fiercely, as if trying to dislodge a bumble-bee. 'Anyone tells you it's a free country, they're full a shit. That's all I can say.' He trudged toward the entrance of the lounge. Erin stayed at his side. She asked him if he'd given any thought to a new name.

'Yeah, as a matter of fact. And I don't want to hear boo about it, OK?'

'Let's have it,' said Erin.

Orly shuffled into the club. Erin wasn't offended that he didn't hold the door. The man was a pig. He couldn't help it. In the office, he went directly to the refrigerator and got a cold Dr Pepper. The thought of offering one to Erin never crossed his mind.

'Tell me the new name,' she said.

'You'll be a big girl? No whining?'

'No whining.'

'All right,' Orly said, slurping his soda. ' "Tickled Pink." How about that?'

'You're joking.'

'I think it's fine.' Orly smacked his lips. 'Feminine. Funny. I like it.'

'It's dreadful,' Erin said. She got up to leave.

'Now don't go making trouble out there—'

'*Tickled Pink?*'

'Hey, this ain't the Christian Science Reading Room, it's a tittie bar. I got a product to sell.'

Erin said, 'You're the boss.'

'Sometimes I think you forget what you do for a living, which is take off your clothes for money. Or maybe it's just you prefer to forget.' Orly rocked back and forth behind the desk. 'It's only a name, honey. Doesn't change the merchandise.'

Erin didn't back down. She wanted to keep Orly on the defensive.

He said: 'Both Moniques love ' "Tickled Pink". They said it sounds like the name of a French boutique.'

'No,' said Erin, 'it sounds like a gynecologist's yacht.'

Orly slammed the soda can on his desk. 'That's all in your head!' he snapped. 'I can't help it you got a filthy mind.'

As Erin walked down the hall, she heard Orly shouting: 'Hell, it's classier than ' "Flesh Farm"! It's classier than those fucking Lings!'

Sgt Al García spent the morning at a rockpit on the outskirts of Hialeah. He was searching for Francisco Goyo's head. Goyo was a gun dealer who'd been kidnapped on Key Biscayne, murdered in Carol City and dismembered in Homestead. Body parts were turning up from one end of Dade County to the other. Al García had put hundreds of bitter miles on the Caprice, collecting Francisco Goyo's hands, feet, torso and limbs. García hated dismemberments because the paperwork multiplied in direct proportion to the number of body parts; it took hours to write up a simple severed thumb. Naturally, the Goyo case had spawned an office pool. To win, one had to match a particular component of Francisco Goyo with the date of discovery. When an anonymous caller reported a possible floating head in Hialeah, a detective named Jimbo Fletcher let out a jubilant roar—if the head was that of the murdered gun dealer, Fletcher stood to make sixty-five bucks. As much as García disliked Fletcher, he found himself hoping that the floating head did belong to the late Señor Goyo. García wanted the case to be over. He had a suspect and a motive; what he needed was a semi-assembled corpse.

While the police divers probed the milky depths of the rockpit, García walked the shoreline. It was so windy that he couldn't light a cigar. Sand from the mountainous limerock dredgings whipped across the wide water, stinging the detective's eyes. Trudging through the chalky dirt, García turned his thoughts to Jerry Killian, and the nearly impossible obstacles to solving that murder. Jurisdiction was a tangle, and it depended on where Killian had died. If he was killed at his apartment, the case belonged to the Fort Lauderdale police. If he was murdered near the river in Montana, the investigation fell to authorities in Mineral County. And if Killian was abducted from Florida to Montana against his will, the FBI should get a piece of the action.

García himself had no jurisdiction whatsoever, no legitimate excuse for pursuing the case except one: nobody else seemed interested. The detective was nagged by an old-fashioned belief that no one should get away with murder so easily. He also wanted to punish the creeps who ruined his family's vacation. The possible involvement of a bigshot politician added urgency to the quest. In fact, García had become so fascinated with the Killian case that he was tempted to take extended sick leave from his Dade County homicide duties. He resented every minute wasted on mundane murder chores, such as bagging fragments of Francisco Goyo. Here was a common shitbird felon with a five-page rap sheet. The world was enriched by his sudden passing. Why, García wondered, am I out here hunting for the man's head? The cosmic purpose eluded him.

At noon, one of the police divers surfaced with a splash. As he paddled to shore, he held an object high out of the water. The object was the shape of a large coconut. Assuming the worst, García retrieved the voluminous Goyo paperwork from the trunk of the Caprice. Returning to the shore, he found the divers gathered around the severed head of a large brindle hog. The hog was wearing a baseball cap: Atlanta Braves.

'Fletcher'll be pissed,' García said.

The divers debated the significance of the find. Animal sacrifice was common among worshipers of Santería, a black magic popular in parts of South Florida. Chickens, goats, turtles and other creatures were slaughtered to appease specific gods; depending on the ceremony, it wasn't unusual to find these grisly offerings in public places. The baseball cap was a riddle, though; none of the cops knew what to make of it. Was the hog beheaded as a curse on the Atlanta Braves, or as a tribute? For guidance the divers turned to Al García. As the senior Cuban, he was presumed most knowledgeable in matters of the occult.

'It's not a religious sacrifice,' García said, winging it. 'It's a family pet.'

'No way,' scoffed the diver who'd found the head.

'Didn't you ever watch '"Green Acres"? They had a helluva pig.'

The diver said, 'Come off it, Al. What kind of people kill their own pet?'

'Hey, *chico*, we're in a recession. All bets are off.' On that somber note, García departed the rockpit. Instead of driving back to the station, he took the turnpike north toward Broward County. On the way, he stopped at a toll plaza, phoned Donna and told her he'd probably be late for dinner.

'What's up?' she asked.

'The usual,' García said. 'Murder. Topless babes. Nude oil wrestling.'

'You poor thing.'

'See you around nine.'

'Good,' Donna said. 'I expect to be regaled.'

Shad was everything that García had expected, and more. The man's musculature was enormous, but typical for his line of work. The detective was more impressed by the cumulative balefulness of Shad's presence—gleaming smooth pate, ferocious overbite, engorged but expressionless eyes. The man's age was impossible to guess. He was not a freak so much as a living dinosaur, slow-blinking and fearless. When he spoke, the voice was low but the tone was hard. When he smiled, which was seldom, he showed no teeth.

Still, Erin Grant seemed to trust him. From this García concluded that, for all his brutishness, Shad was a gentleman toward the dancers. It was a hopeful sign.

They'd found a relatively clean booth near a dance cage. Erin asked Kevin to drop the volume a couple notches so that García wouldn't have to holler over the music. The detective spread several black-and-white photographs on the table. Without prompting, Erin immediately identified the drunk with the champagne bottle.

Except he had a mustache,' she said, pointing.

García looked positively delighted. 'Know who that is? That's our famous Congressman Dilbeck!'

Staring at the picture, Erin thought: Perfect. This is just my luck. 'But he was a maniac,' she said. 'A drunken nut case.'

The detective nodded enthusiastically. 'Is it making sense yet? Your little pal Jerry witnesses the assault, recognizes Dilbeck on stage and immediately grasps the wonderful possibilities. Yet of all the blackmail options available, he chooses the most unselfish of all: arranging for you to get your child back. Or so he thought.'

Erin couldn't take her eyes off Dilbeck's photograph—the starched smile, the smug eyes. He had not looked so dignified while bashing Paul Guber's skull. 'Sonofabitch,' she said.

Al García awaited Shad's confirmation of the lecherous drunk's identity. None came. 'Ring a bell?' he asked.

'Nope,' Shad replied. He would need to consult with Mordecai as soon as possible. Police involvement could screw up the lawyer's plan, and seriously interfere with Shad's retirement.

García selected a picture of Erb Crandall. 'How about him?'

Shad's brow crinkled. 'I'm not sure.'

'I am,' Erin said. 'That's the one who had the gun.'

.'Very possible,' García said. 'Mr Crandall is licensed to carry a concealed weapon. Him and seventy-five thousand other upstanding Floridians.'

Shad asked if Crandall was a professional bodyguard. García said his official title was Executive Assistant to Representative Dilbeck. 'Meaning babysitter,' the detective added, tapping a finger on Crandall's unsmiling face. 'Bagman, too, according to the rumors. But that's of little interest to us.'

García quizzed Erin about the other photographs—assorted aides and cronies of David Dilbeck—but none looked familiar.

'So here's our scenario,' García said, steepling his hands. 'Ms Grant has positively identified Congressman Dilbeck and Mr Crandall as being in the Eager Beaver on the night of September sixth. She's also identified the congressman as the man who jumped on stage and assaulted another customer. The attack ended when Mr Crandall displayed a handgun and escorted Mr Dilbeck out of the club. Is that correct?'

'Right,' Erin said. She shot a suspicious glance at Shad, who shifted uneasily. It bothered him to hold out on Erin. If she and the cop only knew about Mordecai's incriminating photo!

García said, 'It's all right, Mr Shad. If you don't remember, you don't remember. Think on it is all I'm asking.'

'I see assholes every night. They start to look the same.'

'Christ, I know exactly what you mean. Erin, can I have a Diet Coke?'

'She ain't a waitress,' Shad said.

'I'm sorry, you're right. I'll get it myself—'

García started to rise, but Erin motioned him down. 'I've got to dress, anyway. I'll bring three on my way back.'

As Erin headed for the dressing room, Shad began sliding out of the booth. Al García grabbed his elbow and told him to sit tight. He wasn't sure if Shad was stunned or amused by the command.

The detective leaned close. 'Listen, Mr Floor Manager, I don't know your angle, why your memory suddenly is so shitty. That's your business and you sure don't owe me a goddamn thing. But I know you care about that pretty lady, am I right?'

Shad's huge neck throbbed, all veins.

'Here's the deal,' García said. 'She got herself tangled in a blackmail. Not her fault—just some love-crazed customer trying to play hero, trying to get the lady's daughter back from her ex. You're familiar with Mr Darrell Grant, no?'

Shad nodded, barely.

'Ha! Your recall's improving every second.' García let out a grand laugh. 'Anyway, the idea was to put the arm on the congressman, make him pull a string with the divorce judge. The lady gets her little girl, the customer gets to be Sir Galahad. Except somebody whacks him first, which is why I'm sittin' here.'

'You're saying Erin's in trouble.'

'Could be,' the detective said. 'It's an election year, which is no time for a sex scandal. They might figure, hell, who's gonna miss a dead stripper?'

'She ain't a stripper. She dances.'

'Point is, you don't want her to die. Me neither. She's a nice person, works hard, loves her kid, et cetera. So if anything important shakes loose inside that incredible bulbous noggin of yours, gimme a ring.' García stacked the photographs and slipped them into his coat. He said, 'In case you didn't notice, I need all the fuckin' help I can get.'

Shad's expression was stone, but his gut was churning. A keen judge of cops, he knew this one was no bullshitter. Erin might be in real danger, and over what—politics? The woman was a dancer, for God's sake. All she wanted out of life was her daughter.

Insanity is what it was. A world gone mad. Shad felt a strange fever in his breast.

García stood up and laid a five-dollar bill on the table. 'Have my soda,' he said. 'You look thirsty.'

15

Congressman Dilbeck was revived by the sharp tang of Malcolm Moldowsky's cologne. He sat up coughing in spasms. At the foot of the bed stood Moldy and Erb Crandall, appearing dour and unsympathetic.

Moldowsky's greeting confirmed the mood. 'Good morning, shit-for-brains.'

'Hello, Malcolm.'

'Erb told me about your evening.'

'I'm sorry, Malcolm. I got swept away.'

'Know what we need to do? We need to teach you to masturbate creatively. Then maybe you wouldn't bother women.'

Crandall said, 'Those blow-up dolls might do the trick. We'll order him an assortment, all shapes and colors.'

Dilbeck felt dizzy. Slowly he lowered his pounding head to the pillows. He was relieved to see that he was in his own bedroom, not a hospital. From this he concluded, perhaps prematurely, that his injury wasn't so serious. Touching the bruise, he moaned melodramatically; the knot was huge.

He said, 'Don't I need a doctor?'

'Been here and gone,' Crandall reported. 'You're a very lucky man—no concussion, no brain damage.'

'As if we could tell,' Moldy said.

The congressman pleaded for them to lay off, his head was killing him.

'But you've got a fund-raiser tonight, David.'

'No way, Malcolm. Look at me. *Look at me!*'

Moldowsky moved to Dilbeck's side and hovered gravely, like a dentist. 'Under no circumstances will you miss this function, understand? The marquee is Bradley, Kerry and Moynihan, who don't wish to be stood up. More important, we've got six potential sugar votes coming down from the Hill.'

'Those fellows, they're still pissed about the pay raise—'

'Extremely pissed,' said Moldowsky. 'That's why we're flying them first class. That's why we've got Dom and fresh citrus waiting in their suites. It's suck-up time, Davey. Everyone's counting on you to make things right again.'

'What's that supposed to mean?'

'It means the senior Rojos called, among others.'

Overwhelmed by Moldowsky's musk, Dilbeck began to sneeze violently. Moldy backpedaled, shielding his mouth and nose from flying germs. When the congressman regained normal respiration, he announced that he wouldn't be seen in public looking as pitiable as he did.

Erb Crandall said, 'It's not the public, David, it's thousand-dollar-a-plate suckers. Tell them whatever you want. Tell them you got hit with a fucking golf ball.'

'We're locking out the media,' Moldy added. 'Feel free to lie your ass off.'

David Dilbeck grimaced as he fingered the bruise. 'What about X-rays?' he asked. 'How can they be sure about concussions if they didn't take X-rays?'

'The doctor checked your ears,' Crandall explained, 'for fresh blood.'

'Jesus, Mary and Joseph!'

Dilbeck's whining grated on Moldowsky's nerves. 'We'll ice your fucking head, all right? Spend the day on your back, and by tonight the swelling's gone.'

'Exactly,' Crandall said. 'You'll be as dashing as ever.'

'Stop making light of the situation.'

Moldowsky twisted the cap off a pill bottle and tapped out two orange tablets. He instructed Dilbeck to swallow them for his headache: 'Erb told me what happened. In my view, you're lucky that girl didn't stomp on your balls.'

As usual, the congressman remembered almost nothing of the incident. He asked, 'What was her name?'

'Jeanne Kirkpatrick,' said Erb Crandall. 'A very hot number.'

'Seriously, I can't recall a damn thing. Her name. What she looked like. Was she blonde or redheaded, Lord, it's all a blank.'

'Keep it that way,' Moldy said. He closed the drapes to darken the room. 'Get some rest. You've got a big night.'

'Malcolm?'

'What is it, Dave?'

'This is the last time, I swear to God. I'm cured.'

'I'd love to believe you, I dearly would.'

'On my mother's grave, Malcolm. Never again. Never! I hurt so damn bad.'

Moldowsky said goodbye and left the room. His aroma, however, lingered like an industrial smog. Crandall packed a towel with ice cubes and placed it on the congressman's forehead.

'Erb, you believe me?' Dilbeck asked. 'It's out of my system for good.'

'Sure it is,' said Crandall. 'I'll be in the hall if you need me. Try to sleep.'

As David Dilbeck slept, psychedelic visions flashed and popped behind twitching eyelids. Eventually, jumbled starbursts gave way to soothing scenes. The congressman dreamed of a lovely dancer with rich brown hair and small round breasts and a smile that could stop an executioner's heart.

When Dilbeck awoke, the ice in the towel was melted and the pillowcase was soaked against his cheek. His breathing was hot and irregular, but his head no longer throbbed. He bolted upright, energized by the knowledge that the woman dancing in his sleep was real, that he couldn't have dreamed such a smile.

He had seen that dancer somewhere: a radiant moment, buried deep in submemory by a drunken blackout.

Yes, he'd seen her. And she most definitely smiled.

'What did she mean?' In a sing-song tone, the congressman addressed silent walls. 'Who is this lovely?' He shook off the sheets and hopped from the bed. The room rolled under his legs. He stumbled to the bathroom and flipped on the lights. Anxiously he examined both ears for signs of blood, but found nothing but clotted wax.

'Who is she?' he cried to the mirror. 'What does she want with me?'

After less than a week, Marvela quit the club and defected to the Flesh Farm. The enticement was a $500 signing bonus, Mondays off and a new wardrobe. Orly was livid. To all who would listen, he declared that the Ling brothers henceforth were dead men— gator bait, orchid fertilizer, breakfast sausage, D-E-A-D. Orly said he was calling Staten Island and arranging a murder contract. Nobody stole his dancers and got away with it!

The next day, he installed a wind machine among the foot- lights on the main stage. He said it was part of a new campaign to make the Tickled Pink a classier joint—new name, new spiffy image. Erin and the other dancers suspected that Orly was upgrading mainly to compete with the hated Lings.

The wind machine was a hooded electric fan, aimed at an angle to blow and swirl the dancers' hair. The desired effect was an untamed, sultry look. 'I got the idea from Stevie Nicks videos,' Orly told Erin. 'You go on and try.'

She danced a short set in front of the wind machine. The air hitting her face made her blink continually. She didn't feel particularly sexy.

Afterwards, Orly said, 'It's your hair.'

'Oh, here we go.'

'Just listen for once. Would it kill you to grow it down past the shoulders? Or at least get a perm?' He knew better than to suggest a dye job.

Erin said, 'Stevie's got her look, I've got mine.'

'I also bought smoke cannisters and a neon blue strobe.'

'You're really trying,' Erin said, 'and we all appreciate it.' Now if he'd only eighty-six the damn oil wrestling.

Orly opened a box of the new cocktail napkins—pink, nat- urally. 'Notice anything?' he said. 'Lookie. No tits. No snatch.'

The club's previous napkins had featured drawings of saucy nudes in feathered hats and spiked heels. Erin favored the plain pink. 'These are elegant,' she said, 'relatively speaking.'

Orly was pleased. 'It occurred to me, why overdo it with the tits and so forth? No sense staring at poon on a napkin when the real McCoy is wiggling right in front of your nose.'

'Good thinking,' Erin said. Orly was hopeless, but at least he was making an effort. In fact, the long-haired dancers and those with lush wigs did seem to enjoy performing in front of the wind machine. Only Urbana Sprawl declined to use it, complaining that the fan aggravated her allergy to dust mites. She said there was no tactful way for a naked person to cope with a runny nose, especially while dancing. Orly grudgingly agreed.

Discussion of the new wind machine continued all evening in the dressing room. Most of the dancers considered it a worthwhile investment; it was heartening to see Orly spend on capital improvements. Preliminary feedback from customers was positive, too, judging from the tips. For club regulars, windblown hair was an exotic diversion from leaden footwork and half-hearted pelvic thrusts.

'Speaking of customers,' Erin said, 'remember Mr Peepers?'

The two Moniques said they did. Erin asked if they recalled seeing him on the night of the champagne-bottle attack. Monique Jr said yes, she was giving him a private dance at table three when the fighting broke out. She remembered it well because Jerry Killian had scurried to the main stage to see the commotion, leaving her unpaid and dancing on an empty table.

'I was pissed,' Monique Jr said, 'but he came back later and gave me a whole ten dollars.' She rolled her eyes in disdain.

'Did he say anything?' Erin asked.

'He said I had bold nipples, whatever the hell that means.'

'No, did he talk about what he saw—the fight?'

'He asked did I know the guy with the bottle, and I says no. Then he asked do I know what chivalry is, and I said sure I know what chivalry is. ' "Well," he goes, ' "you'll be glad to know it's not dead." And I said great, glad to hear it. Then he started on again about my nipples.'

Urbana Sprawl was impressed by the junior Monique's detailed recollection of a three-week-old conversation; most dancers ignored the idle babble of customers.

'I always remember the shitty tippers,' Monique Jr explained, 'just like I remember the good ones.'

Erin fluffed her hair, touched up her lipstick and headed for a three-dance set in the cage. Kevin cued up one of her favorite Allman Brothers cuts, and Erin blew him a kiss. Long songs were bad for business, but occasionally she needed one to help her disconnect from the routine, drift away with the music.

Tonight she used the time to think about murder. The facts seemed to fit Sgt Al García's scenario: Killian was in the audience when the horny congressman sailed off the deep end. The little guy probably recognized Dilbeck, ratty mustache and all, and hatched the idea for a blackmail.

And days later he was killed . . .

Erin was so absorbed that she didn't spot the customer right away. He stood below the cage, staring at her bottom, waiting for her to spin in his direction. Finally he called Erin's name, and she danced up to the bars. He reached up and folded some money in her garter. It was a fifty-dollar bill. Erin smiled and crossed her arms over her breasts, teasingly lovestruck. Later she sat down at his table to say thanks, a strip-joint ritual when a customer gives an exceptional tip. A three- or four-minute visit was considered sufficient; any longer took precious time off the dancer's clock. Chatty friendliness inevitably gave way to salesmanship, and experienced strippers were masters of the blend. A good table dancer could work the same customer for a half-dozen private numbers between performance sets. That was how most of them made their money; Erin was the only one who got by on stage tips alone.

This big tipper was in his mid-fifties, and dressed like a senior loan officer. He was sipping a Jack Daniels too carefully, and hadn't bothered to loosen his necktie. Obviously he had plans for the evening. When Erin thanked him for the money, he reached for her hand: 'If that's how much I'll pay just to look, imagine how much I'll pay to touch.'

Another smoothie, Erin thought. She tried to pull away, but the man wouldn't let go. She said, 'Obviously this is your first time here.'

'How'd you know?'

'I'm guessing the Midwest—Chicago, Minneapolis?'

'St Paul,' the man said. 'You're pretty good, Honey Pie.'

'Honey Pie? That's the best you can do?' Erin wasn't in the mood for dumb banter. It had been many months since she'd been groped by an out-of-town creep—Sweetie Pants, he'd called her. That one was from Syracuse: the hairiest arms she'd seen outside a zoo.

'Please let go,' she said to St Paul.

'Dance for me.'

'I did.'

'Not here. I've got a room on the beach.' His grip was dry and firm. 'A room with a sauna.'

'No, thank you.'

'For two thousand dollars?'

'I'm not worth it, believe me.' Erin dug her fingernails into the soft underside of the man's wrist. He yelled angrily and let go. As she pushed back from the table, the man's leg shot out and kicked her chair. Erin went over backward.

The customer's laughter died with an epiglottal peep. Erin rose to see the man's face pinched in the crook of Shad's arm. The face was bloody and full of deep remorse. Shad was punching in his usual calm and methodical way, but in his expression Erin saw genuine rage, which was rare.

'That's enough,' she told him.

Shad let the man fall, face down. The customer rolled onto his back and blubbered something about a lawsuit.

'Really?' Shad said. 'You wanna call your wife? I'll bring the phone.' He nudged sharply with a boot. 'Well?'

Ten minutes later, the man from St Paul was strapped in his rented black Thunderbird. He adjusted the rear-view mirror to check the condition of his nose and lips, which were swollen to the size of wax party gags.

Shad propped himself on the door of the car. 'Don't ever come back,' he advised.

'I meant no harm.'

'She look like a hooker?' Shad's barren orb filled the window. 'Answer me, bud. Did the lady look like a whore?'

The man from St Paul was shaking. 'I'm really sorry.'

Shad called Erin to the car and told the man to apologize again, which he did with all his heart.

Erin said, 'You should learn some respect.'

'I'm so sorry. I swear to God.'

Shad said, 'What kinda place you think this is? Does it look like a whorehouse?' The man shook his head tensely.

'This is a classy operation,' Erin chimed in. 'Surely you noticed the napkins.'

The man from St Paul drove swiftly into the Florida night. Erin put an arm around Shad's waist. 'You're in a lousy mood tonight,' she said. 'What's the matter?'

'I'm just worried about you is all.'

'Why?'

'There's bad people in the world, that's why.'

She laughed. 'But you're here to protect me.'

'Right,' Shad said. First thing tomorrow he would go see Mordecai and tell him the deal was off. The stakes had gotten too damn high.

Down the street came the wail of sirens. Soon a police cruiser raced past the Tickled Pink; then an ambulance, two more police cars, another rescue truck. Shad and Erin walked to the curb to see if there was a traffic accident. Moments later they were joined by Orly, bubbling with mirth.

'There *is* a God!' he said.

'Now what?' Erin asked.

'Just listen.'

As if on cue, the sirens began winding down, one at a time. The flashing lights had converged a half-dozen blocks away, on the opposite side of the highway.

'Must be some wreck,' Shad said.

Orly giggled. 'Ain't no wreck. It's the Flesh Farm!'

'What'd you do?' Shad asked. 'Did you pull something?'

'Wasn't me, it was Marvela. She just called, bawling her pretty eyeballs out.' Orly was jubilant. 'She wants her old job back. Haw!'

Shad said, 'Something bad happened.'

Orly grinned. 'Yeah, very bad. Guy dropped dead at the table.'

Erin thought: Poor Marvela.

'And not just any guy,' Orly said. 'A goddamn judge.'

Erin heard herself say: 'Which judge?'

'Who cares? A dead judge is a dead judge. Those fucking Lings, I hope they're pissing razor blades . . .'

Erin started down the road toward the winking blues and reds. Orly called her name but she kept walking. Traffic slowed and a few drivers honked salaciously. Erin clicked along in her tall heels, sequined G-string and black lace bra, aiming for the flashing lights, walking faster, telling herself: maybe, maybe, oh maybe Mr Orly is right.

Maybe there is a God.

The judge considered Marvela a sleek and delicious archangel. She was the only one at Orly's club who flirted properly. The other dancers were detached, perfunctory, even chilly; some refused to perform for him at all. The judge suspected that Erin had poisoned the others against him—they probably despised him for separating their friend from her only child. How unfair! The justification was there in the Bible, plain as day, but none of the dancers wanted to hear him explain it, no matter how heavily he tipped. Everybody had a gift, the judge would say. Everybody had a special purpose on this earth. Motherhood was one, he would say, dancing naked was another.

Being new, Marvela wasn't aware that the judge had been unofficially ostracized. She gave him some terrific table dances, and in a matter of days he was infatuated. When she quit Orly's club, the judge eagerly followed her to the Flesh Farm and the brave new world of friction dancing.

The distance between the clubs was half a mile, but the drive seemed to take for ever. The judge found a parking spot far from the streetlights to avoid being recognized by a passing motorist. Discretion was extremely important until he was confirmed for the federal bench. After that, he was free to recreate as he pleased; to his knowledge, no one had ever been impeached for patronizing a tittie bar.

As the judge turned off the ignition, his heart hammered against birdlike ribs. He felt light-headed, but attributed the feeling to raw excitement. Before entering the steamy house of Ling, he recited a silent prayer, thanking God in advance for the blessings he was about to receive. To be able to lay hands on the beautiful Marvela, to feel her rub those velvet loins against him—these would be fantasies come true!

Sadly for the judge, they did not. Anticipation killed him moments before friction was to begin. He died with his tongue on the table, the Bible balanced on his knees. One hand was fastened to his crotch like the claw of a lobster; it remained attached throughout vigorous rescue maneuvers, including cardiopulmonary massage.

Death had taken the form of a massive cerebral hemorrhage: a significant part of the judge's brain had more or less exploded when the prancing Marvela had draped her *bustier* across the crown of his head. A quick-thinking bouncer had removed the garment before paramedics showed up.

Considering the traffic, their response time was out-standing. The frantic Lings had no opportunity to move the corpse off the premises; all they could do was whimper at the mayhem. Within moments of the first policeman's appearance, the Flesh Farm emptied as if there were a toxic gas leak. The bartenders and dancers were the last to flee.

When Erin arrived, she saw an old man stretched out on the floor. He was surrounded by young medical technicians in blue jumpsuits. One of them knelt beside the lifeless form, thumping the man's chest in perfect time to Janet Jackson's 'Rhythm Nation', which was playing on the club speakers. The Lings stayed well back from the scene, yammering about bad publicity, loss of revenue and a possible visit from state beverage agents.

Erin casually walked up and positioned herself between paramedics. Lifesaving efforts were winding down, along with the music. The man on the floor was plainly deceased. Erin leaned over to examine the face; he looked like the right judge, but she wasn't certain. 'Can you take off the oxygen mask?' she asked.

One of the paramedics, smitten by Erin's attire, cheerfully obliged. He asked if she knew the victim.

'In passing,' she replied.

Marvela, who had changed into street clothes, was being interviewed by two uniformed officers and a detective. She chain-smoked furiously, tapping her ashes into a beer stein. Erin sat at the bar and waited for the cops to finish. Shad came in and joined her. He said, 'You oughta see the helicopter outside.'

'Waste of fuel,' said Erin. 'He's dead as a flounder.'

'It's not from the hospital. It's from Channel 7.'

'No kidding?' Erin laughed darkly. 'Shad, I'm enjoying this. I hate to admit it, but I am.'

'Well, the guy was a prick.'

'And such a hypocrite.'

'Maybe now you can get your girl back.'

Erin said, 'That's what I'm thinking. It's awful, I know, under the circumstances—'

'Forget it. The man was puke.' Shad reached behind the Lings' well-stocked bar and got two glasses. He unhooked the fountain gun and squirted each of them a Coke. Erin watched the paramedics place the dead judge on a stretcher, strapping him under a brown woolen blanket.

'My lawyer,' she said, 'will be amazed.'

'So will your ex.' Shad's lips cracked into a cold smile. 'I'd love to be there when you tell him.'

'I doubt if I'll get that pleasure,' Erin said.

When the police were done with Marvela, she came to the bar and sat with Erin. 'I never even touched him,' she confided, her voice raw with disbelief. The weeping began, and Erin gave her a hug. She didn't know Marvela well, but she could appreciate the trauma of seeing a customer keel over.

Shad hopped the bar and fixed a Dewar's for Marvela, who continued sobbing intermittently. She said she didn't know what happened—she'd barely gotten her top off. 'I can't believe he fucking died. *Died!* I wasn't even down on his lap—'

'That's enough,' Erin told her. 'It wasn't your fault.' She stroked Marvela's hair, which smelled like Marlboros and mousse. Marvela's tears dripped freely on Erin's bare shoulder.

'Look at it another way,' Shad said. 'The man died staring at pussy. There's worse ways to go.'

Marvela was not consoled. She drained her drink and fumbled for another cigarette. 'I should've stuck to straight modeling. Swimwear and teddies, that's it.'

Shad held out a lighter and said, 'For Christ's sake.'

'It's all my fault. He's dead because of me!'

'Hush,' Erin told her. 'You were only doing your job.'

16

Rita and Alberto Alonso agreed to keep Angela while Darrell Grant drove a load of stolen wheelchairs to St Augustine. Alberto was fond of the girl, but Rita preferred the company of canines; Lupa's pups were getting big and frisky. Darrell Grant told his sister to keep Angie inside the trailer, away from the damn wolves. Rita asked where was the kid's toys, and Darrell said there wasn't room in the van for no toys. Alberto said don't worry, there's plenty around here for a girl to play with. He brought out a bag of golf balls and dumped them on the floor. Angela amused herself as best she could.

Alberto slept all day while Rita spent much of the time in the yard with the animals. Angela was fascinated by her aunt's eccentric appearance—catcher's mask, cigarette, logger mitts, baggy housedress. The little girl sat for hours at the window, watching Rita work with her high-strung pets. Once, alone in the trailer, Angela picked up the phone and dialed her mother's number, which she had memorized. There was no answer, but Angela let it ring for twenty-five minutes. Rita came inside and pitched a fit. She snatched the telephone and placed it on top of the refrigerator, out of the little girl's reach.

Darrell Grant was glad to leave town, even for a short time. Free of parental responsibility, he no longer had to be discreet about gobbling speed, upon which he was increasingly reliant. The drugs gave him the nerve to steal, and the guile to lie about it. They also helped him cope with Merkin and Picatta, who hassled him relentlessly. The detectives were vicious nags, always after hot tips. Darrell didn't mind snitching on other criminals, especially since the alternative was prison, but sometimes there simply was nothing to snitch. Merkin and Picatta didn't seem to understand that many crooks were chronically lazy; weeks, even months might pass between crime sprees. Yet the detectives were always demanding fresh stats and warm bodies. If there were no serious felonies afoot, they expected Darrell Grant to hit the streets and get the ball rolling.

The trouble was, Darrell didn't have time to hang out with dirtbags. Dealing wheelchairs was a full-time gig. The St Augustine run, for instance, promised to net three grand—a nursing home was waiting, COD. Then Merkin and Picatta called, harping at him to go see some Cuban bartender in frigging Hallandale who might or might not be dealing kilos. Darrell Grant needed to think fast, and that's where the speed saved his ass. It helped him remember the name of Tommy Tinker, the heroin man. Darrell knew how much the cops in South Florida loved a scag case. Not only was it a refreshing change of pace from crackheads, it was a guaranteed commendation, usually officer-of-the-month. So Darrell pitched Tommy Tinker as the Number One Heroin Dealer east of I-95, and told Merkin and Picatta exactly where on Sunrise Boulevard they could find him.

'Grams or ounces?' Picatta asked.

'Ounces,' Darrell Grant said quickly, 'but he don't sell to white guys. Otherwise I'd be happy to make the score.'

And off went the two detectives in search of a black snitch, while Darrell made tracks for St Augustine. He was passing the Vero Beach city limits when his brain decelerated just enough to remember that Tommy Tinker had been fatally firebombed in New Orleans back in 1987. Darrell Grant experienced a brief flush of panic, but at no time considered turning back or making a call. He popped three more beauties, and stepped on the pedal. Soon the van was racing as fast as his heart, and life seemed fine.

The congressman rallied in time for the gala fund-raiser. He was able to dress without assistance, shave with a dull blade and comb his own hair. Tan makeup camouflaged the bruise, which had shrunken to a greenish marble in the center of his brow.

Erb Crandall drove him to the hotel, and hung near his side throughout the evening. The dinner was well attended and the speeches flattering. The most effusive testimonial came from Senator Moynihan, who'd never met David Dilbeck and was therefore unencumbered by sour memories.

After dessert, Dilbeck himself rose to the podium and managed to speak for eleven minutes without repeating himself. He was careful to lavish absurd praise on colleagues whose votes were crucial to renewing the price supports for domestic sugar. Dilbeck inwardly prayed that his remarks would begin to thaw the ill feelings—after all, how often did such small-timers get compared to the Roosevelts and Kennedys! Erb Crandall said the other congressmen seemed genuinely moved. Dilbeck hoped so, since he'd practically gagged on the compliments he'd dished out.

Later he pinballed from table to table, thanking the paying guests for their generosity. Normally Dilbeck adored being the center of attention, but tonight the limelight was excruciating; the vision in his left eye was blurry, and both ears pounded with an invisible orchestra of steel drums. He sustained himself by silently repeating Erb's mantra: each handshake is worth one thousand dollars.

At a far table, the congressman was greeted by a rotund fellow with flushed cheeks and jumpy rodent eyes. The man was dressed for a funeral. He said he was a lawyer, and introduced a stern female companion as his cousin. Dilbeck noticed a slight family resemblance.

'Remember me?' said the lawyer.

'Well, you certainly look familiar,' Dilbeck lied.

'San Francisco. The Mondale Express.'

'Of course, of course.' Dilbeck didn't have the faintest recollection; he'd spent much of the convention on a barstool at Carol Doda's topless revue. 'I saw Fritz about three weeks ago,' Dilbeck improvised. 'He looks absolutely fantastic.'

The lawyer invited the congressman to sit for a few minutes, but Dilbeck said no thanks, they've got me on a tight schedule. That's when the lawyer handed him the photograph.

'For your album,' he said.

'Jesus, Mary and Joseph!' said the congressman.

Dilbeck cupped his bad eye and gazed at the color print of his drunken self, swinging a bottle at a stranger's head. Dilbeck had no distinct memory of the raunchy scene, except for the woman on the stage. It was the dancer in his dream—by God, she was real! The congressman experienced a tingle that was grossly inappropriate for the moment.

The lawyer said, 'We had the photo enlarged from a slide, which I'm keeping in a very safe place.' He paused, running a finger along his upper lip. 'If I may say so, sir, you look better without the mustache.'

Dilbeck smiled anemically. Erb Crandall, craning over the congressman's shoulder, was comforted not to see his own likeness in the background of the photograph. He wondered, though, if there were other pictures in sequence—pictures of him pointing the gun, for example. Jesus, what a lousy night that was.

'It's peculiar,' Dilbeck said, 'how I don't remember this.'

'But it's you, isn't it?' The lawyer gloated.

Crandall curtly demanded to see identification. Mordecai handed him a business card and said, 'I'm sure you're curious about Joyce's interest. The fellow being assaulted is her betrothed.'

Crandall put his lips to Dilbeck's ear. 'Don't say another word.'

'It's all right, Erb. I honestly don't remember.'

The lawyer went on: 'You're probably wondering about the young man's condition. Unfortunately, the news is not good. He suffered grievous injuries in this attack.'

Dilbeck slumped. 'What can I say? I'm terribly sorry.'

'Shut up,' Crandall hissed.

Joyce spoke up. 'Sorry is fine and dandy, but my Paul will never be the same.'

'Severe head trauma,' the lawyer added. 'That's a champagne bottle you've got there. Korbel, if I'm not mistaken.'

The congressman gave the photograph to Crandall and said, 'You were there, Erb. What the hell happened?'

From the corner of his eye, Crandall spotted a ragged line of well-wishers, including several prominent Rojos, moving across the ballroom toward David Lane Dilbeck. Crandall deftly concealed the dangerous photo in his tuxedo jacket, and told Mordecai to meet him upstairs in the hospitality suite.

The lawyer said, 'Good, we were hoping for some privacy.'

'Fifteen minutes,' Crandall said. Then he rushed off to find Malcolm J. Moldowsky.

Strength fading, David Dilbeck managed to finish his rounds—shaking hands, feigning recognition, chuckling at lame jokes, bowing at banal flattery . . . and thinking only of the sleek dancer whose honor he'd so nobly defended that night at the Eager Beaver. Did she think of him, too?

Joyce paced the lobby while Mordecai met Moldowsky alone, in the hospitality suite. There were no formalities. The lawyer stated his demands; Moldowsky took a few notes. The photograph, creased by Crandall's tuxedo, lay on the coffee table between them.

'Extortion,' Moldy said, thoughtfully.

'In my game, it's called negotiating a settlement. Do you suppose I'm joking about filing a civil action? The picture speaks for itself, Mr Moldowsky.'

'I disapprove of shakedowns.'

Mordecai shrugged. 'Other attorneys would've sued first, then offered to settle. Of course a lawsuit instantly puts the matter in the public eye. Considering Mr Dilbeck's position, I assumed he wished to avoid the publicity.'

'Thanks for being so damn considerate.' Moldowsky got up and fixed himself a drink. His eyes flickered toward the incriminating photo of the Honorable David Lane Dilbeck—homicidal, out-of-control, crazed by lust. It would make quite a splash on the front pages of the newspapers.

The lawyer said, 'I'll understand if you need some time. It must be quite a shock.'

'Not really,' Moldy said. 'The man's name is Paul Jonathan Guber. He spent five days at Broward General with cuts, bruises and a mild concussion. He's doing just fine now, but I guess that's beside the point. Right?' Mordecai was stunned into a momentary silence. After a few seconds, he said, 'Am I to assume that you called the hospital out of concern for my client's health?'

Malcolm Moldowsky tapped his polished fingernails on the side of his glass. 'We look out for the congressman,' he said. Erb Crandall had been keeping tabs on young Mr Guber since the night of the assault.

'I'm impressed,' said Mordecai. 'However, your interest in my client's medical condition could be perceived as an acknowledgment of responsibility. A jury might be curious to know why Mr Dilbeck never voluntarily came forward. So might the State Attorney.'

Moldy was amused. 'Who do you think you're dealing with?'

'That's what I came to find out. I was hoping for a civilized discussion.' Mordecai rose and smoothed the wrinkles from his suit. 'I'll be at the courthouse first thing in the morning. Prepare the congressman for the worst.'

Moldowsky said, 'Sit down, hotshot.'

'No, sir. I've said my piece.'

'Three million is too high.'

'Really?' Now it was Mordecai's turn to be amused. 'Do you know what Sweetheart Sugar grossed last year?'

Moldy made a sucking noise through his front teeth. In slow motion he placed his glass on the table. The lawyer remained smug. He wished that Joyce could see him in action, cutting the nuts off the big boys.

Moldowsky said, 'You know a man named Jerry Killian?'

The lawyer said he'd never heard of him. Moldy could tell he was being truthful. Leave it to Dilbeck to get blackmailed twice for the same fuckup—three times, if you counted the mystery woman who phoned his Washington office.

'I need to know who else is involved.'

Mordecai said, 'My clients are Joyce and Paul.' He didn't mention that Paul Guber, having disassociated himself from the scheme, would never be told about the money. Nor did Mordecai reveal that a modest slice of the settlement would be shared with a violent bouncer named Shad.

'The check,' the lawyer said, 'should be made out to my firm's trust account.'

'A check?' Malcolm Moldowsky laughed harshly.

'Surely you don't intend to pay in cash.'

'No. Wire transfer.'

'From Overseas?'

'Nassau,' Moldy said. 'Possibly the Caymans. Is that a problem?'

'Not as long as it's US dollars.' The lawyer fancied himself the portrait of slick.

Moldowsky said, 'Three million won't fly. Try two-point-five.'

'You're playing games, Mr Moldowsky. We both know the price of sugar, and how it stays so high.'

'Don't push your luck, hotshot. According to my information, Paul Guber is completely recovered.'

'Never know about the human brain,' Mordecai mused. 'One day the man could be fine. The next day it's intensive care.'

'Oh, you're a pistol.'

'The prospect of a trial would be most stressful for the young man and his bride-to-be. I'd recommend some long-term counselling.'

Moldy flicked a hand in the air. 'Cut the bullshit. I'll talk to some people and get back with you.'

'Of course.'

'In the meantime, have a chat with Joyce. Explain the importance of confidentiality.'

'Don't worry,' Mordecai said, 'she's a smart lady.'

And soon to be a rich one.

The Rojos' boat was called the *Sweetheart Deal*. It was ninety feet long, made in the Netherlands. All three staterooms had wet bars and Dolby sound.

The yacht was docked at Turnberry Isle, on the Intra-coastal Waterway. By the time Moldowsky arrived, it was almost two in the morning. The elder Rojos, Joaquin and Willie, offered a cup of Cuban coffee to their guest. Moldy didn't need it; he was wide awake. Two young women were taking a bubble bath in the jacuzzi. Christopher was passed out on the carpet, next to a spotted ocelot in an emerald-studded collar. The wild cat groomed its paws and rumbled.

The Rojos led Moldowsky upstairs to a small sitting room on the captain's deck. Willie asked about David Dilbeck.

'I didn't invite him,' Moldy said, 'for his own protection.'

'Tell us the problem, Malcolm.'

He kept it simple: The congressman had gotten himself into an unsavory situation. A compromising photograph had been taken. Now a lawyer had come forward, demanding three million dollars.

The Rojos were deeply concerned, and conferred quietly in Spanish. Moldowsky noticed that the brothers wore matching robes with the name of the boat stitched over the left breast. One of Joaquin's earlobes was white with dried soap bubbles.

Moldy said, 'The options are limited.'

'Three million dollars,' said Willie, 'is not possible.'

'I'm sure he'll settle for two.'

Joaquin Rojo whispered a curse. The timing of the lawsuit threat couldn't be worse—Dilbeck should hustle the sugar legislation out of committee immediately, so that the full House of Representatives could vote on it before the November election.

Impossible, Moldowsky said. 'Those jerks couldn't pass a kidney stone right now. Everybody's home campaigning.' Besides, he added, the Speaker didn't want the bill on the floor so soon—too controversial. Ralph Nader had gone on 'Nightline', making a stink about subsidies for Big Agriculture. The tobacco and rice lobbies panicked, which caused their stooges in Congress to do the same. A House vote now would be dicey; the smart thing to do was to wait. Which meant the Rojos were forced to rely on David Dilbeck for several more months—and they needed him squeaky clean.

Willie asked, 'How bad is the photograph?'

'Fatal,' said Moldy.

'*Mierda*. Let's pay the goddamn money.'

'No!' Joaquin said. 'I will not be blackmailed.'

'Do we have a choice?' Willie turned to Moldowsky. 'Well, Malcolm?'

Without mentioning Jerry Killian by name, Moldy confided that a similar problem had arisen a few weeks earlier. 'I handled it myself. But this one is more complicated.'

'Because of the photograph?'

'And the fact it's a lawyer.'

Willie Rojo nodded. 'That's what worries me, too. Let's just pay the bastard and forget it.'

His brother rose, shaking a pale fist. 'No, Wilberto. You want to pay, do it with your own children's inheritance. I'm out!'

Spanish erupted again, and this time the brothers' voices escalated in argument. Moldowsky picked up a word here and there. Finally, Joaquin Rojo sat down. 'Malcolm,' he said, 'how much do you know about cane farming?'

Moldowsky shrugged and said he didn't know much.

'We plant in muck,' Joaquin said. 'Mostly sawgrass muck, sometimes custard apple. They call it black gold because it produces such rich sugar. A farmer might get ten good seasons out of a field, then the tonnage starts to drop. Why? Because with each crop, the layer of muck shrinks.' He dramatized with a thumb and fore-finger. 'Eventually the soil isn't deep enough for cane, and the land becomes useless. Underneath is solid limestone.'

Willie said, 'When the muck is gone, Malcolm, it's gone for ever. Our people are telling us five, maybe six more seasons.'

'Then what?'

Joaquin turned up his hands. 'Rock mining. Condominiums. Golf resorts. That's not important right now.'

'Later, yes,' said his brother. 'But for now, our business is sugarcane. We need these last few years to be good ones.'

'A legacy,' Moldowsky agreed.

'Please make Mr Dilbeck's problem go away.'

'I assume you're not paying off the lawyer.'

'My brother and I have decided against it.'

The emerald-collared ocelot trotted up the steps and crouched at Willie Rojo's slippered feet. The old man dug into the folds of his monogrammed robe and produced a gooey chicken drumstick. The brothers watched fondly as the animal devoured the piece, bone and all. The crunching bothered Malcolm J. Moldowsky, who was not much of a cat person.

Joaquin yawned and announced it was time for bed. 'Call us when it's done,' he told Moldowsky.

'This'll still be expensive.'

Willie Rojo giggled as he let the ocelot lick chicken grease off his fingers. 'How expensive?' he asked. 'Not three million dollars, I'm sure.'

'Not even close,' Moldy said; 'but there's a certain risk.'

'Not to us, I hope.'

'No, gentlemen. Not to you.'

Darrell Grant sold the wheelchairs for $3,200 cash and drove straight from St Augustine to Daytona Beach. There he purchased an assortment of colorful pills, and picked up two prostitutes on the boardwalk. Later, when they thought he was asleep, the hookers let their pimp enter Darrell's motel room and pick through his belongings. Darrell waited a suitable interval, then slipped his hand under the pillow where he kept the dagger. With a ghoulish screech, he sprung from the bed and stabbed the pimp in the fleshy part of a thigh. While the man wriggled on the floor, the hookers straddled him and frantically tried to stanch the bleeding. Darrell Grant calmly yanked the sheet from the bed and sliced it into long strips. Then he tied up the thrashing pimp and the two hookers, and stuffed dirty socks in their mouths. The women didn't struggle, as they had gotten a close-up glimpse of Darrell Grant's microdot pupils.

As he worked on the pimp, Darrell hummed a tune from *The Jungle Book*, which Angela had on video cassette. Gaily, he lathered the man's curly black hair and shaved him bald. Then he took the dagger and cut a perfect capital G on the scalp. The pimp moaned and grunted into the filthy gag. Blood trickled in twin rivulets down both sides of his head. The women watched silently, fearing they were next.

Darrell Grant said: 'Now I'm going to teach you people a lesson.'

He got his keys and ran to the van. Two minutes later he returned, carrying an electric staple gun that he'd stolen from a construction site in Boca Raton. At the sight of the stapler, one of the hookers began to sob. Darrell Grant walked over to the pimp and untied one of his arms.

Still panting, he said, 'Were you going to rob me?'

The pimp shook his head violently.

'Liar, liar, pants on fire,' Darrell sang.

He plugged the staple gun into a wall outlet, and said, 'Next time you want money, ask polite.' He grabbed the pimp's hand and stapled a one-dollar bill to the palm. He held the trigger down a long time—ping ping ping—until the staple gun was empty. The pimp's eyelids fluttered and he lolled unconscious. The women shivered with fright.

Suddenly Darrell Grant felt spent. He stretched on the bed and dialed Rita's house. She growled at him for phoning so late, three-goddamn-thirty in the morning. Her brother apologized and said, 'Listen, I might take a few extra days up here. That OK?'

'Suit yourself. Erin's coming tomorrow.'

'What?'

'Visitation day,' Rita said.

'No!'

'That's what she told us.'

'Jesus, Rita, did you tell her Angie was there? How the hell did she know?'

'I can't help it your daughter knows how to use the phone. And she climbs, too, like a little monkey.'

'Angie called her?' Darrell Grant pounded a fist on the bare mattress. 'Goddamn, I can't believe you let this happen.' He was too overmedicated to concentrate on two crisis situations simultaneously. He didn't notice that one of the tied-up hookers had managed to twist an arm free, and was working covertly on the other knots.

Darrell choked the telephone receiver and cried: 'Don't let that cunt in the house, you understand?'

'It's visitation day!' Rita repeated.

'It ain't fucking visitation day!'

'Then *you* come back and deal with it. I got wolves to train.'

'Lord Christ.'

'Another thing, it was on the news—what's the judge that got your divorce?'

Darrell Grant told her the name.

'Yep, Alberto said it was him. He's dead, Darrell.'

'Now hold up—'

'It was on the TV,' Rita said. 'He died last night at a nudie joint.'

Darrell Grant rested his cheek on the foul-smelling mattress. It was definitely time for more pills.

On the other end of the line, Rita was telling the story. 'His family said he went there to preach gospel at the naked girls. You believe that shit? They found a Bible on his lap—it was all on the television.'

'I'll be home by morning,' Darrell Grant said thickly.

'What about Erin?' Rita asked. There was no answer from Daytona Beach. 'Darrell? Whoa hey, little brother, wake up!'

But he was out cold, sapped on the skull by a hooker swinging a staple gun. They made off with the cash, the drugs, the dagger, and of course the van. They did not take Darrell Grant's dirty socks, which were the first things he tasted when he regained consciousness four hours later.

17

On the morning of September twenty-eighth, Sgt Al García drove through a light drizzle to the Flightpath Motel, two hundred yards due west of the main commercial runway of Fort Lauderdale–Hollywood International Airport. The motel manager, an amiable Greek named Miklos, led the detective to Room 233. As Miklos fit the key in the door, García said, 'I bet the carpet is brown.'

'How you know that?'

'It came to me in a dream,' García said. Miklos opened the door and pointed gleefully at the carpet, which was a cocoa-brown shag.

The detective said, 'Sometimes I scare myself.' The Mineral County coroner had found three brown carpet fibers under Jerry Killian's left thumbnail.

'What else you dream?' Miklos asked.

'A man named Killian was murdered in this room.'

'Oh no,' Miklos said. 'Don't tell me.' He said the maid found Killian's checkbook beneath the bed.

'He probably threw it there on purpose,' García said, 'so the bad guys wouldn't get it.' People did weird things on the verge of dying.

Miklos said, 'I send it back right away, next day.'

'You did the right thing.'

'Who called the police?'

'Nobody,' Al García said. 'I opened Mr Killian's mail. There was the checkbook, and your note.'

Miklos frowned. 'Is that OK? To open his letters?'

'Oh sure. I'm an officer of the law.' García got on his knees and crawled under the bed. His fingers probed the ratty shag in search of other clues. All he found was a petrified pizza crust and a nickel. García got up and brushed the fuzz off his trousers.

Miklos said, 'Since I work here, seven people die. It is very sad. Seven in seven months.'

'Guests?'

'Yes, sir. Drugs, guns, stabs, problems with the heart. The police come many times. Always we are replacing carpets and sheets.'

'Maybe it's the location,' García said, his voice rising over the roar of an incoming jet. The place was ideal for customers wishing not to be overheard. He took out a photograph of Jerry Killian.

'I never see him before,' Miklos said. 'You say this man was a murder?'

'Yeah. In the tub is my guess.'

'The bathrooms we clean three times a week.'

'Wow,' García said. 'Your Lysol bill must be outta sight. Can I have a look?'

Miklos sat on the bed and waited. He heard the detective fiddling with the faucets in the bathtub. 'Mr Miklos, what happened to the hot-water knob?'

'Somebody broke.'

'How?'

'I dunno. Maybe two weeks ago.'

The detective came out, drying his hands on a towel. Another jet howled overhead. García said, 'Looks like somebody kicked that fixture right off the wall.' The drowning Jerry Killian had put up a pretty good fight.

Miklos said, 'You say murder but the maid didn't find no dead body.'

'That's because the killer drove the dead body to Montana and dumped it in a river.'

'Why?'

'To mess up my vacation,' Al García said. 'Can I see the guest register?'

Miklos took him back to the office, which wasn't much larger than the bathroom. Killian's name did not appear on the check-in sheets; García would've been shocked if it had. He made notes on everyone who'd rented Room 233 during the previous two weeks. One name showed up five times.

'He's a local,' Miklos said.

'Local what?'

'Businessman. He entertains.'

'Oh,' said García. 'You mean he's a pimp.'

Miklos squirmed. 'Boy, I dunno.'

The detective asked if any of the other guests in 233 had made an impression. Miklos said yes, one man checked in with a bag of live gerbils and a video camera.

'And you find that unusual?' García smiled. 'Go on.'

'Another night was three Jamaicans. I tell them there's only one bed but they say it's OK, *mon*. Three big guys in that room—you saw how small it is.'

García tapped the guest register. Miklos found the name: 'John Riley'. Conveniently generic. The address was a post-office box in Belle Glade, of all places. Lake Okeechobee.

'Big strong guys,' Miklos reported. 'They check out before midnight.'

'Paid cash, I'm sure.'

'We don't see many credit cards,' Miklos said.

'Remember what they were driving? Was there anybody else in the car?'

'Boy, I dunno.'

'What else?' García asked. 'You said they stood out.'

'They all have scars. Very bad scars.'

'On the face?'

'Legs.'

'Do tell,' García said.

'They were in short pants. Red, green, I dunno, but was very bright colors.'

'Gym shorts,' the detective said.

'That's how I saw the scars.' He reached down and patted his shins. 'All down here.'

'You've been a big help, Mr Miklos.'

The friendly motel manager offered to show Al García the

other rooms where guests occasionally died. The detective said no thanks, maybe another time.

'So maybe it was Jamaicans who killed the man who lost his checkbook.'

'It's a thought,' García said.

Miklos winked. 'Maybe your dreams will tell you who did it.'

The detective laughed. 'I deserve that.'

The motel manager accompanied him to the car. Miklos said he'd applied to be night clerk at a Ramada near the beach. He said the waiting list was two pages long.

'But I got more experience than most.'

'You're not kidding,' García said. 'Good luck with that job.'

'Thank you,' said Miklos. 'Good luck with your murder.'

Erin got to the trailer park at seven. Rita was already out in the backyard, yelling at the wolf dogs. It was Alberto Alonso who opened the front door. He'd just returned from the nuclear plant, and still wore his gabardine security-guard uniform. Erin was shocked that he was allowed to carry a gun.

'Coffee?' Alberto said. He unbuckled his holster and casually hung it over the back of a chair. Erin felt sick to her stomach; she had a flashing image of her daughter picking up Alberto's pistol, thinking it was a toy.

'Where's Angela?' she said tensely.

'Asleep, I think.'

Erin checked both bedrooms, which were empty. She returned to the kitchen, where Alberto was tending the coffee maker.

'Where is my daughter?' Erin said.

'Better touch base with Rita.'

'No, I want an answer from you.' She felt her arms shaking with anger. 'Alberto, it's visitation day.'

He poured a cup of coffee at the dinette. 'I remember last time you stopped over. Took off without even saying so long.'

Erin said, 'I didn't feel so well.'

'Rita sure was pissed about the mail.'

'I sent it all back.'

Alberto Alonso eyed her over the rim of the coffee cup. 'You look good in blue jeans,' he said. 'How's the job? I hear they changed the name of the place.'

Erin felt short of breath. What had these two cretins done with her daughter? She said, 'OK, I'll go ask Sheena of the Jungle.'

'Hold on there.' Alberto snickered nervously. 'Maybe we can work something out, just the two of us.'

They heard Rita shouting curses outside. It sounded as if she was being dragged through the shrubbery. 'Lupa don't take to the leash,' Alberto explained.

Erin steadied herself; outmaneuvering Alberto shouldn't be hard. He moved to a window and peeked through the blinds. 'Rita's got her hands full,' he reported in a furtive voice. He jostled back to the kitchen, and swept the dishes and silver off the table.

'How about a little show?' he whispered to Erin.

'Just like you do at the club, only private.'

She thought of that final night, dancing on the table at Jerry Killian's apartment—he'd been so sweet and shy about it. Alberto Alonso was a different story.

He said, 'One little number, OK. Then I'll show you where Angie's at.' He sat on a stool, and excitedly motioned for Erin to climb on the dinette.

'Music would be helpful,' she said.

'Just pretend,' said Alberto. 'Rita hears the stereo, she'll want to know what's up.'

Erin wasn't sure she could dance just then, with or without her songs; all she could think about was finding Angela. Darrell Grant must've called and warned Rita to hide the child. If he knew that the judge was dead, then surely he knew Erin's plan. That he would disregard an emergency injunction, or any court order, was a foregone conclusion. The man would skip the country before surrendering custody of his daughter. To Darrell, it wasn't an issue of rightful parenthood, it was competition—a game of keep-away, with Angela as the prize. Erin knew she had to strike fast, before her ex-husband got back to town.

Stepping up on the table, she almost bumped her head on the drop-ceiling of the trailer. She began humming 'Brown-eyed

Girl', slowly moving her hips, waiting for Alberto's inevitable grope.

'Faster,' he said.

Erin put on her stage smile. As she danced, her sneakers skated on the Formica. After a minute or so, she started to hear the music, clear and tender, in her head. Alberto's coffee-stained leer seemed far away and harmless. She didn't flinch when he clamped his hands around her ankles.

'Go faster,' he said again.

Erin thought: Everything will be all right. Softly she sang the first verse.

'Not too loud,' said Alberto, glancing toward the screen door.

'It's such a great song,' Erin said, to no one.

Alberto dropped his voice. 'How about some titties?'

Erin raised her eyebrows.

'Just a peek,' he said. 'Maybe take off your top.'

Still smiling, Erin undid the top two buttons. Then she said, 'You do the rest, OK?'

A blissful glow came to Alberto Alonso's face. He rose off the stool and reached for her, his fingers wriggling like night crawlers. Erin knew that Alberto would never locate, much less master, the tiny buttons of her blouse; in such extreme states of desire, men tended to lose their fine-motor skills. Alberto's paws ultimately settled upon Erin's chest, and began to massage in rhythmic circles. His coarse touch gave her an ugly chill, but Erin kept dancing like a pro. Alberto's groans intensified with the pace of his fondling; the tip of his tongue emerged between his teeth, a sluglike sentinel of arousal.

Erin's next move was to tousle Alberto's hair, which was more than he could stand. He got a clumsy grip on her breasts and tried to pull her down, toward his waiting mouth. It presented Erin with an irresistible target. She brought her right knee up, majorette-style, high and hard against the point of Alberto's unshaven chin. The crack was like a rifle shot.

Suddenly Alberto lay flat on his back, gargling blood. Erin stood over him. The stage smile was gone. Her blouse was fully buttoned. In one hand she held the coffee pot; Alberto could see steam curling off the sides.

'I intend to pour this on your balls,' Erin said.

Alberto attempted to speak, but the words came out in bubbles.

'I'm not sure this'll kill you,' Erin said, taking aim, 'but you'll wish it had.'

A squeal rose from Alberto: 'Neth doe! She neth doe!'

'Next door?'

He nodded hysterically. Erin put down the coffee pot and dashed out of the trailer. Alberto began gagging on the severed chunk of his tongue. Rita burst in the screen door; at her heels stood Lupa, ears pricked.

'Aiyeeee!' cried Alberto, shielding himself with both arms. But the wolf dog had already picked up the primal scent of the freshly wounded.

Erin held Angela's hand the whole way back to Fort Lauderdale.

'What's wrong?' the girl asked.

'I'm just glad to see you, baby.' It had been fourteen months since she and her daughter had been alone, without Darrell Grant hovering nearby—the worst year of Erin's life. She wondered what had been lost.

Angela said, 'Mrs Bickel has an aquarium. She let me feed her eels.'

Mrs Bickel was the elderly next-door neighbor of Rita and Alberto Alonso. She had been microwaving glazed donuts for Angela's breakfast when Erin arrived to collect her daughter.

'I didn't notice an aquarium,' Erin said.

'It's in the bedroom near the TV. The eels are green and they ate all her pretty fish.'

'I see,' said Erin. It sounded like Mrs Bickel fit perfectly in the demographic strata of the trailer park.

Angela said, 'Are we going to your house now?'

'We sure are. *Our* house.'

'For all day?'

'Better than that,' Erin said.

Angela looked worried. Erin's heart sank at the thought that her daughter might rather be with Darrell, or Rita, or the old lady with the eels. It was Erin's most dreadful nightmare, a year's worth of nightmares. Now she felt paralyzed, afraid to say something that might prompt a lacerating burst of candor from Angie. *I want Daddy!* Erin couldn't have endured it.

The little girl broke the silence with one word: 'Pajamas.'

She was wearing her favorites, starring Big Bird and the Cookie Monster. 'But they're dirty,' Angela said. She pinched a sleeve to show her mother. 'All my clothes are at Daddy's. And what about clean underpants!'

Erin said, 'We're going to buy you some new clothes.'

'Good!'

'You like to shop?'

'I don't know. Daddy only takes me to hospitals.'

'Right. To ride in the wheelchairs.' Erin thought: How will I ever explain that man to his daughter? At what age is a child capable of understanding that her father is irredeemable scum?

Angela said, 'One time I saw a boy riding a wheelchair.'

'At a hospital?'

'Yep. Daddy said the little boy was very sick, so we couldn't race.'

'Your daddy was right,' said Erin.

'When they put the boy back in his room, Daddy got the wheelchair and took it home.'

'Oh?'

'To fix it,' Angela said proudly. 'It needed a new brake.'

'Is that what Daddy said?'

'And new wheels. Wasn't that nice of him?'

Erin sighed. 'Angie, I'm glad you called last night.'

'Me too.'

To Mordecai, the term 'blackmail' was a melodramatic way to describe what he was doing to Congressman David Lane Dilbeck. Playing hardball is what it was. Strip away the tedious formalities of a lawsuit and the essence was no different: give me money—

or else. In or out of court, the seminal element of negotiation was the threat. It was an art, the core of Mordecai's chosen livelihood.

Man falls in supermarket, hires attorney; supermarket settles for six figures. Happens all the time and nobody calls it blackmail. Here an innocent man gets mauled by a drunken congressman, hires an attorney—and they're calling it a shakedown! Mordecai was amused by the double standard.

The attack on Paul Guber was vicious and indefensible; any personal-injury lawyer would've jumped at the case. Of course, most lawyers wouldn't have arranged a secret settlement against their client's wishes, or devised to keep the bulk of the money for themselves. It wasn't Mordecai's proudest moment as a member of the Bar, but these days a fellow did what he must. In fifteen years of practice, youthful fantasies of immense personal wealth had evaporated in disappointment. The Delicato cockroach fiasco was a prime example of his recurring foul luck. Now, the horny congressman loomed as Mordecai's first realistic chance at collecting a seven-figure lump. He proceeded on the assumption that it would be his only shot.

In the early 1970s, Mordecai was among the hundreds of idealistic young law-school graduates who rushed to South Florida with the dream of defending drug smugglers for astronomical cash fees. He'd even studied Castilian Spanish in anticipation of his Colombian clientele! But Mordecai arrived in Miami to discover a depressingly small number of imprisoned South American drug barons; defense lawyers seemed to outnumber the defendants. An attorney of modest talents stood little chance of landing a billionaire narco-trafficker as a client; Mordecai was lucky to get the occasional mule or offloader. Before long, he moved to Fort Lauderdale and opened a personal-injury practice.

The strategy had seemed sound: Broward County was growing much faster than Dade County, and most of the new arrivals were elderly. The elderly tended to fall down more often than younger people, Mordecai noticed, and their injuries usually were more complicated. Better still, there was an inexhaustible supply of old folks, thousands upon thousands, with more on the way each winter. Condos sprouted from the beach to the edge of the Everglades—high-rise bank vaults, in Mordecai's view.

He set up shop and made plans to become absurdly rich. It didn't happen. Mordecai's income was respectable but not profane. He got by on minor negligence cases, insurance litigation and probate, which he hated. He told his secretary that they could both retire to Bermuda if his clients spent half as much time falling down as they did drawing up new wills.

Still, Mordecai was in no position to be picky. South Florida was swarming with young lawyers who prowled the courthouses in a feral hunger, scrabbling like jackals for the tiniest morsel. Competition in all specialties was savage because there wasn't enough work to go around. Desperation was manifested in an epidemic of oily latenight advertising. Once the exclusive province of negligence lawyers, television now attracted all fields of the profession: immigration, divorce, adoption, even traffic violations. One of Mordecai's former classmates had become famous touting himself as 'Doctor D.U.I.' It was survival of the slickest.

Mordecai refused to make a commercial, as it involved the unpalatable prospect of trimming down for the cameras. His mother nagged doggedly—she was dying to see her son on television!—but Mordecai held firm against it. Maybe that had been a mistake. Maybe his career would've taken a loftier trajectory had he chosen the glitter of self-promotion. Then again, what was worse: shaking down a sleazy politician, or putting drunk drivers back on the road?

'I've got to live with myself,' he confided to Joyce.

'You did the right thing,' she said.

They were going to see Malcolm J. Moldowsky, who had called first thing that morning. Moldowsky said there was good news; he wanted to meet both of them in an hour. Mordecai told Beverly to reschedule his morning appointments, and euphorically thundered from the office. Crossing the lobby, a flash caught the lawyer's attention—a ray of sun, glinting off Shad's enormous head. The bouncer was waiting tight-lipped at the west elevator. Mordecai nearly stumbled: What did the lunatic want today? Had he somehow gotten wind that a deal was imminent? The lawyer slipped unseen through the eastern-most exit.

When he picked up Joyce, she said, 'You're excited. Let me drive.'

'No, I'll be fine.'

Joyce warned him about the wet roads and checked the fit of her seatbelt. 'Are you sure you got this right?'

'House of Pancakes. That's what he said.'

'In Davie? Why so far?'

'I don't know, Joyce, but that's what the man said.' Mordecai's voice was tight. 'Do you seriously think I wouldn't write it down—something this important?' He pulled the note from his pocket and thrust it toward her.

'Eyes on the road,' she said. Then, skimming her cousin's scribble: 'All right, so it says Pancake House. We'll see.'

Mordecai was silent for several miles while Joyce searched for a radio station that suited her taste. Mordecai wondered why Moldowsky had requested her presence at the meeting.

'Joyce, I'm going to ask a favor. When we get there, let me do the talking.'

'You don't have to get nasty.'

'Now listen—'

'Besides, it was my idea. Cutting Paul out.'

Mordecai took a deep breath. 'So it was.'

'Maybe, I'm not so stupid then?'

'I didn't say you were stupid. It's a delicate situation, that's all. These are serious people, and we both need to be mindful of what we say.'

Joyce flipped the visor and examined her makeup in the vanity mirror. 'I'm a serious person, too,' she said. 'Slow down, there's the exit.'

They pulled off the interstate at Davie Road and quickly spotted the International House of Pancakes. In his excitement, Mordecai mistakenly parked the Lincoln in a handicapped zone. Before he could back out, a man in blue tapped on the wind-shield. Mordecai rolled down the window.

'I work for Mr Moldowsky,' said the man. The blue was a bowling shirt. 'He's waiting at the country club.'

'Who are you?' the lawyer asked.

'Messenger,' the man replied. 'Part-time. You want to see an ID?'

Mordecai shrugged and said, 'Hop in.'

The man told Mordecai to take Orange Drive west to Flamingo Road. 'How far?' asked the lawyer.

'Not far.'

Joyce wore a cocky smirk. She reached across and poked her cousin in the arm. 'I told you,' she said. 'House of Pancakes! I knew that couldn't possibly be right.'

'Enough,' said Mordecai.

Joyce turned to the stranger in the backseat. 'What's the name of the country club? Is it Brook Run or Pine Abbey?'

The man hesitated, but not long enough for Joyce to notice. 'Brook Run,' he said.

'I hear it's just lovely.'

'Yeah,' the man said. 'That's what I hear, too.'

'Do they have a brunch?'

Mordecai said, 'Joyce, for God's sake.'

The man in the bowling shirt sat forward. 'Yeah, they got a helluva brunch,' he said. 'Slow down and make the next turn.'

18

Erin moved out of her apartment on the same day that she snatched Angela. She found a place in a suburban development called Inverarry, where Jackie Gleason once lived in a luxury mansion with a billiard room. Erin was in a bind, so she took what was available—a two-bedroom town house that was too expensive. The security deposit was a thousand dollars plus first and last month's rent. She paid in cash and signed the lease under her maiden name. She and Angela relocated the entire household by themselves in three trips. The only casualty was the Jimi Hendrix poster, which ripped when Erin removed it from the wall.

The next day, she withdrew another two thousand dollars from her savings account, drove to her lawyer's office and gave him the money—which (by his secretary's tabulation) reduced Erin's outstanding balance from eleven thousand dollars to nine thousand dollars. That afternoon, the lawyer asked the new judge in Erin's divorce case to remove Angela from Darrell Grant's custody because he had dumped the child with dangerously unreliable relatives. Alberto's pistol and Rita's wolves figured prominently in the judge's decision. Neither Darrell nor his attorney showed up to argue. The judge ordered a full hearing on the case in four weeks. He was curious to know more about Erin's occupation.

The other dancers congratulated Erin and doted on Angela in the dressing room of the Tickled Pink. They took turns playing with the little girl until she dozed off on the floor. Erin wasn't happy about the arrangement; the club was no place for a child. The new judge would take a dim view.

Dancers with children customarily worked the day shift so

they could be home at night. Erin couldn't afford to work days because the money was lousy, and she was now nearly broke— the apartment, the lawyer, Angie's new wardrobe.

'The shoes are adorable,' said Urbana Sprawl, fingering the tiny Reeboks. 'Where'd you find these?' She spoke in a whisper, trying not to wake the girl.

Erin said, 'I'm doing tables tonight. So don't fall off the stage when you see me.'

'Damn, you *must* be tapped.' Urbana knew how Erin hated table dances. 'But you'll make money,' she told her. 'Real good money.'

'First one that touches me—'

'No, girl. You call Shad. That's what he's there for.' Urbana removed her top and studied her breasts critically in the mirror. 'Mosquito got me on the left one,' she reported.

Erin said you could hardly see it.

'Hardly ain't good enough.' Urbana found a jar of dark makeup and touched up the bite. 'Don't you worry,' she told Erin. 'Everybody does tables. Fact, you're the only one I ever knew who didn't. That's how fine a dancer you are. Most girls'd starve to death on stage tips.'

'Well, now I'm dancing for two,' Erin said.

Monique Sr came in and announced that Keith Richards was sitting at table five. 'I told Kevin to play some Stones,' she said excitedly. 'Next set, I'm gonna knock his socks off.'

'Keith Richards,' Erin said, failing to conceal her amusement.

'What—you don't believe me?'

Urbana asked what he was drinking.

'Black Jack and water.'

'Then it ain't Keith. What he drinks is Rebel Yell, straight up.' Urbana was an encyclopedia of trivia when it came to the Rolling Stones.

Monique Sr looked crestfallen. Erin, feeling guilty, said: 'Hey, maybe he switched labels.'

'It's *him*,' Monique Sr insisted. 'Come see for yourself.'

Erin said, 'We believe you.'

'No, we don't,' said Urbana. 'Anyway, what's the difference?

The Stones don't use dancers. What could he do for us, even if it was really him?'

Monique Sr started to tell Urbana to go fuck herself, but then she spotted Angie, sleeping. She would not swear in the presence of a child.

'Now, say it was Rod Stewart,' Urbana went on, 'then we got us some possibilities. He uses dancers in all his videos. That's when you got my attention, when Rod the Bod takes table five.'

Erin cut in: 'Monique, you want us to come look?'

'Keith would be thrilled,' she said icily.

'Let's go then.' Erin opened the door and there stood Orly, looking gassy and dour. Monique Sr curtly excused herself and hurried back to the lounge.

Orly trudged in and closed the door. He glared at Angela, curled on the carpet. 'I could lose my license,' he said to Erin. 'Tell me that's not a minor on the premises. Tell me it's a midget stripper in tennis shoes. Otherwise I lose my fucking liquor license.'

Erin apologized for bringing Angie to the club. She told Orly it was a family emergency.

'Shit,' he muttered, and sagged down in a folding chair.

Urbana Sprawl said: 'Don't you wake that child, Mr Orly.'

'Don't worry,' Erin said. 'She doesn't sleep, she hibernates.'

Overcome by cosmetic fragrances, Orly immediately fell victim to an allergy attack. He stifled his sloppy sneezes as best he could.

'Hush,' Urbana said. 'You ain't even supposed to be in the dressing room. Or did you forget?'

'Forgive me,' Orly said. 'See, I couldn't control myself. It's been at least ten minutes since I seen your fat ass naked, so I snuck back here to cop a peek. You don't mind if I whack off now, do you?'

Erin said, 'God, you're in a lousy mood.'

'Damn right.' Orly grabbed a handful of tissues from a box on the vanity. 'The Ling brothers are doing standing-room, on account of that old judge croaking in their club. They got so much business, they're takin' reservations. *Reservations*, at a god-damn tittie bar!'

Erin said, 'The TV news is what did it. You can't buy that kind of publicity.'

Orly began to fulminate obscenely, then caught himself. He glanced irritably at the sleeping girl. In a bitter rasp: 'We're talking about a dead body, a stiff—just about the worst thing you can imagine. And people are lined up around the block to see where it happened. I don't understand human nature, I honestly don't.'

Urbana's eyes were full of mischief. She said, 'Let's keep our fingers crossed. Maybe somebody famous will die here, too.'

'Not the way these girls dance,' said Orly. 'The only thing my customers might die of is sheer goddamn boredom.'

'That's enough,' Erin said sharply. 'I mean it.'

Urbana hustled off to do a set in the cage. Orly shrunk deeper in the folding chair, which pinched his torso like an oversize clothespin. 'Even Marvela's cashing in,' he complained.

'She's overcome her grief, has she?'

'The Lings got her name in big letters on the marquee: come see the pussy that killed the judge!'

'Is that what it says?'

'I'm paraphrasing,' Orly admitted. 'Bottom line, my business is down fifteen percent.'

Bracing for the worst, Erin said, 'So what do you want from us?'

'Reconsider friction dancing.'

'Absolutely not. We took a vote, Mr Orly.'

'Yeah, yeah.' He dismissed the idea with a brusque wave. 'Then how about this: creamed corn.'

Erin said nothing. She wanted him to choke out every depraved detail, with no help or encouragement. She wanted him to be as uncomfortable as possible.

'Instead of Wesson oil,' he said. 'What do you think?'

Erin's face gave nothing away; she didn't even blink. Orly's hands fidgeted on his belly like two fat crabs.

'Wrestling!' he blurted. 'For God's sake, that's what I'm talking about. Creamed corn instead of oil. There's a place in West Palm where it started. First the guys climb in and wrestle the girls. I'm thinking twenty bucks a pop.'

Finally Erin spoke. 'Just so I understand. You want me to

jump into a puddle of creamed vegetables and roll around nude with a bunch of drunk slobs.'

'Not nude. Topless.' Orly gnawed off a hangnail and spit it on the floor. 'Health department won't go for nude. Not with food products.'

'What happened to classy?' Erin demanded. 'New name, new image—what happened to that?'

'Those fucking Lings is what happened to that.' Orly looked despondent. His words carried a tinge of genuine shame. 'You want the truth, I'm hurting. I need a goddamn gimmick, Erin. This creamed corn thing is what they call camp. I'm told the yuppies are suckers for it.'

She said, 'So it's come to this.'

'I can't force you to do it.'

'No shit,' she said. 'With a shotgun you couldn't force me to do it.'

Orly straightened and put on his businessman's face. 'What's the part that gripes you—is it the wrestling or the corn itself? Because something else occurred to me.'

'I can hardly wait,' Erin said.

'How about this? Forget the creamed corn—'

'Bravo.'

'Consider pasta.' Orly's eyebrows danced. 'You mention class, well, there you are. What's classier than pasta?'

'Pasta wrestling?' Erin was tumbling through space.

'Egg noodles, linguini, take your pick.'

'I've got to undress now, Mr Orly. Could I have some privacy please?'

When he stood up, the chair fell off his ass with a clatter. Angie stirred but did not awaken.

'Think about it,' Orly told Erin. 'Like I say, it's a smash in West Palm.'

In the mirror she watched him go out the door. 'What happened to just plain dancing?' she said.

Sabrina came in to keep an eye on Angie while Erin performed. 'I heard you're doing tables tonight,' Sabrina said, combing a jet-black wig. 'It's not so bad.'

'Unless they grab you,' said Erin.

'They won't grab tonight. Shad's in one of his moods.' Sabrina's hairbrush hit a snag and the wig jumped off her lap. 'Damn,' she said.

Erin fastened her G-string and checked her butt in the mirror, to make sure the strap was lined up. She said, 'The thing is, I need the money.'

'You'll do good,' Sabrina said. 'Just be careful not to fall.'

Kevin was playing 'Honky Tonk Woman' when Erin went on stage. The song brightened her mood nearly as much as the sight of Monique Sr dancing wildly on the table of a man who actually looked like Mr Keith Richards, if you used your imagination.

Which is all that was keeping Erin sane.

Visions of Valium tablets danced in Beverly's head. The phones were beeping off the hook, the mail had piled up, and that horrid bald man was reading *National Geographic* in the waiting room, for the second straight day—the same man she'd tried to stab with a letter opener! Seeing him again was awkward; in sixteen years as a legal secretary, she'd never assaulted a client. Half in terror, Beverly had offered a meek apology.

For what? the bald man said. He'd already forgotten about it. Beverly felt more afraid of him than ever.

'I do need to see the boss,' Shad had said.

'You just missed him.'

That was yesterday. The lawyer had rushed to a meeting and failed to return. He hadn't even phoned in for messages. Today, Beverly's exasperation was turning into concern: Mordecai could not be found. So far he'd skipped four office consultations, two depositions and an important hearing in Circuit Court. The court hearing was significant because it involved the awarding of attorney's fees, an occasion that Mordecai never missed.

Beverly was mystified. Now a bank officer was on the line, seeking to verify the number on Mordecai's client trust account. The officer recited the account number and Beverly told him it was correct. 'All deposits usually go through me,' she said.

The bank officer said it wasn't a deposit, it was a withdrawal.

A substantial withdrawal. He said Mordecai had called with instructions to close out the account immediately.

Beverly didn't like the sound of that one bit. Another line lighted up—Paul Guber, mildly worried. He hadn't heard from his fiancée in two days. It was unlike Joyce not to pester him hourly. Did Mordecai happen to know where she was?

Poor Beverly had no answers. Now Shad loomed in front of her desk. Today he wore camo fatigues. 'This is getting ridiculous,' he said.

'I know, I know,' the secretary agreed. 'I can't imagine where he's gone.'

Shad said, 'Let me check around.' He stepped past her and opened the door to Mordecai's office. Afraid to protest, Beverly followed.

'Did you turn all these lights on?' Shad asked.

The secretary said no, the lights were on when she got there. 'He might've worked late last night,' she said. The phones resumed beeping, but she didn't pick up. She was determined not to let Shad out of her sight.

He circled the desk, touching nothing. 'Someone's been through this.'

'How can you tell?'

'It's too damn neat,' Shad said. A man working late hours would leave some clutter, but Mordecai's desk was abnormally tidy, not a pencil out of place. Even the trash can looked as if it had been vacuumed.

Shad asked if there was a drop safe. Beverly said no—Mordecai kept all sensitive files in a lock box at a bank.

'How many keys?' Shad asked.

'Two, I think.'

'Where are they?'

'I don't know,' said Beverly. 'He won't tell me.'

'This is good,' Shad said.

'He won't even tell me which bank.'

'Figures.'

Beverly speculated that maybe the janitors had left the lights on. That might explain why the place was so orderly.

Shad shook his head. The place had been gone over by pros. 'I seem to remember a Rolodex.'

Beverly scanned Mordecai's desk. 'A locked Rolodex, yes. He kept it by the telephone.'

'Well, somebody got it,' Shad said. Damn, this was shitty news.

'Shall I call the police?'

'Suit yourself,' he said. 'My guess is, they'll be calling *you*.'

A man followed Erin home from work. It was three in the morning and the streets were empty. The man was careful to keep a distance of three or four blocks between his car and Erin's smoky old Fairlane. He did a good job, because Erin never suspected that she was being tailed.

She parked beneath a streetlight and led Angela across the lot toward the town house. The man parked not far away, turned on the car radio and napped until dawn. He kept watch on the apartment until ten in the morning. When Erin didn't reappear, the man drove away.

This happened two days in a row. On the third morning, Erin came out of the town house carrying a basket of laundry, Angela scampering close behind. Together they got in the Fairlane and went to a laundromat off Oakland Park Boulevard. Again the man followed, parking at a video store directly across the street. Through binoculars he watched Erin loading the washing machines. An hour later, he watched her loading the dryers. After she was done, the man didn't tail her back to the apartment. Instead he hurried on foot across the street to the laundromat. He was thinking: This is the sickest thing I've ever done . . .

The congressman had been adamant.

'Erb,' he'd said, waving the photograph of the stripper, 'I want her.'

'No, you don't,' Erb Crandall said.

'I've never felt like this before.'

'Yes, you have.'

'I want her in all the wondrous ways that a man can want a woman.'

'Give me a fucking break,' said Erb Crandall.

'If you don't help me find her, I'll do it myself.'

'After the election.'

David Dilbeck said, 'I can't wait that long. I'm under a spell, Erb. I am . . . driven.'

'Sorry,' Crandall said, 'I've got my orders.'

They were riding first class on a Delta flight from Miami to Dulles; a one-day quickie. Somebody was giving a bullshit party for Tip O'Neill. Dilbeck paced the aisle, clutching the incriminating photograph to his breast. He simply would not shut up and sit down.

'Did you see the picture? Did you see what she looks like?'

'Very attractive,' Erb Crandall said.

'I want you to find her and offer her a job on my staff.'

'Have some breakfast,' said Crandall. Other passengers were starting to murmur. The next time Dilbeck came within range, Crandall grabbed the Eager Beaver photo and stuffed it inside a flight magazine, which he placed in his briefcase.

Soon Dilbeck tired. He sat down and said, 'Erb, I won't get through the campaign without her. She haunts my dreams.'

'Really. You know who haunts *my* dreams? Malcolm J. Moldowsky.'

'I need to learn everything about her. Everything.'

'We don't even know her name,' Crandall lied.

'Find out, dammit. Find out everything.' Dilbeck's eyes were on fire. 'Erb, she's not like the others.'

'Yeah, I can tell from the picture. For a minute I thought it was Julie Andrews, dancing in the Alps. Except she was naked with some guy's face between her legs.'

The congressman seized Erb Crandall's arm and said, 'God, I am hopelessly possessed.'

You're half right, thought Crandall. The hopeless part. 'Eat your omelet,' he told David Dilbeck.

'After the election, you said?'

'Right.'

'Maybe I can endure it, Erb. Maybe I could get by if I had something of hers. Something to cherish!'

'Keep your voice down,' Crandall said. 'I'll see what I can do.'

The congressman tugged his arm again. 'No, not like the others. No panties or garters or bra cups.'

'What then?'

He couldn't believe it when Dilbeck told him. 'You are deeply warped,' Crandall said.

'Now, what harm could it do? Seriously, Erb.'

So Crandall found himself in a laundromat, surreptitiously scraping the lint from the filter of a dryer. Not just any lint—the lint from the beautiful nude dancer's personal laundry. Crandall wrapped the sheath of pink fuzz in a handkerchief. He saw a customer peeking over a stack of folded linens, and flashed a phony FBI badge that he kept handy for odd occasions.

When Crandall returned to the house, the congressman met him in the foyer. Dilbeck's hair was freshly combed and his cheeks shone. He received the lint gratefully, in cupped hands. 'My God,' he said. 'You did it.' Then he disappeared into the master bathroom for a long time.

Erb Crandall locked the front door, went to the den, and lay down on a sofa. He turned on a game show and got drunk on gin. He closed his eyes and tried to remember when politics was fun.

19

Shad called Sgt Al García and said it was time to talk. García picked him up at noon and took the new interstate west, out of the city. Shad wondered where they were headed. He told the detective about Mordecai's plan to shake down the congressman. García wanted to hear about the photograph.

'Who's in it, besides Dilbeck?'

'The guy he's whaling on,' Shad said, 'then me and Erin.'

'Where's the original?'

'It's a color slide. The lawyer's got it, probably in a bank box but I don't know where. Not even the secretary knows.'

García asked about Mordecai. How had Shad met him? What was he like? Shad recounted everything, starting with the cockroach scam. The detective chuckled at the business about the temp eating Shad's yogurt, but otherwise listened seriously. He said: 'So it's your guess the lawyer braced Dilbeck with a copy of the picture.'

'That's the way he laid it out.'

'And he promised you a cut of the payoff?'

'Yeah. Because I was a prime witness.'

'And because he screwed up your roach case.'

'Royal,' said Shad, spitting out the window.

'Now he's missing and you're finally worried. You think maybe the same thing happened to your lawyer that happened to poor Jerry Killian. And you're thinking you might be next.'

Shad said, 'It's not me I'm worried about.'

'Me neither, Cueball. It's your stripper friend.'

'Dancer friend.'

'Right. She's a nice lady.' Shad blinked straight ahead. 'She got her daughter back. That ups the stakes.'

'I see your point.'

They came to a tangle of converging highways.

García bore north on US 27. On both sides was a rolling horizon of water and sawgrass.

'The hell are we going?' Shad asked.

'Beautiful downtown Belle Glade. How about a cigar?'

Shad said sure. Al García was pleased. They both lit up and the car filled with smoke. The detective rolled down the windows.

'Good?' he asked.

'All right,' Shad said.

'Hey, *chico*, you inhaling?'

'Yeah. I like it.'

'Damn,' García said. 'That doesn't burn like hell?' Shad said he didn't feel a thing. 'I got what they call a high threshold.'

They rode about ten miles working on their cigars, not saying a word. Eventually García asked what it was like to work at a nude dance club.

Shad puffed out a heavy grunt. 'After a while, you don't notice.'

'Come on.'

'Really. I'm to the point where I get excited when they put their clothes *on*. That's what happens after too long.'

García said, 'I know guys would kill for your job.' 'They can have it. Being around naked women all day is bad for your outlook. After a while it's just tits and ass and nothin' special. Like if you worked an assembly line making Ferraris—before long, they're just cars and that's all. You understand?'

'Everything gets boring.'

'Damn right,' Shad said, teething the cigar, 'and when pussy gets boring, it's time for a career move.'

'I know exactly how you feel.' Al García jerked a thumb over one shoulder. 'Guess what I got in the trunk? An Igloo cooler. And guess what's in the cooler? A human head.'

Shad violently expelled the cigar out the window. He wiped his mouth on the sleeve of his camo jacket.

'No joke,' García said. 'Property of one Francisco Goyo,

deceased. I can't begin to tell you how much gas I've wasted on the case. The fat prick got dumped in a dozen different zip codes.'

'Why,' Shad asked, 'do you got his head in an Igloo?'

'So it won't stink up the car.'

'That ain't what I mean.'

The detective said that a windsurfer on Key Biscayne had found the gruesome item by accident that morning. 'I gotta drop it by the morgue on the way home. They got a Frigidaire full of Señor Goyo.'

'Goddamn,' Shad said, gravely.

'But I know what you mean about boring. Same old shit, day in day out.' García flicked the ash from his cigar. 'You want to trade jobs?'

'Goddamn,' Shad said again.

García drove directly to the Belle Glade post office. He asked Shad to wait in the car so as not to terrify bystanders. At the desk, García showed his police badge and asked about the box number given by the three mysterious Jamaicans at the Flight-path Motel. The clerk, a handsome woman with thick gray hair, said the box indeed belonged to a Mr John Riley, but that Mr Riley had not picked up his mail in six months. There was an excellent reason.

'He's passed on,' the clerk said.

'I'm very sorry.'

'Then you're in the minority.'

García said, 'Who could tell me about it?'

'Anybody,' the clerk replied. 'Riley was a crew boss at Rojo Farms. He was shortin' his cutters and they all knowed it. One morning he got runned over by a migrant bus.' The clerk paused. 'It was a accident, accordin' to the state patrol.'

'But maybe not,' García said.

'Misself, I lean toward a act of God. Riley was a bad man. Bad things happen to bad men.'

'And this was six months ago?'

'At least. And they still curse his name, the cutters do.'

'Anybody curse it more than others?'

The clerk said, 'I don't follow.'

'Did any of the men have a special reason to hate Riley, besides the money he was stealing?'

The clerk was greatly amused. 'What other reason would they need?' She began sorting the mail, arranging it in neat stacks. Many of the envelopes bore scriggly printing and foreign stamps; Belle Glade was a migrant town. The clerk said, 'Sounds like you're after somebody in particular.'

'Don't laugh,' García said. 'It's three Jamaicans.'

'Oh my.'

'I asked you not to laugh.'

'But his whole crew was Jamaicans.'

'I figured,' García said. 'And they all hated him, right?'

'Worse than a snake.'

Back in the car, García asked Shad if he wanted to ride over to Clewiston and see a sugar mill. Shad said he had no earthly interest.

'It'll help make sense of all this,' García said.

'Save your gas and tell me about it on the way back to Lauderdale.'

'Why the hurry?'

Shad's neck inflated. 'Because there's a goddamn Cuban head in the trunk!'

'Señor Goyo was Panamanian.'

'Jesus!' said Shad.

A marsh rabbit appeared in the middle of the road. Al García weaved around it without braking. 'This congressman,' he said, 'his balls belong to the sugar companies. They need him up in Washington, to keep things right. So when dorky little Killian threatens a blackmail, the sugar people's people get nervous. You with me?'

Shad pointed ahead and said, 'Speed trap.'

García said, 'For Christ's sake, I'm a cop. Remember?' He blinked his dashboard light at the state trooper as they flew by. 'You aren't even listening,' he said to Shad.

'Yeah, I am. Sugar money.'

'Killian makes his demand, which is so weird it probably freaks out Dilbeck's people. Fix a custody case? they're thinking. Lean on a judge? We're dealing with a crackpot, they're thinking. So somebody—not Dilbeck, but somebody close—makes a phone call.'

'And so long, crackpot.'

'Right. Three cane cutters show up and snatch Killian, probably out of his apartment.'

'How do you know they're cane cutters?'

'Scars, man. They've got the scars on their legs. Cutters are always whacking themselves by accident with those damn machetes; even the good ones do it. Anyway, they haul Killian to a cheap motel and—as a sick joke—register in the name of a dead boss man. The motel is where they drown him. Then they put him on ice—'

'Don't tell me,' Shad said. 'Another fucking Igloo.'

'Not likely,' said García, steering with one hand, waving the dead cigar stub with the other. 'Anyway, they ice him down and drive straight to Missoula, Montana. Or maybe they use the Rojo corporate jet, who knows—'

Shad said, 'Why Montana?'

'That's where Killian vacations. See, it was set up to look like a fishing accident.'

Finally Shad cracked a smile. His colossal white dome bobbed as García heard him swallow a laugh.

'What is it?'

'Man,' Shad said, 'three Jamaicans cruising through Montana.'

'Yeah, I know.'

'Holy Christ. Is that a riot? Jamaican cowpokes.'

'They had nerve,' Al García said. 'Whoever it was.'

'You'll never get 'em.'

'You're right.'

'Never in a million years.'

'I'm quite sure,' García said, 'they're already back in Kingston. Or dead.'

The temperature light on the dashboard flashed red, so he steered the Caprice to the shoulder of the road. He opened the hood and checked the hose fittings, which seemed tight.

There was no sign of a leak from the radiator. 'Wires,' the detective muttered, and slammed the hood.

Shad was gone from the car. Al García found him forty yards away, three rows deep in a field of tall cane.

'So this is it,' Shad said. A fat blue horsefly gorged on his gleaming scalp. The fly was so big it looked like a tattoo.

García snapped off a stalk of cane and sniffed it. 'What a deal these bastards get. All the water they want for practically nothing. Imported slave labor for the harvest. Then they get to sell the crop at jacked-up prices, courtesy of the US Congress. And when they're all done, they're allowed to dump the stink straight into the Everglades.'

Shad was impressed. 'Land of opportunity,' he said, probing the black muck with the tow of his boot.

'Millions and millions of dollars,' García said. 'Killian had no idea what he was dealing with. Same goes for your ace attorney.'

They got back in the car. Shad declined the offer of another cigar. The horsefly remained attached to his head. García reached over and brushed it away.

Five miles later, Shad said, 'So where's your jurisdiction on this deal? I don't see a Miami connection.'

The detective smiled ruefully. 'Dilbeck's congressional district is in Dade County. That's the best I can do.'

'Pitiful,' Shad remarked.

'Nobody else is much interested. I can't just let a homicide slide.'

'Other words, you're doing this off the clock.'

'That's why I need your help,' García said.

'Think they'll come after Erin?'

'I think they'll come after everyone in that photograph, if necessary. I think they won't even hesitate.'

Shad turned to look out the window. They were out of farm country now. The Everglades shimmered west to the horizon. 'She's got her little girl back.'

'So you said.'

'I guess that don't count.'

'Not with these people.' García stopped at a fishing camp to buy another bag of ice for Francisco Goyo's severed head. Shad frowned when he heard the trunk pop open, the cubes pouring out of the plastic. He hoped García wouldn't try to show him the damn thing. Some cops got off on shit like that.

When they were back on the road, Shad told the detective that he'd done some state time.

'Oh, I know. Manslaughter.'

'Manslaughter *two*,' Shad said.

'That was the plea. The crime was manslaughter.' García saw that the temperature light had come on again. He thumped the dashboard with a fist, and the light went out. 'God bless General Motors,' he said.

Shad asked if he knew about the agg assaults, too. García said sure.

'My boss, Mr Orly, he'd hit the fucking roof,' Shad said. 'Hiring a felon and all. He could lose his license.'

García kept his eyes on the road. 'Don't worry about your boss,' he said. 'I needed to know. He doesn't.'

'I appreciate that.'

'Here's another thing: I'd prefer not to be informed if you've got a piece, OK? Because if I see it, then I gotta do something. Like arrest your ass, OK? That's the law, felons can't carry a gun. So don't feel obliged to take it out and play, because then we got a problem.'

Shad said, 'I'm with you. Let's talk about Erin.'

'Yeah.' The detective drummed his fingers on the steering wheel. 'We gotta figure something out.'

'Shouldn't be hard,' said Shad. 'With my good looks and your brains.'

Malcolm J. Moldowsky prowled the penthouse restlessly. The ocean view did not soothe him, nor did the fine cognac. He was a resentful man, deeply resentful that a person of his stature should be forced to worry.

Moldy was at the top of his game: insidiously powerful, obscenely wealthy and largely untouchable. Up until now. Lately his hard-earned arrogance had lost some of its starch. He was feeling vulnerable, even shaky. Others were to blame. Free-floating incompetence threatened to destroy an artifice that Moldowsky had spent years constructing. He knew how his hero, John Mitchell, must've felt when those idiots bungled a simple burglary. A life's work destroyed by unspeakable stupidities.

In protecting David Dilbeck's career, Moldowsky had breached a realm far beyond the mere peddling of influence. Committing illegal acts was nothing new. It was the nature of the recent felonies that concerned Moldy: a superb white-collar criminal, he'd been forced out of his element. Diverting election funds was a breeze. Unlawfully compensating an elected official was child's play. Falsifying campaign finance reports was a routine chore.

But this! Goddamn that Dilbeck.

For the first time in many years, Moldowsky was second-guessing himself. He hated the feeling because he hated all forms of introspection. In Moldy's line of work, a man's worst enemy was a functioning conscience. He poured another cognac and resumed his idle pacing through the apartment. Passing a mirror, Moldowsky saw that he'd skipped a belt loop in the back of his pants. Also, he had misbuttoned the cuff of his left sleeve. God, was he rattled!

It was the sudden death of the divorce judge that did it. The judge who couldn't be persuaded to help a congressman and fix a lousy custody case. The judge who didn't need a favor because he was already coasting on his merry way to the federal bench.

Jerry Killian was killed because the judge wouldn't budge. Moldowsky had seen no other solution; eliminating the black-mailer removed the threat to David Dilbeck. It was simple, logical, expedient—but had it really been necessary? Moldowsky was annoyed at himself for fretting about it. The Killian decision made perfect sense at the time. Who could've predicted that the judge would obligingly croak?

Moldy was a man who appreciated cruel irony. Normally he would've been amused by the seedy circumstances under which the pious little shit had expired—his brain detonating in a sea of bare breasts. The TV crews swarming the Flesh Farm had left little to the imagination.

Yet the only thing that had entered Moldowsky's mind was an unfamiliar stab of doubt: Maybe I acted too precipitously. If I'd stalled Killian, jerked him around for a couple weeks, then the judge would've solved both our problems by dying. *Grant* v. *Grant* automatically would've been reassigned, and Killian would've backed away from David Dilbeck.

Oh well, Moldy thought. What's done is done. The three Jamaican cane cutters have gone home. Next month there would be a terrible truck accident near Montego Bay; no survivors. And the flight logs for the Rojos' *Gulfstream II* would show a trip to Aspen, not Missoula. Push came to shove, the FAA would back him up with tower tapes. The daughter of a deputy assistant administrator owed her job to Malcolm J. Moldowsky . . .

The phone beeped twice and Moldy picked it up. He stood at the broad window and gazed across the Atlantic. Under cloudy skies, the water was foamy-gray and unalluring. Just over the horizon, in Nassau, was the man on the other end of the phone call. He was a banker who'd been educated in London, but whose speech had retained its soothing island cadence. He told Moldowsky that the wire transfer had been completed.

'What shall we do with the balance?'

'It's entirely up to you,' Moldowsky said.

'We can put it in trust,' the banker suggested.

'Hell, you can keep it, for all I care. Buy yourself a new Hatteras.'

The banker chuckled nervously. 'Certainly, Mr Mordecai left some instructions.'

'As a matter of fact, he didn't.'

'But, sir, the account is in excess of eighty thousand dollars. I'm sure he expects the money to be properly invested.' The banker paused. 'Is there a problem I should know about?'

'Not that you should know about, no. A trust is fine, Mr Cartwright.'

'Unless he needs frequent access.'

'No,' Moldy said. 'That's one thing he definitely won't need.'

He thanked Cartwright and hung up. Immediately the phone rang again. It was the lobby—Erb Crandall was coming up for a visit. Moldowsky took out another glass, just in case the bagman was in a mood to unwind. He wasn't. He said he was ready to quit David Dilbeck's campaign.

Moldy said, 'Now slow down, Erb.'

Crandall stood rigid, arms folded. 'I've been telling you he's a time bomb. Well, the fuse is finally lit.'

Moldowsky was glad he'd had the foresight to start drinking early. 'What's he done?' he asked.

Crandall told him about the clandestine lint mission to the laundromat.

'Lord,' Moldy said. 'That *is* bad.'

'It's only the beginning, Malcolm. He wants more.'

'More what?'

'He's crazy for this stripper. The one in the picture.'

Moldowsky squinted. 'So he wants more lint?'

'Not just lint.'

He described the congressman's current fantasy. Malcolm Moldowsky rocked on his heels, the brandy boiling up in his throat.

'He's off the deep end,' Moldy said hoarsely. 'Completely insane.'

'Thank you, Dr Freud.' Erb Crandall went to the bar and got an ice-cold can of ginger ale, which he rolled back and forth across his throbbing forehead. He slumped in an armchair, his back to the ocean. 'What now Malcolm?'

'The girl,' Moldowsky said. 'Obviously.'

Urbana Sprawl was right about the money. Erin made an extra ninety bucks on her first night of table dancing. Shad stayed close, and nobody touched her. Still, she hated it. The tables at the club were so small that the dancers couldn't move their feet without kicking the customer's drink in his lap. The performance itself wasn't dancing so much as wiggling in place, which was fine for the girls with large breasts—gravity did all the work. But Erin's strong suit was choreography, and there simply was no room to show off. On the tables she was just another stripper, bouncing up and down for tips.

Another drawback was the music. The dancer on the main

stage got to pick the songs, which was only fair, but it meant that the table dancers never knew what was coming next. Most of Kevin's play list was disco, techno, fusion, dance-club, hip-hop and rap, all of which Erin detested. There was no heart to any of it, and pretending otherwise was an ordeal. She smiled so intractably that her facial muscles soon became numb; toward the end of the shift, she looked in the mirrored walls and saw a rictus grin, earnest but unsexy. The tabletop customers never noticed, since their eyes were riveted on her crotch.

On the second night, Erin made two hundred and ten dollars on the tables; the third night, one-eighty-five. On the fourth night, the homicide detective showed up. He and Shad sat down and began to talk. Erin watched curiously from table five, where she was dancing against her better judgment to an extremely long number by Paula Abdul—or, as Mr Orly called her, Kareem Abdul Paula. Erin was eager to finish the dance so she could find out why Al García had come to the club. As the song thumped to an end, the customer reached up and folded a bill into Erin's garter. She thanked him as he helped her step off the table. While reattaching her G-string, Erin saw that the man had given her a hundred-dollar bill. She thanked him again, this time with the standard hug and peck reserved for overly generous customers.

'How about another one?' the man said. He was a handsome young Latin, doing his smoothest Jimmy Smits. His clothes were expensive and his hair was raked back and there were knobs of gold on both hands. He wasn't yet drunk enough to present a problem, so Erin said sure and got back on the table. Shad and García were still hunched in conversation at the bar—she hoped they'd be there for a while. A smart dancer didn't walk away from a heavy tipper, not when she still owed her lawyer nine grand.

Erin did five table dances for the young Latin, and he gave her a hundred each time. She was excited about the money, but also suspicious. The guy wanted something else. Had to.

Eventually it came her turn to dance on the main stage. Kevin put on a cut by the Black Crowes, which woke up the whole joint. The song was fast and nasty, and Erin loved it—she kicked and whirled and double-clutched, working out lots of unspent energy. At the bar, Shad sat alone; Al García was on the pay phone near the front door, with his back to the stage. Oblivious, Erin thought, thoroughly unmoved by my spirited performance. It was funny.

The young Latin customer came to the footlights and waved Erin over. He slipped two hundred dollars in her garter. When Erin leaned down to thank him, he put a hand on her shoulder and whispered something.

Shad tensed, watching Erin's expression. He was ready to move fast, if the creep made a grab. Erin seemed puzzled, but not upset, by the young man's words. When she moved back to the middle of the stage, her smile looked solid and her eyes were calm. She even took a languid, Stevie Nicks-style twirl in front of the wind machine. Shad held steady.

After the set, Erin returned to the young Latin's table. Shad didn't see her stand up for another dance. Before long, the Latin man rose and left the club. Erin appeared at the bar and said: 'I would like a martini.'

Shad asked what was wrong.

'Nothing,' Erin replied. 'Show business.'

'Quite a fan there.' It was Al García. He sat down on the other side of Erin. 'You know who that was?'

'Said his name was Chris.'

'Christopher Rojo,' the detective said. 'Of the sugar Rojos.'

Erin said, 'That would explain all the money. But it doesn't explain this.' She spun on the stool, and swung her right leg across Shad's lap.

'Where's your shoe?' he asked.

'Young Christopher just purchased it,' Erin said, 'for one thousand dollars.'

The bouncer's vast brow crinkled in astonishment. Erin herself was in a mild daze. The money was a godsend, but it wasn't the career of her dreams—selling used footwear to wealthy perverts.

'A fucking shoe,' Shad muttered. 'What for?'

Erin covered her face. 'I don't want to think about it.'

'Love,' said Al García. 'Ain't it grand?'

20

Merkin cupped the receiver and asked Picatta if they should accept a collect call from Darrell Grant.

Picatta said, loudly, 'I don't know a Darrell Grant. How about you?'

'Never heard of him.'

'Where's he calling from?'

'The Martin County jail,' Merkin said. He grinned and held the phone away from his ear. Darrell could be heard, pleading with the long-distance operator to put him through.

Picatta leaned close to the receiver and boomed: 'The only Darrell Grant I know is a lying cocksucker who's getting his probation yanked the second he's back in Broward County!'

Merkin said, 'Is that the same misfortunate Darrell Grant that's about to lose custody of his kid, due to his felony records suddenly showing up on the courthouse computer after being lost all those years?'

'The damnedest thing,' said Picatta, 'after all those years. That new judge was real surprised, is what I heard.'

On the other end, Darrell Grant fell silent. The longdistance operator, an angel of patience, again asked if Detective Merkin would accept the call.

'No, ma'am,' he said. 'You tell Mr Grant if he needs to chat, he should phone up Mr Thomas Tinker, that so-called big-time heroin dealer he told us about. The switchboard at the graveyard will patch you right through. Goodbye now.'

Merkin hung up. The operator clicked off. Darrell Grant glumly handed the telephone to the patrolman, who put it back on the jailhouse wall.

'They're playin' a joke,' Darrell Grant said.

'Didn't sound like a joke.' The patrolman pulled Darrell's arms behind him and snapped on the handcuffs.

'You're makin' a big-time mistake. I work for those boys.'

'Really? They told you to come all the way up here and steal Miss Brillstein's wheelchair?'

The cop marched Darrell Grant to the holding cell. He said someone from the Public Defender's Office would stop by later to discuss a plea.

Darrell Grant found an empty place on a steel cot, between two sleeping drunks. 'You let me know when Merkin calls back,' he told the patrolman.

'In your dreams.'

'I work for the goddamn Broward County Sheriff!'

'Maybe once upon a time,' the cop said, disappearing.

Darrell Grant rocked miserably on the cot, grinding his molars, picking his cuticles, tapping his feet. Was Merkin bluffing, or had they really cut him loose? Worse, had they given his rap sheet to Erin's lawyer? Darrell couldn't believe the detectives could be such bastards. He had to get back to Lauderdale and see what's what. Meanwhile, he needed something to clear the brain and settle the nerves. He asked the other prisoners where he could score some crack. They were not particularly helpful.

A burly redhead with twin cobra tattoos stepped forward. 'Hey, beach boy. True you stole a wheelchair off a cripple?'

'I didn't know she was a cripple,' Darrell said. 'I thought she was just old.'

The Palm Lake Rest Home—he'd cased it pretty carefully, considering he was still foggy from when the hooker had clobbered him . . .

Noon sharp. There's the cute Filipino nurse wheeling Miss Elaine Brillstein down the driveway toward the van. Nurse chatting as she pushes Miss Brillstein, who squints into the sunlight and clutches a fuzzy white sweater across her lap. *'Scuze me, ladies.* Who's that? says Miss Brillstein, squinting harder. *Excuse me, y'all need a hand?* Well, all right, says Miss Brillstein, thank you very much. *I'll get the door.* Hold my sweater, please. *Here, let me help with that.* My, what a nice young man.

Soon as Miss Brillstein's up in the van—the nurse half in, half out, wrestling with the old lady's seat belt—Darrell Grant hijacks the wheelchair and off he runs. Two blocks later, the brake switch drops a bolt and Darrell goes ass-over-teakettle in the middle of a school zone. There's a black-and-white parked on the median, clocking speeders. Darrell Grant can't fucking believe his lousy luck.

From the redheaded prisoner with the snakes on his arms: 'The cop said the old lady had polio.'

Darrell Grant's eyes felt raw and swollen. He experienced an urge to sleep. 'I thought polio was extinct,' he said.

The redhead moved closer. 'My aunt's got polio.'

'Yeah?' said Darrell. 'Is her name Brillstein?'

'No, it ain't.'

'Then mind your own goddamn business.' Without his drugs, Darrell often got pissed at the whole universe.

The redhead said, 'I bet you'd look good in a wheelchair.'

'Not as good as you,' said Darrell Grant, 'with a two-foot donkey schlong up your ass.'

Later, when he awoke in the county hospital and saw that they hadn't bothered to cuff him to the gurney, Darrell Grant congratulated himself for such a bold and brilliant plan.

In South Florida, the disappearance of a lawyer was seldom front-page news. It happened often enough, usually coinciding with the theft of a client's money. The man from the Florida Bar used the term 'misappropriation' when he described the scenario to Beverly.

'How much?' the secretary asked.

'Approximately eighty-five thousand dollars.'

'No way,' she said. 'I can't believe it.'

'Then what do you think happened? Where is he?'

'Maybe he was kidnapped.' Beverly told him that burglars had gone through Mordecai's office one night—even the Rolodex had been stolen! The man from the Florida Bar asked if she'd called the police. Beverly admitted that she hadn't.

'Because you were afraid,' the man said, 'that the clues would point toward Mordecai himself.'

'I kept hoping he'd show up.'

The man from the Florida Bar was sympathetic, but firm. 'The trust account was emptied on his direct instructions. The assets were transferred out of the country three days ago.'

'Yes,' she said glumly. 'The bank called.'

The man from the Florida Bar sat before an open briefcase at Mordecai's desk. The law office was closed—temporarily, according to a note on the front door. Beverly wasn't optimistic. She let the answering service take all the angry calls.

The man from the Bar asked, 'Do you know the number-one cause of disbarment in Florida?'

'Moral turpitude?'

'Good guess, but no. Misuse of client trust funds. Some lawyers simply cannot resist.'

Beverly was in the high-backed chair where Mordecai's clients normally sat. She tolerated the arrangement only because she was curious about what the Bar might know of her boss's whereabouts.

The man said, 'Did he have many elderly clients?'

'Not enough,' Beverly said. 'Why?'

'It's part of the pattern. Older clients tend to be conservative with their money. They put it somewhere and let it sit. Years and years might go by.'

Beverly said, 'Like in their lawyer's trust account.'

The man from the Florida Bar nodded. 'Meanwhile the balance keeps growing. Some lawyers dip in, call it borrowing. Some even go through the motions of trying to pay it back. Others just flat out grab it all.'

Beverly didn't particularly like Mordecai, and had no illusions about his sterling character. But she'd never pegged him as the sort to skip town with clients' money. He seemed more of a small-time chiseler and cutter of corners. Embezzlement seemed too ambitious for Mordecai.

The man from the Florida Bar said, 'Who knows what triggers the impulse. A financial setback, gambling problems, a secret love affair. Which brings us to the obvious question—'

'We were *not* involved,' Beverly cut in. 'Give me a little credit, please.'

'Looks aren't everything. Even a physically . . .'—the man groped for the right word—'*daunting* fellow can have his charms.'

'Not Mordecai,' Beverly said. 'Believe me.'

'Tell me: How did he feel about his cousin?'

The secretary acted confused. 'Which cousin—Joyce?'

'Yes. We believe they're together. Did he ever discuss an attachment?'

'Joyce and Mordecai!' It was so twisted that Beverly almost hoped it was true. Joyce was an avaricious bitch, always angling for the big score. Maybe she'd romanced Mordecai into the swindle. No man was immune to seduction, but Mordecai (who hadn't dated in years) was exceptionally vulnerable. Beverly imagined the two cousins entwined, and it made her shiver.

The man from the Florida Bar said: 'Joyce's fiancé doesn't think much of the theory but, I must tell you, stranger things have happened.'

'Maybe it wasn't a love affair,' Beverly said. 'Maybe it was a straight business deal.'

The man from the Bar folded his hands across his chest. 'What would he need her for? Mordecai alone had access to the trust account. He didn't require an accomplice.'

'No, I suppose not.'

'In many of these cases, these sudden disappearances, the lawyer brings a woman along on the adventure. Frequently, it's his own secretary.'

'Well, I'm still here,' Beverly said sourly. 'And he owes me two weeks' pay.'

'Could be worse. You could be one of those clients.' 'Is that who called you? Was it a client?' The investigator's arrival at the law office had surprised Beverly. The Florida Bar was not renowned for swift and aggressive pursuit of errant members.

The man said, 'We received a tip. That's all I can say.' He gave her a business card with an 800 number in Orlando. 'If you should hear from him, please encourage him to return swiftly and make restitution. The longer he's gone, the worse it will be.'

Beverly felt more abandoned than ever. 'What do I tell everyone about the office being closed? What should I put on the door?'

The man from the Florida Bar shut his briefcase and crisply snapped the brass locks. 'We recommend ' "Death in the family." Most clients won't press the issue.'

They moved from the lounge to Orly's office: Orly, Al García, Shad, and Erin. Angela was in the dressing room with one of the fully clothed Moniques.

García had Orly in a sweat. 'I want to know more about the phone calls.'

'Me, too,' said Erin.

'Some guy, I don't know.' Orly was slurping a Dr Pepper. 'He's asking about a certain customer—'

'Jerry Killian.'

'Yeah, so big deal. There was a fight on stage and this Killian is in the audience, like I give two shits. Man calls and I tell him what he wants—'

'How'd you know Killian's name?'

'Credit card slips,' Orly said. 'Anyway, this guy who calls, he says to keep him posted if the customer shows up again.'

Al García said, 'Why'd you agree?'

'Because I got a license to consider, and this guy says he can give me problems. Says he works for a congressman. So . . . a few nights later, Killian shows up again. This time he's outside, hanging around Erin's car. You remember?'

Shad and Erin nodded together.

'See,' Orly continued, 'I can't have customers hassling my dancers. The guy on the phone says he'll make sure it doesn't happen again. That's it. End of story. I don't hear from him anymore, until today.'

García had a notebook in his hand, but he wasn't writing much. 'Why won't you tell me the man's name?'

'Because you don't understand. The nature of my business, I don't need any grief. I got a liquor license to protect.'

Erin told Orly that Jerry Killian had been murdered.

'Shit,' Orly said, sucking air. He looked at García. 'Is that why you're here?'

'What a sharpie you are. Now give me the damn name.'

Orly looked cornered. 'Maybe I should check with my lawyer. Maybe you should come back tomorrow.'

García said, 'If I have to come back tomorrow, I'm bringing beverage agents. You follow? We'll board the place up, *chico*.'

'Screw you.' Orly was feeling worn out and reckless.

Shad stirred. 'Mr Orly, you better listen. This is no bullshit.'

Al García tapped a ballpoint pen on his knee. 'The deal is, Erin's life is in danger. I've advised her to get out of town, but there's a complication.'

The new judge had forbidden Erin from taking Angela out of Florida. 'As long as I'm stuck here, I might as well work,' she said, 'considering I'm broke.'

Orly's puzzlement deepened. 'Who'd want to kill *you*? I mean, besides your ex.'

Someone knocked sharply on the door. Before Orly could respond, Sabrina burst in. She wore a thin sleeveless T-shirt and pink bikini bottoms. She was splattered with yellowy goop that Erin despondently recognized as creamed corn. Random kernels clotted Sabrina's platinum wig, which she clutched in one fist.

'I can't do this!' she cried.

'Later,' Orly said. 'We got a meeting here.'

'But it got up my nose—'

'Later, I said.'

The dancer ran out. A brief silence followed. Finally Orly said, 'Erin's the best of the bunch.'

'So you wouldn't want anything to happen to her,' García said.

'No, I sure wouldn't.'

Erin said she was deeply touched. Orly scratched at a scab on his arm. 'Plus your little girl. That's a factor.'

'You're all heart,' the detective said.

'The guy's name is Moldowsky. And don't ask me to spell it. Melvin or some damn thing.'

García said, 'Excellent. What did he want today?'

Orly jerked a thumb toward Erin. 'He asked about her. What kind of person she is. Has she got a drug problem. Is there a boyfriend.'

Erin felt a bolt of fear. She'd never heard of this person.

'Another thing,' said Orly. 'He knows about the kid. Knows there's a problem with your ex-husband. The guy, he knows lots.'

'He mentioned Angie?' Erin's voice cracked. She sat forward, balling her fists. 'What did you say?'

'Not a damn thing,' he said. 'I swear, I told him zippo.' Erin's glare was scalding. Orly angrily jabbed a finger in the air. 'You tell her, Shad. Tell her how I handled it.'

Shad backed up Orly's version. 'I was there when the asshole called. Mr Orly didn't give him shit.'

'OK,' Erin said, leaning back. 'I'm sorry.'

'He's a heavy hitter,' said Orly. 'He dropped a few names to get my attention. Otherwise I'd say fuck off.' His piggy eyes narrowed on García. 'I lose my license and there's hell to pay. Bottom line, there's some serious people I answer to.'

'Don't worry, Mr Orly. You cooperate and everything'll turn out just beautiful.'

'Cooperate?' Orly sprayed the word. 'Sweet Christ Almighty, what more you want? I gave up the goddamn name.'

'Yeah, you did,' García said. 'If only there was a phone number to go with it.'

Orly adopted the impatient pose of a man with better things to do. 'Yeah, Moldowsky left a number. I got it here somewheres.' He pawed halfheartedly at the clutter on his desk.

The detective said, 'Excellent. I want you to call him.'

Orly frowned. 'What the hell for? I'm not callin' nobody.'

'Come on,' said Al García. 'Let's find that number.'

Shad winked at Erin, as if to say: This part might be fun.

García stayed at the club until closing time. He waited in the parking lot until Erin came out with Angie. The detective tried to make friends, but the little girl was tired and cranky. She climbed in the backseat of the Fairlane and lay down. García said it was a lousy arrangement, letting Angie stay at the club.

Erin said, 'Sorry you disapprove.' She was in no mood for a male lecture. 'The other girls are terrific with her. And, no, she's not allowed in the dance lounge to see what her bimbo mom does for a living.'

'Easy now,' García said. 'I'm not talking about the atmosphere, I'm talking about the child's safety.'

He held the door while Erin got in the car. She turned the key and revved the engine noisily. 'I want her near me at all times,' she said, 'as long as Darrell's out there.'

From the backseat: 'Momma, can we go home now?'

García lowered his voice to a whisper. 'Think about it. If someone's after you, where's the first place they're gonna come? Right here. Say the shit hits the fan—you want that little girl asleep in the dressing room?'

'Fine,' Erin said. 'Then you find me a kindergarten that's open at three in the morning.' She slipped the car in gear. 'Besides, what's there to worry about? We got you and Shad to protect us.'

Erin drove away fast, burning rubber on the corner. Very childish, she thought, but wonderful therapy. She gunned it all the way home.

When Al García arrived at the town house, twenty minutes later, Erin and Angela were still sitting in the Fairlane. Erin's face was taut as she stared at the front of the apartment. When the detective approached the car, he saw a small pistol on the dash. In the backseat, Angela was as still as a porcelain doll.

García asked Erin to put the gun away. She pointed at the second-story window and said, 'The bedroom light's on.'

'You didn't leave it that way?'

'No lights,' Erin said. She'd shut off everything before leaving for work. It was an old habit; the electric bills were murder.

They watched the window for signs of a shadow. Nothing moved behind the half-drawn drapes.

'Give me the key,' García said.

'It's probably open.'

'And the gun, please.'

Erin gave him the keys and the .32. 'The safety's on,' she said.

'Thanks. If things break loose, lean on the horn.'

The front door was locked. The detective opened it softly and went inside. For several interminable moments, nothing happened; it was as if Al García had been swallowed up in the darkness. Erin scanned the windows and braced for the sound of a muffled gunshot, but all she heard was Angela's gentle breathing in the backseat. Eventually the other windows lit up, one by one, as García moved from room to room. When he reappeared at the front door, he waved for Erin to come in.

The place looked untouched. The detective accompanied her and Angela through the kitchen, the living room, up the stairs to the bedrooms. Nothing seemed to be missing.

So I made a mistake, Erin thought. I left the damn light on.

'This is all your stuff?' García asked.

'Angie and I travel light.' It felt strange to have the detective in her bedroom. Erin caught him smiling at the rock posters on the wall.

She said, 'I'm saving for a Van Gogh.'

'No, I like it.'

Angela ran down the hall and returned with a crayon drawing. 'I drew this myself,' she said, thrusting it at García.

'What a pretty dog.'

'No, that's a wolf. Aunt Rita's.' Angela traced the outline with a finger. 'See the bushy tail? And here's the baby wolves under the tree.'

'Right,' said the detective. 'Wolves.'

Erin took the drawing from his hands. She said, 'That's Darrell's side of the family. I need some aspirin.'

The bathroom was the last place she expected to find signs of an intruder. At first she didn't notice. She got a bottle of Advils from the medicine chest and swallowed three. Standing at the sink, looking in the mirror, Erin sensed something was out of place. She turned and saw what it was.

'God,' she said. A prickle went down the back of her neck.

García walked in. Erin told him to look at the shower curtain, which was pulled open along the length of the bathtub.

'You didn't leave it that way?'

'Never,' Erin said.

Angie squeezed between the grown-ups' legs and said: 'Because of mildew.'

'That's right,' said her mother. 'It mildews if you leave it bunched up that way.'

García smiled. 'Every day I learn something new.'

Erin gave Angie a glass of chocolate milk and put her to bed. Then she and the detective went through the medicine chest, the cabinets, the vanity. They found nothing missing or even disturbed, yet Erin was sure that someone had been there.

Inside her house.

Not Darrell Grant, either. He wouldn't have come and gone without leaving tracks. His ego couldn't abide an anonymous entry. No, Darrell would've mangled something intimate and left it on display.

Erin sat on the edge of the tub and fingered the shower curtain, as if it held the clue.

'Weird,' García said. 'Not your average burglar.'

'I can't afford to pack up and move again. I just can't.'

García leaned against the bathroom sink. He was dying for a cigar. 'I wonder what he wanted,' he said.

Erin said she was too tired to keep looking.

'One more try,' the detective said. 'I got an idea that might help. Tell me everything you do to get ready for work.'

'Please,' said Erin.

'I'm serious. Everybody's got a routine when they get up in the morning. Tell me yours.'

'I'd say the high point is flossing my teeth.'

'Whatever. Walk me through it.'

Erin agreed, out of pure exhaustion. 'Well, first I shower, do my hair, shave my legs. Then I touch up my nails . . . Wait a second.' She was looking at the window sill where she kept her bath articles.

'God, this is sick. Now I know what's missing.' She stood up, shaking. 'Angela can't stay here,' she said, 'not another single night!'

The detective put an arm around her. 'Tell me what they took.'

'You won't believe it,' Erin whispered. '*I* don't believe it.'

21

The congressman lay flat on the bed. He wore a black cowboy hat, a white towel around his waist and a pair of green lizardskin boots. The surgical scar on his breastbone pulsed like a worm in the ultraviolet light.

Erb Crandall said: 'What've you done here?'

'Created a mood.' David Dilbeck opened his eyes. 'Did you get what I wanted?'

'Yeah, I got it. Where's the wife?'

'Ethiopia, courtesy of UNICEF. Then Paris and probably Milan. Do you like the black lights?'

'Brings back memories.'

'Pierre found them at a head shop in the Grove. Let me see what you've got, Erb.'

Crandall stepped tentatively through the purple glow. He said. 'Geez, look at you.'

Using handkerchiefs, the congressman had tied one arm and both feet to the bedposts. Above the boots, his pale shins gleamed, as if shellacked.

'Vaseline,' Dilbeck explained. 'First I warmed it in the micro-wave—it's best to use the sauce setting.' Erb Crandall's disgusted expression prompted Dilbeck to add: 'This is what happens when you won't let me go out and play.'

'David,' Crandall said, 'tell me you've been drinking.'

'Not a drop, my friend.'

So he was insane, Crandall thought; downhill from downhill. He wondered what the chairman of the Florida Democratic Party would say if he could see the senior congressman at this moment.

Dilbeck thrust out his free arm. 'Come on. I've been waiting all night.'

'Crandall dropped it—the thing he had stolen from the stripper's apartment—in Dilbeck's open palm. The congressman squirmed on the bed as he examined the illicit treasure; a pink disposable razor.

'Now, this is the genuine article?'

'From her very bathroom,' Crandall said, listlessly.

Dilbeck twirled it between his fingers. With an edge of excitement, he said. 'I bet she used it this morning.'

'I wouldn't know.'

'I can see the little hairs!'

'Be careful, Davey.' With any luck, the dumb shit would slice his own wrists.

Dilbeck's chest rose and fell heavily. 'Erb, do you like Garth Brooks?'

'Is that who you're supposed to be?'

Dilbeck smiled dreamily. 'My boots are *full* of Vaseline.'

Well, thought Crandall, enough's enough. He took one of the burglar tools from his pocket—a small screwdriver—and put the blade to Dilbeck's neck. The congressman seemed surprised, but not particularly afraid.

Crandall pressed firmly and said, 'I'd be doing us both a tremendous favor.'

'Erb, please. This is harmless sport.'

'You're a sick puppy.'

Dilbeck said, 'Stop that right now.'

'This isn't why I went into politics, David—to pimp and steal for a perverted old fuck like you. Believe it or not, I once had ideals.'

Crandall was romanticizing; he was not a man of ideals so much as a man of instinct. He had been drawn to politics by the sweet scent of opportunity. The bitter backlash from Watergate had guaranteed a landslide for the Democrats, so that's when Crandall invested his loyalty. The choice was not between good and evil, but between winning and losing. Occasionally, Erb Crandall was compelled to question the wisdom of his allegiance, but never had it been so tested as it was now.

'Know what?' he said to the prone and bound congressman.

'Even that jizzbag Nixon wouldn't have pulled something like this.'

'Maybe he'd have been a better President if he had.' Dilbeck arched his silvery eyebrows. 'Ever think of that?'

Dispiritedly, Crandall put the screwdriver away.

'That's a good boy,' David Dilbeck said.

'Moldy's coming in an hour. If I killed you, there wouldn't be time to clean up the mess.'

Dilbeck studied the plastic razor from all angles, as if it were a rare gem. 'What's her name?'

'Erin,' Crandall said.

'That's beautiful. Irish, obviously. Erin what?'

'Never mind.'

'Come on, Erb. I won't try to find her, I promise.'

Crandall walked to the door. 'I need a drink. By the way, you look absolutely fucking ridiculous.'

The congressman paid no attention. 'Erb, one more small favor.'

'Let me guess. You want me to tie your other arm to the bed.'

Dilbeck cackled. 'You better not!'

'What then?'

He wiggled the pink razor in the air. 'Shave me, Erb. Shave me all over.'

Crandall glared loathsomely as he stalked from the room.

David Lane Dilbeck was the only son of Chuck 'The Straw' Dilbeck, once the foremost pumper of septic tanks in Dade, Broward and Monroe counties. In the early boom days of South Florida, before sewers were available, nearly every family relied on a septic tank buried in the backyard. The massively squat cylinders were vital components of the average household, and a frequent source of whispered anxiety. A septic-tank backup was the secret nightmare of every rural husband, as dreaded as a hurricane or a heart attack. Cleaning clogs was a vile business, and only a few hardy entrepreneurs had the will to compete.

The Dilbeck name was widely known in the solid-waste indus-try, and its prominence endured long after most South Florida septic tanks had rusted out. Young David never spent a day pumping sewage (he insisted it gave him a rash), but early on he recognized the value of having a notable father. In 1956, at the age of twenty-four, he boldly announced his candidacy for the Hialeah city council. Many of the town's citizens were lifelong customers of Chuck Dilbeck, and were glad to support his son's ambitions. Speedy response was critical in a septic-tank crisis, so it was important to stay on The Straw's good side. Hundreds of local septic-tank owners enthusiastically volunteered to help in young David's first political campaign, which he won handily.

Even by Florida standards, Hialeah was—and remains—egregiously corrupt. For council members, the easiest graft was the fixing of zoning cases in exchange for cash, real estate and other valuables. David Dilbeck was fortunate to be in Hialeah during the salad years, when there was still plenty of land to be carved up and paved. He spent four fruitful terms listening, learning and successfully avoiding indictment. He excelled at negotiating bribes, and carried the skill with him when he went to Tallahassee as a junior member of the state senate.

The atmosphere in Florida's capital was different, and the pace of life was faster. Corruption was a sociable affair, rich with tradition; the stakes were higher, as well. Because of occasional scrutiny by pesky news reporters, it was unwise for legislators to be seen drooling openly on the laps of private lobbyists. David Dilbeck worked hard to polish his rough edges. He learned to dress and talk and drink like a country gentleman. The senate was loaded with self-cultured rednecks, and most were unabashedly crooked. But the pecking order was rigid, and newcomers who ignored protocol paid dearly for the mistake. Dilbeck adapted smoothly, and was soon studying at the knees of some of Florida's most prolific thieves. He was rewarded in the usual ways.

It was in Tallahassee where he first learned that some women were attracted to politicians and would actually have sex with them. Dilbeck gained this pleasant knowledge episodically, and with each conquest he became more obsessed. He'd always anticipated that public service would make him wealthy, but he never dreamed that it would get him laid. For eight years, Dilbeck wallowed promiscuously and then—in fine Southern tradition—married a phosphate tycoon's gorgeous, semi-virginal daughter, who seldom consented to sleep with him. Pamela Randle Dilbeck was more interested in new fashions and social causes. Her husband encouraged her to travel often.

By the mid-1970s, Dilbeck's career had stalled in the halls of state government, where he had authored exactly two pieces of legislation. Neither could be described as landmark. One of the bills made it illegal for sporting-goods stores to sell machine-gun clips to minors on Sunday. The measure passed narrowly, despite staunch opposition from the National Rifle Association. Dilbeck's only other achievement was a joint resolution naming the Okaloosa dwarf salamander as Florida's official state amphibian; a special limited-edition license plate was made available to the motoring public for thirty-five dollars, plus tax. The salamander tag was designed by a vivacious art instructor from Florida State University, who was paid $40,000 from the general revenue fund, and who also happened to be screwing a certain senator on Thursday afternoons.

Dilbeck's big break was the passing, at age eighty-two, of Congressman Wade L. Sheets of South Miami. The venerable old Democrat had been mortally ill for the better part of three terms, and was rarely seen on Capitol Hill. Those close to Sheets sadly reported that his numerous health problems were complicated by fast-advancing senility; toward the end, he refused to wear pants and demanded to be addressed as 'Captain Lindbergh.' By the time Sheets died, a score of local politicians had positioned themselves to make a run for his seat in the House of Representatives. Among the hopefuls was David Lane Dilbeck.

At Sheets's funeral, Dilbeck delivered a eulogy that was uncharacteristically graceful, bringing fond laughter and tears from the huge assembly of mourners. The emotional speech was even more remarkable, considering that Dilbeck had met Wade Sheets only twice in his life and on both occasions the ailing congressman appeared not to be conscious. Dilbeck's remarkable panegyric (written by an eager young staffer named Crandall) borrowed heavily from old John F. Kennedy scripts, which had borrowed heavily from everybody else. No one in the hushed church picked up on the plagiarisms. The other candidates for the dead Sheets's seat also presented eulogies, but none were as moving or as memorable. The others knew they were sunk when all the TV stations led the news with a video snip of David Dilbeck in the pulpit. That single maudlin oratory ensured his selection as Wade Sheets's successor. Hands down, Dilbeck had given the best damn sound bite at the funeral.

He was thrilled to travel all the way to Washington; the farther one got from one's constituents, the harder it was for them to keep an eye on you. Again, Dilbeck modified his style of larceny to fit local custom. Outright cash-in-a-bag bribery was rare on Capitol Hill; special-interest groups were more subtle and sophisticated. A compliant congressman might receive four skybox seats to a Redskins game in exchange for a key vote. Such arrangements were virtually impossible to trace, much less prosecute. Another quick way to a politician's heart was by exorbitant campaign donations; in this manner, David Dilbeck was seduced by the powerful sugar lobby. Other industries found him equally receptive to their attentions. For two decades he was content to coast along as a well-lubricated lackey. He weathered several stiff Republican challenges and numerous negative news stories, but always managed to get re-elected. Those who owned Dilbeck's soul remained silent because they were satisfied with his favors. Consequently, he was never threatened by a scandal.

Until now.

'Good evening, deacon.'

'Hello, Malcolm.' The congressman shrank in Moldowsky's presence. Erb Crandall could be handled, but Moldy was something else. The man held no loyalties beyond the contractual.

He said, 'Where's the cowboy suit, Davey?'

'So Erb told you.' Dilbeck had ditched the boots and the cowboy hat for a maroon jogging suit. He stood casually in the den, sipping an iced tea.

'Erb is concerned,' Moldowsky said. 'Frankly, so am I.'

As always, Dilbeck found himself admiring Moldy's elegance. He wore a gorgeous dove-colored Italian suit with an indigo necktie. Tonight's cologne was particularly memorable; Moldowsky smelled like an orange grove.

'David,' he said, pacing, 'I hear talk of Vaseline.'

'I'm trying to cope—'

'—and laundry lint. Is this possible?' Moldy's fulsome pucker suggested that he was about to spit on the carpet.

'Malcolm, I wish I could explain. These are forces rising up in me, animal urges . . . and it's simply a matter of coping.'

'Sit down,' Moldy barked. No taller than a jockey, he hated staring up at the person he was berating. 'Sit, goddammit.'

Dilbeck did as he was ordered. Moldowsky moved slowly around the den, occasionally pausing to scowl at the photographs and laminated press clippings that hung on the wall. Without glancing at Dilbeck, he said, 'Erb found a lady's shoe in your desk. Where did that come from?'

'Chris bought it for me.'

'From this stripper?'

'Yes, Malcolm.' Dilbeck took a gulp of tea. 'These little things— they help me get by. It's harmless sport.'

Moldy felt a jolt of desperation. Insanity was one thing he could not fix, spin, twist or obscure. And David Dilbeck was plainly nuts.

'What did Erb do with the shoe?' the congressman demanded. 'He didn't throw it away, did he?'

Unbelievable, thought Moldowsky. He's like a damn junkie.

'My inclination,' Moldy said, 'is to haul your ass back to Washington and lock you in my apartment until the sugar vote. Unfortunately, we've got a campaign to worry about. It would be poor form for you to vanish.'

'I suppose,' Dilbeck said, absently.

'David, you do understand what's at stake?'

'Of course.'

'What if I brought in a woman, to be here just for you—for when you got in these moods. Maybe two women . . .' Dilbeck thanked Moldowsky for the offer but said it wouldn't solve the problem. 'Love has swept me away,' he said.

'Love?' Moldy laughed acerbically.

'It's frightening, Malcolm. Haven't you ever felt so passionately about someone?'

'Never,' Moldowsky said, truthfully. He stuck to call girls. They spoke his language.

'Don't worry, it'll be all right,' Dilbeck told him. 'I'll make it to the election just fine.' He rested his glass on the arm of the chair. 'Erb says Flickman wants a debate. I'm ready.'

'Ignore the little fuck,' advised Moldowsky.

Eloy Flickman was Dilbeck's hapless opponent in the congressional race. Under ordinary circumstances, a debate might've been productive, since ideologically Flickman stood slightly to the right of Attila the Hun. Among his campaign promises: televised executions of drug dealers, free sterilization of welfare mothers and a US military invasion of Cuba. Even the state GOP was leery, providing the shrill appliance salesman with only nominal support.

Dilbeck said, 'I could destroy him, Malcolm.'

'Why bother? He's destroying himself.'

'I worry about that Cuban thing. It's loony enough to catch on.'

'No debate!' Moldowsky said. He stopped pacing and planted himself in front of Dilbeck's face. 'Davey, we've got a more pressing matter—this goddamn stripper you're so taken with.'

The congressman bowed his head. 'What can I say? I'm no longer in control of my impulses.'

In Malcolm Moldowsky's grand vision of the future, David Dilbeck already was a goner. The day the sugar bill moved out of committee, he was finished. A stiff. Moldy and the Rojos would get him dumped from the chairmanship. Other congressmen would be elated to assume Dilbeck's special role; surely not all of them were so conspicuously deranged. In the meantime, Moldowsky had formed a plan. It was not without risk.

'I'll make you a deal,' he told Dilbeck. 'First you've got to promise: no more collecting her laundry lint and razors and her goddamn shoes. Is that understood?'

'All right. But what do I get?' The congressman sounded skeptical.

'A date.'

Dilbeck rose slowly, eyes widening. 'God, you're serious.'

'Her boss called me tonight. He said she might be up for it, if the price is nice.'

'When?' Dilbeck's voice jumped. 'You mean, right now?'

Incredible, Moldowsky thought. He's about to come in his pants. 'Tie a knot in it,' he told the congressman.

'A date, you said.'

'I'm working out the details.'

Dilbeck showed no curiosity about Moldy's relationship with the owner of the nudie bar. He held Moldowsky by the shoulders. 'If you can arrange this, honest to God—'

Moldy brushed Dilbeck's hands away. 'Then you'd behave until the election? This crazy shit'll stop?'

'On my father's grave, Malcolm.'

'Very funny.'

The Straw—a showman to the end—had been buried in a silk-lined septic tank. Moldowsky thought: His lunatic son should have so much class.

Dilbeck rubbed his damp palms on the knees of his jogging suit. 'Malcolm, are we talking about a *date* date, or the other kind?'

'Meaning, do you get to screw the girl? That's between you and her. Hell, I can't do everything—'

'You're right, you're right—'

'—I can't get it hard and put it in for you. Some things you've gotta do for yourself.'

The congressman was on a cloud. 'My friend, you've got no idea what this would mean to me.' He raised his glass to Moldowsky. 'Another coup, Malcolm.'

'Try miracle,' Moldy said. 'A fucking miracle.'

'Your specialty!'

'Oh yeah,' Moldowsky mumbled. Rep. David Dilbeck had no inkling of the drastic steps that had already been taken to save his worthless hide.

By the 1970s, the once-dazzling underwater reefs of Miami and Fort Lauderdale were dead, poisoned by raw sewage dumped into the ocean from the toilets of swank waterfront hotels. Submerged pipes carried the filth a few hundred yards offshore, so beachgoers wouldn't see the billowing brown spumes. It was assumed that even the most dogged tourist might think twice about snorkeling in a torrent of shit.

Decades of rancid outfall eventually killed the delicate corals and drove the glittering fish away. The reefs became gray escarpments, barren and manifestly untropical. Drift-boat captains and dive-shop operators complained of losing customers to the Florida Keys and the Bahamas, where the water was still clear enough to see one's hand in front of one's face. A few South Florida coastal cities took modest measures to reduce the offshore pollution, but the reefs failed to regenerate; once dead, coral tends to stay that way.

Biologists theorized that it was possible to attract fish without real coral, and thus was born the concept of 'artificial reefs', which was neither as exotic nor as high-tech as it sounded. Artificial reefs were created by sinking old ships; once nestled on the bottom, the ghost hulks attracted schools of baitfish which in turn attracted barracudas, jack crevalles, sharks, groupers and snappers. The drift boats and scuba captains were happy, as they no longer had to travel forty miles to find an actual fish to show their customers.

From a public-relations standpoint, the artificial reef program was a grand success—a sort of living junkyard of the deep. For once, human practices of waste disposal could be passed off legitimately as a benefit to the environment. Every few months another derelict freighter would be towed offshore and blown up with dynamite. Local TV stations swarmed the event, as it gave them an opportunity to use their expensive helicopters for something other than traffic reports. Predictably, the highly publicized demolitions became a regular South Florida tourist attraction, attended by hundreds of boaters who cheered wildly as the rusty vessels exploded and disappeared under the waves.

On the morning of October second, an eighty-six-foot Guatemalan banana boat called the *Princess Pia* was towed from Port Everglades to a pre-selected site off the Fort Lauderdale coast. The *Princess Pia* had been salvaged meticulously from the inside out: gone were the melted twin diesels, the corroded navigational gear, the radio electronics, the bilge pumps, the ropes, the hoses, the pipes, the fixtures, the hatch covers, the windshield, even the anchor—every item of value had been stripped from the boat. What remained essentially was a bare hull, degreased to minimize the purple slick that inevitably would form when the *Pia* went down.

The preparation of the ship had taken nearly a month, and was supervised by a Coast Guard inspector, a Broward County environmental engineer and an agent from the US Customs Service, which had seized the vessel fourteen months earlier. Once the Customs agent was satisfied that the *Princess Pia* had no more hidden cargo compartments and carried no more hidden hashish, he signed off on the project. The Coast Guard inspector and the county environmental expert walked through the old heap one last time on the evening of October first. Much later, both men would testify that, except for the explosives, the *Pia* was empty that night; specifically, the aft hold was bare.

A single guard, hired by the demolition company, was posted at the ship's mooring to prevent the dynamite from being stolen from the hull. The guard kept watch dutifully until approximately three in the morning, when a group of friendly stevedores invited him aboard a Japanese lumber barge to play cards and watch pornographic videotapes. In all, the *Princess Pia* was unguarded for at least three and possibly five hours, depending on whose testimony one believed.

This much was undisputed: At dawn the next day, two tugs hauled the *Pia* out to sea on a falling tide. Three Florida Marine

Patrol boats and a Coast Guard cruiser led the way, positioning themselves between the celebratory armada and the dynamite-laden freighter. The site for the new artificial reef was only three miles offshore, but it took a full hour for the *Princess Pia* to get there. The ocean was choppy, with northeast winds kicking to twenty knots; the tug captains kept a cautious pace.

By 9 a.m., the *Pia* was tethered in place, bow facing into the breeze. The police boats raced in widening arcs, clearing a buffer zone. At precisely 10 a.m., a radio signal detonated twin explosions in the ship's hull and stern. Tall blasts of dirty smoke rose from each end, and the ship listed dramatically starboard. She sunk in nine minutes flat. Boaters clapped and howled and sounded air horns.

Nobody suspected that there was a 1991 Lincoln Continental chained to the beams of the aft cargo hold. Nobody knew, until much later, what was in it.

22

The wrestling pit was in the back room, which had its own stage and a small horseshoe bar. Erin was dancing tables while Urbana Sprawl wrestled members of a bachelor party in ninety gallons of Green Giant niblets. The bachelor of honor was a young mortgage banker with many pallid, out-of-shape companions. They stood no chance against Urbana, who played rough and employed her formidable cleavage to maximum advantage. She specialized in pinning opponents without using her arms.

Erin remained baffled by the success of the nude wrestling exhibitions, which had become a red-hot fad in upscale strip joints. There was nothing erotic about grappling with a topless woman in a vat of cold vegetables, although the sodden realization came too late for most customers. By the time the bell rang, few were able to climb from the ring without assistance. The young bankers appeared especially whipped after their sessions with Urbana Sprawl.

Working table to table, Erin paid little attention to the comic slaughter in the wrestling pit. She was thinking about politics, which suddenly had touched her life in a dramatic way. Erin couldn't remember the last time she'd stood in a voting booth. Campaigns bored her. Every politician wore the same horseshit smile and gave the same horseshit speech. Erin was amazed that anyone would believe a word. She recalled being stricken by severe intestinal cramps while trying to watch the Bush–Dukakis debates.

Agent Cleary, bless his buttoned-down heart, used to scold her for being so cynical. On election day he'd lecture the office staff, telling them that democracy is futile without 'an informed and participatory electorate'. He'd say that people get exactly the kind of government they deserve, and those who won't vote have no grounds to complain. He was right, Erin thought. This is what I get for not paying attention. Thieves like David Lane Dilbeck couldn't get elected dogcatcher without the gross apathy of the masses.

And this is my punishment, Erin thought. I've got to date the asshole.

Al García had laid out the situation in his maddeningly laconic way. Erin, who was seldom shocked at the depth of human sordidness, found herself stunned by what she heard: Jerry Killian had been murdered over *sugar*. The lovestruck little nerd was killed because he'd threatened the career of a crooked congressman. According to García, the congressman's principal contribution to the governing of the republic was to direct jillions of dollars in aid to the sugar cartels. Poor Mr Peepers jeopardized that arrangement, so he was swatted as dead as a fly.

García said he wanted to catch the killers before they came looking for Erin. She said that was an excellent idea, and agreed to help in any way possible. Self-preservation was the main motivation; guilt was another. Erin couldn't forget that it was her sexy dancing that had fatally infatuated Jerry Killian.

Men were so helpless, she thought, so easily charmed. Monique Jr was right: they'd do anything for it. Anything.

That's what Erin's mother didn't understand about yuppie strip clubs; it wasn't the women who were being used and degraded, it was the men. Her mother thought these places were meat markets, and indeed they were, the meat being the customers. Experienced dancers always kept one eye on the front door, scouting for the next mark. If you knew your stuff, you could work a guy all night and get every last dollar out of his wallet. You didn't have to blow him or screw him or even act like you might. A girlish smile, a sisterly hug, a few minutes of private conversation—Urbana Sprawl said it was the easiest money in the world, if you could get past being naked.

Because men were so easily charmed. That was a fact.

But Erin was apprehensive about the congressman. He wouldn't be shy and polite like Killian and the other regulars.

No, Dilbeck would be pushy and crude and probably kinky. Al García warned her to be prepared.

'You think he's the one who took my razor?'

'Ask him,' García had said.

Fear wasn't the worst part for Erin; the worst part was sending Angela away. It was the sensible move, because certainly Angie couldn't stay in the new apartment—couldn't stay anywhere near her mother—until the danger was over. Erin felt terrible about it. She didn't like being alone again. She dreaded the silent afternoons, the dinners for one. Angie was safe, and at least Darrell Grant wouldn't find her. But still . . .

'Hey, babes.'

A hand clamped on Erin's leg. She snapped back to reality— Urbana rolling in the creamed corn, Aerosmith blaring on the speakers, her own bra and G-string in a lacey mound between the Michelob bottles at her feet. Three young bankers sat at the table, trying to appear cool and unimpressed. The drunkest of them kept snapping Erin's garter, where the cash tips were folded. She asked him to stop but he didn't. She brushed his hand off her leg and spun a circle on the table, making evasion part of the dance; when she stopped spinning, the banker's hand returned, crawling like a mantis up her thigh. Erin looked across the room for Shad, but couldn't see him.

'That's enough,' she told the banker.

The next thing she felt was his tongue. He was licking vertically from ankle to knee, long, sloppy Popsicle licks.

Erin snatched the man's hair and lifted his head. 'You behave,' she said sharply.

But he wouldn't.

That morning, a small item had appeared on page 6-D of the Fort Lauderdale *Sun Sentinel*, under the headline: BAR TO PROBE MISS-ING LAWYER. The four-paragraph story said the Florida Bar was investigating whether a lawyer named Mordecai had looted his client trust account and fled the country. The article said the man had not been seen for several days, and was believed to have flown to the Bahamas with an unnamed female companion.

Sgt Al García clipped the story and put it with his homicide paperwork in his briefcase. Then he drove to a street corner in Liberty City, where two crack dealers had done the planet a tremendous favor by killing each other in a pre-dawn shootout. Witnesses were as scarce as mourners, but García took out his notebook and went to work.

Another man who clipped the *Sun Sentinel* item was Erb Crandall, sitting in the lobby of the Sunshine Fidelity Savings Bank on Galt Ocean Mile. Crandall was about to commit a minor crime for major stakes. He was about to forge a false name on a vault-room ledger, and use a stolen key to open a stranger's safe-deposit box. Crandall was searching for a Kodak color slide that Malcolm Moldowsky urgently sought to possess. The slide was the original photograph of Congressman David Lane Dilbeck assaulting Paul Guber with a champagne bottle on the stage of the Eager Beaver lounge. Erb Crandall's plan to obtain the incriminating picture began smoothly in the vault room. He signed a well-practiced version of Mordecai's name to the ledger, and handed the key to the clerk. The clerk pulled the steel box from the wall and unlocked it. He led Erb Crandall to a windowless cubicle and left him alone.

When Crandall opened the lid, he found no Kodak slide. Mordecai's box had been cleaned out. In the bottom, face up, lay only a business card:

> SGT ALBERTO GARCÍA
> Metropolitan Dade County Police
> Homicide Division (305) 471–1900

Erb Crandall's fingers were shaking as he carried the safe-deposit box to the clerk's desk. It was all he could do not to run from the bank.

That evening, over dinner, Sgt Al García took out the news clipping and read it again. He was impressed that anyone would go to the trouble of framing a lawyer who most likely was dead. The trust account ruse was very nifty.

Andy asked: 'Al, did you catch 'em yet? The guys who killed that man in the river?'

'Not yet,' García said. The boy talked about the floater all the time; it was the highlight of the family vacation.

'Any suspects?'

'No, Andy. It's a tough one.'

Donna said: 'That's enough, both of you. Remember our rule.'

The rule was: no talk of dead bodies at supper. Al's work was to be discussed only after the dishes were cleared.

'Sorry Mom,' Andy said.

Lynne, the little girl, asked if they could go to Sea World next summer. She wanted to see some turtles and sharks. Andy said he'd rather go back to Montana and hunt for clues.

Donna chased the children from the table and brought her husband a pot of coffee. He said, 'Look what I've gotten you all into.'

'It's all right. She seems like a nice person.'

'Of course she's a nice person. Next question: How come she's working at a nudie bar? Right?'

Donna shrugged. 'It's no great mystery. Have a slice of pie.'

García was intrigued. 'Could you do that—take off your clothes in front of all those drunken strangers?'

'If I had to,' Donna said. 'For the kids.'

'Jesus, there's only about a million other jobs. The girl's not stupid. She can type seventy words a minute.'

'You said she owes her lawyer.'

'Yeah,' García said. 'Who doesn't?'

'So maybe she wants a nest egg. Where's the crime in that?'

'You're right, sweetheart.'

'I like her.'

'Me, too,' he said. 'But it's the job that's got her into so much damn trouble.'

'No, honey, it's the men.' Donna cut a piece of apple pie and put on a plate. 'So what does she look like, Al?'

'You saw her.' He teased with a long pause. 'Oh, you mean with her clothes off? Tell you the truth, I didn't notice.'

Donna smiled. 'You are a pitiful liar. Eat your dessert.'

The phone rang. Donna didn't bother to get up. Only cops

called at dinner time. García went in the kitchen to take it. He looked grim when he came back.

'That was the Broward sheriff's office,' he said.

'They still don't want the case?'

'I knew they wouldn't.' García sat down heavily. 'Hell, I can't even get that cowpoke coroner to say Killian's death was a homicide. Meanwhile I got no weapons, no witnesses and no suspects.' He took a large bite of pie. 'I don't blame BSO for taking a pass.' Another huge bite. 'Least they were decent about it. I mean, they didn't laugh too hard.'

Donna said, 'Slow down. You'll choke to death.'

'It's good pie.'

'Not *that* good. Now tell me what else is wrong.'

'I end up on a speaker phone with two brain-dead detectives. See, the girl's ex was a CI for Broward Robbery.' García didn't need to translate police jargon for Donna. She'd learned plenty from her first husband, the dope dealer.

'The ex is still an informant?'

García, chewing mechanically: 'Nope, they cut him loose after he got busted for grand theft up the coast.'

Donna shook her head. 'I don't get it. If the ex got arrested, isn't that good news for Erin?'

'Oh, great news,' García said, wiping his mouth, 'if they'd managed to keep the bastard in jail.'

'You're kidding.'

'Nope, he escaped. From a county hospital! Stole a wheelchair and rolled out the fucking door!'

Donna told her husband to keep his voice down. 'We've got company,' she reminded him. 'Where's your cigar?'

'Wait, there's more.' García slashed the air with both hands. 'The girl's ex-husband—the kid's father—he's not only mean, he's not only violent, he's got a frigging drug problem. Isn't that a hoot!'

Andy dashed into the dining room and asked what Al was hollering about.

'Work,' Donna said. 'What else.'

Andy clambered up on García's lap. 'Maybe you need another vacation.'

Donna turned away, smothering a laugh. 'So everybody's a smart-ass,' García said, tickling the boy until he howled.

Shad was at the bar in the main lounge. He was distracted by a management problem.

Orly had connived to hire Lorelei, the fabulous python princess, away from the Ling brothers. Tonight was to be her first stage performance at the Tickled Pink, but she'd arrived in puffy-eyed hysterics. Orly could not decipher the problem, and delivered the distraught dancer to Shad, who was on break, reading a large-type edition of *The Plague* by Albert Camus. The book made Shad feel slightly better about living in South Florida.

He was interrupted by Lorelei's convulsive sobs. Her snake was missing, and she suspected the vengeful Lings of abduction. When Orly was informed, he ordered Shad to find another snake for his new star. Shad noted there were no all-night reptile stores in the neighborhood. Unfortunately, Lorelei refused to dance without Bubba, which is what she called her nine-foot Burmese python.

'She says they're a team,' Shad reported. 'She says the snake is trained.'

Orly crumpled an empty can of Dr Pepper and lobbed it grenade-style behind the bar. 'First, there's no such thing as a trained snake, OK? And Item B, did you see the fucking marquee? LORELEI in great big letters—I got customers drove all the way from Miami. Tell her she's got ten minutes to get her boobs on stage.'

Shad glanced toward the hallway, where the weeping python princess now huddled in grief. 'She'll need more than ten minutes,' he said. 'She looks like hell.'

Orly cursed and hacked and massaged his nostrils. 'You don't know anyone with a goddamn snake?'

'Not a big snake,' Shad said. 'I know some guys who breed diamondbacks.'

'Sweet Christ Almighty.'

'They're not much good for dancing.'

'OK,' said Orly. 'Here's what you do. Go see those fucking Lings. Find out how much they want for the girl's python.'

'Bubba is the name.'

'Whatever. Offer five hundred.'

Shad said the Lings likely would tell him to fuck off and die. 'They hate your guts,' he told Orly.

'No, this is business. Now hurry it up.'

Shad put the book by Camus behind the bar, under the popcorn platters. Then he drove up to the Flesh Farm, where the Ling brothers kept him waiting an hour—a nervy move. Shad passed the time drinking Virgin Marys and surveying the dance talent in case Orly demanded a scouting report. Shad's ominous bald presence quickly thinned the audience and further irritated the Lings. Shad finally got his meeting, but the brothers reacted to the python proposition more biliously than anticipated.

He returned to find the Tickled Pink in an uproar. Erin seemed to be in the thick of it. Paramedics were fitting a neck brace on a pale and dazed young man. The victim was encircled by a dozen equally wan companions with corn kernels stuck in their hair. From a distance it looked as if they'd been bombed by sparrows. The men shouted high-pitched questions at the paramedics, over the jack-hammer music. As a protective measure, Urbana Sprawl had stationed her insurmountable breasts between Erin and Orly, who was red-faced and raving.

'Damn,' said Shad, and waded into the chaos.

Later, in the office, Orly blustered about liability and lawsuits and his liquor license.

'You aren't listening,' Erin said. 'The man touched me.'

Urbana Sprawl, showered and fully dressed, spoke out in support of her friend: 'I saw the whole thing, Mr Orly. He got what he deserved.'

Orly snorted. 'A sprained neck. Is that what he deserved? A trip to the hospital, for copping a feel!'

'He touched me,' Erin said, 'between my legs.'

'Aw, he was drunk.'

Erin turned to Urbana. 'This is why I hate table dances.'

Orly said, 'You could've crippled the guy, kickin' him in the head like that.'

'And what's she supposed to do?' Urbana said. 'Give him a nice friendly finger fuck?'

Orly flinched, turning his head. 'Christ, that's enough. No more a that talk.'

'So it's OK for Shad to beat a customer's ass, but not us. Is that the deal?'

'I said, that's enough.'

'Urbana's right,' Erin said. 'It's not fair.'

'Screw fair,' said Orly, puffing his cheeks. 'Shad's job is keeping the peace. Your job is to dance. That's the bottom line.'

Standing by the office door, Shad reluctantly abandoned his silence. 'I got sent up the street,' he said. 'Otherwise it wouldn't have happened.'

Orly gave a corrosive laugh. 'Wonderful. Now it's all my fault. Well, fuck the whole bunch a you.'

Urbana was livid. She leaned her double-wide bosom across his desk and shook a Day-Glo fingernail in his face. 'Nobody touches me 'less I wanna be touched, especially down there. I don't care who it is or how shitfaced they are or how much money they got, I won't stand for it. That little shit's lucky to get out with a sprained neck, because if it was me, I'd rip his damn balls off with my bare hands, just like this—'

Orly gaped as Urbana simulated her technique, snatching imaginary testicles off an imaginary oaf.

'—and don't think I can't!'

Then she was gone. Nobody moved for several moments.

Orly said: 'That girl gives big tits a bad name.'

Erin stood up. 'Well, I'm through for the night.'

'Now wait a second—'

'No. I'm going to visit my daughter.'

After Erin left, Shad came to her defense. He told Orly that Erin had many good reasons to be jumpy—the custody case, the burglary of the apartment, and now a congressman in hot pursuit. 'It's a bad time for her right now. That's how come she blew up tonight.'

Orly wiped his neck with a soiled handkerchief. 'You and me are the only ones in this joint that don't get PMS, and sometimes I'm not too sure about you.'

'It's the music,' Shad said. 'It makes my head hurt.'

'Talk to Kevin.'

'Kevin says talk to you.'

Orly said, 'I don't know rap from reggae. You know my secret? I don't even listen.' He twisted an invisible knob at his right earlobe. 'Just turn it off. I don't hear a damn thing.' He asked how it went with the Lings.

'Lousy,' Shad said.

'They don't have the girl's snake?'

'Yeah, they got it. They just won't ransom it.'

Orly raised his palms. 'Why the fuck not? Business is business.'

'Mainly because they hate your guts.'

'Because of me hiring Lorelei?'

'Because of everything,' Shad replied.

'So the answer is no. It took you two damn hours to get a simple N-O from those jerkoff Japs. Meanwhile I got a crazed stripper doing a Chuck Norris routine on my customers—'

'The answer wasn't only no,' Shad said. 'It was this, too.' He placed an oblong package on Orly's desk. 'The Ling brothers wanted you to have it.'

Orly eyed the crude parcel wrapped in Flesh Farm cocktail napkins and bound with masking tape. 'What the hell is it?' he asked Shad.

'About twelve inches of dead Bubba.'

Orly yelped and pushed away from the desk, away from the unopened package. 'Did I tell you they were animals? Did I? Jesus, what else did they say, those goddamn Lings?'

'They said there's plenty more where that came from.'

23

On the morning of October third, under a hard blue sky, Perry Crispin and Willa Oakley Crispin went down to the beach.

The attractive young couple spread out towels from their suite at the Breakers Hotel, and lay side by side in the bleached sand. They took turns smearing number 29 sunblock all over each other: Perry spelled out 'I Luv You!!!' on his wife's tummy. Willa drew an oily heart on the small of her husband's prodigiously freckled back.

A strong breeze put a salty tang in the air, and made the waves bite raggedly against the shore. The Crispins planned a brief swim later, when they were sweaty. They wore matching black Ray-Bans and pink terrycloth tennis visors. They smiled and whispered and touched each other frequently, as is the habit of newlyweds. Willa and Perry were from large, wealthy families in Connecticut, so the wedding had been suitably extravagant. Palm Beach was the first leg of a four-week honeymoon that would take them to Freeport, St Bart's and finally Cozumel. The sun was high and bright, and the Crispins glistened on their towels. They were unabashedly romantic, totally relaxed and not at all apprehensive about their future together. Substantial trust funds awaited both of them.

By noon, Willa's adorable nose had turned pink. Perry noted it with alarm; his father was a limited partner in four dermatology clinics, and skin cancer had been a recurrent topic at family gatherings. From an early age, Perry showed an eagle eye for discolored moles and suspicious lesions. He told his bride that it was time to get out of the UV rays.

'I came to get a tan,' she protested.

'Darling, we've got four whole weeks.'

As they crossed the beach toward the hotel, the Crispins were followed by a slender blond man in dirty jeans and cowboy boots. Perry and Willa didn't notice the stranger—they were engrossed in discussing the poor quality of the sunblock ointment, and the possibility of trying zinc oxide instead, at least on their noses.

The man behind them said, 'Scuze me, folks.'

Perry and Willa turned. The man wasn't dressed for Palm Beach. His blue eyes were bloodshot and jumpy. His hair was matted on one side, as if slept on.

'You got a car?' he said.

Willa looked frightened. Perry sized up the stranger and took a small step forward. The man displayed a rusty steak knife and said, 'Don't make me ask twice.'

The Crispins led Darrell Grant to their rental car, a candy-apple Thunderbird. Darrell Grant said he approved. He took the keys from Perry and ordered the couple to hop in the backseat.

'Why?' Willa asked.

'Till we get across the bridge,' Darrell said.

The Intracoastal Waterway separated the town of Palm Beach from West Palm Beach. Two more disparate worlds would be hard to find; West Palm was for normal humans, Palm Beach for the eccentric rich. The cops on the island were notorious rousters of unwanted visitors—blacks, Hispanics, and anyone not wearing Polo. If you worked in one of the mansions, fine. Otherwise, get your ass over the bridge. Darrell Grant figured he might need the Crispins to talk him out of a Palm Beach traffic stop.

'You got a purse?' he asked Willa.

The newlyweds squeezed each other's hands. Perry was relieved to see that Willa had left her two-carat diamond wedding band in the hotel room. He hoped she'd done the same with the traveler's checks.

'Halloo?' Darrell Grant said.

'Yes, I've got my purse.'

'Thatta girl.'

'All I carry is forty dollars.'

Darrell snorted. 'How about you, sport?'

'Credit cards is all I've got,' Perry said.

'Figures.' Darrell barreled through a red light on Worth Avenue. He liked the way the T-bird handled. 'All right, honey, gimme the cash. And your medicines, too.'

Willa looked confounded. Her husband motioned gravely at her purse. She took out two twenties and nervously extended them over the headrest, as if feeding a bear at the zoo.

'I don't have any pills,' she told Darrell Grant. 'Except my birth control.'

'That'll do fine.' He grabbed the money with his steering hand. The other hand held the steak knife, running the stained blade through the stubble on his jawline. From the backseat, Willa said: 'I'm sorry but you can't take my pills.'

'Oh yeah?' Darrell was heartily amused.

'You'll get sick,' said Willa. 'They're not made for men.'

'Sick?'

'They're made of hormones!'

'No shit,' Darrell Grant said. 'So, like, I might grow knockers. Is that what you mean? Or maybe even a love muffin.'

'No, I didn't—'

'Be a good girl and hand over the fucking pills.' Darrell's arm came down and speared the rusty knife into the white upholstery. He ripped a long sibilant gash in the stiff vinyl.

Perry Crispin said: 'Willa, give the man what he wants.'

'No.'

'My God,' said her husband. 'Don't be foolish.'

'Fine, Perry. And what're we supposed to do for the next four weeks—hold hands?' Willa protected the purse with both arms. 'Our pharmacy is in Westport, remember?'

Perry Crispin said: 'I'm not believing this.'

'What—you want me to get pregnant?'

In the front seat, Darrell Grant was humming the theme from *The Sound of Music*, which was his sister Rita's favorite movie of all time. Or maybe that was *Mary Poppins*, he always got the two mixed up. 'Which is the one with Dick Van Dyke?' he asked. 'Did I get it right?'

The Crispins had no clue what he was talking about. A dope

fiend, jabbering. Willa leaned forward to plead her case. 'Please, don't take the birth-control pills. It's our honeymoon.'

Ahead was one of the drawbridges leading to West Palm. Finally, thought Darrell, I can dump these brainless puppies. He goosed the accelerator.

'My sister's a nurse,' Willa was saying. 'These pills are very strong. They *will* make you sick.'

Ahead, the crossing gates swung down and a tinny bell rang. The bridge began to rise. Darrell Grant cursed vehemently and hit the brakes.

Perry Crispin's feeble voice: 'It's just a sailboat going through. It shouldn't take long.'

Darrell Grant whirled in the driver's seat. He thrust a calloused palm at Willa and said: 'The pills.'

She shook her head adamantly. Her husband was dumbstruck.

Darrell said, 'Listen, you silly cunt. I ain't gonna eat the damn things, I'm gonna sell 'em. You understand? I'm gonna go across this bridge and scam me some stoners who don't know birth control from LSD. Get it?'

Tears appeared in Willa's eyes. She blinked down-heartedly at her husband. 'Perry, he called me a cunt.'

Perry Crispin felt horrible. He felt he should attack the crazed dope fiend in defense of his wife's honor. On the other hand, he was crippled with terror. He expected his bladder to fail at any second.

'Don't you worry,' he told Willa. 'We'll get more pills.'

'How? My prescription is in Westport.' Despair fogged her voice.

'FedEx, darling. Now do as the man says.' The drawbridge began to go down, one side at a time. Darrell Grant announced that he would count to five, then hack out Willa's heart and make Perry eat it on a hoagie for lunch. Willa immediately opened the purse and gave the madman her pills. Darrell drove across the bridge and parked at a Mini-Mart. He took Perry Crispin's Ray-Bans and also the hot pink tennis visor. Then he told the couple to get their sorry butts out of the car.

The pavement scorched the soles of the Crispins' bare feet, and they hopped like palsied flamingos to a triangular patch of shade. Darrell Grant adjusted the side mirror of the Thunderbird so he could admire the fit of his new sunglasses. The Crispins watched morosely, waiting for the criminal to drive away. Willa remained very angry. 'Thank you very much,' she called out acidly, 'for ruining our honeymoon.'

Darrell Grant scowled and revved the engine. 'You people ever heard of rubbers? It's a new thing, sport. Fits right on your dick.'

'Perry won't use them.' Willa's tone was reproachful. Perry Crispin turned away.

'Figures,' Darrell said. He waved tootle-oo with the steak knife before speeding off. It took two hours to find a junkie bent enough to buy birth-control pills and believe they were Belgian Dilaudids. Darrell only got thirty bucks from the scam but, added to Willa Crispin's forty, it was enough to gas up the T-bird and score some reds. He had a good buzz on by the time he made the interstate, which carried him south in blazing pursuit of his precious little girl and her worthless mother.

The Rojos were in Santo Domingo, so Malcolm Moldowsky was given use of the yacht. Erb Crandall dropped off the congressman at nine sharp, and went directly to a dockside bar to drink alone. He had already delivered the bad news about the lawyer's safe-deposit box. Moldy had taken the homicide detective's card delicately, like a butterfly, between two fingers. 'This changes things,' he'd said, turning the card back and forth, as if marveling at a hologram. 'I guess it's time for Plan B.' Erb Crandall didn't ask for an explanation. The time had come to forsake party loyalty and begin thinking of one's own situation, and of covering one's own ass. Crandall was grateful that Moldy didn't ask him to stay for the meeting on the yacht.

When David Dilbeck stepped into the master stateroom, the first thing he saw was The Photograph from the Eager Beaver. Moldowsky had tacked it on the wall, over the wet bar.

'A reminder,' he said, pouring Dilbeck a drink.

The congressman's eyes riveted on Erin's face. 'Isn't she something,' he said, breathlessly.

Moldy said, 'Don't look at her, David. Look at yourself.'

'It was a bad night.'

'You don't say.' He shoved a tumbler into Dilbeck's gut. 'Sit down and have a drink.'

The congressman obeyed. 'Ginger ale? That's precious, Malcolm.'

Moldowsky climbed into a canvas director's chair. He wore rubber-soled deck shoes, pressed white slacks and a navy pull-over. It was one of the few times Dilbeck had seen him in casual clothes.

'I want you sober,' Moldy began. 'I want you to remember every goddamn word I say. Whatever arrangement you and this girl reach, that's fine. But you're to talk to her, David. There are certain things we need to know.'

'Good Lord, she's not a spy. She's only a stripper—'

'Bring her here tomorrow night,' Moldowsky said. 'It'll be safe.'

'Safe from what?'

'From blackmailers, David.' Moldy pointed up at the photograph. Again Dilbeck's gaze settled on Erin, shielding herself from the bottle attack.

'What if she doesn't like me?' Dilbeck asked.

Moldowsky cracked an ice cube in his molars. 'She'll love you, trust me. Two thousand dollars buys serious love.'

'And what do I get for that?'

'Two hours of dancing.'

'That's all?'

'It's a start.'

David Dilbeck sipped at the ginger ale, which tasted flat. 'I want sexy music, champagne, candles, the whole nine yards—'

Moldy said it was all arranged. He went through a series of questions that Dilbeck was to ask the nude dancer. Dilbeck said no way, it would spoil the mood.

'Come on,' said Moldowsky. 'You're the slickest sonofabitch I ever saw. Go easy. Be cool.'

The congressman was reluctant. 'Malcolm, I do not wish to

scare her off. This may be my only shot.' Once more his eyes wandered to the grainy photograph on the wall. 'Fantastic,' he whispered, to no one.

Moldy shot to his feet and tore the picture down. He charged up to David Dilbeck's chair and confronted him, nose to chin. 'You *will* do this,' he growled at the congressman. 'There are things we need to know. It's *essential*, David'—spraying the word *essential*—'considering what's happened the last month.'

Moldowsky's breath smelled like bourbon and peppermint mouthwash. The mixture clashed fiercely with his cologne. Dilbeck turned away and huffed for fresh air. The yacht rocked gently on the wake of a passing speedboat.

'You will do this,' Moldy repeated in the congressman's ear.

'But I don't understand—'

Moldowsky whirled away. He snatched his glass of bourbon off the bar and took a slug. He noticed a small rectangular outline in the fabric of his pocket—the homicide detective's card, taken from the lawyer's safe-deposit box. Moldy said, 'People are trying to harm you, David. We need to be sure she's not one of them.'

Dilbeck shook his head. 'You're completely paranoid.'

'Humor me.'

'But she's just a stripper.'

Malcolm Moldowsky grabbed Dilbeck's shirt. 'Fannie Fox,' he said, 'was ' "just a stripper." Donna Rice was just a model-slash-actress. Elizabeth Ray was just a secretary who couldn't type. Gennifer Flowers was just a country singer. Don't you get it? Ask Chuck Robb. Or that horny idiot Hart. Teddy Kennedy, for pity's sake. They'll all tell you the same: in politics, stealing is trouble but pussy is lethal.'

Moldy released his grip. Exhausted, he wilted on a bar stool. 'Those who ignore history,' he said, 'are doomed to get their nuts cut.'

David Dilbeck said, 'All right. I'll talk to the girl.'

'Thank you.'

'I'm smarter than those others.'

Moldowsky could scarcely contain himself.

'I'm also stronger,' Dilbeck added.

'Yeah,' said Moldy. 'A rock, that's what you are. A regular Rock of Gibraltar.'

The congressman sidled to the bar and disposed of the ginger ale. Keeping his back to Moldowsky, he poured himself a very sturdy rum-and-Coke. 'Malcolm,' the congressman said, 'is it possible she would let me shave her?'

Moldowsky fell to his knees and gagged spectacularly on the Rojos' carpet.

Al García heard music in Erin's apartment. He knocked loudly and rang the bell. When he got no answer, he took out the key she had given him and let himself in. On the bed Erin lay motionless, a pillow wrapped like a helmet around her head. She wore pink panties and a matching bra, and appeared to be breathing just fine. Half a pitcher of martinis perspired on the nightstand, and the stereo was cranked up full blast. García turned it down.

Erin's voice, muffled: 'What d'you think you're doing?'

The detective sat on the edge of the bed. 'We need to talk.'

'Orly won't let me dance to Jackson Browne any more.'

'How come?'

'Or Van Morrison. He says it's too slow. He says I'm pissing off the girls on the tables.'

'Erin, how you doin' on gin?'

'That's the first time you called me Erin.' Her face peeked out of the pillow. 'By the way, I want my gun back.'

'It's in the dresser,' García said.

'Loaded?'

'Yes, ma'am.'

'Good. What time is it?'

'Noon.' García tried to cover her with a sheet. Erin kicked it off and gave a gravelly laugh.

'Don't tell me you're embarrassed,' she said.

The detective reddened. Erin reminded him that he'd seen her nude several times at the club.

'That's different,' he said.

'Oh?' Erin unsnapped her bra and lobbed it at him. It landed on his right shoulder. Then she squirmed out of her panties and tossed them on the floor. 'There you are,' she said, spreading her arms.

The detective stared at his shoes. 'Let me take a wild guess here. You're upset about meeting the congressman.'

'Upset is a good word for it. Nervous, disgusted, terrified, and pretty much all alone. The only thing in the world I care about, I can't have—'

'Angela's doing great,' Al García said. 'You'll be together soon.' He took the bra off his shoulder and folded it on the bed.

Erin enfolded herself listlessly in the bedsheets. She looked too worn for her age. 'Some guy grabbed me last night.'

'Christ.'

'I came unglued. Nothing in particular.'

'Did you kill him?'

'Nah.'

'So what's the big deal?' The detective pulled a cigar from his shirt. He put it in his mouth but didn't light it.

Erin stared at the ceiling. 'I had a dream about the other man in that picture, the one who's hugging me on his knees. I had a dream they killed him, too, just like Mr Peepers.'

García told her not to worry. 'His name is Paul Guber and he's safe and sound. He went to New York for a few weeks.'

'At your suggestion?' Erin poked him playfully with a toe.

'His firm's got an office on Wall Street. It seemed like a good time for a visit.'

She said, 'You take care of everyone, don't you?'

The detective shook his head unhappily. He told Erin about Darrell Grant's ludicrous escape from the Martin County authorities. She received the news more passively than he expected; then again, she'd had the benefit of several martinis.

'Darrell,' she declared, 'is off the fucking rails.'

'Is he crazy enough to show up at the club?'

'Possibly.' Erin rolled on her belly. 'I can sure pick 'em, huh?'

García left the room to make a phone call. When he returned, Erin had put on a white T-shirt and jeans. She stood at the mirror, brushing her hair. The martini pitcher was empty.

'I poured it out,' she said. shooting him a sharp look. 'I'm not as bombed as you think.'

They went to a Friday's and ordered cheeseburgers. García had a beer. Erin drank coffee. They were conducting a perfectly amiable conversation until the detective asked if she had a boyfriend.

She said, 'Shit, don't do this.'

'What?'

'You know what.'

García chewed thoughtfully. 'My interest is purely professional. I need to cover all the angles.'

'You're not trying to ask me out?'

'Nope.' He raised his right hand, cheeseburger and all. 'I swear to God.'

'You sure?'

'For Christ's sake, Erin, I took you to meet my wife.'

She apologized, sheepishly. She felt like the queen bitch of all time. 'It's not that I've got such a red-hot opinion of myself—'

'I understand,' García said, 'believe me.'

'It's the damn job.' She was so accustomed to being propositioned that she was automatically suspicious of any man who didn't try. It made for a relentlessly cynical view of the opposite sex. Having Darrell Grant in one's past contributed to Erin's attitude.

She said, 'The answer is no, there's no boyfriend. But you knew that, right?'

'Just a hunch.'

'At the end of the night, I don't have much energy left for men. Or much interest, for that matter.'

'Occupational hazard,' said García, attacking a pile of french fries. 'Is there any man you trust completely?'

'Don't laugh,' Erin said. 'I trust Shad.'

Al García grinned. 'Me, too.'

After lunch, he drove out to the ocean. Erin said that she

wanted to stand in the sunshine and bleach out the gin. The detective parked at Bahia Mar, and they walked across the overpass to the beach. García wished he'd taken off his coat and tie; people were giving him odd looks.

Erin walked down far enough to get her toes wet. The detective stopped a few feet from the waves. He lit the cigar and blew the smoke over his right shoulder, safely downwind from Erin.

She said, 'You think I'm a whore?'

'Don't be ridiculous.'

Erin stepped back from the water. 'But you wouldn't want your daughter doing what I do.'

'My daughter,' said García, 'is not leaving the house until she's thirty years old.'

Erin smiled. 'Angie is fascinated by Mommy's costumes.'

The detective said, 'The time comes, she'll understand.'

Erin stretched. The sun felt glorious on her face and arms. She said, 'I tell myself it's just dancing.'

'And I tell myself I'm an ace crime fighter. So what?'

Erin had an urge to jump in the ocean. She got a running start and dove in. She swam fifty yards and stopped. Floating on her back, she blinked the salty sting from her eyes. The swells lifted the T-shirt, billowing around her breasts. Seagulls kited above the surf and cawed raucously. Silver mullet jumped and skittered toward deeper water. She heard the whoosh of a windsurfer and a lewd whistle from the teenager riding the board. Erin serenely flipped him the finger.

When she waded from the water, Al García offered his coat. Erin thought: How can you not like this guy? She said, 'I guess you don't go for the wet look.'

'Please.' He cloaked the jacket around her shoulders. 'Be kind to a shy old fart.'

In the parking lot, García searched the Caprice for a clean towel. Erin spotted the Igloo cooler and said she hoped there was a cold six-pack inside. The detective said the ice chest was for human body parts, not refreshments.

'Yum,' said Erin. She picked up a clear bag of blue hospital masks. 'I bet you looky snazzy in one of these.'

García said they came in handy. He tossed her a striped beach towel that belonged to Donna.

Erin said, 'I'll ask you what you've been dying to ask me: How in the world can you do it?'

'Do what?'

'Your job. Dead bodies day after day—I couldn't take it.'

The detective said, 'Hey, it's a growth industry. The state could sell fucking bonds.'

On the drive home, they talked about Erin's date with the congressman. She had plenty of questions. Would he be alone? How long did she need to stay? What should she do if he went crazy again? Some of García's answers were more comforting than others.

The detective's car phone beeped. He spoke for less than a minute and hung up, frowning.

Erin said, 'Duty calls.'

'Trunk job,' García muttered. 'Miami International.'

'That's ninety minutes away.'

'No hurry. The guy's been there since Labor Day.' He said the stink wasn't so bad if you dabbed Old Spice inside your hospital mask, before popping the trunk. To Erin, it was the stuff of nightmares.

Back at the apartment, she waited by the front door while Al García checked for signs of intruders. He came back out and told her it was safe. He didn't tell her that he'd emptied her bottle of Beefeater's down the bathtub drain.

At the door, the detective told her to think some more about meeting David Dilbeck alone. If she wanted to change her mind, he'd understand. It was a risky deal.

'I won't change my mind,' she said.

'Then be ready for the worst. For two grand, he'll want more than a peek.'

'Oh, he'll definitely get more than a peek,' Erin said. 'Just one thing: Can I bring my own music?'

Al García said sure, absolutely.

24

Orly asked Shad where he got the scorpion. Shad said he bought it off a guy at Dania jai-alai.

'Dead or alive?'

'Alive,' Shad said.

Orly leaned in for a closer look. 'Is it sick or what?'

Shad said, 'No, I drowned it.'

'How?'

'Johnnie Walker.'

Orly laughed, sucking air through his teeth. 'Red or black?'

'Red,' Shad said. He used his tweezers to lift the dead scorpion from the jar.

'Big fucker,' Orly observed. 'So the idea is to make it look like the company's fault?'

'Sure.' Shad placed the dead scorpion in an eight-ounce carton of cottage cheese. He spooned curds over the soggy corpse except for the stinger, which he purposely left exposed.

Orly said, 'And they'll pay off? The company, I mean.'

'Wouldn't you?' Shad placed the lid on the container and pressed firmly on the edges. He hadn't yet decided whether to sue the cottage-cheese manufacturer or the national supermarket chain that carried the product.

'The guy who sold you the scorpion, is he the same one that sold you the snake?'

'No,' Shad said.

'Because Lorelei ain't thrilled with the snake.'

'I heard.'

On short notice, Shad had located a half-blind boa constrictor for two hundred bucks. The seven-foot reptile was mean, restless and extremely difficult to handle on the dance floor. Even with its mouth taped, the boa intimidated Lorelei.

'She's scared to hang it around her neck,' Orly said.

'So tell her don't hang it on her neck.'

'Then where? She's buck naked, man.'

Shad gave a shrug. 'You wanted a new snake. I got one.'

'It peed on her,' said Orly.

'I heard.'

'Now she's threatening to quit on me. Go back to the Flesh Farm.'

Shad said, 'What the hell, Mr Orly. Snakes pee.' It felt like a chainsaw was cropping the top of his skull. He placed the cottage cheese in the refrigerator and wrote a note in block letters warning the dancers not to touch it. Orly watched quietly, his back to the mirror. Monique Jr limped into the dressing room with a broken heel, which Shad fixed with Crazy Glue. A new hire named Danielle dashed in for a cosmetic emergency; a sharp-eyed customer had spotted the incision marks from her recent surgery. While the dancer lifted her round new breasts, Shad applied Maybelline powder to the scars.

When they were alone again, Orly said: 'The Lings don't know who they're dealin' with.'

'I sure told them.'

'About Fat Tony? Nicky Scarfo?'

'The works,' Shad said. 'They don't particularly give a shit. By the way, Fat Tony croaked. The Lings saw it in *The Herald*.'

Orly planted his elbows on the vanity. 'America's going down the shitter, that's my theory. Why? Because these goddamn foreigners don't respect our national institutions—not Detroit, not Wall Street, not even the Mafia.'

Shad didn't like the direction of the conversation. Soon Orly would ask him to sabotage the Flesh Farm; the subject had arisen often.

'I'd like to help,' Shad said, 'but I can't.'

'What's the big deal?'

'I just can't.' He was hesitant to tell Mr Orly about his rap sheet, as the liquor commission frowned on the practice of hiring convicted felons. 'Call up North,' Shad said. 'Get a real torch artist.' Of course the phone call would never be made; Orly didn't know a soul in the mob.

The club owner picked up a hairbrush and tapped a beat on the dressing table. 'Those Lings,' he said. 'I can't believe they'd hack up a perfectly good snake.'

Shad said they were definitely making a statement.

'They broke the girl's heart,' Orly said. 'Hey, see if there's a cold drink in the fridge.'

Shad found him a cream soda.

'I was thinking,' said Orly, lapping the rim of the can. 'Remember when the business was mainly bikers? Back when we were The Booby Hatch and The Pleasure Palace? Biker girls, biker clientele, biker fights. Those days you knew the rules.'

'It was a pit,' Shad said, unsentimentally.

'Yeah, but we knew what was what. The strippers hooked. The customers dealt dope. Everybody carried a knife or a piece.'

Shad said, 'The good old days. I might just cry.'

'Bottom line, yes, it was a dive. Yes, it was a sewer. But there was a logical fucking order to things.' Orly took a gulp of soda, sloshed it around both cheeks and swallowed. 'Those days I never had to worry about crooks like the Lings. Competition? There wasn't none. DJs. Play lists. Wind machines. Trained fucking pythons, forget it! Back then, the girls couldn't dance worth a lick, and I'll also say they were in no danger of getting hired off by *Playboy*. You remember Thin Lizzie?'

Shad couldn't help but chuckle. Lizzie was a biker dancer who stood five-foot-four, weighed a hundred and seventy-seven pounds and had a stock car tattooed on her back. Who could forget? A red-and-blue Dodge, Number 43. King Richard Petty hisself.

'Remember?' Orly said, glowing. 'So maybe she did suck off half of Fort Lauderdale in my parking lot. The lady was no trouble to me. No trouble at all. I tell her to dance fast, she danced fast. I tell her to dance slow, she goes slow. That was long before this wrestling thing caught on, but lemme say—if I'd told Lizzie to wrestle in transmission fluid, she'd by God wrestle. The girl was a trouper and she understood the rules.'

Shad opened a bottle of Bayer aspirins and chewed up five. Orly offered a swig of cream soda, which Shad declined.

'Now look how the business is changed,' Orly went on. 'My dancers are practically unionized, thanks to your friend Erin. They pick their own songs, pick their own hours. Meanwhile my liability premiums are tripled on account of all the bankers and lawyers and CPAs hanging out at the joint. Every time there's a fight I nearly have a fucking coronary, wondering which yuppie asshole's gonna sue me next.'

Shad said, 'One thing about the bikers. They don't sue.'

'Damn right.'

'On the other hand, you're makin' real good money now. We're selling four, five times the booze.'

Orly crumpled the soda can and pinged it off the wall. 'Prosperity,' he said, 'ain't all it's cracked up to be.'

Shad was disillusioned, too, but for other reasons. He knew better than to share his innermost feelings with the boss.

Orly said, 'I had a chance to get into a Taco Bell franchise up in Orlando. Fifteen minutes from fucking Disney World—did I tell you? This was October last year.'

'You told me,' Shad said. Orly's wife had vetoed the deal because Mexican food aggravated her colon.

'So there goes my best chance to get out,' Orly said, 'all because Lily gets the runs from *fajitas*.'

'She'd rather have you runnin' a strip joint?'

'It's crazy, I know, but she's never said a word.' Orly lowered his voice. 'Between you and me and the four walls, I'm so tired of naked poon I can't stand it. It's been years since I had a serious boner, I swear to God.'

Shad agreed it was a draining job. Lord, didn't he know!

Orly said, 'I'll ask straight up. What happens you hit it big on this scorpion deal? Say the cottage-cheese company comes through with a couple hundred grand. I guess I'll be needing a new bouncer.'

'Maybe. Maybe not. I like you all right, Mr Orly.'

'Hey, you could even buy a piece of this joint. We could be goddamn partners!'

'To be honest,' Shad said, 'I don't like you that much.'

'Whatever. That's OK, too.'

In eleven years it was the longest conversation that the two men had ever had. Orly was plainly over-wrought about something. Shad asked what had happened to put him in such a mood.

'Not a damn thing,' he snapped.

'Moldowsky called again, right? About Erin.'

'On top of everything else, yeah.' Orly became subdued. 'He's looking for a picture of this horny congressman. A picture from right here at the club. I'm sure you wouldn't know anything about that.'

'Nope,' said Shad. 'What else?'

'He had a message for Erin.' Orly pulled a shred of paper from his damp breast pocket and gave it to Shad. 'Ten o'clock tomorrow night down at Turnberry. Here's the name of the yacht.'

Shad struggled to decipher Orly's scribble; his sweat had made the ink run. '*Sweetheart* something,' Shad said. He didn't like the idea of Erin meeting Dilbeck on a boat.

Orly said, 'So I suppose she's gonna screw this guy.'

'Why?'

''Cause he's a politician, for God's sake.'

Shad said, 'You know her better than that.'

'A United States congressman, you're telling me it's just a private dance party? No sex is what you're telling me?'

'I'd be very surprised.'

Orly did a poor job of masking his disappointment. Shad did an equally poor job of masking his anger; the stare he leveled at Orly was harrowing.

'Fuck the liquor license,' he said.

Orly stiffened. 'But the guy's busting my balls.'

'Then *you* sleep with him.'

'Take it easy, take it easy.' Nervously Orly chucked Shad on the forearm. 'See, this is what I mean. This is my exact point. In the old days we never worried about evil shit like this. Rednecks, bikers and whores—that was the tittie business. Now look out there, you see beepers and cell phones at every fucking table. Blow-dried dorks in designer suspenders, honest to Christ! The parking lot's full of Beemers and Blazers but, shit, I can't sleep nights. No, you keep your fucking upscale clientele.'

'And politicians,' Shad said. The impulse to choke Mr Orly had ebbed slightly.

'Bikers are better customers,' said Orly. 'I swear to God, Shad, I'd rather have a barful of bikers than one shitfaced congressman. The fights we could handle, remember? Hell, I'd take a stabbing every night over evil shit like this. Some guy I never met, busting my balls about the license.'

In five minutes Urbana Sprawl was due to wrestle in a vat of cooked linguini. Shad planned to supervise. He stood up and said, 'What's done is done. We'll fix things right.'

'How?'

'Don't worry about it, Mr Orly.'

They walked through the main lounge together. Rap music pounded pneumatically from the walls. On stage, Lorelei was struggling with the new snake, which had coiled itself the full length of her right leg. Even the most drunken customers realized it was not part of the act.

Orly cupped a hand to Shad's ear and shouted: 'Maybe I'll put a sign at the door: No politicians allowed! Ax murderers and perverts welcome, but no goddamn politicians!'

Shad faked a smile. He was grumpy enough to bite the head off a kitten.

'Give me bikers any day,' Orly was saying. 'No more congressmen in my joint . . .'

On stage, Lorelei gimped stoically out of the spotlight. She yelled something about her leg turning blue.

Shad thought: I've got to get out soon. Before I do some damage.

*

Malcolm J. Moldowsky knew that the congressman couldn't be blackmailed by a geek bouncer with a felony rap sheet. More problematic was the younger stockbroker, Paul Guber, but he had abruptly left town. It was the third person in the scandalous bachelor-party photograph who most worried Moldy: the stripper.

If so inclined, Erin Grant could singlehandedly destroy the congressman's fragile reputation. Which is precisely why Moldowsky had arranged for the two of them to meet.

Moldy spent the morning of October fourth in a high-level strategy session, by himself. He neither needed nor sought the counsel of others. Silence bred clarity of thinking, and solitude restored one's perspective. It was important to set aside his personal contempt for David Dilbeck and concentrate on the mission for which he was being paid. Many fires burned out of control. It was time to focus.

He needed ammunition, but there wasn't much in Erin's past. The custody file was loaded with juicy accusations, but Moldowsky was skeptical of the ex-husband's veracity; Darrell Grant came off as a despicable creep. No sense opening that particular can of worms.

Moldy decided to treat Mrs Grant very gently indeed. Look but don't touch, he'd warned the congressman. Do nothing to frighten or anger this woman. If she says no, don't argue. If all else fails, try to make friends.

If only Dilbeck could be trusted to stick to the script. The subject of the deceased Jerry Killian was to be avoided. Subtle inquiries were to be made about the stripper's daughter. If Mrs Grant complained about the custody litigation, Dilbeck was to offer his assistance. *I know the new judge quite well*—something mild like that, not pushy or boastful. If Mrs Grant brought up Dilbeck's bloody outburst at the Eager Beaver, the congressman was to appear remorseful but offer nothing. Moldowsky drilled him on these points. He tried to keep things simple because he knew Dilbeck's brain would be fogged with lust. Precautions had been taken to protect the stripper from lewd assault, but risk was unavoidable. The congressman was coming apart. It was a race against time.

Malcolm Moldowsky studied his reflection in the bay window. He liked what he saw—a portrait of elegant confidence under stress. Even at home, Moldy was rarely comfortable wearing anything but a coat and tie. He'd read that Nixon was the same way, but so what? Casual attire impeded Moldy's genius; he simply didn't feel powerful in a tank top and a pair of wrinkled Dockers. On this morning he wore a three-piece charcoal suit, tailored in Paris. The necktie was burgundy with a gray diagonal stripe.

Moldowsky sat at the cherry desk in his den. The phone rang often, but he let the machine answer. He made notes on a legal pad. He wrote: 'What does she want?' Then he jotted a list of possible scenarios, from worst to best.

Worst: The stripper could sink the congressman. She could do it on her own, or at an enemy's behest. She wouldn't necessarily need the photograph, either; an afternoon press conference would do nicely. The revelation would be an instant catastrophe. If it didn't cost Dilbeck the election, it certainly would imperil the sugar subsidies. The Rojos stood to lose millions. Malcolm Moldowsky would do anything to prevent such a calamity. He had painstakingly mended Dilbeck's political fences, and the committee vote was all but nailed down. The single remaining hurdle was a Republican named Tooley from northern Alabama who claimed to be a born-again Christian and railed tirelessly against R-rated movies, all forms of rock music, and the annual *Sports Illustrated* swimsuit edition. Moldowsky happened to know that Congressman Tooley was a syphilitic old fraud, but it didn't matter. The sonofabitch would repudiate David Dilbeck immediately if a seedy sex scandal came to light. Tooley wouldn't vote in the same column as a philandering pagan—not for farm subsidies or any other damn fool thing. If Dilbeck was exposed, the sugar vote would be in grave jeopardy.

At the bottom of Moldy's list was his dream scenario: What if the stripper let the whole thing slide? Maybe she had no hard feelings about the champagne-bottle attack, no interest in blackmailing the hot-blooded congressman, no secret doubts about Jerry Killian's death. Perhaps she just wanted to be left alone to dance her heart out.

Not likely, Moldowsky thought. The woman surely needed money, and surely understood how deeply she could wound David Dilbeck by opening her mouth. Moldowsky guessed that Erin Grant's silence was available for purchase. He figured she'd be content to accept a large sum and leave town quietly with her little girl. That would be fine. A payoff carried its own risks, but arranging a permanent disappearance was no longer viable. Not with a homicide cop hovering in the shadows.

Moldy was vexed by Al García. How did his card turn up in the lawyer's safe-deposit box? Was the detective looking into Mordecai's disappearance? Moldy made a note to check with the Florida Bar. It was he, after all, who had tipped investigators to the missing lawyer's trust-fund 'scheme'.

There were more riddles: Why would a Dade County homicide cop be snooping around Fort Lauderdale? Was García investigating Jerry Killian's death, too? More important, was it he who removed the Kodak slide from Mordecai's safe box?

Experience had taught Malcolm Moldowsky to brace for the worst. Assume García was hot on the trail. Assume he'd gotten wind of the blackmail plots. Assume he suspected foul play in the death of Killian and the disappearance of Mordecai . . .

Let him assume his fool head off, Moldowsky thought.

There's no proof, no evidence, no thread linking these unfortunate coincidences to the congressman. Homicides? A lonely bachelor has a fishing accident in Montana, a slimy lawyer skips town with embezzled accounts. What homicides? What the hell was García doing? Moldy wondered if the detective was playing a little game of his own—maybe the business card was left as bait. If so, the only smart move was to ignore the bastard. Play it cool.

Moldowsky's problem was a pathological lack of restraint. He owned a huge ego, a short temper and no patience. He was unaccustomed to doing nothing. He had so many connections and so much sway that his reflex was to grab the phone and ream some ass. That's what fixers did, they spotted trouble coming and headed it off. But an influence-peddler was only as good as his information, and Moldy didn't know jack about this pushy Cuban cop. It gnawed at him all morning. Two, three phone calls would do the trick . . . but why panic? He'd been so thorough, so careful—a mistake was flatly impossible, ridiculous even. Señor Detective García didn't have squat. Nobody could've put it together so fast.

Yet Moldy found himself eyeing the telephone. Buffed nails tapped restlessly on the cherrywood. He needed to know more. His hand shot across the desk toward the Rolodex. His fingers tripped lightly through familiar index cards. It was an astounding trove of sources. Names and numbers, numbers and names. And they each owed Malcolm J. Moldowsky a favor.

It was like a drug, this power he had.

25

The two goons guarding the Rojo yacht were dazzled by Erin's arrival. She wore blood-red lipstick, gold hoop earrings, a white miniskirt, fuck-me pumps and a sleeveless salmon blouse. She looked great, she smelled great. A walking fantasy. The hired goons envied David Lane Dilbeck.

'You're Mrs Grant?'

'No,' Erin said. 'I'm Tipper Gore.'

'Who's your friend? He's not invited.'

Shad emerged from the shadow. The goons shifted uneasily in their shiny black suits. They clenched their fists and swelled their chests, but the stripper's bodyguard seemed unimpressed. He was as broad as a meat locker, and wore a red beret that barely covered the crown of his lumpy bald dome. His mouth was a cruel-looking beak. He blinked with bulging eel eyes. He had a .38 tucked in his belt, and a South American kinkajou on his left shoulder. The kinkajou was eating a candy bar.

'Relax,' Shad told the goons. 'He's on a leash.'

'Who the hell are you?'

Erin said, 'He's a Guardian Angel. Can't you tell?'

'Get lost,' said one of the goons.

Erin took Shad's hand. 'He goes, I go,' she said.

The goons stepped away and conferred briefly. One of them disappeared into the yacht. He returned with a decision: 'OK, Mr Guardian Angel, you can stay out here with us. But your monkey goes back to the zoo.'

Shad said, 'It ain't a monkey.' The kinkajou chittered through a mouthful of nougats. When Shad stroked its neck, the animal turned and bit him on the wrist. The goons jumped but Shad showed no reaction. He wiped the blood on his camouflage trousers and said, 'I got him off a guy at jai-alai. He loves chocolate.'

'Crazy fuck,' muttered one of the goons.

Two couples came strolling down the dock in the moonlight. The men wore white dinner jackets and the women, both blondes, wore shiny evening gowns. They drank Rum Runners and laughed. The women were impressed by the tall fishing boats and gleaming yachts, and the men seemed to be expert mariners. They were much older than their dates. When they reached the slip where the *Sweetheart Deal* was moored, conversation stopped. The men eyed Erin, who smiled tolerantly. On deck the pinheaded Rojo goons stood shoulder to shoulder, steroid bookends. Shad adjusted the angle of his red beret.

One of the blondes: 'Say, can I pet your monkey?'

'It ain't a monkey. It's a kinkajou.'

'Oh, I love kinkajous.'

'Then what the hell. Pet away.'

One of the dinner jackets: 'He doesn't bite, does he?'

Shad looked insulted. 'No, sir, he doesn't.'

'See you later,' Erin said. She slipped between the two goons and opened the cabin door.

Al García's boss in Homicide was Lt William Bowman, who once played linebacker for the University of Florida. Billy Bowman hated cigars and was eleven years younger than García, but García didn't mind because Bowman was a decent cop, for an Anglo. Most of the time, he left García alone.

On the night that Erin was to dance for the congressman, Bllly Bowman called García into the office. There was the traditional discussion of the wretchedness of the Miami Dolphins offense, followed by a cursory inquiry about the late Francisco Goyo.

'We found everything,' García told Bowman, 'except four toes and a buttock.'

'Nice work.'

'Billy?'

'Yeah.'

'Why am I here?'

Bowman cracked his knuckles. 'Is that a cosmic question? Such as: What's the point of it all? What is God's grand plan?'

García, grumbling: 'No, *chico*, I mean why the fuck am I *here*? In your office. Shooting the shit for no apparent reason.'

'How about closing that door.'

García extended a leg and kicked the door shut.

Bowman said, 'I got an interesting phone call from the chief, who had an interesting call from one of the county commissioners.'

'Do tell,' said García.

'Are you working a case with Broward?'

'Several, Billy.'

'A missing lawyer?' 'This is fascinating,' García said. 'Let's have some coffee.'

Over the next half-hour, he told Lt Billy Bowman the whole story, beginning with the floater in Montana. Bowman was a good listener and he asked sharp questions. When García finished, the lieutenant said he was very impressed. 'You got 'em to drill a lock box without a court order.'

García said, 'I knew a girl at the bank, she's a vice-president now. We set a little trap.'

Billy Bowman winced. 'I didn't hear that.'

'Whoever opened the lawyer's safe box found my card. And whoever found my card got on the phone.'

'Which is exactly what you wanted.'

Al García was generous about handing out his business cards during murder investigations. Frequently he'd give one to a prime suspect, just to gauge the reaction.

'So,' said the lieutenant, 'under whose ass did you light this particular fire?'

'If I had to guess,' García said, 'it's Malcolm Moldowsky.'

Bowman said he'd never heard of the guy. García told him he wasn't supposed to. Political fixers were like vampires, the way they avoided daylight.

'This is how it went: Moldowsky calls the commissioner, who probably owes him a big favor. Maybe several big favors, who knows? So the commissioner calls the chief and says who's this guy García, why's he mucking around up in Broward? The last thing Metro needs is some jurisdictional beef with BSO.'

'Believe it or not,' Bowman said, 'the commissioner was almost clever about it. He claims to be a dear friend of the missing lawyer. Says they met at a Dukakis fund-raiser and he can't believe—what's the dickhead's name?'

'Mordecai.'

'Yeah. The commissioner can't believe Mordecai would take off to the islands with embezzled money.'

García laughed. 'That's very slick, making it personal. Like he was upset about his pal and that's all.'

'Right. And anything we could tell him would be greatly appreciated—and very confidential, of course.'

Bowman took a call on the speaker phone while García poured the last coffee. A uniformed road officer had shot a burglar after a chase down the Palmetto Expressway. Bowman took notes and said he was on the way. He hung up swearing because the dead burglar was a drag queen, which meant that the local TV stations would go wild. The lieutenant said, 'My whole career, I never shot a guy in a strapless cocktail dress. How about you?'

'The world's changing, William.' García lifted a salute with the coffee cup.

Billy Bowman swung his size-thirteen Reeboks up on the desk. 'About this lawyer—you figure he's dead, too?'

'Most likely,' García said.

'And dumped, like the other guy.'

'Yeah, but who knows where.'

'The Everglades is perfect,' Billy Bowman said. 'Why go all the way to Bumfuck, Montana, when you got the Everglades in your own backyard? Hell, a dead body decomposes faster here than anywhere else in the country. That's a known fact, Al.'

'Don't tell me they've done a study.'

'Seriously. Miami's got the fastest rot-rate, because of the heat.'

'Really?' García mused. 'I thought it was the humidity.'

'The point is, Montana makes no sense.' 'It does if your

victim's supposed to be on vacation. Killian was a trout fisher-man, remember? This shitbird lawyer, who knows where they put him? The nearest landfill, probably.'

The lieutenant said nothing for several moments. Then: 'Al, you can't just go out and bust a fucking congressman.'

'I'm aware of that.'

'Unless you catch him in the act. Preferably on video-tape, with the pope and Mary Tyler Moore as eyewitnesses.'

'Bill, I'm aware of that.'

'Where's the Kodak slide? I'm curious is all.'

García let the question hang. Bowman was a smart guy; it wouldn't take him long to see the problem. About eleven sec-onds, in fact.

'You're right,' he told García. 'I don't want to know.'

'Tell the chief there's no missing-lawyer case with Broward.'

'You were just checking out a tip.'

'Right,' García said. 'Dry hole.'

'Sorry we couldn't be more help.'

'Yeah,' García said. 'We're very sorry.'

'And this'll go straight back to Moldowsky?'

'You can bet on it.'

'Then what happens, Al? Can we look forward to an actual arrest in our lifetime?'

García rubbed his chin. 'Frankly, I got shit for evidence. But I got some beautiful theories.'

Bowman liked Al García because he was an excellent detective with no ambition to be anything more. Bowman himself wished to be chief some day, and cops such as García often made him look brilliant. Consequently, he wanted García to be happy and productive, not bored or burned out. Al enjoyed challenges, and the lieutenant usually tried to oblige. But this . . .

'Where's our jurisdiction?' Bowman asked.

'It's iffy,' García admitted. 'Dilbeck lives in Dade County. So does Moldowsky.'

'But the crimes took place elsewhere, right?' Bowman cracked his knuckles again. 'Al, would you hate my guts if I said you're on your own?'

'You'd be crazy not to. Maybe I'll take some sick days.'

'But, as your friend, let me also say I'd love to see you pull this off.'

'It's a long shot, Billy.'

'Yeah, but I got a personal stake here. I voted for the dumb bastard.'

'No shit?' Al García couldn't believe that Bowman was a registered Democrat.

The lieutenant pulled his feet off the desk. 'I remember what you told me a long time ago—'

'The world is a sewer and we're all dodging shit.'

'Very uplifting, Al. I'm surprised Hallmark hasn't bought up the copyright.'

'Words to live by,' García said.

'You know what's sad? I'm beginning to think you're right. I'm beginning to think there's no hope.'

'Of course there's no hope,' García said, 'but don't let it get you down.'

'I'm pissed, Al. I voted for the asshole.'

'Here's what you do: First thing tomorrow, sign up for some range time. Check out an Uzi, one of the fully automatics, and go nuts for about an hour. Shoot the living shit outta the place. You'll feel a thousand percent better.'

Billy Bowman said it sounded like a good idea. He tossed a notebook and a Pearlcorder in his briefcase. 'Well, I better get a move on.'

'Good luck with the drag-queen burglar.'

'Thanks, Al. Good luck with the degenerate congressman.'

David Lane Dilbeck greeted Erin timidly. He wore a blue blazer, a white shirt, pleated camel trousers and expensive cordovan loafers; no socks. His silver hair had a grooved look, as if it had been combed about twenty times in the past hour. Additionally, the congressman reeked of Aramis.

Erin was accustomed to overdoses of cologne, but she wasn't sure if she could hack the comical distraction of a turtleneck.

She said, 'This is a gorgeous boat.'

'Belongs to a friend,' Dilbeck said. 'I use it any time I please.'

'For this?'

Dilbeck stammered in the negative.

'What's that on the stereo?' Erin asked.

'Dean Martin. Music for lovers.'

He's serious, Erin thought. That *is* Dean Martin. 'Well, it's pretty,' she said, 'but I brought my own.'

'Fine.' Dilbeck sounded disappointed. 'It's your show.'

Erin had never spoken with an actual United States congressman. She expected a smoother presentation, an air of self-assurance if not downright conceit. But David Dilbeck struck her as just another jittery old lech.

'Let's try this.' Erin handed him a cassette. 'I put it together myself.' She went to the head and changed to a dance outfit. It wasn't easy; the bathroom was fiendishly small. Erin wriggled into a white teddy. Underneath she wore a lace brassiere and a matching G-string. She was betting that Dilbeck would go for the honeymoon look.

When she came out, ZZ Top was playing on the Rojos' sound system. She balanced the bass and cranked up the volume a couple of notches. The stage was a captain's table that had been moved to the center of the room. The congressman sunk into a canvas director's chair. He crossed his ankles and entwined his hands. A silver champagne bucket sat at his right elbow.

Erin stepped on the table and tested it for traction. As she began to dance, she felt vaguely claustrophobic; the yacht's salon had a low roof, and the paneled walls had no mirrors. Erin never performed without mirrors, and now she was uncomfortable. Mirrors helped her concentrate on the footwork, helped her detach from the stares.

Dilbeck's chin bobbed a half-beat behind the music; he was trying his damnedest to look like a rocker. Erin removed her top and dropped it on his lap. He gazed reverently at the undergarment, his mouth parted. He breathed a low growl. When he raised his eyes, Erin flashed her million-dollar smile. She unsnapped the G-string and slipped it down around the garter. The congressman's neck went limp, and his body swayed.

Scary, Erin thought. A genuine sexual trance. She felt she was witnessing a rare phenomenon, like a total eclipse.

'Legs' faded into 'Brown-Eyed Girl', which blended into 'Under My Thumb'. With each song the dance tempo slowed, and so did the congressman's pulse. His eyes rolled and his jaw fell open, exposing a fortune in capped teeth. A large man, he seemed to shrink visibly as the music played—a marionette cut loose from its strings. Performing for a catatonic was lonely. Erin missed Orly's mirrors.

When the set ended, David Dilbeck snapped upright and began to clap. Erin was startled at his rapid recovery. The congressman folded two hundred-dollar bills in her garter and offered to pour the champagne. She put on the white teddy and turned off the tape deck. Dilbeck had a chair waiting.

He said, 'You are positively amazing.'

'So are you.'

'The most incredible blue eyes!'

'They're green,' Erin said, 'but thanks, anyway.' Dilbeck handed her a glass and made a toast to new friendships. 'Do you remember me?' he asked. 'The last time we met, I wore a mustache.' Already he'd deviated from Moldowsky's script.

Erin said, 'How could I forget. You nearly bashed me in the skull.'

'I'm so sorry.'

'What in the world came over you?'

Dilbeck looked away. 'Truly I don't remember. It was inexcusable.' He tossed back the champagne. 'I hope you can forgive me.' It was, he thought, a cunning way to elicit Erin's frame of mind. If she let the subject drop, she probably wasn't planning to shake him down.

'Come on,' she said, 'how about another number?'

The congressman relaxed. 'Wonderful,' he said, peeling off his blazer.

By the fourth set, he was helpless, exhausted and bombed. Erin had done some of the best dancing of her life. Dilbeck sat cross-legged on the floor of the salon. He'd kicked off his loafers and unbuttoned his shirt. Erin perched topless on the edge of the captain's table. Dilbeck clutched at her knee but she nudged his hand away.

'I love you,' he said. 'Desperately I do.'

'I love you, too, sweetie.'

'Be my girlfriend.'

'Your what?'

'How would . . .'His eyes fluttered. 'How would you like an apartment on the Intracoastal? And a car—what'd you think of the new Lexus? You can quit your job and live like a queen.'

'You're kidding. All that, just for being your girlfriend?'

'Whatever you want.'

'Wow.' Erin saw an opportunity to have some fun. 'Davey, can I ask a question?'

'Anything, darling.'

'I wouldn't have to screw you, would I?'

Dilbeck squinted in puzzlement. 'Well now,' he said, working his lips like a plowhorse.

'What I mean,' said Erin, 'is you wouldn't expect sex in exchange for your kindness. I can tell you're not that kind of person.'

The congressman chuckled wretchedly. He groped for the champagne bottle and took a swig.

Erin let her foot brush against Dilbeck's leg. 'You wouldn't believe some men,' she said. 'They're such pigs. They give you a sports car, they expect at least a hand job. Sometimes two!'

'Huh,' said Dilbeck. 'Imagine that.'

Erin gave a convincing sigh of disgust. 'Some guys,' she said. 'I swear to God.'

'But I love you.'

'I'm sure you do, Davey. But I couldn't accept an apartment or anything else. It wouldn't be right.'

'Please. I want your life to be wonderful.'

The congressman watched sorrowfully as Erin put on her bra top. She liked the rush on nights like this, when the dancing was so good. The feeling of control was indescribable. More important, a plan—a wondrously reckless plan—was taking shape.

'What is it you do in Washington?' she asked Dilbeck. 'Give me a job description.'

Dilbeck took several moments to reassemble his thoughts. 'Mainly I help people. My constituents.' He paused theatrically. 'You may not know this, but I once tried to help you.'

'Really.'

'Yes, ma'am. With regards to your daughter.'

Erin stiffened. She said, 'I didn't know.'

'Oh yes, oh yes. I spoke to a certain judge. He wouldn't listen to reason.'

'My divorce judge?'

'The old man, yes. A difficult fellow, God rest his soul.'

Erin said, 'Why did you do that? How'd you know about my case?' She tried to sound curious and not accusatory. This was the important part, and Al García would want every detail. Was Dilbeck drunk enough to blab about Jerry Killian?

Apparently not. He said, 'A little birdie told me about your case.'

Erin coaxed but he wouldn't budge.

'I was glad to try,' the congressman said. 'I have great compassion for working mothers.'

'Thank you. I had no idea.'

He slid closer to the table. 'I know the new judge, as well.'

Erin said she was impressed that a man as important as Dilbeck would take an interest in her family problems.

'That's my job,' he said. 'Helping people.' One of the congressman's hands came to rest on Erin's thigh. She gave him three, maybe four seconds of thrill before flicking it away.

She said, 'The case is working out fine. My daughter's with me now.'

'I'm glad to hear it. But, remember, if you need anything—'

'Aren't you a sweetheart.'

'Anything at all—'

'Hey, Davey?'

'What is it?'

'Did you steal the razor out of my bathroom?'

David Dilbeck turned gray. Moldy hadn't prepared him for this. He said, 'God help me, I did.'

'You're a sick puppy.'

'That's what Erb says.'

'Who's Erb?'

'Erb Crandall. He works for me.'

Erin said, 'Why'd you take the razor?'

The congressman's jowls quavered. He appeared on the verge of tears. 'That's how much I love you,' he said. 'I took some lint, too.'

'Lint.'

'From your laundry. I'm awfully sorry.'

Erin stood on the table and put her hands on her hips. Dilbeck was sprawled in a wrinkled heap on the wooden floor.

'Davey, I don't mean to pry. But what did you do with my laundry lint?'

'I'm afraid I made love to it.'

The room began to whirl. 'Come closer,' Erin told him.

Dilbeck gripped the corners of the captain's table and pulled himself to his knees.

Erin said, 'Shut your eyes.'

'Oh God.' The congressman's dreams ran wild.

Erin removed one of her shoes and, with all her strength, hammered the four-inch heel into the bones of David Dilbeck's right hand. So much for García's instruction to remain calm.

Dilbeck didn't scream so much as whinny. Erin snatched a handful of oily silver hair.

'Davey, if you ever come into my apartment again, *ever*, I'll shoot you. Is that understood?'

Through his agony the congressman whispered: 'But I love you so much!'

'I know you do, sweetheart.'

The two goons asked Shad if he was really a Guardian Angel. He said yes, but he moonlighted nights at a nudie joint. The goons wanted to know all about it. Shad said the music was terrible and the pay sucked.

'Who cares,' said one of the goons. 'Think of all the pussy.'

Shad said, 'Pussy don't pay the rent.' He plucked an ice cube from his glass and gave it to the kinkajou. The animal snarled as it chewed.

The other goon, who had tiny crumpled-looking ears, asked Shad if he had to pay the dancers for sex. 'Or do you get it free? What's the deal?'

Shad said, 'They pay *me*.'

'Aw, bullshit.'

'It's in my contract.'

The first goon said, 'Yeah, right.'

'Any girl I want.'

Shad transferred the kinkajou from one shoulder to the other. His shirt was sticky with blood, from the animal digging its claws. The crumple-eared goon grimaced when he saw the mess. He and his partner had given Shad and his strange pet a wide berth on the yacht's aft deck. Shad knew that the men feared the kinkajou more than they feared him. That was the plan.

The first goon said, 'So, like, you get to watch all the auditions?'

'Watch, my ass. I do the hiring.'

'Man! So you get to see everything.'

'Everything,' Shad said with a sly smile.

'And you been at it how long?'

'Ten, eleven years.'

'Think of all the titties you've seen.'

'Thousands,' said Shad. 'It boggles the fucking mind.' He couldn't believe what morons they were, these hired guards.

The first one said: 'When you do the auditions, what do you go by? Is it just size? Reason I ask, once I was with this girl who had gigantic boobs but they didn't look so hot when she took off her top. Know what I mean?'

Shad said, 'We got very high standards.'

The crumple-eared goon asked: 'You ever audition anyone famous? I mean, before they got famous.'

'Oh sure,' said Shad, thinking fast. These dolts would believe anything. 'Kim Basinger danced at the club for a while. So did Meryl Streep, only back then she used a different name.'

'No shit?'

'Chesty LeFrance. That's what she went by.'

The first goon said, 'Kim Basinger, sure. But Meryl Streep, man, she ain't exactly stacked.'

'Not now she isn't,' Shad said. 'You should've seen her before the operation. Awesome.'

The kinkajou climbed down his arm and hopped to the deck. Shad gave a sharp tug on the leash. The animal growled and rolled on its back.

'How about that,' said the goon with the bad ears.

Shad said, 'Yeah, I got him trained good.' Truthfully, he wasn't crazy about the kinkajou. He was glad the two hours were almost over, so he could return the animal.

'How about you boys,' Shad said. 'You like this gig?'

The first goon said he'd rather be down below, doing what the old man was doing. The second goon said yeah, the worst part of the job was trying to stay awake. Shad asked how much the old man paid.

'We don't work for the old man. We work for the Rojos.'

'Who's that?'

'Rojo Farms,' said the crumple-eared goon. 'We get two hundred a day.'

'Damn,' Shad said.

'And mostly we just hang out.'

The first goon said, 'They call us drivers but that's bullshit. We're security. The Rojos do lots of entertaining, and we keep an eye on the guests . . . speaking of which.' He motioned to his partner, who stepped to the salon door and listened.

'Music's stopped,' he reported. 'Sounds like they're just talking.'

Shad said, 'So who's the old man in there—some bigshot?'

'Friend of the family.'

The kinkajou began pacing restlessly, tangling the leash around Shad's legs. The Rojo goons were amused by the bald man's efforts to extricate himself. In frustration Shad let go. The kinkajou ambled to a corner and sat down, licking its paws.

One of the goons said, 'I never heard of a stripper with a bodyguard.'

Shad said a woman can't be too careful these days.

The one with the deformed ears motioned toward Shad's gun. 'Is that a .38?'

'Special,' Shad said.

'That's what I want, too. How long before your license came through?'

'I didn't bother with a license. See, I got a slight history.'

'That's rough,' said the goon.

'Fucking computers.' Shad emptied his glass over the rail.

'But still they let you in the Guardian Angels?'

'No problem. I had references.' Shad pointed at his head. 'Plus I already had the hat.'

Erin came out the door. She looked tired but unmolested.

'All set?' Shad said.

'Fine and dandy.'

He held her arm as she stepped from the yacht to the dock.

'Nice night,' she said, smiling up at the teardrop moon.

'Very pleasant,' Shad agreed. He waved goodbye to the halfwit goons.

'Wait,' said the one with the normal ears. 'Don't forget your monkey!'

Al García met them at a bagel joint near the jai-alai fronton in Dania. Erin and Shad were late because Shad couldn't find the guy who'd rented him the kinkajou. After twenty minutes of circling the block, he pulled off the road, opened the door and put the animal out. Shad threw a bag of Snickers bars from the car and drove away. When he walked into the bagel joint, a waitress noticed the bloodied shirt and offered to call 911. She assumed that Shad had been stabbed.

García was waiting at a table near the rear of the restaurant. He was mouthing the nub of a very old cigar. He asked Erin how it went with the congressman.

'Piece of cake.' She gave a slightly edited account. The congressman's lint confession was the highlight. Even Shad was astounded.

'That's some honor,' he said.

García asked Erin if Dilbeck tried anything weird while she was dancing. She said no, just the usual hopeful groping. She left out the part about smashing his hand.

'So what's your impression?' the detective asked.

'One, Davey's not too bright. Two, he probably doesn't know exactly what happened to Jerry Killian.'

García concurred. 'He doesn't have the nerve to do it himself, and the people who did are smart enough not to tell him.'

'In other words,' Shad said, 'we're wasting our goddamn time.'

The waitress brought a platter of bagels and a pot of coffee. Shad took off his shirt and asked the awestruck waitress to please throw it in the garbage. As they ate, Al García peppered Erin with questions.

'Did he say whose yacht it was?'

'A friend,' Erin said. 'That's all he'd tell me.'

García smiled. 'Remember the Cuban kid who paid a thousand bucks for your shoe? His family owns the *Sweetheart Deal*.'

'The sugar people?'

'Yeah. They got Dilbeck's balls in a vault somewhere.'

Erin drummed her nails on the table. 'So the kid bought my shoe as a present for Davey.'

'A nice gesture,' Shad remarked. 'Fetish-of-the-month.'

García said, 'Are either of you history buffs? Me, I love American history.' He leaned forward, dropping his voice. 'I'm trying to imagine what Thomas Paine would think of a congressman who has sex with old shoes and laundry lint.'

Erin agreed that the republic was doomed. She said Tasmania was looking pretty good as an alternate homeland.

Al García asked if David Dilbeck had mentioned the crucial photograph. Erin said he'd barely talked about that night at the Eager Beaver, except to apologize.'

'What about Angela?'

'He offered to help with the new judge,' Erin said. 'That's the only time I was nervous. He seemed a little too interested.'

Shad got up to call the club and make sure no disasters had occurred in his absence. Orly got on the line and bitched about him taking the night off. A British sailor had almost choked to death in the pasta pit—Monique Sr saved him with a modified Heimlich.

'Sorry I missed it,' Shad said. Orly hung up.

Shad returned to the table and said he'd better go, Mr Orly was pissed. García offered Erin a ride home.

In the car, she said: 'So tell me.'

'What?'

'You're humming, Al. You never hum. What happened?'

'Progress!' The detective waggled the cigar nub. 'A very nice lady at the Missoula Holiday Inn remembers three Jamaicans getting a room and ordering a half-dozen rib-eye steaks sent up. This happened a few weeks back. Apparently not a multitude of Jamaicans cruise through Montana this time of year. Anyhow, the nice lady punched their bill up on the computer and read me the charges.'

'And?'

'There was a twenty-two-minute phone call,' García said, cigar bobbing, 'to a certain residence in Miami, Florida.'

Erin said, 'Dilbeck?'

'God, how I wish,' said García. 'No, darling. It was Malcolm Moldowsky—the congressman's fairy godfather. The guy who keeps hassling your boss.'

So there was no doubt about it, Erin thought. They'd murdered Mr Peepers.

'I'll never prove it,' García said, 'but I can sure raise some hell. Did Davey Boy happen to mention Moldowsky's name? Between hard-ons, I mean.'

'He talked about a guy named Crandall.'

'But no Moldowsky?'

'Not tonight,' Erin said. 'I'll try again next time.'

The detective's foot came off the accelerator. 'Did I miss something?'

'I'm dancing for Davey again.'

'Like hell—'

Erin cut him off. 'He tipped me a thousand bucks, Al. That's three grand I walked with. A couple more nights like this, my lawyer's paid off and I've got cash in the bank.'

'Too risky.'

'He's harmless. Trust me, he's a little boy.'

She didn't tell the detective what she had in mind, because he couldn't help. In fact, he probably would've stopped her from going through with it. Likewise, Shad would be an unsuitable accomplice; too impulsive, too volatile. If things got hot, he'd wind up in the back of a squad car. Maybe Erin would, too. She couldn't take the chance.

'Where,' García asked, archly, 'is the next rendezvous?'

Erin shrugged. 'It's entirely up to him.'

'Oh, for God's sake.'

They rode in prickly silence for several miles before she said, 'Al, tell me what's wrong.'

'Nothing.' He spit the spent cigar out the window. 'I think you liked it. Am I right?'

'It was easy tonight. I like it when it's easy.'

He slapped the steering wheel with both hands. 'Christ, it's not a game. I pulled your dead pal out of the river, remember?'

She thought: He wasn't there tonight. He didn't see for himself. Dilbeck was completely helpless.

García warned her that it was bound to get hinky. He said she was pressing her luck, seeing the congressman again. She told him he didn't understand.

'Sure I understand,' he said. 'It's not about the money, is it?'

'Not entirely.' Erin's eyes flashed.

'It's about power. Pure and simple.'

'Al,' she said, 'you've been watching too much ' "Oprah." '

26

The next day, Erin took her daughter to see *101 Dalmatians* at a mall in South Miami. After the movie, they stopped at an ice cream shop, where Erin ordered two scoops of chocolate pistachio for both of them.

Angela, licking a cone: 'Can we get a dog someday?'

'Sure,' said Erin.

'Not like Aunt Rita's, either.'

'How about a Dalmatian? Just like in the movie.'

Angela said, 'No, I want a Great Dane. But not one that bites, OK?'

'Then we'll get a puppy. We'll train it together.'

'What about Daddy?'

Erin crunched hard on a pistachio. 'Good question,' she said.

'He doesn't like dogs. He likes birds.'

'I remember,' Erin said. 'The dog'll be yours and mine.'

Angela wore a thoughtful expression. 'Is Daddy in trouble?'

'Yes, baby, I'm afraid so.'

'Are you in trouble, too?'

'No, Angie, I'm doing just fine.'

Later they walked around Burdine's and looked at the clothes. Erin bought her daughter two dresses, two overalls and a pair of white Nike sneakers with pink slashes.

Angela said, 'Momma, it's not my birthday.'

'I know, honey.'

'What's the matter?'

'Nothing's the matter,' Erin said. 'I love you, that's all.'

'I love you, too, Momma. But don't cry.'

'I'm not crying. It's my allergies.'

Angela looked doubtful. She said, 'Allergies make you sneeze, not cry.'

'For your information, little lady, there are many different types of allergies.'

They held hands, strolling the mall. Coming toward them, a handsome Latin man pushed a girl in a small wheelchair. The girl was pale with jet-black hair, done in braids. She wore a steel brace on one of her legs.

Quickly Erin tugged her daughter toward the doorway of a toy shop. 'Remember all those Barbie dolls you lost—'

'But, Momma—'

'Let's pick out some new ones.'

'But, Momma, look!' Angie had spotted the wheelchair going by. 'It's an Everest-and-Jennings.'

Great, thought Erin. He even taught her the names.

Angela said, 'That's like Daddy does, pushing me. Only why are they going so slow?'

'Because that little girl is hurt. It's not safe for her to go fast.'

'Maybe when she's all better?'

'Yes, baby. When she's all better.'

Erin considered explaining to her daughter the saddest of truths—that some sick people never get better. It would've been a convenient segue back to the subject of Angela's father, and why Angela could never be with him again.

But Erin let it slide. The child was only four years old; she had a whole lifetime to learn about sadness. Today was for Dalmatians, ice cream and new dolls. At the toy store, Erin bought two new Barbies, plus swimsuits and evening gowns. She said no to the fur stoles, but Angie didn't make a fuss.

In the car, she asked, 'Momma, when can I go home?'

'It won't be long.' Erin prayed that Angie meant 'home' with her, not Darrell Grant. 'You mean the new apartment, right?'

Angela nodded excitedly. 'I liked the stairs. That was fun.' She paused. 'Where will Daddy go?'

Erin thought: What do I tell her—Daddy's off to prison? No, *prison* is a scary word. How about: A special place for grown-ups who get in trouble. Or better: A big building that looks just like a hospital, except for the barbed wire. Again, Erin chose to dodge the topic of Darrell's fate.

'He'll be taken care of,' she said.

'Does he have another girlfriend?'

'I don't know.' The question caught Erin by surprise.

''Cause I don't want him to be lonely.'

'He won't be lonely, baby. I promise.' Erin had a depressing vision of Angela as a young woman, loyally visiting her father on weekends at Raiford. Darrell undoubtedly would try to recruit her in the smuggling of cigarettes and pills.

'Where are we going now?' Angie asked.

'Victoria's Secret.'

'What's that?'

'That's where Mommy buys her outfits for work.'

'Your waitress clothes?'

'Right,' Erin said, with a sigh. 'My waitress clothes.'

It was nearly five o'clock when they got back to Miami. Erin didn't want to say goodbye, but she only had one hour to drive back to the club, and the traffic northbound was hell.

Angela kissed her on the nose and pinched her chin; it was a game they played.

'Momma, thank you for the new Barbies.'

'Remember to be nice, and share.'

'I promise.' Angie hopped out of the car, carefully clutching the shopping bag that contained her dolls. She stood on the sidewalk and waved.

'You run on inside,' Erin said. She blew a kiss and tapped the tip of her nose. As Angela started toward the house, Erin slowly drove away. Halfway down the block, she glanced in the rear-view and saw her daughter running after the car. Erin braked hard, making the tires squeal.

'Momma!' Angela was on tiptoes at the window. Her cheeks were pink, and she was out of breath. She hugged the bag of dolls to her chest.

Erin said, 'What is it, baby?'

'I'm scared.'

'Of what?' She opened the car door and Angela clambered

onto her lap. Erin turned to see if someone else was on the street, someone who might have frightened the girl. She saw nothing.

'Angie, what's the matter? What are you scared of?'

'Please don't get in trouble like Daddy.'

'Oh, honey. Is that it?'

'Please!'

'Don't worry,' Erin said, holding her daughter to her breast. 'Don't you worry about me.'

Darrell Grant phoned his sister from the Wal-Mart and said, 'Where's the nearest water from your place?'

Rita said, 'Don't tell me you got a boat.'

'A car,' Darrell said, 'but I need to dump it.'

'Not in the water.'

'Yeah, in the water.'

'A brand-new car?'

'Lord Christ, Rita, can't you just answer a simple question?'

Darrell Grant ditched the stolen Thunderbird in a drainage canal at Turkey Point, where Alberto Alonso worked. Then he hitchhiked to the trailer park and enjoyed one of Rita's peanut butter-and-plantain sandwiches.

She said, 'They's been cops calling, all hours. Alberto says you must've fucked up.'

'You got any Gatorade? The green kind?' Darrell asked.

'It ain't cold.'

'That'll do.'

Rita poured him a tall glass. 'We lost a pup to an eagle.'

'No shit,' said Darrell. 'A real eagle?'

Rita said it damn sure looked like an eagle when it swooped into the backyard. 'Also, your wife kicked the Christmas out of Al. Then Lupa got after him, too . . .'

Darrell Grant waved the sandwich and said, 'Hold up now—'

'He's up to the Veterans' Hospital this afternoon. His tongue's all infected.'

'Goddamn, Rita, you don't mind if I finish my lunch.' Darrell puffed his cheeks to dramatize his urge to vomit.

Rita apologized. Then she said: 'You can't stay here.'

'I know.'

'The cops, they drive by all the time.'

Darrell said, 'I need to borrow your car.'

'The axle's broke.'

'What about that Pontiac across the way?'

'Mrs Gomez,' Rita said. 'We ain't speakin' on account of the wolves got her Siamese.'

Darrell said his idea was to steal the Pontiac, not borrow it. Rita asked since when did he know how to hotwire a car.

'I don't,' Darrell Grant said. 'But I surely know how to use a key.'

From the backyard came a raw chorus of yowls. Rita scooped up her catcher's mask and hurried out through the screen door. Darrell darted to the bathroom and explored the medicine chest; it was cluttered with gauze, adhesive tape and antiseptic ointments. Quickly he spied a bottle of codeine Tylenols, prescribed for the recently mangled Alberto Alonso. Darrell emptied the pills into a front pocket of his jeans.

He was fixing another sandwich when Rita returned. She said, 'So what's the plan, little brother?'

'Well, listen,' he said, wiping his mouth. 'I intend to collect my beautiful daughter and get the hell pronto out of Florida. How's that sound?'

'Start a new life.'

'Exactly.'

'Because you're too smart for this shit.'

'I know it, Rita. I sure do know it.'

She always said her brother should've been an actor, he was so handsome. She could easily picture him on one of her soaps— maybe a charming young drifter on 'All My Children'.

'What about your wife?' she asked.

Darrell Grant laughed caustically. 'Erin will be very lucky,' he said, 'if I don't hurt her before I go.'

Rita poured more Gatorade. This time she tossed in a handful of ice cubes. 'Raising a child by yourself, I don't know.'

Her brother shot her a cold look. 'What's your point?'

'I'm just sayin' it might be easier by yourself. To get a fresh start and all.'

'I'm a super father, Rita.'

'Who said you wasn't?'

'And, besides, Angie and I are partners.'

'That's the part I don't like,' Rita said. 'Usin' that little girl the way you do.'

Darrell said, 'Hey, she has a ball with it. Just ask her if Daddy shows her a fun time.'

'Lord, I'm sure. Stealin' wheelchairs.'

'Hey, you should hear how she laughs when we're rollin' down the halls. The way her hair flies all back, looks just like silk. Nurses wave and say, '"See that pretty little angel!" 'He smiled. 'And out the door we go.'

Rita said, 'You're too good for that, Darrell. That's gypsy shit.'

'Well, it works,' said Darrell Grant, 'whatever the fuck it is. Now—where you figure old Mrs Gomez keeps her keys?'

The morning after Erin danced on the yacht, David Lane Dilbeck gave one of the most magnificent performances of his political career. It began with a rally in Little Haiti, where the congressman excoriated the US Immigration Service for its heartless treatment of black Caribbean refugees. He declared that America owed its strength and heritage to courageous boat people, and that the Founding Fathers would be shame-stricken to see us now rebuff the neediest and most desperate. The only awkwardness arose when Dilbeck, speaking in fractured Creole, badly mistranslated the Emma Lazarus inscription from the Statue of Liberty ('Give me your oxen, your seedless guavas, your broken truck radiators . . .'). Though perplexed, the Haitian crowd remained enthusiastic.

Next the congressman raced to an American Legion barbecue, where he recounted the Battle of Inchon so vividly that many of the rapt veterans assumed that he'd seen action in Korea. He had not, for an undescended testicle had kept David Dilbeck out of the army. The congressman told his story with chin held high. His voice cracked as he poignantly described a young man's private heartbreak, denied a chance to fight for his nation. Leaving the enlistment center on that sad autumn day in 1951, Dilbeck said, he had vowed to overcome his handicap and serve America as devotedly as any man with two normally descended testicles. Patriotic fervor led him first to municipal government, then to Congress! Let me keep my dream, David Dilbeck boomed. Let me serve again! Cheers rose from the vets, who put down their spareribs and waved, with sticky fingers, dozens of miniature American flags. The congressman placed a bandaged hand over his heart and led the Legion crowd in 'The Star-Spangled Banner'.

The final stop was the Sunset Bay condominium, and here Dilbeck hit his peak—lucid, heartfelt and damn near eloquent. Erb Crandall was flabbergasted. He called Malcolm Moldowsky from a phone booth outside the rec room, where the congressman was addressing three hundred retirees.

'Malcolm, it's unbelievable,' Crandall said. 'He's got 'em in tears.'

'The Israel thing?'

'Yeah, but he shitcanned the script. It's all off the top of his head.'

'Oh Jesus,' Moldy said. 'You see any reporters?'

'Just Channel 10, but it's all right. He's a major hit, Malcolm. They're bawling all over their bagels.'

Moldowsky tried to envision the scene. 'Erb, I want an honest answer. Does David know anything at all about the Mideast?'

'He's weak on the geography,' Crandall conceded, 'but he's gangbusters on the Palestinian question. I counted four standing ovations.'

Moldowsky clicked his teeth. 'And he looks OK?'

'Like a million bucks. The best part, Eloy Flickman showed up for an ambush debate. That's how come the TV crew was here.'

'Sneaky bastard.'

'Davey tore him apart,' Crandall said. 'It was fantastic. Flickman took off like a scalded chihuahua.'

'Is that right?' On Crandall's end, in the background, Moldowsky heard a wave of fresh applause. It seemed too good to be true. He thought: What happened last night between Dilbeck and the stripper? She must've screwed him silly.

Moldowsky wanted a full debriefing. 'Put David on the line.'

'He's on a roll, Malcolm. He's into his Holocaust material.'

'I'll wait.'

Six minutes and two ovations later, the congressman got on the phone.

Moldowsky said, 'So tell me about your hot date.'

'A delight,' said Dilbeck, short of breath.

'No shakedowns? I want the truth. What about the photograph?'

'The subject never came up. She was a perfect lady.'

'And you were the perfect gentleman.'

'A monk, Malcolm. By the way, I'll need the yacht again in a few days. Erin's coming back to dance.'

'Why?'

'Because she enjoyed herself.' The congressman's tone was defensive. 'She's very fond of me, Malcolm. Oh, and I'll need more cash.'

'David, I want my people there.'

'That won't be necessary—' A gaggle of crowlike voices drowned Dilbeck's words. 'Malcolm, I've got to sign some autographs. Talk to Erb, OK?'

Moldy fidgeted until Crandall's voice came on the line: 'Malcolm, you should see. They got him in a yarmulke!'

'Stick close for a few days.'

'No, I'm afraid not.' From now on, Crandall was steering clear of Dilbeck's glandular adventures. 'I'm going to Atlantic City.'

'Like hell,' Moldy said.

'Malcolm, let me explain something. I don't work for you, I work for David. And David thinks it's terrific if I take a few days off and fly to Atlantic City.'

'That's because David's got big plans.'

'Well,' said Erb Crandall, 'I got front-row seats to see Cher.'

'Really? I hope your plane hits a fucking mountain.'

'Thanks, Malcolm. I'll be sure to send a postcard.'

'Could you at least find out when he's meeting the girl? Or is that too much to ask?'

'I'll see what I can do,' Crandall said. 'Whatever happened last night, Davey's a new man on the stump. He sparkles, Malcolm.'

'I suppose that's good.' Sparkles?

'Kennedy-esque, according to the Hadassah ladies.'

'Very funny.'

'Gee,' Crandall chided, 'we thought you'd be pleased.'

'The man is ill. You know it, I know it.'

'He carries her shoe in his briefcase.'

'And you're off to the fucking casinos.'

'Malcolm?'

'What?'

'I'll miss you.'

Erb Crandall reached the parking lot just as the congressman's limousine pulled out. Crandall waved pleasantly. Pierre, the driver, tipped his cap in reply. David Lane Dilbeck remained invisible behind tinted windows.

A nasty canker bloomed on Orly's lower lip. Erin couldn't look at him, even though they were deep in argument. She scanned the imitation red velvet walls while Orly told her no fucking way could she take Saturday night off.

'That's twice this week!'

Erin said, 'I can count.'

'The answer is no fucking way. I'm thinking maybe you got another gig.'

'I do,' she said. 'Congressman Dilbeck.'

'Shit.' Orly had no choice but to back down. He didn't want to piss off a congressman, and he definitely didn't want more heat from that ballbuster Moldowsky.

'I'll work a double on Monday,' Erin promised.

'Bet your ass.' Orly picked pensively at the cold sore. 'I'm curious,' he said. 'What's he like?'

'Nothing special.'

'Big tipper?'

'Fair,' Erin said. She knew where Mr Orly was headed. 'I didn't sleep with him,' she said. 'You can ask Shad.'

'I already did.'

'And what did he say?'

'He said you just danced.'

'Don't act so surprised.'

Orly shrugged one chubby shoulder. 'He's a bigshot. Those guys usually want the full treatment.'

Erin's arms began to itch. It happened whenever she sat too long in Orly's office.

He said: 'Lorelei's got phlebitis. She's flying home to Dallas.'

'I'm sorry,' Erin said.

'It was that fucking snake, squeezing on her legs.'

Bravely Erin sneaked a glance at Orly's face. He looked downcast and subdued. Of course the canker didn't help. She nearly felt sorry for him.

'How was the yacht?' he asked.

'Fine, except there's no mirrors. I'm dancing blind.'

Orly said, 'I'll need Shad here at the club. For the noodle wrestling—last night some guy nearly cacked.'

'I'll be fine by myself,' Erin said. 'Look, I know it's still early but why don't I get started on my sets?'

Orly said great, but no slow stuff. 'Not to beat a dead horse, but I'm serious. You can't strip to fucking Jackson Browne.'

'Congressman Dilbeck would disagree.' Erin stood up and pushed the chair away. 'Here's the part he liked best.'

Singing now: ' "Down on the boulevard, they take it hard." ' Dancing in baggy jeans and sneakers. A kick-boxing move—punch, punch, right leg out, then spin. ' "They look at life with such dis-regard." ' Punch, kick, kick and split.

When she finished, Orly whistled and said, 'Damn.'

'I told you.'

'That's Jackson Browne?'

'The table dancers,' said Erin, 'don't know what they're missing.'

*

Urbana Sprawl said that there was a guy jerking his weenie in a green Pontiac. Shad went to the doorway and scanned the cars in the lot. The green Pontiac was parked far away, near the road; Shad could make out a silhouette behind the wheel. He went behind the bar to fetch his tire iron, but then Orly called him over to break up a fight between two men at the Foosball table. Men in suspenders! Orly bellowed. By the time Shad got out to the Pontiac, it was empty. He decided to prowl around.

Darrell Grant already had broken into the club through the fire door. He was sitting in the dressing room when Monique Sr arrived to freshen her makeup. She gave him a radiant smile and said, 'Are you Kiefer Sutherland?'

'That's me.' Darrell was cooked on codeine and Halcions and some unidentified lemon-yellow capsules that he'd purchased from a newspaper vendor on Dixie Highway. Darrell's eyelids hung half-mast and his tongue stuck to his teeth. He said, 'I'm looking for Missus Erin Grant. She works here in a nude capacity.'

Monique Sr told him to put the knife away. Darrell Grant was unaware that he was holding it.

'You lost some weight,' Monique Sr said, 'since your last movie. My name is Monique.' When she held out her hand, Darrell flicked it with the blade. The dancer cried out and pulled away. A stripe of blood appeared on her fingers.

'Hush up,' Darrell said. He grabbed her arm and yanked her into his lap. Monique Sr told him to stop and balled her fist, to stanch the bleeding.

Darrell Grant rubbed the stubble of his beard on the nape of the dancer's neck. He bounced her on his knees and said, 'Here's a news flash, sweetie. I ain't Keith O'Sutherland.'

'I kind of figured.'

He cut the strap of her bra top, which dropped to the carpet. In the mirror, Monique Sr studied the man's slack leer and fogged eyes. She felt him getting hard beneath her.

'Let me go,' she said. 'I'll find Erin.'

'What's the hurry.' He'd spotted the wad of bills in her black garter. 'How much you got there?'

'I don't know. Maybe a hundred.'

'Excellent.' He slid the flat side of the knife down Monique Sr's leg, under the elastic of the garter. He twisted his wrist and the garter broke. The cash fell in a clump. It landed in one of her bra cups.

Darrell Grant said, 'Pick it up.'

As she bent over, he said, 'Those are some tits you got.'

'Please let me go.'

He propped the steak knife behind his right ear, like a pencil. Then he reached around Monique Sr and slapped a hand on each breast. 'I would estimate,' he said, 'these are about three times bigger than my ex-wife's.

Monique Sr said, 'Shit. Now I know who you are.'

She threw an elbow that caught Darrell Grant flush in the right temple. No pain registered in the lifeless blue eyes. He locked both arms around the dancer's rib cage and squeezed. He gave a grunt that started low in the throat, then rose to a musical hum.

Monique Sr, who'd taken eight years of piano, recognized the note as a high C-sharp. She was equally startled by the man's strength, and watched herself go pale in the mirror. The walls pulsed as the man's eerie humming filled her head. Within moments she passed out.

When she regained consciousness, Monique Sr heard Darrell Grant say: 'Wake up, Little Dorothy.' She felt the man's kneecaps bouncing her bottom and realized that he still held her on his lap. She opened her eyes and saw, in the mirror, that he'd cut off her G-string.

She said, 'You want a screw, get it over with.'

Darrell squirmed beneath her. 'I'd like to, but I sorta lost momentum.'

'Then let me go. I was due in the cage ten minutes ago.'

'Just hold up,' he said. 'Maybe if I squeeze them titties again.'

'Nope,' said Monique Sr. 'You're done for the night. I can feel it.'

'Shut up!'

'It's not your fault, sweetheart. It's the drugs.'

Darrell Grant fumbled one-handed at his fly. There was no point. 'Look what you did,' he whined.

'Wasn't me.'

He traced the point of the blade along her bikini lines. 'How about a tattoo down there? Be the first on your block.'

Monique Sr said, 'Please don't cut on me again.' A dancer with scars didn't get much work—not at the good clubs, anyway.

When Darrell stung her with the knife, she promised to do whatever he wanted. 'Thatta girlie,' he said.

The door opened and Erin came in. It took a few seconds to absorb the scene: Her ex-husband sitting in the makeup chair, Monique Sr trembling on his lap, the glint of steel against her tanned belly.

Darrell Grant giggled. 'This is perfect. Shut the damn door and pull up a seat.'

Erin could see he was wrecked. She regretted leaving the pistol at home.

He said, 'I'm gonna give this lady the ride of her life, and you're gonna watch.'

'Hot damn,' said Erin. She sat down and winked at Monique Sr, who was not reassured. She raised her hand to show Erin the blood.

Darrell Grant said, 'We're gonna give you a peep show.'

'Anytime you're ready,' Erin said, crossing her legs.

Darrell's tipsy smile disappeared and his lips pursed in childlike concentration. He commanded Monique Sr to touch him. She said she was. He told her to *grab* him, then.

'I am,' she said.

'I don't feel a damn thing.'

'That makes two of us,' Monique Sr said.

Erin folded her arms. 'I'm waiting, Mr Sex Machine.'

Darrell Grant squinted and strained and bared his teeth.

Erin said, 'Maybe you need a laxative.'

Monique Sr caught herself laughing. Darrell's muscles—legs, arms, neck—went limp in defeat. 'Goddamn you,' he said to Erin.

'Fine. Now let Monique go, and we'll discuss the problem like grown-ups.'

'Not until you take me to Angie.'

Erin said, 'You better talk to the judge.' She couldn't resist: the exact line he'd used on her so many, many times.

He touched the knife to Monique Sr's neck. Teardrops and runny mascara streaked the dancer's cheeks. Erin knew it was important to keep her ex-husband confused and off guard. Any sign of weakness would embolden him.

She said, 'Monique, I apologize. Darrell makes a shitty first impression.'

'He cut my goddamn hand!' the dancer cried, displaying the wound again. 'It's not funny, Erin. Give him what he wants.'

'I want my daughter,' Darrell Grant snarled.

'Well,' said Erin, 'I don't have her any more.'

Darrell took the news poorly. He shoved Monique Sr to the floor and lunged wildly at Erin. The swiftness of his fury caught her by surprise. She tried to raise her legs to push him away, but he was already on top. The chair collapsed, and they went down simultaneously. Darrell Grant dug his knees into Erin's chest. He screamed and cursed until he was breathless. She lost track of how many times he called her a dirty rotten cunt.

She was worried about the knife: where was it? Darrell's arms hung at his side. Pinned flat on the floor, Erin couldn't see her ex-husband's hands, couldn't raise her head to try.

Darrell Grant, panting: 'I want Angie back tonight.'

'You're crushing me,' Erin said.

Monique Sr must have gotten out, because the door was ajar and the dressing room flooded with dance music from the lounge: something brassy by Gloria Estefan. Not an ideal tune to die by, Erin thought.

'Who's got her?' Darrell said.

Erin, wheezing: 'I'll take you there.'

His right arm came up with the rusty steak knife. He held it by the tip of the blade, between his thumb and forefinger.

Darrell Grant, weepy, slurring: 'I lost my baby girl.'

'That's not true,' Erin said.

'All because of you.'

'Darrell, it's not too late.'

He turned the knife in his fingers, closed his palm around the handle. 'Don't you understand? I escaped from jail. That means I got no future to speak of.'

Erin said, 'Everyone fucks up occasionally.'

'My plan was me and Angie hittin' the road. Not any more. Is that a fair statement?'

One of his eyelids had closed. Erin prayed that it would affect his accuracy with the knife. 'If you kill me,' she said, 'you'll never see her again.'

'And if I don't kill you,' he said, 'I'll hate myself for not tryin'.'

Erin had always believed that her ex-husband was incapable of homicide, except by accident. Now, watching Darrell Grant fondle the cheap cutlery, she realized she might've misjudged him. What if he stabbed her? Erin thought, ludicrously, of how disappointed her mother would be. When one's only daughter is hacked to death wearing a sequined bra top and a G-string—well, there's really no way to explain it to one's friends at the orchid club.

'Darrell,' Erin began.

'Shut your eyes. I can't manage if you're lookin' at me.'

But Erin wouldn't close her eyes. She scorched him with a glare. 'I won't let you do this to Angela.'

'Hush up,' he cried. 'Who's got the knife, huh?'

'I *won't* let you.'

'Shut your goddamn green eyes!'

'Why?' Erin said. 'They remind you of somebody?'

'Oh, Lord Christ.' He raised the knife with both hands.

Erin said, 'Put it down, Darrell.' A breathless whisper.

'No way.'

'Darrell, please. For Angie's sake.'

'I said, shut your eyes.'

'Drop the fucking knife!' A man's voice at the door. Erin felt Darrell Grant go rigid. He cocked his head, waiting. He did not drop the fucking knife.

'Junior,' said the voice, Shad's voice. 'I'm counting to three.'

Erin watched her ex-husband mouthing to himself: One Mississippi, two Mississippi . . . and then a branch snapped. That's what it sounded like.

Darrell flew off Erin as if launched by a spring. A plangent wailing now accompanied the melodies of Gloria Estefan. Erin sat up, covering her breasts with her hands. There was Shad with his tire iron, Mr Orly clutching a can of Dr Pepper, and Darrell Grant screaming.

Darrell—his arm hanging crooked and splintered at the elbow, a blond spike of a bone poking through the gray skin, dripping darkness down the front of his jeans.

Shad said, 'Junior, you count too slow.' He whipped off the beret and bowed his shiny dome in Darrell Grant's direction. 'You remember carving this punkin? I'll bet you do.'

'Take him outside,' Orly muttered, and disappeared down the hall.

Erin got to her feet, wobbling. The faces in the mirror were a blur. She pointed at the reflection that most closely resembled her ex-husband. 'Darrell,' she said. 'I knew you couldn't do it.' Then: 'God, I don't feel so good.' Shad caught her in one arm as she sagged. The whimpering Darrell Grant somehow lurched to his feet and stumbled from the dressing room. Shad placed Erin on a small divan and tucked a musty pillow under her head.

'I'll be right back,' he told her. 'Junior forgot his knife.'

27

Shad searched the property but he couldn't find Darrell. He stalked next door and checked the fried-chicken joint, and then the restrooms of the video arcade down the street. When he returned to the Tickled Pink, the Pontiac was gone. The asshole had escaped again.

Erin was surprisingly calm. She borrowed Orly's phone and dialed the Martin County Sheriff's Office to report the sighting of her fugitive ex-husband. She described his gruesome injury, and hinted that Darrell might soon surface at a local emergency room. The cop on the other end was no Al García. He took the information haltingly, and asked numerous vague questions. Erin had to spell her name three times because he kept asking her if it was 'Aaron—like the baseball player.'

When she got off the phone, Orly said, 'We got a policy against husbands and boyfriends at this club.'

'Darrell is neither,' Erin said, 'and I didn't invite him.'

'He crazy enough to come back?'

'That's hard to say, Mr Orly. The police are after him.'

'Lovely. Maybe we'll have a shootout in the pasta pit.'

Shad said, 'The boy's in no shape to fight. I busted his ulna to smithereens.'

Orly frowned. 'His what?'

Erin announced that she was going home to take a hot shower. Shad got the .38 Special and followed in his car. There was no sign of a lurking green Pontiac. He parked by Erin's apartment until the lights went out. Then he circled the complex four times and drove back to the club. Orly was waiting at the front bar.

'Those fucking Lings,' he fumed, 'they're trying to steal Urbana. A thousand bucks they offered her!'

Shad said nothing. He had a feeling there was more.

Orly, dropping his voice: 'Plus they ratted me to the Health Department.'

'You mean Beverage.'

'No, Health.' Orly unfolded a yellow paper and smoothed it violently with the heels of his hands. He pushed it down the bar toward Shad. 'Read it,' he said.

The complaint charged Orly with using 'contaminated food products in a manner that poses a direct and compelling threat to the public safety.' Shad assumed it referred to the topless pasta wrestling.

Orly said, 'It's a damn lie.'

'I know,' Shad said. 'The stuff is always fresh. I check the packaging dates myself.'

'That's exactly what I told the little creep.'

'And?'

'He claims he got a sample of bad vermicelli from the wrestling pit—I forgot when, last Tuesday or something. It says right there on the paper. He put it in a jar and hauled it to some goddamn lab in Miami.'

Three types of nasty-sounding bacteria—*Escherichia coli, Shigella dysenteriae* and *Staphylococcus*—were listed on the health inspector's complaint. 'This is bullshit,' Shad said. 'We been set up.'

'Keep reading,' Orly told him.

'Hey, what's this about orifices?'

The report stated: 'During the so-called wrestling matches, several male customers were observed attempting to insert said contaminated food product into the mouths and other body orifices of the female performers.'

Shad pushed the paper back at Orly. 'It doesn't happen every night. Guys get drunk, you know how it goes.'

Orly turned away from the bar. 'They make it sound so disgusting. Bottom line, it's just fucking noodles.'

The two men sat wordlessly. Sabrina was on the main stage, Monique Jr was in the cage and a new girl named Suzette was dancing tables in the front row. Suzette's claim to fame was a cameo in a recent George Michael video. Orly said she had played a nun in bicycle pants.

Every song Kevin put on was by Prince or Madonna or Marky Mark; the severity of Shad's headache made him wonder if the music had caused his brain to swell. He removed the beret and balanced a bag of ice cubes on his twitching scalp.

'Where's Urbana?' he asked.

Orly said she went to the Flesh Farm to negotiate with the Lings. 'So much for loyalty.' He paused. 'They got a wind machine over there? Because Urbana won't dance near a wind machine.'

'That's right,' Shad said.

'What'm I saying? A grand is a grand.'

Shad told him not to worry. 'She won't do friction. Not for a million bucks.'

'You ever think,' said Orly, 'that maybe they don't want her for friction?'

Shad signaled the bartender to bring the boss a fresh Dr Pepper. Orly continued: 'The Ling brothers aren't stupid. They know a liability potential when they see one. With those tits, she could kill a man easy.' He tongued the rim of the soda can. 'Here's my theory: They're getting out of friction dancing and aiming upscale. They're trying to buy some class, you know? Be respectable like us.'

'Respectable,' Shad said. Mr Orly could be very amusing at times. Shad adjusted the ice bag to fit the contour of his skull. 'You sure it was them who ratted?'

'Who else? They're still pissed about the snake dancer, what's-her-name.'

Kevin approached the bar and buoyantly asked for a Perrier. His expression darkened when he felt Shad's glare. Quickly the disc jockey backed away. Shad lunged for him, but missed. Kevin scurried back to the sound booth.

Orly was saying: 'That damn health inspector, he went through the whole joint. I mean brick by brick.'

'Yeah?'

'The thing is, I panicked slightly. I dumped your cottage cheese in the toilet.'

Shad shut his eyes. 'Damn,' he said.

'I had to,' said Orly. 'The guy was relentless. He finds that goddamn scorpion and then what? Already he's threatening to shut us down.'

'So you flushed it.'

'Get yourself another one. Send me the bill.'

Shad was downhearted. 'I'm fucking jinxed. That's all.'

Orly motioned for the bouncer to follow him outside. Shad couldn't have been more pleased. The traffic noise was a Brahms lullaby compared to the mindless shit that Kevin was blasting on the sound system.

In the parking lot, Orly selected a Volvo sedan and centered himself heavily on the hood. 'So—what do we do about these Lings? I'm open to ideas.'

Shad said, 'My brain hurts.'

'You're the only one I can trust.'

'I ain't no arsonist, Mr Orly. I can't light a fuckin' barbecue.'

'Well, then, let's you and me think.'

A charcoal Acura pulled in and parked near the front awning. Urbana Sprawl got out. She was dressed for a Palm Beach cancer ball. Orly and Shad had never seen her in such sumptuous clothes.

'So, how'd it go?' Orly's voice was tight.

The dancer said, 'I'm here, right? So let it drop.'

Shad glanced at Orly. 'I told you.'

With a squeak, Orly slid his butt off the hood. 'Wait a minute, girl. You turned down a thousand dollars to stay here and work for me?'

'Don't be a dick,' Urbana said, irritably.

Shad squeezed her hand. 'You don't have to talk about it.'

'He wanted to play ' "windshield wiper" with my boobs.'

'Who?' Orly said.

'Ling. He tried to pull down my straps and—'

'Which Ling?' asked Shad.

'The little one. I broke two nails on his face.' Urbana displayed her damaged manicure. 'I wouldn't work for those bastards in a zillion years.' She slipped between Orly and Shad and hurried into the club.

Orly said, 'One of us should've got the door.'

Shad gazed down the street, toward the distant winking neon of the Flesh Farm. 'Mr Orly,' he said, 'which Ling is the little one?'

'Does it matter now?'

'Nope. It truly doesn't.'

The *Princess Pia* began attracting fish the day it settled in seventy-nine feet of water off Fort Lauderdale beach. Dive-boat captains such as Abe Cochran scouted the junked freighter regularly, particularly on those mornings when they were low on fuel and energy, and didn't wish to travel far from port. Where in the Atlantic they took their customers depended on the customers themselves. Well-traveled scuba divers wouldn't settle for exploring such an obvious tourist scam as a newly sunken banana boat. Tourists, however, were suckers for it. They were delighted merely to be blowing bubbles, and vastly enthralled by any fleeting glimpse of marine life. Many of them didn't know a queen angelfish from a sturgeon, leaving Captain Abe Cochran free to embellish the underwater sights.

On the morning of October sixth, Kate Esposito and her boyfriend climbed aboard Abe Cochran's thirty-five-foot charter boat, the *Alimony III*. They were joined by four young travel agents who were visiting Fort Lauderdale for a convention. Abe Cochran recognized the group for what it was, and set a true course for the wreck of the *Princess Pia*. The seas were calm, and the anchor held on the first drop. The travel agents were badly hung over, so Abe Cochran handed out snorkels and instructed them to swim close to the stern, where he could keep an eye on them. This left Kate Esposito and her boyfriend to dive the freighter alone.

Kate had learned to scuba dive as a teenager in a YWCA swimming pool in Boston, but her lifelong dream was to visit the tropics. She was greatly anticipating her first moray eel; her boyfriend had purchased an inexpensive underwater camera for the occasion.

As they tumbled backward off Abe Cochran's boat, Kate Esposito noticed that the water was murkier than she expected. 'Gin-clear' is what the tourist brochures had advertised, but Kate could barely see ten feet in front of her face. Her disappointment ebbed as she approached the wreck of the *Princess Pia*, which lay unbroken on its starboard side. To Kate, it seemed as awesome and eerie as the *Titanic*. Together she and her boyfriend swam the length of the bare freighter. Clouds of small aqua-striped fish swam in and out of the dynamite gashes, and once a pair of leopard rays winged gracefully out of the wheel-house. Each sighting brought bubbles of excitement from Kate and her boyfriend, who attempted to snap pictures of every sea creature they encountered.

Kate was the better diver, and it was she who decided to investigate the interior of the hull. She knew, from documentaries on the Discovery Channel, that moray eels preferred dark and remote crevices; perhaps one had taken up residence inside the scuttled *Princess Pia*. Kate tapped on her boyfriend's tank and signaled her intentions. He waved lamely and handed her the camera. Through the dive mask, Kate's eyes flickered in annoyance. Alone she swam through an open hatch cover on the aft deck. Her boyfriend watched the orange flippers disappear into the ship. He checked his wristwatch: ten minutes, then he was going after her.

Milky shafts of pale light broke the darkness of the cargo hold. Kate Esposito moved slowly, feeling her way. The surface of the metal was smooth and unencrusted because the wreck was so new. Seaweed hung in cinnamon tendrils from the braces, and schools of small fish were abundant, shards of glitter in the fuzzy penumbra. As Kate worked her way deeper into the hold, the water felt cooler and heavier against her legs. A saucer-shaped object shone against the freighter's dull iron skin. Kate reached for the shining disc, knowing that it couldn't be anything precious or valuable, but still not expecting a wire-spoked hubcap. Laughing into her regulator, she let the hubcap fall from her hands.

A long gray form took shape in front of her. Swimming closer, Kate Esposito discerned sharp angles of chrome and glass—a car, chained to the spine of the hull! Not a clunker, either, but a late-model American sedan.

Very weird, Kate thought. On a fender panel, she located a plastic nameplate: Lincoln Continental. Why would someone sink a brand-new Lincoln? Maybe it was a gag, she thought, a publicity stunt by one of the radio stations. With one finger, she wrote her first name in the algae film growing on the puckered vinyl roof. Then she snapped a picture of it for her boyfriend.

Except for a cracked driver's window, the Continental was in remarkably good shape. Even the bumper sticker was intact: HAVE YOU HUGGED YOUR LAWYER TODAY?

Kate Esposito saw that the trunk of the car was slightly ajar: *Now there's an ideal place for a moray eel.* From a mesh dive-bag she retrieved a handful of frozen pilchards, which Abe Cochran had given her to feed the marine life, such as it was. Kate picked up one of the stiff minnows and dangled it gingerly above the crack of the Lincoln's trunk. No sinewy green eel emerged to gobble it. After a minute or so, the pilchard came apart in her fingers. Kate got another one and tried again, wiggling the dead fish as enticement. Nothing moved for it.

No one home, Kate thought. With the toe of a flipper she nudged the lid of the car trunk. It opened in slow motion.

Kate Esposito's boyfriend was trying to catch a baby sea turtle when Kate rifled out of the freighter's hatch and kicked freneti-cally for the surface. Kate's boyfriend followed the trail of bubbles to Abe Cochran's boat, where Kate had crawled up on the teak dive platform. Now she was on all fours, coughing up breakfast. The travel agents, treading water near the bow, warbled excitedly through their snorkels.

Abe Cochran laconically ordered all hands into the boat. Kate's boyfriend yanked off his mask and asked her what she'd seen inside the *Princess Pia.*

'Crabs,' she sobbed, 'eating a dead lawyer.'

*

It took the Broward sheriff's divers four hours to recover the bodies of Mordecai and his cousin Joyce. Preserving an underwater crime scene proved too much of a challenge, especially when a school of aggressive lemon sharks arrived. The Lincoln Continental was left for another day.

At noon the TV news reported the discovery of two bodies inside the wreck of the *Princess Pia*. Captain Abe Cochran refused to talk with reporters, and emphasized his reluctance by hoisting a scuba tank to bludgeon a Channel 7 cameraman. Kate Esposito's boyfriend was more voluble. In a live dockside interview, he graphically recounted Kate's discovery of the dead lawyer in the new Lincoln. Sgt Al García, who had a television in his office, immediately phoned a friend at the Broward Medical Examiner's Office and asked permission to sit in on the autopsy. The doctor said sure—there wouldn't be much of a crowd, considering the unpleasantly advanced condition of the deceased.

García, who stopped first at Mordecai's bank, was the last to arrive at the coroner's office in Hollywood. The luckless contingent assigned to the postmortem included two forensic pathologists, three Broward sheriff's detectives and a pair of first-year medical students from the University of Miami. The Florida Bar had declined to send a representative.

Before entering the autopsy room, García stubbed out his cigar and sprinkled the traditional Old Spice cologne inside his disposable surgical mask. The body bag containing Mordecai was the first to be unzipped, and the crabs had been thorough. The skull was practically picked clean, making it easier for pathologists to track the three small-caliber bullet holes. The Broward detectives made notes, and pointed here and there with yellow No. 2 pencils. No one glanced up when the nauseated medical students bolted out the door.

The doctors labored to cut away the dead lawyer's sodden pin-striped suit. García edged up to the table and asked if he could check the pockets. The doctors shrugged and kept cutting.

García held his breath while he pretended to search Mordecai's suit. One of the Broward detectives grumpily asked what the hell he was looking for.

'This,' said Al García. He held up a small key.

Malcolm J. Moldowsky missed the noon news on TV because he was having lunch with two jittery state senators and an overconfident New York bond underwriter. Moldy also missed the six o'clock news; this time he was in the bathroom, grooming himself for an important dinner with the governor. Lately the state of Florida had been pestering operators of phosphate mines about dumping their radioactive sludge into the public groundwater. The phosphate industry regarded as subversive the idea of cleansing its own waste and burying it safely. Malcolm Moldowsky had been hired at a six-figure fee to plead the cause with his old pal, the governor, so that the regulatory climate at the mines might return to normal.

Moldy always dressed by meticulous routine, beginning with his socks. Then came the underwear, shirt, cuff links, necktie, pants and finally the shoes. It was not uncommon for him to spend twenty minutes working a Windsor knot to perfection, and it was at this critical stage that someone knocked on the front door. Moldowsky was irritated, and puzzled, by the interruption; the guard in the lobby was supposed to buzz when a visitor arrived. Moldy strode bare-legged to the door, where he was met by a stocky Cuban with a thick mustache, a damp cigar and a cellular phone under one arm.

'Yes?' Moldowsky made it a demand.

Al García flashed his badge and strolled in. He grinned at the portrait of John Mitchell. 'Either you got a great sense of humor,' he said to Moldy, 'or you're one of the sickest fuckers I ever met.'

Moldowsky said, 'I didn't catch the name.'

García told him.

Moldy felt himself pucker. 'And you're with?'

'Metro Homicide.'

'Is there trouble in the building?'

'I'm sure there is,' García said, 'but that's not why I'm here. How about putting on some pants?'

Malcolm J. Moldowsky nodded coldly, disappeared into the bedroom and robotically finished dressing. He came out brushing the lint from his wool-blend jacket. His mind swarmed with a hundred possibilities, none of them good. He had gambled too recklessly, leaning on the county commissioner; putting the heat on Sgt Al García had backfired.

Moldowsky said, 'I'm meeting the governor for dinner, so I'm in a bit of a hurry.'

'Me, too,' said García. 'I'm going bowling with Ivana Trump.'

The detective's mocking stare was too much. Moldy found a chair. He told himself to shut up, be careful, pay attention!

García said, 'You know a lawyer named Mordecai?'

'No, I don't.'

'He got murdered. Hey, I know what you're thinking and you might be right. Maybe it was a public service. Maybe we should give the killer a medal. A dead lawyer is a dead lawyer, right?'

Moldowsky said nothing. His throat felt like he'd been swallowing razor blades.

'Without going into gory details,' García said, 'here's the scenario. In the dead lawyer's pocket they find a key to a safe-deposit box up in Lauderdale. And in the safe box they find a Rolodex card with your name and phone number—'

'That's impossible,' said Moldowsky, thinking: *You sneaky prick.* 'Sergeant, I never met this man.'

'I think you're lying, Malcolm, but that's for another day. Don't you want to hear what else they found in the bank box?'

'It doesn't concern me.' Moldy didn't recognize his own voice.

'They found a Kodak slide.' Al García paused to measure Moldowsky's reaction, a flurry of blinks. García said, 'The picture was taken at a nude dance club. Features a certain well-known congressman.'

Moldowsky stoically pretended to know nothing about it. He was afraid to look in the wall mirror; he suspected that his upper lip was moist and curling.

García took out a notebook and uncapped a Bic pen. 'This dead lawyer, you sure he didn't try to blackmail you? He and a woman named Joyce Mizner.'

Moldy stood up and shot his cuffs. 'Sergeant, I'm running very late. Come by the office tomorrow.'

The detective, fishing merrily, cast out a name that Erin had picked up from the congressman: 'You know a guy named Erb Crandall?'

'Of course,' Moldowsky said. His facial muscles were cramping, from trying to appear calm.

'Where do you know him from?' the detective asked.

'From politics. We can talk about this tomorrow.'

'You bet.' García slapped the notebook shut and crammed it crookedly into his coat. He took out a piece of paper and ran his finger down a column of numbers. Then he picked up his cellular phone and dialed.

The telephone on Malcolm Moldowsky's desk began to ring. He stared at it rigidly, hatefully.

Al García said, 'Answer it.'

Moldy didn't move. 'I'm not fond of games.'

The phone kept ringing. 'It's for you,' Garcia said.

'What's your point?'

García turned the cellular off. Moldowsky's phone fell silent. García smiled; he felt like Columbo. 'You got a non-pub number,' he said.

'Of course I do,' said Moldy. 'But you're a police officer. All you need to do is call Southern Bell.'

'That's not how I got it.' García showed the paper to Moldowsky. It was a copy of the itemized bill from the Holiday Inn in Missoula, where the killers had stayed after they dumped the late Jerry Killian into the Clark Fork River.

García said, 'Somebody in Room 212 called here that night. Talked for quite a while.'

'I recall no such conversation.' Moldy's cheeks were on fire. He had assumed the Jamaicans had dialed on a credit card, not direct from the room. *Direct!*

'Maybe you want to contact your lawyer,' García said.

Moldowsky laughed harshly and said don't be ridiculous.

'Your choice,' said the detective. 'One more question, *chico*. Where can I find David Dilbeck tonight?'

Moldowsky said he had no idea.

'Really? I'm told he doesn't wipe his ass without your permission.'

Moldy's composure finally shattered. He bellowed and stomped around the apartment and pounded on the credenza and vowed that Al García would be writing parking tickets for the rest of his miserable career.

'So,' García said, 'you're a man of some influence.'

'Goddamn right.'

'And I've insulted you?'

'Worse than that, Sergeant.'

'Then please accept my sincere apology.' García rose. 'I'll find the congressman on my own.' He straightened Moldowsky's necktie and told him he looked like a million bucks. 'But that cologne of yours could gag a maggot,' he said. 'Personally, I go for the domestic stuff.'

The moment the detective was gone, Malcolm Moldowsky lurched to the desk and seized the phone—the tool of all his genius, the instrument of his betrayal. He was comforted by its feel, the familiar way it fit in his palm, but he was uncertain of his next play. Whom could he call to fix this terrible trouble? Who would have the power to cover it up?

Nobody, Moldy decided gravely. The lawyer's body had been found, and so had the dreaded photograph from the Eager Beaver. The bank box had been opened, emptied, then opened again and salted with evidence—the Rolodex card was a cute touch. At least this prick García had a sense of irony . . .

Moldowsky's gaze fell on the portrait of the great one, John Newton Mitchell—the hooded eyes, the jowly arrogant smirk. What would *he* do, the canny old toad? *Stonewall the bastards.* Naturally. Admit nothing, deny everything. It would have worked, too. Watergate would have dried up and blown away like a chicken turd, if only . . . if only Nixon, that paranoid gnome, had listened.

Sweet Jesus, thought Moldowsky. I've got to find David before that goddamn Cuban does.

He dialed the congressman's private line. It rang twice before the machine picked up. Moldy left a curt message but gave no instructions, as it would only confuse David Dilbeck. Next Moldy tried to locate Erb Crandall in Atlantic City, but none of the big hotels showed him on the register. Either Erb was staying in a dive, or lying about his destination.

Moldowsky felt a cold, crushing weight on his heart. He hung up the telephone and groped for his car keys.

When was Dilbeck meeting the stripper? Was tonight the night?

28

Erin stopped at the club with a present for Monique Sr. It was a sheer silk blouse from Neiman's.

'Sorry about the other night,' Erin said. 'Darrell is Darrell. It's a hopeless situation.'

Monique Sr liked the blouse. She buttoned it over a Day-Glo dance bra. 'Oh, Erin, it's beautiful.'

'That's not for work. That's for somebody special.'

'Special? I wish.' She twirled in front of the mirror, first one way, then another. 'Guess who's ringside at the pit? Garrick Utley.'

Erin said, 'You can't wrestle. Not with your hand cut up.'

'I'm wearing pink evening gloves till it's healed. Mr Orly says I look like Mamie Van Doren.' Monique Sr told Erin about Urbana Sprawl's dispiriting encounter with the Ling brothers.

Erin said, 'Pitiful. I always heard they were gropers.'

There was more unsettling gossip from the dressing room. Once more, Orly surreptitiously had lowered the thermostat to sixty-eight degrees, to promote nipple erections on stage. Also, the multi-wigged Sabrina had been offered three thousand dollars to make a porn film on South Beach.

'She's gonna do it,' Monique Sr said.

'Where is she?'

'The cage.' Monique Sr took off the blouse and put it on a hanger. 'You're too dressed,' she said to Erin. 'I'll go out and tell her you're here.'

Sabrina was her usual sweet-tempered self. She felt a kinship with Erin because both of them had smallish breasts and felonious ex-husbands.

Erin said, 'Tell me about this so-called movie.'

'They said I've got to screw two guys in a hot tub and that's all.'

'Why are you doing this?'

Sabrina seemed puzzled by the question. 'They're paying me,' she said.

'You need money, I'll give it to you.'

The dancer's eyes widened in amusement. 'Three grand? Come on.'

'Whatever you want.'

'Erin, you don't understand. I can't take any more of this wrestling shit. The pasta is just as gross as the creamed corn.'

'But once you do porn—'

'Hey, you don't know what it's like up there. Drunks trying to cram cold niblets up your crack—Jesus, you ought to try it some time.' It was one of the few times Erin had seen Sabrina angry.

'I'll talk to Orly. We'll put a stop to it.'

'Look, the movie can't be worse than wrestling.'

'You ever seen one?'

Sabrina admitted that she hadn't.

'Well, I have,' Erin said. 'When I worked at the FBI, they seized a truckload of tapes at the airport. The agents had a private screening one night in the basement.'

Sabrina's curiosity was earnest. 'What's it like? Are they really so bad?'

'You know what a cum shot is?'

Sabrina said she did not. Erin explained.

'Yukky.' Sabrina reddened. 'The director didn't tell me.'

'I'll bet he didn't.'

'Let me think about this.'

'Take your time,' Erin said.

Sabrina freshened her lipstick and returned to the lounge. Urbana Sprawl came to the dressing room and showed Erin her broken fingernails. She said, 'Men are the scum of the earth.'

'As a general rule,' Erin agreed.

'I think you like that Cuban cop.'

'He's solidly married.'

'Another heartbreaker.'

'His wife's taking care of my daughter,' Erin said. 'She's terrific, too.'

'And here you sit on a Saturday night.'

'Oh, I've got big plans,' Erin said. 'Tonight I dance for the congressman.'

'Mercy,' said Urbana. 'Just answer me why.'

Erin yawned and stretched her arms over her head. 'Because it's my civic duty.'

Rita patiently cleansed her brother's wound.

'I can't do much with this fracture,' she declared.

'Don't even try.'

'What's the goo on your shirt?'

'Mozzarella,' Darrell Grant said. 'Don't ask.'

Rita created a splint for his broken left arm. She used an Ace bandage, hurricane tape and Alberto Alonso's nine-iron. The blade of the golf club stuck out the same end as Darrell Grant's fingers.

'All set,' Rita told him, biting off the last piece of tape. 'Now get a move on before Alberto comes home.'

Darrell's skin was the colour of oatmeal, and his breathing was rapid. 'I could use some morphine,' he said.

'We don't have no morphine. How's about Nuprin?'

'Lord Christ.'

'They say it's better than Tylenols.'

'Rita, I swear to God—'

'All right, how's about this? I got some special pills for Lupa. The vet gave me a bottle for when she had the puppies.'

Darrell Grant looked hopeful. 'Dog morphine?'

'Yeah, I guess.'

She found the bottle and tried to decipher the name of the drug. Neither she nor her brother had heard of it.

'It says two capsules every six hours.'

'That's if you're a fucking poodle,' Darrell said. 'Gimme four and a cold Busch.'

Afterward he vomited for twenty-five minutes. Rita kept daubing his chin and telling him to hurry—Alberto was on the way home from the nuclear plant. Darrell said he was in no shape to travel. Rita assisted him down the front steps and showed him where to hide, in the crawl space under the mobile home.

'Where'd you park the Pontiac?' she asked. 'In case Mrs Gomez puts her glasses on.'

'Down behind the Circle K.' Darrell Grant shimmied beneath the doublewide. He dragged the splinted arm like a chunk of lumber; the blade of the nine-iron made a groove in the dirt.

Ritz said, 'I'll bring a blanket.'

'What about the damn wolves?'

'Don't you worry. They den on the lee side, strictly.'

'Rita, I can't stay down here!'

A car rolled into the driveway. Rita put her fingers to her lips, then she was gone.

Darrell Grant heard Alberto Alonso's voice, the crunch of gravel under his work boots, the screen door slamming . . .

Trapped! Darrell thought. He turned his head slowly, left then right, to assess conditions in the bunker. He wondered about the chances of Rita's trailer falling off the foundation and crushing him like a bug. Unlikely, he decided; the thing was practically brand new, replacing the one that Rita and Alberto had lost to the hurricane. Darrell Grant pressed his good arm against the aluminum—it seemed as sturdy as a mobile home could be. Yet he felt edgy in his underground refuge. The air was as cool as a tomb and smelled sharply of rodents. Still, it was better than spending another night in a dumpster behind the Pizza Hut.

The pain in his mangled arm was piercing and unremittent; chills racked his other limbs. His whole life, Rita always told him how smart and handsome and fortunate he was. 'You can do anything you want in this world,' she'd say. 'You got the looks and the vocabulary.' In retrospect, Darrell Grant realized that marrying Erin had been the high point, the main window of opportunity. If ever he was going to turn things around, she was his big chance. Hell, he'd struggled to please her, too. He'd tried the conventional life: sobriety, monogamy, a day job, the whole ball of wax. It simply wasn't meant to be. He was chronically ill-suited for the responsibilities that come with lawful behavior. Erin didn't even try to understand. When the marriage broke up,

Rita was disappointed. Darrell explained: 'I need a girl that's more of a short-range thinker. Like myself.'

Now, in the short range, Darrell Grant focused on a pair of problems: stopping the flaming agony in his arm, and snatching Angie away from his ex-wife.

After supper, Rita came out and peeked under the trailer. She was ready for an outing with the wolf-dogs—catcher's mask, logger's mitts, the frayed housedress. Darrell noticed that she'd added plastic shin guards to the uniform.

'I brought some fried chicken,' Rita said. 'Extra crispy.'

She placed a cold drumstick in his mouth. Darrell tore off a huge bite and spit the bone. He said, 'Is it Mrs Gomez that's got the cancer?'

'No, her husband. He passed in August.'

'I bet she's still got his pills.'

'Darrell, no!'

'In the bathroom cabinet, I'll bet.' He lifted his head. 'Rita, I'm damn near crazy from the pain. Please?'

'You already stole the poor woman's car.'

'But her husband's croaked, right? So what's the sense of letting good medicine go to waste? Tell me, Rita.'

'I dunno what all to look for.'

'Demerol, Dilaudids, codeine—shit, bring me everything with the old man's name on it.'

'But then you gotta go,' Rita persisted, 'before the damn cops come by again.'

'That's a promise,' said Darrell Grant.

There was something else he needed, but he couldn't ask his sister because she'd never agree. Never in a month of Sundays.

But that's all right, Darrell thought, because I know where it is. I know exactly where Alberto keeps it—the same place as every other macho meathead in Miami.

In the glove box of his car. Fully loaded.

Canceling the dinner engagement was easy. In fact, a less distracted Malcolm J. Moldowsky would have noticed the edge of relief in the governor's voice. Stomach problems? he'd said.

That's too bad, Malcolm. Give me a ring when you're feeling better. When he hung up, the governor had turned to an aide and said: 'Let's pray it's a tumor.'

As he drove toward the towers of Turnberry Isle, Moldowsky's mind was preoccupied with thoughts contrived to stave off panic. The cop had nothing, really, but a Kodak slide and a motel bill.

The phone call from Missoula could be explained. Moldy would claim he had houseguests that night. Lots of long-distance calls in and out. It wouldn't be difficult to find someone who would say (for a price): *Yes, come to think of it, so-and-so's boyfriend's foster uncle called from Montana. Drunk as a skunk, yakking his fool head off . . . what was his name again?*

The photograph from the tittie bar was something else. Clearly, that goddamn García knew the story behind it. Malcolm Moldowsky gripped the steering wheel ferociously, zigzagging through the traffic. A ghastly scene played over and over in his head . . .

The congressman, wearing only cowboy boots and boxer shorts, downcast and bleary on the bow of the yacht.

The Cuban cop, puffing maliciously on his cigar, circling like a starved panther, waving the Kodak slide, firing brutal questions faster than David Lane Dilbeck could possibly invent credible answers.

Dilbeck—tremulous, wilting, caving in. Yes, Sergeant, that's me in the picture. Me with the champagne bottle. Please understand, I'm not well. I need help controlling my animal urges. Ask the lady, go ahead. I never meant to harm a soul . . .

Moldy drove faster. For consolation he clutched at the fact that Dilbeck had no knowledge of what had happened to the blackmailers, Killian and the lawyer. The congressman didn't know what drastic steps had been taken to shield him from scandal. This prick García could interrogate him all day long and come up empty. There were many crimes to which a badgered David Dilbeck might legitimately confess, but murder wasn't one of them.

Traffic came to a stop at the Golden Glades cloverleaf, where a truck hauling limerock had jackknifed on a ramp. Moldowsky cursed, snarled, raked his polished fingernails on the dashboard. He couldn't understand García's interest in a drowned fisherman gand a murdered lawyer. The cases belonged in Broward County, not Dade. What did he want? What was he after? The way the crazy bastard had come at him, with no pretense of respect or civility. Taunting him, fucking with him—like it was personal.

The cars inched along in maddening spurts. As therapy, Moldowsky jammed both fists on the horn. In the station wagon ahead of him, a frizzy-haired young woman flipped him the finger. The man on the passenger side held a MAC-10 out the window as a hint for Moldy to be patient and shut the fuck up.

For diversion Moldowsky tried the radio, and found a call-in program where the guest happened to be Eloy Flickman, Dilbeck's Republican opponent in the congressional race. Moldy was soothed by what he heard. Flickman now was advocating mandatory tubal ligations for all single mothers applying for food stamps. To another caller, Flickman submitted that Cuba's nascent tourist industry was luring too many European visitors away from Miami, and that only a direct nuclear strike on Havana would remove the burgeoning economic threat. Moldy thought: Wonderful! The man's a certifiable loon. Dilbeck's a lock to win re-election, as long as nothing breaks loose in the headlines.

The traffic jam slowly started to unclog. Malcolm Moldowsky switched to a classical music station, and tried to relax. Tonight's mission was uncomplicated: remove the congressman from the Rojos' yacht, and far away from all naked women.

If the detective got there first, well . . . Maybe a bribe was in order. Maybe that's all García wanted.

Moldy hoped so; it would make life so much easier.

When darkness fell, Darrell Grant snatched the gun from Alberto's car and crawled back under the mobile home. Later Rita showed up with three prescription bottles belonging to the late Rogelio Gomez. Darrell Grant poured the pills into the palm of his good hand, and ate three of everything. An hour later, the whole world was a blur, but Darrell felt marvelous. The pain in his arm was gone, along with much of his short-term memory. Rita had to remind him where he'd hidden the stolen Pontiac.

Once he located the turnpike, Darrell Grant drove northbound at a geriatric pace. His vision and reflexes were abominable. Rita's splint proved sturdy but cumbersome: the nine-iron got in the way of Darrell's driving. He had to hang it out the window of the car, as if permanently signaling for a left turn. Since it was Dade County, no one paid the slightest attention.

The trip to Fort Lauderdale took ninety minutes. Darrell Grant spent most of it in the draft of a slow-moving Pentecostal church bus. Miraculously, he spotted the Commercial Boulevard exit in time to steer off. He stopped at a fast-food restaurant next door to the Tickled Pink, and parked obliviously in the drive-through lane. Rousted by a surly assistant manager, Darrell Grant found a new spot. This one offered a clear view of Orly's strip joint; Erin's shitheap Fairlane was parked near the front awning between a Porsche and a Cadillac.

Like she was somebody special, Darrell thought.

He broke out laughing. Everything seemed hilarious tonight; the sight of a dead opossum on the highway had made him giggle all the way from Okeechobee Road to Miramar. These were absolutely top-notch drugs. 'God bless you, Señor Gomez!' he said, saluting the heavens with his nine-iron.

Before long, a limousine appeared at Orly's nightclub. Darrell Grant thought his eyes were playing tricks.

The driver, a black man wearing a cap, got out of the limo and opened one of the doors. In the Pontiac, Darrell leaned forward and tried to squint the blur from his eyes. He was hoping to catch sight of a celebrity. Rock stars were known to hang out at nudie bars; Darrell had seen a video once on MTV.

But it was his ex-wife who walked out of the club toward the limo. She wore blue jeans, a baggy white T-shirt and sandals. She carried a shoulder bag and a shoebox. It looked like she was heading home early. She was alone, too. No trace of Angela.

Darrell Grant was astounded when she got into the limousine.

'The cunt,' he said, turning the key in the Pontiac. Who the fuck does she think she is? Who?

Then he started to laugh again.

When the limousine pulled out of the club, the Pontiac was close behind.

29

Shad went to Sears and purchased two jumbo outdoor garbage buckets with clip-on lids. Then he drove to a snake farm near the Tamiami Airport, west of Miami. The man who owned the snake farm called himself Jungle Juan. He told Shad that most of his reptile stock had been wiped out by the hurricane. His insurance company still hadn't paid off.

'They say I padded the claim,' complained Jungle Juan, 'but I had papers on every damn snake. Certified papers!'

'Like they do for dogs,' Shad said.

'*Exactamente.*'

'And they all got killed in the storm?'

'Hard to say.' Jungle Juan thoughtfully fingered his diamond ear stud. 'They was mostly just gone from sight. I'll assume some escapes, I'll assume some mortalities.'

Shad tried to strike a hopeful note. He said, 'Snakes are tough customers.'

'Some are, some ain't. One old diamondback, the wind picked him up and snapped him like a bullwhip. I seen this myself.'

Shad said, 'But the rats and mice made out OK.'

'By and large, yessir. How many you need?'

'A hundred ought to do it. Rats only.'

Jungle Juan said, 'Now, these ain't white. These are semi-wild Norways.'

'Perfect.'

The cage was eight feet long and four feet high. It was fashioned of plywood and chicken wire. Inside was an undulating mass of vermin, two and three deep. Anticipating food, the rats swarmed noisily toward the cage door when Jungle Juan approached. Deftly he bare-handed the squealing animals, and dropped them one by one into the jumbo garbage pails.

Shad watched impassively. He had no particular aversion to rodents. 'Looks like you got a surplus,' he remarked.

Jungle Juan snorted. 'Rats up the ass, and no snakes to eat 'em. There's your hundred.' He slapped the lids on the garbage cans and said, 'Thank God there's a shipment of boas due Monday. I expect they'll be hungry.'

Shad said, 'We had a dancer that tried a boa.'

'How big?'

'The snake? Seven feet.'

Jungle Juan said, 'Your ball pythons are better for entertainment purposes. They don't bite so damn much.'

Shad asked how much he owed. Jungle Juan said fifty bucks.

'Man, that's cheap.' Shad handed him the cash.

'Hurricane discount,' Jungle Juan explained. 'I gotta move these buggers before they fuck me into Chapter 11. Every day they's a dozen new litters and what happens is, I swear, they start to consume one another.'

He and Shad carried the garbage buckets out to Shad's car. The sound of many rat paws could be heard, scratching feverishly against the heavy plastic. As they loaded the animals into the backseat, Jungle Juan inquired about the dancer with the boa constrictor. Shad told him that she'd taken ill and gone home to Texas.

'What about the snake?' asked Jungle Juan, shrewdly.

'I got him in a stockroom at the club.'

'Healthy?'

'A little farsighted, but otherwise OK.'

'Well, I could sure use him,' Jungle Juan said, 'if you ever wanted to sell.'

'Not just yet,' said Shad.

When he returned to the club, Mr Orly asked to see the rats. Shad let him peek in one of the pails.

'Goddamn,' said Orly, crinkling his face.

'We all set?'

'Yep,' Orly said. 'I just wish I could be there to see it. Those fucking Lings.' He laughed venomously. 'I'd love to get the whole thing on video!'

Shad asked about Erin. Orly said she'd left to meet that goddamn horny no-good congressman.

'Where?' Shad asked.

'I'm assuming the boat. Who cares?'

Shad called Al García's office and left a message. Then he went into the stockroom and emerged with a large dirty pillowcase, knotted at the neck. Orly wished him good luck.

'You come right back,' he told the bouncer. 'It's gonna get busy as hell around here.'

'How long since she took off?'

'Erin? Half-hour, tops.' Orly studied him warily. 'Don't you worry about her. You just get your ass back here, OK?'

Shad circled the Flesh Farm until he spotted the health inspector's car, a gray Dodge Aries with yellow state plates. Monique Jr had been recruited to make the phone call, because no man could resist her helpless little-girl voice. *The rats, they're everywhere!* she'd exclaimed. *They're biting me, they're biting me!* The health department had kept its promise to send someone right over. The inspectors, Shad knew, trampled each other for such an assignment.

Shad parked the car, threw a ladder against the side of the building and hauled the jumbo garbage pails to the roof. The air-conditioning vents rose like squat chimneys at each end of the building. Shad pried off the rusty grids and poured the rats into the duct system. The little guys seemed grateful to be free.

The Lings were hunkered in the office, dodging the health inspector. They had ordered one of the table dancers to get him drunk and compromised. Then they would talk.

Shad barged in and caught the two brothers by surprise.

'What's in the bag?' asked the one wearing a black tuxedo and a Yankees cap. Shad knew him as the Flesh Farm's floor manager. He sat on a torn Naugahyde sofa that was the color of ox blood. Behind the desk was the other Ling, who wore a gray pullover and two ropey gold chains on his neck. He, too, inquired about the contents of the pillowcase.

'Stand up,' Shad said.

Both Lings displayed the identical annoying mannerism of laughing through their teeth, hissing on the inhale. Shad took out the .38 Special and shot three ragged holes in a family portrait on the wall. One of the bullets sensationally disfigured the likeness of the Lings' paternal grandmother; the brothers seemed horrified.

'Bingo,' Shad said. 'Who's next?'

The Lings stood up quickly. Shad arranged them back-to-back in the center of the floor.

One of them said, 'You gone shoot us?'

'Nope,' Shad answered, 'I'm gonna measure you. Take off the damn cap.'

He quickly determined that the tuxedoed Ling was at least two inches taller than the gold-chained Ling. 'You're the one,' Shad said to the shorter brother, 'who grabbed my friend's tits.'

The smaller Ling frowned in vexation. Urbana's fingernail tracks were plainly visible on one cheek. Somebody knocked on the door, and Shad concealed the gun in his belt.

A frantic voice of indistinct gender. 'Mr Ling, come quick! Come now!' A woman's scream cut through the dance music. The brothers glanced at one another in alarm. Shad ordered the one in the tuxedo to go check on the trouble.

The larger Ling said, 'Maybe we should call police.'

'Try an exterminator,' Shad advised.

With both hands the larger brother fitted the Yankees cap tightly on his head, the visor practically touching his nose. Wordlessly he slipped out of the office. Shad locked the door and shoved the smaller Ling into a swivel chair.

'This no business of yours,' the brother protested. 'It's that boss you got. Mister Hotshit Mafia Man.'

Shad twisted Ling's wrist to check the time on the phony Rolex. It was getting late.

Ling pulled his arm away. 'Fat Tony, my ass,' he said, spitting unintentionally. 'Orly must think we stupid, huh? They got Mafia in Japan, too. Plenty fucking Mafia!'

Shad untied the knot in the pillowcase. He felt serene and contented—a rare moment of moral clarity.

Ling said, 'I didn't grab nobody's titties.'

Shad opened the pillowcase and angled it toward the overhead light, so he could see down into the corners. 'I feel good about this,' he said, to no one.

Ling noticed the sinuated movement in the bottom of Shad's sack. He could see the shape of heavy, muscular coils shifting against the fabric.

'You better not!' he shouted.

Shad commanded Ling to stand up and drop his jeans. Ling refused. Shad drew the pistol and poked the barrel in the man's navel. The brother set his jaw and said, 'I rather be shot dead. Make it quick, too.'

Shad thought: What an actor, this guy.

Ling regarded the pillowcase anxiously. 'You sick man,' he said to Shad.

'Really? You're the ones cut poor Bubba to pieces.'

The brother scowled in confusion. 'Bubba?'

Shad clubbed him in the temple with the butt of the .38. Ling fell briefly unconscious. He awoke naked, hot and discomfited. Shad had hung him from the office door, securing his wrists to the coat hook.

The smaller Ling cursed and writhed, his heels and elbows banging against the wood. From the hallway outside came the sounds of mounting chaos. Stretched on the Naugahyde sofa, Shad tended to the liberated boa constrictor; before leaving town, Lorelei had neglected to remove the tape from the snake's mouth.

'What you doing?' Ling demanded.

Shad said, 'This old boy's half-starved.' He piled the reptile on the floor, beneath the dangling and helpless Ling. As the tan-and-brown mass unraveled itself, the brother's upper lip curled in fear. The boa, being naturally arboreal, searched for something to climb. In the absence of a tree, it chose Ling's bare leg. The more vigorously the brother kicked, the tighter the snake drew its coils.

'You know what?' said Shad. 'Your schlong looks just like a hamster.'

After a short contemplation, Ling issued a series of high-pitched screams. The boa's tongue feathered against his quaking skin. He cried: 'It's gone bite my wee-wee!'

Shad thought it was very funny. 'Your what? Is that what it's called in Japan?'

'Get it off me, goddammit.'

The snake continued its ominous ascent.

'You were very rude,' Shad said, 'to grab my friend's boobs the other night.'

'I'm s-s-sorry. I couldn't help it.' Ling had lapsed into a pathetic whine. 'Some girls don't mind,' he said.

'Oh, I doubt that seriously.' Shad wondered how long the coat hook would hold fast under the brother's weight.

Ling struggled to make himself motionless. Fighting, he feared, would agitate the creature. 'Please,' he whispered morosely, 'get it off me. I'll do anything you want.'

Shad yawned. He removed his beret and brushed the lint off the crown. The boa's tongue flicked in and out. It had drawn a vague bead on Ling's shriveling organ.

'Oh-oh,' said Shad. The poor thing *was* starved.

Ling went slack on the door. He let out an involuntary whimper. 'It's gone eat me,' he asserted. The boa's clouded eyes followed every tremble and sway of Ling's luckless member.

Shad said, 'You act like an animal, you get treated like one. Remember that.'

'I s-s-said I sorry.'

Shad smirked bitterly. 'Sorry is the word for it.'

The snake's head rose in a fluid arc, as if levitated by hydraulics. Its creamy neck banded to muscle in the shape of an S.

'Get ready,' Shad warned.

'Oh my God!'

'Don't be such a pussy. It ain't even poisonous.'

'But my wee-wee!'

The boa's strike was too rapid for the human eye. Ling felt the needle sting of teeth before his mind registered the image of the snake's open jaws, lashing. He passed out mid-scream.

When the brother regained consciousness, he found himself face down on the moldy shag carpet. There was no sign of Shad or the farsighted boa constrictor. When Ling rolled over, the effort ignited a burst of pain between his legs. He allowed one hand to explore the jeopardized zone. The brother sighed gratefully: he was punctured but intact, and fully attached.

In exhausted relief, Ling closed his eyes. 'Sick man,' he said. 'Very sick man.'

A faint noise in the ceiling caught his attention. He opened his eyes just in time to see a fat brown rat jump from the air-conditioning vent. It landed, with a perturbed squeak, squarely on Ling's sad and astonished face.

Some of the Flesh Farm's customers were so drunk that the infestation didn't bother them. The performers and waitresses, however, reacted more intelligently: they fled. All friction dancing ceased. The larger Ling armed his two bouncers with aluminum softball bats and directed a violent but ineffective counterattack. The rodents proved quick-footed and elusive. As if by destiny, one vaulted from the Michelob display to befoul the health inspector's whiskey sour.

Shad watched from a bar stool. He thought things went pretty well. As sabotage, it wasn't exceptionally clever, but Mr Orly couldn't expect miracles on short notice. Orly, after all, had wanted to torch the place! A four-alarm blaze might have been more satisfying, visually, but it wouldn't have put the Ling brothers out of business. They'd have simply rebuilt with the insurance money, and probably upgraded—new marquees, new decor, a new sound system. Orly didn't like that prospect one bit, and endorsed the impromptu rat plague as an alternative. Rodent publicity would be fatal to the Flesh Farm.

The TV crews beat the police by five minutes. Onstage, a beautiful nude Brazilian was on her knees, hammering at a lump of lifeless fur. The weapon was a standard high-heeled shoe.

With each blow, the dancer's breasts swung back and forth in tandem, like church bells. Shad wondered how the TV people would edit the tape to make it presentable for the eleven o'clock news.

He went to the parking lot to watch the squad cars arrive. He stopped counting at nine. A busload of orphans could plunge off a bridge and you wouldn't see so many cops. Shad smiled cynically. Nothing brought out the cavalry like strippers in distress.

One of the dancers, a petite brunette, recognized Shad in the gathering crowd. She said, 'You work down the street.'

'Until tonight.'

'I auditioned there about two months ago. When it was the Eager Beaver.'

Shad said he remembered, although he didn't. The dancer put on a long pink sweatshirt to cover her diaphanous stage costume. Shad found her extremely attractive. He had come to adore women in clothes.

The brunette noticed the pillowcase. 'Whatcha got there?'

'A boa constrictor,' Shad said. 'Want it?'

'For what?'

'For your act.'

The brunette said no thanks. One snake dancer in town was plenty.

'But Lorelei's gone,' Shad told her. 'It's wide-open territory.'

'I don't know. I'm not crazy about snakes.'

'Who the hell is?' He handed her the boa in the pillowcase. 'Think about it,' he said. 'Work up a routine.'

He returned to the Tickled Pink and told Orly that the rats were a huge hit. Orly said he figured as much; the place was filling with customers spooked from the Flesh Farm. Orly wanted to know if Urbana's honor had been avenged, and Shad told him the story of the smaller Ling. Orly laughed so hard that he blew cream soda out of his nose.

'Those fuckers,' he gurgled, 'are finished!'

'Congratulations,' Shad said, turning away.

Orly told him to go check on table four. 'It's a bunch of coked-up roofers. One of 'em brought a goddamn dildo.'

Shad said, 'I need to go see about Erin.'

'Like hell. You're on the floor tonight.'

'No, Mr Orly. I've pretty much had it.' He jumped the bar, punched open the cash register and removed sixty-four dollars. 'Yesterday's pay,' said Shad, fanning the cash. 'What I did tonight, that's for free.' He found the Camus paperback and wedged it into his waistband.

Orly said, 'Hell, don't quit on me.'

'It's time.'

'The fuck does that mean? *It's time.*' Orly blocked Shad's path. 'You want a raise? Is this your way of hitting me up?'

Shad gripped him by the soft meat of the shoulders. 'I'm suffocating,' he said, 'in this world.'

'Get serious,' said Orly, pulling free. 'Wall-to-wall pussy, and you're suffocating? 'Scuze me if I don't break down and cry.'

'It's not your fault, Mr Orly. I seen too much.'

Orly suggested a vacation. He told Shad to take a week off, fly to the islands, get laid repeatedly. Shad shook his head. 'A week won't do it,' he said.

'Then make it ten days.'

'You don't understand, Mr Orly. I gotta get out completely. I've lost my sense of wonderment.'

'Oh, for Chrissake,' Orly said. He led Shad to a quiet corner, away from the dance floor. 'When you were a little boy, what'd you want to be when you grew up? I mean, was your life plan to break heads in a nudie joint?'

Shad said, 'I wanted to play for the Forty-niners.'

'Right! And what happened?'

'I got fucking busted in the ninth grade.'

Orly rolled his eyes. 'Point is, almost nobody gets where they want in this life. Everybody's dream takes a beating. Me, I wanted to be an obstetrician.' He waved a pudgy pale hand at the strobe-lit scene behind him. 'This is as close as I got. You follow? It's called facing reality.'

Shad was sidetracked by the laughable notion of Mr Orly aspiring to a medical career. It was one of the most spectacular lies he'd heard in a long time.

'There's different kinds of reality,' he told Orly. 'I want the mystery back in mine.'

'Fuck mystery. Let's talk loyalty. When I hired you, hell, you still had eyebrows. That's how long ago.'

Shad was unmoved by the sentimentality. He could not recall a single Christmas bonus.

Orly said, 'Like it or not, this is God's plan for you. This is what you're cut out for—'

'You should've been a preacher,' Shad said, 'on TV.'

'If it's the scorpion thing, I said I was sorry. Bottom line, I freaked when the inspector showed up.'

Shad said it was no big deal.

'Then what the fuck else can I say?'

'Just *adios*,' said Shad.

Orly's chest sagged in defeat. He shook Shad's enormous hand and said, 'I suppose you got prospects.'

'Nope, but I got some interesting ideas.' Shad said goodbye. Orly watched, dejectedly, as the huge pearly orb floated above the crowd, toward the door.

Urbana Sprawl hopped off a table and intercepted Shad with a tender hug. 'My hero,' she purred.

'That's me, babe.' Shad took the red beret from his pocket and arranged it at a sly angle on Urbana's head. 'Is Erin at the yacht?' he asked.

'Dancing her pretty heart out.'

'What the hell's she up to?' Shad was forced to holler over a rap number that Kevin had sadistically cranked to ninety decibels.

Urban, shouting in his ear. 'I think she's out to do some damage!'

The music seemed to affect Shad's focus and equilibrium; each bass beat fell like a sledge on his brainpan. He wondered how many bullets would be required to take out the wall speakers.

'Onward and upward,' he said to Urbana Sprawl, and elbowed his way out of the lounge.

The penthouse condominium of Malcolm J. Moldowsky was twenty minutes by automobile from the two-bedroom tract house owned by Jesse James Braden and his wife. It might as well have been a whole other universe, as far as Al García was concerned.

The murder of Jesse James Braden was precipitated by two connected events. At exactly 5:10 p.m. on the sixth of October, Jesse James Braden spilled a shaker of Bloody Marys on the freshly laundered upholstery of his wife's Toyota Camry. That was the first event. At exactly 5:11 p.m., Jesse James Braden laughed uproariously at what he'd done. That was the second event.

At exactly 5:12 p.m., the wife of Jesse James Braden dragged him from the Toyota and shot him fatally in the genitals.

Neighbors were divided on the question of whether Mrs Braden had been excessive in her reaction. Witnesses agreed that Jesse had been a prodigious sinner and often conducted himself in a manner that invited homicide. The shooting itself was not so much at issue as Mrs Braden's selection of anatomical targets. The men in the crowd, sober and otherwise, felt that the mere spilling of an alcoholic beverage—and subsequent insensitive laughter—failed to justify three bullets through the penis. The women of the neighborhood, however, asserted that the decedent got exactly what he deserved—a just punishment for years of piggish whoring, drunken violence and general bad behavior. Jesse James Braden, they said, did not respect his wife or her personal belongings.

Into this boisterous debate waded Al García at precisely 6:47 p.m. He didn't want to be there; he wanted to be setting an ambush for a genuine United States congressman—flashing the badge, barking out the Miranda, scaring the piss out of the bastard. He had a gut feeling that the guy would fall apart, start blabbering. García had been looking forward to the moment.

Instead, the detective stood on a front lawn no different from a million other front lawns, except that the man who had mowed it was lying agape in the bromeliads, with his pecker shot off. The paramedics said Jesse James Braden bled out in three minutes flat. It's like a fire hose, they said, the way it leaks.

García hoped to finish the interviews in an hour, since the witnesses concurred on every detail except the precise final utterance of Jesse James Braden—a brief but vituperative tirade. His wife, now safely handcuffed, insisted on showing García the tomato-juice stains on the seat of her car. She demanded that the police photographer get a picture, so that the judge could see what that worthless Jesse had done. When Al García inquired about the murder weapon, Mrs Braden led him indoors to the kitchen. She had placed the pistol in the refrigerator with her dead husband's booze.

The detective's work proceeded smoothly until Jesse's grief-stricken brother arrived at the crime scene and opened fire with a 16-gauge shotgun. Francis Scott Braden missed Jesse's wife by twenty feet, but he grazed a patrolman and blew the rear window out of Al García's unmarked Caprice. The chaotic interruption meant two hours of extra paperwork for García, who again was reminded how much he hated domestic homicides. It wasn't detective work—it was purely janitorial.

García didn't receive Shad's message until he was back in the car, rolling on the interstate, the air whipping through the busted window, scattering his police papers. He drove the Caprice as fast as it would go, cursing the Saturday night traffic because he was missing the big show: Erin, dancing up a storm.

30

Erin fixed a drink from the mini-bar in the back of the limousine. She wondered about the dream she'd had the night before: making love to a man in an orchard of coconut palms. The man looked vaguely like Al García. In the dream it was daytime, the lemon sun arcing high and scorching. The man was nude but Erin wore a black dress, cut high to the neck. She remembered getting on top, telling the man to hush now, relax. She remembered her knees stinging on the rough bed of dry fronds. In the dream there was music, too; Linda Ronstadt, singing 'Carmelita'. It was magical. Erin couldn't remember coming, but she did recall rolling over, gently pulling the man along as if he weighed no more than a child. He lay his head on her breasts and closed his eyes, and mysteriously he no longer resembled Al García. Now it was someone new, a stranger, but Erin didn't push him away. She let him rest. In the dream, she was still aroused. A sea breeze whisked through the orchard, and the porcelain sky filled with bright tropical birds—macaws, cockatoos, parrots, cardinals and flamingos. Erin remembered kissing the man's forehead to wake him, so he could see the flaming colors dip and scatter overhead. The man stirred and murmured in Spanish, but didn't open his eyes. In the dream, the radiant migration seemed to last all morning. Finally Erin spotted her daughter running barefoot, in and out of the mop-topped trees. Angela was wide-eyed and intent, laughing as she followed the kaleidoscopic train of birds. Erin slipped from beneath the sleeping stranger and ran through the palm orchard after her daughter. In the dream, the bald trunks of the palms stooped and swayed malevolently to obstruct her path. Angie's laughter grew unfamiliar and distant. Erin remembered stopping, breathless, and turning her face to the sun—the sky was empty, the birds had vanished. She had awakened in a hot sweat.

Now, in the limousine, the Beefeater's provided no insight to the dream's meaning. It did, however, fortify Erin for an evening with David Dilbeck. She was impelled by the certainty that the congressman would escape implication in Jerry Killian's murder, that he was out of Al García's reach. The idea of the arrogant old drooler going scot-free was unacceptable, so Erin had made up her mind to destroy him. Dilbeck wouldn't be harmed, crippled or killed—just destroyed. It seemed the least she could do, and it had to be done alone. Women's work.

She finished the martini and began dressing for the congressman. She hooked on a lace bra top and a matching G-string, the one with the red seahorses. Her shoes, too, were candy-apple red. A wine-colored minidress completed the package. Around her neck she hung two long strands of imitation pearls. As Erin dressed, she noticed the Haitian driver, Pierre, watching her in the rearview mirror. Erin stuck her tongue at him.

'I'm sorry,' he said, and looked away instantly.

Erin scooted forward to one of the jump seats. She put a hand on the driver's shoulder. 'You speak English?'

'At times,' he said.

Erin poured him a cola from the mini-bar. Pierre accepted it graciously.

'Is there a phone in this car?' she asked.

The driver nodded at a cellular receiver under the dashboard. Erin turned on the vanity light and opened her purse. She wrote something on a piece of paper and handed it to Pierre. Without reading it, he placed the note in his breast pocket.

'That's a phone number,' she told him. 'Things may get strange tonight. Say, at eleven sharp.'

Pierre said, 'It will not be the first time.'

'I'll understand if you can't help me,' Erin told him. 'But I need to know now, before I get started.'

'You overestimate my sense of loyalty.'

'A job is a job,' Erin said. 'I wouldn't want to jeopardize your situation.'

The guard booth of Turnberry Isle came into view. Pierre flashed the headlights and coasted toward the gate. Without turning, he said to Erin, 'But a phone call could come from anywhere, couldn't it?'

She smiled. 'You're a decent guy, Pierre.'

'*Oui*,' he said, touching the brim of his cap.

Congressman David Lane Dilbeck glistened with excitement, and a light application of petroleum jelly. He put on the Garth Brooks getup, shined his boots, dabbed on some designer-cowboy cologne, tweezered the stray hairs out of his nose . . .

The dancer had phoned that morning with an intriguing request. A bit frightening, really. Not all men would've agreed to it.

But Dilbeck instantly consented because he felt an incipient carnal connection with the woman. Something was sparking between them, a promise of lust. The first time, she'd acted so tough, all business—hands off, buster, and so forth. But as the night had worn on, Dilbeck had detected a softening of attitude, traces of affection. The signs were subtle, to be sure; she had, after all, mortared his hand with one of her spiked heels.

Yet even that made sense later, when he took the dancer's phone call. Perhaps pain was a necessary ingredient of her love. The prospect excited Dilbeck; he felt adventuresome and bold. The congressman had frequently heard of such wild women. Now was his chance to tame one and possess her.

He arrived at Turnberry shortly after dusk. He brought, in addition to the item Erin requested, two magnums of Korbel champagne, three dozen red roses, a gold bracelet and a shopping bag of assorted compact discs: Smithereens, Pearl Jam, Toad the Wet Sprocket, Boyz II Men, REM, Wilson Phillips. Dilbeck had no inkling about the nature of the music, nor did he care. He had dispatched an eager young assistant to load up at Peaches, in the hopes that one or more of the selections might prove to be a dancing favorite of Erin's. If crass gift-giving failed, he would endeavour to dazzle her with gossip from inside the Washington Beltway.

That first night on the yacht, it had seemed to Dilbeck that Erin was stubbornly unimpressed by his title. Most of the women who slept with him did so mainly because he was a member of the House of Representatives, and therefore he qualified (marginally) as a power fuck. Erin, however, treated him as just another horny rich guy. She displayed no interest in his position or his grossly embellished achievements, and resisted every conversation that might have led to Washington name-dropping. The relationship could not blossom, Dilbeck decided, until the woman was properly enlightened about his importance. In anticipation, he'd been polishing some of his most trusty cocktail-party yarns. Also, for purposes of documentation, he brought photographs.

Erin came aboard the *Sweetheart Deal* at about eight-fifteen. Entering the salon, she again felt claustrophobic, incarcerated. 'Where's Frick and Frack?' she asked.

'Who?'

'The guards.'

'Grand Bahama,' the congressman said, 'with the Rojos.' The sight of the minidress caused another mild spasm beneath the scar of his double-bypass.

Erin complimented Dilbeck's country-western outfit. 'Dwight Yoakam?' she guessed.

'Garth Brooks, actually.'

'Well, it certainly flatters you.' Erin was pleased at how sincere she sounded. The man looked absurd. And what was that peculiar sheen to his skin?

Dilbeck handed her the gifts. He said, 'I brought some pictures, as well.'

'Of what?' She wasn't in the mood for porn.

'Pictures of me,' said the congressman, 'on the job.'

'Really?' said Erin, swallowing a yawn.

She thanked him politely for the roses and the bracelet, but Dilbeck thought she wore the expression of one who had received such things before, in the course of commerce. She picked through the stack of CDs and rejected all but the Smithereens. As before, she'd brought her own songs for dancing. In honour of Jerry Killian, she again put on ZZ Top.

The congressman said, with an air of masculine accomplishment: 'It took some doing, but I found what you were looking for.'

Erin squeezed his arm. 'Sweetie, I knew you would.'

Her touch made him shiver pleasantly. For a moment, Dilbeck regarded the arm-squeeze as significant, a preliminary to full body contact. Then he realized that Erin was only using him as a brace, to steady her ascent to the captain's table. In a flash she was out of the minidress. The pearls remained.

'What's the hurry?' Dilbeck said. 'I thought we might chat for a while.'

Erin started dancing. Off came the red bra.

'Jesus,' murmured the congressman.

'Sit back, cowboy,' Erin told him. 'Enjoy.'

Malcolm J. Moldowsky approached the docks casually, as if out for an evening stroll. He removed his necktie to look more like a yachtsman.

Twice he walked past the *Sweetheart Deal*. There was no sign of the Cuban detective. Moldy boarded quietly. He heard thumping from inside: drums, heavy guitar licks. The congressman's tastes leaned toward crooners, so Moldowsky knew that David Dilbeck wasn't alone. The show had begun: Erin Grant was there.

Moldy congratulated himself for beating García to the yacht. He put his ear to the door, but heard no human noises mixed with the rock music. He took it as an encouraging sign; silence was always preferable to the sounds of a struggle.

He had this hands on the doorknob when a shadow passed across the deck. Malcom Moldowsky wheeled to see a man balanced on the transom, backlit by the docklights. The man rocked from one leg to the other, in time to the muffled backbeat.

'What do you want?' Moldowsky said.

The man hopped down and stepped toward him. 'I want my daughter,' he said.

Moldowsky smiled with forced patience; the man was too young to be the dancer's father. Moldy said, 'There's been some mistake. Your daughter's not here.'

'Then I might as well shoot you,' the man said.

At the sight of the pistol, Moldowsky raised his hands high. The intruder seemed crazed and displaced. The knees of his jeans were filthy, and his oily blond hair was matted to one side. The eyes were foggy and moist. A golf club was strapped imposingly to a crudely bandaged arm. Moldy figured the man was a hurricane victim, made homeless and insane. They were still out there, addled wanderers, dredging for pieces of scattered lives.

'She's not here,' Moldowsky said, 'your little girl.'

Darrell Grant armed the pistol and squinted one eye. 'Say goodnight, Shorty.'

Moldowsky let out a gasp and covered his face. Expecting to die, his blackening thoughts turned egotistically to the aftermath. Slain on a yacht with a drunken congressman and a stripper—that's the headline! What photo would they choose to accompany the story? A studio portrait, Moldy hoped, not crime-scene gore. And how would he be described in the press coverage—political consultant? Power broker? Fixer? Jesus, and the quotes. There'd be no shortage of grief-stricken testimonials, all fulsomely insincere. Moldy assumed he would soil himself, dying. What a laugh the cruel bastards would get from *that*. The dapper Malcolm Moldowsky, pissing in his Perry Ellis.

In bitter dread, he waited for the flat crack of the gunshot. Nothing happened.

The problem was Darrell Grant's unfamiliarity with firearms. He didn't like guns, never carried one, never even fired one. Now, steadying himself on the deck of the yacht, he couldn't find the damn trigger. His finger probed intently but was obstructed by a disc of hard plastic. Darrell Grant held the pistol in the light and scrutinized the impenetrable device.

'Fuck me,' he said.

It was a lock. Darrell couldn't believe the rotten luck. The goofy Alberto had to be one of the few citizens in all Dade County with the brains to buy a trigger lock. The advertised purpose of such devices was to prevent dirtbag thieves like Darrell Grant from using a stolen handgun against the innocent citizenry. Darrell, however, suspected that Alberto Alonso harboured other concerns, such as Rita shooting him in his sleep.

In any event, the locked pistol was about as lethal as a doorstop. Darrell Grant hurled it over the wheelhouse, into the Intracoastal Waterway. 'Un-fucking-believable,' he said, with a dry giggle.

Malcolm Moldowsky peeked through his fingers when he heard the splash. The gun was gone. Why? Moldy didn't care. The action confirmed his assessment that the intruder was deranged.

'Out of my way,' Darrell Grant said. He gestured with the blade of the golf club, which protruded from the makeshift splint.

Moldowsky feigned concern. 'You really banged up that arm.'

'Gee, I hadn't noticed.' Darrell Grant hoisted the jerry-rigged limb and poked Malcolm Moldowsky in the belly. 'Double compound fracture,' Darrell said, 'but you know what? I had hangnails hurt worse.'

'Let me drive you to a doctor.'

Darrell Grant lowered his voice and spoke very slowly, as if giving street directions to a foreign tourist: 'Get . . . the . . . fuck . . . out . . . of . . . my . . . way. *Por favor?*'

Moldy flattened himself against the cabin door. ZZ Top pounded up and down the bumps of his spine. 'I can't let you in,' he said to the stranger. It was imperative that the public, lunatics included, remain unaware of the congressman's runaway debauchery.

'But my daughter,' Darrell said, thickly.

'I told you, she's not here. You've made a mistake.'

Darrell's face broke into a crooked smile. 'Hey, I followed her mother, OK? All the way from the tittie bar. And I saw her walk on this boat not fifteen minutes ago. Now some asshole midget's gonna tell me I made a mistake?'

Beautiful, thought Moldowsky. The stripper's ex-husband. Tonight of all nights.

He said, 'Let's go up to the restaurant. I should buy you a drink.'

'A drink?' Darrell Grant threw back his head and yowled at the stars. 'Man, I don't need a drink. I'm full a drugs, OK? I mean *tanked*. Best fucking drugs known to mankind!'

'Fine,' Moldowsky said, tensing.

'These pills are so damn good,' Darrell said, 'I came out here searching for pain. Understand? I'm here to go one-on-one with pain, because I *cannot* be hurt. It ain't humanly possible. I had a railroad spike, I'd give it to you this very minute—'

'Settle down,' Moldy said.

'—and I'd make you hammer that fucking railroad spike straight into my skull, say about here—' Darrell Grant touched the centre of his forehead '—and you know what? I wouldn't feel a damn thing, that's the quality of narcotics I'm talkin' about.'

'Please,' Moldowsky said, 'keep your voice down.'

'I never killed a midget before.'

'Let's discuss this.'

'No, sir, you just move your tiny little ass outta the way. I'm here to fetch my daughter.'

'For the last time,' Moldy said, 'she's not on this boat.'

Darrell Grant grabbed him by the sleeve. 'You're right about one thing, Shorty. It's the last fucking time.' He hurled Malcolm Moldowsky to the deck and stepped on his chest.

Moldy wriggled impotently but did not scream. Ludicrously, he still believed it was possible to avoid a public scene. It wouldn't do to attract a nosy crowd to the Rojos' yacht—not with David Dilbeck inside, doing God knows what to a naked dancer. Fearing a repeat of the Eager Beaver debacle, Moldowsky sought to placate the intruder with promises.

'If you let me up,' he told the crazed ex-husband, 'I can help you find your girl.'

'Weeee-heeeee!' exclaimed Darrell Grant.

'I've got,' Moldy panted, 'all kinds of connections.'

The first blow was not a punch but a chip shot. Moldy felt his nose explode. Through the mush he saw the ex-husband, poised in a one-armed backswing. This time the blade of the club caught Malcolm Moldowsky flush in the throat. Madly he gulped for a breath.

'Fore!' Darrell said.

Moldowsky shut his eyes. This was worse than being shot; the newspapers would have a field day.

He clawed uselessly at the madman's legs. The next two swings dislocated Moldy's lower jaw. His cheeks filled with warm blood, spit and broken orthodonture. Even if he'd decided to cry for help, he couldn't. His face was a divot.

God, he thought, what a sorry way to die.

Is it a nine-iron or a wedge? Those fuckers in the press would make a point to find out. Oh, definitely.

The congressman offered Erin a job as his executive secretary in Washington.

'What would I do?' she asked, twirling her pearls.

'Keep my spirits up,' said David Dilbeck. 'Forty-five grand a year, plus major medical.' He cradled the champagne bottle like a doll.

Looking down from the captain's table, Erin said, 'You're so cute.' She tapped a foot on his shoulder, teasing. Dilbeck tried to kiss it. Erin reminded herself to stay alert; the dirty old geezer was halfway gone.

He said, 'Is it time for the jungle toy?'

'Not just yet. You like this song?'

'Yes, ma'am.' The congressman's head lolled, and the cowboy hat fell to the floor. He picked it up and replaced it.

Erin said, 'It's called ' "Whipping Post".'

Dilbeck perked up. 'Is that right?'

'By the Allman Brothers.'

'Well, I've been such a naughty boy,' he said, 'I believe I could use a whipping.'

Erin continued dancing. Apparently there would be no sexual catatonics tonight; Davey was fully conscious, primed for action.

He said, 'Wouldn't you care to whip me? I'm a bad, bad boy.'

'It's just a song, sweetie.'

'But I love you so much.'

'Of course you do.'

'Here, let me prove it.' He shoved the champagne bottle into the ice bucket, and began fumbling with the buttons of his jeans.

Erin spun away, shaking her ass to the blues rhythm. She thought: Off we go!

The congressman said, 'Look here.'

She turned back, smiling the 500-watt smile. 'It's adorable,' she said.

He stood up, wobbly, and wiggled the limp thing in his hand. 'Please touch it,' he said.

'I'm a dancer, sweetie, not a urologist.' Erin kicked him lightly in the sternum, and he sagged back into the canvas chair.

He said, 'God, I've had too much to drink. Did I give you your money?'

'You sure did.'

'And did I show you my pictures?'

'Put your little friend away,' she said.

'Then you'll look at my pictures?'

Erin said sure. She needed a break, anyway. While David Dilbeck tucked himself in, she stepped off the table and put on her dress. She turned down the stereo, poured a ginger ale over ice and pulled up a chair. She made sure her purse was within arm's reach.

Dilbeck opened a photo album across his lap. He tapped at an eight-by-ten picture of himself with a corpulent white-haired man. 'Know who that is?'

'Tip O'Neill,' said Erin.

Dilbeck was astounded. 'You *are* something special.'

'Former Speaker of the House.'

'Right!'

'So what do I win,' Erin said, 'a dinette set?'

Beaming, the congressman said, 'Tip and I are very close.'

'I can see that. It looks like you're scratching his balls.'

Dilbeck flushed. 'Please! We were at a prayer breakfast.'

Erin reached over and flipped the page. The next photograph had been taken outside the White House: Dilbeck with an arm around General Colin Powell. The general wore an expression that suggested recent taxidermy.

'This was during the Gulf War,' said Dilbeck, matter-of-factly. 'Colin and the President invited certain members of Congress for a briefing. Classified, of course.'

Erin asked if they'd given out balloons. Dilbeck nearly lost his temper. 'Darling,' he said, 'you should have some respect.' His tone had turned chilly.

'I'm sorry, Davey.'

Rapidly he flipped through the album, jabbing at significant memories. 'See here: Bill Bradley, Chris Dodd . . . and there's Al D'Amato—we were on a fact-finder together in Riyadh. This one is me and Newt Gingrich—remind me to tell you my Gingrich story.'

Erin said, 'I hope that's just cheese dip on his tie.'

'You listen,' Dilbeck said, lecturing with a champagne slur, 'these are important goddamn people. *I'm* an important person.' He slapped the album shut and raised it with both hands, as if it were a holy tablet. 'These are the men who run this nation,' he said, 'the men who control the fate of the world!'

Erin tried not to laugh. The poor schlub truly believed himself to be a pillar of state.

The congressman said, 'It's difficult to describe the raw power. It's intoxifying, darling. Completely addictive. If you came with me to Washington, you'd feel it immediately. You would also understand its seductions.'

Erin said she didn't mean to poke fun. Dilbeck laid the album on the table, and placed a hand upon it. Again he said, 'These are important men.'

'Chuck Norris?'

'That was a charity benefit in Georgetown—'

'Come on, Davey—'

'For polio or something.'

'I know, but—'

'Look, Erin, it's a matter of appreciating who I am. It's a matter of respect.' 'Davey, you know whose picture I'd really like to see? Malcolm Moldowsky. Is he in your album?'

Dilbeck's jaw tightened. 'No, he's not.' Then, suspiciously: 'Do you know Moldy?' Was it possible? Had the little ratfucker been holding out on him? Hurriedly Dilbeck reframed the question: '*How* do you know Moldy?'

'By reputation only,' Erin said with a wink.

The congressman, more perplexed than ever, cursed in a shaky drunken voice: 'Stop, goddammit! Stop making fun and show some goddamn respect.'

'Respect?' Erin smiled. 'Aren't you the same gentleman who had sex with my laundry lint?'

'Let's change the subject.'

She took him by the wrists and guided his slack hands to her breasts. Dilbeck seemed wary and apprehensive, as if anticipating an electric shock.

Erin wouldn't let him pull away. She said, 'Thrilling, huh? Two pleasant handfuls of fat.'

'Jesus—'

'That's your basic human breast, Davey. Ninety-eight percent fat, with a cherry on top. What's the big attraction?'

He yanked away, clenching his fists to his gut.

'Thousands of dollars,' Erin said, 'just for a peek and a jiggle. It baffles me, sweetie.'

'That's enough.' The congressman was gray, despondent. 'You're killing me. You're killing the whole evening. Is that the plan?'

Erin said, 'I'm curious, that's all.' She told herself to settle down, hold her temper.

Dilbeck was saying, 'I struggle with fleshly temptations. All men do.'

'You have a wife, Davey.'

He lunged for the champagne bucket. 'Congratulations,' he snapped. 'The night is officially ruined.'

Erin put on her favorite Van Morrison tape. She stripped off the dress, got on the captain's table and began to dance again—this time, slowly. Soon David Dilbeck and his afflicted moans faded from her consciousness. The songs washed over her soul. She felt euphoric and energized. Every move was perfect—every kick, every fluid turn, every thrust of the hip. She took the pearls in her teeth and closed her eyes, imagining moonlight.

Outside on the deck, something made a sharp noise. Erin blocked it out of her mind. She was far away, dancing on a sugary beach in the islands. Above the dune was a palm orchard, and the only sound was a soft chorus of wild birds.

Darrell Grant couldn't recall the last time he'd seen his ex-wife without clothes. He was pretty sure it had been in the bathroom—she, washing her hair in the shower; he, covertly looting the medicine cabinet for Darvons. Long fucking time ago, Darrell thought. He'd forgotten what a nice body she had. A little puny up top but, God, what great legs! Swaying in the doorway of the cabin, crutching with the nine-iron, he felt an intriguing tingle in his groin. Amazing, really, considering the high-octane pharmaceuticals he'd ingested. The male plumbing was truly an engineering marvel.

Inside the yacht was an old man wearing stiff new jeans, a striped shirt and a black ten-gallon hat. He looked shitfaced or sick, possibly both. Darrell Grant walked into the salon and sat next to the old cowboy. With his unbroken arm, he waved mischievously at his former spouse, up on the table. Darrell felt himself hardening. He leaned forward and said, 'Hey, you're pretty damn good. Let's have a look at that sweet little pussy!'

The sight of her ex-husband hit Erin like a blast of frigid air. She thought Shad had run Darrell off for good, but here he was, fucking things up again. Amazing. His presence greatly enhanced the potential for fiasco. Erin kept dancing and stared straight through him while she weighed her next move.

Darrell Grant felt a leafy hand at his shoulder. It was the old cowboy, pulling himself up in the chair. He put his lips to Darrell's ear and said, 'You know who I am?'

The man's breath made Darrell grimace. 'Ever heard of Listerine?'

'I'm in love with this lady,' the congressman confided.

'You poor old fuck.'

'And my boots, they're full of Vaseline.'

'I loved her once, too,' said Darrell Grant, 'but all she did was cut me down.'

Dilbeck looked sympathetic. Darrell said, 'Call it a basic clash of philosophies. She can be hell on your self-esteem.'

'A hard one,' the congressman agreed, 'but still I'm swept away.'

He said there was plenty of club soda in the liquor cabinet, in case Darrell Grant wanted to work on those bloodstains in his shirt. Darrell said no thanks. His shattered bones had begun to throb; whaling on the well-dressed midget hadn't helped. Darrell feared that the late Señor Gomez's painkillers were finally wearing off. He tapped out a half-dozen more, tossed them into his cheeks and guzzled lukewarm champagne until his eyes watered.

The congressman said, 'I've got some Extra-Strength Tylenols.'

'Lord Christ.'

The Van Morrison tape ended. Erin kept going. She started singing 'Carmelita', to herself. The song was almost too slow for table dancing.

Darrell Grant attempted to hook her ankles with the nine-iron. 'Where's Angie?' he demanded. Erin eluded him.

Dilbeck said, 'Let her finish. This is so beautiful.'

'Yeah, it's a fucking ballet.' Darrell Grant grubbed in his pockets. 'Hey, beautiful, this is for you!'

He lurched halfway out of the chair, and slipped something under the elastic of Erin's lace garter. It was a nickel. Erin stopped singing and dancing. She removed the coin and held it in the palm of one hand. The two men waited to see what she would do next.

Erin was smiling in a private way as she stepped off the table, still smiling as she got dressed.

The congressman said, 'I suppose we're done for the night.'

Darrell pounded the nine-iron sharply on the table. 'Erin, I want my daughter. No more goddamn games.'

'It's over,' she said, adjusting the pearls.

'Fuck the courts,' Darrell declared. 'Angie and me are headed to Arizona. Retirement Capital of North America!'

Erin opened her handbag and dropped the nickel inside. Then she took out the .32.

'Let's go for a drive,' she said.

Darrell Grant cursed under his breath. The congressman felt a subtle contraction in his chest.

Some Saturday night, Erin thought. Me and the two men in my life. Aren't I a lucky girl.

31

Predictably, Shad was detained at the guard booth outside Turnberry Isle. The security men remembered his earlier visit with the monkey creature on his neck; tonight they said his name appeared on no guest lists. Shad averted an unpleasant argument by producing coupons for free rum drinks and nude pasta wrestling at Orly's club; the security men couldn't have been more appreciative. Sgt Al García arrived as they were waving Shad through the gate. The detective flashed his badge and coasted into the compound. He parked next to Shad, and the two men hurried together to the *Sweetheart Deal*.

The first thing they noticed was the blood on the deck. In the salon, García inspected the empty champagne bottles, the congressman's photo album, and a pile of compact discs, still in their wrappings. Shad thumbed through a stack of cassettes left on the stereo cabinet.

'These are hers,' he said.

They searched the staterooms and found no bodies, no other signs of violence. Erin and the congressman were gone.

'*Mierda*,' said Al García. He went out to the deck and examined the brownish splatters. Apparently the victim had been dragged, then lifted off the deck. García felt a shudder of nausea; it wasn't the sight of the blood, but the thought of whose it might be. Shad was on the dangerous edge of cold rage. He gripped the rail and stared hauntedly into the tea-colored water. His pinkish skull glistened with perspiration, and he hissed ominously when he inhaled.

García said, 'Don't assume too much.'

A rumble came from Shad. 'Yeah. What's a little blood.'

The detective stepped across to the dock. On his knees: 'There's more here. Know what that means?'

'He didn't dump her over the side. So what?'

A fifty-three-foot Hatteras convertible was moored next to the Rojos' yacht. García wanted to check it out. Shad located a flashlight on the bridge of the *Sweetheart Deal*. They boarded the fishing boat together and found more freckles of blood in the cockpit, near the fighting chairs. There was also the smudge of a partial footprint: the rounded heel of a man's boot.

Morosely, Shad said, 'That's our boy.'

'Maybe, maybe not.' Al García pointed at the fishbox. 'You want me to do the honors?'

'If you don't mind.' Shad looked away.

The detective unfastened the latches and threw open the lid. Buoyant with relief, he said: 'Surprise, surprise!'

Shad turned to see. 'Who the hell is that?'

'One of the most powerful men in Florida.'

'Not any more.'

'No,' Al García said. 'He be deceased.'

Malcolm J. Moldowsky had fit easily into the fishbox, which he shared with three glassy-eyed bonitos. The aroma of the dead fish failed to overpower Moldy's imported cologne.

'I don't get it,' Shad said.

'The bonitos probably are shark bait for tomorrow,' García speculated. 'Mr Moldowsky is a late addition to the buffet.'

Shad leaned in for a closer look. 'This is the famous Melvin Moldowsky?'

'Malcolm,' García said, 'in the past tense.'

'Nice threads.'

'Feel better now?'

'About a million percent,' said Shad. 'Who did it?'

García shook his head. 'Maybe Dilbeck went batshit.'

'Don't say that.'

They were worried about Erin. Whoever had bludgeoned Moldowsky owned a monstrous temper. Shad frowned at the mutilated corpse. 'I guess you gotta call somebody.'

'Not right this minute.' Al García closed the fishbox. 'He'll keep.'

They returned to the *Sweetheart Deal* and searched the salon more carefully. Based on the volume of champagne consumed, García calculated that the congressman was too drunk to drive. 'He's got the limo,' Shad said. 'The girls saw it at the club.'

'So the question,' said the detective, 'is where are they now.'

The clue was in the head, where Erin had written in lipstick on the narrow mirror: BELLE GLADE. Shad growled profanely while García fished a gold bracelet from the toilet. Watching the jewelry drip, he said, 'She's got a temper, doesn't she? A simple ' "no thanks" would've done the trick.'

As they hustled to the cars, Shad asked García to radio ahead for help. García told him he'd been watching too much TV. 'First off, that's Palm Beach County, which is way out of my territory. Second, what do I tell 'em, *chico*?' Facetiously he rehearsed the phone call: 'See, guys, there's this stripper who's been abducted by this congressman who's taking her to fucking Belle Glade, of all places, in a goddamn stretch Cadillac. Yes, I said ' "congressman". Yes, Belle Glade. Why? Well, we ain't too sure. But we'd appreciate six or seven marked units, if you can spare 'em . . .'

'Fuck it,' Shad muttered.

'As much as cops love strippers, they hate politicians,' García said. 'They hear it's Dilbeck, they'll all be oh-six. Off duty and unavailable.'

'So we're the whole damn cavalry.'

'Mind if I drive?'

'Sure,' Shad said, 'you're the one with the siren.'

Darrell Grant had never ridden in a limousine. He was enjoying it so thoroughly that the circumstances seemed irrelevant. He accepted the fact that his former wife was holding him at gunpoint.

Darrell said to Dilbeck: 'This your car?'

The congressman nodded. 'It's made available for my use.'

'What do you do? What's your gig?'

'I'm a member of the House of Representatives.'

'Which means . . .?'

'I represent the people of South Florida in Congress. And yourself?'

'I steal wheelchairs,' Darrell Grant replied.

Dilbeck glanced plaintively toward Erin, who sat on the bench seat across from the two men. The congressman's roses lay next to her. She held the gun steady in her right hand.

'Darrell and I were married for a time. What else can I say?' Erin felt an inexplicable calm, heightened by the cool soft ride.

Dilbeck asked Darrell Grant what happened to his arm. He said Erin's motherfucking boyfriend broke it with a motherfucking crowbar. Then: 'Hey, driver, does the TV work?'

In a wounded tone, Dilbeck whispered to Erin: 'What boyfriend?'

Erin iced him with a glare. Pathetic, she thought, both of them. She nonchalantly reached under her minidress to unfasten the G-string and the scalloped dance top. She stuffed them in the shoulder bag. Still holding the gun, she gymnastically attempted to put on a plain cotton bra and white panties. It was a crucial detail; Erin didn't want to be found dressed as a stripper. As she changed underclothes, the congressman watched inquisitively.

With an oily trace of a smile: 'Why the white?'

'For you, baby,' she said.

Darrell Grant braced his sloshing head against the window. They were on the interstate, racing away from the downtown skyline. The snaky scroll of lines on the pavement, the stream of headlights made him woozy. 'I'm seriously loaded,' he remarked.

Erin said to the congressman: 'My ex-husband has a drug problem, in case you were curious.'

'I wish you'd put the gun away,' Dilbeck told her.

'You're not listening, are you?'

Darrell Grant, sleepily: 'I never saw you dance before. That was damn good.'

'Aw, shucks,' Erin said.

'Sorry about that business with the nickel.'

'I'd almost forgotten,' she said, 'your scathing wit.'

Darrell Grant basked in the limousine's spaciousness. 'I could get used to this,' he said, stretching his legs. 'Climate-controlled comfort. Yessir!'

David Dilbeck, speaking as if Darrell couldn't hear him: 'That fracture looks bad, Erin. He should see a doctor.'

'Rita's the one who done up my arm,' Darrell said, hoisting it in pride. 'My big sister.'

'She cares about you,' Erin told him. 'She's the only one left.'

'No, Angie cares for me. Angie loves her daddy.'

'She finds you entertaining,' said Erin. 'There's a difference.'

'She loves me!'

Erin dropped the subject. Maybe Darrell was right. She didn't want to think about it now.

The congressman said, 'How much longer till we get there? I have to relieve myself.'

Erin ignored him. Her ex-husband said, 'I killed a guy tonight.'

'Really?'

'On the boat back there.'

'Any particular reason?'

'I'm trying to remember.'

Erin assumed that he had hallucinated the incident. Darrell Grant said, 'It didn't feel the way I thought it would. Killing a guy.'

'You fell for the hype,' Erin said, 'as usual.' She wondered what to do with him. He was screwing up her plans for the congressman.

'I'm serious about Angie,' he said.

'You kidding? You're headed for prison, Darrell.'

'Nope, Arizona. Wheelchair Capital of North America!'

'Crazy bastard.'

'And I'm taking our daughter.'

'I'll shoot you first,' Erin warned.

David Dilbeck abruptly began sobbing and groping for the door handle. He settled down when Erin jammed the .32 into the hollow of his cheek.

Darrell Grant said, 'Since when do you carry a piece? Jesus, I hate guns.'

'My prostate is acting up,' the congressman announced.

'Quit whining,' Erin snapped. 'Both of you.'

Darrell scratched his shin with the head of the nine-iron. 'At least tell us where the hell we're headed. Hey, driver, you speakee American?'

Pierre gave no reaction.

'I'll tell you where we're going,' Erin said. 'We're going to see our congressman in action.'

By early October, the sugarcane near Lake Okeechobee is green, bushy and ten feet tall. The bottomland is the flattest part of Florida; from a passing car, the fields seem to reach and define all horizons. Within a month, nearly two thousand Caribbean migrants arrive to start the cutting, and the mills run twenty-four hours a day. In early October, though, machines do much of the harvesting. An improbable crablike contraption called a cutter-windrower downs the cane and piles it in rows. More machines then retrieve the harvest for transportation to the company mills, where the sugar is made.

Congressman David Lane Dilbeck didn't give much thought to the science or mechanics of cane farming. It was enough that the Rojos were nice people, well-bred and so generous. The mountainous campaign donations were important, of course, but Dilbeck would have traded his congressional vote for just the occasional use of that gorgeous yacht. He also valued the social company of young Christopher, who shared his tastes in bawdy entertainment and never failed to pick up the tab. For David Dilbeck, the attention of wealthy, powerful people was a flattering fringe benefit of the job.

The congressman saw no injustice in the price supports that had made multimillionaires of the Rojos. The grain, dairy and tobacco interests had soaked taxpayers for years by melodramatically invoking the plight of the 'family farmer'. Why not sugar, too? Similarly, Dilbeck lost no sleep over the damage done to the agricultural economies of impoverished Caribbean nations, virtually shut out of the rigged US sugar market. Nor did the congressman agonize over the far-reaching impact of cane growers flushing billions of gallons of waste into the Everglades.

Dilbeck didn't understand what all the fuss was about. In truth, he didn't much care for the Everglades; it was torpid, swampy, crawling with bugs. Once, campaigning at a Miccosukee village, the congressman consented to an airboat ride because Erb Crandall saw it as a sensational photo opportunity. The airboat ran out of fuel on the Shark River, and Dilbeck spent two wretched hours picking blood-swollen mosquitoes out of his ears.

'And I've seen prettier water,' he told Erin, 'in a pig trough.'

She was giving him a hard time about whoring for the Rojos. 'Where do you think our drinking water comes from?' She pointed through the window of the limousine. 'Out there, Davey. And your pals are pissing fertilizer into it.'

Darrell Grant was bored silly. He repeatedly sought to engage Pierre in conversation, with no success. The highway narrowed to two unlit lanes that Darrell recognized as US 27. Blackness engulfed the limousine; the only trace of the city was a fuzzy sulfurous glow, far to the east. Darrell couldn't figure out where Erin was taking them, or why. The geezer in the cowboy getup remained a riddle. Was this a rich new boyfriend? The idea of Erin as a gold digger engaged him—like mother, like daughter? Anything was possible.

Darrell struggled to hatch a plan, but the drugs interfered with his concentration. What he really wanted to do was sleep for about six months.

It was half-past ten when they arrived in Belle Glade ('Her Soil Is Her Future,' proclaimed a welcome sign). Pierre turned off the main highway and drove slowly through an empty migrant camp. David Dilbeck was alarmed by what he saw. He told Pierre to step on the gas before desperadoes swarmed from the slum and trashed the limo. 'It's a leaser,' he explained to Erin.

'Don't tell me you've never been out here.'

'What's your point?' the congressman groused. The warm embrace of the Korbel had dissipated into a staggering migraine.

Pierre got back on the highway and drove until the town gave way to more green cane fields. Erin asked him to pull over.

'He doesn't understand English,' Dilbeck said, impatiently.

'Is that so?'

Pierre steered off the pavement and stopped on the shoulder of the road. He left the engine running.

'Out we go,' Erin said, brightly. 'And, Davey, don't forget our jungle toy.'

Dilbeck peered into the night suspiciously.

Before harvest, sugarcane is burned to consume the leafy tops, which are useless, and to drive the animals from the fields. In the heart of the season, smoke roils off the stalks in prodigious columns that sometimes block out the sky. Tonight, though, was crystalline—washed with constellations that one never saw in the city. A waning yellow moon hung low.

Pierre got out and opened the back door of the limo. The congressman emerged first, holding a slender brown package. He was followed by Darrell Grant, unsteadily; the protruding nine-iron dinged noisily off a rear fender panel. The last to emerge from the car was Erin, stepping gingerly in her heels. Pierre gave her a small flashlight to go with the pistol.

Darrell Grant complained of a gassy stomach. 'Let me stay here and crash.'

'Sure. In the trunk.' Erin motioned with the gun. 'Pierre, prepare Mr Grant's *boudoir*.'

The Haitian driver obliged. He popped the trunk and moved the spare tire, making room.

'The trunk?' Darrell Grant slapped the congressman on the back. 'Didn't I tell you she's fucking murder on the ego?'

David Dilbeck looked worried. 'Erin, I've got a heart condition.'

'Who doesn't? Darrell, get in the damn trunk.' She shined the flashlight in his eyes.

'You gonna shoot me?' He gave a dopey laugh. 'Somehow I don't think so.'

Erin told him to lie down and take a nap.

Darrell Grant, slouching against the fender of the limousine: 'One thing I been dying to ask: How do you do it? I mean shakin'

your poon at strangers.' He jabbed the congressman contemptuously with the golf club. 'Sick old fucks like him, I don't see how
you do it.'

'The music takes over. That's all.'

'You mean it's an act? I ain't so sure about that.'

'Men are easily dazzled.'

An urgent moan from David Dilbeck: 'I have to pee.'

Erin waved the flashlight toward the cane rows. 'So pee,' she
said. Dilbeck waddled off, clawing at the buttons of his jeans.

Darrell Grant snorted drunkenly. 'I never thought of you as a
stripper. It's actually funny as hell.'

Erin said, 'You emptied the savings account. I had a lawyer to
pay.'

'Plus you figured out the hustle at these nudie joints, am I
right? You mess their hair, play with their necktie, tell 'em how
good they smell.'

'Maybe that's why they call it a tease.'

'God, you're a cold one.'

The congressman could be heard irrigating the sugarcane.
From over his shoulder, he called: 'I truly *do* love her!'

'Pity-ful,' Darrell said.

Erin smiled. 'I rest my case.'

'Know what I think? I think you get off on it.'

'Darrell, you're just *full* of theories tonight.' Was this a sermon,
she wondered, from a wheelchair thief? 'Get in the trunk,' she
told him, 'you like the damn car so much.'

He ignored her. 'I ain't givin' up on Angie. Just so you know:
I'll track the both of you to hell and back.' He brushed past her
and headed into the cane fields.

'Darrell, stop.' She raised the .32 in one hand, the flashlight in
the other.

Her ex-husband turned. The beam of light caught him grinning. 'You won't kill me. Not the father of your only child!'

Erin was considering it. She pictured him hacking up Angie's
dolls, and her gun arm stiffened. 'You told the judge I was an
unfit mother. Is that what you believe?'

'It was lawyer talk, for Chrissakes. You always take shit so personally.' Beseechingly he spread his arms, the shaft of the nine-iron glinting. 'Hell, you were a good mother. Same as I was a good daddy. It was lawyers talkin', that's all.'

At that moment Erin knew she wouldn't fire. She didn't need to; the sorry bastard was already finished. Broke, strung out, maimed, running from the law—Darrell Grant was history. Killing him would be redundant.

'Come back,' she told him. 'I've got plans for you.'

'You mean ' "plans" as in jail? No thanks, cutie pie.' He gave a cocky wave and resumed his getaway.

Erin remembered what Shad advised her about the gun: when in doubt, shoot at something, *anything*.

She fired twice at the ground near Darrell Grant's boots. The crack of the shots was absorbed by the thickets of high cane. She heard her ex-husband yell the word *cunt*. When she aimed the flashlight where he'd been standing, he was gone, crashing like a deer through the crops. She panned the beam in a slow circle until it landed on the congressman, nervously buttoning his fly. He waded from the tall grass and asked, 'Are you all right?'

The gun felt hot in Erin's fist. She thought, Goddamn that Darrell. Maybe he'll step on a rattler.

She wheeled on David Dilbeck. 'Take off your clothes,' she told him.

'I knew it. You're going to make me dance.'

Erin said, 'You wish.'

After cane is cut and stacked, a machine scoops the stalks, thins the excess vegetation and dumps the load into a field wagon. When the wagons become full, a mechanical belt feeds the cane into long steel-mesh trailers attached to truck cabs. Each bin holds twenty tons and dumps from the side. The trailers are parked at intervals along the farm roads bordering the Okeechobee sugar fields.

At first Darrell Grant thought he had come upon the fence of a medium-security prison, a nightmare of ironies. Weaving closer, pawing at the darkness as if it were fog, he saw that the mesh edifice actually was the side of a long truck rig. Using a jumbo tire as a foothold, Darrell began to climb.

The cane trailer offered dual enticements: it looked like a safe place to hide from a homicidal ex-spouse and also a fine place to nap. It was important for Darrell to lie down soon, before he fell. The cancer pills had blown his circuit breakers; he accepted the likelihood that he'd guessed wrong on the dosages, seriously misjudged his tolerance. Oh well.

After scaling the mesh, he flopped into the damp sheaths of smoky cane and burrowed like a worm; he felt clever, invisible and safe. Had he been sober, he might have anticipated the destination of the truck and the disposition of its contents.

Once loaded at the fields, the trailers are driven to the mill and emptied on conveyors. The first stage of processing is the shredding of the cane, which is accomplished by many rows of gleaming, turbine-driven knives. The fiber then is mashed beneath five hundred tons of pressure. In this way the essential liquids are removed. Evaporators convert the purified cane juice into a syrup, which is heated carefully until it forms a mixture of sweet molasses and crystals. Separation is achieved using a high-speed centrifuge.

Usually it takes half a ton of cane to produce a hundred pounds of raw sugar. However, both weight and purity can be markedly affected by the introduction of foreign substances, such as human body parts.

Darrell Grant had medicated himself too heavily and concealed himself too well. He was deep in a junkie nod at dawn, when the cane trailer in which he'd hidden began rolling toward the sugar mill. Darrell did not awaken, at least not in a meaningful way. No cries, shrieks or moans halted the sugar-milling process; rather, it was the nine-iron strapped to Darrell Grant's arm that jammed the turbine-driven blades and brought the boys from Quality Control scurrying toward the shredders.

The mill shut down for three hours while local police collected and bagged the remains. The Palm Beach Sheriff later issued a press release saying that a vagrant had died in a freak milling accident at Rojo Farms. Authorities appealed to the public for help in identifying the victim, who was described as a white male, early 30s, with blond hair. No composite sketch of the man was provided, as the shredder left precious little for the police artist to work from. The press release said that the victim wore jeans and boots, and was possibly a golf enthusiast. The Sweetheart Sugar Corporation was reported to be cooperating fully in the case.

At the mill, a memo went up assuring employees that the unfortunate mishap had not compromised the superb quality of the company's product. In private, however, workers anxiously wondered exactly how much of the dead vagrant had ended up in the day's tonnage. The consensus was that one drop of blood, one lousy pubic hair, one microscopic sliver of a wart was too much.

Distasteful rumors spread wildly, and many workers stopped putting sugar in their coffee and tea. Rojo Farms, like most cane processors, maintained a long-standing rule against the use of artificial sweeteners by employees on company property. Violation was regarded as an act of disloyalty—the agribusiness equivalent of a Chrysler salesman buying himself a Toyota. However, within days after Darrell Grant's gruesome death, a clandestine network of body carriers began smuggling packets of Sweet 'n Low into the Rojo company cafeteria. An internal investigation failed to identify the culprits or shut down the pipeline. To avoid the publicity of a labor confrontation, mill management quietly dropped the matter and rescinded its sugar-only policy. The Rojos themselves were never told.

32

Shad punched the dashboard, hard.

'Enough!' said Al García. 'Christ, have a smoke.'

'Some fucking heroes we are.'

García was doing ninety-four on the interstate. Shad's slick dome whimsically reflected the blue strobe of the dashboard light. The highway wind howled through the shotgun-shattered window. Shad spit scornfully into the night.

'Easy,' García said. 'Hey, I gave up on being a hero a long time ago. Sometimes the best you can do is set things in motion.' The detective puffed expansively on a fresh cigar. 'That's why I put my card in the dead lawyer's bank box. I had a hunch it would motivate Mr Moldowsky toward foolish behavior.'

Shad said, 'This ain't a game. You said yourself.'

'Still, there's plays to be made. We made ours.'

'And look what happened. Erin gets snatched.'

'Don't underestimate the lady.' The detective lowered the window and tapped out an inch of dead ash. 'You notice anything odd about the writing on that mirror? Besides it was lipstick?'

Shad hunched sullenly. He occupied himself with devising a suitable fate for the congressman. He thought in terms of muriatic acid and gaping facial wounds.

'Here's what jumped out at me,' García went on. 'The words on the mirror weren't printed in block letters, they were done in cursive. The style was beautiful, no? So tell me, *chico*, who writes perfect longhand when they got a gun to their head and they're about to be kidnapped? Nobody, that's who.'

Shad's naked eyebrows crinkled in concentration. In the

shadows, his silky pink orb suggested the head of a 250-pound newborn. 'You're saying she planned it all?'

García said, 'It's possible, yeah.'

'No way did she whack that guy in the fishbox.'

'I agree.' The detective's expression was obscured by a swirling shroud of blue smoke. 'Still, she had a game plan.'

Shad remembered what Urbana Sprawl had said: that Erin was out to do some damage.

'In these situations,' the detective said, 'I ask myself who's holding the high cards? And it's definitely Erin, not Dilbeck. Here's this arrogant old fart who thinks he's God's gift to pussy, but all he wants in the whole wide world is the love of this one gorgeous dancer. I mean, he'd be in heaven if this girl just *smiled* in the general direction of his dick. You follow?'

Shad plucked a cigar from Al García's shirt pocket. He tore off the wrapper with his teeth.

García chuckled. 'All that champagne, I'll bet old Davey couldn't get it up with a block-and-tackle tonight. And Erin, she's got thirty IQ points on him, easy.'

Shad said, 'Men get crazy over her. I seen it before.'

'Dilbeck's not your typical rapist, he's too full of himself.'

'He don't need to be typical,' said Shad, biting the nub off the stogie. 'He just needs the idea to take hold.'

García said nothing for several miles. The traffic thinned as they headed west.

Shad mumbled, 'Belle Glade, shit. *Where* in Belle Glade?' He turned toward García. 'I suppose you got some ideas.'

'What I said before about setting things in motion—see, people have this concept of justice. They talk about ' "the system", meaning cops, judges, juries and prisons. If only the system worked, they say, there wouldn't be a crime problem! The streets would be safe, the bad guys would be locked up for life!'

Shad gave a desolate laugh. He pulled the lighter from the dented dash and fired up the cigar. He said, 'Look at Erin's crazy fucker of an ex-husband. That's how terrific the system works.'

'Exactly,' García said, chopping the air with his hand. 'Darrell Grant was a snitch for the cops. Good guys putting bad guys on the payroll, in the name of almighty justice. Your average tax-payer can't understand. See, ' "the system" is a game and that's all. Guy like Moldowsky, I can't touch him. Same goes for the congressman. So what I do then, I try and set things in motion. Make the shit fly and see where it sticks.'

'Because you got no case,' Shad said.

'None whatsoever. But it doesn't mean there can't be justice.'

'Man, you're a dreamer.'

'Maybe so,' said Al García, 'but I'm sure Moldowsky arranged the murders of Jerry Killian and that sleazoid lawyer and the lawyer's cousin. And I'm also sure I couldn't put the case together in a trillion years.' He

arched a shaggy black eyebrow. 'But this much I also know: Tonight I open a stinking fishbox and find Mr Malcolm J. Moldowsky permanently expired. Fate, irony, call it whatever. Least now I got something to tell my boy.'

'Your boy?' Shad said.

'He's the one that found the body in the river.'

Shad grunted somberly.

'Least I can tell him it's over,' said García. 'For once the bad guy got what he deserved.'

Shad said, 'I ain't ready to celebrate. I want to see Erin alive.' He took a loud, noxious drag on the cigar. 'You better hope you didn't set the wrong damn thing in motion.'

'Yeah,' the detective said quietly. 'There's always that chance.'

Shad settled in for the ride. He felt better, kicking around the possibility that Erin was on top of the situation.

'Just promise me one thing,' he said to Al García. 'Promise you ain't got another human head in the Igloo.' He jerked a thumb toward the trunk of the Caprice.

García grinned. 'The night is young,' he said.

The congressman stripped to his boxer shorts and cowboy boots. Erin's flashlight played up and down his gelatinous physique. She was mildly embarrassed for him, but the feeling passed quickly.

'What now?' Dilbeck said, swatting at the bugs.

'Time for you-know-what.'

'Ah.' His tone changed. Excitedly he unwrapped the brown package. He held the machete with both hands, the blade flat across his palms, to show Erin. 'Willie Rojo loaned it to me. It hangs on the wall of his private study.'

'Very tasteful,' she said.

The congressman ran a finger along the squared-off blade. With a coy smile: 'I think I understand what you're after.'

'Doubtful,' Erin muttered.

'You're into games,' Dilbeck said, hopefully.

'Oh, please.'

'Role playing—'

'No, sweetie.'

'You're the master, I'm the slave!'

Erin thought: The creep is really getting turned on.

Dilbeck said, 'So how does it work, your little game?'

'Here's how it works: I want you to cut some sugar.'

He chuckled anxiously. 'But I don't know how.'

'Oh, give it a try,' Erin said. 'For me.'

'I'd feel much better if you put the gun away.'

'Soon,' she said. 'That's a promise.'

With the flashlight she directed the congressman to a row of maturing cane. He stepped forward and swung the machete sidearm. The stalks shook but didn't fall.

Erin said, 'You do better with a champagne bottle.'

David Dilbeck snorted. 'Just watch,' he said, and began whaling. Each blow brought a high-pitched grunt that reminded Erin of Monica Seles, the tennis star. The congressman's reaping technique needed improvement, too; the cane wasn't being cut so much as pulverized. Erin kept the flashlight aimed at the crop row, so Dilbeck could see what he was hacking. She didn't want him to harvest his own toes by accident.

After less than a minute, the congressman stopped. His face was flushed, his chest heaved and the blotched flab of his belly was sprinkled with sweat. The boxer shorts had slipped below his waist, exposing the crack of his marbled buttocks. He was panting like a toothless old lion.

Erin said, 'Sweetie, don't quit yet. You're giving new meaning to the term ' "public servant".'

Dilbeck bent at the waist, sucking to catch his breath. Momentarily he said, 'You've still got your dress on.'

'I certainly do.'

'Fine, fine.' He wiped his palms on his underwear. 'How much more till we can play?'

'I was thinking at least a ton.'

'Very funny—'

'A migrant,' Erin said, 'cuts eight tons a day.'

'Eight tons,' the congressman murmured. That's what Chris Rojo had told him, too. It seemed absolutely impossible.

'One cutter, all by himself,' said Erin. 'I read up on cane farming so we could have a meaningful discussion.' She kicked off her high heels. 'I figured you knew all there was to know about sugar, considering the Rojos own your ass.'

'That's a damn lie.' Dilbeck stiffened.

Erin put the flashlight on him—he was pissed, all right. It wasn't easy to look indignant in boxer shorts. She said, 'Guess what the Rojos pay their cutters.'

'I couldn't care less,' the congressman snapped. 'It's better than starving to death in the *barrios* of Kingston.'

'So that's it—a humanitarian enterprise!' Erin dabbed an imaginary tear. 'Please forgive me, Congressman, I misunderstood. Here I assumed your pals were just greedy businessmen, taking advantage of poor desperate souls. Now I find out they're saints!' She motioned with the gun. 'Keep cutting, sweetheart. And by the way, Jamaica doesn't have *barrios*. They're called slums. You're getting your Third World cultures mixed up again.'

Reinvigorated by anger, Dilbeck went at the sugar cane like a dervish. Between grunts: 'Who are you to lecture me!'

'Merely a constituent,' Erin said. She reminded him that his drinking buddy, young Señor Rojo, had given her a thousand dollars for one of her shoes. 'But I guess he can afford it,' she remarked, 'considering what he pays the migrants.'

The congressman paused in his cutting: 'That's a very simplistic view, young lady. Very simplistic.'

'Davey, when does your committee vote on the sugar subsidies? I wonder what the Rojos would do if you didn't show up.'

Dilbeck couldn't understand how an evening that had started with such promise had deteriorated to this: a stripper with a pistol, in the middle of fucking nowhere—and him, up to his sweaty aching balls in sugarcane. Ruefully he concluded that wild cowboy sex was no longer on the agenda; more harrowing scenarios began to streel through his imagination. All this talk of slave labor, the Rojos, the House committee vote . . . why would a woman speak of such things?

He swung at the cane until his arm was numb. He dropped to his knees, braced himself upright with the machete.

'Good work,' said Erin. 'Only nineteen hundred pounds to go.' She wondered what her mother, the cruising opportunist, might make of this scene. David Dilbeck was the sort that Mom would view as a matrimonial prize—wealthy, prominent and presentable, when properly attired.

He said, 'What is it you really want?'

Erin crouched beside him. 'You remember a man named Jerry Killian.'

Dilbeck nodded guardedly. 'He's the one who tried to blackmail me. That's when I spoke to the judge about, uh, ' "reconsidering" your custody case.'

'And what happened, Davey?'

'Judge said no deal. Got on his high horse.'

'And what about Killian?'

'Was he a boyfriend of yours?' The congressman spoke hesitantly. 'I don't know what happened. Malcolm said it was taken care of. We never heard from the man again.'

'That's because he was murdered.'

Dilbeck fell forward to his hands and knees. 'My God,' he said. 'Is that true? It can't be.'

'Oh, it's true.' Erin stood up. 'All because of you, because of the Rojos'—waving the handgun—'because of all this sugar out here.' She watched him struggle to a sitting position. 'A man's dead, Davey, all because you're a crook.'

The congressman looked ashen and haggard. He told Erin to

get the damn light out of his eyes. 'Nineteen years,' he said, hoarsely. 'Nineteen years I've served in Washington, DC. Don't you dare belittle me.'

Erin said, 'A man is dead.'

'Go look up my record, young lady. I've voted for every civil rights bill that's come through Congress. The vital issues of our time—Social Security, equal-opportunity housing, lower cable TV rates—go look up my votes. And farmers, yes, you're damn right. I support the family farmer and I'm not ashamed to say so!'

Erin sighed inwardly. Dilbeck was parroting a boiler-plate campaign speech.

'—and who singlehandedly blocked the last congressional pay raise? Me! I cast the deciding vote. You don't think that took courage?'

Hastily Erin moved to derail the monologue. She said, 'I phoned your office once myself.'

Dilbeck paused. 'In Washington? Why?'

'To ask about Jerry Killian. You were busy.'

The congressman said, 'If I'd known—'

'What did the Rojos do for you? Parties, girls, boat rides—what else? Las Vegas? The occasional vacation to the islands?' Erin circled him. 'I think you're a man who can't say no to anything that's free.'

Dilbeck dragged a forearm across his brow. 'My father,' he said with well-practiced reverence, 'was an ordinary working man with ordinary dreams. Know what he did for a living? He pumped septic tanks!'

Erin said, 'We could sure use him now.' She walked back to the limousine to double-check a detail with Pierre. She returned carrying a martini in a plastic glass.

'Bless you,' the congressman said, slurping like a hound.

She unzipped the minidress, tugged it down to her heels and kicked it away. A pleasant confusion returned to David Dilbeck's face; sunken eyes flickering with hope. In a simple white bra the dancer looked virginal, scrumptious. The congressman felt a familiar tremor of lust. The woman was an angel in the night.

'You are diabolical,' he murmured. 'I truly love you.'

'Do you have,' she asked, 'the foggiest clue what's happening here?'

Dilbeck shook his head placidly. 'It's all in the hands of the Lord.'

'Oh brother.'

He discarded the empty glass and said, 'I'm a deacon in the church!'

'Yeah, and I'm the singing nun. Stand up, Davey.'

Raising himself proved to be a long-term project, the congressman top-heavy with exhaustion. Using the machete as a crutch, he eventually levered himself erect, arms slack, while Erin made a final inspection with the flashlight. Sprouting from the silly boots were knobbly blue-veined legs, still slick with Vaseline. The light moved up his body: red and wrinkled knees, the droopy boxers, the pendulous gray belly, the engorged surgical scar, the expectant patrician face and the silvery hair, now a ragged thatch garnished with flecks of jet muck and diced cane.

Erith said, 'You are a sight.'

She guessed the time as between eleven and eleven-thirty. Now or never, she thought. She threw the flashlight as far as she could into the tall cane, where it landed without a sound. Then she did the same with the gun.

I must be nuts.

Dilbeck said, 'Well, well.'

In the yellow moonglow, Erin could see his widening smile.

'So I was right about you,' he said.

I must be crazy.

'David,' she said, 'do you want to talk, or dance?'

'Friction?'

I must be totally insane.

'Whatever you like, sweetheart.' Somewhere in the night, Jackson Browne began to sing.

Where the hell are they?

Seventeen minutes away, on a two-lane road skirting the Loxahatchee wildlife preserve, three cars sped northwest toward the

town of Belle Glade. Each of the cars was a slate-gray, late-model
Ford. Each was driven by a clean-cut man in a dark suit. There
were six in all—two in each sedan—and an attractive dark-
haired woman with a young girl. The men all carried guns in
shoulder holsters under their suit jackets. The little girl held two
Barbie dolls, one blonde and one brunette. The woman sat next
to the small girl in the back of the third sedan. She told the girl
not to worry, everything was going to be all right.

Angela Grant said she wasn't worried one bit.

Sgt Al García was stuck behind a slow-moving station wagon
that was plastered with upbeat religious slogans. The driver
either failed to see the flashing blue light in the mirror, or was
unfamiliar with its purpose. García wondered why people with
jesus stickers on their bumper always drove twenty miles per
hour under the speed limit. If God was *my* co-pilot, he thought,
I'd be doing a hundred and twenty.

Shad was sucking the cigar and telling sad tales of lost opportunity—the roach in the yoghurt, the scorpion in the cottage
cheese. 'It was all worked out,' he lamented. 'It was fucking
golden.'

García said, 'That sounds a lot like fraud.'

'Shit. You got a soft spot for insurance companies?'

García mashed the accelerator and passed the Christian station
wagon on the shoulder. A few minutes later, the unmarked
Caprice rolled into the modest commercial district of Belle Glade.
The detective turned off the dashboard light and slowed down,
scouting for the congressman's limousine. He expected it to stand
out dramatically.

Shad continued to describe the art of concealing an adult
cockroach in a refrigerated dairy product. The secret, he confided
to García, was a good pair of tweezers.

The detective, ever eager for insight to the criminal mind,
asked: 'What about the roach itself? Anything special?'

'The fresher the better,' Shad advised.

Just then, a convoy of three gray Fords whipped past in the
opposite direction. 'So that's the deal!' said García, digging the

Caprice into a grinding U-turn. Smart girl, he thought. Gotta give her credit.

Shad said, 'Who the hell are they?' For purchase, he planted both hands on the dashboard. 'Lemme ask something,' he said, cigar bobbing with the bumps. 'Suppose you were an ex-con and you happened to be packin' a piece right now.'

Al García said, 'I believe I'd toss it.'

'Yeah?' Shad rolled down the window. 'Close your eyes,' he told the detective.

Erin said, 'Relax, sweetie.'

'How can I?' She pressed lightly against him, swaying, dreaming that she was with someone else. She tried to remember the last time she'd been held by a man, in a way that meant something.

'Now I get it,' the congressman said. 'You're trying to kill me. You're trying to give me a damn heart attack.'

Erin said, 'Don't be ridiculous. I could give you a heart attack anytime I choose.'

Damp arms enfolded her waist. One hand still gripped the machete.

'Careful,' Erin whispered.

David Dilbeck said, 'We could go away together in a few weeks. We could take the yacht.'

'Sounds interesting.'

'I could make you happy,' he said. 'After the election, you could come with me to Washington.'

'I don't think so, sweetheart.'

Dilbeck, playing sugar daddy: 'You'd like it there. The shopping is phenomenal.'

Erin resisted the urge to bite. 'Tell me about that night at the club,' she said, 'the night you attacked the young man.'

The congressman said, uneasily, 'I remember so little of it.' He tightened his hold. 'I was overcome, dazed, powerless—normally I'm not a violent person. I think that's obvious.'

'You frightened me,' Erin said. The seconds ticked away so slowly. Gazing into the rows of cane, she thought of Darrell

Grant, wondered if he was planning a counterstrike. What would he do if he saw the congressman molesting her? Applaud, probably.

Dilbeck said, 'Malcolm tells me the young fellow is just fine, the one who got hurt with the bottle.'

'You didn't even send a fruit basket.'

'How could I?' The congressman stopped dancing and took her by the elbows. 'You still don't understand, do you? The position I hold is significant and sensitive and powerful. It's an election year, darling.'

'You nearly killed a man,' Erin said.

'Look, I do not wish to be remembered in the same snickering breath with Wilbur Mills and Gary Hart and the rest. Can't you appreciate my situation?' He hugged her fiercely to his sticky chest. 'It's an unforgiving world we live in, angel.'

How right you are, she thought. 'Davey, please don't put your hands in my panties.' The blade of the machete was cool against her thigh.

He said, 'Well . . . I'm waiting for the friction.'

'This is it.'

'No, dear, this is slow dancing.'

'Sorry,' said Erin, maintaining the sway.

'I didn't come all this way for a dry hump.'

'Davey, you're so romantic.'

'Don't be like this!' Again Dilbeck's arms locked around her. Clumsily he began to grind his pelvis against her belly. 'There! What about that?' he demanded.

'Stop it,' Erin said, inaudibly. The moist hairs of Dilbeck's chest felt like moss against her cheek. In a way, she was grateful for the darkness, so she wouldn't have to see every awful detail, if things went wrong.

'I'm tired of this game,' the congressman declared. Abruptly he embarked on his own convulsive rendition of an erotic dance—jerking, jumping, his greased flab slapping against Erin's body. She felt the bra peel up, the plastic pearls indent her breasts. With both hands she held her panties in place, thinking: So much for being in control.

David Dilbeck's haphazard thrusting lifted Erin's toes off the ground. Beating on his shoulders proved futile, so she tried a scream.

The congressman displayed no alarm; rather, her panic seemed to please him. 'Finally,' he said, 'you're beginning to understand.' He grabbed the pearl necklaces and began to twist them into a noose. Gradually they came tight on Erin's throat.

She screamed again—not her best effort—and again until it hurt. Finally the strands snapped and the pearls scattered down her breasts, falling into the cane like tiny hailstones.

33

While waiting, Pierre leaned against the door of the Cadillac limousine. He plugged his fingers in his ears because, at the young woman's instruction, the stereo was full blast. The song was something about lawyers in love. Pierre didn't understand, suspected he never would.

When he spotted the oncoming cars, he reached into the limo and shut off the music. Gravel dust swirled as three gray sedans braked to a stop in a triangle. The headlights sliced up the night, moths whirling like confetti in the hot white beams.

Pierre slapped his hands on his head, crumpling the chauffeur's cap. He counted six men in dark suits, like pallbearers. They drew guns as they emerged from the sedans. The tallest one, who had neat sandy hair and tortoiseshell glasses, approached Pierre and asked if he was the man who called.

'M-pa konprann,' Pierre said, repeating it twice in a chatter intended to convey incomprehension. It worked temporarily.

The armed strangers held a short huddle in which it was determined that none of them spoke Creole. The sandy-haired man took Pierre firmly by the collar. 'Where is she?' he asked, formidably. 'You know who I mean.'

His hands still fastened to the cap, Pierre pointed urgently with an elbow. At that moment a scream broke the stillness, followed by more. The sandy-haired man and three others disappeared into the cane rows. Pierre was impressed by how fast they could run, dressed as they were for a funeral.

The congressman frictioned himself into a trance. His eyelids drooped half-staff, and the sallow folds of his throat quivered when he moaned. Yet his grip on Erin was cast-iron. He pushed her deeper into the fields, the stalks leaning and shaking with the surge. Erin fought to keep her footing, because she certainly didn't want to go down. Dilbeck was a large man; once he got on top, there would be little to do but grit her teeth, close her eyes, ride with the music . . .

She attempted another scream, but only a faint cry came out. She was suffocating on the man's acrid heat, his foul panting, the rankness of his sweat. A stubby but determined stiffness poked at her from his boxer shorts.

'Baa-aby,' he whimpered for the hundredth time.

Erin attempted a death grab for the congressman's testicles. Not knowing there was only one, she came up empty-handed. Dilbeck tightened his hug and toppled slowly, like a rotted oak, taking Erin with him. Falling, she reflected on what a bad idea the machete had been—clever, sure, but not terribly smart. Because now she stood a fair chance of being speared by the damn thing when they hit the ground.

Fortunately it was the congressman who landed first, Erin bouncing on top. The impact roused Dilbeck from his reverie. He began smooching the crown of her head, murmuring about how sexy she smelled. The white bra remained bunched above her breasts, her cheek flattened against his ribs. She no longer heard the music from the limousine. Maybe the cane was too deep; maybe it had swallowed her screams as well.

Then she thought: Will they ever find me out here?

Suddenly, brutally, the congressman bucked her off. She landed hard on her neck and shoulders. The damp muck gave her a chill. Dilbeck crawled on top, awkwardly, subdued her with dead weight. Erin felt the blade of the machete sliding flat up her hip, sawing the elastic of her panties.

Fumbling at himself with the other hand, Dilbeck was saying: 'Now *this* is true love.'

Erin turned and pressed her lips softly to his chest.

'Oh, that's it,' he said.

Then her tongue, teasing—

'Heaven,' said the congressman.

—exploring, until she tasted the tracks of the scar—

'Circles,' he said. 'Do circles.'

—biting down with all her strength, tearing at him like a cat until he pushed away, keening, groping feebly at the ragged wet hole in his chest . . .

Erin got up spitting blood, meat and hair. 'True love,' she said, wiping her mouth violently. 'So how was it?'

Incredulous, Dilbeck struggled to his feet. 'You little b-b-bitch.'

'Fair enough.' Erin covered herself with her arms. 'You owe me a new pair of undies,' she said.

In the violet darkness, amid the broken matted cane, the congressman somehow relocated Willie Rojo's machete.

'Oh, don't be ridiculous,' Erin told him.

Dilbeck's breath came in hydraulic gasps. With both hands he raised the blade. 'You tried to chew my heart out,' he said, coiling for the swing.

Erin turned and dashed barefoot through the fields. She imagined Dilbeck suddenly imbued with Olympian swiftness, crashing the cane in his boots; imagined spiders, worms, moccasins, vermin writhing underfoot; imagined Darrell hiding in the tall grass, awaiting revenge. But she ran on, imagining a cool deep pool in which she would dive, wash herself clean, then vanish like an otter. She imagined Angela, waiting with her dolls on the shore, and ran harder.

Straight into the arms of a familiar sandy-haired man.

Special Agent Thomas Cleary.

The congressman said: 'I can explain.' The three men ordered him to drop the weapon and raise his hands. They had already identified themselves, definitively, as FBI. David Dilbeck was positively relieved.

'Do you know who I am?' he asked, blinking into the sharp cones of light. He tossed the machete away; it landed upright, twanging in the black marl. 'Gentlemen, please,' he said, 'I can explain.'

The FBI trained its agents in many tasks, but memorizing the faces of all 535 members of Congress was not one of them. Moreover, Dilbeck's closest friends and colleagues might not have recognized him in baggy boxer shorts and boots; radish-eyed, shirtless, semi-erect, his trademark silver mane dirty and spiked. An agent's flashlight lingered on the congressman's grisly bite wound, scabbing in the scraggly opposum fur of his chest. Standing nearly nude in a farm field, Dilbeck looked nothing like the distinguished fellow on his campaign billboards. To the agents, he looked very much like a common degenerate, captured mid-rape.

'Thank God you're here,' the congressman said warmly. He thought he was being rescued. Wasn't that the FBI's job?

An agent informed him of his right to remain silent.

'Jesus, Mary and Joseph,' Dilbeck hissed. 'Don't you know who I am?' He told them, repeating it vehemently as they put him in handcuffs.

The FBI men remained polite, firm and unflappable, even when Dilbeck addressed them as junior Nazi brown-shirts.

'Sir, is this yours?' One of the agents had come upon the black cowboy hat. He propped it on Dilbeck's head.

'That's backward,' the congressman groused.

'Naw,' said the agent. 'It looks good. Who are you s'posed to be—George Strait? Dwight Yoakam?'

'Nobody!' Dilbeck barked. 'For God's sake!'

The FBI men bandaged his bleeding wound, gave him four aspirins for the pain and locked him in one of the sedans. Squinting out the window, Dilbeck was engulfed in bewilderment. The gathering commotion revealed more FBI agents, his driver Pierre, a dark-haired woman, a small girl in pajamas being hoisted on the shoulders of an enormous bald Cro-Magnon. At one point a gruff-looking Cuban lowered his face to the glass and grinned, blue smoke seeping from between his teeth.

It's a goddamn circus! the congressman thought.

He ached for a telephone so he could call Moldy. Straighten out this whole damn mess.

Al García kissed his wife and said, 'Fancy meeting you here.'

'They came for Angie,' Donna explained. 'I wouldn't let them take her alone—Al, what's going on?'

García knew that his wife had busted the agents' balls, phoning downtown to verify the IDs. Boy, they hated that. He asked Donna about Andy and Lynne.

'They're at your mother's, and don't change the subject. Tell me what's happening out here.'

'Chaos, near as I can tell.' García introduced his wife to Shad, who'd been galloping through the cane rows with Angela whooping on his shoulders.

'Where's Momma?' the girl wanted to know.

'She'll be here soon,' García said, hoping it was true. The Feebs, as usual, were saying nothing. They eye-balled his sergeant's badge, the same as they'd eyeballed the shot-up Caprice, with minimal curiosity and zero tolerance.

Shad remarked on their snotty attitude. 'Why'd she call *them*?' He kept his voice low. 'The hell they got that you don't?'

'Jurisdiction,' García said. His feelings weren't hurt too badly; by calling the FBI, Erin had saved him a ton of paperwork.

Shad lowered Angie to the ground so that she could retrieve her dolls. He strolled to one of the gray sedans and scrutinized the face at the window: a disheveled old lech in a backward rodeo hat. David Dilbeck wore the agitated look of a stray dog being hauled to the pound.

'Pervie,' Shad muttered. He remembered the asshole from that night at Orly's club.

'Have some respect.' It was García, standing next to him. 'The man is a United States congressman!'

'Un-fucking-believable,' said Shad. Maybe it was time to get a voter's card.

They stood together in the sugarcane. Agent Cleary wrapped Erin in his suit jacket. He looked anxious and a little embarrassed. It rattled him, seeing her this way.

'Where's Angie?' Erin asked. 'Didn't you bring her?'

Cleary nodded, wiped the condensation from the lenses of his eye-glasses. 'I'm not sure why. I'm not sure what we've got here.'

'A kidnapping, more or less.' Erin gave an abridged account of the evening. She was tempted to tell all she knew about the congressman, starting with the Eager Beaver, but there was no point. Cleary was a linear thinker, not a dreamy conspiracist. He wanted overt acts and provable crimes.

In a tight voice he said, 'So you're a dancer.'

'Until tonight,' said Erin. 'Lawyers are expensive, Tom. I told you before, Darrell was running me in circles. By the way, he's out here somewhere'—sweeping an arm toward the fields—'my darling ex-husband.'

At the mention of Darrell Grant, the agent's expression darkened. Erin knew that Cleary felt rotten about not helping with the Darrell problem on the night she'd come to his house. Rules were rules. Now here they were, out in the sugar fields.

Cleary said, blankly, 'Seems you've had quite a time.'

His well-ordered brain was downshifting, trying to find traction in the mayhem. He struggled briefly with the image of his wholesome ex-secretary dancing naked on tables. Then out came the notebook, and the questions: Did Mr Dilbeck rape you? 'No.' Did he assault you? 'Yes.' Did he attempt penetration? 'Sort of.' Did he have a weapon? 'Yep.' Did he threaten you? 'Definitely.' Did he expose himself? 'Tried.'

The agent scribbled and ruminated simultaneously. 'I'm still not entirely comfortable with our authority here.' Scribble, scribble. 'He didn't take you across the state line, so technically we've got a gray area.' More scribbling. 'On the other hand, he did use a weapon so that's a possibility.'

Erin impatiently snatched the ballpoint pen. 'Tom, the man is a congressman. That's your damn jurisdiction.'

'Yes,' said Cleary. No getting around it.

'You look pale,' she said, 'or maybe it's the moonlight.'

The pallor was genuine. Tom Cleary had become nauseated, anticipating the fallout—the daily inquiries from Justice, the not-so-subtle pressure for investigatory details, the maddeningly accurate media leaks. It was a field agent's nightmare, a sex case against a prominent politician. Cleary envisioned paperwork as high as the Washington Monument, and the turning point of a once-promising career. 'I need the whole story,' he told Erin dourly, 'if you expect us to prosecute.'

Laughing, she touched his arm. 'Tom, I definitely don't expect you to prosecute.'

'Then what?' Anger came to his voice. 'This isn't a lark, Erin. We're talking about a member of the House of Representatives.'

'The sleazy old shit tried to boink me.'

When Cleary closed the notebook, Erin returned the pen. She said, 'The man is sick.'

'You want your name all over the newspapers?'

'Not particularly,' she conceded. Not before the final custody hearing.

'Then we're stuck, aren't we?'

She told him to quit thinking like an FBI man, think like a guy who's running for office. Cleary puffed his cheeks and pretended to gag.

Erin said, 'You don't have to arrest him, Tom. Just explain the facts of life.'

They talked for a few minutes, then started back toward the cars. 'I've still got loads of questions,' Cleary complained.

'There's a guy you need to talk to. A detective.' She took the agent's hand, leading him between the cane rows. 'Hasn't Angie gotten tall?'

'She's beautiful,' Cleary said. 'Has her mom's pretty green eyes.' Moments later, quietly: 'Did the bastard hurt you?'

'No, Tom, I'm fine.'

The roadside scene was like a drug raid: the sweep of lights, the bustle of armed men, the broken gargle of police radios. Cleary had pulled out all the stops. Erin was touched, and told him so. She didn't recognize the other agents, but made a point of thanking each one. They were unfailingly courteous, and tried not to be obvious when peeking at her breasts beneath the loose-fitting jacket.

When Angela spotted Erin, she thrust her dolls at Shad and ran, darting through the legs of the FBI men. Erin scooped her up, tweaked her chin and kissed the top of her nose. Angela, giggling, did the same to her mother.

Sgt Al García watched, a relaxed spectator on the hood of the Caprice. He was out of cigars so he'd resorted to bubble gum. Donna was retrieving two beers from the mini-bar in David Dilbeck's limousine. Erin walked up, bouncing Angela in her arms. The detective said she certainly had a flair for the dramatic.

'Now don't be mad,' Erin said.

'Who the hell's mad?'

'Al, I didn't want to get you in trouble. Shad, either.'

'Whatever,' García said, chiding. 'I'm just grateful for the invitation. This is more fun than Wrestlemania.' He pointed at the doughy figure hunched in the government sedan. 'So that's your guy. Congressman Romeo.'

Dilbeck rapped his cuffed wrists against the glass, beckoning Erin. She waved airily over one shoulder.

'Will you speak to Agent Cleary?' she asked García.

'A genuine FBI man! I would be greatly honored.' García offered Angela a stick of grape-flavored gum.

Erin said, 'I think there's a way to pull this off.'

'I think you're absolutely right.'

Shad lumbered to the car, holding the Barbie dolls like two sticks of dynamite. 'You owe me,' he said to Erin, who couldn't help but laugh.

He took her aside and told her about finding Malcolm Moldowsky dead in the fishbox. Erin was stunned. In a whisper she recounted Darrell Grant's mad narco-escapade. Shad generously offered to hunt him down and beat him into puppy chow. Erin said no thanks, she and Angie were out of danger for now.

'We're taking a vacation, starting tonight.'

'You deserve it,' Shad said, thinking how much he would miss her.

David Lane Dilbeck, believing himself a master of supple oratory, assumed that he could talk his way out of the trouble. To bolster his credibility, he audaciously scoffed at the suggestion that he call a lawyer. So the FBI agents perched him on the bumper of the car and gathered in a tribal semicircle to listen. Cleary allowed Al García to join them.

The detective was tickled by the spectacle—the moon, the crickets, the rustling cane fields. 'All we need is a campfire,' he whispered to Cleary, 'and some marshmallows.'

Dilbeck told quite a story. The agents took notes by penlight. García pitied their secretaries.

When the congressman was finished, Cleary said: 'Let's get this straight: You are the victim here, not the perpetrator.'

'Absolutely, yes, abducted at gunpoint.'

'Hmmm,' Cleary said. Al García thought the moment called for a stronger response, something along the lines of hooting and derision.

David Dilbeck said, 'She's been after me for weeks.'

'So you're alone on the yacht,' said Cleary, 'working on a campaign speech, when all of a sudden this crazed woman breaks in and attempts to seduce you.'

'Forcefully,' Dilbeck added, 'and when I rebuffed her, she became enraged.'

'And for this attempted seduction she wore a nine-dollar cotton bra from Kmart?'

'No, she wore red. Lace cups. P-p-paisley G-string! Later she changed all into white, when we were in the car.'

Agent Cleary realigned his glasses. 'So we're to believe that Ms Grant kidnapped you for sexual purposes. Is that a fair summary?'

'She was infatuated,' said the congressman. 'Certainly you've heard of such sad cases.'

García piped in: 'Politicians have groupies, too? I thought it was just rock stars and homicide cops.'

Cleary, keeping order: 'Mr Dilbeck, explain the injury to your chest.'

'She bit me,' he said, 'like a wild animal!'

The agent asked Dilbeck who might verify that he was being stalked by a nude dancer. 'One person,' he replied. 'His name is Malcolm J. Moldowsky. He'll confirm every detail.'

'Unlikely,' said García.

'What do you mean?' the congressman bleated.

García turned to Cleary. 'May I tell him? Please?'

'Yeah, go ahead.'

'Tell me what?' Dilbeck demanded.

'Your friend Malcolm,' said the detective, 'he sleeps with the fishies.'

The congressman slumped sideways off the bumper. The agents dutifully rushed forward to pick him up out of the dirt.

Cleary sighed, frowning at Al García. 'Was that really necessary?'

The two men sat alone in the Caprice. García balanced a bottle of beer on one knee. He jangled the gold bracelet in the congressman's face.

'You lose this?'

Dilbeck turned away coldly. He said, 'I've changed my mind about contacting a lawyer.'

'Too late.' García popped his gum. It didn't taste too bad with Beck's dark. He coiled the bracelet in the palm of his hand. 'You're cooked,' he told Dilbeck.

'Now listen—'

'Just shut up,' suggested the detective, 'and try to comprehend what's happened here. The FBI gets an anonymous call about a kidnapping in progress. The alleged suspect is a US congressman. The alleged victim is a former employee of the Bureau. You with me?'

'Erin worked for them?'

'Ain't it a hoot. Anyhow, the agents arrive to find the suspect—that's you—stripped to his skivvies and armed with a machete. You're chasing the alleged victim across farmland belonging to Joaquin and Wilberto Rojo. Subsequent investigation will reveal that the weapon used in the assault also belongs to this prominent and influential family. Congressman, I want you to imagine all this on the front page of the *Miami Herald*.'

Dilbeck rocked sideways, tugging absently on his lower lip. Al García wondered if he was lapsing into autism.

'Now if I'm you,' the detective said, 'I'm trying to guess how my version of the story is going to play with the Rojos and also the voting public—namely, that I was kidnapped by a nympho stripper. Remember there's no gun, no evidence, not a single witness to back you up. Even your driver says the lady is telling the truth.'

'Impossible,' Dilbeck said, thickly. 'He speaks no English.'

García smiled. 'Your driver is a modest guy. He's got a degree in hotel management from FIU. Didn't he tell you?'

The congressman stopped rocking. He wrapped both arms around his head, as if bracing for incoming mortars. 'There was another man on the yacht,' he said, a dry rasp. 'Durrell something.'

'You mean Mr Darrell Grant, currently a fugitive on several violent felonies.' García spoke from behind a fat purple bubble. 'I were you, I wouldn't count on a junkie for my alibi.'

'But what about this!' David Dilbeck slapped at his bandaged chest. 'I've been viciously attacked—any damn fool can see.' He clawed at the tape and gauze until the bloody crater was exposed. 'Look!' he said. 'My goddamn nipple is gone! I mean *gone*.'

Al García said, 'I hate to be negative, *chico*, but that's your basic defensive bite wound. Man's got a woman pinned, what else can she do?'

The congressman gathered up the mangled bandage and, half-wittedly, attempted to replace it.

'Prosecutors love bite wounds,' García elaborated. 'One time we had a victim chomp some guy's pecker half off. That's how we caught him, too—turned up in the ER at Jackson, said it was a freak gardening accident. Anyhow, we got forensics to match the punctures in the guy's schlong with the bite pattern of the victim's teeth. The jury was out maybe thirty seconds.'

Bereft, Dilbeck stared at his mutilation as if branded. 'What will happen now? The campaign and all.'

García said, 'It was up to me, I'd throw your fat ass in jail. Lucky for you, it ain't.' He took the empty beer bottle and slid from the car. Erin Grant got in. She crossed her legs and adjusted

Agent Cleary's suit jacket to make sure her breasts weren't showing; she wanted Dilbeck undistracted.

'David,' she said, 'what a mess you're in.'

The congressman pulled back like a scalded snail, huddling against the opposite door. His voice cracked with reproach: 'You even called me ' "sweetie".'

'Maybe I call everyone ' "sweetie".'

He shouted: 'I don't love you any more!'

'Oh yes you do.'

After a few moments of silence, Dilbeck offered a squirmy apology for his coarse behavior. He inquired whether Erin intended to press charges.

'That's Plan B,' she said.

'And Plan A?'

'You go home tonight,' she told him, 'and have yourself a heart attack.'

The congressman sneered. 'That's not the slightest bit funny.'

'A mild one,' Erin proposed, 'requiring weeks of bed rest, bland dieting and seclusion.'

'In other words, tank the election.'

'Davey, I'm trying to cut you a break. Now if you'd prefer Plan B, that's fine. Have you ever been on ' "Hard Copy"?' The last of Dilbeck's hope drained away. 'A heart attack, for God's sake. Is there more?'

'Sweetie, of course there's more.' Erin reached up and turned the congressman's cowboy hat, so it wasn't backward on his head.

Breakfast, predawn. A truckstop on old Route 441, jammed with semis, dump trucks, dairy tankers, pickups, flatbeds hauling farm equipment. The place smelled like a diesel fart.

Shad, Donna García and her detective husband sat three abreast in the front of the unmarked Caprice. Donna nursed a black coffee, Shad inhaled his seventh glazed donut and Al García attacked spicy pork sausages with the hope of scouring multiple layers of grape, beer and stale cigar from his palate.

'Disney World,' the detective mused, munching steadfastly.

'I think it's sweet,' said his wife, 'though I'm not sure about the driver.'

Shad said don't worry, the driver's cool.

Pierre was gassing up the limousine at the high-test pump. He felt the weight of the gold bracelet in the left pocket of his trousers; a gift for your wife, the cop had said. Very strange, Pierre thought. The whole evening.

Angela was curled asleep in the jump seat. Erin had changed into her jeans, T-shirt and sandals; her hair was tied in a ponytail. She stood at the door of the limo and chatted with Cleary, the FBI man, finishing his notes. He looked haggard, rumpled, eager to leave. It pleased García to see another lawman labor in that familiar hollow-eyed condition, particularly a Feeb.

Donna asked, 'Where are the others?'

'They escorted the congressman home,' her husband said. 'He wasn't feeling so great.'

Shad interrupted his donutfest to complain that Dilbeck was getting off easy. 'I vote for jail,' he said, 'or a bullet in the brain. That's what the sonofabitch deserves.'

García disagreed good-naturedly. 'For politicians, some fates are worse than death. Erin came up with a beaut, no?'

Donna said that Angela was excited about the Disney World trip. 'Her favorite ride is the teacups. She says it's fun to get dizzy.' Donna paused. 'On the way here, she asked about her father.'

García said that Darrell Grant remained at large in the cane. 'He'll come out when they burn the fields. Him and the rest of the critters.'

Shad, his cheeks stuffed bulbously: 'Any luck, he'll sleep through the goddamn fire.'

Donna told him to stop, don't take another bite. She lifted a half-crescent of donut from his hand. 'This is so gross,' she said. 'A darn bug!'

Shad snatched it away, flipped on the dome light and examined the find. His hopeful expression faded.

'It's awful damn small,' he observed, doubtfully. He extracted the culprit from a dry crumb of donut—a centipede with a shiny, cocoa-colored carapace. It drew into a protective ball at Shad's touch.

'Long shot,' García remarked. 'You'll need a jury of total suckers.'

'Yeah?' Shad placed the bug on the tip of his pinkie and held it near the light bulb.

'It was me,' said García, 'I'd wait for another jumbo cockroach.'

Donna, annoyed: 'What in the world are you talking about?'

'Dreams,' said Shad. 'Nothing important.' He flicked the centipede out the window and inserted the remainder of the donut in his glaze-crusted lips.

Agent Cleary had trundled his notes to a pay phone, where he was deeply absorbed in official conversation. Pierre backed the Cadillac away from the gas pumps. Erin Grant stuck her head out the window and gave a high-spirited wave. Shad and Donna waved back; Al García pantomimed operatic applause.

'Great smile,' he said, as the limo drove away.

'She looks sixteen,' said Shad, 'I swear.'

García eased the Caprice up to the gas pumps to top off the tank before the long drive home. He had one leg out the door when the car shuddered violently. He heard the tinkle of tail-lights breaking, and said, 'Aw, shit.'

A tractor-trailer had crunched the rear of the unmarked police car. The driver stood sheepishly over García's crimped bumper. Damage to the Caprice was minor, but the detective was not consoled: another lengthy accident report would be required, in triplicate. Witnesses interviewed. Tedious diagrams sketched. Polaroids snapped for the insurance company and Risk Management. Hours of useless department bullshit.

'Congratulations,' he told the trucker. 'You just hit a cop.'

'Sorry.' The man was a wiry redhead with twitchy Dexedrine eyes. 'I never saw you guys.'

'That was my guess, too,' García said. He popped the trunk of the Caprice to search for the proper goddamn forms. Donna and Shad got out to see what had happened.

After circling the rig, Shad said, 'Hey, Al. Guess what.'

'What?' García was bent over, rummaging fiercely.

'My neck hurts,' said Shad.

Pad in hand, García slammed the trunk lid. He said, 'You don't *have* a fucking neck.'

The bouncer gave a crafty wink, nodded slightly toward the trailer. 'No kidding, man, I'm in serious pain.'

Donna stood on tiptoes to scout the injury. 'Show me where it hurts.'

'Everywhere,' Shad said, with a theatrical grimace.

Gingerly Donna rubbed the taut slopes between his skull and shoulders. She said, 'Come back to the car. You'd better sit down.'

'Yeah,' Shad agreed, 'I'm pretty damn traumatized.'

The worried truck driver excused himself, creeping off to improve his blood readings with black coffee. Al García walked back to the tractor-rig for a close look. Soon Donna heard him laughing, although she couldn't imagine why; hearty laughter that boomed raw and carefree. Other truckers began to stare, irritated by the disruption of their early morning routine. García sounded daffy and stoned.

Donna found him holding the trailer, his fingers hooked in the steel mesh. He was shaking hysterically. The bin was full of sugarcane. A blue-and-white sign bolted to the side said: ROJO FARMS.

Donna said, 'Now I get it.'

'Well, go ahead,' said her husband, wheezing. 'Call Mr Shad an ambulance.'

'Really, Al.'

'Sweet justice,' the detective said. He wiped his eyes, tried to compose himself, act like a grown-up. Then he felt the laughter rising again like a grand tide. It was one fine moment.

Epilogue

Three weeks before the election, DAVID LANE DILBECK was reported to have suffered a minor heart attack while reading in bed. Although missing the remainder of the campaign, he pulled fifty-two percent of the vote and easily won re-election to the House of Representatives. The following day, he stunned political supporters by resigning his seat, citing chronic health problems. The congressman's chiropractor, cardiologist and urologist issued an unusual joint statement endorsing his decision to retire.

Dilbeck's opponent, ELOY FLICKMAN, gave up politics and became a right-wing radio commentator in South Florida. Within months he was leading the daytime Arbitrons, touting himself as 'the weight-watcher's Rush Limbaugh.' One day after signing a contract with the Liberty Radio Network, Flickman was accidentally killed while picketing an abortion clinic during a live remote broadcast. The driver of the death car lost control when one of her seven children got his sneakers tangled in the steering wheel.

In January, the agricultural committee formerly chaired by Congressman Dilbeck approved a bill renewing multimillion-dollar subsidies for US sugar growers. The measure passed the House 271–150 after a brief floor debate. Speaking eloquently in its favor was REP. BO TOOLEY, the Republican from northern Alabama, who had never before sailed on a yacht as long or luxurious as the *Sweetheart Deal*, and was delighted that its shortwave radio picked up all his favorite Bible stations.

Shortly after its mysterious rat infestation, the FLESH FARM was shut down for multiple health-code violations. Two weeks later, the building burned to the ground. The LING brothers claimed that the blaze started when a dancer's trained snake became entwined in the electric wiring. Indicted later for insurance fraud, the Lings fled to western Canada and opened a chain of massage parlors with a hockey motif.

The remains of DARRELL GRANT were identified from a single fingertip. Three days later, the SWEETHEART SUGAR CORPORATION discreetly notified wholesalers that it was recalling all granulated sugar milled between October 6th and October 9th, due to 'possible rodent contamination during processing'.

After interviewing PAUL GUBER and other clients, the Florida Bar issued a harsh public reprimand of ATTORNEY JONATHAN PETER MORDECAI for 'gross ethical misconduct'. The effect of the discipline was minimal, since Mordecai was dead and no longer practicing law. Paul Guber quit his brokerage firm and entered rabbinical college in Chicago. He never spoke of his brief engagement to the late JOYCE MIZNER, or of his ill-fated bachelor party at the EAGER BEAVER lounge.

ERB CRANDALL did not return to Florida. Instead he settled in Atlantic City, accepting a job as the top political aide to a popular but recklessly overextended city councilman. The following summer, after collecting a large cash bribe on behalf of his boss, Crandall was accosted by three muggers demanding the paper bag he was carrying. His dead body—the shredded sack clutched loyally in one fist—was found by German tourists beneath the legendary boardwalk. The city council promptly named a street in Crandall's memory.

The group of orthopedic surgeons who owned the TICKLED PINK sold the nightclub to a group of dentists, who chose a saucy new name (Bare Essentials II) and bold new management (Johnny 'Three Toes' Spladiano). Mr Spladiano's first three business decisions were to fire ORLY, add valet parking, and enlarge the wrestling pit. Considering himself more fortunate than his predecessor, Orly closed out a modest IRA account and moved to Pensacola, where he and his wife opened a topless oyster bar called Eat Me Raw.

URBANA SPRAWL continued to dance at Bare Essentials II until the day Mr Spladiano replaced creamed corn with sardines in the wrestling arena. She is now premed at Emory University in Atlanta. SABRINA left dancing and worked briefly in adult films before landing the role of Lucette, the perky Parisian spokesmodel for Thigh Diver exercise equipment. The two Moniques also retired from nude dancing, each marrying one of her customers. MONIQUE JR, whose real name was Loretta Brickman, wed a seventy-four-year-old wholesale diamond broker who had outlived three previous wives. MONIQUE SR, whose actual name was Frances Cabrera, married a middle-aged pottery instructor who was, in her adoring eyes, a dead ringer for Keith Richards.

The man known as SHAD, whose real name was Gerard L. Shaddick, sued Rojo Farms, Rojo Trucking and the Sweetheart Sugar Corporation for injuries allegedly sustained when the loaded cane trailer rear-ended Sgt Al García's police car. In the lawsuit, Shad complained of neck pain, migraines, blurred vision, vertigo, sexual dysfunction and chronic anxiety. The case was settled out of court for $2.3 million. Shortly afterward, Shad purchased a split-level condominium in Telluride, Colorado, and became engaged to his physical therapist, a recent emigrant from Norway.

RITA GRANT also sued Rojo Farms, seeking $5 million compensation for the accidental mulching of her brother, Darrell. The lawsuit was swiftly abandoned when Rita was forced to flee Dade County with Lupa, her beloved wolf hybrid. Animal-control officers had ordered her to surrender the animal after it jumped a nine-foot wall at the Metrozoo and brought down a full-grown African springbok.

The murder of MALCOLM J. MOLDOWSKY remains unsolved. In the days following his death, news stories described the crime scene in gruesome detail, revealing that the murder weapon was a nine-iron made by MacGregor. A local columnist characterized Moldy as a ruthless and shady political fixer who had finally crossed the wrong person. Moldy's eulogist, Congressman Bo

Tooley, angrily denounced the story as a 'damnable lie'—a quote lovingly borrowed from Moldowsky's Watergate idol, John Mitchell. The funeral was brief and sparsely attended. From his sickbed, David Dilbeck sent profound regrets.

CHRISTOPHER ROJO was arrested during a late-night disturbance at the Kennedy compound in Palm Beach. Witnesses claimed that he attempted to demonstrate his oil-wrestling prowess upon Maria Shriver, Daryl Hannah and other female guests. Threatened with the loss of several trust funds, Christopher voluntarily entered a facility for treatment of drug and alcohol abuse. There he met his future wife, a copy editor at *Vanity Fair*.

The elder ROJOS remain prominent in Florida's sugar industry, while secretly optioning vast tracts of cane acreage for future development as condominiums and golf resorts. A few days before Congress voted new price supports for sugar growers, Wilberto and Joaquin Rojo announced the funding of two full scholarships at Georgia State University. The student recipients were KATHERINE and AUDREY KILLIAN, whose father had recently perished in a rafting accident in Montana.

PIERRE ST BAPTISTE resigned from Gold Coach Limousines to become catering manager of a new Sheraton in Key West. In the evenings he teaches English to the children of Haitian exiles.

A Broward County judge awarded ERIN GRANT permanent custody of her daughter, ANGELA. They moved to Orlando, where Erin took a night dancing job as Cinderella's eldest stepsister in Disney World's famous Main Street Parade. During the day she works as a data-entry specialist for the local office of the FBI. Her application to the academy at Quantico is currently under review.

STORMY
WEATHER

For Donna, Camille, Hugo and Andrew

Acknowledgements

For their expertise on the most esoteric subjects, I am deeply grateful to my good friends John Kipp (the finer points of skull collecting), Tim Chapman (the effects of canine shock collars on human volunteers) and Bob Branham (the care and handling of untamed South American coatimundis). I am also greatly indebted to my talented colleagues at the *Miami Herald*, whose superb journalism in the aftermath of Hurricane Andrew provided so much rich material for this novel.

C.H.

1

On August 23, the day before the hurricane struck, Max and Bonnie Lamb awoke early, made love twice and rode the shuttle bus to Disney World. That evening they returned to the Peabody Hotel, showered separately, switched on the cable news and saw that the storm was heading directly for the southeastern tip of Florida. The TV weatherman warned that it was the fiercest in many years.

Max Lamb sat at the foot of the bed and gazed at the color radar image—a ragged flame-colored sphere, spinning counter-clockwise toward the coast. He said, 'Jesus, look at that.'

A hurricane, Bonnie Lamb thought, on our honeymoon! As she slipped under the sheets, she heard the rain beating on the rental cars in the parking lot outside. 'Is this part of it?' she asked. 'All this weather?'

Her husband nodded. 'We're on the edge of the edge.'

Max Lamb seemed excited in a way that Bonnie found unsettling. She knew better than to suggest a sensible change of plans, such as hopping a plane back to La Guardia. Her new husband was no quitter; the reservations said five nights and six days, and by God that's how long they would stay. It was a special package rate; no refunds.

She said, 'They'll probably close the park.'

'Disney?' Max Lamb smiled. 'Disney never closes. Not for plagues, famines, or even hurricanes.' He rose to adjust the volume on the television. 'Besides, the darn thing's three hundred miles away. The most we'll see up here is more rain.'

Bonnie Lamb detected disappointment in her husband's tone. Hands on his hips, he stood nude in front of the TV screen; his pale shoulder blades and buttocks were streaked crimson from a day on the water flumes. Max was no athlete, but he'd done fine on the river slide. Bonnie wondered if it had gone to his head, for tonight he affected the square-shouldered posture of a college jock. She caught him glancing in the mirror, flexing his stringy biceps and sizing up his own nakedness. Maybe it was just a honeymoon thing.

The cable news was showing live video of elderly residents being evacuated from condominiums and apartment buildings on Miami Beach. Many of the old folks carried cats or poodles in their arms.

'So,' said Bonnie Lamb, 'we're still doing Epcot tomorrow?'

Her husband didn't answer.

'Honey?' she said. 'Epcot?'

Max Lamb's attention was rooted to the hurricane news. 'Oh sure,' he said absently.

'You remembered the umbrellas?'

'Yes, Bonnie, in the car.'

She asked him to turn off the television and come to bed. When he got beneath the covers, she moved closer, nipped his earlobes, played her fingers through the silky sprout of hair on his bony chest.

'Guess what I'm not wearing,' she whispered.

'Ssshhh,' said Max Lamb. 'Listen to that rain.'

Edie Marsh headed to Dade County from Palm Beach, where she'd spent six months trying to sleep with a Kennedy. She'd had the plan all worked out, how she'd seduce a young Kennedy and then threaten to run to the cops with a lurid tale of perversion, rape and torture. She'd hatched the scheme while watching the William Kennedy Smith trial on Court TV and noticing the breath-less relief with which the famous clan had received the acquittal; all of them with those fantastic teeth, beaming at the cameras but wearing an expression that Edie Marsh had seen more than a few times in her twenty-nine action-packed years—the look of those who'd dodged a bullet. They'd have no stomach for another scandal, not right away. Next time there'd be a mad stampede for the Kennedy family checkbook, in order to make the problem go away. Edie had it all figured out.

She cleaned out her boyfriend's bank account and grabbed the Amtrak to West Palm, where she found a cheap duplex apartment. She spent her days sleeping, shoplifting cocktail dresses and painting her nails. Each night she'd cross the bridge to the rich island, where she assiduously loitered at Au Bar and the other trendy clubs. She overtipped bartenders and waitresses, with the understanding that they would instantly alert her when a Kennedy, *any* Kennedy, arrived. In this fashion she had quickly met two Shrivers and a distant Lawford, but to Edie they would have been borderline fucks. She was saving her charms for a direct heir, a pipeline to old Joe Kennedy's mother lode. One of the weekly tabloids had published a diagram of the family tree, which Edie Marsh had taped to the wall of the kitchen, next to a Far Side calendar. Right away Edie had ruled out screwing any Kennedys-by-marriage; the serious money followed the straightest lines of genealogy, as did the scandal hunters. Statistically it appeared her best target would be one of Ethel and Bobby's sons, since they'd had so many. Not that Edie wouldn't have crawled nude across broken glass for a whack at John Jr., but the odds of *him* strolling unescorted into a Palm Beach fern bar were laughable.

Besides, Edie Marsh was nothing if not a realist. John Kennedy Jr. had movie-star girlfriends, and Edie knew she was no movie star. Pretty, sure. Sexy in a low-cut Versace, you bet. But John-John probably wouldn't glance twice. Some of those cousins, though, Bobby's boys—Edie was sure she could do some damage there. Suck 'em cross-eyed, then phone the lawyers.

Unfortunately, six grueling months of barhopping produced only two encounters with *Kennedy* Kennedys. Neither tried to sleep with Edie; she couldn't believe it. One of the young men even took her on an actual date, but when they returned to her place he didn't so much as grope her boobs. Just pecked her good night and said thanks for a nice time. The perfect goddamn gentleman, she'd thought. Just my luck. Edie had tried valiantly to change his mind, practically pinned him to the hood of his car, kissed and rubbed and grabbed him. Nothing! Humiliating is what it was. After the young Kennedy departed, Edie Marsh had stalked to the bathroom and studied herself in the mirror. Maybe there was wax in her ears or spinach in her teeth, something gross to put the guy off. But no, she looked fine. Furiously she peeled off her stolen dress, appraised her figure and thought: Did the little snot think he's too good for *this*? What a joke, that Kennedy charm. The kid had all the charisma of oatmeal. He'd bored her to death long before the lobster entrée arrived. She'd felt like hopping on the tabletop and shrieking at the top of her lungs: Who gives a shit about illiteracy in South Boston? Tell me about Jackie and the Greek!

That dismal evening, it turned out, was Edie's last shot. The summer went dead in Palm Beach, and all the fuckable Kennedys traveled up to Hyannis. Edie was too broke to give chase.

The hurricane on the TV radar had given her a new idea. The storm was eight hundred miles away, churning up the Caribbean, when she phoned a man named Snapper, who was coming off a short hitch for manslaughter. Snapper got his nickname because of a crooked jaw, which had been made that way by a game warden and healed poorly. Edie Marsh arranged to meet him at a sports bar on the beach. Snapper listened to her plan and said it was the nuttiest fucking thing he'd ever heard because (a) the hurricane probably won't hit here and (b) somebody could get busted for heavy time.

Three days later, with the storm bearing down on Miami, Snapper called Edie Marsh and said what the hell, let's check it out. I got a guy, Snapper said, he knows about these things.

The guy's name was Avila, and formerly he had worked as a building inspector for Metropolitan Dade County. Snapper and Edie met him at a convenience store on Dixie Highway in South Miami. The rain was deceptively light, given the proximity of the hurricane, but the clouds hung ominously low, an eerie yellow gauze.

They went in Avila's car, Snapper sitting next to Avila up front and Edie by herself in the back. They were going to a subdivision called Sugar Palm Hammocks: one hundred and sixty-four single-family homes platted sadistically on only forty acres of land. Without comment, Avila drove slowly through the streets. Many residents were outside, frantically nailing plywood to the windows of their homes.

'There's no yards,' Snapper remarked.

Avila said, 'Zero-lot lines is what we call it.'

'How cozy,' Edie Marsh said from the back seat. 'What we need is a house that'll go to pieces in the storm.'

Avila nodded confidently. 'Take your pick. They're all coming down.'

'No shit?'

'Yeah, honey, no shit.'

Snapper turned to Edie Marsh and said, 'Avila ought to know. He's the one inspected the damn things.'

'Perfect,' said Edie. She rolled down the window. 'Then let's find something nice.'

On instructions from the authorities, tourists by the thousands were bailing out of the Florida Keys. Traffic on northbound U.S. 1 was a wretched crawl, winking brake lights as far as the eye could see. Jack Fleming and Webo Drake had run out of beer at Big Pine. Now they were stuck behind a Greyhound bus halfway across the Seven Mile Bridge. The bus had stalled with transmission trouble. Jack Fleming and Webo Drake got out of the car—Jack's father's car—and started throwing empty Coors cans off the bridge. The two young men were still slightly trashed from a night at the Turtle Kraals in Key West, where the idea of getting stranded in a Force Four hurricane had sounded downright adventurous, a nifty yarn to tell the guys back at the Kappa Alpha house. The problem was, Jack and Webo had awakened to find themselves out of money as well as beer, with Jack's father expecting his almost-new Lexus to be returned . . . well, yesterday.

So here they were, stuck on one of the longest bridges in the world, with a monster tropical cyclone only a few hours away. The wind hummed across the Atlantic at a pitch that Jack

Fleming and Webo Drake had never before heard; it rocked them on their heels when they got out of the car. Webo lobbed an empty Coors can toward the concrete rail, but the wind whipped it back hard, like a line drive. Naturally it then became a contest to see who had the best arm. In high school Jack Fleming had been a star pitcher, mainly sidearm, so his throws were not as disturbed by the gusts as those of Webo Drake, who had merely played backup quarterback for the junior varsity. Jack was leading, eight beer cans to six off the bridge, when a hand—an enormous brown hand—appeared with a wet slap on the rail.

Webo Drake glanced worriedly at his frat brother. Jack Fleming said, 'Now what?'

A bearded man pulled himself up from a piling beneath the bridge. He was tall, with coarse silvery hair that hung in matted tangles to his shoulders. His bare chest was striped with thin pink abrasions. The man carried several coils of dirty rope under one arm. He wore camouflage trousers and old brown military boots with no laces. In his right hand was a crushed Coors can and a dead squirrel.

Jack Fleming said, 'You a Cuban?'

Webo Drake was horrified.

Dropping his voice, Jack said: 'No joke. I bet he's a rafter.'

It made sense. This was where the refugees usually landed, in the Keys. Jack spoke loudly to the man with the rope: '*Usted Cubano*?'

The man brandished the beer can and said: '*Usted* un asshole?'

His voice was a rumble that fit his size. 'Where do you dipshits get off,' he said over the wind, 'throwing your goddamn garbage in the water?' The man stepped forward and kicked out a rear passenger window of Jack's father's Lexus. He threw the empty beer can and the dead squirrel in the back seat. Then he grabbed Webo Drake by the belt of his jeans. 'Your trousers dry?' the man asked.

Passengers in the Greyhound bus pressed their faces to the glass to see what was happening. Behind the Lexus, a family in a rented minivan could be observed locking the doors, a speedy drill they had obviously practiced before leaving the Miami airport.

Webo Drake said yes, his jeans were dry. The stranger said, 'Then hold my eye.' With an index finger he calmly removed a glass orb from his left socket and placed it carefully in one of Webo's pants pockets. 'It loosed up on me,' the stranger explained, 'in all this spray.'

Failing to perceive the gravity of the moment, Jack Fleming pointed at the shattered window of his father's luxury sedan. 'Why the hell'd you do that?'

Webo, shaking: 'Jack, it's all right.'

The one-eyed man turned toward Jack Fleming. 'I count thirteen fucking beer cans in the water and only one hole in your car. I'd say you got off easy.'

'Forget about it,' offered Webo Drake.

The stranger said, 'I'm giving you boys a break because you're exceptionally young and stupid.'

Ahead of them, the Greyhound bus wheezed, lurched and finally began to inch northward. The man with the rope opened the rear door of the Lexus and brushed the broken glass off the seat. 'I need a lift up the road,' he said.

Jack Fleming and Webo Drake said certainly, sir, that would be no trouble at all. It took forty-five minutes on the highway before they summoned the nerve to ask the one-eyed man what he was doing under the Seven Mile Bridge.

Waiting, the man replied.

For what? Webo asked.

Turn on the radio, the man said. If you don't mind.

News of the hurricane was on every station. The latest forecast put the storm heading due west across the Bahamas, toward a landfall somewhere between Key Largo and Miami Beach.

'Just as I thought,' said the one-eyed man. 'I was too far south. I could tell by the sky.'

He had covered his head with a flowered shower cap; Jack Fleming noticed it in the rearview mirror, but withheld comment. The young man was more concerned about what to tell his father regarding the busted window, and also about the stubborn stain a dead squirrel might leave on fine leather upholstery.

Webo Drake asked the one-eyed man: 'What's the rope for?'

'Good question,' he said, but gave no explanation.

An hour later the road spread to four lanes and the traffic began to move at a better clip. Almost no cars were heading south. The highway split at North Key Largo, and the stranger instructed Jack Fleming to bear right on County Road 905.

'It says there's a toll,' Jack said.

'Yeah?'

'Look, we're out of money.'

A soggy ten-dollar bill landed on the front seat between Jack Fleming and Webo Drake. Again the earthquake voice: 'Stop when we reach the bridge.'

Twenty minutes later they approached the Card Sound Bridge, which crosses from North Key Largo to the mainland. Jack Fleming tapped the brakes and steered to the shoulder. 'Not here,' said the stranger. 'All the way to the top.'

'The top of the bridge?'

'Are you deaf, junior?'

Jack Fleming drove up the slope cautiously. The wind was ungodly, jostling the Lexus on its springs. At the crest of the span, Jack pulled over as far as he dared. The one-eyed man retrieved his glass eye from Webo Drake and got out of the car. He yanked the plastic cap off his head and jammed it into the waistband of his trousers.

'Come here,' the stranger told the two young men. 'Tie me.' He popped the eye into its socket and cleaned it in a polishing motion with the corner of a bandanna. Then he climbed over the rail and inserted his legs back under the gap, so he was kneeling on the precipice.

Other hurricane evacuees slowed their cars to observe the lunatic scene, but none dared to stop; the man being lashed to the bridge looked wild enough to deserve it. Jack Fleming and Webo Drake worked as swiftly as possible, given the force of the gusts and the rapidity with which their Key West hangovers were advancing. The stranger gave explicit instructions about how he was to be trussed, and the fraternity boys did what they were told. They knotted one end of the rope around the man's thick ankles and ran the other end over the concrete rail. After looping it four times around his chest, they cinched until he grunted. Then they threaded the rope under the rail and back to the ankles for the final knotting.

The product was a sturdy harness that allowed the stranger's arms to wave free. Webo Drake tested the knots and pronounced them tight. 'Can we go now?' he asked the one-eyed man.

'By all means.'

'What about the squirrel, sir?'

'It's all yours,' the stranger said. 'Enjoy.'

Jack Fleming coasted the car downhill. At the foot of the bridge, he veered off the pavement to get clear of the traffic. Webo Drake found a rusty curtain rod in a pile of trash, and Jack used it to hoist the animal carcass out of his father's Lexus. Webo stood back, trying to light a cigaret.

Back on the bridge, under a murderous dark sky, the kneeling stranger raised both arms to the pulsing gray clouds. Bursts of hot wind made the man's hair stand up like a halo of silver sparks. 'Crazy fucker,' Jack Fleming rasped. He stepped over the dead squirrel and threw the curtain rod into the mangroves. 'You think he had a gun? Because that's what I'm telling my old man: Some nut with a gun kicked out the car window.'

Webo Drake pointed with the cigaret and said, 'Jack, you know what he's waiting for? That crazy idiot, he's waiting on the hurricane.'

Although the young men stood two hundred yards away, they could see the one-eyed stranger grinning madly into the teeth of the rising wind. He wore a smile that blazed.

'Brother,' Jack said to Webo, 'let's get the hell out of here.' The tollbooth was unmanned, so they blew through at fifty miles an hour, skidded into the parking lot of Alabama Jack's. There they used the one-eyed man's ten-dollar bill to purchase four cold cans of Cherry Coke, which they drank on the trip up Card

Sound Road. When they were finished, they did not toss the empties from the car.

A noise awakened Bonnie Lamb. It was Max, snapping open a suitcase. She asked what in the world he was doing, fully dressed and packing his clothes at four in the morning. He said he wanted to surprise her.

'You're leaving me?' she asked. 'After two nights.'

Max Lamb smiled and came to the bed. 'I'm packing for both of us.'

He tried to stroke Bonnie's cheek, but she buried her face in the pillow, to block out the light. The rain was coming harder now, slapping horizontally against the windows of the high-rise hotel. She was glad her husband had come to his senses. They could do Epcot some other time.

She peered out of the pillow and said, 'Honey, is the airport open?'

'I don't honestly know.'

'Shouldn't you call first?'

'Why?' Max Lamb patted the blanket where it followed the curve of his wife's hips.

'We're flying home, aren't we?' Bonnie Lamb sat up. 'That's why you're packing.'

Her husband said no, we're not flying home. 'We're going on an adventure.'

'I see. Where, Max?'

'Miami.'

'That's the surprise?'

'That's it.' He tugged the covers away from her. 'Come on, we've got a long drive—'

Bonnie Lamb didn't move. 'You're serious.'

'—and I want to teach you how to use the video camera.'

She said, 'I've got a better idea. Why don't we stay here and make love for the next three days. Dawn to dusk, OK? Tear the room to pieces. I mean, if it's adventure you want.'

Max Lamb was up again, stuffing the suitcases. 'You don't understand. This is a once-in-a-lifetime chance.'

Right, Bonnie said, a chance to drown on our honeymoon. 'I'd rather stay where it's warm and dry. I'll even watch *Emmanuelle VI* on the Spectravision, like you wanted last night.' This she regarded as a significant concession.

'By the time we get to Miami,' said Max, 'the dangerous part will be over. In fact, it's probably over already.'

'Then what's the point?'

'You'll see.'

'Max, I don't want to do this. Please.'

He gave her a stiff, fatherly hug. She knew he was about to speak to her as if she were six years old. 'Bonnie,' Max Lamb said to his new wife. 'My beautiful little Bonnie, now listen. Disney World we can do anytime. Anytime we want. But how often does a hurricane hit? You heard the weatherman, honey. "The Storm of the Century," he called it. How often does a person get to see something like that!'

Bonnie Lamb couldn't stand her husband's lordly tone. She couldn't stand it so much that she'd have done anything to shut him up.

'All right, Max. Bring me my robe.'

He kissed her noisily on the forehead. 'Thatta girl.'

2

Snapper and Edie Marsh got two rooms at the Best Western in Pembroke Pines, thirty miles north of where the storm was predicted to come ashore. Snapper told the motel clerk that one room would be enough, but Edie said not on your damn life. The relationship had always been strictly business, Snapper being an occasional fence of women's wear and Edie being an occasional thief of same. Their new venture was to be another entrepreneurial partnership, more ambitious but not more intimate. Up front Edie alerted Snapper that she couldn't imagine a situation in which she'd have sex with him, even once. He did not seem poleaxed by the news.

She went to bed covering her ears, trying to shut out the hellish moan of the storm. It was more than she could bear alone. During the brief calm of the eye, she pounded on the door to Snapper's room and said she was scared half to death. Snapper said come on in, we're having ourselves a time.

Somewhere in the midst of a hurricane, he'd found a hooker. Edie was impressed. The woman clutched a half-empty bottle of Barbancourt between her breasts. Snapper had devoted himself to vodka; he wore a Marlins cap and red Jockey shorts, inside out. Candles gave the motel room a soft, religious lighting. The electricity had been out for two hours.

Edie Marsh introduced herself to the prostitute, whom Snapper had procured through a telephone escort service. Here was a dedicated employee! thought Edie.

The back side of the storm came up, a roar so unbearable that the three of them huddled like orphans on the floor. The candles flickered madly as the wind sucked at the windows. Edie could see the walls breathing—Christ, what a lousy idea this was! A large painting of a pelican fell, grazing one of the hooker's ankles. She cried out softly and gnawed at her artificial fingernails. Snapper kept to the vodka. Occasionally his free hand would turn up like a spider on Edie's thigh. She smashed it, but Snapper merely sighed.

By dawn the storm had crossed inland, and the high water was falling fast. Edie Marsh put on a conservative blue dress and dark nylons, and pinned her long brown hair in a bun. Snapper wore the only suit he owned, a slate pinstripe he'd purchased two years earlier for an ex-cellmate's funeral; the cuffed trousers stopped an inch shy of his shoetops. Edie chuckled and said that was perfect.

They dropped the prostitute at a Denny's restaurant and took the Turnpike south to see what the hurricane had done. Traffic was bumper-to-bumper lunacy, fire engines and cop cars and ambulances everywhere. The radio said Homestead had been blown off the map. The governor was sending the National Guard.

Snapper headed east on 152nd Street but immediately got disoriented. All traffic signals and street signs were down; Snapper couldn't find Sugar Palm Hammocks. Edie Marsh became agitated. She kept repeating the address aloud: 14275 Noriega Parkway. One-four-two-seven-five. Tan house, brown shutters, swimming pool, two-car garage. Avila had guessed it was worth $185,000.

'If we don't hurry,' Edie told Snapper, 'if we don't get there soon—'

Snapper instructed her to shut the holy fuck up.

'Wasn't there a Dairy Queen?' Edie went on. 'I remember him turning at a Dairy Queen or something.'

Snapper said, 'The Dairy Queen is gone. *Every* goddamn thing is gone, case you didn't notice. We're flying blind out here.'

Edie had never seen such destruction; it looked like Castro had nuked the place. Houses without roofs, walls, windows. Trailers and cars crumpled like foil. Trees in the swimming pools. People weeping, Sweet Jesus, and everywhere the plonking of hammers and the growling of chain saws.

Snapper said they could do another house. 'There's only about ten thousand to choose from.'

'I suppose.'

'What's so special about 1-4-2-7-5?'

'It had personality,' Edie Marsh said.

Snapper drummed his knuckles on the steering wheel. 'They all look the same. All these places, exactly the same.'

His gun lay on the seat between them.

'Fine,' said Edie, unsettled by the change of plans, the chaos, the grim dripping skies. 'Fine, we'll find another one.'

Max and Bonnie Lamb arrived in Dade County soon after daybreak. The roads were slick and gridlocked. The gray sky was growling with TV helicopters. The radio said two hundred thousand homes were seriously damaged or destroyed. Meanwhile the Red Cross was pleading for donations of food, water and clothing.

The Lambs exited the Turnpike at Quail Roost Drive. Bonnie was stunned by the devastation; Max himself was aglow. He held the Handycam on his lap as he steered. Every two or three blocks, he slowed to videotape spectacular rubble. A flattened hardware store. The remains of a Sizzler steak house. A school bus impaled by a forty-foot pine.

'Didn't I tell you?' Max Lamb was saying. 'Isn't it amazing!'

Bonnie Lamb shuddered. She said they should stop at the nearest shelter and volunteer to help.

Max paid no attention. He parked in front of an exploded town house. The hurricane had thrown a motorboat into the living room. The family—a middle-aged Latin man, his wife, two little girls—stood in a daze on the sidewalk. They wore matching yellow rain slickers.

Max Lamb got out of the car. 'Mind if I get some video?'

The man numbly consented. Max photographed the wrecked building from several dramatic angles. Then, stepping through the plaster and broken furniture and twisted toys, he casually entered the house. Bonnie couldn't believe it: He walked right through the gash that was once the front door!

She apologized to the family, but the man said he didn't mind; he'd need pictures anyway, for the insurance people. His daughters began to sob and tremble. Bonnie Lamb knelt to comfort them. Over her shoulder she caught sight of her husband with the camera at his eye, recording the scene through a broken window.

Later, in the rental car, she said: 'That was the sickest thing I ever saw.'

'Yes, it's very sad.'

'I'm talking about you,' Bonnie snapped.

'What?'

'Max, I want to go home.'

'I bet we can sell some of this tape.'

'Don't you dare.'

Max said: 'I bet we can sell it to C-SPAN. Pay for the whole honeymoon!'

Bonnie closed her eyes. What had she done? Was her mother right about this man? Latent asshole, her mother had whispered at the wedding. Was she right?

At dusk Edie Marsh swallowed two Darvons and reviewed the plan with Snapper, who was having second thoughts. He seemed troubled at the idea of waiting weeks for the payoff. Edie said there wasn't much choice, the way insurance worked. Snapper said he planned to keep his options open, just the same. Edie Marsh took it to mean he'd bug out on a moment's notice.

They had picked a house in a flattened development called Turtle Meadow, where the hurricane had peeled away all the roofs. Snapper said it was probably one of Avila's routes. He said Avila had bragged of inspecting eighty new homes a day without leaving the truck. 'Rolling quotas,' is what Avila called them. Snapper allowed that Avila wasn't much of a roof inspector, as he was deathly afraid of heights and therefore refused to take a ladder on his rounds. Consequently, Avila's roof certifications were done visually, from a vehicle, at speeds often exceeding thirty-five miles an hour. Snapper said Avila's swiftness and trusting attitude had made him a favorite among the local builders and contractors, especially at Christmastime.

Scanning the debris, Edie Marsh said Avila was damn lucky not to be in jail. That's why he quit when he did, Snapper explained. The bones told him it was time. That, and a grand jury.

Bones? said Edie.

You don't want to know, Snapper said. Honestly.

They were walking along the sidewalk, across the street from the house they had chosen on the drive-by that morning. Now the neighborhood was pitch black except for the erratic flicker of flashlights and the glow of a few small bonfires. Many families had abandoned the crumbled shells of their homes for nearby motels, but a few men had stayed to patrol against looters. The men wore pinched tense expressions and carried shotguns. Snapper was glad to be white and wearing a suit.

The house he and Edie Marsh had chosen wasn't empty, dark or quiet. A bare light bulb had been strung from the skeletal remains of the roof, and the gray-blue glow of a television set pulsed against the plaster. These luxuries were explained by the rumble of a portable generator. Edie and Snapper had seen a fat man gassing it up earlier in the day.

The street was either Turtle Meadow Lane or Calusa Drive, depending on which of the fallen street signs was accurate. The number '15600' was sprayed in red paint on an outside wall of the house, as was the name of the insurance company: 'Midwest Casualty.'

A big outfit, Edie noted. She'd seen the commercials on television; the company's symbol was a badger.

'A badger?' Snapper frowned. 'The fuck does a badger have to do with insurance?'

'I dunno.' Edie's mouth was dry. She felt sleepy. 'What does a cougar have to do with cars? It's just advertising is all.'

Snapper said, 'The only thing I know about badgers is they're stubborn. And the last goddamn thing we need's a stubborn insurance company.'

Edie said, 'For heaven's sake—'

'Let's find another house.'

'No!' Weaving slightly, she crossed the street toward 15600.

'You hear me?' Snapper called, then started after her.

Edie wheeled in the driveway. 'Let's do it!' she said. 'Right now, while it's quiet.'

Snapper hesitated, working his jaw like a dazed boxer.

'Come on!' Edie tugged her hair out of the bun and mussed it into a nest in front of her face. Then she hitched her dress and raked her fingernails up both thighs, tearing tracks in her nylons.

Snapper checked to make sure none of the neighborhood vigilantes were watching. Edie picked a place on the driveway and stretched out, facedown. Using two broken roof trusses, Snapper did a superb job setting the scene. Edie was pinned.

From under the debris, she said, 'Blood would help.' Snapper kicked a nail toward her left hand. 'Take it easy.'

Edie Marsh held her breath and scratched the point of the nail from her elbow to her wrist. It hurt like a bitch. She wiped her arm across one cheek to smear the blood for dramatic effect. On cue, Snapper began shouting for help. Edie was impressed; he sounded damn near sincere.

Max Lamb congratulated himself for stocking up on video supplies before they drove down from Orlando. Other tourists had not come so prepared for the hurricane and could be seen foraging through luggage in a manic search for spare tapes and batteries. Meanwhile, pausing only to reload, Max Lamb was compiling dramatic footage of a historic natural disaster. Even if C-SPAN wasn't interested, his friends in New York would be. Max was a junior account executive at a medium-sized advertising firm, and there were many persons whom he yearned to impress. Max was handy with the Sony, but it wouldn't hurt to seek professional assistance; he knew of a place on East Fiftieth Street that edited home videos and, for a small extra charge, added titles and credits. It would be perfect! Once Bonnie settled down, Max Lamb would ask her about throwing a cocktail party where they could screen the hurricane tapes for his clients and his colleagues at the agency.

Max trotted with predatory energy from one wrecked home-stead to another, the video camera purring in his hand. He was so absorbed in recording the tragedy that he forgot about his wife, who had stopped following three blocks ago. Max had wanted to show Bonnie how to use the camera so he could pose amid hurricane debris; she'd told him she would rather swallow a gallon of lye.

For editing purposes, Max Lamb kept a mental inventory of his best shots. He had plenty of rubble scenes, and felt the need to temper the visual shock with moments of poignancy—vignettes that would capture the human toll, spiritual as well as physical.

A mangled bicycle grabbed Max's attention. The hurricane had wrapped it, as snug as a wedding band, around the trunk of a coconut palm. A boy no older than eight was trying to remove the bike. Max dropped to one knee and zoomed in on the youngster's face as he tugged grimly on the bent handlebars. The boy's expression was dull and cold, his lips pressed tight in concentration.

Max thought: He's in shock. Doesn't even know I'm here.

The youngster didn't seem to care that his bicycle was destroyed beyond repair. He simply wanted the tree to give it back. He pulled and pulled with all his might. The empty eyes showed no sign of frustration.

Amazing, Max Lamb thought as he peered through the view-finder. *Amazing.*

Something jostled his right arm, and the boy's image in the viewfinder shook. A hand tugged at Max's sleeve. Cursing, he looked up from the Handycam.

It was a monkey.

Max Lamb pivoted on one heel and aimed the camera at the scrawny animal. Through the viewfinder he saw that the mon-key had come through the storm in miserable shape. Its auburn fur was matted and crusty. A bruise as plump as a radish rose from the bridge of its broad velvet nose. The shoe-button eyes were squinty and ringed with milky ooze.

Swaying on its haunches, the monkey bared its gums in a woozy yawn. Listlessly it began to paw at its tail.

'See what we have here—a wild monkey!' Max narrated, for the benefit of future viewers. 'Just look at this poor little fella. . . .'

From behind him, a flat voice: 'Better watch it, mister.' It was the boy with the broken bicycle.

Max, the Handycam still at his eye, said, 'What's the matter, son?'

'Better watch out for that thing. My dad, he had to shoot one last night.'

'Is that right?' Max smiled to himself. Why would anyone shoot a monkey?

'They're real sick. That's what my dad said.'

'Well, I'll certainly be careful,' said Max Lamb. He heard footsteps as the strange boy ran off.

Through the viewfinder, Max noticed the monkey's brow was twitching oddly. Suddenly it was airborne. Max lowered the camera just as the animal struck his face, knocking him backward. Miniature rubbery fingers dug at Max's nostrils and eyes. He cried out fearfully. The monkey's damp fur smelled awful.

Max Lamb began rolling in the dirt as if he were on fire. Screeching, the wiry little creature let go. Max sat up, scrubbing his face with the sleeves of his shirt. The stinging told him he'd been scratched. For starters he would require a tetanus booster, and then something more potent to counteract the monkey germs.

As he rose to his feet, Max heard chittering behind the palm tree. He was poised to run, until he spotted the monkey loping with an addled gait in the opposite direction. It was dragging something by a strap.

Max Lamb was enraged. The damn thing was stealing his Handycam! Idiotically he gave pursuit.

An hour later, when Bonnie Lamb went looking for her husband, he was gone.

*

Two uniformed Highway Patrol troopers stood in the rain at the top of the bridge. One was a tall, powerfully built black man. The other officer was a woman of milky smooth complexion and medium height, with a bun of reddish-brown hair. Together they leaned against the concrete rail and stared down a long length of broken rope, dangling in the breeze over the choppy brown water.

Five motorists had phoned on their cellulars to report that a crazy man was tied to the Card Sound Bridge. That was only hours before the hurricane, when every police officer within fifty miles had been busy evacuating the sane. Nobody had time for jumpers, so nobody checked the bridge.

The black trooper had been sent to Miami all the way from Liberty County, in northern Florida, to help clear traffic for the rescue convoys. At the command center he'd caught a glimpse of the incident notation in the dispatch log—'White male, 40–50 yrs old, 190–220 lbs, gray hair/beard, possible psych. case'—and decided to sneak down to North Key Largo for a look. Technically he was assigned to Homestead, but in the poststorm chaos it was easy to roam and not be missed. He had asked the other trooper to ride with him, and even though she was off duty she'd said yes.

Now motorists crossing the steep bridge braked in curiosity at the sight of the two troopers at the top. *What're they looking at, Mom? Is there a dead body in the water?*

Raindrops trickled from the brim of the black trooper's Stetson as he gazed across Biscayne Bay, leaden and frothy after the dreadful storm. He reached over the rail and hauled up the soggy rope. After examining the end of it, he showed the rope to the other trooper and said, with a weariness: 'That's my boy.'

The rope hadn't snapped in the hurricane. It had been cut with a knife.

3

Tony Torres sat in what remained of his living room and sipped what remained of his Chivas. He found it amusing that his 'Salesman of the Year' award had survived the hurricane; it was all that remained hanging on the rain-soaked walls. Tony Torres recalled the party two months earlier, when they'd given him the cheap laminated plaque. It was his reward for selling seventy-seven double-wide house trailers, eighteen more than any other salesman in the history of PreFab Luxury Homes, formerly Tropic Trailers, formerly A-Plus Affordable Homes, Ltd. In the cutthroat world of mobile-home sales, Tony Torres had become a star. His boss had presented the Chivas and a thousand-dollar bonus along with the plaque. They'd paid a waitress to dance topless on a table and sing 'For He's a Jolly Good Fellow.'

Oh well, Tony Torres thought. Life's a fucking roller coaster. He stroked the stock of the shotgun that lay across his globe-shaped lap, and remembered things he wished he didn't. For instance, that bullshit in the sales pitch about U.S. government safety regulations . . .

The Steens had questioned him thoroughly about hurricanes. So had the Ramirezes and the pain-in-the-ass Stichlers. So had Beatrice Jackson, the widow, and her no-neck son. Tony Torres always said what he'd been coached to say, that PreFab Luxury Homes built state-of-the-art homes guaranteed to withstand high winds. Uncle Sam set the specs. It's all there in the brochure!

So Tony's customers secured their mortgages and bought up the double-wides, and then the hurricane came and blew them away. All seventy-seven. The trailers imploded, exploded, popped off the tiedowns and took off like fucking aluminum ducks. Not one of the damn things made it through the storm.

One minute they were pleasant-looking middle-class dwellings, with VCRs and convertible sofas and baby cribs . . . and the next minute they were shrapnel. Tony Torres had driven to the trailer park to see for himself. The place looked like a war zone. He was about to get out of the car when somebody recognized him— old man Stichler, who began spluttering insanely and hurling jagged debris at the salesman. Tony drove off at a high rate of speed. Later he learned that the widow Jackson was found dead in the wreckage of the trailer court.

Tony Torres was unfamiliar with remorse, but he did feel a stab of sorrow. The Chivas took care of that. How was I to know? he thought. I'm a salesman, not a goddamn engineer.

The more Tony drank, the less sympathy he retained for his customers. They goddamn well *knew*. Knew they were buying a tin can instead of a real house. Knew the risks, living in a hurricane zone. These were grown-ups, Tony Torres told himself. They made a choice.

Still, he anticipated trouble. The shotgun was a comfort. Unfortunately, anybody who wanted to track him down had only to look in the Dade County phone book. Being a salesman meant being available to all of humanity.

So let 'em come! Tony thought. Any moron customers got a problem, let 'em see what the storm did to *my* house. They get nasty, I turn the matter over to Señor Remington here.

Shouts rousted Tony Torres from the sticky embrace of his BarcaLounger. He took the gun and a flashlight to the front of the house. Standing in the driveway was a man with an unfortunate pin-striped suit and a face that appeared to have been modified with a crowbar.

'My sister!' the man exclaimed, pointing at a pile of busted lumber.

Tony Torres spotted the prone form of a woman under the trusses. Her eyes were half closed, and a fresh streak of blood colored her face. The woman groaned impressively. The man told Tony to call 911 rightaway.

'First tell me what happened,' the salesman said.

'Just look—part of your damn roof fell down on her!'

'Hmmm,' said Tony Torres.

'For Christ's sake, don't just stand there.'

'Your sister, huh?' Tony walked up to the woman and shined the flashlight in her eyes. The woman squinted reflexively, raising both hands to block out the light.

Tony Torres said, 'Guess you're not paralyzed, darling.'

He tucked the flashlight under one arm and raised the shotgun toward the man. 'Here's the deal, sport. The phones are blown, so we won't be calling 911 unless you got a cellular in your pants, and that looks more like a pistol to me. Second of all, even if we *could* call 911 we'll be waiting till Halloween. Every ambulance from here to Key West is busy because of the storm. Your "sister" should've thought of that before her accident—'

'What the hell you—'

Tony Torres took the pistol from the man's waist. 'Third of all,' the salesman said, 'my damn roof didn't fall on nobody. Those trusses came off the neighbor's house. That would be Mister Leonel Varga, next door. My own personal roof is lying in pieces somewhere out in the Everglades, is my guess.'

From beneath the lumber, the woman said: 'Shit, Snapper.' The man shot her a glare, then looked away.

Tony Torres said: 'I'm in the business of figuring people out quick. That's what a good salesman does. And if she's your sister, sport, then I'm twins with Mel Gibson.'

The man with the crooked jaw shrugged.

'Point is,' Tony said, 'she ain't really hurt. You ain't really her brother. And whatever fucked-up plan you had for ripping me off is now officially terminated.'

The man scowled bitterly. 'Hey, it was *her* idea.'

Tony ordered him to lift the wooden trusses off his partner. When the woman got up, the salesman noticed she was both attractive and intelligent-looking. He motioned with the shotgun.

'Both of you come inside. Hell, inside is pretty much outside, thanks to that goddamn storm. But come in, anyhow, 'cause I'd love to hear your story. I could use a laugh.'

The woman smoothed the front of her dress. 'We made a bad mistake. Just let us go, OK?'

Tony Torres smiled. 'That's funny, darling.' He swung the Remington toward the house and pulled the trigger. The blast tore a hole the size of a soccer ball in the garage door.

'Hush,' said the drunken salesman, cupping a hand to one ear. 'Hear that? Dead fucking silence. Shoot off a twelve-gauge and nobody cares. Nobody comes to see. Nobody comes to help. Know why? Because of the hurricane. The whole place is a madhouse!'

The man with the crooked jaw asked, more out of curiosity than concern: 'What is it you want with us?'

'I haven't decided,' said Tony Torres. 'Let's have a drinky poo.'

A week before the hurricane, Felix Mojack died of a viper bite to the ankle. Ownership of his failing wildlife-import business passed to a nephew, Augustine. On the rainy morning he learned of his uncle's death, Augustine was at home practicing his juggling. He had all the windows open, and the Black Crowes playing on the stereo. He was barefoot and wore only a pair of royal-blue gym shorts. He stood in the living room, juggling in time to the music. The objects that he juggled were human skulls; he was up to five at once. The faster Augustine juggled, the happier he was.

On the kitchen table was an envelope from Paine Webber. It contained a check for $21,344.55. Augustine had no need for or interest in the money. He was almost thirty-two years old, and his life was as simple and empty as one could be. Sometimes he deposited the Paine Webber dividends, and sometimes he mailed them off to charities, renegade political candidates or former girlfriends. Augustine sent not a penny to his father's defense lawyers; that was the old man's debt, and he could damn well settle it when he got out of prison.

Augustine's juggling was a private diversion. The skulls were artifacts and medical specimens he'd acquired from friends. When he had them up in the air—three, four, five skulls arcing fluidly from hand to hand—Augustine could feel the full rush of their faraway lives. It was inexplicably and perhaps unwholesomely exhilarating. Augustine didn't know their names, or how they'd lived or died, but from touching them he drew energy.

In his spare time Augustine read books and watched television and hiked what was left of the Florida wilderness. Even before he became wealthy—when he worked on his father's fishing boat, and later in law school—Augustine nursed an unspecific anger that he couldn't trace and wasn't sure he should. It manifested itself in the occasional urge to burn something down or blow something up—a high-rise, a new interstate highway, that sort of thing.

Now that Augustine had both the time and the money, he found himself without direction for these radical sentiments, and with no trustworthy knowledge of heavy explosives. Out of guilt, he donated large sums to respectable causes such as the Sierra Club and the Nature Conservancy. His ambition to noble violence remained a harmless fantasy. Meanwhile he bobbed through life's turbulence like driftwood.

The near-death experience that made Augustine so rich had given him zero insight into a grand purpose or cosmic destiny. Augustine barely remembered the damn Beechcraft going down. Certainly he saw no blinding white light at the end of a cool tunnel, heard no dead relatives calling to him from heaven. All he recalled of the coma that followed the accident was an agonizing and unquenchable thirst.

After recovering from his injuries, Augustine didn't return to the hamster-wheel routine of law school. The insurance settlement financed a comfortable aimlessness that many young men would have found appealing. Yet Augustine was deeply unhappy. One night, in a fit of depression, he violently purged his bookshelves of all genius talents who had died too young. This included his treasured Jack London.

Typically, Augustine was waiting for a woman to come along and fix him. So far, it hadn't happened.

One time a dancer whom Augustine was dating caught him juggling his skulls in the bedroom. She thought it was a stunt designed to provoke a reaction. She told him it wasn't funny, it was perverted. Then she moved to New York. A year or so later, for no particular reason, Augustine sent the woman one of his dividend checks from Paine Webber. She used the money to buy a Toyota Supra and sent Augustine a snapshot of herself, smiling and waving in the driver's seat. Augustine wondered who'd taken the picture and what he'd thought of the new car.

Augustine had no brothers and sisters, his mother was in Nevada and his father was in the slammer. The closest relative was his uncle Felix Mojack, the wildlife importer. As a boy, Augustine often visited his uncle's small cluttered farm out in the boondocks. It was more fun than going to the zoo, because Felix let Augustine help with the animals. In particular, Felix encouraged his nephew to familiarize himself with exotic snakes, as Felix himself was phobic (and, it turned out, fatally incompetent) when it came to handling reptiles.

After Augustine grew up, he saw less and less of his busy uncle. Progress conspired against Felix; development swept westward, and zoning regulations forced him to move his operation repeatedly. Nobody, it seemed, wished to build elementary schools or shopping malls within walking distance of caged jungle cats and wild cobras. The last time Felix Mojack was forced to relocate his animals, Augustine gave him ten thousand dollars for the move.

At the time of Felix's death, the farm inventory listed one male African lion, three cougars, a gelded Cape buffalo, two Kodiak bears, ninety-seven parrots and macaws, eight Nile crocodiles, forty-two turtles, seven hundred assorted lizards, ninety-three snakes (venomous and nonvenomous) and eighty-eight rhesus monkeys.

The animals were kept on a nine-acre spread off Krome Avenue, not far from the federal prison. The day after the funeral, Augustine drove out to the place alone. He had a feeling that his uncle ran a loose operation, and a tour of the facility corroborated his suspicion. The fencing was buckled and rusty, the cages needed new hinges, and the concrete reptile pits hadn't been drained and cleaned in months. In the tar-paper shed that

Felix had used for an office, Augustine found paperwork confirming his uncle's low regard for U.S. Customs regulations.

It came as no surprise that Felix had been a smuggler; rather, Augustine was grateful that his uncle's choice of contraband had been exotic birds and snakes, and not something else. Wildlife, however, presented its own unique challenges. While bales of marijuana required no feeding, bears and cougars did. Lean and hungry was a mild description of the illegal menagerie; Augustine was appalled by the condition of some of the animals and presumed their deterioration was a result of his uncle's recent financial troubles. Fortunately, the two young Mexicans who worked for Felix Mojack graciously agreed to help out for a few days after his death. They stocked the freezers with raw meat for the large carnivores, bought boxloads of feed for the parrots and monkeys, and restocked on white mice and insects for the reptiles.

Meanwhile Augustine scrambled to locate a buyer for the animals, somebody qualified to take good care of them. Augustine was so preoccupied with the task that he didn't pay enough attention to news reports of a tropical storm intensifying in the Caribbean. Even when it bloomed into a hurricane, and Augustine saw the weather bulletin on television, he assumed it would do what most storms did in late summer—veer north, away from South Florida, on the prevailing Atlantic steering currents.

Once it became clear that the hurricane would strike southern Dade County with a direct hit, Augustine had little time to act. He was grimly aware what sustained one-hundred-mile-per-hour winds would do to his dead uncle's shabby farm. He spent the morning and afternoon on the telephone, trying to find a secure location for the animals. Interest invariably dropped off at the mention of a Cape buffalo. At dusk Augustine drove out to fasten tarps and tie-downs on the cages and pens. Sensing the advancing storm, the bears and big cats paced nervously, growling in agitation. The parrots were in a panic; the frenetic squawking attracted several large hawks to the nearby pines. Augustine stayed two hours and decided it was hopeless. He sent the Mexicans home and drove to a nearby Red Cross shelter to wait out the storm.

When he returned at dawn, the place was destroyed. The fencing was strewn like holiday tinsel across the property. The corrugated roofing had been peeled off the compound like a sardine tin. Except for a dozen befuddled turtles, all his uncle's wild animals had escaped into the scrub and marsh and, inevitably, the Miami suburbs. As soon as phone service was restored, Augustine notified the police what had happened. The dispatcher laconically estimated it would be five or six days before an officer could be spared, because everybody was working double shifts after the hurricane. When Augustine asked how far a Gaboon viper could travel in five or six days, the dispatcher said she'd try to send somebody out there sooner.

Augustine couldn't just sit and wait. The radio said a troop of storm-addled monkeys had invaded a residential subdivision off Quail Roost Drive, only miles from the farm. Augustine immediately loaded the truck with his uncle's dart rifle, two long-handled nooses, a loaded .38 Special, and a five-pound bag of soggy monkey chow.

He didn't know what else to do.

Canvassing the neighborhood in search of her husband, Bonnie Lamb encountered the dull-eyed boy with the broken bicycle. His description of the tourist jerk with the video camera fit Max too well.

'He ran after the monkey,' the boy said.

Bonnie Lamb said, 'What monkey?'

The boy explained. Bonnie assessed the information calmly. 'Which way did they go?' The boy pointed. Bonnie thanked him and offered to help pry his bicycle off the tree. The boy turned away, so she walked on.

Bonnie was puzzled by the monkey story, but most of the questions clouding her mind concerned Max Lamb's character. How could a man wander off and forget about his new wife? Why was he so fascinated with the hurricane ruins? How could he so cruelly intrude on the suffering of those who lived here?

During two years of courtship, Max had never seemed insensitive. At times he could be immature and self-centered, but Bonnie had never known a man who wasn't. In general, Max was a responsible and attentive person; more than just a hard worker, an achiever. Bonnie appreciated that, as her two previous boyfriends had taken a casual approach to the concept of full-time employment. Max impressed her with his seriousness and commitment, his buoyant determination to attain professional success and financial security. At thirty, Bonnie was at a point in life where she liked the prospect of security; she was tired of worrying about money, and about men who had none. Beyond that, she truly found Max Lamb attractive. He wasn't exceptionally handsome or romantic, but he was sincere —boyishly, completely, relentlessly sincere. His earnestness, even in bed, was endearing. This was a man Bonnie thought she could trust.

Until today, when he started acting like a creep.

The predawn expedition to Miami seemed, at first, a honeymoon lark—Max's way of showing his bride that he could be as wild and impulsive as her old boyfriends. Against her best instincts, Bonnie played along. She felt sure that seeing the hurricane's terrible destruction would end Max's documentary ambitions, that he'd put down the camera and join the volunteer relief workers, who were arriving by the busload.

But he didn't. He kept taping, becoming more and more excited, until Bonnie Lamb could no longer bear it. When he asked her to operate the camera while he posed on an overturned station wagon, Bonnie nearly slugged him. She quit tagging after Max because she didn't want to be seen with him. Her own husband.

In one gutted house she spotted an old woman, her mother's age, stepping through splintered bedroom furniture. The woman was calling the name of a pet kitten, which had disappeared in the storm. Bonnie Lamb offered to help search. The cat didn't turn up, but Bonnie did find the old woman's wedding album, beneath a shattered mirror. Bonnie cleared the broken glass and retrieved the album, damp but not ruined. Bonnie opened it to the date of inscription: December 11, 1949. When the old woman saw the album, she broke down in Bonnie's arms. With a twinge of shame, Bonnie glanced around to make sure that Max wasn't secretly filming them. Then she began to cry, too.

Later, resolved to confront her husband, Bonnie Lamb went to find him. If he refused to put away that stupid camera, she would demand the keys to the rental car. It promised to be the first hard test of the new marriage.

Two hours passed with no sign of Max, and Bonnie's anger dissolved into worry. The tale told by the boy with the broken bicycle ordinarily would have been comical, but Bonnie took it as further evidence of Max's reckless obsession. He was afraid of animals, even hamsters, a condition he blamed on an unspecified xchildhood trauma; to boldly pursue a wild monkey was definitely out of character. On the other hand, Max loved that damn Handycam. More than once he'd reminded Bonnie that it had cost seven hundred dollars, mail order from Hong Kong. She could easily envision him chasing a seven-hundred-dollar investment down the street. She could even envision him strangling the monkey for it, if necessary.

Another squall came, and Bonnie cursed mildly under her breath. There wasn't much left standing, in the way of shelter. She felt a shiver as the raindrops ran down her neck, and decided to return to the rental car and wait for Max there. Except she wasn't sure where the car was parked—without street signs or mailboxes, every block of the destroyed subdivision looked the same. Bonnie Lamb was lost.

She saw the helicopters wheeling overhead, heard the chorus of sirens in the distance, yet on the streets of the neighborhood there were no policemen, no soldiers, no proper authority to which a missing husband could be reported. Exhausted, Bonnie sat on a curb. To keep dry, she tried to balance a large square of plywood over her head. A gust of wind got under the board and pulled Bonnie over backward; as she went down, a corner of the board struck her sharply on the forehead.

She lay there stunned for several moments, staring at the muddy sky, blinking the raindrops from her eyes. A man appeared, standing over her. He wore a small rifle slung on one shoulder.

'Let me help,' he said.

Bonnie Lamb allowed him to lift her from the wet grass. She noticed her blouse was soaked, and shyly folded her arms across her breasts. The man retrieved the plywood board and braced it at a generous angle against a concrete utility pole. There he and Bonnie Lamb took shelter from the slashing rain.

The man was in his early thirties, with good shoulders and tanned, strong-looking arms. He had short brown hair, a sharp chin and friendly blue eyes. He wore Rockport hiking shoes, which gave Bonnie a sense of relief. She couldn't imagine a psychopathic sex killer choosing Rockports.

'Do you live around here?' she asked.

The man shook his head. 'Coral Gables.'

'Is the gun loaded?'

'Sort of,' the man said, without elaborating.

'My name is Bonnie.'

'I'm Augustine.'

'What are you doing out here?' she asked.

'Believe it or not,' he said, 'I'm looking for my monkeys.'

Bonnie Lamb smiled. 'What a coincidence.'

Max Lamb woke up with a headache that was about to get worse. He found himself stripped to his underwear and bound to a pine tree. The tall man with the glass eye, the man who'd snatched him off the street as if he were a wayward toddler, was thrashing and flopping in a leafy clearing by the campfire. When the impressive seizure ended, the kidnapper gathered himself in a lotus position. Max Lamb noticed a thick black collar around the man's neck. In one hand he held a shiny cylinder that reminded Max of a remote control for a model car. The cylinder had a short rubber antenna and three colored buttons.

The one-eyed man was mumbling: 'Too much juice, too much . . .' He wore a cheap plastic shower cap on his head. Max would have assumed he was a street person, except for the teeth; the kidnapper displayed outstanding orthodontics.

He seemed unaware that his captive was observing him. Deliberately the man extended both legs to brace himself, inhaled twice deeply, then pushed a red button on the remote-control cylinder. Instantly his body began to jerk like an enormous broken puppet. Max Lamb watched helplessly as the stranger writhed through the leaves toward the fire. His boots were in the flames when the fit finally ended. Then the man rose with a startling swiftness, stomping his huge feet until the soles cooled.

One hand went to his neck. 'By God, that's better.'

Max Lamb concluded it was a nightmare, and shut his eyes. When he opened them again, much later, he saw that the campfire was freshly stoked. The one-eyed kidnapper crouched nearby; now his neck was bare. He was feeding Oreo cookies to the larcenous monkey, which appeared to be regaining its health. Max was more certain than ever that what he'd witnessed earlier was a dream. He felt ready to assert himself.

'Where's my camera?' he demanded.

The kidnapper stood up, laughing through his wild beard. 'Perfect,' he said. ' "Where's my camera?" That's just perfect.'

In a hazardously patronizing tone, Max Lamb said: 'Let me go, pardner. You don't *really* want to go to jail, do you?'

'Ha,' the stranger said. He reached for the shiny black cylinder.

A bolt of fire passed through Max Lamb's neck. He shuddered violently and gulped for breath. His tongue tasted of hot copper. Crimson spears of light punctured the night. Max warbled in fear.

'Shock collar,' the kidnapper explained, unnecessarily. 'The Tri-Tronics 200. Three levels of stimulation. Range of one mile. Rechargeable nickel-cadmium batteries. Three-year warranty.'

Max felt it now, stiff leather against the soft skin of his throat.

'State of the art,' said the stranger. 'You a bird hunter?'

Max mouthed the word 'no.'

'Well, trust me. Field trainers swear by these gizmos. Dogs get the message real quick, even Labs.' The stranger twirled the remote control like a baton. 'Me, I couldn't put one of these on an animal. Fact, I couldn't even try it on *you* without testing it myself. That's what a big old softy I am.'

The kidnapper scratched the crown of the monkey's head. The monkey hopped back and bared its tiny teeth, which were flecked black with Oreo crumbs. The kidnapper laughed.

Max Lamb, quavering: 'Keep it away from me!'

'Not an animal person, huh?'

'What is it you want?'

The stranger turned toward the fire.

Max said, 'Is it money? Just take whatever I've got.'

'Jesus, you're thick.' The stranger pushed the red button, and Max Lamb thrashed briefly against his ropes. The monkey skittered away, out of the firelight.

Max looked up to see the psycho, taping him with the video camera! 'Say cheese,' the stranger said, aiming the Handycam with his good eye.

Max Lamb reddened. He felt spindly and pale in his underwear.

The man said, 'I might send this up to Rodale and Burns. What d'you think—for the office Christmas bash? "How I Spent My Florida Vacation," starring Max Leo Lamb.'

Max sagged. Rodale and Burns was the Madison Avenue advertising agency where he worked. The lunatic had been through his billfold.

'They call me Skink,' the kidnapper said. He turned off the Handycam and carefully capped the lens. 'But I prefer "captain."'

'Captain what?'

'Obviously you were impressed by the hurricane.' The stranger packed the video camera in a canvas sleeve. 'Myself, I was disappointed. I was hoping for something more . . . well, biblical.'

Max Lamb said, as respectfully as possible: 'It looked pretty bad to me.'

'You hungry?' The kidnapper brought a burlap sack to the tree where his prisoner was tied.

'Oh God,' said Max Lamb, staring inside the bag. 'You can't be serious.'

4

Filling the BarcaLounger like a stuffed tuna, Tony Torres encouraged Edie Marsh and Snapper to reveal the details of their aborted scam. Facing a loaded shotgun, they complied.

Snapper gestured sourly toward Edie, who said: 'Simple. I fake a fall in your driveway. My "brother" here threatens to sue. You freak out and offer us money.'

'Because you guys know,' Tony said, slapping a mosquito on his blubbery neck, 'I'll be getting quite a wad of dough on account of the hurricane. Insurance dough.'

'Exactly,' Edie Marsh said. 'Your place is wrecked, last thing you need is a lawsuit. So Snapper says here's an idea: Soon as your hurricane money comes in, cut us a piece and we call it even.'

Tony Torres sucked his teeth in amusement. 'How big a piece, darling?'

'Whatever we could take you for.'

'Ah,' said Tony.

'We figured you'd just factor us in the insurance claim. Jack up your losses by a few grand, who'd ever know?'

'Beautiful,' Tony said.

'Oh yeah,' said Snapper, 'fucking genius. Look how good it worked.'

He and Edie sat with their backs to the living-room wall; Snapper with his long legs drawn up, Edie's straight out, kneecaps pressed together. A picture of innocence, Tony Torres thought. The runs in her stockings were a nifty touch.

The carpet was sodden from the storm, but Edie Marsh didn't complain. Snapper felt the wetness creeping through the seat of his dress trousers—the annoyance was sufficient that he might kill Tony Torres, if the opportunity presented itself.

Deep in thought, the salesman slurped at a sweaty bottle of imported beer. He'd offered his captives a quart of warm Gatorade, which they'd refused without comment. A humid breeze blew through the fractures in the walls and rocked the bare sixty-watt bulb on its beam. Edie Marsh tilted her head and saw a spray of stars where Tony's ceiling had once been. The noise from the portable generator gave Snapper an oppressive headache.

Eventually, Tony Torres said: 'You understand there's no law to speak of. The world's upside down, for the time being.'

'You could kill us and get clean away with it. That's what you mean,' Snapper said.

Edie looked at him. 'You're a tremendous help.'

Tony indicated that he preferred not to shoot them. 'But here's my thinking,' he said. 'Tomorrow, maybe the day after, somebody from Midwest Casualty will come see about the house. I expect he'll say it's a total loss, unless he's blind as a bat. Anyway, the good news: I happen to own the place free and clear. Paid it off last March.' Tony paused to stifle a burp. 'I was having a good run at the office, so what the hell. I paid the mortgage off.'

Edie Marsh said: 'Salesman of the Year.' She had noticed the plaque.

'Mister,' Snapper interjected, 'you got somethin' I can put under my ass? The rug's all wet. A newspaper maybe?'

'Oh, I think you'll live,' said the salesman. 'Anyhow, since the bank don't own the house, all the insurance comes to me. As I say, there's the good news. The bad news is, half belongs to my wife. Her name's on the deed.'

Snapper asked where she was. Tony Torres said she'd run off three months ago with a parapsychology professor from the university. He said they'd gotten into crystal healing and moved to Eugene, Oregon.

'In a VW van!' he scoffed. 'But she'll be back for her cut. Of that there's no doubt. Neria will return. See where I'm headed?'

'Yeah,' said Snapper. 'You want us to kill your wife.'

'Jesus, what a one-track mind you got. No, I don't want you to *kill* my wife.' The salesman appealed to Edie Marsh. 'You get it, don't you? Before they cut a check, the insurance company is gonna need both signatures. Me and the missus. And I also believe the adjuster might want to chat face-to-face. What'd you say your name was?'

'Edie.'

'OK, Edie, you wanna be an actress here's your chance. When the man from Midwest Casualty shows up, you be Neria Torres. My loving wife.' Tony smirked at the notion. 'Well?'

Edie Marsh asked what was in it for her, and Tony Torres said ten grand. Edie said she'd have to think about it, which took about one one-hundredth of a second. She needed money.

'What about me?' Snapper asked.

Tony said, 'I always wanted a bodyguard.'

Snapper grunted skeptically. 'How much?'

'Ten for you, too. It's more than fair.'

Snapper admitted it was. 'Why,' he asked, with a trace of scorn, 'do *you* need a bodyguard?'

'Some customers got really pissed off at me. It's a long boring story.'

Edie Marsh said, 'How pissed off?'

'I don't intend to find out,' said Tony Torres. 'Once I get the check, I'm gone.'

'Where?'

'None a your damn business.'

Middle America was what Tony had in mind. A handsome two-story house with a porch and a fireplace, on three-quarters of an acre outside Tulsa. What appealed to Tony about Middle America was the absence of hurricanes. There were tornadoes galore, but nobody expected any man-made structure (least of all, a trailer home) to withstand the terrible force of a tornado. Nobody would blame a person if the double-wides he sold blew to pieces, because that was the celestial nature of tornadoes. Tony Torres figured he would be safe from disgruntled customers in Tulsa.

Snapper said, 'I'm gonna be a bodyguard, I'll need my gun.'

Tony smiled. 'No you won't. That face of yours is enough to scare the piss out of most mortal men. Which is perfect, because the people who're mad at me, they don't actually need to be shot. They just need to be scared. See where I'm headed?'

He took a length of bathroom pipe and smashed Snapper's pistol to pieces.

Edie Marsh said, 'I've got a question, too.'

'Well, bless your heart.'

'What happens if your wife shows up?'

'We got probably six, seven days of breathing room,' Tony Torres said. 'However long it takes to drive that old van back from Oregon. See, Neria won't fly. She's terrified of planes.'

Snapper remarked that money was known to make a person drive faster than usual, or overcome a fear of flying. Tony said he wasn't worried. 'The radio said State Farm and Allstate are writing settlements already. Midwest won't be far behind—see, no company wants to look stingy in a national disaster.'

Edie asked Tony Torres if he intended to hold them prisoner. He gave a great slobbering laugh and said hell, no, they could vamoose anytime they pleased. Edie stood and announced she was returning to the motel. Snapper rose warily, never taking his eyes off the shotgun.

He said to Tony: 'Why are you doing this? Lettin' us walk out of here.'

'Because you'll be back,' the salesman said. 'You most certainly will. I can see it in your eyes.'

'Really?' Edie said, tartly.

'Really, darling. It's what I do for a living. Read people.' The Naugahyde hissed as Tony Torres hoisted himself up from the BarcaLounger. 'I need to take a leak,' he declared. Then, with a hoot: 'I'm sure you can find your way out!'

On the slow drive back to Pembroke Pines, Edie Marsh and Snapper mulled the options. Both of them were broke. Both recognized the post-hurricane turmoil as a golden opportunity. Both agreed that ten thousand dollars was a good week's work.

'Trouble is,' Edie said, 'I don't trust that asshole. What is it he sells?'

'Trailer homes.'

'Good Lord.'

'Then let's walk away,' Snapper said, without conviction. 'Try the slip-and-fall on somebody else.'

Edie contemplated the ugly, self-inflicted scratch on her arm. Posing under a pile of lumber had been more uncomfortable than she'd anticipated. She wasn't eager to try it again.

'I'll coast with this jerkoff a day or two,' she told Snapper. 'You do what you want.'

Snapper configured his crooked jaws into the semblance of a grin. 'I know what you're thinkin''. I ain't no salesman, but I can read you just the same. You're thinkin' they's more than ten grand in this deal, you play it right. If *we* play it right.'

'Why not.' Edie Marsh pressed her cheek against the cool glass of the car's window. 'It's about time my luck should change.'

'*Our* luck,' Snapper said, both hands tight on the wheel.

Augustine helped Bonnie Lamb search for her husband until nightfall. They failed to locate Max, but along the way they came upon an escaped male rhesus. It was up in a grapefruit tree, hurling unripened fruit at passing humans. Augustine shot the animal with a tranquilizer dart, and it toppled like a marionette. Augustine was dismayed to discover, stapled in one of its ears, a tag identifying it as property of the University of Miami.

He had captured somebody else's fugitive monkey.

'What now?' asked Bonnie Lamb, reasonably. She reached out to pet the stunned animal, then changed her mind. The rhesus studied her through dopey, half-closed eyes.

'You're a good shot,' she said to Augustine.

He wasn't listening. 'This isn't right,' he muttered. He carried the limp monkey to the grapefruit tree and propped it gently in the crook of two boughs. Then he took Bonnie back to his truck. 'It'll be dark soon,' he said. 'I forgot to bring a flashlight.'

They drove through the subdivision for fifteen minutes until Bonnie Lamb spotted the rental car. Max wasn't there. Somebody had pried the trunk and stolen all the luggage, including Bonnie's purse.

Damn kids, Augustine said. Bonnie was too tired to cry. Max had the car keys, the credit cards, the money, the plane tickets. 'I need to find a phone,' she said. Her folks would wire some money.

Augustine drove to a police checkpoint, where Bonnie Lamb reported her husband missing. He was one of many, and not high on the list. Thousands who'd escaped their homes in the hurricane were being sought by worried relatives. For relief workers, reuniting local families was a priority; tracking wayward tourists was not.

A bank of six phones had been set up near the checkpoint, but the lines were long. Bonnie found the shortest one and settled in for a wait. She thanked Augustine for his help.

'What will you do tonight?' he asked.

'I'll be OK.'

Bonnie was startled to hear him say: 'No you won't.'

He took her by the hand and led her to the pickup. It occurred to Bonnie that she ought to be afraid, but she felt illogically safe with this total stranger. It also occurred to her that panic would be a normal reaction to a husband's disappearance, but instead she felt an inappropriate calmness and lucidity. Probably just exhaustion, she thought.

Augustine drove back to the looted rental car. He scribbled a note and tucked it under one of the windshield wipers. 'My phone number,' he told Bonnie Lamb. 'In case your husband shows up later tonight. This way he'll know where you are.'

'We're going to your place?'

'Yes.'

In the darkness, she couldn't see Augustine's expression. 'It's madness out here,' he said. 'These idiots shoot at anything that moves.'

Bonnie nodded. She'd been hearing distant gunfire from all directions. *Dade County is an armed camp*. That's what their travel agent had warned them. Death Wish Tours, he'd called it. *Only a fool would set foot south of Orlando*.

Crazy Max, thought Bonnie. What had possessed him?

'You know why my husband came down here?' she said.

'Know what he was doing when he got lost? Taking video of the wrecked houses. And the people, too.'

'Why?' Augustine asked.

'Home movies. To show his pals back North.'

'Jesus, that's—'

'Sick,' Bonnie Lamb said. ' "Sick" is the word for it.'

Augustine said nothing more. Slowly he worked his way toward the Turnpike. The futility of the monkey hunt was evident; Augustine realized that most of his dead uncle's wild animals were irretrievable. The larger mammals would inevitably make their presence known—the Cape buffalo, the bears, the cougars—and the results were bound to be unfortunate. Meanwhile the snakes and crocodiles probably were celebrating freedom by copulating merrily in the Everglades, ensuring for their species a solid foothold in a new tropical habitat. Augustine felt it was morally wrong to interfere. An escaped cobra had as much natural right to a life in Florida as did all those retired garment workers from Queens. Natural selection would occur. The test applied to Max Lamb as well, but Augustine felt sorry for his wife. He would set aside his principles and help find her missing husband.

He drove using the high beams because there were no street lights, and the roads were a littered gauntlet of broken trees and utility poles, heaps of lumber and twisted metal, battered appliances and gutted sofas. They saw a Barbie dollhouse and a canopy bed and an antique china cabinet and a child's wheelchair and a typewriter and a tangle of golf clubs and a cedar hot tub, split in half like a coconut husk—Bonnie said it was as if a great supernatural fist had snatched up a hundred thousand lives and shaken the contents all over creation.

Augustine was thinking more in terms of a B-52 raid.

'Is this your first one?' Bonnie asked.

'Technically, no.' He braked to swerve around a dead cow, bloated on the center line. 'I was conceived during Donna—least that's what my mother said. A hurricane baby. That was 1960. Betsy I can barely remember because I was only five. We lost a few lime trees, but the house held up fine.'

Bonnie said, 'That's kind of romantic. Being conceived in the middle of a hurricane.'

'My mother said it made perfect sense, considering how I turned out.'

'And how *did* you turn out?' Bonnie asked.

'Reports differ.'

Augustine edged the truck into a line of storm traffic crawling up the northbound ramp to the Turnpike. A rusty Ford with a crooked Georgia license plate cut them off. The car was packed with itinerant construction workers who'd been on the road for several days straight, apparently drinking the whole time. The driver, a shaggy blond with greenish teeth, leered and yelled an obscenity up at Bonnie Lamb. With one hand Augustine reached behind his seat and got the small rifle. Bracing it against the doorpost, he fired a tranquilizer dart cleanly into the belly of the redneck driver, who yipped and pitched sideways into the lap of one of his pals.

'Manners,' said Augustine. He gunned the truck, nudging the stalled Ford off the pavement.

Bonnie Lamb thought: God, what am I doing?

They broke camp at midnight—Max Lamb, the rhesus monkey and the man who called himself Skink. Max was grateful that the man had allowed him to put on his shoes, because they walked for hours in pitch darkness through deep swamp and spiny thickets. Max's bare legs stung from the scratches and itched from the bug bites. He was terribly hungry but didn't complain, knowing the man had saved him the rump of the dead raccoon that was boiled for dinner. Max wanted no part of it.

They came to a canal. Skink untied Max's hands, unbuckled the shock collar and ordered him to swim. Max was halfway across when he saw the blue-black alligator slide out of the sawgrass. Skink told him to quit whimpering and kick; he himself swam with the rejuvenated monkey perched on his head. One huge hand held Max's precious Sony and the remote control for the dog collar high above the water.

After scrabbling ashore, Max said, 'Captain, can we rest?'

'Ever seen a leech before? 'Cause there's a good one on your cheek.' After Max Lamb finished flaying himself, Skink retied his wrists and refastened the dog collar. Then he sprayed him down with insect repellent. Max croaked out a thank-you.

'Where are we?' he asked.

'The Everglades,' Skink replied. 'More or less.'

'You promised I could call my wife.'

'Soon.'

They headed west, trudging through palmettos and pinelands shredded by the storm. The monkey scampered ahead, foraging wild berries and fruit buds.

Max said: 'Are you going to kill me?'

Skink stopped walking. 'Every time you ask that stupid question, you're going to get it.' He set the remote on the weakest setting.

'Ready?'

Max Lamb clenched his lips. Skink stung him with a light jolt. The tourist twitched stoically. Soon they came to a Miccosukee village, which was not as badly damaged as Max Lamb would have imagined. Since the Indians were awake, cooking food, Max assumed it would soon be dawn. In open doorways the children gathered shyly to look at the two strange white men: Skink with his brambly hair, ill-fitting eye and mangy monkey, Max Lamb in his dirty underwear and dog collar.

Skink stopped at a wooden house and spoke quietly to a Miccosukee elder, who brought out a cellular phone. As he untied Max's hands, Skink warned: 'One call is all you get. He says the battery's running low.'

Max realized that he didn't know how to reach his wife. He had no idea where she was. So he called their apartment in New York and spoke to the answering machine: 'Honey, I've been kidnapped—'

'Abducted!' Skink broke in. 'Kidnapping implies ransom, Max. Don't fucking flatter yourself.'

'OK, "abducted." Honey, I've been abducted. I can't say very much except I'm fine, all things considered. Please call my folks, and also call Pete up at Rodale about the Bronco billboard project. Tell him the race car should be red, not blue. The file's on my desk. . . . Bonnie, I'm not sure who's got me, or why, but I guess I'll find out soon enough. God, I hope you pick up this message—'

Skink snatched the phone. 'I love you, Bonnie,' he said. 'Max forgot to tell you, so I will. Bye now.'

They ate with the Miccosukees, who declined Skink's offer of boiled coon but generously shared helpings of fried panfish, yams, cornmeal muffins and citrus juice. Max Lamb ate heartily but, mindful of the electric dog collar, said little. After breakfast, Skink tied him to a cypress post and disappeared with several men of the tribe. When he returned, he declared it was time to leave.

Max said, 'Where's my stuff?' He was worried about his billfold and clothes.

'Right here.' Skink jerked a thumb toward his backpack.

'And my Sony?'

'Gave it to the old man. He's got seven grandchildren, so he'll have a ball.'

'What about my tapes?'

Skink laughed. 'He loved 'em. That monkey attack was something special. Max, lift your arms.' He spritzed the prisoner with more bug juice.

Max Lamb, somberly: 'That Handycam retails for about nine hundred bucks.'

'It's not like I gave it away. I traded.'

'For what?'

Skink chucked him on the shoulder. 'I'll bet you've never been on an airboat.'

'Oh no. Please.'

'Hey, you wanted to see Florida.'

It wasn't easy being a black Highway Patrol trooper in Florida. It was even harder if you were involved intimately with a white trooper, the way Jim Tile was involved with Brenda Rourke.

They'd met at a training seminar about the newest gadgets for clocking speeders. In the classroom they were seated next to each other. Jim Tile liked Brenda Rourke right away. She had a sane and healthy outlook on the job, and she made him laugh. They traded stories about freaky traffic stops, lousy pay and the impossible FHP bureaucracy. Because he was black, and few fellow officers were, Jim Tile rarely felt comfortable in a roomful of state troopers. But he felt fine next to Brenda Rourke, partly because she was a minority, too; the Highway Patrol employed even fewer women than blacks or Latins.

During one session, a buzz-cut redneck shot a rat-eyed look at Jim Tile to remind him that Trooper Rourke was a white girl, and that still counted for plenty in parts of Florida. Jim Tile didn't get up and move; he kept his seat beside Brenda. It took the cracker trooper only about two hours to quit glaring.

At the lunch break, Jim Tile and Brenda Rourke went to an Arby's. She was worried about her upcoming transfer to South Florida; Jim Tile couldn't say much to allay her fears. She said she was studying Spanish, in preparation for road duty in Miami. The first phrase she'd learned was: *Sale del carro con las manos arriba.* Out of the car with your hands up!

At the time, Jim Tile held no romantic intentions. Brenda Rourke was a nice person, that was all. He never even asked if she had a boyfriend. A few months later, when he was down in Dade County for a trial, he ran into her at FHP headquarters. Later they went to dinner and then to Brenda's apartment, where they were up until three in the morning, chatting, of all things—initially out of nervousness, and later out of an easy intimacy. The trial lasted six days, and every night Jim Tile found himself back at Brenda's place. Every morning they awakened exactly as they'd fallen asleep—her head in the crook of his right shoulder, his feet hanging off the short bed. He'd never felt so peaceful. After the trial ended and Jim Tile returned to North Florida, he and Brenda took turns commuting for long weekends.

He wasn't much of a talker, but Brenda could drag it out of him. She especially liked to hear about the time he was assigned to guard the governor of Florida—not just any governor, but the one who'd quit, disappeared and become a legendary recluse.

Brenda had been in high school, but she remembered when it happened. The newspapers and TV had gone wild. 'Mentally unstable,' was what her twelfth-grade civics teacher had said of the runaway governor.

When Jim Tile had heard that, he threw back his head and laughed. Brenda would sit cross-legged on the carpet, her chin in her hands, engrossed by his stories of the one they now called Skink. Out of loyalty and prudence, Jim Tile didn't mention that he and the man had remained the closest of friends.

'I wish I'd met him,' Brenda had said, in the past tense, as if Skink were dead. Because Jim Tile had, perhaps unconsciously, made it sound like he was.

Now, two years later, it seemed that Brenda's improbable wish might come true. The governor had surfaced in the hurricane zone.

On the ride back from Card Sound, she asked: 'Why would he tie himself to a bridge during a storm?' It was the logical question.

Jim Tile said, 'He's been waiting for a big one.'

'What for?'

'Brenda, I can't explain. It only makes sense if you know him.'

She said nothing for a mile or two, then: 'Why didn't you tell me that you two still talk?'

'Because we seldom do.'

'Don't you trust me?'

'Of course.' He pulled her close enough to steal a kiss.

She pulled away, a spark in her pale-blue eyes. 'You're going to try to find him. Come on, Jim, be straight with me.'

'I'm afraid he's got a loose wire. That's not good.'

'This isn't the first time, is it?'

'No,' said Jim Tile, 'it's not the first time.'

Brenda brought his hand to her lips and kissed his knuckles lightly. 'It's OK, big guy. I understand about friends.'

5

When they got to Augustine's house, Bonnie Lamb called her answering machine in New York. She listened twice to Max's message, then replayed it for Augustine.

'What do you think?' she asked.

'Not good. Is your husband worth a lot of money?'

'He does all right, but he's no millionaire.'

'And his family?'

Bonnie said her husband's father was quite wealthy. 'But I'm sure Max wasn't foolish enough to mention it to the kidnappers.'

Augustine made no such assumption. He heated tomato soup for Bonnie and put clean linens on the bed in the guest room. Then he went to the den and called a friend with the FBI. By the time he got off the phone, Bonnie Lamb had fallen asleep on the living-room sofa. He carried her to the spare room and tucked her under the covers. Then he went to the kitchen and fixed two large rib-eye steaks and a baked potato, which he washed down with a cold bottle of Amstel.

Later he took a long hot shower and thought about how wonderful Mrs Lamb—warm and damp from the rain and sweat—had smelled in his arms. It felt good to have a woman in the house again, even for just a night. Augustine wrapped himself in a towel and stretched out on the hardwood floor in front of the television. He flipped back and forth between local news broadcasts, hoping not to see any of his dead uncle's wild animals running amok, or Mrs Lamb's husband being loaded into a coroner's wagon.

At midnight Augustine heard a cry from the guest room. He correctly surmised that Mrs Lamb had discovered his skull collection. He found her sitting up, the covers pulled to her chin. She was gazing at the wall.

'I thought it was a dream,' she said.

'Please don't be afraid.'

'Are they real?'

'Friends send them to me,' Augustine said, 'from abroad, mostly. One was a Christmas present from a fishing guide in Islamorada.' He wasn't sure what Bonnie Lamb thought of his hobby, so he apologized for the fright. 'Some people collect coins. I'm into forensic artifacts.'

'Body parts?'

'Not fresh ones—artifacts. Believe it or not, a good skull is hard to come by.'

That was the line that usually sent them bolting for the door. Bonnie didn't move.

'Can I look?'

Augustine took one from a shelf. She inspected it casually, as if it were a cantaloupe in a grocery store. Augustine smiled; he liked this lady.

'Male or female?' Bonnie turned the skull in her hands.

'Male, late twenties, early thirties. Guyanese, circa 1940. Came from a medical school in Texas.'

Bonnie asked why the lower jaw was missing. Augustine explained that it fell off when the facial muscles decayed. Most old skulls were found without the mandible.

Lifting it by the eye sockets, Bonnie returned the spooky relic to its place on the wall. 'How many have you got up there?'

'Nineteen.'

She whistled. 'And how many are women?'

'None,' said Augustine. 'They're all young males. So you've got nothing to worry your pretty head about.'

She rolled her eyes at the joke, then asked: 'Why all males?'

'To remind me of my own mortality.'

Bonnie groaned. 'You're one of *those*.'

'Other times,' Augustine said, 'when I'm sure my life has gone to hell, I come in here and think about what happened to these poor bastards. It improves my outlook considerably.'

She said, 'Well, that makes about as much sense as everything else. Can I take a shower?'

Later, over coffee, he told her what the FBI man had said. 'They'll treat your husband's disappearance as a kidnapping when there's a credible ransom demand. And he stressed the word "credible."'

'But what about the message on the machine? That other man's voice cutting in?'

'Of course they'll listen to it. But I've got to warn you, they're shorthanded right now. Lots of agents got hit hard by the storm, so they're out on personal leave.'

Bonnie was exasperated by the lack of interest in Max's plight. Augustine explained that restless husbands often used natural disasters as a cover to flee their wives. Precious manpower and resources were wasted tracking them to the apartments, condominiums and houseboats of their respective mistresses. Consequently, post-hurricane reports of missing spouses were now received with chilly skepticism.

Bonnie Lamb said, 'For God's sake, we just got married. Max wouldn't take off on a stunt like that.'

Augustine shrugged. 'People get cold feet.'

She leaned across the kitchen table and took a swing at him. Augustine blocked the punch with a forearm. He told Mrs Lamb to settle down. Her cheeks were flushed and her eyes shone.

Augustine said, 'I meant we can't rule out anything.'

'But you heard that man on the answering machine!'

'Yeah, and I'm wondering why a serious kidnapper would be such a smartass. "Don't flatter yourself, Max." And then the guy gets on the line and says, "I love you, Bonnie." Just to needle your husband, see? Make him feel like shit.' Augustine poured more coffee for both of them. He said, 'There's something damn strange about it. That's all I'm saying.'

Bonnie Lamb had to agree. 'To leave his voice all over a telephone tape—'

'Exactly. The guy's either incredibly stupid, or he's got brass balls—'

'Or he just doesn't care,' Bonnie said.

'You picked up on that, too.'

'It's scary.'

Augustine said, 'I'm not so sure.'

'Don't start again. Max is *not* faking this!'

'That stuff about having you call Pete at Rodale, the Bronco billboard—was he talking in code or what? Because some maniac kidnaps *me*, the last thing I'm worried about is keeping up with my ad accounts. What I'm worried about is saving my hide.'

Bonnie looked away. 'You don't know Max, what a workaholic he is.'

Augustine pushed back from the table. Normally he wasn't wild about women who punched for no good reason.

'What do we do now?' She held the cup with both hands, shaking slightly. 'You heard the man's tone.'

'Yeah, I did.'

'Let's agree he's not your average kidnapper. What is he?'

Augustine shook his head. 'How would I know, Mrs Lamb?'

'It's Bonnie.' She stood up, perfectly calm now, tightening the sash on the robe he'd loaned her. 'Maybe together we can figure him out.'

Augustine emptied his coffee in the sink. 'I think we both need some sleep.'

On the way back to Tony Torres's house, Edie Marsh asked Snapper if he had a stopwatch.

'Why?'

'Because I want to put a clock on this jerk,' she said, 'see how long it takes before he tries to screw me.'

Snapper, who had daydreamed of doing the same thing, said: 'I give him two days before he makes a move.' a'I give him two hours,' Edie said.

'So what'll you do? Ten grand's ten grand.'

Edie said, 'You better be joking. I'd shove hot daggers in my eyes before I'd let that pig touch me.' It was a long bleak slide from dating a Kennedy to fucking a mobile-home salesman.

'What if he don't let up?' asked Snapper.

'Then I walk.'

'Yeah, but—'

'Hey,' Edie said, 'you want the money so bad, *you* fuck him, OK? I think the two of you'd make a very cute couple.'

Snapper didn't press the issue. He'd already hatched a backup plan, in case the Torres deal fell apart. Avila was in a happy mood when he'd called the motel. Apparently the *santería* saints had informed him he could become very rich by starting his own roofing business. The saints had pointed out that the hurricane left two hundred thousand people without shelter, and that many of these poor folks were so desperate to get their houses repaired that they wouldn't think of asking to see a valid contractor's license, which of course Avila did not possess.

'But you're afraid of heights,' Snapper had reminded him.

'That's where you come in,' Avila had said. 'I'm the boss, you're the foreman. All we need is a crew.'

'Meaning you won't be joining us up on the roof with the boiling tar in the hot sun.'

'Jesus, Snap, somebody's got to handle the paperwork. Somebody's got to write up the contracts.'

Snapper had inquired about the split. Avila said guys he knew were charging fifteen grand per roof, a third of it up front. He said some home owners were offering cash, to speed the job. Avila said there was enough work around to keep them busy for two years.

'Thanks to you,' Snapper had said.

Avila failed to see irony in the fact that corruptly incompetent building inspections were a chief reason that so many roofs had blown off in the storm, and that so much new business was now available for incompetent roofers.

'You guys plan it this way?' Snapper had asked.

'Plan what?'

Snapper didn't trust Avila as far as he could spit, but the roofing option was something to consider if Torres went sour.

The trailer salesman also happened to be in sunny spirits when Snapper and Edie Marsh arrived. He was sprawled, shirtless, in a chaise on the front lawn. He wore Bermuda shorts and monogrammed socks pulled high on his hairy shins. The barrel of the shotgun poked out from a stack of newspapers on his lap. When Edie Marsh and Snapper got out of the car, Tony clapped his hands and exclaimed: 'I knew you'd be back!'

'A regular Nostradamus,' said Edie. 'Is the electricity up yet? We picked up some stuff for the refrigerator.'

Tony reported that the power remained off, and the portable generator had run out of gas overnight. He was storing food in two large Igloo coolers, packed with ice he'd purchased from gougers for twenty dollars a bag. The good news: Telephone service had been restored.

'And I got through immediately to Midwest Casualty,' Tony said. 'They're sending an adjuster today or tomorrow.'

Edie thought: Too good to be true. 'So we wait?'

'We wait,' Tony said. 'And remember, it's Neria. N-e-r-i-a. Middle initial, G as in Gómez. What'd you buy?'

'Tuna sandwiches,' Snapper replied, 'cheese, eggs, ice cream, Diet Sprite and stale fucking Lorna Doones. There wasn't much to choose from.' He iced the groceries, found a pool chair and took a position upwind of the sweaty Tony Torres. The sky had cleared and the summer sun blazed down, but it was pointless to look for shade. There wasn't any; all the trees in Turtle Meadow were leveled.

Tony complimented Edie Marsh for costuming herself as an authentic housewife—jeans, white Keds, a baggy blouse with the sleeves turned up. His only complaint was the sea-green scarf in her hair. He said, 'Silk is a little much, considering the circumstances.'

'Because it clashes with those gorgeous Bermudas of yours?' Edie glared at Tony Torres as if he were a maggot on a wedding cake. She was disinclined to remove the scarf, which was one of her favorites. She had boosted it from a Lord & Taylor's in Palm Beach.

'Suit yourself,' said Tony. 'Point is, details are damn important. It's the little things people notice.'

'I'll try and keep that in mind.'

Snapper said, 'Hey, Mister Salesman of the Year, can we run the TV off that generator?'

Tony said sure, if they only had some gasoline.

Snapper tapped his wristwatch and said, 'Sally Jessy comes on in twenty minutes. Men who seduce their daughter-in-law's mother-in-law.'

'No shit? We could siphon your car.' Tony pointed at the rubble of his garage. 'There's a hose in there someplace.'

Snapper went to find it. Edie Marsh said it was a lousy idea to siphon fuel from the car, since they might be needing speedy transportation. Snapper winked and told her not to worry. Off he went, ambling down the street, the garden hose coiled on his left shoulder. Edie expropriated the pool chair. Tony Torres perked up. 'Scoot closer, darling.'

'Wonderful,' she said, under her breath.

The salesman fanned himself with the Miami *Herald* sports pages. He said, 'It just now hit me: Men who steal their daughter-in-law's mother-in-law. That's pretty funny! He don't look like a comedian, your partner, but that's a good one.'

'Oh, he's full of surprises.' Edie leaned back and closed her eyes. The sunshine felt good on her face.

The hurricane had transformed the trailer court into a sprawling aluminum junkyard. Ira Jackson found Lot 17 because of the bright yellow tape that police had roped around the remains of the double-wide mobile home where his mother, Beatrice, had died. After identifying her body at the morgue, Ira Jackson had driven directly to Suncoast Leisure Village, to see for himself.

Not one trailer had made it through the storm.

From the debris, Ira Jackson pulled his mother's Craftmatic adjustable bed. The mattress was curled up like a giant taco shell. Ira Jackson crawled inside and lay down.

He recalled, as if it were yesterday, the morning he and his mother met with the salesman to close the deal. The man's name was Tony. Tony Torres. He was fat, gassy and balding, yet extremely self-assured. Beatrice Jackson had been impressed with his pitch.

'Mister Torres says it's built to go through a hurricane.'

'*I find that hard to believe, Momma.*'

'*Oh yes, Mister Jackson, your mother's right. Our prefabricated homes are made to withstand gusts up to one hundred twenty miles per hour. That's a U.S. government regulation. Otherwise we couldn't sell 'em!*'

Ira Jackson was in Chicago, beating up some scabs for a Teamsters local, when he'd heard about the hurricane headed for South Florida. He'd phoned his mother and urged her to move to a Red Cross shelter. She said it was out of the question.

'I can't leave Donald and Marla,' she told her son.

Donald and Marla were Mrs Jackson's beloved miniature dachshunds. The hurricane shelter wouldn't allow pets.

So Ira's mother had stayed home out of loyalty to her dogs and a misplaced confidence that the mobile-home salesman had told the truth about how safe it was. Donald and Marla survived the hurricane by squeezing under an oak credenza and sharing a rawhide chew toy to pass the long night. A neighbor had rescued them the next morning and taken them to a vet.

Beatrice Jackson was not so lucky. Moments after the hurricane stripped the north wall off her double-wide, she was killed by a flying barbecue that belonged to one of her neighbors. The imprint of the grill remained visible on her face, peaceful as it was, lying in the Dade County morgue.

Beatrice's death had no effect whatsoever on the mood of her dachshunds, but her son was inconsolable. Ira Jackson raged at himself for letting his mother buy the trailer. It had been his idea for her to move to Florida—but that's what guys in his line of work did for their widowed mothers; got them out of the cold weather and into the sunshine.

God help me, Ira Jackson thought, tossing restively on the mechanical mattress. I should've held off another year. Waited till I could afford to put her in a condo.

That cocksucker Torres. *A-hundred-twenty-mile-per-hour gusts.* What kind of scum would lie to a widow?

'Excuse me!'

Ira Jackson bolted upright to see a gray-haired man in a white undershirt and baggy pants. Skin and bones. Wire-rimmed eyeglasses that made him look like a heron. In one arm he carried a brown shopping bag.

'Have you seen an urn?' he asked.

'Jesus, what?'

'A blue urn. My wife's ashes. It's like a bottle.'

Ira Jackson shook his head. 'No, I haven't seen it.' He rose to his feet. He noticed that the old man was shaking.

'I'm going to kill him,' he said angrily.

Ira Jackson said, 'Who?'

'That lying sonofabitch who sold me the double-wide. I saw him here after the hurricane, but he took off.'

'Torres?'

'Yeah.' The old man's cheeks colored. 'I'd murder him, swear to God, if I could.'

Ira Jackson said, 'You'd get a medal for it.' Humoring the guy, hoping he'd run out of steam and go away.

'Hell, you don't believe me.'

'Sure I do.' He was tempted to tell the old man to quit worrying, Señor Tony Torres would be taken care of. Most definitely. But Ira Jackson knew it would be foolish to draw attention to himself.

The old man said: 'My name's Levon Stichler. I lived four lots over. Was it your mother that died here?'

Ira Jackson nodded.

Levon Stichler said, 'I'm real sorry. I'm the one found her two dogs—they're at Dr Tyler's in Naranja.'

'She'd appreciate that, my mother.' Ira Jackson made a mental note to pick up the dachshunds before the vet's office closed.

The old man said, 'My wife's ashes blew away in the hurricane.'

'Yeah, well, if I come across a blue bottle—'

'What the hell could they do to me?' Levon Stichler wore a weird quavering smirk. 'For killing him, what could they do? I'm seventy-one goddamn years old—what, life in prison? Big deal. I got nothing left anyhow.'

Ira Jackson said, 'I was you, I'd put it out of my mind. Scum like Torres, they usually get what they deserve.'

'Not in my world,' said Levon Stichler. But the widow Jackson's son had taken the wind out of his sails. 'Hell, I don't know how to find the sonofabitch anyhow. Do you?'

'Wouldn't have a clue,' Ira Jackson said.

Levon Stichler shrugged in resignation, and returned to the heap that once was his home. Ira Jackson watched him poking through the rubble, stooping every so often to examine a scrap. All around the trailer court, other neighbors of the late Beatrice Jackson could be seen hunched and scavenging, picking up pieces.

Her son opened his wallet, which contained: six hundred dollars cash, a picture of his mother taken in Atlantic City, three fake driver's licenses, a forged Social Security card, a stolen Delta Airlines frequent flyer card, and numerous scraps of paper with numerous phone numbers from the 718 area code. The wallet also held a few legitimate business cards, including one that said:

> **ANTONIO TORRES**
> Senior Sales Associate
> PreFab Luxury Homes
> (305) 555–2200

The trailer salesman had jotted his home number on the back of the business card. Ira Jackson kicked through his mother's storm-soaked belongings until he found a Greater Miami telephone directory. The salesman's home number matched the one belonging to an A. R. Torres at 15600 Calusa Drive. Ira Jackson tore the page from the phone book. Carefully he folded it to fit inside his wallet, with the other important numbers.

Then he drove his fraudulently registered Coupe de Ville to a convenience store, where he purchased a Rand McNally road map of Dade County.

6

The vagabond monkey chose to forgo the airboat experience. Max Lamb was given no choice. The one-eyed man strapped him to the passenger seat and off they went at fifty miles an hour, skimming the grass, cattails and lily pads. For a while they followed a canal that paralleled a two-lane highway; Max could make out the faces of motorists gaping at him in his underwear. It didn't occur to him to signal for help; the electrified dog collar had conditioned total passivity.

Riding high in the driver's perch, the man who called himself Skink sang at the top of his lungs. It sounded like 'Desperado,' an old Eagles tune. The familiar melody surfed above the ear-splitting roar of the airboat's engine; more than ever, Max Lamb believed he was in the grip of a madman.

Soon the airboat made a wide turn away from the road. It plowed a liquid trail through thickening marsh, the sawgrass hissing against the metal hull. The hurricane had bruised and gouged the swamp; smashed cypresses and pines littered the waters. Skink stopped singing and began to emit short honks and toots that Max Lamb assumed to be either wild bird calls or a fearsome attack of sinusitis. He was afraid to inquire.

At noon they stopped at a dry hammock, its once-lush branches now skeletal from the storm. Skink tied the airboat to a knuckled stand of roots. Evidence of previous campfires reassured Max Lamb that other humans had been there before. The kidnapper didn't bother to tie him; there was no place to run. With Skink's permission, Max put on his clothes to protect himself from the horseflies and mosquitoes. When he complained of being thirsty, Skink offered his own canteen. Max took a tentative swallow.

'Coconut milk?' he asked, hopefully.

'Something like that.'

Max suggested that wearing the shock collar was no longer necessary. Skink whipped out the remote control, pushed the red button and said: 'If you've got to ask, then it's still necessary.'

Max jerked wordlessly on the damp ground until the pain stopped. Skink caught a mud turtle and made soup for lunch. Tending the fire, he said, 'Max, I'll take three questions.'

'Three?'

'For now. Let's see how it goes.'

Max warily eyed the remote. Skink promised there would be no electronic penalty for dumb queries. 'So fire away.'

Max Lamb said, 'All right. Who are you?'

'My name is Tyree. I served in the Vietnam conflict, and later as a governor of this fair state. I resigned because of disturbing moral and philosophical conflicts. The details would mean nothing to you.'

Max Lamb failed to mask his disbelief. 'You were governor? Come off it.'

'Is that question number two?'

Impatiently, Max fingered the dog collar. 'No, the second question is: Why me?'

'Because you made a splendid target of yourself. You with your video camera, desecrating the habitat.'

Max Lamb got defensive. 'I wasn't the only one taking pictures. I wasn't the only tourist out there.'

'But you were the one I saw first.' Skink poured hot soup into a tin cup and handed it to his sulking prisoner. 'A hurricane is a holy thing,' he said, 'but you treated it as an amusement. Pissed me off, Max.'

Skink lifted the pot off the hot coals and tipped it to his lips. Steam wisped from his mouth, fogging his glass eye. He put the pot down and wiped the turtle drippings from his chin. 'I was tied up on a bridge,' he said, 'watching the storm roll out of the ocean. God, what a thing!'

He stepped toward Max Lamb and lifted him by the shirt, causing Max to drop the soup he had not touched.

Skink hoisted him to eye level and said: 'Twenty years I waited for that storm. We were so close, so goddamn close. Two or three degrees to the north, and we're in business. . . .'

Max Lamb dangled in the stranger's iron clasp. Skink's good eye glistened with a furious, dreamy passion. 'You're down to one question,' he said, returning Max to his feet.

After settling himself, Max asked: 'What happens now?'

Skink's stormy expression dissolved into a smile. 'What happens now, Max, is that we travel together, sharing life's lessons.'

'Oh.' Max's eyes cut anxiously to the airboat.

The governor barked a laugh that scattered a flock of snowy egrets. He tousled his prisoner's hair and said, 'We go with the tides!'

But a despairing Max Lamb couldn't face the prospect of true adventure. Now that it seemed he would not be murdered, he was burdened by another primal concern: *If I don't get back to New York, I'm going to lose my job.*

Edie Marsh was daydreaming about teak sailboats and handsome young Kennedys when she felt the moist hand of Tony Torres settle on her left breast. She cracked an eyelid and sighed.

'Quit squeezing. It's not a tomato.'

'Can I see?' Tony asked.

'Absolutely not.' But she heard the squeaky shift of weight as the salesman edged the chaise closer.

'Nobody's around,' he said, fumbling with her buttons. Then an oily laugh: 'I mean, you *are* my wife.'

'Jesus.' Edie felt the sun on her nipples and looked down. Well, there they were—the pig had undone her blouse. 'Don't you understand English?'

Tony Torres contentedly appraised her breasts. 'Yeah, darling, but who's got the shotgun.'

'That's so romantic,' Edie Marsh said. 'Threaten to shoot me—there's no better way to put a girl in the mood. Fact, I'm all wet just thinking about it.' She pushed his hand away and rebuttoned her blouse. 'Where's my shades,' she muttered.

Tony cradled the Remington across his belly. Sweat puddled at his navel. He said, 'You *will* think about it. They all do.'

'I think about cancer, too, but it doesn't make me horny.' To Edie, the only attractive thing about Tony Torres was his gold Cartier wristwatch, which was probably engraved in such a gaudy way that it could not be prudently fenced.

He asked her: 'Have you ever been with a bald man?'

'Nope. You ever seen venereal warts?'

The salesman snorted, turning away. 'Somebody's in a pissy mood.'

Edie Marsh dug the black Ray-Bans out of her purse and disappeared behind them. The shotgun made her nervous, but she resolved to stay cool. She tried to shut out the summer glare, the ceaseless drone of chain saws and dump trucks, and the rustle of Tony Torres reading the newspaper. The warmth of the sun made it easy for Edie Marsh to think of the duned shores at the Vineyard, or the private beaches of Manalapan.

Her reverie was interrupted by footsteps on the sidewalk across the street. She hoped it was Snapper, but it wasn't. It was a man walking two small dachshunds.

Edie felt Tony's hand on hers and heard him say, 'Darling, would you squirt some Coppertone on my shoulders?'

Quickly she rose from the chair and crossed the road. The man was watching his dachshunds pee on the stem of a broken mailbox. He held both leashes in one hand, loosely. There was a melancholy slump to his shoulders that should have disappeared with the approach of a pretty woman, but did not.

Edie Marsh told him the dogs were adorable. When she stooped to pet them, the dachshunds simultaneously rolled over and began squirming like worms on a griddle.

'What're their names?'

'Donald and Marla,' the man replied. He wasn't tall, but he was built like a furnace. He wore a peach knit shirt and khaki slacks. He said to Edie: 'You live at that house?'

She saw Tony Torres eyeing them from the chaise. She asked the stranger if he was from the Midwest Casualty insurance company. He motioned sarcastically toward the dogs and said, 'Sure. And my associates here are from Merrill Lynch.'

The dachshunds were up, wagging their butts and licking at Edie's bare ankles. The man jerked his double chin toward Tony Torres and said, 'You related to him? A wife or sister maybe.'

'Please,' Edie Marsh said, with an exaggerated shudder.

'OK, then I got some advice. Take a long fucking walk.'

Edie's mind began to race. She looked in both directions down the street, but didn't see Snapper.

The man said, 'The hell you waiting for?' He handed her the two leashes. 'Go on, now.'

Augustine awoke to the smell of coffee and the sounds of a married woman fixing breakfast in his kitchen. It seemed a suitable time to assess the situation.

His father was in prison, his mother was gone, and his dead uncle's wild animals had escaped among unsuspecting suburbanites. Augustine himself was free, too, in the truest and saddest sense. He had absolutely no personal responsibilities. How to explain such a condition to Bonnie Lamb?

My father was a fisherman. He ran drugs on the side, until he was arrested near the island of Andros.

My mother moved to Las Vegas and remarried. Her new husband plays tenor saxophone in Tony Bennett's orchestra.

My most recent ex-girlfriend was a leg model for a major hosiery concern. She saved her modeling money and bought a town house in Brentwood, California, where she fellates only circumcised movie agents, and the occasional director.

But what about you? Mrs Lamb will ask. What do you do for a living?

I read my bank statements.

And Mrs Lamb will react with polite curiosity, until I explain about the airplane accident.

It happened three years ago while flying back from Nassau after visiting my old man in Fox Hill Prison. I didn't realize the pilot was drunk until he T-boned the twin Beech into the fuselage of a Coast Guard helicopter, parked inside a hangar at the Opa-Locka airport.

Afterwards I slept for three months and seventeen days in the intensive care unit of Jackson Hospital. When I awoke, I was rich. The insurance carrier for the charter-air service had settled the case with an attorney whom I did not know and to this day have never met. A check for eight hundred thousand dollars appeared, and much to my surprise, I invested it wisely.

And Mrs Lamb, if I'm reading her right, will then say: So what is it you *do*?

Honestly, I'mnot certain. . . .

The conversation, over bacon and French toast, didn't go precisely as Augustine had anticipated. At the end of his story, Bonnie Lamb looked over the rim of her coffee cup and asked: 'Is that where you got the scar—from the plane crash?'

'Which scar?'

'The Y-shaped one on your lower back.'

'No,' said Augustine, guardedly. 'That's something else.' He made a mental note not to walk around without a shirt.

Later, clearing the kitchen table, Bonnie asked about his father.

'Extradited,' Augustine reported, 'but he much prefers Talladega to the Bahamas.'

'Are you two close?'

'Sure,' said Augustine. 'Only seven hundred miles.'

'How often do you go to see him?'

'Whenever I want to get angry and depressed.'

Augustine often wished that the plane crash had wiped out his memory of that last visit at Fox Hill Prison, but it hadn't. They were supposed to talk about the extradition, about lining up a half-decent lawyer in the States, about maybe cutting a deal with prosecutors so that the old man might actually get out before the turn of the century.

But Augustine's father wanted to talk about something else when his son came to see him. He wanted a favor.

—Bollock, you remember Bollock? He owes me a piece of a shipment.

—The answer is no.

—Come on, A.G. I got lawyers to pay. Take Leaker and Ape along. They'll handle Bollock. Not the money, though. That I want in your hands only.

—Dad, I don't believe this. I just don't believe it. . . .

—Hey, go down to Nassau harbor. See what they done to my boat! Ape says they stripped the radar and all the electric.

—So what. You didn't know how to use it anyway.

—Listen, wiseass, I was taking fire. It was the middle of the goddamn night.

—Still, it's not easy to park a sixty-foot long-liner in nine inches of water. How exactly did you manage that?

—Watch your tone, son!

—Grown man, hangin' out with guys called Leaker and Ape. Look where it got you.

—A.G., I'd love to keep strollin' down memory lane, but the guard says we're outta time. So will you do it? Go see Henry Bollock down on Big Pine. Get my slice and stick it in the Caymans. What's the harm?

—Pathetic.

—What?

—I said, you're pathetic.

—So I'll take that as a 'no,' you won't do this for me?

— Jesus Christ.

—You disappoint me, boy.

—And I'm proud of you, too, Dad. I bust my buttons every time your name comes up.

And Augustine recalled thinking, as he sat in the Beechcraft on the runway at Nassau: He's hopeless, my old man. He won't learn. He'll get out of prison and go right back to it.

A son looks a man square in the eye and calls him pathetic, *pathetic*, any other father would curse or cry or take a punch at the kid. Not mine. By God, not when there's drug money needs collecting. So how about it, A.G.?

Fuck him, thought Augustine. Not because of what he'd done or what he'd been hauling, but because his stupid selfish greed had outlived the crime. Fuck him, Augustine thought, because it's hopeless. He was supposed to raise me, goddammit, I wasn't supposed to raise him.

And then the plane took off.

And then the plane went down.

And nothing was ever the same about the way Augustine saw the world, or his place in it. Sometimes he wasn't sure if it was the accident that had changed him, or the visit with his father at Fox Hill Prison.

At FBI headquarters, Bonnie Lamb spent an hour talking with maddeningly polite agents. One of them dialed her answering machine and dubbed Max's queer kidnap message. They urged her to notify the Bureau as soon as she received a credible ransom demand. Then, and only then, would a kidnap squad take over the case. The agents instructed Bonnie to check her machine often and be careful not to erase any tapes. They expressed no strong views about whether she ought to remain in Miami and search for her husband, or return to New York and wait.

The agents let Bonnie Lamb borrow a private office, where she tried with no luck to reach Max's parents, who were traveling in Europe. Next Bonnie phoned her own parents. Her mother sounded sincere in her alarm; her father, as usual, sounded helpless. He half-heartedly offered to fly to Florida, but Bonnie said it wasn't necessary. All she could do was wait for Max or the kidnapper to call again. Bonnie's mother promised to FedEx some cash and an eight-by-ten photograph of Max, for the authorities.

Bonnie Lamb's last call was to Peter Archibald at the Rodale & Burns advertising agency in Manhattan. Max Lamb's colleague was shocked at Bonnie's news, but vowed to maintain the confidentiality requested by the FBI. When Bonnie passed along her husband's frantic instructions about the cigaret billboard, Peter Archibald said: 'You married a real trouper, Bonnie.'

'Thank you, Peter.'

Augustine took her to a fish house for lunch. She ordered a gin-and-tonic, and said: 'I want your honest opinion about the FBI guys.'

'OK. I think they had problems with the tape.'

'Max didn't sound scared enough.'

'Possibly,' Augustine said, 'and, like I mentioned, he seemed a little too worried about the Marlboro account.'

'It's Broncos,' Bonnie corrected. From the way she winced at the gin, Augustine could tell she wasn't much of a drinker. 'So they blew me off as a jilted wife.'

'Not at all. They started a file. They're the best darn file-starters in the world. Then they'll send your tape to the audio lab. They'll probably even make a few phone calls. But you saw how deserted the place was—half their agents are home cleaning up storm damage.'

She said, angrily, 'The world doesn't stop for a hurricane.'

'No,' Augustine said, 'but it wobbles like a sonofabitch. I'm having the shrimp, how about you?'

Mrs Lamb didn't speak again until they were in the pickup truck, heading south to the hurricane zone. She asked Augustine to stop at the county morgue.

He thought: She couldn't have gotten this brainstorm *before* lunch.

Snapper had neither the ambition nor the energy to be a predator in the classic criminal mold. He saw himself strictly as a canny opportunist. He wouldn't endeavor to commit a first-degree felony unless the moment presented itself. He believed in serendipity, because it suited his style of minimal exertion.

He heard the kids coming long before he saw them. The souped-up Cherokee blasted Snoop Doggy Dogg through the neighborhood, rattling the few windows that the hurricane had not broken. The kids drove by once, circled the block, and cruised past again.

Snapper smiled to himself, thinking: It's the damn pinstripes. They think I'm carrying money.

He kept walking. When the Cherokee came around a third time, the rap music had been turned off. Stupid, Snapper thought. Why not take out a billboard: Watch us mug this guy!

As the Jeep rolled up behind him, Snapper stepped to the side and slowed his pace. He slipped Tony Torres's garden hose off his shoulder and carried it coiled in front of him. The Cherokee came alongside. One of the kids was hanging out the passenger window. He waved a chrome-plated pistol at Snapper.

'Hey, mud-fuckah,' the kid said.

'Good mornin",' said Snapper. He deftly looped a coil of the garden hose around the kid's head and jerked him out of the truck. When the kid hit the pavement, he dropped the gun. Snapper picked it up. He stepped on the kid's chest and, with one hand, began twisting the hose tightly on the kid's throat.

The other muggers piled out of the Cherokee with the intention of rescuing their friend and killing the butt-ugly geek in the shiny suit, but the plan changed when they saw who had the pistol. Then they ran.

Snapper waited until the kid on the ground was almost unconscious before loosening the hose. 'I need to borrow some gas,' said Snapper, 'to watch Sally Jessy.'

The kid sat up slowly and rubbed his neck, which bled from the place where his three gold chains had cut into his flesh. He wore a tank top to show off the tattoos on his left biceps—a gang insignia and the nickname 'Baby Raper.'

Snapper said, 'Baby, you got a gas can?'

'Fuck no.' The kid answered in a raw whisper.

'Too bad. I'll have to take the whole truck.'

'I don't care. Ain't mine.'

'Yeah, that was my hunch.'

The kid said, 'Man, wus wrong wid yo face?'

'Excuse me?'

'I axed what's wrong wid yo mud-fuckin face.'

Snapper went in the Cherokee and removed the Snoop Doggy Dogg compact disc from the stereo. He used the shiny side of the CD like a small mirror, pretending to admire himself in it.

'Looks fine to me,' he said, after several moments.

The kid smirked. 'Sheeeiiit.'

Snapper put the pistol to the kid's temple and ordered him to get on his belly. Then he yanked the mugger's pants down to his ankles.

A Florida Power and Light cherry picker came steaming down the street. The kid shouted for help, but the driver kept going.

Twisting to look over his shoulder, Baby Raper saw Snapper hold the CD up to the sky, like a chrome communion wafer.

Snapper said: 'Worst fuckin' excuse for music I ever heard.'

'Man, whatcha gone do wid dat?'

'Guess.'

Ira Jackson stood with his back to the sun. Tony Torres squinted, shielding his brow with one hand.

The salesman said: 'Do I remember you? Course I remember you.'

'My mother was Beatrice Jackson.'

'I said I remember.'

'She's dead.'

'So I heard. I'm very sorry.' Stretched in the chaise, Tony Torres felt vulnerable. He raised both knees to give himself a brace for the shotgun.

Ira Jackson asked Tony if he remembered anything else. 'Such as what you promised my mother about the double-wide being as safe as a regular CBS house?'

'Whoa, sport, I said no such thing.' Tony Torres was itching to get to his feet, but that was a major project. One wrong move, and the flimsy patio chair could collapse under his weight. '"Government approved," is what I told you, Mister Jackson. Those were my exact words.'

'My mother's dead. The double-wide went to pieces.'

'Well, it was one hellacious hurricane. The Storm of the Century, they said on TV.' Tony was beginning to wonder if this dumb ape didn't see the Remington aimed at his dick. 'We're talking about a major natural disaster, sport. Look how it wrecked these houses. *My* house. Hell, it blew down the entire goddamn Homestead Air Force Base! There's no hiding from something like that. I'm sorry about your mother, Mister Jackson, but a trailer's a trailer.'

'What happened to the tie-downs?'

Oh Christ, Tony thought. Who knew enough to look at the

fucking tie-downs? He struggled to appear indignant. 'I've got no idea what you're talking about.'

Ira Jackson said, 'I found two of 'em hanging off a piece of the double-wide. Straps were rotted. Augers cut off short. No anchor disks—this shit I saw for myself.'

'I'm sure you're mistaken. They passed inspection, Mister Jackson. Every home we sold passed inspection.' The confidence was gone from the salesman's tone. He was uneasy, arguing with a faceless silhouette.

'Admit it,' Ira Jackson said. 'Somebody cut the damn augers to save a few bucks on installation.'

'Keep talkin' that way,' warned Tony Torres, 'and I'll sue your ass for slander.'

Even before it was made a specified condition of his parole, Ira Jackson had never possessed a firearm. In his many years as a professional goon, it had been his experience that men who brandished guns invariably got shot with one. Ira Jackson favored the more personal touch afforded by crowbars, aluminum softball bats, nunchaku sticks, piano wire, cutlery, or gym socks filled with lead fishing sinkers. Any would have done the job nicely on Tony Torres, but Ira Jackson had brought nothing but his bare fists to the salesman's house.

'What is it you want?' Tony Torres demanded.

'An explanation.'

'Which I just gave you.' Tony's eyes watered from peering into the sun's glare, and he was growing worried. Edie the Ice Maiden had disappeared with Ira Jackson's dogs—what the hell was *that* all about? Were they in on something? And where was the freak in the bad suit, his so-called bodyguard?

Tony said to Ira Jackson: 'I think it's time for you to go.' He motioned with the shotgun toward the street.

'This is how you treat dissatisfied customers?'

A jittery laugh burst from the salesman. 'Sport, you ain't here for no refund.'

'You're right.' Ira Jackson was pleased by the din of the neighborhood—hammers, drills, saws, electric generators. All the folks preoccupied with putting their homes back together.

The noise would make it easier to cover the ruckus, if the mobile-home salesman tried to put up a struggle.

Tony Torres said, 'You think I don't know to use this twelve-gauge, you're makin' a big mistake. Check out the hole in that garage door.'

Ira Jackson whistled. 'I'm impressed, Mister Torres. You shot a house.'

Tony's expression hardened. 'I'm counting to three.'

'My mother was hit by a damn barbecue.'

'*One!*' the salesman said. 'Every second you look more like a looter, mister.'

'You promised her the place was safe. All those poor people—how the hell do you sleep nights?'

'*Two!*'

'Relax, you fat fuck. I'm on my way.' Ira Jackson turned and walked slowly toward the street.

Tony Torres took a deep breath; his tongue felt like sandpaper. He lowered the Remington until it rested on one of his kneecaps. He watched Beatrice Jackson's son pause in the driveway and kneel as if tying a shoe.

Craning to see, Tony shouted: 'Move it, sport!'

The cinder block caught him by surprise—first, the sheer weight of it, thirty-odd pounds of solid concrete; second, the fact that Ira Jackson was able to throw such a hefty object, shot-putter style, with such distressing accuracy.

When it struck the salesman's chest, the cinder block knocked the shotgun from his hands, the beer from his bladder and the breath from his lungs. He made a sibilant exclamation, like a water bed rupturing.

So forceful was the cinder block's impact that it doubled Tony Torres at the waist, causing the chaise longue to spring on him like an oversized mousetrap. The moans he let out as Ira Jackson dragged him to the car were practically inaudible over the chorus of his neighbors' chain saws.

7

The Dade County Medical Examiner's Office was quiet, neat and modern—nothing like Bonnie Lamb's notion of a big-city morgue. She admired the architect's thinking; the design of the building successfully avoided the theme of violent homicide. With its brisk and clerical-looking layout, it could have passed for the regional headquarters of an insurance company or a mortgage firm, except for the dead bodies in the north wing.

A friendly secretary brought coffee to Bonnie Lamb while Augustine spoke privately to an assistant medical examiner. The young doctor remembered Augustine from a week earlier, when he had come to claim his uncle's snakebitten remains. The medical examiner was intrigued to learn from Augustine that the tropical viper that had killed Felix Mojack now roamed free. He Emailed a memorandum to Jackson Memorial, alerting the emergency room to requisition more antivenin, just in case. Then he took a Xeroxed copy of Bonnie Lamb's police report down the hall.

When he returned, the medical examiner said the morgue had two unidentifled corpses that loosely matched the physical description of Max Lamb. Augustine relayed the news to Bonnie.

'You up for this?' he asked.

'If you go with me.'

It was a long walk to the autopsy room, where the temperature seemed to drop fifteen degrees. Bonnie Lamb took Augustine's hand as they moved among the self-draining steel tables, where a half-dozen bodies were laid out in varying stages of dissection. The room gave off a cloying odor, the sickly-sweet commingling of chemicals and dead flesh. Augustine felt Bonnie's palm go cold. He asked her if she was going to faint.

'No,' she said. 'It's just . . . God, I thought they'd all be covered with sheets.'

'Only in the movies.'

The first John Doe had lank hair and sparse, uneven sideburns. He was the same race and age, but otherwise bore no resemblance to Max Lamb. The dead man's eyes were greenish blue; Max's were brown. Still, Bonnie stared.

'How did he die?'

Augustine asked: 'Is it Max?'

She shook her head sharply. 'But tell me how he died.'

With a Bic pen, the young medical examiner pointed to a dime-sized hole beneath the dead man's left armpit. 'Gunshot wound,' he said.

Augustine and Bonnie Lamb followed the doctor to another table. Here the cause of death was no mystery. The second John Doe had been in a terrible accident. He was scalped and his face pulverized beyond recognition. A black track of autopsy stitches ran from his breast to his pelvis.

Bonnie stammered, 'I don't know, I can't tell—'

'Look at his hands,' the medical examiner said.

'No wedding ring,' Augustine observed.

'Please. I want her to look,' the medical examiner said. 'We remove the jewelry for safekeeping.'

Bonnie dazedly circled the table. The bluish pallor of the dead man's skin made it difficult to determine his natural complexion. He was built like Max—narrow shoulders, bony chest, with a veined roll of baby fat at the midsection. The arms and legs were lean and finely haired, like Max's. . . .

'Ma'am, what about the hands?'

Bonnie Lamb forced herself to look, and was glad she did. The hands were not her husband's; the fingernails were grubby and gnawed. Max believed religiously in manicures and buffing.

'No, it's not him.' She spoke very softly, as if trying not to awaken the man with no face.

The doctor wanted to know if her husband had any birthmarks. Bonnie said she hadn't noticed, and felt guilty—as if she hadn't spent enough time examining the details of Max's trunk and extremities. Couldn't most lovers map their partner's most intimate blemishes?

'I remember a mole,' she said in a helpful tone, 'on one of his elbows.'

'Which elbow?' asked the medical examiner.

'I don't recall.'

'Like it matters,' said Augustine, restlessly. 'Check both his arms, OK?'

The doctor checked. The dead man's elbows had no moles. Bonnie turned away from the body and laid her head against Augustine's chest.

'He was driving a stolen motorcycle,' the doctor explained, 'with a stolen microwave strapped to the back.'

Augustine sighed irritably. 'A hurricane looter.'

'Right. Smacked a lumber truck doing eighty.'

'*Now* he tells us,' said Bonnie Lamb.

The wash of relief didn't hit her until she was back in Augustine's pickup truck. *It wasn't Max at the morgue, because Max is still alive. This is good. This is cause to be thankful.* Then Bonnie began to tremble, imagining her husband gutted like a fish on a shiny steel tray.

When they returned to the neighborhood where Max Lamb had vanished, they found the rental car on its rims. The hood stood open and the radiator was gone. Augustine's note on the windshield wiper was untouched—a testament, he remarked, to the low literacy rate among car burglars. He offered to call a wrecker.

'Later,' Bonnie said, tersely.

'That's what I meant. Later.' He locked the truck and set the alarm.

They walked the streets for nearly two hours, Augustine with the .38 Special wedged in his belt. He thought Max Lamb's abductor might have holed up, so they checked every abandoned house in the subdivision. Walking from one block to the next, Bonnie struck up conversations with people who were patching their battered homes. She hoped one of them would remember seeing Max on the morning after the hurricane. Several residents offered colorful accounts of monkey sightings, but Bonnie spoke with no one who recalled the kidnapping of a tourist.

Augustine drove her to the Metro police checkpoint, where she contacted a towing service and the rental-car agency in Orlando. Then she made a call to the apartment in New York to get her messages. After listening for a minute, she pressed the pound button on the telephone and handed the receiver to Augustine.

'Unbelievable,' she said.

It was Max Lamb's voice on the line. The static was so heavy he could have been calling from Tibet:

'Bonnie, darling, everything's OK. I don't believe my life's in danger, but I can't say when I'll be free. It's too hairy to explain over the phone—uh, hang on, he wants me to read something. Ready? Here goes:

'"I have nothing to do with the creaking machinery of humanity—I belong to the earth! I say that lying on my pillow and I can feel the horns sprouting from my temples."'

After a scratchy pause: 'Bonnie, honey, it sounds worse than it is. Please don't tell my folks a thing—I don't want Dad all worked up for no reason. And please call Pete and, uh, ask him to put me down for sick leave, just in case this situation drags out. And tell him to stall the sixth floor on the Bronco meeting next week. Don't forget, OK? Tell him under no circumstances should Bill Knapp be brought in. It's still my account. . . .'

Max Lamb's voice dissolved into fuzzy pops and echoes. Augustine hung up. He walked Bonnie back to the pickup.

She got in and said, 'This is making me crazy.'

'We'll call again from my house and get it on tape.'

'Oh, I'm sure it'll jolt the FBI into action. Especially the poetry.'

'Actually I think it's from a book.'

'What does it mean?' she asked.

Augustine reached across her lap and placed the .38 Special in the glove compartment. 'It means,' he said, 'your husband probably isn't as safe as he thinks.'

*

By and large, the Highway Patrol troopers based in northern
Florida were not overjoyed to learn of their temporary reassign-
ment to southern Florida. Many would have preferred Beirut or
Somalia. The exception was Jim Tile. A trip to Miami meant
precious time with Brenda Rourke, although working double
shifts in the hurricane zone left them scarcely enough energy to
collapse in each other's arms.

Jim Tile hadn't counted on an intrusion by the governor, but
it wasn't totally surprising. The man worshipped hurricanes.
Ignoring his presence would have been selfish and irresponsible;
the trooper didn't take the friendship that lightly, nor Skink's
capacity for outstandingly rash behavior. Jim Tile had no choice
but to try to stay close.

In the age of political correctness, a large black man in a crisply
pressed police uniform could move at will through the corridors
of white-cracker bureaucracy and never once be questioned. Jim
Tile took full advantage in the days following the big storm. He
mingled authoritatively with Dade County deputies, Homestead
police, firefighters, Red Cross volunteers, National Guardsmen,
the Army command and antsy emissaries of the Federal Emergency Management Agency. Between patrol shifts, Jim Tile
helped himself to coffee and A-forms, 911 logs, computer printouts and handwritten incident reports—he scanned for nothing
in particular; just a sign.

As it happened, though, madness flowed rampant in the
storm's wake. Jim Tile leafed through the paperwork, and
thought: My Lord, people are cracking up all over town.

The machinery of rebuilding doubled as novel weapons for
domestic violence. Thousands of hurricane victims had stam-
peded to purchase chain saws for clearing debris, and now the
dangerous power tools were being employed to vent rage. A
gentleman with a Black & Decker attempted to truncate a
stubborn insurance adjuster in Homestead. An old woman in
Florida City used a lightweight Sears to silence a neighbor's
garrulous pet cockatoo. And in Sweetwater, two teenaged gang
members successfully detached each other's arms (one left, one
right) in a brief but spectacular duel of stolen Homelites.

If chain saws ruled the day, firearms ruled the night. Fearful of looters, vigilant home owners unloaded high-caliber semi-automatics at every rustle, scrape and scuff in the darkness. Preliminary casualties included seven cats, thirteen stray dogs, two opossums and a garbage truck, but no actual thieves. Residents of one rural neighborhood wildly fired dozens of rounds to repel what they described as a troop of marauding monkeys—an episode that Jim Tile dismissed as mass hallucination. He resolved to limit his investigative activities to daytime hours, whenever possible.

Nearly all the missing persons reported to authorities were locals who had fled the storm and lost contact with concerned relatives up North. Most turned up safe at shelters or in the homes of neighbors. But one case caught Jim Tile's attention: a man named Max Lamb.

According to the information filed by his wife, the Lambs drove to Miami on the morning after the hurricane struck. Mrs Lamb told police that her husband wanted to see the storm damage. The trooper wasn't surprised—the streets were clogged with out-of-towners who treated the hurricane zone as a tourist attraction.

Mr Max Lamb had left his rental car, in pursuit of video. It seemed improbable to Jim Tile that anybody from Manhattan could get lost on foot in the flat simple grid of a Florida subdivision. The trooper's suspicions were heightened by another incident, lost deep in the stack of files.

A seventy-four-year-old woman had called to say she had witnessed a possible assault. It was summarized in two short paragraphs, taken over the telephone by a dispatcher:

'Caller reports suspicious subject running along 10700 block of Quail Roost Drive, carrying another subject over his shoulder. Subject One is described as w/m, height and weight unknown. Subject Two is w/m, height and weight unknown.

'Caller reports Subject B appeared to be resisting, and was possibly nude. Subject A reported to be carrying a handgun with a flashing red light (??). Search of area by Units 2334 and 451I proved negative.'

Jim Tile knew of no pistols with blinking red lights, but most hand-held video cameras had one. From a distance, a frightened elderly person might mistake a Sony for a Smith &Wesson.

Maybe the old woman had witnessed the abduction of Mr Max Lamb. Jim Tile hoped not. He hoped the Quail Roost sighting was just another weird Dade County roadside altercation and not the act of his volatile swamp-dwelling friend, who was known to hold ill-mannered tourists in low esteem.

The trooper made a copy of Mrs Lamb's report and slipped it in his briefcase along with several others. When he had some free time, he'd try to interview her.

There was only twenty minutes left for lunch with Brenda, before both of them had to start another shift. Being able to see her, even briefly, was well worth the ordeal of working the batty streets of South Florida.

Jim Tile was most displeased, therefore, to personally witness the hijacking of a Salvation Army truck while he was driving to the Red Lobster restaurant where Brenda waited. The trooper was obliged to give chase, and by the time it was over he'd missed his luncheon date.

As he disarmed and handcuffed the truck hijacker, Jim Tile wondered aloud why anybody with half a brain would use a MAC-10 to steal a truck full of secondhand clothes. The young man said his original intention was to spray-paint a gang insignia on the side of the Salvation Army truck, but before he could finish his tagging the driver took off. The young man explained that he'd had no choice, as a matter of self-respect, but to pull his submachine gun and, yo, steal the motherfucking truck.

As Trooper Jim Tile assisted the talkative hijacker into the cage of his patrol car, he silently vowed to redouble his efforts to persuade Brenda Rourke to transfer out of this hellhole called Miami, to a more civilized hellhole where they could work together.

Snapper was proud of how he'd acquired the Jeep Cherokee, but Edie Marsh showed no interest in his conquest.

'What's the story?' Snapper pointed at the dachshunds.

'Donald and Marla,' Edie said, annoyed. The animals were pulling her back and forth across Tony Torres's front yard and peeing with wild abandon. Edie was amazed at the power in their stubby Vienna-sausage legs.

'By the way,' she said, straining against the leashes, 'it took that asshole all of three minutes before he grabbed my tits.'

'Big deal, so you win the bet.'

'Take these damn dogs!'

Snapper backed away. Numerous encounters with police German shepherds had left him with permanent scars, physical and mental. Over the years, Snapper had become a cat person.

'Just let 'em go,' he said to Edie.

The moment she dropped the leashes, the two dachshunds curled up at her feet.

'Beautiful,' Snapper said with a grunt. 'Hey, look what I found.' He flashed the chrome-plated pistol he'd taken from the gangsters. Palming the cheap gun, he noticed the chambers were empty. 'Damn spades,' he said, heaving it into the murky swimming pool.

Edie Marsh told Snapper about the tough guy with the New York accent who came for Tony Torres. 'You picked a peachy time to disappear,' she added.

'Shut the fuck up.'

'Well, Tony's gone. Even his damn beach chair. Figure it out yourself.'

'Shit.'

'He won't be back,' Edie said gravely. 'Not in one piece, anyway.'

A concrete block occupied the spot where Tony's chaise had been. Snapper cursed his rotten timing. The ten grand was history. Even in the unlikely event that the salesman returned, he'd never pay. Snapper had fucked up big-time; he wasn't cut out to be a bodyguard.

He said, 'I don't guess you got a new plan.'

A siren drowned Edie's reply, which she punctuated with a familiar hand gesture. An ambulance came speeding down Calusa Drive. Snapper figured it was carrying Baby Raper to the hospital, for some unusual surgery. Snapper wouldn't be surprised to read about it in a medical journal someday.

He spotted Tony Torres's Remington shotgun, broken into pieces on the driveway. Snapper thought: It's definitely time to abort the mission. Tomorrow he'd call Avila about the roofer's gig.

'I'll give you a lift,' he said to Edie Marsh, 'but not those damn dogs.'

'Jesus, I can't just leave 'em here.'

'Suit yourself.' Snapper scooped three Heinekens from Tony's ice cooler, got in the souped-up Cherokee and drove off without so much as a wave.

Edie Marsh tethered Donald and Marla to a sprinkler in the backyard. Then she entered the ruined shell of the salesman's house, to check for items of value.

Skink ordered Max Lamb to disrobe and climb a tree. Max did as he was told. It was a leafless willow; Max sat carefully on a springy limb, his bare legs dangling. Beneath him Skink paced, fulminating. In one hand he displayed the remote-control unit for the electronic training collar.

'You people come down here—fucking yupsters with no knowledge, no appreciation, no *interest* in the natural history of the place, the ancient sweep of life. Disney World—Christ, Max, that's not Florida!' He pointed an incriminating finger at his captive. 'I found the ticket stubs in your wallet, Tourist Boy.'

Max was rattled; he'd assumed everybody liked Disney World. 'Please,' he said to Skink, 'if you shock me now, I'll fall.'

Skink pulled off his flowered cap and knelt by the dead embers of the campfire. Max Lamb was acutely worried. Coal-black mosquitoes swarmed his pale plump toes, but he didn't dare slap at them. He was afraid to move a muscle.

All day the kidnapper's spirits had seemed to improve. He'd even taken Max to a rest stop along the Tamiami Trail, so Max could call New York and leave Bonnie another message. While Max waited for the pay phone, Skink had dashed onto the highway to collect a fresh roadkill. His mood was loose, practically convivial. He sang during the entire airboat ride back to the cypress hammock; later he merely chided Max for not knowing that Neil Young had played guitar forBuffalo Springfield.

Max Lamb believed himself to be blessed with a winning personality, a delusion that led him to assume the kidnapper had grown fond of him. Max felt it was only a matter of time before he'd be able to shmooze his way to freedom. He put no stock in Skink's oral biography, and regarded the man as an unbalanced but moderately intelligent derelict; in short, a confused soul who could be won over with a thoughtful, low-key approach. And wasn't that an advertiser's forte—winning people over? Max believed he was making progress, too, with tepid conversation, pointless anecdotes and the occasional self-deprecatory joke. Skink certainly acted calmer, if not serene. Three hours had passed since he'd last triggered the canine shock collar; an encouraging lull, from Max's point of view.

Now, for reasons unknown, the one-eyed brute was seething again. To Max Lamb, he announced: 'Pop quiz.'

'On what?'

Skink rose slowly. He tucked the remote control in a back pocket. With both hands he gathered his wild hair and knotted it on one side of his head, above the ear—a misplaced mop of a ponytail. Then he removed his glass eye and polished it with spit and a crusty bandanna. Max became further alarmed.

'Who was here first,' Skink asked, 'the Seminoles or the Tequestas?'

'I, uh—I don't know.' Max gripped the branch so hard that his knuckles turned pink.

Skink, replacing the artificial eyeball, retrieving the remote control from his pocket: 'Who was Napoleon Bonaparte Broward?'

Max Lamb shook his head, helplessly. Skink shrugged. 'How about Marjory Stoneman Douglas?'

'Yes, yes, wait a minute.' The willow limb quivered under Max's nervous buttocks. 'She wrote *The Yearling*!'

Moments later, regaining consciousness, he found himself in a fetal ball on a mossy patch of ground. Both knees were scraped from the fall. His throat and arms still burned from the dog collar's jolt. Opening his eyes, Max saw the toes of Skink's boots. He heard a voice as deep as thunder: 'I should kill you.'

'No, don't—'

'The arrogance of coming to a place like this and not knowing—'

'I'm sorry, captain.'

'—not caring to learn—'

'I told you, I'm in advertising.'

Skink slipped a hand under Max Lamb's chin. 'What do you believe in?'

'For God's sake, it's my honeymoon.' Max was on the slippery ledge of panic.

'What do you stand for? Tell me that, sir.'

Max Lamb cringed. 'I can't.'

Skink chuckled bitterly. 'For future reference, you got your Marjories mixed up. Rawlings wrote *The Yearling*; Douglas wrote *River of Grass*. I got a hunch you won't forget.'

He cleaned the bloody scrapes on Max's legs and told him to put on his clothes. His confidence fractured, Max dressed in arthritic slow motion. 'Are you ever going to let me go?'

Skink seemed not to have heard the question. 'Know what I'd really like,' he said, stoking a new fire. 'I'd like to meet this bride of yours.'

'That's impossible,' Max said, hoarsely.

'Oh, nothing's impossible.'

Among the stream of outlaws who raced south in the feverish hours following the hurricane was a man named Gil Peck. His plan was to pass himself off as an experienced mason, steal what he could in the way of advance deposits, then haul ass back to Alabama. The scam had worked flawlessly against victims of Hurricane Hugo in South Carolina, and Gil Peck was confident it would work in Miami, too.

He arrived in a four-ton flatbed carrying a small but authentic-looking load of red bricks, which he'd ripped off from an unguarded construction site in Mobile—a new cancer wing for a pediatric hospital. Gil Peck had caught the festive groundbreaking on TV. That afternoon he'd backed up the flatbed, helped himself to the bricks and driven nonstop to South Florida.

So far, business was booming. Gil Peck had collected almost twenty-six hundred dollars in cash from half a dozen desperate home owners, all of whom expected him to return the following Saturday morning with his truckload of bricks. By then, of course, Gil Peck would be northbound and gone.

By day he worked the hustle, by night he scavenged hurricane debris. The big flatbed conveyed an air of authority, and no one questioned its presence. Even after curfew, the National Guardsmen waved him through the flashing barricades.

Many valuables had survived the storm's thrashing, and Gil Peck became an expert at mining rubble. An inventory of his two-day bounty included: a bagel toaster, a Stairmaster, a silver tea set, three offbrand assault rifles, a Panasonic cellular telephone, two pairs of men's golf spikes, a waterproof kilogram package of hashish, a brass chandelier, a scuba tank, a gold class ring from the University of Miami (1979), a set of police handcuffs, a collection of rare Finnish pornography, a Michael Jackson hand puppet, an unopened bottle of 100-milligram Darvocets, a boxed set of Willie Nelson albums, a Loomis fly rod, a birdcage and twenty-one pairs of women's bikini-style panties.

Exploring the demolished remains of a mobile-home park, Gil Peck was a happy fellow. There was a bounce to his step as he followed the yellow beam of the flashlight from one ruin to another. Thanks to the Guard, the Highway Patrol and the Dade County police, Gil Peck was completely alone and unmolested in the summer night; free to plunder.

And what he spied in the middle of a shuffleboard court made his greedy heart flutter with joy: a jumbo TV dish. The hurricane undoubtedly had uprooted it from some millionaire's estate and tossed it here, for Gil Peck to salvage. With the flashlight he traced the outer parabola and found one small dent. Otherwise the eight-foot satellite receiver was in top condition.

Gil Peck grinned and thought: Man, I must be living right. A dish that big was worth a couple-grand, easy. Gil Peck thought it might fit nicely in his own backyard, behind the chicken coops. He envisioned free HBO for the rest of his natural life.

He walked around to the other side to make sure there was no additional damage. He was shocked by what his flashlight revealed: Inside the TV dish was a dead man, splayed and mounted like a butterfly.

The dead man was impaled on the cone of the receiver pipe, but it wasn't the evil work of the hurricane. His hands and feet had been meticulously bound to the gridwork in a pose of crucifixion. The dead man himself was obese and balding, and bore no resemblance to the Jesus Christ of Gil Peck's strict Baptist upbringing. Nonetheless, the sight unnerved the bogus mason to the point of whimpering.

He switched off the flashlight and sat on the shuffleboard court to steady himself. Stealing the TV saucer obviously was out of the question; Gil Peck was working up the nerve to swipe the expensive watch he'd spotted on the crucified guy's left wrist.

Except for kissing his grandmother in her casket, Gil Peck had never touched a corpse before. Thank God, he thought, the guy's eyes are closed. Gingerly Gil Peck climbed into the satellite dish, which rocked under the added weight. Holding the flashlight in his mouth, he aimed the beam at the dead man's gold Cartier.

The clasp on the watchband was a bitch. Rigor mortis contributed to the difficulty of Gil Peck's task; the crucified guy refused to surrender the timepiece. The more Gil Peck struggled with the corpse, the more the TV saucer rolled back and forth on its axis, like a top. Gil Peck was getting dizzy and mad. Just as he managed to slip a penknife between the taut skin and the watchband, the dead man expelled an audible blast of postmortem flatulence. The detonation sent Gil Peck diving in terror from the satellite dish.

Edie Marsh paid a neighbor kid to siphon gas from Snapper's abandoned car and crank up Tony Torres's portable generator. Edie gave the kid a five-dollar bill that she'd found hidden with five others inside a toolbox in the salesman's garage. It was a pitiful excuse for a stash; Edie was sure there had to be more.

At dusk she gave up the search and planted herself in Tony's BarcaLounger, a crowbar at her side. She turned up the volume of the television as loudly as she could stand, to block out the rustles and whispers of the night. Without doors, windows or a roof, the Torres house was basically an open campsite. Outside was black and creepy; people wandered like spirits through the unlit streets. Edie Marsh had the jitters, being alone. She gladly would have fled in Tony's huge boat of a Chevrolet, if it hadn't been blocked in the driveway by Snapper's car, which Edie would have gladly swiped if only Snapper hadn't taken the damn keys with him. So she was stuck at the Torres house until daybreak, when it might be safe for a woman to travel on foot with two miniature dachshunds.

She planned to get out of Dade County before anything else went wrong. The expedition was a disaster, and Edie blamed no one but herself. Nothing in her modest criminal past had prepared her for the hazy and menacing vibe of the hurricane zone. Everyone was on edge; evil, violence and paranoia ripened in the shadows. Edie Marsh was out of her league here. Tomorrow she'd hitch a ride to West Palm and close up the apartment. Then she'd take the Amtrak home to Jacksonville, and try to make up with her boyfriend. She estimated that reconciliation would require at least a week's worth of blow jobs, considering how much she'd stolen from his checking account. But eventually he'd take her back. They always did.

Edie Marsh was suffering through a TV quiz show when she heard a man's voice calling from the front doorway. She thought: Tony! The pig is back.

She grabbed the crowbar and sprung from the chair. The man at the door raised his arms. 'Easy,' he said.

It wasn't Tony Torres. This person was a slender blond with round eyeglasses and a tan briefcase and matching Hush Puppy shoes. In one hand he carried a manila file folder.

'What do you want?' Edie held the crowbar casually, as if she carried it at all times.

'Didn't mean to scare you,' the man said. 'My name is Fred Dove. I'm with Midwest Casualty.'

'Oh.' Edie Marsh felt a pleasant tingle. Like the first time she'd met one of the young Kennedys.

With a glance at the file, Fred Dove said, 'Maybe I've got the wrong street. This is 15600 Calusa?'

'That's correct.'

'And you're Mrs Torres?'

Edie smiled. 'Please,' she said, 'call me Neria.'

8

Bonnie and Augustine were cutting a pizza when Augustine's FBI friend stopped by to pick up the tape of Max Lamb's latest message. He listened to it several times on the cassette player in Augustine's living room. Bonnie studied the FBI man's expression, which remained intently neutral. She supposed it was something they worked on at the academy.

When he finished playing the tape, the FBI agent turned to Augustine and said, 'I've read it somewhere. That "creaking machinery of humanity."'

'Me, too. I've been racking my brain.'

'God, I can just see 'em up in Washington, giving it to a crack team of shrinks—'

'Or cryptographers,' Augustine said.

The FBI man smiled. 'Exactly.' He accepted a hot slice of pepperoni for the road, and said good night.

Augustine asked Bonnie a question at which the agent had only hinted: Was it conceivable that Max Lamb could have written something like that himself?

'Never,' she said. Her husband was into ditties and jingles, not metaphysics. 'And he doesn't read much,' she added. 'The last book he finished was one of Trump's autobiographies.'

It was enough to convince Augustine that Max Lamb wasn't being coy on the phone; the mystery man was feeding him lines. Augustine didn't know why. The situation was exceedingly strange.

Bonnie took a shower. She came out wearing a baby-blue flannel nightshirt that Augustine recognized from a long-ago relationship. Bonnie had found it hanging in a closet.

'Is there a story to go with it?' she asked.

'A torrid one.'

'Really?' Bonnie sat beside him on the sofa, at a purely friendly distance. 'Let me guess: Flight attendant?'

Augustine said, 'Letterman's a rerun.'

'Cocktail waitress? Fashion model?'

'I'm beat.' Augustine picked up a book, a biography of Lech Wałesa, and flipped it open to the middle.

'Aerobics instructor? Legal secretary?'

'Surgical intern,' Augustine said. 'She tried to cut out my kidneys one night in the shower.'

'That's the scar on your back? The Y.'

'At least she wasn't a urologist.' He closed the book and picked up the channel changer for the television.

Bonnie said, 'You cheated on her.'

'Nope, but she thought I did. She also thought the bathtub was full of centipedes, Cuban spies were spiking her lemonade, and Richard Nixon was working the night shift at the Farm Store on Bird Road.'

'Drug problem?'

'Evidently.' Augustine found a Dodgers game on ESPN and tried to appear engrossed.

Bonnie Lamb asked to see the scar closely, but he declined. 'The lady had poor technique,' he said.

'She use a real scalpel?'

'No, a corkscrew.'

'My God.'

'What is it with women and scars?'

Bonnie said, 'I knew it. You've been asked before.'

Was she flirting? Augustine wasn't sure. He had no point of reference when it came to married women whose husbands recently had disappeared.

'How's this,' he said. 'You tell me all about your husband, and maybe I'll show you the damn scar.'

'Deal,' said Bonnie Lamb, tugging the nightshirt down to cover her knees.

*

Max Lamb met and fell in love with Bonnie Brooks when she was an assistant publicist for Crespo Mills Internationale, a leading producer of snack and breakfast foods. Rodale & Burns had won the lucrative Crespo advertising account, and assigned Max Lamb to develop the print and radio campaign for a new cereal called Plum Crunchies. Bonnie Brooks flew in from Crespo's Chicago headquarters to consult.

Basically, Plum Crunchies were ordinary sugar-coated corn-flakes mixed with rock-hard fragments of dried plums—that is to say, prunes. The word 'prune' was not to appear in any Plum Crunchies publicity or advertising, a corporate edict with which both Max Lamb and Bonnie Brooks wholeheartedly agreed. The target demographic was sweet-toothed youngsters aged fourteen and under, not constipated senior citizens.

On only their second date, at a Pakistani restaurant in Green-wich Village, Max sprung upon Bonnie his slogan for Crespo's new cereal: *You'll go plum loco for Plum Crunchies!*

'With p-l-u-m instead of p-l-u-m-b on the first reference,' he was quick to explain.

Though she personally avoided the use of lame homonyms, Bonnie told Max the slogan had possibilities. She was trying not to dampen his enthusiasm; besides, he was the expert, the creative talent. All she did was bang out press releases.

On a napkin Max Lamb crudely sketched a jaunty, cockeyed mynah bird that was to be the cereal-box mascot for Plum Crunchies. Max said the bird would be colored purple ('like a plum!') and would be named Dinah the Mynah. Here Bonnie Brooks felt she should speak up, as a colleague, to remind Max Lamb of the many other cereals that already used bird logos (Froot Loops, Cocoa Puffs, Kellogg's Corn Flakes, and so on). In addition, she gently questioned the wisdom of naming the mynah bird after an aging, though much-beloved, TV singer.

Bonnie: 'Is the bird supposed to be a woman?'

Max: 'The bird has no particular gender.'

Bonnie: 'Well, do mynahs actually eat plums?'

Max: 'You're adorable, you know that?'

He was falling for her, and she was falling (though a bit less precipitously) for him. As it turned out, Max's bosses at Rodale & Burns liked his slogan but hated the concept of Dinah the Mynah. The executives of Crespo Mills concurred. When the new cereal finally debuted, the box featured a likeness of basketball legend Patrick Ewing, slam-dunking a giddy cartoon plum. Surveys later revealed that many customers thought it was either an oversized grape or a prune. Plum Crunchies failed to capture a significant share of the fruited-branflake breakfast market and quietly disappeared forever from the shelves.

Bonnie and Max's long-distance romance endured. She found herself carried along by his energy, determination and self-confidence, misplaced as it often was. While Bonnie was bothered by Max's tendency to judge humankind strictly according to age, race, sex and median income, she attributed his cold eye to indoctrination by the advertising business. She herself had become cynical about the brain activity of the average consumer, given Crespo's worldwide success with such dubious food products as salted doughballs, whipped olive spread and shrimp-flavored popcorn.

In the early months of courtship, Max invented a game intended to impress Bonnie Brooks. He bet that he could guess precisely what model of automobile a person owned, based on his or her demeanor, wardrobe and physical appearance. The skill was intuitive, Max told Bonnie; a gift. He said it's what made him such a canny advertising pro. On dates, he'd sometimes follow strangers out of restaurants or movie theaters to see what they were driving. 'Ha! A Lumina—what'd I tell ya? The guy had midsize written all over him!' Max would chirp when his guess was correct (which was, by Bonnie's generous reckoning, about five percent of the time). Before long, the car game grew tiresome and Bonnie Brooks asked Max Lamb to stop. He didn't take it personally; he was a hard man to insult. This, too, Bonnie attributed to the severe environment of Madison Avenue.

While Bonnie's father was amiably indifferent to Max, her mother was openly unfond of him. She felt he tried too hard, came on too strong; that he was trying to sell himself to Bonnie the same way he sold breakfast cereal and cigarets. It wasn't that

Bonnie's mother thought Max Lamb was a phony; just the opposite. She believed he was exactly what he seemed to be—completely goal-driven, every waking moment. He was no different at home than he was at the office, no less consumed with attaining success. There was, said Bonnie's mother, a sneaky arrogance in Max Lamb's winning attitude. Bonnie thought it was an odd criticism, coming from a woman who had regarded Bonnie's previous boyfriends as timid, unmotivated losers. Still, her mother had never used the term 'asshole' to describe Bonnie's other suitors. That she pinned it so quickly on Max Lamb nagged painfully at Bonnie until her wedding day.

Now, with Max apparently abducted by a raving madman, Bonnie fretted about something else her mother had often mentioned, a trait of Max's so obvious that even Bonnie had acknowledged it. Augustine knew what she was talking about.

'Your husband thinks he can outsmart anybody.'

'Unfortunately,' Bonnie said.

'I can tell from the phone tapes.'

'Well,' she said, fishing for encouragement, 'he's managed to make it so far.'

'Maybe he's learned when to keep his mouth shut.' Augustine stood up and stretched his arms. 'I'm tired. Can we do the scar thing some other time?'

Bonnie Lamb laughed and said sure. She waited until she heard the bedroom door shut before she phoned Pete Archibald at his home in Connecticut.

'Did I wake you?' she asked.

'Heck, no. Max said you might be calling.'

Bonnie's words stuck in her throat. 'You—Pete, you talked to him?'

'For about an hour.'

'When?'

'Tonight. He's all frantic that Bill Knapp's gonna snake the Bronco cigaret account. I told him not to worry, Billy's tied up with the smokeless division on some stupid rodeo tour—'

'Pete, never mind all that. Where did Max call from?'

'I don't know, Bon. I assumed he'd spoken to you.'

Bonnie strained to keep the hurt from her voice. 'Did he tell you what happened?'

On the other end, Pete Archibald clucked and ummmed nervously. 'Not all the gory details, Bonnie. Everybody—least all the couples I know—go through the occasional bedroom drama. Fights and whatnot. I don't blame you for not giving me the real story when you called before.'

Bonnie Lamb's voice rose. 'Peter, Max and I aren't fighting. And I *did* tell you the real story.' She caught herself. 'At least it was the story Max told me.'

After an uncomfortable pause, Pete Archibald said, 'Bon, you guys work it out, OK? I don't want to get in the middle.'

'You're right, you're absolutely right.' She noticed that her free hand was balled in a fist and she was rocking sideways in the chair. 'Pete, I won't keep you. But maybe you could tell me what else Max said.'

'Shop talk, Bonnie.'

'For a whole hour?'

'Well, you know your husband. He gets rolling, you know what he's like.'

Maybe I don't, Bonnie thought.

She said good-bye to Pete Archibald and hung up. Then she went to Augustine's room and knocked on the door. When he didn't answer, she slipped in and sat lightly on the corner of the bed. She thought he was asleep, until he rolled over and said: 'Not a good night for the skull room, huh?'

Bonnie Lamb shook her head and began to cry.

Edie Marsh gave it her best shot. For a while, the plan went smoothly. The man from Midwest Casualty took meticulous notes as he followed her from room to room in the Torres house. Many of the couple's belongings had been pulverized beyond recognition, so Edie began embellishing losses to inflate the claim. She lovingly described the splintered remains of a china cabinet as a priceless antique that Tony inherited from a great-grandmother in San Juan. Pausing before a bare bedroom wall, she pointed to the nails upon which once hung two original (and very expensive) watercolors by the legendary Jean-Claude Jarou, a martyred Haitian artist whom Edie invented off the top of her head. A splintered bedroom bureau became the hand-hewn mahogany vault that had yielded eight cashmere sweaters to the merciless winds of the hurricane.

'Eight sweaters,' said Fred Dove, glancing up from his clip-board. 'In Miami?'

'The finest Scottish cashmeres—can you imagine? Ask your wife if it wouldn't break her heart.'

Fred Dove took a small flashlight from his jacket and went outside to evaluate structural damage. Soon Edie heard barking from the backyard, followed by emphatic human profanities. By the time she got there, both dachshunds had gotten a piece of the insurance man. Edie led him inside, put him in the Barca-Lounger, rolled up his cuffs and tended his bloody ankles with Evian and Ivory liquid, which she salvaged from the kitchen.

'I'm glad they're not rottweilers,' said Fred Dove, soothed by Edie's ministrations with a soft towel.

Repeatedly she apologized for the attack. 'For what it's worth, they've had all their shots,' she said, with no supporting evidence whatsoever.

She instructed Fred Dove to stay in the recliner and keep his feet elevated, to slow the bleeding. Leaning back, he spotted Tony Torres's Salesman of the Year plaque on the wall. 'Pretty impressive,' Fred Dove said.

'Yes, it was quite a big day for us.' Edie beamed, a game simulation of spousely pride.

'And where's Mister Torres tonight?'

Out of town, Edie replied, at a mobile-home convention in Dallas. For the second time, Fred Dove looked doubtful.

'Even with the hurricane? Must be a pretty important convention.'

'It sure is,' said Edie Marsh. 'He's getting another award.'

'Ah.'

'So he *had* to go. I mean, it'd look bad if he didn't show up. Like he wasn't grateful or something.'

Fred Dove said, 'I suppose so. When will Mister Torres be returning to Miami?'

Edie sighed theatrically. 'I just don't know. Soon, I hope.'

The insurance man attempted to lower the recliner, but it kept springing to the sleep position. Finally Edie Marsh sat on the footrest, enabling Fred Dove to climb out. He said he wanted to reinspect the damage to the master bedroom. Edie said that was fine.

She was rinsing the bloody towel in a sink when the insurance man called. She hurried to the bedroom, where Fred Dove held up a framed photograph that he'd dug from the storm rubble. It was a picture of Tony Torres with a large dead fish. The fish had a mouth the size of a garbage pail.

'That's Tony on the left,' Edie said with a dry, edgy laugh.

'Nice grouper. Where'd he catch it?'

'The ocean.' Where else? thought Edie.

'And who's this?' The insurance man retrieved another frame off the floor. The glass was cracked, and the picture was puckered from storm water. It was a color nine-by-twelve, mounted inside gold filigree: Tony Torres with his arm around the waist of a petite but heavy-breasted Latin woman. Both of them wore loopy champagne smiles.

'His sister Maria,' Edie blurted, sensing the game was about to end.

'She's in a wedding gown,' Fred Dove remarked, with no trace of sarcasm. 'And Mister Torres is wearing a black tuxedo and tails.'

Edie said, 'He was the best man.'

'Really? His hand is on her bottom.'

'They're very close,' said Edie, 'for a brother and sister.' The words trailed off in defeat.

Fred Dove's shoulders stiffened, and his tone chilled. 'Do you happen to have some identification? A driver's license would be good. Anything with a current photograph.'

Edie Marsh said nothing. She feared compounding one felony with another.

'Let me guess,' said the insurance man. 'All your personal papers were lost in the hurricane.'

Edie bowed her head, thinking: This can't be happening again. One of these days I've got to catch a break. She said, 'Shit.'

'Pardon?'

'I said "shit." Meaning, I give up.' Edie couldn't believe it—a fucking *wedding* picture! Tony and the unfaithful witch he planned to rip off for half the hurricane money. Too bad Snapper bolted, she thought, because this was ten times better than Sally Jessy.

'Who are you?' Fred Dove was stern and official.

'Look, what happens now?'

'I'll tell you exactly what happens—'

At that moment, the electric generator ran out of gasoline, dying with a feeble series of burps. The lightbulb went dim and the television went black. The house at 15600 Calusa became suddenly as quiet as a chapel. The only sound was a faint jingle from the backyard, where the two dachshunds squirmed to pull free of their leashes.

In the darkness, Fred Dove reached for his flashlight. Edie Marsh intercepted his wrist and held on to it. She decided there was nothing to lose by trying.

'What are you doing?' the insurance man asked.

Edie brought his hand to her mouth. 'What's it worth to you?'

Fred Dove stood as still as a statue.

'Come on,' Edie said, her tongue brushing his knuckles, 'what's it worth?'

The insurance man, in a shaky whisper: 'What's *what* worth—not calling the police? Is that what you mean?'

Edie was smiling. Fred Dove could tell by the feel of her lips and teeth against his hand.

'What's this house insured for?' she asked.

'Why?'

'One twenty? One thirty?'

'One forty-one,' said Fred Dove, thinking: Her breath is so *unbelievably* soft.

Edie switched to her sex-kitten voice, the one that had failed to galvanize the young Palm Beach Kennedy. 'One forty-one? You sure, Mister Dove?'

'The structure, yes. Because of the swimming pool.'

'Of course.' She pressed closer, wishing she weren't wearing a bra but suspecting it didn't much matter. Poor Freddie's brakes were already smoking. She feathered her eyelashes against his neck and felt him bury his face in her hair.

The insurance man labored to speak. 'What is it you want?'

'A partner,' Edie Marsh replied, sealing the agreement with a long blind kiss.

Sergeant Cain Darby took his weekends with the National Guard as seriously as he took his regular job as a maximum-security-prison guard. Although he would have preferred to remain in Starke with the armed robbers and serial killers, duty called Cain Darby to South Florida on the day after the hurricane struck. Commanding Darby's National Guard unit was the night manager of a Days Inn, who sternly instructed the troops not to fire their weapons unless fired upon themselves. From what Cain Darby knew of Miami, this scenario seemed not entirely improbable. Nonetheless, he understood that a Guardsman's chief mission was to maintain order in the streets, assist needy civilians and prevent looting.

The unit's first afternoon was spent erecting tents for the homeless and unloading heavy drums of fresh drinking water from the back of a Red Cross trailer. After supper, Cain Darby was posted to a curfew checkpoint on Quail Roost Drive, not far from the Florida Turnpike. Darby and another Guardsman, the foreman of a paper mill, took turns stopping the cars and trucks. Most drivers had good excuses for being on the road after curfew—some were searching for missing relatives, others were on their way to a hospital, and still others were simply lost in a place they no longer recognized. If questions arose about a driver's alibi, the paper-mill foreman deferred judgment to Sergeant Darby, due to his law-enforcement experience. Common violators were

TV crews, sightseers, and teenagers who had come to steal. These cars Cain Darby interdicted and sent away, to the Turnpike ramp.

At midnight the paper-mill foreman returned to camp, leaving Sergeant Darby alone at the barricade. He dozed for what must have been two hours, until he was startled awake by loud snorting. Blearily he saw the shape of a large bear no more than thirty yards away, at the edge of a pine glade. Or maybe it was just a freak shadow, for it looked nothing like the chubby black bears that Cain Darby routinely poached from the Ocala National Forest. The thing that he now *thought* he was seeing stood seven feet at the shoulders.

Cain Darby closed his eyes tightly to clear the sleep. Then he opened them again, very slowly. The huge shape was still there, a motionless phantasm. Common sense told him he was mistaken—they don't grow thousand-pound bears in Florida! But that's sure what it looked like. . . .

So he raised his rifle.

Then, from the corner of his eye, he spotted headlights barreling down Quail Roost Drive. He turned to see. Somebody was driving toward the roadblock like a bat out of hell. Judging by the rising chorus of sirens, half the Metro police force was on the chase.

When Cain Darby spun back toward the bear, or the shape that *looked* like a bear, it was gone. He lowered the gun and directed his attention to the maniac in the oncoming truck. Cain Darby struck an erect military pose in front of the candy-striped barricades—spine straight, legs apart, the rifle held at a ready angle across the chest.

A half mile behind the truck was a stream of flashing blue and red lights. The fugitive driver seemed undaunted. As the headlights drew closer, Sergeant Darby hurriedly weighed his options. The asshole wasn't going to stop, that much was clear. By now the man had (unless he was blind, drunk or both) seen the soldier standing in his path.

Yet the vehicle was not decelerating. If anything, it was gaining speed. Cain Darby cursed as he dashed out of the way. If there was one thing he found intolerable, it was disrespect for a uniform, whether it belonged to the Department of Corrections or the National Guard. So he indignantly cranked off a few rounds as the idiot driver smashed through the barricade.

No one was more stunned than Cain Darby to see the speeding truck overshoot the Turnpike ramp and plunge full speed into a drainage canal; no one except the driver, Gil Peck. The sound of gunfire had destroyed his ragged reflexes, particularly his ability to locate the brake pedal. He couldn't believe some peckerwood Guardsman was shooting at him.

What did not surprise Gil Peck, considering his heavy cargo of stolen bricks, was how swiftly the flatbed sunk in the warm brown water. He squeezed through the window, swam to shore and began weeping at his own foul luck. All his hurricane booty was lost, except for the package of hash, which bobbed to the surface at the precise moment the first police car arrived.

Yet the drugs weren't the most serious of Gil Peck's legal concerns. As he was being handcuffed, he declared: 'I didn't kill him!'

'Kill who?' the officer asked.

'The guy, you know. The guy at the trailer park.' Gil Peck assumed that's why the cops were chasing him—they'd found the body of the crucified man.

But they hadn't. Gil Peck's nausea worsened. He should've kept his damn mouth shut. Now it was too late. Pink and blue bikini panties began to float up, like pale jellyfish, from the bed of the sunken truck.

The officer said: 'What guy at what trailer park?'

Gil Peck told him about the dead man impaled in the TV dish. As other policemen arrived, Gil Peck repeated the story, and also his impassioned denials of guilt. One of the officers asked Gil Peck if he would take them to the body, and he agreed.

After the paramedics checked him for broken bones, the thief was toweled off and deposited in the back-seat cage of a Highway Patrol car. The trooper at the wheel was a large black man in a Stetson. On the way to the trailer court, Gil Peck delivered yet another excited monologue about his innocence.

'If you didn't do it,' the trooper cut in, 'why'd you run?'

'Scared, man.' Gil Peck shivered. 'You should see.'

'Oh, I can't wait,' the trooper said.

'You a Christian, sir?'

It was amazing, thought the trooper, how quickly the handcuffs induced spiritual devoutness. 'Anyone read you your rights?' he asked the truck driver.

Gil Peck thrust his face to the mesh of the cage. 'If you're a Christian, you gotta believe what I'm sayin". It wasn't me that crucified the poor fucker.'

But Jim Tile hoped with all his Christian heart that it was. Because the other prime suspect was someone he didn't want to arrest, unless there was no choice.

9

Skink eavesdropped leisurely while Max Lamb made two calls. The phone booth was at a truck stop on Krome Avenue, the fringe of the Everglades. Longbeds overloaded with lumber, sheet glass and tar paper streamed south in ragged convoys to the hurricane zone. Nobody glanced twice at the unshaven man on the phone, despite the collar around his neck.

When Max Lamb hung up, Skink grabbed his arm and led him to the airboat, beached on the bank of a muddy canal. Skink ordered him to lie in the bow, and there he remained for two hours, his cheekbone vibrating against the hull. The howl of the aviation engine filled his ears. Skink was no longer singing harmony. Max Lamb wondered what he'd done to further annoy his abductor.

They stopped once. Skink left the airboat briefly and returned with a large cardboard box, which he set in the bow next to Max. They traveled until dusk. When Skink finally lifted him to his knees, Max was surprised to see the Indian village. They didn't stay long enough for Max to negotiate the return of his video camera. Skink borrowed a station wagon, put the box in the back, and buckled his prisoner on the passenger side. There was no sign of the monkey, and for that Max Lamb was grateful.

Skink put on the shower cap and started the car. Max needed to pee but was afraid to ask. He was no longer confident that he could talk his way out of the kidnapping.

'Is something wrong?' he asked.

Skink shot him a stony look. 'I remember your wife from the hurricane video. Hugging two little Cuban girls.'

'Yes, that was Bonnie.'

'Beautiful woman. You zoomed in on her face.'

'Can we stop the car,' Max interrupted, squirming, 'just for a minute?'

Skink kept his eyes on the road. 'Your bride's got a good heart. That much is obvious from the video.'

'A saint,' Max agreed. He jammed both hands between his legs; he'd tie his dick in a Windsor before he'd wet himself in front of the governor.

'Why she's with you, I can't figure. It's a real puzzler,' Skink said. He braked the car sharply. 'Why didn't you try to phone her tonight? You call your buddy in New York. You call your folks in Milan-fucking-Italy. Why not Bonnie?'

'I don't know where she is. That damn answering machine—'

'And the crap about you and her having a fight—'

'I didn't want Peter to worry,' Max said.

'Well, God forbid.' Skink jammed the transmission into Park and flung himself out the door. He reappeared in the beam of the headlights, a hoary apparition crouched on the pavement. Max Lamb craned to see what he was doing.

Skink strolled back to the station wagon and tossed a dead opossum on the seat next to Max, who gasped and recoiled. A few miles later, Skink added a truck-flattened coachwhip snake to the evening's menu. Max forgot about his bladder until they made camp at an abandoned horse barn west of Krome.

The horses were gone, scattered by the storm; the owners had come by to retrieve the saddles and tack, and to scatter feed in case any of the animals returned. Max Lamb stood alone in the musky darkness and relieved himself torrentially. He considered running, but feared he wouldn't survive a single night alone in nature. In Max's mind, all Florida south of Orlando was an immense swamp, humidly teeming with feral beasts. Some had claws and poisonous fangs, some drove airboats and feasted on roadkill. They were all the same to Max.

Skink appeared at his side to announce that dinner soon would be served. Max followed him into the stables. He asked if it was wise to make a campfire inside a barn. Skink replied that it was extremely dangerous, but cozy.

Max Lamb was impressed that the odor of horseshit could not

be vanquished by a mere Force Four hurricane. On a positive note, the fragrance of dung completely neutralized the aroma of boiled opossum and pan-fried snake. After supper Skink stripped to his boxer shorts and did two hundred sit-ups in a cloud of ancient manure dust. Then he retrieved the large cardboard box from the car and brought it inside the barn. He asked Max if he wanted a cigaret.

'No, thanks,' Max said. 'I don't smoke.'

'You're kidding.'

'Never have,' Max said.

'But you sell the stuff—'

'We do the advertising. That's it.'

'Ah,' Skink said. 'Just the advertising.' He picked his trousers off the floor and went through the pockets. Max Lamb thought he was looking for matches, but he wasn't. He was looking for the remote control to the shock collar.

When Max regained his senses, he lay in wet moldering hay. His eyeballs were jumping in their sockets, and his neck felt tingly and hot. He sat up and said, 'What'd I do?'

'Surely you believe in the products you advertise.'

'Look, I don't smoke.'

'You could learn.' With a pocketknife, Skink opened the cardboard box. The box was full of Bronco cigarets, probably four dozen cartons. Max Lamb failed to conceal his alarm.

The kidnapper asked how he could be sure of a product until he tested it himself. Grimly Max responded: 'I also do the ads for raspberry-scented douche, but I don't use the stuff.'

'Careful,' said Skink, brightly, 'or you'll give me another brainstorm.' He opened a pack of Broncos. He tapped one out and inserted it between Max's lips. He struck a match on the wall of the barn and lit the cigaret.

'Well?'

Max spit out the cigaret. 'This is ridiculous.'

Skink retrieved the soggy Bronco and replaced it in Max's frowning mouth. 'You got two choices,' he said, fingering the remote control, 'smoke or be smoked.'

Reluctantly Max Lamb took a drag on the cigaret. Immediately he began to cough. It worsened as Skink tied him upright to a post. 'You people are a riddle to me, Max. Why you come down here. Why you act the way you do. Why you live such lives.'

'For God's sake—'

'Shut up now. Please.'

Skink dug through the backpack and took out a Walkman. He chose a damp corner of the barn and put on the headphones. He lighted what appeared to be a joint, except it didn't smell like marijuana.

'What's that?'Max asked.

'Toad.' Skink took a hit. After a few minutes, his good eye rolled back in his head and his neck went limp.

Max Lamb went through the Broncos like a machine. Whenever Skink opened an eye, he tapped a finger to his neck—a menacing reminder of the shock collar. Max smoked and smoked. He was finishing number twenty-three when Skink shook out of the stupor and rose.

'Damn good toad.' He plucked the Bronco from Max's mouth.

'I feel sick, captain.'

Skink untied him and told him to rest up. 'Tomorrow you're going to leave a message for your wife. You're going to arrange a meeting.'

'What for?'

'So I can observe the two of you together. The chemistry, the starry eyes, all that shit. OK?'

Skink went outside and crawled under the station wagon, where he curled up and began to snore. Max coughed himself to sleep in the barn.

Bonnie Lamb awoke in Augustine's arms. Her guilt was diluted by the observation that he was wearing jeans and a T-shirt. She didn't remember him dressing during the night, but obviously he had. She was reasonably sure that no sex had occurred; plenty of tears, yes, but no sex.

Bonnie wanted to pull away without waking him. Otherwise there might be an awkward moment, the two of them lying there embraced. Or maybe not. Maybe he'd know exactly what not to say. Clearly he was experienced with crying women, because he was exceptionally good at hugging and whispering. When she found herself thinking about how nice he smelled, Bonnie knew it was time to sneak out of bed.

As she'd hoped, Augustine had the good manners to pretend to stay asleep until she was safely in the kitchen, making coffee.

When he walked in, she felt herself blush. 'I'm so sorry,' she blurted, 'for last night.'

'Why? Did you take advantage of me?' He went to the refrigerator and took out a carton of eggs. 'I'm a heavy sleeper,' he said. 'Easy prey for sex-crazed babes.'

'Especially newlyweds.'

'Oh, they're the worst,' said Augustine. 'Ravenous harlots. You want scrambled or fried?'

'Fried.' She sat at the table. She tore open a packet of Nutra-Sweet and managed to miss the coffee cup entirely. 'Please believe me. I don't usually sleep with strange men.'

'Sleeping is fine. It's the screwing you want to watch out for.' He was peeling an orange at the sink. 'Relax, OK? Nothing happened.'

Bonnie smiled. 'Can I at least say thanks, for being a friend.'

'You're very welcome, Mrs Lamb.' He glanced over his shoulder. 'What's so funny?'

'The jeans.'

'Don't tell me there's a hole.'

'No. It's just—well, you got up in the middle of the night to put them on. It was a sweet gesture.'

'Actually, it was more of a precaution.' The eggs sizzled when Augustine dropped them into the hot pan. 'I'm surprised you even noticed,' he said, causing Bonnie to redden once more.

In the middle of breakfast, the phone rang. It was the Medical Examiner's Office—another John Doe was being hauled to the county morgue. The coroner on duty wanted Bonnie to stop by for a look. Augustine said she'd call him back. He put the phone down and told her.

'Can they make me go?'

'I don't think so.'

'Because it's not Max,' Bonnie said. 'Max is too busy talking to Rodale and Burns.'

'A white male is all they said. Apparent homicide.'

The last word hung in the air like sulfur. Bonnie put down her fork. 'It can't be him.'

'Probably not,' Augustine agreed. 'We don't have to go.'

She got up and went to the bathroom. Soon Augustine heard the shower running. He was washing the dishes when she came out. She was dressed. Her wet hair was brushed back, and she'd found the intern's rose lipstick in the medicine chest.

'I guess I need to be sure,' she said.

Augustine nodded. 'You'll feel better.'

Snapper's real name was Lester Maddox Parsons. His mother named him after a Georgia politician best known for scaring off black restaurant customers with an ax handle. Snapper's mother believed Lester Maddox should be President of the United States and the whole white world; Snapper's father leaned toward James Earl Ray. When Snapper was barely seven years old, his parents took him to his first Ku Klux Klan rally; for the occasion, Mrs Parsons dressed her son in a costume sewn from white muslin pillowcases; she was especially proud of the pointy little hood. The other Klansmen and their wives fawned over Lester, remarking on the youngster's handsome Southern features—baffling praise, because all that was visible of young Lester were his beady brown eyes, peeping through the slits of his sheet. He thought: I could be a Negro, for all they know!

Still, the boy enjoyed Klan rallies because there was great barbecue and towering bonfires. He was disappointed when his family stopped attending, but he couldn't argue with his parents' reason for quitting. They referred to it as The Accident, and Lester would never forget the night. His father had gotten customarily shitfaced and, when the climactic moment came to light the cross, accidentally ignited the local Grand Kleagle instead. In the absence of a fire hose, the frantic Klansmen were forced to save their blazing comrade by spritzing him with well-shaken cans of Schlitz beer. Once the fire was extinguished, they placed the charred Kleagle in the bed of Lester's father's pickup and drove to the hospital. Although the man survived, his precious anonymity was lost forever. A local television crew happened to be outside the emergency room when the Kleagle— hoodless, his sheet in scorched tatters—arrived. Once his involvement in the Klan was exposed on TV, the man resigned as district attorney and moved upstate to Macon. Lester's father blamed himself, a sentiment echoed in harsher terms by the other Klansmen. Morale in the local chapter further deteriorated when a newspaper revealed that the young doctor who had revived the dying Kleagle was a black man, possibly from Savannah.

The Parsonses decided to leave the Klan while it was still their choice to do so. Lester's father joined a segregated bowling league, while his mother mailed out flyers for J. B. Stoner, another famous racist who periodically ran for office. Politics bored young Lester, who turned his pubescent energies to crime. He dropped out of school on his fourteenth birthday, although his preoccupied parents didn't find out for nearly two years. By then the boy's income from stealing backhoes and bulldozers was twice his father's income from repairing them. The Parsonses strove not to know what their son was up to, even when it landed him in trouble. Lester's mother worried that the boy had a mean streak; his father said all boys do. Can't get by otherwise in this godforsaken world.

Lester Maddox Parsons was seventeen when he got his nickname. He was hot-wiring a farmer's tractor in a peanut field when a game warden snuck up behind him. Lester dove from the cab and took a punch at the man, who calmly reconfigured Lester's face with the butt of an Ithaca shotgun. He sat in the county jail for three days before a doctor came to examine his jaw, which was approximately thirty-six degrees out of alignment. That it healed at all was a minor miracle; Snapper was spitting out snips of piano wire until he was twenty-two years old.

The Georgia prison system taught the young man an important lesson: It was best to keep one's opinions about race mingling to oneself. So when Avila introduced Snapper to the roofing crew, Snapper noted (but did not complain) that two of the four workers were as black as the tar they'd be mixing. The third roofer was a muscular young *Marielito* with the number '69' tattooed elegantly inside his lower lip. The fourth roofer was a white crackhead from Santa Rosa County who spoke a version of the English language that was utterly incomprehensible to Snapper and the others. Although each of the roofers owned long felony rap sheets, Snapper couldn't say that his feelings toward the crew approached anything close to kinship.

Avila sat the men down for a pep talk.

'Thanks to the hurricane, there's a hundred fifty thousand houses in Dade County need new roofs,' he began. 'Only a damn fool couldn't make money off these poor bastards.'

The plan was to line up the maximum number of buyers and perform the minimum amount of actual roofing. By virtue of owning a suit and tie, Snapper was assigned the task of bullshitting potential customers through the fine print of the 'contract,' then collecting deposits.

'People are fucking desperate for new roofs,' Avila said buoyantly. 'They're getting rained on. Fried from the sun. Eat up by bugs. Faster they get a roof on their heads, the more they'll pay.' He raised his palms to the sky. 'Hey, do they really care about price? It's insurance money, for Christ's sake.'

One of the roofers inquired how much manual labor would be involved. Avila said they should repair a small section on every house. 'To put the people's minds at ease,' he explained.

'What's a "small" section?' the roofer demanded.

Another said, 'It's fucking August out here, boss. I know guys that dropped dead of heatstroke.'

Avila reassured the men they could get by with doing a square, maybe less, on each roof. 'Then you can split. Time they figure out you won't be back, it's too late.'

The crackhead mumbled something about contracting licenses. Avila turned to Snapper and said, 'They ask about our license, you know what to do.'

'Run?'

'Exactamente!'

Snapper wasn't pleased with his door-to-door role in the operation, particularly the odds of encountering large pet dogs. He said to Avila: 'Sounds like too much talking to strangers. I hate that shit. Why don't you do the contracts?'

'Because I inspected some of these goddamn houses when I was with building-and-zoning.'

'The owners don't know that.'

Chango had warned Avila to be careful. Chango was Avila's personal *santería* deity. Avila had thanked him with a turtle and two rabbits.

'I'm keeping low,' Avila told Snapper. 'B-and-Z's got snitches all over the damn county. Somebody recognizes my face, we're screwed.'

Snapper wasn't sure if Avila was paranoid or purely lazy. 'So where will you be exactly,' he said, 'when we're out on a job? Maybe some air-conditioned office.' He heard the roofers snicker, a hopeful sign of solidarity.

But Avila was quick to assert his authority. 'Job? This isn't no "job," it's an act. You boys aren't here 'cause you can mop tar. You're here 'cause you look like you can.'

'What about me?' Snapper goaded. 'How come *I* was hired?'

'Because we couldn't get Robert Redford.' Avila stood up to signal the end of the meeting. 'Snap, why the hell you *think* you got hired? So people would be sure to pay. *Comprende?* One look at that fucked-up face, and they know you mean business.'

Maybe an ordinary criminal would've taken it as a compliment. Snapper did not.

All the mattresses in Tony Torres's house were soaked from the storm, so Edie Marsh had sex with the insurance man on the BarcaLounger. It was a noisy and precarious endeavor. Fred Dove was nervous, so Edie had to assist him each step of the way. Afterwards he said he must've slipped a disk. Edie was tempted to remark that he hadn't moved enough muscles to slip anything; instead she told him he was a stallion in technique and proportion. It was a strategy that seldom failed. Fred Dove contentedly fell asleep with his head on her shoulder and his legs snagged in the footrest, but not before promising to submit a boldly fraudulent damage claim for the Torres house and split the check with Edie Marsh.

An hour before dawn, Edie heard a terrible commotion in the backyard. She couldn't rise to investigate because she was pinned beneath the insurance man in the BarcaLounger. Judging from the tumult outside, Donald and Marla had gone rabid. The confrontation ended in a flurry of plaintive yips and a hair-raising roar. Edie Marsh didn't move until the sun came up. Then she stealthily roused Fred Dove, who panicked because he'd forgotten to phone his wife back in Omaha. Edie told him to hush up and put on his pants.

She led him to the backyard. The only signs of the two miniature dachshunds were limp leashes and empty collars. The Torres lawn was torn to shreds. Several large tracks were visible in the damp gray soil; deep raking tracks, with claws.

Fred Dove's left Hush Puppy fit easily one of the imprints. 'Good Lord,' he said, 'and I wear a ten and a half.'

Edie Marsh asked what kind of wild animal would make such a track. Fred Dove said it looked big enough to be a lion or a bear. 'But I'm not a hunter,' he added.

She said, 'Can I come stay with you?'

'At the Ramada?'

'What—they don't allow women?'

'Edie, we shouldn't be seen together. Not if we're going through with this.'

'You expect me to stay out here alone?'

'Look, I'm sorry about your dogs—'

'They weren't my goddamn dogs.'

'Please, Edie.'

With his round eyeglasses, Fred Dove reminded her of a serious young English teacher she'd known in high school. The man had worn Bass loafers with no socks and was obsessed with T. S. Eliot. Edie Marsh had screwed the guy twice in the faculty lounge, but he'd still given her a C on her final exam because (he claimed) she'd missed the whole point of 'J. Alfred Prufrock.'

The experience had left Edie Marsh with a deep-seated mistrust of studious-looking men.

She said, 'What do you mean, *if* we go through with this? We made a deal.'

'Yes,' Fred Dove said. 'Yes, we did.'

As he followed her into the house, she asked, 'How soon can you get this done?'

'Well, I could file the claim this week—'

'Hundred percent loss?'

'That's right,' replied the insurance man.

'A hundred and forty-one grand. Seventy-one for me, seventy for you.'

'Right.' For somebody about to score the windfall of a life-time, Fred Dove was subdued. 'My concern, again, is Mister Torres—'

'Like I told you last night, Tony's in some kind of serious jam. I doubt he'll be back.'

'But didn't you say Mrs Torres, the real Mrs Torres, might be returning to Miami—'

'That's why you need to hurry,' Edie Marsh said. 'Tell the home office it's an emergency.'

The insurance man pursed his lips. 'Edie, every case is an emergency. There's been a hurricane, for God's sake.'

Impassively, she watched him finish dressing. He spent five full minutes trying to smooth the wrinkles out of his sex-rumpled Dockers. When he asked to borrow an iron, Edie reminded him there was no electricity.

'How about taking me to breakfast,' she said.

'I'm already late for an appointment in Cutler Ridge. Some poor old man's got a Pontiac on top of his house.' Fred Dove kissed Edie on the forehead and followed up with the obligatory morning-after hug. 'I'll be back tonight. Is nine all right?'

'Fine,' she said. Tonight he'd undoubtedly bring condoms— one more comic speed bump on the highway to passion. She made a mental note to haul one of Tony's mattresses out in the sun to dry; another strenuous session in the BarcaLounger might put poor Freddie in traction.

'Bring the claim forms,' she told him. 'I want to see everything.'

He jotted a reminder on his clipboard and slipped it into the briefcase.

'Oh yeah,' Edie said. 'I also need a couple gallons of gas from your car.'

Fred Dove looked puzzled.

'For the generator,' she explained. 'A hot bath would be nice . . . since you won't let me share your tub at the Ramada.'

'Oh, Edie—'

'And maybe a few bucks for groceries.'

She softened up when the insurance man took out his wallet. 'That's my boy.' She kissed him on the neck and ended it with a little bite, just to prime the pump.

'I'm scared,' he said.

'Don't be, sugar. It's a breeze.' She took two twenties and sent him on his way.

10

On the drive to the morgue, Augustine and Bonnie Lamb heard a news report about a fourteen-foot reticulated python that had turned up in the salad bar of a fast-food joint in Perrine.

'One of yours?' Bonnie asked.

'I'm wondering.' It was impossible to know if the snake had belonged to Augustine's dead uncle; Felix Mojack's handwritten inventory was vague on details.

'He had a couple big ones,' Augustine said, 'but I never measured the damn things.'

Bonnie said, 'I hope they didn't kill it.'

'Me, too.' He was pleased that she was concerned for the welfare of a primeval reptile. Not all women would be.

'They could give it to a zoo,' she said.

'Or turn it loose at the county commission.'

'You're bad.'

'I know,' Augustine said. As legal custodian of the menagerie, he felt a twinge of responsibility for Bonnie Lamb's predicament. Without a monkey to chase, her husband probably wouldn't have been abducted. Maybe the culprit was one of Uncle Felix's rhesuses, maybe not.

Without reproach, Bonnie asked: 'What'll you do if one of those critters kills a person?'

'Pray it was somebody who deserved it.'

Bonnie was appalled. Augustine said, 'I don't know what else to do, short of a safari. You know how big the Everglades are?'

They rode in silence for a while before Bonnie said: 'You're right. They're free, and that's how it ought to be.'

'I don't know how anything *ought* to be, but I know how it is. Hell, those cougars could be in Key Largo by now.'

Bonnie Lamb smiled sadly. 'I wish I was.'

Before entering the chill of the Medical Examiner's Office, she put on a baggy ski sweater that Augustine had brought for the occasion. This time there were no preliminaries to the viewing. The same young coroner led them directly to the autopsy room, where the newly murdered John Doe was the center of attention. The corpse was surrounded by detectives, uniformed cops, and an unenthusiastic contingent of University of Miami medical students. They parted for Augustine and Bonnie Lamb.

A ruddy, gray-haired man in a lab coat stood at the head of the steel table. He nodded cordially and took a step back. Holding her breath, Bonnie lowered her eyes to the corpse. The man was potbellied and balding. His olive skin was covered from shoulder to toe with sprouts of shiny black hair. In the center of the chest was a gaping, raspberry-hued wound. His throat was a necklace of bruises that looked very much like purple fingerprints.

'It's not my husband,' Bonnie Lamb said.

Augustine led her away. A tall black policeman followed.

'Mrs Lamb?'

Bonnie, on autopilot, kept moving.

'Mrs Lamb, I need to speak with you.'

She turned. The policeman was broadly muscled and walked with a hitch in his right leg. He wore a state trooper's uniform and held a tan Stetson in his huge hands. He seemed as relieved to be out of the autopsy room as they were.

Augustine asked if there was a problem. The trooper suggested they go someplace to talk.

'About what?' Bonnie asked.

'Your husband's disappearance. I'm running down a few leads, that's all.' The trooper's manner was uncharacteristically informal for a cop in uniform. He said, 'Just a few questions, folks. I promise.'

Augustine didn't understand why the Highway Patrol would take an interest in a missing-person case. He said, 'She's already spoken to the FBI.'

'This won't take long.'

Bonnie said, 'If you've got something new, anything, I'd like to hear about it.'

'I know a great Italian place,' the trooper said.

Augustine saw that Bonnie had made up her mind. 'Is this official business?' he asked the trooper.

'Extremely unofficial.' Jim Tile put on his hat. 'Let's go eat,' he said.

In the mid-1970s, a man named Clinton Tyree ran for governor of Florida. On paper he seemed an ideal candidate, a bold fresh voice in a cynical age. He was a rare native son, handsome, strapping; an ex-college football sensation and a decorated veteran of Vietnam. On the campaign trail, he could talk smart in Palm Beach or play dumb in the Panhandle. The media were dazzled because he spoke in complete sentences, spontaneously and without index cards. Best of all, his private past was uncluttered by slimy business deals, the intricacies of which taxed the comprehension of journalists and readers alike.

Clinton Tyree's only political liability was a five-year stint as an English professor at the University of Florida, a job that historically would have marked a candidate as too thoughtful, educated and broad-minded for state office. But, in a stunning upset, voters forgave Clint Tyree's erudition and elected him governor.

Naively the Tallahassee establishment welcomed the new chief executive. The barkers, pimps and fast-change artists who controlled the legislature assumed that, like most of his predecessors, Clinton Tyree dutifully would slide into the program. He was, after all, a local boy. Surely he understood how things worked.

But behind the governor's movie-star smile was the incendiary fervor of a terrorist. He brought with him to the capital a passion so deep and untainted that it was utterly unrecognizable to other politicians; they quickly decided that Clinton Tyree was a crazy man. In his first post-election interview, he told *The New York Times* that Florida was being destroyed by unbridled growth, overdevelopment and pollution, and that the stinking root of those evils was greed. By way of illustration, he cited the Speaker of the Florida House for possessing 'the ethics of an intestinal bacterium,' merely because the man had accepted a free trip to Bangkok from a Miami Beach high-rise developer. Later Tyree went on radio urging visitors and would-be residents to stay out of the Sunshine State for a few years, 'so we can gather our senses.' He announced a goal of Negative Population Growth and proposed generous tax incentives for counties that significantly reduced human density. Tyree couldn't have caused more of an uproar had he been preaching satanism to preschoolers.

The view that the new governor was mentally unstable was reinforced by his refusal to accept bribes. More appallingly, he shared the details of these illicit offers with agents of the Federal Bureau of Investigation. In that manner, one of the state's richest and most politically connected land developers got shut down, indicted and convicted of corruption. Clearly Clinton Tyree was a menace.

No previous governor had dared to disrupt the business of paving Florida. For seventy glorious years, the state had shriveled safely in the grip of those most efficient at looting its resources. Suddenly this reckless young upstart was inciting folks like a damn communist. Save the rivers. Save the coasts. Save the Big Cypress. Where would it end? *Time* magazine put him on the cover. David Brinkley called him a New Populist. The National Audubon Society gave him a frigging medal. . . .

One night, in a curtained booth of a restaurant called the Silver Slipper, a pact was made to stop the madman. His heroics in Southeast Asia made him immune to customary smear tactics, so the only safe alternative was to neutralize him politically. It was a straightforward plan: No matter what the new governor wanted, the legislature and cabinet would do the opposite—a voting pattern to be ensured by magnanimous contributions from bankers, contractors, real estate brokers, hoteliers, farm conglomerates and other special-interest groups that were experiencing philosophical differences with Clinton Tyree.

The strategy succeeded. Even the governor's fellow Democrats felt sufficiently threatened by his reforms to abandon him without compunction. Once it became clear to Clint Tyree that the freeze was on, he slowly began to come apart. Each defeat in the legislature hit him like a sledge. His public appearances were marked by bilious oratory and dark mutterings. He lost weight and let his hair grow. During one cryptic press conference, he chose not to wear a shirt. He wrote acidulous letters on official stationery, and gave interviews in which he quoted at length from Carl Jung, Henry Thoreau and David Crosby. One night the state trooper assigned to guard the governor found him creeping through a graveyard; Clinton Tyree explained his intention was to dig up the remains of the late Napoleon Bonaparte Broward, the governor who had first schemed to drain the Everglades. Tyree's idea was to distribute Governor Broward's bones as souvenirs to visitors in the capitol rotunda.

Meanwhile the ravaging of Florida continued unabated, as did the incoming stampede. A thousand fortune-seekers took up residence in the state every day, and there was nothing Clint Tyree could do about it.

So he quit, fled Tallahassee on a melancholy morning in the back of a state limousine, and melted into the tangled wilderness. In the history of Florida, no governor had ever before resigned; in fact, no elected officeholder had made such an abrupt or eccentric exit from public life. Journalists and authors hunted the missing Clinton Tyree but never caught up with him. He moved by night, fed off the road, and adopted the solitary existence of a swamp rattler. Those who encountered him knew him by the name of Skink, or simply 'captain,' a solemn hermitage interrupted by the occasional righteous arson, aggravated battery or highway sniping.

Only one man held the runaway governor's complete trust—the Highway Patrol trooper who had been assigned to guard him during the gubernatorial campaign and later had come to work at the governor's mansion; the same trooper who was driving the limousine on the day Clinton Tyree disappeared. It was he alone who knew the man's whereabouts, kept in touch and followed his movements; who was there to help when Clinton Tyree went around the bend, which he sometimes did.

The trooper had been there soon after his friend lost an eye in a vicious beating; again after he shot up some rental cars in a roadside spree; again after he burned down an amusement park.

Some years were quieter than others.

'But he's been waiting for this hurricane,' Jim Tile said, twirling a spoonful of spaghetti. 'There's cause to be concerned.'

Augustine said: 'I've heard of this guy.'

'Then you understand why I need to talk to Mrs Lamb.'

'Mrs Lamb,' Bonnie said, caustically, 'can't believe what she's hearing. You think this lunatic's got Max?'

'An old lady in the neighborhood saw a man fitting the governor's description carrying a man fitting your husband's description. Over his shoulder. Buck naked.' Jim Tile paused to allow Mrs Lamb to form a mental picture of the scene. He said, 'I don't know about the lady's eyesight, but it's worth checking out. You mentioned a tape you made—the kidnapper's voice.'

'It's back at the house,' said Augustine.

'Would you mind if I listened to it?'

Bonnie said, 'This is ludicrous, what you're saying—'

'Humor me,' said Jim Tile.

Bonnie pushed away her plate of lasagna, half eaten. 'What's your interest?'

'He's my friend. He's in trouble,' the trooper said.

'All I care about is Max.'

'They're both in danger.'

Bonnie demanded to know about the fat man in the morgue. The trooper said he'd been strangled and impaled on a TV satellite dish. The motive didn't appear to be robbery.

'Did your "friend" do that, too?'

'They're talking to some dumb goober from Alabama, but I don't know.'

To Bonnie, it was all incredible. 'You did say "impaled"?'

'Yes, ma'am.' The trooper didn't mention the mock crucifixion. Mrs Lamb was plenty upset already.

Through clenched teeth she said, 'This place is insane.'

Jim Tile was in full agreement. Tiredly he looked at Augustine. 'I'm just tracking down a few leads.'

'Come on back to the house. We'll play that tape for you.'

Ira Jackson's intention had been to kill the mobile-home sales-man and then drive home to New York and arrange his mother's funeral. To his dismay, the murder of Tony Torres left him restless and unfulfilled. Driving through the gutted hurricane zone, Ira Jackson realized what a pitifully insignificant little fuck Tony Torres had been. South Florida was crawling with guys who cheerfully sold death traps to widows. The evidence was plain: Ira Jackson knew shitty construction when he saw it, and he saw it everywhere. Homes in one subdivision came out of the storm with scarcely a shingle out of place; across the street, an equally high-priced development was obliterated, every house blown to pieces.

A goddamn disgrace, Ira Jackson thought. This was exactly the kind of thing that gave corruption a bad name. He recalled the cocky proclamation of Tony Torres: *Every home I've sold passed inspection.*

Undoubtedly it was true. Dade County's code inspectors were as culpable for the destruction as schmuck salesmen like Torres. To Ira Jackson's experienced eye, the substandard construction was too widespread to be explained by mere incompetence; a blind man would have red-tagged some of those cardboard subdivisions. Inspectors most certainly had been paid off with cash, booze, dope, broads, or all of the above. It happened in Brooklyn, too, but Brooklyn didn't get many hurricanes.

Ira Jackson angrily thought of the tie-downs that were sup-posed to anchor his late mother's double-wide trailer. Someone from the county should have noticed the rotted straps; some-one should have examined the augers, to make sure they hadn't been sawed off. Ira Jackson wondered who that someone was, and how much he'd been bribed not to do his job. He drove to the Metro building-and-zoning department to find out.

*

Snapper had sweated through his cheap suit. Mr Nathaniel Lewis was giving him a hard time about the deposit. Out in the truck, the phony roofers were drinking warm beer and arguing about sports.

'Four thousand down is totally out of line,' Nathaniel Lewis was saying.

'All depends on how soon you want a roof. I figured you's in a hurry.'

'Sure we're in a hurry. Just look at this place.'

Snapper agreed that the house was in terrible shape; the Lewises had cut up plastic garbage bags and tacked them to the bare beams, to keep out the rain. 'Look,' said Snapper, 'everybody's roof got blown away. Our phone's ringing off the hook. Four grand puts you top of the list. Priority One.'

Nathaniel Lewis was sharper than Snapper preferred. 'If your phone's ringin' off the hook, how is it you come knockin' on my door like some damn Jehovah. And how is it your crew's sittin' on their butts in the truck, if they's so much work to be done?'

'They're on a break,' Snapper lied. 'We're doing that duplex two blocks over. Save on gas money if we pick up a few more jobs in the neighborhood.'

Lewis said, 'Three down—and that's only if you start right away.'

'We can handle that.'

The crew ascended the skeleton of Lewis's roof. Snapper didn't have to tell the men to take their time; that came naturally. Avila had said it was important to make lots of noise, like legitimate roofers, so the black guys staged a truss-hammering contest, with the Latin guy as referee. The white crackhead was left to cut plywood for the decking.

Snapper waited in the cab of the truck, which smelled like stale Coors and marijuana. Mercifully the sky darkened after about an hour, and a hard thunderstorm broke loose. While the roofers scrambled to load the truck, Snapper told Nathaniel Lewis they'd return first thing in the morning. Lewis handed him a cashier's check for three thousand dollars. The check was made out to Fortress roofing, Avila's bogus company. Snapper thought it was a very amusing name.

He got in the stolen Jeep Cherokee and headed south. The crew followed in the truck. Avila had advised Snapper to move around, don't stay in one area. A smart strategy, Snapper agreed. They made it to Cutler Ridge ahead of the weather. Snapper found an expensive ranch-style house sitting on two acres of pinelands. Half the roof had been torn off by the hurricane. A Land Rover and a black Infiniti were parked in the tiled driveway.

Jackpot, Snapper thought.

The lady of the house let him in. Her name was Whitmark, and she was frantic for shelter. She'd been scouting the rain clouds on the horizon, and the possibility of more flooding in the living room had sent her dashing to the medicine chest. The 'roofing foreman' listened to Mrs Whitmark's woeful story:

The pile carpet already was ruined, as was Mr Whitmark's state-of-the-art stereo system, and of course mildew had claimed all the drapery, the linens and half her winter evening wardrobe; the Italian leather sofa and the cherry buffet had been moved to the west wing, but—

'We can start this afternoon,' Snapper cut in, 'but we need a deposit.'

Mrs Whitmark asked how much. Snapper pulled a figure out of his head: seven thousand dollars.

'You take cash, I assume.'

'Sure,' Snapper said, trying to sound matter-of-fact, like all his customers had seven grand lying around in cookie jars.

Mrs Whitmark left Snapper alone while she went for the money. He raised his eyes to the immense hole in the ceiling. At that moment, a sunbeam broke through the bruised clouds, flooding the house with golden light.

Snapper shielded his eyes. Was this a sign?

When Mrs Whitmark returned, she was flanked by two black-and-silver German shepherds.

Snapper went rigid. 'Mother of Christ,' he murmured.

'My babies,' said Mrs Whitmark, fondly. 'We don't have a problem with looters. Do we, sugars?' She stroked the larger dog under its chin. On command, both of them sat at her feet. They cocked their heads and gazed expectantly at Snapper, who felt a spasm in his colon.

His hands trembled so severely that he was barely able to write up the contract. Mrs Whitmark asked what had happened to his face. 'Did you fall off a roof?'

'No,' he said curtly. 'Bungee accident.'

Mrs Whitmark gave him the cash in a scented pink envelope. 'How soon can you start?' Snapper promised that the crew would return in half an hour. 'We'll need to pick up some lumber. It's a big place you've got here.'

Mrs Whitmark and her guard dogs accompanied Snapper to the front door. He kept both hands jammed in his pockets, in case one of the vicious bastards lunged for him. Of course, if they were trained like police K-9s, they wouldn't bother with his hands. They'd go straight for the balls.

'Hurry,' Mrs Whitmark said, scanning the clouds with dilated pupils. 'I don't like the looks of this sky.'

Snapper walked to the truck and gave the crew the bad news. 'She didn't go for it. Says her husband's already got a roofer lined up for the job. Some company from Palm Beach, she said.'

'Thank God,' said one of the black guys, yawning. 'I'm beat, boss. How about we call it a day?'

'Fine by me,' said Snapper.

Jim Tile rewound the tape and played it again.

'Honey, I've been kidnapped—'

'Abducted! *Kidnapping implies ransom, Max. Don't fucking flatter yourself. . . .'*

Bonnie Lamb said, 'Well?'

'It's him,' the trooper said.

'You're sure?'

'I love you, Bonnie. Max forgot to tell you, so I will. Bye now. . . .'

'Oh yeah,' said Jim Tile. He popped the cassette out of the tape deck.

Bonnie asked Augustine to call his agent friend at the FBI. Augustine said it wasn't such a hot idea.

The trooper agreed. 'They'll never find him. They don't know where to look, they don't know how.'

'But you do?'

'What will probably happen,' Jim Tile said, 'is the governor will keep your husband until he gets bored with him.'

'Then what?' Bonnie demanded. 'He kills him?'

'Not unless your husband tries something stupid.'

Augustine thought: We might have a problem.

The trooper told Bonnie Lamb not to panic; the governor wasn't irrational. There were ways to track him, make contact, engage in productive dialogue.

Bonnie excused herself and went to take some aspirin. Augustine walked outside with the trooper. 'The FBI won't touch this,' Jim Tile said, keeping his voice low. 'There's no ransom demand, no interstate travel. It's hard for her to understand.'

Augustine observed that Max Lamb wasn't helping matters, calling New York to check on his advertising accounts. 'Not exactly your typical victim,' he said.

Jim Tile got in the car and placed his Stetson on the seat. 'I'll get back with you soon. Meanwhile go easy with the lady.'

Augustine said, 'You don't think he's crazy, do you?'

The trooper laughed. 'Son, you heard the tape.'

'Yeah. I don't think he's crazy, either.'

'"Different" is the word. Seriously different.' Jim Tile turned up the patrol car's radio to hear the latest hurricane dementia. The Highway Patrol dispatcher was directing troopers to the intersection of U.S. 1 and Kendall Drive, where a truck loaded with ice had overturned. A disturbance had erupted, and ambulances were on the way.

'Lord,' Jim Tile said. 'They're murdering each other over ice cubes.' He sped off without saying good-bye.

Back in the house, Augustine was surprised to find Bonnie Lamb sitting next to the kitchen phone. At her elbow was a notepad upon which she had written several lines. He was struck by the elegance of her handwriting. Once, he'd dated a woman who dotted her *i*'s with perfect tiny circles; sometimes she drew happy faces inside the circles, sometimes she drew frowns. The woman had been a cheerleader for her college football team, and she couldn't get it out of her system.

Bonnie Lamb's handwriting bore no trace of retired cheerleader. 'Directions,' she replied, waving the paper.

'Where?'

'To see Max and this Skink person. They left directions on my machine.'

She was excited. Augustine sat next to her. 'What else did they say?'

'No police. No FBI. Max was very firm about it.'

'And?'

'Four double-A batteries and a tape of *Exile on Main Street*. Dolby chrome oxide, whatever that means. And a bottle of pitted green olives, no pimientos.'

'This would be the governor's shopping list?'

'Max hates green olives.' Bonnie Lamb put her hand on Augustine's arm. 'What do we do? You want to hear the message?'

'Let's go talk to them, if that's what they want.'

'Bring your gun. I'm serious.' Her eyes flashed. 'We can kidnap Max from the kidnapper. Why not!'

'Settle down, please. When's the meeting?'

'Midnight tomorrow.'

'Where?'

When she told him, he looked discouraged. 'They'll never show. Not there.'

'You're wrong,' Bonnie Lamb said. 'Where's that gun of yours?'

Augustine went to the living room and switched on the television. He channel-surfed until he found a Monty Python rerun; a classic, John Cleese buying a dead parrot. It never failed to make Augustine laugh.

Bonnie sat beside him on the sofa. When the Monty Python sketch ended, he turned to her and said, 'You don't know a damn thing about guns.'

11

Max Lamb awoke to these words: 'You need a legacy.' He and Skink had bummed a ride in the back of a U-Haul truck. They were bucking down U.S. Highway One among two thousand cans of Campbell's broccoli cheese soup, which was being donated to hurricane victims by a Baptist church in Pascagoula, Mississippi. What the shipment lacked in variety it made up for in Christian goodwill.

'This,' said the kidnapper, waving at the soup boxes, 'is what people do for each other in times of catastrophe. They give help. You, on the other hand—'

'I said I was sorry.'

'—you, Max, arrive with a video camera.'

Max Lamb lit a cigaret. The governor had been in a rotten mood all day. First his favorite Stones tape broke, then the batteries crapped out in his Walkman.

Skink said, 'The people who gave this soup, they went through Camille. Please assure me you know about Camille.'

'Another hurricane?'

'A magnificent shitkicker of a hurricane. Max, I believe you're making progress.'

The advertising man sucked apprehensively on the Bronco. He said, 'You were talking about getting a boat.'

Skink said, 'Everyone ought to have a legacy. Something to be remembered for. Let's hear some of your slogans.'

'Not right now.'

'I never see TV anymore, but some commercials I remember.' The kidnapper pointed at the canyon of red-and-white soup cans. ' "M'm, m'm good!" That was a classic, no?'

Unabashedly Max Lamb said, 'You ever hear of Plum Crunchies? It was a breakfast cereal.'

'A cereal,' said Skink.

' "You'll go plum loco for Plum Crunchies!" '

The kidnapper frowned. From his camo trousers he produced a small felt box of the type used by jewelry stores. He opened it and removed a scorpion, which he placed on his bare brown wrist. The scorpion raised its fat claws, pinching the air in confusion. Max stared incredulously. The skin on his neck heated beneath the shock collar. He drew up his legs, preparing to spring from the truck if Skink tossed the awful creature at him.

'This little sucker,' Skink said, 'is from Southeast Asia. Recognized him right away.' With a pinkie finger, he stroked the scorpion until it arched its venomous stinger.

Max Lamb asked how a Vietnamese scorpion got all the way to Florida. Skink said it was probably smuggled by importers. 'Then, when the hurricane struck, Mortimer here made a dash for it. I found him in the horse barn. Remember Larks? "Show us your Larks!" '

'Barely.' Max was a kid when the Lark campaign hit TV.

Skink said: 'That's what I mean by legacy. Does anyone remember who thought up Larks? But the Marlboro man, Christ, that's the most successful ad campaign in history.'

It was a fact. Max Lamb wondered how Skink knew. He noticed that the scorpion had become tangled in the gray-blond hair on the captain's arm.

'What are you going to do with it?' Max asked.

No answer. He tried another strategy. 'Bonnie is deathly afraid of insects.'

Skink scooped the scorpion into the palm of one hand. 'This ain't no insect, Max. It's an arachnid.'

'Bugs is what I meant, captain. She's terrified of all bugs.' Max was speaking for himself. Icy needles of anxiety pricked at his arms and legs. He struggled to connect the kidnapper's scorpion sympathies with his views of the Marlboro man. What was the psychopath trying to say?

'Can she swim, your Bonnie? Then she'll be fine.' The

governor popped the scorpion in his cheek and swallowed with an audible gulp.

'Oh Jesus,' said Max.

After a suitable pause, Skink opened his mouth. The scorpion was curled placidly on his tongue, its pincers at rest.

Max Lamb stubbed out the Bronco and urgently lit another. He leaned his head against a crate of soup cans and said a silent prayer: Dear God, don't let Bonnie say anything to piss this guy off.

Avila's career as a county inspector was unremarkable except for the six months when he was the target of a police investigation. The cops had infiltrated the building department with an under-cover man posing as a supervisor. The undercover man noticed, among a multitude of irregularities, that Avila was inspecting new roofs at a superhuman rate of about sixty a day, without benefit of a ladder. A surveillance team was put in place and observed that Avila never bothered to climb the roofs he was assigned to inspect. In fact, he seldom left his vehicle except for a regular two-hour buffet lunch at a nudie bar in Hialeah. It was noted that Avila drove past construction sites at such an imprac-tical speed that contractors frequently had to jog after his truck in order to deliver their illicit gratuities. The transactions were captured with crystal clarity on videotape.

When the police investigation became public, a grand jury convened to ponder the filing of felony indictments. To give the appearance of concern, the building-and-zoning department reassigned Avila and several of his crooked colleagues to duties that were considered low-profile and menial, a status confirmed by the relatively puny size of the bribes. In Avila's case, he was relegated to inspecting mobile homes. It was a job for which he had no qualifications or enthusiasm. Trailers were trailers; to Avila, nothing but glorified sardine cans. The notion of 'code enforcement' at a trailer park was oxymoronic; none of them, Avila knew, would survive the feeblest of hurricanes. Why go to the trouble of tying the damn things down?

But he made a show of logging inspections, taking what modest graft the mobile-home dealers would toss his way—fifty bucks here and there, a bottle of Old Grand-dad, porno tapes, an eight-ball of coke. Avila wasn't worried about police surveillance on his beat. Authorities were concerned with protecting the upwardly mobile middle-class home buyer; nobody gave a shit what happened to people who bought trailers.

Except men like Ira Jackson, whose mother lived in one.

With the exception of the bus depot in downtown Guatemala City, the Dade County building department was the most disorganized and institutionally indifferent place that Ira Jackson had ever seen. It took ninety minutes to find a clerk who admitted to fluency in English, and another hour to get his hands on the documents for the Suncoast Leisure Village trailer park. Under the circumstances, Ira Jackson was mildly surprised that the file still existed. From what he saw, others were vanishing by the carload. Realizing the hurricane would bring scandal to the construction industry, developers, builders and compromised inspectors were taking bold steps to obscure their own roles in the crimes. As Ira Jackson elbowed his way to an empty chair, he recognized—amid the truly aggrieved—faces of the copiously guilty: brows damp, lips tight, eyes pinched and fretful. They were men who feared the prospect of public exposure, massive lawsuits or prison.

If only it were true, thought Ira Jackson. Experience had taught him otherwise. Bozos who rob liquor stores go to jail, not rich guys and bureaucrats and civil servants.

Ira Jackson thumbed through the trailer-court records until he found the name of the man who had botched the inspection of his mother's double-wide. He fought his way to the file counter and cornered a harried-looking clerk, who informed him that Mr Avila no longer was employed by Dade County.

Why not? Ira Jackson asked.

Because he quit, the clerk explained; started his own business. Since Ira Jackson was already agitated, the clerk saw no point in revealing that Avila's resignation was part of a plea-bargain agreement with the State Attorney's Office. That was a private matter that Mr Avila himself should share with Mr Jackson, if he so desired.

Ira Jackson said, 'You got a current address, right?'

The clerk said it was beyond his authority to divulge that information. Ira Jackson reached across the counter and rested his hand, very lightly, on the young man's shoulder. 'Listen to me, Paco,' he said. 'I'll come to your home. I'll harm your family. You understand? Even your pets.'

The clerk nodded. 'Be right back,' he said.

Snapper was more annoyed than afraid when he saw the flashing blue lights in the rearview. He'd figured the Jeep Cherokee was already hot when he swiped it from the gangster rappers; he didn't figure the cops would be looking for it so soon. Not with all the hurricane emergencies.

Pulling to the side of the road, he wondered if Baby Raper had blabbed when he got to the hospital. No doubt the kid was ticked when Snapper retrofitted that compact disc up his ass, like a big shiny suppository.

But why would the cops care about *that*? Snapper thought: Maybe it's got nothing do with the gangster rapper or the stolen Jeep. Maybe it's just my driving.

The cop who stopped him was a female Highway Patrol trooper. She had pleasant features and pretty pale-blue eyes that reminded Snapper of a girl he'd tried to date back in Atlanta, some sort of turbocharged Catholic. The lady trooper's dark hair was pulled up under her hat, and she wore a gold wedding band that cried out for pawning. The holster appeared oversized and out of place on her hip. She shined a light in the Jeep and asked to see Snapper's driver's license.

'I left my wallet at home.'

'No identification?'

'"Fraid not.' For effect, he patted his pockets.

'What's your name?'

'Boris,' said Snapper. He loved Boris and Natasha, from the old Rocky and Bullwinkle TV show.

'Boris what?' the trooper asked.

Snapper couldn't spell the cartoon Boris's last name, so he said, 'Smith. Boris J. Smith.'

The trooper's pale eyes seemed to darken, and the tone of her voice flattened. 'Sir, I clocked you at seventy in a forty-five-mile-per-hour zone.'

'No kidding.' Snapper felt relieved. A stupid speeding ticket! Maybe she'd write him up without running the tag.

The trooper said: 'It's against the law to operate a motor vehicle in Florida without a valid license. You're aware of that.'

OK, Snapper thought, *two* tickets. Big fucking deal. But he noticed she wasn't calling him 'Mister Smith.'

'You're also aware that it's illegal to give false information to a law-enforcement officer?'

'Sure.' Snapper cursed to himself The bitch wasn't buying it.

'Stay in your vehicle, please.'

In the mirror, Snapper watched the flashlight bobbing as the trooper walked back to her car. Undoubtedly she intended to call in the license plate on the Cherokee. Snapper felt his shoulders tighten. He had as much chance of explaining the stolen vehicle as he did explaining the seven thousand dollars in his suit.

He saw two choices. The first was to flee the scene, which was guaranteed to result in a chase, a messy crash and an arrest on numerous nonbondable felonies.

The second choice was to stop the lady trooper before she got on the radio. Which is what he did.

Some cons wouldn't hit a woman, but Snapper was neutral on the issue. A cop was a cop. The trooper spotted him coming but, encumbered by the steering wheel, had difficulty pulling that enormous Smith & Wesson out of its holster. She managed to get the snap undone, but by then it was good-night-nurse.

He took the flashlight, the gun and the wedding band, and left the trooper lying unconscious by the side of the road. Speeding away, he noticed a smudge of color on one of his knuckles.

Makeup, it looked like.

He didn't feel shame, regret or anything much at all.

Edie Marsh was beginning to appreciate the suffering of real hurricane victims. It rained three times during the day, leaving dirty puddles throughout the Torres house. The carpets squished underfoot, green frogs vaulted from wall to wall, and mosquitoes were hatching in one of the bathroom sinks. Even after the cloud-bursts stopped, the exposed beams dripped for hours. Combined with the cacophony of neighborhood hammers and chain saws, the racket was driving Edie nuts. She walked outside and called halfheartedly for the missing dachshunds, an exercise that she abandoned swiftly after spying a fat brown snake. Edie's scream attracted a neighbor, who took a broom and scared the snake away. Then he inquired about Tony and Neria.

They're out of town, said Edie Marsh. They asked me to watch the place.

And you are . . .?

A cousin, Edie replied, knowing she looked about as Latin as Goldie Hawn.

As soon as the neighbor left, Edie hurried into the house and stationed herself in Tony's recliner. She turned up the radio and laid the crowbar within arm's reach. When darkness came, the hammering and sawing stopped, and the noises of the neighbor-hood changed to bawling babies, scratchy radios and slamming doors. Edie began worrying about looters and rapists and the unknown predator that had slurped poor Donald and Marla like Tic Tacs. By the time Fred Dove showed up, she was a basket of nerves.

The insurance man brought a corsage of gardenias. Like he was picking her up for the prom!

Edie Marsh said, 'You can't be serious.'

'What's wrong? I couldn't find roses.'

'Fred, I can't stay here anymore. Get me a room.'

'Everything's going to be fine. Look, I brought wine.'

'Fred?'

'And scented candles.'

'Yo, Fred!'

'What?'

Edie steered him to a soggy sofa and sat him down. 'Fred, this is business, not romance.'

He looked hurt.

'Sweetie,' she said, 'we had sexual intercourse exactly one

time. Don't worry, there's every chance in the world we'll do it again. But it isn't love and it isn't passion. It's a financial partnership.'

The insurance man said, 'You seduced me.'

'Of course I did. And you were fantastic.'

As Fred Dove's ego reinflated, his posture improved.

'But no more flowers,' Edie scolded, 'and no more wine. Just get me a room at the damn Ramada, OK?'

The insurance man solemnly agreed. 'First thing tomorrow.'

'Look at this place, honey. No roof. No glass in the windows. It's not a house, it's a damn cabana!'

'You're right, Edie, you can't stay here. I'll rejigger the expense account.'

She rolled her eyes. 'Fred, don't be so anal. We're about to rip off your employer for a hundred and forty-one thousand bucks, and you're pitching a hissy fit over a sixty-dollar motel room. Think about it.'

'Please don't get angry.'

'You've got the claim papers?'

'Right here.'

After scanning the figures, Edie Marsh felt better. She plucked the gardenias from the corsage and arranged them in a coffeepot, which was full of lukewarm rainwater. She opened the bottle of Chablis, and they toasted to a successful venture. After four glasses, Edie felt comfortable enough to ask what the insurance man planned to do with his cut of the money.

'Buy a boat,' Fred Dove said, 'and sail to Bimini.'

'What about wifey?'

'Who?' said Fred Dove. They laughed together. Then he asked Edie Marsh how she was going to spend her seventy-one grand.

'Hyannis Port,' she said, without elaboration.

Later, when the Chablis was gone, Edie dragged a dry mattress into the living room, turned off the lightbulb and lit one of Fred Dove's candles, which smelled like malted milk. As Edie took off her clothes, she heard Fred groping inside his briefcase for a rubber. He tore the foil with his teeth and pressed the package into her hand.

Even when she was sober, condoms made Edie laugh. When drunk she found them downright hilarious, the silliest contraptions imaginable. For tonight Fred Dove had boldly chosen a red one, and Edie was no help whatsoever in putting it on. Neither, for that matter, was Fred. Edie's tittering had pretty well shattered the mood, undoing all the good work of the wine.

Flat on his back, the insurance man turned his head away. Edie Marsh slapped his legs apart and knelt between them. 'Don't you quit on me,' she scolded. 'Pay attention, sweetie. Come on.' Firmly she took hold of him.

'Could you just—?'

'No.' It was always bad form to giggle in the middle of a blow job, and Fred Dove was the sort who'd never recover, emotionally. 'Focus,' she instructed him. 'Remember how good it was last night.'

Edie had gotten the condom partially deployed when she heard the electric generator cut off. Out of fuel, she figured. It could wait; Fred Jr was showing signs of life.

She heard a soft click, and suddenly the insurance man's festively crowned penis was illuminated in a circle of bright light. Edie Marsh let go and sat upright. Fred Dove, his eyes shut tightly in concentration, said, 'Don't stop now.'

In the front doorway stood a man with a powerful flashlight.

'Candles,' he said. 'That's real fuckin' cozy.'

Fred Dove's chest stopped moving, and one hand fumbled for his eyeglasses. Edie Marsh got up and folded her arms across her breasts. She said, 'Thanks for knocking, asshole.'

'I came back for my car.' Snapper played the light up and down her body.

'It's in the driveway, right where you left it.'

'What's the hurry,' said Snapper, stepping into the house.

Bonnie Lamb went to Augustine's room at one-thirty in the morning. She climbed under the sheets without brushing against him even slightly. It wasn't easy, in a twin bed.

She whispered, 'Are you sleeping?'

'Like a log.'

'Sorry.'

He rolled over to face her. 'You need a pillow?'

'I need a hug.'

'Bad idea.'

'Why?'

'I'm slightly on the naked side. I wasn't expecting company.'

'Apology number two,' she said.

'Close your eyes, Mrs Lamb.' He got up and pulled on a pair of loose khakis. No shirt, she observed, unalarmed. He slipped under the covers and held her. His skin was warm and smooth against her cheek, and when he moved she felt a taut, shifting wedge of muscle. Max's physical topography was entirely different, but Bonnie pushed the thought from her mind. It wasn't fair to compare hugging prowess. Not now.

She asked Augustine if he'd ever been married. He said no.

'Engaged?'

'Three times.'

Bonnie raised her head. 'You're kidding.'

'Unfortunately not.' In the artificial twilight, Augustine saw she was smiling. 'This amuses you?'

'Intrigues me,' she said. 'Three times?'

'They all came to their senses.'

'We're talking about three different women. No repeats?'

'Correct,' said Augustine.

'I've got to ask what happened. You don't have to answer, but I've got to ask.'

'Well, the first one married a successful personal-injury lawyer—he's doing class-action breast-implant litigation; the second one started an architecture firm and is currently a mistress to a Venezuelan cabinet minister; and the third one is starring on a popular Cuban soap opera—she plays Miriam, the jealous schizophrenic. So I would say,' Augustine concluded, 'that each of them made a wise decision by ending our relationship.'

Bonnie Lamb said, 'I bet you let them keep the engagement rings.'

'Hey, it's only money.'

'And you still watch the soap opera, don't you?'

'She's quite good in it. Very convincing.'

Bonnie said, 'What an unusual guy.'

'You feeling better? My personal problems always seem to cheer people up.'

She put her head down. 'I'm worried about tomorrow, about seeing Max again.'

Augustine told her it was normal to be nervous. 'I'm a little antsy myself.'

'Will you bring the gun?'

'Let's play it by ear.' He seriously doubted if the governor would appear, much less deliver Bonnie's husband.

'Are you scared?' When she spoke, he could feel her soft breath on his chest.

'Restless,' he said, 'not scared.'

'Hey.'

'Hey what?'

'You getting excited?'

Augustine shifted in embarrassment. What did she expect? He said, 'My turn to apologize.'

But she didn't move. So he took a slow quiet breath and tried to focus on something else . . . say, Uncle Felix's fugitive monkeys. How far had they scattered? How were they coping with freedom?

Augustine's self-imposed pondering was interrupted when Bonnie Lamb said: 'What if Max is different now? Maybe something's happened to him.'

Augustine thought: Something's happened, all right. You can damn sure bet on it.

But what he told Bonnie was: 'Your husband's hanging in there. You wait and see.'

12

Skink said, 'Care for some toad?'

The shock collar had done its job; Max Lamb was uncon-ditionally conditioned. If the captain wanted him to smoke toad, he would smoke toad.

'It's an offer, not a command,' Skink said, by way of clari-fication.

'Then no, thanks.'

Max Lamb squinted into the warm salty night. Somewhere out there, Bonnie was searching. Max was neither as anxious nor as hopeful as he should have been, and he wondered why; his reaction to practically every circumstance was muted, as if key brain synapses had been cauterized by the ordeal of the kidnapping. For instance, he had failed to raise even a meek objection at the Key Biscayne golf course, where they'd stopped to free the Asian scorpion. Skink had tenderly deposited the venomous bug in the cup on the eighteenth green. 'The mayor's favorite course,' he'd explained. 'Call me an optimist.' Max had stood by wordlessly.

Now they were on a wooden stilt house in the middle of the bay. Skink dangled his long legs off the end of a dock, which was twisted and buckled like a Chinese parade dragon. The hurricane had sucked the wooden pilings from their holes. Most of the other stilt houses were shorn at the stems, but this one had outlasted the storm, though barely. It lurched and creaked in the thickish breeze; Max Lamb suspected it was sinking with the tide. Skink said the house belonged to a man who'd retired on disability from the State Attorney's Office. The man recently had married a beautiful twelve-string guitarist and moved to the island of Exuma.

Under a swinging lantern, Skink lighted another exotic-smelling joint; marijuana and French onion soup, thought Max Lamb. Something strong and cheesy.

'The toad itself is toxic,' Skink explained. '*Bufo marinus*. A South American import—overran the local species. Sound familiar?' He took a long sibilant drag. 'The glands of Señor Bufo perspire a milky sap that can kill a full-grown Doberman in six minutes flat.'

To Max, it didn't sound like a substance that one should be inhaling.

'There's a special process,' Skink said, 'of extraction.' He took another huge hit.

'What does it do, this toad sap?'

'Nothing. Everything. What all good drugs do, I suppose. Psychoneurotic roulette.' Skink's chin dropped to his chest. His good eye fluttered and closed. His breathing rose to a startling volume; the exhalations sounded like the brakes of a subway train. For fifteen minutes Max Lamb didn't make a move; the notion to escape never occurred to him, such was the Pavlovian influence of the collar.

In the interval of enforced suspension, Max's thoughts drifted to Bill Knapp up at Rodale. The scheming viper undoubtedly had his sights on Max's corner office, with its partially obstructed but nonetheless energizing view of Madison Avenue. Each day lost to the ambivalent kidnapper was a potential day of advancement for Billy the Backstabber; Max Lamb was burning to return to the agency and crush the devious little fucker's ambitions. Brutal humiliation was called for, and Max hoped he was up to the task. Darkly he imagined Billy Knapp a jobless, wifeless, homeless, toothless wretch, hunched over a can of Sterno in a wintry alley, sucking on a moist spliff laced with poisonous toad sweat . . .

When Skink snapped awake, he coughed hard and flipped the butt of the dead joint into the storm-silted water. Not far from the house, the broken mast of a submerged sailboat protruded from the waves. Skink pointed at the ghostly wreck but said nothing. His leathery finger stayed in the air for an exceptionally long time.

'Tell me,' he said to Max Lamb, 'the most breathtaking place you've ever seen.'

'Yellowstone Park. We took a bus tour.'

'Good God.'

'So what?'

'Outside Yellowstone they've got a grizzly-bear theme park. Did you go? I mean, some truly sad cases—no claws, no testicles. They're about as wild as goddamn hamsters, but tourists line up to see 'em. Deballed grizzly bears!'

Rapidly Skink shook his head back and forth, as if trying to roust a bumblebee from his ear. Max Lamb wasn't sure how the conversation had gone so far astray. He did not share the madman's compassion for the altered grizzly bears; removing the claws seemed an entirely sensible procedure, liability-wise, for a public amusement park. But Max knew there was no percentage in arguing. He remained quiet as Skink withdrew into a heap on the planks of the spavined deck. The kidnapper trembled and heaved and cried out names that Max Lamb didn't recognize. A half hour later he was up, scouting the starlit horizons.

'You all right?' Max asked.

Skink nodded soberly. 'The down side of toad. I do apologize.'

'Are you sure Bonnie can find us out here?' 'Why in the name of God would you marry a woman who can't follow simple directions?'

'But it's so dark—'

The trip to Stiltsville had frightened Max Lamb beyond exclamation—full throttle, no running lights, a wet nasty chop in an open skiff. Infinitely more harrowing than the airboat. The hurricane had turned the bay into a spectral gauntlet of sunken yachts, trawlers, cabin cruisers and runabouts. On the way out, Skink had removed his glass eye and pressed it, for safekeeping, into the palm of Max's right hand. Max had clenched it as if it were the Hope diamond.

'Your wife,' Skink was saying, 'will surely hook up with somebody who knows the way.'

'I could use a cigaret. Please, captain.'

Skink groped in his coat until he came up with a fresh pack. He tossed it, along with a lighter, to his captive.

Max Lamb was embarrassed that he'd so quickly become hooked on the infamously harsh Broncos. Around the agency they were jokingly known as Bronchials, such was their killer reputation with anti-smoking zealots. Max attributed his hazardous new habit to severe stress, not a weakness of character. In the advertising business it was essential to remain immune from the base appetites that tyrannized the average consumer.

Skink said: 'What else have you to show for yourself?'

'I'm not sure what you mean.'

'Slogans, tiger. Besides the Plum Crispies.'

'Crunchies,' said Max, tightly.

The dock shimmied as Skink rose to his feet. Max braced himself against a half-rotted beam. There was nowhere to go; the old man who ferried them across the bay had snatched Skink's fifty dollars and hastily aimed the skiff back toward the mainland.

Skink swung the lantern around and around his head. Caught in the erratic strobe, Max said, 'All right, captain, here's one: "That fresh good-morning feeling, all day long."'

'Product name?'

'Intimate Mist.'

'No!' The lantern hissed as Skink put it down.

Max tried not to sound defensive. 'It's a feminine hygiene item. Very popular.'

'The raspberry rinse! Sweet Jesus, I thought you were joking. This is the sum of your life achievements—*douche* jingles?'

'No,' Max snapped. 'Soft drinks, gasoline additives, laser copiers—I've worked on plenty of accounts.' He wondered what had impelled him to mention the Intimate Mist campaign. Was it an unconscious act of masochism, or carelessness caused by fatigue?

Skink sat heavily on the porch, which was canted at an alarming angle toward the bay. 'I do hear a boat,' he said.

Max stared curiously across the water. He heard nothing but

the slap of waves and the scattered piping of seagulls. He asked, 'What happens now?'

There was no reply. Max Lamb saw, in the yellow flicker of the lantern, a smile cross the crazy man's face.

'You seriously don't want any ransom?'

'I didn't say that. *Money* is what I don't want.'

'Then what?' Max flicked his cigaret into the water. 'Tell me what the hell it's all about. I'm sick of this game, I really am!'

Skink was amused by the display of anger. Maybe there was hope for the precious little bastard. 'What I want,' he said to Max Lamb, 'is to spend some time with your wife. She intrigues me.'

'In what way?'

'Clinically. Anthropologically. What in the world does she see in you? How do you two fit?' Skink gave a mischievous wink. 'I like mysteries.'

'If you touch her—'

'What a brave young stud!'

Max Lamb took two steps toward the madman, but froze when Skink raised a hand to his own throat. *The collar!* Max felt a hot sizzle shoot from his scalp down the length of his spine. Instantly he foresaw himself hopping like a puppet. Had he known that the battery in the Tri-Tronics remote control had been dead for the past six hours, it wouldn't have softened his reaction. He was a slave to his subconscious. He had come to understand that the anticipation of pain was more immobilizing than the pain itself—though the knowledge didn't help him.

When Max settled down, Skink assured him he had no carnal interest in his wife. 'Christ, I'm not trying to get laid; I'm trying to figure out man's place in the food chain.' His long arms swept an arc across the stars. 'A riddle of the times, Tourist Boy. Five thousand years ago we're doodling on the walls of caves. Today we're writing odes to fruit-flavored douche.'

'It's a job,' Max Lamb replied petulantly. 'Get over it.'

Skink yawned like a gorged hyena. 'That's a damn big engine coming. I hope your Bonnie wasn't foolish enough to call the police.'

'I warned her not to.'

Skink went on: 'My opinion about your wife will be shaped by how she handles this situation. Whom she brings. Her attitude. Her composure.'

Max Lamb asked Skink if he had a gun. Skink clicked his tongue against his front teeth. 'See the running lights?'

'No.'

'Toward Key Biscayne. Over there.'

'Oh, yeah.'

'Two engines, it sounds like. I'm guessing twin Mercs.'

Somebody aboard the boat had a powerful spotlight. It swept back and forth across the flats of Stiltsville. As the craft drew nearer, the white light settled on the porch of the stilt house. Skink seemed unconcerned.

He began to remove toads from his pockets; gray, jowly, scowling, lump-covered toads, some as large as Idaho potatoes. Max Lamb counted eleven. Skink lined them up side by side at his feet. Max had nothing to add to the scenario, perhaps it was all a dream, beginning with the mangy hurricane monkey, and soon he'd awaken in bed with Bonnie. . . .

The pudgy Bufo toads began to squirm and huff and pee. Skink rebuked them with a murmur. When the beam of the speedboat's spotlight hit them, the toads blinked their moist globular eyes and jumped toward it. One by one they leaped off the dock and plopped into the water. Skink hooted mirthfully. 'South, boys! To Havana, San Juan, wherever the hell you came from!'

Max watched the toads disappear; some kicked for the depths, others bobbed on the foamy crests of waves. Max didn't know what would happen to them, nor did he care. They were just ugly toads, and barracudas could devour them, as far as he was concerned. His only interest was in drawing a lesson from the episode, one that might be employed to handle the cyclopean kidnapper.

But Skink already seemed to have forgotten about the Bufos. Once more he was rhapsodizing about the hurricane. 'Look at Cape Florida, every last tree flattened—forest to moonscape in thirty blessed minutes!'

'The boat—'

'You ponder that.'

'It's flashing a light at us—'

'The gorgeous fury inside that storm. And you with your video camera.' Skink sighed disappointedly. ' "Sin is a thing that writes itself across a man's face." Oscar Wilde. I don't expect you've read him.'

Max's silence affirmed it.

'Well, I've been waiting,' said Skink, 'to see it written across your face. Sin.'

'What I did was harmless, OK? Maybe a bit insensitive, but harmless. You've made your point, captain. Let me go now.'

The speedboat was close enough to see it was metallic blue with a white jagged stripe, like a lightning bolt, along the hull. Two figures were visible at the console.

'There she is,' said Max.

'And no cops.' Skink waved the boat in.

One of the figures moved to the bow and tossed a rope. Skink caught it and tied off. As soon as the rope came tight, the twin outboards went quiet. The current nudged the stern of the boat against the pilings, into the lantern's penumbra.

Max Lamb saw that it was Bonnie on the bow. When he called her name, she stepped to the dock and hugged him in a nurselike fashion, consoling him as if he were a toddler with a skinned knee. Max received the attention with manly reserve; he was conscious of being watched not only by his captor but by Bonnie's male escort.

Skink smiled at the reunion scene, and slipped back into the shadows of the stilt house. The driver of the boat made no move to get out. He was young and broad-shouldered, and comfortable on the open water. He wore a pale-blue pullover, cutoffs and no shoes. He seemed unaffected by navigating a pitch-black bay mined with overturned hulls and floating timbers.

From the darkness, Skink asked the young man for his name.

'Augustine,' he answered.

'You have the ransom?'

'Sure do.'

Bonnie Lamb said: 'Don't worry, he's not the police.'

'I can see that,' came Skink's voice.

The boat driver stepped to the gunwale. He handed Bonnie a shopping bag, which she gave to her husband, who handed it to the kidnapper in the shadows.

Max Lamb said: 'Bonnie, honey, the captain wants to talk to you. Then he'll let me go.'

'I'm considering it,' Skink said.

'Talk to me about what?'

The driver of the boat reached inside the console and came out with a can of beer. He took a swallow and leaned one hip against the steering wheel.

Bonnie Lamb asked her husband: 'What's that on your neck?' It looked like some appalling implement of bondage; she'd seen similar items in the display windows of leather shops in Greenwich Village.

Skink came into the light. 'It's a training device. Lie down, Max.'

Bonnie Lamb studied the tall, disheveled stranger. He was all the state trooper had promised, and more. In size he appeared capable of anything, yet Bonnie felt in no way threatened.

'Max, now!' the kidnapper said to her husband.

Obediently Max Lamb lay prone on the wooden dock. When Skink told him to roll over, like a dog, he did.

Bonnie was embarrassed for her husband. The kidnapper noticed, and apologized. He instructed Max to get up.

The shopping bag contained everything Skink had demanded. Within moments the new batteries were inserted in the Walkman, and 'Tumbling Dice' was spilling out of his earphones. He opened the jar of green olives and poured them into his gleaming bucket of a mouth.

Bonnie Lamb asked Max what in God's name was going on.

'Later,' he whispered.

'Tell me now!'

'She deserves to know,' the kidnapper interjected, spraying olive juice. 'She's risking her life, being out here with a nutcase like me.'

Bonnie Lamb had dressed for a boat ride—blue slicker, jeans

and deck shoes. Good stuff but practical, Skink noticed, none of that catalog nonsense from California. He pulled off the earphones and complimented Bonnie for her common sense. Then he instructed her husband to remove the shock collar and toss it in the sea.

Max's hands quavered at his neck. Skink told him to go ahead, dammit, off with it! Max's lips tightened in determination, but he couldn't make himself touch it. Finally it was his wife who stepped forward, unhooked the clasp and removed the Tri-Tronics dog trainer. She examined it in the light of the lantern.

'Sick,' she said to Skink, and set the collar on the dock.

From his jacket he took a videotape cassette. He tossed it to Bonnie Lamb, who caught it with both hands. 'Your hubbie's home movies from the hurricane. Talk about sick.'

Bonnie wheeled and threw the cassette into the bay.

The girl had fire! Skink liked her already. Nervously Max lighted a cigaret.

His wife wouldn't have been more repulsed had he jabbed a hypodermic full of heroin in his arm. She said, 'Since when do you smoke?'

'If you put the collar back on him,' Skink volunteered helpfully, 'I can teach him to quit.'

Max Lamb told Skink to get on with it. 'You said you wanted to talk to her, so talk.'

'No, I said I wanted to spend time with her.'

Bonnie turned toward the barefoot young man at the helm of the striped speedboat. He apparently had nothing to say. His demeanor was casual, almost bored.

'Where,' Bonnie asked the kidnapper, 'did you want to spend time? And doing what?'

'Not what you think,' Max Lamb cut in.

Skink put on his plastic shower cap. 'The hurricane has set me on a new rhythm. I feel it ticking.'

He put his hands on Bonnie's shoulders, gently moving her to Max's side. From the governor's shadow she felt his stare. He was studying them, her and Max, like they were lab rats. Then she heard him mutter: 'I still don't see how.'

Tersely Bonnie said, 'Just tell us what you want.'

'Watch it,' Max advised. 'He's been smoking dope.'

Skink looked away, toward the ocean. 'No offense, Mrs Lamb, but your husband has put me sorely off the human race. A feminine counterpoint would be nice.'

Bonnie was surprised by a pleasurable shiver, gooseflesh rising on her neck. The stranger's voice was soothing and hypnotic, a wild broad river; she could have listened to him all night. Mad is what he was, demonstrably mad. But his story fascinated her. Once a governor, the trooper had said. Bonnie longed to know more.

Yet here was her husband, exhausted, sunburned, emotionally sapped. She ought to tend to him. Poor Max had been through hell.

'I only want to talk,' the kidnapper said.

'All right,' Bonnie told him, 'but just for a little while.'

He cupped a hand to his mouth. 'You, Augustine! Take Mister Lamb to safety. He needs a shower and a shave and possibly a stool softener. Return at dawn for his wife.'

Skink grabbed Max under the arms and lowered him to the speedboat. He cut the line with a pocketknife, pushing the bow away from the sagging stilt house. He flung one arm around Bonnie and with the other began to wave. As the boat drifted out of the lantern's glow, Skink saw a third figure rise in the stern of the boat—where had *he* been hiding? Then the young man at the wheel brought a rifle to his shoulder.

'Damn,' said Skink, pushing Bonnie Lamb from the line of fire.

Something stung him fiercely, spinning him clockwise and down. He was still spinning when he hit the warm water, and wondering why his arms and legs weren't working, wondering why he hadn't heard a shot or seen a muzzle flash, wondering if perhaps he was already dead.

13

Late on the night of August 27, with a warm breeze at his back and nine cold Budweisers in his belly, Keith Higstrom decided to go hunting. His friends declined to accompany him, as Keith was as clumsy and unreliable a shooter as he was a drunk.

Truthfully there wasn't much to hunt in South Florida, the wild game having long ago fled or died. However, the hurricane had dispersed throughout the suburbs an exotic new quarry: livestock. Mile upon mile of ranch posts in rural Dade County had been uprooted, freeing herds of cattle and horses to explore vistas beyond their mucky flooded pastures. Motivated more by dull hunger than by native inquisitiveness, the animals began appearing in places where they were not customarily encountered. One such place was Keith Higstrom's neighborhood, a subdivision of indistinguishable clam-colored houses, stacked twenty deep and twenty-five across and bordered on every side by bankrupt strip shopping malls.

It was here Keith Higstrom had spent his childhood. His father's family had moved to Miami from northern Minnesota in the early 1940s bringing an affinity for long guns and an appetite for the great outdoors. An impressionable boy, Keith had listened to hunting yarns his entire life—timber wolves and trophy black bears in the north woods, white-tailed deer and wild turkeys in the Florida scrub. The head of an eight-point buck, stoic but marble-eyed, hung over the Higstrom dinner table; the tawny pelt of a prized panther was tacked spread-eagle on the west wall of the den. At age five, Keith began collecting in leatherbound volumes each edition of *Outdoor Life*, *Field & Stream* and *Sports Afield*. His most treasured possession was an autographed photo of the famous Joe Foss, standing over a dead grizzly. At age six, young Keith got a Daisy popgun, a BB pistol at age nine, a pellet rifle at age eleven, and his first .22 at thirteen.

Yet . . . even plinking beer cans at the local rock pit, the boy displayed an unfailing lack of proficiency with firearms. His father was more than slightly disappointed. Young Keith was a pure menace with a gun. Practice brought no improvement, nor did experimenting with different styles of weapons. Scopes didn't help. Tripods didn't help. Recoil cushions didn't help. Even goddamn breathing exercises didn't help.

Often these father–son target practices disintegrated into sulking and tears until the elder Higstrom relented, allowing young Keith to fire a few rounds with a twelve-gauge Mossberg, just so he could have the experience of hitting *something*. Clearly the family lineage of crack dead-eye shots had come to a sorry end. Keith's father returned from these outings looking pale and shaken, although he said nothing to Keith's mother about what he'd witnessed at the rock pit.

Fortunately, by the time Keith was old enough to go out hunting, there was practically nothing left to shoot in Miami except for rats and low-flying seagulls. Every autumn, Keith badgered his father into taking him to the Big Cypress Swamp or private hunting camps in the Everglades, where the deer were chased into high water by airboats and shot at point-blank range. The elder Higstrom dreaded these excursions and found no sport in the killing, but his son couldn't have been happier had he been lobbing grenades at crippled fawns.

It was on one such miserable morning that Keith Higstrom's father swore off hunting forever. They were riding a tank-sized swamp buggy in hot pursuit of a scraggly, half-senile bobcat. Suddenly Keith began firing wildly at an object high in the sky— a bald eagle, it turned out, a federally protected species. The attempted felony was not consummated, due to the young man's shaky aim, but in the fever of the moment he managed to blow off his father's left ear.

Deafened, blood-drenched, writhing facedown in Everglades marl, the elder Higstrom experienced a peculiar catharsis, an unexpected soothing of the soul, as if a cool white sheet were slowly being drawn over his head. Yes, his injury was terrible, and the deafness would (if he came clean about it) cost him his job as an air traffic controller. On the other hand, he could never again be forced to go hunting with his excitable son!

Keith Higstrom couldn't duck responsibility for the accident, nor the guilt that went with it. His father recovered from the gunshot wound, and was kind enough not to bring it up more than once or twice a day. Before long, Keith's remorse gave way to an unspoken resentment, for he perceived that his father was using the missing ear as an excuse to avoid their weekend expeditions. A plastic surgeon had attached a durable polyure-thane facsimile to the left side of the elder Higstrom's head, while a high-tech hearing aid had restored the old man's auditory capacity to eighty-one percent of what it was before the Ever-glades mishap. Yet he stubbornly refused to pick up a gun. Doctor's orders, he squawked.

For Keith, outdoor companionship was increasingly hard to come by. His friends always seemed to have prior commitments whenever Keith invited them to go hunting. Frustrated and restless, he spent long sullen weekends cleaning his guns and watching videotapes of his favorite *American Sportsman* episodes. Whenever his trigger finger got itchy, he'd drive out the Tamiami Trail and park by the canal. As soon as darkness fell, Keith would load a double-barrel shotgun, strap on a headlamp and stalk along the shoreline. His usual targets were turtles and opossums; anything faster or smarter generally eluded him.

Shortly after the hurricane, Keith Higstrom noticed four dairy cows and a palomino mare grazing on his neighbor's front lawn. Everyone on the block was gathered on the sidewalk, laughing and taking pictures; a light moment of relief in the otherwise somber aftermath of the storm. That night, drinking with his buddies at an Irish bar on Kendall Drive, Keith asked: 'How much does a cow weigh?'

One of Keith's friends said, 'I give up, Higstrom. How much does a cow weigh?'

'It's not a joke. More than an elk? Because I got cows loose on my street.'

One of his friends said, 'From the hurricane.'

'Yeah, but how big do you figure? More than a mulie?' Keith Higstrom drained his Budweiser and stood up. 'Let's go hunting, boys.'

'Sit down, Higstrom.'

'You pussies coming or not?'

'Have another beer, Keith.'

With a burp, he charged out the door. He drove home, slipped into the den, and removed his grandfather's old .30–06 from the maple gun cabinet. He dropped a box of bullets, and giggled drunkenly when nobody woke up. He pulled on his boots and his mail-order camo jumpsuit, strapped on the headlamp, and went looking for a cow to shoot.

They were no longer grazing in his neighbor's front yard. Dropping into an exaggerated half crouch, Keith Higstrom weaved down the block. He felt light as a feather, lethal as a snake. The rifle was slick and magnificent in his hands. His plan was to tie the dead cow on the front fender of his Honda Civic and drive all the way back to Kendall, back to the Irish bar where his chickenshit pals were drinking. Keith Higstrom chuckled in advance at the spectacle.

For cover he used mounds of hurricane debris, shuffling noisily from one to another. The street was empty and black and shadowless; the homes on the north side still had no electricity. Passing the Ullmans' house, Keith Higstrom heard something in the backyard—deep raspy snorting. He thought it might be the runaway palomino. As he snuck around the corner of the garage, the beam of Keith Higstrom's headlamp illuminated a pair of glistening indigo eyes, as large as ashtrays.

'God damn,' he exclaimed.

An enormous animal stood next to the Ullmans' half-drained swimming pool. The light from Keith's headlamp played up and down its blue-black flanks. This was no ordinary cow. For starters, it was as big as a tractor. Its sharp horns were lavishly curved and downslung, upside down from those of domestic American stock.

Keith Higstrom knew exactly what he was looking at. Hadn't

he watched Jimmy Dean and Curt Gowdy shoot one of the very same majestic bastards on *The American Sportsman*? But that was in Africa, for Christ's sake. Not Miami, Florida.

It occurred to Keith that he might be suffering the effects of too much alcohol, that the gigantic oval-eyed ungulate glaring at him was merely a Budweiser-enhanced Angus.

Then it snorted again, expelling twin strings of dewy snot. The animal lowered its head and, with hooves the size of laundry irons, decisively pawed a trench in the Ullmans' newly replanted Bermuda sod.

'Shit on a biscuit,' Keith Higstrom said, raising his grand-father's rifle. 'That's a Cape buffalo!'

He fired and, naturally, missed. Twice.

The gunshots awakened Mr Ullman, a banker by trade and a recent arrival from Copenhagen, who looked out the bedroom window just in time to see a tremendous bull galloping across his yard with a thrashing young American impaled on its rack. Mr Ullman quickly telephoned the police and informed them, as urgently as his newly acquired English would allow, that an 'unlucky cowboy is being perforated seriously.' Eventually the police figured out what Mr Ullman was trying to say.

Two hours later, a police dispatcher phoned Augustine's house with a message: His dead uncle's missing Cape buffalo, identified by an ear tag, had turned up in the produce aisle of a storm-gutted supermarket. Unfortunately, there was trouble. The dispatcher requested that Augustine call Animal Control as soon as possible.

Augustine didn't check his answering machine for several hours, because he was out on Biscayne Bay with Bonnie Lamb.

They had borrowed the speedboat from one of Augustine's friends, an airline pilot. The pilot owed Augustine a favor from a long-ago divorce, when Augustine had let him bury $45,000 worth of gold Krugerrands behind Augustine's garage, to conceal them from his future ex-wife's private investigator. After the divorce litigation ended, the airline pilot was left with nothing but the hidden stash of coins. He immediately depleted them on a ninety-one-pound fashion model, who later abandoned him at a five-star hotel in Morocco. Although years had passed, the pilot never forgot Augustine's act of friendship in a time of personal crisis.

The speedboat was on a trailer at a marina in North Miami Beach, untouched by the hurricane. Augustine and Bonnie Lamb met Jim Tile there. His eyes were red and his voice was raw. He told them that a close friend, a female trooper, had been savagely beaten by a car thief, and that he would have preferred to be out on road patrol, hunting for the gutless low-life sonofabitch.

As distracted as he was, Jim Tile also seemed visibly anxious about the boat trip. Even in the dark, the bay looked rough and tricky. Oddly, Bonnie Lamb wasn't worried. Maybe it was the way Augustine handled himself behind the wheel; steering casually with two fingers as he aimed, with his free hand, the spotlight. Smoothly he weaved around massive tree limbs and wind-split lumber and ghostly capsized hulls. The scary ride temporarily took Jim Tile's mind off the image of Brenda on an ambulance stretcher. . . .

Bonnie was anticipating her first sight of the man called Skink. She kept thinking about the bloodied corpse in the morgue—impaled on a TV dish, the trooper had said. Was Skink the killer? To hear the trooper tell it, the ex-governor was not a nut of the certifiable, Mansonesque strain. Rather, he was launched on a mission: a reckless doomed mission, boisterously outside the law. Bonnie was intrigued by bold eccentrics. She wasn't afraid of Skink, not with the trooper and Augustine at her side. In an odd way, although she'd never admit it, she looked forward to confronting the kidnapper almost as much as to reuniting with her husband. . . .

Now Jim Tile and Augustine were struggling to drag the unconscious man over the gunwale of the speedboat. His clothes were soaked, adding to his considerable bulk. Bonnie Lamb tried to help. Augustine got a silvery handful of the man's hair, the trooper had him by the belt loops, Bonnie dug her fingers in the tongues of his boots—and finally the kidnapper was on the deck, vomiting seawater.

From the bow came a whine of disgust: Max Lamb, arms

folded, face pinched, sucking a Bronco cigaret. Bonnie turned back to the tranquilized stranger. The trooper knelt beside him. With a handkerchief he cleaned the foul splatter off Skink's face; the glass eye needed special attention.

Augustine said, 'He's breathing.'

A volcanic cough, and then: 'I saw lobsters big as Sonny Liston.' Skink raised his head.

Jim Tile said, 'Be still now.'

'My Walkman!'

'We'll get you a new one. Now lie still.'

Skink lowered his head with a sharp clunk. Humming, he shut both eyes.

Bonnie Lamb asked, 'What do we do with him?'

Max laughed acidly. 'He's going to jail, what'd you think?'

Bonnie looked at Augustine, who said, 'It's up to Jim. He's the law.'

The trooper had a thermos open, trying to get some hot coffee into his groggy friend. Bonnie put her hands under the kidnapper's head to help him drink. Augustine went to the console and started the boat. Over the noise of the engines, Bonnie asked Jim Tile if she should sit with the man during the ride back, in case he got ill again. The trooper leaned close and in a low voice said: 'He's all right now. Go check on your husband.'

'OK,' Bonnie said. She was glad for the darkness, so the trooper couldn't see her blush. Neither could Max.

The conversation between Gar Whitmark and his wife was not a loving one. That she had handed seven thousand cash to a band of crooked roofers was infuriating enough; that she had failed to ask the name of the one taking the money was unforgivably stupid. The only clue in tracking the thieves was the piece of yellow paper that had been given by the phony roofing foreman to Mrs Whitmark, the yellow paper intended to double as a receipt and an estimate, the yellow paper that Mrs Whitmark had instantly misplaced.

Gar Whitmark's anger had another facet. He was by trade a builder of residential subdivisions, and was therefore personally familiar with every honest, competent roofer in Dade County. The list was not voluminous, but from it Gar Whitmark had intended to select the crew that would rebuild the roof of his gutted home. He'd left messages with a half-dozen companies, and had explained (repeatedly) to his wife that it would take time to line up the job. The hurricane had launched a drooling Klondike stampede among roofers—the best ones were swamped with emergency work and likely would be engaged for months to come. Meanwhile out-of-towners were pouring into Miami by the truckload; some were capable and experienced, some were hapless and inept, and many were gypsy impostors. All arrived to find boundless opportunity.

The typical hurricane victim, frantic for shelter, was forced to trust his instincts when choosing a roof builder. Unfortunately, the instincts of the typical hurricane victim in such matters were not acute. Gar Whitmark, however, had the twin advantages of knowing the cast of characters and possessing the clout to divert the best of them to his own pressing needs. With little trouble he located a top-notch roofer who agreed to put all other contracts aside to tackle Gar Whitmark's roof (Whitmark being one of the most prolific home builders—and employers of roofing contractors—in all South Florida). However, the craftsman whom Whitmark selected first had to replace two other roofs: his own, and that of his wife's mother.

Gar Whitmark gave the man seven days to patch up the family roofs. The delay proved unbearable for Mrs Whitmark, whose roaring anxiety at the chance of more rain-stained Chippendales was no match for her customary palliative dosages of sedatives, muscle relaxants, sleep aids and mood elevators. To Mrs Whitmark, the unexpected appearance of willing roofers at the door had been a godsend. She thought her husband would be grateful for her initiative—it would be one less problem for him to worry about, what with all the nasty threats of negligence suits from customers whose Whitmark Signature homes had disintegrated like soggy cardboard in the hurricane.

Standing in the living room, the rain beating a tattoo on his blue-veined forehead, Gar Whitmark instructed his wife to immediately locate the goddamn receipt or estimate or whatever the goddamn so-called foreman had called it. After an hour's search, the crucial yellow paper turned up neatly folded in Mrs Whitmark's highschool yearbook; Gar Whitmark couldn't imagine why his wife had put it there, or how she found it. Nor could she explain it herself—her brain was too jumbled by the hurricane.

The receipt bore the name of 'Fortress roofing,' which brought a bitter cackle from Gar Whitmark. At least the scammers had a sense of irony! Gar Whitmark dialed the number and got an answering machine. He hung up and called the director of the county building-and-zoning department, who owed his job to seven of the county commissioners, who owed their jobs to Gar Whitmark's generous campaign contributions. As Gar Whitmark anticipated, the building director expressed shock and alarm that a fraud was perpetrated on Gar Whitmark's wife, and promised a thorough criminal investigation.

No, he hadn't ever heard of Fortress roofing—but he'd damn sure find out who was behind it.

Sooner the better, said Gar Whitmark, toweling the rainwater from his stinging scalp, which bristled with fifty pink-stemmed, freshly implanted hair plugs.

Fifteen minutes later, the building director phoned back to report, mournfully, that Fortress roofing had never obtained a valid Dade County contractor's license and was therefore an unknown outlaw entity.

In a fury, Gar Whitmark began contacting roofers he knew—some honest, some not. The name Fortress struck a note with one or two, who said they'd recently lost crew to the new company. The sonofabitch owner, they said, was an ex-inspector named Avila. Dirty as they come, the roofers warned.

Gar Whitmark knew Avila quite well, having successfully bribed him for many years. All those times Gar Whitmark's subcontractors had slipped booty to the greedy bastard! Cash, booze, porn—Avila had a taste for the hard stuff; girl-on-girl, if Gar Whitmark remembered correctly.

He called his secretary, whose fingers swiftly punched up a

highly confidential computer file of corrupt and/or corruptible officials in Dade, Broward, Palm Beach, Lee and Monroe Counties. It was a lengthy roster, alphabetized for convenience. Avila's name and unlisted home phone number winked fatefully at the bottom of the first screen.

Gar Whitmark waited until three in the morning before phoning.

'This is your old friend Gar Whitmark,' he said. 'Your crew of gypsy fakers hit my wife for seven grand. My wife is not well, Avila. If I don't see my money by tomorrow morning, you'll be in the county jail by tomorrow night. And I will arrange for you to share a cell with Paul Pick-Percy.'

The threat brutally jarred Avila wide awake. Paul Pick-Percy was a notorious cannibal. Currently he awaited trial on charges of killing and eating his landlord, who had neglected to repair a leaky ball cock in Paul Pick-Percy's toilet tank. Recently Paul Pick-Percy had also been found guilty of killing and eating a tardy cable-TV repairman and a rude tollbooth attendant.

Avila said: 'Seven thousand? Mister Whitmark, I swear to God I don't know nothing about this.'

'Suit yourself—'

'Wait, now hold on. . . .' Avila sat upright in bed. 'Tell me supposedly what happened, OK?'

'There is no fucking "supposedly."' Gar Whitmark related his wife's pitiable tale.

'And the truck was ours, you're sure?'

'I'm holding the receipt, dipshit. "Fortress roofing" is what it says.'

Avila grimaced. 'Who signed it?'

Gar Whitmark said the signature was illegible. 'My wife said the guy had a fucked-up jaw made him look like amoray eel. Plus he wore a bad suit.'

'Shit,' Avila said. Exactly what he'd feared.

'Is this ringing a bell?' Gar Whitmark's sarcasm was heavy and ominous.

Avila sagged against the headboard of his bed. 'Sir, you'll get your money back first thing.'

'Damn straight. And a new roof as well.'

'What?'

'You heard me, noodle dick. The seven grand your people stole, plus you're picking up the bill when my new roof gets done. By real roofers.'

Avila's stomach pitched. Gar Whitmark probably lived in a goddamn ranch house way down south, with all the other millionaires. Avila figured he'd be looking at twenty thousand, easy, for a new roof job. He said, 'That ain't really fair.'

'You'd rather do dinner with Chef Pick-Percy?'

'Aw, Christ, Mister Whitmark.'

'I didn't think so.'

Avila got out of bed and went to the backyard to round up two roosters, which he took to the garage for beheading. He hoped the sacrifice would be favorably received. After a short scuffle, the deed was done. Avila dripped the warm blood into a plastic pail filled with pennies, bleached cat bones and turtle shells. The pail was placed at the feet of a ceramic statue of Chango, the saint of lightning and fire. The child-sized statue wore a robe, colored beads and a gold-plated crown. Kneeling in beseechment, Avila raised his blood-flecked arms toward the heavens and asked Chango to please strike Snapper dead as a fucking doornail for screwing up the roofer scam.

Avila wasn't sure the ceremony would work. He was relatively new to the study of *santería* and, characteristically, hadn't bothered to research it thoroughly. Avila had begun dabbling in the blood practices when he first learned the authorities were investigating him for bribery; several cocaine dealers of his acquaintance swore that *santería* worship had kept them out of jail, so Avila figured there was nothing to lose by trying. In Hialeah he conferred with a genuine *santero* priest, who offered to teach him the secrets of the religion, rooted in ancient Afro-Cuban customs. The history was infinitely too deep and mystical for Avila, and soon he grew impatient with the lessons.

All he really wanted, he explained to the *santero*, was the ability to put curses on his enemies. Lethal curses.

The priest wailed and told him to get lost. But Avila went home convinced that, from the mumbo jumbo he'd seen, he could teach himself the basics of hexing. For his deity Avila picked the saint Chango, because he liked the macho name. For his first target he chose the county prosecutor leading the investigation against corrupt building inspectors.

Pennies were easy to come by, as were old animal bones; Avila's grandmother lived four blocks from a pet cemetery in Medley. Obtaining blood was the biggest obstacle for Avila, who had no zeal for performing live sacrifices. The first few times, he tried pleasing Chango by sprinkling the coins and bones with steak juices and homemade bouillon. Nothing happened. Evidently the *santería* saints preferred the fresh stuff.

One rainy Sunday afternoon, Avila bought himself a live chicken. His wife was cooking a big dinner for the cousins, so she banished Avila from the kitchen. He put a Ginsu knife in his back pocket and smuggled the victim to the garage. As soon as Avila began spreading newspapers on the floor, the chicken sensed trouble. Avila was astounded that a puny five-pound bird could make such a racket or put up such spirited resistance. The crudely staged sacrifice eventually was completed, but Avila emerged scratched, pecked and smeared with bloody feathers. So was his wife's cream-colored Buick Electra. Her ear-splitting tirade caused the cousins to forgo dessert and head home early.

Two days later, the magic happened. The prosecutor targeted by Avila's chicken curse fell and dislocated a shoulder in the shower. At the time, he was in the company of an athletic prostitute named Kandi, who was thoughtful enough not only to call 911 but to make herself available for numerous press interviews. Given the media uproar, the State Attorney suggested that the fallen prosecutor take an indefinite leave of absence.

The corruption investigation wasn't derailed, merely reassigned. Nevertheless, Avila was convinced that the *santería* spell was a success. Later attempts to replicate the results proved fruitless (and messy), but Avila blamed his own inexperience, plus a lack of suitable facilities. Perhaps, during the sacrifices, he was chanting the wrong phrases, or chanting the right phrases in the wrong order. Perhaps he was performing the ceremonies at a bad time of day for the mercurial Chango. Or perhaps Avila was simply using inferior poultry.

While he ended up plea-bargaining with the replacement prosecutor, Avila's faith in the witchcraft of bones and blood remained unshaken. He decided Snapper's transgression was heinous enough to merit the offering of two chickens instead of one. If that didn't work, he'd invest in a billy goat.

The roosters did not succumb quietly, the clamor awakening Avila's wife, aunt and mother. The women burst into the garage to find Avila singing Spanish gibberish to his cherished ceramic statue. Avila's wife instantly spied red droplets and a waxen fragment of chicken beak on the left front fender of her Electra, and savagely took to striking her husband with a garden rake.

On the other side of Dade County, Snapper dozed peacefully in a dead man's Naugahyde recliner. He felt no pain from the supernatural hand of Chango, nor did he feel the hateful glare of Edie Marsh, who was stretched out on the mildewed carpet and trussed to a naked insurance man.

14

As the candles melted to lumps, Snapper's shadow flickered and shrunk on the pale bare walls. His profile reminded Edie Marsh of a miniature tyrannosaurus.

For laughs, he refused to let Fred Dove remove the red condom.

'That's mean,' Edie said.

'Well, I'm one mean motherfucker,' Snapper proclaimed. 'You don't believe me, there's a lady cop in the hospital you should see.'

When he yawned, the misaligned mandible waggled horizontally, then appeared to disengage altogether from his face. He looked like a snake trying to swallow an egg.

Edie said, 'What is it you want?'

'You know damn well.' Snapper held the flashlight on Fred Dove's retreating cock. 'Where'd you find a red rubber?' he asked. 'Mail order, I bet. Looks like a Santy Claus hat.'

From the floor, the insurance man gave a disconsolate whimper. Edie leaned her head against the small of his back. Snapper had positioned them butt-to-butt, binding their hands with a curtain sash. In Fred Dove's briefcase Snapper found the business cards and policy folders from Midwest Casualty. From that it was easy to figure out—Edie on her knees, and so on. Snapper marveled at the exquisite timing of his entrance.

He said, 'Fair is fair. A three-way split.'

'But you took off!' Edie objected. 'You left me here with that asshole Tony.'

Snapper shrugged. 'I changed my mind. I'm allowed. So how much money we talkin' about?'

'Fuck you,' said Edie Marsh.

Without leaving the recliner, Snapper cocked one leg and kicked her in the side of the head. The sound of the blow was sickening. Edie moaned but didn't cry.

'For God's sake.' Fred Dove's voice cracked, as if he were the one who'd been clobbered.

Snapper said, 'Then tell me how much.'

'Don't you dare.' Edie was woozy, but sharply she dug both elbows into Fred Dove's ribs.

'I'm waiting,' said Snapper.

Edie felt the insurance man stiffen against the ropes. Then she heard him say: 'A hundred forty-one thousand dollars.'

'Moron!' Edie hissed.

'But you won't get a dime,' Fred Dove warned Snapper, 'without me and Edie.'

'That a fact?'

'Yes, sir.'

'Not a goddamn cent,' Edie agreed, 'because guess who's getting the settlement check. *Missus* Neria Torres. Me.'

Snapper aimed the flashlight on Edie's face, which bore a puffy salmon imprint of his shoe. 'Sweetie,' he said, 'it's hard to sign a check if you're in a body cast. Understand?'

She turned away from the harsh light and silently cursed her lousy taste in convicts.

Fred Dove said to Snapper: 'You ought to untie us.'

'Well, listen to Santy Claus!'

Edie's pulse jackhammered in her temples. 'You know what it is, Fred? Snapper's jealous. See, it's not about the insurance money. It's that I was going to make love to you—'

'Haw!' Snapper exclaimed.

'—and he knows,' Edie went on, 'he knows I wouldn't do it with him for all the money in Fort Knox!'

Snapper laughed. Nudging Fred Dove with a toe, he said, 'Don't kid yourself, bubba. She'd fuck a syphilitic porky-pine, she thought there was a dollar in it.'

'Nice talk,' Edie said. God Almighty, her head hurt.

The insurance man fought to steady his nerves. He was flabbergasted to find himself in the middle of something so ugly, complicated and dangerous. Only hours ago the arrangement seemed foolproof and exciting: a modestly fraudulent claim, a beautiful and uninhibited co-conspirator, a wild fling in an abandoned hurricane house.

A bright-red condom seemed appropriate.

Then out of nowhere appeared this Snapper person, a hard-looking sort and an authentic criminal, judging by what Fred Dove had seen and heard. The insurance man didn't want such a violent character for a third partner. On the other hand, he didn't want to die or be harmed seriously enough to require hospitalization. Blue Cross would demand facts, as would Fred Dove's wife.

So he offered Snapper forty-seven thousand dollars. 'That's how it splits three ways.' Snapper swung the flashlight to Fred Dove's face. He said, 'You figured that up in your head? No pencil and paper, that's pretty good.'

Yeah, thought Edie Marsh. Thank you, Dr Einstein.

Fred Dove said to Snapper: 'Do we have a deal?'

'Fair is fair.' He rose from the BarcaLounger and made his way to the garage. Within moments the portable generator belched to life. Snapper returned to the living room and turned on the solitary lightbulb. Then, kneeling beside Fred Dove and Edie Marsh, he cut the curtain sash off their wrists.

'Let's go eat,' he said. 'I'm fuckin' starved.'

Fred Dove rose shakily. He modestly locked his hands in front of his crotch. 'I'm taking this thing off,' he declared.

'The rubber?' Snapper gave him a thumbs-up. 'You do that.' He glanced at Edie, who made no effort to cover her breasts or anything else. She eyed Snapper in a dark poisonous way.

He said, 'That's how you goin' to Denny's? Fine by me. Maybe we'll get a free pie.'

Wordlessly Edie walked behind the Naugahyde recliner, picked up the crowbar she'd left there, took two steps toward Snapper, and swung at him with all her strength. He went down squalling.

Weapon in hand, Edie Marsh straddled him. Her damp and

tangled hair had fallen to cover the bruised half of her face. To Fred Dove, she looked untamed and dazzling and alarmingly capable of homicide. He feared he was about to witness his first.

Edie inserted the sharp end of the crowbar between Snapper's deviated jawbones, pinning his bloodless tongue to his teeth.

'Kick me again,' she said, 'and I'll have your balls in a blender.'

Fred Dove snatched his pants and his briefcase, and ran.

They returned the borrowed speedboat to the marina and went back to Coral Gables. With great effort they carried the man known as Skink into Augustine's house.

Max Lamb was unnerved by the wall of grinning skulls, but said nothing as he made his way down the hall to the shower. Augustine got on the telephone to sort out what had happened with his dead uncle's Cape buffalo. Bonnie fixed a pot of coffee and took it to the guest room, where the governor was recovering from the animal dart. He and Jim Tile were talking when Bonnie walked in. She wanted to stay and listen to this improbable stranger, but she felt she was intruding. The men's conversation was serious, held in low tones. She heard Skink say:

'Brenda's a strong one. She'll make it.'

Then, Jim Tile: 'I've tried every prayer I know.'

As Bonnie slipped out the door, she encountered Max, sucking on a cigaret as he emerged from the bathroom. She resolved to be forbearing about her husband's odious new habit, which he blamed on the battlefield stress of the abduction.

She followed him to the living room and sat beside him on the sofa. There, in sensational detail, he described the torture he'd received at the hands of the one-eyed misfit.

'The dog collar,' Bonnie Lamb said.

'That's right. Look at my neck.' Max opened the top buttons of his shirt, which he'd borrowed from Augustine. 'See the burns? See?'

Bonnie didn't notice any marks, but nodded sympathetically. 'So you definitely want to prosecute.'

'Absolutely!' Max Lamb detected doubt in his wife's voice. 'Christ, Bonnie, he could've murdered me.'

She squeezed his hand. 'I still don't understand why—why he did it in the first place.'

'With a fruitcake like that, who knows.' Max Lamb purposely didn't mention Skink's disgust with the hurricane videos; he remembered that Bonnie felt the same way.

She said, 'I think he needs professional help.'

'No, sweetheart, he needs a professional jail.' Max lifted his chin and blew smoke at the ceiling.

'Honey, let's think about this—'

But he pulled away from her, bolting for the phone, which Augustine had just hung up. 'I'd better call Pete Archibald,' Max Lamb said over his shoulder, 'let everyone at Rodale know I'm OK.'

Bonnie Lamb got up and went to the guest room. The governor was sitting upright in bed, but his eyes were half shut. His ragged beard was finely crusted with ocean salt. Jim Tile, his Stetson tucked under one arm, stood near the window.

Bonnie poured each of them another cup of coffee. 'How's he feeling?' she whispered.

Skink's good eye blinked open. 'Better,' he said, thickly.

She set the coffeepot on the bedstand. 'It was monkey tranquilizer,' she explained.

'Never to be combined with psychoactive drugs,' said Skink, 'particularly toad sweat.'

Bonnie looked at Jim Tile, who said, 'I asked him.'

'Asked me what?' Skink rasped.

'About the dead guy in the TV dish,' the trooper said. Then, to Bonnie: 'He didn't do it.'

'Though I do admire the style,' said Skink.

Bonnie Lamb did a poor job of masking her doubt. Skink peered sternly. 'I didn't kill that fellow, Mrs Lamb. But I damn sure wouldn't tell you if I had.'

'I believe you. I do.'

The governor finished the coffee and asked for another cup. He told Bonnie it was the best he'd ever tasted. 'And I like your boy,' he said, gesturing toward the wall of skulls. 'I like what he's done with the place.'

Bonnie said: 'He's not my boy. Just a friend.'

Skink nodded. 'We all need one of those.' With difficulty he rolled out of bed and began stripping off his wet clothes. Jim Tile led him to the shower and started the water. When the trooper returned, carrying the governor's plastic cap, he asked Bonnie Lamb what her husband intended to do.

'He wants to prosecute.' She sat on the edge of the bed, listening to the shower run.

Augustine came into the room and said, 'Well?'

'I can arrest him tonight,' Jim Tile told Bonnie, 'if your husband comes to the substation and files charges. What happens then is up to the State Attorney.'

'You'd do that—arrest your own friend?'

'Better me than a stranger,' the trooper said. 'Don't feel bad about this, Mrs Lamb. Your husband's got every right.'

'Yes, I know.' Prosecuting the governor was the right thing—a person couldn't be allowed to run around kidnapping tourists, no matter how offensively they behaved. Yet Bonnie was saddened by the idea of Skink's going to jail. It was naive, she knew, but that's how she felt.

Jim Tile was questioning Augustine about the skulls on the wall. 'Cuban voodoo?'

'No, nothing like that.'

'Nineteen is what I count,' the trooper said. 'I won't ask where you got 'em. They're too clean for homicides.'

Bonnie Lamb said, 'They're medical specimens.'

'Whatever you say.' After twenty years of attending head-on collisions, Jim Tile had a well-earned aversion to human body parts. 'Specimens it is,' he said.

Augustine removed five of the skulls from the shelves and lined them up on the hardwood floor, at his feet. Then he picked up three and began to juggle.

The trooper said, 'I'll be damned.'

As he juggled, Augustine thought about the drunken young fool who tried to shoot his uncle's Cape buffalo. What a sad, dumb way to die. Fluidly he snatched a fourth skull off the floor and put it in rotation; then the fifth.

Bonnie Lamb found herself smiling at the performance in spite of its creepiness. The governor emerged from the shower in a cloud of steam, naked except for a sky-blue towel around his neck. His thick silver hair sent snaky tails of water down his chest. He used a corner of the towel to dab the condensation off his glass eye. He beamed when he saw Augustine's juggling.

Jim Tile felt dizzy, watching the skulls fly. Max Lamb appeared in the doorway. His expression instantly changed from curiosity to revulsion, as if a switch had been flipped inside his head. Bonnie knew what he was going to say before the words left his lips: 'You think *this* is funny?'

Augustine continued juggling. It was unclear whether he, or the governor's nudity, was the object of Max Lamb's disapproval.

The trooper said, 'It's been a long night, man.'

'Bonnie, we're leaving.' Max's tone was patronizing and snarky. 'Did you hear me? Playtime is over.'

She was infuriated that her husband would speak to her that way in front of strangers. She stormed from the room.

'Oh, Max?' Skink, wearing a sly smile, touched a finger to his own throat. Max Lamb's neck tingled the old Tri-Tronics tingle. He jumped reflexively, banging against the door.

From the backpack Skink retrieved Max's billfold and the keys to the rental car. He dropped them in Max's hand. Max mumbled a thank-you and went after Bonnie.

Augustine stopped juggling, catching the skulls one by one. Carefully he returned them to their place on the wall.

The governor tugged the towel from his neck and began drying his arms and legs. 'I like that girl,' he said to Augustine. 'How about you?'

'What's not to like.'

'You've got a big decision to make.'

'That's very funny. She's married.'

'Love is just a kiss away. So the song says.' Playfully Skink seized Jim Tile by the elbows. 'Tell me, Officer. Am I arrested or not?'

'That's up to Mister Max Lamb.'

'I need to know.'

'They're talking it over,' Jim Tile said.

'Because if I'm not bound for jail, I'd dearly love to go find the bastard who beat up your Brenda.'

For a moment the trooper seemed to sag under the weight of his grief. His eyes welled up, but he kept himself from breaking down.

Skink said, 'Jim, please. I live for opportunities like this.'

'You've had enough excitement. We all have.'

'You, son!' the governor barked at Augustine. 'You had enough excitement?'

'Well, they just shot my water buffalo at a supermarket—'

'Ho!' Skink exclaimed.

'—but I'd be honored to help.' The skull juggling had left Augustine energetic and primed. He was in the mood for a new project, now that Bonnie's husband was safe.

'You think about what I said,' Skink told Jim Tile. 'In the meantime, I'm damn near hungry enough to eat processed food. How about you guys?'

He charged toward the door, but the trooper blocked his path. 'Put on your pants, captain. Please.'

The corpse of Tony Torres lay unclaimed and unidentified in the morgue. Each morning Ira Jackson checked the *Herald*, but in the reams of hurricane news there was no mention of a crucified mobile-home salesman. Ira Jackson took this as affirmation of Tony Torres's worthlessness and insignificance; his death didn't rate one lousy paragraph in the newspaper.

Ira Jackson turned his vengeful attentions toward Avila, the inspector who had corruptly rubber-stamped the permits for the late Beatrice Jackson's trailer home. Ira Jackson believed Avila was as culpable as Tony Torres for the tragedy that had claimed the life of his trusting mother.

Early on the morning of August 28, Ira Jackson drove to the address he'd pried from the reluctant clerk at the Metro building department. A woman with a heavy accent answered the front door. Ira Jackson asked to speak to Señor Avila.

'He bissy eng de grotch.'

'Please tell him it's important.'

'Hokay, but he berry bissy.'

'I'll wait,' said Ira Jackson.

Avila was scrubbing rooster blood off the whitewalls of his wife's Buick when his mother announced he had a visitor. Avila swore and kicked at the bucket of soap. It had to be Gar Whitmark, harassing him for the seven grand. What did he expect Avila to do—rob a fucking bank!

But it wasn't Whitmark at the door. It was a stocky middle-aged stranger with a chopped haircut, a gold chain around his neck and a smudge of white powder on his upper lip. Avila recognized the powder as doughnut dust. He wondered if the guy was a cop.

'My name is Rick,' said Ira Jackson, extending a pudgy scarred hand. 'Rick Reynolds.' When the man smiled, a smear of grape jelly was visible on his bottom row of teeth.

Avila said, 'I'm kinda busy right now.'

'I was driving by and saw the truck.' Ira Jackson pointed. 'Fortress roofing—that's you, right?'

Avila didn't answer yes or no. His eyes flicked to his truck at the curb, and the Cadillac parked behind it. The man wasn't a cop, not with a flashy car like that.

'The storm tore off my roof. I need a new one ASAP.'

Avila said, 'We're booked solid. I'm really sorry.'

He hated to turn down a willing sucker, but it would be suicidal to run a scam on someone who knew where he lived. Especially someone with forearms the size of fence posts.

Avila made a mental note to move the roofing truck off the street, to a place where passersby couldn't see it.

Ira Jackson licked the doughnut sugar from his lip. 'I'll make it worth your while,' he said.

'Wish I could help.'

'How's ten thousand sound? On top of your regular price.'

Try as he might, Avila couldn't conceal his interest. The guy had a New York accent; they did things in a big way up there.

'That's ten thousand cash,' Ira Jackson added. 'See, it's my grandmother, she lives with us. Ninety years old and suddenly it's raining buckets on her head. The roof's flat-out gone.'

Avila feigned compassion. 'Ninety years old? Bless her heart.' He stepped outside and closed the door behind him. 'Problem is, I've got a dozen other jobs waiting.'

'Fifteen thousand,' Ira Jackson said, 'if you move me to the top of the list.'

Avila rubbed his stubbled chin and eyed the visitor. How often, he thought, does fifteen grand come knocking at the door? A rip-off was out of the question, but another option loomed. Radical, to be sure, but do-able: Avila could build the man a legitimate, complete roof. Use the cash to settle up with Gar Whitmark. Naturally the crew would piss and moan, spoiled bastards. Properly installing a roof was a hard, hot, exhausting job. Perhaps desperate times called for honest work.

'I see,' remarked Ira Jackson, 'your place came through the hurricane pretty good.'

'We were a long way from the eye, thank God.'

'Thank God is right.'

'Where exactly do you live, Mister Reynolds? Maybe I can squeeze you on the schedule.'

'Fantastic.'

'I'll send a man out for an estimate,' Avila said. Then he remembered there was no man to send; the thieving Snapper had skipped.

Ira Jackson said, 'I'd prefer it was you personally.'

'Sure, Mister Reynolds. How about tomorrow first thing?'

'How about right now? We can ride in my car.'

Avila couldn't think of a single reason not to go, and fifteen thousand reasons why he should.

When Max Lamb put down the phone, his face was gray and his mouth was slack. He looked as if he'd been diagnosed with a terminal illness. The reality was no less grave, as far as the Rodale & Burns agency was concerned. On the other end of the line, easygoing Pete Archibald had sounded funereal and defeated. The news from New York was bad indeed.

The National Institutes of Health had scheduled a press conference to further enumerate the health hazards of cigaret smoking. Ordinarily the advertising world would scarcely take notice, so routine and predictable were these dire outcries. No matter how harrowing the medical revelations, the impact on retail cigaret sales seldom lasted more than a few weeks. This time, though, the government had used sophisticated technology to test specific brands for concentrations of tars, nicotine and other assorted carcinogens. Broncos rated first; Bronco Menthols rated second, Lady Broncos third. Epidemiologically, they were the most lethal products in the history of tobacco cultivation. Smoking a Bronco, in the lamentably quotable words of one wiseass NIH scientist, was 'only slightly safer than sucking on the tailpipe of a Chevrolet Suburban.'

Details of the NIH bombshell had quickly leaked to Durham Gas Meat & Tobacco, manufacturer of Broncos and other fine products. The company's knee-jerk response was a heated threat to cancel its advertising in all newspapers and magazines that intended to report the government's findings. That bombastically idiotic maneuver, Max Lamb knew, would itself become front-page headlines if sane heads didn't prevail. Max had to get back to New York as soon as possible.

When he told his wife, she said: 'Right now?'

As if she didn't understand the gravity of the crisis.

'In my business,' Max explained impatiently, 'this is a flaming 747 full of orphans, plowing into a mountainside.'

'Is it true about Broncos?'

'Probably. That's not the problem. They can't start yanking their ads; there's serious money at stake. Double-digit millions.'

'Max.'

'What?'

'Please put out that damn cigaret.'

'Jesus, Bonnie, listen to yourself.'

They were sitting in wicker chairs on Augustine's patio. It was three or four in the morning. Inside the house, Neil Young played on the stereo. Through the French doors Bonnie Lamb saw Augustine in the kitchen. He noticed she was watching, and shot her a quick shy smile. The black trooper and the one-eyed governor were standing over the stove; it smelled like they were frying bacon and ham.

Max Lamb said, 'We'll catch the first plane.' He stubbed out his Bronco and flipped the butt into a birdbath.

'What about *him*?' Bonnie cut her eyes toward the kitchen window, where Skink could be seen breaking eggs at the sink. She said to Max, 'You wanted to file charges, didn't you? Put him in jail where he belongs.'

'Honey, there's no time. After the NIH mess blows over, we'll fly back and take care of that maniac. Don't worry.'

Bonnie Lamb said, 'If they let him go now . . .' She finished the sentence in her head.

If they let him go now, they'll never find him again. He'll vanish like a ghost in the swamp. And wouldn't that be a darn shame.

Bonnie bewildered herself with such sentiment. What's wrong with me? The man abducted and abused my husband. Why don't I want to see him punished?

'You're right,' she said to Max. 'You should go back to New York as soon as you can.'

With a frown, he reached over and lightly smacked a mosquito on her arm. 'What does that mean—you're not coming?'

'Max, I'm not up for a plane trip this morning. My stomach's in knots.'

'Take some Mylanta.'

'I did,' Bonnie lied. 'Maybe it was the boat ride.'

'You'll feel better later.'

'I'm sure I will.'

He said he'd get her a room near the airport. 'Take a long nap,' he suggested, 'and catch an evening flight.'

'Sounds good.'

Poor Max, she thought. He hasn't got a clue.

15

Bonnie Brooks's father worked in the circulation department of the Chicago *Tribune*, and her mother was a buyer for Sears. They had an apartment in the city and a summer cabin on the boundary waters in Minnesota. Bonnie, an only child, had mixed memories of family vacations. Her father was an unadventurous fellow for whom the northern wilderness held no allure. Because he couldn't swim and was allergic to deerflies, he avoided the lakes. Instead he stayed in the cabin and assembled model airplanes; classic German Fokkers were his passion. The tedious hobby was made more so by her father's chronic ham-fistedness, which turned the simplest glue job into high drama. Bonnie and her mother stayed out of the way, to avoid being blamed for disturbing his concentration.

While her father toiled over the model planes, Bonnie's mother paddled her across the wooded lakes in an old birch canoe. Bonnie remembered those happy mornings—trailing her fingertips in the chilly water, feeling the sunlight warm the back of her neck. Her mother was not the stealthiest of paddlers, but they saw their share of wildlife—deer, squirrels, beavers, the occasional moose. Bonnie recalled asking, more than once, why her folks had bought the cabin if her father was so averse to the outdoors. Her mother always explained: 'It was either here or Wisconsin.'

Bonnie Brooks attended Northwestern University and, to her father's puzzlement, majored in journalism. Soon she embarked on her first serious romance, with a divorced adjunct professor who claimed to have won prizes for his reportage of the Vietnam War. The absence of plaques in the professor's office Bonnie naively attributed to modesty. For Christmas she decided to surprise him with a framed, laminated copy of his front-page scoop about the mining of Haiphong harbor. Yet when Bonnie searched the college's microfilm of the San Francisco *Chronicle*, for whom her lover had supposedly worked, she found not a single bylined story bearing his name. Demonstrating the blood instincts of a seasoned reporter, she contacted the newspaper's personnel department and (using harmless subterfuge) was able to determine that the closest her heroic seducer had ever come to Southeast Asia was the copy desk of the *Chronicle*'s Seattle bureau.

Bonnie Brooks acted decisively. First she dumped the jerk, then she got him fired from the university. Subsequent boyfriends were more loyal and forthcoming, but what they lacked in dishonesty they made up for with indolence. Bonnie's mother grew tired of cooking them meals and deflecting their half-hearted offers to help dry the dishes. She couldn't wait for her daughter to graduate from school and find herself a grown-up man.

Good or bad, jobs in journalism were hard to come by. Like many of her classmates, Bonnie Brooks wound up writing publicity blurbs and press releases. She went to work first for the City of Chicago Parks Department and then for a baby-food company that was eventually purchased by Crespo Mills Internationale. There Bonnie was promoted to the job of assistant corporate publicist. The title was attached to a salary that ten tough years in most city newsrooms wouldn't have earned. As for the writing, it was as elementary as it was unsatisfying. In addition to pabulums and breakfast cereals, Crespo Mills manufactured whipped condiment spreads, peanut butter, granola bars, cookies, crackers, trail mix, flavored popcorn, bread sticks and three styles of croutons. In no time, Bonnie Brooks ran out of appetizing adjectives. Attempts at lyrical originality were discouraged by her Crespo supervisors; during one especially dreary streak, she was required to use the word 'tasty' in fourteen consecutive press releases. When Max Lamb asked her to marry him and move to New York, Bonnie didn't hesitate to quit her job.

Max could take only a few days off from work, so they decided to take their honeymoon at Disney World—a corny choice, but Bonnie figured anything was better than Niagara Falls. She knew that a waterfall, no matter how grandiose, wouldn't hold Max's interest. Neither, it turned out, did Mickey Mouse. Two days at the Magic Kingdom and Max was as antsy as a cat burglar.

Then the hurricane blew in, and he just *had* to go see. . . .

Bonnie had wanted to stay in Orlando, stay cuddled under the scratchy motel sheets and make love while the rain drummed on the windows. Why wasn't that enough for him?

She'd almost asked that very question as they sat in the dark on Augustine's patio after the adventure in Stiltsville. And later, on the way to the airport. And again, standing at the Delta gate, when he'd hugged her in a loose and distracted way, his hair and shirt reeking of cigarets.

But Bonnie hadn't asked. The moment wasn't right; he was a man with a purpose. A grown-up man, just like her mother wanted her to find. Except her mother thought Max was an asshole. Her father, well, he thought Max Lamb was a fine young fella. He thought all Bonnie's boyfriends had been fine young fellas.

She wondered what her father would think of her now, on the way to a hospital, scrunched in the front seat of a pickup truck between a one-eyed, toad-smoking kidnapper and a plane-crash survivor who juggled skulls.

Brenda Rourke's head was fractured in three places, and one of her cheeks needed reconstruction. She was bleeding under the right temporal bone, but doctors had managed to stanch it. A plastic surgeon had repaired a U-shaped gash on her forehead, stitching the loose flap above the hairline.

Bonnie Lamb had never seen such terrible wounds. Even the governor seemed shaken. Augustine fastened his eyes on his shoetops—the sounds and smells of the hospital were too familiar. He felt parched.

Jim Tile held both of Brenda's hands in one of his own. Her

eyes were open but unfocused; she had no sense of anyone besides Jim at her bedside. She was trying to talk through the drugs and the pain; he leaned closer to listen.

After a while he straightened, announcing in a low, angry voice, 'The bastard stole her ring. Her mother's wedding ring.'

Skink slipped from the room so quietly that Bonnie and Augustine didn't notice immediately. There was no trace of him outside the door, but a rush of blue and white uniforms attracted them to the end of the hall. The governor was in the nursery, strolling among the newborns. He carried an infant in the crook of each arm. The babies slept soundly, and he studied them with profound sadness. To Bonnie Lamb he appeared harmless, despite the rebellious beard and the grubby combat pants and the army boots. A trio of husky orderlies conferred at a water fountain; apparently a negotiation had already been attempted, with poor results. Calmly Jim Tile entered the nursery and returned the infants to their glass cribs.

Nobody intervened when the trooper led Skink out of the hospital, because it looked like a routine arrest; another loony street case hauled to the stockade: Jim Tile, his arm around the madman, walking him briskly down the maze of pale-green corridors; the two of them talking intently; Bonnie and Augustine dodging wheelchairs and gurneys and trying to keep up.

When they reached the parking lot, Jim Tile said he had to go to work. 'The President's coming, and guess who gets to clear traffic.'

He folded a piece of paper into Skink's hand and got into the patrol car. Wordlessly Skink settled in the bed of Augustine's pickup and lay down. His good eye was fixed on the clouds, and his arms were folded across his chest.

Augustine asked Jim Tile: 'What do we do with him?'

'That's entirely up to you.' The trooper sounded exhausted.

Bonnie Lamb asked about Brenda Rourke. Jim Tile said the doctors expected her to pull through.

'What about the guy who did it?'

'They haven't caught him,' the trooper replied, 'and they won't.' He strapped on the seat belt, locked the door, adjusted his sunglasses. 'Place used to be something special,' he said absently. 'Long, long time ago.'

A feral cry rose from the bed of the pickup truck. Jim Tile blinked over the rims of his shades. 'It was nice meeting you, Mrs Lamb. You and your husband do what's right. The captain, he'll understand.'

Then the trooper drove off.

On the way to the airport hotel, where Max Lamb had reserved a day room for her, Bonnie slid across the front seat and rested her cheek on Augustine's shoulder. He was dreading this part, saying good-bye. It was always easier as a bitter cleaving, when suitcases snapped shut, doors slammed, taxis screeched out of the driveway. He checked the dashboard clock—less than three hours until her flight.

Through the back window of the truck, Bonnie saw that Skink had pulled the flowered cap over his face and drawn himself into a loose-jointed variation of a fetal curl.

She said, 'I wonder what's on that piece of paper.'

'My guess,' said Augustine, 'it's either a name or an address.'

'Of what?'

'It's just a guess,' he said, but he told her anyway.

That night he didn't have to say good-bye, because Bonnie Lamb didn't go home to New York. She canceled her flight and returned to Augustine's house. Her phone messages for Max were not returned until after midnight, when she was already asleep in the skull room.

Shortly after noon on August 28, the telephone in Tony Torres's kitchen started ringing.

Snapper told Edie Marsh to get it.

'*You* get it,' she said.

'Real funny.'

Snapper couldn't walk; the blow from the crowbar had messed up his right leg. He was laid out in the BarcaLounger with his knee packed in three bags of ice, which Edie had purchased for fifty dollars on Quail Roost Drive from some traveling bandit in a fish truck. The fifty bucks came out of Snapper's big score against the Whitmarks. He didn't tell Edie Marsh how much money remained in his pocket. He also didn't mention the trooper's gun in the Cherokee, in the event she blew her top again.

The phone continued ringing. 'Answer it,' Snapper said. 'Maybe it's your Santy Claus boyfriend.'

Edie picked up the phone. On the other end, a woman's voice said: 'Hullo?'

Edie hung up. 'It wasn't Fred,' she said.

'The fuck was it?'

'I didn't ask, Snapper. We're not supposed to be here, remember?' She said it sounded like long distance.

'What if it's the insurance company? Maybe the check's ready.'

Edie said, 'No. Fred would tell me.'

Snapper hacked out a laugh. 'Fred's gone, you dumb twat. You scared him off!'

'How much you wanna bet.'

'Right, he can't stay away, you're such a fantastic piece a ass.'

'You can't even imagine,' Edie said, showing some tongue. Maybe she wasn't hot enough for a young Kennedy, but she was the best thing young Mr Dove had ever seen. Besides, he couldn't back out of the deal now. He'd already put in for the phony claim.

Again the phone rang. Edie Marsh said, 'Shit.'

'For Christ's sake, gimme a hand.' Snapper writhed irritably on the BarcaLounger. 'Come on!'

Bracing a forearm on Edie's shoulder, he hobbled to the kitchen. She plucked the receiver off the hook and handed it to him.

'Yo,' Snapper said.

'Hullo?' A woman. 'Tony, is that you?'

'Hmmphrr,' answered Snapper, cautiously.

'It's me. Neria.'

Who? Frigid drops from the ice pack dripped down Snapper's injured leg. The purple kneecap felt as if it were about to burst, like a rotten mango. Edie pressed close, trying to hear what the caller was saying.

'Tony, I been tryin' to get through for days. What's with the house?'

Then Snapper remembered: The wife! Tony Torres had said

her name was Miriam or Neria, some Cuban thing. He'd also said she'd be coming back for her cut of the insurance.

'Bad connection,' Snapper mumbled into the receiver.

'What's going on? I call next door and Mister Varga, he said the hurricane totaled our house and now there's strangers living there. Some woman, Tony. You hear me? And Mister Varga said you shot a hole in the garage. What the hell's going on down there?'

Snapper held the receiver at arm's length, like it was a stick of dynamite. His bottom jaw shoveled in and out; the joints of his face made a popping sound that gave Edie the creeps.

'Tony?' squeaked the voice on the telephone.

Edie took it from Snapper's hand and said, 'I'm very sorry. You've got the wrong number.' Then she hung up.

At first all Snapper could say was, 'Goddamn.'

'The wife?'

'Yeah. Goddamn.'

Edie Marsh helped him pogo to the chair. The ice crunched as he sat down. 'Where's your Santy Claus boyfriend live?'

'Some Ramada.'

'Goddamn. We don't got much time.'

Edie said, 'Where's Mrs Torres? Is she here in Miami?'

'Hell if I know. Get me to the car.'

'I've got some more bad news. The dogs came back this morning.'

'The wiener dogs?'

'We can't just leave them here. They need to be fed.'

With both hands Snapper choked his throbbing leg and said, 'Never again. I swear to Christ.'

'Oh yeah,' Edie Marsh said, 'like this is some fun picnic for me. Here, give me your arm.'

Avila's new customer took the Turnpike south. Before long the Cadillac was pinned in traffic—construction trucks, eighteen-wheelers, Army convoys, ambulances, sightseers, National Guardsmen, and hundreds of queasy insurance adjusters, all heading into the hurricane zone. Ground Zero.

'Looks like a bombing range,' said the man calling himself Rick Reynolds.

'Sure does. Where's your house?'

'We got a ways yet.' As the car inched along, the man turned up the radio: Rush Limbaugh, making wisecracks about the wife of some candidate. Avila didn't think the jokes were all that funny, but the man chuckled loyally. After the program ended, a news report announced that the President of the United States was flying to Miami to see the storm damage firsthand.

'Great,' said Avila. 'You think traffic sucks now, just wait.'

The man said, 'Yeah, one time I got stuck behind Reagan's motorcade in the Holland Tunnel. Talk about a fuck story—two hours we're breathing fumes.'

Avila inquired how long the man had been in Dade County. Couple months, he answered. Moved down from New York.

'And I never saw nuthin' like this.'

Avila said, 'Me, neither.'

'I don't get it. Some houses go down like dominoes, some don't lose a shingle. How's that happen?'

Avila checked his wristwatch. He wondered if the guy had the fifteen grand on him, or maybe in the trunk of the car. He glanced in the back seat: a crumpled road map and two empty Mister Donut boxes.

The man said, 'My guess is somebody got paid off. There's no other way to make sense of it.'

Avila kept his eyes ahead. 'This ain't New York,' he said. Finally the traffic started to move.

The customer said a trailer park not far from his neighborhood got blown to smithereens. 'Old lady was killed,' he said.

'Man, that's rough.'

'Wonderful old lady. But every single trailer got destroyed, every damn one.'

Avila said, 'Storm of the century.'

'No, but here's the thing. The tie-downs on those mobile homes was rotted out. The augers was sawed off. Anchor disks missing. Now you tell me some inspector didn't get greased.'

Avila shifted uncomfortably. 'Straps rot fast in this heat. How much farther?'

'Not long.'

The customer picked up Krome Avenue to 168th Street. There he turned back east and drove for a mile to a subdivision called Fox Hollow, which had eroded to more or less bare foundations in the hurricane. The man parked in front of the skeletal remains of a small tract home.

Avila got out of the Cadillac and said, 'God, you weren't kidding.'

The roof of the house was totally blown away; gables, beams, trusses, everything. Avila was stunned that Mr Reynolds was allowing his family to remain in such an unprotected structure. Avila followed him inside, stepping over the wind-flattened doors. The place looked abandoned except for the kitchen, where a pack of stray dogs fought over rancid hamburger in the overturned refrigerator. Avila's customer grabbed an aluminum baseball bat and chased the mongrels off.

Peeking into the flooded bedrooms, Avila saw no sign of the customer's family. Immediately he felt the whole day go sour. Just to be sure, he said, 'So where's your ninety-year-old grandmother?'

'Dead and buried,' Ira Jackson replied, slapping the bat in the palm of one hand, 'on beautiful Staten Island.'

As the man from New York prepared to nail him to a pine tree, Avila concluded that Snapper was responsible for hiring the attacker.

Clearly the plan was to murder Avila and take control of his crooked roofers. Where was the mighty fist of Chango? Avila wondered grimly. Had the double-chicken sacrifice misfired?

Then the man from New York explained himself—who he was, what had happened to his mother, and why Avila must die a horrible drawn-out death. At first Avila pleaded innocence, feigning outrage at the fate of Beatrice Jackson. Soon he realized that the survival skills so essential to a county bureaucrat—the ability on a moment's notice to shift blame, dodge responsibility and misplace crucial paperwork—were of no use to him now.

Avila reasoned it was better to tell the truth than to have it tortured out of him. So, out of sheer bladder-shriveling fear, he confessed to Ira Jackson.

Yes, it was he who'd been assigned to approve the mobile homes at Suncoast Leisure Village. And yes, he'd failed to perform thorough and timely inspections. And—yes, yes! God forgive me!—he'd taken bribes to overlook code violations.

'Didn't you see those goddamn rotten straps?' demanded Ira Jackson, who was making a crucifix with fallen roof beams.

'No,' Avila admitted.

'The augers?'

'No, I swear.'

'Never even checked?' Ira Jackson pounded ferociously with a hammer.

'I didn't see them,' Avila said morosely, 'because I never drove out there.'

Ira Jackson's hammer halted in midair. Avila, who was lashed to a broken commode in a bathroom, lowered his eyes in a pantomime of shame. That's when he saw that the toilet bowl was alive with bright-green frogs and mottled brown snakes, splashing beneath him in fetid water.

With a shiver he said, 'I never went to the trailer park. The guy sent me the money—'

'How much?'

'Fifty bucks a unit. He sent it to the office, so I figured what the hell, why waste gas? Instead of driving all the way down there, I . . .' Here Avila caught himself. It seemed unnecessary to reveal that he'd played golf on the afternoon he was supposed to inspect Suncoast Leisure Village.

'. . . I didn't go.'

'You're shittin' me.'

'No. I'm very, very sorry.'

The expression on Ira Jackson's face caused Avila to reevaluate his decision to be candid. Evidently the doughnut man intended to torture him, no matter what. Ira Jackson bent over the crucifix and went back to work.

Raising his voice over the racket, Avila said, 'Christ, if I knew what he was doing with those trailers, he never woulda got permits. You gotta believe me, there's no amount of money would make me take a pass on cut augers. No way!'

'Shut up.' Ira Jackson carried the cross to the backyard and began nailing it to the trunk of a pine. It had been a tall lush tree until the hurricane sheared off the top thirty feet; now it was merely a bark-covered pole.

With each plonk of the hammer, Avila's spirits sank. He said a prayer to Chango, then tried a 'Hail Mary' in the wan hope that traditional Catholic entreaty would be more potent in staving off a crucifixion.

As the man from New York dragged him to the tree, Avila cried, 'Please, I'll do anything you want!'

'OK,' said Ira Jackson, 'I want you to die.'

He positioned Avila upright against the cross and wrapped duct tape around his ankles and wrists to minimize the squirming. Avila shut his eyes when he saw the doughnut man snatch up the hammer. The moment the cold point of the nail punctured his palm, Avila emitted a puppy yelp and fainted.

When he awoke, he saw that Chango had answered his prayers with a fury.

16

At nine sharp on the morning of August 31, an attractive brunette woman carrying two miniature dachshunds walked into a Hialeah branch of the Barnett Bank and opened an account under the name of 'Neria G. Torres.'

For identification, the woman provided an expired automobile registration and a handful of soggy mail. The bank officer politely requested a driver's license or passport, any document bearing a photograph. The woman said her most personal papers, including driver's license, were washed away by the hurricane. As the bank officer questioned her more closely, the woman became distraught. Soon her little dogs began to bark plangently; one of them squirted from her arms and dashed in circles around the lobby, nipping at other customers. To quiet the scene, the banker agreed to accept the woman's auto registration as identification. His own aunt had lost all her immigration papers in the storm, so Mrs Torres's excuse seemed plausible. To open the account she gave him one hundred dollars cash, and said she'd be back in a few days to deposit a large insurance check.

'You're lucky they settled so fast,' the banker remarked. 'My aunt's having a terrible time with her company.' The woman said her homeowner policy was with Midwest Casualty. 'I've got a *great* insurance man,' she added.

Later, when Edie Marsh told the story to Fred Dove, he reacted with the weakest twitch of an ironic smile. Under the woeful circumstances, it was as good as a cartwheel.

Edie, Snapper and the two noisy wiener dogs had moved into his room at the Ramada. No other accommodations were available for a radius of sixty miles, because the hotels were jammed full of displaced families, relief volunteers, journalists, construction workers and insurance adjusters. Fred Dove felt trapped. His fear of getting arrested for fraud was now compounded by a fear that his wife would call the motel room, then Edie Marsh or Snapper would answer the phone and the wiener dogs would start howling, leaving Fred Dove to invent an explanation that no sensible woman in Omaha, Nebraska, would ever accept.

'Cheer up,' Edie told him. 'We're all set at the bank.'

'Good,' he said in a brittle tone.

The long tense weekend had abraded the insurance man's nerves—Snapper, gimping irritably around the small motel room, slugging down vodka, threatening to blast the yappy dachshunds with a massive black handgun he claimed to have stolen from a police officer.

No wonder I'm edgy, thought Fred Dove.

To deepen the gloom, sharing the cramped room with Snapper and the dogs left the insurance man no opportunity for intimacy with Edie Marsh. Not that he could have availed himself of a sexual invitation; the withering effect of Snapper's previous coital interruption endured, as Snapper continued to tease Fred Dove about the red condom.

Also looming large was the question of Edie's aptitude for violence—a disconcerting vision of the crowbar episode was scorched into Fred Dove's memory. He worried that she or Snapper might endeavor to murder each other at any moment.

Edie stretched out next to him on the bed. 'You're miserable,' she observed.

'Yes indeed,' said the insurance man.

With his bum leg elevated, Snapper was stationed in an armchair three and one half feet from the television screen. Every so often he would take a futile swipe at Donald or Marla, and tell them to shut the holy fuck up.

'Sally Jessy,' Edie whispered. Fred Dove sighed.

On the TV, a woman in a dreadful yellow wig was accusing her gap-toothed white-trash husband of screwing her younger sister. Instead of denying it, the husband said damn right, and it was the best nooky I ever had. Instantly the sister, also wearing a dreadful wig and lacking in teeth, piped up to say she couldn't get enough. Sally Jessy exhaled in weary dismay, the studio audience hooted, and Snapper let out a war whoop that set off the dogs once again.

'If the phone rings,' Fred Dove said, 'please don't answer.'

Edie Marsh didn't need to ask why.

'You got any kids?' she asked.

The insurance man said he had two, a boy and a girl. He thought Edie might follow up and ask about their ages, what grades they were in, and so on. But she showed no interest.

She said, 'Cheer up, OK? Think about your cruise to Bimini.'

'Look, I was wondering—'

Snapper, growling over one shoulder: 'You two mind? I'm tryin' to watch the fuckin' show.'

Edie signaled for Fred Dove to follow her to the bathroom. He perked up, anticipating a discreet blow job or something along those lines.

But Edie only wanted a quiet place to chat. They perched their butts on the edge of the bathtub. She stroked his hand and said, 'Tell me, sugar. What's on your mind?'

'OK, the company sends me the check—'

'Right.'

'I give it to you,' said Fred Dove, 'and you deposit it in the bank.'

'Right.'

'And then?'

Edie Marsh answered with exaggerated clarity, like a schoolteacher coaxing an exceptionally dull-witted pupil. '*Then*, Fred, I go back to the bank in a couple days and cut *three* separate cashier's checks for forty-seven thousand *each*. Just like we agreed.'

Undeterred by the condescension, he said: 'Don't forget the hundred dollars I gave you to open the account.'

Edie let go of his hand and brushed it, like a cockroach, off her lap. Lord, what an anal dweeb! 'Yes, Freddie, I'll make absolutely sure your check says forty-seven thousand *one hundred*. OK? Feel better?'

The insurance man grunted unhappily. 'I won't feel better till it's over.'

Edie Marsh didn't inform Fred Dove about the phone call from the real Neria Torres. She didn't want to spook him out of the scam.

'The best part about this deal,' she said, 'is that nobody's in a position to screw anyone else. You've got shit on me, I've got shit on you, and we've both got plenty of shit on Snapper. That's why it's going down so clean.'

Fred Dove said, 'That gun of his scares me to death.'

'Not much we can do. The asshole digs guns.'

Outside, Donald and Marla began scratching at the bathroom door in the frenetic manner of deranged badgers.

'Let's get out there,' Edie Marsh said, 'before Snapper loses it.'

'This is nuts!'

Edie mechanically guided Fred Dove's head to her bosom. 'Don't you worry,' she said, and he was momentarily transported to a warm, fragrant valley, where no harm could ever come.

Then, on the other side of the door, a gun went off, the dachshunds bayed and Snapper bellowed profanely.

'Jesus!' Edie exclaimed.

The insurance man burrowed in her cleavage. 'What're we going to do?' he asked, desolately.

Avila thought: I'm either dead or dreaming.

Because it should hurt worse than this, being nailed to a cross. Even if it's only one hand, it should hurt like a mother. I ought to be screaming at the top of my lungs, instead of just hanging here with a dull ache. Hanging like a wet flag and staring at . . .

It *must* be a dream.

Because they don't have lions in Florida. And that's what that monster is, a full-grown African lion. King of the motherfucking jungle. So real you can see the red-brown stains on its mouth. So real you can smell its piss. So real you can hear the dead man's spine dear God Almighty being crunched in its fangs.

The lion was eating the doughnut man.

Avila was frozen in the pose of a scarecrow. He was afraid to blink. Between bites, the big cat would glance up, yawn, lick its paws, shake the gnats off its mane. Avila noticed a blue tag fastened to one of its ears, but that wasn't important.

The important thing was: He definitely wasn't dreaming. The lion was real. Clearly it was sent to save his life.

And not by the Catholic God—Catholics had no expertise in the summoning of demonic jungle beasts. No, it was a funkier, more mystical deity who had answered Avila's plea from the cross.

Gracias, Chango! *Muchas gracias*.

When I get home, Avila promised his *santería* guardian, I shall make an offering worthy of royalty. Chickens, rabbits. Perhaps I'll even spring for a goat.

In the meantime, Avila implored, please make the lion go away so I can get this fucking nail out of my hand!

The big cat dined leisurely, no more than fifteen yards from the pine tree. Ira Jackson's hammer lay where he'd dropped it, at Avila's feet. From marks on the ground, it appeared that the doughnut man had been jumped from behind, swiftly done in, and dragged to the dry weedy patch where the lion now sat, possessively attending the disemboweled, disarticulated corpse. Ira Jackson's gold chain dangled like spaghetti from the cat's whiskered maw. It disappeared with a flick of the tongue.

Avila's knowledge of lion eating habits was sketchy, but he couldn't believe the animal could still be hungry after devouring the substantial Mr Jackson. Despite the worsening pain in his hand, Avila remained rock steady against the cross until the lion quit munching and nodded off.

Slowly Avila turned his head to examine the nasty puncture. His palm was striped with congealed blood. The nail had penetrated the tough fleshy web between the second and third fingers, which wiggled feebly at Avila's silent bidding. A moral victory, of sorts—Ira Jackson had failed to break any major bones.

Keeping a close watch on the snoozing lion, and moving with glacial deliberation, Avila tugged his good hand free of the duct tape. Slowly he reached across and began to work the nail loose from the punctured palm. The undertaking caused less agony than he'd anticipated; perhaps Chango had anesthetized him as well.

Luckily, the wood of the makeshift crucifix was soft. In less than a minute the nail pulled out, and Avila's hand fell free, with only a modest geyser of blood. He inserted the hand forcefully between his shaking knees, and bit his lower lip to stifle a cry. The lion did not stir. The exhaust of its snore fluttered the bright remains of Ira Jackson's sports shirt, which clung like a lobster bib to the big cat's throat.

While the beast slept, Avila unwrapped the sticky tape from his ankles. As he furtively inched clear of the pine tree, his eyes fell on a partially masticated chunk of bone—a wee remnant of the doughnut man, but a potent talisman for future *santería* rites.

Avila pocketed the moist prize and stole away.

Skink chose to spend the night in the back of the pickup truck. Shortly after ten, Augustine emerged from the house with a hot Cuban sandwich and two bottles of beer. Skink winked appreciatively and sat up. He finished the sandwich in four huge bites, guzzled the beer and said: 'So she stayed.'

'I don't know why.'

'Because she's never seen the likes of you.'

'Or you,' said Augustine.

'And because her husband behaved poorly.'

Augustine slouched against the fender. 'She's here, and I'm glad about it. Which makes me quite the model of rectitude—a woman on her honeymoon, for Christ's sake.'

Skink arched a tangled eyebrow. 'A new low?'

'Oh yes.'

'Her decision, son. Don't beat yourself up.'

Anxiety, not guilt, gnawed at Augustine. On his present course, he would very soon fall in love with Mrs Max Lamb. How much fragrant late-night snuggling could a man endure? And Bonnie was an ardent snuggler, even in platonic mode. Augustine was racked with worry. He had no chance whatsoever, not with her hair smelling like bougainvilleas, not with that velvet slope of neck, not with those denim-blue eyes. He couldn't recall being with a woman who felt so *right*, nestled in his embrace. Even her slumbering snorts and sniffles soothed him—that's how hard he was falling.

It's just a kiss away. Like Mick and Keith said.

A newly married woman. Brilliant.

Unconsciously Augustine found himself gazing at the window of the guest room. Soon Bonnie's shadow crossed behind the drapes. Then the lights went off.

Skink poked him sharply. 'Settle down. Nothing'll happen unless she wants it to.' He stood in the bed of the pickup for a series of twisting calisthenics, accompanied by preternaturally asthmatic grunts. That went on for twenty full minutes under the stars. Augustine watched without interrupting. Afterwards Skink sat down heavily, rocking the truck.

Pointing at the remaining beer, he said: 'You gonna drink that?'

'Help yourself.'

'You're a patient young man.'

'I've got nothing but time,' Augustine said. Why rush the guy?

Skink threw back his head and tilted the beer bottle until it was empty. Pensively he said: 'You never know how these things'll play out.'

'Doesn't matter, captain. I'm in.'

'OK. Here.' He handed Augustine the scrap of paper that Jim Tile had given him at the hospital. On the paper, the trooper had written:

> *black Jp. Cherokee*
> BZQ-42F

Augustine was impressed that Brenda Rourke remembered the license tag, or anything else, after the hideous beating.

Skink said, 'The plate's stolen. No surprise there.'

'The driver?'

'White non-Latin male, late thirties. Deformed jaw, according to Trooper Rourke. Plus he wore a pinstriped suit.'

Skink returned to a sprawled position. He folded his arms under his head.

Augustine peered over the side of the truck. 'Where do we start?' The man could be all the way to Atlanta by now.

'I've got some ideas,' said the governor.

Augustine was doubtful. 'The cops'll find him first.'

'They're all on hurricane duty, double shifts. Even the detectives are directing traffic.' Skink chuckled quietly. 'It's not a bad time to be a fugitive.'

Augustine felt something brush his leg—a neighbor's orange tabby. When he reached to pet it, the cat scooted beneath the pickup.

The governor said, 'I'm doing this for Jim. It's not often he asks.'

'But there's other reasons.'

Skink nodded. 'True. I'm not fond of shitheads who beat up women. And the storm has left me, well, unfulfilled. . . .'

It hadn't been the cataclysmic purgative he had hoped for and prophesied. Ideally a hurricane should drive people out, not bring people in. The high number of new arrivals to South Florida was merely depressing; the moral caliber of the fortune-seekers was appalling—lowlife hustlers, slick-talking scammers and cold-blooded opportunists, not to mention pure gangsters and thugs. Precisely the kind of creeps who would cave in a lady's face. 'Do not,' Skink said, 'expect me to control my temper.'

'Wouldn't dream of it,' said Augustine.

The light in the guest bedroom went on. Augustine found Bonnie Lamb sitting up in bed. For a nightgown she wore a long white T-shirt that she'd found in a drawer: Tom Petty and the Heartbreakers. Augustine had purchased it at a concert at the Miami Arena. The woman whom he'd taken to the show, the psychotic doctor who later tried to filet him in the shower, had bought a black shirt to match her biker boots. At the time, Augustine had found the ensemble fetching, in a faux-trashy way.

'Max call yet?' Bonnie asked.

Augustine checked the answering machine. No messages. He returned to the bedroom and told her.

She said, 'I've been married one week and a day. What's the matter with me?' She drew her knees to her chest. 'I should be home.'

Exactly! thought Augustine. Absolutely right!

'You think my husband's a jerk?'

'Not at all,' Augustine lied, decorously.

'Then why hasn't he called.' It was not a question. Bonnie Lamb said, 'Come here.'

She made room under the covers, but Augustine positioned himself chastely on the edge of the bed.

'You must think I'm crazy,' said Bonnie.

'No.'

'My heart is upside down. That's the only way to describe it.'

Augustine said, 'Stay as long as you want.'

'I want to go along with you and . . . him. The kidnapper.'

'Why?'

'Oh, I don't know. Probably goes back to Max, or my dad and his model airplanes, or my wretched childhood, even though my memories are quite wonderful. It's got to be something. Happy normal little girls don't grow up to dump their husbands, do they?' Bonnie Lamb switched off the lamp. 'You want to lie down?'

'Better not,' said Augustine.

In the dark, her hand found his cheek. She said, 'Here's my idea: I think we should sleep together.'

'But we *have* slept together, Mrs Lamb.' That without missing a beat. Augustine commended himself—a little humor to cut the tension.

Bonnie said, 'Come on. You know what I mean.'

'Make love?'

'Oh, you're a quick one.' She grabbed his shoulders and pulled him down. His head came to rest on a pillow. Before he could get up she was on top, pinning his arms. Impishly she planted her chin on his breastbone. In the light slanting through the window, Augustine was able to see her smile, the liveliness of her eyes and—behind her—the wall of gaping skulls.

Bonnie Lamb said, 'Making love with you might clear my thinking.'

'So would electroshock therapy.'

'I'm very serious.'

'And very married,' said Augustine.

'Yes, but you're still getting hard.'

'Thanks for the bulletin.'

She let go of his arms, took his face in both hands. Her smile disappeared, and sadness entered her voice. 'Don't be such a smartass,' she whispered. 'Can't you understand—I don't know what else to do. I tried crying; it doesn't work.'

'I'm sorry—'

'I feel closer to you than I've ever felt to Max. That's not a good sign.'

'No, it isn't.'

'Especially after a week of marriage. My own husband—and already I feel old and invisible when we're together.' She took his shirt in her fists. 'God, you know what? Forget everything I said.'

'Yeah, right.'

'Then you've thought about it, too.'

'Constantly,' said Augustine. Then, in a burst of foolish virtue: 'But it would sure be wrong.'

Her breasts were lined up just below his rib cage. They rose ever so slightly when she took a breath. Friendship, he reminded himself, could be excruciating.

Bonnie asked, 'What happens now?'

'Oh, my erection will eventually go away. Then we can both get some sleep.'

She lowered her eyes. Blushing? In the shadows it was hard to tell. She said, 'No, I meant with the governor. What're you two guys up to?'

'Hair-raising thrills and high-speed adventure.'

Bonnie nestled closer and settled in for the night. Augustine was severely tempted to stroke her hair, or kiss the top of her head, or trace a finger along that famous velvet slope of her neckline. But, with idiotic decency, he held back.

Mrs Max Lamb fell asleep long before he did. Shortly after midnight, the telephone began to ring in the kitchen. Augustine didn't get out of bed to answer it, because he didn't want to wake his new friend. He probably could have moved her gently to one side of the bed, but he didn't even try.

She was sleeping so soundly, and he felt so good.

17

Bonnie Lamb rolled over at three in the morning, freeing Augustine to rise and answer the phone, which had been ringing intermittently for hours.

Naturally it was Bonnie's husband in New York. Augustine anticipated a lively exchange.

'What's going on!' Max Lamb demanded.

'Bonnie's fine. She's asleep.'

'Answer me!'

'She left you several messages. She wasn't up to the airplane trip—'

'Wake her, please. Tell her it's important.'

As he waited, Max Lamb reflected over the unalloyed rottenness of his long thankless day. The NIH press conference declaiming the hazards of Bronco cigarets made CNN, MTV and all the networks, followed of course by prominent barbs in the Leno and Letterman monologues. The wiseass MTV coverage was particularly aggravating because it struck directly at young female smokers, a key market component of Bronco's booming sales growth. Front-page stories were expected the following morning in the *Times*, the *Wall Street Journal* and the Washington *Post*. The word 'disaster' was insufficient to describe the crisis, as the splenetic chairman of Durham Gas Meat & Tobacco adamantly insisted on a total advertising embargo against all publications reporting the NIH findings—which was to say, all newspapers and magazines in the United States. The atmosphere at Rodale & Burns was sepulchral, due to the many millions of dollars that the agency stood to lose if Bronco's print ads were yanked. Max Lamb had spent the better part of the afternoon attempting to contact DGM&T's chairman in Guadalajara, where he was receiving thrice-daily injections of homogenized sheep semen to arrest the malignant tumors in his lungs. Workers at the clinic said the chairman was taking no calls, and refused to patch Max Lamb through to the old geezer's room.

And if that wasn't enough, Max now had to deal with a flighty, recalcitrant wife in Florida.

Bonnie's voice was husky from sleep. 'Honey?' she said.

Max gripped the receiver as if it were the neck of a squirming rattlesnake. 'Exactly what's going on down there!'

'I'm sorry. I need a few more days.'

'Why aren't you at the motel?'

'I fell asleep here.'

'With the skulls? Jesus Christ, Bonnie.'

When Max Lamb got highly agitated, he acquired a frenetic rasp that his coworkers likened to that of an asthmatic on amphetamines. Bonnie didn't blame her husband for getting upset that she was with Augustine. Trying to explain was point-less, because she didn't yet comprehend it herself. Her attempted seduction—*that* she understood too well. But the urge to go road-tripping with the governor, the lack of interest in returning home to begin her new marriage . . . confusing emotions, indeed.

'I still don't feel very well, Max. Maybe it's exhaustion.'

'You can sleep on the plane. Or in a damn motel.'

'All right, honey, I'll get a room.'

'Has he tried anything?'

'No!' Bonnie said sharply. 'He's been a perfect gentleman.' Thinking: *I'm* the one you've got to worry about, buddy boy.

'I don't trust him.' Max Lamb's normal vibrant voice had returned, indicating a beneficial drop in blood pressure.

Bonnie decided it was safe to point out that if it weren't for Augustine, Max would still be kidnapped.

That provoked a grinding silence on the other end. Then: 'There's something not right about him.'

'Oh, and you're perfectly normal, Max. Driving hundreds of miles to take movies of wrecked houses and crying babies.'

A movement by Augustine caught Bonnie Lamb's attention.

With a mischievous grin, he produced three plump grapefruits and began to juggle, dancing barefoot around the kitchen. Bonnie covered her mouth to keep from giggling into the phone.

She heard Max say, 'I'm flying to Mexico tomorrow. When I get back, I expect you to be here.'

Bonnie's eyes followed the flying citrus.

'Of course I'll be there.' The promise sounded so anemic that her husband couldn't possibly have believed it. Bonnie felt a wave of sadness. Max wasn't stupid; surely he knew something was wrong. She took a slow deep breath. Augustine slipped out of the kitchen and left her alone.

'Bonnie?'

'Yes, honey.'

'Don't you want to know why I'm going to Mexico?'

'Mexico,' she said, pensively. Thinking: He's going to *Mexico*.

Asking: 'Will you be gone long, Max?'

And wondering: Who's this strange, reckless woman who has climbed inside my skin!

Avila didn't tell his wife about his harrowing brush with crucifixion, for she would've massaged it into a divine parable and shared it with all the neighbors. Once, Avila's wife had seen the face of the Virgin Mary in a boysenberry pancake, and phoned every TV station in Miami. No telling how far she'd run with a lion story.

Locking himself in the bathroom, Avila bandaged his throbbing hand and waited for his wife to depart for the grocery store. When the coast was clear, he grabbed a shovel from the garage, crept to the backyard and excavated a Tupperware box full of cash that was buried under a mango tree. The money was his wife's brother's share of a small-time marijuana venture. Avila's wife's brother resided in state prison for numerous felony convictions unrelated to the pot, so Avila and his wife had promised to baby-sit the cash until his parole, sometime around the turn of the century. Avila didn't approve of pilfering a relative's life savings, but it was an emergency. If Gar Whitmark didn't get his seven grand immediately he would call the authorities and have Avila thrown in a cell with a voracious pervert. That's how powerful Whitmark was, or so Avila believed.

He dug energetically for the Tupperware, ignoring the pain of the nail wound. He was spurred by the putrid-sweet stench of rotting mangos, and a fear that one of his many in-laws would arrive unannounced—Avila wanted nobody to know he'd been ripped off by one of his own crooked roofers. He unearthed the container without difficulty, and eagerly pried off the lid. He removed seventy damp one-hundred-dollar bills and wadded them into a pocket. But something wasn't right: Money appeared to be missing from his wife's brother's stash. Avila's suspicion was confirmed by a hasty count; the Tupperware box was short by an additional four grand.

Dumb bitches! Avila steamed. They've been losing at Indian bingo again. His wife and her mother were practically addicted.

To confront the women would have given Avila great pleasure, but it also would've exposed his own clandestine filching. Ruefully he reburied the Tupperware, and concealed the disturbed topsoil with a mat of leaves and lawn cuttings. Then he drove to the Gar Whitmark Building, where he was made to wait in the lobby for ninety minutes, like a common peon.

When a secretary finally led him into Gar Whitmark's private office, Avila spoiled any chance for a civil exchange by asking the corporate titan what the hell was wrong with his scalp, was that a fungus or what? Avila, who had never before seen hair plugs, hadn't meant to be rude, but Gar Whitmark reacted explosively. He shoved Avila to the floor, snatched the seven grand from his hand, knelt heavily on his chest and spewed verbal abuse. Whitmark wasn't a large man, but he was fit from many afternoons of country-club tennis. Avila chose not to resist; he was thinking lawsuit. Whitmark's eyes bulged in rage, and he cursed himself breathless, but he did not punch Avila even once. Instead he got up, smoothed the breast of his Italian suit, straightened his necktie and presented the disheveled con man with an itemized estimate from Killebrew roofing Co. for the staggering sum of $23,250.

Avila was crestfallen, though not totally surprised: Whitmark had selected the best, and most expensive, roofers in all South Florida. Also, the most honest. From his days as a crooked inspector, Avila sourly recalled the few times he'd tried to shake down Killebrew crews for payoffs, only to be chased like a skunk from the construction sites. Killebrew, like Gar Whitmark, had some heavy juice downtown.

Avila pretended to study the estimate while he thought up a diplomatic response.

Whitmark said: 'They start work next week. Adjust your finances accordingly.'

'Jesus, I don't have twenty-three grand.' There—he'd said it.

'You're making me weep.' Gar Whitmark clicked his teeth.

With a bandaged hand Avila waved the Killebrew paper in tepid indignation. 'I could do this same job for half as much!'

Whitmark snorted. 'I wouldn't let you put the roof on a fucking doghouse.' He handed Avila a Xeroxed clipping from the newspaper. 'You either come up with the money or go to jail. *Comprende*, Señor Dipshit?'

The newspaper article said the Dade State Attorney was appointing a special squad of prosecutors to crack down on dishonest contractors preying on hurricane victims.

'One phone call,' said Whitmark, 'and you're on your way to the buttfuck motel.'

Avila bowed his head. The sight of his blackened fingernails reminded him of the buried Tupperware box. Hell, there was only twelve, maybe thirteen grand left in it. He was screwed.

'My wife's still a wreck from what your people did. You wouldn't believe the goddamn pharmacy bill.' Whitmark pointed at the door and told Avila good-bye. 'We'll talk,' he said, ominously.

On the way home, Avila dejectedly mulled his options. How often could he turn to Chango without offending Him, or appearing selfish? Yet the *santero* priest who trained Avila had mentioned no numerical limit on supernatural requests. Tonight, Avila decided, I'll do a goat—no, *two* goats!

And tomorrow I will hunt that bastard Snapper.

*

The Church of High Pentecostal Rumination, headquartered in Chicoryville, Florida, attended all natural disasters in the western hemisphere. Earthquake, flood and hurricane zones proved fertile territories for conversion and recruitment of sinners. Less than thirty-six hours after the killer storm smashed Dade County, an experienced team of seven Ruminator missionaries was dispatched in a leased Dodge minivan. Hotel beds were scarce, so they shared a room at a Ramada Inn off the Turnpike. There was no complaining.

Every morning, the missionaries preached, consoled and distributed pamphlets. Then they stood in line for free army lunches at the tent city, and returned to the motel for two hours of quiet contemplation and gin rummy. The Ramada offered free cable TV, which allowed the Ruminators to view a half-dozen different religious broadcasts at any time of day. One afternoon, in the absence of a pure Pentecostal preacher, they settled on Pat Robertson and the *700 Club*. The Ruminators didn't share Robertson's paranoid worldview, but they admired his life-or-death style of fund-raising and hoped to pick up some pointers.

Toward the end of the program, Reverend Robertson closed his eyes and prayed. The Ruminators joined hands—no easy task, since four of them were on one bed and three were on the other. The prayer was not one they recognized from the Scriptures; evidently Reverend Robertson had composed it personally, since it contained several references to his post office box in Virginia. Nonetheless, it was a pretty good prayer, fervently rendered, and the Ruminator missionaries were enjoying it.

No sooner had Reverend Robertson exhaled the word 'Amen' when the motel room was rocked by a muffled detonation, and the television set exploded before the missionaries' startled eyes. Reverend Robertson's squinting visage vaporized in a gout of acrid blue smoke, and his whiny beseechment faded in a sprinkle of falling glass. The Ruminators scrambled off the beds, dropped to their knees and burst into a hymn, 'Nearer My God to Thee.' That's how the manager of the Ramada found them, fifteen minutes later, when he came to apologize.

'Some asshole downstairs shot off a .357,' he announced.

All singing ceased. The motel manager pushed the broken television away from the wall and pointed to a ragged hole in the carpet. 'From the bullet,' he explained. 'Don't worry. I kicked 'em out.'

'A gun?' cried a Ruminator elder, springing to his feet.

'That ain't the worst of it,' the motel manager said. 'They had dogs in the room! You believe that? Chewin' up the bedspreads and God knows *what*.' He promised to bring the Ruminators another TV set, but warned them to keep their hymn singing at a low volume, so as not to disturb other guests.

'Everybody's on edge,' the manager added, unnecessarily.

After he left, the missionaries locked the door and held a solemn meeting. They agreed they'd done all they could for the good people of South Florida, and quickly packed their bags.

'Well, that was brilliant.'

Snapper told Edie Marsh to shut up and quit beating it to death. What's done is done.

'No, really,' she said, 'getting us thrown out of the only hotel room between here and Daytona Beach. Absolute genius.'

With a gaseous hiss, Snapper sagged into the BarcaLounger. She had some nerve giving him shit, after the way she'd fucked up his leg with that crowbar. Who wouldn't be in a lousy mood, their goddamn knee all swollen up like a Georgia ham.

He said, 'It's your fault, you and them dogs. Hey, get me a Coors.'

On the drive back to the Torres house, they had stopped at a 7-Eleven for gas, ice and supplies. Fred Dove had purchased Tylenol and peppermint Tic Tacs before lugubriously departing for a busy afternoon of storm-damage estimates. He drove off with the hollow stare of a man whose life had abruptly gone to ruin.

Edie Marsh pulled a beer from the cooler and tossed it under-handed at Snapper. 'We're lucky we're not in jail,' she said for the fifth time.

'Dogs wouldn't shut up.'

'So you shot a hole in the ceiling.'

'Damn straight.' Snapper arranged his lower jaw to accommodate the stream of Coors. He reminded Edie of Popeye in the old Saturday cartoons.

'I'm gonna do them fuckin' mutts,' he said. 'Tonight when you're sleeping. That'll leave me three bullets, too, so don't get no ideas.'

'Wow, a math whiz,' said Edie, 'on top of all your other talents.'

'You don't believe me?'

'The dogs are tied outside. They're not bothering anybody.'

When Snapper finished the beer, he crumpled the can and tossed it on the carpet. Then he took out the pistol and started spinning the cylinder, something he'd obviously picked up from a movie. Edie Marsh ignored him. She went to the garage to put more gasoline in the generator—they needed electricity to run the TV, without which Snapper would become unmanageable.

Sure enough, by the time she returned to the living room, he was contentedly camped out in front of *Oprah*.

'Hookers,' he reported, riveted to the screen.

'Your lucky day.'

Edie Marsh felt gummy with perspiration. The hurricane had eviscerated the elaborate ductwork of Tony Torres's air-conditioning system. Even if the unit had worked, there were no doors, windows or roof to keep cooled air in the house. Edie went to the bedroom and changed from her banking dress to a pair of Mrs Torres's expensive white linen shorts and a beige short-sleeved pullover. She would have been inconsolable if the borrowed clothes had fit her, but thank God they didn't; Mrs Torres was easily three sizes larger. The bagginess provided welcomed ventilation in the tropical humidity, and was not entirely unattractive.

Edie Marsh was appraising her new look in the mirror when the phone started ringing. Snapper hollered for her to pick up, goddammit!

Not given to premonitions, Edie experienced a powerful one that proved true. When she answered the telephone, a long-distance operator asked if she would accept collect charges from a 'Neria in Memphis.'

Memphis! The witch was heading south!

'I don't know anybody named Neria,' Edie said, straining to stay calm.

'Is this 305-443-1676?'

'I'm not sure. See, I don't live here—I was walking past the house when I noticed the phone.'

'Ma'am, please—'

'Operator, in case you haven't heard, we had a terrible hurricane down here!'

Neria's voice: 'I want to speak to my husband. Ask her if Antonio Torres is around.'

Edie Marsh said, 'Look, the house is empty. I was walking past and I thought it might be somebody's relative calling. An emergency maybe. The man who stayed here, he's gone. Loaded his stuff in a Ryder truck and moved out Friday. Up to New York, is what he said.'

'Thank you,' said the operator.

'What! What's your name, lady?' Neria asked excitedly.

'Thank you,' the operator repeated, trying to cut the conversation short.

But Edie was rolling. 'Him and some young lady had a rental truck. Maybe his wife. She looked twenty-three, twenty-four. Long blond hair.'

Neria, exploding: 'No, *I'm* the wife! That's my house!'

Sure, thought Edie, now that insurance money is in the air. Dump the granola-head professor and come running back to blimpy old Tony.

'Brooklyn,' Edie embellished. 'I think he said Brooklyn.'

'Sonofabitch,' Neria moaned.

Curtly the operator asked Mrs Torres if she wished to try another telephone number. No reply. She'd hung up. Edie Marsh did, too.

Her heart drummed against her ribs. Unconsciously she rubbed her damp palms on the rump of Mrs Torres's lovely linen shorts.

Then she hurried to the garage and located a pair of small green-handled wire cutters.

From the living room, Snapper called: 'Who the hell was that? The wife again?' When he heard the garage door, he yelled, 'Hey, I'm talkin' to you!'

Edie Marsh didn't hear him. She was sneaking next door to clip the telephone lines, so that Neria Torres could not call Mr Varga to check out the wild story about Tony and the young blonde and the Ryder truck.

The license tag on the black Cherokee was stolen from a Camaro on the morning after the hurricane, in a subdivision called Turtle Meadow. That's where Augustine was headed when Skink directed him to stop at a makeshift tent city, which the National Guard had erected for those made homeless by the hurricane.

Skink bounded from the truck and stalked through rows of open tents. Bonnie and Augustine kept a few steps behind, taking in the sobering scene. Dazed eyes followed them. Men and women sprawled listlessly on army cots, dull-eyed teenagers waded barefoot through milky puddles, children clung fiercely to new dolls handed out by the Red Cross.

'All these souls!' Skink cried, simian arms waving in agitation.

The soldiers assumed he was shell-shocked from the storm. They let him alone.

At the front of a ragged line, Guardsmen gave out plastic bottles of Evian. Skink kept marching. A small boy in a muddy diaper scurried across his path. With one hand he scooped the child to eye level.

Bonnie Lamb nudged Augustine. 'What do we do?'

When they reached Skink's side, they heard him singing in a voice that was startlingly high and tender:

> 'It's just a box of rain,
> I don't know who put it here.
> Believe it if you need it,
> Or leave it if you dare.'

The little boy—scarcely two years old, Bonnie guessed—had chubby cheeks, curly brown hair and a scrape healing on his brow. He wore a sleeveless cotton shirt with a Batman logo. He smiled at the song and tugged curiously on a silver sprout of the stranger's beard. A light mist fell from scuffed clouds.

Augustine reached for Skink's shoulder. 'Captain?'

Skink, to the boy: 'What's your name?'

The reply was a bashful giggle. Skink peered at the child. 'You won't ever forget, will you? Hurricanes are an eviction notice from God. Go tell your people.'

He resumed singing, in a nasal pitch imposed by tiny fingers pinching his nostrils.

> 'And it's just a box of rain,
> Or a ribbon in your hair.
> Such a long, long time to be gone
> And a short time to be there.'

The child clapped. Skink kissed him lightly on the forehead. He said, 'You're good company, sonny. How's your spirit of adventure?'

'No!' Bonnie Lamb stepped forward. 'We're not taking him. Don't even think about it.'

'He'd enjoy himself, would he not?'

'Captain, please.' Augustine lifted the boy and handed him to Bonnie, who hurried to find the parents before the wild man changed his mind.

The pewter sky filled with a loud thwocking drone. People in the Evian line pointed to a covey of drab military helicopters, flying low. The choppers began to circle, causing the tents to flutter and snap. Quickly a procession of police cars, government sedans, black Chevy Blazers and TV trucks entered the compound.

Skink said, 'Ha! Our Commander in Chief.'

Five Secret Service types piled out of one of the Blazers, followed by the President. He wore, over a shirt and necktie, a navy-blue rain slicker with an emblem on the breast. He waved toward the television cameras, then compulsively began to shake the hands of every National Guardsman and Army soldier he saw. This peculiar behavior might have continued until dusk had not one of the President's many aides (also in a blue slicker) whispered in his ear. At that point a family of authentic hurricane refugees, carefully screened and selected from the sweltering masses, was brought to meet and be photographed with the President. Included in the family was the obligatory darling infant, over whom the leader of the free world labored to coo and fuss. The photo opportunity lasted less than three minutes, after which the President resumed his obsessive fraternizing with anyone wearing a uniform. These unnatural affections were extended to a snowy-haired officer of the local Salvation Army, around whom the Commander in Chief flung a ropy arm. 'So,' he chirped at the befuddled old-timer, 'what outfit you with?'

A short distance away, Augustine stood with his arms folded. 'Pathetic,' he said.

Skink agreed. 'Check the glaze in his eyes. There's nothing worse than a Republican on Halcion.'

As soon as Bonnie Lamb returned, they left for Turtle Meadow.

18

Skink had gotten the address from the police report, courtesy of Jim Tile. The mailboxes and street signs were down, so it took some searching to find the house. Because of his respectable and clean-cut appearance, Augustine was chosen to make the inquiry. Skink waited in the back of the pickup truck, singing the chorus from 'Ventilator Blues.' Bonnie Lamb wasn't familiar with the song, but she enjoyed Skink's bluesy bass voice. She stood by the truck, keeping an eye on him.

Augustine was met at the door by a tired-looking woman in a pink housedress. She said, 'The trooper mentioned you'd be by.' Her tone was as lifeless as her stare; she'd been whipped by the hurricane.

'It's been, like, three days since I called the cops.'

'We're stretched pretty thin,' Augustine said.

The woman's entire family—husband, four children, two cats—was bivouacked in the master bedroom, beneath the only swatch of roof that the hurricane hadn't blown away. The husband wore a lime mesh tank top, baggy shorts, sandals and a Cleveland Indians cap. He had a stubble of gray-flecked beard. He tended a small Sterno stove on the dresser; six cans of pork and beans were lined up, the lids removed. The kids were preoccupied with battery-operated Game Boys, beeping like miniature radars.

'We still got no electric,' the woman said to Augustine. She told her husband it was the man the Highway Patrol sent about the stolen license plate. The husband asked Augustine why he wasn't wearing a police uniform.

'Because I'm a detective,' Augustine said. 'Plainclothes.'

'Oh.'

'Tell me what happened.'

'These four kids pulled up and took the tag off my Camaro. I was out'n the yard, burying the fish—see, when the power went off it took care of the aquarium, so we had dead guppies—'

'Sailfin mollies!' interjected one of the kids.

'Anyway, I had to bury the damn things before they stunk up the place. That's when this Jeep comes up, four colored guys, stereo cranked full blast. They take a screwdriver and set to work on the Camaro. Me standin' right there!'

The woman said, 'I knew something was wrong. I brought the children inside the bedroom.'

Her husband dumped two cans of pork and beans into a small pot, which he held over the royal-blue flame of the Sterno. 'So I run over with a shovel and say what do you think you're up to, and one of the brothers flashes a gun and tells me to you-know-what. I didn't argue, I backed right off. Getting shot over a damn license plate was *not* on my agenda, you understand.'

Augustine said, 'Then what happened?'

'They slapped the tag on the Jeep and hauled ass. You could hear that so-called music for about five miles.'

The wife added, 'David's got a pistol and he knows how to use it. But—'

'Not over a thirty-dollar license plate,' said her husband.

Augustine commended David for being so level-headed. 'Let me double-check the tag number.' He took out the folded piece of paper and read it aloud: 'BZQ-42F.'

'Right,' said David, 'but it's not on that Jeep no more.'

'How do you know?'

'I saw it the other day, goin' down Calusa.'

'The same one?'

'Black Cherokee. Mags, tinted windows. I'd bet the farm it's the same truck. I could tell by the mud flaps.'

The woman frowned. 'Tell him about *those*.'

'Mud flaps like what you see on them eighteen-wheelers. You know, fancy, with naked ladies.'

'In chrome,' the woman said. 'That's how we knew it was the same one—'

Augustine said, 'Where's Calusa?'

'—only some white guy was driving it.'

'What'd he look like?'

'Not friendly,' said the husband.

The wife said, 'Watch the beans, David. And tell him about the music.'

'That's the other thing,' David said, stirring the pot. 'He had that damn stereo all the way loud, same as the colored kids. Only it wasn't rap music, it was Travis Tritt. I thought it was weird, this guy in a business suit and a niggered-up Jeep, listenin' to Travis Tritt.'

'David!' The woman reddened with genuine offense. Augustine liked her. He surmised that she was the strength of the outfit.

Her husband, halfway apologizing for the slur: 'Aw, you know what I mean. All that chrome and tint, the guy didn't fit.'

Augustine recalled Brenda Rourke's description of the attacker. 'You're sure about the suit?'

'Clear as day.'

The woman said, 'We figured maybe he's the boss. Maybe the kids who stole our license plate work for him.'

'It's possible,' said Augustine. He sort of enjoyed playing a cop, ferreting fresh trails.

'You say he looked unfriendly. What do you mean?'

David spooned the pork and beans into matching ceramic bowls. 'His face,' he said. 'You wouldn't forget it.'

The wife said, 'We were on our way to the Circle K for ice. At first I thought he had on a Halloween mask, the man in the Jeep. That's how odd he was—wait, Jeremy, that's too hot!' She intercepted her youngest son, lunging for the beans.

Augustine thanked them, on behalf of the Metropolitan Dade County Police, for their cooperation. He promised to do his best to retrieve the stolen license plate. 'I've only got one more question.'

'Where's Calusa?' said David, smiling.

'Exactly.'

'Margo can do you a map. Use one them napkins.'

*

Avila's wife found him writhing on the floor of the garage, near the Buick. He was bleeding from a large puncture in the groin. One of the sacrificial billy goats, anticipating its fate, had gored him.

'Where are they?' demanded Avila's wife, in Spanish.

Through clenched teeth, Avila confessed that both goats had escaped.

'I tole you! I tole you!' his wife cried, switching to English. She rolled Avila on his back and opened his trousers to examine the injury. 'Chew need a tennis shot,' she said.

'Take me to the doctor.'

'Not in *my* car! I done wanno blood on de 'polstery.'

'Then help me to the goddamn truck.'

'Chew a mess.'

'You want me to die right here on the floor? Is that what you want?'

Avila had purchased the billy goats from the nephew of a *santero* priest in Sweetwater. The nephew owned a farm on which he raised fighting cocks and livestock for religious obla-tions. The two goats had cost Avila a total of three hundred dollars, and they didn't get along. They'd butted heads and kicked at each other continually on the return trip to Avila's house. Somehow he had managed to wrestle both animals into the open garage, but before he could attach the tethers and shut the door, a liquid wildness had come into their huge amber eyes. Avila wondered if they'd sensed Chango's supernatural presence, or merely smelled the blood and entrails from past *santería* offerings. In any event, the goats went absolutely berserk and destroyed a perfectly good riding mower, among other items. The larger of the two billies gouged Avila cleanly with a horn before clacking off into the neighborhood.

Avila's wife scolded him zealously on the drive to the hospital. 'Three hunnert bucks! Chew fucking crazy!' When swearing she customarily dropped her Spanish for English, due to the richer, more emphatic variety of profanities.

Avila snarled back: 'Don't talk to me about money. You and

mamí been losin' your fat asses at the Miccosukee bingo, no? So don't talk to me about crazy.'

He checked the wound in his groin; it was the size of a fifty-cent piece. The bleeding had stopped, but the pain was fiery. He felt clammy and light-headed.

Oh, Chango, Avila thought. What have I done to anger you?

In the emergency room, a businesslike nurse eased him onto a gurney and connected him to a glorious bag of I.V. Demerol. Avila told the doctor that he'd fallen on a rusty lawn sprinkler. The doctor said he was lucky it didn't sever an artery. He asked about the dirty bandage on Avila's left hand, and Avila said it was a nasty golfing blister. Nothing to worry about.

As the pain receded, his mind drifted into a fuzzy free fall. Snapper's lopsided face appeared in a cloud.

I will find you, coño! Avila vowed.

But how?

Dreamily he recalled the night they'd first met. It was in a supper club on LeJeune Road. Snapper was at the bar with two women from an escort service. The women wore caked mascara and towering hair. Avila made friends. He had cash in his pocket, having moments earlier collected a bribe from a fellow who retailed fiberglass roof shingles of questionable durability. The hookers told Avila the name of the escort service was Gentle-men's Choice, and it was open seven days a week. They said Snapper was a regular customer, one of their best. They said he was taking them out on the town to celebrate, on account he was going off to prison for three to five years and wouldn't be getting much pussy, professional or otherwise. Snapper told Avila he'd killed some shithead dope dealer that nobody cared about. Prosecutors had let him cop to a manslaughter-one, and with any luck he'd get out of the joint in twenty months. Avila didn't believe a word the guy was saying, but he thought the man-slaughter routine was a pretty good line to use on the babes. He bought several rounds of drinks for Snapper and the prostitutes, in hopes that Snapper might start feeling generous. And that's exactly what happened. When Avila returned from the men's room, the one he liked—a gregarious platinum blonde, Morganna was her name—whispered in his ear that Snapper said it was OK, as long as Avila paid his share. So they'd all gone to a fleabag motel on West Flagler and had quite a time. Morganna proved full of energy and imagination, well worth the shingle money.

Narcotic memories took Avila's mind off the vigorous suturing that was being done on a freshly shaved triangle five inches due southwest of his navel. Then, giddily, it came to him from out of the clouds—one obvious way for Avila to track that cocksucker Snapper and recover the seven grand.

A lead, is what cops would call it.

Not exactly a red-hot lead, but better than nothing.

Another curious neighbor dropped by, asking about Tony. Edie Marsh used the same ludicrous story about being a distant Torres cousin who was watching the place as a favor. She made no effort to explain Snapper, snoring in the recliner, a gun on his lap.

Fred Dove drove up a few minutes later, while Edie was walking Donald and Marla in the front yard. The insurance man looked more cheerless and pallid than ever. From the way he snatched the briefcase off the seat of the car, Edie sensed an urgency to his gloom.

'My supervisor,' he announced, 'wants to see the house.'

'Is he suspicious?'

'No. Routine claims review.'

'Then what's the problem, Fred? Show him the house.'

He gave a bitter laugh and spun away. Edie tied up the dogs and followed him inside.

'The problem is,' Fred Dove said, 'Mister Reedy will want to chat with "Mister and Mrs Torres."' Loudly he dropped his briefcase on the kitchen counter, rousing Snapper.

Edie said, 'Don't panic. We can handle it.'

'Don't panic? The company wants to know why I got kicked out of the motel. My wife wants to know where I'm staying, and with whom. Dennis Reedy will be here tomorrow to interview two claimants that I cannot produce. Personally, I think it's an excellent time to panic.'

'Hey, Santy Claus!' It was Snapper, hollering from the living room. 'You got the insurance check?'

Edie Marsh went to the doorway and said, 'Not yet.'

'Then shut him up.'

Fred Dove dropped his voice. 'I can't stay here with that maniac. It's impossible.'

'His leg hurts,' said Edie. She had given Snapper the last of her Darvons, which evidently were beginning to wear off. 'Look, I'm not thrilled about the setup, either. But it's this or go camp in the woods.'

The insurance man removed his glasses and pressed his thumbs against his temples. A mosquito landed on one of his eyelids. He shook his head like a spaniel until it floated away. 'We can't go through with this,' he said, dolorously.

'Yes we can, sweetie. I'll be Mrs Torres. Snapper is Tony.'

Fred Dove sagged. 'You don't exactly look Cuban. Neither of you, for God's sake.' He punched a cabinet door and cried out, 'What was I *thinking*!'

Snapper declared that Fred Dove was on the brink of dismemberment unless he immediately shut the fuck up. Edie Marsh led the distraught insurance man into Neria's bedroom closet. She shut the door and kissed him with expert tenderness. Simultaneously she unzipped his pants. Fred jumped at her touch, warm but unexpected. Edie squeezed gently, until he was calm and quite helpless.

'This Dennis Reedy,' she whispered, 'what's he like?'

Fred Dove squirmed pleasurably.

'Tough guy? Tightass? What's his deal?'

'He seems all right,' the insurance man said. He'd dealt with Reedy only once, in a flooded subdivision outside Dallas. Reedy was gruff but fair. He had approved most of Fred Dove's damage estimates, with only minor adjustments.

Edie's free hand pulled down Fred's pants. She said, 'We'll go over the claim papers tonight, in case he makes it a quiz.'

'What about Snapper?'

'Let me handle that. We'll have a rehearsal.'

'What are you doing?' The insurance man nearly lost his balance.

'What does it look like, Fred. Will Mister Reedy have our check?'

In stuporous bliss, Fred Dove gazed at the top of Edie's head. Fingers explored her silken hair; his own fingers, judging by the familiar gold wedding band and the University of Nebraska class ring. Fred Dove struggled for clarity. It was no time for an out-of-body experience; for this long-awaited moment, he wanted sensual acuity and superior muscle control.

The insurance man struggled to purge his mind of worry and guilt, to make way for oncoming ecstasy. He inhaled deeply. The closet smelled of old gardenias and mildew: Neria Torres's pre-professor wardrobe, damp and musty from the storm. Fred Dove felt stifled, though a vital part of him was not.

Without using her hands, Edie Marsh leaned him against the wall for leverage. He released her hair and rapturously locked a monkey grip on the wooden dowel. His upturned face was obstructed by the silken armpit of somebody's wedding gown.

Suddenly he had a humiliating flashback to what had happened the last time, when Snapper interrupted them on the floor of the living room. To prevent a recurrence, Fred groped for the doorknob and held it shut.

From below, Edie Marsh paused to inquire again: 'Will Reedy have the settlement check?'

'N-no. The check always comes from Omaha.'

'Shit.'

Fred Dove wasn't sure whether he heard her say it, or felt her say it. The important thing was, she didn't stop.

When Augustine came out to the truck, Bonnie Lamb and the governor were gone. He found them a few blocks away, behind a deserted hurricane house. Skink was kneeling next to a swimming pool, scooping chubby brown toads out of the rancid water and slipping them into his pockets. Bonnie was busy fending off the mosquitoes that hovered in an inky cloud around her face.

Augustine related what he'd learned about the black Jeep Cherokee. Skink said, 'Where's Calusa Drive?'

'They drew me a map.'

'Are we going now?' Bonnie asked.

'Tomorrow,' Skink said. 'We'll need daylight.'

He and Augustine decided to spend the night nearby. They found an empty field and built a campfire from storm debris. Nearby another small fire glowed, flickering from the mouth of a fifty-five-gallon drum—itinerant laborers from Ohio. Two of them wandered over in search of crack. Augustine spooked them off with a casual display of the .38. Skink disappeared with the toads into a scrubby palmetto thicket.

Bonnie said, 'What's DMT?'

'A Wall Street drug,' Augustine replied. 'Before our time.'

'He said he dries the toad poison and smokes it. He said it's a chemical strain of DMT.'

'I believe I'll stick to beer.' Augustine got two sleeping bags from the cab of the truck. He shook them out and spread them near the fire.

She said, 'I'm sorry about last night.'

'Quit saying that.' Like it would have been the worst mistake of her entire life.

'I don't know what's wrong with me,' she said.

Augustine arranged some dead branches on the fire. 'Nothing's wrong with you, Bonnie. You're so normal it's scary.' He sat cross-legged on one of the sleeping bags.

'Come here,' he said. When he put his arms around her, she felt completely relaxed and secure. Then he said: 'I can take you to the airport.'

'No!'

'Because after tonight, you'll be in the thick of it.'

Bonnie Lamb said, 'That's what I want. Max got his adventure, I want mine.'

A reedy howl rose from the palmettos, diffusing into a creepy rumble of laughter.

Bufo madness, thought Augustine. Bonnie stiffened in his embrace. Firmly she said, 'I'm not leaving now. No way.'

He lifted her chin. 'This is not a well person. This is a man who put a shock collar on your husband, a man who gets high off frog slime. He's done things you don't want to know about, probably even killed people.'

'At least he believes in *some*thing.'

'Good Lord, Bonnie.'

'Then why are *you* here? If he's so dangerous, if he's so crazy—'

'Who said he was crazy.'

'Answer the question, Señor Herrera.'

Augustine blinked at the firelight. 'I'm not so tightly wrapped myself. That should be obvious.'

Bonnie Lamb pressed closer. She wondered why she so enjoyed the fact that both of these new men were unpredictable and impulsive—opposites of the man she'd married. Max was exceptionally reliable, but he was neither deep nor enigmatic. Five minutes with Max and you had the whole menu.

She said, 'I suppose I'm rebelling. Against what, I don't know. It's a first for me.'

Augustine rebuked himself for showing off with the skulls; what woman could resist such charm? Bonnie laughed softly.

'Seriously,' he said, 'there's a big difference between your situation and mine. You've got a husband and a life. I've got nothing else to do, and nothing to lose by not doing it.'

'Your uncle's animals?'

'Long gone,' he said. 'Anyway, there's worse places than Miami to be for a monkey. They'll make out fine.' After a rueful pause: 'I do feel lousy about the water buffalo.'

Bonnie said there was no point trying to analyze motivation. Both of them were rational, mature, intelligent adults. Certainly they knew what they were doing, even if they didn't know why.

From the thicket, another penetrating wail.

Bonnie stared toward the palmettos. 'I get the feeling he could take us or leave us.'

'Exactly.' Augustine came right out and asked her if she truly loved her husband.

She answered unhesitantly: 'I don't know. So there.'

Without warning, the governor crashed shirtless out of the trees. He was feverish, drenched in sweat. His good eye was as bright as a radish; the glass one was turned askew, showing yellowed bone in the socket. Bonnie hurried to his side.

'Damn,' he wheezed, 'was that some bad toad!'

Augustine doubted Skink's technique for removing the toxin and processing it for inhalation. Based on the man's present state, it seemed likely that he'd bungled the pharmacology.

'Sit here by the fire,' Bonnie told him.

He held out his hands, which were filled with leathery, lightly freckled eggs. Augustine counted twelve in all. Skink palmed them like golf balls.

'Supper!' he exulted.

'What are they?'

'Eggs, my boy!'

'Of what?'

'I don't have a clue.' The governor stalked toward the laborers' camp, returning five minutes later with a fry pan and a squeeze bottle of ketchup.

Regardless of species, the eggs tasted dandy scrambled. Augustine was impressed, watching Bonnie dig in.

When they finished eating, Skink said it was time to hit the rack. 'Big day ahead. You take the sleeping bags, I'll be in the scrub.' And he was gone.

Augustine returned the fry pan to the Ohio contingent, which was amiably drunk and nonthreatening. He and Bonnie stayed up watching the flames die, sitting close but saying little. At the first onslaught of mosquitoes, they dove into one of the sleeping bags and zipped it over their heads. Like two turtles, Bonnie said, sharing the same shell.

They hugged each other in the blackness, laughing uncontrollably. After Bonnie caught her breath, she said, 'God, it's hot in here.'

'August in Florida.'

'Well, I'm taking off my clothes.'

'You aren't.'

'Oh yes. And you're going to help.'

'Bonnie, we should get some sleep. Big day tomorrow.'

'I need a big night to take my mind off it.' She got tangled while wriggling out of her top. 'Give me a hand, kind sir.'

Augustine did as he was told. They were, after all, rational, mature, intelligent adults.

19

The death of Tony Torres did not go unnoticed by homicide detectives, crucifixions being rare even in Miami. However, most murder investigations were stuck on hold in the frenetic days following the hurricane. With the roadways in disorder, the police department was precariously shorthanded; every available officer of every rank was put to work directing traffic, chasing looters or escorting relief convoys. In the case of Juan Doe #92–312 (the whimsical caption on Tony Torres's homicide file), the lack of urgency to investigate was reinforced by the fact that no friends or relatives appeared to identify the corpse, which indicated to police that nobody was searching for him, which further suggested that nobody much cared he was dead.

Two days after the body was found, a fingerprint technician faxed the morgue to say that a proper name now could be attached to the crucified man: Antonio Rodrigo Guevara-Torres, age forty-five. The prints of the late Mr Torres were on file because he had, during one rocky stretch of his adult life, written thirty-seven consecutive bum checks. Had one of those checks not been made out to the Police Benevolent Association, Tony Torres likely would have escaped prosecution. To avoid jail, he pleaded guilty and swore to make full restitution, a pledge quickly forgotten amid the pressure of his demanding new job as a junior sales associate at a trailer-home franchise called A-Plus Affordable Homes.

Because the arrest report was old, the home address and telephone number listed for Tony Torres were no good. The current yellow pages showed no listing for A-Plus Affordable. Three fruitless inquiries sufficiently discouraged the young detective to whom the case of the crucified check-kiter had been assigned. He was relieved when his lieutenant ordered him to put the homicide file aside and drive down to Cutler Ridge, where he parked squarely in the center of the intersection of Eureka Drive and 117th Avenue, in order to block traffic for the presidential motorcade.

The young detective didn't think again of the murdered check-bouncing mobile-home salesman until two days later, when the police department got a call from an agitated woman claiming to be the victim's wife.

Avila phoned the Gentlemen's Choice escort service and asked for Morganna. She got on the line and said, 'I haven't used that name in six months. It's Jasmine now.'   'OK. Jasmine.'

'Do I know you, honey?'

Avila reminded her of their torrid drunken night at the motel on West Flagler Street.

'Gee,' she said, 'that narrows it down to about ninety guys.'

'You had a friend. Daphne, Diane, something like that. Red-head with a tattoo on her left tit.'

Jasmine said, 'What kinda tattoo?'

'I think it was a balloon or something.'

'Don't ring a bell.'

Avila said, 'The guy you were with, you'd definitely remember. Scary dude with a seriously fucked-up face.'

'Little Pepe that got burned?'

'No, it wasn't Pepe with the burns. Man's name was Snapper. His jaws stuck out all gross and crooked. You remember. It was a party before he went upstate.'

'Nope, still no bell,' said Jasmine. 'What're you doing tonight, sweetheart? You need a date?'

What a cold shitty world, thought Avila. There was no such thing as a friendly favor anymore; everybody had their greedy paws out.

'Meet me at Cisco's,' he told her tersely. 'Nine o'clock at the bar.'

'That's my boy.'

'You still a blonde?'

'If you want.'

Avila arrived twenty minutes late; he had taken a long hot shower following another furtive raid on the buried Tupperware stash. The stitches in his groin still stung from the soaking.

Jasmine sat at the bar, sipping Perrier from the bottle. She wore a subtle scarlet miniskirt and an alarming Carol Channing-style wig. Her perfume smelled like a fruit stand. Avila sat down carefully and ordered a beer. He folded a hundred-dollar bill into Jasmine's empty hand.

She smiled. 'I *do* remember you now.'

'What about Snapper?'

'You're a squeaker.'

'*Cómo?*'

'You squeak when you fuck. Like a happy little hamster.'

Avila flushed, and lunged for his beer.

'Don't be embarrassed,' Jasmine said. She took his left wrist and examined the beads of his *santería* bracelet. 'I remember this, too. Some sorta voodoo.'

Avila pulled away. 'Has Daphne heard from Snapper lately?'

'It's not Daphne anymore. It's Bridget.' Jasmine dug a pack of Marlboros out of her purse. 'Matter of fact, she spent the hurricane with him. Drunk as a skunk at some motel up in Broward.'

Avila made no move to light her cigaret. He said, 'When's the last time she saw him?'

'Just yesterday.'

'Yesterday!'

It was too good to be true! Thank you, mighty Chango! Avila was awestruck and humbled.

Jasmine said, 'That Snapper calls all the time, ever since he got out of Sumter. She's put her meathooks in that boy. By the way, her tattoo—it's not a balloon, it's a lollipop.' Jasmine laughed. 'But you were on the money about which tit.'

'So where's Snapper?'

'Sugar, how should I know? He's Daphne's trick.'

'You mean Bridget.'

Jasmine bowed. 'Touché,' she said, good-naturedly.

Avila produced another hundred-dollar bill. He put it flat on the bar, beneath the Perrier bottle. 'Is he at a motel?' he asked.

'A house, I think.'

'Where?'

'I gotta ask her,' Jasmine said.

'You need a quarter for the phone?'

'She's working tonight. Give me your number.'

Avila wrote it in the margin of the damp C-note. Jasmine put it in her purse.

'I'm hungry,' she said.

'I'm not.'

'What's the matter?' She gave his knee a squeeze. 'Oh, I know. I know why you're pissed.'

'You don't know a damn thing.'

'Yes I do. You're mad 'cause of what I said about the way you are in bed.'

Avila shot to his feet and called for the check. Jasmine tugged him back to the barstool. Pressing her chest against his arm, she whispered, 'Hey, it's all right. I thought it was cute.'

'I don't *squeak*,' Avila said coldly.

'You're right,' said Jasmine. 'You're absolutely right. Come on, honey, couldn't you go for a steak?'

Edie Marsh and Snapper had gotten into a nasty argument over the call girl. Edie had said it was no time for screwing—they needed to practice their husband-and-wife routine for when Fred Dove's boss showed up. Snapper had told her to lighten up or shut her trap. Watching the panel of saucy prostitutes on *Oprah* had made him think about licking the former Daphne's lollipop.

She was delighted to hear from him, the escort service business being slow as molasses after the hurricane. She caught a taxi to the Torres house, but got there late because the driver got lost in the pitch darkness and traffic confusion.

There was no door on which to knock, so Bridget strolled in unannounced. Edie Marsh and Snapper were glaring at each other by candlelight in the living room.

'Hello again,' Bridget said to Edie, who nodded testily.

Bridget scampered to the BarcaLounger and sprawled across Snapper's lap. She scissored her chubby legs in the air and smooched his neck (the disaligned jaws made mouth-kissing problematic).

Snapper said, 'You're sittin' on my gun.'

Bridget wriggled girlishly as he extricated the pistol. She said, 'Baby, what happened to your leg?'

'Ask Little Miss Psychobitch.'

Bridget stared at Edie Marsh. 'He hit me,' Edie said, remorselessly, 'so I hit him back.'

'With a fucking crowbar.'

'Ouch,' said the hooker.

Snapper told Edie to go walk the damn dogs for a couple hours.

Bridget said, 'You got dogs? Where?' She sat up excitedly. 'I love dogs.'

'Just take off your clothes,' Snapper said. 'Where's the Stoli?'

'All the liquor stores were boarded up.'

'Mother of Christ!'

Edie Marsh said, 'Look, Bridget, nothing personal against you. But we've got a very important meeting tomorrow morning—'

'Wait, now,' Snapper cut in. 'You're sayin' there's no vodka? Did I hear right?'

'Baby, the storm, remember? Everything's shut down.'

'Bullshit. You didn't even try.'

'Chill out,' said Bridget. 'We don't need booze for a party.'

Edie Marsh tried once more: 'All I'm asking is that you're gone in the morning, OK? There's a man coming to the house, he won't understand.'

'No problem, hon.'

'Nothing personal.'

Bridget laughed. 'It's not like I had my heart set on staying over in *this* dump.'

Edie said, 'You should see the bathrooms. There's mosquitoes *this* big hatching in the toilets!'

Bridget made a face and pressed her knees together. Snapper said: 'Edie, I'm countin' to ten. Get your lazy ass in gear.'

Donald and Marla began yipping in the backyard.

'Are those your puppies?' Bridget sprang from Snapper's lap and hurried to what once had been French doors. 'They sound adorable—what kind?' She peered expectantly into the night.

Snapper gimped to her side. 'Fertilizer hounds,' he said.

'Fertilizer hounds?'

'When I get done with 'em, yeah. That's the only goddamn thing they'll be good for.' He raised the pistol and fired twice at the infernal yowling. Bridget let out a cry and covered her ears. Edie Marsh came up from behind and kicked Snapper in the crook of his bum right leg. He went down with a surprised grunt.

Outside, the volume of doggy racket increased by many decibels. Donald and Marla were hysterical with fear. Edie Marsh hurried outside to untangle the leashes before they garroted each other. Bridget knelt at Snapper's side and scolded him for being such a meanie.

The way Levon Stichler figured it, he had nothing to lose. The hurricane had taken everything, including the urn containing the ashes of his recently departed wife. The life in which he had invested most of his military pension had been reduced to broken glass and razor tinsel. Hours of painstaking salvage had yielded not enough dry belongings to fill a tackle box. Levon Stichler's neighbors at the trailer court were in the same abject fix. Within twenty-four hours, his shock and despair had distilled into high-octane anger. Someone must pay! Levon Stichler thundered. And logically that someone should be the smirking sonofabitch who'd sold them those mobile homes, the glib fat thief who'd promised them that the structures were government certified and hurricane-proof.

Levon Stichler had spotted Tony Torres at the trailer court on the morning after the hurricane, but the mangy prick had fled like a coyote. Levon Stichler had fumed for a few days, gathering what valuables he could find among the trailer's debris until county workers showed up to bulldoze the remains. The old man considered returning to Saint Paul, where his only daughter lived, but the thought of long frigid winters—and sharing space with six hyperactive grandchildren—was more than he could face.

There would be no northward migration. Levon Stichler considered his life to be officially ruined, and considered one man to be morally responsible for the tragedy. He would know no peace until Tony Torres was dead. Killing the salesman might even make Levon Stichler a hero, at least in the eyes of his trailer-court neighbors—that's what the old man convinced himself. He envisioned public sympathy and national headlines, possibly a visit from Connie Chung. And prison wouldn't be such an awful place; a damn sight safer than a double-wide trailer. Haw! Levon Stichler told no one of his mission. The hurricane hadn't actually driven him insane, but that's what he intended to plead at the trial. The Alzheimer's defense was another promising option. But first he had to devise a convincingly eccentric murder.

As soon as he settled on a plan, Levon Stichler called PreFab Luxury Homes. The phone rang over and over, causing the old man to wonder if the storm had put the trailer-home company out of business. In fact, PreFab Luxury was enjoying a banner week, thanks to a massive requisition from the Federal Emergency Management Agency. Uncle Sam, it seemed, was generously providing trailers to homeless storm victims. Many of the miserably displaced souls who'd been living in PreFab Luxury trailers when the hurricane wiped them out would be living in a PreFab Luxury product once again. Neither the company nor the federal government thought it necessary to inform tenants of the irony.

Eventually a receptionist answered the telephone, and made a point of mentioning how busy they all were. Levon Stichler asked to speak to Mr Torres. The woman said that Tony apparently was taking some personal leave after the storm and that nobody knew when he'd return to the office. Levon Stichler gathered that he wasn't the first dissatisfied customer to make inquiries. The receptionist politely declined to divulge the salesman's home number.

From his sodden telephone directory, Levon Stichler carefully removed the page listing the names and addresses of all the Antonio Torreses in Greater Miami. Then he got in the car, filled up the tank and began the hunt.

On the first day, Levon Stichler eliminated from the list three auto mechanics, a scuba instructor, a thoracic surgeon, a palmist, two lawyers and a university professor. All were named Antonio Torres, but none was the scoundrel whom Levon Stichler sought. He was exhausted, but resolute.

On the second day, Levon Stichler continued to winnow the roster of candidates: a stockbroker, a nurseryman, a shrimper, a police officer, two electricians, an optometrist and a greenskeeper. Another Tony Torres, unkempt and clearly impaired, tried to sell him a bag of bootleg Dilaudids; still another threatened to decapitate him with a hoe.

The third day of the manhunt brought Levon Stichler to the Turtle Meadow subdivision and 15600 Calusa Drive. By then he'd seen enough hurricane destruction to be utterly unmoved by the sight of another gutted, roofless home. At least it still had walls, which was more than Levon Stichler could say for his own.

A pretty Anglo woman met him at the open front doorway. She wore baggy jeans and a long lavender T-shirt. Levon Stichler noticed she was barefoot and (unless his seventy-one-year-old eyeballs were mistaken) she was not wearing a bra. Her toenails were the shade of red hibiscus.

He said, 'Is this the Torres residence?'

The woman said yes.

'Antonio Torres? The salesman?'

'That's right.' The woman held out a hand. 'I'm Mrs Torres. Come on in, we've been expecting you.'

Levon Stichler jerked and said, 'What?'

He followed the barefoot braless woman into the house. She led him to the kitchen, which was a shambles.

'Where's your husband?'

'In the bedroom. Is Mister Dove on the way?'

'I don't know,' answered Levon Stichler, thinking: Who the hell is Mr Dove?

'Listen, Mrs Torres—'

'Please. It's Neria.' The woman excused herself to tend the generator, which was in the garage. When she returned to the kitchen, she turned on the electric coffeemaker and made three cups.

Levon Stichler thanked her, stiffly, and took a sip. The wife would be a problem; he needed to have Tony Torres alone.

The barefoot woman stirred two spoonfuls of sugar into her coffee. 'Is this your first stop of the day?'

'Sure is,' said Levon Stichler, hopelessly puzzled. Having never before murdered anybody, he was full of the jitters. He glanced at his wristwatch so often that the woman couldn't help but notice.

She said, 'Tony's in the shower. He'll be out very soon.'

'That's OK.'

'Is the coffee all right? Sorry there's no cream.'

Levon Stichler said, 'It's fine.'

She seemed like a nice enough person. What was she doing with a crooked slob like Torres?

He heard muffled noises from another room, two voices: a man's guttural laughter and a woman's high-pitched giggle. Levon Stichler reached slowly into the right pocket of his windbreaker. His hand tightened on the cool shaft of the weapon.

'Honey?' the barefoot woman called. 'Mister Reedy's waiting.'

Reedy? Levon Stichler's bold determination began to dissolve in a muddle. Something was awry with this particular Tony Torres. Yet Levon had spied the Salesman of the Year plaque on the wall, *PreFab Luxury Homes*, in raised gold lettering. Had to be the same creep.

Levon Stichler knew he must act swiftly, or lose forever the opportunity to avenge. He removed the concealed weapon from his jacket and raised it, ominously, for the wife to see.

'You better leave,' he advised.

Calmly she set her coffee cup on the counter. Her brow furrowed, but not in fear; more as if she were stymied on a crossword puzzle. 'What *is* that?' Pointing at the thing in Levon Stichler's hand.

'What's it look like?'

'A giant screw?'

'It's an auger spike, Mrs Torres. It was supposed to anchor my trailer in the storm.'

Levon Stichler had choreographed the crime a hundred times in his mind, most recently while sharpening the point of the auger on a whetstone wheel. The fat face of Tony Torres would make an easy target. Either of those cavernous hairy nostrils could be forcibly modified to accept the steel bit, which would (according to Levon's calculation) extrude well beyond the nasal cavity and into the brainpan.

The barefoot woman said, 'Excuse me, but are you fucking nuts?'

Before Levon Stichler could respond, the tall shape of a man materialized in the kitchen doorway. Levon Stichler aimed the spike like a lance, and charged. The woman shouted a sharp warning, and the man threw himself backward onto the wet tile floor. The auger impaled itself in the wooden shelf of a cabinet; with both hands Levon Stichler could not pull it free. Frantically he looked down at his intended victim.

'Oh shit,' he said. 'You're not the one.' He released his grip on the spike. 'You're not the one who sold me the double-wide!'

Another woman—wild-looking and half dressed—burst from the bedroom. Together she and the barefoot one helped Snapper rise to his feet.

In an accusatory tone, Levon Stichler said, 'You are *not* Tony Torres.'

'Like hell,' Snapper said.

Edie Marsh moved between the two men. 'Honey,' she said, facing Snapper, 'Mister Reedy here appears to be nuts.'

'Worse than nuts,' Bridget asserted.

'My name's not Reedy.'

Edie wheeled on the old man. 'Wait a second—you aren't from Midwest Casualty?'

Levon Stichler, who by now had gotten a close-up look at Snapper's feral eyes and disfigured mug, felt his brittle old bones turn to powder. 'Where's Mister Torres?' he asked, with notice-ably less spunk.

Edie sighed in annoyance. 'Incredible,' she said to Snapper. 'He's not Reedy. Can you believe this shit?'

Snapper wanted to be sure for himself. He leaned forward until he was two inches from the old man's nose. 'You're not from the insurance company? You're not Dove's boss?'

Misjudging the situation, Levon Stichler emphatically shook his head no. Edie Marsh stepped out of the way so Snapper could punch him into unconsciousness.

They sat on the rolled-up sleeping bags and waited for the governor to wake up in the palmettos.

Augustine assumed, as men sometimes do when they've had a particularly glorious time, that he should apologize.

Bonnie Lamb said, 'For what? It was my idea.'

'No, no, no. You're supposed to say it was all a terrible mistake. You got carried away. You don't know what got into you. Now you feel rotten and cheap and used, and you want to rush home to your husband.'

'Actually I feel pretty terrific.'

'Me, too.' Augustine kissed her. 'Forgive me, but I was raised Catholic. I can't be sure I've had fun unless I feel guilty afterwards.'

'Oh, it's guilt you're talking about? Sure I feel guilty. So should you, allowing yourself to be seduced by a newlywed.' She stood up and stretched her arms. 'However, Señor Herrera, there's a big difference between guilt and remorse. I don't feel any remorse.'

Augustine said, 'Me, neither. And I feel guilty that I don't.'

Bonnie whooped and climbed on his back. They rolled to the ground in an amorous tangle.

Skink came out of the thicket and smiled. 'Animals!' he bellowed, evangelically. 'No better than animals, rutting in public!'

Bonnie and Augustine got up and brushed themselves off. The

governor was a sight. Twigs and wet leaves stuck to his knotted hair. Gossamer strands of a broken spider's web glistened from his chin.

He tromped melodramatically toward the campfire, shouting: 'Fornicators! Fellaters! You ought to be ashamed!'

Augustine winked at Bonnie Lamb. 'That's one I hadn't thought of: shame.'

'Yeah, that's a killer.'

The governor announced he had a tasty surprise for breakfast. 'Your carnal frolics awoke me last night,' he said, 'so I went walking the roads.'

From his fatigues he produced two small, freshly skinned carcasses. 'Who wants rabbit,' he asked, 'and who wants the squirrel?'

Later they doused the fire and loaded the truck. Using the hand-drawn map that Augustine had been given by the helpful Margo and David, they located Calusa Drive with no difficulty. The black Jeep Cherokee was parked halfway down the street, in front of a badly damaged house; the bawdy mud flaps were impossible to miss. Skink told Augustine to keep driving. They left the pickup half a mile away and backtracked on foot.

Bonnie Lamb noticed, uneasily, that Augustine wasn't carrying either the pistol or the dart rifle. 'Scouting mission,' he explained.

They stayed off Calusa and approached on a parallel street, one block north. When they got close, they cut through a yard and slipped into an abandoned house directly across from 15600. From the broken window of a front bedroom, they had a clear view of the front door, the garage, the black Cherokee and two other cars in the driveway.

Margo and David were right. Their stolen license plate had been removed from the Jeep. Skink said: 'Here's what happened. After the guy beat up Brenda, he pulled the tag from the Cherokee and tossed it. What's on there now probably came off that Chevy.'

The car parked nearest to the garage was a late-model Caprice. The license plate was missing. The second car was a rusty barge of an Oldsmobile with a lacerated vinyl top and no hubcaps. Augustine said it would be useful to know how many people were inside the house. Skink grunted in assent.

Bonnie tried to guess what the next move would be. Notifying the police, she surmised, was not in the governor's plans. Looking around, she felt a stab of melancholy. The room had belonged to a baby. Gaily colored plastic toys were strewn on the floor; a sodden stuffed teddy bear lay facedown in a dank puddle of rainwater. Mounted on the facing wall were wooden cutouts of popular Disney characters—Mickey Mouse, Donald Duck, Snow White. Oddly, they made Bonnie Lamb think of her honeymoon and Max. The first thing he'd bought at the Magic Kingdom was a Mickey golf cap.

I should've known then and there, she thought. Bless his heart, he probably couldn't help it.

She got up to see the baby's crib. A mobile of tropical butterflies, fastened to the rail, had been snapped at the stem. The mattress was splotched with dark greenish mildew. Shiny red ants trooped across the fuzzy pink blanket. Bonnie wondered what had happened to the infant and her parents. Surely they escaped before the roof blew off.

Augustine waved her back to the broken window. Heart skipping, she knelt between the two men. *What am I doing? Where is this heading?*

Another car drives up to 15600 Calusa. A white compact.

Man gets out. Bony and clerical-looking. Gray hair. Brown windbreaker, loose dark trousers. Reminds Bonnie of her landlord back in Chicago. What was his name? Wife taught piano. What the heck was his name?

Standing by his car, the old man puts on a pair of reading glasses. Looks at a piece of paper, then up at the numerals painted on the house. Nods. Takes off the glasses. Tucks them in the left pocket of his windbreaker. Pats the right pocket, as if checking for something.

Awfully hot for a jacket, Bonnie's thinking. Summertime in Miami, how can a person be chilly?

'Where does *he* fit?' said Augustine.

'Contractor. Utility worker. Something like that,' Skink speculated.

Bonnie Lamb watches the old man straighten himself, stride purposefully to the doorway. Into the house he goes.

Augustine said, 'I thought I saw a woman.'

'Yes.' Skink scratched thoughtfully at his beard.

Creedlow! Bonnie thinks. That's the ex-landlord's name. James Creedlow. His wife, the piano teacher, her name was Regina. Chicago wasn't so long ago—Bonnie feels ditzy for not remembering. James and Regina Creedlow, of course.

Augustine said, 'What now, captain?'

Skink settled his bristly chin on the windowsill. 'We wait.'

Two hours later, the old man still hasn't come out of the house at 15600 Calusa Drive. Bonnie's worried.

Then another car pulls up.

20

Neria Torres had no desire to drive all the way to Brooklyn in search of a thieving husband.

'Then fly,' suggested Celeste, the graduate student who shared the Volkswagen van with Neria and Neria's lover, the professor.

The professor's name was Charles Gabler. His field of interest was parapsychology. 'Neria won't fly,' he said. 'She's afraid to death of airplanes.'

'Wow,' said Celeste, cooking on a portable stove in the back of the van. She was in charge of the macrobiotic menu.

Neria said, 'It's not just the flying, it's Brooklyn. How would I find Tony in a place like that?'

'I know how,' Celeste piped. 'Hire a psychic.'

'Great idea. We'll call Kreskin.'

The professor said, 'Neria, there's no need to be snide.'

'Oh yes, there is.'

She and Dr Gabler had been sorely low of funds when he'd proposed that young Celeste join them a week earlier as they prepared to depart Eugene, Oregon, for Miami. Young Celeste had been blessed with a comfortable trust fund, a generous heart and handsome gravity-defying breasts. Neria was under no illusions about the professor's motives, but she tried to put aside her concerns. They needed gas money, and young Celeste kept a world of credit cards in her purse. Somewhere near Salina, Kansas, Neria felt the need to inform Dr Gabler that he was paying too much attention to their travel companion, that his behavior was not only rude but disrespectful, and that the Great Plains in the heat of summer was no place to relearn the basics of hitchhiking. The professor seemed to take the warning to heart.

In truth, Neria was growing bored with Dr Gabler and his absurd blue and red crystals. Mystic healing, my ass—a box of Milk Duds starts to look pretty mystical, you smoke enough dope. Which was how the professor spent most of his waking hours, sluggishly bequeathing the driving duties to Neria and Celeste.

'I'd rather go to Miami anyway,' Celeste said, measuring out two cups of brown rice. 'I'd like to work in one of those tent cities. Cook for the homeless, if they need me.'

The professor regarded Neria Torres through bloodshot hound-dog eyes. 'Darling, it's entirely up to you. We'll go wherever you wish.'

'Wow,' said Neria. The mockery was lost on Celeste, who was immersed in a complex recipe. Neria declared she was going for a walk, and exited the van.

They had parked at a public campground off Interstate 20, outside Atlanta, to discuss which way to go—New York or Miami, north or south. Neria Torres replayed in her mind the upsetting conversation with the stranger who'd answered Tony's telephone. The more Neria thought about it, the more doubts she had. Not that her piggy husband wasn't capable of falling for a twenty-four-year-old blonde; rather, it was highly implausible that one would fall for him. And Brooklyn? Hardly a boomtown for the mobile-home trade. The stranger's story didn't add up.

Neria Torres had tried to confirm the lurid details with Varga, the nosy next-door neighbor, but his telephone was out of order. Neria was certain about two things: She was entitled to half the hurricane money for the house in Miami. And her estranged husband was dodging her.

New York was an astronomic long shot. At least in Florida there'd be a trail. Neria decided they should head for Miami, as originally planned.

She thought of a way to widen the net: Why not let the cops search for Tony, too? They were the pros, after all. Neria back-tracked through the campground to a phone booth, where she used her husband's PIN number to call the Metro-Dade police and make a missing-person report.

After a desk officer took the information, he put Neria Torres on hold. She waited several minutes, growing increasingly impatient. The sky began to drizzle. Neria fumed. She thought of Dr Gabler and young Celeste, together in the back of the Volkswagen van. She wondered if the professor was demonstrating his 'human Ouija board' exercise, the one he'd worked so charmingly on Neria herself.

Around Neria's neck hung a polished stalk of rose quartz, which Dr Gabler had given her to help channel untapped torrents of 'unconditional love.' Dickhead! thought Neria. At that very moment he was probably tuning young Celeste's inner chakras. Until she'd met the professor, Neria Torres hadn't known what a chakra was. Celeste undoubtedly did. She and Dr Gabler seemed to operate on the same wavelength.

The drizzle turned to a hard rain. Under Neria's feet, the red Georgia clay turned to slop. A man with a newspaper over his head came up behind her and stood uncomfortably close. He employed noisy, urgent breathing to emphasize his need for the telephone. Neria cursed aloud and slammed down the receiver.

On the other end, at Metro police headquarters in Miami, the desk officer had been diligently cross-checking the missing husband against a list of unclaimed bodies in the morgue. He was surprised to get a possible hit: One dead man had the same name, same date of birth, same extravagant brand of wristwatch.

The officer immediately had transferred Mrs Torres's phone call to the Homicide division. By the time a detective picked up, nobody was on the line.

Max Lamb flew from New York to San Diego to Guadalajara, where he slept for eleven hours. He woke up and called the airport hotel in Miami. Bonnie hadn't checked in. Max lit a Bronco cigaret and fell back on the pillow.

He chewed over a scenario in which his new wife might be cheating on him with one of two certifiable lunatics, or both. He couldn't conceive of it. The Bonnie Brooks he knew wasn't a free spirit—that was one of the things he loved about her. Steady and predictable, that was Bonnie. To Max's knowledge, the most impulsive thing she'd ever done was to hurl a stale pizza, Frisbee style, out the apartment window in Manhattan. When it came to sex, she was practically old-fashioned. She hadn't slept with *him* until their seventh date.

So it took only minutes for Max Lamb to dismiss his worries about Bonnie's fidelity. The ability to delude oneself on such matters was a benefit of owning a grossly inflated ego. Bottom line: Max couldn't imagine that Bonnie would desire another man. Especially *those* types of men: outlaws and psychos. Impossible! He snickered, blowing smoke at the notion. She was punishing him, that was all; obviously she was still ticked off about the hurricane excursion.

Scrubbing in the shower, Max Lamb refocused on the task at hand: the obstreperous Clyde Nottage Jr, ailing chairman of Durham Gas Meat & Tobacco. Max's orders were to talk some sense into the old fart, make him understand the grievous consequences of withdrawing all those expensive advertisements from print. Before Max Lamb had left New York, four Rodale & Burns executive vice presidents had individually briefed him on the importance of the Guadalajara mission. Success, Max knew, would guarantee a long and lucrative career at the agency. A home run, is how one of the honchos had put it. Turning the old man around would be a grand-slam homer in the bottom of the ninth. Clyde Nottage was one crusty old prick.

A cab took Max Lamb to the Aragon Clinic, a two-story stucco building, freshly painted and lushly landscaped, in a residential sub-division of the city. The lobby of the clinic showed evidence of recent remodeling, which unfortunately had not included central air. Max loosened his necktie and took a seat. On a glass table was a stack of informational pamphlets printed in Spanish. Curious, Max picked one up. On the first page was a drawing of a male sheep with an arrow pointing between its hind legs.

Max returned the pamphlet to the table. He wanted a smoke, but a sign on the wall said 'No Fumar.' A drop of sweat rolled down his jawline. Max dabbed it away with a handkerchief.

A man wearing a white medical coat came out; a pale-eyed

American in his mid-sixties. He introduced himself as Dr Caulk, Mr Nottage's physician.

'When may I see him?' Max Lamb asked.

'In a few minutes. He's finishing his treatment.'

'How's he doing?'

'Better, by and large,' said Dr Caulk, enigmatically.

The chat turned to the clinic, and cancer. The doctor asked Max Lamb if he was a smoker.

'Just started.'

'Started?' The doctor looked incredulous.

'Long story,' Max said.

'Mister Nottage smokes four packs a day.'

'I'd heard six.'

'Oh, we've got him down to four,' said the doctor. He gave the impression it was a contest of wills.

Max Lamb inquired about the unusual nature of the tumor treatments. Dr Caulk took full credit.

'We're really onto something,' he told Max. 'So far, the results have been quite astounding.'

'What made you think to try . . . you know—'

'Sheep semen?' Dr Caulk gave a wise smile. 'Actually it's quite an interesting story.'

As Max Lamb listened, he wondered if the deepening consternation showed on his face. The Caulk therapy was based entirely upon the casual observation that male sheep have a low incidence of lung cancer.

'Compared to . . .?'

The doctor slyly wagged a finger at Max. 'Now you sound just like the FDA.' He folded his hands and leaned forward. 'I suppose you're curious about how we collect the semen.'

'Not in the slightest,' said Max, forcefully.

A mountainous nurse appeared at the doctor's shoulder. She said Mr Nottage's afternoon treatment was completed. Dr Caulk took Max to the old man's room.

Outside the door, the doctor dropped his voice. 'I'll leave you two alone. Lately he's been a bit cranky with me.'

Max Lamb had met Clyde Nottage Jr only once before, on a golf course in Raleigh. The robust, fiery, blue-eyed curmudgeon that he remembered bore no resemblance to the gaunt, gray-skinned invalid in the hospital bed.

Until Clyde Nottage opened his mouth: 'The hell you staring at, boy?'

Max pulled a chair to the side of the bed. He sat down and positioned the briefcase on his lap.

'Gimme cigaret,' Nottage muttered.

As Max inserted a Bronco in the old man's bloodless lips, he said, 'Sir, did the doctor tell you I was coming? How are you feeling?'

Nottage ignored him. He plucked the cigaret from his mouth and eyed it ruefully. 'What they say is true, all true. About these goddamn things causing cancer. I know it's a fact. So do you. So does the goddamn guv'ment.'

Max Lamb was uneasy. 'It's a choice people make,' he said.

Nottage laughed, a tubercular snuffle. With a shaky hand he returned the cigaret to his mouth. Max lit it for him.

The old man said, 'They got you trained good. Look at me, boy—you heard about the sheep jizz?'

'Yes, sir.'

'I got a tumor the size of a Cuban mango in my chest, and I'm down to sheep jizz. My last earthly hope.'

'The doctor said—'

'Oh, fuck him.' Nottage paused to suck defiantly on the Bronco. 'You're here about the ads, right? Rodale sent you to change my mind.'

'Sir, the NIH report was news—bad news, to be sure. But they were only doing their jobs, the newspapers and magazines. They *had* to print the story; it was all over television—'

Clyde Nottage laughed until his nose ran. He wiped it with a hairless withered forearm. 'Christ, you missed the point. They all did.'

The old man's jocular tone gave Max a false burst of hope.

'I yanked those damn ads,' Nottage went on, 'because I was

pissed. That much is true. But I wasn't mad they published the cancer report.'

'Then why?'

An inch of dead ash fell from the old man's cigaret onto the sheets. He tried to blow it away, but the exertion of laughing had sapped him; his lungs moaned under the strain. After regaining his breath, he said: 'The real reason I was pissed, they're fuckin' hypocrites. They tell the whole world we peddle poison, put it on the front page. Yet they're delighted to take our money and advertise that very same poison. Greedy cocksucking hypocrites, and you may quote me to the boys in New York.'

Max Lamb realized the conversation had taken a perilous turn. He said, 'It's just business, sir.'

'Well, it's a business I'm gettin' out of. Right now. Before I leave this sorry world.'

Max waited for a punch line that didn't come. He felt a quaking in his bowels.

Clyde Nottage deposited the smoldering Bronco butt in a plastic cup of orange juice. 'As of this morning, Durham Gas Meat & Tobacco is Durham Gas Meat.'

'Please,' Max Lamb blurted. 'Wait on this, please. You're not feeling well enough to make such an important decision.'

'I'm dying, you fucking idiot. Three times a day some nurse looks like Pancho Villa shoots sheep cum into my belly. Damn right I don't feel well. Gimme Kleenex.'

Max handed him a box of tissues from the bed tray. Nottage snatched one and hacked fiercely into it.

'Mister Nottage, I urge you not to do anything right now.'

'Hell, it's already done. Made the call this morning.' Nottage spit again. He opened the tissue and examined the contents with a clinical eye. 'Last time I checked, I still had fifty-one percent of the company stock. You wasted a perfectly good airplane ticket, boy. The decision's made.'

Max Lamb, queasy with despair, began to protest. Nottage hunched forward, cupped his palms to his face and broke into a volcanic spasm of coughing.

Max jumped away from the bed. 'Shall I get Dr Caulk?'

The old man gazed into his hands and said, 'Oh shit.'

Max edged closer. 'Are you all right?'

'Considering I'm holding a piece of my own goddamn lung.'

'God!' Max turned away.

'Who knows,' the old man mused, 'it might be worth something someday. Put it in the Smithsonian, like Dillinger's dick.'

He drew back his frail right arm and lobbed the rancid chunk of tissue at the wall, where it hung like a gob of salsa.

Max Lamb bolted from the room. Moments later, Clyde Nottage Jr put his head on the pillow and died with a merry wheeze. The expression on his face was purely triumphant.

Dennis Reedy possessed an inner radar for potential trouble. His legendary instincts had saved Midwest Casualty many millions of dollars over the years, so his services as a claims supervisor were prized at the home office in Omaha. Reedy was an obvious choice to lead the Hurricane Crisis Team: South Florida was the insurance-scam capital of the nation, and Reedy knew the territory inside and out.

His radar went on full alert at 15600 Calusa Drive. The injury to the man's jaw was old, and healed. But there was another prospective problem.

'Mister Torres,' Reedy said, 'how'd you hurt that leg?'

Annoyed, the man looked up from the BarcaLounger. 'It was the storm,' he said.

Reedy turned stiffly to Fred Dove. 'You didn't mention this.'

'They're not filing a claim on the injury.'

Reedy suppressed the urge to guffaw in young Fred Dove's face. Antonio Torres was a textbook profile of a nuisance claimant. He was disfigured, morose and unsociable—precisely the sort of malcontent who'd have no qualms about defrauding an insurance company. The notion might not have occurred to Torres yet, but it would.

Dennis Reedy asked him how the accident had happened. Mr Torres shot a look at Mrs Torres, standing next to Fred Dove. Reedy detected nervous animosity in the husband's expression.

Mr Torres began to speak, but his wife cut in to answer: 'Tony got hit by a roof beam.'

'Oh?'

'While he was walking the dogs. Down the end of the street.'

Fred Dove smiled inwardly with relief. Boy, she was good. And quick!

Reedy said, 'So the accident didn't happen here on the property?'

'No,' replied Edie Marsh, 'but I wish it did. Then we'd know who to sue.'

They all chuckled, except Snapper. He stared contemptuously at the emblem of a growling badger, stitched to the breast of Dennis Reedy's corporate blazer.

'I hope you don't mind my asking about the accident,' said Reedy, 'but it's important for us to know all the circumstances— so there's not a misunderstanding later down the road.'

Edie Marsh nodded cooperatively. 'Well, like I explained to Mister Dove, I told Tony don't you walk those dogs in the storm. It won't kill us if they pee on the carpet or wherever. But would he listen? They're like his little babies—Donald and Marla is what he named them. Spoiled rotten, too. We don't have children, you understand.'

She gave Snapper a sad wifely smile. The look he sent back was murderous. She said, 'Tony waited till the eye passed over and the wind died before he went outside. 'Fore long it started blowing hard all over again, and before Tony could make it back with the dogs, he got hit by a beam off somebody's roof. Tore up his knee pretty bad.'

Reedy nodded neutrally. 'Mister Torres, where did this accident occur?'

'Down the end of the street. Like she said.' Snapper spoke in a dull monotone. He hated answering questions from pencil dicks like Reedy.

'Do you recall the address, Mister Torres?'

'No, man, the rain was a mess.'

'Have you seen a doctor?'

'I'll be OK.'

'I think you should go to a doctor.'

Fred Dove said, 'I suggested the same thing.'

'Oh, Tony's stubborn as a mule.' Edie Marsh took Dennis Reedy's arm. 'Let me show you the rest of the house.'

Reedy spent an hour combing through the place. Fred Dove was a jumble of nerves, but Edie stayed cool. Flirting with Reedy was out of the question; she could tell he was an old pro. She steered him away from the hall closet where the crazy geezer with the auger spike was propped, bound and gagged.

Snapper remained sourly camped in front of the television. Edie reminded him that the portable generator was low on gas, but he paid no attention. Donahue was doing a panel on interracial lesbian marriages, and Snapper was riveted in disgust. White chicks eating black chicks! That's what they seemed to be getting at—and there's old Phil, acting like everything's perfectly normal, like he's interviewing the fucking Osmonds!

After inspecting the property, Dennis Reedy settled in the kitchen to work up the final numbers. His fingers were a blur on the calculator keypad. Fred Dove and Edie Marsh traded anticipatory glances. Reedy scratched some figures on a long sheet of paper and slid it across the counter. Edie scanned it. It was a detailed claims form she hadn't seen before.

Reedy said, 'Mister Dove estimated the loss of contents at sixty-five. That's a little high, so I'm recommending sixty.' He pointed with the eraser end of his pencil. 'That brings the total to two hundred and one thousand. See?'

Edie Marsh was baffled. 'Contents?' Then, catching on: 'Oh yes, of course.' She felt like a total fool. She'd assumed the estimate for the house included the Torreses' personal belongings. Fred Dove gave her a sneaky wink.

'One-forty-one for the dwelling,' explained Dennis Reedy, 'plus sixty for the contents.'

Edie said, 'Well, I guess that'll have to do.' She did a fine job of acting disappointed.

'And we'd like your husband to sign a release confirming that he will not file a medical claim related to his knee injury. Otherwise the settlement process could become quite complicated. Under the circumstances, you probably don't want any delays in receiving your payment.'

'Tony'll sign,' said Edie. 'Let me have it.'

She went to the living room and knelt by the BarcaLounger. 'We're in great shape,' she whispered, and placed both documents—the liability waiver and the claims agreement—on the armrest. 'Remember,' she said, 'it's Torres with an *s*.'

Snapper barely took his eyes off the television while he forged Tony's signature. 'You believe these perverts?' he said, pointing at Phil's panel. 'Bring me a damn beer.'

Back in the kitchen, Edie Marsh thanked Dennis Reedy for his time. 'How long before we get the money?'

'A couple days. You're at the top of the list.'

'That's wonderful, Mister Reedy!'

Fred Dove said, 'You've seen our commercials, Mrs Torres. We're the fastest in the business.'

Christ, Edie thought, Fred's really overdoing it. But, with the exception of the chatty cartoon badger, she did recall being impressed by Midwest Casualty's TV spots. One in particular showed an intrepid company representative delivering claims checks, by rowboat, to Mississippi flood victims.

'I've got a laptop at the hotel,' Dennis Reedy was saying. 'We file by modem direct to Omaha, every night.'

Edie said, 'That's incredible.' A couple days! But what about that extra sixty grand?

As soon as Reedy went outside, Fred Dove took her in his arms. When he tried to kiss her, she pushed him away and said, 'You *knew*.'

'It was supposed to be a surprise.'

'Oh, right.'

'I swear! Sixty thousand extra, for you and me.'

'Freddie, don't screw around.'

'How could I steal it, Edie? The check will be made out to "Mister and Mrs Torres." That's you guys. Think about it.'

Irritably she paced the kitchen. 'I'm so stupid,' she muttered. 'Jesus.'

Of course the furnishings would be separate, along with the

clothes and appliances and every stupid little doodad inside the place. Fred Dove said, 'You never filed a big claim before. You wouldn't know.'

'Dwelling *and* contents.'

'Exactly.'

She stopped pacing and lowered her voice. 'Snapper didn't look at the new numbers.'

Fred Dove gave her a thumbs-up. 'That was my next question.'

'I kept my hand over the papers so he wouldn't see.'

'Good girl.'

'Can we get two checks instead of one?'

'I think so, Edie. Sure.'

'One for the dwelling, one for the contents.'

'That's the idea,' the insurance man said. 'An extra sixty for you and me. But don't say a word about this.'

'No shit, Sherlock. He's still got three bullets left, remember?' She pecked Fred Dove on the lips and aimed him out the back door.

21

Skink and Bonnie Lamb kept watch over the house on Calusa while Augustine returned to the pickup truck for the guns. He wasn't in the mood to shoot at anybody, even with monkey tranquilizer. Making love to Bonnie had left him recklessly serene and sleepy-headed. He resolved to shake himself out of it.

First he attempted to depress himself with misgivings and high-minded reproach. The woman was married, newly married! She was confused, lonely, vulnerable—Augustine piled it on, struggling to feel like a worthless low-life piece of shit. But he was too happy. Bonnie dazzled him with her nerve. Augustine hadn't ever been with a woman who would stoically snack on roadkill, or fail to complain about mosquitoes. Moreover, she seemed to understand the psychotherapeutic benefits of skull juggling. 'Touching death,' she'd said, 'or maybe teasing it.'

In the aftermath of passion, zipped naked into a sleeping bag, a lover's groggiest murmurs can be mistaken for piercing insight. Augustine had cautioned himself against drawing too much from those tender exhausted moments with Bonnie Lamb. Yet here he was with a soaring heart and the hint of a goddamn spring in his step. Would he ever learn?

As much as he craved her company, Augustine was apprehensive about Bonnie's joining Skink's expedition. He feared that he'd worry about her to distraction, and he needed his brain to be clear, uncluttered. As long as the governor ran the show, trouble was positively guaranteed. Augustine was counting on it; he couldn't wait. Finally he was on the verge of recapturing, at least temporarily, direction and purpose.

Bonnie was a complication. A week ago Augustine had

nothing to lose, and now he had something. Everything. Love's lousy timing, he thought.

Secret moves would be easier with only the two of them, he and Skink. But Bonnie demanded to be in the middle, playing Etta to their Butch and Sundance. The governor didn't seem to care; of course, he lived in a different universe. ' "Happiness is never grand," ' he'd whispered to Augustine. 'Aldous Huxley. "Being contented has none of the glamour of a good fight against misfortune." You think about that.'

When Augustine got to the truck, he broke down the dart rifle and concealed the pieces in a gym bag. The .38 pistol he tucked in the gut of his jeans, beneath his shirt. He slung the gym bag over his shoulder and began hiking back toward Calusa, wondering if Huxley was right.

As soon as Dennis Reedy and Fred Dove drove away, Edie Marsh hauled Levon Stichler out of the closet. Snapper wasn't much help. He claimed to be saving his energy.

Edie poked the old man with a bare toe. 'So what are we going to do with him?' It was a question of paramount interest to Levon Stichler as well. His eyes widened in anticipation of Snapper's answer, which was:

'Dump him.'

'Where?' asked Edie.

'Far away,' Snapper said. 'Fucker meant to kill me.'

'It was a pitiful try, you've got to admit.'

'So? It's the thought that counts.'

Edie said, 'Look at him, Snapper. He's not worth the bullet.'

Levon Stichler wasn't the slightest bit insulted. Edie pulled the gag from his mouth, prompting the old man to spit repeatedly on the floor. The gag was a dust cloth that tasted pungently of furniture wax.

'Thank you,' he panted.

'Shut up, asshole,' said Snapper.

Edie Marsh said: 'What's your name, Grampy?'

Levon Stichler told her. He explained why he'd come to assassinate the mobile-home salesman.

'Well, somebody beat you to it.' Edie described the visit by the burly fellow with the two dachshunds. 'He took your scumbag Tony away. I'm certain he won't be back.'

'Oh,' said Levon Stichler. 'Who are you?'

Snapper gave Edie a cranky look. 'See? I told you we gotta kill the fucker.'

The old man immediately apologized for being so nosy. Snapper said it didn't matter, they were going to dump him anyway.

Levon said, 'That's really not necessary.' When he began to plead his case, Snapper decided to gag him again. The old man coughed out the dust rag, crying, 'Please—I've got a heart condition!'

'Good.' Snapper ordered Edie Marsh to go fetch the auger spike. Levon Stichler got the message. He stopped talking and allowed his mouth to be muffled.

'Cover his eyes, too,' said Snapper.

Edie used a black chiffon scarf that she'd found in Neria Torres's underwear drawer. It made for quite a classy blindfold.

'That too tight?' she asked.

Levon Stichler grunted meekly in the negative.

'Now what?' she said to Snapper.

He shrugged unhappily. 'You got any more them Darvons? My fucking leg's on fire.'

'Honey, I sure don't—'

'Shit!' With his good leg he kicked Levon Stichler in the ribs, for no reason except that the old man was a convenient target. Edie pulled Snapper aside and told him to get a grip, for Christ's sake.

Under her breath: 'It's all working out, OK? Reedy signed off on the settlement. All that's left is to wait for the money. Kill this geezer, you'll screw up everything.'

Snapper worked his jaw like a steam shovel. His eyes were shot with pain and hangover. 'Well, I can't think of nothin' else to do.'

Edie said: 'Listen. We put old Levon in the car and haul him out to the boonies. We tell him to take his sweet time walking back, otherwise we'll track down each of his grandchildren and . . . oh, I don't know—'

'Skin 'em like pigs?'

'Fine. Whatever. The point is to scare the hell out of him, and he'll forget about everything. All he wants to do is live.'

Snapper said, 'My goddamn leg's near to bust open.'

'Go watch TV. I'll look for some pills.'

Edie searched the medicine cabinets to see if any useful pharmaceuticals had survived the hurricane. The best she could do was an unopened bottle of Midols. She told Snapper it was generic codeine, and pressed five tablets into his hand. He washed them down with a slug of warm Budweiser.

Edie said, 'Is there gas in the Jeep?'

'Yeah. After Sally Jessy we'll go.'

'And what is today's topic?'

'Boob jobs gone bad.'

'How cheery,' said Edie. She went outside to walk Donald and Marla.

After days in a morphine fog, Trooper Brenda Rourke finally felt better. The plastic surgeon promised to get her on the operating-room schedule by the end of the week.

Through the bandages she told Jim Tile: 'You look whipped, big guy.'

'We're still on double shifts. It's like Daytona out there.'

Brenda asked if he'd heard what happened. 'Some pawnshop off Kendall—the creep tried to hock my mom's ring.'

'Same guy?'

'Sounds like it. The clerk was impressed by the face.'

Jim Tile said, 'Well, it's a start.'

But the news worried him. He had unleashed the governor to deal with Brenda's attacker on the assumption that the governor would move faster than police. However, the pawnshop incident freshened the trail. Now it was possible that Skink's pursuit of the man in the black Cherokee would put him on a collision course with detectives. It was not a happy scenario to contemplate.

'I must look like hell,' Brenda said, 'because I've never seen you so gloomy.'

Of course he'd let it get to him—Brenda lying pale and shattered in the hospital. In his work Jim Tile had seen plenty of blood, pain and heartache, yet he'd never felt such blinding anger as he had that first day at Brenda's bedside. Trusting the justice system to deal with her attacker had struck the trooper as laughably naive, certainly futile. This was a special monster. It was evident by what he'd done to her. The guy hated either women, cops or both. In any case, he was a menace. He needed to be cut from the herd.

Now, upon reflection, Jim Tile wished he'd let his inner rage subside before he'd made the move. When Brenda remembered the tag number off the Cherokee, he should've sent it up the chain of command; played it by the book. Turning the governor loose was a rash, foolhardy impulse; vigilante madness. Brenda would recover from the beating, but now Jim Tile had put his dear old friend at dire risk. It would be damn near impossible to call him off.

'I need to ask you something,' Brenda said.

'Sure.'

'A detective from Metro Robbery came by today. Also a woman from the State Attorney. They didn't know about the black Jeep.'

'Hmmm.'

'About the license plate—I figured you'd given them the numbers.'

'I made a mistake, Bren.'

'You forgot?'

'No, I didn't forget. I made a mistake.'

Jim Tile sat on the edge of the bed and told her what he'd done. Afterwards she remained quiet, except to make small talk when a nurse came to dress her wounds.

Later, when she and Jim Tile were alone again, Brenda said, 'So you found your crazy friend. How?'

'Doesn't matter.'

'And he was right here, in this room, and you didn't introduce me?'

Jim Tile chuckled. 'You were zonked, darling.'

Brenda stroked his hand. He could tell she was still thinking about it. Finally she said, 'Boy, you must really love me, to do something like this.'

'I screwed up bad. I'm sorry.'

'Enough already. I've got one question.'

'OK.'

'What are the odds,' Brenda said, 'that your friend will catch up with the asshole who got my mother's ring?'

'The odds are pretty good.'

Brenda Rourke nodded and closed her eyes. Jim Tile waited until her breathing was strong and regular; waited until he was certain it was a deep healthy sleep, and not something else. Before leaving, he kissed her cheek, in a gap between bandages, and was comforted by the warmth of her skin. He felt pretty sure he saw the trace of a smile on her lips.

Skink's forehead was propped on the windowsill. He hadn't made a sound in an hour, hadn't stirred when Augustine left to get the guns. Bonnie Lamb didn't know if he was dozing or ignoring her.

'This was the baby's room. Did you notice?' she said.

Nothing.

'Are you awake?'

Still no response.

A yellowjacket flew through the broken-out window and took an instant liking to Skink's pungent mane. Bonnie shooed it away. From across the street, at 15600 Calusa, came the sound of dogs barking.

Eventually the governor spoke. 'Oh, they'll be back.' He didn't raise his head from the sill.

'Who?'

'Folks who own the baby.'

'How can you be sure?'

Silence.

'Maybe the hurricane was all they could take.'

'Optimist,' Skink grumbled.

Glancing again at the drowned teddy bear, Bonnie thought

that no family deserved to have their life shattered in such a harrowing way. The governor seemed to be reading her mind.

He said, 'I'm sorry it happened to them. I'm sorry they were here in the first place.'

'And you'll be even sorrier if they come back.'

Skink looked up, blinking like a sleepy porch lizard. 'It's a hurricane zone,' he said simply.

Bonnie thought he ought to hear an outsider's point of view. 'People come here because they think it's better than where they were. They believe the postcards, and you know what? For lots of them, it *is* better than where they came from, whether it's Long Island or Des Moines or Havana. Life is brighter, so it's worth the risks. Maybe even hurricanes.'

The governor used his functional eye to scan the baby's room. He said, 'Fuck with Mother Nature and she'll fuck back.'

'People have dreams, that's all. Like the settlers of the old West.'

'Oh, child.'

'What?' Bonnie said, indignantly.

'Tell me what's left to settle.' Skink lowered his head again.

She tugged on the sleeve of his camo shirt. 'I want you to show me what you showed Max. The wildest part.'

Skink clucked. 'Why? Your husband certainly wasn't impressed.'

'I'm not like Max.'

'Let us fervently hope not.'

'Please. Will you show me?'

Once more, no reply. Bonnie wished Augustine would hurry back. She returned her attention to the house where the black Cherokee was parked, and thought about what they'd witnessed during the long hot morning.

A half hour after the old man had arrived, a taxi pulled up. Out the doorway of 15600 Calusa had scurried a redheaded woman in a tight shiny cocktail dress and formidable high heels. Augustine and Bonnie agreed she looked like a prostitute. As the woman had wriggled herself into the back of the cab, Skink remarked that her bold stockings would make a superb mullet seine.

A short time later, a teal-blue Taurus had stopped in the driveway. The governor said it had to be a rental, because only rental companies bought teal-blue cars. Two men had gotten out of the Taurus; neither had a disfigured jaw. The younger one was a trim-looking blond who wore eyeglasses and carried a tan briefcase. The older, heavier one had cropped dark hair and carried a clipboard; his bearing was one of authority—probably ex-military, Skink guessed, a sergeant in his youth. The two men had stayed in the house for a long time. Finally the older one had come out alone. He'd sat in the driver's side of the car, with the door open, and jotted notes. Soon the man with the briefcase had appeared around the corner of the house, from the backyard, and together they'd departed.

While the visitors didn't appear to be violent desperadoes, Skink said that one could never be certain in Miami. Augustine got the hint, and went to fetch the guns from the pickup truck.

Now the governor had his forehead on the sill, and he'd begun to hum. Bonnie asked the name of the song.

' "Number Nine Dream," ' he said.

'I don't know that one.'

She wanted so much to hear about his life. She wanted him to open up and tell the most thrilling and shocking of true stories.

'Sing it for me,' she said.

'Some other time.' Skink pointed across the street. A man and a woman were leaving the house.

Bonnie Lamb stared. 'What in the world are they doing?'

The governor rose quickly. 'Come, child,' he said.

After the Sally Jessy show ended, Snapper made a couple of phone calls to set something up. Exactly what, Edie Marsh wasn't sure. Evidently he'd gotten a brainstorm about what to do with the old man, short of murder.

'Gimme hand,' he said to Edie, and began tearing the living-room drapes off the rods. The drapes were whorehouse pink, heavy and dank from rain. They spread the fabric in a crude square on the floor. Then they put Levon Stichler in the middle and rolled him up inside.

To Edie, it resembled an enormous strawberry pastry. She said, 'I hope he can breathe.'

Snapper punched the pink bundle. 'Hey, asshole. You got air?'

The gagged old man responded with an expressive groan. Snapper said, 'He's OK. Let's haul his ass out to the Jeep.'

Levon Stichler wasn't easy to carry. Snapper took the heavy end, but each step was agony to his shattered knee. They dropped the old man several times before they made it to the driveway. Each time it happened, Snapper swore vehemently and danced a tortured one-legged jig around the pink bundle. Edie Marsh opened the rear hatch of the Cherokee, and somehow they managed to fold Levon Stichler into the cargo well.

Snapper was leaning against the bumper, waiting for the searing pain in his leg to ebb, when he spotted the tall stranger coming toward them from the abandoned house across the street. The man was dressed in army greens. His long wild hair looked like frosted hemp. At first Snapper thought he was a street person, maybe a Vietnam vet or one of those cracked-out losers who lived under the interstate. Except he was walking too fast and purposefully to be a bum. He was moving like he had food in his stomach, good hard muscles, and something serious on his mind. Ten yards behind, hurrying to catch up, was a respectable-looking young woman.

Edie Marsh said, 'Oh shit,' and slammed the hatch of the Jeep. She told Snapper not to say a damn word; she'd do the talking.

As the stranger approached, Snapper straightened on both legs. The pain in his injured knee caused him to grind his mismatched molars. He slipped a hand inside his suit jacket.

'Excuse us,' said the stranger. The woman, looking nervous, stood behind him.

Edie Marsh said, helpfully, 'Are you lost?'

The stranger beamed—a striking smile, full of bright movie-star teeth. Snapper tensed; this was no interstate bum.

'What a fine question!' the man said to Edie. Then he turned to Snapper. 'Sir, you and I have something in common.'

Snapper scowled. 'The fuck you talkin' about?'

'See here.' The stranger calmly pried out one of his eyeballs and held it up, like a polished gemstone, for Snapper to examine. Snapper felt himself keeling, and steadied himself against the truck. The sight of the shrunken socket was more sickening than that of the glistening prosthesis.

'It's glass,' the man said. 'A minor disability, just like your jaw. But we both struggle with the mirror, do we not?'

'I got no problems in that department,' Snapper said, though he could not look the stranger in the face. 'Are you some fuckin' preacher or what?'

Edie Marsh cut in: 'Mister, I don't mean to be rude, but we've got to be on our way. We've got an appointment downtown.'

The stranger had a darkly elusive charm, a dangerous and disorganized intelligence that put Edie on edge. He appeared content at the prospect of physical confrontation. The pretty young woman, tame and fine-featured, seemed an unlikely partner; Edie wondered if she was a captive.

The tall stranger cocked back his head and deftly reinserted the glass eye. Then, blinking for focus, he said, 'OK, kids. Let's have a peek in that snazzy Jeep.'

Snapper whipped out the .357 and pointed it at a button in the center of the man's broad chest. 'Get in,' he snarled.

Again the stranger grinned. 'We thought you'd never ask!' The young woman clutched one of his arms and tried to suppress her trembling.

Augustine noticed a young towheaded boy, rigid in a shredded patio chair outside a battered house. Most of the roof was gone, so a skin of cheap blue plastic had been stapled to the beams for shade and shelter. It puckered and flapped in the breeze.

The towheaded boy looked only ten or eleven years old. He held a stainless-steel Ruger Mini-14, which he raised from his lap as Augustine passed on the sidewalk. In a thin high pitch, the boy yelled: 'Looters will be shot!'

The warning matched a message spray-painted in two-foot letters on the front wall: LOOTERS BEWAIR!!

Augustine turned to face the child. 'I'm not a looter. Where's your father?'

'Out for lumber. He told me watch the place.'

'You're doing a good job.' Augustine stared at the powerful rifle. A bank robber had used the same model to shoot down five FBI agents in Suniland, a few years back.

The boy explained: 'We had looters, night after the hurry-cane. We were stayin' with Uncle Rick, he lives somewheres called Dania. They came through while we's gone.'

Augustine slowly stepped forward for a closer look. The clip was fitted flush in the Ruger; all systems Go. The boy wore a severe expression, squinting at Augustine as if he stood a hundred yards away. The boy fidgeted in the flimsy chair. One side of his mouth wormed into a creepy lopsided frown. Augustine half expected to hear banjo music.

The boy went on: 'They got our TVs and CD player. My dad's toolbox, too. I'm 'posed to shoot the bastards they come back.'

'Did you ever fire that gun before?'

'All the time.' The child's hard gray-blue eyes flickered with the lie. The Mini-14 was heavy. His little arms were tired from holding it. 'You better go on now,' he advised.

Augustine nodded, backing away. 'Just be careful, all right? You don't want to hurt the wrong person.'

'My dad said he's gone booby-trap everything so's next time they'll be damn sorry. He went to the hardware store. My mom and Debbie are still up at Uncle Rick's. Debbie's my half-sister, she's seven.'

'Promise you'll be careful with the gun.'

'She stepped on a rusty nail and got infected.'

'Promise me you'll take it easy.'

'OK,' said the boy. A droplet of sweat rolled down a pink, sunburned cheek. It surely tickled, but the boy never took a hand off the rifle.

Augustine waved good-bye and went on up the road. When he arrived at the house where he'd left Bonnie Lamb and the governor, he found it empty. Across the street, at 15600 Calusa, the black Jeep Cherokee was gone from the driveway.

22

Augustine sprinted across the street. He pulled the pistol when he reached the doorway. There was no answer when he called Bonnie's name. Cautiously he went through the house. It was empty of life. The air was stale; mildew and sweat, except for one of the bedrooms—strong perfume and sex. A hall closet was open, revealing nothing unusual. A plaque on the living-room wall indicated the house belonged to a salesman, Antonio Torres. The hurricane had done quite a number on the place. In the backyard Augustine saw two miniature dachshunds tied to a sprinkler. They barked excitedly when they spotted him.

He sat down in a Naugahyde recliner and tried to reconstruct what could have happened in the twenty minutes he'd been gone. Obviously something had inspired the governor to make his move. Surely he'd ordered Bonnie to wait across the street, but she'd probably followed him just the same. Augustine had to assume they were now in the Jeep with the bad guy, headed for an unknown destination.

Augustine tore through the house once more, searching for clues. In the rubble of the funky-smelling bedroom was an album of water-stained photographs: the salesman, his spouse, and a multitude of well-fed relatives. Brenda Rourke had not recalled her attacker as an overweight Hispanic male, and the pictures of Antonio Torres showed no obvious facial deformity. Augustine decided it couldn't be the same man. He moved to the kitchen.

Hidden in a large saucepan, in a cupboard over the double sink, was a woman's leather purse. Inside was a wallet containing a Florida driver's license for one Edith Deborah Marsh, white female. Date of birth: 5–7–63. The address was an apartment in West Palm Beach. The picture on the license was unusually revealing: a pretty young lady with smoky, predatory eyes. The photo tech at the driver's bureau had outdone himself. Folded neatly in the woman's purse were pink carbons of two insurance settlements from Midwest Casualty, one for $60,000 and one for $141,000. The claims were for hurricane damage to the house at 15600 Calusa, and bore signatures of Antonio and Neria Torres. Interestingly, the insurance papers were dated that very day. Augustine was intrigued that Ms Edith Marsh would have these documents in her possession, and took the liberty of transferring them to his own pocket.

It was an interesting twist, but Augustine doubted it would help him locate Bonnie and the governor. The key to the mystery was the creep with the crooked jaw. He'd be the one carrying Brenda Rourke's service revolver. He'd be the one at the wheel of the Cherokee. Yet the house yielded no traceable signs.

With every passing moment, the creep was getting farther away. Augustine experienced a flutter of panic, thinking of what might happen. It was inconceivable that the governor would be cooperative during an abduction. Resistance was in the man's blood. A .357 aimed at his forehead would only enhance the challenge. And if he screwed up, Bonnie Lamb would be lost.

Augustine ached with dread. His impulse was to get in the truck and start driving; desperate widening grids and circles, in a wild hope of spotting the Jeep. The creep had only a short head start, but also the considerable advantage of knowing which direction he was going.

Then Augustine thought of Jim Tile, the state trooper. One shout on the police radio and every cop in South Florida would know to keep an eye open for the Cherokee. Augustine had made a point of memorizing the new tag: PPZ–350. Save the Manatee.

He picked up the kitchen phone to get the number for the Highway Patrol. That's when he noticed his old friend, the redial button. He'd learned the trick while keeping house with the demented surgical intern, the one who ultimately knifed him in the shower. Whenever he found her gone, Augustine would touch the redial button to determine if she'd been phoning around town to score more Dilaudid, or pawn items stolen from lhis house. Before long he was able to recognize the voices of her various dope dealers and fences, before hanging up. In that way, the redial button had been a valuable tool for predicting his girlfriend's moods and tracing missing property.

So he punched it now, to find out the last number dialed from 15600 Calusa before Skink and Bonnie disappeared. After three rings, a friendly female voice answered:

'Paradise Palms. Can I help you?'

Augustine hesitated. He knew of only one Paradise Palms, a seaside motel down in Islamorada. He gave it a shot. 'My brother just called a little while ago. From Miami.'

'Oh yes. Mister Horn's friend.'

'Pardon me?'

'The owner. Mister Horn. Your brother's name is Lester?'

'Right,' said Augustine, flying blind.

'He's the only Miami booking we've had today. Did he want to cancel?'

'Oh no,' Augustine said. 'No, I just want to make sure the reservation is all set. See, we're supposed to surprise him down there—it's his birthday tomorrow. We're going to take him deep-sea fishing.'

The woman at the motel said the dolphin were hitting off-shore, and advised him to try the docks at Bud 'n' Mary's to arrange a charter. 'Would you like me to call over there?'

'No, that's all right.'

'Does Mister Horn know?'

'Know what?' said Augustine.

'That it's Lester's birthday. He'll be so sorry he missed it—he's in Tampa on business.'

'Oh, that's too bad,' Augustine said. 'I meant to ask—what time's my brother getting in? So we can make sure everything's arranged. You know, for the surprise party.'

'Of course. He told us to expect him late this afternoon.'

'That's perfect.'

'And don't you worry. I won't say a word to spoil it.'

Augustine said, 'Ma'am, I cannot thank you enough.'

*

After a day of inept drinking and arduous self-pity, Max Lamb took a flight from Guadalajara to Miami. There he intended to quit smoking, reclaim his brainwashed spouse and reconstruct his life. Another honeymoon was essential—but, this time, someplace far from Florida.

Hawaii, Max thought. Maybe even Australia.

His head was a cinder block. The tequila hangover fueled vivid, horrific dreams on the plane. Once he awakened clawing at an invisible shock collar, his neck on fire. In the nightmare it was Bonnie and not the kidnapper wielding the Tri-Tronics remote control, diabolically pushing the buttons. An hour later came another dream; again his wife. This time they were making love on the deck of an airboat, skimming across the Everglades under a blue porcelain sky. Bonnie was on top of him with her eyes half open, the sawgrass whipping her cheeks. Clinging to her bare shoulder was a monkey—the same psoriatic pest that Max had videotaped after the hurricane! In the dream, Max couldn't see the face of the airboat driver, but believed it was the quiet young man who juggled skulls. As Bonnie bucked her hips, the vile monkey hung on like a tiny wrangler. Suddenly it rose on its hind legs to display a miniature pink erection. That's when Max screamed and woke up. He was wide-eyed but calmer by the time the plane landed.

Then, at the Miami airport, his tequila phantasms were reignited by a newspaper headline:

Remains in Fox Hollow Identified as Mob Figure;
Believed Mauled, Devoured by Escaped Cat

Max bought the paper and read the story in horror. A gangster named Ira Jackson had been gobbled by a wild lion that broke out of a wildlife farm during the storm. The gruesome details heightened the urgency of Max's mission.

He arrived at Augustine's home with a prepared speech and, if necessary, a legal threat. The lights were off. Nobody answered the door. In the absence of confrontation, Max was emboldened to slip around to the backyard.

The sliding glass door on the porch was unlocked. Inside the house, it was stuffy and warm. Max started the air conditioner and turned on every lamp he could find. He wanted to advertise his presence; he didn't want to be found creeping through the halls in darkness, like a common burglar.

Thrilled by his own daring, Max combed the place for signs of his wife. Hanging in a closet was the outfit she'd worn on the day he was kidnapped. Since the rental car had been looted of their belongings, Max reasoned that Bonnie must now be wearing somebody else's clothes, or her folks had wired some cash— or perhaps Augustine had bought her an expensive new wardrobe. Wasn't that what wife-stealers did?

Max Lamb forced himself to enter the guest room. He purposely avoided the wall of skulls, but shuddered anyway under the dissipated stares. He was pleased to find the bed linens rumpled exclusively on the left side—Bonnie's favorite. A depression in the lone pillow seemed, upon inspection, to match the shape of a young woman's head. The bed showed no manifest evidence of male visitation.

An oak dresser yielded an assortment of female clothing, from bras to blue jeans, in an intriguing range of sizes. Relics of Augustine's ex-girlfriends, Max assumed. One of them must have stood six feet two, judging by the Amazonian cut of her black exercise leggings. Max located several petite items that would have fit his wife, including a pair of powder-blue sweat socks in a tidy mound on the hardwood floor. His outlook improved; at least she was wearing borrowed clothes.

He steeled himself for the next survey: Augustine's room.

The man's bed looked like a grenade had been set off under the sheets. Max Lamb thought: He's either having fantastic sex or horrible nightmares. The disarray made it impossible to determine if two persons had shared the mattress; the cast of *A Chorus Line* could have slept there, for all Max could tell.

Uncertainty nibbled at his ego. He got an idea—distasteful but effective. He bent over Augustine's bed and put his nose to the linens, whiffing for a trace of Bonnie's perfume. Uncharacteristically, Max Lamb couldn't recall the brand name of the fragrance, but he'd never forget its orchard scent.

He sniffed in imaginary grids, starting at the headboard and work-ing his way down the mattress. An explosive sneeze announced his findings: Paco Rabanne for men. Max recognized the scent because he wore it himself (in spite of a near-incapaci-tating allergy) every Monday, for the sixth-floor meetings at Rodale.

Paco and laundry bleach, that's all Max detected on Augus-tine's sheets.

One more place to check: the wastebasket in the bathroom. Grimly Max pawed through the litter: no used condoms, thank God.

Later, stretched out on Augustine's sofa, Max realized that Bonnie's faithfulness, or possible lack thereof, wasn't the most pressing issue. It was her sanity. Somehow they'd snowed her, those madmen. Like some weird cult—one eats road pizza, the other fondles human skulls.

How could such a bright girl let herself be brainwashed by such freaks!

Max Lamb decided on a bold move. He composed a script for himself and rehearsed it for an hour before picking up the phone. Then he dialed the apartment in New York and left the message for his wandering wife. The ultimatum.

Afterwards Max called back to hear how it sounded on the answering machine. His voice was so steely that he scarcely recognized himself.

Excellent, he thought. Just what Bonnie needs to hear.

If only she calls.

Avila's wife snidely announced that his expensive *santería* goats were in the custody of Animal Control. One had been cap-tured grazing along the shoulder of the Don Shula Expressway, while the other had turned up at a car wash, butting its horns through the grillwork of a leased Jaguar sedan. Avila's wife said it made the Channel 7 news.

'So? What do you want *me* to do?' Avila demanded.

'Oh, forget about! Three hundred dollars, chew jess forget about!'

'You want me to steal the goats back? OK, tonight I'll drive to the animal shelter and break down the fence and kidnap the damn things. That make you happy? While I'm there I'll grab you some kittens and puppies, too. Maybe a big fat guinea pig for your mother, no?'

'I hate chew! I hate chew!'

Avila shook his head. 'Here we go again.'

'Chew and Chango, your faggot *oricha*!'

'Louder,' Avila said. 'Maybe you can wake some of your dead relatives in Havana.'

The phone rang. He picked it up and turned his back on his wife, who hurled a can of black beans and stormed from the kitchen in a gust of English expletives.

It was Jasmine on the line. She asked, 'What's all that noise?'

'Marriage,' Avila said.

'Well, love, I'm sitting here with Bridget, and guess where we're going tonight.'

'To blow somebody?'

'God, look who's in a piss-poor mood.'

'Sorry,' Avila said. 'It's been a shitty day.'

'We're driving to the Keys.'

'Yeah?'

'To meet your friend,' said Jasmine.

'No shit? Where?'

'Some motel on the ocean. Can you believe he's payin' the both of us to baby-sit some old-timer.'

'Who?' Avila couldn't imagine what new scam Snapper was running.

Jasmine said, 'Just some yutz, I don't know. We're supposed to keep him busy for a couple days, take some dirty pictures. Five hundred each is what your friend's giving us.'

'Geez, that sucks.'

'Business is slow, sweetie. The hurricane turned all our regulars into decent, faithful, God-fearing family men.'

Avila heard Bridget's giggle in the background. Jasmine said, 'So five hundred looks pretty sweet right about now.'

'You can double it if you give up the name of the motel.'

'Why do you think we called? Aren't you proud of me?'

Avila said, 'You're the best.'

'But listen, honey, we need to know—'

'Let me talk to Bridget.'

'Nope, we want to know what you got in mind. Because both of us are on probation, as usual—'

'Don't worry,' Avila said.

'—and we don't need no more trouble, legally speaking.'

'Relax, I said.'

'You ain't gonna kill this guy?'

'Which guy—Snapper? Hell, no, he owes me money is all. What time are you meeting him?'

Jasmine said, 'Around eight.'

Avila checked his wristwatch. 'You girls ain't gonna make Key West by eight o'clock unless you got a rocket car.'

'Not Key West, honey. Islamorada.'

It was seventy-five miles closer, but Avila still wasn't certain he could get there in time. First he had to make an offering; such a momentous trip was unthinkable without an offering.

He said, 'Jasmine, what's the name of the motel?'

'Not till you promise me and Bridget won't get in trouble.'

'Jesus, I already told you.'

She said, 'Here's the deal, so listen. You gotta wait till we get our money from your friend Snapper. Then you gotta promise not to shoot anybody in front of us, OK?'

Avila said, 'On my wife's future grave.'

'Also, you gotta promise to pay us what you said—five hundred each.'

'Yep.'

'Plus two stone crab dinners. That's Bridget's idea.'

'No problem,' Avila said. Informing the prostitutes that stone crabs were out of season would only have muddled the negotiation.

'The name,' Avila pressed.

'Paradise Palms. I've never been there before. Bridget, neither, but Snapper promised it's really nice.'

'Compared to prison, I'm sure it's the fucking Ritz. What's the room number?'

Jasmine asked Bridget. Bridget didn't know.

'Doesn't matter,' Avila said. 'I'll track you down.'

'Remember what you promised!'

'Yeah, I'll try. It's already been at least seven seconds.'

'Well, sweetheart, we better cruise.'

Avila was about to set the receiver on the cradle when he remembered something. 'Hey! Jasmine, wait!'

'Yeah, what.'

'Did you tell her about me?'

'Bridget? I didn't tell her nuthin".' Jasmine sounded puzzled. 'What's to tell?'

'Nuthin".'

'Oh . . . you mean about—'

'Don't say it!'

Jasmine said, 'Honey, I would *never*. That was between you and me. Honest to God.'

'"Cause the other night you said I was better.' How valiantly Avila had labored to stifle his vocalizing during the lovemaking! What few sounds he'd made were not, by any stretch of the imagination, squeaks.

'The other night you were just great,' said Jasmine. 'Fantastic, even. Better than I remembered.'

Avila said, 'Same goes for you, too.'

Later, driving to Sweetwater for the chickens, he couldn't stop thinking about the call girl's sultry compliment. Whether she meant a word of it or not wasn't worth speculating on; the concept of sincerity was so foreign to Avila's own life that he felt unqualified to pass judgment on Jasmine. He was just glad she'd quit calling herself Morganna—what a clunker of a name to remember in the heat of passion!

The combined effect of marijuana and methaqualone on Dr Charles Gabler's judgment was not salutary. Never was it more evident than late on the night of September 1, at a roadside motel off Interstate 10 near Bonifay, Florida. Overtaken with desire, the professor slipped out of the twin bed he shared with the sleeping Neria Torres, and slipped into the twin bed occupied by the wakeful young graduate student, Celeste. As he ardently attached himself to one of Celeste's creamy breasts, Dr Gabler was becalmed by a warm, harmonious confluence of physical and metaphysical currents. His timing couldn't have been worse.

Neria Torres had been reevaluating the parameters of her relationship with the professor ever since they'd pulled off a highway outside Jackson, Mississippi, so he could take a leak. Sitting in the driver's seat, watching Dr Gabler try to tinkle in some azaleas, Neria had thought: I don't find this cute anymore.

As the professor had tottered back toward the van, the beams of the headlights dramatically illuminated the ruby-colored crystals dangling from the lanyard around his neck.

'Oh wow,' young Celeste had exclaimed, suffused with mystic awe and Humboldt County's finest.

That was the moment when Neria Torres had looked into her future and decided that the professor should share no large part of it; specifically, the insurance settlement from the hurricane. Neria envisioned a scenario in which Dr Gabler might endeavor to sweet-talk her out of a portion of the money—he would probably call it a friendly loan—and then flee in the dead of night with his nubile protégée. After all, that's pretty much what he'd done to his previous lover, a vendor of fine macramés, when Neria Torres entered his life.

Even if the professor harbored no selfish designs on the hurricane booty, Neria had a pragmatic reason to dump him: His appearance in Miami would complicate the duel with her estranged husband over the insurance settlement. Considering the tainted circumstance of her departure from the household, Neria doubted that Tony would be in a mood to forgive and forget. Her inability to make contact in the days following the storm was foreboding—the vindictive bastard obviously intended to pocket her half of the windfall. If the battle went to court, Dr Gabler's bleary presence during the proceedings would not, Neria Torres knew, work in her favor.

These were the thoughts she carried into sleep at the motel in

Bonifay. Had it been a deeper sleep, or had the room's Eisenhower-vintage cooling unit been a few decibels louder, Neria Torres might not have been awakened by the muffled suckling and amorous hmmm-hmmms from the nearby bed. But awakened she was.

Except for cracking her eyelids, Neria didn't move a muscle at first. Instead she lay listening in disgusted fascination, struggling to arrange her emotions. On the one hand, she was vastly relieved to have found a solid excuse for jettisoning the professor. On the other hand, she was furious that the sneaky little shit would be so crude and thoughtless. Over the years, Tony Torres undoubtedly had cheated on her now and again—but never while she was sleeping in the same room!

Eventually, it was the immodest giggling of young Celeste that galvanized Neria Torres. She sprang from the bed, turned on all the lights, snatched up the velvet satchel containing Dr Gabler's special healing crystals and began whaling deliriously on the writhing mound of bedsheets. The satchel was heavy and the stones were sharp, taking a toll on the professor's unfirm flesh. With an effeminate cry, he scuttled to the bathroom and chained the door. Meanwhile the graduate student cowered nude and tearful on the mattress. The stubble on Dr Gabler's chin had left a telltale path of abraded, roseate blotches from her neck to her quivering belly. Neria Torres noticed, with fierce satisfaction, a faint comma of a scar beneath each of young Celeste's perfect breasts; an Earth Mother with implants!

Repeatedly she gasped, 'I'm sorry, Neria, please don't kill me! Please don't . . .'

Neria threw the satchel of crystals to the floor. 'Celeste, you know what I hope for you? I hope that asshole hiding in the john is the highlight of your entire goddamn life. Now where's the keys to the van?'

Hours later, at a busy truck stop in Gainesville, Neria tried another call to Mr Varga, her former neighbor in Miami. This time his phone was working; Varga answered on the third ring. He insisted he knew nothing about Neria's husband and a young blond hussy loading up a rental truck.

'Fact, I haven't seen Tony since maybe two days after the hurricane.'

'Are there still strangers at the house?' Neria asked.

'All the time, people come and go. But no blondes.'

'Who are they, Leon?'

'I don't know. Friends and cousins of Tony, I heard. They got two dogs bark half the night. I figured Tony's letting 'em watch the place.'

Varga shared his theory: Neria's husband was lying low, due to adverse publicity about the mobile-home industry. 'Every damn one blew to smithereens in the storm,' Varga related. 'The papers and TV are making a big stink. Supposedly there's going to be an investigation. The FBI is what they say.'

'Oh, come off it.'

'That's the rumor,' Varga said. 'Your Tony, he's no fool. I think he's making himself invisible till all this cools down, these people come to their senses. I mean, it's not *his* fault those trailers fell apart. God's will is what it was. He's testing us, same as He did with Noah.'

'Except Noah wasn't insured,' said Neria Torres.

Mr Varga was right about one thing: Tony wouldn't stick around if there was heat. His style was to take a nice hotel room and ride things out. In the meantime, he'd have some of his deadbeat relatives or white-trash salesmen pals stay with their bimbos in the house on Calusa. Tony wouldn't be far away; never would he skip town without getting his paws on the Midwest Casualty money.

Neria was buoyed. The story about the young blonde and Brooklyn obviously was bullshit, a ruse cooked up by her husband. Wishful thinking, too, Neria mused. Talking to Mr Varga validated her decision to return to Miami.

'Are you really heading home?' he asked. 'You and the mister give it one more try?'

'Stranger things have happened,' said Neria Torres. She made Mr Varga swear on a stack of Holy Bibles not to breathe a word. She said it would ruin everything if Tony found out she was coming.

23

Snapper instructed Edie Marsh to take the Turnpike, and watch the damn speedometer. He was pressed against the passenger-side door, keeping the stolen .357 pointed at the freak in the army greens. The young woman was no immediate threat.

The stranger blinked like a craggy tortoise. He said: 'How much you get for her ring?'

Snapper frowned. The fucker *knew*—but how?

Edie Marsh didn't take her eyes off the road. 'What's he talking about? Whose ring?'

Snapper spied, in the lower margin of his vision, the wandering prow of his jawbone. He said, 'Everybody shut the fuck up!'

Leaning forward, the longhair said to Edie: 'Your rough-tough boyfriend beat up a policewoman. Ripped off her gun and her mother's wedding band—he didn't tell you?'

Edie shivered. Maybe it was his breath on the nape of her neck, or the slow rumble of his voice, or what he was saying. Meanwhile Snapper waved the police pistol and hollered for the whole world to shut up or fucking die!

He jammed a CD into the dashboard stereo: ninety-five decibels of country heartache. Within minutes his fury passed, soothed by Reba's crooning or possibly the five white pills Edie had given him back at the house.

OK, boy, now *think*.

The original plan was to waylay the nutty old man with the hookers. No problem there. A guy Snapper knew from his Lauderdale days, Johnny Horn, had a small motel down in the Keys. Ideal spot for Levon Stichler to take a short vacation. Snapper's idea was to get one a them cheap disposable cameras, so the hookers could take some pictures, the kind a respectable man wouldn't want his grandkiddies to see. Two or three days tied naked to a motel bed, the old fart wouldn't care to recall he'd ever set foot at 15600 Calusa Drive. If he promised to behave, then possibly the disposable camera would get disposed of. The old man could make his way back to Miami with nothing but a bed rash and a sore cock to show for the experience.

Best of all, Snapper wouldn't have to pay for the motel room in the Keys, because Johnny Horn owed him a favor. Two years back, Snapper had more or less repossessed a Corvette convertible from the freeloading boyfriend of one of Johnny Horn's ex-wives. Snapper had driven the Corvette straight to the Port of Miami and, in broad daylight, parked it on a container ship bound for Cartagena. It was a high-risk deal, and Johnny said for Snapper to call the Paradise Palms anytime he needed a place to crash or hide out or take some girl.

Snapper had dreamed up the plan for old man Stichler all by himself, without Edie's input. He surely didn't want to throw all that cleverness out the window, but he couldn't conceive of how to fit the new intruders into his scheme, and he was too fogged from the pills to improvise. It seemed easier to kill the one-eyed freak and his woman companion—and as long as Snapper was being so bold, why not do loony old Levon as well? That way, Snapper reasoned, he wouldn't have to pay the two whores anything, except for gas money and possibly a seafood dinner.

On the downside: How to get rid of three dead bodies? The logistics were daunting. Snapper suspected that his droopy brain wasn't up to the challenge. Killing took energy, and Snapper all of a sudden felt like sleeping for three weeks solid.

He worked up a pep talk for himself, recalling what a wise guy once told him in prison: *Dumping bodies is like buying real estate— location, location, location.* Snapper thought: Look around, boy. You got your mangrove islands, your Everglades, your Atlantic-mother-fucking-Ocean. What more you want? A fast shot to the head, then let the sharks or the gators or the crabs finish the job. What's so damn difficult about that?

But Jesus, the stakes were high; one measly fuckup and it's back to Raiford for the rest of my life. Probably locked in a ten-by-ten with some humongous horny black faggot weight lifter. Clean and jerk my skinny ass till I walk like Julia Roberts.

And shooting people *is* awful noisy. Edie Marsh wouldn't go for it, Snapper knew for a fact. She'd make quite a stink. And killing Edie with the others was impractical because (a) he didn't have enough bullets and (b) he couldn't cash the insurance checks without her. *Damn.*

'What is it?' Edie shouted over Reba.

Snapper made a sarcastic zipper motion across his lips. He thought: I'm so goddamn tired. If only I could have a nap, it would come to me. A new plan.

The one-eyed stranger began to sing along with the stereo. Snapper scrutinized him coldly. How'd he know about the lady trooper? Snapper's hands had a slight tremor. His lips were as dry as ash. What if the bitch had gone and died? What if first she'd gotten a good look at him, or maybe the Jeep? What if it was already on TV, and every cop in Florida was in the hunt?

Snapper told himself to knock it off, think positive. For the first time in days, his busted-up knee didn't hurt so much. That was something to be glad about.

The young woman in the back seat joined her flaky companion in song. She was winging it with the lyrics, but that was all right with Snapper; her voice was pretty.

Edie Marsh tapped the rim of the steering wheel and acted peeved at the amateur chorus. After about three minutes she reached out and poked the Off button on the CD player. Reba fell silent, and so did the chorus.

Snapper announced that the next selection was Travis Tritt.

'Spare us,' Edie said.

'Hell's your problem?'

The woman in the back seat spoke up: 'My name's Bonnie. This is the governor. He prefers to be called "captain."'

'Skink will be fine,' said the one-eyed man. 'And I would kill for some Allman Brothers.'

Snapper demanded to know what they wanted, why they'd been snooping at the Torres house. The man who called himself Skink said: 'We were looking for you.'

'How come?' 'As a favor to a friend. You wouldn't know him.'
Edie Marsh said, 'You're not making a damn bit of sense.'

Something shifted in the bed of the Jeep. The sound was
followed by a faint quavering moan.

From the woman, Bonnie: 'What are your names?'

Edie Marsh rolled her eyes. Bonnie caught it in the rearview.

Snapper said, 'Fuckin' idiots, the both of 'em.'

'All I meant,' said Bonnie Lamb, 'is what should we call you?'

'I'm Farrah Fawcett,' Edie said. Nodding at Snapper: 'He's
Ryan O'Neal.'

In discouragement, Bonnie turned toward the window. 'Just
forget it.'

A warm hand settled on Edie's shoulder. 'Whoever you are,'
Skink said intimately, 'you make a truly lovely couple.'

'Fuck you.'

Snapper lunged across the seat and stuck the barrel of the .357
in a crease of the stranger's cheek. 'You think I don't got the
balls to shoot?'

Skink nonchalantly pushed the gun away. He eased back in
the seat and folded his arms. His fearless attitude distracted Edie
Marsh. Snapper commanded her to pull off at the next exit. He
needed to find a bathroom.

Having never been abducted at gunpoint, Bonnie Lamb wasn't
as scared as she thought she ought to be. She attributed the
unexpected composure to her resolve for adventure and to the
governor's implausibly confident air. Based on nothing but blind
faith, Bonnie was sure that Skink wouldn't allow them to be
harmed by a deformed auto thief. The guy's erratic gun handling
was nerve-racking, but somehow not so menacing with another
woman in the Jeep. Bonnie Lamb could tell that she wasn't
some dull-eyed trailer-park tramp; she was a sharp cookie, and
not especially afraid of the dolt with the pistol. Bonnie had a
feeling there wouldn't be any killing inside the truck.

She wondered what Max Lamb would think if he could see
her now. Probably best that he couldn't. She felt terrible about
hurting her husband, but did she miss him? It didn't feel like it.

Perhaps she was doing Max the biggest favor of his life. Having waited all of one week to commit adultery with a near-total stranger, Bonnie surmised that she had, in the parlance of pop psychotherapy, 'unresolved issues' to confront. Poor eager Max was a victim of misleading packaging. He thought he was getting one sort of woman when he was getting another. For that Bonnie felt guilty.

She vowed not to depress herself by overanalyzing her instant attraction to Augustine. She wished he were there, and wondered how he would ever find them on the road. Bonnie herself had no clue which way they were headed.

'South,' the governor reported. 'And south is good.'

The man with the pistol snarled: 'Quiet, asshole.'

Suddenly Bonnie got an eerie hologrammic vision of the gunman's naked skull on the wall of Augustine's guest room. The broken mandible caused the bony orb to rest with a sinister tilt on the shelf; a pirate's crooked grin. Then Bonnie had a flash of Augustine, juggling the gunman's skull with the others.

From a pocket Skink withdrew a squirming Bufo toad, which immediately peed on him. The man with the .357 sneered.

The woman who was driving glanced over her shoulder. 'What now?' she grumbled.

'Smoke the sweat,' Skink said, cupping the toad and its amber piddle in his palm, 'and then you see mastodons.'

'Get that stinking thing outta here,' said the gunman.

'Did you know mastodons once roamed Florida? Eons before your ancestors began their ruinous copulations. Mastodons as big as cement trucks!' Skink put the toad out the window. Then he wiped the toad pee on the sleeve of the gunman's pinstriped suit.

'You fuck!' Snapper took aim at Skink's good eye.

The woman at the wheel told him to cool it—other drivers were staring. She turned off at the next exit and pulled into an abandoned service station. The hurricane had blown down the gas pumps like dominoes. Looters had cleaned out the garage. On the roof lay the remains of a Mazda Miata, squashed upside down like a bright lady-bug.

While the gunman left the Jeep to relieve himself behind the building, the woman reluctantly took charge of the .357. She looked so uncomfortable that Bonnie Lamb felt a little sorry for her; the poor girl could barely hoist the darn thing. Surely, Bonnie thought, now was the moment for Skink to make his move.

But he didn't. Instead he smiled at the woman in the driver's seat and said, 'You're truly pretty. And aware of it, of course. The guiding force for most of your life, I imagine—your good looks.'

The woman blushed, then toughened.

'Where'd you spend the storm?' Skink asked.

'In a motel. With Mel Gibson there,' the woman said, nodding toward Snapper, 'and a hooker.'

'I was tied to a bridge. You should try it sometime.'

'Right.'

Bonnie Lamb said, 'He isn't kidding.'

The woman shifted the .357 to her other hand. 'What on earth are you people doing? Who sent you to the house—Tony's wife?' She turned around on her knees, bracing her gun arm on the front seat. 'Bonnie, dear,' she said sharply. 'I'd really appreciate some answers.'

'Would you believe I'm on my honeymoon.'

'You're joking.' The woman glanced doubtfully at Skink.

Bonnie said, 'Oh, not *him*. My husband's in Mexico.'

'Boy, are you ever lost,' said the woman.

Bonnie shook her head. 'Not really.'

The storm had knocked down the traffic signal at Florida City, or what was left of Florida City. A tired policeman in a yellow rainsuit directed traffic at the intersection. Edie Marsh tensed behind the wheel of the Jeep. She told Snapper to make sure the gun was out of sight. As they passed the officer, Bonnie Lamb figured it would be a fine time to poke her head out the window and shout for help, but Skink offered no encouraging signal. His chin had drooped back to his chest.

Most of the street signs remained down from the hurricane,

but Bonnie saw one indicating they were about to enter the Fabulous Florida Keys. Snapper was apprehensive about possible checkpoints along Highway One, so he instructed Edie Marsh to use Card Sound Road instead.

'There's a toll,' she noted.

'So?'

'I left my purse at the house.'

Snapper said, 'Jesus, I got money.'

'I bet you do.' Edie Marsh couldn't stop thinking about what the one-eyed stranger had said: Snapper assaulting a woman cop and swiping her mother's ring.

'How much *did* you get for it?' she asked.

'For what?'

'The ring.' Edie stared ahead at the flat strip of road, which stretched eastward as far as she could see.

Snapper muttered obscenely. He fished in his coat and came out with a plain gold wedding band. He held it three inches from Edie's face.

'Happy?' he said.

The sight of the stolen ring affected Edie in an unexpected way: She felt repulsed, then dejected. She tried to picture the policewoman, wondered if she was married or had children, wondered what dreadful things Snapper had done to her.

Lord, Edie thought. What a small, disappointing life I've made for myself. She wanted to believe it would've been different if only she'd talked that shy young Kennedy into the sack. But she was no longer sure.

'I couldn't pawn it,' Snapper was saying. 'Damn thing's engraved, nobody'll touch it.'

'What does it say?' Edie asked quietly. 'On the ring.'

'Who cares.'

'Come on. What does it say?'

The woman in the back seat sat forward, also curious, as Snapper read the inscription aloud: '"For My Cynthia. Always."' He gave a scornful laugh and hung his bony arm out the window, preparing to toss the ring from the truck.

'Don't do that,' Edie said, backing off the accelerator.

'The fuck not? If I can't hock the goddamn thing, I'm gone dump it. Case we get pulled over.'

Edie Marsh said, 'Just don't, OK?'

'Oops. Too late.' He cocked his arm and threw the ring as far as he could. It plopped into a roadside canal, breaking the surface with concentric circles.

Edie saw everything from the corner of her eye. 'You lousy prick.' Her voice was as hard as marble. The woman in the back seat felt the Jeep gain speed.

Defiantly Snapper waved the heavy black pistol. 'Maybe you never heard of somethin' called "possession of stolen property"— it's a motherfuckin' felony, case you didn't know. Here's another beauty: Vi-o-lay-shun o" pro-bay-shun! Translated: My skinny white ass goes straight to Starke, I get caught. Do not pass Go, do not collect any hurricane money. So fuck the cop's jewelry, unnerstand?'

Edie Marsh said nothing. She willed herself to concentrate on the slick two-lane blacktop, which intermittently was strewn with pine boughs, palmetto fronds and loose sheets of plywood. A regular obstacle course. Edie checked the speedometer: ninety-two miles per hour. Not bad for a city girl.

Snapper, ordering her to slow down, couldn't keep the raw nervousness out of his voice. Edie acted as if she didn't hear a word.

The one who called himself Skink didn't stir from his nap, trance, coma, whatever it was. Meanwhile the young newlywed (Edie noticed in the rearview) carefully removed her own wedding band from her finger.

The tollbooth was empty and the gate was up. Edie didn't bother to slow down. Bonnie Lamb held her breath.

When they blew through the narrow lane, Snapper exclaimed, 'Jesus!'

As the Jeep climbed the steep bridge, Skink raised his head. 'This is the place.'

'Where you spent the storm?' Bonnie asked.

He nodded. 'Glorious.'

Beneath them, broken sunlight painted Biscayne Bay in shifting stripes of copper and slate. Ahead, a bloom of lavender clouds dumped chutes of rain on the green mangrove shorelines of North Key Largo. As the truck crested the bridge, Skink pointed out a pod of bottle-nosed dolphins rolling along the edge of a choppy boat channel. From such a height the arched flanks of the creatures resembled glinting slivers of jet ceramic, covered and then uncovered by foamy waves.

'Just look,' said Bonnie Lamb. The governor was right—it was purely spectacular up here.

Even Edie Marsh was impressed. She curbed the Jeep on the downhill slope and turned off the key. She strained to keep the rollicking dolphins in view.

Snapper fumed impatiently. 'What *is* this shit?' He jabbed Edie in the arm with the .357. 'Hey you, drive.'

'Take it easy.'

'I said fucking *drive*.'

'And I said take it fucking easy.'

Edie was livid. The last time Snapper had seen that hateful glare was moments before she'd bludgeoned his leg with the crowbar iron. He cocked the revolver. 'Don't be a cunt.'

'Excuse me?' One eyebrow arched. 'What'd you say?'

Bonnie Lamb feared that Edie was going to lose her mind and go for Snapper's throat, at which point she certainly would be shot dead. Snapper jammed the gun flush against her right breast.

The governor was unaware. He had everted the upper half of his torso out the window to watch the dolphins make their way north, and also to enjoy a fresh sprinkle that had begun to fall. Bonnie tried to grab his hand, but it was too large. She settled for squeezing two of his fingers. Gradually Skink drew himself back into the Jeep and appraised the tense drama unfolding in the front seat.

'You heard me,' Snapper was saying.

'So that *was* you,' Edie said, 'calling me a cunt.'

Violently Snapper twisted the gun barrel, bunching the fabric of Edie's blouse and wringing the soft flesh beneath it. God, Bonnie thought, that's got to hurt.

Edie Marsh didn't let it show.

'Drive!' Snapper told her again.

'When I'm through watching Flipper.'

'Fuck Flipper.' Snapper raised the .357 and fired once through the top of the Jeep.

Bonnie Lamb cried out and covered her ears. Edie Marsh clutched the steering wheel to steady herself. The pain in her right breast made her wonder briefly if she was shot. She wasn't.

Snapper cheerlessly eyed the hole in the roof of the truck; the acrid whiff of cordite made him sneeze. 'God bless me,' he said, with a dark chuckle.

A door opened. Skink got out of the Jeep to stretch. 'Don't you love this place!' He unfolded his long arms toward the clouds. 'Don't it bring out the beast in your soul!'

Glorious, Bonnie agreed silently. That's the word for it.

'Get back in the car,' Snapper barked.

Skink obliged, shaking the raindrops from his hair like a sheep dog. Without a word, Edie Marsh started the engine and drove on.

24

'What do you mean, no roosters?'

The owner of the *botánica* apologized. It had been a busy week for fowl. He offered Avila a sacrificial billy goat instead.

Avila said, 'No way, José.' The sutures from his goring itched constantly. 'I never heard anyone running outta roosters. What else you got?'

'Turtles.'

'I don't got time to do turtles,' Avila said. Removing the shells was a messy chore. 'You got any pigeons?'

'Sorry, meng.'

'Lambs?'

'Tomorrow morning.'

'How about cats?'

'No, meng, hiss no legal.'

'Yeah, like you give a shit.' Avila checked his wristwatch; he had to hurry, do this thing then get on the road to the Keys. 'OK, Señor, what *do* you got?'

The shop owner led him to a small storage room and pointed at a wooden crate. Inside, Avila could make out a furry brown animal the size of a beagle. It had shoe-button eyes, an anteater nose, and a long slender tail circled with black rings.

Avila said, 'What, some kinda raccoon?'

'Coatimundi. From South America.'

The animal chittered inquisitively and poked its velvety nostrils through the slats of the crate. It was one of the oddest creatures Avila had ever seen.

'Big medicine,' promised the shop owner.

'I need something for Chango.'

'Oh, Chango would love heem.' The shop owner had astutely

pegged Avila for a rank amateur who knew next to nothing about *santería*. The shop owner said, '*Sí, es muy bueno por Chango.*'

Avila said, 'Will it bite?'

'No, my freng. See?' The *botánica* man tickled the coati's moist nose. 'Like a puppy dog.'

'OK, how much?'

'Seventy-five.'

'Here's sixty, *chico*. Help me carry it to the car.'

As he drove up to the house, Avila saw the Buick backing out of the driveway; his wife and her mother, undoubtedly off to Indian bingo. He waved. They waved.

Avila gloated. Perfect timing. For once I'll have the place to myself. Quickly he dragged the wooden crate into the garage and lowered the electric door. The coati huffed in objection. From a cane-wicker chest Avila hastily removed the implements of sacrifice—tarnished pennies, coconut husks, the bleached ribs of a cat, polished turtle shells, and an old pewter goblet. From a galvanized lockbox Avila took his newest, and potentially most powerful, artifact—the gnawed chip of bone belonging to the evil man who had tried to crucify him. Reverently, and with high hopes, Avila placed the bone in the pewter goblet, soon to be filled with animal blood.

For sustenance Chango was known to favor dry wine and candies; the best Avila could do, on short notice, was a pitcher of sangria and a roll of stale wintergreen Life Savers. He lighted three tall candles and arranged them triangularly on the cement floor of the garage. Inside the triangle, he began to set up the altar. The coatimundi had gone silent; Avila felt its stare from between the slats. Could it know? He whisked the thought from his mind.

The final item to be removed from the wicker chest was the most important: a ten-inch hunting knife, with a handle carved from genuine elk antler. The knife was an antique, made in Wyoming. Avila had received it as a bribe when he worked as a county building inspector—a Christmas offering from an unlicensed roofer hoping that Avila might overlook a seriously defective scissor truss. Somehow Avila had found it in his heart to do just that.

Vigorously he sharpened the hunting knife on a whetstone. The coati began to pace and snort. Avila discreetly concealed the gleaming blade from the doomed animal. Then he stepped inside the triangle of candles and improvised a short prayer to Chango, who (Avila trusted) would understand that he was pressed for time.

Afterwards he took a pry bar and started peeling the wooden slats off the crate. The sacramental coati became highly agitated. Avila attempted to soothe it with soft words, but the beast wasn't fooled. It shot from the crate and tore crazed circles throughout the garage, scattering cat bones and tipping two of the *santería* candles. Avila tried to subdue the coati by stunning it with the pry bar, but it was too swift and agile. Like a monkey, it vertically scampered up a wall of metal shelves and bounded onto the ceiling track of the electric door-opener. There it perched, using its remarkable tail for balance, squealing and baring sharp yellow teeth. Meanwhile one of the *santería* candles rolled beneath Avila's lawn mower, igniting the gas tank. Cursing bitterly, Avila ran to the kitchen for the fire extinguisher. When he returned to the garage, he was confronted with fresh disaster.

The electric door was open. In the driveway was his wife's Buick, idling. Why she had come back, Avila didn't know. Perhaps she'd decided to pilfer the buried Tupperware for extra bingo money. It truly didn't matter.

Apparently her mother had emerged from the car first. The scene that greeted Avila was so stupefying that he temporarily forgot about the flaming lawn mower. For reasons beyond human comprehension, the over-wrought coatimundi had jumped from its roost in the garage, dashed outdoors and scaled Avila's mother-in-law. Now the creature was nesting in the woman's coiffure, a brittle edifice of chromium orange. Avila had always believed that his wife's mother wore wigs, but here was persuasive evidence that her fantastic mop was genuine. She shrieked and spun about the front yard, flailing spastically at the demon on her scalp. The jabbering coati dug in with all four claws. No hairpiece, Avila decided, could withstand such a test.

His wife bilingually shouted that he should do something, for

God's sake, don't just stand there! The pry bar was out of the question; one misplaced blow and that would be the end of his mother-in-law. So Avila tried the fire extinguisher. He unloaded at point-blank range, soaping the stubborn animal with sodium bicarbonate. The coati snarled and snapped but, incredibly, refused to vacate the old woman's hair. In the turmoil it was inevitable that some of the cold mist from the fire extinguisher would hit Avila's mother-in-law, who mashed her knuckles to her eyes and began a blind run. Avila gave chase for three-quarters of a block, periodically firing short bursts, but the old woman showed surprising speed.

Avila gave up and trotted home to extinguish the fire in the garage. Afterwards he rolled the charred lawn mower to the backyard and hosed it down. His distraught wife remained sprawled across the hood of the Buick, crying: '*Mamí, mamí*, luke what chew did to my *mamí*!'

Above her keening rose the unmistakable whine of sirens— someone on the block had probably called the fire department. Avila thought: Why can't people mind their own goddamn business! He was steaming as he hurried to his car.

At the very moment he fit the key in the ignition, the passenger window exploded. Avila nearly wet himself in shock. There stood his wife, beet-faced and seething, holding the iron pry bar.

'Chew fucking bastard!' she cried.

Avila jammed his heel to the accelerator and sped away.

'O Chango, Chango,' he whispered, brushing chunks of glass from his lap. 'I know I fucked up again, but don't abandon me now. Not tonight.'

A peculiar trait of this hurricane, Jim Tile marveled on the drive along North Key Largo, was the dramatic definition of its swath. The eye had come ashore like a bullet, devastating a thin corridor but leaving virtually untouched the coastline to the immediate north and south. August hurricanes are seldom so courteous. Its bands had battered the vacation estates of ritzy Ocean Reef and stripped a long stretch of mangrove. Yet two miles down the shore, the mangroves flourished, leafy and lush, offering no clue that a killer storm had passed nearby. A ramshackle trailer park stood undamaged; not a window was broken, not a tree was uprooted.

Phenomenal, thought Jim Tile.

He goosed the Crown Victoria to an invigorating ninety-five; blue lights, no siren. At high speeds the big Ford whistled like a bottle rocket.

Paradise Palms was a lead but not a lock. Augustine had done his best in a tough situation, the trick with the redial button was slick. Maybe the guy who'd beaten up Brenda was in the black Jeep Cherokee. Augustine didn't know for sure. Maybe they were headed to the Keys, maybe not. Maybe they'd stay with the Jeep, or maybe they'd ditch it for another car.

The only certainty was that they were transporting Skink and the tourist woman, Augustine's girlfriend. The circumstances of the abduction, and its purpose, remained a mystery. Augustine had promised to lie back and wait at Paradise Palms, and the trooper told him that was an excellent idea. One-man rescues only worked in the movies.

The old road from Ocean Reef rejoined Highway One below Jewfish Creek, where it split into four lanes. The traffic thickened, so Jim Tile slowed to seventy miles per hour, weaving deftly between the Winnebagos and rental cars. It was the time of late summer when the setting sun could torment inexperienced drivers, but there was no glare from the west tonight. A bruised wall of advancing weather shaded the horizon and cast sooty twilight over the islands and the water. Lightning strobed high in distant clouds over Florida Bay. Its exquisite sparking was wasted on Jim Tile, who dourly contemplated the prospect of hard rain. A chase was tricky enough when the roads were bone dry.

On Plantation Key the highway narrowed again, and as the traffic merged to two lanes, Jim Tile thought he spotted the black Cherokee not far ahead. Quickly he turned off the blue lights. It had to be the same Jeep; the shiny mud flaps were as preposterous as Augustine had described them.

Four vehicles separated Jim Tile from the Jeep—three passenger cars, and a station wagon towing a fishing boat on a wobbly trailer. The boat was tall and beamy enough to make it hard for those in the Jeep to see the marked police car in the stacked traffic behind them. Already the rain was falling, fat drops popping sporadically on the hood of the Ford. The thickening sky promised a deluge.

The station wagon in front of Jim Tile began an untimely, though predictable, deceleration. Bad omens abounded: Michigan license plates suggested unfamiliarity with local landmarks; the driver and a female passenger were gesticulating heatedly, indicating a marital-type disagreement. Most distressing, from Jim Tile's point of view: A third passenger clearly could be seen unfolding a road map as large as a tablecloth.

They're lost, the trooper thought. Lost in the Florida Keys. Where there was only one way in and out. Amazing.

Now the map was being passed to the front seat, where the driver and his wife pawed at it competitively. The station wagon began snaking back and forth, followed somewhat indecisively by the boat trailer. Two McDonald's bags flew from one of the car's windows, exploding unwanted French fries and ketchup packets on the shoulder of the highway.

'Pigs,' Jim Tile said aloud. He scowled at the speedometer: thirty-two damn miles per hour. If he tried to pass, the guy in the Jeep might see him coming. The trooper boiled. As the rain fell harder, he went to his windshield wipers and headlights.

The sluggish station wagon stayed ahead of him for the entire length of Plantation Key, until its sole operative brake light began to flicker. The rig meandered to a dead stop.

Dispiritedly, Jim Tile put the patrol car in Park, thinking: This ain't my day.

Ahead rose the Snake Creek drawbridge. The black Jeep and the three cars behind it easily crossed before the warning gates came down. The moron in the station wagon would have beaten it, too, had he ventured to touch the accelerator.

Now the trooper was stuck. The Jeep was on the other side of the waterway, out of sight. Jim Tile stepped from his car and slammed the door. With raindrops trickling off the brim of his

Stetson, he approached the witless driver of the station wagon and asked for a license, registration and proof of insurance. In the eight minutes that passed before the Snake Creek bridge came down, the trooper managed to weigh the bewildered tourist with seven separate traffic citations, at least three of which would inconveniently require a personal appearance in court.

On the way to the Torres house, Fred Dove stopped to buy flowers and white wine. He wanted Edie Marsh to know he was proud of her performance as Neria, devoted wife of Tony.

When the insurance man pulled up to 15600 Calusa, he saw that the Jeep wasn't in the driveway. His heart quickened at the possibility that Snapper was gone, leaving him alone with Edie. Not that she was fussy about privacy, but Fred Dove was. He couldn't perform at full throttle, sexually, as long as a homicidal maniac was watching TV in an adjoining room. Snapper's loud and truculent presence was deflating in all respects.

Nobody answered when the insurance man rapped on the wooden doorjamb. He stepped into the Torres house and called Edie's name. The only reply came from the two miniature dachshunds, barking in the backyard; they sounded tired and hoarse.

The ugly Naugahyde recliner in the living room was unoccupied, and the television was off. Fred Dove was encouraged—no Snapper. Inside the house, the light was fading. When the insurance man flipped a lamp switch, nothing happened. The generator wasn't running; out of gas, probably. He found Snapper's flashlight and peeked in the rooms, hoping to spy Edie napping languorously on a mattress. She wasn't.

Fred Dove saw her purse on the kitchen counter. Her wallet lay open on top. Inside he found twenty-two dollars and a Visa card. Fred Dove was relieved; at least the house hadn't been robbed. He held Edie's driver's license under the flashlight; her expression in the photograph spooked him. It was not a portrait of pure trustworthiness and devotion.

Oh well, he thought, lots of girls look like Lizzie Borden on their driver's license.

The insurance man returned to the living room, lit a candle and sat in the recliner. He wondered where Edie had gone and why she'd left her purse when she knew the streets were crawling with looters. It seemed like she'd departed in a hurry, probably in the Jeep with Snapper.

Fred Dove settled in for a wait. The candle smelled of vanilla. The cozy way it lighted the walls reminded him of the night they nearly made love on the floor, the night Snapper barged in. The humiliation of that moment still stung; it had invested Snapper with indomitable power over the insurance man. That, plus the loaded gun. Fred Dove could hardly wait until the psycho thug was paid off. Then he and Edie would be free of him.

Every so often the insurance man switched on the flashlight and reexamined Edie's picture on the driver's license. The vulturine eyes did not soften. Fred Dove wondered if it was her deviousness that he found so arousing. The notion disturbed him, so he retreated to innocuous diversions. He hadn't known, for example, that her middle name was Deborah. It was a name he liked: plucky, Midwestern and reliable-sounding. He was willing to bet that if you went through every women's prison in America, you wouldn't find a half-dozen Deborahs. Perhaps the name had been taken from one of Edie's grandmothers, or that of a special aunt. In any event, he regarded it as a positive sign.

He wondered, too, about the apartment listed as her address in West Palm: what kind of art Edie had hung on the walls, what color towels were folded in the bathroom, what sort of homey magnets were stuck on her refrigerator door. Linus and Snoopy? Garfield the Cat? If *only*, Fred Dove thought. He thought about Edie's bed, too. He hoped it was king-sized, brass or a big wooden four-poster—anything but a water bed, which negatively affected his thrusting techniques. Fred Dove hoped the sheets on Edie's bed were imported silk, and that one day she would invite him to lie down on them.

The insurance man stayed in the recliner for more than two hours, long after the neighborhood chain saws and hammers had fallen silent. He finally arose to take a position near a window-pane, in glum preparation to witness the vandalism of his rental car by a group of swaggering, loud-talking teenagers. Mercifully they ignored Fred Dove's drab sedan, but minutes after they passed the house he heard a pop-pop that could have been the backfire of an automobile, or gunshots. In the backyard Donald and Marla dissolved in frenzy, striking up an irksome chorus with half a dozen other vigilant dogs on the block. Fred Dove's nerves were fraying fast. He returned Edie's driver's license to the purse. Hurriedly he arranged the flowers in a vase and placed it next to the unopened wine on the dining-room table. Then he blew out the candle and went outside to check on the dachshunds.

Tangled impressively in their leashes, the animals whimpered out of hunger, loneliness and general anxiety. Their low-density memories still twitched from the near-fatal encounter with the prowling bear. The moment Fred Dove set them free, the dachs-hunds clambered up his lap and licked his chin shamelessly. He was suckered into giving them a short walk.

Admiring the unfettered mirth with which Donald and Marla pranced and peed, the insurance man was bothered by the idea that they might spend the whole night outdoors and unattended. He wrote Edie a note and folded it on top of her purse. Then he led the two wiener dogs to his rented sedan, drove back to the motel and smuggled them in a laundry bag up to his room. It was marginally better than all-night movies on cable.

The motels in the Upper Keys were filling with out-of-town insurance adjusters. The clerk at the Paradise Palms said she felt uncomfortable, profiting off the hurricane.

'But a customer's a customer. Can I have your name?'

Augustine introduced himself as Lester's brother. 'I phoned earlier. What's his room number?'

'He's not here yet.' The clerk leaned across the counter and whispered: 'But your sisters checked in about twenty minutes ago. Room 255. I mean, I'm assuming sisters, on account of they're Parsons, too.'

'Parsons indeed.' Augustine nodded and acted pleased. Sisters? He couldn't imagine.

He paid for his room with cash. The clerk said, 'Those girls know how to dress for a party, I'll sure say that.'

'Oh boy,' said Augustine. 'What have they done now?'

'Don't you go fussing—let 'em have their fun, all right?' She handed him his key. 'You're in 240. I tried to put you in the unit next door, but some wise guy from Prudential, he didn't want to switch.'

'That's quite all right.'

Once inside his room, Augustine put the loaded .38 on the bureau, near the door. He took the parts of the dart rifle from the gym bag and laid them on the bedspread. The muscles of his neck were in knots. He wished he'd brought a few skulls, for relaxation.

Augustine turned up the TV while he assembled the tranquilizer gun. He was surprised that he'd beaten the black Jeep to Islamorada, hadn't even passed it on the eighteen-mile stretch south of Florida City. He wondered if they'd turned on Card Sound Road, or stopped someplace else—and why. His worst fear, the thing he kept pushing out of his mind, was that the creep with the crooked jaw had already killed Skink and Bonnie, and dumped them. There were only about a hundred ideal locations between Homestead and Key Largo; years might pass before the bodies were found.

Well, he'd know soon enough. If the asshole showed up without them, then Augustine would know.

If the asshole showed up at all. Augustine still wasn't sure if 'Lester Parsons' was the man with the crooked jaw.

He stood the dart rifle in a closet and put the pistol in his waistband, under the tail of his shirt. Rain whipped his face as soon as he stepped out the door. He shielded his eyes and hurried along the walkway to Room 255. He knocked seven times in a neighborly cadence—shave-and-a-haircut, two bits—to give the false impression that he was expected.

The door was flung open by a fragrant redheaded woman in high heels and a luminous green bikini. Augustine recognized her as the hooker in fishnets from 15600 Calusa.

An orange sucker was tattooed on the freckled slope of her left breast. In her left hand was a frosty Rum Runner.

She said, 'Shit, I thought you were Snapper.'

'Wrong room,' said Augustine. 'I'm sorry.'

'Don't be.'

Another woman came out of the bathroom, saying, 'Goddamn this rain. I wanted to go in the pool.' She wore a silver one-piece suit, an explosive white-blonde wig and gold hoop earrings. When she saw Augustine in the doorway, she said, 'Who're you?'

'I thought this was my sister's room, but I guess I'm at the wrong motel.'

The redhead introduced herself as Bridget. 'You wanna come in and dry off?'

'Not if it gets Snapper mad.' Augustine was thinking: Snapper—now what the hell kind of name is *that*?

The redhead laughed. 'Yeah, he's quite the jealous maniac. Come on in.'

The blonde said, 'Jesus, Bridget, they're gonna be here any second—'

But Augustine was already inside the room, scouting unobtrusively: an overnight bag, two cosmetic cases, a cocktail dress on a hanger. Nothing out of the ordinary. Bridget tossed him a towel. She said her friend's name was Jasmine. They were from Miami.

'My name's George,' said Augustine, 'from California.' Inanely he shook hands with the hookers.

Bridget held on, examining his ring finger. 'Not married?'

'Afraid not.' Augustine gently tugged free.

Jasmine told Bridget to forget it, they didn't have enough time. Bridget said they wouldn't need much.

'George looks like a fast starter.' She winked somewhat mechanically at Augustine. 'You want some fun until the rain stops?'

'Thanks, but I really can't stay.'

'Hundred bucks,' Bridget suggested. 'Double date.'

Jasmine pulled a long white T-shirt over her swimsuit. She griped: 'Hey, do I get a vote in this? A hundred for what?'

Bridget slipped a milky arm around Augustine's waist and pulled him close. The obvious implant in her left breast felt like a sack of nickels against his rib cage. 'Seventy-five,' she said, dropping her eyes to the bright tattoo, 'and I'll give you a taste of my Tootsie Pop.'

'Can't,' Augustine said. 'Diabetic.'

Jasmine gave a biting laugh. 'You're both pitiful. Bridget, let "George from California" go find his sisters.' She sat cross-legged on the bed and applied pungent glue to a broken artificial fingernail. 'Boy, this weather's suck-o,' she muttered, to no one.

Bridget's motivational hug went slack, and slowly she recoiled from Augustine's side. 'Our man George has a gun.' She announced it with a mix of alarm and regret. 'I felt it.'

Jasmine, blowing on her glue job, looked up. 'Goddamn, Bridget, I knew it! You happy now? We're busted.'

'No you're not.' Augustine took out the pistol and displayed it in a loose and casual way, hoping to quell their concerns. 'I'm not a cop, I promise.'

Jasmine's eyes narrowed. 'Shit, *now* I know. The squeaker sent you.'

'Who?'

'Avila.'

'Never heard of him.'

Bridget backpedaled to the bed and sat next to her friend. Nervously she crossed her arms over her breasts. 'Then who the hell are you, *George*? What is it you're after?'

'Information.'

'Yeah, right.'

'Really. I just want you to tell me about this "Snapper,"' said Augustine, 'and I also want to know if you two ladies can keep a secret.'

25

The professor's VW van ran out of gas two miles shy of the Fort Drum service plaza. Neria Torres stood by the Turnpike and flagged down a truck. It was an old Chevy pickup; three men in the cab, four others sprawled in the bed. They were from Tennessee. Neria wasn't crazy about the odds.

'Looking for work,' explained the driver, a wiry, unshaven fellow with biblical tattoos on both arms. He said his first name was Matthew and his middle name was Luke.

Neria was nervous nonetheless. The men stared ravenously. 'What do you guys do?' she asked.

'Construction. We're here for the hurricane.' Matthew had a spare gas can. He poured four gallons into the van. Neria thanked him.

She said, 'All I can give you is three bucks.'

'That's fine.'

'What kind of construction?'

Matthew said: 'Any damn thing we can find.' The other men laughed. 'We do trees, also. I got chain saw experience,' Matthew added. Neria Torres didn't ask if the crew was licensed to do business in Florida. She knew the answer. The men climbed out of the truck to stretch their legs and urinate. One of them was actually mannered enough to turn his back while unzipping.

Neria decided it was a good time to go. Matthew stood between her and the van. 'I dint ketch your name.'

'Neria.'

'That's Cuban, right?'

'Yes.'

'You don't talk with no accent.'

She thought: Well, thank you, Gomer. 'I was born in Miami,' she said.

Matthew seemed pleased. 'So you're on the way home—hey, how'd you make out in the big blow?'

Neria said, 'I won't know till I get there.'

'We do residential.'

'Do you really.'

'Wood or masonry, it don't matter. Also roofs. We got a helluva tar man.' Matthew pointed. 'That bald guy doin' his bidness in the bushes—he worked on that new Wal-Mart in Chat'nooga. My wife's cousin Chip.'

Neria Torres said, 'From what I understand, you won't have a bit of trouble finding jobs when you get to Dade County.'

'Hey, what about your place?'

'I don't know. I haven't seen it yet.'

'So it could be totaled,' Matthew said, hopefully. Slowly Neria opened the door of the van. Only when it stubbed his shoulder blades did Matthew move out of the way.

Neria got behind the wheel and revved the engine. 'Tell you what. When I get home and see how the roof looks, then I'll give you a call. Where you staying?'

The other workers laughed again. 'Sterno Hilton,' said Matthew. 'See, we're campin' out.' He said they couldn't afford a motel, no way.

Neria fumbled in the console until she found a gnawed stub of pencil and one of the professor's matchbooks, which reeked of weed. She wrote down a bogus telephone number and gave it to Matthew. 'OK, then, you call *me*.'

He didn't even glance at the number. 'I got a better idea. Since none of us ever been to Miami before . . .'

Oh no! she thought. Please no.

'. . . we'll just follow you down. That way, we're sure not to get lost. And if your place needs work, we can git on it right-aways.'

Matthew's plan was well received by his crew. Neria said, uselessly: 'I don't think that's a good idea.'

'We got references.'

She was eyeing the pickup truck, wondering if there was a chance in hell that the professor's van could outrun it.

'We kicked some ass over Charleston,' Matthew was saying, 'after Hurricane Hugo.'

Neria said, 'It's getting pretty late.'

'We'll be right behind you.'

And they were, all the way down the Turnpike.

The truck's solitary headlight, stuck on high beam, illuminated the interior of the VW van like a TV studio. Neria stiffened in the harsh brightness, knowing that seven pairs of inbred male eyes were fixed on the back of her head. She drove ludicrously slow, hoping the rednecks would grow impatient and decide to pass. They didn't.

All she could do was make the best of it. Even if the Neanderthals didn't know a thing about construction, they might be helpful in tracking a thieving husband.

Max Lamb cracked the door to poke his head out. He'd never met an FBI man before. This one didn't look like Efrem Zimbalist Jr. He wore a green Polo shirt, tan Dockers and cordovan Bass Weejuns. He also toted a bag from Ace Hardware.

When it came to name brands, Max was nothing if not observant. He believed it was part of his job, knowing who in America was buying what.

The agent said, 'Is Augustine home?'

'No, he isn't.'

'Who are you?'

'Could I see some ID?' Max asked.

The agent showed him a badge in a billfold. Max told him to come in. They sat in the living room. Max asked what was in the bag, and the agent said it was drill bits. 'Storm sucked the cabinets right out of my kitchen,' he explained.

'Black and Decker?'

'Makita.'

'That's a first-rate tool,' said Max.

The agent was exceedingly patient. 'You're a friend of Augustine's?'

'Sort of. My name is Max Lamb.'

'Really? I'm glad to see you're all right.'

Max's eyebrows hopped.

'From the kidnapping,' the agent said. 'You're the one who was kidnapped, right?'

'Yes!' Max's spirits skied, realizing that Bonnie had been so concerned that she'd called the FBI. It was proof of her devotion.

The agent said, 'She played the tape for me, the message you left on the answering machine.'

'Then you heard his voice—the guy who snatched me.' Max got a Michelob from the refrigerator. The FBI man accepted a Sprite.

'Where's your wife?' he asked.

'I don't know.'

Excitedly Max Lamb related the whole story, from his kidnapping on Calusa Drive to the midnight rescue in Stiltsville, up to Bonnie's disappearance with Augustine and the deranged one-eyed governor. The FBI man listened with what seemed to be genuine interest, but took no notes. Max wondered if they were specially trained to remember everything they heard.

'These are dangerous men,' he told the agent, portentously.

'Was your wife taken against her will?'

'No, sir. That's why they're so dangerous.'

'You say he put a collar on your neck.'

'A shock collar,' Max said gravely, 'the kind used to train hunting dogs.'

The FBI man asked if the kidnapper had done the same thing to Bonnie. Max said he didn't think so. 'She's very trusting and impressionable. They took advantage of that.'

'What's Augustine's role in all this?'

'I believe,' said Max, 'the kidnapper has brainwashed him, too.' He got another beer and tore into a bag of pretzels.

The agent said, 'Prosecution won't be easy. It's your word against his.'

'But you believe me, don't you?'

'Mister Lamb, it doesn't matter what I believe. Put yourself in the jury box. This is a very weird story you'll be asking them to swallow. . . .'

Max shot to his feet. His cheeks were stuffed with pretzel fragments. 'Jeshush Chritht, mahh wife's misshing!'

'I understand. I'd be upset, too.' The FBI man was maddeningly agreeable and polite. 'And I'm not trying to tell you what to do. But you need to know what you're up against.'

Max sat down, glowering.

The agent explained that the Bureau seldom got involved unless a ransom demand was issued. 'There was none in your case. There's been none for your wife.'

'Well, *I* think her life's in danger,' Max said, 'and I think you people are in deep trouble if something happens to her.'

'Believe me, Mister Lamb, I understand your frustration.'

No you don't, Max fumed silently, or you wouldn't talk to me like I was ten years old.

The agent said, 'Have you spoken to the police?'

Max told him about the black state trooper who was acquainted with the kidnapper. 'He said I was entitled to press charges. He said he'd take me down to the station.'

The FBI man nodded. 'That's the best way to go, if you've got your mind made up.'

Max told the agent there was something he definitely ought to see. He led him to Augustine's guest room and showed him the wall of skulls. 'Tell me honestly,' he said to the FBI man, 'wouldn't you be worried? He *juggles* those damn things.'

'Augustine? Yeah.'

'You know?'

'He won't hurt your wife, Mister Lamb.'

'Gee, I feel so much better.'

The agent seemed impervious to sarcasm. 'You'll hear from Mrs Lamb sooner or later. That's my guess. If you don't, call me. Or call me even if you do.' He handed his card to Max, who affected hard-bitten skepticism as he studied it. Then he walked toward the kitchen, the agent following.

'I was wondering,' the FBI man said, 'did Augustine give you a key?'

Max turned.

'To the house,' the agent said.

'No, sir. The sliding door was open.'

'So you just walked in. He doesn't know you're here?'

'Well . . .' It hadn't occurred to Max Lamb that he was breaking the law. For one infuriating moment, he thought the FBI man was preparing to arrest him.

But the agent said: 'That's a swell way to get your head shot off—being in somebody's house without them knowing. Especially here in Miami.'

Max, grinding his teeth, realized the impossibly upside-down nature of the situation. He was wasting his breath. A state trooper is friends with the kidnapper, an FBI man is friends with the skull collector.

'You know what I really want?' Max drained his beer with a flourish, set the bottle down hard on the counter. 'All I want is to find my wife, put her on a plane and go home to New York. Forget about this fucked-up place, forget about this hurricane.'

The agent said, 'That's a damn good plan, Mister Lamb.'

26

Snapper made Edie Marsh pull over at a liquor store in Islamorada.

'Not now,' she said.

'I *got* to.'

'We're almost there.'

A rumble from the back seat: 'Let the man have a drink.'

She parked behind the store, away from the road. Jim Tile didn't see the black Cherokee as he sped past. Neither did Avila, ten minutes later.

Snapper wouldn't be talked out of his craving, and Edie was worried. She knew firsthand the folly of mixing booze with Midols. Double dosed, Snapper might hibernate for a month.

The woman named Bonnie asked for a cold Coke. 'I'm burning up.'

'Welcome to Florida,' said Edie.

Snapper tossed three ten-dollar bills on her lap. 'Johnnie Red,' he said.

'Bad idea when you're full of codeines.'

'Shit, I've handled ten times worse. Besides, it don't feel like codeine you gave me.'

Edie said, 'Your knee quit hurting, right? The bottle said "codeine."'

Snapper switched the .357 to his left hand. With his right hand he twisted Edie's hair, as if he were uprooting a clump of weeds. When she cried out, he said: 'I don't give a fuck if the medicine bottle said turpentine. Go get my Johnnie Walker.'

Edie pulled free and jumped out of the Jeep. She flipped him the finger as she went through the door of the liquor store. Snapper said, 'Stubborn bitch.'

'Feisty,' Skink agreed.

Bonnie Lamb felt like her skin was sizzling. She thought it would be glorious to bury herself in fresh snow. 'Honest to God, it's so hot. I feel like taking off my clothes.'

She couldn't believe she'd said it aloud.

Snapper was startled, and too confused for lust.

'Jesus Christ, what's a matter with you people.'

Bonnie said, 'I'm smothering.'

His eyes wandered to the young woman's chest. Nothing like a pair of tits to fuck up the balance of power. He knew that if she flashed those babies, his position instantly would be weakened, his authority diminished. It was a lost advantage that even the .357 could not restore.

'Keep your goddamn shirt on,' he told her.

'Don't worry.' Bonnie fanned herself in nervous embarrassment. In the back of the Jeep, Levon Stichler mewled inquiringly, trussed in his cocoon of moldy carpet. Skink figured the old man must have been listening, wondering if he was missing something.

Edie Marsh returned from the store. Her hair sparkled with tiny raindrops. She handed Bonnie a can of Dr Pepper. 'The Cokes weren't cold. Here, asshole.' She shoved a brown paper bag at Snapper. He took out the Johnnie Walker bottle and opened it with one hand. He threw back his head and chugged, as if from a canteen.

'Take it easy,' Edie admonished.

Contemptuously he smacked his lips. 'I bet you'd look good completely bald,' he said to her. 'That guy on the new *Star Trek*, Gene Luke—you and him could pass for twins.'

Edie said, 'Touch my hair again. Just try.'

He swung the .357 until the barrel came to rest on the tip of Edie's nose. He cocked the hammer and said: 'Come on. Somebody talk me out of it.'

Bonnie thought: Oh God, please don't. She shivered in sweat.

Snapper took another sloppy swig of whiskey. The one-eyed man reminded him of the ammunition shortage. 'Shoot her, that'd leave only one bullet for the rest of us.'

'There's other ways besides the gun.'

Skink let loose an avalanche of laughter. 'Son, I'm fairly immune to blunt objects and sharp instruments.'

Edie's pitch was more blunt. 'Pull the trigger,' she said to Snapper, 'and kiss your hurricane money goodbye. Forty-seven grand goes out the window with my brains.'

Snapper's bad mandible began to creak; a sign, Skink hoped, of possible cogitation. The moron was deciding between the long-term rewards from the money and the short-term satisfaction from shooting her. Apparently it wasn't an easy choice.

Skink said, 'Consider it an IQ test, chief.'

Impulsively Bonnie Lamb opened the cold Dr Pepper and poured it under her blouse; a fizzing caramel torrent from the cleft of her neck to her tummy.

'Stop!' Snapper yelled. 'You stop that crazy shit!'

'I'm suffocating in here—'

'I don't care! I don't fucking care.'

Bonnie was so light-headed from the heat that Snapper's fury didn't register. 'I'm sorry,' she said, 'I'm really sorry, but it's a hundred degrees in this stupid truck.'

The soda pop soaked through her top, so that Snapper could see the lacy outline of a bra and a pale damp oval of bare belly. Skink asked Edie Marsh to put on the air conditioner.

'I tried. It's broken.' Edie's voice was empty.

'Don't even think about getting naked,' Snapper warned Bonnie, 'or I'll kill you.' His head jangled with loud voices, some his own. In exasperation he shouted: 'You don't think I'd shoot all you crazy shits? You don't believe me? Check the fuckin' hole in the roof a this Jeep!'

Yeah, Edie thought. Matches the one between your ears.

'Can we get on with this?' she said sourly. 'It *is* awfully damn humid.'

As Bonnie's skin cooled off, she heard herself apologizing repeatedly. Yet it was absurd to be ashamed. Why should she care what two common criminals thought of her?

But she did care. She couldn't help herself. It was the way she'd been raised: A proper young woman did not douse herself with soda pop in front of total strangers, even felons.

'It's all right,' Skink said. 'You're scared, that's all.'

'I guess I am.'

Snapper heard her. With a vulgar chuckle, he said, 'Good. Scared is damn well what you ought to be.' He was halfway to shitfaced.

Edie drove slowly, fretfully. The man was a keeling wreck. *How could they possibly pull this off?* She devised a fantasy scenario: If Snapper passed out drunk, she'd push him from the Jeep. Then she'd tell the eccentric couple in the back seat that she was very, very sorry—it was all a terrible misunderstanding. She'd promise them Snapper's share of the Midwest Casualty settlement if they'd forget the whole dreadful evening. She would drive them back to Miami without delay and (to prove she was basically a decent person) offer to replace the gold ring stolen from the lady trooper. The unconscious Snapper would be run over on the highway by a passing shrimp truck and no longer pose a menace to society, or to Edie's future.

Unfortunately, Snapper wasn't nodding off. The Johnnie Walker bottle lay capped on the dashboard. Now he was playing with the gun, spinning the cylinder and humming mischievously.

Edie Marsh said, 'Could you please not do that?'

Snapper gurgled crapulously, his jaw jutting like a window box. 'You're so hot and sweaty, Edie, you oughta do what she almost done. Take off your clothes.'

'You'd like that, wouldn't you.'

'I would *love* it. Wouldn't y'all?' He waggled the .357 at Skink and Bonnie Lamb. 'Come on, wouldn't ya like to see Edie's tits? They're cuties.'

Bonnie felt crummy that she'd given Snapper the idea.

Skink said, 'Speaking for myself, yes, I'm sure they're delightful. But some other time.'

Edie Marsh felt herself blush. Nobody spoke. Snapper began to hum again, accompanied by the metered squeak of the wind-shield wipers. Ahead, on the ocean side of the highway, Edie saw the electric-blue sign for the Paradise Palms Resort Motel.

Skink shook Levon Stichler out of the carpet, dumping him like a sack of flour on the terrazzo. Somebody yanked off the gag and the blindfold.

The old man's eyes watered at the sudden brightness.

A woman's voice: 'You again.'

Levon blinked until a face came into focus—the redhead from the hurricane house at Turtle Meadow. The chiffon scarf, Levon's blinder, dangled from her festively painted fingernails. Standing next to the red-head was a wild-looking blonde. She said, 'What's your name, sweetheart?'

The redhead wore a diaphanous black bustier, fishnet stockings and stiletto heels. The blonde wore a silver lame" teddy that made her shimmer like the hood ornament on a Silver Shadow. The air was sugary with perfume; pure heaven, after three hours of gagging on mildew and carpet fuzz. When Levon Stichler sat up, he found himself in the center of an attentive circle: the two prostitutes, the thug in the pinstriped suit, the pretty long-haired brunette, another young woman, with creamy skin and delicate features, and a large bearded man wearing a flowered shower cap. The bearded man was polishing a glass eye on the sleeve of his jacket. They were gathered in a small motel room.

Levon Stichler said: 'What's this all about?'

The prostitutes introduced themselves. Bridget and Jasmine.

Snapper dropped to a crouch. Roughly he pinched the back of the old man's neck. 'You tried to kill me, 'member?'

'It was a mistake. I told you.'

'Here's the deal: You're gone stay down here two, maybe three days with the girls. They're gone fuck ya and blow ya till you can't walk. Plus they gone take some pitchers.'

Levon was skeptical. The man reeked of liquor and spoke as if he had a mouthful of marbles.

'Just shoot me and get it over with.'

'We're not shooting anybody.' It was the pretty brunette. 'Honest,' she said, 'long as you behave.'

Snapper said, 'Maybe you're too old to get it up or maybe you like guys—I don't fuckin' care. Point is, you stay here with these girls till I call and say it's OK to leave. Then what you do, you take your sweet time gettin' back to Miami. By that I mean, stand on the highway with your thumb out. Unnerstand?'

Levon stammered and blinked. Snapper swatted him twice across the face.

Edie Marsh said: 'I don't think Mister Stichler realizes the alternative. The alternative is we go to the cops and tell how you tried to murder Snapper and rape me with that trailer spike. Your family'll think you've gone senile. The photographs won't help—Grandpa doing pony rides with two call girls.'

Levon glanced up at Bridget and Jasmine. They were large and scary. He could tell they'd worked together before.

'Think of it as a vacation,' said Edie. 'Hey, you're allowed to have fun.'

'I wish I could.'

'Uh-oh.' Bridget knelt beside him. 'Prostate?'

The old man nodded somberly. 'It was removed last year.'

Jasmine told him to cheer up. 'We'll think of something.'

Skink, fitting his glass eye into its socket, advised Levon Stichler to do what he was told. 'It's still better than getting shot.'

Bridget said, 'Gee, thanks.'

Snapper paid the prostitutes from a wad of the stolen roofing money, which they counted, divided and put away. They turned their backs so he wouldn't peek inside their pocketbooks, which bulged with the other cash given to them ten minutes earlier by Avila, and ten minutes before that by the good-looking young man with the .38 Special.

'Is there ice in the bucket?' Bonnie Lamb asked. The hooker named Jasmine told her to help herself. Bonnie scooped two handfuls of cubes and pressed them to her cheeks.

The one-eyed man helped the prostitutes lift Levon Stichler to his feet. Snapper poked the old man's Adam's apple with the barrel of the gun. 'Don't try nuthin' stupid,' he said. 'These young girls can crack coconuts in their legs. Killing a skinny old fart like you is no problem whassoever.'

Levon Stichler didn't doubt it for a moment. 'Don't worry, mister. I'm no hero.'

The redhead pinched his butt playfully. 'We'll see about that.'

Augustine was hiding behind a Dumpster when the black Cherokee with the cheesy mud flaps arrived at the Paradise Palms. His spirits leaped when he saw Bonnie Lamb get out, followed by the governor. The driver was a brown-haired woman in a lavender top; probably the one from the driver's license photo, Edith Deborah Marsh, age twenty-nine. She was the next to get out of the Jeep. From the passenger side: a lanky sallow man in a rumpled suit, no necktie. He carried a gun and a bottle, and seemed unsteady. His crooked jaw was made conspicuous by a street light. Augustine had no doubt. It was him; the one who'd attacked Brenda Rourke, the one the prostitutes had told him about. Snapper in real life, 'Lester Parsons' on the motel register.

The man opened the hatch of the Cherokee and barked something at Skink, who removed a long lumpy bundle and hoisted it across his back. Once the procession disappeared into the motel, Augustine ran to the Jeep, climbed in the cargo well and quietly closed the hatch. He flattened himself below the rear window, placing the .38 at his right side. With both hands he held the dart rifle across his chest.

This, he thought, would be something to tell the old man. Make those fat wormy veins in his temples pop up.

Dad wouldn't dream of risking his neck unless vast sums of money were at stake. Love, loyalty and honor weren't part of the dope smuggler's creed. Augustine could hear the incredulity: *A.G., why the hell would you do such a crazy thing?*

Because the man deserved it. He beat up a lady cop and stole her mother's wedding ring. He was scum.

Don't be an idiot. You could've been killed.

He kidnapped the woman I love.

I raised an idiot!

No you didn't. You didn't raise anybody.

Whenever Augustine wrote his father, he made a point of mentioning how much money he'd given away to ex-girlfriends, obscure charities and ultraliberal political causes. He imagined his father's face turning gray with dismay.

You disappoint me, A.G.

This from a dumb shit who ran aground at full throttle with thirty-three kilos in the bilge and the entire Bahamian National Defense Force in pursuit.

'You disappoint me.'

Right. Augustine listened to the rain thrumming against the roof of the truck. It made him drowsy.

He hadn't expected to see his father waiting when he awoke from the coma, so he wasn't disappointed. Predominantly he was thrilled to be alive. The person at his bedside was a middle-aged Haitian nurse named Lucy. She told him about the plane crash, the months of slumber. Augustine hugged her tearfully. Lucy showed him a letter from his father, sent from the prison in Talladega; she'd read the letter aloud to Augustine when he was unconscious. She volunteered to read it again.

Son, I hope you are alive to read these words. I'm sorry the way things turned out. Dad should've signed off right there, but grace and decency were never his strong suits.

Everything I did was for you, he wrote. *Every move I made, right or wrong.*

Which was crap, an unnecessary lie. It mildly saddened Augustine but didn't embitter him. He was beyond all that. The airplane accident had pruned his emotions down to the roots. Nothing affected him the way it had before, which was fine. He decided everyone could benefit from a short coma. Wipe the slate clean.

So what if it took him years to come up with a new agenda? Here it was. Here *she* was.

Dad would not approve. Fortunately, Dad was not a factor.

Augustine heard the closing of a door, footsteps slapping in the puddles, voices advancing across the motel parking lot. He took three deep breaths. Checked the safety on the dart rifle.

He was glad for the weather, which misted the Jeep's windows and made him invisible from the outside. The voices grew sharper—two men arguing. Augustine didn't recognize them. Perhaps Snapper and somebody else, but who?

Loud words broke through the whisper of the rain. Augustine decided not to give himself away unless Bonnie Lamb was in trouble. The argument moved closer. Then came a deep huff, the sounds of a clumsy struggle; a bottle shattering on the pavement.

One of the men blurted: 'Hold the damn gun while I strangle this fucker.'

Snapper's consternation about the two remaining bullets in the .357 was well founded. A crack marksman he was not.

A police report dated July 7, 1989, showed that one Lester Maddox Parsons was arrested for shooting Theodore 'Sunny' Shea outside the Satellite Grille in Dania, Florida. The victim was not just a garden-variety crack dealer, as Snapper claimed after the incident. In truth, Sunny Shea was his longtime business partner. The scope of their enterprises extended beyond drugs to stolen guns, jewelry, clothing, patio furniture, stereos, even a shipment of baby food on one occasion. Eventually Sunny Shea came to suspect Snapper of cheating him on the proceeds, and confronted him with the accusation one humid summer night in the doorway of the Satellite Grille, before sixteen eyewitnesses.

Snapper's indignant response was to display a 9mm Glock (swiped from the glove box of an unmarked Coral Springs police car) and attempt to empty said weapon into Sunny Shea. In all, Snapper fired eleven times from a distance of eight feet. Only six rounds struck Sunny Shea, and not one nicked a vital organ— quite a feat, considering that Sunny Shea weighed only one hundred thirty pounds and hadn't an ounce of fat on his body. The hapless shooting exhibition was even more remarkable because Snapper was stone sober at the time.

Sunny Shea never lost consciousness, and was extremely

cooperative when police inquired about the identity of his assailant. The two detectives who hauled Lester Maddox Parsons to the Broward County Jail ridiculed him mercilessly about his lousy aim.

The next morning, when they came to his cell to inform him that the charge of attempted first-degree murder had been upgraded, Snapper glowed with vindication. Then he learned it wasn't one of his shots that had killed his scrawny, obnoxious partner—some bonehead in the emergency room had injected Theodore 'Sunny' Shea with an antibiotic to which he was virulently, and fatally, allergic.

Snapper pleaded out to a chickenshit manslaughter and got easy time, but his confidence in the efficacy of handguns was ruined forever. Two bullets in a .357 was scarcely better than no bullets at all.

Which was why he didn't want to waste them on Avila, the whiny spic. He was the last guy on earth that Snapper expected to see at Paradise Palms. He'd materialized like a drowned ghost out of the rainstorm, bitching about the roofing deposit that Snapper had ripped off from Mrs Whitmark.

'You know who she is? You know who she's married to?' Avila was screeching. Skink and the two women retreated to a dry vantage, under the eaves of the motel, while Avila chased Snapper around the parking lot like a terrier. Their conversation was difficult to follow, but Edie Marsh got the substance of it: Snapper had made a seven-thousand-dollar score.

Funny how he'd forgotten to tell her about it. Same as the wedding ring.

The pistol in Snapper's possession worried Avila but didn't deter him. For eighty miles he'd been praying for Chango's protection, and felt moderately imbued. Snapper appeared frazzled and shaky, possibly visited by black spirits.

Avila said, 'Gimme the money.'

'Eat shit,' Snapper growled.

When he turned away, Avila hopped on his back. Snapper shook him off. Avila pounced again, ripping Snapper's suit and knocking the Johnnie Walker from his hand. The two men locked together, spinning in the mist. Ultimately Snapper backed into a sabal palm tree, slamming Avila against the trunk. He made a true squeak as he slid to the ground.

Snapper, panting, weaved toward Edie: 'Hold the damn gun while I strangle this fucker.'

Halfheartedly she took the pistol and held it on Bonnie and Skink. Snapper fell upon Avila and breathlessly beat him. Avila was surprised by the clarity of the pain. When his nose exploded under Snapper's fist, he realized he'd been foolhardy to count on beatific intervention. Evidently Chango hadn't forgiven him for the aborted coati sacrifice.

As Snapper's grimy fingernails closed upon his throat, Avila inventoried the multiple sources of his agony: the fractured nose, the sliver of broken whiskey bottle in his right thigh, the unhealed crucifixion hole in his left hand, the goat-related goring in his groin and, soon, a crushed larynx.

He thought: Forget the seven grand. Screw Gar Whitmark. It's time to run.

Avila brought his right knee hard to Snapper's crotch. Snapper's eyelids fluttered but he didn't release his grip on Avila's neck. Avila kneed him twice more, ultimately producing the desired result. Snapper moaned and rolled away. Avila struggled to his feet. He took three steps and slipped. When he got up again, he heard Snapper rising behind him. Frantically Avila bolted for the road.

The rain made it hard to discern the details of the two men running along Highway One. Neither was large enough to be the governor, or physically fit enough to be Augustine. From where his Highway Patrol car was parked, a hundred yards away, Jim Tile was unable to see if the tall man had a crooked jaw. He might have been any old Keys drunk in a soggy pinstriped suit.

The black Jeep was still parked at the Paradise Palms. The trooper decided to sit still and wait.

Avila made it half a mile before he ran out of strength. He stopped on the Tea-Table Bridge and doubled over, sucking air. He tried to flag passing motorists, but none found room in their icy hearts for a bedraggled, saliva-flecked, blood-spattered hitch-hiker. Avila was further dejected to see, framed in the window of a speeding Airstream, a freckle-faced teenaged girl, snapping his photograph.

What a sick world, he thought, when an injured human being becomes a roadside amusement.

Meanwhile, out of the veil of rain came Snapper. He was shambling like a zombie across the bridge. For a weapon he'd selected a rusty axle from an abandoned Jet Ski trailer.

Avila raised both arms in supplication. 'Let's forget the whole thing, OK?'

'Don't move.' Snapper gripped the axle at one end and brought it high over his head, like a sledgehammer.

With a morose peep, Avila hurled himself sideways off the bridge. The drop was only fourteen feet, but given his dread of heights, it might as well have been fourteen stories. Avila was mildly amazed to survive the impact.

The water was warm and the tide was strong. He let it carry him out the channel toward the ocean, because he wasn't strong enough to swim against it. When the sodden weight of his clothing began to drag him under, he kicked off his shoes and pants, and stripped out of his shirt. Soon the lights from the Overseas Highway were absorbed by darkness and bad weather. Avila could see nothing but the occasional high-altitude flash of heat lightning. When a heavy object thumped him in the small of the back, he was sure it was the snout of a great white shark and that death was imminent.

But it was only a piece of plywood. Avila clung to it like a crippled frog. He thought of a sublime irony—what if the life-saving lumber had blown off one of the roofs that he'd been bribed not to inspect? Perhaps it was Chango's idea of a practical joke.

All night long, adrift in the chop, Avila cursed the hurricane for bringing him such misery: the sadistic doughnut man, Whit-mark and, of course, Snapper. The rainfall stopped at dawn but the sun never broke free of the clouds. It was midafternoon before Avila heard an engine. As he shouted for help, a tall white fishing boat idled within hailing distance. Avila waved. The skipper and his tropically garbed clients waved back.

'Hang in there, *amigo*,' the skipper yelled, and trolled away.

Twenty minutes later, a Coast Guard boat arrived and took Avila aboard. The crew gave him dry clothes, hot coffee and homemade chili. He ate in appreciative silence. Afterwards he was led belowdeck to a small briefing room, where he was greeted by a man from the Immigration and Naturalization Service.

In halting Spanish, the immigration man asked Avila for the name of the Cuban port he had fled. Avila laughed and explained that he was from Miami.

'Then what're you doing out here in your underwear?'

Avila said a robber was chasing him down the road, so he jumped off a bridge in Islamorada.

'Tell the truth,' the immigration man said sternly. 'Obviously you're a rafter. Now where did you come from—Havana? Mariel?'

Avila was about to argue when it dawned on him that there was no faster way to shed his burdens. What could he look forward to in his current life but an unforgiving wife, a traumatized mother-in-law, personal bankruptcy, the wrath of Gar Whitmark and a possible criminal indictment?

He asked the immigration man: 'What will happen to me if I confess?'

'Nothing. You'll be processed at Krome and most likely released.'

'If I am a political refugee.'

'That's the usual procedure.'

'*Sí*,' Avila said. '*Yo soy balsero*.' I am a rafter.

The immigration man seemed so relieved that Avila was left to conclude (as a former civil servant himself) that he'd saved the man mountains of paperwork.

'*Su nombre, por favor?*'

'Juan,' Avila replied. 'Juan Gómez. From Havana.'

'And your occupation in Cuba?'

'I was a building inspector.'

27

They waited in the Jeep—Edie Marsh up front, holding the revolver; Bonnie Lamb pressed against the governor in the back seat.

It was Bonnie who said: 'What if he doesn't come back?'

Edie was thinking the same thing. Hoping it. The problem was, Snapper had the damn car keys. She asked the man in the shower cap: 'You know how to hot-wire one of these?'

'That would be illegal.'

The cinematic smile startled her. She said, 'Why aren't you afraid?'

'Of what?'

'The gun. Dying. Anything.'

Bonnie said she was frightened enough for all of them. The rain slackened; still no sign of Snapper, or Avila. Edie had difficulty keeping her eyes off the man called Skink.

'What is it,' he said. 'My hat?'

She lifted the .357. 'You could take this away from me anytime you wanted. You know it.'

'Maybe I don't want to.'

That's what scared her. What was the point of holding a gun on a person like this?

He said, 'I won't hurt you.' Again with the smile.

Edie Marsh was a sucker for laugh lines around the eyes. She said to Bonnie: 'I think I know what you see in this guy.'

'We're just friends.'

'Really? Then maybe you can tell me,' Edie said, 'what's he got planned?'

'I honestly don't know. I wish I did.'

Edie was all clammy shakes, roiled emotions. In the motel

room, depositing Mr Stichler with the two hookers, she'd caught something on the TV that got her daydreaming—a news clip of the President of the United States touring the hurricane damage. At his side was a tall, boyishly attractive man in his thirties, whom the TV newscasters identified as the President's son. When they said he lived in Miami, Edie Marsh got a whimsical flash. So what if he wasn't a Kennedy? And maybe he was too much of a good young Republican to pick up some hot girl in a bar and get raunchy. Or just maybe he'd been waiting his whole repressed life to do exactly that. And he *was* the President's son. It was something to consider, Edie mused, for the future. Particularly if the hurricane scam continued to unravel at its current pace.

She put Snapper's gun on the seat. 'Get out of here,' she told Skink and Bonnie. 'Go on. I'll tell him you pushed me down and got away.'

Bonnie looked over at the governor, who said: 'Now's your chance, girl.'

'What about you?'

He shook his head. 'I made a promise to Jim.'

'Who the hell's Jim?' asked Edie Marsh.

Bonnie said: 'Then I guess we're staying.'

Skink encouraged her to make a dash for it. 'Go call Augustine. Let him know you're OK.'

'Nope,' Bonnie said.

'And your husband, too.'

'No! Not until it's over.'

Edie was exasperated, her nerves worn ragged. Snapper was right; they *are* nuts. 'Fine,' she said, 'you two fruitballs stay if you want, but I'm outta here.'

Skink said: 'Excellent decision.'

'Tell him I went to use the bathroom.'

'No problem,' said Bonnie.

'I got my period or something.'

'Right.'

Skink leaned forward. 'Could you hand me the gun?'

'Why not,' Edie said. Perhaps the smiler would shoot Snapper dead. There were about forty-seven thousand reasons that Edie wasn't upset at the idea, not including the barrel-shaped bruise on her right breast.

She was passing the .357 to Skink when he waved her off, saying: 'On second thought—'

Edie turned and let out a gasp. It was Snapper's face, dripping wet, pressed to the window of the Jeep. The bent nose and misshapen mouth made him look like a gargoyle.

'Miss me, bay-beeee?' he crooned, pallid lips wriggling like flatworms against the glass.

Jim Tile was tempted to call for backup, though it would spell the end of the governor's elaborate reclusion.

Long ago they'd made a pact: no cavalry, unless innocent lives were in peril. The trooper was thinking of the tourist woman as more or less innocent. She and Skink might be dead already.

Glumly Jim Tile watched the rain drench the passing cars on Highway One. Again he castigated himself for letting his emotions get the better of his brain. Brenda was alive. He should've thanked God, then let it go.

But he didn't. And the governor had had little trouble talking him out of the license-tag number.

'Pest control' was what Skink had called it, as they were leaving the hospital.

'Whoever did that to Mrs Rourke is not a viable member of the species. Not a welcome donor to the gene pool. Wouldn't Darwin himself agree?'

And the trooper had merely said: 'Be careful.'

'Jim, we're infested with these mutant shitheads. Look what they've done to the place.'

The trooper, locked in some cold distant zone: 'The tag's probably stolen off another car. It may lead you nowhere.'

The governor, momentarily shaking loose of his friend's firm grip: 'They're turning it into a sump hole. Some with guns, some with briefcases—it's all the same goddamn crime.'

'Pest control.'

'We do what we can.'

'Be careful, captain.'

Then he'd flashed those movie-star pearlies, the ones that had gotten him elected. And Jim Tile stood back and let him go. Let him stalk the man in the black Jeep Cherokee.

Which was now parked in a windy drizzle outside the Paradise Palms. The trooper counted three figures inside the truck; two of them, he hoped, were Skink and Bonnie Lamb.

A dark shape near the road caught his attention.

The tall man in the suit was hurrying along the gravel shoulder of Highway One. There was a tippiness to his gait; he seemed well challenged to keep a straight course, clear of the speeding cars. He flinched when the high beams of a gasoline tanker caught him in the face.

This time Jim Tile got a good look at the misaligned jaws.

He watched the man pass beneath the bright electric sign in front of the motel. He saw him walk up to the Jeep, lean close to a window. Then the man ran around to the driver's side, opened the door and got in. Smoke puffed from the truck's exhaust pipe. The brake lights flickered.

Jim Tile said, 'Hello,' and started his engine.

Suddenly, all around, the night was diced into blues and whites.

Snapper was backing the Jeep out, chortling about what had happened to Avila: 'Dumb fuck went straight off the bridge, you shoulda seen— Hey! Hey, what the hell . . .'

Bright lights started strobing everywhere. In the reflection of the puddles. On the coral-colored walls of the motel. In the fronds of the sabal palms.

Snapper shoved the Jeep into Neutral. 'Fucking cops!'

'No way,' Edie said. But she knew he was right.

A figure in gray was approaching the Cherokee. Snapper rolled down the window. It was a state trooper; big black sonofabitch, too. He'd parked his patrol car at an angle, to block the exit.

Snapper's mind raced, half drunk, half wired: Christ Almighty, would Momma and Pappy pitch a fit they ever heard I got taken down by a nigger cop. Momma especially.

In a flash Snapper figured out what must've happened: The

lady trooper either was alive, or had survived long enough after the beating to give a description of the Jeep, and maybe even of Snapper himself.

So this was the big black posse.

Snapper knew he should've ditched the Cherokee after it happened. Sure, park the fucker in the nearest canal and call it a deal. But, oh Jesus, how he loved that stereo system! Reba, Garth, Hank Jr., they'd never sounded so sweet. His whole life Snapper had wanted a car with decent speakers. So he'd stayed with the stolen Jeep because of its awesome stereo—and here was the price to be paid.

A big black motherfucker of a cop, coming across the parking lot, drawing his gun.

The one-eyed man tapped him on the shoulder. 'Haul ass, chief.'

'Huh?'

'That's what I'd do.'

'No,' murmured Edie Marsh. 'We've had it.'

Snapper told her to shut up. He snatched the .357 off the seat, pointed it out the window and somehow managed to shoot the trooper in the center of the chest. The man fell backward, landing with a splash.

'Good night, nigger,' Snapper said.

Skink went rigid. Bonnie and Edie screamed. Snapper slammed the Jeep into gear and peeled rubber.

'You see thaa-aatt?' he whinnied. 'One shot, one nigger cop! Whooheee! One shot!'

In the cargo well of the Cherokee, Augustine popped up on one knee. The stubby dart rifle was at his shoulder, the sights trained on the ragged hairline of Snapper's neck. He was surprised when Skink turned and shoved him back to the floor.

That's when the rear window of the Jeep vaporized.

The explosion caught Snapper furrowed in concentration, as he labored to steer around the parked Highway Patrol car, lit up like a Mardi Gras float.

Snapper ducked, peering up at the rearview. He saw the black trooper lying in a puddle, his arm waving but not aiming the smoking gun. Then the trooper went limp, and Snapper cackled.

The Cherokee fishtailed on the rain-slicked asphalt as it entered the highway. Edie Marsh hunched like an aged nun, sobbing into her hands. Skink had pulled Bonnie Lamb into his lap, out of the gunfire's path. Huddled in the cargo hatch, Augustine silently plucked nuggets of safety glass from his clothes.

Snapper was loopy on Midols, Johnnie Walker and pure criminal adrenaline. 'You see that big nigger go down?' he yammered at the top of his lungs. 'You see him go down!'

Christophe Michel spent the night of the hurricane in the safe and convivial atmosphere of Key West. At noon the next morning he put on the television and recognized, with cramps of dread, the bombed-out remains of a luxury housing development called Gables-on-the-Bay. The subdivision had been built by a company called Zenith Custom Homes, which not only employed Christophe Michel as a senior structural engineer but advertised his ecumenical credentials in its sales brochures. Michel had been recruited from one of France's oldest engineering firms, which had not energetically protested his departure. Among the fields in which Michel sorely lacked experience was that of girding single-family structures to withstand the force of tropical cyclones. His new employer assured him there was nothing to it, and FedExed him a copy of the South Florida Building Code, which weighed several pounds. Christophe Michel skimmed it on the flight from Orly to Miami.

He got along fine at Zenith, once he understood that cost containment was higher on the list of corporate priorities than ensuring structural integrity. To justify its preposterously inflated prices, the company had hyped Gables-on-the-Bay as 'South Florida's first hurricane-proof community.' Much in the same way, Michel later reflected, that the *Titanic* was promoted as unsinkable.

All week the news from Dade County worsened. The newspaper hired its own construction engineers to inspect the storm rubble, uncovering so many design flaws that an unabridged listing was possible only in the tiniest of agate type. One of the engineers sarcastically remarked that Gables-on-the-Bay should have been called Gables-*in*-the-Bay—a quote so colorful that it merited enlargement, in boldface, on the front page.

With home owners picketing Zenith headquarters and demanding a grand jury, Christophe Michel prudently planned his departure from the United States. He closed his bank accounts, shuttered the condo in Key West, packed the Seville and set out for the mainland.

The rain did nothing for his fragile confidence in American traffic. Every bend and rise in the overseas highway was a trial of reflexes and composure. Michel finished his last cigaret while crossing the Bahia Honda Bridge, and by Islamorada had gnawed his forty-dollar manicure to slaw. At the first break in the weather, he stopped at a Circle K for a carton of Broncos, an American brand to which he unaccountably had become devoted.

When he returned to the Seville, four strangers emerged from the shadows. One of them put a gun to his belly.

'Give us your goddamn car,' the man said.

'Certainly.'

'Don't stare at me like that!'

'Sorry.' The engineer's trained eye calculated the skew of the man's jawbone at thirty-five degrees off center.

'I got one bullet left!'

'I believe you,' said Christophe Michel.

The disfigured gunman told him to go back in the store and count backward from one hundred, slowly.

Michel asked, 'May I keep my suitcase?'

'Fuck, no!'

'I understand.'

He was counting aloud as he walked for the second time into the Circle K. The clerk at the register asked if something was wrong. Michel, fumbling to light a Bronco, nodded explicitly.

'My life savings just drove away,' he said. 'May I borrow the telephone?'

Bonnie Lamb expected Skink to erupt in homicidal fury upon seeing his best friend shot down. He didn't. Bonnie worried about the listless sag to his shoulders, the near feebleness of his movements. He wore the numb, unfocused glaze of the heavily sedated. Bonnie was sorry to see the governor's high spirits extinguished.

Meanwhile Snapper ranted and swore because the Seville had no CD player, only a tape deck, and here he'd gone to all the goddamn trouble of removing his compact discs from the Jeep before they'd ditched it behind the convenience store.

Bonnie squeezed Skink's arm and asked if he was all right. He shifted his feet, and something rattled metallically on the floorboard. He picked it up and asked, 'What's this?'

It was a red pronged instrument, with a black plastic grip and a chrome key lock.

Snapper looked over his shoulder and sniggered. 'The Club!'

'The what?'

Bonnie Lamb said, 'You know. That thing they advertise all the time on TV.'

'I watch no television,' Skink said.

Snapper hooted. 'The Club, for Chrissakes. The Club! See, you lock it across't here'—he patted the steering wheel—'so your car don't get stolen.'

'Really?'

'Yeah. Lotta good it did that dickhead back at the Circle K.' Snapper's laughter had a ring of triumph.

Edie Marsh was struggling to collect herself after the shooting. Even in the darkness, Bonnie could see fresh tears shining in her eyelashes.

'I had this boyfriend,' Edie sniffled, 'he put one of those on his new Firebird. They got it anyway. Right out of the driveway, broad daylight. What they did, they iced the lock and cracked it with a hammer.'

Snapper said, 'No shit? Froze it?'

'Yeah.' Edie couldn't come to terms with what had happened at the Paradise Palms, the wrongness and maddening stupidity of it. They'd never get away now. Never. Killing a cop! How had a harmless insurance scam come so unhinged?

Skink was impressed with the ingenious simplicity of The Club. He took special interest in the notched slide mechanism, which allowed the pronged ends to be fitted snugly into almost any large aperture.

'See, that way you can't turn the wheel,' Snapper was explaining, still enjoying the irony, 'so nobody can drive off with your fancy new Cadillac Seville. 'Less they put a fuckin' gun in your ribs. Ha! Accept no imitations!'

Skink set the device down.

'Accept no imitations!' Snapper crowed again, waving the .357.

The governor's gaze turned out the window, drifting again. Teasingly, Bonnie said: 'I can't believe you've never seen one of those.'

This time the smile was sad. 'I lead a sheltered life.'

Edie Marsh wondered if Snapper could have picked a dumber location to shoot a cop—a county of slender, connected islands, with only one way out. She kept checking for blue police lights behind them.

Snapper told her to knock it off, she was making everyone a nervous wreck. 'Another half hour we're home free,' he said, 'back on the mainland. Then we find another car.'

'One with a CD player, I bet.'

'Damn right.'

The Seville got boxed in behind a slow beer truck. They wound up stopped at the traffic light in Key Largo. Again Edie snuck a peek behind them. Snapper heard a gasp.

'What!' He spun his head. 'Is it cops?'

'No. The Jeep!'

'You're crazy, that ain't possible—'

'Right behind us,' Edie said.

Bonnie Lamb began to turn around, but Skink held her shoulder. The light turned green. Snapper floored the Seville, zipped smartly between the beer truck and a meandering Toyota. He said: 'You crazy twat, there's only about a million goddamn black Jeeps on the road.'

'Yeah?' Edie said. 'With bullet holes in the roof?' She could see a bud of mushroomed steel above the passenger side.

'Jesus.' Snapper used the barrel of the .357 to adjust the rearview mirror. 'Jesus, you sure?'

The Cherokee was still on their bumper. Bonnie noticed the governor wore a faint smile. Edie picked up on it, too. She said, 'What's going on? Who's that behind us?'

Skink shrugged. Snapper said: 'How 'bout this? I don't care who's back there, because he's already one dead cocksucker. That's 'zackly how many shots I got left.'

In what seemed to Bonnie as a single fluid motion, the governor reached across the seat, wrenched the .357 from Snapper's hand and fired it point-blank into the Cadillac's dashboard.

Then he dropped it on Snapper's lap and said: 'Now you've got jackshit.'

Snapper labored not to pile the car into a utility pole. Edie Marsh's ears rang from the gun blast, although she wasn't surprised by what had happened. It had only been a matter of time. The smiler had been humoring them.

One thought reverberated in Bonnie Lamb's head: What now? What in the world will he do next?

Snapper, straining not to appear frightened, hollering at Skink over his shoulder: 'Try anything, *anything*, I fuckin' swear we're all going off a bridge. You unnerstand? We'll all be dead.'

'Eyes on the road, chief.'

'Don't touch me, goddammit!'

Skink placed his chin next to the headrest, inches from Snapper's right ear. He said, 'That cop you shot, he was a friend of mine.'

Edie Marsh's chin dropped. 'Tell me it wasn't "Jim."'

'It was.'

'Naturally.' She sighed disconsolately.

'So what?' Snapper said. His shoulders bunched. 'Like I'm supposed to know. Fucking cop's a cop.'

To Bonnie, the social dynamics inside the carjacked Seville were surreal. Logically the abduction should have ended once Snapper's gun was out of bullets. Yet here they were, riding along as if nothing had changed. They might as well be on a double date. Stop for pizza and milk shakes.

She said: 'Can I ask something: Where are we going? Is somebody in charge now?'

Snapper said, '*I* am, goddammit. Long as I'm drivin''—'

He felt Edie jab him in the side. 'The Jeep,' she said, pointing. 'Check it out.'

The black truck was in the left lane, keeping speed with the Cadillac. Snapper pressed the accelerator, but the Jeep stayed even.

'Well, shit,' he grumbled. Edie was right. It was the same truck they'd abandoned ten minutes earlier. Snapper was totally baffled. Who could it be?

They watched the Cherokee's front passenger window roll down. The ghost driver steered with his left hand. His eyes were locked on the highway. In the oncoming headlights Snapper caught sight of the man's face, which he didn't recognize. He did, however, note that the stranger definitely wasn't wearing a Highway Patrol uniform. The observation gave Snapper an utterly misplaced sense of relief.

Bonnie Lamb recognized the other driver immediately. She gave a clandestine wave. So did the governor.

'What's going on!' Edie Marsh was on her knees, pointing and shouting. 'What's going on! Who is *that* sonofabitch!'

She was more dejected than startled when the Jeep's driver one-handedly raised a rifle. By the time Snapper saw it, he'd already heard the shot.

Pfffttt. Like a kid's airgun.

Then a painful sting under one ear; liquid heat flooding down through his arms, his chest, his legs. He went slack and listed starboard, mumbling, 'What the fuh, what the fuh—'

Skink said it was a superb time for Edie to assist at the wheel. 'Take it steady,' he added. 'We're coasting.'

Reaching across Snapper's body, she anxiously guided the

Seville to the gravel shoulder of the highway. The black Jeep smoothly swung in ahead of them.

Edie bit her lip. 'I can't believe this. I just can't.'

'Me, neither,' said Bonnie Lamb. She was out the door, running toward Augustine, before the car stopped rolling.

28

Jim Tile once played tight end for the University of Florida. In his junior year, during the final home game of the season, a scrawny Alabama cornerback speared his crimson helmet full tilt into Jim Tile's sternum. Jim Tile held on to the football but completely forgot how to breathe.

That's how he felt now, lying in clammy rainwater, staring up at the worried face of a platinum-haired hooker. The impact of the shot had deflated Jim Tile's lungs, which were screaming silently for air. The emergency lights of the patrol car blinked blue-white-blue in the reflection in the prostitute's eyes.

Jim Tile understood that he couldn't be dying—it only felt that way. The asshole's bullet wasn't lodged in vital bronchial tissue; it was stuck in a layer of blessedly impenetrable Du Pont Kevlar. Like most police officers, Jim Tile detested the vest, particularly in the summer—it was hot, bulky, itchy. But he wore it because he'd promised his mother, his nieces, his uncle and of course Brenda, who wore one of her own. Working for the Highway Patrol was statistically the most dangerous job in law enforcement. Naturally it also paid the worst. Only after numerous officers had been gunned down were bulletproof vests requisitioned for the state patrol, whose budget was so threadbare that the purchase was made possible only by soliciting outside donations.

Long before that, Jim Tile's loved ones had decided he shouldn't wait for the state legislature to demonstrate its heartfelt concern for police officers. The Kevlar vest was a family Christmas present. Jim Tile didn't always wear it while patrolling rural parts of the Panhandle, but in Miami he wouldn't go to church without it. He was glad he had strapped it on today.

If only he could remember how to breathe.

'Take it easy, baby,' the hooker kept saying. 'Take it easy. We called 911.'

As Jim Tile sat upright, he emitted a sucking sound that reminded the prostitute of a broken garbage disposal. When she smacked him between the shoulders, a mashed chunk of lead fell from a dime-sized hole in Jim Tile's shirt and plopped into the puddle. He picked it up: the slug from a .357.

Jim Tile asked, 'Where'd they go?' His voice was a frail rattle. With difficulty he holstered his service revolver.

'Don't you move,' said the woman.

'Did I hit him?'

'Sit still.'

'Ma'am, help me up. Please.'

He was shuffling for his car when the fire truck arrived. The paramedics made him lie down while they stripped off his shirt and the vest. They told him he was going to have an extremely nasty bruise. They told him he was a very lucky man.

By the time the paramedics were done, the parking lot of the Paradise Palms was clogged with curious locals, wandering tourists and motel guests, a fleet of Monroe County deputies, two TV news vans and three gleaming, undented Highway Patrol cruisers belonging to Jim Tile's supervisors. They gathered under black umbrellas to fill out their reports.

Meanwhile the shooter was speeding up Highway One with the governor and the newlywed.

A lieutenant told Jim Tile not to worry, they'd never make it out of the Keys.

'Sir, I'd like to be part of the pursuit. I feel fine.'

'You're not going anywhere.' The lieutenant softened the command with a fraternal chuckle. 'Hell, Jimbo, we're just gettin' started.'

He handed the trooper a stack of forms and a pen.

The body of Tony Torres inevitably became a subject of interest to a newspaper reporter working on hurricane-related casualties.

The autopsy report did not use the term 'crucifixion,' but the silhouette diagram of puncture wounds told the whole grisly story. To avert embarrassing publicity, the police made a hasty effort to reignite the investigation, dormant since the aborted phone call from a woman claiming to be the dead man's widow. Within a day, a veteran homicide detective named Brickhouse was able to turn up a recent address for the murdered Tony Torres. This was done by tracing the victim's Cartier wristwatch to a Bal Harbour jeweler, who remembered Tony as an overbearing jerk, and kept detailed receipts of the transaction in anticipation of future disputes. The jeweler was not crestfallen at the news of Señor Torres's demise, and graciously gave the detective the address he sought. While the police department's Public Information division stalled the newspaper reporter, Brickhouse drove down to the address in Turtle Meadow.

There he found an abandoned hurricane house with a late-model Chevrolet and a clunker Oldsmobile parked in front. The Chevy's license plate had been removed, but the VIN number came back to Antonio Rodrigo Guevara-Torres, the victim. The tag on the rusty Olds was registered to one Lester Maddox Parsons. Brickhouse radioed for a criminal history, which might or might not be ready when he got back to the office in the morning; the hurricane had unleashed electronic gremlins inside the computers.

The detective's natural impulse was to enter the house, which would have been fairly easy in the absence of doors. The problem wasn't so much that Brickhouse didn't have a warrant; it was the old man next door, watching curiously from the timber shell of his front porch. He would be the defense lawyer's first witness at a suppression hearing, if an unlawful search of the victim's residence turned up evidence.

So Brickhouse stayed in the yard, peeking through broken windows and busted doorways. He noted a gaspowered generator in the garage, wine and flowers in the dining room, a woman's purse, half-melted candles, an Igloo cooler positioned next to a BarcaLounger—definitive signs of post-hurricane habitation. Everything else was standard storm debris. Brickhouse saw no obvious bloodstains, which fit his original theory that the mobile-home salesman had been taken elsewhere to be crucified.

The detective strolled over to chat with the snoopy neighbor, who gave his name as Leonel Varga. He told a jumbled but colorful yarn about sinister-looking visitors, mysterious leggy women and insufferable barking dogs. Brickhouse took notes courteously. Varga said Mr and Mrs Torres were separated, although she'd recently phoned to say she was coming home.

'But it's a secret,' he added.

'You bet,' Brickhouse said. Before knocking off for the evening, he tacked his card to the doorjamb at 15600 Calusa.

That's where Neria Torres found it at dawn.

Matthew's pickup truck had followed her all the way from Fort Drum to the house at Turtle Meadow. The seven Tennesseeans swarmed the battered building in orgiastic wonderment at the employment opportunity that God had wrought. Matthew dramatically announced they should commence repairs immediately.

Neria said, 'Not just yet. You help me find my husband, then I'll let you do some work on the house.'

'I guess, sure. Where's he at?'

'First I've got to make some calls.'

'Sure,' Matthew said. 'Meantime we should get a jump on things.' He asked Neria's permission to borrow some tools from the garage.

'Just hold on,' she told him.

But they were already ascending the roof and rafters, like a troop of hairless chimpanzees. Neria let it go. The sight of the place disturbed her more than she had anticipated. She'd seen the hurricane destruction on CNN, but standing ankle-deep in it was different; overwhelming, if the debris once was your home. The sight of her mildewed wedding pictures in the wreckage brought a sentimental pang, but it was quickly deadened by the discovery of flowers and a bottle of wine in the dining room. Neria Torres assumed Tony had bought them for a bimbo.

She fingered the detective's card. She hoped it meant that the cops had tossed her asshole husband in jail, leaving her a clear path toward reclaiming half the marital property. Or possibly more.

She heard a mechanical roar from the garage; the resourceful Tennesseeans had found fuel for the generator. A bare lightbulb flickered on and off in the living room.

Leonel Varga, still in his bathrobe, came over to say hello. He assured her that the police detective was a nice man.

'What did he want? Is it about Tony?'

'I think so. He didn't say.' Mr Varga stared up at the busy figures of the men on the roof beams, backlit by the molten sunrise. 'You found some roofers?'

Neria Torres said, 'Oh, I seriously doubt it.'

She dialed the private number that Detective Brickhouse had penciled on the back of the business card. He answered the phone like a man accustomed to being awakened by strangers. He said, 'I'm glad you called.'

'Is it about Tony?'

'Yeah, I'm afraid it is.'

'Don't tell me he's in jail,' said Neria, hoping dearly that Brickhouse would tell her precisely that.

'No,' the detective said. 'Mrs Torres, your husband's dead.'

'Oh God. Oh God. Oh God.' Neria's mind was skipping like a flat rock on a river.

'I'm sorry—'

'You sure?' she asked. 'Are you sure it's Antonio?'

'We should take a ride up to the morgue. You're home now?'

'Yes. Yes, I'm back.'

Brickhouse said, 'I've got to be in court this morning. How about if I swing by around noon? We'll go together. Give us some time to chat.'

'About what?'

'It looks like Antonio was murdered.'

'How? Murdered?'

'We'll talk later, Mrs Torres. Get some rest now.'

Neria didn't know what she felt, or what she ought to feel.

The corpse in the morgue was the man she'd married. A corpulent creep, to be sure, but still the husband she had once believed she loved. Shock was natural. Curiosity. A selfish stab of fear. Maybe even sorrow. Tony had his piggish side, but even so . . .

Her gaze settled for the first time on the purse. A woman's purse, opened, on the kitchen counter. On top was a note printed in block letters and signed with the initials 'F.D.' The note said the author was keeping the dogs at the motel. The note began with 'My Sexy Darling' and ended with 'Love Always.'

Dogs? Neria Torres thought.

She wondered if Tony was the same man as 'F.D.' and, if so, what insipid nickname the initials stood for. Fat Dipshit?

Curiously she went through the contents of the purse. A driver's license identified the owner as Edith Deborah Marsh. Neria noted the date of birth, working the arithmetic in her head. Twenty-nine years old, this one.

Tony, you dirty old perv.

Neria appraised the face in the photograph. A ball-buster; Tony must've had his fat hands full. Neria took unaccountable satisfaction from the fact that young Edith was a dagger-eyed brunette, not some dippy blonde.

From behind her came the sound of roupy breathing. Neria wheeled, to find Matthew looming at her shoulder.

'Christ!'

'I dint mean to scare ya.'

'What is it? What do you want?'

'It's started up to rain.'

'I noticed.'

'Seemed like a good spot for a break. We was headed to a hardware store for some roof paper, nails, wood—stuff like that.'

'Lumber,' Neria Torres said archly. 'In the construction business, it's called "lumber." Not wood.'

'Sure.' He was scratching at his Old Testament tattoos.

She said, 'So go already.'

'Yeah, well, we need some money. For the lumber.'

'Matthew, there's something I've got to tell you.'

'Sure.'

'My husband's been murdered. A police detective is coming out here soon.'

Matthew took a step back and said, 'Sweet Jesus, I'm so sorry.' He began to improvise a prayer, but Neria cut him off.

'You and your crew,' she said, 'you *are* licensed in Dade County, aren't you? I mean, there won't be any problem if the detective wants to ask some questions . . .?'

The Tennesseeans were packed and gone within fifteen minutes. Neria found the solitude relaxing: a light whisper of rain, the occasional whine of a mosquito. She thought of Tony, wondered whom he'd pissed off to get himself killed—maybe tough young Edith! Neria thought of the professor, too, wondered how he and his Earth Mother blow-job artist were getting along with no wheels.

She also thought of the many things she didn't want to do, such as move back into the gutted husk at 15600 Calusa. Or be interviewed by a homicide detective. Or go to the morgue to view her estranged husband's body.

Money was the immediate problem. Neria wondered if careless Tony had left her name on any of the bank accounts, and what (if anything) remained in them. The most valuable item at the house was his car, untouched by the hurricane. Neria located the spare key in the garage, but the engine wouldn't turn over.

'Need some help?'

It was a clean-shaven young man in a Federal Express uniform. He had an envelope for Neria Torres. She signed for it, laid it on the front seat of Tony's Chevy.

The kid said, 'I got jumpers in the truck.'

'Would you mind?'

They had the car started in no time. Neria idled the engine and waited for the battery to recharge. The FedEx kid said it sounded good. Halfway to the truck, he stopped and turned.

'Hey, somebody swiped your license plate.'

'Shit.' Neria got out to see for herself. The FedEx driver said it was probably a looter.

'Everybody around here's getting ripped off,' he explained.

'I didn't even notice. Thanks.'

As soon as he left, Neria opened the FedEx envelope. Her delirious shriek drew nosy Mr Varga to his front porch. He was shirtless, a toothbrush in one cheek. In fascination he watched his neighbor practically bound up the sidewalk into her house.

The envelope contained two checks made out to Antonio and Neria Torres. The checks were issued by the Midwest Life and Casualty Company of Omaha, Nebraska. They totaled $201,000. The stubs said: 'Hurricane losses.'

Shortly after noon, when Detective Brickhouse arrived at 15600 Calusa, he found the house empty again. The Chevrolet was gone, as was the widow of Antonio Torres. A torn Federal Express envelope lay on the driveway, near the rusty Oldsmobile. Mr Varga, the neighbor, informed the detective that Neria Torres sped off without even waving good-bye.

Brickhouse was backing out of the driveway when a rental car pulled up. A thin blond man wearing round eyeglasses got out. Brickhouse noticed the man had tan Hush Puppies and was carrying a box of Whitman chocolates. High-pitched barking could be heard from the back seat of the visitor's car.

The detective called the man over. 'Are you looking for Mrs Torres?'

The man hesitated. Brickhouse identified himself. The man blinked repeatedly, as if his glasses were smudged.

He said, 'I don't know anybody named Torres. Guess I've got the wrong address.' Speedily he returned to his car.

Brickhouse leaned out the window. 'Hey, who's the candy for?'

'My mother!' Fred Dove replied, over the barking.

The detective watched the confused young man drive away, and wondered why he'd lied. Even crackheads know how to find their own mother's house. Brickhouse briefly considered tailing the guy, but decided it would be a waste of time. Whoever crucified Tony Torres wasn't wearing Hush Puppies. Brickhouse would have bet his pension on it.

*

Augustine parked at a phone booth behind a gas station. The governor had them wait while he made a call. He came back humming a Beatles tune.

'Jim's alive,' he said.

Edie Marsh leaned forward. 'Your friend! How do you know?'

'There's a number where we leave messages for each other.'

Bonnie asked if he was hurt badly.

'Nope. He took it in the vest.'

Augustine shook a fist in elation. Everybody's mood perked up, even Edie's. Skink told Bonnie she could call her mother, but make it fast. It went like this:

'Mom, something's happened.'

'I guessed as much.'

'Between Max and me.'

'Oh no.' Bonnie's mother, laboring to sound properly dismayed, when Bonnie knew how she truly felt.

'What'd he do, sweetie?'

'Nothing, Mom. It's all me.'

'Did you have a fight?' her mother asked.

'Listen, I've met two unusual men. I believe I've fallen in love with one of them.'

'On your honeymoon, Bonnie?'

'I'm afraid so.'

'What does he do?'

'He's not certain,' Bonnie said.

'These men, are they dangerous?'

'Not to me. Mom, they're totally different from anyone I've ever known. It's a very . . . primitive charisma.'

'Let's not mention that last part to your father.'

Next Bonnie phoned the apartment in New York. When she got back to the Seville, she told Skink to go on without her.

'Max left a message on the machine.' She didn't look at Augustine when she said it. Couldn't look at him.

Bonnie repeated her husband's message. 'He says it's over if I don't meet with him.'

'It's over regardless,' Skink said.

'Please.'

'Call back and leave your own message.' The governor gave her the details—the place, the time, who would be there.

After Bonnie finished with the phone, Skink made another call himself. When they got back in the car, Augustine punched the accelerator and peeled rubber.

Bonnie put her hand on his arm. He gave a tight, rueful smile.

They made the 905 turnoff in the nick of time. Already the northbound traffic was stacked past Lake Surprise; Skink surmised that the police had raised the Jewfish Creek drawbridge for their roadblock. He predicted they'd set up another one at Card Sound, as soon as more patrol cars arrived from the mainland.

Edie Marsh said, 'So where are we going?'

'Patience.'

The two of them sat together in the back seat. On the governor's lap was a Bill Blass suitcase, removed from the Cadillac's trunk to make space for the blacked-out Snapper.

Skink said, 'Driver, dome light! *Por favor.*'

Augustine began pushing dashboard buttons until the ceiling lights came on. Skink broke the locks off the suitcase and opened it.

'What have we here!' he said.

The troopers waited all night at Jewfish Creek. As Jim Tile predicted the black Jeep Cherokee never appeared, nor did the silver Cadillac stolen from a customer at a Key Largo convenience store. The French victim had dryly described the armed carjacker as 'a poster boy for TMJ.'

At daybreak the cops gave up the roadblock and fanned through the Upper Keys. It would take three days to locate the Seville, abandoned on a disused smugglers' trail off County Road 905, only a few miles from the exclusive Ocean Reef Club. The police would wait another forty-eight hours before announcing the discovery of the vehicle. They omitted mention of the bullet hole in its dashboard, as they didn't wish to unduly alarm Ocean Reef's residents and guests, which included some of the most socially prominent, politically influential and chronically impatient taxpayers in the eastern United States. Many were already in a cranky mood, due to the inconvenient damaging of their vacation homes by the hurricane. News that a murderous criminal might be lurking in the mangroves would touch off heated high-level communiqués with Tallahassee and Washington, D.C. The Ocean Reef crowd didn't mess around.

As it turned out, there was no danger whatsoever.

Most newly married men, faced with unexpected desertion, would have been manic with grief, jealousy and anger. Max Lamb, however, was blessed by a hearty, blinding preoccupation with his career.

A nettlesome thought kept scrolling across his mind, and it had nothing to do with his runaway wife. It was something the nutty kidnapper had told him: *You need a legacy.*

They'd been riding in the back of a U-Haul truck, discussing unforgettable advertising slogans. Max hadn't anything zippy to brag about except the short-lived Plum Crunchies ditty. Since the failure of the cereal campaign, the sixth floor had deployed him more often for billboard concepts and print graphics, and not as much on the verbally creative side.

Which stung, because Max considered himself a genuinely glib and talented wordsmith. He believed it was well within his reach to write an advertising catchphrase that would embed itself in the national lexicon—one of those classics the kidnapper had mentioned. A legacy, if you will.

Now that Bronco cigarets were history, Max was left to review the potential of his other accounts. The hypercarbonated soda served on the plane to Miami put him in mind of Old Faithful Root Beer. Old Faithful's popularity had peaked in the summer of 1962, and since then its share of the global soft-drink market had fizzled to a microscopic sliver. Rodale's mission was to revive Old Faithful in the consciousness of the consumer, and to that end the eccentric Mormon family that owned the company was willing to spend a respectable seven-figure sum.

Around Rodale & Burns, the Old Faithful Root Beer account

was regarded as a lucrative but hopeless loser. Nobody liked the stuff because one sixteen-ounce bottle induced thunderous belching that often lasted for days. At a party, Pete Archibald drunkenly offered a joke slogan: 'The root beer you'll never forget—because it won't let you!'

Lying there alone in Augustine's house, Max Lamb savored the prospect of single-handedly resuscitating Old Faithful. It was the sort of coup that could make him a legend on Madison Avenue. For inspiration he turned on the Home Shopping Network. Into the wee hours he tinkered determinedly with beverage-related alliterations, allusions, puns, verses and metaphors. Bonnie didn't cross his mind.

Eventually Max struck on a winner, something that sounded like good silly fun to kids, and at the same time titillating to teens and young adults:

'Old Faithful Root Beer—Makes You Tingle in Places You Didn't Know You Had Places!'

Max Lamb was so excited he couldn't sleep. Once more he tried calling the apartment in New York. No Bonnie, but the answering machine emitted a telltale beep. He punched the three-digit code and waited.

Bonnie had gotten his message—and left him a reply that caused him to forget temporarily about the Old Faithful account. The flesh under Max's shirt collar prickled and perspired, and stayed feverish until dawn.

He wasn't surprised by the symptoms. The downside of seeing his wife would be seeing the deranged kidnapper again. Only an idiot wouldn't be scared shitless.

29

Snapper regained consciousness with the dreamy impression of being someplace he hadn't been in twenty-two years—a dentist's chair. He sensed the dentist hovering, and felt large deft hands working inside his mouth. The last time Snapper had a cavity filled, he'd reflexively chomped off the top joint of the dentist's right thumb. This time he was becalmed by the ejaculate of the dart rifle.

'Lester Maddox Parsons!' The dentist, attempting to wake him.

Snapper opened his eyes in a fog bank. Looming out of the psychedelic mist was a silvery-bearded grin. A dentist in a plastic shower cap? Snapper squirmed.

'Whhaannffrr?' he inquired.

'Relax, chief.'

The dentist's basso chuckle rolled like a freight train through Snapper's cranium. His jaws were wedged wide, as if awaiting the drill. Come on, he thought, get it over with.

He heard buzzing. Good!

But the buzzing wasn't in his mouth; it was in his ears. Bugs. Fucking bugs flying in his ears!

'Hrrrnnnff!' Snapper shook his head violently. It hurt. All of a sudden he was drenched by a wave of salty water. What he didn't cough up settled as a lukewarm puddle in his protruded mandible, which functioned as a natural cistern.

Now he was completely awake. Now he remembered. The fog cleared from his mind. He saw a campfire. Edie, sweaty and barefoot. And the young broad, Bonnie, with her arms around the asshole punk who'd shot him.

'Yo, Lester.' It was the giant one-eyed fruitcake, holding an empty bucket. There was no dentist.

But Snapper definitely felt a cold steel object bracing his jaws open, digging into the roof of his mouth, pinching the tender web of flesh beneath his tongue; something so heavy that it caused his head to nod forward, something that extended diagonally upward from his chin to beyond his forehead.

A heavy bar of some type. Snapper crossed his eyes to put it in focus. The bar was red.

Oh fuck.

He wailed, trying to rise. His legs tangled. With rubbery arms he flailed uselessly at the thing locked in his mouth.

Skink held up a small chrome key and said, 'Accept no imitations.'

'Nnnnngggggoooo!!'

'You shot my friend. You called him a nigger.' Skink shrugged in resignation. 'You beat up a lady, stole her momma's wedding ring, dumped her on the roadside. What choice have you left me?'

He took Snapper by the hair and dragged him, blubbering, to the shore of a broad milky-green creek.

'What choice?' Skink repeated, softly.

'Unngh! Unnnggghhhh!'

'Sure. *Now* you're sorry.'

Edie, Bonnie and Augustine appeared on the bank. Skink crouched in the mud next to Snapper.

'Here's the deal. Most any other species, you'd have been dead long ago. Ever heard of Charles Darwin?'

Mosquitoes tickled Snapper's eyelids as he nodded his head.

'Good,' Skink said. 'Then you might understand what's about to happen.' He turned to the others. 'Somebody tell Mister Lester Maddox Parsons where we are.'

Augustine said: 'Crocodile Lakes.'

'Yes indeedy.' Skink rose. Once more he displayed the chrome key, the only thing that could unlock The Club from Snapper's achingly prolongated jowls.

Skink threw it in the water. He said, 'Crocodile Lakes Wildlife Refuge. Guess how it got its name.'

Mournfully Snapper stared at the circle of ripples where the key had plopped into the creek.

They'd stopped once along County Road 905, so Skink could snatch a dead diamondback off the blacktop.

'Don't tell me,' said Edie. 'It tastes just like chicken.'

The governor, coiling the limp rattlesnake at his feet, pretended to be insulted. He told Edie she was much too pretty to be such a cynic. He snapped off the snake's rattle and presented it to her for a souvenir.

'Just what I always wanted.' She dropped it in the ashtray.

After ditching the car, Skink made a torch from a gummy stump of pine. For nearly two hours he led them through a shadowed canopy of buttonwoods, poisonwoods, figs, pigeon plums and mahogany. He'd slung Snapper over his shoulder like a sack of oats. In his right hand he held the torch; in his other was the Bill Blass suitcase. Edie Marsh followed along a path hardly wide enough for a rabbit. Bonnie went next, with Augustine close behind, carrying (at Skink's instruction) the tranquilizer rifle and The Club. The .38 Special was in his belt.

Eventually they entered a small clearing. In the center was a ring of sooty stones; a campfire site. A few yards away sat a junked truck with freckles of rust and a faded orange stripe. Bolted to the roof was a bar of cracked red lights. Bonnie and Augustine stepped closer—it was an old Monroe County ambulance, propped on cinder blocks. Augustine opened the tailgate and whistled appreciatively. The ambulance was full of books.

The governor deposited Snapper on the ground, propped against a scabby tree trunk. He went to a spot on the other side of the clearing and kicked at the leaves and loose twigs, exposing an olive-drab tarpaulin. Rummaging beneath it, he came out with a tin of bread crumbs, a jar of vegetable oil, a five-gallon jug of fresh water and a waxy stick of army insect repellent, which he passed around.

While he collected dry wood for the fire, Edie Marsh came up beside him. 'Where are we?'

'Middle of nowhere.'

'Why?'

'Because there's no better place to be.'

They gathered to watch him skin the rattler. Edie was impressed by his enormous hands, sure and swift and completely at ease with the knife.

As the fire sparked up, Augustine pulled Bonnie closer and buried his face in the silkiness of her hair. He was soothed by the soft crackle of tinder; the owl piping on a distant wire; raccoons trilling and fussing in the shadows; the whoosh of nighthawks scooping insects above the firelit treetops. The sole discordant note was the stuporous snore of Lester Maddox Parsons.

The air tasted fresh; the rain was done for a while. Augustine wouldn't have traded places with another soul. Crocodile Lakes on a warm September night was fine. He kissed Bonnie lightly, having no special plans beyond the moment. He willed himself not to worry about Max Lamb, who would be coming tomorrow on a mission to retrieve his bride.

Skink began spooning out chunks of pan-fried snake. Edie Marsh facetiously said it was impolite not to save some for Snapper. Skink declared that he wouldn't so dishonor the memory of a dead reptile.

That's when he'd asked Augustine for The Club.

He turned his back to the others while he fitted it under Snapper's papery gray lips. Bonnie believed the procedure would have been physically impossible, were it not for the preexisting crookedness of those saurian jawbones. Afterwards nobody said a word, until Snapper made a groggy inquisitive murmur.

Skink bent over him. 'Lester?'

'Mmmmmfrrrtthh.'

'Lester Maddox Parsons!'

Snapper's eyelids fluttered. The governor asked Augustine to take a bucket down to the creek and get some water to wake up the sorry sonofabitch.

The pink-orange parfait of dawn failed to elevate Edie's spirits. She was sticky, scratched, hot, parched, filthy, as wretched as she'd ever been. She wanted to cry and pull at her hair and scream. She wanted to make a scene. Most of all she wanted to escape, but that was impossible. She was trapped on all sides by humming crackling wilderness; it might as well have been a twelve-foot wall of barbed wire. Her hands and feet weren't shackled. The governor held no gun to her head. Nothing whatsoever prevented her from running, except the grim certainty that she'd never find her way out, that she'd become blindly lost in the woods and starve, and that her emaciated body would be torn apart and devoured by crocodiles, rattlers and ravenous tropical ants. The prospect of an anonymous death in the swamps offended Edie's dignity. She didn't want her sun-bleached bones to be found by hunters, fishermen or bird-watchers; pieced together by wisecracking medical students and coroners; identified by X-rays from her childhood orthodontist.

She approached the governor. 'I want to talk.'

He was mumbling to himself, feeling around in his shirt. 'Damn,' he said. 'Out of toad.' He glanced at Edie: 'You're a woman of the world. Ever smoke Bufo?'

'We need to talk,' she said. 'Alone.'

'If it's about the suitcase, forget it.'

'It's not that.'

'All right, then. Soon as I finish chatting with Lester.'

'No, now!'

Skink cupped her chin in one of his huge, rough palms. Edie Marsh sensed that he could break her neck as effortlessly as twisting the cap off a beer. He said, 'You've got shitty manners. Go sit with the others.'

Bonnie and Augustine were kneeling in the back of the junked ambulance, poring through Skink's library. Edie couldn't understand how they could seem so unconcerned.

She said, 'We've got to do something.' It came out like a command.

Augustine was showing Bonnie a first edition of *Absalom, Absalom*. He glanced up at Edie and said, 'It's a ride. When it's over, it's over.'

'But who *is* he?' She pointed toward Skink. Then, facing

Bonnie: 'Aren't you afraid? God, am I the only one with brains enough to be scared?'

'Last night I was,' Bonnie said. 'Not now.'

Augustine told Edie to quiet down. 'It'll be over when he says so. In the meantime, please do your best not to piss him off.'

Edie was jarred by the harshness of Augustine's tone. He jerked a thumb toward Snapper, agape by the campfire. 'What're you doing with that shitbird, anyway?'

Bonnie cut in: 'Let's drop the whole thing.'

'No, it's all right. I want to explain,' said Edie. 'It was just business. We were working a deal together.'

'A scam.'

'Insurance money,' she admitted, 'from the hurricane.'

She caught Bonnie staring. 'Welcome to the real world, princess.'

'So when's the big payoff?' Augustine asked.

Edie laughed ruefully. 'The adjuster said any day. Said it was coming Federal Express. And here I am, lost in the middle of the fucking Everglades.'

'It's not the Everglades,' said Augustine. 'In fact, this is Saint-Tropez compared to the Everglades. But I can see why you're upset, watching two hundred grand fly away.'

Edie Marsh was dumbfounded. Bonnie said, 'You're joking. Two hundred thousand dollars?'

'Two hundred and one.' Augustine chided Edie with a wink.

She asked, almost inaudibly: 'How'd you know?'

'You left something in the house on Calusa.'

'Oh shit.'

He unfolded the pink carbons of the Midwest Casualty claim— Edie recognized the cartoon badger at the top of the page. Augustine ripped the carbons into pieces. He said, 'I were you, I'd come up with a clever excuse why your pocketbook might be in that particular kitchen. The police'll be mighty curious.'

'Shit.'

'What I'm saying is, don't be in such a rush to get back to civilization.' He turned back to the governor's books.

Edie bit her lower lip. Lord, sometimes it was tough to stay cool. She felt like breaking down again. 'What's this all about—some kind of game?'

'I don't think so,' Bonnie said.

'Jesus Christ.'

'Ride it out. Hang on till it's over.'

Not me, thought Edie. No fucking way.

The Club exaggerated Snapper's pre-exaggerated features. It pushed the top half of his mug into pudgy creases, like a shar-pei puppy; the eyes were moist slits, the nose pugged nearly to his brow. The rest was all maw.

'An authentic mouth-breather,' Skink said, studying him as if he were a museum piece.

'Fhhhrrrggaaah,' Snapper retorted. His elbows stung from scrapes received when the lunatic had dragged him to the creek.

Now the lunatic was saying: 'God, I hate the word "nigger." Back at the motel I considered killing you when you said it. Blowing your three pitiful teaspoons of brain matter all over the Jeep. Even if you hadn't shot my friend, the thought would've crossed my mind.'

Snapper stopped moaning. Worked at controlling his slobber. Watched gnats and mosquitoes float in and out of his mouth.

'Nothing to be done about that.' Skink flicked at the insects. He'd already spread a generous sheen of repellent on his captive's neck and arms. ' "Not to be taken internally." Says so right on the package.'

Snapper nodded submissively.

'Lester Maddox Parsons is the name on your license. Wild guess says you're named after that clay-brained Georgia bigot. Am I right?'

A weaker nod.

'So you started out two strikes against you. That's a shame, Lester, but I expect even if your folks had called you Gandhi, you still would've grown up to be a world-class dickhead. Here, let me show you something.'

The governor yanked the Bill Blass suitcase from under his butt. He positioned it in front of Snapper and opened it with a gay flourish. 'Drool away,' he said.

Snapper rose to his haunches. The suitcase was packed with money: bank-wrapped bundles of twenties.

'Ninety-four thousand dollars,' Skink reported. 'Plus assorted shirts, socks and casual wear. Two packs of French condoms, a set of gold cuff links, a tube of generic lubricant—what else? Oh yes, personal papers.'

He probed in the luggage. 'Bank statements, newspaper clippings about the hurricane. And this . . .'

It was a glossy color sales brochure for a real estate project called Gables-on-the-Bay. Skink sat next to Snapper and opened the brochure.

'There's our boy. Christophe Michel. "Internationally renowned construction engineer." See, here's his picture.'

Snapper recognized him as the dork at the Circle K.

'What would you do,' Skink mused, 'if you designed all these absurdly expensive homes—and they fell down in the first big blow. I believe a smart person would grab the money and split, before subpoenas started flying. I believe that was Monsieur Michel's plan.'

Snapper didn't give two shits about the Frenchman. He was transfixed by the sight of so much money. He would have gaped rapturously even if his jaws weren't bolted open. He remembered a Sally Jessy, or maybe it was a Donahue, with some hotel maid from Miami Beach who'd found like forty-two grand under a bed. The maid, for some reason, instead of grabbing the dough she'd turned it in to the manager! That's how come she'd got on Sally Jessy; the theme that day was 'honest people.' Snapper remembered shouting at the TV screen: What a dumb cunt! They'd showed a picture of the cash, and he'd almost come in his pants.

And here he was staring at twice as much. In person.

'Whhrrrrooognnn? Whhhaaakkkfff?'

'Good question, Lester.'

Without warning, the one-eyed freak stood up, unbuttoned

his army trousers, whipped out his unit and—to Snapper's mortification—urinated prodigiously upon the hurricane money.

Woefully Snapper rocked on his heels. He felt sick. Skink tucked himself in and went for the monkey rifle. He opened the chamber, peered inside. Then he strolled over to Snapper, flipped him on his belly and shot a tranquilizer dart into his ass. Right away the fog rolled in and Snapper got drowsy. The last thing he heard came from Skink.

'Who wants to go for a swim?'

Bonnie and Augustine stayed to look at the books while the governor took Edie to the creek. She wanted to talk; Skink wanted to get wet. He stripped, starting with the shower cap.

As he stepped into the water, she said: 'What about the crocodiles?'

'They won't bother us. There aren't enough of them left to bother anybody. I wish there were.'

Serenely he sank beneath the surface, then burst into the air, shaking bubbles and spray from his beard. He was as brown as a manatee, and so large he seemed to bridge the creek. Edie was unprepared for the sight of his body: the lodgepole arms and broad chest, his bare neck as thick as a cypress trunk. The baggy army fatigues had given none of it away.

'Coming in?'

'Only if we can talk,' she said.

'What else *would* we do?'

Edie thought: There's that damn smile again. She asked him to turn around while she took off her clothes.

He heard her slip into the creek. Then he felt her slender arms and legs; she was clinging to his back. As he moved into deeper water, she wrapped herself around his thighs.

'I'm a little scared,' she said.

'Haw! You and I are the scariest beasts in the jungle.'

Edie's mouth was at his ear. 'I want to go back to Miami.'

'So go.'

'But I don't know the way out.'

The governor was treading against the push of a strong tidal current. It cleaved around their bobbing heads as if they were dead stumps in the creek.

Edie's breath quickened from the thrill of being in fast water. She said, 'From the minute you and Pollyanna showed up at the house, I knew it was over. Snapper's gun—it meant nothing. We didn't kidnap you; you kidnapped us!'

'Nature imposes hierarchy. Always,' Skink said.

Edie, in a taut whisper: 'Please. Show me the way out of here.'

'And I was so sure you'd be angling for that suitcase.'

'No way,' she said, although it fleetingly had crossed her mind. Instead she'd decided to concentrate on getting out of the Keys alive.

A small silver fish jumped nearby. Playfully Skink swiped at it. He said, 'Edie, your opinion of men—it's not good. That much we share. Christ, imagine what Florida would look like today if women had been in charge of the program! Imagine a beach or two with no ugly high-rises. Imagine a lake without golf courses.' He clapped his hands, making a merry splash.

Edie said, 'You're wrong.'

'Darling, I can dream.' He felt her lips feather against his neck. Then a tongue, followed by the unsubtle suggestion of a nibble. He said, 'And what was that?'

'What do you think.'

When she kissed him again, they went down. The saltiness burned her eyes, but she opened them anyway. He was smiling at her, blowing bubbles. They surfaced together and laughed. Carefully she repositioned herself, climbing around him as if he were a tree—hanging from his rock-hard forearms and shoulders, bracing her knees against his hipbones as she swung to the front. All the time she felt him easing toward a shallower spot in the creek, so he could stand while holding her.

Now they were eye-to-eye, green water foaming up between them. Edie said, 'Well?'

'Weren't you the one worried about crocodiles?'

'He'd have to eat both of us, wouldn't he?'

'At the moment, yes.'

'That means he'd have to be awfully big and hungry.'

Skink said, 'We should be quiet, just in case. Certain noises do attract them.' He sounded serious.

'How quiet?' Lightly she brushed her nipples along the lines of his ribs.

'Very quiet. Not a sound.'

'That's impossible.' She felt his hands on the curve of her bottom. He was lifting her, keeping her in a gentle suspension. Then he was inside her. Just like that.

'Hush,' he said.

'I can't.'

'Yes you can, Edie.'

They made love so slowly that often it seemed they weren't moving a muscle. All sense of touch and motion came from the warm summer tide that rushed past and around and between them. In the mangroves an outraged heron squawked. More silver mullets jumped toward the shallows. A long black snake drifted by, indifferently riding the slick of the current as if it were floating on jade-colored silk.

Edie Marsh was good. She hardly made a sound. For quite a while she even forgot the purpose of the seduction.

Afterwards she wanted to dry off and take a nap together, but Skink said there was no time. They dressed quickly. Without a word he led her through the tangled woods. Edie saw no particular trail; at times it seemed they were hiking in circles. Once they reached a paved road, he took her arm. They walked another mile to an intersection with a flashing traffic light. A sign said that one road went to Miami, the other toward Key West.

Skink told her to wait there.

'For what?'

'Somebody's taking you to the mainland. He'll be coming soon.'

Edie was caught by surprise. 'Who?'

'Relax.'

'But I wanted *you* to take me.'

'Sorry,' said Skink. 'This is as far as I go.'

'It's going to rain again.'

'Yep.'

'I heard lightning!' Edie said.

'So don't fly any kites.'

'When did you plan this? Dropping me out here . . .' She was angry now. She realized he'd always meant to let her go—which meant the sex-in-the-creek had been unnecessary.

Not that she hadn't enjoyed it, or wouldn't love to try it again, but still she felt tricked.

'Why didn't you tell me last night?'

Skink flashed her the politician's smile. 'Slipped my mind.'

'Asshole.' She picked a leaf out of her wet hair and peevishly flicked it into the wind. Swatted a horsefly off her ankle. Folded her arms and glared.

He leaned down and kissed her forehead. 'Look on the bright side, girl. You got over your fear of crocodiles.'

30

At half past noon, a police cruiser stopped at the intersection of Card Sound Road and County Road 905. A broad-shouldered black man in casual street clothes honked twice at Edie Marsh. As he motioned her to the car, she recognized him as the cop whom Snapper had shot outside Paradise Palms.

'You might not believe this,' she said, 'but I'm really glad you're OK.'

'Thanks for your concern.' His tone was so neutral that she almost didn't catch the sarcasm. He wore reflector sunglasses and had a toothpick in the corner of his mouth. When he reached across to open the door, Edie glimpsed a white mat of bandage between the middle buttons of his shirt.

'You're Jim, right? I'm Edie.'

'I figured.'

He took the road toward Miami. Edie assumed she was being arrested. She said, 'For what it's worth, I didn't think he would shoot.'

'Funny thing about morons with guns.'

'Look, I know where he is. I can show you where he is.'

Jim Tile said, 'I already know.'

Then she understood. The trooper had no intention of trying to find Snapper. It was over for Snapper.

'What about me?' she asked, inwardly speculating on the multitude of felonies for which she could be prosecuted. Attempted murder. Fleeing the scene. Aiding and abetting. Auto theft. Not to mention insurance fraud, which the trooper might or might not know about, depending on what the governor had told him.

'So what happens to me?' she asked again.

'Last night I got a message saying a lady needed a ride to the mainland.'

'And you had nothing better to do.'

From miles behind the sunglasses: 'It was an old friend who called.'

Edie Marsh kept trying to play tough. It wasn't easy. No other cars were in sight. The guy could rape me, kill me, dump my body in the swamp. Who'd ever know? Plus he was a cop.

She said, 'You didn't answer my question.'

The toothpick bobbed. 'The answer is: Nothing. Nothing's going to happen to you. The friend who left a message put in a good word.'

'Yeah?'

' "Jail will not make an impression on this woman. Don't waste your time." That's a quote.'

Edie reddened. 'Some good word.'

'So you get a free ride to Florida City. Period.'

After crossing the Card Sound Bridge, the trooper stopped at Alabama Jack's. He asked Edie if she wanted a fish sandwich or a burger.

'I'm barefoot,' she said.

Finally he broke a smile. 'I don't believe there's a dress code.'

Over lunch, Edie Marsh tried again. 'I got sick when Snapper pulled the trigger,' she said, 'back at the motel, I swear. It's the last thing I wanted.'

Jim Tile said it didn't matter one way or the other. To appear friendly, Edie asked how long he'd been assigned to Miami.

'Ten days.'

'You came for the hurricane?'

'Just like you,' he said, letting her know he had her pegged.

On their way out of the restaurant, he bought her an extra order of fries and a Coke for the road. In the car, Edie tried to keep the conversation moving. She felt more secure when he was talking, instead of staring ahead like a sphinx, working that damn toothpick.

She asked if she could see the bulletproof vest. He said he'd had to turn it in at headquarters, for evidence. She asked if the bullet made a hole and he said no, more of a dimple.

'Bet you didn't think hurricane duty would be so hairy.'

Jim Tile fiddled with the squelch on the radio.

Edie said, 'What's the craziest thing you've seen so far?'

'Besides your geek partner shooting at me?'

'Yeah, besides that.'

'The President of the United States,' he said, 'trying to hammer a nail into a piece of plywood. Took him at least nine tries.'

Edie straightened. 'You saw the President!'

'Yeah. We had motorcade duty.'

Thoughtfully she munched on a French fry. 'Did you see his son, too?'

'They were riding in the same limo.'

'I didn't know he lived in Miami, the President's son.'

'Lucky him,' the trooper said.

Edie Marsh, sipping her Coke, trying not to be too obvious: 'I wonder where his house is, somebody like that. Key Biscayne probably, or maybe the Gables. Sometimes I wonder about famous people. Where they eat out. Where they get their cars waxed. Who's their dentist. I mean, think about it: The President's kid, he still has to get his teeth cleaned. Don't you ever wonder about stuff like that?'

'Never.' Fat raindrops slapped on the windshield. Still the trooper stayed camped behind the sunglasses.

Edie didn't give up. 'You got a girlfriend?' she asked.

'Yes.'

Finally, Edie thought. Something to run with. 'Where is she?'

'In the hospital,' Jim Tile said. 'Your buddy beat her to a pulp.'

'Oh God, no. . . .'

He saw that she'd spilled the Coke, and that she didn't even know it.

'God, I'm so sorry,' she was saying. 'I swear, I didn't—will she be all right?'

Jim Tile offered a handful of paper napkins. Edie tried to sop the soda off her lap. Her hands were shaky.

'I didn't know,' she said, more than once. She recalled the engraving on the mother's wedding band, the one that Snapper had stolen. 'Cynthia' was the name on the ring, the mother of the trooper's girlfriend.

Now Edie felt close to the crime. Now she felt truly sick.

Jim Tile said, 'The doctors think she'll be OK.'

All Edie could do was nod; she was tapped out. The trooper turned up the volume of the police radio. When they reached the mainland, he stopped at a boarded-up McDonald's. The hurricane had blown out the doors and windows.

A teal-blue compact was parked under a naked palm tree. A man in a green Day-Glo rain poncho was sitting on the hood; from the sharp creases, it appeared that his poncho was brand-new. The man hopped down when he saw the Highway Patrol car.

'Who's that?' Edie asked.

'Watch out for broken glass,' Jim Tile said.

'You're leaving me here?'

'Yes, ma'am.'

When Edie Marsh got out, the man got in. The trooper told him to shut the door and fasten his seat belt. Edie didn't back away from the car; she just stood there, crossing her arms in a halfhearted sulk. The effect was impaired by the slashing rain, which caused her to blink and squint, and by the stormy wind, which made her hair thrash like a pom-pom.

Through the weather she shouted at Jim Tile: 'What am I supposed to do now?'

'Count your blessings,' he said. Then he made a U-turn and headed back toward Key Largo.

Bonnie gave Augustine a nervous kiss before she left camp with Skink. Her husband was on his way. They were to meet at the road.

Alone, Augustine tried to read, huddled in the old ambulance to keep the pages dry. But he couldn't concentrate. His imagination was inventing dialogue for Bonnie and Max's reunion. In his head there were two versions of the script; one for a sad good-bye, one for I'm-sorry-let's-try-again.

Part of him expected not to see Bonnie again, expected her to change her mind and fly back to New York. Augustine had accustomed himself to such letdowns.

On the other hand, none of his three ex-fiancées would have lasted so long in the deep woods without a tantrum or a scene. Bonnie Lamb was very different from the others. Augustine hoped she was different enough not to run away.

Despite his emotional distress, Augustine kept a watch on Snapper, still zonked from the monkey tranquilizer. It wouldn't be long before the dumb cracker woke up blathering. Except for the cheap pinstripe suit, he reminded Augustine of the empty-eyed types his father used to hire as boat crew.

Another thing that got him thinking about his old man was the lousy weather. Augustine recalled a gray September after-noon when his father had dumped sixty bales overboard in the mistaken belief that an oncoming vessel was a Coast Guard patrol, when in fact it was a Hatteras full of hard-drinking surgeons on their way to Cat Cay. The marijuana bobbed on seven-foot swells in the Gulf Stream while Augustine's father frantically recruited friends, neighbors, cousins, dock rats and Augustine himself for the salvage. Using boat hooks and fish gaffs, they retrieved all but four bales, which were snatched up by the agile crew of a passing Greek tanker. Later that night, when the load was safe and drying in a warehouse, Augustine's father threw a party for his helpers. Everybody got stoned except Augustine, who was only twelve years old at the time. Already he knew he wasn't cut out for his old man's fishing business.

Augustine climbed out of the ambulance and stretched. A redtailed hawk hunted in tight circles above the campsite. Augustine walked over to the place where Snapper slept. The governor had left the hurricane money lying in the suitcase, reeking of urine. Augustine nudged Snapper with his shoe. Nothing. He grasped The Club and turned the man's head back and forth. He was as limp as a rag doll. The motion caused a slight stir and a sleepy gargle, but the eyelids remained closed. Augustine lifted one of Snapper's hands and pinched a thumbnail, very hard. The guy didn't flinch.

Dreamland, thought Augustine. No need to tie him up.

He found the sight and sound of Lester Maddox Parsons particularly depressing when married to the fear that Bonnie Lamb wasn't coming back. Sharing camp with a shitbird criminal had no appeal. The smell of fast-moving rain, the high coasting of the hawk, the cool green embrace of the hardwoods—all spoiled by Snapper's sour presence.

Augustine couldn't wait there anymore. It was worse than being alone.

Jim Tile said, 'Where's the young man?'

'Library,' said Skink.

They were in the trooper's car, near the trail upon which Skink had led Bonnie to the road. She and her husband were sitting side by side on one of the metal rails that ran the perimeter of Crocodile Lakes. The police car was parked seventy-five yards away; it was the best that Jim Tile and Skink could offer for privacy. Even from that distance, in the rain, Max Lamb was highly visible in the neon poncho.

'His old man's in prison.' Skink was still talking about Augustine. 'You'll love this: She says he was conceived in a hurricane.'

'Which one?'

'Donna.'

Jim Tile smiled. 'That's something.'

'Thirty-two years later: another storm, another beginning. The boy's star-crossed, don't you think?'

The trooper chuckled. 'I think you're full of it.' There was affection in the remark. 'What's the story with the father?'

'Smuggler,' Skink said, 'and not a talented one.'

Jim Tile considered that for a moment. 'Well, I like the young man. He's all right.'

'Yes, he is.'

The trooper put on the windshield wipers. They could see—by

the movement of the poncho—that Bonnie's husband was up and pacing.

'*Him* I don't envy,' Jim Tile said.

Skink shrugged. He hadn't completely forgiven Max Lamb for bringing his Handycam to Miami. He said, 'Lemme see where you got shot.'

The trooper unbuttoned his shirt and peeled away the bandage. Even with the vest to stop it, the slug had raised a plum-colored bruise on Jim Tile's sternum. The governor whistled and said, 'You and Brenda need a vacation.'

'They say maybe ten days she'll be out of the hospital.'

'Take her to the islands,' Skink suggested.

'She's never been to the West. She loves horses.'

'The mountains, then. Wyoming.'

The trooper said, 'She'd go for that.'

'Anywhere, Jim. Away from this place is the main thing.'

'Yeah.' He turned off the wipers. The heavy rain gathered like syrup on the windshield. They did not speak of Snapper.

'Which one is it?' Max Lamb asked.

He hoped it was the kidnapper, the wilder one. That would bolster his theory that his wife had lost her mind; a weather-related version of the Stockholm Syndrome. That would make it easier to accept, easier to explain to his friends and parents. Bonnie had been mesmerized by a drug-crazed hermit. Manson minus the Family.

Bonnie said, 'Max, the problem is *me*.'

When she knew it wasn't, not entirely. She'd watched him, after stepping from the police car, jump at the sight of a puny marsh rabbit as if it were a hundred-pound timber wolf.

Now he was saying, 'Bonnie, you've been brainwashed.'

'Nobody—'

'Did you sleep with him?'

'Who?'

'Either of them.'

'No!' To cover the lie, Bonnie aimed for a tone of indignation.

'But you wanted to.'

Max Lamb rose, raindrops beading on the plastic poncho. 'You're telling me that this'—with a mordant sweep of an arm—'you prefer *this* to the city!'

She sighed. 'I wouldn't mind seeing a baby crocodile. That's all I said.' She was aware of how outrageous it must have sounded to someone like Max.

'He's got you smoking that shit, doesn't he?'

'Oh please.'

Back and forth he paced. 'I can't believe this is happening.'

'Me, neither,' she said. 'I'm sorry, Max.'

He squared his shoulders and spun away, toward the lakes. He was too mad to weep, too insulted to beg. Also, it had dawned on him that Bonnie might be right, that perhaps he didn't know her very well. Even if she changed her mind and returned with him to New York, he constantly would be worrying that she might flip out again. What happened out here had sprained their relationship, probably permanently.

Turning to face her, his voice leaden with disappointment, Max said, 'I thought you were more . . . centered.'

'Me, too.' To argue would only drag things out. Bonnie was determined to be agreeable and apologetic, no matter what he said. She had to leave him with *something*—if not his pride, then his swollen sense of male superiority. She figured it was a small price, to help get him through the hurt.

'Last chance,' Max Lamb said. He groped under the bright poncho and pulled out a pair of airline tickets.

'I'm sorry,' said Bonnie, shaking her head.

'Do you love me or not?'

'Max, I don't know.'

He tucked the tickets away. 'This is unbelievable.'

She got up and kissed him good-bye. Her eyes were rimmed with tears, though Max probably didn't notice, with all the raindrops on her face.

'Call me,' he said bitterly, 'when you figure yourself out.'

Alone, he walked back to the patrol car. The kidnapper held the door for him.

Max was quiet on the drive back to the mainland; an accusatory silence. The state trooper was friends with the maniac who'd kidnapped Max and brainwashed his wife. The trooper had a moral and legal duty to stop the seduction, or at least try. That was Max's personal opinion.

When they got to the boarded-up McDonald's, Max told him: 'You make sure that nutty one-eyed bastard takes care of her.'

It was meant to carry the weight of a warning, and ordinarily Jim Tile would have been amused at Max's hubris. But he pitied him for the bad news he was about to deliver.

'She'll never see the governor again,' the trooper said, 'after today.'

'Then—'

'I think you're confused,' said the trooper. 'The young fella with the skulls, that's who she fell for.'

'Jesus.' Max Lamb looked disgusted.

As Jim Tile drove away, he could see him in the rearview—stomping around the parking lot in the rain, kicking at puddles, flapping like a giant Day-Glo bat.

They were a mile from the road when Augustine appeared on the trail. Bonnie ran to him. They were still holding each other when Skink announced he was heading back to camp.

Augustine took Bonnie to the creek. He cleared a dry patch of bank and they sat down. She saw that he'd brought a paperback book from the ambulance.

'Oh, you're going to read me sonnets!' She clasped both hands to her breasts, pretending to swoon.

'Don't be a smartass,' Augustine said, mussing her hair. 'Remember the first time your husband called after the kidnapping—the message he left on the answering machine?'

Bonnie no longer regarded it as that—a kidnapping—but she supposed it was. Technically.

Augustine said, 'The governor had him read something over the phone. Well, I found it.' He pointed to the title on the spine of the book. *Tropic of Cancer*, by Henry Miller.

'Listen,' said Augustine:

' "Once I thought that to be human was the highest aim a man could have, but I see now that it was meant to destroy me. Today I am proud to say that I am *inhuman*, that I belong not to men and governments, that I have nothing to do with creeds and principles. I have nothing to do with the creaking machinery of humanity—I belong to the earth! I say that lying on my pillow and I can feel the horns sprouting from my temples." '

He handed the novel to Bonnie. She saw that Skink had underlined the passage in red ink.

'It's him, all right.'

'Or me,' said Augustine. 'On a given day.'

The sky was turning purple and contused. Overhead a string of turkey buzzards coasted on the freshening breeze. In the distance there was a broken tumble of thunder. Augustine asked Bonnie what happened with Max.

'He's going back alone,' she said. 'You know, it's crossed my mind that I'm cracking up.' She took out her wedding ring. Augustine figured she was going to either slip it on her finger or toss it in the creek.

'Don't,' he said, covering both possibilities.

'I'll send it back to him. I don't know how else to handle it.' Her voice was thin and sad. Hurriedly she put the ring away.

Augustine asked, 'What do you want to do?'

'Be with you for a while. Is that OK?'

'Perfect.'

Brightening, Bonnie said, 'What about you, Mister Live-for-Today?'

'You'll be pleased to know I've got a plan.'

'That's hard to believe.'

'Really,' he said. 'I'm going to sell Uncle Felix's farm, or what's left of it. And my house, too. Then I intend to find someplace just like this and start again. Someplace on the far edge of things. Still interested?'

'I don't know. Will there be cable?'

'No way.'

'Rattlesnakes?'

'Possibly.'

'Boy. The edge of the edge.' Bonnie pretended to be mulling.

He said, 'Ever heard of the Ten Thousand Islands?'

'Somebody counted them all?'

'No, dear. That would take a lifetime.'

'Is that your plan?' she asked.

Augustine was familiar with the partner-choosing dilemma. She was deciding whether she wanted an anchor or a sail. He said, 'There's a town called Chokoloskee. You might hate it.'

'Baloney. Stay right here.' Bonnie hopped to her feet.

'Now where are you going?'

'Back to camp for some poetry.'

'Sit down. I'm not finished.'

She spanked his arm away. 'You read to me. Now I'm going to read to you.'

What Bonnie had in mind, dashing up the trail, was Whitman. Somewhere in the rusted ambulance was a hardbound volume of 'Song of Myself,' a poem she'd loved since high school. One line in particular—'In vain the mastodon retreats from its own powder'd bones'—reminded her of Skink.

As she entered the campsite, she spotted him motionless on the ground. Snapper craned over him, making throaty snarls. He was coming down from a sulfurous rage. In one hand was a piece of burnt wood that Bonnie recognized as the governor's hiking torch.

She stood rigid, her fists balled at her sides. Snapper wore a contorted expression made no less malignant by the red-and-chrome bar clamped to his face. He was unaware of Bonnie watching from the tree line. He dropped the torch, snatched up the suitcase and began to run.

Insanely she went after him.

31

Snapper had been awakened by a cool drizzle. The campsite was still. The one-eyed lunatic was asleep, stretched out in his grubby army duds beneath a tree. There was no sign of Edie Marsh, or the sharpshooter, or the weird broad who'd doused herself with soda pop in the Jeep.

Slowly Snapper sat up. His eyes were crusty and his mouth was ash dry. A clot of black dirt stuck to one eyebrow: For the umpteenth time he tried unsuccessfully to wrench The Club out of his gums. The pain was hideous, as if the bones of his face were spring-loaded to blow apart. He was grateful he couldn't see himself; he must've looked like a fucking circus freak. Bucket-Mouth Man. Dorks lining up to toss softballs down his gullet.

Jesus H. Christ, he thought, I gotta clear the cobwebs.

There on the ground was the suitcase full of cash, yawning, where Skink had left it. The smell pungently reminded Snapper that it hadn't been a nightmare: The asshole had actually pissed on ninety-four thousand perfectly good U.S. dollars.

Snapper tested his legs; left, right, together. Next he clenched his hands, flexed his arms. So far, so good. The second tranquilizer dart finally had worn off.

He rose to his feet. Tenuously he took one step toward the cash. Then another. The iron bar on his jaws was so cumbersome that he almost lost his balance and toppled forward. He tried to hold his breath while he latched the suitcase, but the aroma was unavoidable. Snapper found the water jug and emptied it into his throat. His spluttering failed to disturb the dozing lunatic.

Snapper spied a handy weapon—a length of gummy wood, one end charred.

The big dork must've heard him coming, because he tried to roll away when Snapper swung. The blow caught the man in a shoulder instead of the head, but Snapper heard bones crack. He knew it hurt.

'Ahhheeegggnnn!' he brayed, swinging again and again until the fucker quit rolling and just lay there making a faint hiss, like a tire going flat.

Bonnie had always been scrappy for her size. In junior high she had chased down a boy who'd lifted her skirt in the school cafeteria. The boy's name was Eric Schultz. He was almost six feet tall, foul-mouthed and cocky, a star of the basketball team. He outweighed Bonnie by eighty pounds. When he tried to run away, she tackled him, held him down and punched him in the testicles. Eric Schultz missed the first and second rounds of the basketball playoffs. Bonnie Brooks was suspended from class for three days. Her father said it was worth it; he was proud. Bonnie's mother said she overreacted, because the boy Eric had been held back twice for eighth grade. Bonnie's mother said he'd probably done what he had to Bonnie because he didn't know any better. *He does now*, Bonnie had said. She agreed with her father: Stupidity was an overworked excuse.

With his bum knee, Snapper was easy to catch. His speed was further hindered by the unwieldy facial contraption, which snagged in the vines and branches. He went down in the same basic configuration as had Eric Schultz—limbs splayed, nose down. It took only a moment for Snapper to realize it was a woman hanging off his shoulders, and not a large one. The casual manner in which he shook free suggested to Bonnie that her rabbit punches were ineffective. Unlike young Eric Schultz, Lester Maddox Parsons had been to prison, where he'd learned much about dirty fighting. He wasn't about to let a one-hundred-pound girl get a clear shot at his jewels.

With both arms he swung the Frenchman's suitcase, knocking

Bonnie sideways against the gnarled trunk of an old buttonwood. She landed flat on her back, punching frenetically. The red steel bar across Snapper's cheeks blocked her best jabs. He quickly pinned her wrists, but she stopped kicking only when he dug a knee into her pubic bone.

Beneath the dull deadening weight of his torso, she gradually lost sight of the buzzards and the gathering clouds. Her next view was a glistening, pink, fistulous cave—his mouth, stretched in the shape of a permanent scream. He panted from exertion; hot, necrotic gusts. Bonnie wanted to gag. Something wet and wormy settled on the cleft of her chin.

A lip.

She took it in her teeth and bit hard. Snapper yowled and pulled away. A half second later, Bonnie was stunned by a sharp blow to her temple. The Club. The bastard was trying to beat her with it, using frenzied, snorting sweeps of his head. She had no way to protect herself. Snapper wouldn't release her arms because he didn't need his own for the attack; his gourd was doing all the work. Bonnie was dazed by another white burst of pain. She shut her eyes so she wouldn't have to see his goggling wet hole of a face. She made herself go limp, thinking that unconsciousness would be fine and dandy.

Snapper imagined himself a wild bull in the ring; goring at will. The bitch was helpless beneath him, hardly twitching. He paused to catch his breath, spit blood, and congratulate himself for so cleverly converting a handicap to a martial asset. The cop on the TV commercial was right; The Club was indestructible! Despite the stinging of his lip and the burning in his knee and the electric throbbing in the joints of his jaw, Snapper didn't feel so bad. His pride outweighed the pain. Certainly he'd earned the rights to the Frenchman's hurricane money.

That's when a hand moved between his legs; lightly, like a sparrow on a branch.

'Nnnngggguuuhhh!!'

The bitch grabbed him. Snapper bellowed. He thrashed his head, trying to pummel her with the heavy end of The Club. Then he realized it couldn't be the girl squeezing his balls, because both her wrists remained pinned in the dirt. She wasn't moving a muscle. It had to be somebody else.

Then, from a distance, he heard: 'No! Don't do that.'

He tried to hold still. Tried to breathe without whimpering. Tried to turn ever so slightly, to see who the fuck had at least one (and possibly both) of his nuts in their fingers.

Again the voice, this time closer: 'Don't do it! Don't!'

The one-eyed freak, calling out.

Who's he talking to? Snapper wondered. Don't do *what*?

Then the gun went off at his head, and he knew.

Max Lamb was surprised to find a woman sleeping in the front seat of his rental car. He recognized her as the one whom the state trooper had dropped off in the parking lot earlier that afternoon.

She sat up, brushing her long brown hair from her eyes. 'It was raining. I had no place to go.' Not the least bit bashful.

'That's OK,' Max said. He wormed out of the Day-Glo poncho and tossed it in the back seat.

'My name is Edie.' She reached out to shake his hand.

He took it, stiffly. She had a strong grip.

'I'm Max,' he said. Then he heard himself saying: 'You need a lift back to Miami?'

Edie Marsh nodded gratefully. That's what she'd been counting on. One way or another, all rental cars ultimately returned to Miami.

She said, 'I would've tried hitching a ride, but there was lightning.'

'Yeah, I heard.'

Somehow Max missed the ramp to the Turnpike; it wasn't easy, but he did. Edie didn't complain. A lift was a lift. All the roads went the same direction anyway.

'Where are you from, Max?' He looked perfectly harmless, but still she wanted to get him talking. Silent brooding made her edgy.

'New York. I'm in advertising.'

'No kidding.'

And off he went. During the next hour, Edie learned a great deal about Madison Avenue. Max was absolutely elated to discover that she'd been a glutton for Plum Crunchies cereal. And she remembered his slogan, word for word!

'What others have you done?' she asked brightly.

Max was tempted to tell her about Intimate Mist but thought better of it. Not everyone felt comfortable on the subject of douches.

'Bronco cigarettes,' he said.

'Really!'

'Speaking of which, would you mind if I smoked?'

'Not at all,' said Edie Marsh.

He offered her a menthol. She declined politely. As smoke filled the car, she rolled down the window and tried not to cough herself blue. 'When are you going back to New York?'

'Tomorrow,' Max said. He grew quiet again.

Edie said: 'If you tell me, I'll tell you.'

Max looked perplexed.

She said, 'You know—what we were doing with that cop. Me coming, you going.'

'Oh.' After a pause: 'I'm not in any kind of trouble, if that's what you mean.'

Dryly she said, 'I had a hunch you're no Ted Bundy.'

What eyes! Max thought. What an interesting woman! He had reason to believe she was aware of her impact.

He said, 'How about this: If you don't tell me, I won't tell you. What's over is over.'

'I like that approach.'

'Let's just agree we've had a bad day.'

'And how.'

In South Dade they hit heavy traffic where the storm had blown ashore, taking down everything. Edie Marsh had seen the destruction the day after the hurricane, but it seemed much worse to her now. She was surprised to find herself fighting back tears.

Out of nowhere Max said: 'Hey, I bet I can guess what kind of car you drive.' Apparently trying to take their minds off what they saw: two unshaven men, on a street corner, fighting over a five-gallon jug of fresh water. Their wives and children watching anxiously from the sidewalk.

'Seriously,' Max was saying. 'It's a knack I've got. Matching people to their cars.'

'Based on . . .?'

'Intuition, I guess you'd say.'

Edie said, 'OK, give it a try.'

Max, eyeing her up and down, like he was guessing her weight: 'Nissan 300?'

'Nope.'

'A 280Z?'

'Try an Acclaim.'

He winced. 'I had you figured for a sports import.'

'Well, I'm flattered,' Edie said, with a soft laugh.

There was a brutal truth at the heart of Max's silly game. Eligible young Kennedys and even sons of sitting presidents did not customarily flag down women in 1987 Plymouths.

Later, after Max had found the Turnpike extension and made his way downtown, he said: 'Where can I drop you?'

'Let me think about that,' said Edie Marsh.

'Captain, have you got a mirror?'

'No.'

'Good,' Bonnie said.

She felt a raw knot rising on her forehead, another on a cheekbone. Augustine assured her that she didn't look as bad as she thought. 'But you could use some ice.'

'Later.' She was watching Skink. 'I know somebody who ought to be in a hospital.'

'No,' said the governor.

'Augustine says your collarbone is broken.'

'I believe he's right.'

'And several ribs.'

'I shall call you Nurse Nightingale.'

'Why are you so stubborn?'

'I know a doctor in Tavernier.'

'And how do you plan to get there?'

'Walking upright,' Skink replied. 'One of the few commendable traits of our species.'

Bonnie told him to quit being ridiculous. 'You're in terrible pain, I can tell.'

'The whole world's in pain, girl.'

She looked imploringly to Augustine. 'Talk to him, please.'

'He's a grown man, Bonnie. Now hold still.'

He was cleaning her face with his shirt, which he'd wadded up and soaked in the creek. Skink perched on a nearby log, his arms crossed tightly. Moments earlier they'd watched him gobble a dozen Anacins from a plastic bottle he located under the camp tarpaulin. Bonnie boldly swallowed three.

No aspirins were offered to Snapper, who was bound with a corroded tow-truck chain to the buttonwood tree. He was caked with soggy leaves, mulch and dried blood. His cheap suit was filthy and torn. During the struggle, Augustine had made him dig a short trench with his mandible, so his maw was full of stones and loose soil, like a planter. In addition, he was missing an earlobe, which Augustine had shot off at point-blank range. It was inconceivable to Snapper that such a chickenshit wound could be so excruciating.

Skink said to Augustine: 'I thought sure you were going to kill him.'

'It was tempting.'

'My way's better.'

'After what he did to Jim's girlfriend?'

'Yes. Even after that.' The governor bowed his head. He was hurting.

Augustine was drained. The adrenaline had emptied out in a clammy torrent. He no longer entertained the idea of murdering Snapper, and doubted if he was even capable of it. An hour ago, yes. Not now. It was probably a good time to leave.

Bonnie studied his expression as he tended her cheeks and brow. 'You OK?' she said.

'I don't know. The way he hurt you—'

'Hey, I asked for it.'

'But you wouldn't be out here if it weren't for me.'

Playfully she jabbed a finger in his side. 'What makes you so sure? Maybe I'm here because of *him*.'

Skink grinned but didn't look up. Augustine had to laugh, too. That's why we're both here, he thought. Because of him.

'Would it be bad manners,' Bonnie said to Skink, 'if I asked what you plan to do with the money.'

His chin came off his chest. 'Oh. That.' Grimacing, he rose from the log. 'Lester, you awake? Yo, Lester!'

'Ghhhnungggh.'

The governor used his feet to push the Frenchman's suitcase across the clearing to the buttonwood tree, where he kicked the latches open. Snapper regarded the bundled cash with a mixture of undisguised longing and suspicion. He wondered what sick stunt the fucker was cooking up now.

Only the bills on top were wet. Skink swept them aside with his hands. Bonnie and Augustine walked over to see.

The governor said, 'You guys want any of this?' They shook their heads.

'Me, neither,' he muttered. 'Just more shit to lug around.' He addressed Snapper: 'Chief, I'm sure there was a time in your sorry-ass life when ninety-four grand would've come in handy. Believe me when I tell you those days are over.'

Skink took a matchbook from his pocket. He asked Bonnie and Augustine to do the honors. Snapper spewed dirt and thrashed inconsolably against the chains.

The money gave off a rich, sweet scent as it burned.

Later he unlocked the truck chain holding Snapper to the tree. Plaintively Snapper pointed at the red brace fastened in his mouth. Skink shook his head.

'Here's the deal, Lester. Don't be here when I get back. Do not fuck with my camp, do not fuck with my books. It's about to rain like hell, so lie back and drink as much as you can. You'll need it.'

Snapper didn't respond. Augustine stepped up. He took out the .38 Special and said, 'Try to follow us out, I'll blow your head off.'

Bonnie shuddered. The governor removed a few items from beneath the tarpaulin and placed them in a backpack. Then he lighted the torch and led the others into the trees.

Snapper had no desire to follow; he was glad the crazy fuckers were gone. A gust churned the cinders at his feet, blew a flurry into his lap. He ran his fingers through the ashes, brought a handful to his nose. It didn't even smell like money anymore.

Later he awoke to the hard rustle of leaves. The rain came driving down. Snapper took the man's advice. He filled up on it.

At daybreak he would start his march.

They broke a fresh trail through the hardwoods. Bonnie was worried that Snapper would be able to use it to find his way out. 'Not across a lake,' Skink said.

She hooked her fingers in Augustine's belt as they swam. The governor hoisted the torch, his boots and the backpack over his head, to keep them dry. Augustine was astounded that the man could swim so well with a fractured collarbone. The crossing took less than fifteen minutes, though it seemed an eternity to Bonnie. She was unable to convince herself that crocodiles shunned firelight.

Afterwards they rested on shore. Skink, struggling into his laceless boots: 'If he gets out of here, he deserves to be free.'

Augustine said, 'But he won't.'

'No, he'll go the wrong way. That's his nature.'

Then Skink was moving again, an orange flame weaving through the trees ahead of them. Bonnie, hurrying to keep up: 'So something'll get him. Panthers or something.'

Augustine said, 'Nothing so exotic, Mrs Lamb.'

'Then what?'